the Boy I Love

Lynda Bellingham

**SIMON &
SCHUSTER**

London · New York · Sydney · Toronto · New Delhi

A CBS COMPANY

First published in Great Britain by Simon & Schuster UK Ltd, 2014
A CBS COMPANY

Copyright © Lynda Bellingham, 2014

1 3 5 7 9 10 8 6 4 2

Simon & Schuster UK Ltd
1st Floor
222 Gray's Inn Road
London WC1X 8HB

www.simonandschuster.co.uk

Simon & Schuster Australia, Sydney
Simon & Schuster India, New Delhi

A CIP catalogue record for this book
is available from the British Library

Hardback ISBN: 978-1-47114-897-2
Trade paperback ISBN: 978-1-47114-901-6
Ebook ISBN: 978-1-47110-286-8

Typeset by M Rules
Printed and bound by CPI Group (UK) Ltd, Croydon, CR0 4YY

A Tribute to Lynda

We are so very proud to be the publishers of Lynda's fiction. Lynda was brimful of ideas born of her lively imagination and her own experiences. She knew instinctively how people of every generation interact and had – of course! – a wonderfully keen eye for drama, and for emotion and love in all guises. She wrote of joy and sadness, conflict and union, old and young, past and present, with tenderness and wisdom. *Tell Me Tomorrow*, Lynda's first novel, has three generations of women at its heart – a grandmother, a mother and a daughter – and Lynda dedicated the novel to mothers everywhere. These wonderful characters shone out on every page, to be joined, in *The Boy I Love*, by an equally memorable and delightful cast. On every page, in every description, in every word of dialogue, readers will hear Lynda's voice loud and clear. How fortunate we are that Lynda completed her second novel this summer so that we can all rejoice in the talents of a truly gifted storyteller.

Suzanne Baboneau
Lynda's editor
November 2014

The boy I love is up in the gallery,
The boy I love is looking now at me.
There he is, can't you see, waving his handkerchief
As merry as a robin that sings on a tree.

George Ware, 1885, sung by Marie Lloyd

Act 1

Enter stage left

Chapter 1

Oh, Mr Porter, what shall I do?
I want to go to Birmingham
And they are taking me onto Crewe.
Send me back to London
As quickly as you can.
Oh, Mr Porter, what a silly girl I am!

September 1982

Sally Thomas swallowed hard and smiled bravely as the whistle blew and the train began to pull out of the station. She gave a final wave to her family, standing at the barrier and already a blur, and sat down with a bump as the train picked up speed.

'Oh, Mr Porter, what shall I do …' The old Victorian music-hall song rang in her ears as she gazed out at the beautiful cream stone buildings of Cheltenham, her home town. It looked so picture-perfect in the early-morning sun. Traces of autumn tinged the leaves in red and gold, and there were flashes of burnt orange from the creepers that draped themselves over the houses like garlands.

The girl could not help but think how different the landscape would be in Crewe. From gold to grey. Still, she would learn to love the difference between the two and make it her home for the next six months. Her first professional job as an actress! In July, Sally had managed to get an early audition for the upcoming season by physically taking herself to meet the director in Crewe, rather than waiting in line down in London with hundreds of other hopefuls. Her temerity had gained her a place in the company, and now as she fell asleep to the rhythm of the train, she dreamed of bright lights and velvet curtains, and her first introduction to Crewe Theatre just two short months ago . . .

July

She was shaken awake as the train shuddered to a halt at Platform One, Crewe station. As she stepped down from the train, Sally was overwhelmed by the size of the place. High above her, steel girders rose in Gothic splendour just like a cathedral. Her ears were bombarded with a cacophony of noise: engines grinding, whistles blowing, brakes screeching and the endless rumble of humanity – a river of people flowing towards the exit or breaking through to platforms to find their trains. Sally began to think she might have misjudged Crewe as just a town 'up north'. The station, at least, seemed to be the centre of the universe!

She joined the other passengers and was swept along to the exit and out to the taxi rank, where things were much calmer and quieter, thank goodness. She hailed a taxi and asked for the theatre.

'Is it far?' she enquired, hoping the answer would be negative as her finances were tight to say the least.

'No, lass, just up the hill. Hop in. You working there?' asked the cab driver, looking at her in his driving mirror as she sat back in the seat.

'I hope to be, yes,' Sally replied shyly. 'I have got an audition today, as a matter of fact. So – fingers crossed.'

'Well, good luck to you, lass. You will do just fine.'

No more than five minutes later, the taxi slowed and stopped outside a beautiful Victorian theatre. It shone like a beacon to Sally. No matter the street was a little shabby, and next door there was a very run-down Chinese takeaway, to Sally it was the gateway to all her dreams. She paid the driver and thanked him for his good wishes, then got out and turned to the front doors. Putting down her suitcase, she pulled on the handle, only to discover that it was locked. She pressed her nose to the glass, shielding her eyes with her hand to peer into the darkness. There were no signs of life.

'Great,' sighed Sally. 'Now what?'

She looked up the street and was greeted by grey stone terraced houses, and a stray dog checking out a lamp-post. Stepping back from the entrance, she told herself, 'There has to be a stage door round the back somewhere.' Sure enough, she spotted an opening at the end of the front of the theatre building, so picking up her things, she set off to investigate. The gap proved to be a narrow alleyway, and halfway down was a battered sign hanging from the wall: *Stage Door*.

With a sigh of relief Sally pushed open the door and stepped into a dimly lit corridor. She ventured further in, expecting to meet a stage doorman – or woman, for that matter.

'Hello? Anybody around?' she called out. There was a small kiosk with a sliding glass window and an empty chair. It was lit by a table lamp with a red silk shade which had long since seen better days in someone's boudoir. Sally thought it looked very incongruous, stuck in this little corner. A two-bar electric fire was glowing gaily and piles of newspapers lay on the floor – but nobody was there to answer her call.

She followed her nose, and then the sign in big red letters painted on the wall leading down the stairs: *to The Stage. Silence!*

The staircase wound round and down, and at the bottom there was a heavy wooden door. Sally pulled on the handle, opened it and stepped into the almost-darkness onstage. She could just make out a dim light in the far corner, presumably from the prompt corner. She tiptoed towards it, keeping an ear out for any sounds of life. She caught the odd word from someone whispering somewhere nearby ... but could not quite make out who was talking. She moved between two black curtains and found herself right out on the stage. Suddenly a light hit her between the eyes like a laser, and she was completely blinded for a few seconds.

'Sorry, sorry,' she called out. 'Is there someone there? My name is Sally Thomas and I have come for an audition. Please take the light off me as I can't see a thing!' She moved towards the front of the stage, trying to get out of the spotlight, and peered out into the auditorium – but could see nothing because she still had spots in front of her eyes.

Then, as her vision slowly adjusted, she felt a presence up to her left – and there in the box, she could make out a figure standing just inside the doorway. There was a red glow burning in the dark and the faint hint of cigar tobacco – but before she could speak, a voice filled the theatre with liquid gold. Sally had never heard such an incredible voice.

'Sorry, young lady. Didn't mean to frighten you. We have trouble with the lighting board. Who did you say you were again?'

'Sally Thomas. Are you Giles Longfellow, by any chance?' Sally was regaining her composure and feeling ready to present herself. After all, she had come a long way for this audition and had no intention of messing it up.

'Yes, indeed I am. Eric, are you still up there?' Giles Longfellow called up to the gods, to where his lighting man was perched on a follow spot trying to adjust the bulb.

A voice wafted out from the darkness. 'Yes, guvnor. All sorted. Be down in a tick.'

'Thank you, Eric. Now, young lady, what are you going to do for me?' The man in the box leaned over the rail towards Sally and she felt she could almost reach up and touch him.

Suddenly, all the house-lights came on and the full beauty of the theatre revealed itself. It was like a wedding cake of pink and white stucco. The red plush seats and the gleaming brass rails set off the intricate plasterwork on the walls and the boxes, rising to a ceiling that was covered in cherubs and flowers. A huge crystal chandelier sent shafts of light down onto the seats below like rays of sunshine piercing a dark forest.

Sally gasped and looked back up to the box, from whence came Giles's richly mellow voice again: 'Young lady, did you hear me? You look like a frightened rabbit.' He stepped back and sat down.

Sally gave him her full attention at once and announced with as much aplomb as she could muster, 'I would like to do

Portia's speech from *The Merchant of Venice*: "The quality of mercy is not strained . . ."'

'Very well, continue.'

The girl walked to the centre of the stage and took a deep breath. This was the moment she had trained for and lived for. Her first proper audition for the professional theatre.

Sally had left drama school six months ago, and had spent the intervening time writing to dozens of repertory theatres throughout the country. Some responded but most never did. It had proved very disheartening in the main, but Sally was determined and driven, and was not going to give up easily. She had managed to get a job at the British Drama League in Fitzroy Square, London. It was an extraordinary place, a cross between a library and advice centre for foreign students, offering drama courses and training for stage management. It also had offices for various departments in theatre, from the technical staff to visiting directors, and was a popular venue for theatres to hold auditions. Sally manned the ancient telephone switchboard, which was like a puzzle for wiring aficionados. Each line had a connection, but oh! – how often did she put the wrong plug in the wrong hole!

'Bear with me, caller,' was her cri de coeur all day long. 'I am so sorry, sir, you have been disconnected.'

By the end of a busy day, Sally would be distraught – but her boss, a lovely man called James Langton, was ever ready to offer her encouragement. James had always been associated with the theatre in some way. Sally was never sure if he had been an actor himself, years ago. He certainly had theatricality about him – and great charm. James ran the Drama League like an historic institution and had taken Sally and another young actor, Jeremy Sinclair, under his wing. Every time a theatre booked the rehearsal rooms to hold auditions, he would ring down and inform them both. This meant that the two actors could ensure that at some point, they were able to insinuate themselves into a position to get an audition.

Sally used to wait until the director had seen everybody, and then she would appear at the door and announce that – what a coincidence! She was an actress and not a telephone operator, after all, and would they please let her audition? Most of the time it worked a treat, but so far she had not managed to get a job. Then one afternoon Mr Langton had come down to her little booth and informed her that Crewe Theatre would soon be holding auditions for its new season, starting in September, and that she should write or phone. Sally wasted no time: she immediately rang the theatre and was told that the director, Giles Longfellow, would indeed be coming down to London to the BDL to hold auditions, but if she was able to come up to Crewe before then, he would be delighted to see her 'in situ' as it were. Seizing this opportunity to get in early, she made an appointment for the following week.

Now here she was, standing on the stage at Crewe, launching into her audition piece with gusto.

Halfway through, however, Giles Longfellow called down from the box, 'Thank you, my dear, that will do. Can you sing?'

Sally was completely thrown by this question. Not because she couldn't sing, but because he had not let her finish her speech. She stammered a, 'Y-yes, I can.'

'Then away you go,' came the response from above.

Sally sang the Victorian music-hall song called 'The Boy I Love', made famous by the great Marie Lloyd. It was a good choice as she could sing it unaccompanied. Her strong, clear soprano voice filled the auditorium with the sweet, affecting melody, and was rewarded by a handclap from the director.

'Well done! Delightful. Stay there – I am coming down.' And Giles disappeared.

Sally admired yet again the elegance of the box and noted that there was a coat of arms on the front. The Royal Box – how very appropriate for the flamboyant Giles Longfellow, she decided. Maybe one day *she* would be singing to Royalty in the box! Her daydreams were interrupted by the arrival of the Director.

'You did well, my dear, and I am very pleased to say I think we can offer you a place in our company next season. You are not experienced enough to play leads, but depending on how well you adapt, and how hard you work, I can certainly promise you some decent roles – and thanks to your fine singing voice I see you in some of our musical productions. It does mean you will have to accept some stage-management work, but at least you will get your forty-two weeks in the theatre, which will make you eligible for your full Equity card. Do you have an agent, by the way?'

Sally had not managed to attract the attention of an agent so far, but she had discussed this with Mr Langton and he had offered to advise her, should the need arise, on the financial side of things. So bearing this in mind, she replied, 'No, but I have a manager called James Langton and he has said he will deal with the fee, if that is convenient to you, sir.'

'James Langton as in the British Drama League?' Giles looked amused.

'Um, yes. Do you know him?' asked Sally.

'Absolutely, my dear! We are old friends. But what is his interest in you, may I ask?'

Sally was not sure which way this conversation should be going, but decided that honesty was the best policy.

'I work in reception at the BDL,' she explained, 'and Mr

Langton very kindly helps me find auditions, et cetera, while I am working there. He has been so supportive, and told me that any time I needed advice, he would help me. So I just thought to mention him to you with respect of salary or whatever. I hope that is all right?'

'Of course, no problem at all. I will talk to him asap. Thank you for coming all this way, dear, and I look forward to welcoming you to the new company in September.'

'Oh, thank you so much, Mr Longfellow, I am thrilled to be working for you and I—'

But he had gone. Disappeared like a magician, without the puff of smoke, although the smell of his cigar drifted across the footlights like a longlost memory. Sally's heart was thumping. She had her first job! Going to the footlights, she took in the auditorium one last time from top to bottom. She loved it! And then she looked up to the Royal Box – and blew a kiss.

Chapter 2

Giles Longfellow was ambitious, but he was also weak. He had talent, but lacked the iron will to pursue his dreams to their ultimate conclusion. All his life he had been led by his heart – well, his nether regions, to be absolutely blunt. He would fall wildly in love and indulge every emotional level of his intellect and physical need. This would last for months, or sometimes only weeks, but it drained him of all his energy and left him reeling. In his youth it had cost him a promising career as an actor because he would lose all interest in a job if the mood for love took him over, and employers soon realized he was a liability. Not only because his stagecraft suffered as his concentration wavered, but on one particular occasion his pursuit of happiness with one individual had led to accusations of rape and he had only just escaped jail.

James Langton was remembering the incident now. He and Giles did not know each other that well, but had agreed to meet after James had rung Giles's secretary to discuss Sally Thomas's contract for the upcoming season.

'You went through a very bad patch a few years back, I

seem to recall,' mused James over a very fine dinner at the Garrick Club.

'Oh God, yes, it was a pretty close thing, but I was bailed out by the lovely Lord Graham. We have been friends ever since.' Giles did not add that they were also lovers, on and off. After the police arrested Giles for indecently assaulting a young man, Lord Edward (Teddie) Graham had stepped in and paid off the boy and his parents and pulled strings with the Commissioner of Police. He and Giles had then had an affair, but unlike most of Giles's romantic attachments it had not fizzled out or ended dramatically, but every now and then had renewed itself.

Lord Graham was married to money and had managed to father three children, most importantly an heir and a spare, as they said in those rarefied social circles. This secured the marriage, and the family seat, which was a beautiful hundred-room stately home in Cheshire. Teddie was able, in the main, to keep his preferences under wraps, but when the need arose he would stay down in London at his club and seek out Giles Longfellow, who after his run-in with the authorities had also had to keep himself in check. Both men enjoyed each other's company and although it was hardly a relationship based on passion it served them both well.

Giles finally started to focus on his career as a director and was offered the post at Crewe five years ago. Edward Graham's country pile was just up the road so it seemed the perfect post – for the time being, at any rate. As he became more confident as a director, thanks to his work at Crewe, so Giles's ambition returned. This season he wanted to make his mark, and head for the West End and perhaps a post with the Royal Shakespeare Company. He had proven himself with several productions at Crewe, and surprisingly, run the financial side at a profit with the help of an Arts Council grant. However, in order to achieve the kind of production that would turn heads in his direction, he was going to need extra cash to lure some exciting talent up to Crewe. Lord Graham was his golden ticket. Teddie had become a patron of the arts, in particular of Crewe Theatre, and had pledged financial support to Giles for his new season. So, Giles was down in London to court a young actor called Rupert Hallam, who was making waves in theatrical circles, to persuade him to come to Crewe to do *Hamlet*. The rest of the cast would soon fall into place if Giles secured the young man. God knows, there were enough actors to choose from, and he had already chosen Sally Thomas.

'I liked her because she showed pluck coming all the way to see me. She gave a consummate performance, maybe not glittering, but she has a good singing voice and I need that in the company, as I am hoping to do two or three music-based productions: a revival of *The Boyfriend*, a Victorian music-hall show, and of course, a pantomime at Christmas. I have told the girl that she will have to do some stage management at first until I can really see her strengths, but I promised her she would get her chance. And, of course, she would be official understudy too.' Giles took a sip of very expensive Bordeaux. As James was paying the bill, he had offered to choose the wine!

James couldn't hide his pride and delight for his protége.

'Oh, believe me she is thrilled, and quite understands the situation. I am very grateful to you, Giles. Actually I have another young actor I would be very pleased if you could audition and give me your thoughts. His name is Jeremy Sinclair and he works for me part-time in the reference library.' James refilled Giles Longfellow's glass.

Giles regarded the other man for a few moments and then said, 'Is it love, James?'

James Langton blushed deeply and spluttered, 'Good God, no! I am not like that, you know I am not. Whatever gave you that idea? I have a wife and I am a respectable married man. Giles, you are outrageous to suggest such a thing.'

Giles burst out laughing. 'All right, calm down, for goodness sake, man. It was just a thought. You don't have to hide things from someone like me . . . ' but James interrupted him.

'Please, stop this at once. I will not tolerate such accusations. I try to help some young actors, male *and* female, because it is such a tough profession, and I see them every day at the Drama League struggling to survive. My interest is purely artistic patronage, if you will, nothing more.'

'Fine, we will leave it at that, and I apologize if I have offended you, James. Now drink up, and let's order another bottle and you can give me some suggestions for a drama.'

Later that evening, James let himself into his neat, suburban terraced house in Finchley. He crept into his tiny study, closing the door behind him, and opened the bottle of brandy on the sideboard. He poured himself a large one and went to sit in his favourite armchair. Taking a generous sip of the golden nectar, he closed his eyes and daydreamed of young buttocks in rugby shorts. Jeremy was a beautiful specimen he had to admit. If only . . .

Sally could hardly contain her excitement when she turned up for work at the British Drama League on Monday morning. She was the first to arrive after Geordie, the caretaker, who could be heard in the kitchen at the back of the building whistling a Beatles tune. She called out to him, 'Geordie, did you pick up the post?' She switched on the light in the hallway as it was always dark. The combination of Victorian tiles and dark green paint made the whole place very depressing, and a tad Dickensian. Sally imagined Uriah Heep appearing in a doorway, smiling unctuously at her and rubbing his hands!

Instead, she was greeted halfway down the hall by the rather portly figure of Geordie in his russet-brown overalls and flat cap.

'Morning, miss, how are you this morning?' he asked her as he handed her the post. 'You seem right chirpy, if I may say so. Good weekend, was it?' He gave her a very theatrical wink and tapped the side of his nose. He looked so ridiculous Sally could not help bursting into laughter.

'Oh, Geordie, you really are the pits. You have such a dirty mind!'

Geordie feigned offence. 'Now, miss, please – how can you say that to me? I mean no harm, just trying to be friendly-like, that's all.' He turned and disappeared into the gloom on his way back to the kitchen to put the kettle on, for the first of the many cups of tea and coffee, consumed throughout the day by the inhabitants of number 9, Fitzroy Square.

Sally unlocked her tiny cubicle and found herself feeling quite nostalgic. No more early mornings on the number 13 bus to work. No more Geordie and his nudge nudge, wink wink greetings; from next month she would be a professional actress, working in repertory. She sat in front of her switchboard with her chin resting in her hands and dreamed of applause, and footlights, and bells ringing ... ringing bells meant ... oh Lord! She grabbed a plug and pushed it into the blinking light on the board in front of her.

'British Drama League, good morning, how may I help you?' The answer came rapidly and impatiently. 'Yes, of course. I am putting you through now.' Sally pulled out the plug and placed it in the appropriate connection. She breathed a sigh of relief as the connection was made and she could hear the recipients talking through her headphones on the desk. She had not even had time to put them on. It was going to be one of those Monday mornings, she could tell, but she did not give a hoot because life had turned a corner, and she was on her way up !

Chapter 3

Sally arrived home with her assorted bags and boxes – and promptly burst into tears in the kitchen! Her mother, Patricia, swept her into her arms, plonked her down at the table and handed her a clean white cotton hankie. No tissues for her!

'Whatever is the matter, my darling girl?' she asked.

'Oh nothing, Mum. I am just being stupid and dramatic.' Sally hesitated before blowing her nose on the virgin square of crisp cotton. 'It's just, everything is going to change and I am scared and excited all at the same time, and coming home just makes me realize how much I will miss you all.'

Sally's parents lived in Cheltenham in an old Victorian terraced house. Patricia Thomas had always yearned for one of the Georgian houses in the city, but knew it would have to remain a pipe dream. Her husband, Douglas, was a teacher and part-time collector of antiques, and unless he suddenly discovered a masterpiece in an attic somewhere, they were never going to be able to afford such a property. Patricia had studied at the Slade School of Art in Bloomsbury in the 1950s, and had actually been rather good. When she married

Douglas Thomas in 1950, she was still studying in her final year at the Slade. She had met him at one of the notorious Chelsea Art Club balls. Douglas was taking his finals in History at Oxford, but hoping to become an art teacher in one of the big public schools. He was a very confident young man veering on the arrogant, and saw teaching as a means to express himself in ways he could never have achieved as an artist, firstly because he did not have the talent, and secondly because his parents had refused to let him go to art school. Patricia thought him the handsomest man she had ever set eyes on, and as they danced the night away she fell madly, wonderfully, completely in love with him. Douglas was pleased and flattered. After all, she was very beautiful, and someone who would complement his image perfectly. The pair had spent the summer in passionate embraces, with wild parties at the Arts Club by night and picnics beside the Serpentine by day. Douglas took his young love to Oxford and showed her off to all and sundry. By the end of the summer they had announced their engagement, and life changed very dramatically for the young couple.

Douglas had secured a teaching post at Stowe – a very prestigious public school in Buckinghamshire. He had been offered a small cottage in the grounds, and the newlywed couple set up home. All hopes Patricia may have had of a life as a carefree artist floated out of the tiny latticed window of the damp cottage in which she was now a prisoner. She was alone for long hours of the day while her husband taught privileged, but mostly untalented, boys how to wield a paintbrush. For most of the class it was a period when they could play up, chat and tell dirty jokes. Douglas very soon became disenchanted with the notion of his special calling as a teacher. His power was almost non-existent, and he soon turned his frustration onto his wife. Oh, they were still madly in love, and Patricia did everything in her power to make life easy and smooth for her darling husband, but he would often be quite patronizing and cold towards her.

Slowly, over the coming years she learned to ignore his jibes about her intellect and abilities. She would laugh delightedly in front of guests as he berated her for some tiny misdemeanour or other, and he would eventually step down from his high horse and wallow in her adoration. It was a strange marriage but it somehow worked. They spent the school holidays travelling round Europe, and Patricia was in her element then, giving Douglas endless sermons on the History of Art. She became his part-time researcher, doing most of his homework for him. He would always return from one of their trips abroad full of information for his classes, and presenting the students with reams of slides and photos. He became quite renowned for his 'out of hours devotion' to duty. Obviously, Patricia had no idea just how useful she was to her husband. It was a mutually agreeable arrangement though, because Patricia loved feeling superior in some small way to her gorgeous lovely husband, who was so bright and witty. In turn, Douglas was more than happy to praise his eager young wife and accept all the teachings she threw at him while enjoying the respect and attention from his pupils and peers.

The couple had a good life in many ways, and it was a few years before the idea of children entered their togetherness. Patricia was almost ambivalent to the idea. She was quite happy playing muse, mistress and even mother to her darling husband. Douglas, however, decided the time was approaching when they should try for a family. Two years later, in 1962, Sally was born – and two years after that, her sister Dora arrived. They were both dear little girls and Douglas loved

them. In fact, he thrived, surrounded by all the female
adoration. He gained a good reputation at Stowe, and was
eventually head-hunted and moved to Cheltenham Ladies
College as Head of Department. He loved his job and revelled
in the attention from his young female students, feeling god-
like as he strode down the corridors acknowledging the
admiring looks from the girls. He also had more time to spare,
and began to collect and deal in Fine Art.

Patricia surprised herself and the family by completely falling
in love with her babies. They filled every minute of her life; she
gloried in their growth, and grasped every tiny morsel of her
daughters' love. She was a wonderful mother, and worked tirelessly to make their home a warm and welcoming place.
However, as the girls grew up and their need of her grew less,
so Patricia's own need for self-esteem returned. Douglas was, as
ever, completely self-absorbed, and although he appreciated
how lucky he was to have such a seemingly perfect family, it
never occurred to him that he should contribute anything
more to the general well-being of his wife and daughters.

Patricia yearned for another kind of self-fulfilment. There
was a part of her that felt empty and unused. She would sometimes creep away when the children were asleep, taking her
paints and easel outside, weather permitting, and she would sit
and paint her frustrations away. Other times she grabbed a
sketchbook and pencils, or charcoal, and as she watched her girls
in the garden, or playing in their front room, she would draw
them quickly and deftly, capturing precious moments. She loved
her family with all her heart, but her soul was in her art. Very
rarely did she dare to imagine what life might have been like if
she hadn't married so young and devoted her energies to her
family. She sometimes thought that Douglas was so much luck-
ier to have been born a man. He had another life outside the

family. She knew he thrived on female attention, and she sometimes allowed a moment of doubt to creep into her thoughts
when he did not come home till very late. She never questioned
him – that would have been asking for trouble – and anyway,
she didn't want to know the answer. As long as he came home
to her, and still made love to her, she was able to cope. She had
known only her husband sexually, having been a virgin when
they met. He had been a very good and practised lover. Well,
that was how it should be, in her view. Men were very different
animals – and boys would be boys, wouldn't they?

As the girls matured and Patricia had more time of her own,
she decided to look for a part-time job as a teacher. Douglas
found this highly amusing.

'Dear God, Patricia darling! What could you possibly teach
anyone? You haven't painted for fifteen years. Who would
have you, my sweet?'

Much to Patricia's delight, and Douglas's amazement, the
local council took her on to teach adult art classes. She proved
a great success, and the job gave her a whole new take on life.
She started to make new friends, and while Douglas was busy at
the college Patricia now had a social life of her own. She
ignored her husband's little digs and put-downs, and filled her
days with laughter and colour. She had hoped one of her
daughters might have inherited her artistic talents, but it was not
to be, although when Sally announced she was going to be an
actress Patricia felt a tingle of excitement. Dora, who was two
years younger and had just left school, was much more practical and had applied to do Business Studies at uni. Both girls had
the security of a stable home background which gave them a
certain amount of confidence with which to face life. Sally was
sometimes critical of her father's rather patronizing attitude to
his wife, and would encourage her mother to answer back.

'Oh, Sally dear, that is just his way. He doesn't mean anything by it. I just ignore it.'

'But, Mum, he has no right to put you down like he does.
Where would he be without you?'

Patricia would laugh her girlish laugh, toss her hair and
gaily announce: 'Oh, probably with some gorgeous woman
with lots of money!' She always tried to sound nonchalant,
but deep in her heart she had always feared the day Douglas
would announce he was leaving. Once the girls no longer
needed her attention fulltime, her sole concern was keeping
her husband happy. As she had grown older she knew that he
wanted her to be the gay young thing he had danced with all
those years ago. She kept her hair long and dyed it regularly
to keep the grey at bay. She had retained her figure and knew
she was attractive. Sometimes one of her pupils would make
an advance towards her and she would laugh it off with a
rebuke: 'Don't be so silly! I am very happily married to the
man of my dreams!' Patricia really did think that, and
Douglas had no idea just how fortunate he was to have her.

Sally always felt she was a bit of a disappointment to her
parents. Her mother was very glamorous in her way, but a bit
too girly for her liking, and certainly Sally had inherited
none of that coquettishness. She was a good cross of her
mother and father, and had strong attractive features, but she
could not be described as beautiful. Her tutors at drama
school had told her she would never play the young heroines
as she was just not pretty enough. She had initially been
upset, but commonsense had soon taken over, and Sally knew
that especially onstage, a good actress could convince an
audience that she was beautiful. It almost made her feel more
confident, knowing she did not have to rely on her looks and
would never have to worry about getting old. She would

always be able to play the interesting characters until she fell off the twig. Dora was probably better-looking than her, but that was fine. There was no jealousy between the girls, and they had always been very close. Dora managed their father brilliantly, and could put him in a good mood with a click of her fingers. While she was still living at home Dora was a good foil for him, and their mother did not have to worry about his dark moods.

Sally had been looking forward to spending time with them all over the month of August. Now here she was, feeling sorry for herself. She got up and gave her mother a hug, saying, 'I am so stupid, really. I'm just so happy to be home. Come on, let's get these boxes sorted out and then we can go and have a large glass of wine with Dad.'

The two women attacked the bags, sorting the rubbish from the washing and from the 'keep forever' memorabilia that gathers through three years of college. It was a gorgeous summer's day and all the windows were open. The sweet perfume of honeysuckle and mown grass wafted through the house, along with the call of a blackbird above the constant hum of buzzing bees. Sally was always caught unawares by the clarity of these sounds compared to London, where everything was lost in the general drumming of city noise, sliced through with the occasional siren. Here in her parents' loving home, surrounded by trees and blue sky, she revelled in a sense of complete well-being. It gave her strength.

'Come on, darling, stop daydreaming and get a move on,' her mother urged. 'It's nearly lunchtime and your dad will be expecting a visit.' She gathered all the bags ready to go and went to fetch the car keys, adding, 'We can celebrate having our daughters home for the summer.'

Chapter 4

There was a letter from Crewe Theatre waiting for Sally the next morning. It contained a digs list and a reminder that under the Esher Standard Contract issued by Equity, the actors' union, the artiste (Sally in this case) was obliged to provide an evening dress for the season, and to use her own clothes as and when required. The management was only obliged to provide period costumes.

'Oh my God!' she gasped over her boiled egg and soldiers. 'I have to wear my own clothes!'

'What do you mean?' asked Dora. 'What does the letter say?' She grabbed it from her sister and read the instructions issued therein. Then: 'My God, Sally, there isn't a play written that could possibly include your wardrobe,' she said, and burst out laughing.

'Shut up, Dora! What do you mean by that? There is nothing wrong with the way I dress, is there?'

Dora laughed even louder and Patricia came into the kitchen to find out what all the fuss was about.

'Mum, tell Sally what is wrong with her dress sense,

please. Can one even begin to describe the lack of sartorial savvy?'

'Dora, please stop cackling, it is very unbecoming. What is the problem here?'

'I have had a letter from the theatre,' explained Sally, 'telling me I have to provide my own clothes, except where period costume is required – *and* I have to take an evening dress. I don't own a dress, never mind an evening one!' she wailed.

'Oh dear,' sympathized her mother. 'I do see your problem. Dora, will you stop giggling! Sally dresses very individually, I will grant you, but she is not completely without taste.' This response drew further sniggers from Dora.

'Oh, do shut up, Dora!' snapped Sally. 'The joke wears thin, methinks. So what am I going to do?'

'Well, we will have to sort you out. There is a fantastic vintage clothes shop in Cheltenham, and lots of jumble sales we can rummage through. If the worst comes to the worst, Dora can make you an evening dress, can't you, dear?' Patricia turned to her youngest daughter. 'Let's make a list of useful clothes you might need in a season. Do you have any idea what plays they are going to do? That would help enormously.'

Dora jumped up from the table, saying, 'Listen, sis, we can have a great time putting your wardrobe together. We will turn you into a style icon, don't you worry.'

'I don't want to be a style icon, thank you very much,' responded Sally rather grumpily. 'I am an actress.'

'We know, but there is no reason why you can't be a smartly dressed actress. Come on, let's get down the town and do a bit of shopping.'

Dora was practically out of the front door. Patricia stopped her with, 'Hold on, darling, just a moment.' She went out of the kitchen and across the hall to the study, and came back two minutes later with her purse. 'I want to give you both a little something to spend.' She handed them both some cash.

The girls protested but she went on, 'I don't often get the chance to spoil you, and now seems as good a time as ever. I actually sold a painting last month and I have another commission, so please let me share my good fortune with my beautiful daughters. And listen, if you can't find an evening dress, Sally, get a pattern and Dora and I will make it for you. Dora knows where to buy gorgeous material, don't you, darling?'

'Oh yes, absolutely. Thank you so much, Mum, this is fantastic of you. Oh my God, I am so excited. Shopping – and with some money for a change.' And she was off once more towards the front door.

Sally picked up her bag and started to follow, then stopped and gave her mother a big hug. 'Thank you so much for this. I will make you proud.'

'Go on, you have made me proud already.' Patricia kissed her and shooed her off, 'Now get going or your sister will grab all the best buys first.'

The girls made straight for the vintage clothes shop. Dora knew the owner, Jackie, who was the mother of a girl she had been at school with. Jackie was very interested to hear all about Sally's job and the theatre.

'Please take my number in case you need anything later in the season,' she said to Sally. 'Maybe the wardrobe department at Crewe will be interested in some of my stock. Do you know what plays you are doing yet?'

'No, not yet, but I can certainly let you know,' said Sally.

Dora was already going through the rail of dresses. 'Ooh, look. This is beautiful, Sal, and would really suit you. Come on, try it on.'

The girls spent the best part of half an hour trying on dresses until poor Sally was bug-eyed.

'I can't remember what I have tried on!' she cried. 'It is exhausting.'

Dora had narrowed the choice down to two dresses. One was a 1950s satin dress, very fitted at the waist with a low neckline and off the shoulder. The other was a simple satin dress cut on the bias, so very flattering for the figure, and rather sexy. It was black.

'This one needs some sparkly jewellery to set it off,' announced Dora, holding the black satin up.

'I have no idea which one to choose,' sighed Sally, who had really had enough and was thinking about a glass of wine and some shepherd's pie in the pub.

Jackie suggested they took both.

Well,' agreed Dora, 'that is the obvious answer, but I don't think the budget will stretch that far.'

Jackie checked the tickets on both dresses and said, 'Look, why don't you buy the satin one and I will give you a twenty-five per cent discount? And I will let you have the other dress on loan, so take it up to Crewe with you, and if you decide you can use it, we will re-negotiate.'

'Oh, that would be fantastic,' said Sally. 'If you are really sure?' And when Jackie nodded her assent: 'Thank you *so* much. Actually, it could be very useful for Crewe because we might well need some period stuff and we could liaise with you. That is brilliant, Jackie.'

The girls were on a high as they left the shop and danced down the street.

'How amazing is that?' said Dora. 'Come on, we will celebrate with a quick glass of wine in the wine bar, then onto more mundane attire like trousers and tops. I want to take you to this terrific boutique that has opened recently. They have really unusual stuff and it is cheap.' With that she was off across the street, skipping towards the wine bar, followed by an equally excited Sally clutching her bag of goodies in her hands.

By the end of the day, the sisters returned home worn out. They flopped down on the sofa surrounded by bags. Patricia made them a cup of tea and then sat down and waited for the fashion parade to begin.

Dora took charge and explained about the two evening dresses. Much against her will, Sally made one last effort and modelled them for her mother.

'Oh yes, girls, you have done well. They are both beautiful and so different. I remember having a dress like this for one of the Chelsea Arts balls,' Patricia said softly, remembering the joy of dancing all night and feeling so beautiful in her dress. 'The fifties one is gorgeous, Sally, and has a very flattering neckline because it shows off one's shoulders as well as a bit of bosom.'

Sally laughed at her mother's rather coy choice of word for the old cleavage.

'Bosom? Oh, Mother, that is so ladylike!' she chortled.

'Well, I suppose it is, but it was what we called it in my day. Now the black dress is very sexy, isn't it? Let's hope the theatre does some Noël Coward and then you will have the perfect outfit. It needs some jewellery though, doesn't it?'

Dora chipped in, 'Exactly what I said, so we should go jumble-sale hunting on Saturday and pick up a bit of sparkle.'

'Good idea,' agreed Patricia. 'Now show me what else you have bought, please.'

Sally was secretly thrilled that her sister had sorted out her wardrobe for her. She knew she had no real flair and was not at all interested in fashion. She lived in a couple of pairs of trousers, a few shirts and jumpers, and a standard navy jacket for every occasion. Dora had found her some great-fitting jeans, and some lovely suede boots to go with them. 'But also handy when it gets cold with some thick tights and a short skirt,' Dora had suggested.

There was a very useful three-quarter-length wool jacket which looked great over T-shirts, and also a couple of long tops which just covered the bum, and were simple yet attractive. Dora was able to mix and match and put several outfits together for Sally with ease.

'I don't know how you are able to see these things so easily,' remarked Sally. 'Thank you, Dora, you really have been an enormous help.'

Dora turned to face her, and said in a deliberately casual tone: 'Sally, I was thinking that maybe I could see if there was a job going in the wardrobe at Crewe. I would really love to come and learn all about costumes and design. I have already applied for uni next autumn to do Business Studies, and rather than take a gap year it would be great to actually earn some money and learn other stuff, you know? Who can tell: I may even decide to be a designer instead of an entrepreneur. Shall I telephone and see what the state of play is, do you think?' Dora sighed happily. 'It would just be so great if we could work together, and get a flat or something, wouldn't it?'

Sally felt a flicker of guilt. It *would* be lovely to have Dora with her – but then again, there was a part of her that wanted to have this adventure by herself. It was her first real job and there would be so much to learn. She wanted it to be her experience, her own personal journey. Dora was so different from her. She was extrovert and outgoing and up for anything. Sally sometimes felt outshone by her sister's joie de vivre. But that was so selfish of her. How mealy-mouthed can I be? she rebuked herself.

'Yes,' she replied aloud. 'Why not ring them and see what they say.'

As it happened, things worked out rather well. Giles Longfellow's PA, Susan Chambers, explained to Dora that there was a resident wardrobe mistress called Mrs Enid Weaver who lived locally in Crewe. However, Giles had decided that he needed someone younger for this season, so he had hired a lady called Gwendoline Stewart who would do most of the work while Enid would come in twice a week to supervise. It would have been very difficult for Giles to sack Enid as she was a stalwart of the theatre, so he was treading very softly. It had been suggested that for the beginning of the season, things should be left to Enid and Gwendoline to organize, and then perhaps a few weeks later there might be a vacancy for an assistant. Would it be possible for Dora to hang on and join later?

Dora was thrilled, and as far as Sally was concerned, it was perfect because it gave her a chance to establish herself in the company and find her feet. She would be able to sort out her living arrangements with an eye to being able to offer Dora a home there eventually. But it would be *her* place. She needed to feel secure in herself, and her work, before her sister came and joined her. This way it was her territory.

Sally had thought hard about all this, and decided it was natural to feel territorial. She and Dora were very close and rarely argued, but they had never lived together since school, and certainly never worked together in such a closed environment. Sally knew from her drama-school days just how insular actors could be. They were very cliquey, and could make outsiders feel very uncomfortable. She would obviously ensure that Dora did *not* feel like an outsider – but she could only do that successfully if she was in control of her own surroundings. By the time Dora arrived, Sally hoped, she would be Queen of all she surveyed . . .

Chapter 5

Sally was determined to catch up with her best friend from school while she was at home. Muriel McKinney was a teacher in a school for handicapped children, and Sally admired her enormously. She was a rare and special person. The response to her telephone call was immediate and excited.

'Sally! How fantastic to hear your voice. Where are you? How are you?' Muriel screamed down the phone.

Sally couldn't help laughing. 'God, Muriel, that voice could launch a thousand tugs! I am home for two or three weeks so we have to have a catch-up. When is a good time for you?'

'Oh, there is so much to talk about. I am getting married in December,' her friend announced out of the blue.

'Well, that has shut me up for a start. Married? How long have you known the guy? You haven't mentioned him to me.' Sally was taken aback. It only seemed like a few weeks ago that she had been talking to Muriel and discussing a girls' night out.

'Sally, you are hopeless! We have not spoken for months. I feel terrible that I have not been in touch to keep you posted, but you know what it's like with work and everything. His name is Dave and he is a folk singer with a band. In fact, he is doing a gig on Saturday night at the Hen and Chickens – remember where we always used to go? Well, he will be there doing his bit, so why not come with me and Mack. You remember Mack, don't you?' she teased.

'Oh please, come on. How *is* your hunky brother?' Sally recalled how she had always been a little flustered around her friend's big brother. Mack had seemed very moody and mysterious to a young girl like Sally. She could picture him now with his incredibly blue eyes smiling down at her.

'Doing really well. He is a successful photographer and sculptor. I know he would love to see you, Sal. Shall we meet up at the pub at seven on Saturday then, and you can vet my beloved. Not that I will listen to a bad word against him!' Muriel said happily.

'Great. I will see you there. It is so lovely to hear your voice, my dear friend. Bye!' Sally replaced the receiver, beaming with well-being. Life was good.

The rest of the week passed all too quickly as Sally put her house in order. She arranged with Douglas to drive up to Crewe on Sunday morning.

'Is that a good idea?' ventured Dora. 'We are all going out on Saturday night, don't forget. Do you want to be looking for digs with a hangover?'

'Mmmm. You have a point, sister dear. But I don't think I will have any choice. Dad won't want to spend a weekday up there, will he? I will just have to practise self-control.'

In fact, Saturday night proved very jolly, and not at all as raucous as it might have been. Dora didn't join them at the pub in the end as she decided to go to the movies with an old friend. (Or a new beau, if the truth be known!) So Sally met

Muriel and Dave and the lovely Mack in the Hen and Chickens by herself. It was strange to be back on her old turf having a night out like normal folk. Sally always distinguished people who were not in the acting profession as normal. Actors were a breed apart, and a group of them together was like a flock of starlings continually screeching and pecking and jostling for position. Sitting in the pub that Saturday night was pleasantly soothing, and Sally felt very relaxed. Mack was good fun and very attentive. It almost felt like a date.

'So, what do you think of Dave?' Mack asked when Muriel had gone to the cloakroom.

'He seems very nice,' Sally replied truthfully. 'Why do you ask? And Muriel seems very happy.'

'Well, he *is* my future brother-in-law, so I have a vested interest in the success of the romance.' Mack got up to go to the bar. 'Another cider?'

'Yes, please.' Sally passed him her glass and watched him lope off to get the drinks. He really was very attractive – and such a lovely man, she thought to herself. How good would it be to find someone like him to share things with? But she knew it was pointless even considering a relationship while she was pursuing her goals in the theatre. She was going to need every ounce of concentration to do a play every two weeks, and work on the stage management team. At drama school they had had a few classes on stage management, but nothing much. The biggest challenge had been to build a set to scale with all the scenery and furniture. It was fun, but no one took it very seriously. Certainly Sally herself had never expected in a million years that she would be employed as an Assistant Stage Manager, for goodness sake! Like most actors her ego was sufficiently healthy that she had assumed she would be playing roles, not making props.

'Penny for them?' Mack startled her as he sat down and put the drinks on the table.

'Oh blimey, you gave me a fright. I was miles away,' Sally told him.

'In sunny Crewe, by any chance?' he asked.

'Yes, as a matter of fact. How did you guess?' Sally asked, taking a sip of her cider.

'Well, I do know you a little bit, Miss Thomas, and as I recall you are a very committed young lady. Therefore I would imagine that you are already trying to work out what it is all going to be like up there.'

Sally grinned sheepishly. 'Well, yes, I am a bit distracted. Sorry, but it is all rather scary.'

'Of course it is, but you will be great. By the way, have you got a spare hour next week for me to do a photo and a piece about you? The local rag is very keen to support their first true celebrity.'

'Oh, please don't embarrass me!' laughed Sally. 'I am hardly anything near that status. But I would love to do the article with you. Thank you for putting it together.'

Their conversation was halted by the opening number of the band and Dave's voice filling the room. He was rather good actually, and Sally looked round to see where Muriel had got to. She spotted her at the front of the stage, joining in the chorus with great gusto.

By the end of the evening, Sally was singing along to 'Come On, Irene' the big hit by Dexy's Midnight Runners. It was the perfect end to a great night. They all ended up in the local Indian and then Mack offered to walk her home.

'Shall I ring you Monday, to set up our photo opportunity?' he asked as they reached Sally's front door.

'Yes, that's fine, but could you make it at the end of the afternoon because we might not be back from Crewe?'

'Sure thing. Maybe we could go and get something to eat afterwards if you fancied it?'

Sally was suddenly very aware of Mack's lips. They seemed very kissable. How much did she want him to kiss her? Before she could answer that question, Mack had pulled her to him and was giving her the answer. He tasted so good despite the curry and beer.

She returned his kiss with more passion than she had intended. Finally they broke apart.

'That was very unexpected,' said Sally breathlessly.

'Not for me. I have been longing to do that all night, Miss Thomas. However, I know you have to get up early so I won't detain you. I look forward to Monday.' He winked, then turned and walked away, leaving Sally in a bit of a tizz.

She let herself into the house, went to the kitchen to make a cup of tea and sat at the table there to gather her thoughts. Why did this have to happen now, on the eve of her big adventure? Here she was, going off into the unknown to seek her fortune – and all she could think about was her next date with Mack. Maybe it was because he seemed so solid and secure and she was feeling the exact opposite. Sitting here now in the family kitchen, surrounded by all the familiar objects from her childhood, the girl was aware of just how much her life was about to change – and she had little choice in which way it would turn.

'What will be will be,' she sighed, as she switched off the lights and tiptoed up to bed. Roll on tomorrow – and let the play begin!

Sally was up early on Sunday morning and doing breakfast for everyone when her father appeared in the kitchen doorway.

'That's what I like to see,' he said, 'enthusiasm. Good on

you, girl. We will get you sorted you out in no time.' He sat down and tucked into the eggs and bacon Sally had placed in front of him.

'Is Dora awake?' she asked. 'I wasn't sure whether she was going to come with us or not today.'

Before Douglas could answer, Dora herself came bounding down the stairs, saying, 'Course I am coming with you. I wouldn't miss it for the world. Ooh, breakfast! Did you make me some, Sally?'

Sally smiled and presented her sister with a plate of eggs and bacon.

'Oh, great! You really do cook the best "full English" in the world. If you don't make it as an actress you could always open a café.'

'Hmm, it's good to know I have a talent for something,' replied Sally, finishing her mug of tea and clearing up the pans. 'Where's Mother this morning? Is she still in bed?'

'Good Lord no,' snorted Douglas. 'She has gone off to teach a water-colour class. She sent her love, wishes us luck and says she will see us back at the ranch. Come on then, girls, we had better get a move on or we won't make it up to Crewe before lunch.' He swiped his plate with a piece of bread, devoured it hungrily and then placed the plate in the sink. 'Delicious. Thanks, Sally. See you outside.'

The girls rushed round doing the final clear-up in the kitchen, and Sally made sure she had all her addresses and phone numbers, and the maps and sheets of theatrical info she had been sent, and then they were off.

It was still early so the roads were clear, and by ten o'clock they were bowling up the M6 making good headway. It only took them about two and half hours and by ten thirty they found themselves outside the theatre.

Thank God the sun is shining, thought Sally because Crewe was certainly not the most welcoming town on a Sunday morning. The street was deserted and the theatre looked very shut, although Susan had assured her when she had rung that the stage door was always open from 10 a.m. until 5 p.m. every day.

'Let's go round to the stage door,' Sally suggested. 'You can leave the car here, Dad. Come on.'

Dora and Douglas followed Sally down the alleyway at the side of the theatre. The big red sign was still there, pointing into the doorway, and Sally pulled on the handle, relieved as it opened.

'Hello! Anybody around?' she called out.

'Hello, dearie, you must be Sally Thomas. Susan said you were coming today. Welcome.' The greeting came from a cheery, round-faced lady who filled the entire cubicle that was the stage-door entrance. 'Lovely to meet you, pet. I am Mrs Edge – Gladys – and I am mostly front of house but I fill in – you know, when needed. We all muck in here.'

Sally took her hand and shook it, saying, 'Lovely to meet you too, Gladys. This is my sister Dora and my father Douglas.'

There was no room to shake hands so Sally backed up to the outside door and let Gladys come out to them.

'Now, dearie, have you got a list?' Gladys went on. 'I can give you some recommendations if you like, but the trouble is, most of the good stuff has gone. We have a couple of leading actors who come back every year, you see, and obviously they take the same places each time. Let's look at your list.'

Sally handed her the digs list which she had marked up herself with possible addresses near the theatre. Gladys peered at it.

'Well now, I can tell you straight away, luv, none of these are

any good because they are either taken or no longer available.'
She looked up and saw Sally's face drop. 'No, don't despair.
'Cos I knew you was coming, I have had a ring round, and
there are a couple of "possibles". Would you like a flat eventually, do you think? Because there is a very nice
two-bedroom up near the station. It's only fifteen minutes'
walk away, and the lady who owns it is very decent and won't
overcharge, and she prefers females. She has got someone until
October, but if we can get you in a room until then that
would suit, wouldn't it, dearie?'

'That would suit perfectly, Gladys. You see, my sister Dora
here is hoping to come and join me in October, so it couldn't
be better.'

'Can we go and see it now though, do you think?' chimed
in Dora, who was hovering excitedly.

'Well, I can ring her and see,' said Gladys. 'I have also got
the number for a room in a house in the next road. I don't
know the people, but you could go and see it now while I sort
out the flat.'

'Sounds like a plan,' joined in Douglas. 'But before we set
off, do you think I could use a toilet, Gladys? It has been a
long drive this morning.'

'Of course, dearie. Silly me, I should have offered you the
convenience sooner. Go in and follow the passage down and
round the corner. Do you girls want the Ladies?' Sally decided
she had better go in case the opportunity did not arise again,
and left Dora to Mrs Edge's administrations. By the time she
returned, Dora seemed to have the whole plan down pat.

'Right. The landlady of the flat can see us this afternoon
about two, and the room round the corner is available to see
now – so shall we do that, and then go and have a coffee or
something and look round the town?'

'Absolutely. Thanks so much, Gladys, for your help. What is the address again?'

'Number 2, Stanley Terrace – it's the next road on the left and the lady's name is Mrs Blacklock. I have no idea what it's like, mind. But if it doesn't suit, come back here. I have got one more suggestion up me sleeve.' She winked and went back to her guard duty.

The Thomases set off for Stanley Terrace.

'You can see this used to be a miners' town, can't you?' remarked Douglas. 'Rows and rows of back-to-backs. It is a unique landscape to Britain and completely different from the south, eh?'

Sally was feeling a little apprehensive. These houses were so tiny. They could only be two up two down, and the thought of sharing with complete strangers was daunting.

They found number 2 and knocked on the front door.

A dog barked, and a second later the door opened and a short bald man stood filling the narrow doorway.

'Aye?' was all he said.

'Oh hi, I am Sally Thomas. I believe Gladys at the theatre called you about me coming to look at a room here? I hope this is not an inconvenient time or anything. I mean, we can come back later if . . . ' Sally was rapidly running out of steam as she met the relentless grimace of the man, and now behind him a huge Alsatian dog was panting eagerly. Sally was not awfully sure if it was panting with delight or hunger!

'Oh, right. Aye, the wife said. She deals with all that. Come in, luv. Get back, Fred, out the road. Nora, come here.' He stood back to let Sally in, and she tentatively squeezed between the doorjamb, and Fred's dribbling jaws, into the front parlour. Dora followed with no qualms at all, and Douglas was left on the doorstep neither in nor out.

'How do you do. I am Douglas Thomas – Sally is my daughter.' Douglas held out his hand and the bald-headed man looked confused.

'Eh, we don't stand on ceremony here. Come in and sit thissen down. I am Arthur Blacklock. Fred – out to the back wi' thee.' He shoved the drooling dog through the parlour and out of a door on the other side of the room. Douglas inched his way into the room and joined his daughters on the hearth-rug. They could just about all fit in the room. There was an open fire made up ready to go, and two huge chairs either side covered in an array of antimacassars. In the far corner under a 1950s standard lamp was a folding table with two chairs and a bowl of plastic flowers on top. The door leading to the kitchen was shut to keep Fred out, so it was very dark in the room, and the three of them could hardly make out Nora as she appeared at the bottom of the stairs to greet them.

'Goodness, what a crowd! We have not seen the like of so many people in here since me mam's wake.' She laughed. 'I shall put the kettle on and we can have a chat. Which one of you is the young lady who wants the room?'

'Oh, that's me,' said Sally, holding out her hand. 'Pleased to meet you, Mrs Blacklock. This is my father Douglas Thomas, and this is my sister Dora. I am sorry, we didn't mean to invade you like this on a Sunday morning, but I am very keen to find somewhere to stay before the season starts.'

'No worries at all. Why don't you sit down where you can and I will get some tea. Arthur, where have you got to? Get the kettle on, will you?' She opened the door to the kitchen and Sally could see through to a back yard, where Arthur was sitting with Fred smoking a cigarette.

'Oh, you are useless! Stay out the road then and let me get on with it.' Nora went to the sink and filled a kettle. There was an old-fashioned range affair for the cooker, red tiles on the floor and a fine example of a Victorian kitchen sink. Sally felt as if she was in a chapter of a D.H. Lawrence novel. Any minute now, a swarthy miner would appear and start to wash himself at the window. She should be so lucky! Thinking about baths though, where the hell was the bathroom here? And indeed, was there even one?

'Um, Mrs Blacklock, before you go to all the trouble of making tea, would you like to show me the room? I don't have much time today as my father has to get back to Cheltenham, so if we could see the room that would be great,' she said politely.

'Oh yes, of course, my dear. How stupid of me. Well, follow me then. It is not much, I grant you, but it is clean, and I am happy to cook you an evening meal as well as breakfast.' The kindly woman made her way back to the stairs and up they went to a tiny landing, off which were three doors.

Mrs Blacklock threw open the far door with a flourish to reveal what could only be described as a large cupboard. There was the tiniest of windows, letting in a glimmer of hope for the inhabitant who would be sat literally under the window-ledge on the single bed pushed up against the wall. On the other side there was just room to squeeze between a pine wardrobe with no handle, and a bedside table only big enough to hold a single lamp. Sally's heart sank. It was everything she had dreaded and more.

'Is there a bathroom?' she whispered.

'Oh yes, though we would have to organize when you had a bath because of the water-heater. Would twice a week suit, do you think?' The lady of the house was now standing in the middle of a piece of cracked lino beside a free-standing tin bath wedged against a basin, barely clinging to the brackets that held it to the wall. 'The toilet is downstairs in the back yard. We keep meaning to get round to doing something about bringing it in, but it is what we are used to really.'

Sally caught Dora's eye and had to cough to cover her near-outburst of the giggles. Could this be real?

'Um, right. Well, thank you very much, Mrs Blacklock, for showing me round. I think the best thing is for me and my family to go away and have a think, and we will get back to you this afternoon. Is that OK?'

'Yes, if you like, love.' Nora did not seemed bothered one way or the other. Dora was already out of the door, and Douglas was steering his eldest eagerly towards the light.

'Come along, Sally, we must get on,' he was waffling. 'Goodbye, Mrs Blacklock, regards to Mr Blacklock.'

As the door of number 2 closed behind them, the three of them were almost bent double with laughter, trying to put as much distance as possible between them and the house of horrors.

'Oh dear, I cannot believe what I have just witnessed,' groaned Douglas. 'What in hell's teeth was that all about, Sally? Are you seriously telling me that you actors live in these places?'

Sally and Dora were holding onto each other for support. In fact, their hysterical laughter was very nearly tears as far as Sally was concerned. Was this going to be her fate?

'Oh Dad, please don't! I don't know, do I? What on earth am I going to do?'

Chapter 6

The trio found Gladys back in the alleyway, now ensconced in her chair outside. The morning had blossomed into a perfect summer's day, with a clear blue sky and a slight breeze gently moving the August heat across the rooftops. Gladys had her skirt rolled up and was exposing quite a large amount of very white leg to the sun's rays, while negotiating a bottle of stout in one hand and a folded *Sunday People* on her lap. A small table stood to one side on which was a large plate of pie and chips.

'Back again, luvs? How was it then?' she asked.

'Not really big enough, I am afraid,' replied Sally. 'They were very nice and everything, but I wouldn't have felt comfortable sharing their home at such close quarters.'

'I understand, dearie. Those terraces can be really poky, I know. Not like down south, is it?' she added. 'When I first come up here I couldn't get me head round it either. It was like being in *Coronation Street*. I'm from Dagenham, see? Cars to coal. Met my old man on a day trip to Blackpool and ended up here. Anyway, enough about me, you'll be needing another plan.'

'We don't want to ruin your Sunday morning completely,' said Douglas, 'but if you have any other suggestions we would be very grateful.' The three of them stood in front of Gladys expectantly. She hauled herself out of the chair and waddled in through the stage door, returning almost immediately with a number on a piece of paper.

'Here you go. Ring this number and see if they can help. You know Susan, Mr Longfellow's PA?' Sally nodded her head in acknowledgement. 'Well, her niece Janie is coming to work at the theatre this season front of house, because her boyfriend is an actor, and he has got a job in the company. Can't remember his name but he seems like a nice enough lad. So anyway, Susan has got them a little house up the hill behind here. I believe it has two bedrooms, and she did say to me that they would have to rent out the other room to help with the rent. If you ring this number, it is the niece's home and you could have a word. She doesn't live in Crewe but I know they are coming down next week to move stuff in ready to start at the beginning of September. Go in and use the theatre phone now – see if you get any joy. I will eat me pie, if you don't mind, duck, before it gets cold.'

She sat down again and lifted the plate off the side table and proceeded to devour the contents.

'Oh yes, please, do carry on. Thank you so much.' Sally turned to the others. 'Shall we go and find somewhere to sit and have a drink or something and ring this number?'

'Well, you might as well do that here first, as the phone is right there,' Dora reminded her. 'Come on, give me the piece of paper.' She took it from her sister and disappeared into the gloom.

'I'll wait here,' Douglas said. 'Go on, dear.'

Dora had already dialled the number as Sally joined her.

'Give it to me,' said Sally, leaning across and grabbing the phone.

'Patience!' admonished Dora, annoyingly.

Before they could start bickering, a voice at the other end of the line answered, 'Hello? Nantwich 7451.'

'Oh hi, sorry to bother you on a Sunday morning but I have been given your number by Gladys, at the stage door of the theatre in Crewe. Are you Susan's niece, Janie, by any chance? I am so sorry – you must think me very rude.' Sally was trying to squeeze closer to the telephone while Dora was enjoying being obstructive. A small shove and Sally gained the advantage, leaving Dora no option but to get out of the way. She disguised her defeat by pretending to show enormous interest in the faded black and white photos pinned all over the back wall of the cubicle.

'No, not at all, that is fine. Yes, I am Janie Bell, Susan's niece. How may I help you, Miss . . . ?'

'Thomas – Sally Thomas. Well, I am an actress and I am starting the new season at Crewe in two weeks' time and my father has driven me up here today to try and find digs. So far it has been a bit of a disaster, but Gladys on the stage door has just suggested I might try to talk to you, as I believe you and your boyfriend are coming to join also, and have a house with a possible spare room. I would be so grateful if you might consider letting it to me.'

'Well, we haven't really got that far yet but I could talk to my bloke and my aunt, and call you back. Have you got a number?'

Sally tried not to sound too pushy. 'Well actually, I was wondering if there was any way I could see your place today, while I am here in Crewe, because we have to drive back to Cheltenham later today, and then I won't be back until we start. I am just so worried about having somewhere to stay, if you can see what I mean. It is my first job and I am a bit nervous.' Sally caught her sister making boo hoo signs and pretending to cry.

'Go away!' mouthed Sally.

There was a pause the other end of the line and then the sound of a hand being placed over the receiver. Sally held her breath. Eventually the line cleared and a new voice came on the receiving end.

'Hello, Sally? This is Susan Chambers here. I know we have talked on the phone, and corresponded, and I hope you are not having too difficult a day. Janie has just explained the situation to me and I have assured her that I think it would be quite all right for you to go and see the house. Gladys has a set of keys. Are you with anyone?' she asked.

'Yes,' replied Sally, 'my father and my sister Dora. That would be brilliant if we could. I mean, we can ring you later to discuss rent, et cetera, but if I could at least get an idea of the place it would help so much.'

'I quite understand,' the woman replied. 'Call us when you have been to see the house. Good luck.' The line went dead and Sally breathed a sigh of relief.

She then turned to Dora with, 'Why do you have to be such a pain! This is important to me. You are always so quick to take the mickey.'

'Oh, keep your hair on, sis,' retorted Dora, unbothered. 'Come on, let's get on, I am bloody starving.' They got the keys from Gladys, and the address, and set off up the hill towards the station. It was not far, and Sally's spirits rose as they turned into a well-maintained street with a row of Victorian houses. The latter were noticeably larger than the previous terrace, though not huge by any means.

'This looks more like it,' commented their father as he turned the key in the lock. They all stepped gingerly over the threshold, feeling like intruders.

'Hope there are no squatters lurking,' whispered Dora.

'Trust you to think the worst,' Sally whispered back.

'Why are you whispering, girls?' Their father's voice resounded round the room and made them both jump.

'Oh, Dad!' they shouted in unison.

He laughed and turned on the light, revealing a delightful room, simple and welcoming, with a small sofa and dining table and chairs in the corner. There was a gas fire with a new rug in front of it. Someone had cleaned it all and painted it very recently. A door led into the kitchen, which was bright and airy, containing a cooker, sink and kitchen table and chairs. Unlike the last house they had visited, this was clean and light and more spacious. In the back yard was a tub of flowers which had recently been watered.

They moved back into the living room and went up the stairs to the landing. It was similar again to the other house but this time, thank God, the door to the bathroom revealed a reasonable-sized room with bath, basin and toilet – maybe not exactly Habitat, but perfectly decent. They examined the two bedrooms and it was obvious which one was for the lodger, although it was still larger than the last disaster, and so much more pleasant.

'Oh, I could make this lovely!' exclaimed Sally. 'And there is more than enough room to sit in here at night. It would be great if I could get an old telly though.' She threw a sideways glance at her father.

'We will see what we can do,' he muttered.

'It's perfect,' agreed Dora. 'And anyway, it's only until I get here, then we will have our own flat.'

'Oh yes, of course,' said Sally. 'Once *you* arrive, everything will be just fine and dandy, won't it?'

'Stop it, you two,' ordered Douglas. 'Come on, let's go and get some lunch. It might improve your tempers.'

'So what's the plan then?' asked Dora as they made their way down to the city centre. 'We go and see our flat after lunch, and then go back to the stage door and ring Susan?'

'"Our flat"' – what are you like?' said Sally. 'Well, yes, OK, let's do that. Agreed, Dad?'

'Absolutely,' responded Douglas. 'Now for heaven's sake, let's get something to eat!'

The town centre offered them very little. There was a market square around which clung the usual suspects – Woolworths, Smiths and Boots. There was hardly a soul in sight, and not a café or restaurant to be seen. They finally found a pub up a narrow alley which boasted Sunday lunch for £1.50. Douglas went to the bar while the girls found a table. It was quite busy, and there was a darts match going on in the corner which was attracting great speculation from the regulars. A few gave the threesome a sideways glance, and a nod and a smile.

'Natives seem friendly enough,' commented Dora as she smiled back.

They ordered roast beef and Yorkshire pudding and settled back to watch the action. The landlady arrived a few minutes later with their order.

'Hey up, chuck, here's yer dinners.' They were confronted with the biggest Yorkshire puddings they had ever seen in their lives.

'Oh my goodness, that is *huge*!' gasped Sally. 'How on earth am I going to eat all that?'

'Aye, we like 'em big up here,' said the landlady proudly.

'That's fuel, that is. You get that little lot down yer, and you'll keep goin' all day. Enjoy.'

Dora was in fits of laughter as she tried to tackle the basin of batter atop her pile of beef.

'It's a like a Desperate Dan cowpat!' she squealed, as gravy oozed over the side of her plate. 'Oh help! It's going everywhere.' She managed to shove a forkful into her mouth, and was rendered speechless for the next five minutes as she worked her way through her plateful. All three of them had to concentrate hard to achieve inroads into their meals.

Finally Douglas wiped his chin and said, 'Well, I have to say that was delicious. I have never tasted Yorkshire pudding like that in my life, and the beef just melts in your mouth.'

'Absolutely,' agreed Sally. 'I won't go hungry up here, will I? Even if I can only afford one meal a week, this is all I need.'

They finished their food, complimented the chef and promised to come again. They had instructions from the landlady on how to reach the flat and set off. It was now two o'clock and Douglas was hoping to get away by four. They walked back up the hill, passing their car and the theatre. There was no sign of Gladys.

'Maybe she is having a nap inside,' said Sally. 'Let's hope she doesn't shut up shop before we get back.'

As they approached the road to the station there were a few more signs of life. A couple with a push-chair were wending their way towards the park to the right of the station entrance. A group of kids were kicking a football around, and there was a family eating hamburgers on a bench. The sounds of the station came wafting across on the breeze and Sally remembered her arrival, that hot day in July, for her audition.

'The station is enormous, you know,' she remarked to no

one in particular. 'It is very beautiful in an iron kind of way.'

Dora snorted. 'What does that mean, an iron kind of way?'

'Well, it is an amazing building almost like a cathedral, with huge iron girders like arches above the lines. It is quite famous, isn't it, Dad?' Sally turned to her father.

'Oh yes. It is a famous Victorian construction and when the railways were being built, Crewe was very much at the centre of it all. Everybody changed trains at Crewe. Now come on, girls, let's get a move on. I reckon it is this road on the left.' Douglas strode off towards a block of shops on the corner of a square at the side of the station.

Sure enough, they arrived at the door of number 7, Ridgeway Road. Next door was a shop selling all things to do with needlework.

'Oh, this could be handy for you, Dora,' said Sally.

'What do you mean?'

'Well, you will be needing supplies for your job in the wardrobe, won't you?'

Dora didn't look very convinced. 'I suppose so,' she said.

There were half a dozen shops in the parade – a newsagent's, a little tearoom at the end, an insurance office and what looked like a travel agent, and a shop selling second-hand clothes.

The door opened to the turn of the key and they made their way to the upstairs flat, having picked up the usual pile of junk mail from inside the door.

'Is someone living here at the moment?' asked Dora.

'Yes, I think so, but Gladys said they are away for the week-end so hopefully we won't find anyone at home. That would be embarrassing, wouldn't it?'

At the top of the stairs was another door which had a Yale lock. Douglas started to open it.

'Maybe we had better knock first, just to be sure there is no one here?' Sally said anxiously.

'Good idea,' answered her father and he knocked briskly. After a couple of minutes he opened the door and popped his head in, calling out, 'Is there anyone at home?'

Dora had a fit of the giggles and Sally sighed with impatience.

'Oh, do come on, Dora, you are being pathetic. What's the matter with you?'

'It's like *Goldilocks and the Three Bears*,' the girl laughed. 'We three bears are back from the picnic and someone's been sleeping in our beds!' This set her off again. Sighing, Sally left her to it and followed her father along a corridor to the end where he was already opening doors and examining cupboards.

The room at the end was the living room – a huge room with one side all windows. The view left a bit to be desired though, as it overlooked the shunting yards at the back of the station, however, it held a certain quaint interest. The furniture was old and a bit shabby, but clean. There was carpet on the floor which could do with a bit of Shake n' Vac, and some new curtains wouldn't go amiss, thought Sally. However, in the main, there was a nice atmosphere, and it was lovely and light and airy.

Dora had arrived in the room and announced, 'This is lovely, sis! We can do things with this.'

The girls left their father investigating the meter in the corner of the room and went to find the bedrooms, which were in a row off the long corridor. The first bedroom was like the front room, a large, airy space with a huge double bed and big walnut wardrobe. The curtains were in need of attention and the rug at the bottom of the bed was faded and bedraggled, but there was nothing that couldn't be fixed. The second room was only slightly smaller; it too had a double bed and a wardrobe and chest of drawers. Both rooms overlooked small gardens leading to the next row of houses in the road beyond. It was very quiet.

'This is great, isn't it, Dora?' said Sally. 'It will suit us perfectly.'

Their father joined them and agreed it was a find. 'We need to make sure you can afford it though, Sally,' he warned. 'Come and see the kitchen and bathroom and then we must go.'

The bathroom was a big room as well, functional rather than fashionable, but so what? The kitchen was very 1960s, with lots of Formica-topped cupboards and plastic handles, but all perfectly clean. There was a cooker and even a washing machine!

They locked up and set off back to the theatre, Sally desperately trying to work out how much it would all cost.

'Listen, don't fret, we will sort it all out,' Douglas reassured her.

They arrived back at the stage door just before four o'clock, and were relieved to find Gladys back in her corner, no doubt refreshed from her nap.

'Any luck?' she enquired as Sally handed her back the keys.

'Oh, Gladys, the flat was perfect. I love it. I just wish I could move in straight away. But the other little house is lovely too, and I would definitely like to rent a room there with Janie. Is it OK to use your phone again and call Susan so I can confirm things before I leave?'

'Course you can, dearie. There you go. Have you still got the number? That's it then, get to it. Now would you two like a cuppa while you wait?' She turned to Douglas and Dora in the doorway.

'Ooh, yes please,' said Dora. 'I could really do with a cuppa. Thank you, Gladys.'

Sally dialled the number and waited, crossing her fingers.

'Hello, Nantwich 7451.'

Sally recognized Susan's voice. 'Susan? It's Sally Thomas here, from the theatre.'

'Oh yes, hello again. How did it go?' Susan asked.

'Oh, it's perfect,' said Sally. 'I would so love to take a room if it's possible. Is Janie still up for it?'

'Yes, I know they both decided they would have to have an extra person to share the rent. Now do you know the terms?'

'No, I know nothing at all.' Sally held her breath for the umpteenth time that day.

Giles's PA gave Sally all the details.

Sally signalled to her father to come and see what she was writing down. He did a few calculations and nodded his approval. Sally turned back to the phone.

'Hello, Susan? Are you still there? That would be fine. Do you want a deposit? I can send you a cheque if you like.'

'Yes, that's a good idea. Send a month's rent in advance, and address it to me at the theatre, and I will post you a receipt. You have got my number, and if you need to ask any further questions you can ring me. I know you and Janie will get on well, and Pete is very easygoing. I am so pleased things have worked out and I look forward to meeting you on the twelfth of September.'

Sally put the phone down and did a little dance for joy. 'Oh, that is great! I am so relieved I have found somewhere. Thanks so much, Dad. You are a star!' She hugged her father and they went into the alleyway to find Dora and Gladys demolishing a large packet of chocolate digestives.

'We're so grateful, Gladys, for all your help. Just one last thing and we will leave you in peace. How do I secure the other flat for October?'

'Oh, you can leave all that with me, dearie,' said Gladys comfortably. 'Miss Morris is an old friend. I will talk to her and explain everything, and she'll be in touch.'

'How do you know she'll approve of me?' asked Sally.

'Oh, she'd love you, dearie. Well brought-up girl like you.' This last comment elicited a snort of derision from Dora, who was stilled by a black look from her sister.

'Well, if you are sure, that would be fantastic. I can't thank you enough. I will make it up to you, I promise,' Sally added.

'And *I* will be here in October to help you as well,' added Dora self-importantly. 'I will make sure you and me eat cake all day long, Gladys.'

'Goodness me, pet, that won't do me any good at all. But bless you for thinking of me. So you had better all get going now. I have to shut up shop and get home to cook my Ronnie's tea.'

'Yes, of course. We are so sorry to keep you. Take care, and we will see you in a couple of weeks.' Sally gave the large woman a big hug and they left her at the stage door waving the biscuits at them by way of farewell.

They climbed into the car as the sun was beginning to dip behind the rooftops, casting long shadows on the cobbled street.

'I like it up here,' announced Dora from the back seat. 'What it lacks in boutiques it makes up for in heart, don't you think?'

'Oh yes,' agreed Sally. 'It seems so friendly that I'm really looking forward to moving here. And quite frankly I won't have any time or money for boutiques. It's going to be really tough doing a new play every two weeks, as well as learning the lines and doing all the stage management stuff they are going to throw at me.'

'Well, it is what you wanted,' said Douglas, 'and you will give it your best shot, Sally, you always do. Now let's get home to your mother and a second Sunday dinner!'

Chapter 7

The days flew by as Sally gathered herself and her belongings together. Dora was fantastic and made it her mission to provide her sister with even more clothes, to create the most comprehensive wardrobe she could find. Sally gained several more pairs of trousers, one pair of which was velvet, two jackets, three shirts and two pairs of court shoes.

'God, I will never wear these!' Sally shrieked as she wobbled round the shoe shop.

'You may not, but lots of characters in your plays will, dopey,' replied Dora. 'Just think of all those young ladies who need rescuing in those Agatha Christie dramas.'

'You are so right,' Sally said. 'I suppose I was thinking more along the lines of Shakespeare and Chekov. But of course, we will be doing farces and thrillers, won't we?' She sighed and handed the shoes to the assistant, saying, 'Thank you, I'll take these.'

Dora also excelled in the sewing department and she made Sally two beautiful evening dresses using patterns similar to the dresses they had seen in the vintage shop. The girls had decided to go back to Jackie and return the dresses they had originally bought, and use the money to buy some costume jewellery. Dora had promised that she would liaise with Jackie once she was working at Crewe and knew a bit more about the budgets and what might be required. Sally ended up with a black satin sheath dress that made her look really slim and very sexy!

'Oh my, look at you,' said her mother admiringly. 'This is a new Sally I am seeing here.'

'Oh Mum – don't, please, it is embarrassing and not me at all.' Sally wriggled uncomfortably and got a slap on the leg from Dora.

'Keep still or you will get a pin in your bum. Don't be so daft, Sally – you are an actress. This is half the fun, being able to dress up and be something you are not. So just shut up!'

Dora had made the second dress much more demure. Like the one in Jackie's shop, it was a 1950s-style, with a full skirt and petticoats in a gorgeous peacock blue.

'Dora, you are amazing! Thank you so much. I could never have done this by myself.' Sally beamed at her sister.

'Well, I am pleased you appreciate me. In return, you must make sure the wardrobe department see what I can do, so they realize they can't possibly manage without me. Now give me one of those pairs of shoes we bought because I am going to dye them to match this dress.'

Sally sat down one evening with her father and they went through her finances. Her salary was modest, but there'd be enough to live on. There was only one more favour to be asked. A TV!

'Well now, young lady, this is a bit of a luxury, but your mother has persuaded me that you might need the company at first, and it is cheaper than going to the pub every night. So I have invested in a new portable TV for your room.' Douglas lifted a huge box up from behind his desk.

'Oh Dad, you are generous – thank you so much. I promise it will all be worth it in the end. I will make it up to you and Mother, just wait and see.' Sally hugged her father and went in search of Patricia.

'Thank you, Mum,' she said, throwing her arms around her mother's waist.

'Whatever for?' Then light dawned. 'Ah, the TV, I am guessing. Well, it is important you keep up with what is on telly, isn't it?' Patricia said gaily.

'Quite right, Mum, you are a wise old bird and no mistake.'

'Less of the old, thank you,' scolded Patricia. 'Now let's go and find you a suitcase and start putting things in piles. You know how much I like a nice neat pile.' They both laughed and went in search of bags.

Despite her days being full-on, Sally did manage to arrange a photo-shoot with Mack. She went to his studio and they spent a couple of hours taking different shots in different locations. Mack was easygoing and made her feel very comfortable.

'I usually hate having my photo taken,' she ventured as she sat on a chair in the middle of several unfinished sculptures in Mack's studio. Everything was white, even the floors, but whatever Mack had done with the lighting had suffused the whole room in a soft haze. It was very restful, and when Sally saw the Polaroids he had taken as tests, she was pleasantly surprised by how pretty she looked.

'Lighting is the most important factor in photography, I think,' Mack was saying as he snapped away. 'And not just in photography. It obviously makes a huge difference when I am painting or sculpting. I love being in this space and it changes all the time depending on the seasons.' He grinned. 'I get completely carried away in here some days, and Muriel has to come and remind me that there is a world out there.'

'I envy you your solitude,' said Sally. 'It must be wonderful to practise your art without having to rely on other people. As an actor, I need an audience for a reaction. Spouting Shakespeare in my lonely attic is not going to get me a job. I have to be out there in front of people.'

'Yes, I suppose you are right,' replied Mack. 'I have never thought about it from that perspective, although ultimately I am also reliant on someone commissioning and the public buying my work.'

'Yes, but you can create it first without a reaction from anyone. Acting requires a response – especially comedy. As an actor I also need someone objective watching over me. It is all about the director at the end of the day, especially in TV and films. Although at the theatre, the actor is the master onstage. He can rehearse for weeks and the director can give notes all day long – but once that curtain goes up, it is his domain. For those two hours he is in control. What a great feeling that is!'

Sally had risen to her feet with excitement, then realized she had ruined the pose. 'Oh, I am so sorry, but surely you have enough photos by now, Mack? Please let's go and have a drink.'

'OK, you are right. Come on, let's go and have a slap-up dinner. The paper is paying.'

Mack took her to a French bistro near the river. It was very exclusive and Sally guessed that it was also very expensive.

'I told you the local rag is paying for this,' said Mack when Sally raised an eyebrow at the prices. 'You are worth it, Miss Thomas, a potential star in the making!'

They both laughed then got down to the serious business of

eating and drinking. It was a lovely evening. Mack was so easy
to talk to, and funny as well. With the rosy glow of a bottle of
Beaujolais inside her, Sally was brave enough to suggest that he
might like to come and visit her in Crewe.

'You could bring Muriel and Dave and make a weekend of
it. See me perform even!' She giggled, thinking to herself, I
can't believe I am doing this.

'I would love that,' replied Mack. 'Would it matter if I came
on my own?' He was looking at her very intensely now and
Sally began to feel a little warm.

'Not at all,' she said shyly.

Mack got the bill and they left, finding each other's hands as
they walked home. It felt so good and so right to be there with
Mack. Sally was in a state of shock. What was this all about?
They stopped at the bottom of the street near her house and
Mack kissed her deeply, drawing her into him. He then
stepped back and held her face in his hands.

'I am going to miss you, Sally Thomas. I want to come and
see you very soon, if that is OK with you?'

'Yes, please,' whispered Sally and kissed him again. She had
never felt so alive. She wanted to make love to Mack so badly,
but this was just not the right time. She was leaving in a couple
of days and he would think badly of her, surely?'

'Mack, I want to say . . .' she began, but he put a finger to
her lips.

'You don't have to say anything, Sally. I understand this is
not the right time for you to start a love affair with me or anybody. But believe me, I would love to see you again and I
don't want to lose this moment however fragile it may be. Let
us just try to meet as soon as we can, and see what develops.
You are a very special lady, Sally Thomas. I need you but your
public needs you more.'

'Oh thank you, Mack!' Sally hugged him hard. 'I can't wait to show you my new life when you come up.'

Mack leaned down and planted a chaste kiss on her cheek, then turned and walked away. As Sally watched him go he turned round briefly, with a wave, and was gone.

Sally began to feel tears welling up and chided herself yet again on being foolish. She was doing what she had always wanted to do. She must not get sidelined.

'Get a grip, girl!' she told herself. 'This is what you want and you are going to make the most of it.'

By Saturday night Sally was ready to go. She had decided to catch an early train on Sunday morning even though her parents had offered to drive her. It seemed important that she made the break this end and showed some spirit.

Now as the train shuddered to a halt and a whistle pierced her dreams, Sally awoke with a start and realized she had arrived at Platform One, Crewe station. Giving a little yawn, she stood up and began to collect her bags. Excitement surged through her.

Let the adventure begin!

Act 2

Take centre stage

Chapter 8

My old man said, 'Foller the van,
And don't dilly dally on the way.'
Off went the van wiv me 'ome packed in it,
I followed on wiv me old cock linnet.
But I dillied and dallied, dallied and I dillied
Lorst me way and don't know where to roam.
Well, you can't trust a Special like the old time coppers
When you can't find your way 'ome.

'Good morning, everyone, and welcome to my wonderful world of theatre!' Giles Longfellow's voice reverberated around the theatre and bounced off the chandelier to land smack bang in the centre of the stage. Sally was reminded of her first visit to Crewe and her gaze immediately flew to the Royal Box. Sure enough, she could see the shadowy figure of their employer hovering behind a gilded pillar. He appeared like a conjuror at the finale of his act and looked down upon the assembled cast.

'Forgive my theatricality, folks, but I love this theatre, and I am determined that this season will be the best ever. I have gathered a great cast and some wonderful entertainment for the next nine months, and together we will ensure that live theatre lives on in the provinces despite the government's best efforts to curb our budget. Heather, please hand out the schedule of works while I come down and join you.' He disappeared through the curtain at the back of the box, and the company turned expectantly to Heather, the stage manager.

Sally had met her at nine o'clock that morning as she arrived at the stage door.

'Hi. I am Sally Thomas – ASM, small parts and understudy,' she had announced rather nervously. 'I am not quite sure what to do first, or who to ask for . . .'

Heather had slapped her on the back and steered her towards the stage, saying, 'Oh, well done for getting here early. That bodes well for the first day. I am Heather Rollings, and I am the stage manager here. It's my third year so I pretty much know how it all works. Come and have a cup of tea in the office and I will fill you in.'

Sally followed her down to the basement and along a narrow corridor lined with huge heating pipes. There was a door at the end and Heather ushered her into a musty room with a light bulb swinging from the ceiling and a desk with a lamp and piles of paperwork on it. A broken armchair stood in the corner next to a side table, on which was a kettle and some cracked mugs, and containers of tea and coffee. There was a half-full bottle of milk that Heather quickly emptied into a tiny basin in the corner. She left the bottle on the floor by a bin as she produced a fresh one from her rucksack.

'We waste so much milk here, but without a fridge what can I do? Tea or coffee?' she asked, filling the kettle.

'Oh, tea please,' said Sally, looking round.

'Not exactly the Theatre Royal, Haymarket, is it?' remarked Heather. 'To be honest I am hardly ever in here, as I'm too busy running round like a blue-arsed fly. Have you done any stage management at all?' She posed the question as if she already knew the answer.

'Well, I did a bit at drama school, but this is my first professional job actually and—'

'Oh crap, I thought so.' Heather cut her off. 'Sorry, Sally, but Giles does this to me every year. Hires would-be actresses to do stage management. You are not in the least bit interested in lighting or props, you just want to perform!' She threw a tea bag into a mug and banged it down in front of Sally. 'It drives me mad. There is another girl in the cast down as ASM as well – Sarah something. I just hope she is the genuine article.'

'I am so s-sorry,' stammered Sally. 'I really am. But please don't think I am not going to pull my weight. I fully expect to do my share, and I am eager to learn, honestly.'

Heather sat down at her desk and studied her for a few minutes. Sally waited for her assessment.

'Fair enough,' came the sighed response. 'At least you tipped up on time today. Let's see how we get on. Now today can go as smooth as treacle, or turn into bedlam. First thing you need to know, my girl, is all about the pecking order. But first, I'll do the tea.' She got up and poured boiling water into the mugs.

'Pecking order?' repeated Sally. 'How do you mean?'

Heather came back and took a list from her bag; she placed it between them. 'This is the cast, and it's important that you learn who is at the top of the list, and who is at the bottom. And let me tell you that very often, some of these buggers shouldn't be on any list at all!' Her good humour restored, over the next half an hour Heather took Sally through the cast, and then led her up to the stage to lay out chairs ready for the 'Meet and Greet'. Two large chairs stood in the centre, and then the smaller fold-away chairs fanned out on each side into a semi-circle.

Heather laid a cast list on the two main chairs, saying, 'These are for Peggy and Percy, our leading artistes – a couple off stage as well as on, known behind their backs as Pinky and Perky.' She snorted. 'They rule the roost, so watch out. Don't tell Peggy anything she can use against you, and keep out of Percy's way unless you are prepared to be a slave to his demands.'

'How many of the cast have been here before?' Sally asked as she put a typed list on each chair.

'Let's see . . . well, Geoffrey Challis has done a few seasons here. He is lovely, by the way. He has a wife and three kids and I really don't know how he makes ends meet, but I suspect his missus has money. Charmaine Lloyd was here last year. She's OK most of the time, but I get the impression she feels she should be leading the Royal Shakespeare Company. As far as I know, everyone else is a newcomer.'

'I am staying with Peter and Janie at the moment. I met them last night and they seem very pleasant.' Sally followed Heather across the stage to the pass door. Heather held it open for her, and then they both climbed the stairs to the Green Room, which was inevitably at the top of the building.

'This will keep you fit,' puffed Heather. 'I keep trying to give up the fags but it's hopeless.'

The Green Room was the heart of any theatrical company. So-called because it was invariably painted green, it was the communal dumping ground and meeting place for the actors and stage management. Here, there was tea and coffee, a kettle, a fridge and a microwave. The fridge, Heather said, was usually crammed with every type of food imaginable, from salad to Pot Noodles, to mouldy cheese. The room always had that faint aura of curry and burnt toast. This morning was no exception.

Heather went straight to the little window in the corner and opened it, saying, 'Oh God, it always stinks in here. Look at the sink! No one ever washes up the plates or anything. I am going to put up a notice for the new company, and let's try to get them to at least clear up their own mess. We have enough to do without taking that on as well. Now as you will discover, the tea and coffee need constant replenishing – it goes so fast. The management pays for that, and milk, and sometimes biscuits for special occasions, like today. First day we always have biscuits, which I have brought with me, so if you could find a clean plate and put them out, I will make a start on washing up mugs. We are about twenty today.'

'Blimey, as many as that,' said Sally, hunting for plates.

'Yes. The lighting designer comes and the designer, the wardrobe and the carpenter, et cetera. Plus we are quite a big cast, you know,' added Heather. 'Twelve, I think, and more to come later.'

By the time they had sorted out the refreshments and carried them back to the stage, the first arrivals were standing around looking lost.

'Morning, all. There is tea and coffee on the way, so please find a seat and read your production notes and call sheets,' announced Heather authoritatively. 'Sally, let's set up a table in the prompt corner – there is a socket there for the kettle.'

Sally followed her over to the corner and dumped her load, then turned back to the stage to watch the arrivals. Janie and Peter had just come in and waved in her direction. Sally went to join them.

'Morning, you two. Sorry I was in such a state last night but it was such a nightmare journey. I never thought I would make it.' Sally had, indeed, had a terrible time yesterday. Having fallen asleep as the train sped through the Cotswolds, she was rudely awakened by a very loud announcement that due to works on the line, the train was delayed. Sally was not particularly bothered as she had all day, so she decided to find the buffet car and get herself some supplies. To her horror there was a queue right down the train! Thirty minutes later she arrived at the counter only to find there was nothing left except crisps and water or wine.

'I'll have a white wine and a packet of plain crisps, please.' She took her meagre purchases back to her seat and gazed out of the window. It had started to drizzle, and the landscape was definitely no longer as pleasant. She could see two huge concrete silos in the distance, and smoke was billowing from giant chimney-stacks on the other side of the tracks, sending great white fluffy clouds into the grey mass of sky above. Like daubs of paint on a palette, she thought. Further announcements came and went, until two and a half hours later the train squealed to life and shuddered forward slowly, finally gathering speed – but not for long. Thirty minutes later the voice of doom announced from the Tannoy in a fine Black Country burr that, 'This train will shortly be stopping at Rugby. Would passengers please alight and wait on Platform Three for the next train to Crewe.'

By the time the train had spat them all out, the passengers were mutinous, but there was no one to complain to, so they fell back on each other. Sally escaped to the waiting room and found a corner seat. It was now mid-afternoon and she could see her whole day disappearing fast. She wondered if there was any way she could warn Janie and Peter that she would be late.

If they decided to go out she was completely snookered, as she had no keys. But they had no phone in the digs, as she remembered. Maybe she could ring Gladys at the stage door – but then what could *she* do? No, Sally did not want to cause trouble so early in the day; she would just trust to luck. Hearing a commotion, she looked out to see a group of irate passengers accosting a guard. She went to the door of the waiting room and opened it to listen to his excuses.

'Ladies and gentlemen, *please* let's have some calm. We are doing our best to make alternative arrangements for your onward journey. Would you kindly make your way to the ticket office where my colleague will give you details of your onward transport.'

This sounds ominous, thought Sally. She gathered up her things and joined the crowd as they crossed the platform over the bridge to the ticket office. After waiting in the queue, she finally made it to the grille where a very harassed-looking lady was taking down information.

'Destination?' she enquired curtly.

'Crewe, please,' replied Sally.

'Right, there will be a coach outside here in forty-five minutes to take you to Crewe. Sorry for any inconvenience.'

'How long will the journey take, do you think? I am not from round here, and I have no idea where I am really.' Sally tried to smile her way into the woman's affections.

'Oh dear, well, this is Rugby so if the traffic is OK on the motorway you should be there in an hour and a half. Here's your ticket. Good luck, love.' Her parting shot to Sally came with an attempt at a smile.

Great, thought Sally. I am not going to get to my digs much before eight o'clock tonight.

In fact, she arrived on the doorstep of her new home at

seven thirty, and almost burst into tears of relief when her knock was answered, and Janie was standing there.

'Goodness – we thought you must have got lost!' the other girl cried.

'I am so sorry, but I couldn't ring you, could I?' replied Sally as she practically fell through the door with her bags. 'I have been on a train or a coach since ten o'clock this morning. Great British Rail, how do they manage it?'

'You poor girl. Here, let me take your bags and you go and sit by the fire with Pete. I expect you're starving. We have only got the basics in so far, but I can make you some cheese on toast and a cup of tea or a hot chocolate.'

'Oh, that sounds like heaven,' sighed Sally. 'Thank you so much. Hello, Pete, nice to meet you.' She leaned down to take Peter's hand but he politely jumped up.

'Sally, welcome. It is lovely to meet you too. What a bummer, eh? Still, you are here now, and Janie will have you settled in before you know it. She is a real mother hen, and I can't believe I have been so lucky to find her. She rules my life!' They sat down and let Janie fuss around them. Sally felt instantly at home, and the day's woes faded fast as she ate her cheese on toast and wrapped her hands around a steaming mug of hot chocolate.

'Have you got any idea what happens tomorrow morning?' she asked Peter. 'I am actually ASM, small parts and understudy so I am expecting to be in early doing chores, unfortunately.' She grinned. 'Not like you, Pete – a proper actor.'

'Now, we are not having any distinctions between stage management and artistes in our company. We are all in it together, aren't we, sweetheart?' Peter grabbed Janie's hand as she stood beside him and pulled her onto his lap. She let out a squeal of delight.

'Oh yes definitely, we are all in it together.' She giggled and wrapped her boyfriend's hands around her. 'I have every intention of getting myself a small part in some of the plays as well as making the costumes,' she announced. Then: 'Stop that, you wicked boy! Sorry, Sally, but he is very naughty.' She turned on his lap and kissed him full on the lips.

Sally took this as her cue to go to bed. 'Good night, guys. I will leave you to it. I need to get to the theatre tomorrow for nine, so I will creep out and see you there later. Thanks for the lovely welcome.' She made her way upstairs and left the lovebirds clasped in each other's arms. They hardly seemed to notice Sally's exit.

Her little room looked so cosy as she opened the door. Dear Janie had made up her bed and put a bulb in the lamp for her. The curtains only just made it across the window but it was only a temporary home, so it didn't matter for now. She found her wash-bag and made her way to the bathroom. There was a gorgeous smell of lavender from a candle burning in a saucer on the edge of the bath. Sally would have loved a long soak but decided to wait until she had got the feel of the place and how everything worked. She cleaned her teeth and had a quick wash, then fell into her little bed and was asleep in moments.

'Sally, are you there? Come in, Houston?' Heather broke through Sally's reverie. 'Can you make some drinks, please. Our leading actors have arrived.'

'Sorry, Heather, I was miles away. No problem – I am on it.' Sally crossed the stage and took note of two larger-than-life people standing centre stage.

'Percy, my darling boy, take my bag.' The voice belonged to a large-bosomed lady with lots of jewellery swathing her ample chest. Her head was decked with a turban of exotic material. The make-up was thick but immaculately applied, and the nails were long and scarlet.

'Miss Delamaine?' enquired Sally. 'Can I get you a tea or coffee? I am Sally Thomas, one of the ASMs this season.'

'Oh hello, dear, how kind of you to ask. Yes, a white coffee with a sweetener, if possible. There should be some around from last season. If not, I have some in my bag. And do we have biscuits, or have there been cut-backs already?' She laughed and looked around for a response from her audience. Sally obliged with a chuckle and Percy let out a snort.

'Peggy, you are a card! How do you do, dear? I am Percival Hackett, leading man to Miss Delamaine's leading lady. I would like a strong white tea, please, and a glass of water for the meeting.' With that he turned with a flourish and made his way to the centre seats.

Sally went to the wings and prepared the refreshments as requested. She couldn't find any sweeteners but she put a selection of the biscuits onto a separate plate for her 'leading actors' and took them over.

'Thank you, dear girl. Put them on the floor here, would you?' Percy pointed to a spot and Sally obliged, thinking to herself that this could all end in tears. But time enough for all that. First day, just be lovely and get through it, Sally.

There was a clap of hands and all went quiet. Giles Longfellow had taken centre stage and was preparing to address his company. Sally quickly crossed to the wings and fetched him a chair which she placed to the side of him. He acknowledged the gesture with a quick smile then waved her away.

'So, ladies and gentlemen – welcome, and let us begin.'

Chapter 9

While Giles explained his plan of action, Sally sat at the edge of the semi-circle with pen and paper and, while taking the odd note, mostly concentrated on sizing up the cast. Jeremy had seemed pleased to see her, although when Giles arrived he quickly made his excuses and went off to join him. Giles was deep in conversation with a rather handsome young man called Robert, she discovered from Heather, the font of all knowledge.

'That is Robert Johnson, an actor; he has been around a couple of years and done a bit of telly. I think he is a personal friend of Giles Longfellow's as he came to work here last season and then left. I think he was having a bit of a fling with Giles – don't know much about him though.'

Sally watched as Jeremy was introduced to Robert by Giles, and the three of them had an earnest chat about something. Jeremy certainly looked the part of the young actor. He was wearing flared coral-coloured jeans and a floral shirt, and had grown his hair so he could flick it provocatively. His orientation seemed in no doubt whatsoever now to Sally, and by the way that Robert was touching his arm and leaning towards him as they spoke, she guessed it would not be long before they were very good friends. A loud burst of laughter drew her attention towards Peter, her landlord, who was joking with Simon Day and Geoffrey Challis. Simon was a real Jack the lad and seemed full of fun. He had already winked several times at Sally during the course of the morning. Geoffrey was charming, just as Heather had told her, and seemed to fit in with everyone. She did not have a chance to talk to Charmaine or Sarah until they broke for coffee, when Sarah came over to the prompt corner and introduced herself.

'Hi, I am Sarah Kelly the ASM. Can I do anything to help?' she offered.

Heather gave her two mugs of coffee and said, 'Hi, Sarah. Take these to Giles, please. This is Sally, by the way. She is also an ASM and small parts, I believe.'

'Nice to meet you,' said Sarah and went off with the coffees.

Sally took the next two mugs and asked, 'Pinky and Perky, I presume?'

Heather burst into a fit of giggles. 'Ssh! For God's sake don't let anyone hear you say that! But yes – spot on, Sally, you learn fast. I think we are going to get along. Better take some more biscuits, by the look of it. They are probably stocking up for later, or eating them now so they don't have to buy any lunch.'

As Sally was coming back for another mug or two, Charmaine Lloyd approached her.

'Hello, and what is your title in our esteemed little band? I am Charmaine, by the way,' she drawled rather theatrically.

'Yes, I realized,' replied Sally. 'I am Sally Thomas, ASM and small parts – lovely to meet you. Would you like a coffee or tea?'

'No, thanks. I don't suppose there is any Perrier water, is there? No, of course not, how silly of me. I suggested to Giles

last year that he get a water-cooler thing, like the Americans
have. Don't suppose that has materialized though. God, I feel
depressed already ...' She wandered off across the room trail-
ing her coat behind her like a catwalk model.

Interesting, thought Sally. Wonder if she is any good?

Giles had announced the first three productions by the end
of the morning, and there was great excitement because the
opening show was going to be Joan Littlewood's *Oh, What a
Lovely War!* and everybody had to sing. Much to Sally's amazement she was in the production as a Pierrot and had two solo
songs!

Heather slapped her on the back and feigned a disgruntled
voice. 'Well, that's you out of service as far as my management
is concerned. You will be faffing around singing and dancing
instead of chasing up props for me.'

'Oh no, I promise I will do all my stage-management stuff
as well. Please don't think you can't rely on me,' Sally assured
her.

'I am only joking,' said Heather more gently. 'Don't worry,
we will manage, and I think it is great you have got the songs.
You must have a good voice.'

'Not bad,' said Sally modestly. She hid her true excitement
for the time being. But boy, wait till she rang home and told
them!

The other two productions were to be *A Man for All Seasons*
by Robert Bolt, starring Percy Hackett as Sir Thomas More
and Peggy Delamaine as his wife. Percy was in his element,
and had already cornered the poor wardrobe mistress to discuss
his many and varied outfits. Charmaine was to play the daughter, and Jeremy had the role of More's betrayer, Richard Rich.

The third production in the line-up was to be a musical
version of the famous Aristophanes' play *Lysistrata*.

'This will be, in essence, a world première, ladies and gentlemen, so it will attract great interest, we hope. It will also be the production to launch a three-day conference that this theatre will be hosting, for the Association of Repertory Theatres throughout the UK; so an important time for us all. Now the lead in this production will be our own, very lovely Charmaine Lloyd. I would like Sally Thomas to understudy you and play one of the neighbours in the town. So you will be very busy, Sally, combining all your posts. Heather, I am sure, will give you as much help as she can, although it will be a tough one for you, Heather, as all the girls will be in the show in some form or other. Sarah, that includes you.'

Giles turned his gaze upon the young ASM who perked up considerably and said, 'Oh, that's great. I will really enjoy being part of the company. Thank you, sir.'

'So now you all have your work cut out, we will break for a quick lunch and then everyone back here for two o'clock. I will start with a musical rehearsal taken by our musical director Mr Timothy Townsend. Take a bow, Tim.' The musical director stood for his applause. He was a very unprepossessing little man with a bald head and ample paunch, which must get in the way of him playing the piano, thought Sally.

The company broke, and Sally was about to suggest a bag of chips when Heather took her arm and led her towards the cluster of folk in the corner who had not been part of the cast list as such, but consisted of the designer and lighting crew and the chief carpenter.

'There's no time to stop. You have to join the production meeting now, my girl. Though I suspect it will be held in the pub?' Heather addressed this last word to a huge man in overalls with shoulder-length hair and a fine beard and very twinkly eyes.

'Pub is right on, Heather my lass, and is this fine-looking young lady my dinner for today?' He peered down at Sally, who fleetingly felt a shiver of panic before the giant burst into a huge guffaw and introduced himself. 'Will Black at your service, chief carpenter and maker of magic. You are Sally, are you not? ASM and not so small parts, I gather. You will be a busy little bee. Come on, let's get to the pub so we can start our very important production meeting.' He gave her a big wink and turned away to the rest of the group to chivvy them up. Sally followed on feeling like Alice in Wonderland. Nothing seemed real any more.

The pub was opposite the theatre and a world away from the picturesque Cheltenham scene. This was a drinking pub and nothing else. The tables were stained and chipped, and the chairs hard and uncomfortable. There was scarcely a female in sight, as men stood shoulder-to-shoulder at the bar, their arms lifting their pints almost in unison, like some sort of tribal dance. Will caused a parting of the ways and they all followed him through to a back room.

'Fetch a few more chairs and I'll get the drinks in. Pints all round, is it?' He paused when he caught Sally's eye. 'Ah well, maybe not quite. What are you having, my dear, gin and tonic?' Sally would have given her right arm for a gin and tonic but had the good sense not to rise to the taunt.

'Pint of cider, please,' she said. 'Draught if they have it.'

Will gave one of his guffaws and disappeared into the bar. Once everyone was settled, the plans came out on the table and design took over while Sally and Heather, notepads at the ready, awaited instructions. Sally was in a complete state of giddy excitement about her roles in *Oh, What a Lovely War!* and trying to fathom out just what her duties were going to be backstage. Because they did a new production every two weeks the sets all had to be very adaptable, and Will had his work cut out to keep new ideas coming. The lighting designer had a standard rig, but subject to finance would try and give each production a little extra something. What struck Sally very clearly was just how passionate everyone was about their jobs. She began to feel a sense of pride in being part of the team. But then suddenly it was five to two and Sally had to put her actress's hat on and get back for the music call.

'I am sorry but I have to go,' she whispered to Heather.

'Yes, go on. Don't worry, we are nearly done here anyway, and when the pub shuts that is definitely the end of the meeting,' the other girl laughed. 'Go! Or you will be late and that will not look good.'

'Tell Will I shall get the next round in when I see him.' Sally rose and nipped out before anyone could pass comment. She just made it to the stage as Timothy was handing round the music sheets.

'Now I think the best way to go about this is to start with an ensemble number so we can all warm up our voices, and then I am going to listen to each one of you in turn, and put you in the correct place for your range. So please all look at the title song "Oh, What a Lovely War!"'

The company spent the next half an hour belting out the tune and feeling very uplifted.

'There is nothing like a good singsong to lift the spirits, is there?' a voice whispered in Sally's ear. It was Simon and she laughed and nodded.

Timothy was a wonderful pianist despite his paunch and was soon putting people in different spots next to each other.

'We are going to have to learn harmonies. Have any of you got tape machines? If so, I can play your harmonies for you and you can record them and learn them at your leisure.'

Robert and Jeremy put their hands up, and surprisingly, Sarah did too. The rest of them all looked a bit pathetic. Percy and Peggy laughed it off, announcing that they would pick up the tunes soon enough. Charmaine looked pained and said, 'I don't really *do* singing. Can't I just stick with the tune?'

Timothy looked a little taken aback. 'Well, that is not quite the spirit, Charmaine, but we will see how we get on. Sally, what are you going to do, especially about your solos? I won't have much time to spend with you on your own. Would you be able to get hold of a cassette, do you think?'

Sally was already thinking what to do. 'Um, yes, of course – I will see what I can do. Sorry I am not prepared. I had no idea I would be used so soon.' She looked round the room, embarrassed, feeling very unprofessional.

'Well, I understand you have a beautiful voice,' encouraged Timothy, 'so we must make use of it. Now I want us to have one more go at all the company stuff then we can call it a day, because some of you have to go to Wardrobe now, I understand.'

After the rehearsal was finished Sally went to find Heather for further instructions. It was already five thirty and she was exhausted. All she wanted to do was go back to the digs, have a hot bath followed by some baked beans on toast and go to bed – which reminded her: she would have to do some shopping on the way home, because she had bought no supplies, and could not expect Janie to cater for her again.

Heather was in her office printing out the next day's calls.

'Listen, love, you have had a long day so I won't go through all this now. Let's meet tomorrow at nine and I'll show you the schedule, et cetera. But if you wouldn't mind just handing these out to those still left in Wardrobe and pinning one on the noticeboard at the stage door when you leave, that would be great.'

'Oh thank you, Heather, so much. I must say I am knackered. I will get the milk and biscuits for tomorrow so you don't have to worry.'

'OK, but remember – no more biscuits now until the next special event. Don't spoil them. If this lot have them every day they will never appreciate the treat. Plus it will cost you an arm and a leg, and believe me you will find your wages go quick enough without feeding the five thousand.'

'OK thanks, point taken. Just milk then. See you in the morning,' Sally called back over her shoulder. She found Janie in a tiny room off the wardrobe going through baskets of costumes and said, 'You still at it, you poor thing? What time are you going to finish?'

'Oh, I am just filling in time while Pete has his fitting. He is nearly done. Shall we walk back together? I have made a stew for tonight. It only needs heating up, and we can get a loaf on the way home from the corner shop. Thank God it stays open late because we have discovered nothing much stays open in Crewe after five.' Janie closed the lid of a trunk and stretched her back.

'Oh Janie, I can't eat your food,' replied Sally. 'You can't cook for me all the time.'

'I won't, don't worry. You can cook sometimes, and Pete is pretty good at certain things. Curry, curry and curry,' the other girl laughed.

'OK, that's great. We can set up a rota. I have to buy milk for tomorrow, so I will get the bread at the same time – and how about a bottle of wine to celebrate our first day?' Sally suggested, warming to the plan.

'Good idea. Oh, here he comes, my little Pierrot. Sally, you will have to be fitted for your Pierrot costume, as we are hiring them. Do you want me to do it now while you are here?'

Sally sighed. It was the last thing she wanted to do, but needs must. 'I suppose it is a good idea to get it over with,' she agreed.

'Pete, why don't you go to the pub and we will pick you up on the way out?' Janie gave him a kiss and sent him on his way.

They went into the wardrobe and Sally was properly introduced to the wardrobe mistress Gwendoline Stewart. She looked very proper, and had big black glasses and her hair in a bun, of all things. Sally had an instant image of some man removing her glasses and taking down her hair, then ravaging her over the sewing machine. It made her giggle, which caused Gwendoline to give her a straight look.

'Something funny?' she asked crisply.

'No, sorry, I am just hysterical with tiredness. It has been a long day.'

'Huh, you think this is long, just you wait until the dress rehearsal and technical days. They are flipping murder.' Gwendoline seemed to enjoy imparting this piece of information. She took her tape measure from around her neck and started to measure Sally's waist, saying, 'Right, Janie, take down these measurements, please, then we can all go home.'

Once they were finally out of the building and making their way to the pub, Sally ventured to ask Janie about Gwendoline.

'Oh, she's OK when you get to know her. She is a bit of a goer by all accounts – at the Christmas party last year she came dressed as a Moulin Rouge dancer. I think though that normally she is just a bit shy and finds actors intimidating. I get on with her fine and am even allowed to call her Gwen. She is supposed to be second-in-command to Enid, but I think Giles feels that Enid is past it now, so he is easing Gwen in, hoping Enid won't notice!'

Sally laughed and decided she would work on Gwendoline, if nothing else than for Dora's sake, because it could be awkward for her sister if they didn't get on.

The two girls dragged Pete away from Simon, Robert and Jeremy, and trudged up the hill to their little house. The corner shop was just closing, but Sally managed to get her milk and a white sliced, and a bottle of white wine, though God knows what it would taste like. At home, Janie got the stew on and Pete helped her while Sally went and had her bath. It was heaven and she vowed to make sure there were always candles and bath goodies for them all.

They ate the stew at their little dining table by candlelight.

'Well, saves on electricity, doesn't it?' remarked Janie. 'And we all look so much prettier. This wine is hitting the spot, Sally, thank you.'

They all washed up and then made a beeline for their beds.

'So much for the sex, drugs and rock 'n' roll life of a wandering actor,' called out Peter as he switched off the landing light. 'Night night, everyone. Sweet dreams.'

But there was only silence!

Chapter 10

'Again, please, everyone.'

'Oh! Oh! Oh! It's a lovely war!'

The piano was jumping off the boards as Timothy banged out the rhythm. For three days the music rehearsals had taken over everyone's lives. Wherever one went inside the theatre someone could be found hunched in a dark corner singing to themselves, or tapping out the tune on the kettle in the Green Room. Two or three of the actors would break off in the middle of a hasty bite of a sandwich and burst into their harmonies, then fall back against the battered old sofa exhausted.

'This is ridiculous,' announced Charmaine. 'I am *not* going to be bullied like this. I am an actress, not a music-hall turn!'

Peggy, who was standing in the doorway, stopped her in her tracks with: 'Charmaine, my dear, shut up. You only have to sing the tune once. God only knows, it is obvious you are not a singer, but be grateful for small mercies and *just get on with it.*'

Sally wanted to giggle out of sheer nerves: the whole thing had become a nightmare. She had never worked so hard in her life. Not only was she trying to learn her two solos, but she was running all the errands for Heather on the props side with Sarah. The girls took it in turns to go round the town begging and borrowing whatever was needed. In fact, the props on this production were not too bad as the set was minimal. It was more a question of the actors setting the scene. The lighting was going to be important in giving each scene its own atmosphere. Sally had managed to buy a second-hand cassette machine in a charity shop, and every minute she was not working on set she was playing back her songs. Sarah had proved quite a dark horse. She seemed to know every song backwards – and all the harmonies. For a girl who professed to be committed to stage management, she was showing an uncanny interest in the show. Sally made a little note to keep an eye on her.

The whole theatre had come alive in this first week. Even the front-of-house staff seemed to appear out of nowhere. Posters went up in the foyer, and Evie in the Box Office was like the fairy on the Christmas tree. She was always immaculately dressed in something bright and sparkly, her make-up in perfect order, and her hair coiffed to within an inch of each sprayed peak, like a lemon meringue pie. People daring to pass the front doors of the theatre were somehow drawn into her web, like insects into a Venus fly trap.

In the wardrobe department, Gwendoline, Enid and Janie were lost behind lines of clothes and piles of shoes, and great mountains of black velvet used as curtains to hide the wings at the side of the stage. Huge baskets called skips filled the corridors outside.

Poor Heather was not only having to deal with the set designer, lighting rig and carpentry demands, but also the constant demands of the cast. Pinky and Perky were up in arms because their dressing rooms were not ready. Percy's over-trained vowels could be heard echoing down the stairs, 'Heather dear, I need a light in here!'

Peggy would grab Sarah and force her to drop whatever important job she was doing on the production so that she could bring the mistress a small armchair from the store.

'I have to get my feet up, darling, when I can,' she would wheedle. 'See if you can't find me a little velvet cushion to go on top, there's a dear.'

Charmaine was in Dressing Room 3 and wanted Sally to clean it from top to bottom before she would unpack.

'Honest to God, it is *filthy*, Sally. I will contract some dreadful disease if I set foot in there now. Please, can't you just spare me an hour or so and give it a good wash-down?'

Sally had sought Heather's advice on this and received a very concise answer: 'Tell Madam to Foxtrot Charlie off!'

The boys, Simon, Peter and Jeremy, were having a ball. Sally envied them their carefree camaraderie. They were up and down the stairs all day long, singing their soldier chorus. Jeremy had to be reminded every so often that he too was an ASM, and Sally would suddenly have to go and pull him out of the pub to help with the prop-building. Robert and Geoffrey stayed on the sidelines. Robert was never far away from Giles Longfellow, who would appear in the Royal Box from time to time and check that all was moving in the right direction. He had announced to the cast that first day, that he would rehearse the scenes only once the actors had mastered the songs. Timothy was on a mission for sure, and suddenly by Thursday the light seemed to dawn and the whole thing came together. It was so exhilarating to stand there and sing out in joyful harmony. Everyone clapped and hugged each other at the end of the run-through. Even Charmaine's solo sounded all right, as she had a sort of warble to her voice that was very much of the period of the First World War.

'You'd think she had created it especially,' whispered Peggy to Percy. 'Bloody woman has the luck of the devil.'

Sally had performed her two songs well, if somewhat tentatively. Timothy took her aside afterwards and gave her some suggestions.

'You have a beautiful voice, Sally – now you must add some emotion. *Act* the songs. When you sing "Keep the Home Fires Burning" we want to feel your pain, your loss. I want them to be sobbing in the stalls. With the other number, "I'll make a Man of You", I want you to be saucy and seductive. You need to twinkle more. You know the songs perfectly, so forget about the mechanics and just enjoy. Speak to Wardrobe about getting you some kinky boots or something for that second number.'

Sally was slightly miffed that somehow she was not sexy enough, and decided to have a word with Janie. She found her as usual with her head in a skip.

'Honestly, Sally, I stink of mothballs! It's my new perfume. What can I do for you?'

'Timothy has basically just told me I am not sexy enough in my number. I need some help with my costume, Janie. I know you are up to your eyes, but can you give me an idea of what I am going to be wearing?'

'Oh God, Sally, I haven't a clue. But Gwen is in the other room – we can ask her.' Frankly, Sally would rather have avoided the issue and not bothered Gwendoline, who was still a bit stand-offish as far as Sally was concerned. However, needs must.

'Hi, Gwendoline, we have a small problem with our artiste here,' breezed Janie. 'Timothy wants her sexier, and as we don't have a costume as yet, this could be a problem – though I suppose you could go on naked, Sally, and that would do the trick!'

Janie laughed throatily, and Sally felt sick at the thought. 'I am really sorry to be a pain, Gwendoline, but if there is anything I can do to help, I will. I could go and see if I could get some black boots – long ones, you know – to glam up a bit.'

Gwendoline studied Sally for a few moments and then decided. 'Yes – good idea, Sally. That would be a great help, then I will make you a sort of drum majorette-type outfit with a little soldier hat, and we will give you a cane to play with – and away you go! Oh, and get some fishnet tights as well. Can you afford all this, because I am not sure the budget will stretch?'

Sally's heart sank. More expense, but if it helped get her in with Gwendoline it could all be worthwhile, especially when Dora arrived. At least then she would have back-up and her own personal dressmaker!

'OK then, I will go out right now, and find those boots,' Sally declared. 'Tell Heather I have gone on an emergency mission.'

It was a relief to get out into the fresh air. Sally had been coming in to work every day at eight thirty and leaving after dark. The theatre was dirty and full of dust, only made worse by all the scenery-building going on. Suddenly she was walking in September sunshine, the light playing on the autumn leaves rustling above her. She could almost pretend she was out on a day's shopping spree without a care in the world. Almost. She was plonked back into reality by a shout from behind.

'Fancy a good time then, girlie?' Simon and Jeremy were descending on her with a huge plant between them. She burst out laughing.

'What is that? You idiots!'

'Please don't mock, it is very unbecoming,' pouted Jeremy. 'This is our palm tree for the camel scene.'

'But it's an aspidistra,' hooted Sally.

'It may well be, but it is all we could find at the market so bog off, Miss Noddy Know-it-all!' replied Simon. 'Look, it's green, and it will wave in the breeze so it will be fine. Just have to use your imagination. Where are you skiving off to anyway?'

'I have got to find a pair of boots for my costume as the drum majorette,' said Sally.

'Ooh, lovely! Kinky boots,' growled Simon. 'I knew you'd got it in you, Sally Thomas.'

'Oh please, give me a break,' she retorted. 'Jeremy, keep your friend under control, and don't forget, by the way, we have to pick up that chaise longue from the junk shop later. Did you manage to get a trolley from the scene dock?'

Jeremy looked crestfallen. 'Oh shit, I forgot all about it. I am so sorry, Sal. I know, I'll ask Robert if he can help me pick it up in his car. We could tie it on the roof.'

'OK, but please get it done.' She turned and left them to it.

Sally decided to make for Freeman Hardy & Willis round behind the market. She vaguely remembered seeing some boots in there in the course of her travels. This was the thing about looking for props all day long – one passed so many windows and stores, it was hard to remember what was what. She arrived at her destination and peered into the shop window. It all looked rather dismal, but nothing ventured . . .

Through the gloom inside Sally detected a young girl sitting on a bench below shelves of shoeboxes, filing her nails.

'Hi. I am looking for some black knee-high boots. Can you help me at all?' she asked.

The girl jumped up with a start. 'Sorry, what did you want?'

'Black boots.' Sally repeated the question.

'Oh right. Well, yes, we have got these really nice black-patent-leather ones. What size are you?'

'Six,' said Sally, sitting down on the bench and starting to take her shoes off.

The girl disappeared into the back, leaving Sally to ponder on why some shops put yellow cellophane in the windows to make the shop even darker. The girl returned with a large box and proceeded to unpack the promised boots. They were in fact rather impressive, thought Sally. She slid her leg into the boot and started to zip it up, only to find a gentleman kneeling at her feet, his hands deftly taking over from hers, and moving up her leg with alacrity.

'Oh, sorry – who are you?' stammered Sally, trying to gain back her leg from his grasp.

'Mr Leslie Tibbs at your service, miss. These are our top-of-the-range boot for this winter. Just a penny under thirty pounds, and cheap at the price.'

Oh blimey, thought Sally. That is a fortune.

'Actually, I was wondering if you might be able to help me a bit here,' ventured Sally. Holding her leg as seductively as she could in front of Mr Tibbs's nose, she put on her best, most dazzling smile, and whispered, 'I am an actress here at the Crewe Theatre, and we are doing this wonderful show called *Oh, What a Lovely War!* I am playing a drum majorette, and singing this big number, and it would be so fantastic if you could lend me the boots for the run of the show. The trouble is, we have so little money for costumes but this would just make my outfit perfect.'

Mr Tibbs released her leg and let it drop unceremoniously to the floor.

'Oh, I am not sure we can do that, my dear. These are expensive boots, you know. What if they get damaged?'

'Well, obviously the theatre would have insurance to cover anything like that. But I would take such good care of them, honestly. I could get you and the shop some publicity, probably in the local paper, and we would be able to give you front-row tickets for the first night and the party afterwards. I would be so grateful.' Sally forced herself to lean in close and bat her eyelashes.

'Hmm, I see. Maybe we could come to some arrangement. Local paper, you say? That would be very good for business. Very well, you find out what can be done about publicity, and I will hold these boots for you until the end of the week.'

'Oh, you are so kind. Thank you. I will go right away and sort it out.' Sally nearly kissed him, but thought better of it as she could see the twinkle in his eye at the thought of rewards from 'this actress'. She knew exactly who to contact at the local press office, as Evie in the Box Office had already instructed her on the power of the press at all times.

'Court them at all times, luv, shamelessly. We need every bit of publicity we can get. Make friends with Tommy Nuttall. He is also their photographer and the bloke is a sucker for a pretty face.'

Here I come, Tommy! Sally found him in the Crewe *Chronicle* office, feet up, having a fag.

'Well, well, to what do I owe the honour of a visit from one of the local talent? How is it going up at the dream factory?'

'Fine, thanks, Tommy. Look, I have an idea for a photo opportunity. The manager at Freeman Hardy & Willis has agreed to donate a pair of boots to me for my number in the show if he can have some publicity. So I thought it would make a nice picture if I get my costume on and he fits the boots. Bit of leg, you know?' Sally couldn't believe she was saying this rubbish!

'Well, listen to you, sensible girl. I like someone with a bit of nous about her. Yes, spot on. Can we do it tomorrow morning so I can get it in for next Wednesday's show page?'

'Well, I can try. The costume has got to be made yet. Leave it with me and I will ring you this afternoon. Have you got a number?'

'Here's my card, darling, I await your call.'

Sally practically ran back to the theatre and up to Wardrobe.

'Gwendoline, I think I have cracked it! I have secured a great pair of patent-leather boots on condition I have my photo taken with the manager of the shoe shop tomorrow morning. Can we get a costume together by then?'

Gwendoline gave a huge sigh and leaned dramatically on the door. 'Oh my goodness, to be taken for granted like this. Let me see. Very well – give me half an hour then come back and I may just have something for you, darling.'

Sally forced a smile of thanks and disappeared downstairs, thinking the bloody woman was far more theatrical than any actress in the company!

Heather grabbed her at the stage door and pulled her into the stalls. 'Where have you been? Giles was looking for you to rehearse a scene with the chorus. I lied and said you were out on a job for me.'

'Well, it was not really a lie. I was out on a job for Wardrobe, trying to get myself a costume for the show. I did ask Janie to tell you. Honestly, Heather, it is a nightmare trying to do all these different jobs at once. I am never going to get my bloody act together for the first night,' she wailed.

'Don't fret, hon. You will be fine. I promise you, when that curtain goes up you will be there dazzling the punters. Now get over to the rehearsal room and do your thing. By the way, have you had any lunch? I thought not. Here, take this Kit-Kat to keep you going.' Heather handed it to her and patted her on the back. 'Go on, get going.'

Sally chucked the chocolate gratefully down her throat and sped off to find Giles. The rehearsal room was next door to the theatre and had been a bar once, as part of the original foyer. It had just a few bulbs for lighting and some rickety chairs. The actors were all huddled round a two-bar fire.

'Aah, at last you have deigned to join us, Miss Thomas,' bellowed Giles.

'I am so sorry, Giles, I had to go and get some boots for Wardrobe. I had no idea we were going to rehearse this afternoon,' she stammered.

'Fine, leave it for now. Just get your script and we can run through the first chorus scene. It is going to be tight, luvvies, but we will get there. Now from the beginning, please.'

Sally sat down next to Jeremy, who whispered, 'Don't worry, Sal, it will all come right in the end.' And he squeezed her hand.

Sally felt like bursting into tears. She had never felt so out of control. She hardly knew what day it was, never mind what her first line in the play might be. Still, if she got those boots she had a pretty good chance of pulling off that number and showing the guys a thing or two!

Chapter 11

'Oh wow, it is amazing! Gwendoline, you are brilliant.' Sally stood in front of the cracked old mirror in the wardrobe department, transfixed by her appearance. She was staring at a sparkly, sexy drum majorette, dressed in black fishnets, with patent-leather boots to the knee, short gold hot pants, a sequinned tunic with gold tasselled epaulettes, and all topped off with a peaked helmet with a huge black feather. She turned and gave Gwendoline a hug.

'I can't thank you enough. This has just made everything possible. I will perform to the costume now, don't you see? I can't let you down after all this.'

Gwendoline was still recovering from the hug but managed a weak smile.

'Well, I am certainly glad to be of assistance, and I must say it does make a change to be appreciated. Now if you'll excuse me I must get on as I have to sew pom-poms on twelve Pierrot outfits.'

Sally went in search of Mr Tibbs from Freeman Hardy &

Willis who was waiting in the foyer with Tommy the photographer to have his photo taken for posterity.

'Oh I say!' said the shoe-shop manager, on seeing Sally's outfit. 'That is certainly eye-catching, Miss Thomas. You look splendid, and the boots finish it all off a treat.'

Tommy set up the photo with Sally seated with acres of leg and thigh on display, while Mr Tibbs knelt at her feet adjusting the zipper and smiling at the camera.

'Great shot, great shot. Lift your leg a bit more, Sally.' This last request was met with a black look from Sally who had had enough of being exploited for one day.

'OK OK, no problem,' added Tommy quickly, 'I have got the shot. Thank you very much, Mr Tibbs. This will be in the *Chronicle* on Wednesday and I will try to get it in the *Manchester Evening News* as well.'

'Much appreciated, Mr Nuttall. Thank you, Miss Thomas, for all your help, and my wife and I look forward to the opening night. Give us a wave, won't you?' He winked and was gone.

'Well, there goes a happy customer,' said Tommy, packing up his equipment. 'Well done, girl, that was a result all round. Keep it up, and you and I will make a few bob.'

Sally laughed. 'You mean *you* will. Still, it has been a good result, I must say. The boots really make the outfit. I will certainly keep in touch, Tommy, and thank you. Now I must fly or I will get the sack. See you later.'

Backstage was becoming a 24-hour hive of activity. It was as if the theatre had been asleep for months and now the light had been switched on and every nook and cranny was lit up. Sally imagined it like a doll's house. As she pulled open the front she could see every room in the place, and in each room there was a story unfolding, with each of the characters creating their own dramas within their elected spaces. The cast hardly left the theatre for the next week so they all retreated to their dressing rooms. Heather and Sally had spent a morning allocating dressing rooms, and checking lights, plumbing, radiators and electric fans. There was so much rubbish piled behind curtains and cupboards. Dust and grime curled around every knob and knocker.

'I just can't understand why Giles never spends any money on getting all this sorted,' sighed Heather, trying in vain to apply a spanner to a radiator tap. 'It's classic, isn't it? They spend thousands doing up the front of house, and gilding the lily, but completely abandon the real heart of the place and the people who work here. I can't get this bloody thing to turn. Do us a favour, can you? Go and ask Gladys at the stage door if her Ronnie could come in and repair this, and maybe her daughter Cheryl might like to come and clean for a couple of hours with a mate and earn a few bob. I can probably fiddle it from petty cash and then at least there will be some semblance of organized chaos and Peggy and Percy will shut up for five minutes. Have you been in their rooms lately? It is real home from home.'

Sally went off to find Gladys and then decided to pay Peggy a visit. The door to the dressing room was shut, and as Sally went to knock she noticed the brightly polished brass number 1 nailed in the centre of the door.

'Enter!' Peggy invited the caller in. 'Hello, darling! How is it going? Would you like a cuppa and a biscuit? I bet you haven't had time to spend a penny, never mind drink a cup of tea. That's showbiz, my dear.'

While Peggy got out cups and saucers Sally had a chance to take in the room. It was like a grotto in a circus or a carnival. Every inch of space was filled with 'stuff', from the beaded trim round the ceiling light to the fairy lights around the mirror lights. Everywhere twinkled. Goodness knows what the electrician would have to say about the safety aspect! In front of the dressing-table lights and mirror was an elaborate hand-embroidered mat covering all the tatty and chipped paintwork of the wooden dressing table. Laid out in neat rows were sticks of make-up, all of them in the original gold and black paper carefully folded down as the greasepaint was used. At drama school the students had been given a couple of lessons in stage make-up and Sally had bought the obligatory sticks of five and nine from Fox's of Covent Garden, which was the famous make-up supplier to the theatre. Five and nine were sticks of greasepaint which, when applied together, formed a base for the face. It was thick and glutinous and looked terrible close up, but from a distance and under the lights gave the face a reasonable colour and skin quality. There were hundreds of variations of colour, and depending on the kind of parts one got to play, the quantity of sticks required would vary. However, for the juvenile lead there was really just the basic five and nine plus a carmine stick which doubled as lipstick and rouge – and, as Sally discovered from Peggy, provided the dot in the corner of the eye!

'What is that?' Sally had asked one evening when she was delivering groceries to the dressing room.

'This, dear girl, is called definition. When one is playing to the gods it is vital that they see one's eyes, and this creates a point of reference.' Sally watched transfixed as Peggy applied the bright red dot to each eye. This was followed by a thick black line along the eyelid, finishing in a tick at the edge of the eye. Greens and blues had been applied in sweeping strokes to the eyelid, each brush-stroke reaching for the outer corner of the eyebrow with alarming insistence, and joining the thick black eyebrow in its final quest to hit the hairline! Uplift was an understatement, thought Sally. The result was two huge orbs of multicoloured delight. If they didn't see that in the Upper Circle, they must be blind indeed.

Over the next few months, Sally came to appreciate that in terms of make-up, Peggy's routine was unchanging and resulted in all her performances bearing the same basic look – that of an aging Cleopatra. It worked fine for most of the time, but when she came to play Sir Thomas More's wife in *A Man for All Seasons* it was down to Percy to quietly take her aside and suggest she wipe it off immediately! To her credit she did as she was told – all but for the red dots. Some things would never change.

'Here's your tea, love.' Peggy broke through Sally's thoughts, and she took the cup.

'Gosh, Peggy, this room is miraculous. You've completely transformed it. Do you do this wherever you go?'

'Do what, darling?' asked Peggy, sitting down in front of her mirrors.

'Well, bring all this stuff with you. I mean, you must have so much to haul around with you all the time.'

'Oh, I couldn't travel without my things. This is my life, darling. You will soon come to realize that an actress's dressing room is her real home. This is my sanctuary. As long as I am surrounded by my bits and pieces, I feel safe. Percy is the same. Have you seen his room?' Peggy got up and made towards the door which led to the adjacent dressing room. When Sally had first been going round with Heather sorting rooms, she had commented on the fact that these two rooms were connected.

'Surely Pinky and Perky don't like this arrangement much, do they?' she had questioned.

'Ah well, hereby hangs a tale,' replied Heather. 'These two

rooms were originally just Dressing Room number one. In the old days the leading actor was often also the actual manager of the theatre and the company, so he had the big plush room. Apparently there was one season where the two leading actors both thought they were entitled to Dressing Room number one, and it got so heated that a compromise had to be found. So they split this into two and put the actors' names on the doors rather than numbers. So everyone was happy.'

Sally watched Peggy now as she moved to open the connecting door. What did Percy make of that? she wondered.

'Actually maybe we had better not intrude into his room while he is not there.' Peggy stopped suddenly and turned back to Sally. She looked sheepish. 'I mean, here's me going on about an actor's dressing room being his sanctuary, and I am about to invade the privacy of a fellow artiste. No, you will have to wait and ask Percy yourself to show you his bits.'

Peggy returned and took up her place again in front of the mirror.

'Now where were we? Oh yes, my things. Well, as you can see, I have collected from all over the place. Those little bells hanging over the lampshade came from China, you know. I had a dear friend who sent them to me. All the ornaments have a meaning. Mostly they are First Night presents given to me for luck, so naturally one would never get rid of them. It is a wonderful feeling to come into the theatre of an evening and wipe away the outside world. I am always in at least two hours before a show and will spend my time just pottering, you know? If I have been out during the day, to lunch or the cinema or something, I like to clear my head of all these events and just breathe in the atmosphere in my room – the make-up and the candles and the costumes. It makes me feel secure. Life is so full of insecurities, don't you think? Things we can't control, people we don't understand. Well, here in my world I am secure and safe, and in control.'

Peggy looked through the mirror at Sally sitting behind her and smiled a little sadly. 'Don't mind me, darling, just a silly old actress doing "her thing".'

'Don't be silly,' said Sally, who was genuinely moved. 'I find it all really interesting. I have so much to learn yet. Thanks for the tea, Peggy. I will leave you in peace now and go and find Percy, because Giles wants you both for the last scene. Will you be down in five?'

'Of course, and tell that Sarah to make sure my prop chair is placed stage right. She got it wrong this afternoon and I couldn't find it. Threw my scene completely, and then she had the nerve to give me a note! Bit above herself, that one, I might say – I'll have to make sure she knows her place.'

Sally left before she got embroiled in backstage diplomacy. So far she had managed to keep her nose clean.

Chapter 12

The run-up to the first night was like a roller-coaster gathering pace as it reached the top of the incline and hung there for a few seconds before dramatically plunging down again. The cast ate, drank and slept their allotted parts. Giles finally pulled them all together, casting his magic from the front of the Royal Circle, or whispering from the box. He seemed to feed them all energy. Sally could no longer feel her feet as she stomped out the beat with the rest of the cast for the finale. Every bone in her body was crying out for release from the pain of spending eighteen hours on her feet. On the Sunday night, when the technical rehearsal threatened to go on until the early hours, succour came from an unexpected source. About midnight, Mrs Wong from the Chinese takeaway next door appeared at the side of the stage with a huge box of food. Delicious aromas were wafting across the stage and everyone was transfixed by the thought of sweet and sour pork balls.

'Who dares to interrupt my rehearsal?' bellowed Giles from the auditorium.

But Mrs Wong was not cowed. 'Mister Giles, you terrible

man make all work too hard! Mrs Wong bring food and all will go better. Come, come, everybody, eat now. Mister Giles, you come too and take a break.'

The cast let out a spontaneous cheer and fell upon the food, tearing off the foil and stuffing their mouths.

'Oh my God, this is so good!' mumbled Sally through a spoonful of chicken in black bean sauce. It was the turning point of the night, and Mrs Wong became the heroine of the hour. For the rest of the season the cast would turn to her sweet and sour sauce and chunky chips for inspiration. It became the one constant in their schedule: technical rehearsal and Mrs Wong's takeaway.

They finished the run at around three o'clock in the morning. Janie and Pete and Sally staggered up the hill to the house and fell into bed. Next morning came round in a flash and they all appeared in the kitchen, bleary-eyed but ready for the next onslaught. Pete had cooked them a huge 'full English', since Janie, efficient as ever, had cannily found the time to stock the fridge for such occasions.

'This will probably be the last thing we eat today,' she warned them.

Sally felt guilty that she herself was so behind in organizing things in real life. For the last week all she could think about was the show. How would she ever survive when she moved to her flat? And what on earth would Dora make of it all?

The three of them gathered everything they needed for the rest of the day and set off for the theatre. The dress rehearsal was scheduled to start at two, but Sally had so much to do before she could even start thinking about her own performance.

Heather was waiting for her at the stage door.

'Listen,' she said. 'Before you get stuck in here, can you

whip down to Woolworth's and buy some balloons and those party-popper things? Bloody Giles has decided he wants the cast to set them all off at the end of the show. Here's some petty cash – I hope it's enough.'

Sally dumped her stuff with Gladys and set off. She practised her numbers as she sped along the road, until she caught the eye of some youths hanging out on the corner of the street, pointing at her, and laughing and hollering along with her. Oh well, so they thought she was potty – who cared!

When she got back to the theatre there was a traffic jam at the stage door as the band appeared to have arrived. Frank, George, Terry and Gil – double bass, trumpet, piano and drums all on loan from Crewe's very prestigious brass band.

'Hi, can I help at all?' she asked.

'Frank Masters, at your service,' said a tall jolly man with a fine head of hair, extending his hand from behind his double bass.

'Sally Thomas,' said Sally, taking his hand. 'Pleased to meet you. Shall I show you to the Band Room?'

Frank laughed. 'Oh, I think we know the way there by now, don't we, lads? This is our tenth year playing for this lot.'

'Oh sorry, how stupid of me,' apologized Sally, feeling very foolish. 'I am the new girl, of course. But let me help you at least, and organize some tea or coffee.'

'Don't you mither yourself, my girl, we are fine. You get on and we will see you in the pub later.' Frank managed to make a space for Sally to squeeze past. She went straight to the props corner and presented Heather with her purchases.

'Well done. Now can you make sure that everyone has their opening costumes and that all their props are checked on the prop tables either side, please? I will be calling the half in five minutes, God help us.'

The half was called twenty-five minutes before curtain up and it was legally binding that every member of the cast be in the theatre when it was called. This allowed stage management to keep tags on anything untoward or any latecomers. The biggest problem would be a no show from an actor, so the understudy would have to be informed and dressed and ready to go. If the actor arrived after the half had been called, he would still not be allowed on; it was down to the understudy.

Five minutes! Sally rushed to complete her tasks. She was desperate to get to her dressing room and practise a little with her make-up. She took the stairs to the top of the theatre two at a time. That would have to be her warm-up for the show. She was sharing one of the dressing rooms with Sarah; it was usually reserved for the chorus so it was slightly larger, with several dressing tables and a couple of basins in the corner. The boys were next door in an identical room. Needless to say though, theirs was in a hell of a mess. The boys had hung a makeshift clothes-line across the room, from which hung a huge variety of underwear, some cleaner than others. Odd socks and shoes lay where they'd been chucked in the corner. Smelly trainers and the odd football and soggy towels lay in piles, and books and magazines were scattered all over the floor.

It was horrible to see!

Not my problem, thought Sally as she passed the ever-open door and moved to her own dressing room. There had been no time to personalize it at all, so everything was rather cold and pristine. Sarah had managed to put up a couple of posters her end of the dressing table and laid out her make-up and towel, but poor old Sally's end was decidedly bare. Oh well, time enough for all that later. She had picked up her opening costume on the way up and hung it carefully on the rail then quickly unpacked her bag of goodies. She sat down in front of the mirror and finally drew breath.

The face that stared back at her through the rather grubby glass was wide-eyed and pale. She had bags under her eyes for the first time in her life, and her hair needed washing. Was this an actress in the making? Too bloody right it was! She had fifteen minutes to get ready. She stuck her head under the tap in the basin and pinched some of Sarah's shampoo. The water was cold but did the job. She had actually bought herself a little hairdryer so she attacked her wet locks with vigour for five minutes and then stuck it up in a roll ready for her nifty hat! She then whacked on the five and nine and a good dollop of scarlet on the cheeks, but no time for the red dots this show. She gave her lips a good outline though, with the old lipstick and some awful gloss stuff she had seen on offer in Woolies. It tasted disgusting, and when she smiled she had it smeared all over her front teeth. Not a good look.

She started to haul herself into her black fishnets as the Tannoy over the dressing-room door suddenly crackled into life, making her jump.

'Five minutes to curtain up, ladies and gentlemen. Five minutes, please. Could Miss Thomas come to the prompt corner immediately, please?'

'Oh shit!' Sally swore as she got her boot-zip stuck. 'I am not going to be ready.' But she managed it. Took a quick look in the mirror and was amazed how a bit of theatrical make-up and sparkle had transformed her from tired ASM to cheeky drum majorette, and sped down the stairs.

She made the prompt corner just as Heather was calling beginners.

'Well done, girl, you look great. Now just make sure they

all line up in the right order and stand by to raise the curtain, please.'

Crewe was still waiting for its automated Tabs (curtains) so they had to be raised by hand on pulleys. Sally assumed the position, and was ready to haul away, much to the delight of the boys who were all lined up behind her ready to go on, and had the perfect view of her fishnets. As she raised her arms to pull the curtain, her rather short tunic was beyond the realms of decency.

'Oh shut up, you losers!' she hissed and then got an attack of the giggles.

Suddenly there was only bright lights and the sound of the drums beating out their entrance, and they were off and running. Well, nearly . . .

'Stop! Stop, hold the tabs! We have a problem with the follow spot!' Giles was screaming from the centre of the circle. 'Go back and reset and start again.'

Unfortunately, dress rehearsals are notoriously fraught with danger. The old adage 'Bad dress rehearsal great show' is always there to adhere to, cling to – pray to!

They managed to get through the whole show just about intact, but it was now nearly six thirty and the show was to open at seven thirty! The cast were gathered in the stalls for their notes. Some had managed to grab a cup of tea, or an apple, just to keep them going. Giles gave each actor their notes, ticking them off his pad theatrically with a grand gesture of his pen.

'Well, it is the usual kick bollock and scramble,' he said, 'but the basic show is there, and we are going to get out there tonight and sell it one hundred and fifty per cent. We want our audience to come back again and again. So, I know you are tired and hungry, but this is it, guys! This is why we do it and we are going to do it well. Good luck – and see you upstairs in the bar afterwards for a glass of bubbly.'

They all clapped and hugged each other and suddenly disappeared. Sally was just clearing final pieces of paper from the stage and was aware of the silence in the auditorium. It was as though the theatre had taken a deep breath and was waiting. She could almost hear the walls whispering with all those voices from so many shows over so many years. The air was filled with a hidden energy, waiting for the spark to ignite the show; it was a bit like being in a church. She tiptoed off the stage, not wanting to disturb the setting before it was time.

As she made her way upstairs to the dressing room she was reminded of her impression that the theatre was like a doll's house. If she opened any of the doors now as she passed there would be a slice of life taking place. An action, a word, all in miniature, captured behind these doors. The sounds of laughter, a high note soaring out. Someone gargling, a thumping of feet on the floor followed by a cheer. Every corner of the building was alive and throbbing with anticipation, and then suddenly it was released.

The band played out and Sally felt the thrill of hearing the pure chords of a live trumpet against the beat of a drum. The audience started to clap along with the band. Then as quickly as the crowd was cheering they went quiet, hushed as the lights went down, and the huge embroidered curtain rose above the stage with a swish. Momentary blackness, then white light bursting onto the stage as the cast seemed to spring from the wings in their bright Pierrot costumes, singing, 'Oh! It's a lovely war!'

The two hours went past like a shot and suddenly it was over. The cast were all standing in a row in front of the footlights taking their bows to an ecstatic audience who were on their feet, and the balloons were floating above them, and the poppers were popping!

Sally thought she would burst with happiness. Nothing in her drama training had prepared her for this. She waved at Mr and Mrs Tibbs, and hugged Charmaine who was standing next to her.

'Isn't this fantastic,' she shouted above the cheering to a rather bemused Charmaine.

'Well, it is certainly different from the Royal Shakespeare Company,' replied the actress.

Once the curtain was down, after several encores, the cast tore back to their rooms and whipped off the make-up and costumes and made their way to the bar. They had been promised champagne, which had been a bit misleading on Giles's part, but there was free beer and a glass of warm white wine. No one cared: it was alcoholic, and there were even some sausage rolls and crisps. The cast did their bit and chatted to the local dignitaries. Sally got stuck with Mr and Mrs Tibbs for a while but was then moved on to the Mayor, who was very chatty.

'Wonderful show, Miss Thomas. And your number was a triumph. What a costume, eh?' He almost did a nod nod, wink wink routine, but a pat on the arm from his wife silenced him.

The cast slowly began to withdraw as was usually the way. The actors needed their space to come down from the high. Word spread round the room that it was all back to Janie and Pete's for some of Mrs Wong's chips and sweet and sour sauce, and bring a bottle if you had one. The pub was closing in five minutes so suddenly the theatre bar was empty, save for the few remaining programme-sellers and bar staff. Sally had actually managed to remember to buy a bottle on her way in that day, so she set off home with Simon and Jeremy, who were in charge of the chips.

They sang all the way home and fell into the front room in a pile of hysteria.

The little terraced house shook and shivered for a good two hours until the inhabitants could stay awake no longer. There was not a spare inch on the floor that was not inhabited by a body. Had anyone ventured to open the door they would have been knocked back by the pungent odours of stale beer, sweet and sour sauce and greasepaint. But the floor was covered with smiles!

Chapter 13

Jeremy woke up as an elbow nudged him in the ribs. For a moment he was completely thrown as he slowly sat up and found himself surrounded by bodies. What the hell . . . ? He eased himself out from under a leg or two and made his way gingerly across the room to the kitchen. Slowly the previous evening was coming back to him. He searched the debris scattered across the draining board and decided to risk a half-full pint glass to rinse under the tap. He ran the cold water and splashed his face, then filled the glass and drank like a man returning from the desert. The beginnings of a headache tapped on his forehead but he refused to acknowledge it. He had work to do. Cursing his stupidity, and regretting the last two shots of vodka he had downed the night before, he wiped his hands on his trousers and beat a retreat from the sleeping house, closing the door quietly on gentle snores.

It was still early and the sunrise was just completing a fiery red blaze across the rooftops. Crewe looked almost beautiful. There had been a frost and Jeremy shivered in his thin jacket. He quickened his pace and practically jogged to the theatre.

Not great news for the headache! He arrived at the stage door numb with cold to discover it was locked. Of course it would be. It's eight thirty in the bloody morning, you pillock! Jeremy admonished himself. Now what? His digs were a bus-ride away, and by the time he had gone home and come back again, the morning would be gone and he had to get this script under his belt. He had arranged to meet Robert at the theatre at eleven to go through his part in *A Man for All Seasons*. This was to be his first decent role of the season and Jeremy was determined that Giles would see his potential. There was so little time to rehearse that any help he could get was a bonus, and Robert's offer was a godsend.

Jeremy would just have to wait until nine thirty to get into the building when the cleaners arrived. He had no choice but to hang around outside the theatre. By the time Alice, the cleaner, arrived he was almost frozen on the spot.

'Oh chuck, you poor thing. Come on, pet, get inside and I'll make you a cuppa. Bless your heart.' Alice clucked and fussed as she led Jeremy through the foyer and upstairs to the Green Room where she put the kettle on and produced a bottle of milk from her bag. 'Let's get the fire on and you thaw out a bit. You look terrible – are you going down with summat?' she asked.

'No, but I do have a bit of a hangover,' admitted Jeremy. 'Nothing a paracetamol won't cure.'

Alice laughed. 'Nothing changes, does it? You lot will never learn.' She was busy putting tea bags in mugs. 'There is some bread here, still edible. Do you want me to make you some toast and Marmite? It's just the ticket for a hangover.'

Jeremy nodded a yes, and stuck his bum in front of the two-bar electric fire kindly donated by the management to keep the actors alive in the coldest months. Five minutes later he was finally able to feel his hands again, which were now wrapped round a mug of hot sweet tea. The cleaner brought him a plate of Marmite on toast and he almost felt human again.

'Thanks so much, Alice. I owe you one. Perhaps I can treat you to a Mrs Wong's Special one night. How does that sound?'

'Lovely, pet, anytime. Now I must get on. Clear this up a bit in here when you've finished, will you? It is not my job to wash up after you mucky lot!' With that admonishment she was gone.

Jeremy finished his toast and washed up his plate and mug, and the rest of the mugs strewn around the room. He then wiped down the table, emptied the ashtrays and filled the bin with whatever he could pick up. He then made his way to the boys' dressing room, where his heart sank. From one mess to another! The room was a tip. Costumes from last night were tossed over chairs. Underwear was draped over hooks, and socks scattered like confetti all over the floor.

Christ, what was it with these guys? Why couldn't they just show a modicum of thought for others? Why was it commonly accepted that blokes had to live like pigs? That somehow it was OK – almost manly, in fact? That real men don't bother to tidy up? Jeremy pondered these facts as he automatically went into tidy-up mode. He could not live in chaos, and he certainly would not be able to sit here and work surrounded by his fellow actors' debris. Locating a large black bin bag, he filled it with all the dirty washing, took it down to Wardrobe and filled the two washing machines there. Just great, doing the washing for all those lazy bastards on a Sunday morning! Jeremy then spent an hour cleaning all the dressing tables and the basins, asking himself if this was going to happen every week. Did his attention to cleanliness make him a figure of ridicule? Would he become the resident poof because he was tidy?

All through drama school Jeremy had had to cope with the jibes and innuendos about his sexuality. He took it all on the chin and could even laugh about it sometimes, but deep down it niggled at him. He had never really paid much attention to his sexuality; it was not a priority for him. Only his career as an actor mattered; only his development as a performer. He had never been bothered about 'pulling birds' when his schoolmates had discovered the joys of the opposite sex. He would rather go to the theatre and watch one of his heroes such as Peter O'Toole or David Warner. Most weekends he went to Stratford upon Avon, to the home of the Royal Shakespeare Company, where he'd sit in the gods and feed on the glorious words of the Bard. His parents, who were not theatrical in any way, were rather puzzled by their son's obsession with the theatre. But to give them their due, they supported him every step of the way and when he announced he wanted to go to drama school they did not object.

Jeremy had imagined that when he joined the ranks of the other drama students they would all be of a like mind. He was disappointed. Most of them were like every other student – there for the sex, drugs and alcohol. Acting was a mere sideline to the main event, which was having a good time. Once again he found himself the butt of the jokes and everyone assumed he must be gay, except Sally. It was her interest and dedication that drew them together as friends. Not that either of them was particularly mad on socializing, but they did form a pact and would often rehearse together. Sally possessed a kind of reserve that Jeremy could identify with; they both seemed to share the same sense of reserve about their bodies too, which somehow disappeared when they were acting. They could lose themselves in a character.

When Sally had got her job at the British Drama League she introduced Jeremy to James Langton and he had found a place for Jeremy as well. It was a slightly strained relationship, as Jeremy suspected that James had a soft spot for him, and although he knew James Langton was married, his gut feeling was that he might well have a penchant for young men. This instinct had taken Jeremy by surprise. Why would he think like that? Was he being naïve about his own sexuality? Yet if, and when, he had these thoughts, they did not linger long enough for him to really give them proper consideration. Basically, he was just not interested in anything else except acting. All his physical and emotional energy was geared to honing his skills as a performer. Everything else could take a back seat.

So deep in his own thoughts was Jeremy that he was unaware of Robert standing in the doorway until he heard him comment, 'Well, well, Cinderella, you poor thing. Left to do all the housework and not a fairy godmother in sight! Allow me to wave my wand and take you away from all this drudgery.' Robert had a knack of making everything he said sound bored or insulting. He didn't so much speak as drawl his comments.

'Oh hi, Robert, thanks so much for arranging to meet me. I am sorry about this but I just can't work in a mess. Please, have a seat. Can I make you a coffee?' Jeremy pulled out a chair.

'Oh, don't worry on my account. I have actually just had a coffee, so not a problem. Do you want to work here or on the stage?' Robert asked.

'Oh – well, I hadn't really thought about it. It would be

great to go onstage eventually maybe, but I think for now it would be good to just read through it here, if that is OK?' Jeremy suddenly felt nervous under Robert's scrutiny.

'Sure. No problem. Let's get down to business,' the other man replied, taking off his coat and sitting down.

They spent the next two hours going through all the scenes Jeremy was in as Rich. The character was a very intense young man who was opinionated and a little pompous. Robert talked Jeremy through the obvious pitfalls and pointed out various key moments. Jeremy listened to every word and absorbed all he could, making notes as they went along for future reference.

Finally, Robert sat back and lit a cigarette, saying, 'Well, I think we have covered just about everything you need to bring young Rich to life, don't you?'

'Yes. Thank you so much, Robert. I really appreciate this. There is so little time, as you know. I feel I can go into rehearsals tomorrow with confidence.' Jeremy tidied his notes.

'Don't hesitate to come and ask me anything else that you might discover. I am going to be around quite a lot as I am assisting Giles on this, and we will be working together on *Hamlet*, which as you probably know is his pet project. Now, shall we adjourn to the pub and warm our cockles with a pint?' He rose and started to put on his coat.

'Oh yes, what a good idea,' agreed Jeremy. 'The drinks are on me – it is the least I can do to thank you for this morning. Oh, I just remembered the washing! You go ahead and order while I just pop and empty the machines.'

Robert burst out laughing. 'Oh, the glamour of it all! Showbiz, eh?' He swept out and left Jeremy to his chores.

Later in the pub, Robert regaled Jeremy with stories of fellow actors and various productions he had been in over the years.

'How did you meet Giles?' asked Jeremy.

'Oh, we go back a few years,' replied Robert airily. 'We were lovers for a time – oops, I mustn't be wicked, must I?' He gave Jeremy a wink. 'Has he tried out his charm on you yet?'

Jeremy suddenly felt uncomfortable. 'No, why would he?' he returned.

Robert studied him for several minutes. 'No particular reason, I suppose,' he mused. 'Of course, one should never make assumptions, but I had wondered if you were gay. Is that not the case?'

'No – not that it is anyone's business,' retorted Jeremy. Here we go again, he thought to himself. Why does sex always have to come into everything?

Robert smiled. 'Now, now, there is no need to take umbrage. There is nothing wrong with being gay, you know. There are a lot of us about – doesn't make one a bad person.'

'Sorry,' said Jeremy. 'I didn't mean any offence. It is just I find it so frustrating that everyone in this business wants to know about one's sex-life. What business is it of anyone's? What difference does it make? I want to be judged on my talent, not my sexual orientation.'

Robert clapped his hands slowly. 'Bravo. Well done, young man.'

Jeremy was not awfully sure if the other man was being sarcastic or not. So he changed the subject. 'Would you like another drink?' he asked, rising from his seat.

'Thank you, but no. I must get off to my next appointment. It has been a most enlightening sojourn, dear Jeremy. You are, indeed, a very serious young man and I wish you well in your search for integrity in this fickle profession.'

Robert stood up and leaned across and kissed Jeremy on both cheeks.

'Never say never,' he whispered in Jeremy's ear and was gone.

Jeremy sat down and finished his pint. Bloody poofs! Why did they all assume he was gay? He just wasn't interested in relationships; he was completely content in himself, and with his own company. Falling in love seemed fraught with danger and best left alone. Let others fall in love with *him* – and preferably onstage. He would stay out of all the messy emotional stuff.

But then he met the love of his life – and everything changed.

Chapter 14

The cast quickly learned that they had to pace themselves very carefully in order to survive the schedule. Struggling in on Monday morning after having only a few hours on Sunday to recover from Saturday night's hangover, and trying to do washing and weekly chores, plus prepare their heads for the next play was no easy task. It was a shock to the system, and all the newcomers to the game acknowledged the fact in the pub Monday lunchtime.

'Bloody hell,' announced Simon, taking a swig of his pint. 'I don't know what day it is now, let alone in two months' time. I can't believe I have got to learn another play, and we have only done one night of *Oh, What a Lovely War!* My brain is fried.'

'We will have to curb our drinking,' said Pete. 'Either that or increase it.' He laughed. 'Come on, Si, don't be such a wimp. We can do it. Now let's get the pies in.'

Sally was certainly struggling to get through the day. Like everyone else she had over-indulged on Saturday night, and spent most of Sunday trying to get rid of her hangover. Jeremy had appeared in the afternoon wondering if she would read through the script with him.

'Oh my God, Jeremy, I haven't given it a thought!' she wailed.

'Well, don't worry. It is just I worked with Robert this morning, and it really helped me to go through the words with someone,' he said, feeling a bit of a swot now when confronted by his friend's agonized face.

'No, you are right. Come on, let's do it. But can I make a cup of tea, please?' Sally went and put the kettle on and then they settled down in her room to read the play.

The rest of Sunday was gone in a flash and Monday loomed. The cast had a read-through of the play and various discussions with Costume and Design and suchlike, and then Giles started to block the play. Sally was running round organizing fittings and set-design meetings and making tea for all and sundry. By five o'clock, when they broke for supper, she was exhausted but she still had to prepare all the props for the evening show and sort out her own costumes.

Heather could see that she was having problems. 'Don't worry, pet, you will soon get into a routine and forget how tired you are,' she said kindly. 'It is tough, but you will need to learn to take little naps when you can. Have you finished checking the props?' Sally nodded. 'Then go and get something to eat and try to close your eyes for ten minutes. It will really help you,' she advised.

Sally thought it highly unlikely she would be able to sleep just like that but she was starving so she went next door to Mrs Wong's and got some lunch, then went back to her dressing room. Sarah was there reading the play so there was a pleasant silence. Before she knew it, Sally was asleep and only woke when Sarah shook her awake.

'Sally, wake up! It is nearly the half and you will feel awful if you don't get yourself together.'

'Oh, thank you so much. Gosh, I can't believe I fell asleep so easily,' Sally said drowsily. 'I'd better have a shower to wake me up.'

She was soon back up to speed and dressed in her opening costume, standing in the wings waiting to raise the curtain.

The show was definitely a little subdued on the second night and Giles was less than pleased. Before starting rehearsals the next morning he gave the company a lecture on the danger of second nights, and never letting the standards drop.

'You have to try extra hard the second night,' he pronounced. 'The audience have paid their money just the same as the first-night audience: why should they get second-best just because you lot had too much beer and not enough sleep? I will come down hard on you all if I see any more signs of slacking. Understood?'

There were murmurs of 'Yes, sir' and the cast all sat up straighter. It was going to be a tough nine months!

That afternoon, Sally rang home to check on everyone, and Dora came on to inform her that she would be arriving next week.

'Oh my goodness! I haven't even given you a thought,' said Sally.

'Well, that is charming I must say,' replied Dora. 'Aren't you moving into our flat this weekend?'

'I don't know,' said Sally, dismayed that all this information was coming at her. 'What date did we agree? Honestly, I am so sorry, Dora, but you have no idea what it has been like, the last few weeks. I just have not had a minute to do anything else except come to work and sleep. But yes, I guess you are right – we were going to move in the second week of October, weren't we?'

'Yes, exactly, dummy. So is that still the plan?' asked Dora.

Sally tried to think what the schedule was going to be like for this weekend. In fact, if they were going to move it would have to be this weekend, because the following one was the Get-in when they worked all hours.

'Dora, listen. Let me ring the landlady Miss Morris and see what she had in mind. It might not be possible now until the beginning of next month because I am not sure I have the time. I am really sorry to mess you about,' she added, knowing her sister would not be pleased.

'You are hopeless,' came the expected reproach. 'Why do I bother to try and support you? You are so selfish, Sally.'

Sally sighed and waited for a pause in the tirade.

'Look, I have told you, I will ring the landlady right now and do my best to sort it. I am really sorry, Dora, but I can only do my best, so just give it a rest. Can you put Mum on the phone now, please?'

Sally heard a loud snort the other end of the line as the phone was banged down and Dora shouted to their mother to come to the phone.

'Hello, darling, how's it going?' The sound of Patricia's voice made Sally feel desperately homesick.

'Oh Mum, it is so good to hear your voice,' she said, trying not to burst into tears. 'I am so sorry about Dora, but honestly you have no idea how hard I have been working. It is a nightmare.'

'Don't worry, my darling. Dora will calm down. She has just got so over-excited about coming to live with you. It is all she talks about. I am worried about you though, Sally. Are you eating properly? Do you get enough sleep?' she fretted.

'The answer is no, and no – but honestly, Mum, it is fine really. It is just a shock to the system after not doing very much, and it is certainly nothing like drama school. God, we didn't know how lucky we were just playing at acting. But it is great fun, and when I am actually performing, it is completely magical!'

'Well, please look after yourself, dear. Is there anything you need?' asked her mother. 'We can send supplies with Dora. But don't worry about arranging the flat right now if you are so busy. Dora will have to be patient.'

'No, I understand how she feels,' said Sally. 'It is just that I have had so much on my mind it was a shock when she launched into the plan. I will ring her later, tell her, when I have spoken to the landlady. Now I had better get on. Give my love to Dad and of course to you.'

'All right, my dear. Lots of love to you – and ring any time won't you? Bye.' Her mother hung up.

Sally took a deep breath and went to find the number for the landlady of the flat.

As it turned out, Dora was quite right and Miss Morris, the landlady, *was* expecting them the coming weekend. Sally agreed she would pick up the keys during the week from the agent's office, which was only down the road from the theatre, and move in on Sunday.

Sally went to find Janie and break the news of her imminent departure.

'Oh no – I will miss you so much. It is going to be just me and the boys all the time. Promise you will come round some-times and give me some female support,' Janie pleaded.

'Of course I will. And you can come to me to get away from them all. Honestly though, I am not sure I am ready for this at all. I haven't given it a thought since I came up in the summer. I just hope it is all going to be OK – with Dora and everything, I mean. I need to talk to Gwendoline as well, about letting my sister work in Wardrobe. Will she pay her, do you think?'

'Well, we could certainly do with some help, and if she is willing to do some laundry et cetera as well as the sewing, I am sure Gwendoline will find the money from somewhere.'

Sally went to Wardrobe as soon as she got to the theatre that night for the show. As usual Gwendoline was surrounded by washing. Crossing her fingers, Sally reminded her about Dora.

'Yes, I remember Susan mentioning your sister,' Gwendoline said. 'I think she could be just what we need. When would she want to start?'

'Well, we are moving into the new flat on Sunday so she could start Monday if you wanted. We have got a washing machine as well so she could always do stuff for you at our place,' suggested Sally.

Gwendoline laughed. 'Perfect. Not sure your sister will thank you for volunteering that information, but still, it sounds good to me.'

'Thank you so much, Gwendoline. It is very kind of you. I will go and ring her now and tell her she is hired.' Sally went down to the stage door to use the phone.

Gladys was sat in front of her ever-glowing electric fire and greeted her warmly. 'All right, dearie? You coping with it all? I know it is hard the first few weeks adjusting to the long hours. Bless yer heart, you look worn out already. When's that sister of yours turning up then?'

'You must be psychic, Gladys. I am just about to ring her and arrange for her to arrive on Sunday when we move into our new flat.' Sally pressed the button to the tinkle of coins dropping in the box. 'Mum? Can I speak to Dora please? Yes, it is all arranged. No, I'll manage, don't worry.' Sally smiled at Gladys who was pretending to look busy with her knitting, while eavesdropping on Sally's phone call.

'Sally? What's happened? Is it OK for me to come on Sunday?' Dora hardly drew breath.

'Yes, it is all sorted. Miss Morris is expecting us to move in then. Good job you are on the ball, Dora. Listen – are you coming by train or is Dad bringing you?'

'Dad has offered to drive me and I think Mum would like to come as well and see where we are going to be living. Is that OK?' Dora sounded unsure.

'I suppose so, but the trouble is, it will be quite a rush if they want to stay for lunch because we have to move everything and unpack and I only have Sunday, plus I will have to work on my lines. It is all a bit overwhelming really,' sighed Sally.

'Don't get your knickers in a twist, sis. Mum and Dad will understand and you will be in need of a free lunch by then. We can go to that place we went to before and have a Sunday roast, then Ma and Pa will go and we'll have all afternoon to sort ourselves out. Then I can make the supper while you do your lines. How's that sound?'

Sally could not help but think it sounded great. 'Perfect,' she replied. 'You are a star, baby sister. I can't wait to see you. So you will be arriving mid-morning, do you reckon?'

'Absolutely. See you then, sis.' And Dora was gone.

Sally had a sneaky feeling her life had been taken over, but at the moment it didn't seem such a bad thing.

The rest of the week was full on, as on Wednesday they had a matinée and an evening show. Thursday, Giles finalized the cast for the next production, the musical version of *Lysistrata*, a Classic Greek comedy about women withholding their sexual favours from their husbands until the latter agree to stop going to war. Charmaine was to take the lead of Lysistrata, and Sally was to understudy and also play one of the other neighbours, plus she had a great solo. Fortunately it was all set on an empty stage, with few props, so that was something less to concern her. However, the thought of Greek women and sexual favours was a lo-o-o-ng way from Sir Thomas More and his troubles. One thing at a time, please!

Chapter 15

Dora let out a scream of delight and hugged her sister.

'We are here! Isn't this great? Dad is unpacking as we speak. Oh sorry, Mother, here you go. Big hugs all round.' Dora moved aside so Patricia could take her place in Sally's arms.

'Oh darling, you look exhausted. Come on, let's bring everything in and then we can sit and talk. Douglas, don't unpack anything yet, please. We need a plan.'

Sally looked at her family standing there in the road beside a car loaded with stuff. Where to start?

'OK, guys, first things first – let's go to the new flat. Is there room for me in there as well, or shall I walk?' She already had her coat on.

'You can sit on Dora's lap,' suggested Douglas. 'It's only up the road, isn't it?'

'Yes, come on, Sally. We can squeeze in the front and Mum has a little spot in the back between the pillows and the laundry basket.'

They all piled in and set off up the hill. Sally produced the keys to their new home, opened the front door, and she and

Dora jockeyed for position. Both girls managed to reach the inner door at the top of the stairs together. Breathless and flushed with excitement, Sally finally managed to open the door and they practically fell into the hallway. Thank goodness the sun was shining and the flat looked bright and welcoming. As the girls went from room to room, it was clear that someone had taken the time to clean the place very thoroughly.

'Oh, it is fantastic,' said Dora. 'Much nicer than I remember.'

'You are right, sis,' replied Sally. She made her way to the kitchen and found a potted plant and a note. 'Hey, come in here, Dora. Look – the last tenants left us a note and a plant.' Sally read it aloud.

> *'Dear new tenants,*
>
> *Hope you will be as happy as we were in the flat. See other note for instructions for hot water, etc.*
> *Miss Morris likes to collect the rent herself and have a poke around. But she is no trouble!*
> *Good luck.*
>
> *Jean and Trevor*

'Oh, that is so sweet of them,' remarked Patricia, making an entrance through the door with a laundry basket full of groceries. 'Now come on, girls, get this unpacked asap, then we can go and have lunch.'

They all got down to work, making beds and unpacking food. The flat very soon looked like a home, especially with the added touches of big cushions made by Patricia, and a secondhand rug or two. The pièce de résistance was finally brought up from the car by Douglas and given pride of place in the lounge.

'Oh Dad, you are a star!' Sally rushed to give him a hug as her father set down the TV.

'Well, I am glad you are appreciative, my girl. But it will be useful for you both on a cold Sunday afternoon.' He fiddled and faffed with the tuning until it all worked perfectly. 'Good job there is an aerial. How did you find out?' he asked.

'I rang Miss Morris, of course. She is such a lovely lady and quite understood the need for a TV. "I wouldn't be without mine," she told me. Listen, everyone, are we nearly finished? Only it is already one thirty and I have got work to do this afternoon. I am sorry to be so boring.'

'No, darling, don't worry,' said her mother, coming into the room with a bowl of pot pourri. Everyone looked at her. 'What? Why not? It might have been awful when we got here and this would just help things smell a bit more pleasant.' She plonked it slap bang in the middle of the rather scratched coffee table and the rest of the family burst into laughter.

'Only you, Patricia,' chuckled Douglas. 'Now come on, get your coats and let's get going.'

Fifteen minutes later the family were sat round a table in the pub, ordering the infamous Yorkshire puddings.

'You wait till you see the size of these suckers, Mum,' announced Dora, already tucking into a packet of pork scratchings.

The meal was a big success and Sally relished the food and the company of her family. She realized how much she had missed them. Still, at least now she had Dora with her which would give her so much support.

'It is lovely to see you, Mum,' she whispered as Douglas was paying the bill. 'I do love you.'

'I know, darling, and we love you. Try not to get too tired and make sure you eat properly. We will come and visit you whenever you want. Which show would you like us to see?' asked Patricia.

'Blimey, Mum, I haven't given it a thought, to be honest,' replied Sally. 'Let me get through the next couple of weeks and then I will have a better idea. I don't know if I am going to get a really good part yet. *Hamlet* should be marvellous, but I am only playing the Queen in the Dumb Show. But I am directing that, by the way, which will be very interesting.'

Her mother gave her arm a squeeze. 'I know you will do your best at whatever is put before you,' she murmured. 'We are so proud of you, Sally. We just want you to be happy.' Then Patricia leaned over and kissed her daughter. Douglas had paid the bill and farewells were exchanged in the pub, and then Sally and Dora were dropped off at their new front door.

The girls waved their parents out of sight and stood on the doorstep. It had turned chilly now the sun was going down, and dusk was spreading its blanket over the rows of terraced houses with their identical red-brick chimneys and their gently curling smoke signals evaporating into the darkening sky.

Sally opened the door and they both stepped inside without a word. They climbed the stairs to the landing, and then walked slowly into their new home. Dora turned on an overhead light which needed a shade, while Sally went and plugged in the electric fire. It was soon glowing like a fairground ride thanks to their father's donation earlier to the meter in the kitchen. Sally switched on a table light with a warm pink shade, again donated by the parents, its rosy light spreading tranquillity through the room.

'Look what Mum has left us,' announced Dora, coming in from the kitchen with a bag of crumpets and a plate of cream cakes.

Sally sank into the battered armchair and let out a sigh of contentment. 'Dora, this is perfect, our very own space. It is so cosy already. I love it. Would you be an angel and put the kettle on while I start to attack this script?' she asked.

Dora looked slightly miffed. 'Well, I suppose so, just this once. But don't think I am going to wait on you hand and foot, once I start working, sister dear.'

Sally looked up at her, checking for signs of real bad temper and found none. She grinned.

'No, of course not, silly – just today. I am so behind, and it has all been a hell of a learning curve. You wait till tomorrow, Dora – you won't believe the hours!'

Dora went into the kitchen to fill the kettle.

'I can't wait,' she said to herself with a big grin on her face. 'I simply cannot wait.'

Chapter 16

The inhabitants of the upstairs flat at number 7, Ridgeway Road were a little stressed the next morning. Sally was up bright and early, but her sister proved more of a problem. The coffee failed to raise her, so did the radio on full blast, so finally Sally was forced to resort to pulling the covers off, hardening her heart to the moans and groans of protest.

'Dora, I am sorry, but this is the reality. We have to be at the theatre by nine, so come on, move your arse, please. You've got fifteen minutes.'

Dora let out a scream and leaped from the bed. She made a dash to the bathroom, wailing, 'It's *sooo* cold!'

Sally couldn't agree with her more, but there was no central heating, and the idea of getting up even half an hour earlier to put the electric fire on was too much, not to mention the electricity bill. So Sally had got used to the morning dash to the ablutions, and often didn't bother until she got to the warmth of the theatre.

She made Dora another coffee and a piece of toast to make amends, and when Dora appeared at the bathroom door wrapped in her huge fluffy dressing gown, Sally explained the problems, and suggested that her sister do the same and just make sure there were lots of woollies to hand each morning to slide into at speed. Dora's answer was a bleary-eyed nod.

They managed to leave on time and jogged down the hill to the theatre which warmed them up a little. They arrived just after nine, in fact, so the wonderful Gladys was there to greet the new recruit.

'Morning, Sally, and good morning to you, Miss Dora. We have been expecting you. It is a pleasure to have your lovely face gracing my stage door, and I wish you every success with the season. Anything you need or any problems, come to Gladys.'

Dora puffed up with pride and plonked a big kiss on Gladys's cheek. 'Thank you, darling, I will.' And with that she flounced off down the stairs.

'Quite the actress, eh?' said Gladys with a wink. 'You wanna watch yourself, duckie. She will be after your job next.' She laughed so hard she had a coughing fit. Sally left her to it and hurried after Dora. She found her talking to Heather outside the wardrobe department.

Heather was already doing her recruiting speech but Sally interrupted her with; 'Hang about, Heather. Gwendoline has first refusal, you know.'

Heather sighed. 'I know, I know, but it would be great if Dora can spare me a bit of time to get some props when you are doing your acting. You know what it's like now, Sally – every bit of help is needed.'

Sally nodded in sympathy, but added, 'Yes, you are right – but can we just start Dora where she was supposed to be and then take it from there?'

Heather laughed. 'Yeah, of course. Good luck, Dora – but

remember me, please.' And the stage manager was off up to the stage to begin the day.

Gwendoline was inside the wardrobe department with her head in the washing machine as usual.

'Hi guys, be with you in five minutes,' she said. 'Why don't you make us all a coffee? I even brought some buns in this morning as a special treat to welcome Dora.'

'Oh thank you so much, Gwendoline,' gushed Dora, ignoring the signs from her sister indicating that she should lay off the creeping.

Sally said, 'That is lovely of you and we will get started. Come on, Dora, take at least one of those cardigans off and let's get to work. I will make coffee while you acquaint yourself with where everything is.' Dora took the hint, and slipped off her coat and top cardigan then went to join Gwendoline.

Sally made coffee and put the buns on a plate, not before stuffing one in her mouth. Then she called out to the others: 'Coffee's ready. I am off to set up with Heather. Come and find me later, Dora, when Gwendoline has finished with you – if she finishes with you at all!'

Up onstage the actors were all gathering for the first scenes. Sally found Jeremy in a corner as usual.

'I am so sorry I was not around yesterday,' she told him, 'but my family arrived with my sister Dora, and we moved into our new flat. Do you want me to read a couple of scenes with you now, before we start? Is there time?'

Jeremy looked relieved. 'Yes, come on, let's whip up to the Green Room and you can take me through these two scenes.'

Sally told Heather where she was going, and Heather waved her off, saying, 'See you in half an hour.'

The two friends left the stage and went upstairs. After they had finished and were on their way back down, they passed

Geoffrey Challis's dressing room and Gwendoline came out, looking a little ruffled. Just before she managed to shut the door, Sally caught a glimpse of Geoffrey very much in a state of undress.

Her surprise must have registered on her face enough for Gwendoline to feel the need to stammer: 'Just sorting Geoffrey out with a costume that needs adjusting. The poor man is hardly awake.' And she scuttled off.

Sally looked at Jeremy and said, 'Well, that was a bit odd at this time of day, don't you think?'

He looked perplexed. 'What do you mean exactly?'

Sally laughed. 'Oh Jeremy, you are useless. You miss everything. The wardrobe mistress coming out of an actor's dressing room, before nine thirty in the morning, looking a little flustered. And the actor with only his pants on. One could be forgiven for suspecting a bit of hanky panky!'

Jeremy eyed his friend a little crossly. 'Oh, for goodness sake – not you as well, Sally. Why does everyone have to bring sex into everything? Maybe she was just fitting him.' He marched on down the corridor followed by a giggling Sally. Fitting him for what though? she thought to herself, and made a mental note to find out what was bugging her friend about sex.

On stage, Giles was clapping his hands and calling for quiet.

'I need to tell you all a couple of things about the next two productions. Is everyone here? Where are Sally and Jeremy and Geoffrey? Heather, can you give them a call over the Tannoy, please. In the meantime, I will start with Act Two this morning so if everybody would be kind enough to hang around the theatre or at least keep close by – preferably *not* in the pub, Percy.'

This drew a groan from Percy and a snort from Peggy, who said, 'He will be in my dressing room with me, sir, doing his lines.'

Sally and co arrived with apologies and the cast was complete.

Giles took the floor.

'There are a couple of problems with *Lysistrata* and the chorus. We have some wonderfully strong voices already but we need to swell the numbers. I have two thoughts. First, is to engage a couple more actresses from local sources if possible, and second, we pre-record the songs and then play the choral numbers on speakers from the wings to increase the volume. I would appreciate any suggestions for the actresses and I have, in fact, already contacted the stage school to see if any of the teachers fancy a go.

'The second point is to give you all a heads-up on the casting for *Hamlet*. We are very excited to be able to announce the arrival of Rupert Hallam who is making a name for himself on the small screen in the very popular *Up at the Big House* which is in its second series, and I know he is going to do a wonderful job as Hamlet. Opposite him I have engaged another rising star, Isabelle James, fresh from her first film, playing a part in a new Woody Allen movie, as yet untitled. I hope you will all make them most welcome. With regards to the rest of the casting, I would like to see Jeremy, Simon and Peter tomorrow lunchtime, and can you all be prepared to read different scenes and different parts for me, please? Right, that is housekeeping over, now let's get back to good old Sir Thomas, shall we?'

The boys all went off to a corner to discuss their chances, and Jeremy found his way to Robert who had been standing behind Giles throughout, as usual.

'Could I have a word please, Robert?' Jeremy asked a little tentatively.

'Of course you can, my dear. Fire away.' Robert turned and fixed Jeremy with his very blue eyes which seemed to bore into him like a laser.

Jeremy took a deep breath and said, 'I would very much like to have a stab at Laertes, and if you think I am in any way suitable for the part, would you put in a good word for me with Giles?'

Robert looked at Jeremy, appraised him, and took his time. Jeremy held his ground and waited.

It seemed an age before Robert finally gave his response. 'Yes, of course I will. Leave it with me.'

'Thank you very much,' replied Jeremy and left Robert watching him depart to join the boys.

Sally in the meantime had dashed up to Wardrobe to grab Dora.

'Listen, sis, I think there may be a job for you in the next production, singing in the chorus. Maybe even a couple of lines. What do you think?'

Dora was on her sewing machine already and had to stop production to take all this in.

'Oh my God, you really think so? But can I do it, Sally? I am not an actress.'

'Oh, don't be ridiculous,' scoffed Sally. 'You have an amazing singing voice – nearly as good as mine. That's a joke, by the way. You can do it standing on your head and you have got me to help. Giles wants suggestions and then he will audition you.'

'Audition me?' yelped Dora. 'I will be so nervous though. What will I sing?'

'Anything you like. A Beatles song, a folk song – you know

loads of them – and I can always take you through some of the actual chorus from the play. You must have a go, Dora – please!'

'OK, OK I will do it. Now let me get on with this, or I will get the sack before the end of my first day!'

Sally went to find Giles and talk to him about her sister. He seemed pleased and impressed by the Thomas family's talent.

'That is good news, Sally. Tell your Dora that I will see her next Saturday morning at ten o'clock onstage.'

Thrilled to bits, Sally spent the rest of the morning working her way through the props. Simon, Peter and Jeremy had gone off to Wardrobe to check out the new girl, and were all very happy: there was a sudden rush to be measured for their costumes. Gwendoline came to Dora's rescue by informing them that the costumes were all hired, and if there were any alterations, she and Janie would be doing them, as Dora was assigned to making the girls' costumes for *Lysistrata*. Knowing they were going to be very flimsy, this only increased the boys' interest in design, and Dora was invited to the pub at lunchtime for a chat.

'Oh, go away, you horrible lot and let me get on,' scolded Dora. 'But I shall expect the drinks to be on you later, or my mouth is sealed.'

Sally laughed and made a mental note not to worry too much about her sister; she could obviously take care of herself. There were far more important things to concentrate on, like finding a throne for the play and doing another performance of *Oh, What a Lovely War!* tonight. As the actors all traipsed downstairs Sally felt obliged to remind them of this and suggested they rest between the rehearsal and the show. Fat lot of good it would do.

Heather was coming towards her brandishing a notepad.

'Oh, this looks like bad news,' sighed Sally. 'Where do you want me to go?'

Heather was apologetic. 'We need to nail this throne as it is the main prop really. Lord Edward Graham has offered to lend us one. Amazing, eh? He is a great friend of Giles's, apparently. Anyway, if you could go with Peter in the van and pick it up this lunchtime, it would be perfect. I know you will probably miss lunch but I will treat you both to a McDonald's on the way back.' She handed Sally some cash. 'Is that a fair deal?'

Sally knew she had no choice but that was OK – all part of the job. 'Your wish is my command,' she said brightly. 'Just one favour, will you keep an eye on Dora in the pub? You might have to remind her that she has to come back at two and work.'

'Will do,' replied Heather, hurrying off to her next assignment.

Sally stood in the corridor for a minute trying to remember what she was going to do next. Oh, yes of course – she needed a pee!

Chapter 17

Sally and Peter drove through massive black wrought-iron gates, topped with a crest and a motto in Latin. Before them stretched a road winding its way between two lines of beautiful conifers; spreading back across the adjacent lawns were huge oaks and chestnut trees which had obviously been planted hundreds of years ago. The road twisted for at least a mile and a half and then suddenly, over the brow of a little hill, Crewe Hall came into view.

'Wow!' breathed Peter.

'Yes, indeed,' Sally managed to stutter. 'Golly, this is stunning and it must be very old. All that half-timbering is fifteenth-century Tudor, isn't it?'

They drove round the sweeping courtyard past an impressive fountain which, despite the winter frosts, was spouting happily. While they were wondering if they could leave their rather tatty van outside the front entrance, a man in a pinstriped suit appeared.

'Good morning, folks,' he said pleasantly. 'I am Chester, the butler. You must be from the theatre. You can leave the van here and we can go and fetch the throne. It is quite heavy, I should warn you, young man.'

Sally made the introductions and then they followed Chester inside the enormous pile. She wished her father could be here to see this magnificent entrance hall, with its high vaulted ceiling soaring over a huge oak staircase that wound its way down from heaven above to the ground floor. All the wood was in such good nick and polished to perfection that Sally couldn't help but comment, 'Gosh, you must have quite a staff working here to keep this in such good condition.'

Chester answered quite naturally, 'Oh yes indeed, we have a team of cleaners on a rotation scheme. Crewe Hall is like the Forth Bridge: by the time you get to the other end you have to start again. I am sure His Lordship would be happy for you to have a tour at some point. We do official tours in the summer, but yours would be private. I will mention it to him at the next Housekeeping meeting. Now here is the throne. We brought it down from the throne room for you to save time. Can you hold the cushions, Sally? And, Peter, if you take the other arm, hopefully we can lift the chair or drag it outside.'

The two men managed to make it to the front of the house, but then hit the problem of the gravel driveway.

Peter had a suggestion. 'I will back the van up so we can lift it in without damage.'

This accomplished, the three of them managed, with the help of a rope or two, to get the throne into the van, laid carefully on its side on top of a rug.

'Well done,' said Chester rather breathlessly. 'I can see you both have some commonsense. I would just remind you again, and please pass this on to your colleagues, that this throne is very old and very valuable.'

'Absolutely understood, sir,' replied Sally. 'Is His Lordship coming to watch the play?' she added.

'Yes, I believe he will be attending with his son and daughter. He is very keen on history, as you can imagine, and likes to encourage that interest in his children. After all, they will inherit all this eventually, so it is important they understand the historical background of Crewe Hall and where they come from.'

Sally and Peter thanked the friendly butler and set off down the beautiful drive once more. They drove much more slowly on the way home, aware of the priceless item that was on board. When they queued at the drive-in for their McDonald's, they both giggled at the thought of what they carried in the back of the van. It was a long jump from Tudor lords to travelling players like themselves, partaking of an American hamburger!

Heather was waiting back at the theatre worrying about her most precious prop. She had the scene dock open for easy access and Peter drove the van straight in. They managed to unload the throne with no difficulty, and placed it, wrapped in its blankets, in a safe corner.

Heather announced: 'This is now my responsibility for the whole of the run. Giles has informed me that the throne is insured for thousands of pounds. So if it goes missing or gets damaged, I am in deep doo-doos!'

During the tea break, Sally went to find Percy to suggest he come and take a look at his magnificent throne – maybe sit in it and get the feel of it. She also thought it might be a good idea to make sure he understood how valuable it was before he had his mid-morning coffee and biscuits while seated in it! She knocked on Percy's dressing-room door but, as was often the case, it was Peggy's lilting voice that called out, 'Come in! Oh Sally my dear, how lovely of you to come and see us. The kettle has just boiled, and I am making a pot for Percy and me, but we can add another cup.' She rose from her chair and went to the cabinet of crockery to find another china cup and saucer. It was always china cups for tea, with Peggy.

'I don't want to be a bother,' said Sally. 'Is Percy OK? He has such a mammoth part in this play, he must be working all the hours God sends.' She took the cup and saucer from Peggy and laid it on the tray with the others next to the matching milk and sugar bowl. There was also a china stand with some rather delicious-looking biscuits laid out. Definitely the place to come for tea, thought Sally to herself.

Peggy had warmed the teapot and was now measuring heaped teaspoons of tea leaves into the pot and adding boiling water. 'This will put hairs on your chest,' she teased. 'Mind you, it hasn't done a lot for Percy. Talking about Percy,' Peggy lowered her voice, 'I am a bit concerned about him, to be honest with you. He has taken to staying late in his dressing room, saying he is doing his lines. Now that is all well and good, as long as he stays off the sauce, but he can't always do that on his own. So I offered to stay with him but got short shrift. He said he was fine, thank you, and didn't need me spying on him. Well, I must admit that hurt me somewhat, but then again I am used to the other side of his tongue. Anyway, the other night I stayed in my room catching up on some letters, et cetera, and time went on. Then I heard voices next door. This was now about midnight. Well, I was curious, to say the least, and knocked on the door. Percy called out, "Hold on a minute!" so I assumed he was in the toilet. But when he finally unlocked our dividing door he looked very dishevelled, and sitting in his armchair as happy as Larry was Sarah, with a copy of the play conveniently placed on her lap.

'"What's all this," I asked,' continued Peggy, pouring out their tea.

'"Nothing, my sweet, just a bit of work on my lines and young Sarah is very kindly taking me through them."'

'So I said, "Well, when I offered, you refused. But I can see the attraction of going through lines with a pretty young thing like Sarah and not a raddled old bag like me."'

'"Oh come on now, my girl, you are being daft. I just wanted to save you having to stay up late. I know how much your beauty sleep means to you. So when Sarah offered I took the opportunity. I was only thinking of you, my love."'

'What could I do but leave them to it?' Peggy asked Sally. 'So I said something like: "Well, you need your beauty sleep as well, Prince Percy, preferably on your own. I will see you back at the digs in an hour."'

Peggy passed Sally her cup of tea and proffered one of the delicious biscuits.

'What do you make of Sarah?' she enquired, watching Sally very closely.

'I'm really not quite sure what to make of her, to be honest. She doesn't really muck in with the rest of us, and I do get the feeling sometimes that she thinks she is above us. I suspect she is quite ambitious too, but with all due respect to Percy, can he really help further her career?'

Just as Peggy was about to reply, the dividing door opened and there was the man himself.

'Ah, we have company – and beautiful it is too. Hello, Sally. To what do we owe the honour of this visit?'

Peggy had jumped up to allow Percy to seat himself in his own armchair and wait for his tea and biscuits to be placed on the little table beside him. Peggy did the honours, then went and sat back at her dressing table, occasionally turning to the mirror and checking her hair. Occupational hazard with actors, thought Sally. They cannot resist a mirror!

'Oh, I was just passing, and thought you might be having a heavy week with all your lines and wondered if you needed anything done,' she said. 'Also, I wanted to let you know that Peter and I just went to pick up your throne from Crewe Hall. What an impressive place, and what a magnificent throne you will be having, Percy. It is insured for many thousands of pounds. So do sit carefully.'

'Blimey, that is some responsibility, isn't it, my little flower?' Percy smiled at Peggy. 'I have never had to deal with an expensive antique on stage. Children and animals are one thing, but furniture? What do you say, old girl?' he chuckled.

'Oh indeed my dear, we really don't like animals or children. Not onstage anyway,' Peggy added with a sad little smile through the mirror to Sally.

'Well, that was the perfect cup of tea. Thank you so much, Peggy, and I am glad that you both seem to have the script well and truly under your belts. I think it is going to be a really super show, and you will hold it all together as the leading man you are, Percy.'

'Don't flatter him any more, dear, or he will be impossible to manage. Now get off and have a sit-down before tonight, love.'

Sally left them to it, feeling a stab of apprehension for poor old Peggy. What on earth was Sarah up to? For the second time in the season so far, Sally was wondering the same thing and she resolved to pay more attention. As for Gwendoline and Geoffrey – that also required some serious investigating.

*

Sally now had the setting up for the evening show and was wondering where Dora might be and whether she might be in the mood to help her rather hard-pressed sister. Sally found her in the boys' dressing room holding court with a variety of the rather filthy jokes that she liked to tell – usually in the pub after a few drinks, but they were going down very well this afternoon, it would seem.

'Sorry to interrupt, but can you come and give me a hand if you have finished your sewing for the day, sis?' Sally ventured.

'Oh, must I? Sally, I am exhausted, and it has been my first day. I wanted to go home and get a couple of songs sorted. I will cook something for when you get back tonight though.' This raised a cheer from the boys, who all wanted to come back for supper. 'You have to ask the boss,' Dora told them, smiling sweetly at Sally. 'She has a lot more to do than me.'

Sally felt a bit miffed. 'I really don't know what state I will be in tonight, so can we take a raincheck, everyone? If you are not coming to help me now, Dora, I need to get on, so see you some time later.' Sally nodded to the room and left wondering why she felt so annoyed.

Can't worry about it now though, I've got too much to do, she thought to herself, and disappeared into the Props Room to find the rifles for a very lovely war.

Chapter 18

The rest of the week was the usual stressed mix of rehearsing all day in one play, then clearing one's head ready for performing the evening show – then if one was really stupid, clearing one's head the next morning from the pub the night before! Sally succumbed to Dora's invitation to the boys to come to supper after all. The trouble was, once they had all performed together at night, and the show had gone well, one quick drink in the pub before closing was not enough to bring them all down to a normal level where they could go home and go to sleep.

It turned out to be a fun evening. Simon was on very good form, as was Peter, and even Geoffrey came – followed discreetly half an hour later by Gwendoline.

'Not too late, am I?' she asked at the door, carrying a bottle of wine. 'Had to wait for the dryer to finish, as usual.'

Sally led her upstairs. 'Not at all, it is lovely to see you.' She watched Gwendoline look around the room until she found Geoffrey sat in a corner talking to Janie, and with no further comment she was off like a greyhound from the traps. Well, thought Sally, we know where *that* is going.

Dora was holding court in the kitchen where she was dishing up her famous chilli con carne.

'It is actually the only thing I can cook so you may get a little bored after nine months,' she giggled. Simon was in her thrall and helping pass bowls.

'Well, it must be love if Simon has anything in his hand other than a bottle of beer,' remarked Sally.

'Oh now come on, that is a bit unfair, Sal. I do my share of clearing up when needs be.'

This last remark brought a howl from Jeremy, who was busy at the sink washing up cutlery to be used again.

'Jesus, Simon, you talk absolute bullshit sometimes. You don't pick up anything in the dressing room, not even your pants, which I wash for you!'

'Ooh, now come on, girls, put your claws away!' laughed Dora. 'People will talk.'

'They talk anyway,' replied Jeremy disconsolately. 'Story of my life.'

'Tell me, I am all ears,' said a voice from the kitchen door, and they all looked up to see Robert standing there with one of his sardonic looks and a huge box of wine in his arms. 'I thought tonight I would get down and dirty with the artistes. Here, someone take this. I will exchange this box of wine for some of Dora's wonderful chilli, and, Jeremy, you can come and tell me your life story while I eat.'

It almost sounded like an order, and everyone hesitated slightly, but Jeremy nobly faced up to the challenge. He opened the box of wine and poured two large glasses, then collected a bowl of Dora's chilli and swept out of the kitchen, passing Robert in the door, with a, 'Follow me.' And then they were gone, leaving everyone in the kitchen to carry on.

Simon turned to Sally with the question on everyone's lips. 'Is Jeremy gay?'

Sally felt cornered. She didn't want to be put in a position where she had to comment on her friend, but could not see a way out.

'I honestly don't know, and that is the truth, guys. But if he is, does it matter? He is one of the kindest people I know and a bloody good actor. I'm aware that he gets really pissed off because he feels there is too much emphasis on someone's sexual orientation and not enough on their talent.'

'Well, I agree with him there.' Geoffrey had come into the room and joined in the discussion. 'In the end it is about talent, not your sex-life, isn't it?' The room went silent while they all looked at Geoffrey, who was a bit the worse for wear.

'How's your wife and family?' asked Peter suddenly.

'None of your business,' shot back Geoffrey. 'Have *you* learned your lines properly for that last scene? And don't say it is none of my business, because it is; you cock up on the night, we all suffer. So I suggest you make bloody sure you are line-perfect, young man. Good night, everyone.' And with that, Geoffrey turned on his heel and was gone, wending his way across the sitting room to their front door where Gwendoline was conveniently waiting with his coat over her arm.

The kitchen brigade quickly dispersed into the other room, leaving Sally and Dora alone.

'Wow – is it like this every time you have a party?' asked Dora, pouring herself a glass of the boxed wine.

'God, no, it would be a nightmare. No, I think though that as time goes on one has to be very careful not to get caught up in all the dramas. Are you listening to me, Dora? Seriously, anything you might get involved with – or anyone, for that matter – you need to make sure that it doesn't come back to haunt you. That goes for me too,' she added almost to herself.

'The trouble is,' she went on, 'we all live in each other's pockets and people need to feel secure in the environment they are living in. Actors especially get far too close to each other, far too quickly, and create these false relationships. I mean, look at us now. We have only been here a month and suddenly it is all kicking off.'

Dora came over and gave her big sister a hug. 'Listen, don't get your knickers in a twist, Sally dear. We are here to have a good time and help you up the ladder of success, and for me to discover what I really want. Speaking of which, I must confess I am really keen to pass my audition for *Lysistrata*, so you will help me, won't you?'

'Of course I will, you daft girl, but don't take things too fast. Establish your usefulness first, and you can do that by helping me more.'

'Agreed,' said Dora. 'Now come on, let's finish the chilli. I am absolutely famished!'

The party turned out to be lovely. Everyone mellowed and relaxed, and the talk ended up on Rupert Hallam and Isabelle James, the two newcomers, and how their arrival would affect the rest of them.

'Do we have any idea how the casting will go?' asked Peter. 'I mean, there are obvious choices for characters like Polonius and the King and Gertrude, aren't there?'

Robert was sitting on the sofa with Jeremy and Janie, who piped up: 'Not necessarily, Peter. What do you think, Robert? You are assisting Giles, after all – you should have some ideas?'

Robert looked round the room and realized it was time to

go. Speculation could often become very negative, and he didn't want to lose his credibility.

'Ah, now I think it is my bedtime.' He rose and gave them all his best, most reassuring smile. 'All will be revealed in good time – and never forget, there are several plays in the offing this season. It is not all about *Hamlet*, you know.' The room let out a communal sigh.

Sally decided to move things along. 'Come on, guys, it's late and never mind the Dane – Sir Thomas More has to be sorted out first. Jeremy, do you want the sofa tonight?' Sally was giving her friend a way out of a walk home with Robert. She could see the gratitude in his eyes.

'Yes, that would be great. Thanks, Sal. And you can take me through my lines first thing, can't you?' This elicited a sigh from Sally and a groan from the rest of the room.

'OK, coats on – it's bedtime, everyone. We have still got three more days of *Oh, What a Lovely War!* and then our leap back in time to Henry the Eighth. Then we have sex, drugs and rock 'n' roll from the Greek girls!' This sent up a huge cheer and moved everyone out of the door. Sally, Dora and Jeremy cleared up and then made some hot chocolate.

'We will survive, you know,' remarked Jeremy. 'Your sister and I have a lot in common, Dora. We want to succeed on our merits and we are in it for the long game.'

'I can see that,' said Dora, 'and I think you will succeed. I have only just arrived, but from the outside you both seem so much more focused than most of the cast. I have to confess I have been bitten by the bug though. If I can get that part in the chorus, who knows where it may lead next? Can't I play Ophelia in your Dumb Show, Sally? I mean, you are directing it, and I am your sister. Nepotism is acceptable, isn't it? I just have to make sure I am one hundred per cent more talented than anyone else.'

Sally laughed. 'You are incorrigible, sister dear. There is no Ophelia in the Dumb Show, but let's wait and see.'

She looked across at Jeremy, who was busying himself making up the sofa, and caught his eye. He tapped his nose and mouthed, 'Watch out!'

Lying in bed later, Sally tried to gather her thoughts. There suddenly seemed to be a great deal going on behind the scenes. She thought back to Peggy and Percy and their situation. Then there was Geoffrey and Gwendoline – what was going on there? Geoffrey had seemed the most stable of all the company, with a happy marriage and a loving wife and three beautiful children. Not that anyone had seen them so far this season. Even Jeremy seemed unsettled, and Sally was suspicious of Robert's motivation for helping him with his script. She tried to work out what she was doing in all this. Just getting on with the job, she hoped.

But was this enough? Even her sister was making plans already. Was this how it was going to be? Nine months of people vying for position. She thought about Charmaine, who so far had kept her distance from the rest of the cast. Did she learn to do this during her two years spent at the Royal Shakespeare? Sally had heard many actors moan about the politics of the company and how unfair it was. You joined the chorus, fully intending to work your way up through the ranks, only to discover that the powers-that-be could bring in whoever they wanted along the way to play the leads, and even the smaller roles. So what was the point of dedicating your early career to a company that showed no loyalty?

Well, it was still early days, and Sally had every intention of making her stage presence well and truly felt. Dora might have her own agenda, and as long as it did not cross Sally's path, they would be fine.

She finally fell asleep wondering what Rupert was going to be like and whether his Hamlet would achieve the notoriety that Giles so craved for his theatre.

Chapter 19

By midnight on Saturday night *Oh, What a Lovely War!* was but a distant memory, and as the set of *A Man for All Seasons* sprang up around them, and the speakers played a harmonious selection from the Franciscan Monks collection, the crew and cast seemed to become quieter and more serious. Well, they did for about half an hour, until Mrs Wong's sweet and sour chips arrived, and the carpenter opened the beer! Then it was all hands to the deck as usual, and a race to get through it all before dawn.

Sally and Dora and Janie finished the washing and then went back to Janie and Peter's house for a quiet bottle of wine and a bit of a gossip.

'So come on then, Janie, what's with Gwendoline and Geoffrey?' asked Sally, hunkering down in a comfy chair with her glass of red and a packet of crisps.

'How did you find out, you wicked girl? It is supposed to be the secret of the century.' Janie looked at Sally's surprised face and groaned. 'Oh God, you don't really know, do you? You guessed and I fell for it. I am such a klutz! Please don't say anything to anybody as I could get the sack. Gwendoline has sworn me to secrecy, Sally. Please—'

'Oh blimey, Janie, stop panicking – of course we won't say anything,' Dora interrupted. 'Calm down and enjoy your drink. Listen, it is just interesting though, isn't it, those two? I thought Geoffrey was happily married – or so you said, Sally.'

'Well, I thought he was, wasn't he, Janie?' Sally and Dora turned and waited for their friend to fill in the gaps.

'Yes, he was. Certainly, last season things seemed fine – but Gwendoline has been hanging around on the edge of his marriage for quite a while, I am beginning to suspect. She tells me that she and Geoffrey were an item at college years ago and then, when he went off to be an actor, they lost touch for a couple of years. She had no idea he had even become an actor; she thought he had gone to teach drama at some school up north. Anyway, they bumped into each other at a school reunion, and it was as if they had never parted, except he announced that he had a wife and three small children – these daughters who are the apple of his eye. Gwendoline is completely obsessed with Geoffrey and decided to get him into the cast last year so she could "work on him" – her words, by the way. I have no idea what went on last year, but this year, so far, there is no sign of the wife and kids, and Gwendoline is on a mission. Believe me, it is embarrassing for me because they are always touching each other up and disappearing into the laundry room, and I dread going to his dressing room in case I catch them at it.' Janie stopped and looked at the other two girls, who were helpless with laughter.

'What is so funny, may I ask? It is not funny if you are involved even if you don't want to be. Stop laughing!' she ordered.

'Sorry, Janie, really but I have got this mental image of

tight-arsed Gwendoline whipping off her glasses and her Alice band and grabbing Geoffrey in his Pierrot costume and breathing into his ear "Take me, Geoffrey darling" and Geoffrey peering at her and saying those immortal words: "God but you are beautiful behind your glasses. Come to me, Gwendoline!"' This resulted in more squeals of laughter from Dora and Sally, while poor Janie looked on aghast.

'Please stop it, guys. What am I going to do?' she pleaded.

The two sisters finally calmed down and tried to offer helpful suggestions.

'Just try and stay out of their way,' advised Sally. 'I was only talking about this the other day to Dora, explaining that it's fatal to get involved with all the goings-on. Why can't we all just muddle along like the boys do? Go to the pub, have a few drinks and don't ask any questions. Classic male behaviour. Sorry, didn't mean to be quite so sexist.'

'Do we think Charmaine is gay?' asked Dora, completely changing the subject.

'Gay? No, why do you ask that?' said Janie, pouring more wine for them all.

'I don't know really,' replied Dora. 'It's just a feeling I have and she came on to me yesterday.'

Sally looked quite shocked. 'Came on to you how? And anyway, how would you know what coming on from a woman was like, Dora?'

'Oh please, Sally, give me a break! I am not a child. We had gay relationships at school. Didn't you?' retorted Dora.

There was silence while Sally took this all in. 'Um, no actually, I wasn't aware of anything like that at school. I just never noticed, I suppose.'

Dora sighed and said to Janie, 'That is so typical of my sister. She lives in a little world of her own. I think that's why she and Jeremy get on so well. They just never notice anything except maybe their acting roles.'

Sally felt rather foolish. 'Maybe Charmaine just likes to keep things close to her chest,' she suggested, 'as does Sarah. What do we think about Miss Kelly then?' To her relief this brought all manner of speculation from the other two girls.

'She is quite hard, I think,' said Janie. 'And she uses people. I have noticed she is all over Percy Pig, helping him with his lines. Mind you, I am not sure Percy can pull any strings for her.'

'Except,' said Sally, 'Giles does listen to him quite a lot about casting, and they have worked together for many years. If Sarah can get to Giles through Percy and land herself a good juicy role this season, she can get agents to come and see her. God, listen to us! The poor girl is probably just lonely and shy, and it is easier to make friends with Percy and Peggy than us lot of witches.'

'Actually, I think you were right the first time, Sally. You have always been a good judge of character and having come into all this after you and Janie, I think I can say I have noticed things as a bystander. Sarah is not to be trusted and I suspect she is after taking parts away from you, Sal. She is always sidling up to Robert and asking about characters. She has learned all the songs for *Lysistrata* and I wouldn't be surprised if she angles for the part you are lined up for – and to understudy the lead. Just keep an eye on her, sister dear.'

'Well, you're a dark horse, Dora,' commented Janie, gathering up their glasses. 'Did you know you had such an observant sibling, and with such a cynical heart, Sally? I think you should go home and sleep on these things, girls. But please, can I remind you that these dark thoughts are a secret between us.'

Sally got her coat and bag and Dora said to Janie: 'Thank you for the wine. I am really sleepy now and my little bed is calling. Come on, Sally, it is Sunday tomorrow – how cool is that? A lie-in!'

As they walked home, arm-in-arm, the sisters did not speak, each deep in their own thoughts.

The next morning, Sally woke to a grey blustery November day, and decided that it was the perfect Sunday to stay in and watch telly and eat toast. Dora, however, had other ideas, and came bouncing into the kitchen humming a song from *Lysistrata*.

'Can we go through some songs for my audition today?' she asked through a mouthful of cereal. 'I thought I could sing the main one that old Charmaine sings to gather all you ladies together. It is quite funky and I know I could sing it well.' She proceeded to demonstrate her point.

'Oh please, Dora, not just yet. Let me wake up first,' shouted Sally, putting her hands over her ears.

'Sorry,' said Dora, looking rather forlorn. 'Just want to get on with it.'

Sally looked at her sister across the table for a good few minutes, wondering where this sudden desire to act had come from. Dora had never shown any interest in acting while Sally was at college, and certainly did not pursue it through school plays or anything as Sally had done. Why now?

'I hope you don't mind me asking, Dora, but why all this sudden wish to be an actress? I thought you had come up here to Crewe to help with the wardrobe department and learn a bit about design? Now all of a sudden you want to perform.'

Dora didn't reply immediately. She finished her cereal in silence, then got up and rinsed the bowl in the sink and left it

on the draining board. Wiping her hands on the tea towel, she
turned round and leaned against the sink.

'To be honest, I really don't know. But watching you all
these last two weeks has awoken something in me, sis. I just
feel so alive and I want to join in. Listen, I may be hopeless,
and it will all come to nothing, but I need to have a go at least.
Do you mind?' she asked Sally, holding her gaze.

'Why should I mind?' her sister answered, a little too
quickly. 'You can do what you like, but don't expect too
much, will you? I mean, Giles is no pushover and he has his
cast already.'

'Oh, I know that, of course. But there is this opportunity in
Lysistrata, isn't there? Why not go for it?' Dora's eyes were
bright with excitement. 'Can we just run through the song a
couple of times, please? *Please?*'

Sally laughed. 'Come on then, let's get it out of the way
then I can relax for the rest of the afternoon.'

The girls worked on the song and Sally had to admit that
her sister was pretty impressive. It was very strange to be in this
situation, and she felt a niggle of uncertainty. After the conversation last night about the other actresses and their
ambitions, Sally wondered if she was taking things too much
for granted. She just assumed she had her place in the company. Giles had promised her some decent roles and he seemed
pleased with her work so far. But maybe she should be more
pushy. She decided to talk to Jeremy and find out what he
knew about future casting from Robert.

The sisters spent the rest of the day lying on the sofa and lis-
tening to the wind and the rain lashing against the windows.
They had ham sandwiches for tea and were in bed by nine.
Fast asleep by five past . . .

Chapter 20

The opening night of *A Man for All Seasons* was a great success. To give him his due Percy Hackett turned in a more than adequate Thomas More. Sally watched from the wings for most of the performance as she did not have too many props to deal with, and Heather had wanted her to learn the book and be able to prompt and give cues to the actors and crew. It was a scary job initially, as everyone relies on the prompt corner and basically the buck stops there. However, Sally soon managed to deal with six different things at once and actually enjoyed the power she had in her hands during a show. Tonight had gone without a hitch, and Sally was smiling as the cast took their bows.

There had been great excitement at the opening of the play as Lord Graham had arrived with his son and daughter. They took their places in the Royal Box just as the lights were going down. Giles was faffing around in the interval organizing champagne for the guests.

'Lord Graham is a very dear friend,' he explained to Sally. 'He does so much for this theatre, and I don't know what we would do without him.'

After the play, the cast were invited to meet His Lordship in the bar.

'Is there a free pint in it?' asked Simon as they came offstage.

'Absolutely,' said Sally, who was in charge of passing on the invitation. 'Glad to see you have got your priorities right as usual, Simon.' She grabbed Jeremy by the arm as he was leaving and asked: 'Are you going up to the bar?'

'Wouldn't miss it for the world, my dear. Nothing like a bit of landed gentry, is there?' He winked at her. 'I'll see you in the bar.'

Jeremy was feeling terrific. He had nailed the role and knew he had given a good performance. As he was changing, Robert had come in and slapped him on the back, saying, 'Congratulations! You managed to make that character watchable for a change. He is written as such a prig but you made him human – even gave him some charisma, dare I say it?'

Jeremy glowed with pride. This was what he wanted. This was what he lived for. He was going to show the world what a great actor he could be. He arrived in the bar feeling fantastic and in control of his destiny – and then he saw the boy, and everything fell away. There was only silence and the space between him and the young man standing at the bar smiling at him.

'Hi, I loved your performance. Can I get you a drink?' The young man shook Jeremy's hand and then placed an arm round his shoulders and steered him towards the drinks. It seemed the most natural gesture in the world, yet so intimate that Jeremy could hardly get his breath.

'I am Eddie Graham, by the way, son of the Lord.' The boy made a face and laughed. 'It is always embarrassing at first. Hopefully you won't hold it against me. Here, have a glass of champagne. You look done in.'

Jeremy took the glass and desperately tried to pull himself together. What was the matter with him? He was trembling.

'Um, thanks very much,' he said, taking the glass and throwing the contents back in one gulp. 'Yes, I am sorry to be so slow but it has been a long day. Could you pass me another drink, do you think?' Jeremy handed Eddie the empty glass and waited for the replacement. He couldn't move from the spot. Eddie laughed and his whole face lit up. It was such an open, beautiful face, thought Jeremy, losing himself once again in the moment, only to come back down to earth with a bump as he felt a hand on his arm moving him away from the bar – and there was Giles, beaming down at him.

'Well done, Jeremy. Fantastic performance! You've met Eddie? Good, lovely, well let me introduce you to his father, Lord Graham.' Giles spun Jeremy round to face a tall hand-some man, who rather spookily resembled an older version of Eddie. Well, he would, wouldn't he? *Pull yourself together, Jeremy, for God's sake.*

'How do you do, sir,' he managed to mumble and shook the proffered hand.

'Pleased to meet you, my boy. Thoroughly enjoyed the evening. This is my daughter Tilly, by the way.' His Lordship stepped aside to reveal a strikingly pretty girl with the same open face as her brother, and mountains of golden hair.

'Hi,' she said. 'Congratulations on the play – it was fab.'

Jeremy was now completely at a loss as to where to go with any of this. The bar was so crowded and the noise level had reached epic proportions, and he felt a bit dizzy.

'Do you mind if I just sit down for a moment?' he asked no one in particular and Eddie jumped to attention.

'Of course, sorry. There is a chair. I'll get it.' And he had gone off before Jeremy could stop him.

Jeremy turned to the girl and tried to explain: 'You must think me very odd just standing here, but the thing is, it is always rather overwhelming coming up to all these people after just finishing a show. It is like coming out of one world and into another.'

'Oh, please don't apologize. I think it's great you even bothered to come. I am not sure I would.' Tilly smiled at him and he basked in the glow.

Eddie was suddenly at his side, saying, 'Here you go. Please sit and relax. We rather bombarded you, didn't we? Sorry, but it is so exciting being here and seeing all the actors and everything.'

The two siblings spent the next few minutes chatting and generally being very pleasant. Jeremy still couldn't quite bring himself up to speed and was desperate for some help to get him out of his coma.

'There you are – I have been looking everywhere for you. Oh, sorry, didn't mean to interrupt.'

It was Sally.

She stopped and acknowledged the two guests.

Jeremy finally found his tongue. 'Sally, this is Eddie and Tilly Graham. They have been to see the show tonight with their father Lord Graham.'

'But don't let that put you off,' laughed Eddie. 'We are quite nice really, aren't we, Tilly?'

Sally smiled and shook their hands.

'How lovely to meet you. I am sorry I barged in, but when my best friend goes missing I am always a bit concerned. He is not safe out on his own!' They all laughed and Jeremy started to relax for the first time in the evening. Thank goodness Sally was here to rescue him. But rescue him from what, exactly?

The bar was finally emptying out as the audience left. As

usual the cast and crew had their eye on the pub and most of
them had already left. Giles and Lord Graham were deep in
conversation at the other end of the bar so Jeremy ventured to
invite their new friends for a drink with them.

'Oh, that would be terrific, but I think Dad is on a bit of a
mission to get back tonight as he has to be in London tomorrow,' replied Eddie. 'But it would be great if we could meet up
sometime. I would love to see backstage – but I don't want to
be a nuisance.'

'No, no, of course you wouldn't be a nuisance. We work
every day until about five so if you wanted to turn up then we
could show you round. It would be a pleasure,' said Jeremy,
turning to Sally for confirmation.

'Oh yes, absolutely,' she agreed. 'Listen, I hate to be a party-
pooper but we need to get going, Jeremy.'

'Oh yes, please don't let us keep you. It has been a pleasure
meeting you and I look forward to my guided tour.'

This little speech from Eddie was directed solely at Jeremy
and it was picked up by Sally, who made a mental note to ask
Jeremy all about it later. In the meantime she grabbed his arm
and joked, 'Don't you know that a clean exit is always best?
Stop dithering and say goodbye.'

'Goodbye,' Jeremy said obediently, watching the two beautiful young things cross the bar towards their father.

He felt the butterflies in his stomach again and turned
guiltily to see if Sally was watching him. Fortunately she had
her head down and was concentrating on dragging him across
to the door. He swallowed hard and tried to pull himself
together. He needed to be alone to examine what had happened to him tonight. One thing he knew for sure: it had
nothing to do with acting or his performance.

Act 3

Exit stage left

Chapter 21

The boy I love is up in the gallery,
The boy I love is looking now at me.
There he is, can't you see, waving his handkerchief
As merry as a robin that sings on a tree.

Jeremy arrived at the stage door the next day to be greeted by a very excited Gladys, who handed him an envelope. The woman was desperately hoping he would open it there and then, and put her out of her misery. Needless to say she had examined the envelope extensively, but it had given her no clues, except that it was expensive stationery. She watched Jeremy disappear upstairs with a frustrated sigh. Oh well, you couldn't win 'em all.

Once in the dressing room, which mercifully he had to himself, Jeremy tore open the missive. The card was also expensive and matched the envelope. The handwriting was smooth and flowing.

Dear Jeremy,

It was so wonderful to meet you last night and be a small part of your celebrations.

I was so disappointed when we had to leave.

You very kindly suggested you might meet with me one day soon and show me round the theatre.

I just wanted to make sure that you understood how much I would appreciate your offer. Here is my telephone number and you can leave a message if I am not around. I am working on my father's estate at the moment so am out most of the day, but you will always find me in after 5 p.m.

I do so hope you will call.

Kind regards,

Eddie Graham
01270 998662

Jeremy could feel his heart pounding, and realized that he was holding his breath. He let it go with a big sigh, wondering what this was all about. Did Eddie feel the same way, or was this just a polite note showing a mild interest in the theatre? Surely it was more than that. Deep down inside him a little voice was telling him that there *had* been a connection last night – he was not imagining it. What should he do now? He put the card back in the envelope and pushed it down inside his bag. He would go and ask Sally.

He found his friend folding clean washing in the wardrobe department with Dora and Gwendoline and Janie. Now was obviously not a good time to discuss his life.

'Hi, Jeremy,' said Dora gaily. 'You are looking a bit stressed.'

Sally crossed to Jeremy and took his arm. 'Is something wrong?' she whispered. 'Come outside.' She pushed him through the door into the corridor.

'I have had a card from Eddie,' replied Jeremy. 'He wants a guided tour of the theatre.'

'Well, that's great. Say yes, you numpty, and get him here and then you can see how the land lies.' Sally gave him a hug and said, 'I have to work, let's talk about it later.'

Jeremy went back to the dressing room and reread the note, then lay on folded arms at his dressing table, trying to control the swirling thoughts going round in his head. Finally he fell asleep, and was awoken an hour later by the lads arriving for the evening show.

Sally meanwhile had finished the laundry and had gone off to set the stage and check props. Dora called after her, 'Hey, wait for me, sis! I need a favour. Giles has asked to see me tomorrow during the lunch-hour to audition for the chorus, so will you just listen to my song a couple of times?'

'Sure,' replied Sally, making her way onto the stage. 'Why don't you sing for me now, onstage, while no one is around?'

Dora stopped in her tracks and looked around. 'OK then, if you think it is all right.'

'Yes – go on, go for it. I will whip up to the box - just give me a minute.' And she disappeared out of sight.

Left on her own in the middle of the stage, Dora was suddenly very aware of the whole theatre. The auditorium in front of her, with the rows of red velvet seats creating a crimson sea, calm now, but which would soon be rippling with life. She gazed upwards to the balcony, a distant land, and let out a small sound, aiming for the back of the theatre. Her tiny note floated away and was lost in the crimson velvet tiers above her.

'You will have to do better than that,' came Sally's voice from the semi-darkness. She sounded so close but when Dora looked up she could see her sister away in the box. It was deceptive.

'Sorry, I was just suddenly overwhelmed by the whole building. It really is so beautiful, isn't it?' murmured Dora as she moved to the front of the stage and peered over the edge into the pit.

'Come on, Dora, stop messing about and give me a blast,' ordered her sister, and her voice chased the shadows round the theatre.

Dora cleared her throat and launched into a gutsy rendition of the opening number from the new musical *Lysistrata*. Her voice was strong and clear, and she really gave the high notes a blasting. It was very rousing and just right emotionally for the scene, in Sally's opinion. She was just about to say as much when she was stopped in her tracks by the sound of clapping. The hands were very slowly coming together and each clap reverberated round the auditorium.

'Encore! Bravo! You are hired, my girl, is she not, Timothy?'

The two sisters were trying to gauge where the voice was coming from. Sally left the box and came down to join Dora on the stage, by which time Giles and Timothy Townsend, the musical director, were leaning on the edge of the pit in the stalls looking up at them.

'Are you serious?' asked Dora, unable to keep the excitement out of her voice.

'Absolutely, my dear,' replied Giles. 'We have two talented sisters in our midst. Marvellous! Sally, I have been looking for you, because I want you to talk to Timothy here about taking a solo number in the next show. At the moment it belongs to the leading character, but Tim and I agree you have a wonderful soprano voice and it would be a shame not to use it. So if you are game, he can give you the song now so you have time to get it under your belt for rehearsals tomorrow. As for you, Dora – that is your name, I believe?'

Dora nodded her head so hard Sally thought it would drop off!

'Well, if you could come with us now,' Giles continued, 'we will take you through the role and Timothy can check out your range, et cetera. See you in the rehearsal room in five.'

The two girls were left standing staring into an empty theatre and silence prevailed. For a few seconds!

Then: 'Oh my God!' screamed Dora. 'I am going to be in the show. I am going to be an actress. Oh my God!' She grabbed her sister and proceeded to waltz her round the stage.

'Well done,' said Sally, trying to catch her breath and at the same time work out what exactly had just happened and where she herself fitted into all this. A solo in the next show, that was great – but how would Charmaine feel about losing a number to Dora, of all people? What would she have to say about that?

'Hang on, can we stop, please? I need to think.' Sally escaped from Dora's arms and went across to the prompt corner to find a script of *Lysistrata*. 'I just want to check how all this fits together,' she explained to Dora.

'Does it matter?' the other girl asked. 'All we need to do is wait to be given our new roles – and away we go. I can't believe I am going to be in *Lysistrata*. Come on, let's go and tell everyone.'

'*No*. Hang on, Dora, that is *not* a good idea. People are very sensitive about their roles and it is not your place to announce cast changes. Leave it to Giles to tell everyone tomorrow morning. Please trust me on this.' Sally took hold of Dora's arm and looked her straight in the eye. 'Do you understand? You do not want to start out at the beginning of the rehearsals on the wrong foot, believe me. Promise me you will not say a word?'

Dora made a zip movement across her mouth with her fingers.

'Mum's the word, sis!'

Chapter 22

The next morning at ten o'clock sharp the company was assembled in the rehearsal room waiting with anticipation for their next roles. It was freezing, despite the efforts of the two big blow-heaters that had been brought in, and everyone was hidden behind scarves and mufflers and woolly hats. Giles was pacing back and forth as the last stragglers tumbled in, landing in a heap on the floor. Simon and Peter had had a heavy night!

'Thank you, gentlemen, for deigning to grace us with your presence,' boomed Giles sarcastically. 'You can in fact pick yourselves up and go and get coffee for the rest of us as a punishment. You have very little to do in the next production, but I shall expect to see your support in other areas.'

The boys mumbled apologies and scrambled off to make the coffee.

'Now, ladies and gentlemen, before I go through the casting, I want to explain about the conference that is going to be held here the week our production opens, and the part we will be playing as hosts. It is the annual conference of the

Association of Repertory Theatres, and they hold it every year in a different theatre. They also like to open with a bit of a bang, so *Lysistrata* has appealed to them enormously, and they have announced that the conference proceedings will coincide with our first night. There will be a "Do" afterwards, which they fund, I am delighted to say, and all they ask of us is that we stay after the show, and chat to all the dignitaries and such. In my experience, from past events, it can be very handy for you actors, because you get to meet all the directors of almost every theatre in the country, and having given your audition on stage during the evening, you just have to be charming – and your career is in the bag.'

There was a collective groan from the cast. Actors are notoriously bad at schmoozing. Very few learn the art of chatting up producers and securing a job. Same thing with the casting couch: it is never as simple as just being chased round an office by a large amorous producer with a big fat cigar!

Giles clapped his hands and put a stop to any chat that was threatening to bubble up under the scarves. Everyone had a story to tell about some famous actor who had slept their way to the top.

'Now as far as the lead is concerned, Charmaine, you already have your instructions. However, I have made one slight change to the role and given the battle song to a new recruit called Dora Thomas.' There was a murmur amongst the ranks at this, and Charmaine scanned the room until she found Dora. The latter was not difficult to spot, as she was sitting bolt upright in the centre of the actors, looking bright-eyed and bushy-tailed.

'Secondly,' Giles boomed on, 'Sally will be singing a big new number at the top of Act Two, and I have combined the parts of the neighbour and the council member who opposes

Lysistrata into one role, which will be Sally. Peggy, you are the oldest woman in the village.'

This brought much laughter from the cast and a howl of displeasure from Peggy, though she turned it into a superior smile as she explained: 'Listen, you toe rags, it is the best part in the play and I will wipe the floor with you all – wait and see!'

Giles continued to read out the names. Out of the corner of her eye Sally watched Sarah's reaction since she had been given a very minor role as the servant to Percy's senator. Surprisingly, the girl was smiling and was hanging onto Percy like a limpet. Watch this space.

Geoffrey was also a senator and a hard-done-by husband. He winked across the room towards Gwendoline, who blew him a kiss. No discretion there then, observed Sally.

Simon and Peter returned with the coffees just as Giles was announcing that they would be playing general riff-raff and crowd, and everyone burst out laughing again. The maestro raised his hand and the room went quiet.

'I know it is a play for the women, in the main, but guys, that does not mean you must sit back and just let it roll along. I want you all to have real characters. I want to be able to understand how this strike of sexual favours, by your wives and mistresses, affects you and your lives. There is a serious message in the play even though we are doing it as a musical. So I don't want to see any slacking – and remember, you will be on show not just to our audiences but to every repertory director in the country.'

Giles broke up the group and called Timothy Townsend, the musical director, to talk to the actors about the music rehearsals.

Sally was making her way across to the piano when she was joined by Charmaine.

'I am not quite sure how to take these changes,' the other actress challenged Sally. 'Am I not good enough to sing those numbers?'

Cringing inwardly, Sally replied as positively as she could, 'Oh no, I just think Giles needed to spread the music a bit so we all got a go. You have that lovely song to your husband, and I expect Giles thought that as you have so many more lines to learn than the rest of us, you could concentrate on them and not worry about all the numbers. Which let's face it, do take up a great deal of time.'

'I suppose so,' said Charmaine, but she sounded less than convinced.

Fortunately the conversation did not continue as they had reached the piano, and Timothy was very busy handing out sheets of music.

The rest of the morning was spent learning the songs. By the end of the session, coats and scarves had been tossed aside, and everyone was rosy-cheeked and full of *con brio*.

Singing did that to people, thought Sally, who was having the time of her life, as was her sister. Dora had sung her number note-perfectly, and the room had responded with a round of applause. The girl was in her element.

It was only when they broke for lunch that Sally realized that Jeremy had not been in rehearsals. How odd, she thought. She went to the Props Room to find Heather who was the font of all knowledge – after Gladys at the stage door, of course.

'He had a dentist appointment,' announced Heather, 'but he did ask me if he needn't come back until after lunch. As he is not in the play I thought there would be no harm – and he did have a list of props he was going to pick up for me.'

Sally wondered what was going on with her friend. Still,

there was plenty of time to find out later. For the moment, she had work to do, starting with keeping her sister's feet on the ground.

The next few days were full on for the girls. The songs had to be learned before Giles could really tackle the emotional content of the play. The other big challenge was the costumes. Giles and Gwendoline had this idea of flimsy and sexy to enhance the idea of women's femininity while at the same time showing that the women themselves were not flimsy in any way, and as far as sex was concerned, they would use every trick in the book to make their husbands' lives hell until they agreed to stop going to war.

Gwendoline had all the girls round the table in her office while she produced sketches of each character's costume.

'Oh Charmaine, look at yours!' yelped Dora, holding up a drawing of the skimpiest costume they had ever seen. 'It's more of a handkerchief than a dress.'

Charmaine looked a little taken aback but Gwendoline was ready.

'Charmaine, don't look so worried. It will all be very tasteful and I will only work to your requirements. But I do want you to look incredibly sexy. I have also got some gorgeous wigs to show you. Listen up, everyone. We want a feeling of this hot Greek island full of lushness and sensuality, against the horrors of war. These women have had enough of months and months without their husbands, who went away fighting while they had to tend the fields and work hard to make ends meet. They want to be feminine again, and enjoy the fruits of their labours. So by withdrawing their sexual favours from their husbands when the men get back from fighting, they are making a strong statement, not just about peace, but the needs and importance of women on every level. By emphasizing their physical appearance and attractiveness, I want not only the men in the audience to really understand what it must be like for the poor homecoming husbands, but I want women to realize that being attractive is not about being a victim. We do not make ourselves gorgeous just for our men, and we can use our attributes for important issues, not just to please our husbands.' She paused for breath.

'So we will start with Charmaine and then I will fit Sally, then Dora. Sarah has gone on an errand with Percy so I will fit her last. We have got a teacher joining us from the local stage school. Apparently, she used to be an actress years ago, and she is happy to be in the chorus, and I think our very own Janie is going to join you onstage.' She turned to Janie who was busy ironing costumes as usual, and Sally gave a cheer and was joined by the others. Janie did a curtsey and looked very pleased.

'Just don't expect me to sing by myself because I am tone deaf,' she warned them.

'Hmm, that doesn't bode very well for the company numbers,' said Charmaine, looking displeased.

'Oh don't worry, I am only kidding. I can hold a tune OK, I just don't want to sing on my own.' And unruffled, Janie went back to her ironing.

'Right, come on, ladies – let's get down to business. Charmaine, try this, Sally take this one and Dora, you try the red one.'

Dora screamed with delight. 'Oh, how brilliant! I have always wanted to be a redhead.'

Sally and Charmaine took their wigs to the dressing room and sat next to each other in front of the mirrors.

'I must say, I had hoped my debut leading role this season might have been something a little more serious,' lamented

Charmaine, as she pulled the mass of strawberry-blonde curls onto her head. 'When Giles mentioned *Lysistrata* originally to me, I thought he meant the play. He never mentioned music or singing . . . Oh my giddy aunt!'

Charmaine had been stopped in her ramblings by the image staring back at her from the mirror. Sally had to turn away and pretend to be struggling with her wig, so as not to laugh out loud. There was so much hair one could hardly make out Charmaine underneath. She resembled Jane Fonda in *Barbarella*.

'This is ridiculous! Where's Gwendoline?' the actress snorted, and steamed off. Sally recovered herself and adjusted her wig which was actually rather nice. It was several shades of auburn, and although it was full, it did not have the abundance of curls that Charmaine's wig had sported. She turned round to see Charmaine stomping back followed by Gwendoline with an armful of hair.

'There is no need to panic,' Gwendoline was saying, trying to soothe the troubled waters. 'Of course we want you to look beautiful. Now sit down and try this one on.' She presented the actress with a much smoother head of hair though still on the blonde side, this time veering to platinum.

'I just don't see myself as a blonde,' said Charmaine. The wig was better than the last but did not enhance her features. Unfortunately, Charmaine had a long face which could look a little horsey. She did really need a few curls to lift her face.

Sally was sitting in her auburn wig quite happily taking all this in when she felt the hair being removed.

'This could work really well for me, I think,' announced Charmaine, donning the filched wig.

'But that is mine,' began Sally, knowing only too well it would make no difference when push came to shove.

'Here, you try the strawberry blonde,' said Charmaine, passing it across.

Sally put on the blonde abundance of curls and burst out laughing. 'I look like a Shetland pony,' she giggled.

'Well, how appropriate. I myself have always been compared to a thoroughbred racehorse,' stated Charmaine rather grandly.

Everyone in the room looked at each other to check whether this woman was actually serious or not, realized she was, and had to avoid eye-contact in order not to gag.

'Thank you so much for that, Charmaine. It is good to know where I stand in the breeding stakes of horses. I wonder where we are in the acting profession?'

'Now, come on, ladies, please let us try and resolve this because I need to get on,' intervened Gwendoline before things got out of hand. 'I must say the auburn wig is very good on you, Charmaine, and actually, Sally, if we trim that wig, it will be rather fetching. You look very sexy, as a matter of fact,' she added for good measure.

Sally looked at her hard to see if the wardrobe mistress was taking the mickey and decided she was being serious.

'OK, fine, I bend to your taste and you are the designer, after all.'

'Thank heavens for that,' said Gwendoline. 'Now wish me luck, girls. I have to go and break it to Peggy that she is wearing a bald cap.'

Chapter 23

'How does your mouth feel now?'

'OK, except I can't stop dribbling.'

'Yes, I must say it is not a pretty sight. Here, take my napkin.'

Jeremy took the proffered napkin and briefly touched Eddie's fingers. It sent a shiver through him. He wished the dentist had anaesthetized his whole body, he was trembling so much. Could Eddie tell? He could hardly believe he was sitting opposite the cause of his angst, in a tearoom in Nantwich. He had rung Eddie first thing this morning, having written down a message for the answer machine in case he had to speak into it. It had taken him several attempts to get the tone just right. Not too friendly, but warm and inviting at the same time.

Hi, this is Jeremy Sinclair here. We met the other night at the theatre. You said you would like a tour backstage at some time. I have spoken to our general manager who says that is absolutely fine, so any time you and your sister would like to come, just give me a call. The number at the stage door is 01270 377555. I look forward to your call.

He had dialled Eddie's number and tried to do vocal

exercises while he waited to calm himself down. He was totally caught offguard when he heard Eddie's voice answer, 'Hi, Eddie Graham here, how can I help you?'

'Oh, um, hi, is that Eddie? Blimey, I wasn't expecting your voice at all! Sorry, you have completely thrown me.' Jeremy could feel his cheeks burning and was so glad the recipient of this call could not see him at this moment.

'Is that Jeremy, by any chance?' asked Eddie.

'Yes – yes, it is. I am so sorry. Please forgive me for being so pathetic. I just assumed you would be out in the fields some-where, as you told me you were working on the estate.' Jeremy was trying very hard to pull himself together and sound like a grown-up.

'Well, normally I am, but I was waiting for a delivery of animal feed – fascinating life I lead, don't you think?' Eddie laughed and Jeremy had a mental picture of his beautiful face lighting up. 'So what can I do for you?' Eddie continued.

'Well, I was just wondering if you and Tilly still wanted to come and look round the theatre. I am actually free this week, as I am not in the next production so I have plenty of spare time,' explained Jeremy.

'Oh wow, that would be tremendous, thank you so much. I will have to check with Tilly, as she has school. If she can't make it, could I come on my own?' Eddie asked.

Jeremy felt his heart leap into his mouth and he desperately fought to keep control of his tongue which was trying to tie itself in knots.

'Yes, not a problem, just give me a ring at the stage door. Have you got a pen? The number is 01270 377555.'

'Got it, right. Fantastic, thank you,' Eddie said. 'How is it all going? Are you getting good audiences? My father mentioned that you had a good write-up in the local rag this week.'

'Yes, really good, thanks,' replied Jeremy. 'I am just off to the dentist in Nantwich to have a filling done. Not looking forward to that, I can tell you. But it is fortunate I am not working this week so I can get it sorted out.'

'Nantwich? Whereabouts? I have to go into town this lunchtime to pick up some tools. We could meet and have a coffee. What time are you going to be finished with the dreaded dentist?' asked Eddie.

'About noon, I guess,' whispered Jeremy in a fever of excitement. Why couldn't he pull himself together? 'Where shall we meet? I don't know the town at all, but the address of the dentist is 126 Chester Way. Do you know where that is?'

'Oh yes, I know exactly where you are going. I tell you what the best thing to do is: you wait there and I will pick you up and we can find a coffee place somewhere around there. How does that suit you?'

Jeremy agreed. The phones went down and he was left in a state of complete panic. What was he doing? This was madness.

And here they were, three hours later, sitting in a quaint little tearoom, and Jeremy was trying not to dribble on the tablecloth! They found so much to talk about, amazingly. The conversation flowed and they had laughed and joked like old friends.

'I guess I had better make a move or I will get the sack,' Jeremy said finally, remembering he had some shopping to do for Heather for the theatre. 'Can you tell me how to get back to Crewe? I came by train, but I can't remember where the station is now.'

'Don't worry, I will take you. It is only round the corner, and there are loads of trains. Come on.' They both got up and Eddie paid the bill.

'You don't have to do that,' protested Jeremy. 'Let's split it.'

Eddie laughed. 'I think I can afford a teacake or two. You can pay next time, and we will go out to dinner.'

They were standing on the pavement outside the café and Eddie took Jeremy's arm. 'Please say we can meet up soon.' He held onto Jeremy's arm as if his life depended on it, and Jeremy had an overwhelming desire to take Eddie into his arms and hold him.

'Yes, of course we can. Whenever you want.' Jeremy held Eddie's gaze until the boy let go of his arm and they both seemed to relax back into the world around them.

'We'd better get a move on,' mumbled Eddie and strode off to the van he was driving. Jeremy hurried after him. The station was, indeed, just around the corner, and as Jeremy was searching for the door handle he felt Eddie move towards him. He turned slightly and was caught by a kiss from him. He started to respond and then gasped and broke the moment. Eddie pulled back and Jeremy could see fear in his eyes.

'I am so sorry, please forgive me. Please don't say anything. I—' Jeremy took his hand and stopped him. 'You have done nothing wrong, Eddie, but now is not the right time or place. Please, leave me a message at the stage door, or come and meet me after the show one night if you can and we will talk. But we have to be careful.'

He squeezed Eddie's hand and climbed out of the car. He turned and waved, and then walked to the platform. He could hardly put one foot in front of the other, for his legs felt as numb as his mouth – but he couldn't blame the dentist for this. Oh God no, this was completely of his own making, yet he felt out of control. Suddenly his life was about to change forever, and Jeremy really was not sure if this change was for better or worse.

Chapter 24

When Jeremy got back to the theatre it was getting on for four o'clock. He had brought the bits and pieces that Heather had asked for, and was about to go and find her when he was stopped in his tracks by a piercing scream. He ran towards the sound, leaping up the steps to the dressing room two at a time. What the hell was going on? The screams grew louder as he neared the girls' dressing room, and as he flung open the door he was greeted by a terrible sight.

There were several women – well, they seemed to be women, but they were covered in copious amounts of hair of all different colours and in the middle was one horrible grotesque creature with a bald head and wisps of hair straggling down her neck. She was semi-naked, as were the other women, clad only in skimpy veils of transparent silk. As Jeremy ran in they screamed again, and then burst into hysterical laughter.

'What the fuck is going on?' he demanded. He was slowly beginning to realize that these creatures were in fact the girls he knew and loved. 'Sally, what has happened? What is going on here?' He had finally managed to recognize his friend under her mountain of blonde hair.

Sally was laughing so much she could hardly speak.

'Oh, my God, Jeremy, can you believe these wigs and costumes? Gwendoline is having a breakdown. She must be to create this. Look at poor Peggy . . .' Sally turned to point at the bald crone and collapsed into fits of mirth again.

Peggy was indignant. 'Pipe down, Sally! It is bad enough I have to look like this without your mockery. Come on, girls, we have got to see a way through this.'

At this point, Charmaine appeared at the dressing-room door looking stunning in a long diaphanous robe with her auburn locks cascading down her back.

'Hi, everyone – isn't this just wonderful? I am so thrilled with my costume – and look at Sarah.' She turned and let Sarah come forward. She was dressed in a white silk Grecian-style dress which hung from her shoulders in very flattering folds. A hairpiece at the back gave her thick golden-brown tresses, and the false hair had been braided into her own hair at the front. The whole dressing room went quiet.

'Sarah is going to play my maid and the sort of Vestal Virgin of the town,' Charmaine informed them. 'She represents love and purity, and all that was good before the men started going to war and causing grief and famine.'

Sally was the first to find her voice and she half-whispered, 'Sorry, but I don't remember any of this in the script I have been reading from.'

Sarah glided towards her with a triumphant gleam in her eye.

'Oh, I know – it has only just been added,' she said. 'The thing was, Percy had been talking to Giles about the play because he did it years ago, and mentioned a scene that was not in this translation. Well, Giles loved it when he read it, and as I have so little to do in this play, and because Percy has been helping me with audition speeches and knows what I can really do, he persuaded Giles to put me in the scene. Isn't that fantastic?'

Sally sat down slowly and looked at Sarah through the mirror. 'Yes, fantastic,' was all she could muster for fear of giving the girl a real piece of her mind. Clever little minx, she thought. That'll teach us to take our eyes off the ball.

Jeremy could sense that the atmosphere in the room had dropped several degrees; it was feeling positively frosty, so he beat a hasty retreat. 'Sally, I have to go and deliver this stuff to Heather, but can we talk later, please?' He was gone before she answered.

Gwendoline was gathering wigs from the ladies, telling them, 'Look, girls, please don't panic. By the time we have dressed the wigs they will look gorgeous.'

'How can you dress a bald pate?' whined Peggy. 'Do I really have to play this old hag? What have I ever done to Giles to deserve this? I will never work again.'

Dora came to the rescue and put her arm round the distraught actress.

'Now listen to me, Peggy. You are a fantastic actress and you will make this work. In fact, you are the only one who *can* make this work. Think of that scene where you get us all in the square and talk about women, and what we do for society, and how beauty is but a fleeting distraction ... all that stuff anyway. Your voice and strength onstage will be fantastic, and maybe, Gwendoline, Peggy can wear a robe of some sort that has a regal quality to it, to balance the head and the baldness; something in a wonderfully rich colour.'

Gwendoline responded with the perfect answer.

'Absolutely! You are quite right, Dora. Peggy's character should have a regal quality about her. Time has ravaged her looks, but not her mind.'

Everyone waited to see Peggy's reaction. The woman knew how to hold a moment, and she milked it for all it was worth. Slowly she raised her head and wiped away a tear. Slowly she rose from her seat and walked to the door and then turned back to the room. A straggling wisp of hair strayed across her face and she blew it away, declaring, 'Onwards and upwards, girls. I have never been beaten by a role yet. This will be my greatest challenge, and I shall embrace it with all my being. Bald is beautiful!' With that she turned and swished out.

Everyone let out a sigh of relief. Sally turned to Dora and said, 'Come on, sis, let's go and get some tea and take these bits of hankie off. I take it we will be wearing a bit more than this on the night, Gwendoline?'

'Oh yes, of course. I was just trying to get a general feel of the thing. Goodness knows where Sarah got her costume. It certainly didn't come from this wardrobe.'

'I bet she made it herself,' ventured Janie. 'She is always up to something, isn't she?'

'I wonder what Peggy makes of all this?' mused Sally, thinking that she was no doubt fully aware of Sarah's machinations, and watching her progress very closely.

'Well, there is a lesson for all of us,' announced Dora. 'Go for what you want in life.'

No one in the room was cheering.

Chapter 25

Sally found Jeremy in the pub.

'Not drinking before a performance, I hope?' she scolded.

'No, don't be daft. I take my career way too seriously to do that,' replied Jeremy. 'Would you like a drink?'

'Just an orange juice, please,' said Sally. 'So how are things? I have hardly seen you this week. Is it strange not being in the next play? Mind you, the way things are going you should be grateful you are not in it. What about those wigs and costumes, eh? I can't believe Gwendoline is going to get away with her whole concept. And we have got all the bloody repertories coming to watch us make fools of ourselves.'

Sally was in full flood when she suddenly realized she was getting no response from her friend at all. He was staring off into space, fiddling with a card.

'Hey! Hello, earth calling, anyone at home? Jeremy, whatever is the matter with you?' Sally shook his arm and finally Jeremy focused on her.

'I am so sorry, Sally. I have a lot on my mind. There is so much to tell you, but I am not sure we should talk about it now as we have got a show in an hour. Can I come to your place tonight, after the play finishes? I really need to talk to you.'

'Yes, of course you can, silly. We'll get some fish and chips or something on the way home.' Sally gave him a hug, finished her orange juice and went back to work, leaving Jeremy once more gazing into space. At the stage door Sally bumped into Giles and Robert deep in conversation. She nodded as she passed but didn't stop. She was curious as to what their relationship actually was. Were they lovers? She didn't think so, but maybe they had been once. Robert certainly kept close to the man at the top, and played all sorts of political games that Sally could only guess at. She really didn't care, unlike Sarah; the latter, it would seem, was on a mission to make herself the leading lady. She really was something else, and Sally wasn't sure she had much respect for the girl. Success at any cost? Not for Sally anyway. She wanted to be able to face herself at all times, and know she had shown integrity and respect to herself and others. She adored being an actress and just wanted to be able to do the work, knowing she had fulfilled those criteria.

Sally went down to the Props Room to find Heather, who was as usual surrounded by an assortment of props, dirty coffee mugs and always one member of the crew asleep in her chair or eating her biscuits.

'Sally, the very person I do want to see!' exclaimed the stage manager happily. 'Can you be on the book tonight? I need to have a meeting with all the heads of departments about our next offering. I gather you actors or rather actresses are not happy with your costumes?'

Sally chuckled. 'Well yes, that would be an understatement, but to be honest with you, Heather, I don't think anyone much cares what the actresses think. Giles has a vision of sex and Ancient Greece that he is going to parade before the residents of Crewe and the directors of the Repertory Organization, whether we like it or not. We will either be run out of town, or never work again – or both! Yes, I will be on the book tonight, no problem. Is everyone in and on the job who should be?' she added.

'All present and correct. Thanks, Sally, I owe you one.' Heather gave her a smile and set off to find her team.

The evening show went without a hitch until Act Two, when Percy, in his robes as Sir Thomas More, got the edge of the huge coat he wore caught in the great oak door. Obviously the great oak door was only plywood cleverly disguised by the scene builders and painters as solid oak. If one opened or closed it too vigorously, it shook, or was in danger of snapping. Percy was trying very hard to extricate himself while giving a rather moving speech to Mrs More. Peggy was also trying to hide the problem from the audience by standing sideways, and holding out her long dress. Word spread backstage and suddenly the wings were full of actors bent double with laughter. Percy kept looking into the wings towards Sally, desperate for help, but even she was trying hard not to laugh. It was just one of those awful things that happen onstage sometimes. Suddenly there was a ripping sound which Peggy covered with a wrenching cough, as she fell upon Sir Thomas and tried to get him out of the great oak door. But the bloody door was stuck fast. Peggy was now so determined to get them off the stage that all reason and logic left her – and the next thing, she was climbing out of the window, pulling Sir Thomas with her. Bearing in mind they were supposed to be in a castle, even if they were lucky enough to have been on the ground floor, it was still a leap to terra firma. But Peggy could not care less about the reality of the scene, she just wanted out. So Sally brought the curtain down as Sir Thomas More disappeared, arse over tit, out of the castle window. Happy days!

Percy and Peggy came charging into the wings absolutely furious.

'Why didn't you do something, Sally? How could you leave me there struggling?' Percy demanded. 'I have *never* been so humiliated in all my life. Come on, Peggy, let's get changed for the last act, though God knows if anybody has bothered to stay and watch. My performance was *ruined.*'

Percy was off up the stairs followed by a placatory Peggy clutching a packet of digestives that she always kept in the wings for emergencies. The rest of the play passed without incident and the cast took an extra curtain call, so Percy was mollified.

Everyone decided it was definitely a night for the pub.

'You coming, Sally?' asked Simon, giving her bum a squeeze as he passed. Truth be told he rather fancied Sally, but the opportunity had never presented itself yet. Maybe tonight.

'Get off my bum, you pervert,' Sally laughed. 'Sorry, Simon, not tonight. I have got a date with fish and chips and Jeremy.'

'Oh Gawd, more line learning and intellectual discussion about his "Acting",' mocked Simon. The boys often took the mickey out of poor Jeremy now, because he did take his work so seriously. 'Well, more fool you is all I can say,' Simon went on. 'You could have had a fabulous evening with me in the pub. A few pints then a quick trip to Mrs Wong's and back to my place for a shag. What more could you want?'

Sally shook her head as she took a swipe at the incorrigible boy and told him to get lost. She finished clearing up and switching off all the lights, then went upstairs to get her stuff

from the dressing room. As she passed Peggy and Percy's dressing room she heard a stifled giggle. She paused and knocked
on Peggy's door.

'Are you OK, Peggy? Can I get you anything before I go?'

There was the sound of shuffling and someone moving
around and then Percy's voice rang out loud and clear.

'She has gone home already, my dear. Thank you for your
concern. Let us just hope the great oak door opens tomorrow
night, shall we? Good night.'

Sally called back a good night as she climbed the stairs to
her room. Well, what was that all about? No doubt young
Sarah doing some more work on her part . . . Just then, Jeremy
came out of the boys' dressing room and interrupted her
musings.

'Hi. Are you ready to go?' he asked.

'Just getting my bag and stuff,' she replied.

As they went downstairs Sally tried to listen for any sounds
from Percy's room. Jeremy looked at her as if she had gone
mad as she tiptoed past the door.

'What the . . . ?' he started to ask, but she put her finger to
her lips and mouthed, 'Tell you later.'

Outside, Sally took Jeremy's arm and started to explain all
about the incident with Sarah and the dresses and her new
role. Jeremy, however, was only half-listening as he tried to
work out exactly what he was going to tell his friend tonight.
He had spent the whole day trying to get Eddie out of his
mind. All through his preparations for the evening performance, all he could concentrate on was Eddie's kiss. His
mouth. There had been a moment onstage tonight when he
had dried, forgotten his lines. It is every actor's worst nightmare. One minute everything is going swimmingly then
suddenly there is a pause. Jeremy had a vision of Eddie's smile

in front of his eyes, he was leaning in to touch his face and all around was silence, deafening silence. Silence! Christ, who was supposed to be talking? The face in front of Jeremy was Percy's, panic in his eyes, begging Jeremy to come up with his next line. The moment seemed to last for hours though it was only a few seconds, but Jeremy wanted to die. Never had this happened before. He was mortified. He apologized to Percy when they came off stage but the older man just laughed it off.

'Don't worry, mate, happens to the best of us. Doesn't half give you a kick in the bollocks though, eh?'

'Jeremy?' Sally's voice was concerned. 'You keep going off into another place, and I have no idea what you are thinking. Are you worried about work, because if you are, don't be. You are a marvellous actor and I am sure they are going to give you Laertes in *Hamlet*. It will be so exciting and—'

'Sally, please.' Jeremy literally stopped Sally there and then in the street and took both her hands in his as he faced her.

'Please stop. I have to talk to you. I am going mad. Sally, I have fallen in love!'

Chapter 26

When the two friends got back to Sally's flat, she put the fire on, opened a bottle of wine and made poached eggs on hot buttered toast, while Jeremy poured his heart out. Once they were settled in front of the fire Sally offered her opinion.

'Why is it so terrible that you have fallen in love? You should be over the moon,' she managed to say through a mouthful of toast.

'I know, I know,' groaned Jeremy, 'but it is not part of my plan. I do not want to get involved with anything other than my work. You know we have talked about this so often, Sally. I feel it is important that I focus completely on my job. We have got *Hamlet* coming up, and that will be tough for all of us.'

'But dearest, life can never really be ordered and controlled like you are suggesting, and in fact, having someone in your life can add to your understanding of yourself and others, and help you with your performances.' She watched her friend fiddle unenthusiastically with his food. 'Don't you want that?' she couldn't resist asking.

Jeremy smiled. 'Not really hungry – here you are, I know you are dying to have it.' He passed her his plate. 'The other thing we haven't mentioned is the whole issue of being gay. I don't understand how this has happened to me, when I have never fancied a man before. Why now, suddenly?'

Sally thought about this as she ate the last piece of toast. 'But have you ever really fancied a girl? Anyone?' she asked.

Jeremy finished off the wine in his glass and poured another. After a couple of sips he answered Sally with a sigh. 'No.'

Sally suddenly had a vision of Mack for some bizarre reason. She had fancied him when they had met again when she was home in Cheltenham. He had never got in touch afterwards, and yet Sally had felt there was a real connection between them. But then like Jeremy she was not really interested in anything at the moment except acting. So whose fault was it that Mack had not been given sufficient reason to call?

'It is so hard to deal with these intense emotions, isn't it?' she said softly. 'But I really believe you must go with your heart. Eddie obviously feels the same about you. But what will his parents say? Surely they will not understand their son and heir being gay? Oh Jeremy, I just don't want to see you get hurt. Go gently and don't rush things – and be careful.'

Jeremy leaned over and gave Sally a big hug. He felt so safe with her. He loved the fact they could talk about anything and share intimate secrets about themselves. Would he have that with Eddie? Just the thought of him made Jeremy's stomach do a somersault. It was no good, he knew, trying to discuss anything rationally; he had to pursue this thing to whatever conclusion occurred. He was completely smitten.

He left Sally with a promise to go slowly and embrace his newfound love with caution. However, as he walked home in the cold November night, he was already planning how he could meet up with Eddie as soon as possible.

After Jeremy had left, Sally cleared up and started to take her make-up off when the door opened and her sister bounced into the flat, followed by Simon carrying a bag of beers.

'Hi, Sally, didn't expect you to be up. Still, just as well you are, as we would probably have woken you up anyway. Sit down, Simon, and give me the beers, and I will stick them in the fridge. Would you like some scrambled eggs on toast?' Dora suggested as she made her way to the kitchen. But before Simon could answer, Sally piped up, 'Actually I just used up all the eggs. Jeremy came back for a drink and we had poached eggs. Sorry.'

Dora made a face. 'Oh pooh. Well, that is a bummer. Have we got any bread left? We can have toast and Marmite or something then.'

Simon flicked open the top of a can and joined in the discussion. 'Don't worry about me, darling. Beer is fine. Come on, don't fret. Come and sit with me.'

Sally could guess where this was leading and she followed Dora into the kitchen as her sister went to put the beers in the fridge.

'What are you doing?' she whispered. 'You are surely not considering letting Simon stay the night by any chance?'

Dora turned and studied her. 'What is this all about – the older sister taking care of her younger sibling's moral welfare? I don't know if he is going to stay the night yet. It depends. But if he does, that is really my business, don't you think? Come on, Sally, I am old enough to decide these things for myself.'

Sally snorted. 'You are eighteen, for God's sake! I was still a virgin then.'

'Well, I'm not,' replied Dora, relishing the dropping of this bombshell.

Sally was absolutely dumbfounded, but one look at her sister's smug expression made her determined not to reveal the extent of the horror she felt.

'Oh I see. Well then, I guess you know what you are doing. How many men have there been in your short life?' she asked with no attempt to hide the sarcasm.

Uncomfortable now with where this conversation might go, Dora did not answer immediately. While she was deciding how to deal with this rather tricky subject, luck intervened, and Simon appeared in the kitchen doorway.

'Come on, girls, give it a break, I am trying to chill out here. Are we going to have a cosy threesome?' he sniggered.

'Oh grow up, Simon,' snapped Sally. 'I will leave you both to it. Good night.'

She marched off to her bedroom and slammed the door, then regretted the gesture. They probably thought she was jealous. Simon was always trying it on with her, and now he was hanging around her sister. How pathetic was that? And what the hell was Dora up to? Had she really lost her virginity already? Sally was outraged and yet she realized that it truly was none of her business, was it? She thought about their parents and wondered if they knew about Dora. Thinking about them made Sally feel so homesick and alone. Talking to Jeremy earlier had caused her to start thinking about her own life and what she really wanted from it. Now she began to feel there was a chasm between her and Dora. Their lives were no longer under the auspices of their parents. The family had changed and she had to change also – but how? She suddenly felt very tired and resolved to have a long talk to Dora about everything and get things straight between them. Life was difficult enough without arguments with her sister.

As she hit the pillow, Sally heard music coming from the other room and Dora's throaty laughter. Oh God, how was she going to face them both in the morning if Simon stayed? Sally accepted that she was being ridiculous and getting herself in a tizzy for no good reason – except there *was* a reason: Dora's welfare. Just because she had had a few drinks, did her sister really have to stoop so low as to sleep with a slob like Simon? The answer was probably yes. If that was the case, then the less she knew about it the better. She would get up early, and if Simon was here she would make herself scarce and get out quick.

Sally managed to smile to herself as she felt sleep starting to take her away from all this pettiness. *Come on, girl, you have dealt with worse than this in your life*, she told herself. *Get a grip . . .* but her body was gone, drifting into blissful unconsciousness. She would save the gripping for another day.

Chapter 27

A Man for All Seasons ended this coming Saturday, which would mean a busy night for everyone getting the old set out, and the new one in. However, it was a little easier this weekend as they had three weeks' rehearsal for *Hamlet*. The actors were given a special dispensation to have the night off, and Sunday and Monday morning too. Several of the cast had decided to go home to family and loved ones.

Jeremy immediately rang Eddie and told him the good news.

'Fabulous.' Eddie was pleased. 'I have such a plan for the weekend you will not believe your eyes. How about I come over Saturday morning and pick you up? Presumably you will finish even earlier because you are not in *Lysistrata*, are you?'

Jeremy had not even thought of that! 'Yes, you're right – I will check today just to make sure. I can't wait. Talk to you later.'

'Oh yes, my lovely man, this is the beginning of a beautiful thing. Bye!'

The phone went dead in his hand but Jeremy held on a

little longer, trying to feel Eddie through the handpiece. 'Silly me,' he whispered. He then set off to find Heather, and as usual found the poor woman struggling with piles of props in her room.

'Oh, Jeremy – perfect timing. Can you help me get these boxes off my desk, and find a space in a corner somewhere? It's murder in here on Get-out Weekends. Would you like a coffee? The kettle has boiled – it's over there by the sink, and there is fresh milk in the fridge.'

Jeremy agreed to all demands and five minutes later the pair of them were sipping coffee on a relatively empty props table.

'So how is the world treating you, my dear?' asked Heather, who liked to keep tabs on everybody if she could. 'I notice you have not been in the pub much lately. Are the lads giving you a hard time still?'

'No, thank God, they have learned to leave me alone, especially as I am the official cleaner of the boys' dressing room in return. So we are all happy. No, it's just because I wasn't in this week's production, and you didn't overload me with prop-finding or other such chores that I have been getting out and about a bit. There is some lovely countryside outside Crewe.'

Jeremy took a swig of coffee before asking his question. Crossing his fingers under the table for luck he went on, 'Heather, I don't want to appear cheeky but as I am not in the last performances on Saturday, and if I make sure I have done all my duties, is there a possibility I could leave lunchtime on Saturday?'

'Cor, you are pushing your luck, mate,' chuckled Heather. 'However, in my great wisdom I see no reason why not. But how will you make it worth my while?'

Jeremy stood up and went and rinsed his mug in the sink, creating a moment of drama with the silence. He then turned

slowly and announced, 'You have a choice of chocolates, cig-
gies or wine. Name your price, Heather Rollings.'

'Chocolates, please – and make it a nice big box,' she added.

'Naturally, my dear, that is a deal.' Jeremy blew her a kiss
and practically skipped out of her office. He then went to
the Green Room to call Eddie back, hoping there was no
one around while he did so. With luck, the others were all
still in bed. He was in luck; the room was empty, though it
smelled of last night's stale ready meals, and Pot Noodles.
But for once Jeremy didn't notice: he was a man on a mission. He dialled the number and waited nervously, picturing
an enormous entrance hall and the butler, as described by
Eddie, gliding serenely across the marble floor to answer the
telephone.

'Crewe Hall, who is calling, please?' The tone was perfect.

'Oh, good morning, it is Jeremy Sinclair here. I am one of
the actors at Crewe Theatre this season. I was hoping to talk to
Eddie if that is possible?'

'I am afraid he is out with His Lordship, sir. They have a
shooting party this morning followed by lunch. Can I take a
message?'

'Yes, thank you. That would be great. If you could just tell
Eddie I have arranged a tour of the theatre for him on
Saturday, if that is convenient, and could he ring me as soon as
possible and confirm.'

'Of course I will do so, and thank you for your call, Mr
Sinclair.'

The phone went down. Well, I have done all I can,
thought Jeremy. It is now in the hands of the gods. Two more
days to wait – and oh, the anticipation! He made his way back
upstairs to the dressing room thinking to have a clear-up but
also to look at *Hamlet* and start to accustom himself to the

script. To his joy and delight he had been summoned to Giles Longfellow's inner sanctum a few days ago and Giles had offered him the role of Laertes. Jeremy was over the moon and said so.

'Thank you so much, sir. I am very excited about the production and will not let you down.'

Giles looked at Jeremy from across his huge mahogany desk, which was his pride and joy, and steepled his fingers under his chin. This was his favourite pose, denoting thoughtfulness and good nature, the all-giving master.

'I hope not, Mr Sinclair. I hope not.' He bestowed a smile upon his minion, and then turned to the papers on his desk. Jeremy had been dismissed.

He went back to the dressing room and did his usual clean around and collected dirty mugs. Bloody boys! He got his script and a couple of bits and pieces he would need at the weekend, then took the mugs up to the Green Room, where he tried to call Sally at her flat. There was no answer but as Jeremy came back down, they met mid-stair.

'Hi, darling, what are you up to this morning?' he greeted Sally. 'I just tried to ring you to take you for an early lunch or brunch, what do you say?'

'Actually, that would just hit the spot, Jeremy. Thank you. Can you wait while I dump this laundry back for Janie for ironing? Dora was supposed to do it last night but she had a visitor.' Sally sounded fed up and weary.

'Ooh, tell all,' said Jeremy eagerly.

'Wait till we are sitting down,' said Sally and went on up to the wardrobe department with her bundle while Jeremy carried on down to the stage door to wait for her. Gladys was ensconced in her corner with her knitting as usual.

'Morning, young sir. How are you doing, my son? You've

had a bit of time off this last couple of weeks. That must have been nice for you.'

'Yes, it was lovely, Gladys, and I will be off early Saturday too. I am waiting for Sally to take her to lunch as the poor girl will be working non-stop.'

'She's a lovely lass, that Sally – so different from her sister. Chalk and cheese, that pair.' She sniffed. Gladys's sniff was infamous and could tell a thousand tales. Jeremy was just about to ask her to illuminate, but Sally appeared at his side.

'Ready when you are. Hi, Gladys, we are going into town: do you want anything brought back?' asked Sally.

'Nah, you are all right. Enjoy your lunch. See you later.'

The pair set off down the hill to the town square.

'Where shall we go?' asked Sally.

'I know,' said Jeremy, looking very pleased with himself. 'They have opened a lovely little café just off the square. It does amazing all-day breakfasts. Follow me.'

Once they had got sat down and Sally had ordered a 'full English', and Jeremy scrambled egg and smoked salmon – a real luxury – the pair attacked a pile of toast washed down with huge mugs of tea. Jeremy let Sally settle down before he asked, 'So what's the trouble?'

'Why do you think there is trouble?' replied Sally still munching her hot buttered toast.

'Well, you look tired and stressed, which is understandable with these schedules, but getting to act in between is usually the sweetener – and you don't seem very sweet, my love,' noted Jeremy, sitting back as his food arrived.

There were a few moments' silence while the plates were put on the table, and Sally took advantage of the time to try and get her thoughts in order.

'When Dora came to stay with me it was partly for support,

but also a way for her to discover new things she might like to do in the future if she abandons this idea of Business Studies. She was always very keen on design and fashion, and very good at drawing and art. It was her idea to try and get a job in the wardrobe department, which she did. But now she has decided she wants to be an actress.' Sally took a big mouthful of bacon and sausage.

'Well, that is OK, isn't it?' responded Jeremy, trying to understand. 'You won't be in competition. You are both very different.'

'That may be so out in the big, wide world, but here in a small company like this, we all knew where we stood when we took the job. There were parts we would like to do, and hopefully if we proved ourselves, those parts would follow. I know there are people in this company who will play dirty, given half a chance, to get what they want, but I just didn't expect it from my sister.' Sally could feel tears pricking the back of her eyes and took another mouthful of food to distract her.

Jeremy looked shocked. 'What are you talking about, Sally? What has happened to make you say this?'

'Obviously you have not been around for any of this production. In fact, did you even come to the first night? Oh yes, of course you did – you wouldn't miss hob-nobbing with the great and the good of the repertory system in this country. Did you get any work offered to you?' She waited for his reply.

'No, I didn't as a matter of fact, and I left early anyway. But come on, Sally, don't start having a go at me again. I am in love for the first time in my life – cut me a bit of slack.'

Sally smiled at her friend. 'Yes, yes, OK, you are right – now is not the time. Well, on that first night it was a riot. You saw what we looked like. All that hair and see-through costumes. I felt like a stripper, to be honest. Charmaine looked rather fetching though, because her wig was dark and she asked for a bit more coverage with the costume. So there we were, Dora and I, in our matching strawberry-blonde wigs and diaphanous gowns, doing our thing. I was thrilled because I got a round of applause for my song, and I know I made the best of a bad job of a rather dull character.

'Anyway, we all go upstairs to meet the bigwigs – pardon the pun – and to work the room. But of course, now we are without our hair no one recognizes us, so we have to be very clever and make sure at the top of any conversation that the director in question knows exactly who we were. I was doing OK, but you know me, I get so intimidated by all that stuff, and after half an hour I went and sat down with Janie and we just watched all the shenanigans. Suddenly I saw my sister giving this man the full beam of her headlights; he was obviously completely smitten and hanging on her every word. They chatted for quite a while, and then Dora turned and spotted me watching, and suddenly she was kissing him on both cheeks and was off to the other side of the room. Call me suspicious but I smelled a rat, and decided to go and ask Dora what she was up to. I caught her about to leave for the pub with Simon and Peter.

'"Hi, Sally, we are off to the pub. Why don't you come with us?" she said, practically pushing the boys out of the door.

'"Yes, I will. OK, let's go," I said and followed her out.

'We didn't talk much until we got to the pub, and while the boys were getting the drinks we found a table at the back. It was very busy and all the locals were congratulating us and blowing wolf whistles, et cetera. I had to stop Dora doing a tour of the room otherwise we would have been there all night, and I was knackered and still needed to find out what she had been up to before the boys came back.

'"Who were you talking to in there?" I asked. "It all looked very intense and then suddenly you left him. Who was he?"

'"Oh, some director – nobody important, I don't think. Anyway, he was telling me how much he loved my song and what I had made of a difficult part. He was basically suggesting I might like to go and do a season at his theatre, which was nice. I just can't remember which theatre though. I am hopeless."

'Then the boys arrived with the drinks and Simon congratulated Dora on her performance in the bar! I asked him what he meant and he started telling me that Dora had nailed this director from Nottingham Playhouse no less, and he had offered her a job. Well, you can imagine how my ears pricked up.

'"Was that the man you were talking to – and you said you couldn't remember his name?" I asked, and Dora looked really nervous.

'"Um, yes, I guess so – but it was no big deal. He won't remember my name."

'"Oh yes he will," said Simon, "because he checked you on the programme and everything. Mind you, he was looking at the wrong name, wasn't he, Dora?"'

Jeremy looked at Sally and said, 'I don't think I want to hear what is coming next.'

'Can you believe it? Simon goes on to tell us that the guy had got the wrong actress – it should have been me – and that Dora made no attempt to put him straight. Dora then pretends it was all a big mistake and says that she was going to tell the man, but she couldn't find him later on. It was so embarrassing, and Simon was loving every minute, so I just told Dora we had to go and made her leave.'

As Sally ate her breakfast she remembered the walk home to the flat and the scene that followed. They had gone into the flat, stuck some money in the meter and got the fire going. Both then went and changed into their big woolly dressing gowns and Sally had put the kettle on. Tea made, the girls had huddled in front of the fire and Sally had challenged her sister.

'You let that director from Nottingham Playhouse think you were me, didn't you, Dora?'

'Well yes, but I wouldn't have kept it up. I was going to tell him at some point.' But Dora could not look her sister in the eye.

'And at what point would that have been, I wonder? On the first day of the new season when you had signed and sealed the contract? How could you do that to me? I am your sister, Dora! I brought you here to Crewe to help you find yourself, and you have done nothing but try to muscle in on my job. And now you have taken a job away from me. What is your problem? What have I ever done to you to deserve this?' Sally had been shouting and pacing the floor.

Dora waited a few moments before giving her explanation.

'Sally, this is not personal. I do love you, and I am grateful for everything you have done for me. But I do want to get on in my life, and I have decided that acting is something I love doing. But unlike you, Sal, I am the sort of person who goes for it, no matter what. I grab what I can in the moment. You are very happy to troll along with everything and everybody, enjoying the whole company thing. Well, that is not me, I am sorry. I want to be Numero Uno, the centre of attention, and if an opportunity presents itself to me like tonight, I take it. Does that make me a bad person?' She had looked up at Sally who was still pacing. Sally was so confused and hurt and angry, she barely knew how to answer.

'At this moment, I don't know what to think, Dora. But I am your sister, and I would have thought, in this case, there might have been a degree of loyalty?'

'But, Sally, you will get so many offers from this season, I know it. This one just seemed to have my name on it, and I honestly thought you would be pleased for me.'

Sally had felt her anger rising like bile in her throat, and had shocked herself by how much dislike she was feeling for Dora. Her sister was playing the manipulative card, turning it all onto Sally. It was late, and Sally had the good sense to know that this problem was not going to go away any day soon. She needed to really think about the consequences, not just with regards to her position in the company and how to maintain that position, but her relationship with her sister, which could be damaged irrevocably.

'Let's leave it there for now, shall we?' Sally had said. 'Goodnight, Dora, see you in the morning.' She had gone to her room and quietly closed her door, just catching Dora's rather faint, 'Night.'

Sally finished her story, including what had happened at the flat the previous night, and her 'full English' all at the same time. Picking up her mug of tea she regarded Jeremy over the rim as he sat back in his chair. He looked a little shell-shocked.

'And on top of all this she slept with Simon?' was his first comment.

Sally burst out laughing. 'Oh, Jeremy, I do love you! Trust you to pick up on the least important issue of the whole mess. Yes, she brought him back to the flat. I was so cross, and then she had the gall to brag that she had lost her virginity much sooner than me!'

'She is a right little hussy in the making,' tutted Jeremy. 'But seriously, she is something else, Sally. I am disgusted and absolutely on your side. Where *is* the loyalty? But you are right, this problem is not going to go away, and you don't have many choices. Can't we send her home?'

'With what excuse? I can't tell my parents we have had a big falling-out. It will destroy them, especially my mum. I think I am just going to have to keep a sharp eye out and unfortunately learn to fight for my corner.' Sally gave a long sigh. 'It feels so much better to have someone to talk to about it all. Thank you. At least if you share the knowledge, you might have some suggestions as we go along. Now I must go and give my Welsh mountain pony impersonation with my traitor of a sister at my side. Oh dear. What next, eh? Are you OK though? Sorry it has been all about me. Taking things slowly, I hope?'

Sally peered into Jeremy's face, looking for signs of a lie, but he just gave her a charming smile that told her nothing, and said, 'Don't you worry about me, my pet. I am doing fine, but will be away this weekend in Manchester, so do try and keep everything together until I get back.'

'Yes, sir! But please remember, Jeremy, I want you to play Hamlet in my Players piece, and I would appreciate some input from you when we rehearse, although I know you are going to be up to your eyes with fight scenes, and mad scenes, and what-have-you. Gosh, it is going to be so exciting. So just go easy and make sure you are rested and raring to go.'

Jeremy laughed and gave his friend a big kiss and a hug. If the truth be known, he was feeling very guilty, because the last thing he would be on Monday morning was fit and raring to go after a weekend of wild lovemaking – he hoped!

Chapter 28

Lying in bed on Saturday morning, enjoying the luxury of not having to get up early, Jeremy had slept dreamlessly, but now his head was filled with the weekend ahead. What was going to happen? How would it happen? Did he really want it to happen? He had tried to focus on his scenes in *Hamlet*, but Eddie's face would spring up in front of his eyes. Jeremy knew in his heart that he had to go with these feelings, no matter what. He would worry about everything else later.

He got up and dressed in record time in an old T-shirt and jeans because he had decided to go to the theatre and get ready there as it was warmer. He had already packed his holdall – a new one he had splashed out on for the occasion. Good luggage said a lot about a man. He had a fleeting memory of his mother standing at their front door with an old suitcase done up with string, and frayed on the leather corners. They were all going on holiday to Devon. He had had a little leather case as well, which he had filled with crayons and paper and his favourite toy cars. He could see his mother's face beaming at him as he climbed into the family Ford, his dad already at the wheel studying an atlas of Great Britain, and sucking on a boiled sweet.

'They are for the journey,' scolded his mother. 'Your dad is dreadful, Jeremy, he eats all the sweets before we have even started the trip. Now come on, let's get going.'

Jeremy felt a pang of guilt as he shut his front door and set off for the theatre. God knows what his parents would make of him now.

The front of the theatre was still locked as it was early, but Jeremy made his way round to the stage door and found that the cleaners were already in.

'Hi, Alice, how goes it?' He waved to the girl on the stairs scrubbing away. He squeezed past her and went on up to the dressing room. The familiar smells hit his nostrils as he ascended on high: greasepaint and sweat, and cheap perfume, with the added touch of fried food. Lovely!

Alice had already cleared up the dressing rooms, so Jeremy was able to shower and change at a leisurely pace. He dried his hair and regarded himself in the mirror. His hair had grown quite long, as he had intended for Laertes, and he liked the fact that it softened his face. He was by no means handsome, but he was attractive and, as his mother would always say to people, 'He will grow into his face!'

He checked his overnight bag and squeezed in the bottle of very expensive aftershave he had bought himself for this weekend. A tingle ran down his spine, a tremor of nerves. *Please make everything go well*, he prayed, to no one in particular. It was hardly a matter for the dear Lord, he reminded himself.

Just then, he heard a shout from downstairs and recognized Eddie's voice.

'Coming!' he yelled, and took the stairs two at a time.

Eddie was standing in the stage doorway with the sun

glinting on his immaculately cut hair. He looked like an angel to Jeremy.

'Hi, Eddie, how are you?'

Jeremy moved towards him but stopped when he heard a wheezy voice comment, 'Lovely morning, Mr Jeremy. You're in early, aren't you?'

'Gladys! Gorgeous Gladys, good morning to you. Yes, I am up bright and early so that I may show Mr Graham here the wonders of our theatre before the horde arrive. Is that OK with you?' Jeremy gave her his most brilliant smile and Gladys grinned back.

'Of course, you go ahead. Be careful when you go onstage though because the lights are not on yet. Do you know where the workers are?' she asked.

'Yes, I do. I can switch them on easily. Thanks, Gladys. Come on, Eddie, follow me down to the land where magic is made.'

'Magic, my arse!' Gladys commented under her breath as the two young men bounded off.

By the time they arrived at the pass door it was indeed absolutely pitch black. Eddie grabbed Jeremy round the waist and pulled him towards him.

'Not here,' whispered Jeremy. 'There may be someone from the crew here already. Just hang on. OK, grab my hand and follow me across the stage. I have got a surprise for you.'

Jeremy felt his way along the back wall of the stage and down to the corner where there was a pass door leading out to the auditorium and the boxes. A door on the right opened to some steps winding round a corner to another door on which was written in gold embossed letters *Royal Box*.

Jeremy gently pulled Eddie inside. 'I thought this was very appropriate for an aristocrat like you. I have often wondered just how many secret trysts must have taken place in here over the years.'

Eddie moved closer to Jeremy. 'Are you suggesting a tryst right here, right now?' he murmured as they stood facing each other, breathing hard. Then, very slowly, each started to undress the other. Not a word was spoken. And finally they faced each other completely naked. Their eyes had hardly left each other's. Jeremy wanted to scream with anticipation. He was shaking now. The two young men were standing nose to nose, but Jeremy was completely frozen like a statue. Eddie traced the line of Jeremy's jaw with his thumb, and when he took his face in both hands and drew him into a kiss, Jeremy thought his head would explode. Colours whirled before his eyes and he struggled to catch his breath; he seemed to have been holding it for hours. Eddie pulled back just enough to give Jeremy some space, and then his tongue gently teased its way between his lips once again. Oh, so slowly . . . Eddie pursued his probing, becoming more insistent; demanding attention. Jeremy could feel his whole body pulsating with the passion he was feeling, this overwhelming need. Slowly, so slowly . . . he unfolded his whole being to Eddie's will, and sank to the ground.

'Are you OK?' murmured Eddie, gently releasing his arm from underneath Jeremy's back. 'Ooh, ouch! Sorry, but my arm has gone to sleep.' He giggled and sat up. 'We had better make a move, hadn't we, J? Someone is bound to be down soon.' He reluctantly stood up and started to sort out his pile of clothing.

'Shit – yes, you're right. What am I thinking, lying here like an idiot.' Jeremy pulled himself up to a sitting position and rubbed his face. He sighed, 'Oh my God, Eddie, I am in such a daze I can hardly function. Help me!' He looked up at Eddie standing on the edge of the blue circle of light coming from the stage, and put out his hand. He couldn't see Eddie's face and he felt a momentary slither of panic down his back. It was gone in a moment, as Eddie pulled him to his feet and planted a big smacker on his lips.

'Stop it, you! We must get out of here quickly.' Jeremy pulled on the rest of his clothes just as a voice boomed out from the lighting gallery.

'Who's there? That you, Eric?'

Jeremy recognized the voice of the Will Black, the head carpenter.

'No, sorry, Will – it's me, Jeremy. I lost the bloody switch. I am such an idiot – I was showing my friend round and couldn't find the switch for the working lights, but it is done now though.' He had managed to get to the back of the stage by this time and find the switch.

'Everything OK with you, mate?'

Jeremy searched the darkness above them and then heard Will coming down the ladder at the side. He quickly improvised for Eddie. 'See, Eddie, this is where all the hard work is done. Will Black is the man who makes it all happen up there in the gods. Will, may I introduce Eddie Graham. He is a friend who wanted to see how everything works backstage.'

Will Black shook Eddie's hand and slapped Jeremy on the back, saying, 'Bloody actors are useless! Still, you do all right, matey. Nice to meet you, Eddie. Now if you will excuse me, lads, I need to get on.' He strolled off across the stage like a huge bear.

'God, he is enormous,' whispered Eddie. 'Wouldn't want to bump into him on a dark night.'

'Come on, you,' said Jeremy. 'Let's get out of here, for goodness sake.'

They arrived at the stage door to find Gladys happily sat with her knitting and a huge mug of tea.

'Right, we will be off now then, Gladys,' announced Jeremy.

'It was very interesting seeing everything onstage,' added Eddie. 'Thank you for giving me a tour, Jeremy.'

'Well, you have a nice weekend, won't you,' said Gladys. 'Going somewhere nice, are you, boys?'

Jeremy gave her a second look to see if she was suggesting something else, but her face was inscrutable.

'Oh, just a trip to Manchester. Eddie is returning the favour by giving me a tour of the city.'

'Lovely, dears. Well, see you later – and be good.' The big woman could not resist a huge wink which made Jeremy wince with embarrassment.

'Thanks,' he stammered. 'Yes – right. Come on then, Eddie, let's go!'

Once they got down the road they burst into a fit of giggles.

'She is a witch, I swear it,' chuckled Jeremy. 'Will she tell everyone, do you think?'

'Oh, who cares. We are not doing anything wrong, are we? Come on, let's get this weekend started.' Eddie grabbed Jeremy's hand and pulled him up the street warbling a rendition of Doris Day singing 'Once I Had a Secret Love'.

Chapter 29

Sally yawned and stretched, then sighed. She could hear Dora banging about in the kitchen making coffee. God, I would love a cup, thought Sally, but that means facing my sister. It is too early for discussions of any sort, let alone family confrontations. Although as she lay here, this morning, Sally wondered if there was any point in bringing up the whole thing again. It was a fait accompli as far as Dora was concerned. Would it not be better if Sally just got on with her own life? And if that meant being less than open with her sister, so be it. She thought about home, and her parents, and how trusting and loving her childhood had been; Dora's too, for that matter. When had things changed? Why did they change? Sally loved her sister and would always love her, of course, but now there was a beat missing somehow, and she wasn't sure she could find her way back to how it was before. Her thoughts were interrupted by a knock on the door and Dora's head appeared.

'Fancy a coffee?' she said, and came into the room with coffee and toast.

'Wow, what a treat, Dora! Thank you. To what do I owe this attention?' asked Sally, sitting up in bed.

Dora looked contrite. 'I have behaved badly, I know, sis, but I honestly didn't mean to cause you grief. I just didn't think as usual, I suppose.'

'No, you did not, and yes, it has upset me quite a lot, as a matter of fact. But I have decided to leave things be, because to be honest, Dora, there is too much going on in my life at the moment and I don't want to fall out with you on top of everything else. But please do try and think about other people's feelings and remember that you are here because of me.'

'I know, you are right and I will try harder – but please understand, Sally, I am serious about wanting to try a career as an actress, and hopefully that will not mean we are in competition.'

Sally caught a look in Dora's eye. What was it, a challenge?

'What are you doing today – apart from two shows, I mean?' asked Sally. 'Only I was wondering if we should try and set up a rehearsal for my Dumb Show asap, and I have just remembered that Rupert and Isabelle arrive some time this weekend.'

Dora looked at her blankly. 'Who?'

'Our stars! How could you forget? I think Giles wanted me to greet them and make sure they are OK. Mind you, I have got enough to do as usual with two shows, plus the get out, and preparing for the big "meet and greet" on Monday morning. Can you help me at all, do you think?' Sally gave her sister her best pleading look.

'Oh well, I suppose so, but Simon has organized for us all to go to Manchester tonight to a club, and I have invited Mack up for the night – thought it would be a nice surprise for you, actually.'

'Mack? As in Mack McKinney – Muriel's Mack?' Sally was stunned by this news. 'Whatever brought this on?' she pressed. 'And what has Mack to do with me?'

'Oh come on, Sally, don't pretend you didn't fancy him when you were there in the summer. I suggested he might like to come up and visit one day and he seemed really chuffed to be asked.' Dora disappeared into the other room, leaving Sally to gather up her thoughts.

Mack here? She had to admit the idea was not unattractive to her, but she couldn't quite work out how Dora was involved in all this. She followed her sister into the kitchen.

'Did you see Mack then, when I had gone?' she asked. 'I didn't know you knew him that well.'

'No, I don't know him that well, but Muriel told me you had got on well, and I thought as you have been a bit tense the last couple of weeks, it might do you good to see someone from home. Simon was organizing this club thing and it occurred to me that you might like someone to go with. Oh for goodness sake, Sally, it is no big deal, just a bit of fun.'

'Keep me happy and out of your way, you mean?' snapped Sally, suddenly feeling very manipulated again. 'I really do not need you to organize my life, Dora. Please stop!'

'Fine,' returned Dora. 'You are such a drama queen, Sally. It doesn't matter. You stay here and practise your little Dumb Show while the rest of us have a life. Blimey, even Jeremy has gone away this weekend – and good on him.'

Sally was suddenly reminded that indeed she really was on her own this weekend, as Jeremy was away finding true love. So there you go, Sally! Miss Goody Two Shoes again trying to do the right thing. Well, sod it! She would at least have a heads-up before Monday on what to expect from the new 'stars'. Avoiding any more conversation with Dora, she got dressed and made her way to the theatre, just stopping at the corner shop for milk and biscuits and a bottle of wine for later. Come midnight they would be gagging for a drink.

As she was crossing the square she saw Peggy struggling with her weekend shopping and went to relieve her.

'Oh bless you, darling,' Peggy huffed and puffed. 'Bloody shopping always does my head in on a Saturday, but if I don't do it now there will be nothing for Sunday lunch, and His Lordship would be very cross indeed. Come on, let's have a coffee and a bun before we shut ourselves away for the rest of the day.'

Sally followed Peggy across to the tearoom round the back of the Memorial.

'You are so right, Peggy,' she said, putting the bags on the floor and plonking herself down at a corner table. 'There is something about Saturdays that is really depressing, because everybody else seems to be getting ready for a night out, and they are out and about shopping, and having fun, and the likes of you and me are preparing to hide away in the dark until ten thirty tonight doing two shows. I mean, don't get me wrong – I love performing – but sometimes it would be lovely to have a normal weekend, wouldn't it?'

Peggy chuckled. 'There is nothing normal about this game, dearie. Now what are you going to have?'

Once they had ordered coffee and two Eccles cakes, Peggy had a confession to make.

'I suppose you have noticed that young Sarah has been hanging about round Percy, haven't you?' she said.

Sally answered carefully, 'Well yes, she does seem to be overly attentive, but I suppose that is normal in younger actresses. She is probably learning a good deal from Percy.'

Peggy snorted. 'She is taking the silly old fool for a ride, and

I am getting fed up with it. Listen, Sally, I have had to deal with this all my life with His Lordship. Always young women, and that is why I even tried to put a stop to it by spreading rumours that he liked the boys! But it never worked. Normally I turn a blind eye, but this one just won't give up, and I think that Percy must be going through a midlife crisis because he is besotted. I have to admit it is getting to me, Sally, and I don't know what to do.' Peggy sniffed and held her paper serviette to her nose.

Sally wanted to reach across the table and give the woman a big hug. Instead she said gently, 'Oh now, Peggy, I think you are getting your knickers in a twist for nothing. I know she is pushy, that Sarah, but Percy is not a fool. He knows the score.'

'Well, you would think so, wouldn't you, dearie? But there is no fool like an old fool.' Peggy popped the last morsel of her Eccles cake in her mouth and chewed thoughtfully. 'What can I do?' she whispered.

Sally was suddenly very angry with all these girls making waves. Well, two girls – Sarah and Dora as it happened.

'Do you want me to have a word?' she suggested. 'I am very happy to warn her off – and maybe we can turn her attention elsewhere. Who else can help her career? What about Robert?'

'Huh! He is another one who spends all his time playing games,' said Peggy. 'He's not to be trusted at all, dearie.'

Sally thought about Jeremy and his little secret and made a mental note to warn him to be careful.

'OK then,' she said aloud. 'I will deal with this, Peggy, and don't you worry – we will get Miss Sarah Kelly to see sense.'

When Sally got to the theatre she was accosted by Heather, who was going mad trying to find one of the blonde wigs which had gone missing.

'If those boys have had it away as a joke I will kill the little sods.' She shook a finger at Sally. 'Do you know anything about this?'

'No, you daft thing,' laughed Sally. 'Give me a break, Heather, I have got enough on my plate. Do you know where Giles is, by any chance?'

'Yes, he is in his office – but he is with Lord Graham, so watch out . . .'

Sally made her way to the front of house and up the stairs to the Royal Circle where Giles's office was situated. She knocked on the door and waited. After a few moments Giles himself opened the door. He seemed less than pleased to see her.

'Yes?' he barked. 'I am very busy, so if it isn't important can it wait until later?'

Sally heard the sound of someone clearing their throat and a waft of cigar smoke curled round the door.

'No, it is fine, I will come back later but I do need instructions about the arrival of Rupert and Isabelle.' She turned and went away feeling very miffed. What on earth was the matter with everyone? They all seemed to have agendas that had nothing to do with getting the show on the road. She decided to seek out Sarah and give her a job to do. It might not ultimately help keep her away from Percy, but it would make Sally feel better! She found the young lady in the Green Room making coffee. Sally noted there were two mugs.

'Hi, Sarah, are you busy?' she asked.

Sarah stirred the coffee and smiled sweetly. 'I was just going to take this to Percy, as a matter of fact.'

'OK then, when you have done that, can you go down to the stage and help Heather find a lost wig? She is going mad.'

'Actually, I know where the wig is,' answered Sarah. 'I

caught Simon wearing it after the show last night, so I took it off him and kept it in my dressing room.'

Sally was rather nonplussed. 'Oh right, good. Well, can you take it to Heather and then see if Janie needs help to start putting costumes in skips?'

Sarah nodded and set off with her two cups of coffee. Sally couldn't resist calling after her, 'I don't think you have time to drink that with Percy, do you? Best get a move on.'

The sound of voices coming from the stage door reminded Sally that it was nearly time to get ready for the afternoon performance. She ran up to the dressing room and spent five minutes doing a warm-up for her voice. Suddenly, she found she could forget all the petty ups and downs and focus on herself. She must not forget this was what she was here for; to learn to grow as an actress. She had a great deal to get through in the next three weeks, so no distractions.

Her serenity was interrupted by the arrival of her sister. 'Sally, look who is here!' yelled Dora and stepped back to allow the surprise guest to enter the dressing room.

'Hello, Sally,' said Mack.

Sally was struck dumb. The room was full of this gorgeous handsome man who was smiling at her and moving forward to give her a kiss on the cheek.

'Mack – what a surprise! Oh my goodness, I am gobsmacked. Why are you here?' The question was out before she could stop herself.

'Charming,' he laughed. 'I am not quite sure how to respond to that.'

'No, sorry, I didn't mean to be rude, it is just such a surprise. Actually Dora did mention it this morning, but I have been so busy it completely went out of my head. It is lovely to see you. Are you going to watch the show? Shall I get you a ticket?' Sally could feel herself wittering on and tried to pull herself together. Bloody Dora had done it again!

But Mack seemed to be taking it all in his stride. 'Don't worry about me,' he said. 'I will have a wander round the town, and probably get something to eat, and then we can either meet between the shows or after. It is not a problem. I know you are very busy, so just do your thing and we will see what happens later.'

'Thank you, Mack.' Sally breathed a sigh of relief. 'I must say there is a lot to do, and, Dora, you should have been here an hour ago.' She turned her attention to her wayward sister. She was not going to let her get away with this disruption. 'You had better get up to the wardrobe department a bit quick.'

Dora had the grace to do as she was told, and Sally left Mack wending his way back to the stage door. By the time she had changed and got her make-up on she was exhausted!

Chapter 30

By the end of the second performance Sally was feeling like death. She was so tired, and the last thing she felt like doing was going clubbing.

'Oh come on, sis, don't be a spoilsport. You have got to come.' Dora was standing in the doorway dressed to the nines. 'What will poor Mack think? He has come all this way to see you and you are being a party-pooper.'

'You invited him, Dora, not me,' Sally retorted. She was well aware that Mack was waiting downstairs with the others, but she just couldn't face him. 'Tell him I am truly sorry, and that we can go and have a pub lunch or something tomorrow. I presume he is sleeping on our sofa tonight?'

'Who knows?' Dora giggled. 'Things might change in the night, sister dear.'

'Oh, don't be so stupid and childish. What is the matter with you, Dora? I hardly know the guy, for Christ's sake. Why are you pushing him in my face?'

Dora just waved her hand and disappeared down the stairs, calling, 'See you later!'

Sally was in a really grumpy mood now. Left on her own, she almost wished she had gone with them all. Almost. Then Janie appeared in the doorway with a load of dirty washing. 'Anything for me?' She stopped and noticed Sally's long face. 'Everything all right?' she asked.

'Oh yes, fine. It is just Dora is getting on my nerves. She sort of set me up tonight with this old friend from home. He is the brother of my best friend from school, but I don't really know him that well. Anyway, he is very nice and everything, but she invited him up here for the weekend, and then expects me to drop everything and go out clubbing. She can be very irritating at times.'

Janie nodded. 'She is still very young, Sally. Don't let it get to you. Come on, come and have a glass of wine with me and Heather while we finish clearing up. Gwendoline left early tonight with Geoffrey, so work that one out. Mark my words, it is all going to end in tears.'

After Janie had left, Sally pondered on her situation. Why was she being so dismissive of Mack? The last time she had seen him she was full of passion and longing, and now suddenly she was talking about him as if he was a complete stranger. Yet if truth be told, Mack had crept into her thoughts many times over the last few weeks. She had gone over and over their last evening together. She had even managed to pluck up the courage to send him the odd postcard of Crewe, with a reasonably bland comment like *So this is show biz!* but he had not replied, and as the days passed Sally had put him to the back of her mind and concentrated on the job in hand. Now he was here and she was just too tired to respond.

Sally finally crawled into bed about 1 a.m. and fell instantly asleep, not waking until nine the next morning. Wondering what was going to greet her on the other side of her bedroom door, she donned a dressing gown and pulled open the door quietly, creeping into the sitting room to find a body filling the sofa. She had left out a pillow and blankets last night, hoping that Mack would feel welcome. He had made full use of the sofa, and was sprawled over it with his feet hanging over the edge.

Sally tiptoed into the kitchen and put the kettle on. She was hoping that she could get some work done before everyone woke up, and then enjoy the rest of her Sunday with Mack, catching up on news from home. She made herself coffee and toast and honey, and crept back to her room. Now that Giles had done her the honour of offering her the job of directing the Dumb Show in *Hamlet*, Sally was determined to make her mark and do him proud. She had discussed masks with Gwendoline, who was happy to oblige, and Dora had promised to make white robes for the actors – though whether that offer still held was anyone's guess.

Sally spent the next couple of hours reading the text, and also acquainting herself with the part of Ophelia, since she was the official understudy, as well as director of the Dumb Show. Her thoughts turned to *Hamlet* and Rupert Hallam, who had been in the news a good deal lately as the new heart-throb, due to his role in an ongoing series on TV. Isabelle James, his opposite number, had just won a BAFTA for her performance in a very moody film about incest. Sally had not seen it but all the reviews raved about her performance, and there was much comment made about her nude scenes. She had apparently had to undress through most of her scenes. Well good luck to her, thought Sally. If you've got it, flaunt it! The phone rang suddenly and she was up and out to the hall, quick as a flash.

'Sally? It's Giles Longfellow here. I am sorry to trouble you on your day off, but I think I did mention I might need your help today with our new arrivals. I am still in the countryside, but apparently Rupert has arrived at the theatre and no one knows what to do with him. Can you get down there and ask Gladys to open my office so you can pick up the keys to his flat, which are on top of my desk. The address is number 1, Greenbanks – you know that block of new flats down by the river? Take a taxi and keep the receipt, and I will reimburse you. If you could just get him milk and bread and stuff and see him in safely, I would appreciate it.'

'Yes, that's fine, Giles. I will go now.' Sally put the phone down with a sigh. So much for her day off and a pub lunch in the country.

'Problems?' A voice at her elbow startled her.

'Oh gosh, Mack, you made me jump! Sorry, did I wake you? I have got to go to the theatre and play host to our new arrival, Rupert Hallam. Help yourself to tea and coffee, et cetera. I should be back within the hour. I was going to suggest a pub lunch, but I don't know how much time we will have left. It's eleven o'clock now.'

'Don't worry, I will hang out here and wait for you,' he said. 'I take it Dora is still asleep? Shall I wake her up in a bit so we can all meet up together?'

'Yes, why not,' replied Sally, without much enthusiasm. 'I'll see you later. Oops, I had better get dressed,' she added, realizing she was still in her pyjamas.

Sally threw on an old jumper and some jeans and gave her hair a quick brush. Looking at her reflection in the mirror, she could see the brush had done nothing useful, so found her favourite hat and hid the mess underneath. A tiny voice did hint she might have wanted to try a bit harder as Mack was here and they might go out later, but it was quickly squashed

by a glance at the time. Sally grabbed her bag and left the flat
as Mack was putting on the kettle.

When Sally arrived at the stage door she was greeted by
Gladys looking very overexcited and decidedly pink in the
cheeks.

'Oh, Miss Sally, thank goodness you got here. Poor Mr
Hallam has been waiting so patiently and me not knowing
what to do for the best. Mr Hallam, this is Sally. She is the
ASM and knows all about everything.'

Rupert Hallam turned to shake Sally's hand, saying lan-
guidly, 'Thank God you have arrived. I was starting to think
that everyone had forgotten about me.' He stuck his nose in
the air.

Sally replied, 'Oh, not at all – and I'm so very sorry you've
had to wait.' She turned immediately to Gladys. 'I need the
keys to Mr Longfellow's office, please, so I can get the keys to
Mr Hallam's accommodation. If you don't mind waiting a few
more minutes, Rupert, we will sort this out, and I will take
you to your flat. Can you also get me a taxi, please, Gladys, to
Number 1, Greenbanks.' Inside, Sally was fuming. This guy
was so aloof and full of himself. Well, we'll soon bring him
down a peg or two, she promised herself.

By the time she got back to the stage door the taxi had
arrived and she and Rupert were able to set off immediately.
He did not say a word on the journey over and Sally was in no
mood to try and be friendly. The taxi dropped them off and
Sally made her way to the front entrance of Greenbanks. It
suddenly occurred to her that she had no means of transport
back to her flat, so that meant more grief. She managed the
locks, and finally opened the front door to a very smart and
obviously expensive first-floor flat. It had a glass window right

across one wall and a leather sofa, and a glass dining table and four chairs. Sally couldn't help thinking, 'Oh, this is lovely!' Then realized she had spoken out loud.

'Yeah, not bad, I must say,' agreed Rupert Hallam, putting his bag down and going into the bedroom. Sally decided to investigate the kitchen, which was very modern and had every gadget imaginable. Lucky sod, she thought to herself. She dumped the carrier bag with the groceries on the counter.

'Well, I will leave you to settle in then,' she declared frostily. 'I have written out a list of useful numbers for you, including mine and the stage manager's. Her name is Heather Rollings and I am sure she will be calling you later.'

She had started to make her way to the door when Rupert stopped her.

'Listen, I apologize if I was a bit curt earlier. It's just all a bit overwhelming, to tell you the truth. Don't suppose you know where to get some food? Is there a pub you all go to? I guess there is no one about because it's Sunday.'

Sally suddenly felt a bit sorry for him. He looked very forlorn standing there.

'Yes, absolutely right. Sunday is a dead day but we all love it. It is the only time we have off, really – the rest of the week is full on.' Sally wasn't quite sure what to do next. Leave, or invite him to join them in the pub. Her good nature getting the better of her, she decided to give Mr Hallam a second chance.

'As a matter of fact, we were thinking of going for a pub lunch so you are welcome to join us. I share a flat with my sister Dora, and we have a friend visiting from home, so please – do come if you would like.'

Rupert gave her a beaming smile that completely changed his face from moody and mean to young and boyish – and *very* good-looking, Sally had to admit.

'That would be really cool. Thank you so much.' He picked up his rucksack, found his wallet and started to leave. Sally remembered his keys and handed them to him at the door.

'Won't get far without them,' she grinned. 'Oh actually, can we use your phone to call a taxi? It is not far but a pain to walk it, and time is marching on if we want to get to a pub before it closes.'

'Be my guest,' replied Rupert, pointing to the phone.

Sally rang the cab company then tried her flat and luckily got hold of Dora.

'Listen, can you and Mack be ready to come down when I ring the doorbell? We can take this taxi on to the pub and charge the theatre. I thought we could go to the Cross Keys on the Nantwich Road.' Dora agreed and Sally put the phone down. 'Right – all sorted, let's hope the taxi gets here quickly.'

While they waited Sally explained who she was exactly, and how she was the understudy for Ophelia, and about her Dumb Show ideas. Rupert seemed genuinely interested and admitted that this was his first theatre role since drama school and he was very nervous.

'Do you know Isabelle?' asked Sally.

'Not really. I have met her at a couple of film things, but that's all,' replied Rupert. 'She is scarily beautiful though,' he added. Sally caught the admiration in his voice and thought that was par for the course; two beautiful young things together. She knew where that would lead.

When the two of them arrived at Sally's flat Dora was at the front door with Mack, bursting with excitement.

'Hi there! I rang Janie and Peter and they are joining us, and Simon may raise himself from his pit, so we should have a good laugh.' Dora clambered into the car leaving Mack to find his own place in the front, as it happened. It was only as Dora settled back in the seat that the penny dropped and she recognized Rupert. For one blissful minute there was silence and then she was off again.

'Oh wow, hi! You are Rupert Hallam, aren't you? I am such a fan and I think it is brilliant that you have given up your career to come here and do *Hamlet*.'

Rupert burst out laughing. 'Hang on a minute – give up my career? I do hope that is not how the rest of the world sees it, or I am finished. I have given up nothing, if you don't mind. It is an honour to be doing this production, and part of my heritage as an actor.'

Dora had the good grace to apologize profusely, and then shut up, as indicated to her by Sally making a zipping gesture across her mouth. The rest of the journey passed in relative silence, apart from Mack asking the driver various questions about local sights. The pub was on the edge of town so was nearly like a country pub. It served good wholesome dishes like shepherd's pie or Sunday roast with all the trimmings, and it was cheap. The gang were just in time to order food, and while they were doing that, Rupert went and bought everyone drinks, plus a couple of bottles of wine for later.

Sally joined him to help carry the drinks to the table. 'Nothing like bribery to get the cast on your side,' she quipped.

'Oh now, come on, Sally, don't have a go at me. I am trying my best to get off on the right foot, that is all.'

Rupert paid the bill and followed Sally back to the others. Janie and Peter were there already and had commandeered a table. Introductions were made and everyone got down to serious drinking. It turned out to be a lovely afternoon. Actors very rarely have trouble making friends. In fact, they tend to love everyone instantly, and it is only later that they see the cracks and start bitching. Rupert was very good company, Sally noticed. The aloofness she had seen at the beginning of the day had gone completely, and in its place was a joky, open young man enjoying the company, and loving the limelight – which was inevitable, thought Sally as she watched Dora hanging on his every word and flirting outrageously. Even Janie was doing her best to get his attention with all her talk of costumes and fittings.

'One of the perks of my job,' she piped up. 'Measuring the inside leg of handsome young actors.'

Peter pretended mock horror and everyone laughed. 'No leg could match up to that of your beloved boyfriend, Janie, my dear,' he leered, and he gave her a squeeze.

Simon arrived just as last orders were being called and found himself getting a round. Dora offered to go halves with him but he refused. Sally's sharp eyes picked up a look between them and suspected that things were not very happy. Sally had spent quite a good deal of the lunchtime observing everyone. She loved people-watching and would always try and sit in a corner if she could. She had inevitably found herself comparing Mack and Rupert. Both were good-looking, confident men, yet so different. Mack was impressive just by his physical presence. He was by far the tallest of the bunch, and seemed like a gentle giant. His hair was thick and long and very shiny, and when he laughed he revealed strong white teeth. He was a very attractive man and not at all cowed by a load of actors wittering on about themselves. On the contrary, he seemed to really enjoy their anecdotes and stories, and even added a few of his own. Sally wondered if she was being foolish not getting to know him better. He had come all the way to visit her, after all.

By comparison, Rupert was very much the face of the

moment. He seemed much slighter than he appeared on the television screen. He was not quite as tall as Mack, but still about five foot eleven. He had a perfectly chiselled jaw, and his mouth and lips were perfect – almost like a girl's. His face was saved from being too pretty by an aquiline nose and high cheekbones, and those deep, penetrating dark eyes. He had the long floppy hair of an actor which he constantly kept flipping back out of his eyes. For all his good looks Rupert was definitely one of the lads, and seemed immune to Dora's attempts at flirting. Just as well, thought Sally, noticing Simon getting grumpy in the corner. Even Mack tried a couple of times to attract Dora's attention, to no avail.

As soon as they were thrown out of the pub Dora invited everyone back to the flat.

'But we have work to do and washing to sort, so let's leave it for now,' said Sally.

'Sis, what have I told you about being a party-pooper. We have got to finish Rupert's lovely wine he bought and the football will be on soon so the boys can put their feet up and watch telly just like being at home.'

This brought a roar of approval from the male contingency and Sally knew she was defeated. The afternoon passed very quickly, with lots of cheering and rowdy jokes. Janie managed to drag Peter away at five, and Rupert called a cab.

'Mustn't mess up my first day with a hangover,' he grinned to Sally at the front door. 'Thanks so much for today, Sally. I feel as if we have known each other for ever. Promise you will keep an eye on me? I sometimes find it hard to stay focused and then I fuck up.' For a moment he looked very serious.

'We won't let you fuck up, don't worry,' she promised. 'I will be your shadow, never fear.' She leaned over and gave him a kiss on the cheek and Rupert responded by giving her a big hug.

'Thanks again, Sally.' And he was gone.

'Well, aren't you the dark horse, getting a snog in so soon.' Dora was standing behind her in the hallway.

'Don't be stupid,' Sally sighed. 'Let's just get an early night, shall we, as it is a busy day tomorrow.'

'Oh yes, miss, whatever you say, miss. Actually, Mack and I might go out for a drink later, seeing as how you have ignored him most of the weekend, and he goes back to Cheltenham tomorrow.' The girl turned and flounced off into the sitting room.

Sally suddenly felt very tired and decided enough was enough. She went into the sitting room and started to clear away. Simon was asleep on the floor and Mack was dozing on the sofa.

'Where's Dora gone now?' asked Sally, working her way round the room. 'We need to tidy up and send people to their homes ... Simon!' She gave him a nudge in the ribs which produced a groan of protest.

'Time to go home, Simon. Come on, please.'

Dora appeared at her bedroom door. 'Actually I am knackered now. Do you mind if I just have a quick nap before we go out, Mack?'

Mack stood up and then realized there was nowhere to go.

'Sure thing, whatever,' he said. 'If Sally doesn't mind me watching TV, and taking up space in her sitting room tonight.' He turned to her, looking like a lost dog.

'Of course I don't mind, Mack, you are our guest. Though God knows we have hardly been the most attentive hosts, have we?' she said loudly enough for her sister to hear.

Simon had dragged himself to his feet and was looking for his shoes. When he had finally left, and there was silence from Dora's bedroom as she took a nap, Mack sat back and fixed

Sally with his big brown eyes. He had a way of looking at one very directly; his gaze was like his camera lens, thought Sally.

There was a long pause and Mack seemed to be gathering his thoughts together. Finally he said, 'Are you pleased to see me? It is just that I feel I am intruding on your life somehow. Dora made me think it is what you would have wanted. She can be very persuasive at times.' He smiled shyly. 'We have had a couple of nights out together since you left, and to be honest I am not sure that was such a good idea.' He hesitated.

'What do you mean?' asked Sally with a growing sense of foreboding. 'When you say you went out together, do you mean as friends or . . . something more?'

'That's just it, Sally. You see, she invited me to come and stay here when we were out one night in Cheltenham, and I think I misunderstood the situation – and now I don't know how to extricate myself without embarrassment all round. Shit, I feel such a fool.' Mack ran his fingers through his hair with frustration.

'I am sorry, Mack, but I don't understand what you are trying to say. Are you and Dora an item?' Sally nearly choked on the word. Surely this could not be happening? Had Dora managed yet again to crash through her life and create chaos? Could Mack be such a bastard, able to replace one sister with another? Sally wanted to get up and rush out but Mack seemed to read her thoughts and placed his hand on her arm.

'No, Sally. I thought Dora was trying to help. I have wanted to contact you so many times over the last few weeks but I just couldn't pluck up the courage. I know how much this job means to you and I didn't want to get in the way. But to be honest I can't stop thinking about you and our date together. I thought you and Dora had devised this plan between you so we could meet up again, but the way Dora has been behaving

I think she thinks I fancy *her*. I am sorry if that sounds arrogant or offensive but it is not at all what I intended. I just wanted to see *you* again, Sally.' Mack seemed to run out of steam then and sat back looking wretched.

Sally's heart took a huge leap and wiped out any fatigue she had been feeling.

'Oh Mack, I *am* pleased to see you – you have no idea. I am sorry I have been so grumpy and dull, but I really have had a hell of a time, and I apologize for not ringing you. But as you have so rightly understood I am trying hard to get to grips with this job and my career. I have so many mixed feelings about it all now, and no one to talk to about it all.'

Mack suddenly got up, came round and took Sally in his arms. He then kissed her with such ferocity she was completely taken aback, and when he stopped she practically dropped into her seat again.

'What happens now?' asked Mack slightly breathlessly.

Sally looked up at him and felt a surge of excitement. She wanted to drag him into her bed right now – but the thought of her sister in the other room was not conducive to her sense of romance. *Dora.* She could not bring herself to think about what her sister had had in mind. Certainly nothing as unselfish as helping Sally find love. But these thoughts were for another time. She stood up and gave Mack a hug.

'Much as I would like to seal our pact, I really don't think now is the right moment, Mack. Can we arrange for you to come up to stay another time, and maybe we could go and spend a night somewhere away from Crewe. Away from Dora,' she added.

Mack looked disappointed but he answered with a smile in his voice, 'I will wait for as long as it takes, Miss Thomas. Meanwhile, I will dream of you tonight and of things to come.'

They took their time saying good night. Sally loved kissing Mack – he was so good at it! Finally he drew back breathless and shaking slightly with desire.

'That's enough, Sally. I can't take any more. It is torture not being able to make love to you. I want you so badly. Are you sure I can't change your mind?' He moved towards her and Sally put out her arms to stop him.

'No – please, Mack. I want us to be alone and private. That will not be the case when Dora wakes up, believe me.'

'OK, I concede defeat but if you don't mind I will go now and get the late train back to Cheltenham. It will give me time to cool off and have a good think.'

They shared one last lingering kiss and then he was gone. Sally ran a bath; she lit lots of candles and soaked in the sooth-ing water until she was prune-like. Not a good look, she smiled to herself, and stepped out into her towel. She was so tired she just lay down on top of her bed and fell fast asleep. She woke later and crawled under the covers, going straight back to the Land of Nod, dreaming that Mack was in bed beside her, wrapped in her arms . . .

Chapter 31

'Good morning, everyone. May I take this opportunity to extend a special welcome to our two newcomers, Rupert Hallam and Isabelle James.' Giles Longfellow paused long enough for the cast to recognize their new stars, and sensing that there was not going to be a round of applause forthcoming, started one himself.

He then continued, 'It is no secret that this production of *Hamlet* is my pet project, and one I have dreamed of creating for a long time. But I also hope that you, the cast and crew, will become as enthused as I am and realize the importance of the production's success. Not just for me or you, but for the future of Crewe Theatre. You see, I want this theatre to be firmly on the map as an important contributor to the arts in the UK. I am hoping to take this production to the West End eventually, and with luck, it will be the start of many such transfers and collaborations with different producers. Thanks to Lord Graham and his enormous generosity, we have been able to get the ball rolling with *Hamlet* – and may this be just the beginning of a new golden age for this theatre.'

Giles paused again, this time to compose himself. He really did feel quite emotional about the whole thing and, if the truth be known, he was also a little fearful of the outcome. This was his opportunity to shine. He had been working towards this moment for many years now, and was only too aware that the one thing that could let him down was himself. He and Teddie had been seeing a good deal more of each other, due to the fact that they were in close proximity and able to meet easily under the pretext of discussing the finances of the theatre. This had led to many a late-night supper, and the two men had grown closer in every way. His Lordship was still obliged to keep a low profile in his personal dealings with Giles, as he still had Her Ladyship to consider. Lady Tanya Graham knew the score only too well. She had fallen in love with Teddie Graham when they were both still at their boarding schools. Her family owned a huge estate in Northumberland, and over the years several of the landed gentry in and around the area would entertain each other and naturally keep an eye out for any of the younger members' future couplings. Same old, same old . . . Put the right two together, create an heir and a spare, and then all would be hunky-dory.

Tanya had always adored Teddie. He was such fun, and somewhat less pedestrian and conventional than some of the other suitors she was forced to endure. The two of them shared a sense of humour and did not take any of the rigmarole too seriously. They managed to laugh their way through the hunt balls, croquet parties and polo meets, and became firm friends. Inevitably they became lovers, and then engaged and married. It was a smooth transition and they were a very glamorous couple for the first few years on the circuit. Teddie loved to party, and there were many occasions recorded in *Vogue* and *Tatler* to keep his reputation going. But then they had their two children, Edward and Tilly, in quick succession, and suddenly Tanya found herself settled in Crewe Hall up north, while her husband spent a good deal of time at their flat in Chelsea. She actually quite enjoyed the early years with the children. They had a wonderful life in the countryside, and there were always holidays to look forward to: a chalet at Klosters for the winter ski season, or a villa in the South of France for the summer. Tanya was well aware of the situation. She would always be Lady Graham, and as such would enjoy a life of luxury forever – but she would no longer enjoy her conjugal rights with her husband. He would discreetly pursue another avenue. Should she decide to take a lover, that was acceptable, as long as it was never discovered or flaunted in public; appearances were everything.

The couple had lived this way for years, and mostly it worked very well, especially as Teddie tended to keep his other life down in London. Recently, however, he was spending a great deal of time at Crewe Theatre – and when Tanya was introduced to Giles Longfellow at the first night of *A Man for All Seasons*, she immediately knew the reason why. Her heart sank. The saying not on your own doorstep echoed in her head. She was far from pleased, and resolved to keep her distance from the theatre as much as possible. As far as Giles Longfellow was concerned, Tanya was polite but distant, and Giles very much understood his place in the scheme of things; he kept a low profile with the lady of the house.

Giles's relationship with Lord Graham was a distraction that he could have done without really, as he had a good deal on his plate and his career was very much at stake with this season at Crewe. But as usual, his emotional needs overruled his commonsense and he could not resist his trysts with Teddie, be they in a club in Manchester, or late at night in his office. He could no longer live without the thrill of being with his lover.

The only person who knew what was going on was Robert, who had once been the object of his affection. Their romance had almost ended before it began last year, here at the theatre, because Robert could not handle the intensity with which Giles fell in love. For the first few weeks the two men had shared every living moment together. They locked themselves away in Giles's office every lunchtime and ate each other for lunch! They became the laughing stock of the cast and crew, who got fed up with interrupting them in dark corners of the theatre, the most popular being the Royal Box, no less. Finally it was Percy and Peggy who took control and told them it had to stop as it was affecting the whole company, and not for the good. Giles accepted the ultimatum quite easily, and was soon back in his old routine, and directing the next production with great aplomb. Robert, however, was not so easily consoled, and disappeared back to London, never to be seen again.

Percy had announced his relief to Peggy, saying, 'I could never get me head round the lad – something not quite straight there. Very ambitious too, you know. Wouldn't surprise me if we see him again one day, Peggy. I get the feeling he won't let Giles off the hook that easily.'

So it was no surprise when Robert appeared at the first read-through this season, having been introduced as the director's assistant.

Robert was indeed using his power and knowledge to further his career. He got on fine now with Giles, and no longer fancied him, but he was going to use him as much as he could to gain advantages in the pursuit of his theatrical career. *Watch and learn* was his motto these days.

Giles rounded off his introductory speech by explaining that Robert would be taking rehearsals in the rehearsal room next door at the same time as Giles directed the play on the main stage.

'Robert will take individual scenes with you as required, and also oversee the fight sequences. May I also remind you that the lovely Sally Thomas will be directing the Dumb Show, and she will give you your calls accordingly. So now, no more talking, let us read this wonderful play. Heather, start the clock.'

Sally listened intently to the read-through, not just as an actress and understudy, but out of a natural curiosity to see how the company coped with the language of Shakespeare.

Rupert Hallam was a joy. He had obviously worked hard already on the text, and he had a fine sense of the play. He made the words jump off the page, and even found the humour in *Hamlet*, and what he could not find he managed to create. Isabelle, however, seemed completely lost and over-whelmed by the dialogue. She read her lines like a child, in a dull monotone. When she was not actually in a scene she spent the time playing with her hair and fidgeting with a cigarette, which she smoked intensely, sucking in the smoke as if her life depended on it. Rather the other way round, thought Sally to herself, having given up smoking at college, after realizing that the people in the know were right, and not only did smoking ruin your voice, but it could basically kill you.

Percy Hackett was in his element as Polonius, and it was obvious Peggy would have her work cut out supporting him through the play. Sadly, Peggy was too old to play Gertrude, which was a role she had played several times over the years. 'Still, it means I will be nice and free to keep an eye on my

Percy, if you know what I mean,' she said with a big wink in Sally's direction. Geoffrey was playing Claudius the King, and Charmaine was Gertrude, his queen.

'Now we will see all the Royal Shakespeare training coming to the fore,' said Gwendoline, with a touch of sarcasm in her voice. She and Geoffrey were now a definite item, but Sally knew she was very insecure. Geoffrey's wife had appeared at the theatre last week with their three daughters and made a very public scene; she had basically banned him from seeing his little girls. He was clearly very upset and Gwendoline was not able to easily distract him. She was also painfully lacking in any understanding about how a father feels about his children, and she and Geoffrey were finding things very difficult.

'He will go back to the wife, you mark my words,' commented Percy in the Green Room one morning. 'All the sex in the world can't wash away the guilt of leaving the children.'

Peggy turned round and studied her wayward partner. 'Oh? And you are such an expert then, are you, dearie?'

'Well, I don't have kids but I do know a bit about life, Peggy, and in the end loyalty and family count for a lot, don't they?'

Peggy held his look and smiled slowly. 'It is good to hear you say that, my old ducks, because sometimes I do wonder,' she said.

Percy crossed to her and gave her a hug. 'We are all right, girl, don't you fret. Now get my coffee and let's do some line learning.'

Sally had had a little time to study Ophelia and was keen to have a go. Hopefully there would be a chance for her to stand in for Isabelle over the next two weeks of rehearsal when the actress had costume fittings and suchlike. Sally was also very curious to see how Robert conducted his rehearsals. She found him difficult to pin down. Sometimes he was very friendly and rather camp, and yet at other times he was very aloof and cold. He certainly had the ear of Giles Longfellow, and Sally had tried to discover the nature of their relationship. Peggy had told her all about last season, but Sally wondered if Robert still held a torch for Giles.

'He watches Giles all the time,' she commented to Peggy. 'I find him quite tricky to communicate with, don't you?'

'Doesn't bother me, darling, I just get on and do my own thing. All the shenanigans that carry on after hours go over my head.'

Except those related to Percy, Sally thought to herself. That is a very different kettle of *poissons*!

Sally's attention turned to Jeremy. Her dear friend looked decidedly the worse for wear today. He was very pale and sweating profusely. She caught his eye and smiled encouragingly, but he just shook his head slowly and pointed to his glass of water. When they broke for lunch Sally went straight over to him and asked him if he was OK.

'No, I feel terrible and want to be sick, quite frankly. Oh God – I will be back in a minute!' And he was gone. Sally decided to get the full story later. She crossed to the props table which had been set up ready for the afternoon rehearsals and found Dora deep in conversation with Rupert.

'But does *Hamlet* know for sure that his mother is involved with murder?' she was asking him.

'Hi, guys. How's it going?' Sally decided to intervene.

Rupert turned to her with a big smile on his face and said, 'Sally! How are you? Do you want to discuss anything with me? Dora is grilling me on my motivation already,' and he laughed.

'I like to know everyone's motivation,' responded Dora, flirting outrageously with the leading man. She addressed her sister. 'How about you, Sally dear?'

'Some people would call that being nosy,' replied Sally, a little more tartly than she had intended. 'Dora, would you like to help me with the masks? I want to be able to explain to the cast what I will be doing with the Dumb Show when we discuss the play in a minute.'

'Oh, isn't it lunchtime yet?' sulked Dora. 'I'm starving, aren't you, Rupert?' She fluttered her eyelashes at the young man, who was just about to be accosted by Isabelle.

'Rupert, darling,' she practically purred. 'Can we go through some lines as soon as possible? I am *sooo* scared.' She took his arm and leaned into him, flicking her mane of hair out of her gorgeous green eyes to look up at her co-star invitingly.

Oh dear, thought Sally very ungraciously. You have serious competition for the femme fatale role, Dora! To the group she said, 'Come on, Dora, we have work to do. Good luck, you two – see you later.' And she dragged her sister away.

'Oh wow!' grumbled Dora. 'That Isabelle really is a piece of work. She can't act for toffee, but she certainly knows how to get the blokes going with all that bloody hair-tossing business.'

Sally stopped and took her by both shoulders. 'Dora, look at me and listen very carefully. Don't start all that sort of nonsense. You are very minor in all this, and if you want to continue in this company you need to know your place. You do *not* chat up the leading man or slag off the leading lady. Do you understand? You get on with the job and mind your p's and q's.'

'Oh, please don't treat me like a child, Sally. I know my place, but believe me, by the time I have finished here, and people see what I can do, my place will be very different. I just think it is unbelievable that girls like Isabelle get jobs when they blatantly can't act!'

'Well, that is the nature of the beast and always has been, to a certain extent. So the sooner you accept that fact, the happier you will be about it all.'

'But it is so unfair,' wailed Dora dramatically.

'Oh please. Who said anything in life was fair? You just have to work with it. Believe me, if life was fair I would be playing Cleopatra at the National!' Sally snapped.

'Ooh Sally, dear, your mask has dropped. Surely my mild-mannered sister is not showing signs of malice?'

Dora sensed revenge, but was stopped in her tracks when Sally turned and pulled her towards the exit with, 'Ah yes, talking of masks, come with me and find them.' That finished the conversation for the time being, but Sally knew her sister only too well: during the weeks to come, Dora would be on the war-path, and the fight for Rupert's affections would be fierce, she had no doubt. He was very lovely though, Sally had to admit, and her own heart gave a little flutter at the thought of his smile.

Jeremy felt much better after he had been sick. He had left Sally in such a rush, leaving his poor friend wondering what was going on, not that he didn't think for one minute that Sally was not on to him. It was just a question of how much he actually told her about Eddie. Jeremy whispered his name: Eddie . . . He looked at himself in the mirror above the basin, and saw the desperate longing in his eyes. 'What a pathetic sight,' he told himself. 'God, you need to pull yourself together.' He splashed cold water over his face and laughed quietly. Oh boy, had he fallen hard. One minute he had been a man with no emotional ties – now he was in knots!

'What's so funny, Jeremy?' Simon asked as he came into the Gents and went for a pee. 'What do we think about our leading lady then? Bit of all right or what?' He joined Jeremy at the basins and washed his hands.

'A tad out of your league,' teased Jeremy. 'But you never know, she might be into a bit of rough trade.' He made his way out of the door followed by Simon still doing up his flies as they bumped into Robert.

'Well, well, what have you two been up to? Simon, I didn't know you were that way inclined!' Robert said, noting Simon's zip.

'Yeah, very funny,' muttered Simon, pushing past him.

'Charming,' said Robert to Jeremy as he too tried to pass. 'How was your weekend, Jeremy? From what I saw, it was very full on.' He gave a theatrical wink. Jeremy cringed. He and Eddie had bumped into Robert in a bar on Sunday night and it had all been very awkward. All he needed was someone like Robert knowing his private affairs.

He just nodded and said, 'Yes, it was quite a weekend,' and carried on past him.

Robert watched him go with a smile on his face. Knowledge was power, he reminded himself.

Jeremy decided to go up to the dressing room for the duration of the lunch-hour and keep well away from anyone likely to interrogate him. He felt bad about not going to find Sally to explain his behaviour, but he knew she would understand, and he would talk to her later. He just needed a bit of time to sort out his thoughts and feelings. Everything had happened so fast that he was still reeling.

Chapter 32

When they left the theatre on Saturday afternoon, Eddie had
driven them to Manchester.

'This is going to be a sort of Magical Mystery Tour,' he had
announced in the car. 'Just sit back and enjoy the ride!'

Jeremy was in heaven. He watched the countryside speed
past on the motorway, and every now and then he would turn
to Eddie and catch his eye, and they would smile at each other.
Their brief coupling in the theatre was still lingering. Jeremy
could smell Eddie on his T-shirt. He was tingling with the
need to touch his new lover. As if he could read his thoughts,
Eddie put a hand on Jeremy's thigh and caressed him. His hand
was gentle at first then more urgent, travelling further up his
leg, kneading his flesh beneath his jeans. He finally found
Jeremy's hard-on and laughed gently.

'Oh, so you want more, do you? That is good to know.
Shall we stop somewhere and sort you out?' Jeremy was
embarrassed and did not quite know how to react. Eddie
seemed so experienced and well versed in all this seduction
business, yet he was so young.

They had come off the motorway at the next junction and found a field. Eddie parked behind a hedge and made swift work of taking Jeremy to heaven. Jeremy could not have imagined the excitement of this fast love in a car, in a field, in the middle of the countryside. It made him want to scream with pleasure. His whole body was on fire and wanting more and more.

'Now come on, J, you will just have to wait until we get to our destination. Let's get back on the road or we will be late for the other delights I have in store for you.' And with that Eddie backed out of the gate and set off once more for the bright lights of the big city. They arrived in Manchester an hour later, and Eddie displayed a comprehensive knowledge of the back streets. They finally arrived at the front of a huge Victorian house, in a quiet street very near the city centre.

'Follow me,' he ordered, bounding up the front steps and ringing the bell.

'What about our bags?' Jeremy called out.

'Just leave everything and someone will come and deal with them,' replied Eddie. 'Come on, J – hurry up!' Just at that moment, the door was opened and a young man dressed like a butler appeared on the threshold. 'Welcome to the Queen's Hotel,' he said. 'Do you have luggage?'

'Just a couple of bags,' Eddie told him.

'Very well, we will collect those and bring them to your room. Would you like me to park your car, sir? We have a car park at the back for residents.'

'Yes, please.' Eddie took Jeremy's arm. 'Come on, you. Just wait till you see this.'

The butler stood back and let them pass, and then followed them inside.

The place was like a film set, thought Jeremy. The hall was

straight out of the television series *Upstairs Downstairs*. A graceful staircase led upwards from an original black and white tiled floor. A massive chandelier hung over the proceedings, the hundreds of crystal teardrops sparkling above them. But the most bizarre sight was of a huge gilt-framed portrait of the Queen, in her ceremonial robes, which hung above the fireplace to the right of the door.

Jeremy could hardly stop himself from bursting into laughter. He tugged Eddie's sleeve and pointed at the painting, sniggering, 'You can't be serious. That is outrageous! Our poor monarch would die if she knew she was presiding over a gay hotel in Manchester.'

'Oh, never mind that. Come on, we need to sign in.' Eddie skipped off down the corridor ahead.

Jeremy dutifully followed him, and like Alice in Wonderland found himself in another world. The reception desk was vast and had once been mahogany, he guessed. Now, however, it had been gilded to within an inch of its life. It sat in a sea of deep red wallpaper and twinkling rococo fixtures and fittings. No one in this house had ever heard the expression 'less is more'.

The butler handed Jeremy a quill pen with peacock feathers and said, 'Please fill in your details, sir. It is for two nights, I understand?'

'Oh here, let me,' said Eddie, taking over. Jeremy was still open-mouthed at his surroundings.

'Shall I give you a credit card?' added Eddie, taking out his wallet. 'By the way, is George around yet?' he enquired.

'Not yet, sir, but he sent his regards and looks forward to seeing you later in the bar for a cocktail. Now would you care to follow me, please?' The butler glided off towards the staircase, the two lovers in his wake.

At the top of the stairs they turned left and stopped at the first door. Written on it in very elegant gold script was *The Blue Room*. The door opened to reveal a blue room indeed. It was like being in the centre of a Wedgwood plate! There was a roomy canopied double bed with silk sheets, and an enormous blue and gold eiderdown. Jeremy had not seen an eiderdown since he visited his granny as a schoolboy. The lampshades either side of the bed were blue and gold silk, and the wardrobe and dressing table had been painted Wedgwood blue with white trimmings, as were the walls and all the plasterwork. It was incredibly ornate. The butler opened the door to the bathroom to reveal a classic Victorian bathroom, with black and white tiles and a large free-standing slipper bath with all the brass fittings. The toilet had the obligatory mahogany seat, and the pull chain was a twisted rope of fine coloured silks, with a huge tassel to finish it off.

The butler then explained where the fridge was hidden inside a tallboy, also painted blue and white. The matching TV looked most incongruous perched on top of the chest of drawers. Jeremy wondered what Josiah Wedgwood would have made of it!

'If there is anything else you require, please do not hesitate to ring the bell,' the butler said smoothly, and he indicated yet another bell-pull with the attendant tassel.

'Thank you, that is fine,' said Eddie, giving him a generous tip.

'Thank you, sir,' said the butler solemnly, then added with a wink and a wiggle, 'Have fun, you guys.'

Jeremy threw himself on the bed and let out a scream of delight. 'Eddie, this is unbelievable! How did you know about this place?'

Eddie was busy opening a bottle of champagne which had been left for them in a splendid silver bucket.

'Ah, I have friends in high places. Or should I say low places,' he laughed. 'Here, let's have a toast. To love at first sight.' And they touched glasses with a very satisfactory ping from the crystal flûtes provided.

'Everything is so over the top, yet somehow fits,' remarked Jeremy. 'Who owns it?'

'A lovely man called George Delaware. He and his partner Dale have been here for yonks. I don't really know the details, but apparently George used to be a bit of a gangster in the old days – part of the Manchester mafia. Did you know that in the fifties and early sixties, George Raft – an actor and alleged gang member in America – came over to Manchester to see if there was room for his lot up here, and they were sent packing by the good old northerners, who had their own mafia, thank you very much, and didn't need the likes of the Americans to help them make their millions. George told me all this once when I was here.'

Eddie took a swig of champagne then put down his glass and turned to his lover. 'Now, Mr Sinclair, I require you to make slow passionate love to me before dinner.'

And Jeremy was only too happy to oblige.

The rest of the afternoon and early evening were spent making love or drinking champagne. Jeremy decided to try the bath and lay up to his neck in bubbles. There was an extraordinary array of toiletries in the bathroom and he was determined to work his way through the lot. While he was soaking, Eddie watched TV or came into the bathroom to annoy his lover with attempts to seduce him.

'Leave me alone! I can't take any more!' cried Jeremy.

'Oh really? I don't believe that for a minute.' And Eddie whipped off his clothes and joined him beneath the bubbles.

After several of these forays Jeremy finally managed to finish his bath and get ready for the night ahead.

'What exactly do you have in store for me?' he asked delightedly. Eddie was proving to be full of surprises and all of them good, so far.

'Well, we will have drinks with George, then dinner in the restaurant, and then we will adjourn to the club next door, which is also part of the hotel and owned by George. So basically, we do not have to stray far to take our pleasure,' grinned Eddie. 'Pretty clever, don't you think, Mr J? Everything close at hand.'

'It is wonderful. *You* are wonderful. But you still haven't told me how you knew about this place,' said Jeremy.

Eddie looked at him for a minute and then seemed to make a decision. He sighed and said, 'My father has several queer friends. Obviously it is not something he wants to advertise and my mother does not allow them at the house.' Jeremy was about to interrupt but Eddie stopped him. 'Yes, I know what you are going to say, J – that she is a bigot and that it is not for her to judge people, et cetera. Unfortunately, the world is a cruel place, and people *are* ignorant and bigoted, including my mother. When you think it has only been since 1967 that homosexuality was made legal. That is a mere fifteen years ago, Jeremy, and it is still a big thing for a lot of people. You are lucky because you work in a profession where people don't care about things like that. Well, obviously there are a lot of queers in the theatrical profession, which helps, but in the big world outside there is still a great deal of prejudice. My father has started a campaign against discrimination of homosexuals, but it is a real uphill struggle and none of his so-called 'posh' friends want to know.'

'Is your father a homo then?' asked Jeremy. Eddie paused very briefly before he answered.

'No, definitely not – which makes it incredibly difficult for
me. I mean, how can I tell him I am queer?' There was a catch
in Eddie's voice and Jeremy took his hand.

'In fact, I don't think I will ever be able to be open about it,
Jeremy. Well, certainly not in my family circles. I am expected
to marry, and have an heir to carry on the Graham title. I have
seen it with some of my father's friends. They are really queer
but all married. I have seen them here in this hotel, but no one
says anything. You wouldn't believe it in this day and age, but
there is still a terrible stigma about being homosexual.'

Jeremy took Eddie in his arms and held him close. 'Come
on, mate,' he said tenderly. 'Don't get upset. You have a friend
in me now, and we will sort it out. Meanwhile, you have
promised me a good time, so let's go and get a few cocktails
inside us then we won't care about anything.' They kissed passionately and almost succumbed to their growing lust but
broke away laughing, promising each other to save it all for
later.

When they arrived in the bar it was already buzzing. Unlike
a normal cocktail bar in a small hotel where couples sit discreetly chatting in whispers, here the conversation was loud
and frequently interspersed with whoops of delight and
screeches of laughter.

The barman was naked except for a jockstrap and a black
bow tie. Jeremy could hardly contain himself and each new
revelation was fuel to the fire. He wanted to be shocked or
surprised. He certainly had had no idea that hotels like this
existed. He was still wrestling with his feelings for Eddie
which had sprung from nowhere seemingly. What would his
father think, he wondered, if he announced he was queer? His
father enjoyed comics like Larry Grayson, but just dismissed
them in general as 'poofs'. Did his dad even know what a

homosexual was? He had never had a conversation with his parents about things like this. It had been bad enough when his father brought up the subject of sex and 'taking precautions'. Jeremy had begged him not to continue, assuring him that they did all this kind of stuff at school and he really did not have to bother. Even at school no one mentioned homosexuality as such. There was gossip about a boy who had just joined their class from a private school where there had been a big scandal about abuse. But all that meant to Jeremy and his mates was that a teacher had been a paedophile. Even this expression was not totally clear to them. Girls got flashed at by dirty old men, so the assumption was it must be the same dirty old men who did whatever they did to girls *and* boys. But it was not regarded as anything to do with their take on life in general. Certainly not a life choice a young man might make.

'Jeremy, did you hear me?' Eddie's voice cut through his musings.

'Sorry, I was miles away. What did you say?'

'Would you like to try the house cocktail? I am assured by this charming barman that it is excellent.' Eddie gave the barman his most alluring smile and it occurred to Jeremy that he might have been flirting with him. He felt a flash of unease. Jeremy was discovering emotions he had never felt before. So maybe this 'unease' might better be described as jealousy. This was certainly not an emotion he wanted to feel too often.

He shook himself mentally then turned to Eddie and said, 'Yes, a cocktail would be lovely. This bar is pretty amazing.'

The bar was not large but it felt womb-like as the walls were a dark pink flock with the ubiquitous wall lights and drapes of silk where necessary. The bar was mirrored glass, and mirrors lined the wall behind it so customers sitting in the cubicles were reflected in them, doubling the amount of people, which made the room feel even fuller. Everything glowed in a pink light. Life was rosy!

'Good evening, you young things.' The voice told a tale of cigarettes and red wine and late nights.

'George, how lovely to see you.' Eddie jumped off his bar stool and embraced the man in front of him. Jeremy thought he was pretty impressive. He was tall, over six feet, and broad in the shoulders. He had a fine head of black hair but the black was out of a bottle and rather overused, Jeremy decided. The man was dressed in a dark red velvet smoking jacket with a white shirt underneath sporting a large frill down the front. He had black trousers and what appeared to be velvet mocassins with a coat of arms in gold thread sewn on the fronts.

'So this is Jeremy,' said the deep throaty voice. 'Pleased to meet you.' Jeremy took the outstretched hand and shook it. The hand was big and warm, and the handshake almost painfully strong.

'Great to meet you, George. Eddie has been telling me some fantastic stories about you.'

George looked at Eddie and then back to Jeremy and lowered his voice to say, 'Hopefully not too many stories – always better to keep things close to the chest. Careless talk costs lives, as they used to say during the war.' He paused for a fraction of a second and then burst into laughter. 'Only kidding, chuck, only kidding. My bad boy days are long gone.'

Jeremy was not so sure, and had the distinct feeling that he would not want to cross Mr Delaware. However, it was smiles all round now and the drinks flowed. Jeremy explained to George some of his life as an actor and invited him and Dale to come to the first night of *Hamlet*.

'We'll see,' said George. 'Dale is not very good at sitting still for long. You'll meet him later – he is DJ tonight in the club. He loves it, up and down like a sailor on shore leave. Well, my pretty babies, I am going to leave you to have your dinner, and then maybe we can meet up later with Dale for a nightcap. Have a good night and be happy, boys.' He kissed them both farewell and drifted off to a table of screaming queens who were obviously regular guests of the hotel.

Eddie and Jeremy adjourned to the restaurant which was yet another fantasy of colour and bad taste. This time it was about black walls and lamps that hung from the ceiling above each table, creating a pool of light by which to eat. However, it was incredibly difficult to see anything and Jeremy got quite hysterical with laughter as he peered through the darkness trying to talk to Eddie.

'Stop it, J, you will offend our host. It is supposed to be very atmospheric,' said Eddie, trying very hard to read the menu.

'It is certainly that – to the point of being almost stratospheric.' Jeremy groped for Eddie's leg under the table. 'Very good for touching up your date though, which I guess is what it is all about really.'

Eddie giggled and moved closer to Jeremy and they spent dinner behaving outrageously under the table. It added a whole new meaning to the words 'table manners'.

'God – if my parents could see me now they would disown me,' said Jeremy, stuffing his face with avocado dip. 'Have you eaten here before?' He was beginning to think that Eddie had been living this life for quite a while.

'Only once, with a friend from school,' Eddie replied. 'But nothing romantic like this.' He leaned across the table and licked some dip off Jeremy's cheek. 'Can't wait for the strawberries and cream,' he whispered.

Jeremy had another pang of unease. Something made him think that Eddie was telling him what he knew Jeremy wanted to hear. But he brushed aside the still small voice of suspicion. After all, what did the past matter? This was now, and he knew that Eddie was in love with him and they would be together for ever. This was his destiny. It was meant to be.

By the time they had finished dinner both of them were very tipsy. They arrived back at the cocktail bar to find George and friends equally well oiled.

'Here they are, love's young dream,' announced George to the table. 'Boys, meet my Dale,' and he practically shoved poor Dale in front of them for inspection. He was not at all what Jeremy had imagined, if indeed he had imagined anyone at all, but it certainly would not have been anywhere close to the vision in front of them. Dale was tall and elegant as a willow, with long blond hair nearly to his shoulders. He had piercing blue eyes, and very defined cheekbones. He was like a model, thought Jeremy.

'Hi, pleased to meet you,' said Dale in a soft voice, almost lisping. 'I hear you are coming to the club later. I will play a song for you if you tell me what you would like to hear.' He lifted a long delicate hand to his face and brushed some hair from his eyes. Then he turned and pranced off like a race horse.

'Don't mind Dale,' said George. 'I told you he can't keep still. Now sit yourselves down and have some of this champagne.'

They sat down and introduced themselves to the rest of the table. Eddie seemed to be in his element, and entertained them all with jokes and stories for the next hour. The irony was not lost on Jeremy, who for all his training as an actor, now felt completely useless. Yet somehow it didn't matter. His ego did not feel threatened and he was happy to bask in his lover's reflected glory. He was on a high, not just from the champagne, but from Eddie's attention. He had never felt so complete as a man. He just wanted to spend every minute with this guy and feel his energy inside him. He was lost to the world that night. When they got to the club Jeremy danced for hours. He gave himself to the thudding bass beat and just let rip. He had never really danced in his life, and he made Eddie laugh with his attempts at Disco dancing. There were bodies all around him and he could feel their heat. Different men passed by, and would kiss him or touch him up as they danced past. He loved the attention and yet always looked for Eddie for assurance. Eddie was equally busy moving around the dance floor flirting and touching up dancers. The two of them danced with another boy for quite a long time. It got very steamy and there was talk of going back to the room for a threesome, but Jeremy suddenly got cold feet and backed off. Eddie danced him into a corner and kissed him passionately.

'Don't fret, J, you are the only thing in my life now. We don't have to have any diversions or side orders if you don't want them. I am happy with just you and me. Let's go back to the room now and make love all night. Come on, you gorgeous man, I am feeling so randy!'

Jeremy was so drunk by this time he could not have done anything much in the way of dancing or flirting. When they got to their room he fell across the bed and passed out. The next thing he knew, Eddie was undressing him very slowly and whispering in his ear, 'You are gorgeous and wonderful and useless and drunk, but I love you, Jeremy Sinclair. Just get your clothes off and you will soon feel better because you will be feeling me beside you.'

Jeremy giggled and freed his foot from his trousers and

made a grab for Eddie who rolled away off the bed and out of reach.

'That's more like my J. There is hope for you yet. OK, I am going to take my clothes off now, and then we will see who is too drunk to screw.'

'Not me!' cried Jeremy, suddenly coming back to life. 'Ready or not, here I come,' and he sprang up, grabbed Eddie and threw him down on the bed, pinning him against the bedhead. He searched Eddie's face for several moments, trying to read every little tic or twitch. He looked deep into his lover's eyes and saw himself reflected there. He was giddy with lust and every muscle was taut with anticipation.

'I love you, Eddie,' he said very slowly, then lowered himself down and found Eddie's mouth for a deep kiss that took him away to paradise.

Chapter 33

Sunday was indeed a day of rest for our two young lovers. They missed breakfast and lunch, and finally opened an eye around two o'clock. Several glasses of juice and two pots of coffee later, Eddie announced that they should go for a walk.

'It's cold out there,' grumbled Jeremy, still snuggled under the sheets.

'But it is not raining, and the sun is visible. Come on, you wuss, get your kit on. I want to take you by the canal, and then I thought we could have an early dinner at an amazing Chinese restaurant I know called the Mandarin. It is incredibly famous in these parts and has been going for years.'

Jeremy really had no say in the matter and decided to succumb to whatever Eddie had in mind. His brain no longer seemed to function on a practical level any more. It was all about sensations and emotional highs, and living every moment with this incredible boy. Jeremy felt so old compared with Eddie, and yet there was only two years between them.

Eddie, however, seemed to have lived more lifetimes in those two years than Jeremy would ever do in twenty.

The boys set off in their winter woollies and walked briskly along the canal. It was pretty bleak even with the sun shining on the dark water, but Eddie seemed to love it.

'I reckon this will be very popular one day,' he said. 'The old warehouses and cottages will all get gentrified – you just wait and see.' By five it was dark, and they made their way into the centre of Manchester to the Chinese restaurant, which was packed already even at this early hour.

'Everyone here is Chinese!' exclaimed Jeremy.

'Exactly,' replied Eddie with a grin.

The menu was extensive and Jeremy lost the will to live just trying to read it, so once again he put himself into the capable hands of his lover. Eddie went to town and they really had trouble finishing the banquet, especially when it came to the chicken feet – a 'speciality of the house'.

'Oh, Eddie, this is really stuck in my craw,' groaned Jeremy, practically gagging. 'I can't eat it, I am sorry,' and he virtually spat it out into his napkin.

'I must say, you do look rather purple,' chuckled Eddie. 'Don't want to kill you off so soon in the relationship. Come on, let's go grab a taxi to the hotel and have a cocktail.'

By the time they got back, Jeremy was so full of Chinese he just wanted to lie down and go to sleep.

'Oh, don't be such an old misery guts,' retorted Eddie. 'Get in the shower and you will soon feel like a new man.'

Jeremy did as he was told and stood for a good ten minutes letting the hot water caress his back and shoulders. He suddenly called out to Eddie, 'You are right, I do feel like a new man. Got anyone in mind?!'

The next thing he knew, he was being scrubbed with a

loofah and Eddie was whispering in his ear, 'Haven't got any new men, but this one has plenty of wear left in him, so shut up and enjoy!'

Later, they strolled into the bar feeling on top of their game. As per usual the bar was full to bursting, and the conversation as loud and shrill as ever. Eddie waved to George, who was holding court at a big centre table. They decided to sit at the bar for a while and ordered champagne cocktails.

'Oh, this is slipping down a treat,' said Jeremy. 'Please order me another immediately.' He leaned across and was about to plant a kiss on Eddie's cheek when a familiar voice stopped him in his tracks.

'Well, well, what do we have here, love's young dream? I didn't think you had it in you, Jeremy. I was obviously completely wrong.'

Jeremy turned to look up from his bar stool into the amused eyes of Robert Johnson.

'Robert! What a surprise. This is my friend Edward. Eddie, this is Robert Johnson our assistant director.'

'Hi, would you like a drink, Robert?' asked Eddie innocently enough.

'No, I am fine, thanks. I am joining some friends here in a minute. Actually, Jeremy, I am joining Giles and his friend Lord Graham.' He had turned to Eddie as he said this. Eddie kept his cool but Jeremy just froze. 'Do you know Lord Graham, Edward?' asked Robert, pointedly holding the boy's gaze.

'I should do,' replied Eddie. 'He is my father. Can't think what he would be doing here of all places.'

'I am sure he would be saying exactly the same about your presence here, don't you think?' taunted Robert.

'In that case, maybe it's a good idea we keep this meeting to ourselves. Come on, Jeremy, we were just going anyway. We only stopped by for a quick drink, looking for an actor friend of Jeremy's.'

Jeremy rose and squeezed past Robert, who was standing very close to both of them.

'Sorry, excuse me,' he stuttered. 'See you tomorrow at the read through.'

Robert's smile was practically reptilian. 'You certainly will, my dear. Enjoy the rest of your evening. A pleasure to meet you, Edward,' he called back over his shoulder – and then he was gone.

Once back in their room, Jeremy and Eddie discussed the seriousness of their situation.

'We haven't done anything wrong, for God's sake. We are both over age, and why shouldn't we be having a drink here. Doesn't mean we are queer necessarily?' suggested Eddie.

'Oh come on, Ed. Did you see a single straight man in that room? I don't really mind because no one will care what I get up to, but you are a different matter. Your father will go mad if he discovers his son and heir is a homosexual.'

Eddie thought about this for a few minutes. 'Yes, you are right. But then what was my father doing there?' he added.

'I suppose Giles must have suggested they come here and your father's curiosity got the better of him. You said he is fairly relaxed about the queer thing, and maybe he wanted to see a bit of the life for himself.'

'Suppose so,' pondered Eddie, but he did not sound convinced. 'However, it's not a conversation I want to pursue at this point in time, so let's hope Robert keeps his mouth shut.'

'I wouldn't bank on it,' said Jeremy. 'He is a weird one and very difficult to read. He was quite pleasant to me at the beginning of the season but has cooled off since it became clear I did not fancy him. Having said that, he never really comes on to anybody too strongly, and he spends quite a lot of time flirting with the girls, so maybe he is playing a game all round. He definitely has Giles's ear though. Not quite sure why yet. Maybe when we see what he does as a director on *Hamlet* with Giles, we will spot the talent. Who knows? I will keep a very close eye on him in future. That's all we can do for now. Come on, let's watch some TV. I am knackered, and tomorrow is a big day for me.'

'Ah, my poor baby. OK, we will chill tonight, and you can show me your version of "An Actor Prepares" – as long as it involves lots of sex!'

The weekend ended perfectly for Jeremy on Sunday night with, indeed, not much sleep but lots of lovemaking.

'This has to last me a while,' he murmured to Eddie as they started to drift into blissful sleep. 'Good night, you beautiful man.'

Eddie turned and kissed him on the forehead. 'Sleep, perchance to dream . . .'

The next morning they ate a huge cooked breakfast in rather a subdued mode.

'Will you be around at all this week?' asked Eddie.

'I doubt it very much. Rehearsals will be full on because there is a hell of a lot to get through. Mind you, after I am killed there may be some time. But don't worry – I will ring you whenever I can.' Jeremy smiled across the table.

'Well, just remember I will mostly be out in the middle of nowhere on a bloody tractor. Best time to get me is before seven or after five. But then you are onstage. Shall I call you at your digs around eleven?' Eddie suggested.

'Yes, that might be best. Oh Eddie, this has been so wonderful I don't want it to end.' Jeremy took Eddie's hand across the table.

'Don't fret, there will be many more weekends – and even better than this,' Eddie promised, squeezing his lover's hand. 'But come now, we must get you back to the state of Denmark, where something is rotten and where princes come from. You have battles to fight, my love.'

Chapter 34

'We have battles to fight, literally and figuratively,' announced Giles after lunch. 'So I would like Rupert, Jeremy, Simon and Pete to go with Robert to practise sword-fights next door. Isabelle and Sally, we will make a start on all Ophelia's scenes, and Charmaine, Percy and Geoffrey – please be standing by to do your scenes. I am sorry if there is a bit of a wait, but it would be good just to run through what we are going to do with Polonius, and the whole ghost scenario. Everyone else, please do not wander far from the theatre as Gwendoline will want to do some fittings. It is going to be a very difficult show from the point of view of costumes, as many of you are doubling up in parts. I may have to employ one extra actor to play the ghost and cover. Still, that's enough to be getting on with for now, so off you go.'

Sally gathered her script and made her way down into the stalls to sit with Giles, but he had decided to stay onstage as Isabelle was already starting to cause concern with her nerves.

'I feel so vulnerable, Giles. The stage seems vast at the

moment and I am worried I will not be able to fill it.' She was clutching her script tightly to herself and puffing on the inevitable fag.

'That's OK, darling, we have plenty of time. Sally and I will join you, do not worry.'

The three of them sat in a huddle and started to work through the dialogue. It was painfully obvious, after only a few minutes, that Isabelle did not have a clue what she was saying, or indeed what any of the play was about. Sally's heart sank as she envisaged days spent with their leading lady giving her instruction on Shakespeare and his dialogue. Thank God she herself had learned the part already.

In the coming days it became very apparent to everyone that Giles was right: the production was going to be incredibly complicated with so many people doubling up as courtiers and small characters who came and went. Simon and Pete were hysterical, standing in the wardrobe with Gwendoline and Janie trying to fit them.

'Why don't we just wear different hats, or wigs?' joked Simon. 'Why, look yonder, sirrah! Behold, there is the watchman in his pink hat!' He then pulled on another hat from the pile in front of them. 'Nay, sir, this is not your hat. This belongeth to old Yorick, methinks.'

Pete by this time had pulled on a long robe and answered in a falsetto voice, 'Oh dearie me, alas alack, poor Yorick is long gone. But looketh over there, I see a ghost naked. What? Is it come to this? A naked ghost? Bringeth me the wardrobe mistress that she may see the error of her ways!'

By this time they were all laughing so much they did not see Robert watching from the doorway.

'I am glad you are all so confident about your performances that you can afford to stand around making jokes. Simon and

Peter, I want you onstage in five minutes to go through the fight scene.' He turned on his heel and left the room.

'Oops!' said Pete.

Sally was in a complete panic. She had had no idea how much work would be involved in setting up the Dumb Show with such a shortage of actors. In fact, she was forced to take some theatrical licence and have ladies playing men. She even had to put herself in the piece, which meant having to learn a huge speech. This did not last long, however, as she was wanted almost all the time to rehearse with Rupert. Isabelle was proving a complete nightmare. She could not seem to learn the lines at all. Rupert was having trouble going through each scene as they had to stop all the time, so he too was starting to panic, and relied more and more on Sally to provide his lines. At one point they were in the ridiculous position of Rupert and Sally rehearsing in one room, and Giles and Isabelle in another so that Giles could help the girl learn the lines as she went along. Truth be known, Sally was in seventh heaven; she loved every minute of her time with Rupert. He was so giving as an actor and warm and affectionate that by the end of the first week, she was truly smitten. But it was not to last. Giles called her into his office on Saturday morning and said, 'Sally, you are going to have to put Dora on the book with Rupert and get on with your Dumb Show. I need to know that that is one thing that is sorted.'

Sally was gutted. 'But I can do both,' she pleaded. 'I can get Dora on the case, and I have been thinking that she will have to do my big speech anyway, as I am tied up with Rupert and his scenes.'

'Sally, you are not tied up at all. May I remind you that *Isabelle* is playing Ophelia, and will shortly be taking her rightful position opposite her leading man. She has come on in leaps and bounds and I have to say, with no disrespect to you at all, that when Rupert and she are together, the chemistry is phenomenal. Now, please can you call Dora to the stage.'

Sally had to hold back the tears that were threatening to spill down her cheeks. She knew Giles was right, and she was only the understudy, but it still hurt that all her hard work was dismissed in a minute. Bloody Isabelle would step in, and thanks to everyone around her, holding her up and supporting her, she would come out of this with glory. She started to run up the stairs to the dressing room to have a good cry.

'Sally, are you OK?' asked Rupert as he came down the stairs towards her.

Oh God, no, this is all I need, thought Sally. *Please leave me alone.*

'Are we not going through the scene again?' he went on, unaware of any problems.

'Yes, I think you are going to do it with Isabelle. I need to get to my rehearsal for the Dumb Show. Sorry, Rupert, I must dash.' Sally tried to ease past him but he took her arms and stopped her.

'What's wrong? You are crying. Here, have a tissue.' He produced one like magic and gave it to her.

'I am so sorry, Rupert, you shouldn't have to concern yourself with me. You have enough going on in your life. It's just all getting to me, I guess. There is so much to do and not enough time. Please don't worry, just concentrate on your role.'

'Well, I was hoping you might have me round to your place tonight so we could consolidate everything we have worked on, and then I can introduce Isabelle to the scenes tomorrow.'

Sally sighed. She could not think of anything more perfect, but it was not to be.

'I think Giles wants to do that now, Rupert. But find me

later if you have any problems.' She pulled away and ran upstairs.

Sally spent the rest of the day gathering her cast together and nailing the Dumb Show. She was determined to sort it out and get back to Rupert and Ophelia. A nagging voice inside her was pointing out that she was not giving her Dumb Show the attention it required. The whole project had been so exciting at the beginning, and her debut as a director had fired her up. Now, however, all she wanted to do was get it over with so she could return to the intimacy of the rehearsal room and Rupert. She had put Dora in her role, but soon realized that it did not work, as her sister just did not have the vocal ability to hold the speech together. She herself would have to do it. She reluctantly told Dora to go off and join Rupert and Giles.

'Oh my God! This is brilliant,' enthused the other girl. 'I can't wait to work with Rupert – he is so gorgeous. Maybe Isabelle will be taken off, and *I* will be there to take over. I must make sure I know the part inside out. You will have to help me, Sally.'

'I will do no such thing,' her sister retorted angrily. '*I* am the official understudy, and if Isabelle was off *I* would take over. Just remember, Dora, you are only filling in for me while I sort out the Dumb Show, then I will take over again. You are just there to read the lines, thank you, so don't get any ideas above your station.'

'Ooh sorreee!' mocked Dora. 'Talk about getting on your high horse.' And she flounced off.

Sally went to find Jeremy as much for moral support as for his input into the Dumb Show.

'Now calm down and let's go through this slowly,' he said wisely. 'You are short of actors, are you not? Well, I had a thought this morning while chatting to the redoubtable Peggy. She would be perfect as the Player Queen. Let's face it, she may be getting on in years but her voice is very youthful, and one won't see the rest of her because she will have the mask on. Then you have got me as the Player King, so that will all work. You have Sarah and Dora – and even Robert if needs be. You will have to be First Player, and if you did have to cover Isabelle, then I guess I could learn the bloody speech.'

Sally gave her friend a grateful hug. 'I knew I could rely on you. Thanks so much, Jeremy – that is perfect. So can we rehearse now, do you think, or what about I cook lunch on Sunday and you come round and we go through all the speeches, and then I can put everyone else in next week, as and when they are free?'

'Ah now, weekends are going to be a problem from now on, I am afraid,' said Jeremy, looking sheepish. 'I will be seeing Eddie every weekend so will not be around.'

Sally looked at him. 'Wow, is it that serious? You have only known him a few weeks. Don't you think you should take things slowly?'

'No, I really don't,' he replied. 'This amazing thing has happened to me, Sally, and I am going to run with it. We are in love and I have found my soulmate. Nothing else matters.'

'What about your acting?' asked Sally carefully, remembering all their late-night discussions about their career prospects.

'What about it? As you said, it can only help me as an actor to have experience of these incredible emotions I am going through just now.'

'Yes, I can see that,' she agreed, 'but won't you feel the pressure of work if you are out gadding about all weekend? You were certainly in no fit state last week after your time off. I just don't want you to screw up this part, Jeremy. You have been longing for this job, so don't blow it because you are too exhausted to give it your best shot. Remember, all the agents are coming, and the producer of Isabelle's film and God knows who else. This is the moment you have been waiting for. We both have,' she added, suddenly reminded that she too had been working towards this production and now found herself pulled in all directions.

'Please don't worry, Sal. I am fine – I couldn't be happier. Now come on, let's go and find Peggy and talk to her.'

That night, everybody seemed to have the same idea and ended up in the pub. It was one of those spontaneous evenings that always go well. The one consolation during these two weeks of intense activity was the fact that there was no evening show. The actors could afford a night on the tiles and still recover, though some took longer than others, as Simon liked to point out every so often.

'I am a delicate little flower really,' he would say. 'I only drink because I am so insecure and fragile.' He would then spend the rest of the night trawling the pub for an unsuspecting female to massage his ego! Dora had long ago given up on him, and was far too busy pursuing her career as an actress through foul means or fair. Sally watched her sister now, flirting at the bar with Robert. Lately she had spent a good deal of time with him, much to Sally's dismay. She waved to Dora, who came bouncing over to where Sally was sitting waiting for Jeremy.

'Hi, everything OK, sister dear? It is good fun tonight, isn't it? Must go – Robert has got the drinks in, see you later.'

'Just be careful,' warned Sally. 'He is very slippery and will sell you out as soon as look at you.'

'I don't know why you are so against him,' replied Dora. 'He has been very kind to me, and given me lots of good advice about theatre and directors and stuff. He is quite sexy too, in a dark, brooding kind of way.'

She giggled and Sally looked up sharply. 'Oh Dora, please don't tell me you have slept with him.'

'No, he's gay, silly – well, I think he is. Maybe he swings both ways. I wouldn't say no if he asked me.' Then she added, 'Oh, don't be so stuffy, Sally. Relax. It is only a bit of fun. Haven't you slept with someone for a laugh?'

Sally sat there in the pub with her half a lager and lime and tried to understand what had happened to Dora to turn her into this frivolous wayward girl.

'I can't believe you are saying these things, Dora, I really can't. Is no one safe from your clutches? Why would I sleep with anyone just for a laugh? I am not a prude, but I am not a tart either. You sound like a slapper!'

Dora laughed. 'Oh come on, please – it's 1982. I am my own woman and I do what I like, when I like, with whom I like. It doesn't mean anything and that's the way I like it. I don't want to fall in love and find myself committed to a deep relationship with all its problems. I want to be a star, Sally. There – I have said it. I want to be a huge star and I am going to do it, you just watch me.'

Sally suddenly felt very old and tired. She dismissed Dora's declarations as typical youthful bravado. Her sister was just going through a phase. But she could not help but feel hurt and alienated by Dora's behaviour. She was still miffed about Mack, but had chosen not to bring up the subject because she didn't want to make matters worse. A part of her felt she was over-reacting. Dora had meant no harm. However, another part of Sally felt betrayed by her sister, who would probably have slept with Mack without a second thought, had she had the chance.

The more she thought about it, the more she felt betrayed. Best to forget all about it and hope that one day it would all be water under the bridge. But now, here Dora was again, challenging Sally's integrity and career as an actress. Sally had to admit she was a little overwhelmed by her sister's ambition.

Was that what it was all about – naked ambition? But then she remembered Jeremy's face today when he was talking about being in love, and how vulnerable he had seemed. That was also a dangerous route to take, in her book. The two of them had always agreed that emotional stability was important to survive the pressures of the business, but that stability could come from friendship, which was more reliable than using precious energy on romantic involvement. Sex was important, but not vital. Sally smiled wryly to herself; she should be so lucky! She had hardly been feeding her emotional or artistic soul in the last three months. Even the excitement of the first nights, and going onstage to face the audience had faded under the weight of everyday life in a repertory theatre. It was mostly drudgery, if the truth be known. Where was the spark?

She had often thought about Mack since their last meeting, but somehow she was still not ready to add him into the equation. It would just complicate matters. Better that she deal with the job to the best of her ability, and then meet Mack with a clean slate. She had rung him and they had chatted happily about general stuff in their lives. In fact, Mack was not going to be able to visit for a few weeks anyway as he had been commissioned to deliver three large sculptures for an exhibition in Italy.

'My first real international showcase,' he said happily. 'I am gutted we can't meet up yet, but believe me, when we do, we can celebrate in style.'

She smiled dreamily to herself at the thought of being with him.

'Penny for them?' Rupert broke into her thoughts as she finished her lager and lime.

'Oh, just trying to work out how to fit everything in. It's a

nightmare, isn't it? How did your rehearsal go with Isabelle?'
Sally asked, curious to know the answer.

Rupert made a rueful face. 'Well, all right, I suppose, but
there is a long way to go. She is trying really hard, and she is
so sweet one can't get angry with her.' He turned to look
round the bar and spotted Isabelle, who was surrounded by
adoring males, all hanging on her every word. She looked a
little the worse for wear.

'She should really go home to bed by the looks of her,' said
Sally, feeling deflated. She had hoped that Rupert might suggest coming back to her flat to go through the lines as he had
mentioned earlier.

'I think I had better be the gent, don't you? Get her home.
Hopefully we can run some lines tomorrow, Sally. Thank you
for being such a brick.' He kissed Sally on the cheek, and she
got a brief whiff of his cologne, and then he was gone. She
watched him scoop Isabelle up and carry her, in a fireman's
lift, out of the pub. Everyone was whooping and hollering and
cheering. Sally decided she had had enough for the night and
left soon afterwards. She had to admit she was exhausted, and
as her mother always used to say: 'Things always look better in
the morning after a good night's sleep.'

As she lay awake in bed that night, restless and unable to
drop off, Sally tried to stop the negative thoughts from spilling
over her sleepy head. Then very slowly, her thoughts turned to
Rupert. But what about Mack? She tried to focus on him, but
it was Rupert's face that floated before her. In fact, her whole
body tingled, and she felt herself falling into his arms as he
lifted her up and carried her away.

Chapter 35

By the end of the week Sally was seriously pissed off. She felt completely abandoned by everyone. Giles and Robert were always having private meetings in the office, and the cast were fretting about all the costume changes and paying very little attention to the text. Jeremy was really irritating her, as he gazed endlessly into space with an inane grin on his face. As soon as he could after rehearsals, he was on the phone at the stage door to Eddie. She had hoped he would be around to support her, not just as a fellow actor, but as a friend. She was also aware that Dora had completely taken over her duties as understudy, and every time Sally visited the rehearsals she watched with growing anger as her sister flirted with Rupert. The only consolation was that Isabelle stood between Dora and the object of her desire. The actress might not have the means to absorb the text of one of Shakespeare's greatest plays, but she sure knew how to fend off female competition. Sally had hardly had a chance to talk to Rupert as he was spending every minute of the day, and possibly the night, with his co-star. This was the nub of the matter. To Sally's dismay it

seemed that romance had blossomed between the two leading
actors and she was devastated by the thought. How could
Rupert fall for such an obvious ploy? He had seemed so sensitive and caring when they had talked, and now here he was
blatantly indulging his carnal needs like any other bloke. The
trouble was that for all the sexual chemistry that might be
going on offstage, the onstage performances were still
lacklustre, and it seemed to Sally that Giles was not able to
inspire the actors to do better. This was the other problem for
Sally. She could see that Giles was losing his grip, and Robert
also was very anxious. The two of them seemed to have lost
the plot. Well, it was a bit late now!

Sally decided to corner Robert and see if she could find out
what was going on. She met him at the stage door one morning early and offered to make him a coffee.

'Thank you, that would be very welcome,' he said and
followed her up to the Green Room.

'I think I may even have some chocolate biscuits squirrelled
away for emergencies,' said Sally as she put the kettle on.

'Is there an emergency?' asked Robert. Sally turned and
caught him watching her very carefully.

'No, not exactly, but things do seem a little – how shall I
say? A little fraught.' Sally busied herself with the coffee. She
did not want to overstep the mark. Robert could be very
tricky and she had no wish to jeopardize her position.

'Fraught?' Robert rolled the word round his tongue.
'Fraught. Yes, you could say that, I suppose.' He pulled out a
chair from the table in the centre of the room and sat down
slowly. Suddenly he seemed frail; all the swagger and postur-
ing was gone. Sally finished making the coffee and placed a
mug on the table in front of him. She fetched her own mug
and the biscuits and sat down beside him. They remained in

silence for a good five minutes, then Robert seemed to gather himself together. He picked up the coffee, took a few sips and then turned to Sally.

'So, do you have any bright ideas as to how we can ease the situation?'

Sally was not quite sure how genuine the question was, or whether there was a hint of sarcasm. She decided to opt for the positive.

'Oh, I didn't mean to criticize or anything. It is just that obviously we all want the play to be a great success – for Giles and the theatre – and if there is anything I can do to help, then I am very happy to be of service. I have managed to nail my Dumb Show at last, though what will happen when we get onstage with that truck, God only knows.' The designer had decided that a part of the scenery would be built on a moving truck which could be wheeled on and off. This was going to be particularly dramatic in the grave-digging scene as there was a grave built into the truck part so *Hamlet* could jump into it. However, the truck was also onstage during the Dumb Show and, in fact, Sally was contemplating using it as a way to get her actors off at the end of the scene. She had in mind a final tableau which would then disappear as the truck was pulled off the stage in a blackout. However, in order for this to work it was imperative that all the actors were firmly on the correct bit of the stage, or someone might well get left behind or worse still, disappear into the grave!

Robert smiled and agreed that, 'It would indeed be interesting to see what happens. But what exactly do you feel is not working as far as the play is concerned?'

Sally knew she was on the spot. It was not her place to pass comment on the directorial skills of Giles Longfellow. She weighed her words very carefully.

'Oh goodness, I wouldn't dream of suggesting there is anything not working, not at all. But I have spent quite a good deal of time with Giles and Rupert and Isabelle, and it has been quite frustrating at times when the text is not clear, or the lines are slipping. You know what it's like, Robert.' She tried to put the ball back in his court, but he was refusing to co-operate.

'Yes, I understand it has not been easy, but Giles tells me Isabelle is finally making progress and hopefully with a few runs of the play under her belt she will pull it out of the bag.'

Sally decided to change the subject. 'I gather we have a few important folk coming to the first night?' she said. 'Even a West End producer, with a view to taking the play into Town?'

Suddenly Sally saw Robert shut down in front of her. She had gone too far. There was no way he was going to share with her – a mere ASM – any information like that.

'We will have to wait and see. Now I must get on. Thank you for the coffee, Sally, and I look forward to seeing your Dumb Show.' He stood up and was once more in control as he left the room without a backward glance. She had been dismissed. That is all very well, she thought, but it does not change the fact that things are not right, and I am going to make sure my actors are given the best chance there is to shine.

She went in search of Jeremy, who was usually in early. Sure enough he was up in his dressing room going through his lines.

'Hi, how are you?' he asked as Sally stomped through the door.

'Not happy!' she exclaimed. 'Jeremy, if we don't pull our fingers out, this production is going to sink without trace. What are the fight scenes like? Are you happy with what Robert has done with them?'

'What has brought all this on?' asked Jeremy. 'Since when have you been in charge?'

'Oh, stop it! I am not in charge but I am worried that we are not up to speed. I have just tried to get Robert to give me a clue as to what is going on, but he was very tight-lipped.'

'Why do you think there is something going on?' replied Jeremy. 'Has something happened?'

'No, not really, it is just that Giles and Robert seem to be constantly whispering in corners, and I know that there are problems with Isabelle which do not seem to be getting any better.'

'Oh really? I thought she *was* getting better. Dora seems to think she is going to surprise us all on the night.'

'Huh,' replied Sally, unable to hide her disapproval. 'What does *Dora* know about anything?'

Jeremy laughed. 'Oh dear, sisterly affection, eh? Are you sure it is not you who is seeing the world through very jaded glasses at the moment?'

'What is that supposed to mean?' retorted Sally. 'I have been working my butt off to make this play work and no one appears to notice or care. Dora seems to think she is now Isabelle's understudy, which is ridiculous, and Giles won't let me get back to the job I started. I was helping Rupert, and it was going really well until . . .' She stopped suddenly, aware that she wanted to burst into tears.

Jeremy got up and gave her a hug. 'Come on, Sal, don't give up now. You are being brilliant and once we have opened the play it will all calm down. I know you must be upset about Rupert and Isabelle, but—'

Sally cut him off. 'What do you mean? Why would I be upset? Upset about what? Just because the two stars are shagging each other? It is just a shame they don't put the same energy into their performances as they do in bed.' Sally knew she was being unfair but she just could not help herself.

'Well, well, Miss Thomas, I never thought I would see you crack. Don't tell me you have become emotionally involved with a fellow actor. That is not how we decided it worked. Were you not giving me hell just last week, for not focusing on my performance?'

'Oh, don't be ridiculous, Jeremy,' Sally snapped. 'That was a completely different thing. You are madly in love with Eddie and risking everything else. What is there to compare with me? I am not madly in love with anybody.'

'No, but you are infatuated with Rupert, and don't try and deny it. I am your best friend, remember?'

Sally opened her mouth to protest and then changed her mind. It was the truth. Jeremy had got it right. Everything she was feeling was down to Rupert. She felt so stupid and angry with herself for letting her feelings get the better of her. The ridiculous thing was that Rupert had no idea how she felt about him. As far as he was concerned they were great mates, and that was all. How could he know she was so destroyed by his affair with Isabelle? How could she feel so betrayed by him? There was nothing *to* betray. She had created the whole thing in her head and now it was spoiling everything.

'Oh, Jeremy, I feel such a prat.' Fortunately, she managed to stop the tears. The last thing she wanted at this moment was to let Jeremy or anyone else know how she felt. She would deal with it in private.

'Come on you, cheer up. You have done a fantastic job with the Dumb Show, and everyone knows how much you have contributed to Isabelle's performance. With any luck she will go missing and you will get a go. Imagine that.' Jeremy kissed her on the cheek and turned back to his script.

'Are you going away this weekend again?' asked Sally.

'Yes, of course. Why do you ask?' Jeremy waited.

'Oh nothing really, except I thought I might have a big Sunday lunch to get everyone together for the last week before we open. Bit of bonding, you know.' She smiled.

'Sorry, got my own bonding to do.' Jeremy grinned meaningfully back at Sally.

'Great,' said Sally to herself and left the dressing room. She decided to go and visit the girls in Wardrobe for a cheer-up and a gossip. She found Gwendoline sewing beads onto a gorgeous silk gown.

'Is that for our leading lady?' enquired Sally as she came in the room.

'Yes, and she is thrilled with it,' said Gwendoline, looking up at Sally. 'I just hope she stays thrilled enough not to lose any more weight because I have to keep taking it in.'

'Blimey, if she lost any more weight she would disappear when she turned sideways,' snorted Janie, who was ironing in the corner. 'Mind you, I joke – but bloody hell, girls, she is something else isn't she? You know she keeps making herself sick. Practically every time I go in her dressing room she is puking in the toilet. I reckon she has got a problem.'

'What sort of problem?' asked Sally.

'You know what I mean – an eating-disorder type of thing. Anorexia, I think they call it. I was reading about it the other day in a magazine. Lots of film stars have it because they have to be so thin for the films. They either don't eat at all, or eat and then make themselves sick afterwards. Some people have even died, it gets so bad.' Janie was warming to her subject. 'Mind you, she probably gets sick from all that dope she smokes as well. What?' Janie looked up from her ironing to see Gwendoline and Sally staring at her open-mouthed. 'Oh, don't tell me you didn't know? She is always rolling joints and stashing them in her make-up bag for later. Pete reckons that is why she can't learn the lines. He says she is basically stoned all the time. I am surprised Giles hasn't noticed – or Rupert, for that matter. Let's face it, he is such a lovely guy and so obviously not into drugs, yet he spends all his time with her. Did I tell you I caught them at it in the dressing room the other day? God, it was so embarrassing.'

'I thought you said she spent all her time with her head down the toilet,' Sally said rather sullenly. 'What a busy girl she is.'

Janie laughed. 'Go on, Sally, tell it how it is!'

'Sorry, but it does make me cross, Janie. People like her always seem to get away with murder, don't they? Not much talent but all the luck in the world, and mugs like us prepared to cover for her. Anyway, enough of all that, I came here to be cheered up and get the gossip. How is Sarah these days?' For some reason Sally had suddenly thought about the girl and her dealings with Percy. Peggy seemed happier of late so maybe things had gone back to normal.

'Funny you should mention her,' said Janie. 'She is not my favourite person and she owes me money as it happens, but she is very quiet these days. I think something has happened.'

'She owes me money as well,' joined in Gwendoline. 'And I believe she has had money off most of the boys. She seems to have eased off on Percy, I noticed.'

'I know Peggy was worried about all that,' said Sally. 'Do you think Sarah was actually sleeping with him?'

'Yes, I do. She is a right little madam,' blasted Janie. 'And I tell you what I think, that she tried to get money out of Percy because he was in a right state a while back and asked Pete about loans and such from the bank, and when Pete asked him why he needed the money, Percy got all tearful and admitted he was a bad boy sometimes and girls took advantage – but he wouldn't actually own up to it being Sarah. But let's face it, we all know she has been all over him like a rash. Even Peggy knows the score. I reckon Peggy has fronted her up and told her to get lost and that is exactly what she has done. Can't blackmail Percy if the wife knows all about it, can she? So now she is keeping her head down – looking for the next victim, I expect.'

'I always suspected it was Sarah who told Geoffrey's wife he was having an affair.' Gwendoline let this statement hang in the air and all three girls digested the information.

Sally found herself thinking what a sad world it was when people spent so much time and energy being horrible to each other.

The silence was broken by the arrival of Dora.

'Hi, guys! Just been told I have to try on Isabelle's costumes in case I have to go on. How cool is that . . .' She stopped as she caught her sister's glare across the room.

'You have to go on? Dora, how many times do I have to tell you *I* am Isabelle's understudy?'

'Don't blame me, sis. Giles sent me here. Talk to him.' Dora crossed to Gwendoline and started to undress.

'Oh, don't worry, I will,' Sally hissed and marched out of the room.

Chapter 36

Sally was fuming as she strode across the stage towards Giles Longfellow's office. This was beyond endurance. Never mind the fact that her bloody sister was trying to usurp her role, Sally had a contract with the theatre that stated that *she* was the official understudy. As she approached the door to Giles's office she could hear raised voices. She knocked loudly and the shouting stopped immediately. There was a pause and then the door was opened by Robert who looked at her briefly and then pushed past her and left.

'Sally, come in, come in.' Giles looked decidedly ill at ease and was mopping his brow with a silk handkerchief. 'Please sit down, dear. What can I do for you?'

Sally took a deep breath and jumped straight in. 'I am very disappointed to discover that somehow my sister Dora seems to have replaced me as the understudy for Ophelia. I have a contract which states I am employed as an ASM, and to play small parts and understudy. Why have you not allowed me to continue in this capacity?'

Giles let out a long sigh. 'Oh, Sally, my dear, do we have to go through all this now? I am so stressed, as you can appreciate. I value your time and your talent enormously, but you can't do everything. You have been engaged with the Dumb Show, which I hear is fabulous, and you have had your usual duties to perform finding props, et cetera. I felt it was impossible for you to understudy as well.'

'But you could have talked to me about the situation,' said Sally. 'You agreed I could put Dora on my other jobs, and once I had set up the Dumb Show I would have been free once again to work with you and Isabelle. I have arranged the whole thing to fit round my duties, and there is not a problem. Please, Giles, it is only fair you give me back the job. Apart from anything else, Dora is not experienced enough to hold the performance together, no matter what she thinks.'

Giles regarded Sally for a few moments and then remarked, 'Do I suspect a trace of filial jealousy?'

'Oh, for goodness sake!' cried Sally. 'I am so sick of people always resorting to that old chestnut. I brought Dora here to work. I am proud of what she has achieved and happy for her, but that is not the point. I am the understudy *and I want my job back.*'

Giles laughed, a deep throaty sound that resounded round the room.

'Well done, you! OK, Sally, you win. You are the official understudy and I will check with the printers that your name is in the programme. Make sure you let Gwendoline know about costumes and then meet me onstage to go through all the Ophelia scenes with Isabelle. I might as well tell you now that there is every possibility that you *will* have to go on at some point, as the girl has some medical problems that may need attention. Obviously we just hope and pray she is fine for the first night. Please keep all this to yourself,' he added.

'Of course,' replied Sally, trying to keep calm and hoping Giles would not notice the flush of exaltation she could feel spreading over her whole face. 'Thank you, Giles, I am very grateful.' She moved as swiftly as possible, without looking as though she was rushing, to the door. She just wanted to get away before he changed his mind!

Once outside, and out of earshot, she let out a whoop of delight and went to find her dear sister. Dora was still in the wardrobe department trying on costumes. Sally made sure she was very calm and businesslike. It would not do at all for her to look as though she was enjoying her assignment.

'Dora, can I have a word outside? Would you excuse us for a minute, ladies?'

Dora followed Sally out and up to the dressing room. 'So what is so secretive we have to come up here?' she asked.

'I have just been talking to Giles and we have agreed that it is only right and proper that I get my job back as understudy to Isabelle. So I—' Sally was interrupted by a very petulant Dora.

'Oh come on, Sally, that is not fair! I have worked really hard the last couple of weeks. I am perfect for the part, and Rupert and I have a very special bond.'

'I am sure that is true, sister dear, and nobody is denying you have worked hard, but unfortunately you do not have a contract, as I do, stating that you are the understudy. I too have worked hard for the last few months with this company, and it is only right and proper I get the perks of the job. Your turn will no doubt come one day if you continue to pursue your chosen career with the zeal you have shown so far.'

The two sisters stood facing each other eyeball to eyeball; neither wanted to be the first to break the spell. Finally they both had to turn to face Janie, who announced breathlessly,

'Sally, you have to come quickly. Isabelle has collapsed!'

They all rushed downstairs to the stage where a very dramatic scene awaited them. Rupert was bent over Isabelle, who was lying on the floor surrounded by various members of the cast and crew. Robert was pacing back and forth, and Giles was standing at the edge of the group looking lost.

'Has someone called an ambulance?' ordered Sally. 'Come on, guys, move out of the way. Give the girl some breathing space.' She knelt down beside Rupert and tried to work out what was happening.

'The ambulance is on its way,' called Gladys from the pass door. 'I will bring them straight down luvvie, don't you fret.'

Sally displayed her First Aid technique to great effect, and having felt Isabelle's pulse and established there was nothing too serious going on, she announced, 'I think she has just fainted. Someone get me a towel soaked in cold water . . . Oh, you got one – thanks, Heather.' She took the towel from the stage manager and laid it across Isabelle's forehead just as the actress started to stir.

'There you go . . . Everything is all right, Isabelle, you just fainted.' Sally spoke softly to the girl as she slowly came to, and became aware of her surroundings.

There was a commotion from the other side of the stage and two paramedics marched across to them.

'Is this the lady? Can we have her name, please? Isabelle. OK, Isabelle, can you hear me?' The two medics proceeded to put Isabelle back together again, and everyone drifted away. Sally took Rupert by the arm and led him towards the edge of the stage.

'Would you like me to make you a cup of tea?' she murmured. 'What happened?'

'Don't worry about me – I'm all right. It was just a surprise.

One minute she was fine and the next she was on the floor. God, I hope she is going to be OK.'

'I am sure she will soon recover.' Sally had a thought. 'Has she eaten anything today?' she asked.

'I don't know. No, I don't think so. We didn't have time for breakfast this morning.'

Sally gritted her teeth at the thought of the two lovebirds tumbling out of bed. 'Does Isabelle eat properly, Rupert?' Sally wondered if he had any idea about the girl's eating problems.

'Yes, I guess so. I mean, we all eat at strange times here, don't we? I haven't really noticed, to be honest. Why do you ask?' He looked at Sally enquiringly.

'Oh, no reason, just that Isabelle is very thin, and you know what actresses are like about their figures. You can never be too thin. But sometimes it can be dangerous. She needs all her strength at the moment with the hours we are working.'

'Yes, I suppose you are right,' said Rupert, looking as though he had no idea what Sally was going on about.

'Now come on, let's go and find Giles and get some work done. I can take up my role again as understudy.'

Giles, Rupert and Sally worked all afternoon. It was a fabulous rehearsal and by the end of the day Rupert was flushed with excitement.

'Let's go to Mrs Wong's and get some chips,' he said. 'That was fantastic, Sally. I really feel as if I have turned a corner and I know I will be able to help Isabelle too.'

Oh great, thought Sally. All this effort for someone else to get the glory. But out loud she agreed. 'You certainly have cracked it now. That last scene is going to be so moving.'

Before they left the theatre they got an update on Isabelle. Apparently the hospital was going to keep her overnight for tests but she would be back tomorrow.

'I suppose I should go and visit her,' said Rupert as they made their way next door to Mrs Wong's.

'I am sure she will be fine and probably sleeping, so I don't think you need worry too much,' Sally reassured him. 'Heather has gone to the hospital with her stuff for the night, so I would relax and just enjoy your chips. Shall we get a bottle of wine as a treat?' They got takeaway in the end, and bought a bottle on the way to Sally's flat where they spent a wonderful evening chatting about nothing in particular. They really did get on so well and Sally was glowing with contentment.

Suddenly the door opened and Dora appeared, weaving her way across the room.

'Oh wow, what are you two up to, eh? When the cat's away in hospital? You are a quick worker, Rupie boy.' Dora plonked herself down on the sofa and started to take off her boots.

'Dora, you are drunk. What have you been up to?' said Sally, trying to change the subject.

'Oh, just drowning my sorrows with the lads, now I have been relegated to general dogsbody again by my scheming sister. So Rupert, what are you doing here? You didn't answer my question.' Dora had managed to get her boots off and was now splayed across the sofa watching Rupert who was sitting nearby on the carpet with his glass of wine.

'I am enjoying a glass of wine with your lovely sister. Is that not allowed?' asked Rupert, completely unaware of the under-currents swirling around him.

'Do you want a sandwich or something, to mop up the booze?' Sally was hovering at the kitchen door, desperate to create a diversion. She knew what Dora was like in this mood.

'No, thanks. I am going to bed in a minute. What are you two going to do?'

Dora leered at Rupert who quite innocently replied, 'I am off

too in a minute – got another hard day tomorrow. Isabelle is
going to be back in the morning, so we are all good to go.' He
got up and finished off the last of his wine. 'I will see you tomorrow, Sally, and thanks again for today. You have been a star.'

He went to kiss Sally on the cheek and Dora chimed in, 'I
bet you are disappointed, aren't you, Sal? Isabelle is going to be
OK. How very annoying!'

Sally was leading Rupert to the door as quickly as she dared.
She tried to sound light-hearted as she replied, saying, 'Oh,
Dora, stop it! Of course I am delighted that Isabelle is recovering. We had a lovely time this afternoon but that is all part of the
job. Thank you, Rupert, for working with me today. I look forward to putting it together with Isabelle tomorrow.' She closed
the door with a sigh of relief, and then turned to her sister.

'What the hell is the matter with you? Why are you being
such a bitch? I am beginning to wonder whether you should
think about leaving, because quite frankly I have had enough
of your machinations, and insults, and bad behaviour.'

'Oh, give me a break,' responded Dora, sitting up now and
ready for a fight. 'Who are *you* to decide whether I leave or
not? I have the theatre to think of, and my responsibilities to
the rest of the cast. I happen to care about them, you know,'
she said hotly.

'Oh really? So then why don't you get on with the jobs in
hand and stop giving me a hard time? I don't want to fight,
Dora. I don't understand what has gone wrong between us.
We were having such fun in the beginning.' Sally went to sit
beside her sister on the couch.

Dora looked sullen.

'It is just so frustrating sometimes watching you at work and
wanting to be doing it myself. I just want to get on, Sally, and
you are so happy to plod along and take things as they come.

I want to *make* things happen. Then you have taken away the one thing I was really into, and now I am back to square one.' Dora was pacing the room now like a cat. She is very beautiful, thought Sally. Much more like an actress ought to be than me. Maybe she is right and I am ruining her chances but not making the best of my own.

Out loud she said, 'I am sorry about the understudy thing but you have to understand I have looked forward to that since the beginning of the season. I didn't know you were going to come here and turn into an aspiring actress overnight. I don't want to be the enemy.' Sally suddenly felt exhausted. 'Look, please let's try and have fun like we were before. You will get a great part in the next production, I am sure. Giles really likes you, and I will remind him you are keen to work as an actress.'

'We are doing Victorian music hall next, you idiot! So I get a couple of solos. Big deal – that is not going to show off my acting skills, is it?' Dora complained.

Sally was defeated. 'OK, sorry, I forgot – but please just be patient, like we all have to be. Why should you get everything all at once?' With that, she took the wine glasses into the kitchen and left Dora to ponder life's foibles.

As she crossed the living room to go to bed Dora stopped her and gave her a hug. 'OK, sis, a truce. I will try not to wind you up or give you a hard time.'

Sally gave her a hug back and said, 'Thank you, dear, that makes me very happy. Now I need to sleep. I will be so glad when this production finally opens. Night night.'

But as she undressed in her room, Sally wished she felt better about her situation with Dora. She still loved her sister, but she didn't like or trust her very much, and that felt so sad. Her every instinct told her things were never going to be the same between them again when this job finally came to an end.

FINALE

The walk down

Chapter 37

Let's all go down the Strand –
Let's all go down the Strand!
I'll be leader, you can march behind
Come with me and see what we can find!

The first dress rehearsal of *Hamlet* was an absolute disaster. It lasted four hours, and by the time the curtain came down, everybody had lost the will to live. Giles told everyone to go home and sleep on it. 'It' being any version of terrible acting that any one of them could muster.

Sally had a nightmare that she was buried in the grave onstage and nobody could hear her shouting to be set free. She woke the next morning in a terrible sweat, trembling with panic. It took half the morning for her to shake herself free of the sense of doom that hung over her. When she got to the theatre for the note session she could almost smell the clods of earth descending on top of her again.

'All right, Sally?' The familiar voice of Heather cut through the day dream.

'Oh God, Heather, I had the most terrible nightmare last night,' started Sally, but Heather broke in with: 'Me, too. I was the stage manager of this awful production of *Hamlet*.' She burst out laughing and after a couple of seconds Sally joined her, relieved to be able to understand, finally, that it had only been a nightmare.

'Oh dear God, what a night! What are we going to do, Heather? Four hours of unadulterated crap. The bloke playing the ghost was like something out of a Disney cartoon, and when Peggy nearly did the splits as the truck went off – well . . .'

It had, indeed, been an unforgettable moment. Having warned everybody so many times that they must make sure they were standing on the upstage part of the truck, behind the carefully drawn luminous line, it was with growing horror that Sally watched Peggy take up her final position for the Dumb Show tableau, with one foot on one side of the line and one on the other. As the truck slowly moved back upstage, so did Peggy's legs move apart, one going upstage, the other down. Just as disaster seemed inevitable, the actress hauled her downstage leg from the ground and toppled slowly into the gap where the grave would have been. As the black-out descended Heather rushed onto the stage and dragged her off. The incident would definitely go down in the annals. Poor Peggy was hysterical, refusing to go onstage ever again.

This morning, Sally went straight to her dressing room with a box of chocolates she had bought on the way in.

'Oh bless you, darling, what a lovely thought. I must say I was beside myself last night, but I am back to my old self today. Nothing like a good night's sleep and a few whiskeys to put me straight. Percy said he thought I was going to lose my virginity all over again, cheeky sod!'

At that moment, Percy appeared at the connecting door, saying, 'Bit of a no go last night, eh? Reckon we will have a few cuts, don't you, love?'

'Oh Percy, who knows? Maybe it will all come together. It was the first dress, after all,' said Sally, trying to be optimistic. 'Come on, let's go and hear what our director has to say.'

Giles Longfellow faced his cast and crew with remarkable stoicism.

'It was not good,' he began. 'However, there were moments when I could see the light, and although we have a good deal to embrace I think we can do so with positivity. I am not going to give individual notes just yet. The first thing we are going to do is run the play sitting here now and get the lines right. You have to understand that there is no way in a Shakespeare play that you can make up the words if you forget them. Everyone has got to be word-perfect. After that I will decide what to rehearse first this morning. Right, Heather, start the clock.'

After the word run Robert took the boys away to practise the fights and Giles got hold of Henry Hooper who had been cast to play the ghost. He was an old actor who lived locally and had been delighted to be asked to appear. It was an unmitigated disaster, however, and Giles was forced to ask him to leave.

'It has just not worked out. I am sorry, Henry, but we will give you your wages and hopefully there will be another opportunity to use you.' Giles had no alternative but to play the part himself.

It was also agreed that some of Sally's dialogue in the Dumb Show would be cut. She was not surprised and set to work chopping and changing the script as subtly as she could. In the midst of all the activity, Isabelle announced to Giles that she had to go to London for a medical issue and would be away for the night. It would mean she was not available for the second dress rehearsal.

'It is fucking unbelievable!' Giles raged to Edward Graham. The only light in Giles's life at the moment was his meetings with Teddie. They had arranged to have dinner in the Queen's Hotel in Manchester. It was rare for Lord Graham to allow himself to stay in such places, but being midweek it was relatively quiet and George Delaware, the owner, was very discreet and made sure he chose the staff on duty who would deal with the room service. He just loved the fact that his hotel entertained a Lord and nothing was too much trouble. Discretion was very much the order of the day with His Lordship, and George had been rather thrown when his son Eddie had tipped up. The first few times George had assumed the boy was with friends of a certain persuasion, but when he had spent his first long weekend with a rather attractive young actor called Jeremy, George began to think he might have a problem with the father and son.

George had opened his club after his last stint in prison. He was well known to the Manchester police as a villain of long standing, but few people on either side of the fence knew George was homosexual. Had anyone in the police known this before 1967 they would no doubt have added that felony to the list. Fortunately for George, the Sexual Offences Act was passed in 1967 and it was no longer illegal to be a homosexual. However, George realized it would be many years before certain sections of society were ready to accept gay men. 'Gay' was a word that for many years had suggested someone with a racy lifestyle. Slowly it became a more pleasant way of describing a man – or woman, for that matter – who was homosexual, which was such a clinical term. George had spent the last twenty years defending his gay customers and yet at the same time promoting them. His club became a refuge in the late 1960s for men who could not 'come out' as it were. It was unbelievable that even now in 1982, men like Lord Graham had to hide their true sexuality. But the Queen's Hotel had also become a leading light in gay clubs. Men from all over the world would visit and stay in one of the elaborately decorated rooms. Nowadays the police regularly visited too, either for personal reasons or for information. George had retained his ability to keep his ear to the ground. What he didn't know about what went on in his city wasn't worth knowing.

George's latest campaign was to bring to the attention of the gay community a very dark and forbidding phenomenon that had first reared its ugly head in America last year. It was an unknown disease which presented itself in the early stages as flu, but as the months and sometimes years went on, it developed and attacked the immune system, until the patient ultimately died. The *New York Times* had reported in July last year that there appeared to be a new form of illness which presented among gay men. There was a rush of young gay men turning up at hospitals in the city of New York all with the same symptoms. They dubbed it the 'gay cancer'.

George knew only too well how ignorance could cause panic, and the public always reacted before knowing the facts. He himself had witnessed an incident recently in a gay club in London where a young man was eating in the restaurant and another customer called the manager and suggested there was a problem because the young man in question had lesions on his skin and could infect the rest of the customers. It had been a very unpleasant situation and in the end the young guy was forced to leave. George had followed him out and they had

gone for a drink, and the young man told George his sorry
tale. His name was Barry and he was twenty-three. He had
been on a holiday in New York four years ago, and as is usual
for a young guy, had spent many hours in the clubs. About
two months after he returned to England, he developed flu-
like symptoms and went to his doctor, who basically just told
him to take aspirin and hot drinks. Then two years later he
noticed that his glands were swollen and he kept getting
mouth ulcers and night sweats. He was referred to a hospital
and after several blood tests was told he had HIV or AIDS.
There was no cure, the doctors informed him, and they could
not estimate how or when death would occur, except that
research to date was indicating the disease attacked the
immune system so he should be careful not to go anywhere
near people with infections of any sort. The boy was distraught. His family had thrown him out when they discovered
he was gay. Other friends said he had brought it on himself for
being a 'poof' and would have nothing to do with him in case
they caught it. He was in such a state he was talking about suicide.

George took Barry back to Manchester and put him to
work in the hotel. He then sat down and found out as much
as was possible about the disease so far. He quickly realized it
was a deadly foe and that there was going to be a huge outcry
as more and more men and women died. He was appalled that
the gay community were attacked for bringing it upon themselves, and it was only after hours of reading reports and
actually speaking to doctors in the USA, that George got the
real facts, or as many as were available at the time. AIDS was
the general term used to cover the illness, though it was a
much more complicated scenario involving the immune
system. The disease was capable of infecting anyone, but

because it entered the body through the blood it was passed on through sexual encounters, or infected needles as used by drug addicts. Obviously those most at risk would appear to be gay men and addicts who used dirty needles.

George was now on a mission to educate the gay community. He started with his own staff and explained all he knew about the disease. He tried to impress on all his friends the need to wear protection when having sex. This was not just another venereal disease: this was a death sentence. He watched over his customers like a shepherd with his flock. Sadly, and tragically, so many of the younger guys just did not listen, and brushed off the advice as old men panicking. 'It won't happen to me,' was the inevitable cri de coeur.

One man who was beginning to face up to his fate was Robert Johnson. George had known Robert for several years and they had once been lovers. Robert had contracted HIV three years ago and was made very aware that his time was limited. He and George had spent many hours talking about his dilemma, and George had watched helplessly as his friend became more and more bitter and disillusioned with life – or the life he had left.

Last year, Robert went to work at Crewe Theatre and began an affair with the director there called Giles Longfellow. The couple seemed well suited, and when Robert brought Giles to meet George they had all got along very well. George had begged Robert to tell Giles about his illness but he refused, saying it would only mess things up for him. Robert seemed so much more positive about his situation and was talking about going to London with Giles and becoming a director. George let his pleasure in seeing Robert feeling better take over his commonsense, which was to advise Robert to come clean. But suddenly everything changed again. Robert turned up at the Queen's one night in a terrible state. It was all over with Giles and he was heartbroken. George spent days with Robert cajoling him into a better frame of mind. Slowly Robert responded, but he was never the same again. He remained withdrawn and watchful. He was cynical and aloof. He liked to stir things up for people. Why should they be happy when his life was so fucked up, was how he described his motives to George.

Now another problem was looming on the horizon. Robert was back at Crewe, working as assistant director to Giles Longfellow, who was currently having an affair with Lord Graham – whose son Eddie was also turning up at the Queen's with a young actor based at Crewe. None of this boded well, and George was on the alert to pick up the pieces . . .

Chapter 38

'Shall we make the first night black tie?' mused Giles, as he and Robert sat having a sandwich for lunch in his office. 'It would make it a really special occasion, the like of which has never been seen before in Crewe.'

'I think that is pushing your luck, my dear,' replied Robert. 'How many men own a dinner-jacket these days? Why not just put "dress glamorous" and they can decide for themselves? We tell them to come dressed in style for our Victorian music-hall shows, don't we? The audience always love dressing up for that.'

'Oh God, we have got that to contend with in two weeks' time!' exclaimed Giles. 'I can't believe the time goes so quickly.'

'Except during our production of *Hamlet*,' commented Robert, bringing Giles back down to earth with a horrible bump.

'Christ, yes, we must lose another fifteen minutes, Robert. Have you got any suggestions? Actually, I have one: to cut down the sword-fight between Hamlet and Laertes, I do think it goes on too long for that point in the play. We are nearing the home run and we should be speeding up the pace. I also feel that the boys need to pick up their cues in all those bitty scenes with Fortinbras and stuff.'

'Marvellous overview of the great play by our director,' sneered Robert with a big dollop of sarcasm. '"Bitty scenes with Fortinbras and stuff." What the fuck does *that* mean?'

Giles regarded Robert across the desk and sensed there was more to this outburst than appeared on the surface.

'Is something wrong, Robert?' he asked.

'Where to start?' the other man returned. 'The production stinks, Giles, and it is *your* fault because you have taken your eye off the ball and spent too much time shagging His Lordship.'

Giles finished chewing his sandwich, wiped his mouth on his paper serviette and took a sip of coffee. When he finally spoke, his voice was almost a whisper.

'How *dare* you talk to me like that. Who the fuck do you think you are? You are only here because I felt sorry for you after everything that happened last year. You have no qualifications to direct and certainly no right to talk to me as you do. What is your problem, Robert? You ponce around being patronizing to the actors most of the time, you nitpick at every opportunity, and to be honest, your directorial skills are pretty shabby – and now you have the gall to blame me for mistakes in this production!'

Robert held his ground. 'Yes, I do blame you, Giles. Who else is there to blame? I have done my bit, whether you like it or not, and as for my personality faults – well, tough, no one is perfect. But you are the director at the end of the day. You cast the play, you agreed design, and you are the head of this whole caboodle. So yes, the buck rests with *you*.'

Giles absorbed the blows and contemplated his next move. He knew he had failed miserably to pull the production together, and he also knew that his emotional life had once again distracted him from the job in hand. This was to have been his big chance. How ironic was it that, years ago, Teddie Graham had bailed him out of trouble so he could pursue his career once more, and now it was Teddie who was the cause of the trouble. Robert knew too much about him for Giles not to acknowledge some of these facts, but it would make him weak, and Robert needed no encouragement to take advantage of him in the vulnerable position he had put himself. He chose his words carefully.

'I am truly sorry that you feel this way and maybe I have made mistakes, but now is not the time to upbraid me for them. We have two days to the first night, Robert – can we not work together to put the show on, and then discuss our differences? I am assuming you will not want to work with me after this and do not see a future for the play in London?' He looked questioningly at Robert, who was still standing tense and straight-backed in front of his desk. Robert now relaxed and moved to the big wing-chair in the corner of the room and sat down slowly. He took out his cigarettes and lit one, inhaling the blue curling smoke and holding it in his lungs for a moment before releasing the smoke in a thin stream through pursed lips.

'Ah, now we come to the crux of the matter, Giles, my dear. If you are happy to admit mistakes so am I happy to admit lack of experience in the directorial stakes. You and I know I will not get employed by anyone else after this, so we are stuck with each other. I have every intention of going to the West End with this production, and you and I will do everything in our power to make that happen, won't we?'

Robert took another drag of his cigarette and waited for Giles to answer.

'Robert, is this a game of some sort? What are you trying to say? On the one hand you think I am useless as a director, yet on the other you are suggesting we can pull this off between us and continue to work together. I really don't see how that is going to happen. I have to be completely honest and say I am not sure I want to work with you any more after this.'

'I don't think you have a choice,' said Robert very quietly. 'Giles, you and I were once in love, and then you dropped me for the sake of idle gossip and your career prospects. Pretty pathetic excuses for destroying someone's life, don't you think? But to be fair when I came to you this year and suggested we work together, you gave me the opportunity to follow my dream and become a director. I am not going to let you drop me again as casually as you did last time. Especially as you seem intent upon ruining your chance of a lifetime for romance. So if you need a little persuasion, let's talk about Lord Graham and his son Eddie, shall we? Eddie has followed in his father's footsteps and I am not talking about agricultural college. Young Edward is proving quite the "gay young thing" in social circles in Manchester, especially in the Queen's Hotel. I know you enjoy the delights of this venue as I introduced you to George and his happy band. I also know that you enjoy many a night with His Lordship under the protection of George. All well and good, you may say. But I do not think His Lordship would be happy to know his son is indulging his passion for young men's flesh under the same roof, and risking the family name in doing so. I would be happy to have a word in his ear should you and I not find a way to carry on. Surely it is much better all round, that we keep these things in the family, so to speak. We should all be looking after each other and our reputations, don't you think?'

Robert sat back and waited for Giles to respond. He gleaned enormous satisfaction from watching the man sweat. He could see the thoughts running through Giles's head. The panic and fear in his eyes. Let someone else feel helpless and abandoned like he had been. He lived every day now with the promise of death and it made him intolerant of those who took life and good fortune for granted. Those people who walked through life taking what they wanted with no thought of what havoc they might wreak on others' emotions. Giles was a weak man who always managed somehow to wriggle out of trouble. Well, lucky him! This time he would find it a little more difficult and maybe his misfortune would be lucky for Robert. It was too late to save him from the fate that so cruelly awaited him, but not too late to make whatever was left of his life worth living.

Robert saw Giles swallow hard and his Adam's apple rose and fell in contradiction to the feigned outward calm he was presenting across the desk. Giles then rose and came round to the front of the desk and leaned against it.

'Well, well, life *is* full of surprises. Why don't you and I go now and get this play ready for a spectacular first night in Crewe? Who knows where it may lead us.' He walked to the door and held it open for Robert, who rose from the chair like a bird of prey and crossed the room in one fell swoop, to pause and peruse his prey before making his exit.

Chapter 39

The first night was a huge success, much to the amazement of the cast. The run-up to the big night had been unbelievably fraught with drama, never mind the drama onstage. The biggest problem had been Isabelle, who just seemed to go to pieces. Sally and Rupert spent every minute with her encouraging her and feeding her and trying to make sure she kept the food down. She would use any excuse to get to the toilet, but Sally would refuse to budge from her elbow. Rupert was remarkably calm and together. He was obviously besotted by his leading lady, much to Sally's disgust, but she understood that without him beside her, there was no way Isabelle was going to get on that stage.

The rest of the cast had come together in the last two days, and decided that in spite of their director's lack of guidance, they were bloody well going to do this, and the energy onstage was terrific. Jeremy was sick with nerves, not just because the audience was full of important people from the world of theatre and film, but because Eddie was going to be sitting in the Royal Box with his family. His Lordship was coming with his whole family, Tanya and Tilly and Eddie. He and Eddie had talked about the night and how they would keep their affair under wraps.

'For God's sake, you must not come too close to me or I will give the game away. I know I will just want to kiss you!' exclaimed Eddie. 'We must make sure we are always in a group together. Will you peep through the curtain at the beginning and blow me a kiss?'

Jeremy laughed. 'Oh yes, that would be just great, me standing behind the curtain blowing kisses. "What are you doing, Jeremy?" "Oh, just waving at my lover in the Royal Box!" Can you imagine how that would go down with Giles Longfellow?'

'Well, frankly, he is the one person who *would* understand. Did you see him in the bar at the Queen's last weekend, by the way? I was wondering who he was with that night. I asked George, but he didn't seem to know. Perhaps he has a secret assignation sometimes. We could investigate.' Eddie giggled.

'We have enough trouble keeping our own assignations secret without worrying about other people,' said Jeremy.

Dora, meanwhile, was obsessed with the guest-list for the evening, and how she was going to get herself introduced to the producer of Isabelle's new film.

'If I can just get him in front of me, I know I can win him over. And did you know there is a casting director from *Coronation Street* coming, Sally?' Dora looked at her sister, who was busy trying to make posies of wild flowers for Isabelle to carry on in her mad scene.

'Why would you think I care about *Coronation Street*? I do not want to be in a long-running series – it would ruin my career. You just get typecast.'

'Oh, don't be so bloody pompous, Sally. Work's work – and

it's better to be out there being seen. No point in sitting in your little garret room acting to the mirror. Where is that going to get you?'

Sally did not bother to answer her sister. They did not agree on anything these days. She had not had the time to work things out between them, but she knew that something would have to be done. She was nervous about seeing their parents while the situation was like this. It would only take a minute for their mum to realize that something was wrong, and she would be so upset. Sally had actually put their parents off coming to see *Hamlet*, telling them it was not much good, and that she and Dora were just too busy to enjoy their visit.

'All right, my darling,' Patricia had said. 'But we really do want to see you both very soon. We miss you!'

Giles and Robert worked together, and it had been agreed between them that Giles would discuss the future with Robert after the opening night. In his heart Giles knew it was make or break time, and he would do anything to keep Robert quiet. If he had to agree to giving him a job once the play went to London, so be it. It was worth it to prevent Teddie from finding out about his son. Of course it would all come out eventually, but now was not the time.

The curtain went up and *Hamlet* hit the stage. Rupert was magnificent, and whenever she had a minute during the play, Sally watched him from the wings. He soared, there was no other way to describe his performance. The scenes with Ophelia were magical. Rupert seemed to imbue Isabelle with all his energy and magic. She looked amazing with her golden hair like a waterfall down her back, and with her long slim legs draped in fine silk which clung to her body, she resembled a young fawn. Charmaine was another surprise on the night. Her Gertrude was full of hidden depths and feral sexuality.

Sally was also impressed with her friend Jeremy. His Laertes shone a brilliant light. Sally had never seen him so strong onstage. He had grabbed the role and brought a new dimension to the stage.

'I do so hope he gets a wonderful job from this tonight,' she remarked to Heather. 'He deserves a break.'

'Don't we all,' the woman sighed.

It was a strange evening for Sally because she did not have much input as an actress, and all the fuss about being seen by the right people was out of her reach. But she didn't feel envy or jealousy. She just wanted the team to do well. Her time would come, she felt sure. The more she watched Dora's intense quest for recognition, the less she craved it. She just wanted to be taken seriously as an actress and play wonderful parts in great plays. Not much to ask!

The curtain came down to thunderous applause. In the bar afterwards the actors mingled with the regular audience and tried their best to present themselves to anyone of importance who might give them a job. The big producer had left straight after the performance, but not before going to visit Isabelle in her dressing room to congratulate her. Sally happened to be passing her dressing-room door and heard Isabelle say, 'Thank you, darling, but it was nothing. I just love Shakespeare and adore working on text. I guess I have a natural instinct for words.'

Sally wanted to be sick! What a load of old tosh. She went to congratulate Rupert who was surrounded by a group of schoolgirls getting his autograph.

'Look at you, you big Hamlet you,' she laughed. 'I can see your head getting bigger by the minute.'

'Sally! Give me a kiss, it is all down to you. You have been my guiding light. Come here, I love you!' He wrapped his arms around Sally in a big hug and then planted a kiss on her lips. She longed to cling to him forever. He felt so good.

She pulled away, however, and said, 'See you in the bar?'

'You bet, lovely lady. I will see you there.'

Sally looked for Jeremy to congratulate him but he had already gone to the bar apparently, according to Geoffrey who was making his way up to the Dress Circle bar.

'Great night, Sally. We pulled it off!'

'Yes, we did. Congratulations, Geoffrey.'

Sally made her way through the crush to the bar to grab a drink. Suddenly Dora was in front of her flushed with excitement.

'Hi, Sally, isn't it great? Everyone loved it. I have just met the casting director lady and she is going to call me about doing an audition for *Coronation Street*. Isn't that fantastic?' Dora didn't wait for an answer, but carried on past Sally, waving at someone across the bar. Jeremy was just ahead of Sally, about to lean into the bar and grab a glass of champagne.

'Get one for me,' she called out. The noise was unbelievable and she had to shout her request a second time. Jeremy smiled at her and passed her a glass and then got one for himself, and turned to give her a kiss.

'Well done, Sally, the Dumb Show was a triumph.'

'Well done you, more like. Jeremy, you were amazing – you were on fire!' They hugged each other.

'Oh, look at the luvvies,' sneered Robert. 'Daaarling, you were maaarvellous! God, nothing changes.'

'Oh, shut up, Robert. Just for once stop posing and join in. It was bloody marvellous and you know it,' said Jeremy. 'Here, let me get you a glass of champagne.' As Jeremy turned back to the bar, someone pinched his bum.

'What the . . . ?' he started, only to stop immediately as

Eddie appeared at his side. 'Don't do that,' Jeremy hissed. 'That is exactly what we discussed we would not do, you stupid boy!'

'Hello, Eddie, and how are you this evening?' enquired Robert, stepping between the two men. 'Did your family enjoy the play?'

Eddie gave him a charming smile and replied: 'Yes, thank you so much, Robert. You must be so proud of your very talented cast.' He turned and beamed at Jeremy. 'You were wonderful.'

'Oh yes, they were *all* wonderful. Well, I must go and mingle. No doubt we will meet again – soon, I expect,' Robert held them both in his gaze for a moment and then moved off.

'He is impossible,' said Sally. 'Here, Jeremy, can you nab me another drink. So how are you, Eddie? Oh, here is your father.' Sally stepped aside to allow Lord Graham to get to the bar. 'Please, Your Lordship, let Jeremy do the honours. Jeremy, make that two glasses of champagne, please,' she shouted over the hubbub. 'Sorry, we haven't been introduced. My name is Sally Thomas. I am a member of the company, and Jeremy is my best friend.' She turned back to take the glasses from Jeremy, who having realized who they were for, was panicking silently.

Eddie made the introductions, again formally, and they all politely chinked glasses.

'The sword-fight was wicked,' enthused Tilly. Then: 'Have you ever made a mistake and stabbed each other?'

Jeremy laughed. 'Not yet, touch wood. And thankfully Rupert and I get on very well, so there is no danger he will stab me on purpose. I am sure there must have been times when actors didn't like each other and things could have got a little . . . difficult.'

Eddie joined in. 'Well, we always hear about actors being bitchy to each other, don't we?'

'Oh, I think that aspect is exaggerated,' replied Sally. 'Certainly in this company we all pull together, don't we, Jeremy?'

'Really?' said Eddie. 'That's not what Jeremy told me the other day. Your leading lady has been a nightmare, I gather.' Suddenly realizing he had said too much, he whipped round to see if his father was listening. Lord Graham had, in fact, been accosted by a local dignitary and missed the conversation. Breathing a sigh of relief, Eddie took his sister's arm and said smoothly, 'Well, we have to go, don't we, Tilly? Where is Mother? Lovely to meet you all and well done. Come on, Father.' They disappeared into the throng and left Jeremy and Sally staring at each other.

'Do I suspect a faux pas here?' asked Sally. 'I take it Lord Graham does not have any idea that you two are an item?'

'Oh my God, no! That would be a disaster. Can you imagine the repercussions? Poor Eddie would probably be disinherited.'

'But surely he is going to have to come out one day?' said Sally. 'He can't pretend for the rest of his life.'

'Lots of people do,' replied Jeremy sadly. 'I don't know what is going to happen – I just know I love Eddie so much I couldn't live without him.'

Sally squeezed his hand and said kindly, 'Come on, let's go and join the others. I feel a Mrs Wong coming on.'

They crossed to where the rest of the company were beginning to assemble ready for a mass exodus to the pub.

'Hi, guys,' said Pete. 'We cracked it, didn't we? No thanks to the management, but—'

'Ssh, Pete!' cautioned Janie. 'The management is about to give a speech.'

Giles Longfellow was tapping his glass and getting nowhere in his attempts to silence the crowd, until finally Simon put two fingers in his mouth and produced an ear-splitting whistle. The rest of the cast whooped with delight.

'Ladies and gentlemen, it gives me great pleasure to stand here tonight and express my delight and gratitude to the citizens of Crewe for making this evening possible. To the members of the council who work with us on a daily basis to keep our theatre running. To all the members of staff front of house for their hard work, and to all the wonderful cast and crew for their tireless commitment. It has not been easy but I think I can honestly say tonight has made it all worthwhile. And finally I would like to extend a huge thank you to Lord Graham for his support. Nothing would happen without his generosity. Thank you, sir, and thank you, everyone. Enjoy the rest of your night!'

Jeremy looked across the room to see Eddie, flanked by his mother and father, shaking hands with Giles and making their goodbyes. He caught Eddie's eye and his lover flashed him a heart-melting smile.

'Quite a boy, isn't he?' said a voice at his elbow. Jeremy looked at Robert and tried to gauge what he was driving at, but it was impossible to read the man. Jeremy was always left with a feeling of unease, as if Robert were about to divulge a terrible secret. But then it was true, wasn't it? He did know a terrible secret and if he did divulge it they would all be ruined.

'Coming to the pub, Robert?' was all he said and he made his way to the door.

Chapter 40

Sally sat opposite Giles in his office and tried to take in what he was telling her.

'I am afraid Isabelle will be leaving at the end of the week. This, of course, means a huge upheaval for the cast, and we will have to rehearse you in. For you it is an even bigger challenge, but one I know you will embrace with your usual professional approach. It is an extraordinary situation, I must say, and I feel very frustrated that my hands are tied.'

'But what about her contract? Can she legally just bunk off like this?' Sally could feel her anger bubbling up.

'Legally it is not credible, but the circumstances are so unusual I have agreed to her dismissal. The trouble is, Sally, between you, me and the gatepost, Isabelle is a liability. The fact we managed – *you* managed – to get her on at all is a miracle. Her agent can provide a letter from a specialist confirming that she needs medical attention as soon as possible, so what can I say?'

'But she is going off to Hollywood to make a film,' protested Sally. 'Is that a euphemism for "medical attention" or is that simply taking the mickey? I can't believe people can get away with these things.' She was growing angrier by the minute, and Giles was irritating her as well, because he was being so pathetic.

'I know, I know, it is a hard pill to swallow. But the good news is, you are going to be playing Ophelia! Now I have called the company for two o'clock to explain everything, and by then we will have a rehearsal schedule worked out. It is going to be very tough for everyone, as we have to start the next production at the same time. Thank God it is Victorian Music Hall. Not too much to rehearse, just learning the songs really. Timothy is so good he will soon have everybody off their song-sheets, and Sarah is going to help me stage some of the numbers.'

'Sarah?' said Sally. 'Why Sarah?'

'Oh, she has done a lot of Music Hall and I went to see her at the Leeds Variety last year. She was wonderful. She came to me earlier in the season and asked if she could assist, and now it will be a great help, because I will be rather busy for the first week sorting out your performances. By the way, I have given Dora your big number since I thought you will not be so free to rehearse. So I hope you don't mind that I have given her "Burlington Bertie". Is that OK with you, dear?'

'Yes, of course.' But Sally wanted to weep. She had been so looking forward to doing that number and had already learned it. She was going to be sidelined again. Still, it wasn't all bad. She was going to play Ophelia with Rupert for a whole week! The thought drove everything else from her mind.

'Right – well, I had better get off to Wardrobe and sort out costumes. Thank you, Giles, I will not let you down,' she told him.

'I know you will be marvellous, and by way of reparation I

have invited a top London agent up next week to cover your performance. He is going to come with James Langton, who I know is an old friend of yours.' Giles looked very pleased with himself.

'Oh, that *is* fantastic news!' exclaimed Sally. 'Thank you so much, Giles.' And she practically hopped with joy out of his office.

The rest of the cast were thrilled with her news, although they were not so thrilled by the thought of more rehearsal.

'I will do my best to learn it all quickly,' Sally promised them. 'Listen, I know most of the play because I have been working on it.'

'Can I take over all your stuff then?' chimed in Dora, always quick to jump on an opportunity.

'Yes, you can,' said Sally. 'We will need to work on that, obviously. We will have to co-ordinate times with Timothy and his rehearsals. Congratulations, by the way, Giles has told me you are going to do "Burlington Bertie".'

Dora had the grace to look slightly sheepish. 'Oh thanks, Sally. I am sorry you have missed out but you are going to be brilliant as Ophelia.'

'I hope so,' her sister said.

Rupert was beside himself when Sally found him in his dressing room.

'How can she do this to me?' He was nearly in tears. Sally wanted to console him but she was actually annoyed that he seemed more upset for himself than for the situation, and the fact that the stupid cow had dumped everyone in the proverbial, not only him, for her own selfish reasons.

'How can she do this to *us*, you mean,' she chided. 'Come on, Rupert, the girl is a mess and has completely lost the plot. She has got away with murder. Giles has released her from her contract so she can gallivant off to Hollywood. She is completely selfish.'

'I know that, Sally, but I love her. We were going to get a place together. We had the West End production to look forward to – what will happen to that now?'

'I am sure they will find it very easy to engage another actress. Hopefully one with more talent than Miss Isabelle James.' Sally no longer cared what Rupert thought of her harsh words regarding the love of his life.

'Please don't be mean about her, Sally. This is very hard for me. I know you will be brilliant as Ophelia, and believe me, I will give you all my support, but just understand how I am feeling right now.'

Sally looked at Rupert sat there feeling bereft. She longed to hold him and comfort him, but the actress in her took over. There was no time for all that now. She had a performance to create, and he was going to help her no matter how heartbroken he was. This was her time now, and she was going to make the most of it.

'Come on, you. Time enough to weep later – we have work to do,' she told Rupert.

Isabelle had the good sense to keep well out of everyone's way, and only came into the theatre at the last minute to get changed and ready for the show. She seemed to sleepwalk through her performance, as though she was already on the plane to La La Land.

'Good riddance, I say,' remarked Gwendoline. 'You are going to be so much better, Sally. Now try this dress on and let's see what has to be altered.' The alterations were all straightforward but when it came to the floaty number there was an underwear problem.

'The thing is, whatever you put on by way of underwear

will show through this material. Isabelle didn't wear anything underneath. Are you happy to do that, Sally?' asked the wardrobe mistress.

Truth be told, Sally was horrified at the thought of wearing a see-through dress with nothing on underneath. But a little voice was telling her to get over herself. She was an actress, and she would do whatever it took for the good of the scene. She could quite clearly see the benefit of being naked under the dress, not just for the line of the dress, but basically for the whole atmosphere of the scene. She would feel so much more vulnerable, and it would help the madness and the feeling of loss somehow; she knew she had to do this.

'Yes, that's fine,' she said firmly, hoping to convince herself in the meantime.

The rest of the week was crazy. Sally hardly ate or slept. She started to watch Isabelle from the wings but decided it did not help her. She was better off just creating her own performance without any other influences. Rupert was wonderful as ever and they were able to create a real energy between them. By Saturday night everyone was quite happy to bid farewell to Miss James. There was even relief for Rupert, who had struggled all week knowing she was leaving but needing to keep everything smooth as they had to work together. Isabelle had a studio car coming to pick her up after the show and drive her to London, as she was booked on a flight the next day to LA.

'I won't have time to shop or anything,' she whined to Sally, who wanted to be sick.

To save Rupert facing a lonely Sunday in Crewe Sally had invited him to lunch. Dora decided she would cook and let the actors chill out as she put it. It turned out to be a very good idea as Sally was so nervous she could think about nothing except the play, and Rupert was beyond conversation as he wallowed in his misery. Dora drank copious amounts of red wine as she stirred her chilli con carne and couldn't care less about anything. Every now and then she would burst into a chorus of 'I'm Burlington Bertie, I rise at ten thirty,' and strut around the living room. She even managed to glean a smile from Rupert.

'That's better!' she exclaimed. 'Right, you guys, come and eat my chilli, and all will be well.'

Sally watched Dora flirting with Rupert and tried to be generous of spirit. Her sister was not a mean or malicious person. She was just young maybe? Sally thought back to their childhood and how most of the time they had been very happy as sisters. Sally was always the sensible one though, the older sister in charge. She had a mental picture of Dora standing on a low wall outside a holiday cottage singing at the top of her voice, and their parents rushing out and blaming Sally for letting her sister climb up and put herself in danger. Looking at her sister over the table at lunch, Sally felt a surge of love for Dora and made a mental note to make sure that once she had opened next week, she would talk to Dora about all the goings-on so far, and try to mend some bridges.

By seven o'clock on Monday night Sally was a wreck. She could not stop shaking. She sat in her new dressing room, recently vacated by Isabelle, and brushed her hair slowly, trying to restore some calm. The cast had all been round with little gifts and cards, which had made her cry!

'Five minutes, everyone. Five minutes.' Heather's voice through the Tannoy was strangely reassuring. There was a knock on the door.

'Come in,' she called out.

The door opened to reveal Giles Longfellow with an enormous bunch of lilies followed by Robert with a huge box of chocolates.

'Good luck, my darling,' Robert said as he leaned over and kissed her on both cheeks.

'Yes, good luck, dear. I know you will be marvellous.' Another set of kisses from Giles and they were gone.

'Beginners for Act One, please. Beginners for Act One.'

Sally was not on straight away, but she could not bear to sit up here in the dressing room on her own, so she decided to go and stand in the wings. She stopped at Rupert's door and knocked.

'Come in.'

Sally popped her head round the door. 'Just wanted to wish you good luck and apologize in advance for any cock-ups.'

Rupert rushed to the door and opened it and gave her a big hug. 'Oh Sally, I am sorry, I should have come to you, but I have been going through my lines again. Please don't worry about tonight – you are going to be wonderful. You have been all along, let's face it. I am so looking forward to acting with you. Good luck.' He planted a huge smacker on her lips.

Sally stood in the darkness of the wings and wrapped her cloak around her. She could feel the audience like a living breathing creature waiting out there to devour her. From where she was standing she could see the first few rows, and the lights onstage shone on the faces of the people watching. Eventually she heard her cue and walked into the light. She was hit by the warmth onstage after the draughty wings. It was the heart of the building, its soul – and she was slap bang in the middle! She had a split second of sheer panic as she opened her mouth to speak and her mind went blank. It felt like an eternity, a huge empty space and everything seemed to be moving in slow motion. She saw Jeremy, as Laertes, her brother, coming towards her, his mouth moving but no sound coming out. She wanted to scream and as she took a breath . . . her words flowed out with ease. She was off and running!

'You did it! Well done – it was terrific!' Jeremy was hugging her and Sally was numb. She could hardly remember anything about the play.

'I am just so relieved I got through it,' she said. 'Oh Jeremy, was I really all right?'

'You were better than all right, you were brilliant – such a relief after Madam. Suddenly the play makes sense.' He kissed her on both cheeks, lifted her off the ground and twirled her round. 'Come on, get changed. We are taking you to the pub!'

When they arrived at the pub everyone was there including Giles and there was a bottle of champagne on ice waiting for her to open. Bob, the landlord, came and gave her a kiss and opened the champagne for her, saying, 'Well done, lass, I hear you were grand.'

There were cheers all round, and Sally was completely overwhelmed by everyone's kindness.

'What it is to be loved,' remarked Dora at her side. 'Well done, sis, you were brill.'

Sally found Rupert sitting at a table with Geoffrey and Charmaine and Peggy and Percy. They all congratulated her, and she bought everyone a drink before finally sitting down. Suddenly she was completely exhausted.

'Oh my goodness, I am so tired all of a sudden,' she said.

'That is normal, my dear,' offered Peggy. 'It is all the adrenalin you have used tonight. Worse than a car crash, they say. You will soon get used to it. It was a bloody good night though, wasn't it, Percy?' She nudged him into a response.

'Not half, my love. You played a blinder, no doubt about it. Now come on, drink up, and I will get you another.'

'No, not for me, thank you, Percy. I am going to go home and sleep. Hopefully Giles will let me have a late call tomorrow, just for once. Rupert, I have to thank you most of all for being so kind and helpful despite your broken heart.' Sally looked across at her leading man, who was getting quietly sozzled. He grinned at her and blew her a kiss.

'See you tomorrow.'

She found Dora, who was not yet ready to go, and gave her instructions not to wake her in the morning. Then she bade a final farewell to her companions at arms and went home. It was a clear and starry night. There was frost already on the trees, and all the cobbles were twinkling as she walked across them. It looked like fairyland. Snatches of Ophelia's song ran through her mind and she hummed to herself. She wanted to do it all over again, right now, even though she was practically dead on her feet. She had loved being onstage and feeling the audience with her; almost leaning in to her to catch her words. She had reached out to the back of the circle, and sensed the back row. Every corner of the auditorium was hers to play. She had given her all, and the audience had embraced her and taken her to their hearts. She loved being an actress!

By the time she climbed the stairs of the flat she was freezing cold and could not stop shivering. She made a hot chocolate and undressed as quickly as she could, donning a jumper over her pyjamas and a thick pair of socks on her feet. Slowly she calmed down, and the warmth of the drink spread through her body, right down to her toes. She didn't even bother to clean her teeth as her head hit the pillow and she fell deeply asleep – with no 'perchance to dream' about it!'

Chapter 41

Giles watched the frozen fields speed past through the window of the train. The sun was coming up a deep red splashed across the horizon, cracking daybreak like a golden egg across the landscape. Robert was sleeping opposite him and Giles took the opportunity to study him. They had been lovers for a while last year, but Giles had found Robert to be very intense, and rather negative in his approach to their relationship. Giles had tried to talk to him, and get to know what he was like, underneath the rather cold and brittle exterior, but did not get very far. Certainly Robert had secrets and held them very close to his chest. They had decided to part and Giles did not see Robert again for months, until he turned up at the theatre one morning, and basically asked for a job. Giles felt guilty enough to agree, and thus began Robert's new career as assistant director. Giles had regretted his decision almost immediately, as it was obvious that Robert did not have the intuition or natural instincts that make a good director. He was also difficult with the actors, who did not respond favourably to his patronizing, and often plain rude, remarks.

Since their confrontation in his office last week Giles had done some serious thinking. He knew just how serious the situation would be if Teddie discovered his son was gay: the repercussions would spread across his own life as much as the Graham family's. Over the past months Giles had fallen deeply in love with Teddie Graham, and as so often happens when one is blinded by emotion, he had hidden his head in the sand as to where they were going with their relationship. Giles could not think beyond the now. He just wanted things to stay the same forever. Robert had brought him up short with a jolt. Not only was his personal life threatened, but his professional life too was in jeopardy. So here he was on his way to sign a contract with one of the biggest producers in the West End for a three-month run of his production of *Hamlet*. Robert would also get a credit as assistant director and work with him on the production. Teddie would remain in blissful ignorance of his son and heir's sexual proclivities, and Giles could enjoy his lover's attentions indefinitely.

Robert coughed and stirred. 'Oh sorry, I must have dropped off. What time is it?' he asked.

'Not a problem, we have two hours to go yet. Go back to sleep, dear boy.'

'I have a headache, as a matter of fact. I think I will go and see if I can get an aspirin.' Robert rose and started for the buffet car. 'Do you want a coffee or anything?' he asked.

'Lovely idea – yes, please, and a ham and cheese roll would be even more perfect.' Giles grinned. 'A secret treat of mine.'

'Coming up,' said Robert and set off in search of supplies. He returned later with the coffees and two rolls, and as he sat down he grimaced.

'Something the matter?' asked Giles, taking his roll and greedily unwrapping it.

'I think I must be getting the flu or something. I ache all over and I have got terrible mouth ulcers. I am going to see my doctor on the way back to the station this afternoon, as a matter of fact – see if he can give me something to stave off the worst of the symptoms.'

They lapsed into silence as they ate their breakfast, and shortly after that Robert was asleep again. Giles continued to watch the world go by, until he also dropped off. Both men were awoken at the same time as the train hooted its arrival into Euston. They took a cab to the Charing Cross Road, to Wyndham's Theatre, which also housed the offices of their producer. Robert was still struggling to feel better, and Giles suggested he go straight to his doctor.

'Listen, it is not as though you really need to be here with me,' he pointed out. 'You have seen the contract and you know the contents. I am not going to have you written out at the last minute or anything.' Giles laughed tightly. 'Can't afford to do that, can I?'

Robert nodded. 'Very well then, I will accept your suggestion and go now – and then meet you at the station this afternoon at four fifteen at the barrier.'

'Absolutely. See you then,' acknowledged Giles, and strode off towards the theatre.

Robert hailed a cab. 'St Thomas' Hospital.'

'Right you are, guv.' The taxi driver looked in his mirror and decided this was not a passenger who wanted to chat, so he put his foot down and kept his mouth shut!

Robert sat back in the cab and tried to stop the thoughts from swirling round in his head. It was always like this when he went to the hospital for tests. Nothing could stop the rot, he knew that. Would the doctor be able to tell him how long he had? He decided he would go to the Terence Higgins Trust after the hospital. This was basically an advice centre set up in July by the partner of a man called Terence Higgins, who had died of this disease. No one really knew what caused it, or how to cure it. The doctors could only monitor patients like himself and struggle to find a solution. But Robert knew he was getting worse. Soon he must take himself away somewhere to die.

The counsellor had told him last time that he *must* tell all the men he had had sex with what was going on, but he just couldn't do it. And yet, he had to tell Giles, for Christ's sake. Now there was this stupid business with Lord Graham and his son. Robert had not intended to involve them in his campaign to make Giles employ him. It had been a spur-of-the-moment thing because he was angry. He had watched Giles and Lord Graham being fêted at the Queen's Hotel by George Delaware and he had been jealous. After all, it was he who had introduced Giles to the hotel, and now he had been swept aside by titled gentlemen. Then he had seen Eddie at the hotel, and they had got together one night. The boy was uncontrollable. Robert had given him a serious talk about protection and too much careless sex, but who was he to talk? They had all partied together that night. It had been wild. None of these guys seemed to know anything about the disease that was stalking them. He had had a couple of conversations with some friends about the symptoms, and yet there was nothing concrete to work from.

Robert had never, in the whole of his life, felt so alone and abandoned. He would tell Giles tonight when they got back to Crewe, he decided, and if Giles was unable to find any compassion for him, so be it. He was fucked anyway.

Giles lifted the glass to his lips and savoured the moment; another wonderful lunch with his colleague Mr Langton, courtesy of the British Drama League.

'Here's to Hamlet, Prince of Denmark. May you be the Prince of Shaftesbury Avenue!' announced James Langton, enjoying the toast. 'It is good to see you, Giles, and how delightful that I will be seeing my protégés on Friday night at your theatre.'

'Yes, it all turned out very well, did it not?' replied Giles. 'Sally has proved invaluable as a company member and Jeremy is a splendid actor with a formidable career ahead, I think.'

'But you had problems with your leading lady, I gather?' asked James, who loved the gossip. 'She was on drugs and all sorts, I hear.'

'Well, I don't know about all that side of it, but as far as her acting skills went she was a non-starter. She had no idea about text or stagecraft. Los Angeles is welcome to her, as far as I am concerned. We are already inundated with suggestions for Ophelia for the production in Town. I hope we can use some of the cast from Crewe as well, although it is always difficult with London producers as they want to be in control of everything. Mmm . . . this wine is absolutely first-class, James. Good choice. Now tell me your news. How is your wife?'

Giles meandered through lunch getting pleasantly pissed and arrived at the barrier in Euston station in good time to meet Robert and get the train home. To his dismay Robert never appeared, and he was forced to board the train alone. He was concerned at first, but shortly after Watford Junction he was lost to the world in an alcohol-fuelled coma and did not wake until the guard announced their arrival at Crewe.

Robert lay in his hospital bed staring at the ceiling. He had asked the nurse if she would be so kind as to call Crewe Theatre and explain that he would not be returning for some time due to ill-health, and to ask Giles Longfellow to call him as soon as possible, on the hospital number. So here he was, waiting for death to come. The doctor had looked at the lesions which had appeared on his legs and taken more blood tests.

'I am so sorry, but there is nothing we can do for you except keep you comfortable, and in as little pain as possible. Do you have anyone you would like us to contact in the meantime?'

Robert told him that all that was being taken care of by the nurse, and said that hopefully, his friend from Crewe would ring, and would be able to make a visit. No, there was no family member he wished to inform.

So now he was alone, and acutely aware of his body. There is something about lying in a hospital bed with few distractions that encourages self-examination. Robert could feel a tingling in his toes and in his mind's eye he traced a route up his legs past the lesions, which he had tried to ignore, up through his groin which was aching, no longer with lust or love, just regret at what had been. Across his stomach which was churning with fear, up through his chest and heart, which was hurting with sadness and self-pity, up through his neck which ached, and into his mouth which was ulcerated and dry with panic. His brain was jampacked with too many thoughts jostling for position. He tried to swallow and drew in a sharp breath of pain. Then the tears flowed, slowly at first and then in a torrent – unstoppable, like his demise. Did anyone care?

Chapter 42

Sally spent the week in a dream. It flew by way too quickly for her. Every night she learned something new about a scene or an emotion, and every night she drew closer to Rupert. Her initial nerves, about being naked under the dress, were soon forgotten, but there had been one moment in the wings when Rupert had come up behind her and put his arms around her, and she could feel him hesitate as he became aware of her nakedness through the dress.

'Wow!' he whispered in her ear. 'You feel amazing. I could stand here all evening and explore you.'

Sally shivered and moved away quickly, wrapping her cloak around her. 'It is so cold in these draughty old wings,' she whispered back. 'I can think of better places to be.' *In my bed, she thought. Holding me, making love to me. All thoughts of Isabelle expunged from your mind.*

Onstage, she and Rupert were a good team, and had created a chemistry between them, even if it was not quite as charged as before. Friday night had been a scary evening, when James Langton arrived with the agent from William

Morris. The latter was a very charming urbane man who pulled no punches. After the show they met in the bar. Giles had arranged a light supper to be served, and had gone to town with smoked salmon and oysters, and champagne. Jeremy and Sally and Rupert were invited with Giles, James and Peter Stone, as he was introduced to them. He was very laidback and looked just like Sally had imagined a big London agent would: wearing a trendy, expensive suit, handmade shoes and silk shirt, and with distinguished grey hair and a slight Californian tan.

'A pleasure to meet you both, Sally and Rupert. And you are Jeremy – that's right, Laertes. A very exciting and enlightening performance, if I may say so, young man. You have a future ahead of you. Would you like to do more Shakespeare?'

'Oh, absolutely,' enthused Jeremy. 'I would love to get into the RSC and do a season at Stratford. That is my goal.' He laughed nervously, wondering if he had gone too far, but Peter seemed to be genuinely interested.

'And you, Sally, what are you hoping to do after your season here?'

Sally found it more difficult to express her desires. She had been so sure when she left drama school that she would work her way up through rep to a play in the West End, or maybe join the company at the National, but since she had been watching Dora work the system here, and all her talk about exposure on TV, she was not so sure where she belonged. Did she have enough talent, as Jeremy seemed to possess, to crack the big companies? She suddenly felt very shy, and hesitated before she replied. She looked at them round the table waiting for her to speak.

'I am not sure, to be honest. In the last three months working here, so much has happened to me, and I probably need time to absorb everything I have experienced. I know I am a good actress, but maybe not good enough.' She looked round the table and smiled. 'Not exactly selling myself, am I?' she said.

Peter Stone answered her. 'No, you are not, but I like your honesty, and you have an understanding of yourself and the business which is intelligent and useful. Too many young actresses just think their looks will see them through. There are many ways of getting a foot on the ladder, young lady, but many of those ladders lead to nowhere. If you are really serious about staying in the game you have to want it more than life itself, and accept that it is ultimately down to luck. You must have heard the cliché "right time, right place" – but that is exactly what it boils down to in this game. Now enough talk, let's eat this delicious supper you have provided, Giles.'

Everyone relaxed and the evening seemed to go well. Giles and James were an odd couple, and Sally wondered if they had ever had a relationship, but when she whispered her query to Jeremy, he giggled into his napkin, replying, 'He would never come out of the closet, Sally. Do you remember when we were at the British Drama League? He went on and on about the wife, even though he was desperate to get into my knickers, I now realize.'

'I am so naïve,' sighed Sally. She watched Rupert talking to Peter Stone about films in the pipeline, and casting opportunities, and could see how well he played the game. He was flirting with Giles and Jeremy, and at the same time being the serious Young Pretender to the throne. Everybody put on a face – except her! Once supper was done, Sally was more than ready to leave, glad of the excuse of two shows tomorrow as it was Saturday, and tomorrow night was her last performance.

She thanked Giles for the lovely dinner and the opportunity

to see James again. Made her farewell to Peter, who gave her his card and said, 'Ring me and make an appointment when you are back in Town and we can see what's on offer.' Well, at least she had not been a complete failure. She gave Jeremy a big kiss and said goodbye. Thank God Giles had ordered her a taxi, and she was able to sit back on the short journey home and try to assess the night. She started to fall asleep and decided to leave it all for the morning. Too much to cope with now.

She was relieved to find Dora in bed asleep, as she had wondered whether her sister would wake up and give her a grilling about the night. Needless to say, Dora had begged Sally to ask if she could come to the supper as well to meet Peter Stone, but Sally had refused point blank.

'You will just have to wait your turn. I am sure it will come soon enough. Isn't that casting woman coming to watch you next week?' she had asked.

'Well yes, but that is not the same as a top London agent, is it?' Dora sulked. 'Anyway, I get the message.'

Sally woke early on Saturday. She got up and made a cup of tea then sat in the kitchen trying to sort out her thoughts. She found the card Peter Stone had given her and turned it over and over in her hand. She would go and see him, she decided, as soon as she finished here. She needed an agent, that was for sure, because she was not capable of doing all the chat-up stuff. Yet she just had a gut feeling that Peter Stone found her a little dull for his style of agency, and maybe Dora would be more to his liking. She got up to go and get ready, leaving the card on the table.

When she arrived at the theatre, she found a huge bunch of flowers at the stage door.

'Here, you must have a secret admirer, love,' grinned

Gladys. 'I can't find a note anywhere.' It was accepted by
everyone in the theatre that there were no secrets from her, at
least not anything that could be pried open to divulge a name.
It was all fair game to Our Lady of the Door.

'Oh wow! How lovely. I will have another look and let you
know,' said Sally with a wink. She also had several cards in her
pigeonhole which was a new experience for our budding
actress. She loved opening them. They were all so different
and always kind. She made sure she responded wherever there
was an address, and sent one of the little postcard-sized photos
she had had printed before she left home. It was her mother
who had suggested she do them.

'Oh, Mum, don't be daft!' she had retorted. 'Who is going
to want a picture of me?'

'Your fans, you stupid girl. You wait and see, they will be
thronging round that stage door like bees to a honey pot.'

Well, that hadn't quite happened, but Patricia had been
right about the fan letters and Sally was very glad she had
taken her mother's advice. The thought of her mother suddenly made her very homesick. Unfortunately, her parents had
not been able to come this week as Dad could not get the time
off from school, and Mum was nervous about coming up on
her own. It was a big blow, but Sally had stuffed her disappointment to the back of her mind and got on with the job.
There would be other times. In fact, it now looked like they
would come up to watch the Christmas show, *Wind in the
Willows*, because both Sally and Dora had lovely parts. Sally
had been cast as the water rat and Dora was the gaoler's sexy
daughter. So the plan was for her parents to come to the last
show on Christmas Eve which finished early so they could
drive home and be back for Midnight Mass, followed by
champagne and hot mince pies; then a bit of a sleep-in, before

indulging in a perfect family Christmas Day. Jeremy was going to pick them up on the motorway somewhere very early on Boxing Day morning so they would be back for the two o'clock matinée. God forbid anything went wrong, as most of the leading players would be in the car. Short and sweet though the holiday might be, it was worth every wink of sleep lost to Sally, who could not conceive of Christmas anywhere else on earth. She was also secretly hoping that she might be able to see Mack. He had rung her to wish her luck, explaining that he would be away until Christmas, but would make sure they met at some point during the holiday. Her Christmas reverie was interrupted by Jeremy, who was in early, as usual.

'Good night last night, wasn't it?' he said. 'That Peter Stone seems to have his finger on the pulse. And guess what? Giles has invited me and Eddie to have dinner with him tonight in Manchester, so I will be off for another night of debauchery.'

'Not with Giles, surely?' asked Sally. 'He wouldn't let himself be that vulnerable to a cast member, would be?'

'Well, he already has to a certain extent, because we have seen him several times in the club with His Lordship and Robert.' He stopped short. 'Oops, I have just committed a huge boo boo! Sally, you must swear on your life not to tell anyone. Please swear. It is the best-kept secret in the gay world that Lord Graham and Giles Longfellow are a couple.'

Sally was completely dumbstruck. 'I can't believe it,' she whispered. 'But what about his wife, Tanya, and his daughter? What about Eddie? Oh my Lord, Jeremy, does his father know his son is gay? What happens to the Graham line if Eddie is the only son and heir? Difficult to continue if you are gay.'

It was something that Jeremy and Eddie tried not to think about too often.

'Will he get married and have an heir and a spare like his

father has done, do you think?' she continued. The complications were growing by the minute. 'Would he have to give you up for the time being?'

Jeremy sighed and ran his fingers through his hair. 'I just don't know, Sal. It is my worst nightmare. Let's face it, the aristocracy have their own rules. It is a bit like the mafia. They have the money and the power. Eddie may well be forced to make decisions against his will, and you can bet your bottom dollar I will be out of the picture.'

'So why do you think Giles wants to see you this weekend?' asked Sally.

'Probably to warn me off, I don't know. Maybe he is going to talk to Lord Graham – who can tell? It is a bit scary, I admit, and I haven't been able to get hold of Eddie since yesterday to see if he knows anything. In fact, I am going to the pub now to use their telephone. Gladys does not need to know about this conversation. I am hoping to catch Eddie at lunch. I'll see you later.' He kissed her on the top of her head and left.

What a tangled web we weave, thought Sally.

She made her way up to Wardrobe to search out Janie. They had decided to give a party tonight by way of saying goodbye to Rupert and 'well done' to Sally. It was going to be hard for Sally but she was prepared – had been all along in a way. Through this week she had wondered if there was a smidgeon of hope that she might be in with a chance, as ever since their moment in the wings when Rupert had put his arms around her, she had felt a frisson between them. Maybe tonight she would ply him with drink and seduce him. The problem was, she would have to have had a few drinks herself to find the courage!

After the show tonight Pete and the boys planned to go back to her flat and get everything ready for the party. Sally had made a big shepherd's pie, and there were lots of nibbles, and they had all clubbed together for the booze, but the champagne that Sally had bought was going to be the surprise. Janie had also hinted that she had a surprise too, so it was going to be fun.

The matinée was full of schoolchildren, which was always hard work, because they would chatter all the way through the play, and whoop and holler at any suggested sexual innuendo. Sometimes the actors just longed to go to the front of the stage and yell 'SHUTUP!' But this company had mostly been very good about their behaviour, although the skeleton of Yorick was sometimes written on, and displayed to the rest of the cast onstage by Rupert turning his back on the audience. The first time he did it, Pete and Simon giggled so much they both jumped into the grave and stayed there until they could control themselves. The Ghost, while waiting in the wings one day, had decided to lift his gown and flash his parts at Charmaine, who was just about to go onstage. She was so shocked she practically leaped ten feet in the air and landed with a bump on the stage. There had been strict instructions from Giles that there were to be no dirty tricks on the last night as it was very unprofessional, and the audience tonight had paid their money like everyone else and deserved a good show.

Well, we will see, thought Sally nervously.

Sally spent the time between the shows packing up. She would be out of this dressing room and back up with the girls next week. She wondered if Dora would be in here as she was headlining in the music hall. They were certainly chasing each other. Maybe they would share a dressing room for *Wind in the Willows*, although the role of the rat was considerably bigger than the washerwoman's daughter, so it would seem fair Sally got the dressing room to herself. Oh stop it, you silly cow, you are turning into a right old diva. This is Crewe Repertory Theatre, not the Haymarket.

'Beginners Act One, please,' came the call. Everybody involved in the play came down to the stage and had a group cuddle. It was such a lovely moment, and the kind of thing that only happened in the theatre – real company spirit. Sally went to her usual corner to catch the beginning of the play and Rupert came to give her his customary hug.

'Mmmm, you feel better than ever tonight, Miss Thomas. The vibes are positively jumping.' He kissed her ear, and Sally had to hold herself together so as not to melt in his arms. It must be all the adrenalin coursing through her body that created this sensual thrill. *Use it well, Sally, make it work for you onstage.*

She turned round and embraced Rupert, clinging to him so he would remember her through her thin silk dress. 'Good luck. It has been an amazing experience for me, I will never forget this moment.' She kissed him gently on the lips and then pulled away. 'Off you go – the curtain is rising!'

The performance went like clockwork. Everybody upped their game. The only mishap was that having never injured each other in the duelling scene, Rupert nicked Jeremy on the neck. There was real blood! Although it looked very dramatic from the wings, and poor Heather was trying to get first aid organized *and* stay on the book, disaster was averted as Jeremy pulled a silk hankie from his pocket and used it to good effect to stop the blood. Thank God for the hankie. Later that night, a toast was proposed to the indomitable Gwendoline, who had a policy of always secreting hankies on her actors for just such emergencies.

As soon as the curtain came down, the boys were off to set

up the shindig. The crew were in, already tearing down the walls of Elsinor. It was an easy get out tonight as there was no real set to erect for the Victorian Music Hall. So they had high hopes of making the party before all the food and drink had gone, which is what usually happened, though Sally and Janie had made a pact to hold some back for the workers.

It took Sally a bit longer than usual tonight to get ready. She had a shower and reapplied her make-up, because she wanted to look her best. She had saved a new dress for tonight and even managed to hide it from Dora. It was a little low at the front, and Sally was not sure about flashing her cleavage – but it was now or never! She waited for Janie and Gwendoline to finish putting the washing in, so they could walk up the hill together.

'Where's Geoffrey? Isn't he going to escort us ladies then?' enquired Sally as she appeared at the door. Gwendoline managed a tight smile and replied, 'He has escorted his opposite number, the Queen of Denmark, to the party. Felt he couldn't leave her to walk on her own. So come on, girls, let's give it all we've got.'

Chapter 43

The party was in full swing when they got back to the flat. The music was very loud, and could be heard halfway down the street, but everyone reckoned that for one night only, Crewe and their downstairs neighbours would have to put up with it. Sally put her shepherd's pie in the oven to warm up, with mountains of garlic bread to sop up the drink later. She dropped her stuff in her bedroom and then went to find Rupert. She should have known he would be pinned in a corner by her dear sister. Where Sally had gone for cleavage, Dora had gone for a plunging backless dress. She looked stunning, and Sally's heart sank. *Here we go again. I can't compete with that.* She went to the kitchen to get a drink and Janie caught her grim expression.

'Not fed up already, surely?' she commented.

'Oh no, just feeling inadequate as usual. Darling Dora has set her sights on Rupert tonight – she obviously has intentions of giving him a good send-off.'

Janie came and gave Sally a hug. 'Listen to me. You have a bond with Rupert, you always have, and that counts for a lot.

I don't know if it can go anywhere – let's face it, a week ago he was wildly in love with Isabelle – but don't let Dora muscle in on your night, and it *is* your night, Sally. You have been a triumph in every way on this production, and saved a lot of people's arses. You go for it and enjoy. You look gorgeous. Now please find my errant boyfriend, and tell him I need him for five minutes.'

Sally did as she was told and sent Pete to the kitchen. She then made her way to the corner.

'Hi, guys! Wow, Dora, you look amazing. That dress is almost finished,' she quipped.

'Yes, very funny, sister dear. But I could say the same about yours,' Dora threw back.

'Now, girls, please no scrapping. This evening is all about feeling the "lurve" in the room.' Rupert was laughing at them.

'Can I get you another drink?' suggested Dora.

'Or would you like some of my homemade shepherd's pie? You must be starving,' ventured Sally.

Rupert raised his hands in surrender. 'I give in! Both, please.'

Sally and Dora exchanged murderous looks and went off to the kitchen. Rupert meanwhile went in search of male support and found Geoffrey and Jeremy in deep conversation about the play.

'Oh, we will miss you, Rupert,' said Geoffrey, 'even though the competition has been gruelling, hasn't it, Jeremy?'

'Indeed it has – from both sides of the fence,' teased Jeremy. 'You had the pick of the bunch.'

'Oh don't,' groaned Rupert. 'Sally and Dora have been on the attack already. I am beginning to wonder if this would be my chance to have a random night with two sisters. What do you reckon?'

'Oh, too much information!' chorused the other two. 'We will await the results, like two sad old farts.'

'Actually, I must say my farewells, Rupert, as I am off to Manchester tonight,' Jeremy told him. 'So good luck, mate, and I hope we meet again very soon. Maybe even in the West End, fingers crossed.'

'Absolutely – wouldn't that be great? We could knife each other to pieces every night!'

Jeremy went to find Sally and accosted her on the way to the kitchen. 'Hey, Sal. Sorry I have to go so early, but Eddie is picking me up in five minutes. Have a great night and see you Monday morning. Love you.' He gave her a kiss and loped off.

Peggy and Percy were tucking into the shepherd's pie at the kitchen table when Sally came in to get her share for Rupert.

'This is spot on, girl,' mumbled Percy through a large mouthful. 'You're not only a lovely actress, but a consummate cook. You'd better watch out, Peggy, you have got competition.'

'Yes, dear – in your dreams. Well done, Sally, it is lovely. Come over here, I want to ask you something.' She beckoned to Sally, who crossed the kitchen and knelt down at Peggy's side.

'What's up?' she asked.

'Have you see that Sarah tonight anywhere?' Peggy whispered.

'No – come to think of it, I haven't. Did she say she couldn't come?'

'No, but I tell you what, she is up to something. Every Saturday night I notice she is gone a bit quick, and I just wondered where she goes. You mark my words, there is something going on.'

Sally filled her plate and went in search of her man. Rupert was surrounded by the boys and they seemed to be having such a wonderful time she felt a smidgen of guilt at breaking it up, but once the boys saw the grub they were off!

'Well, you certainly know how to clear a room,' laughed Rupert. 'Ooh yummy, is this for me? Sally, you have been so outstanding on everything to do with this job. I really couldn't have coped without you. I hope we can stay in touch. Do you think Giles might ask you to understudy in the West End? Wouldn't that be great? Maybe I should mention it to him.'

'Well, it is a kind thought,' agreed Sally, 'though it would be great to have a real part in something next. Who knows?' She knocked back her drink, and decided now was the time for the champagne before everyone was too plastered to enjoy it. 'Will you excuse me a minute, I have a hostess job to perform,' she said and reluctantly turned away to see Dora bearing down on him with a bottle of champagne, no less, tucked under her arm.

'Um, just a minute, my girl. That belongs to me and is going to be opened when *I* say the word and not before. So give it here and go and find some other form of alcohol with which to seduce your prey.'

'My word, aren't we the Diva tonight? Here, take your miserable champagne. I don't need any help to seduce a man.' Dora sashayed across the room and joined Rupert and the boys, who had returned with their spoils.

Well, that should keep her out of trouble till I return, thought Sally.

When Sally got back to the kitchen she was greeted by the sight of Janie and Gwendoline laying out an incredibly beautiful cake onto a plate.

'Oh my goodness, where did *that* come from?'

'Oh no! You were not supposed to come in here until we

were ready to present this to you and Rupert. Janie made it and I supplied the ingredients,' said Gwendoline.

'Oh, girls, what a wonderful idea. And it's great timing, because I was just about to open the champagne I have bought as my surprise. So we can have cake and champagne to finish off the evening with a bit of class.'

Sally got all the glasses laid out on the side while the girls finished arranging the cake.

'Shall we carry the cake in last?' said Gwendoline.

'Absolutely,' nodded Sally, 'and I will now go and give everyone a glass of champagne and prepare them for your entrance.'

She managed to get everyone next door to be quiet, and not sip the champagne until she had said her few words, but first she went to the kitchen door and announced, 'Ladies and gentlemen! Pray silence for that talented duo in the wardrobe department, with yet another side to their talent. Let them eat cake!'

The girls entered to wild cheers, and applause at the sight of this huge cake. On top they had written:

To Rupert and Sally
What a pair!
With love from the cast and crew, November 1982

'Would Rupert and Sally please like to come and cut the cake,' said Janie, producing two big knives, one for each of them.

Rupert spoke first, saying, 'I never imagined it was going to be as good as this. All the ups and downs – and that was just my sex-life! No, seriously, we have had our problems, but you have all been so supportive to me and I hope we all meet again one day in the future. But can I say a special thank you to Sally here. She has been my rock.' Rupert leaned over and gave Sally a big smacker on the lips as everyone cheered with delight. Perhaps Dora less so!

Sally responded with a short and sweet: 'Thank you so much, everyone. I am completely overwhelmed. No job will ever compete with this. Thank you.' She swallowed hard, and raised her glass of champagne to the room. 'Cheers, everyone, and good luck always!'

The toast resounded around the room, and then in a flash all was back to normal and the business of eating and drinking was resumed.

'Let's hope once the champagne dries up they will start to leave,' said Sally, who was feeling a little tipsy.

'Oh, don't worry, they will go soon enough, but you and I have some serious drinking to do,' Rupert said. 'I have never seen you drunk. It could be quite a surprise, a bit like your lack of underwear in your Ophelia costume. That was so arousing – but you already know that, don't you?' He held her gaze.

Sally did not look away but murmured, 'Yes, it was very exciting – one of those rare unexpected moments. I love them, and I love to be surprised.' She turned away to give someone a piece of cake.

Rupert slipped his arm around her and drew her to him, whispering, 'Perhaps I can surprise you again tonight?' It took all of Sally's self-control not to let out a whoop of delight right there. Instead she looked him straight in the eye and whispered back, 'Show me.' And then she walked away, hoping Rupert could not see how her legs were trembling. The next half an hour seemed like an eternity, but eventually everyone was gone except Sally and Rupert and Dora. Oh yes, Sally had forgotten about Dora!

'This is cosy,' the girl said, opening the last bottle of champagne – the one Sally had been saving to take to bed with Rupert.

'Where did you find that bottle, Dora?' she asked carefully.

'In your bedroom, for some reason in an ice-bucket ready to go.'

There was a deafening silence. Then Rupert spoke very quietly, but steadily. He said, 'Ah yes, Dora, you have caught me out. I was going to spend some time drinking that with Sally tonight before we say our goodbyes. We have been through a great deal, as you know. So no offence to you, but we will say good night now and go in the other room, if you don't mind.'

Dora was dumbstruck, probably for the first time in her life. She had nowhere to go with this. So she stood up and put the bottle down on the table, but kept her own glass in her hand.

'Good night then. I am sure you won't begrudge me this one glass. I raise it to you both, and wish you health, wealth and happiness.'

And with that she went to her room without a murmur.

Sally turned and looked at Rupert. 'I can't believe you did that,' she breathed.

'Needs must sometimes. Now come on, take me to your room so we can have that talk, or whatever ...' There was a very naughty twinkle in his eye, or so Sally hoped, because quite frankly she was two sheets to the wind and her own eyesight was blurred. She hoped Rupert's sight might be similarly incapacitated for the rest of the evening, should she have to take her clothes off. But stop! She was getting above her station.

They adjourned to the bedroom with the bottle. Rupert placed it by the side of the bed and proceeded to take his clothes off.

Sally was taken aback. 'What are you doing?' she asked rather foolishly.

'Isn't it obvious? I hardly think lying in your bed in my brown boots and Levis is very suitable.' He had stripped to his pants, and then pulled back the sheets and got into bed.

'Come on then, chop chop, we haven't got all night. Well, we have – but I have no doubt that at some point you will fall asleep on me.'

Sally was now completely thrown. She had never undressed in front of anyone before. All her drunken sessions had been with as little light as possible, and as many clothes on as she could reasonably get away with. This was a nightmare. She sat on the edge of the bed and turned on the lamp her side of the bed.

She had pulled off her dress before she realized she would have to go and turn off the main light, thus exposing her fat stomach and unattractive tights. But at least the tights kept the fat on her legs enclosed and gave them a nice smooth shine. So she was going to have to make a dash for the switch and hope he wasn't looking. Fat chance of that: he was sitting up sipping his champagne waiting for the floorshow!

Oh well, here goes nothing, she thought. She had a gorgeous bra on at least, which she had had to go and buy to complement the low dress and get a good cleavage. Janie had chosen it, otherwise she would have been in her usual Marks & Spencer white matching sensible underwear. It was a black lace half-cup bra and she wore a matching black lace thong, which had been annoying her all night, because it was right up her bum! She tried to walk with her stomach turned away from the bed, which gave her a strange look of a lost spider! When she got to the light-switch she lifted her arms above her head in a kind of mock stretch, which gave her the opportunity to breathe in deeply, and hold her stomach in for the final moment in the light. Then, thank God, the light was off and there was only the rosy glow from her little bedside light. She managed to hold her breath all the way back to the bed, where she slipped niftily between the sheets.

'Well, they weren't exactly the most seductive moves I have seen in a bedroom, Sally,' came Rupert's voice, 'but I guess you have yet to perfect them for professional purposes.'

'What do you mean by that!' she exclaimed, stung. 'You think I do this all the time? How dare you suggest I am a slapper – like some girls you know,' she said pointedly, then regretted it.

'No,' Rupert said calmly, 'I mean when you have to do love scenes on camera, you twit. It is horrible, believe me, Sal. You feel such an arse in front of the crew, and everyone is scrutinizing your bits, et cetera. It's a nightmare. So all I am saying is you should practise a bit more and have your moves ready.'

'Sorry, I didn't understand what you were driving at, but I can assure you, Rupert, I will not be asked to do those sorts of scenes. I am just not pretty enough. I know my limitations. I am a character actress – I will always be the fat friend, or the mixed-up one who is useless. Honestly, I don't mind. As long as I can play good parts in prestige productions I will be happy. Give me some champagne, you greedy pig, you have already drunk half the bottle. It was me who was supposed to show you I can get drunk.' She grabbed the bottle, poured herself a glass and threw it back, then poured another.

Rupert was leaning on one elbow watching her with a smile on his face. 'You are such good value, Sally, do you know that? I love being with you, it makes me smile all the time. Isabelle was hard work and I am supposed to be in love with her.'

Sally sighed inwardly. Oh god, I knew *she* would have to come up eventually, but how am I going to get rid of her from the conversation.

'Don't you think, maybe, it was more lust than love? I mean, she is a gorgeous girl and everything, but she is so self-obsessed, Rupert – how could she love anyone back? And all the anorexia and bulimia and the drugs; it is not good for her certainly, nor you. You don't need that kind of image just as you are about to crack it big on the West End stage. You need a nice calming influence – like me.'

Sally couldn't believe she had just come out with that statement, and was about to take it back when Rupert leaned over and kissed her. She waited for him to draw away again, but he didn't. Instead he moved over to her and slowly began to explore her with his tongue. It was bliss. Sally loved kissing and was always disappointed when boys used to stop as quickly as they could, in order to get to the next part of the proceedings, which was usually to grab a breast. Not so young Rupert. They seemed to kiss for hours, only coming up now and then for air. But suddenly everything changed, for both of them. Sally could feel her need growing inside her. All the doubts and hurts and worries were disappearing, and leaving in their place a hunger. A huge desire to feel another human being. To touch skin and taste salty kisses and burn from his touch. Rupert had slipped on top of her and seemed to have discarded his pants on the way.

'What about precautions?' she managed to mumble through the kisses.

'Taken care of,' Rupert's voice was low and urgent. 'Sally, you are a beautiful person.' He gently found her g-string and removed it, and then unclasped her expensive lacy bra with one deft flick of his fingers. But he did not clutch at her boobs, he just kissed her all over, exploring her body. Sally was shy at first because she did not want him to be disappointed. Isabelle she most certainly was not! But whether it was down to the champagne, or Rupert's power of seduction, slowly she opened up to him. She wanted to explore his body, was hungry for more.

'Hey, take it easy,' he panted, 'we have got all night, you know. I want to savour this. Miss Sally Thomas, a tiger in bed.'

'Stop, Rupert, you are embarrassing me now. Please let's just do it!'

'What a quaint turn of phrase for the excellent lovemaking I had in mind. Do it! Sally Thomas, just lie back and enjoy, you deserve it . . .'

Chapter 44

'You will both have to have blood tests.' Giles sat back from the table in a private sitting room of the Queen's Hotel and watched the two young lovers try to absorb the devastating information he had just imparted to them. There was no other way of doing this except with the brutal and honest truth. All of them, including himself, were in mortal danger. He had discussed it endlessly with Teddie, who had gone off to London immediately to see his private doctor. But this was not something that could be cured with money.

'So is Robert going to die?' whispered Eddie.

'I am afraid he is very close to the end, and I was going to suggest you both went to visit him to say goodbye. I will pay the train fares for you. You could go down tomorrow and come back Monday morning. Do you have anywhere you can stay tomorrow night? If not, I will pay for a B&B – there are plenty in the vicinity of the station. Now, is there anything you want to ask me?' Giles was acutely aware that Eddie was going to have to talk to his father, and God knows how Teddie Graham was going to deal with the fact that his only son and heir was gay; or indeed, that his own secret life was now threatened with exposure.

'Are we going to die?' Jeremy was holding himself ramrod straight, and his face was white and pinched. He let out a little moan and then covered his mouth with his hand. 'Oh God, what am I going to tell my parents!'

'I suggest you say nothing to anyone at this juncture,' advised Giles. 'First things first. You will go and have blood tests on Monday morning, and then once we have the results we will know better what we have to do. I am so sorry, boys. It is the most frightening and threatening thing to happen to any of us. Everyone in the gay community is going to have to stick together and beat this.'

He got up from the table and bade them both good night. It was already the early hours of Sunday morning and the boys were exhausted.

'Come on, Eddie, let's go to bed and try to get some sleep,' Jeremy said. 'I will look up the trains for tomorrow.'

They passed the bar on the way to their room, and heard all the laughter and screams of delight that accompanied a Saturday night at the Queen's Hotel. How different was life going to be for so many people if this terrible disease got a grip?

They undressed and prepared for bed in silence. Once under the covers they lay side by side, each with his own thoughts racing through his head. Then very softly Eddie began to cry, just sniffles at first as he brushed away a tear, but then he could not hold in the sobs that racked his body. Jeremy took him in his arms and rocked him gently, ignoring his own tears, wet on his cheek.

'Shush now. Come on, Eddie, all is not lost. We may be OK. Come on, be strong. We will fight this together. Please don't cry, my love.' Jeremy held his lover until finally Eddie fell asleep. Jeremy turned over and tried to fall asleep himself, but his mother's face was right there in front of him; her warm, lovely smile reassuring him when he was frightened, or insecure as a child.

'It is all right, Jeremy dear. You will be fine. Mummy loves you very much. You are a very good boy.'

The boys found themselves a room in a B&B near Euston the next evening. It was not the most salubrious of areas, but this particular establishment was down a side street up near Camden Town in a shabby Georgian terraced house. The room was clean and the landlady a very jolly lady, born and bred locally.

'Just make sure you have no visitors. All right, darlings?' She wagged her finger at them. 'There are plenty of "ladies" out there willing to oblige you with a bit of fun, but they do not belong in my house. Do you understand?' She stood in front of them with her hands on her hips waiting for their response. It would have been funny if things had been different, thought Jeremy. He smiled at her and promised.

'Oh absolutely. We have no intention of bringing anyone back. We just needed a place to sleep tonight before we get the train back to Crewe tomorrow morning.'

They had arranged to go and visit Robert that evening. Neither of them could talk about it or what they were going to do or say. Jeremy had so many questions for Eddie, as he had had no idea that Robert and Eddie had once had an affair. Or was it just a one-night stand? How many others were there? But he could not bear to open that can of worms just yet. There was too much at stake. For now they were simply doing what Giles told them.

They had been given the number of a new organization

called the Terence Higgins Trust, which offered advice to anyone who needed it regarding the disease.

'Let's see Robert first and then we can ring them and ask questions,' said Jeremy.

'I hate hospitals,' muttered Eddie as they made their way through Reception on the ward at St Thomas'. It was not a good place to be, Jeremy had to agree. The neon lighting was harsh against the dark windows and outside, a cold damp December evening was pressing up against the glass. The nurse showed them to a side room on a ward.

At first, Jeremy thought the bed was empty as there was no sign of a body under the covers, but as he moved further into the room and round the corner of the end of the bed, he gasped, and pulled back. Robert's head was just visible above the sheet but it was more like a skull. The skin was stretched so thinly across the cheekbones and the eyes were sunken, lost under the brow, like two black stones at the mouth of a cave.

Jeremy had to use every ounce of strength to pull himself together.

'Hi, Robert.' He tried to smile. 'We have come to say hello, and to wish you better. I am so sorry this has happened.'

Robert opened his mouth and tried to speak but there was nothing. He then pushed the covers down and struggled to lift his arm.

'What do you want?' asked Jeremy. 'Water? Hang on, I will get it for you.' He went to the cabinet at the side of the bed and found a beaker with a spout. He leaned in to Robert and tried to place the spout in his mouth. He felt so clumsy and was terrified he would break Robert's arm trying to sit him up, as it was as thin as a twig, and covered in sores. He could feel the revulsion in himself, then the fear that he would, somehow, be infected. He pulled back and said, 'Shall I get the nurse? Sorry, I am being useless, aren't I?'

Robert shook his head, and a ghost of a smile brushed his lips. He looked past Jeremy to Eddie, who was transfixed. He could not move from the end of the bed.

'Robert . . . I am so sorry. I . . . Sorry, I can't cope with this, I . . .' Eddie turned and fled from the room.

Taking a deep breath, Jeremy took Robert's hand in his and squeezed very gently.

'Take care, lots of love.' He could feel Robert trying to squeeze his hand back, but the tiny, bony sticks that were his fingers just lay inert. It was like touching a skeleton, and Jeremy had to grit his teeth to stop a scream pushing its way up from the pit of his stomach. This was his worst nightmare. He managed to extricate his hand and step back. Every fibre of his being was pulling him towards the door. He just wanted to follow Eddie and run. Run for his life, literally.

'Goodbye, Robert,' was all he could murmur, and he slowly moved backwards towards the door, keeping his eyes on the man in the bed until the very last moment, when he turned and staggered from the room. Eddie was nowhere to be seen so Jeremy went to the exit, hoping to find him on the way. He discovered Eddie outside, sitting on a wall, hugging himself for warmth.

'I am so sorry, but I just couldn't take it, J,' he said hoarsely. 'He was like a skeleton, there was nothing left of him. Oh my God, what a horrible way to die. It's like he just disintegrated. Fuck this!' He stood up and paced in circles.

'Come on,' said Jeremy. 'Let's get out of here. We need to eat.'

They found a little trattoria and had a plate of pasta and a carafe of red wine.

'So tell me about you and Robert. When did that happen? Before me or after me?' Jeremy was determined to keep calm and objective, although his heart was pounding. What other secrets had Eddie been keeping from him?

Eddie did not answer straight away but sat very still staring at Jeremy. Finally he said, 'I love you, Jeremy, I really do. You are the first person I have ever felt really close to in my life. But I love sex. I love the excitement of pulling someone. That first kiss. I can't help myself, and it is going to destroy everything for me in the end. Robert was just a fling. He was at the Queen's one night with a whole load of faggots, and they were all such fun and there was lots of champagne flowing and we had an incredible night. It is what I love, Jeremy, and I have basically been doing it for the last three years. I am not proud of who I am or what I am becoming, and my love for you has made me realize it is not the way to live my life. So now I am going to reap the terrible rewards of my actions, aren't I? I am probably going to die a horrible death like Robert.' He took a sip of wine to stop himself from bursting into tears.

Jeremy pushed his plate away. He felt sick. Sick and incredibly hurt and shaken. How could he have not seen what Eddie was like? He had had his suspicions when Eddie had first taken him to the Queen's and everybody seemed to know him. But this was a whole different person talking now in front of him. The boy was in a different league. Jeremy had thought theirs was a romance. A love story. The two of them finding each other and building a life together. But how could that ever happen if Eddie needed these 'diversions'? It was never going to happen now anyway, because they could both be infected with this deadly virus.

'I cannot understand how you can say you love me and then go and have an orgy with other men. Sorry, Eddie, I am obviously not in your world. I am disgusted. I feel betrayed and demeaned and very foolish. How naïve am I? You must have had a laugh about good old Jeremy coming out of the closet.'

'Stop it, J! Please, I love you. I know I am a mess but I can change. I *want* to change – that is the most important thing. If you are there for me, I can do anything. Please, Jeremy, don't abandon me now,' he implored.

Jeremy could not deal with any of it; he was just lost. He called for the bill and they went back to the digs. Jeremy lay on top of his single bed and tried to put his thoughts in order. Eddie lay beside him on the other bed, waiting.

'Look, I am sorry, Eddie, but I don't know what to think at the moment,' he said in the end. 'Let's just get through the next twenty-four hours and then we can see where all this is going. It's a fucking nightmare at the moment, that's for sure. Good night.' Then he turned off the light and lay in the London night feeling as though he was hurtling down a ravine into nothing but blackness.

Chapter 45

Sally woke with a start and lay still, listening in the dark for a few seconds before she dared move, or dared to remember last night. Had it really happened? Suddenly the bed shook as something heavy beside her moaned softly and then settled down once again. Sally turned over as slowly as she could so as not to disturb the covers, and came face to face with the sleeping Rupert. Her heart did a somersault and she had to stop herself from planting a kiss right there on his luscious lips.

Then the panic set in. What must she look like? Last night's make-up streaked the pillow and she could smell her own stale breath. This was not how she wanted Rupert to see her when he opened his eyes.

She slid from the bed and tiptoed round the bedroom collecting her dirty washing, and then opened her chest of drawers very carefully and retrieved her one pretty nightdress. She slipped through the bedroom door, closing it silently behind her, and set up camp in the bathroom. It was still early so she had time to make herself look presentable before Rupert or Dora surfaced. She had a lovely scented bath, washed her hair and lavished half a pot of Dora's body lotion over herself. She even put some mascara on as her eyes were looking decidedly piggy this morning. When she felt presentable, she went into the living room, tidied up a bit and washed up last night's debris, by which time she was wide awake and starving. However, she didn't want to start breakfast without Rupert. Yes, Rupert – right. She crept back into the bedroom to find him quietly snoring in blissful ignorance of the world around him. Sally climbed back into bed and moved as close as she dared so that when he did awake, she would be in grabbing distance. She lay there for ages and finally dozed off herself, to be suddenly awoken by a yelp as Rupert jumped out of bed.

'Oh shit – what time is it?' he said, looking round the room and trying to understand where he was. 'Sally, are you awake? Listen, what time is it? I have to get the train to London this morning, and I have probably missed the only direct one there is!' He was pulling his jeans on and searching for his socks and shoes. Sally scrambled from the bed feeling her world beginning to crumble.

'But you never said anything last night. You never said you were leaving today. What about all your packing and everything?' Sally stood in front of Rupert and took his arm to keep him still. 'Why didn't you tell me?' Her eyes were bright with tears.

Rupert stopped and looked at the girl in front of him in her crisp white nightie, and light dawned.

'Sally, I am so sorry – it never occurred to me. I have been packing all week and I have got a mate at the Manchester Library Theatre who was driving down this weekend to take a load of my stuff for me, so now I just have a couple of cases. The thing is, I wasn't expecting to be here – you know, this morning. So I need to get back to my flat and pick up my stuff, and leave the keys, et cetera.' He looked again at Sally's face and realized he had made a huge mistake. Completely misread the situation. He took Sally's hand and led her to the bed, and they sat down on the edge.

'Sweetheart, I had a fantastic time last night, it was a hoot. You are my best mate and I know we will be friends forever, but I hope you feel the same, and that you didn't think there was anything else . . . well, anything stronger. I mean, last night was great but maybe we shouldn't have confused the issue – you know . . .'

Sally was hardly listening to him. There was just a loud buzzing in her head. Why didn't he just go? She hated him, hated herself for being so stupid. God, she must look ridiculous sitting here in her fucking virginal white nightie! She wanted to scream and kick and punch him, and everyone! *Just leave me alone*, she wanted to shout, but she only managed to stammer, 'Don't be daft, of course I understand. It was great fun. Thanks. But you must go. I think you will be OK for the train if you hurry. Do you want to ring for a taxi? I can do it.' Sally went and dialled for a cab and managed to pull herself together. She put the kettle on and filled mugs with coffee.

Rupert joined her in the kitchen.

'Five minutes for the cab. Here, have a sip of coffee while you're waiting.' Sally wandered into the lounge and plumped a few cushions and generally made sure there was a huge space between her and Rupert.

'Sally, I do hope we will keep in touch. You've got my number, and hopefully you might consider understudying in the play? It would be great to have you in the company.' Rupert waffled on until he was saved by the doorbell. 'Ah, that will be the taxi. Well, goodbye for now, Sally, and thank you again for last night.'

He advanced towards her and Sally felt herself go as stiff as a board. She practically pushed him away from her, saying as brightly as she could, 'Yes, it has been a wonderful experience all round. Thanks, Rupert, and good luck.' She turned to open the front door, and as he passed her Rupert leaned in and gave her a kiss on the lips.

'Maybe another time, another place?' And he was gone.

Sally turned and ran to the toilet, where she threw up. She sat there on the bathroom lino for a long time, sobbing into the roll of toilet paper. If only I could throw up my heart and start again, she thought to herself. It can't get much lower than this. How did I get it so wrong?

Chapter 46

'Good morning, everybody. It's another Monday, and another opening of another show. I hope you are all well rested and ready to raise the roof with our Victorian Music Hall delights!'

'Blimey, whatever she's on, I want some,' whispered Simon to Pete as they swigged their habitual post-weekend Lucozade.

Sarah continued with obvious delight, revelling in her new-found role as director.

'There is an air of the Butlin's Redcoat about her though,' commented Charmaine, none too kindly.

'I have been asked by Giles to mention a couple of things this morning. Sadly, Robert will no longer be with us for the rest of the season due to ill-health. We will be sending him some flowers from the company, and Heather will be coming round with a card for you all to sign. We wish him well. Secondly, Giles will be commuting between London and Crewe a good deal, finalizing the plans for the production of *Hamlet* in the West End. He apologizes profusely, but what with the run-up to Christmas, and losing Robert as his assistant, he is very pressed for time. However, I will be stepping in wherever possible, so if you have any queries, please feel free to ask me. Finally, I have the casting for *Wind in the Willows* which I will pin on the noticeboard. So now, down to business. There will be a vocal warm-up with Tim, and then we will start the technical dress rehearsal and work through the numbers. Hopefully there will be time for a dress rehearsal tonight, then one tomorrow afternoon as is normal, and then – curtain up! Throughout the day Gwendoline will see you about your costumes, and anything you have offered from your own wardrobe should be given to her today. Thank you! I will be in the Royal Box if anyone wants me.'

Sarah swept off the stage as though she had owned and run the theatre all her life. Sally watched her take her large briefcase and script up to the box, calling to Heather to bring her a coffee.

Sally followed Heather to the props room. 'Blimey, this is a bit of a turn-up, isn't it?' she asked Heather, who was trying to find a clean mug in the sink.

'Bloody Lady Muck,' grumbled Heather. 'It has been a nightmare taking orders from her. She has got Giles wound round her little finger. Mind you, that was not difficult as he is in a terrible state. Have you seen him? I don't know what the matter is, but something is up. He was in Manchester all weekend, only got back this morning, and now he is holed up in his office with Lord Graham. Anyway, Sarah has taken over and that's that. Be interesting to see if she really does know what she's doing. Tim says she is spot on with all the musical stuff, so let's hope so. Now how are you, my little flower? You are looking a bit forlorn this morning.'

Sally really did not want to tell anyone of her humiliation, so she explained away her abject misery as a bit of a cold.

'Well, take care of yourself because we are going to need

every hand on deck this week with all the comings and goings.'

Sally then went to find Jeremy who had seemed very distracted at the company meeting. He was in his dressing room, clearing up as usual after the others.

'God, Jeremy, do you never stop tidying up?' Sally embraced her friend.

'It makes me feel better,' he explained. 'I need to have calm and structure in my surroundings, especially when my life is falling down round my ears.' He crumpled suddenly and sat down with his head in his hands.

'Whatever is the matter?' asked Sally, alarmed, pulling up a chair beside him.

Jeremy began to cry. He was taking in air in great gulps, trying but unable to stem the flood. Sally held him, and passed him a tissue from time to time, but there was nothing else to be done except let the man cry it all out. Finally, Jeremy sat back exhausted. Sally fetched him some water and he drank it gratefully. They rested for a few moments in silence until Jeremy seemed to make a decision and started to speak, his voice thin and shaky.

'Sally, have you by any strange coincidence heard of HIV or AIDS?'

'No, I don't think so. What are they?'

'Basically it is a disease a bit like cancer. It attacks the cells in the body and destroys its immune system. It is relatively new in this country and doctors don't know much about it at this stage, but the trouble is, it is a killer. Once infected, a person will almost surely die.' Jeremy bit back another surge of tears. 'It seems to be transmitted sexually, but they don't know for sure, so everyone is panicking and frightened to touch anyone or share anything. It is horrific, Sally. They think it is spread by gay men, but I have been talking to doctors in London and they are saying this is not true, and people must have all the facts before they accuse people of causing such havoc. But so far it seems to be only gay men who are dying, and . . .' He started to weep again.

Sally stopped him, saying, 'Hang on a minute, Jeremy. Please, just slow down. What are you trying to say – that you have caught this virus? And what about Eddie – is he involved in all this? Come on, just take it slowly, and tell me everything.' She held Jeremy's hand and did not let go until he had finished talking her through everything that had happened, including the visit to see Robert.

Sally tried to understand exactly what Jeremy was saying. 'So you have both had a test and it is highly likely that you could develop this virus and die?' Her voice petered out to a whisper.

'They have to monitor us over the next few weeks,' replied Jeremy.

'What about your parents?' ventured Sally. 'Have you talked to them?'

'No, of course not! How can I, Sally? They don't even know I am gay, never mind a potential victim of some fucking killer disease. And can you imagine what it is like for Eddie? If Lord Graham finds out his son is gay, he will go crazy! It is the worst possible mess, and I have no idea what we are going to do.' Jeremy broke down again.

'What are we going to do, Giles?' Edward Graham was sitting opposite Giles Longfellow in his office. Giles was clasping his head in his hands, wishing it would stop thumping.

'I will be ruined!' Teddie went on. 'Never mind dead! Oh Christ Almighty. We are not promiscuous, Giles, so how did this happen?'

The other man groaned. 'How many more times do you want me to have to grovel, Teddie? I had an affair with Robert last year, and I had no idea he was infected. For whatever reason, he didn't see fit to tell me. Please God we are clear. We will know soon enough. Just try and hold yourself together until we know for sure.'

'If Tanya found out I had been having this affair with you, she would divorce me,' said Edward, running all the possible disasters through his head.

'I doubt it,' retorted Giles. 'I think you will find she knows all about you, Teddie, dear boy, and chooses to look the other way. She has no intention of rocking the family boat because of your peccadillos!'

'You may well be right,' sighed Edward. 'But what about the children? Poor Eddie will never forgive me.'

This was the moment Giles had been dreading. He had discussed the matter with Jeremy and Eddie, and they had all decided that it would be Giles who broke the news to Lord Graham of his son's affair with Robert and his subsequent relationship with Jeremy – and where that left them in this horror story.

Giles was often criticized for being a weak man in many respects, but he accepted his responsibility to his friends and loved ones, and in this case his love for Edward Graham overcame any qualms he might have had about facing this head on.

'Teddie, there is no easy way to tell you this. But I want you to know how much I love you and will always be there for you and Eddie. You are going to have to spend a good deal of time with your son over the next few days and weeks, and it is going to hurt you so much I can hardly imagine how you will cope. But you will because you are a strong and loving man. Teddie, my dearest heart, your son is also gay. He is having a relationship with the young actor from our company here called Jeremy – you have met him. Tragically, last year Eddie had a fling with Robert Johnson, so he too is under threat of this insidious disease, as is his lover.' He was stopped by a bloodcurdling cry and groans from Lord Graham. The sounds were primeval. He was like a wounded animal at bay.

Giles went to get him a brandy. The man was rocking backwards and forwards in the chair, moaning and whimpering, and calling out his son's name. Giles made him drink the brandy and waited for it to take effect. He was trying to decide the best plan of action. Should he take Lord Graham home, or keep him in a hotel or his flat, until he was calm and in control, and they knew for certain what their futures were going to be? Eddie was back at Crewe Hall, he knew from Jeremy, and it was probably not a good idea for father and son to meet there. So there were not many options. He had not had time to consider his own predicament, which was pretty grim by any standards. But he refused to think about that now. He had to sort out Edward.

'He can't be gay,' Edward was muttering to himself. 'I won't let him be gay. The Graham name must go on. He will do as I tell him and marry, and have a son and heir as I did. He will stop this nonsense right now.' The more he talked himself up, the angrier he was becoming.

Giles took him by the shoulders. 'Teddie, look at me. Look at me! Can you hear yourself? Really hear? Your son may be dying – *you* may be dying. Right this minute we all need each other. We need to love and support each other, do you hear me?' He looked into his friend's eyes and could see only panic and fear and loathing.

'Damn you, Giles! I blame you for this. You are a weak man who has always followed his cock! Why couldn't you just keep

your dirty habit to yourself? We could have been so happy forever with our secret. Now my son has fallen, and it is your
bloody company of actors who have done this. They have
seduced him!' He started to moan and berate Giles again.

Giles took no notice of the accusations because they were
so ludicrous, but he could not help but feel a tinge of sadness
at how quickly Teddie resorted to type, and how quick he was
to stereotype actors. Theatre was to blame for corrupting society with the gay community. All ills rested at their door. The
hypocrisy made him sick.

'Listen, Teddie, you have to pull yourself together and
decide what to do for the next couple of days. I don't think
you should go home. Why don't we go down to London and
stay in your flat until we are sure of the outcome of the tests,
et cetera, and let Eddie and Jeremy cope with their situation.
And then we will have to face whatever life is going to throw
at us.'

Giles suddenly felt so tired, and defeated, and sad for them
all.

It was Life or Death, simple as that.

Chapter 47

Sally went and sat at the back of the stalls in the dark to think. She was overwhelmed by the events taking place around her. Her own heartbreak seemed so unimportant in the great scheme of things, and yet it had left her feeling vulnerable and useless. All confidence in herself was gone. Yet now she was faced with the possibility of losing her closest friend and was completely incapable of helping him in any way. Everything was out of control; even their work was in danger from an ambitious young woman who was the Pretender to the throne. Sally watched her shouting commands to Jeremy onstage. Sarah Kelly was like an eagle in her eyrie swooping down every now and then to chivvy the actors along. Poor Jeremy, thought Sally, how can he concentrate on singing at a time like this? How long would he have to wait for the results? And what on earth would happen when Eddie was discovered to be gay by his father? Sally thought about Eddie and his promiscuous lifestyle. Jeremy was completely out of his depth on that score. Could the two of them ever have had a chance in the long run?

Her mind turned to Dora and her life, and suddenly Sally had a terrifying thought. What if Dora had slept with Robert? She could be in danger of this dreadful virus as well. Sally got up and immediately went in search of her sister. She found her in the wings, waiting to go on for her number. Now was not the time to ask intimate questions.

Jeremy was coming off shaking his head and swearing to himself.

'That was good,' said Sally, hoping to encourage him, but he was having none of it.

'It was crap. Look, I need to get to a phone and find out if there is any news.' He started towards the exit and the stage door.

'Why don't you come and use Heather's phone? It is more private and I can stand guard,' suggested Sally. 'Let me help where I can. I know I can't do much, but I love you, Jeremy, and want to be there for you and Eddie.'

'Thanks, Sally, I appreciate it. Lead on.' He followed Sally out of the wings to the office.

After several attempts to find Eddie, to no avail, Jeremy decided to go and see Giles. 'Do you know where he is?' he asked Sally.

'Not for sure, but I assume he must be in his office because I have seen him in the building,' she answered.

'OK, I will go and see if I can find him. If anyone calls for me I will be back in fifteen minutes or so. Can you cover for me, please, Sally?'

'Of course. Go on – go.' Sally went back to the stage.

'Ooooh! What a beauty, I've never seen one as big as that before.
Oh! What a beauty, it must be two foot long or even
more . . .'

Simon was giving his all to a huge marrow which was being constructed onstage by the crew as he was rehearsing. Geoffrey and Charmaine were standing by waiting to go on next, and Sally overheard them discussing their new director.

'I think she reckons she is running the National,' moaned Charmaine. 'She keeps giving me detailed notes about my motivation. My motivation is to sit quiet and still while you sing to me! Do I need to have a discussion about what my thoughts are as you warble away?'

'Probably best not to know,' replied Geoffrey solemnly. 'I can only imagine what *you* must be thinking about. What you are going to eat for tea? Why you are here at all?'

Charmaine laughed at this. 'Oh now, Geoffrey, don't be so hard on yourself. I enjoy listening to your voice, I really do.'

Sally could not help but stifle a giggle and the other two turned round guiltily.

'Oh, Sally, don't do that! You gave us a fright.' The two of them looked like naughty school children.

'Sorry, guys, but you are a hoot. Sarah is certainly making her mark though, isn't she? Are you coping with it OK?'

'Oh God, yes!' exclaimed Geoffrey. 'We have been doing this too long to be put off by anything less than an earthquake. We do it ourselves most of the time anyway, don't we?' They all laughed and Sally watched as the two of them went onstage to set up for their number.

Heather appeared at her side and said, 'Sally, can you go over to the workshop and oversee the marrow? It needs adjusting or something, according to Simon. See what he wants, will you?'

Sally saluted and disappeared.

'Has anyone seen my tiddler?' Pete's voice whispered in Heather's ear. She spun round. 'I beg your pardon?' she gasped. 'What on earth do you mean – and is it rude?'

'That is the name of my song,' chuckled Pete. 'I need a jamjar and a stick with a long bit of string attached to it with a little fish on the end of it. And yes, it *is* rude.'

'Blimey, bring back *Hamlet*,' said Heather. 'All I had to find was a skull! Right, come with me, young man and we will sort out your tiddler, if you'll excuse the expression.'

On the way to the workshop Sally suddenly remembered Dora and did an about-turn towards the dressing rooms instead. She found her sister pacing up and down going through her song.

'Sorry to interrupt,' said Sally, 'but can I have a word?'

Dora stopped singing and faced her. 'Yes, but make it quick. I have to go and do a chorus number in a minute.'

Sally took a deep breath. 'Dora, I am sorry to pry but it is important. Did you sleep with Robert?'

The girl sighed heavily. 'God, Sally, we are not still on that, are we? For Christ's sake, what does it matter to you?'

'Nothing.' Sally pushed on. 'It is just something I need to check. Please just trust me on this – it is important.'

Dora said very slowly and clearly, 'No, I did not have sex with Robert Johnson. There, are you happy now? I can't believe I am even bothering to answer you.'

Sally gave her a quick nod and sped out of the room before Dora could ask any awkward questions. She still needed to see how Jeremy was getting on, but Heather found her first, and asked about the marrow.

'Oops, I forgot. I am so sorry – I will do it now. It is just there is so much going on I can't keep up with it all!'

'Tell me about it,' said Heather grimly. 'It is supposed to be the season of comfort and joy, but there seems little evidence of that around here. By the way, just to add to the chaos, we have to get someone to organize a "secret Santa" jobbie for between the shows on Christmas Eve. We always have a bit of a tea and buns and prezzies. I know, I know, now is not ideal but it is only three weeks away. Shit – look at the time! I need to call the company onstage, excuse me.' She hurried off like the white rabbit in *Alice in Wonderland*, shaking her head and muttering to herself.

Sally was forced to follow her to the stage where Sarah was waiting with a sheaf of notes in her hands.

'Right, everyone, I am pleased to say we are in good nick. So I propose we break for lunch then start the technical rehearsal at two o'clock. As I said before, with a bit of luck we may get a dress rehearsal in tonight, or at least half a one. So tomorrow morning around eleven we can finish it and then break, and then start the proper Dress at two o'clock, ready to open the show at seven thirty. Thank you, everyone, it is going to be fabulous.'

Sally had hardly rehearsed her number at all, but she was not too bothered as she knew exactly what she was doing with it and did not need Sarah Kelly's input. She did, however, need a dress – and a period dress at that. She knew Janie had put one aside for her but she had not yet tried it on and it might be a good idea to do that now. She met Janie coming down the stairs with an armful of costumes.

'Can I try on my dress any time soon?' Sally asked her.

'Yes, of course. Do you want to do it now? If so, just follow me.' Sally did as she was told and followed Janie to the wardrobe department, where Gwendoline was overseeing Pete while he tried on a pair of short trousers for his Tiddler number.

'Pete, you look most fetching,' chuckled Sally. 'What do you think, girls? Could you have that in your bed?'

'Please spare me,' Janie replied. 'It is bad enough having to listen to him playing with his tiddler!' They burst into fits of the giggles.

'Yeah, yeah, very funny, girls. Mock a man trying to do the best for his art.'

'Art!' screeched Janie, and this brought about further squeals of laughter.

'Sorry to interrupt, but could I have a word please, Sally.' Giles Longfellow was standing in the doorway and the whole room went silent.

'Yes, of course,' said Sally. She followed Giles out of the room without a backward glance.

Not a word was spoken all the way to Giles's office. He showed Sally into the room and shut the door.

'Please have a seat. Would you like something to drink?' He was pouring himself a very large brandy as he said this.

'No, thank you,' said Sally, and waited for Giles to speak.

He sat down opposite her slowly. He looked old and grey, and there was none of the dashing entrepreneur about him today. He swirled the golden liquid round the brandy glass and peered into it like a fortune-teller hoping for inspiration.

'You are Jeremy's closest friend, he tells me.' Giles spoke without looking at her. 'I understand he has told you about Robert and his illness.' He paused and took a sip of brandy. 'He has also told you of his involvement with Eddie Graham and the obvious problems this creates. Do you have any idea how serious the situation is for everyone?' He gave Sally a piercing look and Sally held his gaze. She could see the pain in his eyes but also something else. Giles was frightened. Deep down to his bones he was scared. The fear was rolling off him, Sally could almost smell it.

Why was she here? She could not understand why he had asked her to see him.

'I am a little confused as to why you have asked me here, Giles. Yes, I understand that there are serious issues concerning Jeremy and Eddie and possibly yourself, but what can I do exactly?'

There was a long silence and then a groan from Giles.

'Because Eddie has contracted this virus and he will probably die, and he is your best friend's lover. Jeremy is devastated and you are the only person he has in his life to turn to, so I am asking you to take care of him through this. We are all devastated and the whole dreadful business touches so many lives. I won't go into the details if you don't mind, as they are confidential, but I would also ask you to keep this private. I know you can be trusted, Sally, and I value your discretion enormously, and your support. It is going to be exceedingly tough on Jeremy for the next few weeks so I just wanted to make sure you would be there for him.'

'Of course I will. Thank you so much for telling me and for trusting me. I do hope you all get through this and I am so sorry to hear about Eddie.'

Sally decided the best thing to do was to get out quick. She left the office and ran down the stairs as fast as she could. She was so shocked she really could not take it all in. Where was Jeremy now? She needed to talk to him. She went straight to the boys' dressing room but only Simon and Pete were there.

'Have you seen Jeremy?' she asked.

'He had gone to the shop to get some lunch,' said Pete.

'Thanks,' replied Sally and was gone. She raced down the stairs and out to the stage door. 'Gladys, have you seen Jeremy?'

The big woman was eating a hot pie and could not answer immediately. Much to Sally's frustration she had to wait while Gladys chomped her way, huffing and puffing, through her mouthful of steak and kidney.

'Pardon me, luv, sorry 'bout that. Blimey, it was 'ot! Now then, what was you asking? Oh yes, young Jeremy. Well, he came running out looking something terrible. White as a sheet. I told him to go to the pub and buy himself a brandy. So I think that is where he has gone. Nothing serious is it, luv?' But she was talking to herself because Sally had already gone.

Sally found Jeremy sitting in the corner by the fire surrounded by hearty happy lunchtime drinkers. He was hunched over his glass, staring into the flames. Sally managed to grab a spare stool and dragged it across to sit down beside him. He hardly acknowledged her presence.

'Jeremy, I am so sorry. What is there to say? It is terrible news. Please look at me, come on, you need to talk. Shall we go somewhere more private?'

'Eddie is going to die and I can't take it in. Why has this happened? Am I being punished? Sally, I am OK, I am not infected, and nor are Giles or Lord Graham. I can't comprehend it. We are spared, yet Eddie has to die. What am I going to do? I can't tell my parents and I have got to get through Christmas Day. Oh God, I can't do it.'

Sally could feel his shoulders starting to shake and knew she had to get him out of the pub. She hauled him up, saying, 'Come on now, let's just go somewhere private. Hang on a few more minutes, and then you can cry all you want, my friend.' She literally dragged him out of the pub and managed to get him to walk back to the theatre.

'Now let's get past Gladys without an enquiry. You just have to hold your breath and stand up straight and walk quickly.' Jeremy did everything he was told and the two of them hurried past Gladys with a wave. The latter was not too bothered as she was now engaged with a large portion of steamed roly poly pudding, which was also very 'ot!

Sally got Jeremy sat down in her dressing room and shut the door so they would not be disturbed. There was still half an hour before the technical rehearsal started.

'Look, we are going to have to find a way to get you through this show starting with two o'clock today unless I tell Sarah you are ill. I could do that and then you could go home.'

'I don't want to be on my own,' cried Jeremy. 'I want to see Eddie but his father has forbidden it. Sally, they have taken Eddie away to a nursing home somewhere. They are telling people he has terminal cancer, but he might live for ages yet. I don't know much about the illness, but Giles had been telling me and George Delaware that the virus could lie dormant for years before it presents itself. I want to talk to Eddie and make him see that we can still be together. I won't leave him. I love him, for God's sake.'

'OK, let's get this straight. Lord Graham won't let you see Eddie ever again?'

'Yes – he is crazy! He told Giles it was my fault his son was gay, never mind caught this terrible virus. Nothing could be further from the truth, Sal. I feel like a teenager compared to Eddie. He has betrayed me and our love. He has been having affairs for the last three years. He says he wants to stop now he has met me, but who knows. Anyway, all that is irrelevant now. I just want to see him and talk.'

'Can't Giles help you see him? Surely if he and Lord Graham are so close he would have some influence?' she suggested.

Jeremy blew his nose and sat up, trying to pull himself together.

'To be honest, I think this whole thing has split them up. Giles seems completely lost. Lord Graham is battening down the hatches and closing all possible means of this leaking out to the press. Can you imagine what they would make of it? I reckon Giles has been given his marching orders as well. So one way or another, we are all fucked.'

'I think Eddie will find a way to contact you,' said Sally thoughtfully. 'He will not want to leave it like this. Just try and sit tight for the time being and see what happens. You have got so much on your plate, these next three weeks, Jeremy. I know it is tough but you must be strong and you must not let it stop you doing your work. You know what we have always told each other. Work comes first.' Sally stopped as she saw the tears welling up again in Jeremy's eyes. She gathered him to her and held him tight. 'You can do this,' she whispered. 'We will do it together.'

Chapter 48

'Ladies and gentlemen, for your delectation and delight please put your hands together and welcome a young and perfectly formed songstress born to soar to the heights of sublime ecstasy . . . Miss Sally Thomas!'

The audience cheered and whistled as Sally was lowered on a swing to the centre of the stage where she sang 'The Boy I Love is Up in the Gallery'. She wore a gorgeous pale blue and cream lace dress with mountains of petticoats, and little leather boots which peeped through the folds of her gown as she swung backwards and forwards. With all the drama that was going on in real life it was a relief to be here for five perfect minutes every night and sing her heart out to an adoring crowd. She had had more fan letters this week than any other time. It certainly helped her through the days rehearsing with Jeremy, who wandered about in a coma.

His poor performance as the all-important character, Badger, was so disappointing for her, and the rest of the cast, because they had all been so looking forward to *Toad of Toad*

Hall. Simon was creating a wonderfully evil leader of the weasels, and Percy was sublime as Toad.

'This part was made for you,' said Sarah, clapping her hands after a particularly good run-through.

'Don't know whether to take that as a compliment or not,' whispered Percy under his breath to Peggy.

She gave his arm a squeeze and whispered back, 'You are too good-looking for the role really, my darling!' and they both laughed.

Sally was having a ball playing the water rat, Ratty. She was strutting about with a false moustache on, much to everyone's amusement. Pete was the perfect Mole because he was quite small anyway but he had already devised an amazing face make-up which blended down his neck and chest into his costume. It was a pain to put on every night, but the effect was incredible because it gave the animals real characters. Pete had to give lessons to everyone else in the cast and even got his name in the programme as animal make-up designer.

'Can't be bad to have another string to his bow,' commented Janie. 'We need all the help we can get in this game.'

Dora was a dream as the gaoler's daughter who disguises Toad as a washerwoman so he can get out of gaol. Gwendoline had made her a frock with the lowest bodice imaginable, and Dora's cleavage was very much on show, to the delight of the boys.

'Are you sure she can go in front of children dressed like that?' asked Sally. Janie and Gwendoline had a fit of the giggles.

'Well, it will make all the dads happy, won't it?' chuckled Janie. 'It's a laugh – children don't worry about a bit of cleavage.'

'A bit!' yelped Sally.

Jeremy, however, was giving a decidedly lacklustre performance as Badger.

'I am so sorry, Sally, I just can't stop thinking about Eddie. If only I could see him and talk to him.'

After a few days of this Sally had had enough and went to see Giles.

'Please, Giles, can you persuade Lord Graham to at least let Jeremy say goodbye properly,' she pleaded. 'We need him up to speed for this show.'

'I will do my best, but His Lordship will hardly give me the time of day either.'

If truth be known, Giles was at his wit's end. He and Teddie had had a meeting in London to discuss the finances of the theatre, and Edward Graham had basically told Giles that after this season he was withdrawing his support.

'But why, for God's sake? Just because you and I can no longer be together doesn't mean the theatre has to suffer. You know how much it means to me to keep Crewe going, and all my dreams for the future, and we are going to open *Hamlet* in three months' time, which will be a fantastic achievement. Please, Teddie, don't destroy everything I have. I have lost you, which is enough to bear.'

But Giles was wasting his breath. Lord Graham had shut down and was immune to all pleading. From the moment he had heard that his son had HIV and his predicament was life-threatening, something inside Edward Graham had also died. He could hardly face Tanya and Tilly, so he spent most of his time in his apartment in London. He rarely went out socially. Gossip was rife in the inner circles, but he had managed to keep it all from the press. He had sent Eddie away to stay with some friends in New York and had arranged for his son to see a doctor there who was an authority on this new disease. Any hope that could be offered would be welcome. But there had been none.

He was expecting Eddie home for Christmas and intended to keep him well away from that boy he thought he was in love with. Love! He was so bitter and angry with poor Jeremy for no good reason. He knew he was being illogical, and he even felt remorse at the pain he must be causing the boy by not allowing him to see Eddie. But he also felt repelled by him, by them both, for their obvious passion and pleasure with each other. Not his son! How did it happen? He could see the hatred and loathing in his wife's eyes and he knew she blamed him for everything. But then had he not been similarly overwhelmed with a passion for Giles? Did he not support being gay? It was no longer against the law. Society recognized it as acceptable now. Why did he feel this guilt? He must stand proud and face the world for himself, for his son. But in his heart he knew he was weak and that his life would be a hell on earth if he admitted his sexuality. Tanya had promised to stand by him for Eddie and Tilly's sake, but only if he never saw Giles again, or engaged in any extra-curricular activity. They would live the lie to the end and if, God forbid, Eddie's 'illness' should develop, then it was to be known as cancer and left at that.

If Eddie died . . .

'I have had a postcard from Eddie!' Jeremy was beside himself with delight when he cornered Sally early one morning. 'He has been in New York but gets back this weekend and wants to meet. Oh my God, I am so happy, Sally. I am so sorry I have been such a pain, and I promise I will make it up to you guys and give the performance of my life for you all. Old Badger will rise up and strike the Wild Wood!' He gave Sally a big kiss and skipped off to the dressing rooms.

Thank goodness, thought Sally. The euphoria may not last when reality sets in, but at least if it gets us through the play, that is something to be thankful for at least. And maybe the Christmas spirit will imbue us all with a little hope.

Christmas was bearing down upon them fast and the cast were becoming quite demob-happy. All the dressing rooms were festooned with paperchains and tinsel. Even Sarah had put some holly round her mirror and was hanging silver balls along the edge when Sally came into the dressing room one morning. The two girls were not exactly enemies but not friends either, but Sally had decided that Sarah had her feet under the table and if Sally wanted certain parts after Christmas she needed to stake her claim.

'Morning, Sarah, that looks very festive,' she smiled her greeting.

'Thank you,' replied Sarah, standing up and turning to face Sally. 'How are you finding life on the water bank? I must say, all of you have really taken to your characters.'

'Oh, we love it! Ratty was always my favourite as a child. Actually, Sarah, I have been meaning to ask you about the next couple of plays after Christmas. Will you be directing them?'

'Yes I will, as a matter of fact. Giles, as you know, has a lot on his plate with *Hamlet* so he asked me to take over. As you can imagine, I am thrilled. It is what I have always wanted to do.' Sarah said this as though in answer to any questions anyone might have had who was in doubt as to her intentions from the beginning of the season.

Sally nodded in agreement. 'Oh yes, that is obvious from the work you have done so far. So that's great then, you have your heart's desire, lucky you.' She couldn't help her last comment and it was out before she could stop it.

'It is not all luck, you know.' Sarah's answer was sharp. 'You have to fight sometimes for what you want. I take it you have not found *your* heart's desire, Sally. But have you really worked out exactly what that is yet?'

Sally began to feel uncomfortable. What did this woman want from her? It was really none of her business what her heart's desire was anyway. Deciding to change the subject, she put on a big cheesy grin and said, 'I would love to play Sandy in *The Prime of Miss Jean Brodie*. I take it Charmaine will be playing Jean Brodie? I would also love to play the lead in *The Boyfriend*. I am very committed to this season at Crewe, Sarah, and feel quite strongly that I can bring a good deal to the productions as an actress and a company member.'

Sarah watched her without any expression. She was giving nothing away.

'Well, it is good to know where you stand, and I am glad to see you still have ambition after the ups and downs so far. What about Dora? She is very popular with the audiences and very keen to make her mark.' Sarah could not resist throwing a small spanner into the works.

'Absolutely right,' agreed Sally, refusing to be drawn. 'There are certain roles she will be perfect for in the coming plays. However, she still has to get more experience before she can take responsibility for a leading role. But that is just my opinion,' she added with her most charming smile. 'Well, I had better get going or there will be no props ready for the dress rehearsal. See you later.'

Sally breathed a sigh of relief as she went down the stairs. Sarah was tricky, there was no doubt about it, and she really kept her cards close to her chest. But Sally was determined not to be put off. She had had a shitty time since Rupert left, and the only good thing was, they had all been so busy she had had little time to feel sorry for herself. But every now and then she thought about their night together and her stomach tied in knots. He had sent her a card from LA saying he was having a wonderful time. There was no mention of Isabelle, but why would he be that cruel to her? She was not a fool, and just wished he would leave her alone now. She could never be friends after what had happened, and she certainly did not want to understudy in *Hamlet* in the West End. That really would be going nowhere fast. The lowest of the low, watching *his* star ascend to great heights. They had asked Jeremy to go, and that was quite right. His Laertes was a brilliant piece of work. Sally was so happy for him, and hoped it would make up a little for his problems. He was still very quiet and withdrawn, and she spent any spare time she had keeping an eye on him and trying to raise his spirits.

Sally was concentrating on making *Toad of Toad Hall* a huge success, and she was looking forward to going home for Christmas Day. She was also hoping to catch a few moments with Mack. Everything that had happened with Rupert had rather taken over her thoughts . . . but Sally still needed to resolve her feelings about Mack. Somehow, he represented another way of life. But was that what she wanted? There was so much going on around her that was affecting her in so many different ways . . . and it was difficult to put it all together. She was longing to see her parents and just bask in their warmth and security.

Sally had managed to get gifts in between rehearsals and prop-collecting, and tonight she sat in the flat in front of the fire and played Christmas carols on the radio while she wrapped them all up. Dora had come home one night from the pub and interrupted her reverie.

'Oh my God, sis, don't tell me you have done all your presents already? What are you like?' She had slumped down onto the sofa, squashing some Christmas paper and decorations as she did so.

'Oh, for goodness sake, Dora, look what you are doing! Get up – you have wrecked my wrapping stuff. Come on, please, move your fat arse.'

'Excuse *me*,' huffed Dora, dragging herself off the sofa. 'I do not have a fat arse, if you don't mind. Oh come on, Sally, chill out a bit. You are no fun these days. Still pining for Rupie? Let's face it – that was never going anywhere.'

Sally refused to rise to the bait. She was just too tired and fed up with everything. She and Dora did nothing but bicker these days, and Sally was hoping that on Christmas Day they could keep it pleasant for their parents' sake.

'Have you heard from the casting woman at *Coronation Street* yet?' she asked, changing the subject.

Dora let out a scream of delight. 'Oh shit, yes! How could I forget to tell you? I have got an audition for a character in *Corrie* – a possible regular character. Can you believe it?' Dora was now jumping up and down, dangerously close to Sally's wrapped gifts.

'Hey, that is wonderful news, but please mind my parcels. Sit down over there, can't you, there's a good girl.' Dora actually did as she was told, and sat in the chair hugging herself. 'I can't believe it, but it would be so amazing if I got it. I go next week. What a Christmas present that would be, wouldn't it?'

Sally went and gave her sister a hug. 'I am really happy for you. Good luck.' She then went to the kitchen and started to make some hot chocolate.

Dora stood in the doorway and watched her. 'Are you really pleased for me?' she asked.

Sally looked at her. 'Yes, of course I am. Why do you ask?'

'Oh, I don't know. These days I just seem to annoy you all

the time, and things have not been going very well for you, have they? Did that agent ever get in touch, by the way?'

Sally concentrated hard on the hot milk. 'No, he didn't, but to be honest I didn't expect him to really. I was not his type of actress. He has offered Jeremy a contract, did you know? I think that is great news – just what Jeremy needs at the moment.' She forced a bright smile in Dora's direction and poured out the drinks, adding, 'Don't you worry about me, Dora, I will soon be catching you up. Think hare and tortoise.'

They laughed and said good night and each went to her own room.

Sally undressed, desperately trying to keep all thoughts of agents and jobs at bay. She did not want to think about any of that for the time being. She had received the letter from the agent Peter Stone with resignation. She had known it would be a no. She had not even expected him to contact her, and when she had had a moment of daring and decided to write to him, she couldn't find his card. Last time she had seen it was on the kitchen table, the night they had all met. So when she couldn't find it she took it as a sign it was not to be and let it go. She had been thrilled for Jeremy and decided she would tackle the whole agent thing after Christmas. If she got a couple of good parts she would write to various theatres and casting directors and agents, and take it from there. For now she just wanted to go home and sit in front of the familiar Christmas tree and pretend she was ten years old again.

Chapter 49

Giles scanned the room but could see no sign of Edward. Why would he? This was a crematorium in North London and Giles was here out of respect for his ex-lover and friend, Robert Johnson. Why the hell did he think Edward would be there? He shivered and pulled his scarf tighter round his face. It was a bitterly cold day, bleak and depressing, with a sky full of rolling black clouds. They seemed angry. Was that in support of the man lying in the coffin in front of them? Was Robert's anger creating this dark presence around them?

There were only a handful of people sitting there, and Giles did not know any of them, although he vaguely recognized a counsellor from the Terence Higgins Trust who gave him a nod. Please let it be over! Giles could not stop shaking and he knew it was not just the cold. These last few weeks had seemed a lifetime. A lifetime spent surrounded by unhappiness and betrayal. He just wanted to get through this. He would survive, of that he had no doubt. There was a tiny part of Giles that he never gave away to anyone, not even Teddie. Call it hope or ego or just plain self-preservation, but this tiny part of him was the spark that kept him going. He would rise up again from the ashes. Ashes – Christ, now was not the time to bring up ashes. The director of the funeral parlour had contacted him and suggested that he, Giles, might like to take Robert's ashes. Not in a million years! There did not seem to be any relatives until today, when apparently, a distant cousin had turned up and was happy to take the urn. She was a thin, grey little woman sitting at the back. Giles wondered if he should speak to her and offer his condolences. But what would be the point?

Poor Robert, he had been so flamboyant when he first arrived at the theatre. His particular sense of humour had appealed to Giles, the cutting, slightly sarcastic comments he would make about people. But their union had been awkward from the start and Giles had always had the feeling that Robert had another agenda. He was a closed book as far as his emotions were concerned. But then Teddie and Giles had become close once more, and these last six months had been the happiest time of his life. To have a partner to share things with and a job that he adored made for the perfect life. He knew he would never be able to find that again. He had to face the production of *Hamlet* on his own and he was not sure he had it in him any more. Large tears were rolling down his cheeks and Giles hastily wiped them away. He wanted to leave, but the service, such as it was, had begun. Someone sat down next to him and his heart sank. Who would sit down next to a total stranger when there were plenty of empty pews? He tried to shift away but that someone grabbed his arm.

'It's OK, Giles, it's only me, Jeremy. Are you all right? You look as if you want to run away,' he whispered.

Giles looked up and saw Jeremy smiling at him and he let out a huge sigh of relief.

'Oh my God, am I glad to see you. I just can't do this on my own. Thank you for being here. Did you come down by train? How are you going to get back?' he fretted.

'Don't worry about that now. Let's just get through this and then we can go and have a drink somewhere,' replied Jeremy.

In fact, Jeremy was on cloud nine as he was going to meet Eddie this afternoon at some flat in St John's Wood. When Eddie had rung and suggested they meet this Sunday it was ideal, as Jeremy already knew about Robert's cremation from George Delaware, who had called him.

'I am sorry to say we are not going to be able to come to the cremation as Dale and I are away that weekend, abroad. I do so hope you will go, Jeremy, and say a prayer for Robert on our behalf.' It was more a command than a request.

'Yes, of course, I will go,' he promised.

When Jeremy saw Giles sitting all alone, and looking so forlorn he was glad he was there.

After the service, the two men made a hasty retreat, found a pub and sank a couple of vodkas each.

'Poor Robert,' muttered Giles. 'He has died in vain so far. No one seems to want to address this terrible problem of HIV, do they?' He took Jeremy's hand. 'And yet his death has destroyed so many lives around him. Yours and mine, to name but two. Are you coping OK, dear boy?'

Jeremy thought it best to keep his visit to Eddie to himself, but it was difficult not to share his joy because he had been unhappy for so many weeks.

'I am surviving, Giles, but it is very hard. What about you?' he asked.

Giles stared into his vodka then threw it back and ordered another. 'I am bereft, dear boy. Rock bottom. I just don't know how I am going to pull it all together after Christmas.'

'But we have *Hamlet* to look forward to. Please remember, Giles, how important this production is going to be. It is everything you have worked for and it is going to be fantastic. Please, Giles, you have to make it work for the likes of me. I am relying on you to make me a star!'

'You are right, of course, my boy. I will do my best. With your help, I hope?' He looked into Jeremy's face for confirmation. Suddenly Jeremy thought of Sally, how they always talked about their work, and how it should always come first, and he suddenly did feel stronger and more positive.

'Bloody right you will succeed, Giles. Failure is *not* an option. Broken hearts are one thing, but broken dreams are not allowed. We will overcome!'

Jeremy left Giles having one for the road, and boring some poor barman with his version of *Hamlet*, and made his way to the address he had been given in St John's Wood. He arrived outside a rather impressive block of flats which must have been built sometime in the 1930s. He took the lift to the fourth floor and, catching sight of himself in the glass panelling, became aware of just how nervous and excited he was, as he had pink cheeks! He paused at the front door and took a few deep breaths before finally ringing the bell. He then stared straight ahead of him, not moving a muscle, until the door was flung open and Eddie was there before him, alive.

'J, I can't believe it is you at last!' Eddie pulled Jeremy through the door and they closed it with their bodies as they leaned against it to embrace. They kissed long and deep, and when they finally broke away both men were flushed and breathless.

Eddie led Jeremy into a beautiful 1930s-style living room full of period furniture and antiques.

'Wow, this is fantastic. Who does it belong to?' Jeremy

wandered around examining everything and picked up a photo in an Art Deco frame. 'Oh, I see,' he said softly. 'It belongs to your father, doesn't it?' He turned to face Eddie. 'Does that mean he has forgiven you your heinous crimes?' The sarcasm was not lost on his lover.

'I am so sorry about everything, Jeremy. Please let me explain things properly. That's why we are meeting, isn't it?' He turned away, and had a coughing fit. It was a horrible sound and Jeremy suddenly felt frightened.

Eddie went on breathlessly, 'Please, sit down. Would you like a drink or coffee or something?'

'A glass of white wine would be good, thank you,' said Jeremy and he sat down on the edge of one of the perfectly upholstered sofas as though he was waiting to be called into the doctor's surgery.

Eddie brought him the glass of wine and put the bottle in a silver wine-cooler on the side.

'One glass is never enough,' he smiled. He coughed again and it racked his body. Jeremy noticed for the first time that his friend had lost weight.

'Are you ill?' he said curtly, trying to hide his terror at what Eddie was about to tell him.

'Gosh, J, you sound like a headmaster,' Eddie laughed.

'I am sorry, Eddie, but this is agony. You obviously have something to tell me and I am guessing it is not good news, because apart from anything else you look bloody awful. And sorry, I didn't mean . . .' Jeremy could go no further; he could not stop the tears from flowing.

Eddie came and sat beside him and held him. 'Don't, Jeremy, please. Don't make this any harder than it is. I love you so much, it just does not seem right that we cannot be together, but the truth is, my dearest love, I am dying and—'

'*Nooo*, don't say that!' wailed Jeremy. 'You can't die, Eddie! Please don't say that!'

'Listen to me, J, please. This is very important to me and to you. There is nothing we can do. My father will not let me see you again after this. My mother actually arranged this for me. She hates the whole mess but she understands how much I love you and that I need to say goodbye.' Jeremy tried to speak but Eddie stopped him. 'No, please, you must let me finish. I have presented with the first symptoms and now who knows? It could be months or years before the next phase. But the prognosis is not good. I don't want you to spend the next years of your life worrying about when I am going to pop my clogs. You have a fantastic career in front of you, Jeremy, and if you love me you will make sure you do everything in your power to embrace your success. I will hear all about it, believe me. I will be following you all the time. My father will never let us be together and we will never be reconciled. His hypocrisy is beyond belief. The pain he has caused my mother all these years, and now he castigates me! However, it is something we aristocrats have to do . . . stick together. So they will all gather round me and that will be that. It is shit, there is no other word for it. A wasted life, but *please*, Jeremy – promise me you will not waste yours.'

Jeremy sat there on the sofa in his lover's arms and just wanted to die, right there. If there had been a poisoned chalice he would have drunk deep and died happy.

'Do you promise me then?' Eddie's voice hung in the air.

Jeremy shuddered and gathered himself up off the sofa. There was nothing more to say; he was exhausted. He stumbled against a chair and reached out to Eddie, who took his arm and steadied him.

'You will write to me or phone me sometimes?' asked

Jeremy, clutching his stomach as if it were going to drop on the floor. He was just full up with pain and hurt, and wanted to scream his agony to the world.

Eddie held him tight and steered him to the front door. 'I will always love you, Jeremy. You showed me what real love is, and for that I thank you. Please be strong for me, and remember wherever you are I will be watching you.'

They kissed one last time – a gentle, tender kiss – and Jeremy drew strength from his lover and was able to ride the lift down to the ground floor with dignity. He went out into the freezing December evening grateful for the darkness to hide his tears. So many tears and so much pain. Jeremy walked all the way to Euston, by which time it was nine in the evening. He was too cold to care, but once on the last train back to Crewe he started to unthaw and as he grew warmer, his heart grew colder. *Life's a bitch and then you die!* Except the wrong people seem to die, always the wrong people.

He would work hard for Eddie; he would make him proud, and show his fucking father what his son loved about him. He hoped Lord Graham suffered for the rest of his life the guilt of destroying his only son's chance of happiness. Please let Eddie live a long life, prove them all wrong. He was a shining star, he couldn't die!

Chapter 50

Christmas Eve was finally here! Sally woke early with just the same sense of excitement she had had as a child. She was all packed and ready to go. Her parents would be arriving during the day and then they would watch the last show before driving their daughters home for the holiday. Christmas morning in her own bed! It was almost too much to bear, thought Sally happily. The week had flown by, and everyone at the theatre had been in a constant state of goodwill. Presents appeared on dressing tables and the boys bought everyone a chocolate Father Christmas. Sally had organized the girls' presents to the crew and front-of-house staff. She had found a stall in the market which sold homemade soap. So everyone got a little bar of soap in the shape of Santa Claus and a sack of gold money. Chocolate, of course.

Dora had had an early Christmas present in the form of an offer from Nottingham Playhouse for their next season.

'The job that should have been mine,' remarked Sally to Janie as they were ironing costumes.

'Do I detect a hint of the green-eyed monster?' teased Janie.

'No, not really. It's just I wish she showed a bit more

gratitude. Let's be honest, she did lie to the director of Nottingham Playhouse at that repertory conference and lead him to believe he was talking to me! She seems to be blissfully unaware of just how bloody lucky she is. Even the powers that be at *Coronation Street* are willing to wait for her to get her Equity ticket and then give her a job.'

Sally suddenly realized how curmudgeonly she sounded and stopped herself, saying contritely, 'Oh, I am sorry, Janie. I must sound like a right old miserable twisted sister. But each time I give Dora the benefit of the doubt, she goes and does something else. She pinched that business card of the agent Peter Stone that I had left on the kitchen table a while back and rang him and made an appointment to see him. I know she is perfectly entitled to do so, but it is so insensitive of her. She could have asked me first if I minded.'

'And do you mind?' ventured Janie.

'Do you know what? Yes, actually, I do ...' Sally was pleased for Dora, of course, but she could not deny a touch of envy. Her younger sister's life seemed to just progress with such ease. Everything always falling into place.

'I suppose the thing that galls me is that she just takes it all for granted.'

'Oh, come on, Sal. Everyone hits a bad patch eventually and it is how you deal with the knocks that counts.'

'I don't wish her any bad patches,' sighed Sally. 'Just wish she was a bit more grateful. I am sick to death of being the second-class citizen – the sad sister who is always one step behind. I seem to be getting nowhere fast.' Sally was very close to tears and Janie knew it.

'Hang on a minute, girl. You have gone from ASM to leads in three months. Not bad going, is it, eh? I am thrilled you will be playing Sandy in *The Prime of Miss Jean Brodie* – and has not Miss Sarah Kelly hinted that you could be leading the ensemble in *The Boyfriend?*'

Sarah had, indeed, told Sally that she and Giles thought she was the best person for the role of Polly Browne in *The Boyfriend*, the last production of the season. Sally had been thrilled to bits at the time, so why was she feeling so down now?

'Listen, we are all tired and emotional. A day off and some Christmas pud and you will be feeling as right as rain,' advised the ever-optimistic Janie.

On the quiet, Sally was also very worried about Jeremy. He had told her about his trip to London and she had had to admit it was very hard on him.

'You poor thing, it does seem as though the rich close ranks under fire, doesn't it?' she had consoled him. 'All I can say is that time *will* heal. You will survive – and you *must* survive because you have an incredible career ahead of you. A new agent, a role in the West End – what more did you ever dream of? I wish I was so lucky.' Sally couldn't resist her small moment of self-pity.

'Oh, Sally, don't say that. You are doing fine. You have made the right decision to stay at Crewe and play proper parts instead of understudying. It would have driven you mad, and you would have had to put up with Rupert.'

'I suppose you are right,' she replied a little sadly. 'I wonder who will play Ophelia this time?'

'Forget it! Whoever it is will be a one-hit wonder and forgotten about by the time you are accepting your first Emmy. Now come on, let's clear up the Green Room because, let's face it, no one else will.'

Patricia and Douglas Thomas arrived at the theatre just before curtain up on the matinée. Dora and Sally met them with shrieks of delight at the stage door.

'It is so good to see you,' said Sally, running into her dad's arms. 'We have to go and do the show now, but you know how to get to the flat, don't you?'

'Yes, of course,' replied Douglas. 'We can go and start packing the car with Dora's stuff, can't we? Then your mother and I will be at the stage door at four o'clock to take you to tea before the final show. She wants to go and buy some supplies for the journey home as well, I think.'

'OK, then we will see you later,' called Dora over her shoulder, already on the way to the dressing room to get changed. She added to Sally, 'I will never get all my stuff in the car, so do you mind hanging on to some of it until I get a place in Nottingham, then I will come and get it?'

'No, not all,' said Sally, carefully putting on her moustache. 'You know, I will miss being Ratty, but maybe not the facial hair. Perhaps that is why I can't get an agent, because they think I am a hairy actress!' She burst out laughing, and Dora joined in, until they were both laughing so much their make-up was running.

Sally gave her sister a hug and said, 'I will miss you, Dora, even though you have been a pain in the butt. Just try and think about other people sometimes before you go off on one.'

'Yes, sister dear,' Dora giggled. 'I love you too, and I am truly sorry for all the grief I have caused.'

Sally smiled, and they left it at that. However, in her heart of hearts Sally knew that things between them would never be the same again. She would never be able to fully trust Dora, and she knew that Dora would be living on a different planet this time next year. It was sad but true, and Sally surprised herself by her cynicism. Probably best to get on and take everything with a pinch of salt.

The rest of the day went like clockwork. The girls took their parents to the pub for tea, and had pie and chips, and then did the last show to a full house of screaming children. As the curtain fell there was a stampede for the dressing rooms, with poor Heather trying to remind people that they must be back on Boxing Day for the half, at two o'clock.

'Why do I bother?' she shouted over the noise to Sally. 'Have a great Christmas Day, pet.'

Sally went to find Jeremy, who was struggling to the stage door with a huge bag.

'We will see you at Junction Six bright and early on Boxing Day. Have a lovely Christmas Day, my darling.' She gave him a big kiss.

'You too, Sally. I hope Santa brings you something gorgeous!' Then: 'Bye, Gladys, don't eat too many mince pies or you won't fit through the stage door!' Jeremy planted a smacker on the big woman's cheek and was gone.

Sally found her parents waiting by the car which was piled high, but with room for them all to squeeze in.

'I have got all the food and drink with me in the front,' explained Patricia. 'Just ask me when you want something. Now come on, let's get going. I loved your moustache, Sally.'

They all climbed in, and Douglas tooted a farewell to whoever might be listening, and they were off!

The comings and goings on a Saturday night in the theatre were always chaos. No one would have noticed anybody slipping through the big dock doors at the back of the auditorium where all the scenery was kept. Gladys had already gone home and locked the stage door. The remaining crew would switch off all the lights except the safety ones, and then leave through the small door in the dock doors.

Gradually the noise died down, and after the final calls of

'Good night' and 'Happy Christmas' had floated past the stage door, silence fell like a huge blanket over the theatre. The figure in the dark anorak and hood sat for some time in the Royal Box, just listening to the silence. The stage was lit by a vague blue light, casting a sheen across the floor, making it look like a lake. The rows of red velvet seats appeared tiny from the box. The figure brushed the nap of the ledge, and his skin tingled as the velvet pricked his fingertips. A door banged and made him jump but soon there was silence once more. It was a dead silence, with no reverberations, echoes or resonance. The figure closed his eyes and tried to imagine he could hear the audience; the murmuring of an expectant and excited crowd, a laugh ringing out now and then. But there was nothing. The theatre had shut down for the holidays. It was sleeping now, dreaming of all the shows and drama that had filled its walls. It was resting, ready for the next onslaught.

'Life goes on,' murmured the man. He took a swig from the bottle of champagne he had by his side, and coughed as it went down the wrong way. His cough bounced off the walls of the auditorium like a joke from the stage and came back to hit him like a stone, reminding him of the evil that was inside him. He grasped the brass railings of the box until the hacking cough stopped raking across his chest. He was left breathless and feeling sick. He tried another sip of the bottle, this time taking it more slowly. The bubbles made his nose itch and he smiled to himself in the darkness. He reached into his pocket for the envelope, and as he pulled it out, he realized it was all scrunched-up. He laid it on the edge of the box and tried to flatten it out. Then from his other pocket he took the bottle of pills and put them on one of the little gilt chairs. He suddenly clasped hold of the envelope again, thinking that no, it wasn't safe to leave it there. One gust of air would send the missive fluttering down into the stalls below, and it would be lost.

I need a table. He looked around the box. It was like a toy house with the tiny gilt chairs and the heavy brocade curtains either side, held open with gold and silver tassels. Then he spotted a table near the door, beautifully inlaid with pale wood, and carried it down to the front of the box. He placed the pills and the bottle of champagne on it and then sat down again, holding the envelope. Careful not to tear the letter inside, he pulled out the headed notepaper and began to read:

> *Hi, everyone!*
>
> *Well, I certainly messed up, didn't I, but who was to know there would be a bloody virus that could kill you just for having a good time!*
> *The trouble with contracting a terminal disease is that you have to live with it until you die, and I am not prepared to do that. Sorry, guys, but why should I stay alive a bit longer to keep you happy?*
> *Mind you, my father probably can't wait to get rid of me as I am such an embarrassment to the family, but I know Jeremy will be upset, and for that I am truly sorry. J, my darling, you are the one reason I would choose to stay alive. But it would be no life, Jeremy. You taught me how to love another person more than myself and I am so grateful. But now I can see the horizon, I just want to get on with it and not hang around and disintegrate before your very eyes.*
> *Enjoy your lives!*
> *I do love you, Mother, and I am sorry if I have disappointed you.*

I love you, Tilly, and say again: enjoy your life. Grab it and hold it tight. I know you will be OK and I will be watching over you, never fear.

Dad, I do love you and I know you love me. Why couldn't you have been honest? With me, with Mother, with Tilly – but most of all with yourself? There is no shame in loving a man, you must believe that. But what you did was lie and cheat to do it. Please learn from me. Ha! That would be something, wouldn't it? A lesson learned from your promiscuous gay son? But I have been honest, in the end, with everyone, and God knows I have enjoyed my life, albeit short and sweet.

Now there is just this bloody death business, so the sooner I get it over with, the better.

Lots of love to everyone,

Eddie x

The young man carefully folded the letter and put it back in the envelope addressed to Jeremy Sinclair. He laid it on the table, then unscrewed the bottle of pills and tipped them out. With the help of the champagne, he managed to wash down the entire pile of white tablets. Then, feeling tired, he folded his arms on the edge of the balcony, slowly laid down his head and closed his eyes. He wanted to remember his visit to this box with Jeremy. It had been the happiest moment of his life when they first touched each other. He could smell the scent of Jeremy's skin and feel the softness of his lips as he kissed Eddie . . .

Chapter 51

'Ladies and gentlemen, it is with enormous sadness and regret that I have to tell you that Lord Edward Graham's son, Eddie, committed suicide on Christmas Eve, here in this theatre. It is for this reason that the police are still here, as some of you may or may not have noticed. The theatre will be closed until further notice. I apologize for getting you back here, but I did not know myself until last night when I returned from the break. I suggest we use the time wisely though, and start with a read-through of *The Prime of Miss Jean Brodie* in the rehearsal room. Heather, if you would be kind enough to organize some coffee. I will need the whole company to stay in the theatre, as the police may want to speak to you all, at some point, regarding this dreadful business.'

After Giles had left the Green Room, no one spoke for ages. Heather bustled round getting mugs and coffee sorted, but most people just stood or sat in a daze. Suddenly Sally asked, 'Has anyone seen Jeremy?'

There was no answer.

She left the room and rushed to his dressing room where she found him sitting with a bottle of vodka open beside him.

'Oh, Jeremy, I am so sorry. You must be devastated. Come here.' She made to take him in her arms but Jeremy stopped her.

'Please, Sally, I know you mean well, but just leave me alone for now. Giles has given me permission to miss the read-through.'

'But I am worried you . . .'

'Please, Sally – just go. I promise you I am not going to do anything foolish. I just need to absorb this, and work my way through it.'

Sally nodded and backed away. She was desperate to console him, he looked so frail, but she did as she was told and left Jeremy to his mourning.

She called into Wardrobe to see Janie and find out if she knew any more details.

'Well, not really. We only came in this morning. Apparently he was just sitting in the Royal Box dead. They don't know exactly for how long, or anything. There was a suicide note, which the police took away.'

'Oh God, how sad. Anyway, I had better get going. See you later.'

The read-through was a disaster. Jeremy was not there, and nobody was concentrating, so Giles broke early.

'I think we can leave this for today. But I want everyone here tomorrow morning bright-eyed and bushy-tailed.'

Sally managed to grab Giles by the arm as he was leaving. 'Sorry to bother you, Giles, but do you have any more information? I am so worried about Jeremy, you understand. Someone said there was a suicide note?'

'Yes, Sally, of course you are worried. I do understand, but

I can't help really. You need to speak to the police about the suicide note, I should imagine. Come with me and I will introduce you to the man in charge.'

Sally followed Giles down to the stage, where there were police and people in white boilersuits everywhere. He went to find Detective Sergeant Derek Bush, who was in charge. While she was waiting, Sally glanced up at the Royal Box, and the memory of her first encounter with Giles floated into her mind. How happy and excited she had been that day. Giles had looked so grand and formidable up there in his eyrie. Why had Eddie chosen that particular spot to die, she wondered. How unbearable it must be for his loved ones. But not only was he dead, he had killed himself. He had chosen to die. He must have felt so alone.

Sally wondered if Jeremy would blame himself somehow. She must help him to understand it was nothing to do with him. He could not have prevented it.

'But if I hadn't left him on his own! I should have made him come with me, that day I saw him at his father's flat. I knew he was going to end up on his own. Oh Christ, why did I leave him!' he cried.

Sally and Jeremy were sitting in his dressing room. Everyone else had gone to the pub for lunch so it was quiet, and private.

'But, Jeremy, Lord Graham would never have let you take Eddie away. What would you have done, kidnapped him?'

'I know, I know you are right, Sally, but I feel so useless – like I let him down.'

'Jeremy, may I remind you that it was because of Eddie, and his behaviour, that you too could have been facing a death sentence. You haven't let anyone down!'

Jeremy looked at Sally for a few minutes and then got up and gave her a hug.

'You are a very special person, Sally, and a good friend. I can only say these things to you. I knew Eddie would take his life, because from the moment he was diagnosed I could feel it in him, sense his desire to do something positive about the situation. I know that must sound ridiculous because to most people suicide is a very negative response. However, to someone like Eddie, he was being positive. There was no cure for his illness so he would have had to spend the rest of his days waiting for the dreaded signs to appear, warning him of his approaching death. Does anyone want to live like that? I know one day they may find a cure and all the rest of it, but for now Eddie had nothing to do but wait. I have thought a good deal about him while I have been at home, and I have almost cried myself through it, Sally. My poor parents did not know what to make of me, I was so down. I know how lucky I am to be in the clear, and it has made me even more determined now to make a success of my career. I don't need anyone in my life any more. I loved Eddie more than life itself, and I don't regret a single moment I spent with him, but now I am on my own and going to make the best of it.'

He gave Sally another hug and said huskily, 'Come on — let's join the others in the pub.'

Everyone was a bit subdued, and the word was out that Jeremy and Eddie had been an item, so when they arrived at the pub no one quite knew what to say. Jeremy cleared the air by announcing that the drinks were on him, and they were going to toast his lover and wish him well, wherever he was. A big cheer went up and everyone's spirits rose. They were a team and would move on together.

Sally sat in the corner and watched the proceedings. Dora caught her eye and waved to her. Sally smiled and waved back and was reminded that they were back in action again now, so anything could happen. Dora had taken over Christmas Day with her high spirits, and wonderful news. Of course Mum and Dad were absolutely over the moon, and could not believe things had changed so much in just a few months. Sally could not help but feel that she herself had somehow let them down. She had stayed in much the same place, as far as they were concerned. Never mind that she had fallen in love and had her heart broken, discovered that she and her sibling were worlds apart, and decided that maybe she was not cut out to be an actress after all.

When Patricia had come to tuck her up on Christmas Eve, she said, 'I know we joke about things sometimes and you may feel we don't take you seriously enough, but you know you can tell us anything, my darling. We just want you to be happy.'

Happy! Wasn't that what everybody wanted in life? Was Eddie looking for happiness when he popped those pills? Was he searching for happiness when he was partying hard, and taking all those men inside him? Was Sally happy when she woke up beside Rupert?

Yes, I was, I suppose, Sally thought to herself. But I was also happy because deep inside me, I felt good about myself. Surely I can achieve that contentment without having to rely on other people all the time? I am quite content at Crewe, and I am going to enjoy each minute as it happens, and see where I go. As that agent Peter Stone said, it is all luck and karma, and being in the right place at the right time.

'Sorry to interrupt your day dream, sweetie, but I need you to help me clear the wing space for the next show,' Heather said.

'Just coming,' answered Sally and went to find Jeremy.

He was surrounded by the lads so she pulled him to one

side, saying, 'I just wanted to tell you I love you, and that we *can* do this!'

That afternoon, Giles assembled the cast and crew once again to tell them that the police had finished their investigation of the theatre and they were now free to continue their rehearsals. There was a round of applause and people wandered off to sort themselves out and get back to life as normal.

'Oh, Jeremy,' Giles called to him as he was leaving with the others. 'This is for you. The police no longer need it and it is addressed to you.' He handed Jeremy the envelope.

'But what about his family? Surely you should give it to his father?' Jeremy ventured.

'I have tried to contact Lord Graham on several occasions, but to no avail. It has been made very clear to me that neither he, nor the Graham family, want anything to do with me – or the theatre for that matter.' Giles smiled at Jeremy sadly. 'God only knows what is going to happen to us next season when His Lordship's grant is withdrawn.'

'I am sure we can think of something, Giles, and everyone will rally round. Don't give up hope yet, and just think: once *Hamlet* has had rave reviews, you will be flavour of the month!'

'Thank you for your vote of confidence, young man, it is much appreciated.' Giles watched the young actor join the gang, and thought for the umpteenth time how much he missed Teddie. But once again, Lady Luck had not left him completely. He had his production of *Hamlet* to keep him busy and he could do without romance for the time being.

Sally had invited Jeremy to supper at the flat. She had made proper dinner, and the two of them were sitting at the kitchen table finishing their bottle of wine when Jeremy produced the envelope.

'What's that?' asked Sally.

'It's the note Eddie left for me, and I thought I would share it with you.' Jeremy smiled shakily and squeezed her hand. 'I am not sure I could have read it on my own anyway.'

He slipped his finger inside the envelope, took out the sheet of notepaper and began to read his lover's last words aloud.

Chapter 52

April 1983

Sally gazed out across the rooftops of Venice. The beauty of the scene was overwhelming. It was another world. She thought back to Christmas, just three months ago. So much had changed in her life. When the season had finished at Crewe she had retreated home still reeling from Eddie's suicide and Jeremy's despair. She had so wanted to help her dear friend get through this terrible time, but in the end it had to be down to him. They had parted with promises to catch up after a break, Jeremy to his parents' home and Sally to hers. Dora had left to go to Nottingham and suddenly Sally was back to her childhood days being cosseted by her parents.

And then there was Mack. She could not believe how happy she had been to see him. He had come to the house and they had gone for a walk, and to her amazement Sally had poured out all her hopes and fears to him. He had wrapped her up in his love and coaxed her back to her usual sunny self.

She still had not decided what she wanted to do next though, and suddenly fate had taken over.

'I have been offered a three-month tour of Europe to teach and advise on sculpture for a new generation of city-dwellers,' announced Mack one day in the pub. 'God knows what it means, but I get paid to work my way round Europe. Why don't you come with me and give yourself a real break, Sally.'

Sally could not think of one reason not to say yes. And here she was in Venice, looking across St Mark's Square, feeling as if she was in a Canaletto painting. She was the happiest she had ever been in her life, but sometimes a nagging little voice would remind her that she had to decide what she wanted to do with her life. Her career. She suddenly thought of Jeremy and all the conversations they used to have about commitment to the theatre and dedication. She must send him a postcard. Maybe when she got back, she would ring him and see if he wanted to share a pad together. They had discussed it at one point . . .

'Hey, you – come back to bed. I need you.'

Sally turned and looked at the huge double bed, then the head of glossy black hair, beneath which she could see a pair of piercing blue eyes smiling at her.

Domani, domani – tomorrow, tomorrow – what would tomorrow bring?

Final Curtain

Read on to discover
Lynda Bellingham's
first novel

Tell Me Tomorrow

Chapter 1

Hertfordshire, Spring 1910

John and Alice Charles had three sons, loud, strapping lads always up to mischief, but only one daughter. She was called Mary, and she was the youngest of the family. John was the vicar of St James' Church in a small village called Allingham, not far from the historic town of St Albans in the county of Hertfordshire.

It was on a church outing to St Albans that Alice Cooke entered the young would-be curate's rather lonely life, and love blossomed. Alice was the daughter of a wealthy landowner in Buckinghamshire, and her marriage to John was deemed a drop in the social scale. Once it was clear to Alice's parents that she was determined to marry beneath her station, they sent her packing, albeit with a quite substantial dowry. However, Alice never saw her parents again. They regarded her as feckless, and a disappointment, and concentrated their hopes and ambitions on their two sons instead. As the only child of elderly parents who died when he was embarking on his career in the clergy, John was alone in the world. Alice was now abandoned, so the two young lovers made their world themselves, and thanks to Alice's optimistic nature and goodness of heart, between them they created a loving family.

Their daughter Mary had the advantages of being brought up with three brothers – and the disadvantages. She was protected and spoiled, but also very innocent, and unaware of life outside her family. But she had a lively mind and had inherited her mother's warmth and optimism. She loved to learn, and if truth be told she was the brightest of them all. However, life in those days was ruled by the men. Mary had to play a secondary role to her brothers even though she often taught them herself, as school was not something they went to willingly. There was many a day when cries could be heard from the scullery as one or other of the boys was beaten for playing truant.

But not today; nobody was going to be shouted at today. It was Sunday, Mothering Sunday to be precise, and it was a beautiful morning, with the promise of spring in the air. Mary had been waiting for this special day to arrive for ages. She had made a card for her beloved mother and helped her brothers to make one from them. The back door of the scullery was wide open as the girl searched the garden for early snowdrops and budding daffodils to put on her mother's breakfast tray. She could hear a lark showing off in the field behind the house, and paused to listen to the clear notes soaring above her. It was hard not to enjoy the promise of the day, outside here on the step.

But Mary was under a dark cloud that morning. Her mother, Alice Charles, lay upstairs grievously ill with pneumonia.

Mary was only ten years old but was already taking on the

household chores. With her father and three brothers in the house, the work never ended. Mrs Edge came in every day to help. She was a lovely round lady who lived in the village. Her duties covered everything from cooking a hearty tea for Mary and the boys, to arranging all the flowers in the church and leading the ladies of the village in the cleaning of the brass. She was a great comfort to Mary as her mother's illness took hold. The little girl was very much alone as John Charles did not seem able to cope at all with his wife's decline. He had always been a rather distant figure to Mary. He worked very hard, dividing his time between the church and his parish duties, and spent hours shut away in his study. He always had time for his wife, of course, for Alice was the light of his life, and she tried to ensure that the house was calm and tranquil. Not an easy task with three sons around. Now Mary was trying to ease the burden of her mother's care, so that her father could write his sermons, and perform his pastoral duties. But the house had lost its brightness since her mother had taken to her bed.

Mary had spent most of the night beside her mother, tending to her and trying to keep the fever at bay. She had just changed the bed-linen and Alice's nightgown. Having washed the other sweat-soaked sheets by hand and stuffed them through the mangle, she was hanging them out in the morning sunshine to dry. She felt a little faint from lack of sleep but paid no heed. Time enough to sleep when her mother was on the mend.

Back inside the kitchen, she put her posy of flowers in a tiny glass vase and placed it on the tray. Then she went to the range to pick up the heavy black iron kettle that was boiling on the top. She made some tea and spooned plenty of sugar into a cup. Mrs Edge said sweet tea could cure anything. This would make her mother feel better. She was not supposed to touch the heavy kettle, but these were difficult times, and all the child knew for sure was that she had to do her very best. She cut a slice of bread very carefully, with the sharp bread-knife threatening to do her mischief at any moment, and spread some butter and jam on the extra thick slice. How she loved the sweet-smelling sticky jam her mother made. It smelled of summer and strawberries and fun.

She carried the tray upstairs to her mother's bedroom. The curtains were closed and the room was dark and stuffy, and it smelled sour. Mary put down the tray and tiptoed to the bed-side. Alice was propped up against the pillows, her eyes closed, breathing with great difficulty. The little girl took her hand and squeezed it gently.

'Happy Mothering Sunday. I've got your breakfast, Mother. A nice cup of tea, and some bread and jam. Now you must eat it all up to make you strong.'

Alice Charles opened her eyes and smiled wanly at her daughter. 'You are a wonderful nurse, Mary,' she managed to whisper. 'I'll have it in a minute. But first, will you open the drawer in my bedside table, please, dear?'

The little girl did as she was told. Inside the drawer were some lovely lace hankies and a lavender pouch. Mary picked it up and smelled the wonderful fragrance. As she did so, Alice tried to turn her head but the effort was too much. She breathed hard and it caught in her throat as a gasp. Mary was frightened by the sound.

'Mother, please be still,' she implored. 'Please get better.' And she tried in vain to stop the tears that were desperately forcing their way down her cheeks.

Alice drew herself up, praying silently for the strength to do what she had to do, and said, 'Mary, dear, now don't cry. It is going to be fine. Inside that drawer you will find my prayer book. Please pass it to me.'

Mary found the book and put it in her mother's trembling hands. Alice opened the book at the first page and showed it to her daughter.

'Look here – see? I've written you a note. Promise me you will keep this prayer book with you always, and every night when you go to sleep, you will say your prayers and think of me. I'll be watching over you all the time, my dearest daughter. You will have a lot to do, but your father and your brothers need your help. Please don't be sad, I will be with you always in your heart.'

The dying woman made a last superhuman effort as she gasped, 'Now be a good girl and go and call your father to come quickly. I need to speak to him.' Then she fell back on the pillows, exhausted.

To Mary it seemed as if she had fallen asleep.

'Mother, please wake up, you haven't eaten your breakfast.' She shook her mother's arm and it dropped heavily off the bed and just hung there. The little girl slowly backed away from the bed and a scream rose in her throat.

'Father! Come quick!'

The funeral service seemed very long to Mary. She tried hard to sing all the hymns well for her mother, but she wanted to cry all the time. As she sat in a pew with her prayer book clutched in her hands, and her eyes screwed tightly shut, she prayed and prayed to God to make her mother come back. But He didn't. Mary would often talk to Him at night, after that. She never gave up asking, and she always kept her prayer book close by, along with the card she had made that day for her mother.

Mary now became a mother to her brothers even though she was the youngest. It was a lonely life, for her father could offer her little comfort as he was grieving himself, and the boys were busy growing into men. Mrs Edge still came in every day and helped with the chores, but it was clear to everyone in the village that the vicar wanted to be left alone. He performed his duties with care and diligence, but the spark of life had gone out of him.

Mary never really had time to make friends at school because as soon as the bell went, she was off home to cook and clean for the household. But it was not all bad. There was a farm just up the road from the vicarage owned by a couple called Ernest and Olive Cooper. They had two sons of their own who went to school with the Charles boys, and all the lads loved to play on the farm. Haystacks and cowsheds made great hiding places, and every summer the boys would spend long hot days in the fields. For Mary it was a magical place to go and be with all the animals. She loved the smell of Olive's kitchen where there was always an animal of some description in front of the range. Cats, dogs – even baby lambs. One afternoon there was a sheep giving birth and Mary sat with Olive who was keeping an eye on it, because it had been having difficulties. At last the lamb dropped to the ground as Mary watched in awe. The farmer's wife picked up the lamb and placed it under the mother's nose, rubbing it with the afterbirth.

'They need a bit of help sometimes, to understand what it is all about, God bless 'em!' she explained to the little girl.

But the ewe did not want to know. She butted the still wet and bloody lamb, and walked away. Mary was so distressed to see this that she burst into tears.

'Don't fret yourself, dearie,' said Olive kindly. 'I will take the lamb indoors and put it by the fire, and you can help me feed it by hand.'

Sure enough, they carried the lamb indoors and soon it was lying in Mary's lap in front of the fire, while she fed it from a glass baby bottle. It was love at first sight. Mary was round at the farm every minute she was free. The lamb grew bigger and bigger each day. Mary called her Alice after her mother. Her brothers teased her mercilessly and ran round her singing the old nursery rhyme:

> *'Mary had a little lamb*
> *Its fleece was white as snow.*
> *And everywhere that Mary went*
> *The lamb was sure to go.'*

She even took it to school one day to show her class. Mary could never quite get over the way the mother sheep had rejected and abandoned her baby, but the farmer's wife was very matter-of-fact about it. She said it happened quite often.

'But how could you not love your baby?' whispered Mary.

'Well, there are some women as have the same problem, dearie. There's naught you can do about it though. You can't *make* people love you.'

Having three brothers meant that Mary was always learning all sorts of things, not all of them good either. They taught her to spit and she was really good at it. In addition, she could skim a stone across the pond with the best of them and ride a horse and drive a cart like a champion. Her happiest memories were of sitting on the hay cart at the end of a hot summer's day. The sun would be setting as they rolled back to Coopers Farm full of fresh air and cider and homemade pies. The boys would be fighting and scrapping on top of the hay like young lion cubs. She would sit up front with her eldest brother Joseph, lulled by the swing of the horses' rumps in front of her and the jangling of the harness and the screeching of the bats swooping around them in the dusk.

As they reached the farm gates, the last streaks of the red sunset collapsed on the horizon, and darkness would fall. The boys would walk Mary back to the vicarage and then they would go to the pub. The landlord of the Wheatsheaf in Allingham was well aware that the boys were not only too young to be drinking but also the vicar's sons, so the boys were given non-alcoholic ginger beer and big plates of shepherd's pie. At home, Mary would creep in and check on her father, who was usually sitting at his desk preparing a sermon or writing letters to do with parish matters. Sometimes she would find him fast asleep with his head on his arms. The Reverend Charles made Mary feel a little frightened because he was always sad and often stern with them. He just could not give his children the affection they needed, and while the boys had each other for comfort, it made the girl miss her mother so much, especially at bedtime when she could remember so vividly her tender embrace as she tucked Mary in, with loving words to help her dream wonderful things. Just before she fell asleep, Mary would remember her mother's words and slip out of bed to kneel on the floor and say her prayers, because she knew her mother was watching.

One morning Mary got out of bed and was horrified to see blood on the bed-sheets and on her nightdress. She checked herself all over for cuts and could find nothing wrong. In the bathroom, she suddenly felt her stomach contract in pain. She sat down on the lavatory and bent over to ease the cramps, but felt a rush of liquid between her legs and heard it splash into the bowl below. Looking down, she cried out in panic as the water in the bowl turned pink. Sobbing now with fear and disbelief, she grabbed a flannel and held it between her legs. What was happening to her?

There was a knock on the door and she heard Joseph's voice outside. 'Mary? Come on, girl, we want our breakfast. What are you doing in there?'

Mary tried to rise from the seat, but another trickle of blood stopped her in her tracks. She called out, 'Joe, something dreadful has happened. I am bleeding and I think I am dying. Please fetch the doctor.'

As a young man of nineteen, Joseph had already picked up a good deal of knowledge about the opposite sex. However, it was one thing to discuss the female anatomy with his friends, but quite another to speak of such delicate matters with his sister.

But he knew someone who could help. Telling his sister to stay calm and to hold on for a few minutes while he fetched help, Joseph sped off to Dr Jeffreys' house two streets away, and banged on the door. The doctor's wife, Lorna, answered his knock. She was a trained nurse and often stood in for her husband when he was too busy to deal with minor ailments that arose during surgery hours.

Blushing, Joseph explained to her what he thought was Mary's problem. Lorna Jeffreys was very understanding, and quite impressed by this young man's grasp of the sensitivity of the situation. Fetching her coat and hat, and an old but clean sheet, she followed Joseph back to the vicarage, where poor Mary was still closeted in the bathroom. Joseph led the nurse upstairs and tapped on the door.

'Mary, dear, don't panic,' he called. 'Mrs Jeffreys is here to help you. Please open the door. I will go downstairs and make us all a cup of tea in the meantime, and don't worry about breakfast. I will see to everything.'

Once Mary had heard her brother go downstairs, she opened the bathroom door and Lorna was soon attending to her, helping her bathe, showing her how to cut up and make a cloth pad and fetching her clean clothes from the bedroom. At the same time she was giving the poor girl a welcome lesson on the female anatomy.

'You must think me very foolish,' said Mary, as Mrs Jeffreys explained about her monthly cycle. 'I am so sorry to cause you all this bother. I just had no idea what was happening to me. Mother died two years ago now and my education mostly consists of housekeeping and reading books that my father suggests to me. There has been no room for girlish talk or another friend or their mother to teach me about such things.'

'Oh, you poor child,' said Lorna. 'Please don't apologize. It is a very natural thing to be worried when you start your cycle. But all is well now – and if you ever need to ask me anything again, anything at all, please do not hesitate to come and see me. I am very happy to talk to you at any time.'

With that the doctor's wife packed her bag and was gone, leaving Mary feeling as if her life had changed forever, and she was still not quite sure why.

Life went on and Mary toiled from dawn till dusk in the vicarage. She was quite content with her life, however, and loved nothing better than to see everyone round the table of an evening, eating the food she had cooked and laughing and animatedly discussing things going on in the world. She still visited the farm all the time to see Alice, her pet sheep. Mr Cooper suggested they might let her ewe have a lamb of its own one day soon.

The Charles boys were finding their feet now. Brother Joseph had been away in London studying to become an accountant and would come home on his rare leaves full of stories of drinking all night and dancing till dawn. Joseph was the only one of the three boys who had left home, albeit temporarily. Reginald was still at school and studying very hard. He had a rather serious side to his nature and his father had great hopes that he would follow him into the Ministry.

John Charles remembered his own years of study with great fondness, even though he had lost his parents so young. His meeting with Alice had changed his life completely. Not just because of her sunny disposition and warm and caring spirit, but due to her inheritance. Although John vowed he would never touch his wife's money, Alice had persuaded him to buy their first home – a small terraced house in St Albans – as a means of securing their future. When they left to take up residence in the vicarage at Allingham, the couple did not sell the house but found a lodger and his family. And to this day, the rent still provided extra income for the family – a welcome boost to the Reverend Charles's modest stipend.

Alice had turned the sombre vicarage into a house full of light and joy, and the sound of happy children. John Charles missed his wife with every fibre of his being every day of her passing.

Stephen was the youngest of the boys and closest to Mary. There were only three years between them. He shared her love of animals and the two of them spent all their spare time at Coopers Farm. Recognizing the lad's love of farming, Ernest Cooper encouraged him to learn all he could about animal husbandry. One day, as they were sitting in the farm's big welcoming kitchen, Stephen announced that he wanted to be a vet when he left school.

When he told his eldest brother of his hopes and dreams, Joseph gave him a friendly punch on the arm and said, 'That's a fine ambition to have, young Stephen, but beware you don't get led astray like me and spend too much time in the pub instead of attending to your studies.'

Their father had just quietly entered the room and overheard this – and they fell silent, waiting for a reproof. But he hardly seemed to see them and just turned and went out again without a word. Mary ran after him to make sure he had everything he needed. She hated to see her father so lost. When she returned to the kitchen, the boys had already forgotten the interruption and were laughing and joking as Joseph continued his tales of life in the big city.

One day, Joseph came home with a friend called Henry Maclean. Henry was in the Army and talked about how there was going to be a war soon, with the Hun, and everyone would have to fight for their country. All the brothers sat round the kitchen table listening to him and drinking beer, which Mary served them. She could only feel dread at the thought of a Europe at war, but the boys were bright-eyed and full of plans to join up. She was secretly entranced by Henry, who seemed different from her brothers somehow. More sophisticated and well-groomed. He had beautiful sandy hair that flopped in his eyes, and he had to keep brushing it out of the way as he talked. His voice was very mellow and he was well-spoken, but not too posh.

When Henry left that night, to return to his regiment, he squeezed Mary's hand and gave her a kiss on the cheek. The spot burned from the touch of his lips. She was so young, but already she felt the catch in her belly, the tightness in her throat – and the pain in her heart.

Henry Maclean was proved right. War did come – and it

spread across Europe like a huge black cloud, covering every-thing in a net of death and destruction. Hundreds of thousands of lives were lost. Stephen Charles was killed in battle, blown up in a German attack on his regiment, three months after he arrived in Passchendaele. Joseph somehow managed to survive but came home a broken man. The carnage he had witnessed left him shell-shocked and staring into a bottle of whisky. Reginald took all the pain and suffering as a sign that he should follow his calling and enter the Church – much to the delight of his father. The Reverend John Charles went straight to his wife's grave to share the good news with her.

Although devastated by the news of Stephen's death, John had somehow found a new strength during the war. He had worked tirelessly, travelling from village to village to take ser-vices in times of need; many of the clergy had joined up to provide spiritual support for the soldiers and to work with the wounded. Often with Mary at his side, Reverend Charles would seek out bereaved families and offer his help and com-fort.

Mary herself felt that she had been pretty much deserted by everyone. She mourned her brother's death and prayed for his soul to that same God who had taken her beloved mother from her. She shed many bitter tears. But life had to go on and there was so much to do and so many people in need that she had to push her own hurt to the back of her mind and just get on with life. She worked with the Red Cross, helping to care for wounded soldiers, and she also taught classes in the village school when necessary. She grew up very quickly, as did so many young people at that time.

One summer evening in 1919, Mary was picking strawberries in the garden when she heard a motor car. This was a rare occurrence. She knew no one who owned a car except the doctor. She ran out to the front of the house and saw Joseph, looking very much the worse for wear, slumped in the front passenger seat of a Bentley. At the wheel was Henry Maclean. He looked just the same as always, if a little tired and lined around the eyes. Mary's heart skipped a beat. Joseph stumbled out of the car and staggered up the garden path, waving his arms in the air and attempting to sing 'It's a Long Way to Tipperary'.

'Joseph, calm down! What are you doing here? Whose car is that?' she asked, dancing excitedly round the two young men as they walked into the house.

'Got any of that homemade sloe gin, Mary?' Joseph hiccupped and fell into the nearest chair.

'I think you have already had quite enough,' she retorted.

'Oh, come on, old girl, don't be such a killjoy. Poor Henry here needs a drink. He has fought a war, for God's sake!'

Mary turned to Henry, who was standing in the doorway with his hat in his hand looking rather bemused.

'I am so awfully sorry,' she said shyly. 'Please do come and sit down. Of course I will fetch you a drink, and some food maybe? You look like you could do with a good meal inside you.'

'That would certainly be very welcome. Thank you, Mary.' He gave her a huge smile and her legs went quite wobbly.

An hour later, Henry and Mary were tucking into homemade soup and bread and cheese, followed by bowls of strawberries just picked from the garden.

'Oh my God, this is heaven,' said Henry through mouthfuls of food. Joseph was sprawled on the sofa now, practically asleep. He was red-eyed and unshaven and stank of whisky.

'I have made a bed up for you in Stephen's room. If you

don't mind, that is, sleeping in his room because he . . .' Mary stopped and felt the tears fill her eyes. She hurriedly left the room and went into the kitchen to compose herself. She was leaning on the sink wiping away her tears with her apron when Henry came to find her.

'Please don't worry,' he said gently. 'It is so hard for everyone. We have lost so many of our friends and loved ones. Joe only gets drunk because he is grieving so much.'

Mary looked into Henry's eyes and could see the pain. 'Was it very bad?' she whispered. Henry didn't answer for a long moment and seemed to be fighting with himself for control.

'Yes,' was all he said, and then he took her in his arms and kissed her. Long and hard. Needing to feel her softness, her goodness and her innocence.

They stood absolutely still, holding each other. Mary wanted the moment to last forever, but it was broken by the sound of Joseph's snores from the other room.

'We'd better get him into bed,' she said, gently breaking away from Henry's arms. 'Would you be kind enough to help me?'

'Of course, come on.' Henry led the way and the two of them hauled Joseph off the sofa and somehow managed to push and heave him upstairs to his room, where Henry virtually threw him onto the bed. Joseph moaned and turned on his side and was fast asleep again before they had reached the door. They laughed and turned to go downstairs. A moment held between them. What now?

There was a bang from the front door downstairs and the Reverend Charles called out, 'Hello? Anybody home? Mary, where are you?'

Mary quickly moved away and went to the top of the stairs, calling out, 'I am here, Father. Henry and I have been putting

Joe to bed.' She ran down to give her father a hug and turned to indicate Henry as he came down to join them.

'Hello, my boy, good to see you home safe and sound,' the minister said. 'Terrible business – thank God it is all over at last. Are you staying the night? Has Mary fed you?'

'Mary has done us proud in every way, sir. She has kindly offered me a bed, and if you will excuse me, I will retire to it now. It has been a long day. Goodnight, Mary, and thank you for everything. Goodnight, sir.' He turned to go up the stairs and Mary put her hand on his arm.

'Wait, let me get you a towel.' She went to fetch it and her father moved off to the kitchen in search of his supper.

Mary came back with a clean towel and handed it to Henry, her eyes never leaving his face.

'Thank you.' He leaned in and softly kissed her on the lips before turning slowly and climbing the stairs. He might have been going to the moon. Mary felt so bereft. What could she do to keep him close?

'My dear, have you got my dinner ready?'

'Coming, Father,' came her reply.

After he had finished his supper, John Charles left the table, kissed his daughter goodnight, and retired to his study, where he shut the door.

Mary cleared away the dishes and went out into the back garden. It was a beautiful summer's night. The sky was so clear she could see every single star.

'Twinkle, twinkle little star . . .' Mary whispered to herself and she looked up at the window of Stephen's bedroom, as if she could transport herself to where Henry lay asleep. At the thought of him, a tremor ran through her entire body. She felt as if she was on fire. What was happening to her?

Sensing movement behind her, she turned – straight into

Henry's arms. He held her very close and she could smell him. Touch his skin with her lips. She caught her breath and tried to look at him but that meant pulling away, and she didn't want to do that. She wanted to stay close to him forever. Oh, but what about her father? She let out a little gasp of fright.

'What is it?' Henry asked.

'My father is in his study. He must not see me this way.'

'He just went to bed. I heard his door shut. I was lying awake thinking of you. I couldn't sleep, Mary. I had to hold you once again.'

Henry took her chin in his hand and slowly pressed his lips to hers. Oh so gently, did his tongue prise her lips apart, and play against her teeth. Oh so gently, did his tongue go deeper, teasing her tongue to respond. She seemed to be melting into his arms her body pressed into his, as he lifted her up in his arms and carried her towards the little summerhouse at the bottom of the garden. Never letting his lips leave hers for a moment, he lowered her onto the garden seat and started to unbutton her dress. Mary could feel nothing but the beating of her heart and a sound like rushing water in her head.

As he kissed her, Henry's hand moved down to touch her breast and then her nipple. He teased it between his fingers, making it hard, and Mary let out a moan of pleasure. Could anything be more wonderful than this? Henry had lifted her dress now and was exploring beneath it. He ran his fingers, feather light, up the inside of her thigh, pausing to stroke the soft skin above her stocking top. Her body jerked involuntarily as he found her secret place. She could not control the waves of ecstasy and opened herself to his fingers as they gently pushed into her warm moist self. With this exquisite sensation, her head lost the battle for logic or reason; her innocent young body responded naturally to his touch, to his closeness, and her very being demanded to be satisfied.

Her legs fell open to take Henry's body between her thighs. Her hands instinctively found his hard erect penis and fondled it. The anticipation was unbearable. She was gasping with need. And suddenly he was inside her, pushing urgently into her warmth and wetness. There was no pain, just the pleasure of being full up with his manhood. He moved and she moved with him. It was so natural, both these young bodies wanting affirmation of life after so much death. As their passion grew, their lovemaking became more intense and he penetrated deep and hard into her, touching her to the core. She followed his rhythm, and felt him spurt into her, her muscles clasping him as if her life depended on it. She let out a cry of pure joy and held him to her until they were spent. He looked down at her and smiled to reassure her all was well. She took his face in her hands and kissed every inch of it, laughing and crying all at once.

Eventually, Henry got up and dressed himself, then helped Mary gather herself together. They did not speak a word as they walked back to the house, under the starry sky, holding hands. Henry kissed her lightly at the kitchen door and went to his room. Mary stood at the kitchen sink drinking a cup of water and feeling every bone and muscle in her body tingle. This was what it felt like to be alive, she knew it! She wanted it to last forever.

But it was not to be. The next morning, when Mary woke up, Henry had gone. Joseph explained to her that he had made his apologies, but said he had to drive back to London to attend a job interview with a City bank. He sent his thanks to Mary for everything, and hoped they would all meet again soon. Mary had to run out of the room, so as not to give herself away. She raced into the garden and was violently sick under a hedge. A terrible blackness swept over her as she seemed to understand her fate.

Three months later, she was sat in front of Dr Jeffreys, white-faced and trembling, as he gave her the results of her night of passion. A baby, due to be born in the spring. Mary left the surgery in a daze. Despite the warm summer sunshine she was shivering and her legs felt weak; she had to sit down on the bench outside the doctor's house.

'Hello, Mary. Are you feeling all right, dear?' Lorna Jeffreys was looking down at her. The doctor's wife remembered so clearly their shared secret of all those years ago – Mary's ignorance of her body. Now she could see the naked shame in the young woman's eyes and her heart went out to her.

Putting her arms round her and lifting her up, Lorna said quietly, 'Come on, let's go and have a cup of tea, shall we?' She led Mary round the side of the house to the living quarters at the back of the surgery.

Neither woman spoke until they were sitting at the kitchen table with their tea in front of them.

Lorna broke the silence: 'Do you remember all those years ago, when I said that if ever there was anything I could do to help, you should call on me?'

Mary sighed deeply and searched Mrs Jeffreys' face. The woman had obviously guessed what was wrong, but there was no reprimand in her voice. No disapproval in her gaze. Mary started to cry. She felt so alone and so ashamed. What could she do? She was a fallen woman. This news would surely kill her father.

Charles had grown quite frail in the last few months, so much so that they had called Reginald down from his Theological College in Hendon in North London. The family hoped that it might be possible for Reginald to do his curate training with his father, at St James' Church in Allingham.

The Reverend John Charles was highly regarded in the Diocese, and the Bishop of St Albans was a close friend. The proposal had been discussed, and as things in the local parishes were still a little disordered since the war ended, it was agreed that John Charles could do with the help, and to have his son close by was the best thing to do for all concerned.

It was a comfort to think that her father would soon have Reg to support him. As Mary's tears slowly subsided, she was able to drink her tea and think more clearly.

'Is there anything I can do to help you?' asked Lorna, taking Mary's hand.

'No, not really. But thank you for all your kindness to me. I don't deserve it.' Mary stood up and made for the door. Turning, she told Mrs Jeffreys, 'I am going to talk to my brother Reginald; he will know what to do for the best. Thank you again. Goodbye.'

Mary walked home, consumed with her guilt and shame and fear. Her father must never find out. How could he ever forgive her? She thought of her dear mother and the tears sprang afresh. How could she have been so foolish? Reg would be coming home in the next few days to make arrangements for his training, and until then, she would have to keep her own counsel.

On reaching the vicarage, Mary went straight to her bed, telling her father that she had a headache. She hated to tell him a lie but needs must. Yet another sin to add to her long list. Before getting into bed, Mary prayed to her mother and begged her forgiveness. She held her prayer book to her heart and fell asleep with it in her hands.

'It's all right, I will help you. We will get through this together,' Reginald told his sister as he handed her a cup of tea; he and Mary were sitting in the front parlour. The vicarage was empty as John Charles had gone to visit a sick parishioner. Mary had poured out her story to her brother and was now once again collapsed in tears in her seat.

Although Reginald had always been the most serious of the brothers, he possessed a very kind heart. Deep down, there was a romantic streak inside him and he was currently in the throes of falling in love, thanks to a meeting with a girl called Leonora Matheson, who came to his college for Bible Studies. But now was not the time to confess these feelings to his poor dear sister.

'Leave things with me and let me have a think,' he said, handing Mary a large handkerchief so she could blow her nose. 'I have an idea already that could be a solution but I need to find out more. Take heart, dear Mary. God will find a way and He will forgive you. Now stop crying and go and make yourself busy.'

Mary did as she was told, but nothing could take away her deep shame and sense of foreboding. What did life have in store for her now, she wondered.

Diversity in Organizations

SECOND EDITION

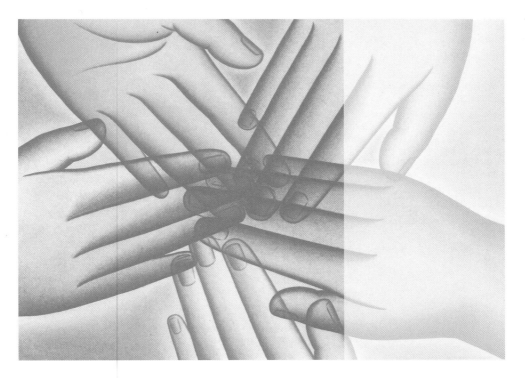

Myrtle P. Bell
UNIVERSITY OF TEXAS, ARLINGTON

SOUTH-WESTERN
CENGAGE Learning™

Australia • Brazil • Japan • Korea • Mexico • Singapore • Spain • United Kingdom • United States

SOUTH-WESTERN
CENGAGE Learning™

Diversity in Organizations, Second Edition, International Edition

Myrtle P. Bell

Vice President of Editorial, Business: Jack W. Calhoun

Editor-in-Chief: Melissa Acuna

Acquisitions Editor: Scott Person

Developmental Editor: Jeffrey Hahn

Editorial Assistant: Ruth Belanger

Marketing Manager: Jonathan Monahan

Content Project Management: PreMediaGlobal

Frontlist Buyer, Manufacturing: Arethea Thomas

Senior Marketing Communications Manager: Jim Overly

Production Service: PreMediaGlobal

Senior Art Director: Tippy McIntosh

Cover Image: iStockphoto (B/W Image); Shutterstock Images/Nicemonkey (Color Image)

Rights Acquisitions Specialist, Image: Deanna Ettinger

Right Acquisitions Specialist, Text: Sam A. Marshall

Library of Congress Control Number: 2011923665

International Edition:

ISBN-13: 978-1-111-82257-6

ISBN-10: 1-111-82257-3

Cengage Learning International Offices

Asia
www.cengageasia.com
tel: (65) 6410 1200

Australia/New Zealand
www.cengage.com.au
tel: (61) 3 9685 4111

Brazil
www.cengage.com.br
tel: (55) 11 3665 9900

India
www.cengage.co.in
tel: (91) 11 4364 1111

Latin America
www.cengage.com.mx
tel: (52) 55 1500 6000

UK/Europe/Middle East/Africa
www.cengage.co.uk
tel: (44) 0 1264 332 424

Represented in Canada by Nelson Education, Ltd.
tel: (416) 752 9100/(800) 668 0671
www.nelson.com

Cengage Learning is a leading provider of customized learning solutions with office locations around the globe, including Singapore, the United Kingdom, Australia, Mexico, Brazil, and Japan. Locate your local office at: **www.cengage.com/global**

For product information: **www.cengage.com/international**
Visit your local office: **www.cengage.com/global**
Visit our corporate website: **www.cengage.com**

AVAILABILITY OF RESOURCES MAY DIFFER BY REGION. Check with your local Cengage Learning representative for details.

Printed in the United States of America
1 2 3 4 5 6 7 15 14 13 12 11

To Earnest, so aptly named.

Brief Contents

Table of Contents

Preface

In the years since I wrote the first edition of *Diversity in Organizations*, many significant events related to diversity have occurred. In 2008, the United States elected its first Black president, the man identified as "Barack Obama, U.S. Senator" in the multiracial chapter of the first edition. Although my prescient Goolsby Leadership students in the spring of 2006 referred to him as "the hope of our generation," when I wrote that feature in 2005, I had no thought that Senator Obama would be elected U.S. president. That he was elected was momentous in and of itself, as were the diverse backgrounds of the people who voted for him.

Obama's election led to claims of a "postracial" America, which have not yet been realized. Even so, the diversity of those who voted for him does speak of immense progress from the point where few believed, even in a time of recession and two wars, that a Black man would ever be elected U.S. president or that women would also be seriously considered candidates during the election.

As I began writing the second edition and investigating the status of each racial and ethnic group, women and men, people with disabilities, and other non-dominant group members, it became even more clear that the need for diversity research and study remains strong. Blacks continue to have nearly twice the unemployment rate of Whites—a problem that persists even at the same education levels. Residential segregation and the fact that Blacks with similar credit histories, personal backgrounds, and in similar residential locations were more likely to be given subprime loans help explain the current higher foreclosure rates among Black Americans.[1] Although women became the majority in the workforce as men's jobs were lost during the recession, the wage gap remains tenacious. Sexual harassment, discrimination, and segregation continue to be severe and pervasive problems for working women. Arizona passed a law that seemed to support racial profiling of Latinos. Employer targeting of Hispanics for discrimination and harassment, while at the same time preferring them to and discriminating against Blacks and Whites for some low-wage, often exploitative jobs continues. Although gays and lesbians have served admirably in the military for years, "Don't Ask, Don't Tell" continued to be the law until very recently, and challenges to it continued to be met with tenacious resistance. For every non-dominant group some disparities persist, and, in some cases, have worsened since the first edition. It is no surprise that discrimination

---

[1] Rugh, J. S., & Massey, D. S. (2010). "Racial Segregation and the American Foreclosure Crisis." *American Sociological Review.* 75(5): 629–651.

charges filed with the EEOC reached their highest number ever, in multiple categories.[2]

Because most people who experience discrimination do not sue, other motivations for fair treatment, non-discrimination, and diversity and inclusion remain important. As a result, organizations are continuing to emphasize diversity and inclusion in recruiting and marketing, funding employee resource groups, supporting diverse family units, and in many other ways. There is still much work to be done, but there is still progress amid retrenchment and there is still hope for a better, fairer, more just future.

CHANGES TO THIS EDITION

As was the first edition, this edition of *Diversity in Organizations* is research-based, using hundreds of articles, chapters, and books from the fields of management, sociology, psychology, economics, criminal justice, and health as resources. This edition contains a general updating of the content of all chapters, including data on population, participation, and employment, legislation, litigation, relevant research, and features. Objectives and Key Facts in each chapter have been updated as well. This edition emphasizes diversity and inclusion and the degree to which "different voices of a diverse workforce are respected and heard"[3] and offers more insight into implications for organizations interspersed throughout the chapters. Each chapter includes new examples of litigation under diversity-related laws, including those recently passed, and new relevant empirical research. Chapter 7 now includes an interview of the

chief diversity executive at a major corporation. The discussion of theories has been concentrated in Chapter 2, which includes more psychological theories and processes that affect diversity and research evidence on reducing bias in selection. Section II has been reorganized such that the topics of sex and gender, work and family, and sexual orientation follow each other, improving flow and cohesion. Chapter 16, "International Diversity and Facing the Future," includes more research on diversity issues in an international context and contains a feature essay focusing on the perspective of an international organization on global diversity and inclusion.

Key changes in this edition include:

- Added an adaptation of Cox's Interactional Model of the Impact of Diversity on Individual Career Outcomes and Organizational Effectiveness.
- New research on structured interviews to reduce similarity bias.
- Discussions of new legislation, including the Genetic Information Nondiscrimination Act (2008), Americans with Disabilities Amendments Act (2008), and Lilly Ledbetter Fair Pay Act (2009).
- The inclusion of research on the effects of diversity in the judiciary on judges' decisions.
- New sections on immigrant Blacks and on Blacks and Hispanics.
- New features on Surgeon General Regina Benjamin and Supreme Court Justice Sonia Sotomayor.
- New research on race and color discrimination across races.

---

[2] http://www.eeoc.gov/eeoc/statistics/enforcement/charges.cfm, accessed November 23, 2010.
[3] Pless, N. M., & Maak, T. (2004). "Building an Inclusive Diversity Culture: Principles, Processes, and Practices." *Journal of Business Ethics*, 54: 129–147.

- New research on discrimination and health care.
- Updated information on participation and employment of older workers since the economic recession.

ACKNOWLEDGMENTS

I thank Jeff Hahn, Scott Person, and the staff at Cengage and its affiliated and support organizations for their patience and perseverance throughout the development of this edition. I thank Pradhiba Kannaiyan and the copy editors at PreMediaGlobal for their editorial assistance. I am especially grateful to Jennifer Ziegler at Cengage, and Margaret Trejo at Trejo Production for their outstanding last minute work and conscientiousness.

I am grateful to the many colleagues who reviewed and offered valuable feedback on the book:

Ronald Bolender
Mount Vernon Nazarene University

Gwendolyn M. Combs
University of Nebraska–Lincoln

Leon Fraser
Rutgers Business School

Diane Hagan
Ohio Business College

Brenda Johnson
Cleveland State University

Hazel-Anne Johnson
Rider University

Beth Livingston
Cornell University

Darcel Lowery
Rutgers University

Sheryl Moinat
University of Wisconsin, River Falls

Dyan Pease
Sacramento City College

Janet Sayers
Massey University

Although not listed by name, I appreciate the many members of the Gender and Diversity in Organizations division of the Academy of Management who offered feedback and support for the first edition, along with suggestions for improving this one. Those colleagues and friends continue to examine important questions in their research, providing the research evidence that is the foundation for this book. I am grateful that they are committed to doing work that matters.

I thank the Diversity Connections Consortium and Terry Howard, its founder and fuel, for keeping me thinking, growing, and encouraged to continue this work. I am fortunate to belong to such a group of people so passionate about equality, diversity, and inclusion and thank Ed McFalls for introducing me to the group.

Many thanks are due to Frank McCloskey, the inaugural vice president of diversity at Georgia Power, for agreeing to be featured in Chapter 7 and for helping me focus on what mattered most to say. I appreciate Josefine Van Zanten, vice president of diversity and inclusion at Shell, for her willingness to share how Shell sees diversity from a global perspective. Thanks also go to Karsten Jonsen for making the connection.

The Society for Human Resource Management and Dr. Shirley Davis, director,

Global Diversity & Inclusion, twice funded a gathering of 100 Global Diversity Thought Leaders to discuss the future of the field and efforts to establish formal credentials for diversity professionals. I am honored to have been part of such a group. As the respected organization that validates the credentials of human resources professionals (e.g., PHR, SPHR, GPHR), having a SHRM certification for those who do diversity work would certainly help bring credibility and legitimacy to the field. I hope SHRM is successful in this important work.

Very special appreciation goes to my wonderful students at UT Arlington, who keep their "diversity hats" on and who e-mail me years later to let me know what a difference the book and course have made for them and to share their continued diversity learning experiences. I thank them for enrolling in my Diversity in Organizations course, for sharing their ideas, questions, and hopes, and for going out into the world of work to make things better, fairer, and more inclusive, helping their organizations, employees, and customers.

I thank Laura Ratcliff Lenoir, Henry Toney, Mingo Johnson, Geylon and Minnie Johnson, and many other ancestors whose lives, love, and sacrifice helped pave the way for me to do this work. I am grateful that my mother, Iris Johnson, instilled in me the value of knowing and opening our home to people from various parts of the world and various parts of town. My heart is open to love and concern for both similar and very different others as a result of early, frequent, and continued lessons from her. Daphne Berry, through the lens of her education in feminist theory and political economy, opened my eyes to aspects of diversity that I may otherwise never have seen; the issues are much bigger than individual acts of discrimination and exclusion. My daughter and son are my inspiration to continue this work, in hopes for a better future and world for them and those who are yet to be born. My husband, Earnest, encouraged me to write this edition and the first, and provided every support imaginable, including well-timed words and cups of coffee when I felt too exhausted to continue. Without him, my work and my life as I know it would not be. Lastly, but most important, I am especially grateful to God for providing me with the tools, courage, and privilege to do this work.

ANCILLARIES

The Instructor's Resource CD includes an instructor's manual, teaching notes, and suggested testing options. PowerPoint files are also available for each chapter of the textbook.

SECTION I

Introduction, Theories, and Legislation

Yuri Arcurs/Shutterstock.com

Introduction

Chapter Objectives

After completing this chapter, readers should have a firm understanding of the importance of diversity in organizations. Specifically, they should be able to:

- ❏ *explain what "diversity" encompasses in the United States and the considerations used in determining the relevant diversity concerns in other countries.*

- ❏ *discuss the historical background for the study of diversity in organizations.*

- ❏ *define key diversity terms, including types of discrimination, productive characteristics, and inclusion.*

- ❏ *discuss research supportive of the individual and organizational benefits of diversity.*

Key Facts

Despite extraordinary corporate and media attention paid to diversity in the past thirty years, discrimination, inequality, and exclusion persist in organizations.

Valuing diversity can benefit organizations in the areas of cost, resource acquisition, marketing, creativity, problem solving, and system flexibility.

If an organization develops a reputation for valuing all types of employees, it will become known as an employer of choice, in which workers from all backgrounds feel they have the opportunity to work, grow, and be treated fairly.

Working in and learning in environments with people who are different can benefit individuals through intellectual engagement, perspective taking, and greater understanding of the implications and benefits of diversity.

A supportive climate for diversity results in benefits for individuals and organizations, but diversity without a supportive climate can result in negative consequences.

3

Introduction and Overview

What Is Diversity?

In this book, **diversity** is defined as real or perceived differences among people in race, ethnicity, sex, age, physical and mental ability, sexual orientation, religion, work and family status, weight and appearance, and other identity-based attributes that affect their interactions and relationships.[1] These areas are differences that are based on power or dominance relations between groups, particularly "identity groups," which are the collectivities people use to categorize themselves and others.[2] **Identity groups** are often readily apparent to others, strong sources of personal meaning, and related to historical disparities among groups in treatment, opportunities, and outcomes.

The definition of diversity includes the terms *real* and *perceived* to acknowledge the social constructions of many areas of difference. In particular, race is socially constructed, yet perceptions of race, beliefs about people of different races, and discrimination on the basis of race strongly affect people's life experiences. Similarly, gender is also socially constructed, representing perceptions of how males and females *should* behave, rather than being representative of biological differences between them that might *cause* them to behave differently. These beliefs about the differences between males and females strongly affect the experiences of men, women, and boys and girls in society and organizations.

In contrast to the categories focused on in this book, some research has explored diversity in terms of functional area (e.g., marketing, finance, or accounting), tenure, values, and attitudes as they affect people's organizational experiences. These categories may also be sources of real or perceived differences that affect people's interactions, outcomes, and relationships at work. For example, engineering, finance, and accounting managers typically earn more and have greater occupational status than human resources managers. However, one's functional area at work is less likely to be readily apparent, a strong source of personal identity, or associated with historical disparities in treatment, opportunities, or outcomes in society at large. Thus, this book does not consider diversity in functional area, personality, learning style, and other sources considered in some research. Focusing on *any* individual difference, rather than differences having strong personal meaning and stemming from or coinciding with significant power differences among groups, would make all groups diverse and would make the entire concept of workplace diversity meaningless.[3]

Employment or **labor market discrimination** occurs when personal characteristics of applicants and workers that are unrelated to productivity are valued in the labor market.[4] **Access discrimination** occurs when people are denied employment opportunities, or "access" to jobs. **Treatment discrimination** occurs when people are employed but are treated differently once employed, receiving fewer job-related rewards, resources, or opportunities than they should receive based on job-related criteria.[5] Access and treatment discrimination are forms of employment discrimination. In cases of access or treatment discrimination, people with identical productive characteristics are regarded differently

---

[1]Dobbs, M. F. (1996). "Managing Diversity: Lessons from the Private Sector." *Public Personnel Management*, 25(September): 351–368.

[2]Konrad, A. M. (2003). "Defining the Domain of Workplace Diversity Scholarship." *Group and Organization Management*, 28(1): 4–17.

[3]Ibid.

[4]Ehrenberg, R. G., & Smith, R. S. (1982). *Modern Labor Economics: Theory and Public Policy*. Glenview, IL: Scott, Foresman and Company, p. 394.

[5]Greenhaus, J. H., Parasuraman, S., & Wormley, W. M. (1990). "Effects of Race on Organizational Experiences, Job Performance Evaluations, and Career Outcomes." *Academy of Management Journal*, 33: 64–86.

because of demographic factors such as race, ethnic origin, sex, age, physical ability, religion, and immigrant status. Productive characteristics include occupational and human capital variables, such as education, skills, and tenure.[6]

Also relevant to how people from different backgrounds are treated is the concept of **inclusion**, which is the degree to which "different voices of a diverse workforce are respected and heard."[7]

In inclusive organizational cultures, employees feel as though they are accepted, belong, and are able to contribute to decision-making processes.[8] In addition to efforts to ensure discrimination is avoided and employees are diverse, efforts to ensure employees are also included and able to fully contribute are critical to organizational success.[9] Thus, throughout the book, "valuing diversity" refers to diversity *and* inclusion. ●

▌ DETERMINING "DIVERSITY" IN AN INTERNATIONAL CONTEXT

Many issues related to inequality, discrimination, and diversity are similar, but it is important not to apply concepts from one area to another in wholesale fashion without considering contextual factors.[10] Race, ethnicity, sex, age, physical and mental ability, sexual orientation, religion, work and family status, and weight and appearance are important differentiating factors in the United States, and some of these factors are also important in many other regions of the world. Depending on national context, culture, political and socioeconomic structures, and history, different factors of "diversity" will be of most importance in the interactions and relationships among people.[11]

Identifying and studying differences based on power or dominance relations, stemming from historical disparities and perpetuated by continued differential and pejorative treatment, can help determine key identity groups in different contexts around the world. For example, although slavery officially ended after the Civil War in the United States, segregation and discrimination continue to affect the experiences, opportunities, and outcomes of American Blacks. Moreover, even in the United Kingdom, where slavery was considerably shorter-lived than in the United States, long-standing differences in the treatment of Black, Asian, and

[6]Rivera-Batiz, F. L. (1999). "Undocumented Workers in the Labor Market: An Analysis of the Earnings of Legal and Illegal Mexican Immigrants in the United States." *Journal of Population Economics*, 12(1): 91–116.

[7]Pless, N. M., & Maak, T. (2004). "Building an Inclusive Diversity Culture: Principles, Processes, and Practices." *Journal of Business Ethics*, 54: 129–147.

[8]Roberson, Q. (2006). "Disentangling the Meanings of Diversity and Inclusion in Organizations." *Group & Organization Management*, 31(2): 212–236.

[9]Nishii, L. H., & Mayer, D. M. (2009). "Do Inclusive Leaders Help to Reduce Turnover in Diverse Groups? The Moderating Role of Leader-Member Exchange in the Diversity to Turnover Relationship." *Journal of Applied Psychology*, 94(6): 1412–1426.

[10]Syed, J., & Özbilgin, M. (2009). "A Relational Framework for International Transfer of Diversity Management Practices." *The International Journal of Human Resource Management*, 20(12): 2435–2453.

[11]Ibid.

minority ethnic immigrants (e.g., Turks, Pakistanis, Indians) and their identifiable descendants compared with Whites in the United Kingdom continue to exist. Racial inequality is also an issue in South Africa where there has been a long history of discrimination against Blacks.[12] In Australia, British and European immigrants shaped restrictive immigration policies toward later, non-White immigrants, particularly Chinese and Pacific Islanders.[13] Similar histories and current disparities exist between "minority" and "majority" racial, ethnic, or religious groups around the world. In addition, the status of women makes sex and gender a relevant difference in virtually all societies. Regardless of region, then, particular factors affecting different groups may be identified and then addressed in order to reduce discrimination and increase equality, inclusion, and organizational competitiveness.

■ MULTIPLE GROUP MEMBERSHIPS AND PERMEABILITY OF BOUNDARIES

People's group memberships affect their outcomes, opportunities, and experiences in society and in organizations. Such things as employment, compensation, advancement, retention, participation, and competitiveness are a few of the outcomes that are related to demographic background. In the United States, those who are White, male, and do not have a disability generally earn higher wages and have higher organizational status than persons who are non-White, female, or have a disability.[14] Whites are more likely to work in the **primary labor market**, which includes jobs in large organizations, with more opportunities for advancement and retirement, vacation, and medical benefits. Blacks and Hispanics are more likely to work in the **secondary labor market** of low-skilled, low-paid, insecure jobs.[15]

The categories of race, ethnicity, sex, age, physical ability, sexual orientation, and religion are not mutually exclusive. Everyone possesses a racial and ethnic background, age, sexual orientation, and, possibly, religion. Some of the categories are immutable, but others are not and

---

[12]Shen, J., Chanda, A., D'Netto, B., & Monga, M. (2009). "Managing Diversity Through Human Resource Management: An International Perspective and Conceptual Framework." *The International Journal of Human Resource Management*, 20(2): 235–251.

[13]Syed, J., & Kramar, R. (2010). "What Is the Australian Model for Managing Cultural Diversity?" *Personnel Review*, 39(1): 96–115.

[14]See, for example, U.S. Department of Labor, Women's Bureau. (2002). "Earnings Differences Between Women and Men." In D. Dunn & P. Dubeck (Eds.), *Workplace/Women's Place: An Anthology*. Los Angeles: Roxbury Publishing Company; Braddock, D., & Bachelder, L. (1994). *The Glass Ceiling and Persons with Disabilities*. Washington, D.C.: Department of Labor.

[15]For a discussion of dual labor markets, see Healey, J. F. (2004). *Diversity and Society: Race, Ethnicity, and Gender*. Thousand Oaks, CA: Pine Forge Press.

may change over one's lifetime. People may be born with or acquire disabilities, and everyone ages. A person may be a member of the majority group in one area but not in another, for example, White and female or male and Latino. A White man may have a disability, be an older worker or of a minority religion, and personally experience job-related discrimination. He may also have a working wife, mother, or sister who has faced sex-based salary inequity or harassment or a daughter or granddaughter whom he would prefer not to have to face such discrimination at work.

White men are considerably more likely to occupy leadership positions (executive, board member, or manager) than other groups. Diversity research indicates that the commitment of top management to diversity increases the effectiveness of diversity initiatives. Therefore, White men are more likely to have the power to implement important changes at the organizational level and to influence behaviors and perspectives about the overall benefits of diversity; their commitment to diversity is essential.

Although data clearly show, and we emphasize here, that members of some groups face more barriers and organizational discrimination, this book stresses the value of diversity to *everyone*. Like Roosevelt Thomas, a pioneer in diversity work, we suggest that "managing diversity is a comprehensive managerial process for developing an environment that works for all employees."[16] At the same time, it is naïve to ignore the fact that membership in some groups or that some combinations of memberships (e.g., minority female) have more negative ramifications for job-related opportunities and success than others.[17] Commitment to diversity requires a concerted effort to recognize, acknowledge, and address historical discrimination, differential treatment, and unearned advantages rather than undermining efforts to address inequities in the name of inclusiveness.[18] The research and recommendations in this book make apparent the need to consider the past and present while working toward a more diversity-friendly future.

Misperception: Diversity is beneficial only to minorities and women.

Reality: Diversity can benefit everyone.

---

[16]Thomas, R. (1991). *Beyond Race and Gender: Unleashing the Power of Your Total Work Force by Managing Diversity*. New York: AMACOM, p. 10.

[17]For a discussion of the intersection of race and sex discrimination and the need to consider both in research, see Reskin, B. F., & Charles, C. Z. (1999). "Now You See 'Em, Now You Don't." In I. Brown (Ed.), *Latinas and African American Women at Work: Race, Gender, and Economic Inequality*. New York: Russell Sage Foundation.

[18]See Roberson (2006).

This book is relevant to large and small companies, colleges and universities, religious organizations, military organizations, and any other organizations in which people work or wish to work or that have clients, customers, or constituents. Although under U.S. laws some organizations (e.g., churches, private clubs) are often allowed to prefer certain types of people over others as employees, many of the concepts in this book also apply to such organizations and can be of benefit to their leaders. For example, religious organizations may legally require that employees be members of a particular faith, yet they will likely have employees with work and family issues or may be wrestling with the issue of ordaining women. Similarly, the U.S. military is a unique, historically male organization, yet its issues with sexual harassment and sexual orientation diversity can help inform other types of organizations. As will be apparent from the variety of organizations discussed in this book, diversity issues affect all organizations at some point.

▊ TERMINOLOGY

In this book, when referring to the U.S. population, the following expressions are used somewhat interchangeably: sex/gender, Blacks/African Americans, Latinos/Hispanics, Asians/Asian Americans/Asians and Pacific Islanders, Whites/Anglos/European Americans/Caucasians, and minorities/people of color.[19] Although the linked terms are not exactly the same (e.g., sex is biological while gender is socially constructed, and not all Blacks consider themselves African American), they are widely recognized, their meanings are generally well understood, and they are often used interchangeably. Even so, there are important differences among them. Indeed, some scholars have argued persuasively that the ambiguity and fluidity of terminology render "race" and "ethnicity" almost meaningless.[20] Some researchers go so far as to use quotation marks at any mention of the word *race* to indicate its lack of meaning.

Like gender, "race is socially constructed to denote boundaries between the powerful and less powerful" and is often defined by the more powerful group.[21] In the United States, these social constructions are reflected by the changes in terminology used by the Census Bureau over

---

[19]Terminology is discussed further in the following chapters. Individuals' different preferences for particular terms are acknowledged and respected.

[20]See Wright, L. (1997). "One Drop of Blood." In C. Hartman (Ed.), *Double Exposure: Poverty and Race in America*. Armonk, NY: M. E. Sharpe.

[21]Healey, J. F., & O'Brien, E. (2004). *Race, Ethnicity, and Gender*. Thousand Oaks, CA: Pine Forge Press, p. 282.

the years and in court rulings about who was or was not White. Latinos may be of any race, and people may be of more than one racial or ethnic background, which adds to the complexity of understanding race and what it means. Although all Latinos are categorized as such, there are substantial differences in the diversity-related experiences of Mexican Americans, Puerto Ricans, and Dominicans and between Black Nicaraguans and White Colombians.

Ethnicity refers to a shared national origin or a shared cultural heritage. Thus, "Hispanic" is an ethnic description, although it is often treated as a racial one. "Asian" is another ambiguous term. Is it an ethnicity, since ethnicity refers to a shared national origin, or is it a race, as the term is often used and understood? As with differences among Latinos, there are also considerable differences among Asians who are from Korea and those from India or Vietnam, and among Black Americans, South African Blacks, and those from the West Indies. These and other contextual complexities related to race, ethnicity, sex, and gender and their effects on individuals in organizations will be explored in later chapters.

As discussed further in Chapter 2, instead of the terms *majority* and *minority,* which reflect population size, the terms *dominant* and *non-dominant* are used at times to distinguish between more powerful and less powerful groups, acknowledging the importance of power in access to and the control of resources. The powerful control more resources and are "dominant," whether or not they are more numerous (such as Whites in South Africa and men in the United States and most other nations).

▌ THE STIMULUS FOR THE FOCUS ON DIVERSITY: WORKFORCE 2000

In 1987, the Hudson Institute published Johnston and Packer's research on the changes in the nature of work and in the demographic background of workers in the twenty-first century.[22] The research shocked organizations and the media and was an impetus for much of today's diversity research. Johnston and Packer noted that by the year 2000, 85% of the *net new entrants* into the U.S. workforce would be women and minorities. Often quoted, this statement was widely misunderstood to mean that by 2000, White men would constitute only 15% of the workforce. However, White men were then, and remain still, the largest single group in the **labor force.** It was the *net new entrants* who were increasingly women and people of color. The phrase *net new entrants* refers to the difference between those who entered the workforce (newcomers to the workforce)

[22]Johnston, W. B., & Packer, A. E. (1987). *Workforce 2000: Work and Workers for the 21st century.* Indianapolis, IN: Hudson Institute.

and those who left the workforce (e.g., via retirements, death). Although women and minorities would comprise 85% of the net new entrants, because of the immense size of the workforce and because White men are the single largest majority in the workforce, it will be a long time before White men are no longer the largest single group. This misunderstanding or misinterpretation of terminology and projections about the increasing diversity of the workforce fueled interest in the topic and prompted concerns about the organizational ramifications of these changing demographics.

In 1997, the Hudson Institute published *Workforce 2020*, which again predicted changes in work and in workforce demographics, but for the year 2020.[23] The report emphasized that about 66% of the workforce would continue to be non-Hispanic White men and women, 14% would be Latinos, 11% non-Hispanic Blacks, and 6% Asians. Most important to the demographics described in *Workforce 2020* was the aging and retirement of large numbers of baby-boomers, resulting in a plateauing of worker age.

What has happened to the U.S. population now that the year 2000 has come and gone and we are proceeding toward the year 2020? Although not exact (because not everyone participates in the workforce), the population demographics are similar to the predictions in *Workforce 2020*. As shown in Table 1.1, White men and women are the majority of the population, followed by Latinos, Blacks, and Asians. The current workforce is indeed more diverse than it was in the prior century, but Whites remain the largest group numerically. The workforce is aging, and younger workers are more diverse in race and ethnicity than in the past. Recession-related economic changes have prevented many aging workers from retiring, resulting in even more age diversity in organizations than in the past. Women are now obtaining more college degrees than men, yet women's earnings continue to be less than men's (see Table 1.1). These issues have important implications for individuals, employers, and organizational diversity.

In addition to the changes in the demographic makeup of American employees, as the Hudson Institute predicted, economic changes and globalization have resulted in more service-oriented jobs and more international customers and business relationships. The loss of manufacturing jobs, where there is less opportunity for contact with dissimilar others, and the growth of service industry jobs, which involve considerable person-to-person interaction with dissimilar others, continue. These changes in types of jobs make awareness of and efforts to understand and learn to interact with those who are dissimilar more

---

[23]Judy, R. W., & D'Amico, C. (1997). *Workforce 2020*. Indianapolis, IN: Hudson Institute.

TABLE 1.1 *Highlights from the U.S. 2000 and 2008 Census Demographic Profiles*

	2000		2008	
	Number	**Percent**	**Number**	**Percent**
General Characteristics				
Total population	281,421,906	100.0	304,059,728	100.0
Male	138,053,563	49.1	149,863,485	49.3
Female	143,368,343	50.9	154,196,243	50.7
Median age (years)	35.3		36.9	
One race	274,595,678	97.6	297,045,856	97.7
White	211,460,626	75.1	228,182,410	75.0
Black	34,658,190	12.3	37,586,050	12.4
American Indian and Alaska Native	2,475,956	0.9	2,443,422	0.8
Asian	10,242,998	3.6	13,413,976	4.4
Native Hawaiian and other Pacific Islander	398,835	0.1	427,810	0.1
Some other race	15,359,073	5.5	14,992,188	4.9
Two or more races	6,826,228	2.4	7,013,872	2.3
Hispanic or Latino (of any race)	35,305,818	12.5	46,891,456	15.4
Social Characteristics				
Population 25 years and over	182,211,639	100.0	200,030,018	100.0
With a disability* (18 to 64 years)	n/a	n/a	18,995,085	10.1
Foreign born (% of total population)	31,107,889	11.1	37,960,935	12.5
Speak a language other than English at home (population 5 years and over)	46,951,595	17.9	55,783,998	19.7
Economic Characteristics				
Participating in labor force (population 16 years and over)	138,820,935	63.9	157,465,113	65.9
Median earnings male full-time, year-round workers	n/a		$45,556	
Median earnings female full-time, year-round workers	n/a		$35,471	

*The Census Bureau introduced a new set of disability questions in the 2008 ACS questionnaire.

Source: Adapted from 2000 and 2008 U.S. Census Bureau, American FactFinder. http://factfinder.census.gov, accessed August 12, 2010.

critical than ever. Further, service industry jobs, often occupied by women, continue to increase, while manufacturing jobs, often occupied by men, continue to decline through layoffs, plant closures, and off-shoring. As a result of these changes, at one point in late 2009, women for the first time comprised the majority of the U.S. labor force. Increasing globalization has also resulted in greater interaction among people from diverse backgrounds. Not only do employees interact with peers from diverse backgrounds in their local environment, they also travel around the world, interacting with people who are from different cultures and belief systems and who often speak different first languages.

Demographic changes are occurring in many countries around the world. In the United States and Canada, where growth of the workforce is slowing, fewer younger workers are being added than in the past. In some European countries and in Japan and China, the workforce is actually shrinking; more people are leaving than joining it. Along with the striking age of Japan's workforce, its underutilization of women workers is notable and has received considerable criticism.[24] As a result of some of the demographic changes, many countries increasingly view developing nations as sources of new employees, even though a number of these countries have historically resisted, and sometimes continue to resist, immigration. Immigrants often have educational backgrounds, language skills, strengths, and weaknesses different from those of native workers, thus requiring special effort to integrate immigrants successfully. This becomes even more difficult when they are also identifiable by appearance, name, or cultural differences. Both the need for these new workers and the resistance to them make paying attention to issues of diversity and inclusion particularly important.

■ DIVERSITY AND ORGANIZATIONAL COMPETITIVENESS

What is the meaning of increasing diversity to individuals and organizations? What should organizations do to ensure that applicants have opportunities to work and workers have opportunities to contribute and succeed? How can organizations integrate new workers into a formerly homogenous organization? How should organizations address resistance to immigration when immigrants are key sources of applicants, employees, and customers? We will examine in this book these and other diversity-focused questions.

In their often-cited article on the implications of cultural diversity for organizational competitiveness, Cox and Blake proposed that there are six specific business-related reasons why organizations should value diversity. They explained that effective management of diversity could benefit organizations in the areas of cost, resource acquisition, marketing, creativity, problem solving, and system flexibility.[25] Numerous management, marketing, and organizational behavior textbooks, as well as news magazines

---

[24]Price, S. (2010). "Women: Most Underused Resource in Japan, Business Case for Gender Diversity." http://www.jef.or.jp/journal/jef_contents_free.asp?c=3766, accessed June 8, 2010.
[25]Cox, T., & Blake, S. (1991). "Managing Cultural Diversity: Implications for Organizational Competitiveness. *Academy of Management Executive*, 5(3): 45–56.

and the popular press, have discussed these benefits of diversity and continue to shape the thinking about its value. Cox and Blake focused on those six reasons in order to highlight areas that had previously received limited research attention, not to imply that they were the only reasons for valuing diversity. Along with the business reasons, we also consider the social, moral, and legal reasons. In addition, Cox and Blake's suggestions focused on diversity as it applies to women and minorities; we apply their suggestions to the effects of different aspects of diversity—such as age, religion, sexual orientation, and others—on an organization's competitiveness.

Cost

Employee turnover and litigation. The costs associated with doing a poor job of integrating workers from different backgrounds can be extremely high: lower job satisfaction and the subsequent costs of turnover among women, minorities, and, likely, people of various religious faiths, gays and lesbians, and others whose contributions are often devalued in organizations. Cox and Blake and other researchers have reported lower satisfaction and higher turnover of women and minorities when compared to men and Whites. This finding is an important organizational concern, particularly as the number of women and minorities in the workforce increases. If, along with women and minorities, workers from other groups (such as those with child and/or elder care responsibilities or people with disabilities) are dissatisfied and quit in response to negative organizational treatment, organizational costs related to turnover may be tremendous. However, researchers have found that, for some employees, organizational efforts to support diversity can enhance commitment and reduce intentions to quit even when employees perceive discrimination.[26] On the other hand, if minority employees feel that their organization's commitment to diversity is insincere, dissatisfaction, lowered commitment, and cynicism can result.[27]

Although the majority of research focuses on the turnover of women and minorities, one study found that increasing organizational diversity was associated with lowered attachment for Whites and males but not for women and minorities.[28] Other research indicates that at times both minorities and Whites experience discomfort in cross-race interactions, with

[26]Triana, M. C., García, M. F., & Colella, A. (2010). "Managing Diversity: How Organizational Efforts to Support Diversity Moderate the Effects of Perceived Racial Discrimination on Affective Commitment." *Personnel Psychology*, 63(4): 817–843.

[27]Chrobot-Mason, D. L. (2003). "Keeping the Promise: Psychological Contract Violations for Minority Employees." *Journal of Managerial Psychology*, 18(1): 22–45.

[28]Tsui, A. S., Egan, T. D., & O'Reilly, C. A. (1992). "Being Different: Relational Demography and Organizational Attachment." *Administrative Science Quarterly*, 37: 549–579.

minorities expecting to be targets of prejudice and Whites fearing being perceived as prejudiced.[29] The possibility that increased diversity is associated with lower attachment, turnover, and discomfort for people of different backgrounds suggests that organizations should take proactive measures to address and circumvent these negative outcomes while maximizing the positive outcomes.

Costs associated with turnover include exit interviews, lost productivity while positions are unfilled, and recruiting costs for replacement employees. Organizations may find replacement more expensive than retaining current employees. This is particularly true when the learning curve and training costs of replacements are also taken into consideration. Specific organizational efforts to address needs of specific workers may minimize turnover. For instance, research indicates that workers with child care responsibilities (commonly, women; increasingly, men) have more organizational commitment and lower turnover when companies provide child care subsidies, on-site day care, or other child care support.[30] In addition, educating all workers about the benefits of increasing diversity may reduce dissatisfaction, detachment, and fear among employees while also communicating that diversity is desirable.

Lastly, many people think of the costs associated with doing a poor job of integrating workers largely in terms of discrimination lawsuits. Cox and Blake did not specifically include litigation expenses among their cost factors, however. Further supporting organizations' concerns over litigation is the media attention surrounding large damage awards involving major companies. As discussed further in Chapter 3, research suggests that large damage awards are indeed effective in improving opportunities for groups that have experienced discrimination, at least in the short term. However, despite the substantial media attention, the likelihood of an organization being sued by an aggrieved individual is relatively small, but the continuing costs associated with low job satisfaction and high turnover are high. For example, the number of discrimination-related charges filed by individuals with the Equal Employment Opportunity Commission (EEOC) between 1997 and 2010 ranged from about 75,000 to nearly 100,000. Although these are substantial numbers, they are quite small relative to the number of firms in the United States and relative to the 139 million people in the workforce. The majority of workers who feel they are treated unfairly, not valued, or discriminated against do not sue. Instead, they may simply leave the organization and tell their family and

[29]Shelton, J. N. (2003). "Interpersonal Concerns in Social Encounters Between Majority and Minority Group Members." *Group Processes and Intergroup Relations*, 6: 171–185.

[30]Youngblood, S. A., & Chambers-Cook, K. (1984, February). "Child Care Assistance Can Improve Employee Attitudes and Behavior." *Personnel Administrator*, 93–95.

friends about their experiences, which affects the organization's ability to attract other workers (e.g., resource acquisition).

Misperception: The risk of being sued by an individual for discrimination is fairly high.

Reality: Overall, an organization's likelihood of being sued by an individual is very small.

Lost business. Costs associated with lost business should be added to the costs of absence, turnover, and discrimination lawsuits that are commonly associated with mismanagement of diversity. When employees or customers learn of or personally experience unfair treatment toward their group by an organization, they are less likely to patronize it. In addition, other groups who were not personally affected may find overt discrimination or other negative behaviors offensive and choose to spend their dollars elsewhere. Dealing with negative publicity and protests against discriminatory policies can be expensive and time-consuming for organizations, as experienced by Cracker Barrel in response to its discriminatory policies toward Black customers and gay and lesbian employees, discussed in Chapters 4 and 11, respectively.[31]

Resource Acquisition

An organization's ability to attract and retain employees from different backgrounds is referred to as *resource acquisition*. Depending on the national context, those who have been overlooked as potential employees often include women, racial and ethnic minorities, workers with disabilities, gays and lesbians, and people from non-dominant religious faiths. Cox and Blake proposed that if an organization develops a reputation for valuing all types of workers, it will become known as an employer of choice, increasing its ability to compete in tight labor markets. Empirical research provides support for the positive effects of heterogeneous recruitment ads on minorities' desire to work for organizations.[32] Conversely, if an organization develops a reputation for valuing

---

[31]Kilborn, P. T. (1992). "Gay Rights Groups Take Aim at Restaurant Chain That's Hot on Wall Street." *New York Times*, http://www.nytimes.com/1992/04/09/us/gay-rights-groups-take-aim-at-restaurant-chain-that-s-hot-on-wall-street.html, accessed June 2, 2010.
[32]Avery, D. R., Hernandez, M., & Hebl, M. R. (2004). "Who's Watching the Race? Racial Salience in Recruitment Advertising." *Journal of Applied Social Psychology*, 34(1): 146–161; Perkins, L. A., Thomas, K. M., & Taylor, G. A. (2000). "Advertising and Recruitment: Marketing to Minorities." *Psychology and Marketing*, 17: 235–255.

only a subset of workers, it may miss out on hiring excellent workers who do not fall into that subset. Other researchers have similarly argued that "talented people may be predisposed to avoid companies that discriminate."[33] Such organizations may also have higher compensation costs because of drawing from a smaller pool of workers (i.e., supply would be lower, making demand costs higher). As discussed in Featured Case 1.1, such an organization may also see lower productivity from both the preferred subset of workers and those who are not preferred.

In addition to *Fortune*'s annual issue on the best companies for minorities, *DiversityInc*, *Working Mother*, *Latina Style*, *Catalyst*, the American Association of Retired Persons (AARP), *Hispanic Today*, and other entities routinely publish lists of best companies for women, minorities, parents, and other groups. These reports are widely read and provide substantial publicity for the companies that make, or fail to make, the lists. The high level of attention from the media may affect applicants' interest in companies as well as companies' ability to market to diverse consumer groups.

Marketing

Cox and Blake proposed that an organization's reputation for valuing all types of workers will also affect its ability to market to different types of consumers. This is accomplished in multiple ways. First, consumers who appreciate fair treatment for everyone will be more likely to patronize an organization known to value diversity and to treat all workers fairly and less likely to patronize organizations known to discriminate. Employers known for contributing to particular organizations (such as the United Negro College Fund or the Human Rights Campaign) receive recognition from those organizations and their patrons. This recognition may translate into purchases and customer loyalty.

Second, having employees who are from various backgrounds improves a company's marketing ability because such organizations will be better able to develop products that meet the needs of and appeal to diverse consumers. After a period of declining sales and profits, Avon Products was able to successfully market to Blacks and Hispanics by increasing their representation among marketing managers. Avon's profitability increased tremendously as a result.

Third, organizations with employees from various backgrounds may also be more likely to avoid expensive marketing blunders associated with

[33]Wright, P., Ferris, S. P., Hiller, J. S., & Kroll, M. (1995). "Competitiveness Through Management of Diversity: Effects on Stock Price Valuation." *Academy of Management Journal*, 38: 272–288.

Case Study of Fictitious Company, Inc.

Assume that people from demographic groups A and B are employed at Fictitious Company, Inc. Both A Workers and B Workers have a similar number of excellent performers and poor performers in their group. Workers from both groups expect fair performance evaluations, pay raises, and promotions based on their performance. After a period of working for and excelling in performance, high-performing B Workers realize that despite their high qualifications and strong performance, their performance is rated lower than that of A Workers, their pay raises are lower, and they are not likely to be promoted. This perception is validated when B Workers consider the management and executive levels of Fictitious Company and see very few people from the B Workers category in those levels. What is the expected result on motivation and future performance of high-performing B Workers? Low- and average-performing B Workers are observing. They realize that high-performing B Workers, despite their high performance, receive low performance ratings and few-to-no raises and promotions. What is the expected effect on the motivation to work harder and the future performance of low-performing B Workers?

After a period of employment at Fictitious Company, A Workers realize that they are continually rated highly and receive pay raises and promotions regardless of their performance. If they make their sales and quality goals, they receive high raises and are promoted. If they miss their sales and quality goals, they

remarkably receive high raises and are promoted. If they are chronically late or absent on Mondays and Fridays, there are few-to-no negative consequences. What is the expected result on future performance and motivation of A Workers who are truly good performers but observe A Workers who miss sales and quality goals still being promoted and rewarded? What is the expected result on the motivation to improve and the future performance of A Workers who are low performers but receive rewards nonetheless?

To summarize, at Fictitious Company, high-performing B Workers receive clear messages that their high performance is not valued. Low-performing B Workers receive messages that there is no reason to strive for high performance because people like them receive no reward for high performance. A Workers receive messages that their low and high performers are valued and rewarded similarly, so there is no need to strive for excellence. What is the result of this scenario for the overall performance and competitiveness of Fictitious Company, Inc.?

Contrast this scenario to that of Fictitious Savvy Company, Inc., in which members of A Workers and B Workers expect, and receive, fair performance evaluations, promotions, and raises. What is the expected result on the future motivation and performance of high, average, and low performers among A Workers and B Workers in Fictitious Savvy Company, Inc.? What is the expected result on the organizational performance of Fictitious Savvy Company?

having homogeneous advertising or marketing teams. In the early history of Frito-Lay's Frito's corn chips, the major focus of its advertising was the character Frito Bandito, who was known for stealing Fritos because they were so good that he was unable to resist. The character had a heavy accent, his appearance was stereotypical, and the portrayal of Latinos as stealing was insulting. Complaints from Latinos resulted in Frito-Lay's discontinuing Frito Bandito.[34]

Though not an advertising blunder, American Airlines' Latin America Pilot Reference Guide, an internal document, once caused the company negative publicity that could have affected its ability to market to Latino consumers (and other groups). The guide reportedly warned pilots that Latin American customers would call in false bomb threats to delay flights when they were running late and that they sometimes became unruly after drinking too much on flights. When news of the statements in the reference guide hit the press, the airline apologized and stated it would revise the manual.[35]

Creativity and Problem Solving

Research indicates that groups composed of people from different backgrounds bring with them differences that result in greater creativity and problem-solving ability. These abilities stem from the different life experiences, language abilities, and education that groups composed of diverse members have. Empirical research also supports the idea that diversity positively affects group performance, creativity, and innovation. In longitudinal research, Watson, Kumar, and Michaelsen investigated the effects of diversity (in race, ethnicity, and nationality) on group performance. Following diverse and homogeneous groups of students over the course of a semester, these authors found that, initially, the homogeneous groups outperformed the diverse groups. By the end of the semester, however, the performance of the diverse groups exceeded the performance of the homogeneous groups. After learning to interact with each other, the diverse groups developed more and higher-quality solutions to problems than homogenous groups, exhibiting greater creativity and problem-solving skills.[36]

McLeod, Lobel, and Cox have empirically investigated the effects of racial diversity on idea generation in small groups. Using brainstorming techniques (which are commonly used in organizations for developing new ideas), they found that groups composed of diverse members produced higher-quality ideas than groups composed of homogenous

---

[34]"Justice for My People, the Hector Garcia Story." https://justiceformypeople.org, accessed August 12, 2010.
[35]Hetter, K., & Mallory, M. (1997). "American: More Apologies." *U.S. News & World Report*, 123(8): 57.
[36]Watson, W. E., Kumar, K., & Michaelsen, L. K. (1996). "Cultural Diversity's Impact on Interaction Process and Performance: Comparing Homogeneous and Diverse Task Groups." *Academy of Management Journal*, 36: 590–603.

members.[37] As global competition increases, the ability to generate superior ideas is vital to success.

In his research on the logic of diversity, Scott Page, professor of Complex Systems at the University of Michigan, used simple frameworks to demonstrate how individuals with diverse problem-solving tools (as a result of diverse backgrounds) are able to outperform others in problem-solving tasks.[38] As an example, two people with diverse backgrounds would choose to test different potential product improvements differently, increasing the probability of finding a useful innovation. In problem-solving experiments, Page demonstrated how groups composed of diverse problem solvers confronting a difficult problem outperformed groups composed of the best individual performers. His research also showed how combinations of different tools can be more powerful than the tools themselves.

System Flexibility

System flexibility is the sixth reason for valuing diversity, in that it provides organizations with a competitive advantage. Cox and Blake argued that women have a higher tolerance for ambiguity than men. Tolerance for ambiguity is associated with cognitive flexibility and success in uncertain situations. Bilingualism and biculturalism are indicative of cognitive flexibility and openness to experience.[39] In the United States, Latinos and Asians are often bilingual and bicultural, Blacks tend to be bicultural, and Native Americans who have lived on reservations among their native culture and also outside learn to navigate between two worlds.[40] In the many regions of the world where the populations are multilingual and multicultural, cognitive flexibility, openness to experience, and navigating between worlds are common and are desirable diversity attributes. In addition, although they are not traditionally perceived as bi- or multicultural, the life experiences of some people with disabilities, gay males, and lesbians may provide them cognitive flexibility and openness to experience similar to that of bi- or multicultural individuals. Exposure to other cultures, languages, or the experiences and challenges of being different from those

[37]McLeod, P., Lobel, S. A., & Cox, T., Jr. (1996). "Ethnic Diversity and Creativity in Small Groups." *Small Group Research*, 27(2): 248–264.

[38]Page, S. E. (2007). "Making the Difference: Applying a Logic of Diversity." *Academy of Management Perspectives*, 21(4): 6–20.

[39]Bell, M. P., & Harrison, D. A. (1996). "Using Intra-national Diversity for International Assignments." *Human Resources Management Review*, 6: 47–73; Cox & Blake (1991); LaFromboise, T., Coleman, H. L. K., & Gerton, J. (1993). "Psychological Impact of Biculturalism: Evidence and Theory." *Psychological Bulletin*, 114: 395–412.

[40]Cox & Blake (1991); Muller, H. J. (1998). "American Indian Women Managers: Living in Two Worlds." *Journal of Management Inquiry*, 7(1): 4–28.

in the majority may help individuals develop the flexibility and openness not possessed by others, which can be beneficial in diverse organizational settings.

Other Areas Where Diversity Can Be Advantageous

Cooperative behaviors. Researchers have found that groups composed of members from collectivist backgrounds (such as Asian, Black, and Latino) instead of individualist backgrounds (such as White/European American) displayed more cooperative behavior on group tasks.[41] In an increasingly global and diverse environment, where cooperation is important to business success and where teamwork is vital, organizational diversity will therefore be an asset.

Interaction effects with organizational strategy. Orlando Richard's study of the relationship between racial diversity and firm performance found a complex interaction effect.[42] Firms with a growth strategy (requiring innovation, idea generation, and creativity) were more successful when employees were diverse. Richard suggested that when firms have a growth strategy, racial diversity increases productivity, which increases firm performance. Thus, organizations might wish to actively seek out diversity as a particular source of a competitive edge when pursuing a growth strategy. Although Richard did not test other aspects of diversity, diversity in gender, age, and other areas may also be advantageous for high-growth firms. In another study, researchers following firms over time found that racial diversity had a positive, linear impact on long-term performance. In companies with more than moderate levels of diversity, there was a positive effect on both short- and long-term performance.[43]

Financial returns. An association between effective management of diversity and stock prices has been established by Wright and colleagues. Using six years of data, they assessed the effect of positive publicity from affirmative action programs (which they used as evidence of valuing diversity) and negative publicity from damage awards in discrimination lawsuits on the stock returns of major corporations. They found positive influences on

---

[41]Cox, T., Lobel, S. A., & McLeod, P. L. (1991). "Effects of Ethnic Group Cultural Differences on Cooperative and Competitive Behavior on a Group Task." *Academy of Management Journal*, 4: 827–847.

[42]Richard, O. C. (2000). "Racial Diversity, Business Strategy, and Firm Performance: A Resource-based View." *Academy of Management Journal*, 43: 164–178.

[43]Richard, O. C., Murthi, B. P. S., & Ismail, K. (2007). "The Impact of Racial Diversity on Intermediate and Long-term Performance: The Moderating Role of Environmental Context." *Strategic Management Journal*, 28: 1213–1233.

stock valuation for firms that received awards from the U.S. Department of Labor regarding their affirmative action programs. In contrast, announcements of discrimination settlements were associated with negative stock price changes for the affected companies.[44] Gender diversity at high levels has also been associated with higher stock prices, firm quality, and financial performance.[45]

Firms that purposely behave in a socially responsive way are rewarded by financial markets. In South Africa, companies that actively resisted apartheid and agreed to be independently monitored for equal and fair employment practices, to maintain unsegregated facilities, to provide training for non-White employees, and to improve employees' lives outside the work environment realized greater growth in stock prices after the end of apartheid than did companies not agreeing to such monitoring.[46] These results indicate that bottom-line concerns and the moral and social reasons for pursuing diversity can coexist.[47]

Moral and Social Reasons for Valuing Diversity

Diversity researchers and practitioners have been criticized for focusing solely on the "business case" reasons for pursuing diversity;[48] these criticisms are often legitimate. Many researchers have argued that economic and commercial reasons for valuing diversity, although they have some merit, should not be the only reasons for supporting diversity.[49] This book is written from the perspective that moral and social reasons can and should work in concert with business reasons for supporting diversity

[44]Wright et al. (1995).

[45]Desvaux, G., Devillard-Hoellinger, S., & Meaney, C. (2008). "A Business Case for Women." *The McKinsey Quarterly* (4): 26–33; Dezsö, C. L., & Ross, D. G. (2008, July). "Girl Power: Female Participation in Top Management and Firm Quality." http://ssrn.com/abstract=1088182, accessed December 10, 2010; Welbourne, T. M., Cycyota, C. S., & Ferrante, C. J. (2007). "Wall Street Reaction to Women in IPOs: An Examination of Gender Diversity in Top Management Teams." *Group and Organization Management*, 12(5): 524–547.

[46]Kumar, R., Lamb, W. B., & Wokutch, R. (2002). "The End of South African Sanctions, Institutional Ownership, and the Stock Price Performance of Boycotted Firms: Evidence on the Impact of Social/Ethical Investing." *Business and Society*, 41: 133–165; Lamb, W. B., Kumar, R., & Wokutch, R. E. (2005). "Corporate Social Performance and the Road to Redemption: Insights from the South Africa Sanctions." *Organizational Analysis*, 13: 1–14.

[47]Bell, M. P., Connerley, M. L., & Cocchiara, F. (2009). "The Case for Mandatory Diversity Education." *Academy of Management Learning & Education*, 8(4): 597–609.

[48]See Litvin, D. (2006). "Diversity: Making Space for a Better Case." In A. Konrad, P. Prasad, & J. Pringle (Eds.), *Handbook of Workplace Diversity*. Thousand Oaks, CA: Sage, pp. 75–94; Mor Barak, M. E. (2005). *Managing Diversity: Toward a Globally Inclusive Workplace*. Thousand Oaks, CA: Sage.

[49]Pringle, J. K., Konrad, A. M., & Prasad, P. (2006). "Conclusion: Reflections and Future Directions." In A. Konrad, P. Prasad, & J. Pringle (Eds.), *Handbook of Workplace Diversity*. Thousand Oaks, CA: Sage, pp. 531–540.

through pursuit of equality and inclusion.[50] For example, the inequality and poverty often experienced by minorities and women due to discrimination and exclusion from work in formal organizations are moral and social issues. Reduction of inequality, poverty, and discrimination can benefit society and future populations as well as organizations.

Difficulties Resulting from Increased Diversity and Organizational Responses

Although the foundation of this book is the positive value of diversity, it is important to consider some of the negative outcomes that may arise from increased diversity. Some of these negative consequences can include dysfunctional communication processes between different group members, discrimination, harassment, perceptions that nontraditional workers are unqualified, and lowered attachment, commitment, and satisfaction.[51] As mentioned earlier, researchers have found that the cross-race interactions required by increasing organizational diversity can at times be taxing for employees.[52] On the other hand, multiple studies have indicated that although increased diversity was associated with negative outcomes initially, this lessened over time.[53] Research suggests that as employees get to know one another and exchange job-relevant information, the negative effects of surface-level differences can be reduced. In other words, people stop attending to outward appearances and begin attending to work-related differences.

Given the complexity of research results on diversity—found to be beneficial at times to interpersonal interactions and organizational functioning and at other times shown to be functionally negative—it is imperative that organizations attend to diversity issues proactively. Leaders should facilitate interactions between people of diverse backgrounds at work, providing communication training if necessary, and monitor dysfunctional behaviors. Managers should directly confront and dispel the

[50]See Cox & Blake (1991), note 3; Bell et al. (2009); Kumar et al. (2002); Lamb et al. (2005).

[51]See, for example, Jackson, S. E., Brett, J. F., Sessa, V. I., Cooper, D. M., Julin, J. A., & Peyronnin, K. (1991). "Some Differences Make a Difference: Interpersonal Dissimilarity and Group Heterogeneity as Correlates of Recruitment, Promotion, and Turnover." *Journal of Applied Psychology*, 76: 675–689; Konrad, A. M., Winter, S., & Gutek, B. A. (1992). "Diversity in Work Group Sex Composition: Implications for Majority and Minority Members." In P. Tolbert & S. B. Bacharach (Eds.), *Research in the Sociology of Organizations*, Vol. 10. Greenwich, CT: JAI Press, pp. 115–140; Harrison, D. E., Price, K., & Bell, M. P. (1998). "Beyond Relational Demography: Time and the Effects of Surface- and Deep-level Diversity on Work Group Cohesion." *Academy of Management Journal*, 41: 96–107.

[52]Tsui, A. S., Egan, T. D., & O'Reilly, C. A. (1992). "Being Different: Relational Demography and Organizational Attachment." *Administrative Science Quarterly*, 37: 549–579.

[53]Harrison et al. (1998); Watson, W., Kumar, K., & Michaelson, L. K. (1993). "Cultural Diversity's Impact on Interaction Process and Performance: Comparing Homogeneous and Diverse Task Groups." *Academy of Management Journal*, 36: 590–602.

common perceptions that certain groups of people are qualified and other groups of people are not and practice zero tolerance of discrimination and harassment. As with any important change, organizations should take proactive steps to minimize negative outcomes resulting from increasing diversity while maximizing the positive ones.[54] Changes in population demographics, globalization, the growth in service jobs requiring considerable interaction with dissimilar people, and other factors make these steps critical to organizational success.

Organizations that are supportive of diversity have faced boycotts and negative publicity from those who are resistant to diversity. *Fortune* magazine reports that in 1962, when Harvey C. Russell, a Black man, was named a vice president at Pepsi, the Ku Klux Klan called for a boycott of Pepsi products, flooding the country with handbills that encouraged customers not to buy Pepsi.[55] More recently, the Southern Baptist Convention led a boycott of Disney because of its inclusive policies toward gay and lesbian employees and customers.[56] After eight years of having little apparent effect, the Convention ended its boycott.

The "Value in Diversity" Perspective versus Negative Impacts of Diversity

Cedric Herring, professor of Sociology and Public Policy at the University of Illinois at Chicago, used data from the 1996–1997 National Organizations Survey (NOS) to test the "value in diversity" perspective that is consistent with portions of Cox and Blake's arguments about diversity and organizational competitiveness.[57] He specifically wanted to determine the validity of questions about the positive impact of diversity on the bottom line. The NOS is comprised of 1,002 organizations drawn from a stratified random sample of 15 million U.S. work establishments, and Herring focused on 506 for-profit organizations that provided information about the sex and race of their workers, sales revenue, customers, market share, and profitability. He also controlled for other important factors, such as company and establishment size, organization age, industrial sector, and region that could have also affected the important variables. Herring found considerable support for the value-in-diversity hypothesis. Racial

[54]For example, see Choi, S., & Rainey, H. G. (2010). "Managing Diversity in U.S. Federal Agencies: Effects of Diversity and Diversity Management on Employee Perceptions of Organizational Performance." *Public Administration Review*, January/February: 109–121.

[55]Daniels, C., Neering, P., & Soehendro, M. (2005, August 22). "Pioneers." *Fortune*, 152(4): 72–88.

[56]Johnson, A. (2005). "Southern Baptists End Disney Boycott." http://www.msnbc.msn.com/id/8318263/ns/us_news/, accessed March 4, 2011.

[57]Herring, C. (2010). "Does Diversity Pay? Race, Gender, and the Business Case for Diversity." *American Sociological Review*, 74(2): 208–224.

diversity was associated with increased sales revenue, more customers, greater market share, and greater relative profits, and gender diversity was associated with increased sales revenue, more customers, and greater relative profits. Herring acknowledged that some of the negative outcomes of increased diversity could concurrently exist in some organizations, but in his sample, using stringent tests, diversity did have a net positive impact on organizational functioning.

■ INDIVIDUAL BENEFITS OF DIVERSITY

In addition to the organizational benefits of diversity, longitudinal research provides evidence of the value of diversity to individuals. The research of Patricia Gurin and her colleagues identifying the benefits of a diverse learning environment for students was used in 2003 by the U.S. Supreme Court in its decision in favor of portions of the University of Michigan's diversity programs.[58] Gurin found that students whose classmates were diverse and who interacted with each other in meaningful ways and learned from each other were more likely to see diversity as not necessarily divisive, to see commonality in values, and to be able to take the perspective of others.

In another longitudinal study, Sylvia Hurtado found similar evidence of the benefits of diversity among college students.[59] Hurtado's study involved 4,403 students from nine public universities across the United States. When students interacted with diverse peers during their first year of college, changes in cognitive and social outcomes followed. By the second year of college, students expressed more interest in poverty, more support for race-based initiatives, more openness to the perspectives of others, and more tolerance for sexual minorities. Students who had taken diversity courses and participated in campus-sponsored diversity learning programs experienced the greatest number of positive benefits. Hurtado proposed that "these results suggest that campus efforts to integrate the curriculum, or adopt a diversity requirement, have far-reaching effects on a host of educational outcomes that prepare students as participants in a diverse economy."[60] In his longitudinal study involving 15,600 students

[58]Gurin, P., Nagda, B. A., & Lopez, G. E. (2004). "The Benefits of Diversity in Education for Democratic Citizenship." *Journal of Social Issues*, 60(1): 17–34. See also Gurin, P. Dey, E. L., Hurtado, S., & Gurin, G. (2002). "Diversity and Higher Education: Theory and Impact on Educational Outcomes." *Harvard Educational Review*, 71(3): 332–366; Gurin, P. Y., Dey, E. L., Gurin, G., & Hurtado, S. (2003). "How Does Racial/Ethnic Diversity Promote Education?" *The Western Journal of Black Studies*, 27(1): 20–29.
[59]Hurtado, S. (2005). "The Next Generation of Diversity and Intergroup Relations Research." *Journal of Social Issues*, 61: 595–610.
[60]Ibid., p. 605.

at 365 universities, Octavio Villalpando found that after four years of college, regardless of the students' race or ethnicity, their level of satisfaction with their college experience was positively influenced by attending cultural awareness workshops, socializing with students from different racial or ethnic groups, taking courses with content on racial or ethnic issues, and campus policies that promote diversity initiatives.[61] Other researchers have also found that compared with a control group, those taking an elective diversity course had positive changes in attitudes toward people with disabilities, racial minorities, and gay, lesbian, and bisexual workers, increased intercultural tolerance, and perceived equality of gender roles.[62]

The increasing diversity of populations and workforces makes preparation for such diversity invaluable. In recognition of this, researchers have argued for mandatory diversity education,[63] and many universities are making taking a diversity-related course a requirement. According to the Association of American Colleges and Universities, 54% of accredited colleges and universities in the United States have instituted diversity requirements and another 8% are developing such requirements.[64] Some schools now offer diversity majors (e.g., the graduate psychology program of Cleveland State University), minors (e.g., the undergraduate business program at Virginia Tech), or certificate programs. Students who are equipped to work effectively in diverse environments reap individual benefits, and the organizations that employ them benefit as well. Of course, societal benefits, in which everyone has the opportunity to contribute and succeed, are also expected outcomes.

▌ DIVERSITY, INDIVIDUAL OUTCOMES, AND ORGANIZATIONAL EFFECTIVENESS

In the previous sections, we defined diversity and discussed how valuing or devaluing diversity can influence organizational effectiveness. We emphasized Cox and Blake's six reasons for valuing diversity: cost, resource acquisition, marketing, creativity, problem solving, and system flexibility. In his pioneering book *Cultural Diversity in Organizations*, Cox included

[61]Villalpando, O. (2002). "The Impact of Diversity and Multiculturalism on All Students: Findings From a National Study." *NASPA*, 40(1): 124–144.
[62]Probst, T. M. (2003). "Changing Attitudes Over Time: Assessing the Effectiveness of a Workplace Diversity Course." *Teaching of Psychology*, 30(3): 236–239.
[63]Bell et al. (2009).
[64]van Laar, C., Sidanius, J., & Levin, S. (2008). "Ethnic-related Curricula and Intergroup Attitudes in College: Movement Toward and Away from the In-group." *Journal of Applied Social Psychology*, 38(6): 1601–1638.

more details in his Interactional Model of the Impact of Diversity on Individual Career Outcomes and Organizational Effectiveness.[65] Cox proposed that the **diversity climate** of an organization (including individual-, group/intergroup factors, and organizational-level factors) affects individual outcomes (affective, achievement, applicant, and customer), which then influence organizational effectiveness.[66] An adapted and broader version of this model is depicted in Figure 1.1, in which additional areas have been included in the diversity climate, individual outcomes, and organizational effectiveness. While the model has not been completely tested empirically, many of its proposed ideas and relationships have been empirically supported, as already mentioned in this chapter and as will be discussed in the remaining chapters.

▌ ORGANIZATION OF THE BOOK

We have introduced the concept of diversity in this chapter and discussed Cox and Blake's six areas in which diversity is beneficial for organizations and the empirical evidence on the relationships between diversity and group and organizational performance. In the remainder of the book, we refer to these areas and to other ways in which diversity is both inevitable and valuable for individuals and organizations, if combined with efforts to ensure equality and inclusion. As much as possible, for each group or topic discussed in the remaining chapters, the same six areas are covered. Although aspects unique to the various groups and topics require variations from this general plan, what standardization is possible should provide cohesion and improve readers' ability to consider and compare similarities and differences across groups. Each chapter begins with chapter objectives and relevant key facts. Where appropriate, we have structured the chapters according to these standard sections: introduction and overview, population (including percentages and growth rates), education, and employment (including **participation rates**—working or looking for work, unemployment rates, income levels, and employment types). Within these sections, we highlight points of particular relevance to diversity in organizations, for example, the role of gender role socialization in women's and men's occupational choices.

---

[65]Cox, T., Jr. (1993). *Cultural Diversity in Organizations*. San Francisco: Berrett-Koehler Publishers, p. 7.
[66]Ibid. See also Kossek, E. E., & Zonia, S. C. (1993). "Assessing the Diversity Climate: A Field Study of Reactions to Employer Efforts to Promote Diversity." *Journal of Organizational Behavior*, 14(1): 61–81.

FIGURE 1.1 ***Adapted Interactional Model of the Impact of Diversity on Individual and Organizational Outcomes***

DIVERSITY CLIMATE	INDIVIDUAL OUTCOMES	ORGANIZATIONAL EFFECTIVENESS
Individual-Level Factors • **Identity** • **Prejudice** • **Stereotyping and Social Categorization*** • **Discrimination***	*Affective Outcomes* • **Job/Career Satisfaction** • **Organizational Identification** • **Job Involvement** • **Organizational Citizenship Behaviors***	*First Level* • **Attendance** • **Turnover** • **Resource Acquisition** • **Creativity/ Innovation** • **Problem Solving** • **System Flexibility*** • **Cooperative Behaviors** • **Work Quality** • **Workgroup Cohesiveness and Communication**
Group/Intergroup Factors • **Racial,* Ethnic,* Gender,* and Cultural Differences** • Ethnocentrism • Intergroup Conflict • **In-group/Out-group bias*** • **Similarity Effect***	*Achievement Outcomes* • **Performance Evaluations** • **Compensation** • **Promotion/ Horizontal Mobility Rates** • **Race and Sex Segregation*** • **Glass and Stained Glass Ceiling***	
Organizational-Level Factors • Structural Integration • Informal Integration • **Bias in Human Resource Systems***	*Applicant Outcomes** • **Employment Opportunities*** ***Customer Outcomes**** • **Customer Satisfaction*** • **Organizational Loyalty*** • **Racial Profiling***	*Second Level* • **Marketing and Market Share** • **Lost Business** • **Profitability** • **Stock Prices*** • **Organizational Attractiveness*** • **Organizational Performance*** • Achievement of Formal Organizational Goals • **Bias in Human Resource Systems***

*Not included in the original model.
Items in bold print examined in this book, including relevant research evidence.

Note: Recall that Cox & Blake's (1993) six reasons for valuing diversity are cost (including turnover), resource acquisition, marketing, creativity, problem solving, and system flexibility.

Source: Adapted from Cox, T., Jr. (1993). *Cultural Diversity in Organizations*. San Francisco: Berrett-Koehler Publishers, p. 7.

It is by use of this general plan as well as the focus on topics unique to each group that we provide a distinct picture of the status and experiences of the various group members, which is important to learning and thinking critically about diversity issues. This approach should also provide readers with a cohesive foundation for understanding the aspects of diversity considered here and for others they may encounter in the future both in the United States and all over the world. For example, although different countries may have different minority or non-dominant groups, readers can use the same approach to learn about and develop understanding of them. The following sections discuss details of the standard sections in each chapter.

Introduction and Overview

Each chapter focusing on a particular group (e.g., racial and ethnic groups, workers with disabilities) begins with an introduction and overview containing information unique to that group to help explain its status in relation to diversity in the United States. For example, in the United States, only Blacks have experienced the historical background of slavery and the subsequent discrimination that continues to shape their position in organizations and in society. Latinos are unique in terms of their diverse backgrounds (e.g., Cuba, Puerto Rico, Mexico, Central America), races, language ability, and youthfulness of population. It is not widely known that even though they were considerably more accepted than Blacks, people of Mexican descent experienced extreme discrimination, segregation, and lynching in parts of California and Texas from the early 1900s to the 1970s. Mexican Americans pursued their civil rights during the same period African Americans fought for theirs, at times alongside African Americans and Asians.[67]

The experiences of Asian Americans as immigrants, refugees, or native-born Americans are unique to them. Perceived as the "model minority," Asians at the same time have encountered the glass ceiling and other forms of discrimination.[68] As we will see, the Asian experience in the United States is not uniform; it comprises an unequal distribution of education, wealth, and success, including poor education, extreme poverty, and welfare dependency.[69] And although many think that Asians choose self-employment as a means of earning high wages, research indicates some Asian entrepreneurs are self-employed as a result of discrimination, a lack of opportunities in formal organizations, and the glass ceiling. As with small businesses in general, many Asian businesses fail and others are only profitable because of long hours and

[67]See Acuna, R. (1988). *Occupied America: A History of Chicanos*, 3rd ed. New York: Harper Collins Publishers. See also "Justice for My People" (2003).
[68]Wood, D. (2000). *Glass Ceilings and Asian Americans: The New Face of Workplace Barriers*. Walnut Creek, CA: AltaMira Press.
[69]Espiritu, Y. L. (1999). "The Refugees and the Refuge: Southeast Asians in the United States." In A. G. Dworkin & R. J. Dworkin (Eds.), *The Minority Report*. Orlando, FL: Harcourt Brace Publishers.

the unpaid labor of family members.[70] Like others of color, in some parts of the United States, Asian Americans make up the bulk of those employed as housekeepers and custodians, neighborhood gardeners, garment workers, and in other low-wage occupations. These jobs are quite different in occupation and earnings from the stereotype of the model minority.

Population

The number of people in a particular group is critical for many different reasons. Large groups have more voice in democratic governmental processes, more consumer buying power, and strength in other areas. These benefits may positively affect their treatment in organizations and result in organizations paying more attention to their needs. However, as "minority" groups grow in size, they may seem more threatening to those in the majority, which may negatively affect their organizational status and treatment.[71] But from a positive viewpoint, the growth in minority group populations may allow majority group members to have more personal experiences with and knowledge of particular individuals, which *may*, therefore, allow them to rely on personal knowledge, rather than stereotypes, particularly if given organizational stimuli, tools, and support for doing so.

Along with the benefits that occur as a result of growth in numbers, as the group becomes a greater percentage of the overall population, its voice, buying power, and other strengths increase, warranting attention from persons interested in diversity issues. Even so, 30 million in a population of 60 million is much different from 30 million in a population of 300 million. Population growth occurs through births and immigration, and population growth rates affect both sheer numbers and the degree of impact that a particular group has. When a minority group is growing at a faster rate than the majority, over time, the minority group will increase its percentage of the population as a whole. When a minority group has both a higher birth rate and greater immigration than the majority group, as do Latinos and Asians in the United States, this leads to a faster shift in the numbers and percentages of the minority group compared with the majority group. These shifts in population require different organizational strategies and perspectives in order to address the needs of diverse consumers, applicants, and employees. As an example, as Latinos have become a larger percentage of the population, some organizations have begun to actively recruit bilingual employees in human resources, customer service, marketing, and management positions.

---

[70]Espiritu (1999).

[71]Kanter, R. M. (1977). *Men and Women of the Corporation*. New York: Basic Books.

Education

Each group's level of education affects whether and where people are employed, their incomes, and their opportunities for and actual advancement. Thus, we provide details for each group on the numbers of people of working age with and without high school, college, and advanced degrees. Comparisons of educational achievements within (between men and women) and across groups provide insights into other factors (e.g., the glass ceiling and walls) that may be influencing the employment, income, and organizational advancement of different groups. Do White men and women have similar levels of education? If so, are they receiving similar returns (e.g., income, status, advancement) on their educational investment? What is the educational status of immigrants? How does this affect their employment? Are there differences in education and employment among immigrants from different countries or from different races but the same country? We investigate these and similar questions for each demographic group.

Employment, Unemployment, and Participation Rates

Levels of employment and participation rates of a group are closely tied to education and provide information about a group's position in organizations. The percentages of people in a group who are employed, unemployed, **underemployed**, and not seeking work compared with those of other groups are important in understanding group status and other diversity factors. We seek to answer questions such as the following:

- Are minorities with similar education more, less, or equally likely as Whites to be employed?
- When laid off, how long do different group members, such as older and younger workers, remain unemployed before finding similar employment?
- What are the participation rates for women from various racial and ethnic groups?
- Why are people with disabilities consistently less likely to be employed than are people without disabilities, even when similarly qualified and able to work?

We investigate what can be done about these issues and why organizations should be concerned about them. We consider what employment rates actually mean, compared with what is commonly reported, and how these figures differ across groups, emphasizing that for certain groups unemployment rates are often understated and deceptive.

In periods of apparent economic success, as well as in more difficult economic periods, the job-related status of people of color, women, and

TABLE 1.2 *Percent U.S. Unemployment by Race and Ethnicity*

	1972	2008
Overall	5.6	5.8
Whites	5.1	5.2
Blacks	10.4	10.1
Latinos	7.5	7.6

Note: These rates are population averages. Similar disparities exist by race at various educational levels.

Source: U.S. Department of Labor, Bureau of Labor Statistics. (2009). *Labor Force Characteristics by Race and Ethnicity*, Report 1020. http://www.bls.gov/cps/cpsrace2008.pdf, accessed August 12, 2010.

people with disabilities may be more negative than is apparent. Because Whites are the majority of the population in the United States, their unemployment levels heavily weight the reported unemployment rates. Unemployment for Blacks is usually about twice the unemployment rate for Whites, but this is not commonly known or widely reported. For example, in 1972, the overall unemployment rate was 5.6%; for Whites, Blacks, and Latinos the rates were 5.1%, 10.4%, and 7.5%, respectively (see Table 1.2). In 2008, when overall unemployment was 5.8%, the rates for Whites, Blacks, and Latinos were 5.2%, 10.1%, and 7.6%, respectively.[72]

These types of differences in unemployment rates have been consistent for decades and are not completely explained by differences in education. Blacks have higher average education levels than Latinos, yet Blacks have higher average unemployment rates. What dynamics of diversity are affecting these unusual relationships?

Many people do not know about other distortions in reported unemployment rates. People who have given up actively seeking work in their field ("discouraged" workers), those working at lower levels than appropriate for their education (the underemployed), or people who work part-time because they are unable to find full-time work are not included in the unemployment rate.[73] In the United States, discouraged and underemployed workers are more likely to be Blacks; in many European countries, they are likely to be immigrants.[74] In the United Kingdom, for instance, Bangladeshis are five times more likely to be unemployed and earn

[72]U.S. Department of Labor, Bureau of Labor Statistics. (2009). *Labor Force Characteristics by Race and Ethnicity*, Report 1020. http://www.bls.gov/cps/cpsrace2008.pdf, accessed June 9, 2010.
[73]Ibid., p. 3.
[74]Bell, M. P., Heslin, P., & Fletcher, P. (2010). "Daring to Care About Hidden Unemployment: Discrimination and Discouragement in Minority Communities." Paper presented at the meeting of the Academy of Management, Montreal, Canada.

considerably less per hour than Whites.[75] Iraqis in Denmark are nearly six times more likely to be unemployed compared to the majority population (27% versus 5%).[76] We discuss discouraged, unemployed, and part-time workers and their relationships to diversity in organizations in later chapters.

Types of Employment and Income Levels

The jobs in which people are employed and their income levels provide much insight into the status of different groups. Comparisons between people with similar qualifications but different group memberships provide even greater insight into diversity-related factors at work (e.g., discrimination, equal opportunity, the glass ceiling). We investigate questions such as the following:

- In what types of occupations and industries do most members of a group work?
- What percentages of the group occupy executive, managerial, professional and administrative, or other positions?
- Are similarly qualified women less likely to be in managerial or executive positions than men?
- How do the pay and the advancement potential of the jobs and industries in which women and minorities are clustered compare with the pay and advancement potential of jobs and industries in which Whites and men tend to be clustered?

Education, employment rates, and types of employment lead logically to income. The more education one has, the more likely one is to be employed and earning higher wages. This is theoretically and practically true; however, returns on education vary by race, ethnicity, gender, physical ability, and other factors. Education does not translate into higher income at similar rates for all racial and ethnic groups. The following chapters explore relationships among education, employment, and income for different groups, along with some startling discoveries about the dynamics of discrimination, stereotyping, and other diversity issues.

Focal Issues

Where appropriate, details are provided on one or more issues of particular relevance to a chapter's focal area or group. Chapter 4 considers

---

[75]Zimmerman, K. F., Kahanec, M., Constant, A., DeVoretz, D., Gataullina, L., & Zaiceva, A. (2008). *Study on the Social and Labor Market Integration of Ethnic Minorities.* I Z A Research Report No. 16. Institute for the Study of Labor, Bonn. http://www.iza.org/en/webcontent/publications/reports/report_pdfs/iza_report_16.pdf, accessed July 22, 2010.
[76]Ibid.

the negative effects of discrimination on the health of Blacks and the persistent effects of slavery and discrimination on their social and financial progress. One focal area in Chapter 9 is the relationship between socialization and women's reportedly lower likelihood of negotiating higher salaries successfully (and its impact upon the wage gap). Such investigations of the details of some of the diversity-related concerns unique to specific groups may be unfamiliar to readers as diversity issues but are actually quite common on a day-to-day basis. For example, many people are aware that male and female children are taught what is appropriate sex-typed behavior, but giving this a name ("gender role socialization") and explaining its relevance should help readers appreciate the everyday influences diversity issues have on individuals and organizations.

Individual and Organizational Recommendations

Relevant to its specific focus, each chapter makes recommendations for individuals and for organizations related to the concerns of the particular group under study as well as for improving the organizations' overall climate for diversity. Although organizational, societal, and systemic factors underlie much of the extant discrimination and resistance to diversity, some individual actions that people may take can influence individual outcomes. What can one person do? Chapter 4 provides recommendations for Black women that can reduce the double-whammy disadvantage of membership in two non-dominant groups. Chapter 9 includes specific recommendations on how organizations can prevent sexual harassment and how individual women can reduce or address individual discrimination. Chapter 13 suggests ways in which older workers can avoid pre-interview exclusion based on high school or college completion dates on a résumé.

International Feature

Many chapters include an international feature that considers some aspects of their main subject from an international perspective. Chapter 10 compares family policies in the United States with those of other developed nations; Chapter 13 explores legislation in Australia that prohibits age discrimination against younger, as well as older, workers. Inclusion of international features clarifies the importance of diversity around the world and demonstrates ways in which readers and organizations may learn from and improve diversity issues in different regions.

Other Features

Each chapter includes at least one case study, individual feature, organizational feature, research summary, or report on litigation or discrimination complaints and an analysis. Reports of research from a variety of disciplines provide understandable discussions of rigorous empirical studies. Organizational features describe examples of diversity programs at actual companies. Descriptions of actual litigation or discrimination complaints against some of the same companies are reports on possibly familiar real-life issues and encourage readers' in-depth analysis and critiquing. Rather than touting any particular company's diversity program as ideal or criticizing organizations that have undergone discrimination claims, the organizational and litigation features provide useful information on real programs and issues in organizations. As well, the descriptions of discrimination charges and settlements, particularly involving companies with long-standing diversity programs, underscore the importance of continued, vigilant commitment to diversity, equality, and inclusion. Organizations must make their stance on diversity widely known and to every employee through repeated training, communication, and monitoring of decision making and employee outcomes. Our inclusion of positive reports as well as reports on charges of discrimination, settlements, and other problems also demonstrates the need to avoid blanket assumptions or judgments about an organization based on limited information.

Suggested chapter-end Actions and Exercises should enhance readers' understanding of the subject matter and help make abstract concepts and discussion more pragmatic. Some of these exercises are interviewing a person working in a job atypical for his or her sex, documenting the race and ethnic makeup of cashiers at a discount store, or constructing an organization chart of a company with which the reader is familiar (for possible evidence of glass ceilings, walls, and escalators). "Misperceptions" and "Reality" points interspersed throughout the chapters highlight common misperceptions about a topic and then provide more accurate information.[77]

Because diversity issues are interrelated, an important feature of the book is cross-references and discussion of the relevant interrelationships. For example, Chapter 11 includes a section on same-sex families that is also referenced in Chapter 10. As important as an individual examination of each group and topic is (i.e., separate chapters on racial groups), the cross-references and discussions of these interrelationships within chapters create a holistic view of diversity in organizations. Diversity issues are relevant to everyone, and to each other.

---

[77]Not every reader will be familiar with every misperception.

SUMMARY

This chapter has introduced the concept of diversity, detailed the organization of the book, and explained what readers may expect. Included are descriptions of protections from employment discrimination provided by U.S. federal regulations as well as areas left unprotected but that are relevant to issues of diversity. Also touched on, from an international perspective, is the importance of not using a one-size-fits-all approach to managing diversity, but instead focusing on the issues most relevant to the particular context. Although some groups have experienced considerably more discrimination, devaluation, and underutilization than others, historically and currently, we take the perspective that diversity is of importance to everyone. The overriding premise of this book is that diversity is valuable to individuals and organizations for moral, social, and business reasons and that people from various backgrounds should be afforded employment opportunities and allowed to reach their potential as employees, managers, executives, and leaders. Research indicates that job applicants, employees, customers, and constituents will respond positively when organizations value diversity, and negatively when they do not. We do not ignore the fact that increasing diversity involves difficulties, but write from the perspective that those difficulties must be addressed so that everyone has opportunities to contribute and that this will be beneficial to individuals, organizations, and society. From this perspective, the book continues its consideration of the past, present, and future of diversity in organizations.

KEY TERMS

Access discrimination — when people are denied employment opportunities, or "access" to jobs, based on their race, sex, age, or other factors not related to productivity.

Diversity — real or perceived differences among people in race, ethnicity, sex, age, physical and mental ability, sexual orientation, religion, work and family status, weight and appearance, and other identity-based attributes that affect their interactions and relationships.

Diversity climate — individual-, intergroup-, and organizational-level factors that comprise the atmosphere for different groups and of support for or resistance to diversity in an organization.

Identity group — the collectivities people use to categorize themselves and others.

Inclusion — the degree to which the different voices of a diverse workforce are respected and heard.

Labor force — all persons age 16 and over working or looking for work.

Labor market discrimination — the valuation in the labor market of personal characteristics of applicants and workers that are unrelated to productivity.

Participation rate — the ratio of persons age 16 and over who are working or looking for work divided by the population of persons age 16 and over.

Primary labor market — jobs in large, bureaucratic organizations that have opportunities for advancement and include lucrative retirement, medical, and vacation benefits.

Secondary labor market — jobs, often in the service sector, that offer few or no opportunities for advancement, nor medical, retirement, or vacation benefits.

Treatment discrimination — when people are employed but are treated differently once employed, receiving fewer job-related rewards, resources, or opportunities than they should receive based on job-related criteria.

Underemployed — workers employed at less than their full employment potential, including those working part-time, temporary, or intermittent jobs but desiring regular, full-time work; those working for lower wages than their skills would imply or in positions requiring considerably lower skills than they possess; and those involuntarily working outside their fields.

Questions to Consider

1. What is diversity?
2. How can relevant diversity issues be identified in different contexts?
3. List and discuss the six reasons that Cox and Blake proposed for valuing diversity in organizations. What else can be given as reasons for valuing diversity?
4. What are some negative outcomes of increasing diversity, and given the inevitability of increasing diversity, what can organizations do to reduce these negative outcomes?
5. What does research say about the importance of diversity to individuals?

Actions and Exercises

1. Begin observing diversity in your work, school, neighborhood, religious, and/or entertainment environments. What is the racial, ethnic, gender, and age distribution of the people in each of these environments? What do you observe that you may not have noticed were you not investigating diversity in organizations? Explain.
2. Identify the relevant diversity categories in two different countries. What are the key factors (e.g., population, participation, poverty, group differences) involved in those categories?

Theories and Thinking about Diversity

CHAPTER 2

Chapter Objectives

After completing this chapter, readers should have a greater understanding of what constitutes minority groups, the processes surrounding people's thinking about and treatment of those who are dissimilar to them, and what organizational processes can help to increase diversity, equality, and inclusion. Specifically, they should be able to:

❑ *discuss the meaning of the terms* minority group *and* non-dominant group.

❑ *explain characteristics used to identify non-dominant groups and be able to use these characteristics to identify the non-dominant groups in one's particular environment.*

❑ *discuss thought processes related to stereotyping, prejudice, and discrimination and theories related to diversity in organizations.*

❑ *examine in-group favoritism and out-group bias.*

❑ *explain what organizations can do to promote diversity and inclusion, given knowledge about reasons for differential treatment, experiences, and outcomes for different demographic groups.*

❑ *have a foundation for synthesizing the material in the remaining chapters.*

Key Facts

Characteristics of minority or non-dominant groups often include identifiability, differential power, discrimination, and group awareness.

Minority, or non-dominant, groups are not necessarily fewer in number than majority, or dominant, groups.

Categorization and stereotyping are often unconscious processes, which alone are not necessarily negative.

People tend to attribute positive characteristics to members of their in-groups and negative characteristics to members of groups to which they do not belong.

In-group favoritism and out-group bias disadvantage non-dominant groups and impede diversity.

Structured interviews can reduce the effects of similarity bias in selection.

Introduction and Overview

In this chapter, we consider some of the many theories and research studies related to psychological processes affecting diversity in organizations. What are prejudice, stereotyping, and discrimination and how do they work to impede diversity? Why is it that diversity is at times a negative attribute of organizational functioning and what can be done to change this? What factors are associated with people's preferences for similar others and hostility and discrimination toward dissimilar others? What can organizations do to address these effects? Knowledge of these factors will provide a foundation for understanding the material in the remaining chapters of the book and for fostering diversity in organizations.

We begin with a discussion of the characteristics associated with minority groups. What defines minority groups? Aside from counting, how does one tell who is the "majority" and who is the "minority" in a society? We examine some of the many theories and concepts related to diversity and investigate how new forms of racism and sexism (and other "isms") affect individuals' behavior toward others. We conclude with suggestions for individuals and organizations to reduce stereotyping and discrimination and to increase fairness in employment decisions and treatment of others at work. ●

■ WHAT IS A "MINORITY"?[1]

Although the term *minority* is generally understood to mean "fewer in number," it does not always refer to groups that are numerically fewer than majority group members. What, then, *is* a minority?[2] Minority or non-dominant[3] groups are those subordinated to majority or dominant group members in terms of power, prestige, and privilege.[4] In South Africa, Whites are the dominant group, although they are outnumbered by people of color. In the United States, women outnumber men, but men are the dominant group. *Non-dominant*, then, is a more accurate term than *minority*, although both are used in this book.

In many of the topics we cover, there are clear dominant and non-dominant groups; in others, the distinction is ambiguous. Of the U.S. racial and ethnic groups discussed in this book, Blacks, Latinos, Asian Americans, American Indians, and multiracial group members represent non-dominant groups, and Whites are the dominant group. Throughout the world, men are the dominant sex, although women often outnumber men. In the United States, Christians are the dominant religious group, and heterosexual is the dominant sexual orientation. People without disabilities are clearly the dominant group. Attractive people are dominant with respect to unattractive people, and thinner people are dominant with

[1] Dworkin, A. G., & Dworkin, R. J. (1999). *The Minority Report*, 3rd ed. Orlando, FL: Harcourt Brace Publishers, pp. 11–27.

[2] Ibid.

[3] Some researchers use the term *subordinate* instead of *non-dominant*.

[4] Schaefer, R. T. (1989). *Racial and Ethnic Groups*, 4th ed. New York: Harper Collins Publishers.

respect to overweight people—although overweight people outnumber thinner people. Whether younger or older workers are the dominant group is not clear, making research and generalizations about age diversity somewhat complicated. Although older workers occupy more of the high-status, high-paid organizational positions than younger workers, stereotypes and misperceptions pervade the workplace experiences, opportunities, and outcomes of many older workers. At times, younger workers are clearly preferred to older workers, but at other times younger people are viewed as irresponsible, not dependable, and lacking in organizational commitment. The answer to the question of whether people with or without families are dominant is even less clear. For men, researchers have found that being married (to a woman) and having children contribute to being viewed positively in organizations, to higher wages, and to greater advancement. For women, as we discuss in Chapters 9 and 10, having a husband and children contributes to perceptions of divided loyalties and, as a result, to lower wages and fewer promotions.

In considering what is a minority, or non-dominant group, social scientists propose that non-dominant group members have distinguishing characteristics across societies and time. Drawing from the seminal work of a group of noted social scientists, Anthony and Rosalind Dworkin propose that minority group members have four common characteristics: identifiability, differential power, the experience of discrimination,[5] and group awareness. Using similar ideas, Edward Sampson offers the following relationships between identifiability, power, and discrimination:

… which types of differences are emphasized and which are ignored is usually a choice made by the social groups that occupy positions of dominance within a society. These are the groups that have the power to make their definitions of who is one of them and who is different stick. Dominant groups not only select the qualities of difference that will be emphasized but also develop the rationale to explain why those differences mean one group should be treated differently from another. (p. 22)[6]

The ways in which identifiability, power, discrimination, and group awareness create subordinating systems are considered in the following sections.

---

[5] Dworkin & Dworkin used the term *differential and pejorative treatment* as well as *discrimination*.
[6] Sampson, E. E. (1999). *Dealing with Differences*. Orlando, FL: Harcourt Brace Publishers.

Identifiability

For subordinating systems to work, minority and majority group members must possess distinguishing physical or cultural traits that make it possible to single them out for differential treatment (such as discrimination and segregation). If members of non-dominant groups were not recognizable, differential treatment would be difficult or impossible. Historical records suggest that dominant groups devise means to identify non-dominant groups if the members have no distinguishing features. As an example, in Nazi Germany, Jews were required to wear yellow armbands to distinguish them from non-Jews.[7]

In the United States, women, Blacks, Latinos, Asians, and American Indians are generally fairly easy to identify, making it easier to single them out for differential treatment. In the past, as in the present, however, many individual members of non-dominant racial groups have been difficult to identify, including those who self-identify as members of a minority group who are attributed to another group by independent observers. If a person's Black, Hispanic, Asian, or American Indian heritage is clearly visible, differential treatment from prejudiced employers, businesses, and even the police (racial profiling) is a potential consequence. But it is also true, as we discuss in later chapters, that non-dominant group members who cannot be clearly identified may experience some problems as well. The group identities of gays and lesbians, some multiracial people, and people with some types of disabilities are invisible, and these group members may experience stress and guilt associated with this invisibility and, at times, fear of disclosure.

Differential Power

Dworkin and Dworkin define *power* as the "actual use of resources to influence and control others."[8] Differential power allows those who have more power to control those who have less power. Although power is associated with numerical dominance, those who are members of groups that are larger in number are not always the most powerful. As examples, native people in what would become the United States were originally greater in number, but they were less powerful than the European newcomers and thus were subject to domination; there are more women than men in many countries, but women as a group are less powerful than men. Through their control of resources, powerful groups also control access to education, employment, food, health care, income, and other things that

---

[7] Dworkin & Dworkin (1999).
[8] Ibid., p. 19.

affect the life chances and futures of those without power. Thus, power helps the dominant remain dominant.

Discrimination

Dworkin and Dworkin include the experience of discrimination as a defining characteristic of minorities. **Discrimination** has been broadly defined as differential and pejorative actions that serve to limit the social, political, or economic opportunities of members of particular groups.[9] Various types of discrimination have limiting effects on its targets. For example, gender-based pay discrimination limits the social, political, and economic opportunities of women. Through access discrimination, the social, political, and economic opportunities of Blacks are limited. For targets of discrimination, according to Dworkin and Dworkin, the experience of being discriminated against leads to group awareness and becomes the focus of protests and activism.[10]

Group Awareness

Group awareness, the final characteristic of minority groups proposed by Dworkin and Dworkin, is one consequence of their subordination by the majority and its discriminatory practices. The unfair treatment minority groups experience leads them to realize that they are subjected to differential treatment simply because of their group membership and that this treatment is a result of the majority's definitions and evaluations rather than to any intrinsic qualities or actions of their group. They may also realize that they can achieve certain goals (e.g., jobs, housing) through cooperative resistance (such as protests, boycotts, and participation in the political process).

Analysis of the Characteristics

Although these characteristics—identifiability, differential power, discrimination, and group awareness—do in many cases help clarify which groups are minority groups, they are by no means definitive. At times, they do not apply to some non-dominant groups or are otherwise insufficient, as for those with invisible identities and for individuals with power who are also non-dominant group members (e.g., a CEO who is a woman

[9] Ibid., p. 98; Frederickson, G. M., & Knobel, D. T. (1980). "A History of Discrimination." In T. F. Pettigrew, G. M. Fredrickson, D. T. Knobel, N. Glazer, & R. Ueda (Eds.), *Prejudice*. Cambridge, MA: The Belknap Press of Harvard University, pp. 30–37.
[10] Dworkin & Dworkin (1999).

of color). In other situations, there are disconnects between the group to which a person appears to belong and his or her self-identity. Taylor Cox labels these situations as incongruence of phenotype (visible identity) and culture identities,[11] such as a Mexican American with Caucasian physical features identifying with the Mexican American culture. This creates cognitive dissonance for observers that may cause discomfort or even negative reactions. In the chapters that discuss individual groups, we will analyze further the applicability of these four criteria to those groups.

▌ CATEGORIZATION AND IDENTITY

As discussed in the previous section, Dworkin and Dworkin's first defining criterion for minority groups is identifiability. Once identified, what factors make groups single out others for discrimination? What factors make otherwise rational people prone to believe stereotypes? Why do prejudicial attitudes sometimes result in discrimination and not in other times?

Although prejudice and discrimination are sometimes viewed as synonymous, they are not. **Prejudice** is "irrationally based, negative attitudes" about certain groups and their members.[12] Prejudice is an attitude, whereas discrimination is behavior based on the attitude. Given the power to act and the absence of sanctions for doing so, discriminatory behavior may result from prejudice. For example, employers may have negative attitudes about overweight people, and these attitudes may result in refusal to hire them (employment discrimination), which is not currently illegal in most parts of the United States.

Stereotypes are the overgeneralization of characteristics to large human groups and are the basis for prejudice and discrimination. **Prescriptive stereotyping** refers to perceptions about how people should behave, based on their group memberships (e.g., women should wear makeup, as discussed in the Ann Hopkins case in Chapter 9), while **descriptive stereotyping** refers to ideas about how people do or will behave, based on their group memberships (e.g., women are caring and are therefore appropriate as nurses and elementary school teachers).[13] Fairly common job-related stereotypes about the groups we consider in the following chapters can be easily called to mind even by those who do not believe

[11] Cox, T. (1993). *Cultural Diversity in Organizations: Theory, Research, and Practice*. San Francisco: Berrett-Koehler Publishers.

[12] Pettigrew, T. (1980). "Prejudice." In T. F. Pettigrew, G. M. Fredrickson, D. T. Knobel, N. Glazer, & R. Ueda (Eds.), *Prejudice*. Cambridge, MA: The Belknap Press of Harvard University, pp. 1–29.

[13] Goldman, B. M., Gutek, B. A., Stein, J. H., & Lewis, K. (2006). "Employment Discrimination in Organizations: Antecedents and Consequences." *Journal of Management*, 32(6): 786–831.

them or who are themselves members of the targeted groups.[14] Some stereotypes reflect interactions between multiple groups, such as race, ethnicity, gender, and parental status. In a job-related context, stereotyping can prevent individuals who would be capable, committed workers from being hired, promoted, or trained. Negative organizational outcomes follow from the individual outcomes.

Although common stereotypes can easily be identified, when prompted to think of someone from each group who does not fit the stereotype, many people can do so. Despite being able to identify people who do not fit them, people often attend to evidence that supports stereotypes they hold and ignore evidence that disconfirms stereotypes. Further, stereotypes can lead to prejudice, which in turn can lead to discrimination, given the right circumstances.

Social Categorization and Stereotyping

Social cognitive theory suggests that people use categorization to simplify and cope with the large volumes of information to which they are continually exposed. Categories allow us to quickly and easily compartmentalize data. Consistent with Dworkin and Dworkin's proposals that minority group members must be identifiable, people often use visible characteristics, such as race, sex, and age, to categorize others. Thus, when one sees a person of a particular race, automatic processing occurs and beliefs about this particular race are activated. When the person is not visible but his or her name is known (perhaps on a résumé), this provides information about the person's sex, which allows categorization: male or female. Mental models of a person suited to a particular job (e.g., bank teller, truck driver) are often associated with sex, and sorting of candidates by sex occurs as a result of such models. A name may also provide evidence of a person's race or ethnic background, which could also allow categorization and discrimination (see Chapter 4). People's propensity to categorize, coupled with the need to then *evaluate* the person categorized, leads to stereotyping.[15]

Along with the tendency to categorize, people have a tendency to perceive themselves and others as belonging to particular groups. This part of categorization, referred to as *social categorization,* involves ordering one's social environment by groupings of persons.[16] Social categorization helps create and define one's place in society. Groups define one's place by separating people: where we belong or do not belong and where others

---

[14] See Cox (1993), p. 91, for a detailed list of common stereotypes about various groups.

[15] Nelson, T. (2002). *The Psychology of Prejudice.* Boston: Allyn & Bacon.

[16] Tajfel, H. (1978). "Social Categorization, Social Identity and Social Comparison." In H. Tajfel (Ed.), *Differentiation Between Social Groups.* London: Academic Press, pp. 61–76.

belong and do not belong. A person's in-group is the group to which he or she belongs, while out-groups are groups to which he or she does not belong. Depending on the situation, and what factor is salient, or distinctive, a person's in-group may be based on his or her race, sex, age, or other factor of importance.[17] Salient characteristics are important to an individual at a particular time, or at all times, depending on how critical the characteristic is to the individual's experiences and life chances. For example, in a department with three women and ten men, the in-group for the women would be women and the out-group would be men. If the department comprised two Blacks (one man and one woman) and eleven White men and women, in-groups and out-groups could instead be determined using racial categories. Which category would be salient would depend on the situation (e.g., if the men were all sitting together on one side of the room, or if the conversation were about racial profiling) and the extent to which people *identified* themselves by their race or sex. For a Black person in the United States, race may be salient in an organization in which there are few Blacks or in an organization in which everyone is Black (if being in such an organization is unusual). Beverly Daniel Tatum's book *Why Are All the Black Kids Sitting Together in the Cafeteria?* explains that the clustering of Blacks in the cafeterias of predominantly White educational institutions is obvious and disturbing to some observers.[18] The similar clustering of Whites is less obvious or disturbing.

Social identity refers to the part of an individual's self-concept that derives from his or her membership in a particular social group and the value and emotional significance attached to that group membership.[19] Using race as an example, social identity describes how much a person identifies as a member of a certain race and how strongly and passionately he or she feels about belonging to that race. Is being Black integral to one's life, experiences, and being? For sex as a characteristic, social identity describes how much a person identifies as a man or woman and how strongly and passionately he or she feels about being a man or woman. Is being a man integral to one's life, experiences, and being? Social identity is similar to Dworkin and Dworkin's conceptualization of group awareness for non-dominant group members. Those who see that they belong to a particular group and that the group receives pejorative treatment by others (out-groups) become aware of their group membership as a collective body able to take resistive action.

[17] McGuire, W. J., McGuire, C. V., Child, P., & Fujioka, T. (1978). "Salience of Ethnicity in the Spontaneous Self-Concept as a Function of One's Ethnic Distinctiveness in the Social Environment." *Journal of Personality and Social Psychology*, 36(5): 511–520.
[18] Tatum, B. D. (1997). *Why Are All the Black Kids Sitting Together in the Cafeteria?* New York: Basic Books.
[19] Ibid., p. 63.

Consequences of Social Categorization and Social Identity

As noted earlier, when we first come into contact with others, we categorize them as belonging to an in-group, or an out-group. These tendencies can affect job satisfaction and the relationships among supervisors, subordinates, and peers.[20] We tend to see members of our in-group as being heterogeneous but out-group members as being homogeneous—having similar attitudes, behaviors, and characteristics (i.e., fitting stereotypes). Researchers propose that these perspectives may occur because of the breadth of interactions we have with people from our in-group as compared with those from out-groups. There also is often strong in-group favoritism and, at times, derogation of out-group members. Favoritism and viewing members of one's group positively bolster one's self-esteem, as does viewing other groups negatively. Alone, favoritism for one's particular group is not necessarily negative. When coupled with power, however, favoritism is associated with negative opportunities and outcomes for the out-group.

In-group favoritism and out-group biases. A likely result of in-group favoritism in a work setting is the hiring, promoting, and rewarding by those in power (i.e., the dominant group) of members of their in-group. Even if no overt derogation of out-group members is involved, the non-dominant out-group is disadvantaged when the dominant in-group is favored. Because women and minorities are typically non-dominant in organizations, social categorization and in-group favoritism work against them, negatively affecting their chances for employment, high-status positions, promotion, and other opportunities when compared with Whites and men. Women and people of color often have relatively little organizational power; thus any favoritism they may feel toward women and people of color is less likely to disadvantage men and Whites. The documented existence of the similarity effect, or similarity bias, in which people are more likely to select or hire demographically similar others, is also a manifestation of in-group favoritism. However, as discussed in Research Summary 2.1, using structured interviews can negate in-group favoritism.

Similar behaviors exhibited by members of the in-group and the out-group are judged differently, in addition to favoring the in-group and derogating the out-group.[21] A man who exhibits a "take-charge" attitude is viewed as assertive (a positive attribute), but a woman who does so is "aggressive" (a negative attribute; see also the Ann Hopkins case in

---

[20] Shen, J., Chanda, A., D'Netto, B., & Monga, M. (2009). "Managing Diversity Through Human Resource Management: An International Perspective and Conceptual Framework." *The International Journal of Human Resource Management*, 20(2): 235–251.
[21] Dworkin & Dworkin (1999).

Using Structured Interviews to Reduce Bias in Selection

Many researchers have investigated the influence of demographic similarity on interview outcomes. Research results have been mixed, with some researchers finding that interviewers favored those who were similar in race or sex while others finding no similarity effects. Julie McCarthy and her colleagues proposed that these mixed results were due to different research settings, different samples, and different types of interviews. Compared with unstructured interviews, in which the interviewer asks various questions to different candidates, properly designed, structured interviews have certain key characteristics that increase the validity of the selection process. One of the key elements is that interviewers ask all candidates the same set of questions that are based on a job analysis—what tasks the candidate will be required to do, and what knowledge, skills, and abilities she or he will need.

McCarthy et al. used the key elements and thirteen others identified by previous research as being critical to successful structured interviews (including behaviorally anchored rating scales and interviewer training). Their sample included nearly 20,000 people who had applied for professional positions with the U.S. government. Demographically, of applicants 59% were men, 34% were women, and 7% declined to provide their sex. Whites, Asians, Hispanics, and Blacks were 79%, 7%, 5%, and 4% of applicants, respectively. Five percent did not report their race or ethnicity. Of 207 interviewers, 58% were men, 37% were women, and 5% did not identify their sex; Whites, Blacks, Asians, and Hispanics comprised 63%, 19%, 4%, and 3% of the interviewers, respectively, with 11% not providing their race or ethnicity.

Each candidate had experience-based, situational, and behavioral interviews. In the experience-based interview, applicants answered questions about their qualifications. In the situational interview, applicants responded to hypothetical questions that they might experience at work. In the behavioral interview, applicants described their behavior in past situations that was relevant to the job for which they were being interviewed. Interviewers were extensively trained on how to conduct and score the interview, on the importance of taking notes during the interview, and on rater errors, and two interviewers evaluated each candidate.

Findings were clear: Applicants' race and sex were not related to their ratings by the interviewers nor was applicant/interviewer similarity related to applicants' ratings. Because the research involved a very large field sample that included significant proportions of White, Black, Hispanic, and Asian applicants and interviewers, the results of no sex and race effects and no similarity effects in applicant ratings have strong implications for selection decisions. The researchers noted that organizations that adopt carefully structured and administered interviews can minimize concerns about discrimination on the basis of race and sex. The use of highly structured interviews will help facilitate the selection of a diverse workforce as well as reduce litigation concerns. Through requiring structured interviews, and monitoring results of human resources activities for fairness, organizational leaders can also reduce the effects of individual prejudice, stereotyping, and discrimination, and bias in HR systems (see Figure 1.1).

Source: McCarthy, J. M., Van Iddeking, C. H., & Campion, M. A. (2010). "Are Highly Structured Job Interviews Resistant to Demographic Similarity Effects?" *Personnel Psychology*, 63: 325–359.

QUESTIONS TO CONSIDER

1. Aside from the diversity-related benefits, what are some other benefits of structured job interviews?

2. For your current job or for your most recent previous job, was your interview a structured interview? What were the race and sex of the last three people with whom you interviewed for a job? Were they similar to or different from you? Do you think the similarity or difference played a role in whether you were hired?

Chapter 9). Again, because men are in positions of power, their propensity is to see this attitude as a positive attribute of men but to judge it as negative when exhibited by women, which disadvantages women.

Fundamental attribution error. The **fundamental attribution error**, the tendency to underestimate the influence of external factors (e.g., situations or circumstances) and overestimate the influence of internal factors (e.g., personal qualities) when evaluating the behavior of others, also occurs during in-group and out-group evaluations. Thus, when in-group members behave positively or are successful, this behavior is attributed to the character or personal attributes of in-group members. When they behave negatively (such as screaming at a subordinate), this behavior is attributed to the circumstances (e.g., being upset because the computer system crashed and records were lost). When out-group members exhibit desirable behaviors, this behavior is attributed to luck or chance rather than to their character. When they behave negatively (such as screaming at a subordinate), this behavior is attributed to the character of the out-group member (e.g., rude, inconsiderate). The entire out-group is also then viewed as being rude, rather than as having one member who behaved rudely at a particular point in time. Future interactions with out-group members will then continue to be shaped by perceptions that they are rude. Ironically, expecting that someone will be rude may lead to treating that person rudely, to which they may respond rudely, confirming the expectation that they (and people like them) are rude.

When confronted with information about an out-group member that is contradictory to stereotypes, people tend to see this is as "unique" ("not like the rest of them"[22]) rather than use it to question and discard their beliefs. When confronted with behavior that confirms a stereotype about an out-group member, people attend to such information and hold to relevant

---

[22] Padilla, L. M. (2001). "But *You're* Not a Dirty Mexican: Internalized Oppression, Latinos, and the Law." *Texas Hispanic Journal of Law and Policy*, 7(1): 58–113.

stereotypes. From a diversity perspective, let us consider the stereotype that Asians lack communication skills and thus prefer to work in technical jobs rather than managerial jobs. Let us assume that a decision maker who is making promotion and succession plans holds this stereotype about Asians. If this person knows an Asian American who was born and reared in the United States (and who speaks English as well or poorly as any other American), he or she is still likely to think Asians as a group do not speak English well and will not make good managers. Rather than use the knowledge that this individual Asian has good communication skills as a reason to question and discard the stereotype, the decision maker is likely to discard the information as unique to this particular Asian. Were that decision maker to encounter an Asian who preferred the technical promotion track over the managerial path, he or she would attribute this preference to the Asian's lack of communication skills (rather than to a genuine personal strength or interest), confirming an existing stereotype.

Taking women as another example, if a decision maker holds the stereotype that women do not have the requisite managerial skills, a woman who expresses interest in advancing in an organization and is highly successful in assessment center exercises would still be disadvantaged by that stereotypical perception. A successful woman would be viewed as an anomaly, and her success would be attributed to external factors (the organization's desire to increase representation of women in management, affirmative action, or physical attractiveness), rather than to her personal strengths and motivation. Were she to enter management and fail, this confirmatory failure would be attributed to her (and women) not having the skills requisite to manage. In actuality, her failure may be related to the failure of management to provide training, mentoring, and encouragement due to stereotypes about women managers.[23]

Again turning to how these attribution errors disadvantage non-dominant groups, imagine that those in positions of power—the dominant group—attribute their own failures to circumstances but their successes to personal strengths and character. Imagine also that they see the failures of non-dominant groups as a result of lack of strength and moral character and the successes of those groups as due to luck, accident, or chance. A likely consequence, then, is the tendency to hire, promote, and reward the in-groups, because they are meritorious, and to not hire, promote, and reward out-groups, because they clearly are not meritorious. Feature 2.1

---

[23] A featured case in Chapter 9 describes a case in which a woman was used as a test to see how women drivers would fare—expectations for her success were low, however. The woman's failure as a delivery driver resulted in the company's decision to not hire any more women drivers, because it was clear that they would not work out.

FEATURE 2.1	*The Media and the Promulgation of Stereotypes*

News reports, television and movies, and commercials communicate stereotypes about perpetrators and victims of crime, gender roles, age groups, and numerous other diversity issues.[24] People tend to believe what they see on television and read on news Web sites, implicitly trusting writers and reporters to be objective conveyors of what is actually occurring. Yet those who write and choose stories are not unbiased. Instead, they are products of a society that views certain groups as more likely to commit crimes, to have large families they are unable to support, to be illegal immigrants, and have other negative biases reflecting racial, ethnic, gender, and other stereotypes. Although Whites commit a greater proportion of drug-related crimes, Blacks and Latinos are more likely to be shown on television being arrested for such crimes. Although most crime is intraracial (e.g., Black on Black or White on White), news reports are more likely to portray Black on White crime.[25] People of color are also more prominently portrayed as perpetrators of crime in the news. One study found that over fourteen weeks, people of color were shown to be crime perpetrators in 20% more cases than would be predicted based on FBI statistics.[26]

Misperception: Blacks and Latinos commit more crimes than Whites.

Reality: Blacks and Latinos are more likely to be arrested than Whites and even more likely to be depicted on television being arrested than their actual representation among arrests.

In addition to biased reporting of crimes, the media's use of divisive or misleading terminology causes resistance to diversity. *Affirmative action* does not mean *quotas*, for example, but if the news media equate them, people will be more likely to equate them also. Women are working at some of the highest participation rates in history, but if *60 Minutes* reports that large numbers of executive women are leaving the workforce to stay at home, people will believe this is true. During the aftermath of the Hurricane Katrina in 2005, Yahoo! News (online) displayed photos of the flooding in New Orleans and people wading through the water with food, drawing the attention of many people of all racial and ethnic backgrounds. Whites were reported to be wading after *finding* food, while a young Black male was reported to be wading after *looting* a store. Explanations that the photos were taken by two different reporters and that the descriptive bylines were the reporters' words did little to reduce the perceptions of bias.[27] After complaints, at the request of the photo owner, Yahoo! removed the photo of the Whites, while the one showing the Black man remained.

QUESTIONS TO CONSIDER

1. In addition to racial, ethnic, and gender stereotyping, what other kinds of stereotypes have you seen in the media? How do frequent portrayals of such stereotypes affect people's perceptions of their veracity?

---

[24] Nelson (2002). See also Anastasio, P. A., Rose, K. C., & Chapman, K. C. (1999). "Can the Media Create Public Opinion? A Social-Identity Approach." *Current Directions in Psychological Science*, 8(5): 152–155.

[25] For a discussion of intraracial crime compared with interracial crime, see Gross, S. R., Jacoby, K., Matheson, D., Montgomery, N., & Patil, S. (2005). "Exonerations in the United States: 1989 Through 2003." *The Journal of Criminal Law and Criminology*, 95: 524–560.

[26] Romer, D., Jamieson, K. H., & deCouteau, N. J. (1998). "The Treatment of Persons of Color in Local Television News: Ethnic Blame Discourse or Realistic Group Conflict?" *Communication Research*, 25(3): 286–305, cited in Nelson (2002).

[27] Ralli, T. (2005, September 5). "Who's a Looter? In Storm's Aftermath, Pictures Kick Up a Different Kind of Tempest." *New York Times*. Section C, Column 1, p. 6.

2. *Choose one week night and one weekend night to watch television during prime time. Document the programs watched. Who are the main characters? Describe their race, sex, approximate age, and other notable factors. What diversity-related factors do you observe?*

3. *One commercial that has attempted to change what was a stereotypical statement is the revised Jif ® peanut butter commercial. Previous commercials said, "Choosy Moms*

choose Jif ®"; the newer one says, "Choosy Moms ... and Dads choose Jif®." What other stereotype-resistant commercials have you observed? What stereotype-supportive commercials have you observed? What messages are being conveyed?

4. *Investigate the circumstances surrounding the 2010 Shirley Sherrod/USDA media-driven disaster. What could have prevented the disaster from spreading with such fervor?*

describes how media portrayals contribute to stereotyping and distorted perceptions of group members.

Chapter 4 examines how the legacy of slavery and discrimination has contributed to wealth disparities between Whites and Blacks. Chapter 7 considers how privileges enjoyed by Whites as "normal" aspects of everyday life contribute to the "myth of meritocracy." For example, when Whites believe that Blacks do not have as much wealth as Whites have because of failing to invest, to become entrepreneurs, or to work hard and that Whites have greater wealth because of hard work, this is an example of the fundamental attribution error. Making such an error does not allow Whites to see how their personal, unearned advantages also disadvantage non-dominant group members. These unearned advantages include such things as networks in organizations that hire them because of in-group referrals, legacy admissions to prestigious universities, and inheritance from ancestors who profited from things denied to Blacks (e.g., union membership and resulting high wages, homes in neighborhoods reserved for Whites that appreciated in value).

Multiple group memberships. Multiple group memberships make relationships between in-groups and out-groups and social identities quite complex. A White male has a racial identity and a sex or gender identity. Depending on the circumstances and particular stereotypes, he may perceive Whites or men as the in-group and non-Whites and women as the out-groups, as appropriate. In some cases, Whiteness may be the most salient identity, and he may display favoritism toward White women. In other cases, his maleness may be more salient, and he may favor a Black man. When stereotyping is included as a factor, he may make different decisions. If Blacks are perceived as not reliable, for example, the White male manager may prefer to hire a White woman. If he views women as likely to quit work to stay at home with children, he may favor a man of color.

Add religion, sexual orientation, and disability to that White male's social identities and the situation becomes even more complex. Imagine that the White man is also Jewish and gay and has a disability. In some circumstances, being Jewish or having a disability may be salient. In other circumstances, his White maleness may be overshadowed by his having a disability or being gay. These factors would reduce his power and the perception that he is a member of the in-group of heterosexual, non-disabled White males. Being gay or having a disability could also affect his perceptions of and actions toward (other) non-dominant group members. If his identity as a member of a non-dominant group is salient, this may increase the likelihood he will see other non-dominant group members less negatively as well. The experience of heterosexism, for example, may cause him to see women as individuals with a variety of characteristics rather than as a monolithic group. Being Jewish may make him view Blacks as experiencing unfair discrimination and to be supportive of Blacks' pursuit of equality. As is evident by these examples, multiple group memberships that include some non-dominant groups add complexity to the social identity equation and highlight the need to avoid painting people with broad strokes.

Non-dominant groups as the in-group. When non-dominant groups are the in-group, the results of the social categorization of people into in-groups and out-groups are different. Women, for example, may view other women as having positive attributes and prefer them to men. They may attribute positive behaviors to the characteristics of women and negative behaviors to circumstances in which women find themselves. They may attribute negative behaviors to the characteristics of men and positive behaviors to circumstances. Similarly, Blacks, Hispanics, Asians, and American Indians may attribute positive characteristics to themselves and negative characteristics to Whites. As discussed earlier, a key difference for women, racial and ethnic minorities, people with disabilities, and other non-dominant group members as in-groups is their access to power. Because they are less likely to be in positions of power, they are less likely to be able to discriminate against men, Whites, people without disabilities, and other dominant group members.[28]

It is also important to note that non-dominant group members may also hold stereotypes about members of their own groups. Instead of favoring members of their own in-groups, they may stereotype them and view the dominant group as more likely to have positive attributes. In research conducted using real teams (rather than those formed in the

[28] See Goldman et al. (2006).

laboratory), Jennifer Boldry and Deborah Kashy found that the status of the group affected perceptions of the homogeneity of out-groups and the heterogeneity of in-groups.[29] Lower-status groups viewed themselves and high-status groups (their out-groups) as having variation in member characteristics. High-status group members saw themselves and their group as having heterogeneous characteristics but saw the out-group members as having homogenous characteristics. Interestingly, the lower-status group rated the high-status group more favorably in terms of leadership, motivation, and character than the high-status group members rated themselves. Boldry and Kashy's sample included undergraduate freshmen and juniors participating in a campus Corps of Cadets, a legitimate group for research purposes but composed of 90% males. The race and ethnicity of the sample were not reported, but it is to be expected that more diversity in status characteristics (e.g., race, ethnicity, or sex) would result in different perceptions of the qualities of in- and out-groups. In addition, the out-group members were striving to become official in-group members as they moved up the status hierarchy (i.e., become senior members of the Corps), which is not likely for those who would differ by race, ethnicity, or sex.

It is possible, however, that non-dominant group members (e.g., Blacks, Latinos) to a certain extent may "buy in" to the negative stereotypes about their group and also prefer members of the dominant group, reflecting internalized racism. **Internalized racism** occurs when members of devalued races accept and believe negative messages about their own abilities and intrinsic worth and those of others of the same race.[30,31] Kenneth and Mamie Clark's "doll studies," which continue to be replicated decades later, and Jane Elliott's "Blue Eyes/Brown Eyes" experiments have been offered as evidence of the power of racism and continued messages that one's group is of low value.[32] While many minority group members resist those negative messages, those who succumb may suffer a host of negative individual consequences (e.g., depression, hopelessness, health problems) that affect organizations and society as well.

....

[29] Boldry, J. G., & Kashy, D. A. (1999). "Intergroup Perception in Naturally Occurring Groups of Differential Status: A Social Relations Perspective." *Journal of Personality and Social Psychology*, 77(6): 1200–1212.

[30] Jones, C. P. (2000). "Levels of Racism: A Theoretic Framework and a Gardener's Tale." *American Journal of Public Health*, 90(8): 1212–1215; Lipsky, S. (1987). *Internalized Racism*. Seattle, WA: Rational Island Publishers; Padilla (2001); Pyke, K., & Dang, T. (2003). "'FOB' and 'Whitewashed': Identity and Internalized Racism Among Second Generation Asian Americans." *Qualitative Sociology*, 26(2): 147–172; Speight, S. (2007). "Internalized Racism: One More Piece of the Puzzle." *The Counseling Psychologist*, 35: 126–135.

[31] Internalized sexism, ageism, heterosexism, and ableism, and associated negative outcomes also can occur.

[32] Clark, K. B., & Clark, M. P. (1950). "Emotional Factors in Racial Identification and Preference in Negro Children." *The Journal of Negro Education*, 19(3): 341–350; Peters, W. (1987). *A Class Divided: Then and Now*. New Haven, CT: Yale University Press.

There are many other negative consequences of stereotyping in addition to people internalizing negative beliefs. As we discuss in later chapters, name-based discrimination, job steering based on who is thought to be suited to certain jobs (e.g., by sex, race, physical appearance), and customer racial profiling are just a few of these negative consequences. Organizational Feature 2.1 provides an example of how perceived racial profiling can result in lost business both from customers who are profiled and from other customers.

Individuals clearly suffer from being stereotyped, but organizations experience negative consequences as well. For example, a common fear is that young people, particularly minorities, are likely shoplifters. In a large study in an Atlanta store, however, unobtrusive observers found that shoppers aged 35–54 were most likely to steal and that non-Whites and Whites were equally likely to steal. Rather than a race, sex, or age category, people who exhibited certain *behaviors* were most likely to be shoplifters: leaving the store without making a purchase, scanning the premises looking for surveillance cameras, and tampering with products.[33] If retailers focused training on avoiding stereotypes and paying attention to behaviors, shrinkage due to shoplifting might be significantly reduced.

▌ AVERSIVE RACISM, AMBIVALENT SEXISM, AND OTHER NEW ISMS

Overt demonstrations of intentional discrimination are considerably less likely in the twenty-first century than they have been in the past. However, researchers have identified contemporary, different forms of racism, including aversive, symbolic, and new racism. **Aversive racism** occurs when those who ostensibly adhere to **egalitarian** values and believe themselves to be unprejudiced still possess negative feelings and beliefs about racial issues and minority group members. Unlike those who practice traditional, overt racist behavior, those who hold aversive racist beliefs do not openly discriminate, but when their actions can be justified by some other factor (e.g., lack of "fit" or some other factor other than race), they are likely to exhibit aversive racist behaviors. Multiple studies have documented the existence of this form of racism across times and settings, and it could be considered more troublesome than traditional racism. People who hold traditional racist beliefs might state them openly, but aversive racists espouse egalitarian beliefs, making efforts to identify and change their true beliefs more difficult.

-----

[33] Dabney, D. A., Hollinger, R. C., & Dugan, L. (2004). "Who Actually Steals? A Study of Covertly Observed Shoplifters." *Justice Quarterly*, 21: 693–728.

ORGANIZATIONAL FEATURE 2.1	*Negative Consequences of Bad Check Accusation*

The appearance of making decisions on the basis of stereotypical beliefs generated considerable negative publicity for Walmart when Reginald Pitts, a Black man and the human resources manager at GAF Materials, went to a Tampa area Walmart to purchase 510 gift cards for company employees and was assumed to be using a bad check.[34] GAF, the biggest roofing systems maker in the United States with $1.6 billion in revenues the year prior to the incident, had been purchasing about $50,000 worth of gift cards at Walmart for several years. The gift cards were typically picked up by a White female administrator, but because she was on vacation, Pitts decided to get the gift cards himself. He phoned in the order and went to Walmart with a $13,000 company check, his driver's license, and his GAF business card. When called, a GAF accounting supervisor assured store managers that the check was good, but the store managers still told Pitts they were having trouble verifying the check. While he waited more than two hours at the customer service desk, two Black Walmart employees told Pitts that similarly large transactions by other customers had been processed without delay and suggested he was being closely scrutinized because he was Black.

When Pitts asked for the check to be returned so he could purchase the cards elsewhere, the store managers refused to return the check and continued stalling. They had called the Hillsborough County sheriff.

When the deputies arrived, one grabbed Pitts, telling him they needed to talk with him about the "forged check" and that Walmart had called them to report a felony. Pitts said he thought he was going to jail.

After nineteen minutes of reviewing the "evidence," the deputies concluded there were no grounds for a criminal charge and returned the check to Pitts. Pitts said that the Walmart store manager told him he "did what he had to do" and "have a great day, sir." "I keep going over and over the incident in my mind. I cannot come up with any possible reason why I was treated like this except that I am black," said Pitts.

GAF and Pitts lodged complaints with Walmart, which opened its own investigation. Walmart conceded the situation was "handled very poorly" but said that Walmart does not tolerate racial profiling or discrimination. Four Walmart officials called Pitts to apologize for the incident, including Lawrence Jackson, the executive VP of Walmart's "People" Division (Human Resources). According to Pitts, Jackson "said that he was apologizing as one HR manager to another and as one African-American to another."

After the "totally humiliating" experience of Mr. Pitts, GAF purchased the employees' gift cards at Target instead. In addition to that lost business, apparently other customers, after significant media coverage, were also incensed and took their business elsewhere. Samantha

---

[34] Albright, M. (2005, December 2). "Racial Profiling Feared at Walmart." *St. Petersburg Times*. http://www.sptimes.com/2005/12/02/Tampabay/Racial_profiling_fear.shtml, accessed July 28, 2010; Albright, M. (2005, December 10). "Ugly Walmart Tale Resonates." *St. Petersburg Times*. http://www.sptimes.com/2005/12/10/Business/Ugly_Wal_Mart_tale_re.shtml, accessed July 28, 2010; "Walmart Apologizes to Man for Bad Check Accusation." *USAToday*, http://www.usatoday.com/news/nation/2005-12-02-walmart-check_x.htm?csp=34, accessed July 28, 2010.

Devine, an office manager at a medical clinic, had planned to go to Walmart to buy holiday gift cards for coworkers. When she heard what Pitts had encountered there, Devine said, "It made me so angry I haven't set foot in a Walmart since."

QUESTIONS TO CONSIDER

1. What assumptions might the store manager have made about Mr. Pitts?

2. Given the risk of retaliation from management if found out, what factors may have motivated the Black store employees to tell Mr. Pitts that other customers had processed large checks without hassle?

3. What specific procedures could be implemented at stores so that this kind of thing does not occur?

In one study, John Dovidio and Samuel Gaertner documented the change in White participants' expression of prejudiced beliefs between 1989 and 1999, finding significantly fewer instances in 1999.[35] Even so, the researchers did find that, when making selection decisions, participants who expressed prejudicial beliefs (i.e., traditional racism) at both points were less likely to select Blacks, regardless of the qualifications of the Black candidates. Those who did not express prejudicial beliefs showed no differences in rates of recommendation when qualifications for either Blacks or Whites were particularly high. When qualifications were ambiguous—neither particularly strong, nor particularly weak—Whites were more frequently recommended than similarly qualified Blacks. Thus, when qualifications were strong and discrimination could be easily identified, aversive racists made similar recommendations for Blacks and Whites. When qualifications were ambiguous and decisions could be attributed to factors other than discrimination (e.g., "fit" or "personality"), aversive racists made fewer selection recommendations for Blacks. Dovidio and Gaertner suggested that this behavior may be based in part on the fundamental attribution error (discussed earlier) and reflective of Whites' tendency to give the benefit of the doubt to ambiguously qualified in-group members but not to out-group members. As we discuss in Chapter 4, Blacks with similar financial qualifications are less likely to be approved for credit (e.g., loans, mortgages) than Whites, which may also indicate in-group favoritism and out-group bias.

In another complex study, Eduardo Bonilla-Silva and Tyrone Forman investigated changes in Whites' reported racial attitudes, hypothesizing that recent changes overstate the amount of positive change in racial attitudes.[36] Using qualitative and quantitative data drawn from 732

[35] Dovidio, J. F., & Gaertner, S. L. (2000). "Aversive Racism and Selection Decisions." *Psychological Science*, 11(4): 315–319.

[36] Bonilla-Silva, E., & Forman, T. (2000). "'I'm Not a Racist, But …': Mapping White College Students' Racial Ideology in the USA." *Discourse and Society*, 11: 50–85. See also Pager, D., & Quillian, L. (2005). "Walking the Talk? What Employers Say Versus What They Do." *American Sociological Review*, 70: 355–380.

university students (who, it has been argued, are less prejudiced than others), Bonilla-Silva and Forman found that students avoided the appearance of holding discriminatory beliefs in surveys, but interview data presented a different picture. "I'm not a racist ... but ..." preceded statements expressing hostile attitudes toward racial minorities; beliefs that minorities, rather than systematic discrimination, were responsible for their own situations; and belief in the existence of reverse discrimination, among other things. The researchers urged caution in concluding that racial attitudes were improving, suggesting that "racetalk" and "colorblind racism" were replacing the expression of traditionally racist attitudes that are no longer widely acceptable.

Symbolic racists use symbols, rather than race, to attempt to explain their resistance to equality.[37] For example, symbolic racists are not against integrated schools but think forced busing is unfair, and they may argue that they are not against affirmative action, per se, but think it provides unqualified people with unearned advantages. "New" and "modern" racism are similar to other contemporary forms of racism and reflect people's decreasing willingness to express overtly racist beliefs, but their propensity is to behave in discriminatory ways when provided a rationale or justification for doing so.[38] Highly structured interviews, mentioned earlier, can be helpful in reducing these problems in hiring decisions.

Ambivalent sexism is the simultaneously holding of both hostile ("women are incompetent at work") and "benevolent" ("women must be protected") sexist beliefs about women.[39] **Hostile sexism** is an antipathy toward women based on faulty and inflexible generalization (e.g., negative stereotypes). **Benevolent sexism** is defined as a set of interrelated attitudes toward women that are sexist (stereotypical) and at the same perceived as positive by the attitude holder (e.g., helping, attraction).[40] Benevolent sexism might be manifested by comments to a female co-worker on her appearance, which could undermine her being taken seriously at work,[41] or by finishing her sentences, which could make her appear timid and unassertive. Although benevolent sexism is viewed less negatively than hostile sexism, it is still detrimental to women.[42]

....

[37] Kinder, D. R., & Sears, D. O. (1981). "Symbolic Racism Versus Racial Threats to the Good Life." *Journal of Personality and Social Psychology*, 40: 414–431.

[38] See Chapter 4 for a discussion of research by Art Brief and his colleagues on new racism and recommendations for hiring.

[39] Glick, P., & Fiske, S. T. (1996). "The Ambivalent Sexism Inventory: Differentiating Hostile and Benevolent Sexism." *Journal of Personality and Social Psychology*, 70(3): 491–512.

[40] Ibid.

[41] Ibid.

[42] Barreto, M., & Ellemers, N. (2005). "The Burden of Benevolent Sexism: How It Contributes to the Maintenance of Gender Inequalities." *European Journal of Social Psychology*, 35(5): 633–642.

Neosexism is similar to aversive racism; it occurs when people's reported egalitarian values conflict with negative attitudes toward women.[43] The existence of neosexism has been documented in studies conducted in the United States, Slovenia, and Croatia, among other areas.[44] It could be argued that similar aversive attitudes exist toward other non-dominant groups. Reporting egalitarian attitudes toward gays and lesbians but resisting equitable work-related benefits for them or reporting egalitarian attitudes toward people with disabilities but resisting accommodations for them as expensive or unfair to people without disabilities are possible examples.

▮ RECOMMENDATIONS FOR INDIVIDUALS AND ORGANIZATIONS

Efforts to combat stereotypes must be purposeful. As we have discussed, when confronted with information that is contradictory to their stereotypes, people tend to see the situation as "unique" rather than using it to question and begin discarding their beliefs. When faced with behavior that confirms stereotypes, people attend to such information instead of recognizing that there is variation among members of all groups. Indeed, it is likely that every stereotype will apply to individuals from many different groups. With concerted effort, motivated people can in some cases deactivate stereotyping and stop automatic categorization and discriminatory actions.

Kerry Kawakami and colleagues have empirically investigated the effects of training on stereotype reduction. They found that practice in negating stereotypes results in reduced activation of stereotypes.[45] Adam Galinsky and Gordon Moskowitz have also found that perspective taking helps to reduce stereotyping and some of its negative consequences.[46] Even without formal training, we can and should work consciously, as individuals, to resist stereotyping, in-group favoritism, and out-group biases. Awareness of these processes is an important step, as is organizational support of equity. We should question ourselves and our beliefs, attitudes, and behavior toward dissimilar others.

[43] Tougas, F., Brown, R., Beaton, A. M., & Joly, S. (1995). "Neosexism: Plus Ça Change, Plus C'est Pareil." *Personality and Social Psychology Bulletin*, 21(8): 842–849.

[44] Frieze, I. H., Ferligoj, A., Kogovsek, J., Rener, T., Hovat, J., & Sarlija, N. (2003). "Gender-Role Attitudes in University Students in the United States, Slovenia, and Croatia." *Psychology of Women Quarterly*, 27: 256–261.

[45] Kawakami, K., Dovidio, J. F., Moll, J., Hermsen, S., & Russin, A. (2000). "Just Say No (to Stereotyping): Effects of Training in the Negation of Stereotypic Association on Stereotype Activation." *Journal of Personality and Social Psychology*, 78(5): 871–888.

[46] Galinsky, A., & Moskowitz, G. (2000). "Perspective Taking: Decreasing Stereotype Expression, Stereotype Accessibility, and In-Group Favoritism." *Journal of Personality and Social Psychology*, 78(4): 708–724.

Because aversive racists are unaware that they hold prejudiced attitudes and genuinely think they are unbiased, efforts to change their prejudices are necessarily different from attempts to change those who openly acknowledge and express overt prejudice. Dovidio and Gaertner suggest several strategies that may be employed to help people reduce their propensities to stereotype and the in-group–out-group categorizations that people seem to make automatically.[47] Their analyses indicate the following measures may be effective:

- Lead aversive racists to see the inconsistencies in their behaviors and their stated values, thereby developing cognitive dissonance and the desire to reduce it. Active efforts to reduce dissonance will help aversive racists reduce and ultimately eliminate automatic activation of stereotypes in interactions with out-group members.
- Engage group members in activities to achieve common, superordinate goals. Doing so will reduce perceptions of competition between in-groups and out-groups while increasing perceptions of cooperation.
- Encourage groups to perceive themselves as members of a single, superordinate group, rather than as two separate groups. Doing so will help create a common identity and result in in-group favoritism that includes both groups.

In an organizational setting, group members who view themselves as part of the organization working for the same employer, pursuing the organization's vision and mission, and competing against others in the industry will be more likely to see their diverse group as the in-group working toward the same goal. In organizations in which diversity is embraced and valued and discrimination and exclusion are not tolerated, those who would exclude and limit based on characteristics such as race, sex, age, religion, sexual orientation, ability, and other irrelevant factors at work should be viewed as undesirable out-groups working against the important organizational goal of diversity, equality, and inclusion.

In addition to working to reduce discrimination based on stereotyping and social categorization processes, organizational monitoring and control measures should be implemented. Diverse recruitment and selection teams, supervisors and managers, and legitimate selection criteria would be helpful at organizational entry. Interviews should be highly structured, and interviewers should be trained in proper procedures and errors and biases. Salary decisions should be made based on job requirements, as should training, development, promotion, and termination decisions, and should be monitored regularly by the human resources staff. Organizational

[47]Dovidio, J. F., & Gaertner, S. L. (1999). "Reducing Prejudice: Combating Intergroup Biases." *Current Directions in Psychological Science*, 8(4): 101–105.

leaders must be willing to implement policies and monitoring and control measures supportive of diversity throughout their organizations. Although some researchers have questioned the efficacy of prejudice reduction programs,[48] what is certain is that organizational leadership, zero tolerance for discrimination, and control and monitoring can and do affect behaviors at work.

SUMMARY

In this chapter, we have considered factors that characterize minority, or non-dominant, groups and have provided a rationale for determining "What is a minority?" yet we have acknowledged that identifiability, power, discrimination, and group awareness vary among non-dominant groups. We have incorporated research from social psychology to help understand prejudice, stereotyping, and social categorization. These social processes were linked to behaviors that support or hinder diversity in organizations and to some specific examples that will be discussed in subsequent chapters. When made on the basis of stereotyping and social categorization, job-related decisions (hiring, firing, compensation, promotion and advancement, training, job placement, etc.) are problematic. We presented measures to reduce stereotyping, aversive racism, and other aversions.

Although it is impossible to consider every theory and psychological process related to diversity, readers should now be aware that along with the deliberate, overt categorization of different others, underlying, unconscious processes are also involved. Behaviors described in some of the lawsuits and settlements presented in the chapters to follow are indicative of overt, conscious differential treatment. Both overt and unconscious discrimination often result from people's propensity to stereotype and see members of certain groups as more or less appropriate for certain jobs (e.g., women as secretaries versus truck drivers). It is these unconscious propensities that are most insidious and difficult to eradicate. As some lawsuits show, some employers verbalize their stereotypical perceptions, but many simply act on them, so the individual affected has little or no concrete evidence of discrimination.

When adopting the idea that diversity is valuable to individuals and organizations, individuals should be aware of both overt discrimination and the unconscious processes that result in discrimination. Willingness to listen, think, understand, and grow in learning about diversity issues will be helpful in improving positive outcomes.

KEY TERMS

Ambivalent sexism — the simultaneous holding of both hostile and "benevolent" sexist beliefs about women; for example, "women are incompetent at work" and "women must be protected."

---

[48] Paluck, E. L., & Green, D. P. (2009). "Prejudice Reduction: What Works? A Review and Assessment of Research and Practice." *Annual Review of Psychology*, 60: 339–367.

Aversive racism — the holding of egalitarian values and beliefs that one is unprejudiced but still possessing negative feelings and beliefs about racial issues and minority group members.

Benevolent sexism — a set of interrelated attitudes toward women that are sexist while they are perceived as positive by the attitude holder.

Descriptive stereotyping — perceptions about how people do or will behave, based on their group memberships.

Discrimination — differential and pejorative actions that serve to limit the social, political, or economic opportunities of members of particular groups.

Egalitarian — one who believes in human equality, particularly regarding social, political, and economic rights and privileges.

Fundamental attribution error — the tendency to underestimate the influence of external factors (e.g., situations or circumstances) and overestimate the influence of internal factors (e.g., personal qualities) when evaluating the behavior of out-group members.

Hostile sexism — antipathy toward women based on faulty and inflexible generalizations (negative stereotypes).

Internalized racism — the acceptance and belief by members of devalued races in negative messages about their own abilities and intrinsic worth and those of others of the same race.

Neosexism — the conflict between people's reported egalitarian values and their negative attitudes toward women.

Prejudice — irrational, negative evaluations of a group.

Prescriptive stereotyping — perceptions about how people should behave, based on their group memberships.

Social identity — the part of an individual's self-concept that derives from his or her membership in a social group and the value and emotional significance attached to that group membership.

Stereotypes — overgeneralizations of characteristics to large human groups.

QUESTIONS TO CONSIDER

1. This chapter discusses many identities and multiple group memberships that people have. If you were to describe the important parts of your identity, what would be on your list? Make a list, and then rank order the most-to-least important aspects of your identity. Which are immediately apparent to others?

2. As a powerful group, elected officials affect the life chances of the populace. How are elected officials in the area in which you live similar to or different demographically from the population in that area?

3. Researchers have found that people are less willing to express "traditionally" prejudiced beliefs than in the past, but their behavior does not agree with espoused beliefs. How can such disparities in expressed beliefs and actions undermine diversity in organizations? What organizational measures can be implemented to investigate whether there are inconsistencies in expressed

beliefs, behaviors, and outcomes related to diversity in organizations?

4. Choose an aspect of your identity in which you are a member of the dominant racial, ethnic, sex, or religious group. Have you experienced being the minority in a situation (e.g., White among many Blacks, Asians, or Latinos; Christian in the United States among many Jews)? If you are a racial minority, have you experienced being a minority among others of color (e.g., Asian among many Blacks; Latino among many Asians) rather than among Whites? If you are a man, have you experienced being the minority in a meeting at work or at school in a class? If you are a woman, have you experienced being the minority in a meeting at work or at school in a class? What were these experiences of being a "minority" like?

ACTIONS AND EXERCISES

1. Discuss stereotypes with a trusted friend or family member. What kinds of job-related stereotypes is he or she aware of? (Note that awareness of stereotypes does not mean belief in the veracity of the stereotype.) Discuss how these stereotypes can negatively affect individuals' job opportunities and advancement. Can you think of a person who is *not* a member of the stereotyped group who fits the stereotypical characteristic? Can you think of a person who is a member of the stereotyped group who doesn't fit the stereotype?

2. Using a local newspaper (*San Francisco Chronicle, Chicago Tribune, Dallas Morning News,* etc.), a campus or university newspaper, and a community or city newspaper, locate stories that include photos of people in the story. Make a table of the type of story (human interest, business news, crime, etc.), race, ethnicity, sex, and estimated age of the subject. What diversity-related observations can be made from the table?

3. Locate a newspaper that has an executive or business section that includes "promotions," "executive changes," or other career moves. If there are photos of the people involved, list their race, ethnicity, and sex. If names only are provided, determine the sex of the person, where possible. What observations can you make from your list?

Legislation

CHAPTER 3

Chapter Objectives

After completing this chapter, readers should have a firm understanding of diversity-related laws, executive orders, and court rulings in the United States and selected diversity-related laws in other countries. Specifically, they should be able to:

❏ *explain the historical background of and rationale behind specific diversity-related legislation in relation to race, sex, religion, age, disability, and work and family status.*

❏ *discuss events in several notable diversity-related lawsuits in the United States.*

❏ *describe components and limitations of diversity legislation and discuss why complying with laws is an important aspect of a diversity program.*

❏ *explain reasons organizations may pursue diversity and inclusion even in the absence of legislation.*

❏ *discuss research on the relationship between race and sex of judges and decision making in discrimination and harassment claims.*

Key Facts

Although the Equal Pay Act has been in existence for five decades, women in the United States still earn less than 80 cents for each dollar that men earn. Sex segregation limits the effectiveness of the Equal Pay Act.

Title VII of the U.S. Civil Rights Act is the country's most comprehensive civil rights legislation, prohibiting discrimination on the basis of race, sex, religion, and national origin, but discrimination persists.

Charges of discrimination reached their highest ever in 2010; retaliation surpassed race as the highest allegation.[1]

In the United Kingdom and Australia, age discrimination against applicants and employees of any age is prohibited, yet in the United States, age discrimination is only illegal against those who are 40 or older.

Compliance with laws is a necessary component of valuing diversity but, alone, is not evidence of valuing diversity.

Minority and female judges look at evidence and make decisions differently than do White and male judges, which strongly establishes the need for diversity in the judiciary.[2]

---

[1] "EEOC Reports Job Bias Hit Record High of Nearly 100,000 in Fiscal Year 2010." http://www.eeoc.gov/eeoc/newsroom/release/1-11-11.cfm, accessed January 12, 2011.

[2] Chew, P. K., & Kelley, R. E. (2009). "Myth of the Color-Blind Judge: An Empirical Analysis of Racial Harassment Cases." *Washington University Law Review*, 86: 1117–1166; Peresie, J. L. (2005). "Female Judges Matter: Gender and Collegial Decision Making in the Federal Appellate Courts." *Yale Law Journal*, 114(7): 1759–1790.

Introduction and Overview

Although equal opportunity laws have existed in the United States for nearly fifty years, a brief review of the recent listing of lawsuits on the Equal Employment Opportunity Commission (EEOC) Web site provides accounts of allegations of discrimination, harassment, and retaliation against employees based on race, sex, age, national origin, disability, and religion. Organizations involved include *Fortune* 100, 500, and 1000 companies, universities, not-for-profit organizations, minority-owned businesses, churches, and other reputable organizations. Ironically, some of these organizations have been recognized as award-winning leaders in diversity, with mentoring programs, employee resource groups, broad nondiscrimination policies, and other programs supportive of diversity. Many of the illegal acts cited in the lawsuits were taken against workers who are unaware of the relevant laws (including young workers in their first jobs and people who have worked for many years), who may not have received diversity training in school or at work, and who may think they have no recourse. Although some employers and managers are fully aware of the illegality of their actions, some who engage in discrimination may also have not received any training and may be unaware of relevant laws.

Refusing to hire valuable workers or terminating or **constructively discharging** (making work so unbearable that people quit) them and failing to follow the organization's guidelines on harassment and discrimination are poor management practices and can result in the negative consequences discussed in Chapter 1. In addition to the moral and social issues involved in such cases, the many potential benefits of diversity delineated by Cox and Blake are not realized. Excluding qualified applicants and continuing to search for similarly qualified applicants wastes organizational resources. Recruiting and training money spent on those hired but terminated for nonperformance reasons is wasted, and the resulting recruitment and training costs incurred for their

replacements are unnecessary. Likely consequences also are lowered productivity of affected workers and their peers and increased medical costs and absence related to stress. Customers who experience discriminatory treatment or learn of discrimination against employees may choose to do business elsewhere. Given these and other problems, why do individuals within companies and organizational practices persist in overt discrimination and exclusion? What can be done to help organizations avoid these unfair, costly, and counterproductive practices?

Chapter 1 considered some of the reasons that organizations should value diversity, for example, financial and marketing advantages, the increasing diversity of the workforce, and globalization, reasons that are the major foci of this book. But the laws, executive orders, and court decisions surrounding and motivating, for some, interest in diversity issues are critical as well. Without such stimuli, many of the diversity-related actions that organizations have taken within the last five decades would not have been taken. It is important to understand the rationale behind such legislation, the specific areas covered, the prohibitions, and the limitations. However, we reiterate that to focus on avoiding litigation is a shallow approach, which is unlikely to reap the benefits associated with truly valuing diversity or to encourage managers to sincerely pursue diversity.

Despite the media and managerial attention generated by large damage awards, relative to the numbers of applicants and employees, few people litigate each year, for various reasons. One reason is that discrimination claims typically must be filed within a certain period after the alleged discriminatory act; another is that people are often unaware that discrimination, whether overt or covert, has occurred. Recall from Chapter 2 that the overt and verbalized discrimination that was quite common in the past is now less likely to be expressed verbally, although discriminatory decisions are still made. When people are aware of discrimination and have some proof, they may not have the resources to sue and the EEOC may be unwilling to litigate individual cases. But compliance with the law is still extremely important, if only by reason of the increasing diversity of the workforce, globalization, and international competition. Yet abiding by the laws, although necessary, is not a sufficient goal.

Those countries that have no antidiscrimination legislation could benefit from learning about the spirit of such laws and the cases derived from them. What can organizations learn that is useful in establishing diversity? What should organizations do to ensure that people have the opportunity to work and be treated fairly in order that the many individual, organizational, and societal benefits of diversity are realized? Similar questions exist for customers— What can organizations learn to ensure that customers are valued, regardless of their demographic background, religion, sexual orientation, or other irrelevant factors? ●

▌ HISTORICAL BACKGROUND

Most of the important U.S. legislative, judicial, and executive branch decisions that have affected diversity in organizations emerged in the early 1960s and continued through the end of the twentieth century. The stimuli for this activity included important societal issues, such as overt social and employment discrimination against women and Blacks as well as against other people of color, those of different religions, older workers, and people with disabilities. The discrimination prevented these people from obtaining or maintaining employment or subjected them to unfair treatment once employed, and it contributed to large wage, income, and quality-of-life disparities between people of color and Whites.[3] Resistance to discrimination, in the form of marches, boycotts, and sit-ins, resulted in the passage of Title VII of the Civil Rights Act in 1964 and numerous subsequent legislation. Over time, as societal issues have evolved, so has legislation, which has responded to the increasing diversity among the population and the clear need to attend to new and different issues.

In this chapter, we consider these laws in chronological order because when they went into effect provides insights into how and when societal recognition of the need for addressing significant diversity issues emerged. We also include examples of EEOC litigation and settlements in some specific areas. The Department of Labor (DOL) and the Department of Justice (DOJ) at times litigate employment and customer discrimination, respectively; some of those cases are discussed in remaining chapters.

----

[3] Because of shared family income, White women married to White men suffered fewer negative economic effects of employment-related discrimination. Never-married, divorced, and widowed White women suffered more of the negative effects of employment discrimination.

After completing this chapter, readers should have a firm and broad understanding of U.S. legislation and enforcement agencies related to diversity in organizations. Later chapters provide more details and cases specifically related to the chapter topic.

■ MAJOR FEDERAL ACTS RELATED TO DIVERSITY IN ORGANIZATIONS

In this chapter, we cover laws, executive orders, and judicial decisions, which, for brevity, we refer to as *legislation* or *acts*. Because U.S. law prohibits discrimination or harassment on the basis of race, color, religion, sex, national origin, age (40 or over), disability, or genetics, every applicant or employee has some recourse if discrimination occurs. Most employers, labor unions, and employment agencies are forbidden to discriminate on the basis of those factors in hiring and firing; compensation, assignment, or classification of employees; transfer, promotion, layoff, or recall; job advertisements; recruitment; testing; use of company facilities; training and apprenticeship programs; fringe benefits; pay, retirement plans, and disability leave; or other terms and conditions of employment. Also prohibited are harassment on the basis of one's demographic group memberships, employment decisions based on stereotypes about ability because of such group memberships, and retaliation for filing a claim of discrimination or complaining about it or marriage to or affiliation with individuals of a particular group.[4] These broad prohibitions imply that people should be allowed to work without regard to their group memberships; they are the foundation of diversity-related legislation. In recent years, people have filed more discrimination charges than ever for violations of these prohibitions. This trend can be attributed to multiple factors, including greater accessibility of the EEOC to the public and changes in its practices, such as requiring fewer steps to file a charge, economic conditions, employees becoming more aware of their rights under the law, and increased diversity and demographic shifts in the labor force.[5]

Figure 3.1 lists the major federal acts regarding diversity issues and their provisions. In the following sections, we discuss the broad categories of protections and sample cases in which the laws were used.

[4] http://www.eeoc.gov/laws/practices/index.cfm, accessed October 2, 2010.
[5] "EEOC Reports Job Bias Hit Record High of Nearly 100,000 in Fiscal Year 2010."

Figure 3.1 **Chronology of Major U.S. Federal Acts Affecting Diversity in Organizations**

Act	Provisions
Emancipation Proclamation (1863)	Freeing slaves allowed Blacks the opportunity to work for wages rather than as slaves.
Executive Order 8802 (1941)	Requires equal employment opportunities for all American citizens, regardless of race, creed, color, or national origin.
Equal Pay Act of 1963	Requires women and men to be paid equally for equal work.
Title VII of the Civil Rights Act of 1964	Prohibits discrimination on the basis of race, color, religion, sex, or national origin in employment-related matters.
Executive Orders for Affirmative Action (EO 11246 in 1965 and 11375 in 1966)	Require employers to take affirmative steps to prevent discrimination in employment, including taking proactive measures to ensure hiring and promotion of minorities (men and women) and women (White and women of color).
The Age Discrimination in Employment Act of 1967	Prohibits employment-related discrimination against persons aged 40 or older. Exceptions can be made for bona fide occupational qualifications. Some countries (United Kingdom, Australia) and states (Michigan) prohibit all age discrimination.
Rehabilitation Act of 1973	Precursor to the ADA. Prohibits discrimination against federal employees with disabilities and requires the federal government and contractors to take affirmative action in the hiring, placement, and advancement of people with disabilities and to make reasonable accommodations to allow them to work.
Vietnam Era Veterans' Readjustment Assistance Act of 1974	Prohibits discrimination against Vietnam-era and other veterans and requires affirmative action for them.
Pregnancy Discrimination Act of 1978	An amendment to Title VII that clarifies Title VII's prohibition against discrimination on the basis of sex, including pregnancy, childbirth, and related medical conditions. Requires employers to treat pregnancy similarly to other temporary disabilities for medical and benefits-related purposes.
EEOC Guidelines on Sexual Harassment 1980	Defines sexual harassment, formally acknowledging it as a form of sex discrimination prohibited by Section 703 of Title VII, and suggests affirmative steps employers may take to prevent sexual harassment. The EEOC uses these guidelines in enforcement, and many courts rely on them in decisions.
Older Workers Benefit Protection Act of 1990	An amendment to the ADEA of 1967. Prohibits employers from denying benefits to older workers but allows reductions in benefits based on age, as long as the employers' costs of providing benefits to older workers are the same as their costs for providing benefits to younger workers.
Americans with Disabilities Act of 1990	Prohibits employment-related discrimination against people with physical and mental disabilities for employers of fifteen or more people in the private sector and in state and local government. Requires employers to make reasonable accommodation for those otherwise qualified to work but does not require affirmative action for people with disabilities.

FIGURE 3.1 *Chronology of Major U.S. Federal Acts Affecting Diversity in Organizations (Continued)*

Act	Provisions
Civil Rights Act of 1991	An amendment to Title VII of the CRA of 1964. Provides for compensatory and punitive damages (limited to $300,000) in cases of intentional discrimination and harassment; allows for jury trials; extends the coverage of act to U.S. citizens working abroad for U.S. companies; established Glass Ceiling Commission (now disbanded).
Family and Medical Leave Act of 1993	Allows certain employees to take up to 12 weeks' unpaid leave to care for a spouse, child, or parent, or for a personal illness. Employers must maintain employees' benefits and offer the same or a substantially similar job upon employees' return from leave. In 2010, broadened the definition of "son" or "daughter" to include those performing parental roles, including same-sex partners, grandparents, and others.
Genetic Information Nondiscrimination Act of 2008	Prohibits the use of genetic information, including family medical history, in employment decisions; restricts the acquisition of genetic information; prohibits harassment based on genetic information; and prohibits the disclosure of genetic information.
Americans with Disabilities Act Amendments Act of 2008	Emphasizes that the definition of disabilities should be construed broadly and should not generally require extensive analysis, making it easier for those seeking protection under the ADA to establish a disability. Expands the meaning of "major life activities" to include episodic impairments or those in remission.
Lilly Ledbetter Fair Pay Act of 2009	Restores the pre-Ledbetter position of the EEOC that with every discriminatory paycheck, a new clock starts for the 180-day (or 300-day) period to file a claim.

The Equal Pay Act of 1963

The Equal Pay Act of 1963, an amendment to the Fair Labor Standards Act (FLSA) of 1938, was the first major act relevant to diversity in organizations. The Equal Pay Act is now enforced by the Equal Employment Opportunity Commission (discussed in the following section) but between 1963 and 1979 was enforced by the U.S. Department of Labor. Because the act covers those who are also covered by the FLSA, virtually all employers are subject to the provisions of the Equal Pay Act, which was an attempt to address pay inequities between men and women. In 1963, at the time the act went into effect, women earned about 59 cents to the dollar that men earned. Nearly fifty years later, women working full-time, year-round still earn less than 80 cents to the dollar that men earn—a substantial improvement, but a significant difference nonetheless.

Jobs are considered to be equivalent, or substantially similar, when they require similar skill, effort, and responsibility, are in the same organization, and are performed under similar conditions. However, these requirements for "equivalence" severely limit the effectiveness of the Equal Pay Act. Men typically work with other men, and women typically work with other women. This phenomenon, termed *sex segregation,* takes place when at least 70% of incumbents in a particular job are male or female. Employer stereotyping and steering are contributors to sex-segregated jobs, the issue in the Polycon Industries case, settled in 2010.

Polycon Industries to Pay $170,000 to Settle EEOC Suit Over Sex-Segregated Workforce[6]

Agency Charged that Merrillville Plastics Manufacturer Refused to Promote Women into Higher-Paying Jobs and Placed Female New Hires into Lower-Paying Posts

A plastics product manufacturer will pay $170,000 to settle a sex discrimination lawsuit brought by the EEOC. The EEOC charged that Polycon Industries violated federal law by refusing to promote female employees into its higher-paying production positions. The EEOC also charged that Polycon considered gender when placing new hires into entry-level positions, to the detriment of female new hires, who were overwhelmingly placed into lower-paying entry-level jobs. In addition to the monetary settlement, the consent decree requires Polycon to affirmatively take action to place new hires and promote females in a nondiscriminatory manner, comply with prohibitions against further discrimination, post and distribute a policy of nondiscrimination, train its employees, and report to the EEOC.

In addition to employer actions like those described in the Polycon case, many other factors contribute to sex segregation of jobs, including **gender role socialization**. Gender role socialization is the process by which social entities—families, friends, organizations, the media—form and shape expectations of acceptable behaviors (and jobs) for men and women. People are socialized to view certain jobs as appropriate for women and others as appropriate for men. Because "women's jobs" (such as receptionist and elementary school teacher) typically pay less than "men's jobs" men's jobs (such as manager and high school principal), this seemingly innocent sorting plays an important role in gender pay inequity.

Seemingly valid exceptions due to merit and seniority that disadvantage women have also limited the effectiveness of the Equal Pay Act. Exceptions

[6] Adapted from EEOC press release at http://www.eeoc.gov/eeoc/newsroom/release/9-15-10.cfm, accessed October 2, 2010.

to the equal pay requirement are allowed when there are differences based on the employees' job seniority, merit (e.g., skill, education), or performance. These exceptions are generally accepted as legitimate by employers, employees, and unions but may serve to reduce the effectiveness of the Equal Pay Act. That an employee who has worked for the company longer, who has more job-related skill, and better performance would earn more than one who has less tenure, skill, and lower performance appears logical to most people. For a variety of reasons, however, men on average have more seniority than do women. Some of those reasons are viewed as being "voluntary," such as intermittent work due to child and elder care responsibilities. Other reasons include past sex discrimination by unions and employers that kept women out of jobs, reserving them instead for (White) men. Although now illegal, such discrimination that occurred in the past has resulted in men having longer tenure and therefore able to enjoy the benefits that go along with it. Those benefits include higher seniority-based pay, more vacation, and, perhaps most important, more protection from layoffs, as the last hired are often the first fired.

In addition to the problems of the apparently neutral practice of favoring those who have more seniority, judgments about skill, merit, and performance are not always objective. This subjectivity, and people's propensity to prefer those who are similar, may disadvantage members of non-dominant groups, including women.

Effectiveness of the Equal Pay Act. Although the effectiveness of the Equal Pay Act has been limited by sex segregation and seemingly legitimate exceptions, it is still credited with helping to reduce the pay gap between men and women. In the early 1960s, pay disparities between men and women were considerably greater than they are now. Women working full-time earned less than 60 cents to each dollar that men earned. The wage gap remained about the same until the early 1980s when women's wages reached about 75 cents to the men's dollar. However, women's wages seem to have plateaued, even though women are obtaining more education and working more hours than in the past. Some researchers argue that the wage gap is largely due to women's "choices" of careers, fields of study, time spent out of the workforce, and fewer hours worked when compared with men. Chapter 9 considers in more detail the role of "choice" in women's and men's careers, fields of study, workforce participation, and hours worked and provides evidence that gender role socialization and societal expectations affect these "choices" to a great degree.

Litigation under the Equal Pay Act. Although sex segregation limits the effectiveness of the Equal Pay Act, it does not negate the act's usefulness. Litigation provides evidence of sex-based pay disparities—as prohibited by the act. Several significant cases have been resolved in the litigants' favor, including those involving women working in male-dominated fields being paid less than similarly situated men. Settlements have been obtained for female engineers, controllers, truckers, machine operators, teachers, university professors, and jail guards in individual or class action cases.

Title VII of the Civil Rights Act of 1964

Title VII of the Civil Rights Act of 1964 (Title VII) is considered to be the most comprehensive act in terms of diversity and civil rights.[7] It prohibits discrimination on the basis of race, color, religion, sex (including sexual harassment or pregnancy discrimination), and national origin in employment-related matters. Title VII covers the great majority of employers, including:

1. all private employers, state and local governments, and educational institutions that employ fifteen or more individuals for twenty or more weeks per year.
2. private and public employment agencies.
3. labor organizations.
4. joint labor-management committees controlling apprenticeship and training.
5. companies incorporated or based in the United States or that are controlled by U.S. companies employing U.S. citizens outside the United States or its territories.

The inclusion of employment agencies and labor organizations in Title VII acknowledges their important role in controlling access to jobs. The EEOC can and does sue such agencies when they engage in discrimination, as described in the following case.

Area Temps Agrees to Pay $650,000 for Profiling Applicants by Race, Sex, National Origin and Age[8]

Temporary Agency Complied with Discriminatory Placement Requests, Fired Employees Who Opposed Unlawful Practices, EEOC Alleged

---

[7] Wolkinson, B. (2000). "EEO in the Workplace, Employment Law Challenges," Module 8. In E. E. Kossek & R. Block (Eds.), *Managing Human Resources in the 21st Century*. Cincinnati, OH: South-Western Publishing p. 75.

[8] Adapted from EEOC press release at http://www.eeoc.gov/eeoc/newsroom/release/7-27-10.cfm, accessed December 12, 2010.

Area Temps, a Northeast Ohio temporary agency, agreed to pay $650,000 to resolve a class discrimination lawsuit filed by the EEOC. The EEOC charged that the temporary agency considered and assigned (or declined) job applicants by race, sex, Hispanic national origin, and age. The EEOC also alleged Area Temps unlawfully complied with discriminatory requests made by its clients based on race, sex, national origin, and age, and unlawfully fired two of its employees in retaliation for their opposition to Area Temps' discriminatory practices and for one employee's participation in the EEOC's investigation.

In addition to monetary relief, the three-year consent decree settling the suit requires the company to post a notice of resolution regarding this lawsuit that is visible to employees. The company must also provide a notice-of-resolution letter to all applicants, management and selecting officials, and outside clients on the obligations of the company under federal antidiscrimination laws, as well as Area Temps' commitment to abide by such laws.

Certain employers are excluded from coverage under Title VII, including private membership clubs, religious organizations, schools, associations, or organizations hiring American Indians on or near reservations. For those organizations operating solely within the confines of the exclusion, certain types of discrimination are not illegal.

Disparate treatment occurs when an applicant or employee is treated differently because of membership in a protected class. Refusing to hire Blacks as restaurant servers or men as child care workers constitutes disparate treatment, also referred to as *intentional discrimination.* Evidence of such treatment would include statements by employers or written policies—items that are often difficult to verify or obtain. Common stereotypes about abilities, traits, or performance of people belonging to certain groups may lead to disparate treatment; for example, the stereotype that women have limited math skills could result in women purposely not being assigned to jobs requiring math skills. Assuming applicants who have Hispanic names will have limited English skills and refusing to interview them is another way that stereotypes could lead to disparate treatment.

Disparate or **adverse impact** occurs when an apparently neutral, evenly applied job policy or employment practice has a negative effect on the employment of people belonging to protected classes. It is demonstrated by statistical evidence showing that people in a protected class were disproportionately affected by a particular "neutral" practice. This type of discrimination, also referred to as *unintentional discrimination,* might occur through educational requirements or height and weight restrictions that may exclude large numbers of certain groups.

Evenly applied, neutral practices that disproportionately exclude members of certain groups should be carefully scrutinized. Are the requirements legitimate for successful job performance? Are there no other nondiscriminatory alternatives that would still allow for successful performance? Title VII does not require employers to hire, promote, or retain people who do not meet job requirements. Instead, Title VII requires employers to pay careful attention to job requirements and employment decisions to ensure that members of certain groups are not excluded by factors that are not clearly related to successful performance. From an employment perspective, constraining the applicant pool through selection requirements that do not help identify those who would be better performers is ineffective, costly, and, often, discriminatory.

The Equal Employment Opportunity Commission. Title VII created the Equal Employment Opportunity Commission (EEOC), which began operating on July 2, 1965. The EEOC's mission is to "promote equality of opportunity in the workplace and enforce federal laws prohibiting employment discrimination."[9] During the first year of operation, the EEOC received 9,000 complaints—four times the number expected, demonstrating the gravity and pervasiveness of discrimination in the United States. A primary role of the EEOC is investigating complaints of discrimination, conciliating when complaints are deemed meritorious, and litigating when efforts to resolve complaints through conciliation are unsuccessful. Instead of litigating, the EEOC may also issue complainants a "Right-to-Sue-Notice," allowing them to file individual actions in court (without the EEOC's involvement).

Although an average of about 85,000 claims have been filed with the EEOC for the past decade, relatively few claims result in resolutions for plaintiffs. As shown in Table 3.1, the percentage of all cases ending with merit resolutions was about 21% over the period. These "merit resolutions" include settlements, withdrawals with benefits, and conciliations; $319.4 million was recovered for affected parties in 2010. On the other hand, about 60% of charges were deemed to have no reasonable cause. Despite media attention and managers' fears, EEOC charges, litigation, settlements, and damage awards are unlikely events. Even so, the EEOC plays a vital role in enforcing various laws, issuing guidelines to assist employers in interpreting and complying with laws, and providing individuals with a voice in employment-related treatment.

---

[9] http://www.eeoc.gov/eeoc/index.cfm, accessed October 7, 2010.

TABLE 3.1 *EEOC Charge Receipts and Resolutions Under Title VII, ADA, ADEA, and EPA for 2000–2010*

	FY 2000	FY 2001	FY 2002	FY 2003	FY 2004	FY 2005	FY 2006	FY 2007	FY 2008	FY 2009	FY 2010
Receipts	79,896	80,840	84,442	81,293	79,432	75,428	75,768	82,792	95,402	93,277	99,922
Resolutions	93,672	90,106	95,222	87,755	85,259	77,352	74,308	72,442	81,081	85,980	104,999
Resolutions by Type											
Settlements	7,937	7,330	8,425	8,401	8,665	8,116	8,500	8,834	8,831	8,634	9,777
	8.5%	8.1%	8.8%	9.6%	10.2%	10.5%	11.4%	12.2%	10.9%	10.0%	9.3%
Withdrawals with Benefits	3,753	3,654	3,772	3,700	3,827	4,072	4,052	4,122	4,790	4,892	5,391
	4.0%	4.1%	4.0%	4.2%	4.5%	5.3%	5.5%	5.7%	5.9%	5.7%	5.1%
Administrative Closures	19,156	18,636	19,633	15,262	15,416	12,659	12,298	12,865	16,615	16,189	17,330
	20.5%	20.7%	20.6%	17.4%	18.1%	16.4%	16.6%	17.8%	20.5%	18.8%	16.5%
No Reasonable Cause	54,578	51,562	56,514	55,359	53,182	48,079	45,500	42,979	47,152	52,363	67,520
	58.3%	57.2%	59.3%	63.1%	62.4%	62.2%	61.2%	59.3%	58.2%	60.9%	64.3%
Reasonable Cause	8,248	8,924	6,878	5,033	4,169	4,426	3,958	3,642	3,693	3,902	4,981
	8.8%	9.9%	7.2%	5.7%	4.9%	5.7%	5.3%	5.0%	4.6%	4.5%	4.7%
Successful Conciliations	2,040	2,365	1,940	1,432	1,217	1,319	1,141	1,137	1,128	1,240	1,348
	2.2%	2.6%	2.0%	1.6%	1.4%	1.7%	1.5%	1.6%	1.4%	1.4%	1.3%
Unsuccessful Conciliations	6,208	6,559	4,938	3,601	2,952	3,107	2,817	2,505	2,565	2,662	3,633
	6.6%	7.3%	5.2%	4.1%	3.5%	4.0%	3.8%	3.5%	3.2%	3.1%	3.5%
Merit Resolutions	19,938	19,908	19,075	17,134	16,661	16,614	16,510	16,598	17,314	17,428	20,149
	21.3%	22.1%	20.0%	19.5%	19.5%	21.5%	22.2%	22.9%	21.4%	20.3%	19.2%
Monetary Benefits (Millions)*	$245.7	$247.8	$257.7	$236.2	$251.7	$271.6	$229.9	$290.6	$274.4	$294.2	$319.4

Note: The number for Receipts reflects the number of individual charge filings. Because individuals often file charges claiming multiple types of discrimination, the number of Receipts for any given fiscal year will be less than the total of the race, sex, sexual harassment, pregnancy, national origin, religion, retaliation (not shown), age, disability, equal pay, and GINA charges shown in Table 3.2.

*Does not include monetary benefits obtained through litigation.

Source: All Statutes, FY 1997 Through FY 2010, http://www.eeoc.gov/eeoc/statistics/enforcement/all.cfm, accessed March 10, 2011.

As with many federal agencies, many of the EEOC's resources are allocated to helping organizations comply with the law, rather than focused on penalizing them for violations. One of these resources is EEOC guidelines issued to educate employers (and thus prevent illegal actions). The EEOC defines **harassment** in employment settings as "bothering, tormenting, troubling, ridiculing, or coercing" a person because of race, color, religion, sex, national origin, disability, or age, all of which forms of harassment are increasing in frequency.[10]

Race and national origin. Under Title VII, it is illegal to discriminate against someone because of his or her race, color, birthplace, ancestry, culture, or linguistic characteristics common to a particular ethnic group. Because of the extreme and pervasive discrimination against Blacks in the United States, they were the primary racial group for whom the protections of Title VII were originally intended. Other racial and ethnic groups, including Latinos, Asian Americans, American Indians, and Arab Americans, have also benefited from the provisions of Title VII. Recently, discrimination on the basis of national origin has been on the increase; many complaints involve low-wage earners and immigrants in the fishing, poultry, and agricultural industries, many of whom have limited English proficiency and few other employment options. As described in the following case, the EEOC often targets multiple acts of discrimination.

Albertsons Agrees to Pay $8.9 Million for Job Bias Based on Race, Color, National Origin, Retaliation[11]

EEOC Says Employees Subjected to Swastikas, Lynching Drawings, Epithets

Albertsons, LLC, a national grocery chain, agreed to pay $8.9 million and furnish other relief to settle three employment discrimination lawsuits filed by the EEOC. The EEOC had charged Albertsons with race, color, and national origin discrimination and retaliation at its Aurora, CO, distribution center. The monetary relief will be distributed among 168 former and current employees. The first case was filed in 2006 and alleged a pattern or practice of workplace harassment and discrimination based on race, color, and national origin. According to the lawsuit, minority employees were repeatedly subjected to derogatory comments, name-calling, and graffiti. Moreover, the EEOC alleged that, the

---

[10] Equal Employment Opportunity Commission, Office of Public Affairs. (1992). *Issue Codes.* Washington, D.C.: EEOC, p. 68.

[11] Adapted from EEOC press release at http://www.eeoc.gov/eeoc/newsroom/release/12-15-09.cfm, accessed October 3, 2010.

offensive graffiti included racial and ethnic slurs, depictions of lynchings, swastikas, and white supremacist and anti-immigrant statements. Some of this graffiti remained for years until the restroom was remodeled in 2005. The EEOC also charged that minority employees were given harder work assignments and were more frequently and severely disciplined than their white coworkers. The EEOC charged that managers were aware of, and even participated in, the harassment and discrimination.

In the second lawsuit, filed in 2008, the EEOC alleged a pattern or practice of retaliation in which dozens of employees who had complained about the discriminatory treatment and harassment were subsequently given the harder job assignments, passed over for promotion, and even fired as retaliation. The third case alleged race discrimination on behalf of a single African American employee at the distribution center who was terminated.

EEOC Acting Chairman Stuart J. Ishimaru said, "Employers simply cannot overlook or tolerate this kind of outrageous discrimination and retaliation." EEOC Regional Attorney Mary Jo O'Neill said, "The graffiti was particularly shocking. Employers need to aggressively criticize such conduct, seek out the culprits and take swift action." Besides the monetary relief, Albertsons agreed to submit to four years of court-ordered monitoring and to institute an extensive training program to ensure that management is aware of and will comply with equal employment opportunity laws in the future.

In addition to prohibiting the kind of egregious harassment just described (disparate treatment), apparently neutral practices, such as English-only rules, may be in violation of Title VII, unless the employer has a business necessity for them. English-only rules are allowable only when needed to ensure the safe or efficient operation of a business and only when implemented for nondiscriminatory reasons. In addition, employment decisions may not be made based on an employee's foreign accent, unless the accent seriously interferes with job performance.[12]

Sex. Under Title VII, it is illegal to discriminate against someone because of his or her sex or gender in all employment-related matters.[13] Overt employment discrimination against women was rampant at the time Title VII

---

[12] National Origin Discrimination, http://www.eeoc.gov/laws/types/nationalorigin.cfm, accessed October 3, 2010.

[13] See Chapter 9 for a discussion of the Ann Hopkins case, in which the U.S. Supreme Court first specified that it was illegal to discriminate on the basis of perceptions about how someone of a particular sex *should* behave (gender).

was passed; some reports maintain that the inclusion of prohibitions against sex discrimination in the act was a last-ditch effort by conservative Southern legislators to ensure that it did not pass. Other research contradicts this claim, noting that feminists had been fighting for such legislation for a long time. Regardless of different beliefs about *why* prohibitions against sex discrimination were included in Title VII, it is clear that *some* aspects of discrimination applied more to women than to Black men, who obtained the right to vote (in theory, if not in practice) before White women did.[14] Despite persistent sex discrimination, harassment, and sex-based pay differences, Title VII has been very beneficial to working women in the United States. Although men who experience sex discrimination are also covered by Title VII, it is women who remain the primary targets. In 2010, $129.3 million was recovered for plaintiffs, as shown in Table 3.2.

Title VII has also been applied to sex-based discrimination against men. One case against Hooters restaurant alleged such discrimination, even though Hooters is known for scantily clad female servers.[15] In another case, Jillian's, a nationwide chain of family dining/entertainment facilities with headquarters in Louisville, Kentucky, agreed to settle a class action lawsuit in which at least 100 men alleged sex discrimination. The EEOC alleged that Jillian's maintained sex-segregated job classifications and failed to hire and/or transfer men to more lucrative server positions because they were men. Jillian's agreed to pay $350,000 in damages to men in Indianapolis, to hire and place employees at all its facilities without regard to sex, to train its managers on Title VII's regulations against sex discrimination, and to post nondiscrimination notices at all facilities and on its employment applications.[16]

Along with prohibitions against sex discrimination in hiring, firing, promotions, and other commonly recognized aspects of employment, Title VII prohibits sex discrimination in the form of pregnancy discrimination and sexual harassment, discussed later in the chapter. Its prohibition against gender discrimination (discrimination due to failure to comply with expected roles for men or women, as discussed further in Chapter 9) has been supported by a Supreme Court ruling.[17]

Religion. Title VII provides people of different or no religious beliefs with protection against employment-related discrimination. Employers are

---

[14] For many years, poll taxes, threats, and intimidation prevented Black men from exercising their right to vote.

[15] http://www.eeoc.gov/eeoc/newsroom/release/11-21-95.cfm, accessed March 13, 2011.

[16] "Jillian's to Pay $360,000 for Sex Discrimination Against Men." http://www.eeoc.gov/eeoc/newsroom/release/archive/8-13-04.html, accessed March 10, 2011.

[17] See the Ann Hopkins case in Chapter 9.

TABLE 3.2 *EEOC Charge Receipts, Resolutions, and Settlements by Statute, 2010*

	Equal Pay	Race	Sex	Sexual Harassment	Pregnancy	National Origin	Religion	Age	Disability	GINA
Receipts	1,044	35,890	29,029	11,717	6,119	11,304	3,790	23,264	25,165	201
Resolutions	1,083	37,559	30,914	12,772	6,293	12,494	3,782	24,800	24,401	56
Resolutions by Type										
Settlements	118	3,325	3,138	1,417	813	917	330	2,250	2,597	3
	10.9%	8.9%	10.2%	11.1%	12.9%	7.3%	8.7%	9.1%	10.6%	5.4%
Withdrawals with Benefits	90	1,567	1,774	1,195	567	535	203	1,322	1,456	2
	8.3%	4.2%	5.7%	9.4%	9.0%	4.3%	5.4%	5.3%	6.0%	3.6%
Administrative Closures	203	5,018	5,727	2,907	1,025	2,008	626	4,167	3,980	11
	18.7%	13.4%	18.5%	22.8%	16.3%	16.1%	16.6%	16.8%	16.3%	19.6%
No Reasonable Cause	614	26,319	18,709	6,393	3,670	7,910	2,309	16,308	15,182	38
	56.7%	70.1%	60.5%	50.1%	58.3%	63.3%	61.1%	65.8%	62.2%	67.9%
Reasonable Cause	58	1,330	1,566	860	218	1,124	314	753	1,186	2
	5.4%	3.5%	5.1%	6.7%	3.5%	9.0%	8.3%	3.0%	4.9%	3.6%
Successful Conciliations	25	377	475	308	102	177	73	252	439	1
	2.3%	1.0%	1.5%	2.4%	1.6%	1.4%	1.9%	1.0%	1.8%	1.8%
Unsuccessful Conciliations	33	953	1,091	552	116	947	241	501	747	1
	3.0%	2.5%	3.5%	4.3%	1.8%	7.6%	6.4%	2.0%	3.1%	1.8%
Merit Resolutions	266	6,222	6,478	3,472	1,598	2,576	847	4,325	5,239	7
	24.6%	16.6%	21.0%	27.2%	25.4%	20.6%	22.4%	17.4%	21.5%	12.5%
Monetary Benefits (Millions)*	$12.6	$84.4	$129.3	$48.4	$18.0	$29.6	$10.0	$93.6	$76.1	$0.08

*Does not include monetary benefits obtained through litigation.

Source: Enforcement and Litigation Statistics, http://www.eeoc.gov/eeoc/statistics/enforcement/index.cfm, accessed January 12, 2011 (see separate links for race, sex, sexual harassment, pregnancy, national origin, religion, retaliation (not shown), age, disability, equal pay, and GINA charges).

prohibited from treating applicants or employees more or less favorably because of their religious beliefs or practices. Employers are also required to make reasonable accommodations for employees' sincerely held religious beliefs or practices, with flexible scheduling, job reassignments, lateral transfers, and other means that do not impose undue hardship.

Lawsuits filed in 2010 by the EEOC against Walmart and Supercuts alleged that after years of accommodating employees' requests not to work on their Sabbath, management began refusing to do so. Statements from employees and the EEOC emphasize the diversity-related contradictions associated with the employers' actions.

Walmart Sued for Religious Discrimination[18]

After 15 Years Observing Sabbath, Employee Required to Work Sundays

On October 1, 2010, the EEOC filed a federal lawsuit against Walmart for disciplining and threatening to fire an assistant manager at its Colville, WA, store when he refused to violate his religious beliefs. Richard Nichols, a devout Mormon, began working for Walmart in 1995, started as a manager at the Colville store in 2002, and observes the Sabbath by doing no work of any kind (including household chores or shopping). From 1995 to 2009, Walmart accommodated his request for leave on Sundays, but in the fall of 2009, the company revised its scheduling system and refused to continue accommodating Nichols.

"For the last 15 years, I have loved working for Walmart," Nichols said. "I enjoy what I do and the people I work with. But this refusal to take into account my religious needs is causing me a great amount of stress. I'm afraid I'll be fired for choosing my religion over my work; it's not a choice I want to have to make."

"Where there is a conflict between an employee's religious beliefs and work rules, the law mandates that employers make a sincere effort to accommodate those beliefs," said Luis Lucero, director of the EEOC's Seattle Field Office. "Walmart's refusal to explore any workable solutions with Nichols is not only illegal but short-sighted. Why would anyone treat a long-time, dedicated employee this way?"

---

[18] Adapted from EEOC press release at http://www.eeoc.gov/eeoc/newsroom/release/10-1-10c.cfm, accessed October 3, 2010.

Supercuts Sued for Religious Discrimination[19]

Hair Salon Refused to Accommodate Stylist's Sabbath

On October 1, 2010, the EEOC filed a federal lawsuit charging Supercuts hair salon with religious discrimination for requiring a stylist employed at their Pleasant Hill, CA, salon to work on her Sabbath and firing her when she refused to violate her religious beliefs. Carolyn Sedar, a stylist and shift manager, observes Sabbath and does not work on Sundays. According to the lawsuit, Sedar began working for Supercuts in 1999 and store managers accommodated her religious beliefs until November 2008 when a new store manager scheduled Sedar for a Sunday shift. Sedar submitted three written complaints to and had several conversations with the store and district managers informing them that she could not work on her Sabbath. Supercuts refused to excuse Sedar from the Sunday schedule, even after she gave officials a copy of the EEOC's guidance on religious discrimination, and fired Sedar after she refused to work two consecutive Sundays.

Sedar said, "the Bible says that I should not work on Sabbath and I could not violate that tenet even though my beliefs cost me a job that I loved." EEOC San Francisco District Director Michael Baldonado noted that "Ms. Sedar worked for the company for nine years under several store managers who accommodated her Sabbath without incident. When a new manager scheduled Ms. Sedar to work on Sundays, she made every effort to inform Supercuts that its actions were unlawful. Now they are facing a lawsuit."

According to EEOC San Francisco Regional Attorney William R. Tamayo, "many of these requests can be handled easily. For example, Supercuts could have permitted Ms. Sedar to swap shifts with coworkers, as they had done already for almost a decade. Supercuts could not show that excusing Sedar from work on her Sabbath would impose an undue hardship."

Although these cases have not been resolved, a similar suit was settled in August 2009 by the EEOC's Memphis District Office against the parent company of Supercuts (doing business as Smartstyle) for failing to accommodate an employee who observed Sabbath on Sundays. In 2003, Supercuts had settled another lawsuit that alleged it had discriminated against a

[19] Adapted from EEOC press release at http://www.eeoc.gov/eeoc/newsroom/release/10-1-10f.cfm, accessed October 8, 2010.

White regional manager who refused to participate in discrimination against Black employees. The company settled the suit for \$3.5 million and said it would train hundreds of managers on nondiscriminatory practices, yet blatant discrimination persisted.[20]

In both the Walmart and Supercuts religious discrimination cases, the EEOC first attempted to reach a prelitigation settlement and, when it was not reached, filed suit seeking back pay and other monetary losses and compensatory and punitive damages for appropriate injunctive relief to prevent future discrimination. Along with avoiding discrimination and making reasonable accommodations of employees' sincerely held religious beliefs, the EEOC encourages employers to put in place antiharassment policies that include religious harassment. Title VII has been helpful, for example, to many Muslims who faced overt discrimination and harassment after the terrorist attacks in the United States on September 11, 2001. As shown in Table 3.2, in 2010, the EEOC received 3,790 charges of religious discrimination, resolved 3,782 charges (including some from previous years), and recovered \$10.0 million in monetary benefits for complainants and other aggrieved parties.[21] The EEOC has issued "Guidelines on Discrimination Because of Religion" and "Guidelines on Religious Exercise and Religious Expression in the Federal Workplace" that may help employers to create a supportive climate for religious diversity.[22]

Exceptions: Bona fide occupational qualifications and business necessity.

In a limited number of situations, discrimination on the basis of sex, religion, and age is not illegal. Bona fide occupational qualifications (BFOQs) refer to certain situations in which employers may require that all employees hold a certain characteristic. For sex as a BFOQ, for example, an employer could legitimately require that women model evening gowns, that a male be hired to play a leading man in a movie, or that women work in dressing or changing rooms in a lingerie shop. Age may be a BFOQ in certain circumstances when it is "reasonably necessary to the normal operation of the business." Mandatory retirement of pilots and age limits for public safety officers are examples of the narrow legal use of age limits. Religion could be a BFOQ for particular religious organizations. An organization may also claim that a particular practice resulting in disparate impact (but not disparate treatment) is a "business necessity." For business necessity to be a valid defense, the employer must

---

[20] "Supercuts to Pay \$3.5 Million for Race Bias and Train Hundreds of Managers, in EEOC Settlement." http://www.eeoc.gov/eeoc/newsroom/release/8-13-03.cfm, accessed October 8, 2010.
[21] "Religion-based Charges, 1997–2009." http://www.eeoc.gov/eeoc/statistics/enforcement/religion.cfm, accessed January 12, 2011.
[22] http://clinton4.nara.gov/textonly/WH/New/html/19970819-3275.html, accessed April 6, 2011.

demonstrate that there is no alternative practice that would serve the same purpose without having the discriminatory effect.

Although the aforementioned situations are cases in which discrimination may not be illegal, organizations should emphasize using legitimate job-related qualifications and attending to what is actually required, rather than simply discriminating when it is not illegal to do so. When organizations are able to remove obstacles to employment for larger proportions of the population, organizations, individuals, and all of society stand to benefit.

Affirmative Action in Employment

In 1965 and 1966, President Lyndon B. Johnson issued key executive orders for affirmative action in employment. These orders are administered and enforced by the U.S. Department of Labor's Office of Federal Contract Compliance Programs (OFCCP). Executive Orders (EO) 11246 and 11375, as amended, prohibit federal contractors with over $10,000 in government business per year from discriminating in employment decisions on the basis of race, color, religion, sex, or national origin. In addition to prohibiting discrimination, these orders require proactive measures—affirmative action—to help ensure equality of employment opportunities for women and minorities. Government contractors having fifty or more employees and at least $50,000 in government contracts are required to develop an affirmative action plan for each of their establishments.

Affirmative action programs. Affirmative action programs (AAP) are written programs or plans that help employers identify areas in which women, minorities, persons with disabilities, and Vietnam-era veterans are underutilized in the employers' workforce. A utilization analysis is a comparison of the population of underrepresented groups in the surrounding or relevant (for recruiting purposes) labor market to how many people from those groups are present in the organization, by particular job categories. If there is a lower proportion of women and minorities in the organization than in the available labor market, underutilization is indicated and the organization should implement plans to correct this. Whereas Title VII is passive, in that it prohibits discrimination, affirmative action requires taking action—taking steps to correct or reduce underutilization.

Legitimate plans to correct underutilization might include additional training programs or different recruitment methods, not "quotas," which are generally illegal. Employers may not legally implement quotas, and only in unique cases of blatant discrimination may a judge impose quotas on an offending employer. Judges are reluctant to do this, however, even in cases of egregious discrimination. Rather than imposing quotas, judges will recommend that employers pay careful attention to recruiting practices and set hiring goals for the group that experienced discrimination.

Misperception: Affirmative action programs require employers to have hiring "quotas" if minorities or women are underutilized.

Reality: Employers should have goals and timetables for correcting underutilization; employer-imposed quotas are illegal and judges are reluctant to impose them.

In a sex discrimination case involving Walmart, the EEOC alleged that the company regularly hired male applicants for warehouse positions while excluding equally or better qualified woman applicants, using gender stereotypes in filling the positions. Hiring officials allegedly told women applicants that such positions were not suitable for women. As part of the settlement of the case, Walmart agreed to fill the next fifty available positions with female class members.[23]

Recruitment is an important and accepted means of increasing numbers of qualified applicants from diverse backgrounds. If an organization is underutilizing women, for example, it might alter recruitment efforts to include universities with a large percentage of women students, such as Smith College, Texas Woman's University, or St. Mary's College in Indiana. Organizations wishing to increase representation of racial and ethnic minorities might include recruiting at universities such as the University of Texas at El Paso, University of California at San Diego, or Baruch College in New York, which have high percentages of Latinos, or historically Black universities such as Southern University, Prairie View A&M University, or North Carolina A&T. Advertising in media that target specific groups, such as *Essence* or *Ebony* magazine (Blacks), *Univision* or *Latina Style* (Hispanics), is a simple and an easy means of increasing the diversity of the applicant pool. By changing recruiting venues or methods, people from diverse backgrounds have more opportunities to compete for job openings.

Periodic compliance reviews by the Office of Federal Contract Compliance Programs (OFCCP—the monitoring agency) can help employers identify problem areas and corrective action. Compliance reviews seek to change personnel routines (e.g., hiring, promotion) that

---

[23] "Walmart to Pay More Than $11.7 Million to Settle EEOC Sex Discrimination Suit." http://www.eeoc.gov/eeoc/newsroom/release/3-1-10.cfm, accessed September 3, 2010.

might result in discrimination.[24] These reviews are different from litigation in response to individuals' complaints. EEOC compliance reviews can result in substantial damage costs to employers, however, as discussed in the following news release about the case against a Coca-Cola bottler.

U.S. Labor Department Settles Discrimination Case with 2nd-largest Coca-Cola Bottler in the Nation[25]

Minority Applicants to Receive Back Wages, Interest, and Job Offers

Coca-Cola Bottling Company Consolidated agreed to pay $495,000 in back wages and interest to 95 African American and Hispanic job seekers who applied in 2002 for sales support positions at a distribution facility in North Carolina. The settlement follows an investigation by the U.S. Department of Labor's OFCCP. In addition to back pay, the company agreed to make offers of employment to those 95 applicants until at least 23 interested applicants are hired. Those hired will receive retroactive seniority benefits they would have accrued from July 1, 2002, had it not been for the discrimination.

This plant is the second largest Coca-Cola bottler in the nation and a major supplier of Coke brand products to military and government installations under a number of federal contracts. As a result of the federal contracts, the bottler was subject to compliance review, during which the OFCCP found that the bottler failed to hire qualified minority applicants at a comparable rate to White applicants. Statistical analysis determined that the disparity in hires was too great to occur solely by chance. In addition, the OFCCP found that the bottler's own records revealed cases in which rejected minority applicants had more experience and education than some White hires.

Persistent or unaddressed problems may result in conciliation agreements, which may include back pay, promotions, or other forms of relief for affected parties. When attempts to conciliate are unsuccessful, sanctions, including loss of government contracts, may be imposed upon employers. As with other diversity efforts, avoidance of sanctions or penalties should not be an organization's primary compliance goal. Nor should the relationship between employers and the OFCCP be assumed as solely an adversarial one. The OFCCP can assist employers in developing

[24] Kalev, A., & Dobbin, F. (2006). "Enforcement of Civil Rights Law in Private Workplaces: The Effects of Compliance Reviews and Lawsuits Over Time." *Law & Social Inquiry*, 31(4): 855–903.
[25] Adapted from OFCCP news release: Release Number 10-1368-ATL, http://www.dol.gov/opa/media/press/ofccp/ofccp20101368.htm, accessed October 8, 2010.

AAPs by offering company seminars and individual consultations on company policies and procedures. When used correctly, affirmative action can be a valuable tool in increasing the representation of underutilized groups in an organization, providing opportunities to benefit from their inclusion and contributions. Researchers have found that employers subject to affirmative action requirements that hire a manager with responsibility for compliance see stronger effects from diversity and equal opportunity programs.[26]

Relationships between affirmative action in education and in employment. Many newspaper and magazine articles and academic publications have discussed issues related to affirmative action in education, contracts with the government, or employment. Because the term *affirmative action* by itself does not indicate what type of activity is under discussion (e.g., increasing representation in elite schools or in employment), people may misunderstand its focus or goals. Indeed, as discussed in Research Summary 3.1, research indicates that opposition to affirmative action is related to lack of knowledge.[27]

We focus here and in this book primarily on affirmative action in employment, but education and employment are clearly related. Professor Patricia Gurin's longitudinal research on the long-term benefits of diversity to students in the learning environment can help clarify this relationship. As discussed in Chapter 1, in several studies, Gurin and colleagues found that many students' experiences with diversity at the University of Michigan increased their sense of commonality with those from different racial and ethnic backgrounds, their ability to take the perspective of other groups, and their understanding that differences are not necessarily divisive.[28] The more contact students had with people from other racial and ethnic backgrounds, the more they engaged in active, critical thinking and the more they embraced democratic values. These benefits occurred for both White students and students of color.

....

[26] Kalev, A., Dobbin, F., & Kelly, E. (2006). "Best Practices or Best Guesses? Assessing the Efficacy of Corporate Affirmative Action and Diversity Policies." *American Sociological Review*, 71: 589–617.

[27] Kravitz and Yun found that opposition to affirmative action in employment is related to the lack of knowledge about the law. Kravitz, D. A., & Yun, G. (2005, August). "Further Development of a Test of Knowledge of Workplace Affirmative Action Law and Regulations." Paper presented at the annual meeting of the Academy of Management, Honolulu, HI.

[28] Gurin, P., Nagda, B. A., & Lopez, G. E. (2004). "The Benefits of Diversity in Education for Democratic Citizenship." *Journal of Social Issues*, 60(1): 17–34. See also Gurin, P., Dey, E. L., Hurtado, S., & Gurin, G. (2002). "Diversity and Higher Education: Theory and Impact on Educational Outcomes." *Harvard Educational Review*, 71(3): 332–366; Gurin, P. Y., Dey, E. L., Gurin, G., & Hurtado, S. (2003). "How Does Racial/Ethnic Diversity Promote Education?" *The Western Journal of Black Studies*, 27(1): 20–29.

RESEARCH SUMMARY 3.1	*Focus on Affirmative Action*

Numerous researchers have investigated the often negative perceptions and attitudes people have about affirmative action programs (AAPs) in employment. Many of these perceptions are obtained from news media and political advertisements, which frequently contain inaccuracies or intentional misrepresentations about the content, requirements, and function of affirmative action. Some of these misperceptions include erroneous beliefs about the requirements of and processes required by affirmative action programs (e.g., quotas) and beliefs that those hired under affirmative action are less competent and qualified than others.[29]

Madeline Heilman and her colleagues have conducted extensive research on stigmatization and presumptions of incompetence about women hired under AAPs. In field and laboratory studies, these women were *perceived* to be less competent than persons not hired under AAPs. These findings occurred when the raters were White men but also when the raters were White women, Black men, and Black women—those from groups who are likely to be helped by AAPs.

Moreover, these findings, are likely to be related to people's general perceptions that affirmative action results in organizations passing over more qualified workers for less qualified or unqualified workers and to other inaccuracies that have been identified by researchers.[30] The perceptions contrast starkly with the actual requirements of AAPs that applicants must first be qualified to be considered and findings of other research that indicate clear preferences for equally qualified or even unqualified Whites over persons of color. Art Brief and his colleagues found that when instructed to discriminate under the guise of a "business justification," research subjects did so, rating Black applicants lower than similarly qualified White applicants. Most disturbing, when given this justification to discriminate, some respondents chose *unqualified Whites* over qualified Blacks.[31,32] A similar study replicated these findings of discrimination against minorities in Germany.[33] Years of covert and overt discrimination against minorities and women have systematically advantaged White men in many contexts.[34]

[29] See Heilman, M. E., Block, C. J., & Lucas, J. A. (1992). "Presumed Incompetent? Stigmatization and Affirmative Action Efforts." *Journal of Applied Psychology*, 77: 536–544; Bell, M. P., Harrison, D. E., & McLaughlin, M. E. (2000). "Forming, Changing, and Acting on Attitude Toward Affirmative Action in Employment: A Theory Based Approach." *Journal of Applied Psychology*, 85: 784–798; and Crosby F. J. (2004). *Affirmative Action Is Dead: Long Live Affirmative Action*. New Haven, CT: Yale University Press.

[30] See, for example, Bell et al. (2000); Kravitz, D., & Yun, G. (2005, August). "Further Development of a Test of Knowledge of Workplace Affirmative Action Law and Regulations." Paper presented at the annual meeting of the Academy of Management, Honolulu, HI.

[31] Brief, A. P., Buttram, R. T., Reizenstein, R. M., Pugh, S. D., Callahan, J. D., McCline, R. L., & Vaslow, J. B. (1997). "Beyond Good Intentions: The Next Steps Toward Racial Equality in the American Workplace." *Academy of Management Executive*, 11(4): 59–72. See also Brief, A. P., Dietz, J., Cohen, R. R., Pugh, S. D., & Vaslow, J. B. (2000). "Just Doing Business: Modern Racism and Obedience to Authority as Explanations for Employment Discrimination." *Organizational Behavior and Human Decision Processes*, 81: 72–97.

[32] More details on this study are provided in Chapter 4.

[33] Petersen, L., & Dietz, J. (2005). "Prejudice and Enforcement of Workforce Homogeneity as Explanations for Employment Discrimination." *Journal of Applied Social Psychology*, 35(1): 144–159.

[34] See, for example, Brodkin, K. (2004). "How Jews Became White." In J. F. Healey & E. O'Brien (Eds.), *Race, Ethnicity, and Gender*. Thousand Oaks, CA: Pine Forge Press, pp. 283–293; "Dedicated Lives" (1997). *Emerge*, July/August, pp. 35–38.

To reduce misperceptions about affirmative action and assumptions that women and people of color are hired solely because of AAPs and that White males are hired because of discrimination against others, it is important for organizations to publicize the qualifications of new hires of all backgrounds. Publicizing the background and qualifications of new hires of all demographic groups would help demonstrate that all employees are hired because of job-related qualifications. Make clear that women and people of color are not hired solely because of affirmative action and that White males are not hired because of the good-old-boys' network and discrimination against women and people of color. Employees should also be educated about the affirmative practices that the organization employs (such as

broad recruitment methods) and the benefits of diversity for all employees. Education is an important tool in reducing resistance against diversity efforts.

QUESTIONS TO CONSIDER

1. *What factors likely contribute to common, erroneous beliefs about affirmative action, even among intended beneficiaries?*

2. *How do perceptions that minorities and women who are hired are unqualified contrast with research indicating that unqualified Whites are sometimes chosen over qualified Blacks?*

Open support of numerous *Fortune* 500 companies for programs to increase acceptance of diversity among students indicates that major corporations are aware of the important relationships between diversity in educational institutions and the subsequent benefits of a well-educated, diverse workforce. During the Reagan administration's efforts to curtail employment-related affirmative action programs, 95% of CEOs of major corporations stated they would continue their voluntary AAPs even if the federal government ended such requirements.[35] A different study in which 94% of CEOs reported perceptions that affirmative action had improved their hiring and marketing programs indicated similarly strong corporate support for affirmative action.[36] Affirmative action has clearly been helpful to its intended beneficiaries as well. In 1973, firefighters in the Los Angeles Fire Department were 94% White and 100% male. By 1995, 55% of the firefighters were White, 26% were Latino, 13% were Black, 6% were Asian, and 4% were women.[37] When employees are more representative of

[35]Reskin, B. (2000). "The Realities of Affirmative Action in Employment." In F. J. Crosby & C. VanDeVeer (Eds.), *Sex, Race, and Merit: Debating Affirmative Action in Education and Employment.* Ann Arbor, MI: University of Michigan Press.
[36]Crosby, F. J., & Herzberger, S. D. (1996). "For Affirmative Action." In R. J. Simon (Ed.), *Affirmative Action: Pros and Cons of Policy and Practice.* Washington, D.C.: American University Press, pp. 3–109.
[37]Rosenthal, S. J. (1997). "Affirm Equality, Oppose Racist Scapegoating: Myths and Realities of Affirmative Action." In C. Herring (Ed.), *African Americans and the Public Agenda.* Thousand Oaks, CA: Sage Publications, pp. 105–125.

the diversity in the population, there can be numerous benefits for the organization and for the population being served. In addition, employees (regardless of race or sex) of affirmative action companies have higher earnings than people employed at nonaffirmative action companies.[38]

Other beneficiaries of affirmative action programs. The Rehabilitation Act of 1973 (RA) prohibits discrimination against employees and applicants with disabilities when they work for or apply to the federal government or government contractors. The RA also requires the federal government to take affirmative action in the hiring, placement, and advancement of people with disabilities, similar to that for women and minorities. The Vietnam Era Veterans' Readjustment Assistance Act (1974) requires federal contractors take affirmative action for disabled veterans and Vietnam war and other veterans.[39] Despite the common misperceptions that affirmative action benefits only minorities and women, about 80% of all veterans, the targets of this affirmative action legislation, are White men.[40]

The Age Discrimination in Employment Act of 1967

The Age Discrimination in Employment Act (ADEA) prohibits employment-related discrimination against persons who are aged 40 and over, which is an important issue for the millions of aging baby-boomers in the United States. Under the ADEA, employers of twenty or more people, including state and local governments, employment agencies, and labor organizations are prohibited from discrimination on the basis of age in employment-related matters. This act also prohibits age-based harassment, retaliation for complaining about or filing a claim of discrimination, and employment decisions based on stereotypes about one's ability based on age. Employers should not intentionally target older workers for layoffs or termination or deny them training because they are believed to be close to retirement or unwilling to learn, which, as discussed in Chapter 13, are common misperceptions about older workers.

---

[38] Ibid.

[39] http://www.dol.gov/ofccp/regs/compliance/ca_vevraa.htm, accessed March 10, 2011.

[40] Wilson, M., Perry, S., Helba, C., Hintze, W., Wright, M., Lee, K., Greenlees, J., Rockwell, D., & Deak, M. A. *National Survey of Veterans (NSV) Final Report, 2001.* http://www1.va.gov/VETDATA/docs/SurveysAndStudies/NSV_Final_Report.pdf, accessed October 7, 2010.

Kmart to Pay $120,000 to Settle EEOC Age Bias Suit[41]

Pharmacist Called "Greedy" for Working at Age 70, Then Forced to Quit, and Threatened with Legal Action in Retaliation for Complaining, Federal Agency Charged

Kmart Corporation will pay $120,000 and furnish other relief to settle an age harassment, constructive discharge, and retaliation lawsuit filed by the EEOC, which had charged that Kmart discriminated against a 70-year-old pharmacist at a Honolulu store. According to the EEOC's suit, over the course of four years, a pharmacy manager openly professed on several occasions that the pharmacist was "too old," "should just retire," and was "greedy" for continuing to work at age 70. The EEOC said that the manager humiliated the pharmacist by saying, "you need to retire from pharmacy work now," in a communication book open to the entire department. According to the EEOC, the manager also purposely scheduled her to work on Sundays—knowing that she attended church those days—to encourage her to quit. The victim complained to a district manager, general manager, and human resources manager regarding the age-based harassment, to no avail. Finally, the pharmacist quit to escape the discrimination, harassment, and retaliation.

In cooperation with the EEOC, Kmart entered into a three-year consent decree and agreed to post a notice on the matter; hire an EEO trainer; review and revise its existing antidiscrimination policy; provide annual ADEA training to all staff; and ensure that performance evaluations reflect discriminatory misconduct by management staff.

A major inadequacy of federal legislation related to age in the United States is its failure to include any workers under age 40 from age-related discrimination. As a result, younger workers, who are the "minority" in many cases, are subject to and experience age-related stereotyping and discrimination. In contrast, as discussed further in Chapter 13, in the United Kingdom, Australia, and some states and cities in the United States, employment discrimination on the basis of any age is prohibited.

The Pregnancy Discrimination Act of 1978

The Pregnancy Discrimination Act (PDA), an amendment to Title VII, clarified that Title VII's regulations against discrimination because of sex

---

[41] Adapted from EEOC press release at http://www.eeoc.gov/eeoc/newsroom/release/3-24-10.cfm, accessed October 8, 2010.

included discrimination on the basis of pregnancy, childbirth, and related medical conditions. The PDA prohibits discrimination in hiring, leave, health insurance, and fringe benefits. In some organizations prior to 1978, pregnant women were required to resign or take leave and could be denied medical benefits that others received. The PDA does not require employers to provide benefits or leave for pregnancy or related conditions. However, if benefits or leave are provided for other temporary medical conditions, the PDA requires that employers provide the same benefits for pregnancy and related conditions. As with employees with other conditions, if pregnant women can still work, they cannot be forced to go on leave. If other employees who are temporarily unable to work because of illness are entitled to return to work once they have recovered, the same opportunities are required for women who are unable to work because of pregnancy or related conditions.

In 2010, the EEOC received 6,119 charges of pregnancy discrimination and resolved 6,293 (some from previous years). Of those, 25.4% were resolved with merit, resulting in $18.0 million in monetary benefits for the charging parties and other aggrieved individuals.[42] The EEOC's litigation against Walmart on behalf of Jamey Stern (see Featured Case 3.1), involved a decade-long case.

Instead of overt pregnancy discrimination, such as refusal to hire pregnant women, some cases involve other issues related to pregnancy. A case involving pension plans was brought by the EEOC against Cincinnati Bell on behalf of 458 employees who took maternity leave that was deducted from their service credit. The service credit reductions negatively affected certain employees' pensions and benefits under early retirement plans.[43] The company agreed to provide service credit adjustments for the majority of the affected women and monetary relief to about 40 of them. Such a case clearly demonstrates the need to understand and attempt to comply with intentions and goals behind diversity-related legislation rather than simplistically agreeing not to discriminate.

EEOC Guidelines on Sexual Harassment (1980)

In 1980, the EEOC issued its first formal guidelines on sexual harassment to provide direction for employers in addressing and curbing this specific form of sex discrimination. **Sexual harassment** is unwelcome sexual

---

[42] "Pregnancy Discrimination Charges EEOC & FEPAs Combined: FY 1997–FY 2009." http://www .eeoc.gov/eeoc/statistics/enforcement/pregnancy.cfm, accessed January 12, 2011.

[43] "EEOC and Cincinnati Bell Settle Class Pregnancy Bias Suit." http://www.eeoc.gov/eeoc/newsroom/ release/6-15-00-a.cfm, accessed October 2, 2010.

FEATURED CASE 3.1	*Pregnancy Discrimination at Walmart—Case Settled When the Baby Is 10 Years Old!*

Although the Pregnancy Discrimination Act has existed for many years and employers should therefore be well aware of it, overt pregnancy discrimination still occurs. One such case began in November 1991, when Jamey Stern applied for a job at Walmart. Stern had worked at Walmart before, as a clothing clerk, and was applying for rehire. When Stern told the assistant manager that she was pregnant, the manager told her to "come back after she had the baby." Stern did not know that refusing to hire someone because of pregnancy was illegal until later when she read a magazine article about pregnancy discrimination while in her doctor's waiting room. Stern then filed a discrimination complaint with the EEOC, which filed a lawsuit in 1994 after attempts to settle the case with Walmart were unsuccessful.

In 1997, a jury found that Walmart had intentionally discriminated against Stern, awarding her $1,700 in back pay, but the issue of punitive damages (available in cases of intentional discrimination) was not addressed in the award. **Punitive damages** are "money damages designed to punish the wrong-doing employer and deter other employers" from discriminating. The EEOC appealed, given the jury's finding that the discrimination was indeed intentional. After multiple setbacks, appeals, and the revelation that Walmart had "fabricated a number of facts during the investigation and the trial," Walmart settled the case. In December 2002, eleven years after the incident, Walmart agreed to pay $220,000 in damages to Stern and to provide comprehensive training on pregnancy discrimination to managers.

After the settlement, Ms. Stern noted that "one person can truly make a difference ... even in the face of such an adversary as Walmart."

Stern also expressed confidence that others would benefit and become educated about their rights and about resources, such as the EEOC, available to protect those rights.

_____

Sources: "Walmart to Pay $220,000 for Rejecting Pregnant Applicant, in EEOC Settlement." http://www.eeoc.gov/press/12-23-02.html, accessed September 26, 2010; "EEOC Litigation Settlements December 2002." http://archive.eeoc.gov/litigation/settlements/settlement12-02.html, accessed September 26, 2010.

QUESTIONS TO CONSIDER

1. *Although the Pregnancy Discrimination Act had been in existence for thirteen years when Jamey Stern applied for the job at Walmart, the assistant manager still refused to hire Stern and did not attempt to hide the reason. What might explain the manager's actions?*

2. *Jamey Stern was unaware that pregnancy discrimination is illegal.*
   a. Speculate on the proportion of the population that is also unaware of this and other areas covered under discrimination legislation. Estimate the proportion of employees in hiring positions at Walmart and other organizations who are not aware that pregnancy discrimination is illegal.
   b. What might Jamey Stern's response have been to being rehired at Walmart while pregnant?

3. *What is the average family income of people who work in low-wage jobs? Without the resources of the EEOC, how likely is it*
   a. that someone like Jamey could have personally brought this case against Walmart,
   b. that the case would have gone to trial, and

c. that Jamey could have engaged in an eleven-year litigation?

4. Had Jamey Stern applied to work at a lesser-known company, speculate on how likely it is that the case would have been taken on by the *EEOC. What, if any, effects might publicity about lawsuits and judgments against large companies have on the actions of managers in smaller companies that may be less likely to be sued?*

advances, requests for sexual favors, and other verbal or physical conduct of a sexual nature that explicitly or implicitly interferes with a person's employment, unreasonably interferes with her or his work performance, or creates an intimidating, hostile, or offensive work environment.[44] Sexual harassment results in numerous negative physical and psychological outcomes for those who are harassed and for bystanders and is expensive for harassment targets and employers.[45]

In **quid pro quo harassment**, managers, supervisors, or others with authority make sexual demands, and submission to or rejection of those demands is used as a basis for employment decisions (such as promotion, termination). In **hostile environment harassment**, unwelcome sexual conduct has the "purpose or effect of unreasonably interfering with job performance, or creating an intimidating, hostile, or offensive working environment."[46] Lewd jokes, sexually explicit posters, or sexual comments could constitute hostile environment sexual harassment. Research indicates that men and women differ in their perceptions of what behaviors constitute hostile environment harassment or innocuous behavior. Clear organizational policies prohibiting sexual harassment and education about what constitutes harassment by managers and supervisors, employees, and customers are imperative.

It is estimated that up to 75% of working women have already experienced or will experience sexual harassment at some point during their work lives; however, most women who are harassed do not file complaints.[47] In 2010, the EEOC received 11,717 charges of sexual harassment, 84% of which were filed by women. Only 27.2% of complaints were resolved in the charging parties' favor. However, more than $48.4 million was recovered for complainants and other aggrieved

---

[44] U.S. Equal Employment Opportunity Commission. "Sexual Harassment." http://www.eeoc.gov/laws/types/sexual_harassment.cfm, accessed March 10, 2011.

[45] Schneider, K. T., Swan, S., & Fitzgerald, L. F. (1997). "Job-Related and Psychological Effects of Sexual Harassment in the Workplace: Empirical Evidence from Two Organizations." *Journal of Applied Psychology*, 82: 401–415.

[46] Guidelines on Discrimination Because of Sex, 29, C. F. R. Section 1604. 11(a). 1995.

[47] See Fitzgerald, L. F., & Ormerod, A. J. (1993). "Breaking Silence: The Sexual Harassment of Women in Academia and the Workplace." In F. Denmark & M. Paludi (Eds.), *Psychology of Women: A Handbook of Issues and Theories*. Westport, CT: Greenwood Press, pp. 553–581; Gutek, B. A. (1985). *Sex and the Workplace*. San Francisco: Jossey-Bass; and Martindale, M. (1990). *Sexual Harassment in the Military: 1988*. Arlington, VA: Defense Manpower Data Center.

parties,[48] not including monetary benefits obtained through litigation. As with other types of equal employment opportunity issues, these figures indicate that, for individual parties, filing a complaint is considerably more likely to result in an unsuccessful claim than in a successful claim. Even so, because of the large collective amount of damage awards and negative publicity associated with such cases, employers are motivated to avoid being one of the companies charged in a high-profile case. Small companies can also be involved, and smaller settlements are also possible, as described in the following case against a family-owned and -operated business.[49]

Finch Air Conditioning Settles EEOC Lawsuit for Sexual Harassment of Young Female Employees

Family-Owned and -Operated Business Pays $80,000 to Settle Class Claims of Sexual Harassment by Owner

Finch Air Conditioning and Heating, Inc., agreed to pay $80,000 to settle claims of sexual harassment and constructive discharge of female employees brought by the EEOC. The EEOC alleged that female employees at Finch were routinely subjected to sexual harassment and discrimination. According to the EEOC, the owner of the family-owned and -operated business used his position and power to harass young female employees, commenting on his own sexual preferences and asking them questions about theirs, touching them inappropriately and without their permission, including forcing one employee's hands on his private parts and menacing and frightening employees into silence about his conduct. The EEOC also alleged that sexual harassment was condoned within the workplace.

The settlement terms required the company to pay $80,000 to compensate class members for the sexual harassment they suffered. The decree also contains provisions to ensure that Finch's owner, managers, and employees are properly trained to fully understand and comply with employment discrimination laws. In addition, Finch is required to maintain policies and procedures for addressing illegal discrimination in the workplace, including effective complaint procedures, as well as guidelines for investigating complaints of discrimination.

---

[48] U.S. Equal Employment Opportunity Commission. "Sexual Harassment Charges. EEOC & FEPAs Combined: FY 1997–FY 2010." http://www.eeoc.gov/eeoc/statistics/enforcement/sexual_harassment. cfm, accessed October 2, 2010.

[49] Adapted from EEOC press release at, http://www.eeoc.gov/eeoc/newsroom/release/8-25-10b.cfm, accessed October 2, 2010.

Customer harassment. Customers can also create hostile environment sexual harassment for which employers may be held liable. Researchers describe such harassment as an occupational hazard and note the negative consequences (such as avoidance that leads to lower productivity, stress, and turnover) on those who experience it.[50] In one such case, Love's Travel Stops agreed to pay to settle a lawsuit involving 18- and 20-year-old female cashiers.

Arizona Truck Stop to Pay $70,000 to Settle EEOC Suit Charging Sex Harassment by Customers[51]

EEOC Says Love's Travel Stops and Country Stores Tolerated Hostile Workplace

Love's Travel Stops and Country Stores, Inc., will pay $70,000 as part of a settlement of a sexual harassment lawsuit filed by the EEOC. The EEOC had charged that Love's subjected two young female cashiers (aged 18 and 20 at the start of their employment) to repeated and serious sex-based abuse by customers. The cashiers detailed extensive sexual harassment by truck drivers, some of whom were regular customers of Love's. The EEOC alleged that this conduct included unwanted sexual touching and pressing; crude and obscene remarks; sexual demands and innuendos; handing one victim an obscene card; and demands for personal information. The EEOC maintained that Love's knew about and tolerated the hostile work environment caused by its customers yet failed to take steps to stop the harassment. Moreover, the EEOC alleged that one manager laughed about the harassment and that another manager said the harassment was to be expected because the workplace is a truck stop. The cashiers were told to "deal with it."

In addition to the settlement requiring Love's to pay $70,000 to the former cashiers, Love's also must investigate complaints of sexual harassment, provide training for managers and supervisors on conducting sexual harassment investigations, and post a warning that harassment of Love's employees will not be tolerated.

Prevention of sexual harassment. As discussed earlier, although damage awards and negative publicity can be costly, the likelihood that an

---

[50] Gettman, H., & Gelfand, M. (2007). "When the Customer Shouldn't Be King: Antecedents and Consequences of Sexual Harassment by Clients and Customers." *Journal of Applied Psychology*, 92(3): 757–770.

[51] Adapted from EEOC press release at http://www.eeoc.gov/eeoc/newsroom/release/8-3-10a.cfm, accessed September 19, 2010.

organization will be sued for sexual harassment is relatively small. Even so, the many negative individual and organizational outcomes of sexual harassment should provide sufficient stimuli for organizations to try to prevent it. The EEOC recommends that organizations take proactive steps against sexual harassment. These steps include having and widely disseminating the organization's policy on harassment, educating employees about sexual harassment and their rights to a harassment-free environment, and having multiple ways to complain if harassment occurs. The employer should investigate promptly and thoroughly any complaint of harassment and, if harassment is found, take immediate action to end the harassment and prevent future harassment. Disciplinary actions against the harasser should be directly related to the severity of the incident. A warning may be appropriate for some incidents and immediate termination may be appropriate for other acts. If the complainant experienced any denial of employment benefits or opportunities as a result of failure to comply with sexual demands, those benefits or opportunities should be restored.[52]

The EEOC issues updates to its guidelines on sexual harassment (and other areas it enforces) when appropriate. These updates are readily available on the EEOC's Web site: http://www.eeoc.gov. Organizations should pay careful attention to these updates, as they provide invaluable assistance to those interested in a discrimination-free environment. The guidelines can also be useful to organizations that are not bound by U.S. laws but that are concerned with creating harassment-free workspaces.

Older Workers Benefit Protection Act of 1990

The Older Workers Benefit Protection Act (OWBPA) is an amendment to the ADEA of 1967. It prohibits employers from denying benefits to older workers but recognizes that it is more expensive to provide some benefits, such as life or disability insurance, to older workers. Thus, this act allows employers to reduce benefits based on age, as long as the employers' costs of providing benefits to older workers are the same as the costs of providing benefits to younger workers.[53] As an example, an employer can provide an older employee with $50,000 of life insurance coverage at an employer cost of $100 per month and a younger employee with $75,000 of life insurance coverage at an employer cost of $100 per month.

---

[52] http://www.eeoc.gov/policy/docs/currentissues.html, accessed February 29, 2004. See also Bell, M. P., Cycyota, C., & Quick, J. C. (2002). "Affirmative Defense: The Prevention of Sexual Harassment." In D. L. Nelson & R. J. Burke (Eds.), *Gender, Work Stress, and Health: Current Research Issues.* Washington, D.C.: American Psychological Association, pp. 191–210.

[53] http://www.eeoc.gov/facts/age.pdf, accessed October 7, 2010.

Although the younger employee has more insurance, because the employer contribution is the same, there is no illegal discrimination.

Americans with Disabilities Act of 1990

Although the Rehabilitation Act (RA) of 1973, discussed earlier, had begun the work of addressing discrimination against people with disabilities, their persistent unemployment or underemployment and the employment discrimination against them led to the passage of the Americans with Disabilities Act (ADA) in 1990, which affects more employers than did the earlier statute. The stated purpose of the ADA is to "establish a clear and comprehensive prohibition of discrimination on the basis of disability."[54] As with Title VII and the ADEA, under the ADA, employers having fifteen or more employees, employment agencies, labor unions, and state and local governments are prohibited from discrimination in employment matters against workers with disabilities: hiring and firing; compensation, assignment, or classification of applicants or employees; transfer, promotion, layoff, or recall; job advertisements; recruitment; testing; use of company facilities; training and apprenticeship programs; fringe benefits; pay, retirement plans, and disability leave; or other terms and conditions of employment. Unlike the RA, the ADA does not require affirmative action.

An individual with a disability is a person who has a physical or mental impairment that substantially limits one or more of his or her life activities, has a record of such an impairment, or is regarded as having such an impairment. The covered impairments, notably, do not include current drug users, persons having "sexual behavior disorders," kleptomaniacs, compulsive gamblers, and certain other issues.[55] To be covered by the ADA, individuals (employees or applicants) must be qualified to perform the essential (but not marginal) functions of the job in question, with or without reasonable accommodation. Reasonable accommodation includes such things as job restructuring, modifying work schedules, providing readers or interpreters, or other accommodations. Importantly, research indicates that accommodations are usually free or cost less than $100.[56]

Misperception: Complying with the ADA is very costly to employers.

Reality: Most accommodations cost less than $100.

----

[54] http://www.eeoc.gov/laws/statutes/ada.cfm, accessed October 7, 2010.
[55] Ibid.
[56] Job Accommodation Network. (1999). *Accommodation Benefit/Cost Data.* Morgantown, WV: Job Accommodation Network of the President's Committee on Employment of People with Disabilities.

Employers are also prohibited from asking job applicants about the existence, nature, or severity of a disability; instead, they may only ask about applicants' ability to perform specific job functions. These questions should be asked of all applicants, not only those with visible disabilities. Guidelines to help small employers with reasonable accommodations are also available.[57]

EEOC charges of disability discrimination. In 2010, the EEOC received 25,165 new complaints of disability discrimination and resolved 24,401. Of the resolved claims, 21.5% were resolved in the plaintiffs' favor. Although a small percentage, the complaints resolved in the charging parties' favor resulted in the recovery of $76.1 million for complainants and other aggrieved parties. In some cases, disability discrimination occurs concurrently with violations of the Family and Medical Leave Act (FMLA), as occurred in the case described next.

Medical Health Group to Pay $125,000 for Disability Bias against Worker with Cancer[58]

EEOC Said Employer Fired Woman Battling Breast Cancer When She Attempted to Return to Work

Medical Health Group (MHG), a Maryland medical practice, will pay $125,000 and furnish significant remedial relief to settle a disability discrimination lawsuit in which the EEOC had charged that the company refused to let an employee who had recovered from breast cancer surgery return to work. According to the EEOC's suit, MHG discriminated against Barbara Metzger, who had worked for the medical practice for 25 years, by firing her when she attempted to return to work after recovering from serious surgical complications.

Metzger was diagnosed with breast cancer in January 2007. About a week before her approved medical leave ended, Metzger was called into work on May 31, 2007. She told her employer that she intended to work without interruption while undergoing her remaining chemotherapy and radiation treatments. The supervisor then cited examples of people she knew whose cancer treatments made them too sick to work. Metzger was presented with a termination letter that stated she was being fired because she was "currently unable to return to work on a full-time basis. Due to the seriousness of her illness, and extended nature of the treatment required … we must exercise our option to permanently fill your position."

---

[57] http://www.eeoc.gov/facts/accommodation.html, accessed October 8, 2010.
[58] Adapted from EEOC press release at http://www.eeoc.gov/eeoc/newsroom/release/7-22-09.cfm, accessed October 8, 2010.

According to the EEOC, "a woman who is bravely battling breast cancer has enough of a challenge without having to lose her job because of unlawful discrimination." The EEOC also commented that employment decisions should not be made based on fears and stereotypes about a person's medical condition. In addition to the monetary settlement, MHG will also provide ADA compliance training to its officers, supervisors, and managers, modify its antidiscrimination policies and distribute the new policy to all employees and managerial staff, and post a notice confirming its commitment to complying with the ADA. Additionally, MHG resolved a Family and Medical Leave Act (FMLA) claim brought by an attorney on Metzger's behalf.

The Civil Rights Act of 1991

The twenty-seven years between the passage of Title VII of the Civil Rights Act of 1964 and the Civil Rights Act (CRA) of 1991 brought numerous and significant changes for employees, employers, and applicants. More people knew what was considered illegal, and the demographic composition of the workforce was changing. Even so, several issues remained, prompting the passage of the CRA of 1991, which had the purpose of strengthening and improving federal civil rights laws, providing for damages in cases of intentional employment discrimination, and clarifying provisions regarding disparate impact.

Some of the changes in the law were viewed as favorable to employees and applicants; others as favorable to employers. The CRA's most commonly discussed change favorable to employees is its provision for compensatory and punitive damages in cases of intentional race, sex, religious, national origin, or disability discrimination or harassment. These damages are intended to punish offending employers and deter future discriminatory conduct. However, the damages any one person can receive are limited to maximums of

- $50,000 for employers having between 15 and 100 employees
- $100,000 for employers having between 101 and 200 employees
- $200,000 for employers having between 201 and 500 employees
- $300,000 for employers having over 500 employees.

Although punitive damages awarded by juries often exceed these amounts, such awards are reduced to those allowable by law. As shown in the following case, punitive damages can nonetheless significantly increase awards to targets of intentional discrimination.

Ninth Circuit Upholds Jury Verdict of $241,708 Awarding Punitive Damages in EEOC Case against "Go Daddy"[59]

EEOC Sued Software Company for Retaliation against Muslim Worker

In September 2009, the EEOC announced that an appeals court upheld a 2006 unanimous federal court jury verdict finding that Go Daddy Software, Inc., had retaliated against Youssef Bouamama when it fired him for complaining about discriminatory comments against him. The court rejected Go Daddy's challenge to the jury's finding that the company had engaged in unlawful retaliation. The jury found that Go Daddy terminated Bouamama, a Muslim of Moroccan national origin, for complaining about religious and national origin discrimination. The jury verdict included punitive damages of $250,000, compensatory damages for emotional distress of $5,000, and a verdict of $135,000 for lost wages. The punitive and compensatory damages award were reduced to $200,000 to conform to the statutory caps under the Civil Rights Act of 1991 and the back pay amount to $36,552 and awarded prejudgment interest in the amount of $5,156. The total amount is $241,708. Go Daddy was also found to have violated federal record-keeping requirements when it failed to retain employment applications relevant to the case.

EEOC Supervisory Trial Attorney David Lopez said that "the jury, acting as the conscience of this community, properly found that Go Daddy engaged in conduct warranting its award of punitive damages. It is important to understand that these damages are designed to deter this employer from again violating federal civil rights laws prohibiting retaliation for opposing discriminatory practices."

In addition to punitive damages, the 1991 CRA allowed for jury trials and the awarding of attorney's fees to the prevailing party; clarified the concept of "business necessity" and "job-related"; extended protection to U.S. citizens working abroad for U.S. companies; and established the Glass Ceiling Commission to study and report on the status of women and minorities in upper-level jobs. Although it has since been disbanded, the Glass Ceiling Commission issued compelling, widely distributed reports on the existence of the **glass ceiling,** garnering considerable attention.

---

[59]Adapted from press release at http://www.eeoc.gov/eeoc/newsroom/release/archive/9-14-09.html, accessed October 8, 2010.

The Family and Medical Leave Act of 1993

The passage of the Family and Medical Leave Act (FMLA) in 1993 was indicative of the changing needs of workers in the United States. Most couples were now both employed, many had minor children, and many families were headed by single working women. The need to allow employees to take time off from work, with continuance of benefits and assurance of jobs upon their return, was clear. Enforced by the U.S. Department of Labor, the FMLA requires employers having at least fifty employees for at least twenty weeks per year to grant eligible employees up to twelve weeks of unpaid leave per year to care for personal or family medical needs. Eligible employees may take leave for the birth and care of their newborn child or for the adoption or placement of a foster child; for the care of a seriously ill spouse, child, or parent; or for their own serious health condition. Eligible employees are those who have worked for the employer for at least 1,250 hours during the past twelve months at a worksite where fifty or more employees work within seventy-five miles of the worksite. Under the FMLA, employees may file complaints with the Department of Labor or file a private lawsuit.

Criticisms of the FMLA include its failure to require pay and to include employers of fewer than fifty people, parents-in-law, other family members, and nonmarital partners. Personal or family illness may increase the need for income—how many employees can afford much time without pay, particularly when illness strikes? Further, because many U.S. workers are employed in small organizations, the requirement for fifty or more employees excludes many people; more than half of Americans do not qualify under the FMLA. Another important criticism is related to gender and family roles; many argue that couples should be able to decide which spouse takes leave and the exclusion of parents-in-law does not allow for this. Finally, many people have relational ties that include those who are not immediate (aunts, uncles, etc.) or biological family (godparents, fictive kin), and committed, but not marital, partners are common. Although the FMLA is indeed helpful to many families who need it, limitations and exclusions make it of little use to many employees. As a result, research indicates that people who most need family leave do not take it.[60]

As family relationships change, so too should relevant legislation; some states are ahead of federal legislation regarding who constitutes family. At the time of this writing, eleven states have enacted statutes that

[60] Gerstel, N., & McGonagle K. (2002). "Job Leaves and the Limits of the Family and Medical Leave Act." In D. Dunn & P. Dubeck (Eds.), *Workplace, Women's Place*. Los Angeles: Roxbury Publishers, pp. 205–215; American Association of University Women, http://www.aauw.org/takeaction/policyissues/familymedical_leave.cfm, accessed September 27, 2010.

are similar to the FMLA: California, Connecticut, Hawaii, Maine, Minnesota, New Jersey, Oregon, Rhode Island, Vermont, Washington, and Wisconsin. Some of these statutes differ in key areas, such as in the definition of "family," with some including parents-in-law and other kin.[61] In 2010, the FMLA was clarified to include those who had served in a parental relationship for a "son" or "daughter," including grandparents parenting grandchildren, uncles or aunts parenting nieces or nephews, or nonmarital partners parenting their partners' children.[62] Some remaining inadequacies of the FMLA, including time off with pay, are discussed further in Chapter 10.

The Genetic Information Nondiscrimination Act of 2008[63]

Title II of the Genetic Information Nondiscrimination Act (GINA) of 2008, which took effect in November 2009, prohibits discrimination against employees or applicants because of genetic information. It is included here as diversity-related legislation because many medical genetic issues are related to race and ethnicity or sex. GINA prohibits using genetic information in making employment decisions, restricts the acquisition of genetic information by employers and other entities covered by Title II, and strictly limits the disclosure of genetic information. This information includes an individual's genetic tests along with an individual's family medical history. Family medical history is included because it is often used to determine whether someone has an increased risk of getting a disease, disorder, or medical condition in the future. Employment decisions on the basis of genetic information, harassment, and retaliation for filing claims of discrimination are all prohibited. Acquisition of genetic information is prohibited except for six narrow exceptions detailed by the EEOC. In 2010, 201 claims were filed and 56 resolved, with 12.5% being merit resolutions.

Americans with Disabilities Act Amendments Act of 2008

In September 2008, President George W. Bush signed the Americans with Disabilities Act Amendments Act (ADA Amendments Act), which emphasizes that the definition of *disabilities* should be construed broadly and should not generally require extensive analysis.[64] These changes make it

---

[61] "U.S. Department of Labor Clarifies FMLA Definition of 'Son and Daughter.'" http://www.dol.gov/opa/media/press/WHD/WHD20100877.htm, accessed December 12, 2010.
[62] Ibid.
[63] http://www.eeoc.gov/laws/types/genetic.cfm, accessed December 12, 2010.
[64] http://www.eeoc.gov/laws/statutes/adaaa_info.cfm, accessed October 7, 2010.

easier for those seeking protection under the ADA to establish having a disability. Importantly, the act expands the meaning of "major life activities" to include those not recognized in the past and makes clear that an episodic impairment, such as multiple sclerosis, or one in remission, such as cancer, is a disability if it would substantially limit a major life activity when it is active.

The Lilly Ledbetter Fair Pay Act of 2009

The Lilly Ledbetter Fair Pay Act of 2009 was the first legislation passed under the Obama administration. This act supersedes a 2007 Supreme Court decision that required discrimination charges concerning compensation be filed within 180 days (or 300 days in some cities and states) of a discriminatory pay decision. It restores the pre-Ledbetter position of the EEOC that with every paycheck that is discriminatory, a new clock starts. Once again, an individual subjected to pay discrimination may file a complaint within 180 (or 300) days of

- when a discriminatory compensation decision or other discriminatory practice affecting compensation is adopted;
- when the individual becomes subject to a discriminatory compensation decision or other discriminatory practice affecting compensation; or
- when the individual's compensation is affected by the application of a discriminatory compensation decision or other discriminatory practice, including each time the individual receives compensation that is based in whole or in part on such compensation decision or other practice.

This ruling also applies to compensation discrimination under Title VII of the Civil Rights Act of 1964, the Age Discrimination in Employment Act of 1967, or the Americans with Disabilities Act of 1990.[65]

▌ OTHER RELEVANT STATE, LOCAL, AND CITY ORDINANCES

In addition to the key federal acts discussed in the previous section, several state, local, and city ordinances relevant to diversity in organizations exist. Although the multitude of such legislation makes it impossible to consider them all, some of the specific ordinances that prohibit employment-related discrimination on the basis of weight or appearance, such as Michigan's Elliott–Larsen Civil Rights Act, will be discussed

---

[65] "Notice Concerning the Lilly Ledbetter Fair Pay Act of 2009," http://www.eeoc.gov/laws/statutes/epa_ledbetter.cfm, accessed September 16, 2010.

later in the book. Where no federal acts prohibit discrimination on the basis of those factors, other ordinances may, and many times state and local fair employment practices are more stringent than federal laws. Therefore, it is imperative that managers be aware of laws in their particular location, especially when the organization has multiple sites of operation. In such cases, implementing company-specific guidelines that apply to the entire organization would provide proactive support for diversity as well as help to avoid violation of state, local, or city ordinances.

▌ Future Federal Acts: What's Ahead?

The extant laws, executive orders, and EEOC guidelines were passed because of discrimination against and inequitable treatment of certain groups. Although these laws have been somewhat successful in improving employment and opportunities for non-dominant groups, many inequities remain. In addition, egregious acts, such as placing condoms in the lockers of women or nooses on the desks of African Americans, rapes, and physical assaults still occur. These acts must be addressed using the existing or additional legislation, as appropriate. Perhaps most important, however, is preventing these discriminatory acts through a sincere organizational emphasis on inclusion and zero tolerance for harassment and discrimination.

As we consider in later chapters, people who are gay, lesbian, bisexual, transgender, or obese face considerable employment-related discrimination, which is not currently illegal in the United States under broad federal legislation. As happened prior to the passage of laws regarding discrimination on the basis of race, sex, age, national origin, religion, and disability, activism and public outcry have drawn attention to discrimination against these groups. More laws are likely to address these areas, but it is unlikely that any new protected classes will be added to major federal laws in the near future. However, individual states may continue to make these changes on their own. In pursuit of diversity and inclusion, individual organizations may also prohibit discrimination on the basis of additional attributes as well.

▌ Effects of Diversity on the Judiciary and on Judicial Decisions

The numerous laws and litigation related to diversity discussed in the previous sections clearly indicate that diversity is needed among managers, supervisors, decision makers, and employees in organizations. Research indicates that diversity is also needed among the judges who make the decisions about plaintiffs' discrimination claims. In their comprehensive study entitled "Myth of the Color-Blind Judge," Pat Chew and Robert Kelley detailed the underrepresentation of minority judges as compared to Whites.[66] About 90% of all federal and state judges are White, and White judges make different rulings in racial harassment cases than do minority judges, even when taking into account the judges' political affiliations or the case characteristics. In racial harassment cases, plaintiffs prevailed in only 22% of cases. Black judges ruled against plaintiffs 54% of the time; White judges ruled against plaintiffs 79% of the time. Although Blacks were more likely to be plaintiffs, both White and Hispanic plaintiffs had higher rates of success than Black plaintiffs. Chew and Kelley concluded that as a group, White judges are less able to identify and empathize with Black plaintiffs and less able to find their arguments plausible and credible, but that Black judges could identify with Black plaintiffs and also with plaintiffs of other races. They also suggested the relatively low rate of plaintiffs' success in litigation is related to the lack of diversity among judges. In another study, Nancy Crowe found that female judges were more likely than male judges to rule for the plaintiffs' in sex discrimination cases. These studies and multiple others provide strong evidence that the judiciary needs to be more representative of the population it serves.[67]

SUMMARY

This chapter has considered the history and details of several key laws and executive orders related to diversity in organizations. These acts formally provide employees with rights to nondiscriminatory treatment and give organizations guidelines on fairness and the protection of all workers. Because it covers a broad range of employment issues and gives recourse to affected applicants and employees, this legislation has been somewhat effective in increasing opportunities, income, and employment for various groups. Many issues remain, however. In addition, many organizations having a strong commitment to equality and inclusion have been charged with discrimination, emphasizing the complexity of diversity issues and the need to avoid blanket generalizations.

As diversity in organizations continues to evolve and needs are identified, other legislation, judicial decisions, and executive orders will be required. Despite the existing laws, relatively few people, compared to the total number of workers, bring complaints to the EEOC, fewer complaints are deemed meritorious, and even fewer result in settlements or judgments for plaintiffs, which is partly due to the lack of diversity in the judiciary. Avoidance of lawsuits is a

---

[66] Chew & Kelley (2009).
[67] Ibid. See also Peresie (2005); Tobias, C. (2010). "Diversity and the Federal Bench." *Washington University Law Review*, 87: 1197, http://lawreview.wustl.edu/commentaries/diversity-and-the-federal-bench/, accessed October 12, 2010.

shallow impetus for compliance with laws; organizations should, instead, use compliance as one of many methods of pursuing diversity. Because many countries do not have specific diversity-related laws, an important first step in such places would be to determine who the non-dominant groups are (Chapter 2), what their organizational experiences and outcomes are, and what barriers to diversity and inclusion exist. Committed compliance with the spirit of laws that exist elsewhere relevant to diversity and inclusion may be beneficial.

Key Terms

Constructive discharge — making working conditions so unpleasant that an employee is forced to quit.

Disparate (or adverse) impact — when an apparently neutral, evenly applied job policy or employment practice has a negative effect on the employment of people belonging to protected classes.

Disparate treatment — when an applicant or employee is treated differently because of membership in a protected class.

Gender role socialization — the process by which social institutions, including families, friends, organizations, and the media, form and shape expectations of acceptable behaviors for men and women.

Glass ceiling — an invisible barrier that prevents women, minorities, and people with disabilities from advancing in organizations.

Harassment — bothering, tormenting, troubling, ridiculing, or coercing a person because of race, color, religion, sex, national origin, disability, or age.

Hostile environment harassment — unwelcome conduct that has the purpose or effect of unreasonably interfering with job performance, or creating an intimidating, hostile, or offensive working environment.

Punitive damages — money damages awarded in cases of intentional discrimination that are designed to punish the employer and deter other employers from discriminating.

Quid pro quo harassment — when managers, supervisors, or others with authority make sexual demands, and submission to or rejection of those demands is used as a basis for employment decisions.

Sexual harassment — unwelcome sexual advances, requests for sexual favors, and other verbal or physical conduct of a sexual nature that explicitly or implicitly interferes with a person's employment, unreasonably interferes with her or his work performance, or creates an intimidating, hostile, or offensive work environment.

Questions to Consider

1. What is the relationship between compliance with legislative acts and valuing diversity? Explain.
2. What approach should organizations take in their pursuit of diversity and inclusion in countries that do not have equal opportunity laws?
3. Do you personally know anyone who has engaged in an employment discrimination lawsuit against an employer and prevailed? Without divulging who the parties are, explain what happened.

4. Many of the EEOC cases presented in this chapter involve acts that are egregious and offensive. Choose three cases and for each speculate on the organizational factors that would allow such practices to occur and, in some cases, to persist for extended periods. Why do you think no one in the management chain intervened? What would you recommend, specifically, to deal with the perpetrators and prevent future occurrences?

5. This chapter discusses multiple lawsuits brought by the EEOC against Supercuts. What factors may be contributing to the persistence of problems within the organization? Make specific recommendations for preventing such problems in the future.

ACTIONS AND EXERCISES

1. Access the press releases on the Equal Employment Opportunity Commission's Web site: http://eeoc. gov/. Document a recent lawsuit or settlement involving race, ethnic, sex, age, disability, national origin, or religious discrimination that was likely to have been covered by the media. Describe the allegations, plaintiffs, and resolution of the cases. Document the time periods between the incidents and the final resolution of the cases. Search the Web for newspaper articles or other media reports relevant to each case. Do the EEOC's presentation and the media's presentation take different perspectives? Discuss.

2. Consider the issues discussed as limitations in federal laws. Pick one issue and then list and discuss the elements that could be included in legislation to address that limitation. What specific steps should employers take according to such legislation to ensure equal treatment of the affected parties?

3. Choose a state in the United States and document two existing state-level diversity-related laws. How are they similar to and different from federal laws in those areas?

4. Choose a particular country outside of the United States and document its major diversity-related laws. In the absence of such laws, what might organizations do to address areas in which there is disparity of treatment and inequality?

SECTION II

Examining Specific Groups and Categories

Andrey Popov/iStockphoto.com

Blacks/African Americans

Chapter Objectives

After completing this chapter, readers should have a greater understanding of Blacks and diversity in organizations. Specifically, they should be able to:

- ❏ *be aware of the historical background and current status of Blacks.*

- ❏ *be able to discuss participation rates, employment, and income levels of Blacks.*

- ❏ *examine differences in earnings by education level for Blacks and other racial and ethnic groups.*

- ❏ *discuss research evidence on employment experiences of native and immigrant Blacks.*

- ❏ *be able to compare similarities and differences between employment experiences of Black men and women.*

- ❏ *explain individual and organizational measures that can be used to improve organizational experiences of Blacks.*

Key Facts

Blacks who are high school graduates are about twice as likely to be unemployed as White high school graduates.

Average earnings of Black men with college degrees are about 32% less than those of White men with college degrees but nearly 60% more than those of Black men with only high school diplomas.

Average earnings of Black women with college degrees are about 80% more than earnings of Black women with only high school diplomas.

Black women have higher workforce participation rates than White women, but White men have higher participation rates than Black men.

The Black population is younger than the overall population; 63% of Black labor force participants are younger than 45, compared with 58% of all labor force participants.

Introduction and Overview

We begin our discussion of racial and ethnic groups in the United States with Blacks because of their unique status as descendants of slaves and the legacy of societal and organizational discrimination that they continue to face.[1] The current status of U.S. Blacks is strongly influenced by the conditions under which the ancestors of most Blacks originally came to this country. Unlike those immigrants who came seeking opportunities or were fleeing persecution in their homeland, most of the first Blacks arrived as slaves, with no options or opportunities for improving their position. Although many other immigrants faced hostility, overt discrimination, and even periods as indentured servants (e.g., the Irish, Italians, and Germans), they were not enslaved. In addition, the discrimination and segregation experienced by and among European immigrants, though significant, was less pervasive, less vehement, and considerably shorter-lived compared to the experience of African slaves and their descendants.[2]

Researchers have documented how Blacks and immigrants of color faced and continue to face more "substantial barriers to assimilating into and full participation in mainstream American society relative to *all* White ethnic groups" (emphasis in the original).[3] Although the Declaration of Independence stated that all men were created equal and endowed with inalienable rights of life, liberty, and the pursuit of happiness, these rights did not apply to Blacks, women, Native Americans, or immigrants of color.[4] The Naturalization Law of 1790, the first federal law to deal with citizenship of immigrants, specifically allowed only *White men* to become citizens, and these racial restrictions on citizenship of immigrants were not repealed until 1952, in the McCarran—Walter Act. The 162-year life of the Naturalization Act of 1790 negatively affected the rights and opportunities of many immigrants of color, and highlights the importance of race-based ethnic differences that persist today.

The absence of clear physical distinctions, such as skin color, to indicate whether a person is of Irish, German, Italian, or English descent, is one impediment to immediate overt discrimination against members of those groups. As discussed in Chapter 2, one characteristic of minority groups is visibility, which facilitates immediate categorization and stereotyping.[5] For the most part, European Americans' country of origin is invisible, which makes discrimination on that basis difficult. As we point out in Chapter 7, high rates of intermarriage between Whites of different ethnic backgrounds and less legal segregation and exclusion also reduced overt and lasting discrimination against White ethnic minority groups as compared to Blacks. Segregation, exclusion, and discrimination against Blacks in the United States have proven to be formidable barriers, shaping people's lives and opportunities for generations.

---

[1]The introduction and history sections of this chapter refer to the experiences of non-Hispanic Blacks, as descendants of slaves, in the United States. Blacks who have come to the United States after slavery also face discriminatory racial barriers in organizations and society. The terms *Black* and *African American* are used interchangeably. Unless otherwise noted, Blacks who are of Hispanic origin are considered in Chapter 5.

[2]Johnson, C., & Smith, P. (1998). *Africans in America: America's Journey through Slavery.* Orlando, FL: Harcourt Brace Publishers; Williams, J. (1987). *Eyes on the Prize: America's Civil Rights Years, 1954–1965.* New York: Viking Penguin.

[3]Reskin, B. F., & Charles, C. Z. (1999). "Now You See 'em, Now You Don't." In I. Browne (Ed.), *Latinas and African-American Women at Work: Race, Gender, and Economic Inequality.* New York: Russell Sage Foundation, pp. 380–407. See also Takaki, R. (Ed.) (1987). *From Different Shores: Perspectives on Race and Ethnicity in America.* New York: Oxford University Press, p. 390.

[4]Herring, C. (1999). "African Americans in Contemporary America: Progress and Retrenchment." In A. G. Dworkin & R. J. Dworkin (Eds.), *The Minority Report.* Fort Worth: Harcourt Brace Publishers, pp. 181–208; Takaki, R. (1987). "Reflections on Racial Patterns in America." In R. Takaki (Ed.), *From Different Shores: Perspectives on Race and Ethnicity in America.* New York: Oxford University Press, pp. 26–37.

[5]Dworkin, A. G., & Dworkin, A. (1999). "What Is a Minority?" In A. G. Dworkin & R. J. Dworkin (Eds.), *The Minority Report.* Fort Worth, TX: Harcourt Brace Publishers, pp. 11–27.

Terminology

In this chapter, consistent with U.S. Census Bureau terminology, *Black* and *African American* are used interchangeably to refer to people whose origins can be traced to any of the African Black racial groups. Thus, despite some differences in their experiences and identity, the terms include American descendants of slaves as well as recent immigrants.[6] Many Hispanics from Central and South America have African origins, and have similarities and differences in experiences and identity when compared with non-Hispanic Blacks.[7] Experiences and diversity of Black Hispanics are considered in Chapter 5. ●

▌ HISTORY OF BLACKS IN THE UNITED STATES

Historical records indicate that Africans were first sold in what is now the United States in about 1619. During the same period, Whites also were bound in servitude by indenture contracts. Over time, White servitude of any sort ended, but African slavery, a "complete deprivation of civil and personal rights," continued for the next 146 years.[8] The formal institution of slavery ended by decree in 1863 with Lincoln's Emancipation Proclamation, but even the end of the Civil War in 1865 did not bring to Blacks the rights and opportunities provided to all Whites at the end of the American Revolution. Between 1865 and 1964, formal, legally sanctioned (or required) segregation in many parts of the country severely impeded the progress of Blacks. "Jim Crow" laws required "separate but equal" accommodations, transportation, education, and even burial for Whites and Blacks; however, "separate" meant unequal, inferior, and often substandard facilities for Blacks.[9]

Misperception: Legalized discrimination and segregation ended with the end of slavery.

Reality: Legally sanctioned (or mandated) discrimination and segregation persisted for decades after the end of slavery, including "separate but equal" schools and other facilities for Blacks and Whites.

[6]See Tormala, T. T., & Deaux, K. (2006). "Black Immigrants to the United States: Confronting and Constructing Ethnicity and Race." In R. Mahalingham (Ed.), *Cultural Psychology of Immigrants*. Mahwah, NJ: Lawrence Erlbaum Associates, pp. 131–150.
[7]See Chapter 5 for research concerning Black Hispanics.
[8]Jordan, W. D. (1962). "Modern Tensions and the Origins of American Slavery" p. 23. *Journal of Southern History*, 28(1): 18–30. See also Jordan, W. D. (1968). *White over Black: American Attitudes toward the Negro, 1550–1812*. Chapel Hill, NC: The University of North Carolina Press, p. 107; Rose, P. I. (1970). *Slavery and Its Aftermath*. New York: Atherton Press.
[9]Herring (1999).

Extremely hostile attitudes toward Blacks in the South and greater employment opportunities elsewhere contributed to large-scale migration to cities like Boston, Chicago, Detroit, and New York. Escape from the South was no panacea to the ills of discrimination, however. Although employment at steel mills, automakers, and railroads provided Black men with higher earnings than sharecropping, cotton-picking, and other low-wage jobs in the South, better-paying, safer, and more prestigious jobs were still reserved for Whites. Inferior housing and education, and overt racial discrimination existed in the North as well. As discussed in Chapter 7, the Black migration from the South to the North improved the social position of lower- and working-class immigrant Whites and reduced discrimination against them. The migrating Blacks stepped into the role of the inferior class and became the targets of the discrimination, harassment, and exclusion that had previously been directed at lower-class Whites.

Focal Issue 4.1 considers differences between Blacks and Whites in the accumulation of wealth, focusing on the influence of slavery, subsequent pervasive discrimination against Blacks, and inheritance.

Blacks in the Military

Segregation and discrimination extended to the armed forces, where fellow White military personnel and nonmilitary personnel alike were openly hostile toward Black servicemen. Black men served in the French and Indian War, the American Revolution, the War of 1812, the Civil War, and the wars of the twentieth century, albeit under many restrictions. The Blacks who fought in the American Revolution helped gain freedom from British rule, but freedom from slavery eluded them. Throughout World War II, Blacks experienced sanctioned segregation and discrimination, as did their nonservice counterparts.[10] For many years Blacks in the military were restricted to jobs such as janitor, clerk, cafeteria worker, and laborer, even when they were qualified for higher jobs.[11] It is not difficult to imagine the consequences of such restrictions: lower pensions, reduced ability to provide for a family, and failure to acquire skills transferable to better post-military positions.

Other overt discrimination took the form of unfounded accusations against Black soldiers for theft, insubordination, and the rape and

---

[10]Astor, G. (2001). *The Right to Fight: A History of African Americans in the Military*. Cambridge, MA: DaCapo Press.
[11]Ibid.

FOCAL ISSUE 4.1	Differences in Black/White Accumulation of Wealth: Effects of Slavery and Generations of Discrimination

Many researchers in various disciplines (e.g., sociology, economics, and finance) have investigated differences between Blacks and Whites in accumulation of wealth. Some suggest that these differences are primarily due to differences in inheritance, rather than differences in saving or spending habits.[12] For the first 250 years of their existence in what is now the United States, Blacks *were* property rather than *owned* property. For decades after being freed in 1865, Blacks were still legally denied the right to own property by various laws across the United States. Whereas Whites had property and wealth to pass on to heirs, Blacks generally did not.[13] Systematic and legal discrimination in employment and earnings exacerbated these disparities for nearly 100 more years, until passage of the Civil Rights Act in 1964, which prohibited race-based discrimination in employment and helped narrow the White/Black earnings gap to some extent. "Put simply, long after legalized discrimination and segregation ceased, their intergenerational impacts persist."[14] Not only was there little or no inheritance to pass on due to slavery and its aftermath, Blacks' wages still suffer effects of discrimination,

which limits their ability to acquire and, thus, pass on wealth.

Black/White differences in wealth have also been partially attributed to discrimination in access to credit, which results in Blacks being less likely to be homeowners or to start their own businesses, both of which contribute strongly to accumulation of wealth.[15] In an analysis of access to business loans, Ando found that Blacks were significantly less likely to obtain credit than were Whites, Asians, and Latinos. After controlling for differences that might have explained Blacks' lower acceptance rates, Ando still found significant differences.[16] Similar disparities in mortgage loan approvals and rates for comparably creditworthy Blacks and Whites also exist.[17] As with employment discrimination, it appears that Blacks with marginal qualifications are rejected or charged higher interest rates, while Whites with marginal qualifications are given the benefit of the doubt.[18]

Compared to 74.4% of non-Hispanic Whites, 45.4% of Blacks owned their own homes in 2010.[19] In the period of 1940 to 1960, while White (male) veterans capitalized on education, employment, and housing benefits after their service, Black veterans were systematically and

[12]Darity, W. A., Jr., & Myers, S. L., Jr. (2000). "Languishing in Inequality: Racial Disparities in Wealth and Earnings in the New Millennium." In J. S. Jackson (Ed.), *New Directions: African Americans in a Diversifying Nation.* Washington, D.C.: National Policy Association, pp. 86–118; "Black American's Wealth Increases—They Still Lag," Reuters, October 29, 2003.

[13]Blau, F. D., & Graham, J. W. (1990). "Black/White Differences in Wealth and Asset Composition." *Quarterly Journal of Economics,* 105: 321–339.

[14]Darity & Myers (2000), p. 104.

[15]Ibid.

[16]Ando, F. (1988). *An Analysis of Access to Bank Credit.* Los Angeles: UCLA Center for Afro-American Studies.

[17]Yinger, J. (1995). *Closed Doors, Opportunities Lost: The Continuing Costs of Housing Discrimination.* New York: Russell Sage Foundation.

[18]See George, C. G. (1991). "Use of Testers in Investigating Discrimination in Mortgage Lending and Insurance." In M. Fix & R. J. Struyk (Eds.), *Clear and Convincing Evidence.* Washington, D.C.: Urban Institute Press, pp. 257–306.

[19]Bureau of the Census. Table 22. "Homeownership Rates by Race and Ethnicity of Householder: 1994 to 2010," www.census.gov/hhes/www/housing/hvs/annual10/ann10t_22.xls, accessed March 18, 2011.

purposefully denied such benefits even though they had earned them.[20] The Federal Housing Authority believed in racial segregation of neighborhoods, publicly promoted segregation, and often denied Blacks loans. Renting instead of owning also contributed to Blacks having less property to leave to subsequent generations; obviously, renters do not will homes to heirs. For Blacks who were able to purchase homes, residential segregation and steering by realtors contributed to continued stratification.[21] Evidence of residential segregation and steering continues to be documented.[22] Homes in predominantly Black neighborhoods are worth less and appreciate more slowly than homes in neighborhoods that are not predominantly Black. In addition, school systems tend to be worse, opportunities for employment are less, and services are lower in such neighborhoods, which also contributes to persistent, enduring gaps in income and opportunities for wealth.[23]

QUESTIONS TO CONSIDER

1. *Prior to reading this section, had you considered the effects of slavery and subsequent continued discrimination on the ability of (a) Blacks and (b) Whites to inherit and earn wealth, savings, and property?*

2. *What factors may affect the higher rejection rates of equally creditworthy Blacks for business and home loans?*

3. *Why might realtors steer Blacks to "Black" neighborhoods?*

4. *What organizational steps can banks, mortgage companies, and realtors take to ensure they do not perpetrate credit and housing discrimination?*

harassment of White women, the latter two of which were life-threatening charges. Accusations often led to biased courts martial and punishments that were far harsher than those faced by similarly charged Whites, including significantly more sentences of life imprisonment and dishonorable discharges.[24] On some military bases in the South, Black soldiers had to drink from separate water fountains while White soldiers and *German prisoners of war* drank from the fountains for Whites only.[25] In some areas of the country, children of Blacks in the military were bused to Black schools in town because the on-base schools were reserved for White children. Outside military bases, Blacks in these areas had to ride in the backs of trolleys and busses and in the "colored" sections of trains; new

----

[20]Brodkin, K. (2004). "How Jews Became White." In J. F. Healey & E. O'Brien (Eds.), *Race, Ethnicity, and Gender*. Thousand Oaks, CA: Pine Forge Press, pp. 282–294.

[21]Ibid.

[22]Oliver, M. L., & Shapiro, T. M. (1995). *Black Wealth/White Wealth: A New Perspective on Racial Inequality*. New York: Routledge; Turner, M. A. (1992). "Limits on Neighborhood Choice: Evidence of Racial and Ethnic Steering in Urban Housing Markets." In M. Fix & R. J. Struyk (Eds.), *Clear and Convincing Evidence*. Washington, D.C.: Urban Institute Press, pp. 95–130.

[23]Massey, D., & Denton, N. A. (1993). *American Apartheid: Segregation and the Making of the Underclass*. Cambridge, MA: Harvard University Press.

[24]Astor (2001).

[25]Ibid.

draftees reported to duty after long rides at the back of segregated busses. Soldiers were denied service in restaurants, theaters, and bars in many cities, and at times faced open hostility, assault, and even lynching by townspeople.[26] Understandably, Black American soldiers, who often fought to support democratic principles in foreign countries, opposed and resisted such hypocritical treatment within their own country. Today, Blacks fare better in the military, and the United States has 2.3 million Black veterans, more than any other minority group.[27] However, Black officers remain rare, particularly at the highest levels. Although 17% of the U.S. military is comprised of Blacks, only 9% of officers are Black.[28]

The Civil Rights Movement

Blacks had resisted discrimination and segregation for many years, but it was not until the civil rights movement of the 1950s and 1960s that substantial social and legal changes and the securing of rights previously denied to Blacks were achieved. Well-known activists and organizers included Medgar Evers, Fannie Lou Hamer, Dr. Martin Luther King, Jr., Rosa Parks, legendary baseball player Jackie Robinson, Dorothy Height, and Malcolm X; but many ordinary Blacks also participated in boycotts, demonstrations, and "sit-ins." In the early 1960s, college students organized sit-ins at lunch counters in stores in the South that refused service to Blacks. The students were often arrested and jailed, but on the following days, other student protesters again sat at the lunch counters. Most of the sit-ins occurred in the South, but stores in the North also faced negative consequences arising from the discriminatory actions of their counterparts in the South (e.g., Woolworth's, a large discount store that had locations in both the North and South). When the Southern locations refused service to Blacks, many Black and White Northerners refused to patronize those stores in the North, putting economic pressure on the entire company. The "Don't buy where you can't work" slogan, used in many effective boycotts, which began as early as 1938 when Black leaders called for boycotts and picketing against organizations that refused to hire Blacks, sums up the potential for lost business when an organization becomes known for not valuing diversity.[29] In 2009, Black buying power amounted to $910 billion and by 2014 it is estimated to be

[26]Ibid.

[27]Facts for Features, Black (African-American) History Month: February 2010. http://www.census.gov/newsroom/releases/archives/facts_for_features_special_editions/cb10-ff01.html, accessed October 13, 2010.

[28]Baldor, L. C. (2008). "After 60 Years, Black Officers Rare." http://www.msnbc.msn.com/id/25809737/, accessed October 13, 2010.

[29]Sewell, S. K. (2004). "The 'Not Buying Power' of the Black Community: Urban Boycotts and Equal Employment Opportunity." *Journal of African American History*, 89(2): 135–152.

$1,137 billion.[30] If this is combined with buying power of potential allies (Whites, Hispanics, and others), the costs to business of discrimination could be tremendous.

Many Whites also participated in the battles for Black equality before, during, and after the civil rights movement. They included Alabaman Virginia Durr and New Yorkers Michael Schwerner and Andrew Goodman. Schwerner and Goodman were murdered in Mississippi along with James Chaney (a Black activist) during the fight for Blacks' civil rights. And despite past (and present) periods of hostility between some Blacks and Jews, estimates are that two-thirds of the Whites who participated in the civil rights movement were Jewish, including Schwerner and Goodman.[31] Whites who supported Black causes in the South risked ostracism, harassment, and murder.

In conjunction with increased societal and governmental pressure, the sit-ins, boycotts, and picketing of the 1960s were successful in achieving results. The combined efforts of the many who fought for justice in the United States during this time secured the passage of the Civil Rights Act of 1964 and executive orders on affirmative action (discussed in Chapter 2). In large part due to these and subsequent laws and executive actions, the 1960s, 1970s, 1980s, and 1990s brought about change and some progress for African Americans and for equality and diversity in the United States. Among other changes, Black poverty rates declined from 41.8% in 1964 to 24.7% in 2008—still a significant one-quarter of the population, but considerably lower than in 1964.

▌ RELEVANT LEGISLATION

Perhaps the most important piece of legislation relevant to the experiences of Blacks in organizations is Title VII of the Civil Rights Act. The existence of overt racial discrimination and the civil rights activities of the 1950s and 1960s preceding passage of Title VII made Blacks the primary focus of Title VII. As discussed in Chapter 3, Title VII, as amended, prohibits discrimination on the basis of race in employment matters and racial harassment, and provides those targeted with some recourse.

Executive orders in support of affirmative action are also particularly relevant to the employment experiences of African Americans because of

[30]Humphreys, J. M. (2009). "The Multicultural Economy 2009." Selig Center for Economic Growth, Georgia Business and Economic Conditions, http://ahaa.org/pdf/GBEC.pdf, accessed October 12, 2010.
[31]Schoenfeld, E. (1999). "Jewish Americans: A Religio-Ethnic Community." In A. G. Dworkin & R. J. Dworkin (Eds.), *The Minority Report*. Orlando, FL: Harcourt Brace Publishers, pp. 364–394. Takaki, R. (1993). *A Different Mirror: A History of Multicultural America*. Boston: Back Bay Books, Little Brown and Company. See also Salzman, J., Back, A., & Sorin, G. S. (Eds.) (1992). *Bridges and Boundaries: African Americans and American Jews*. New York: George Braziller.

the need for proactive nondiscrimination measures, as opposed to the passive provisions of Title VII. As we discuss later in the chapter, Blacks and women who work for affirmative action employers earn more than those who work for nonaffirmative action employers. Despite the more than forty years that Title VII and relevant executive orders have been in place, however, the employment status and income of African Americans continue to lag those of Whites with similar qualifications. Slavery and sanctioned discrimination existed for more than 300 years in the United States; Title VII and affirmative action have existed for fewer than fifty years.

Misperception: The playing field is now level; affirmative action is no longer needed.

Reality: Affirmative action is still needed to combat persistent, pervasive discrimination in hiring, placement, promotions, and advancement.

▌ POPULATION

The 41.1 million Blacks in the United States comprise 13.5% of the population. Blacks are relatively young: 80% of Blacks are under age 50 and 30% are age 18 or younger.[32] This youthfulness reflects the slightly higher-than-average birthrate and the shorter life expectancy of Blacks, both of which are related to diversity in organizations. First, the larger proportion of young Blacks means that a larger proportion of Blacks will enter the workforce in the future. To fully utilize the assets of this large segment of the population, organizations must create environments that welcome and provide opportunities for Blacks rather than fostering discrimination, segregation, and exclusion. Second, although there are many reasons for the shorter life expectancies of Blacks (such as less access to health care and crime and poverty), researchers have suggested that stress related to discrimination, low responsibility and autonomy at work, and underutilization of Blacks' skills at work also contribute to illness and early death.[33] The organizational pursuit of fairness and equity can reduce discrimination-related stress that Blacks experience, while also increasing their access

---

[32]Facts for Features, Black (African American) History Month: February 2010. http://www.census.gov/newsroom/releases/archives/facts_for_features_special_editions/ch10-ff01.html, accessed October 14, 2010.
[33]Sagrestano, L. M. (2004). "Health Implications of Workplace Diversity." In M. S. Stockdale & F. J. Crosby (Eds.), *The Psychology and Management of Workplace Diversity*. Malden, MA: Blackwell Publishing, pp. 122–143; Keita, G. P., & Jones, J. M. (1990). "Reducing Adverse Reaction to Stress in the Workplace: Psychology's Expanding Role." *American Psychologist*, 45(10): 1137–1141; James, K. (1994). "Social Identity, Work Stress, and Minority Workers' Health." In G. P. Keita & J. J. Hurrell (Eds.), *Job Stress in a Changing Workforce: Investigating Gender, Diversity, and Family Issues*. Washington, D.C.: American Psychological Association, pp. 127–145.

to health care and reducing poverty. Lastly, Blacks and other people of color are also often concentrated in occupations with higher risks of injury and death more than Whites (e.g., convenience store clerk, construction worker), which contributes somewhat to shorter life expectancies.[34]

▌ EDUCATION, EMPLOYMENT, AND EARNINGS

Education

During slavery, laws in many states prohibited teaching slaves to read or otherwise providing them with education, although some Whites and many literate Blacks still did so.[35] When slavery ended, Blacks continued trying to obtain education. For nearly ninety years after the Civil War, laws in many communities required Blacks to be educated separately from Whites. At times, no facilities for Blacks were available. Since the 1954 Supreme Court decision in *Brown vs. the Board of Education of Topeka*, which outlawed the "separate but 'equal'" educational system, there have been marked increases in the levels of Black education. In 1940, 7.7% of Blacks and 26.1% of Whites had completed at least high school, but by 2008, 83% of Blacks and 87.1% of Whites had done so.[36] As shown in Table 4.1, Whites have more education than Blacks. These differences provide some explanation for the Black/White earnings and employment gap, but they do not explain it completely.[37]

Misperception: Earnings and employment differences between Blacks and Whites are due to the lower educational attainment of Blacks.

Reality: Blacks with the same level of education as Whites are more likely to be unemployed than Whites and earn less when employed than Whites.

[34]Sagrestano (2004), p. 127.

[35]Pollock, B. H. (2001). "An Act Prohibiting the Teaching of Slaves to Read." In B. H. Pollock (Ed.) (2001), *Zamani to Sasa: Readings on the Black Quest for Freedom, Identity and Power in America.* Dubuque, IA: Kendall/Hunt Publishing Company, pp. 107–108.

[36]Table A-2. Percent of People 25 Years and Over Who Have Completed High School or College, by Race, Hispanic Origin and Sex: Selected Years 1940 to 2004. http://www.census.gov/population/socdemo/education/tabA-2.pdf, accessed August 29, 2010; and Table 226. Educational Attainment by Selected Characteristics: 2008. U.S. Census Bureau, Current Population Survey. http://www.census.gov/prod/2009pubs/10statab/educ.pdf, accessed October 13, 2010.

[37]Herring (1999), p. 187. See also Reskin, B. F., & Charles, C. Z. (1999) for a discussion of how and why the relationship between education and earnings and other labor market outcomes differs between Whites and other groups.

TABLE 4.1 *Educational Attainment by Race, Hispanic Origin, and Sex: 2008*

		High School Graduate or More	College Graduate or More
All Races	Male	85.9	30.1
	Female	87.2	28.8
	Total	86.6	29.4
White	Male	86.3	30.5
	Female	87.8	29.1
	Total	87.1	29.8
Black	Male	81.8	18.7
	Female	84.0	20.4
	Total	83.0	19.6
Asian and Pacific Islander	Male	90.8	55.8
	Female	86.9	49.8
	Total	88.7	52.6
Hispanic*	Male	60.9	12.6
	Female	63.7	14.1
	Total	62.3	13.4

*Persons of Hispanic origin may be of any race.

Sources: Educational attainment for males and females by race drawn from Table 225. Educational Attainment by Race, Hispanic Origin, and Sex: 1970 to 2008. Total figures drawn from Tables 224 and 226. Educational Attainment by Selected Characteristics: 2008. U.S. Census Bureau, Current Population Survey. http://www.census.gov/prod/2009pubs/10statab/educ.pdf, accessed October 13, 2010.

Participation Rates

How likely are African Americans to be in the labor force? Table 4.2 presents actual (1998 and 2008) and projected (2018) participation rates (those who are employed or seeking employment) for men and women, by race. White men have higher participation rates than Black men, and Black women have slightly higher participation rates than White women.

Proportionately, increases in the employment and earnings of Blacks have not matched their increasing levels of education. In the twentieth century and the twenty-first century thus far, Black unemployment levels have been considerably higher than those of Whites.[38,39] As Table 4.3 shows, in every category, Black unemployment is higher than that of every other

[38]Bureau of Labor Statistics. (2009). *Labor Force Characteristics by Race and Diversity*. Report 1020, accessed from http://www.bls.gov/cps/cpsrace2008.pdf, accessed December 14, 2010.
[39]Herring (1999).

TABLE 4.2 *1998 and 2008 Actual and 2018 Projected Participation Rates by Race/Ethnicity and Sex*

	1998		2008		2018 Projection	
	Men	**Women**	**Men**	**Women**	**Men**	**Women**
All groups	74.9	59.8	73.0	59.5	70.6	58.7
White, non-Hispanic	75.0	59.9	72.4	59.8	70.7	59.0
Black	69.0	62.8	66.7	61.3	65.7	61.2
Hispanic	79.8	55.6	80.2	56.2	78.2	56.4
Asian	75.5	59.2	75.3	59.4	73.8	57.4
All other groups*	—	—	71.4	60.1	70.1	63.3

*The "All other groups" category includes (1) those classified as being of multiple racial origin and (2) the race categories of (2a) American Indian and Alaska Native or (2b) Native Hawaiian and Other Pacific Islanders. Dashes indicate no data collected for category.

Source: Employment Projections Program, U.S. Department of Labor, U.S. Bureau of Labor Statistics. http://www.bls.gov/emp/ep_table_303.htm, accessed September 4, 2010.

racial/ethnic group at the same level of education. Black/White comparisons are most striking: Blacks are considerably more likely to be unemployed than Whites who have one and sometimes two fewer levels of education. This persistent unemployment can contribute to discouragement and dropping out of the workforce completely, as discussed in Focal Issue 4.2.

Earnings by Educational Attainment

As Table 4.4 shows, across all education levels (total), the highest to the least average annual earnings are received, respectively, by Asian men, non-Hispanic White men, Asian women, Black men, non-Hispanic White women, Hispanic men, Black women, and Hispanic women.[40] At the bachelor's degree level, White men's earnings are highest, while Black men and Black women remain at the fourth and seventh positions. These figures vary from year to year and were affected by the recession that began in 2007. Despite between-group disparities, as with all groups, Black men earn more than Black women at all education levels and education increases earnings for Blacks.

While Blacks with a high school education are estimated to earn about a million dollars (1999 figures) during their work-life, those with a bachelor's degree would earn $1.7 million, and those with an advanced degree would earn $2.7 million.[41]

....

[40]As discussed in Chapter 6, Asians' higher earnings are also partly reflective of their greater propensity to live in areas with high costs of living, such as California, Hawaii, and New York.

[41]Day, J. C., & Newburger, E. C. (2002, July). *The Big Payoff: Educational Attainment and Synthetic Estimates of Work-Life Earnings*. Washington, D.C.: U.S. Census Bureau. http://www.census.gov/prod/2002pubs/p23-210.pdf, accessed December 12, 2010.

TABLE 4.3 *Unemployment Level by Educational Attainment by Race (2008, 2009) (Percent of Population 25 and Over)*

2008	Total	Men	Women	White	Black	Asian	Hispanic*
Less than high school	9.0	8.8	9.4	8.2	14.5	6.4	8.2
High school graduate	5.7	5.9	5.3	5.1	9.3	4.3	6.2
Some college, no degree	5.1	5.0	5.1	4.5	8.0	3.8	5.4
Associate degree	3.7	3.8	3.7	3.3	6.2	3.8	4.1
Bachelor's and higher	2.8	2.5	2.7	2.4	4.0	2.8	3.4

2009	Total	Men	Women	White	Black	Asian	Hispanic*
Less than high school	14.6	14.9	14.2	13.9	21.3	8.4	13.7
High school graduate	9.7	11.0	8.0	9.0	14.0	7.5	10.4
Some college, no degree	8.6	9.3	8.0	7.9	12.1	8.9	9.6
Associate degree	6.8	7.9	5.9	6.2	10.3	7.5	8.5
Bachelor's and higher[†]	4.6	4.7	4.5	4.2	7.3	5.6	5.7

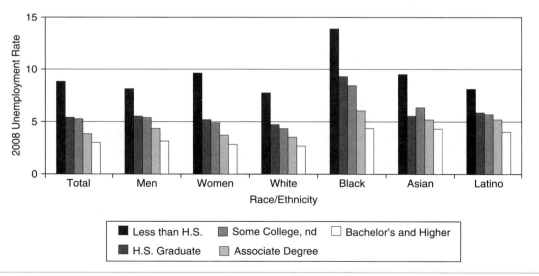

*Persons whose ethnicity is Hispanic are classified by ethnicity as well as by race.
[†]Bachelor's and higher includes persons with bachelor's, master's, professional, and doctoral degree.

Source: http://www.bls.gov/cps/cpsaat7.pdf, accessed October 12, 2010.

FOCAL ISSUE 4.2	*Unemployment, Underemployment, and Discouraged Workers*

Unemployment levels published by the U.S. government and reported in the media understate the true levels of employment as well as completely excluding people who are "underemployed" and those who are "discouraged workers." Under the official definition of unemployment, an individual must be actively seeking work to be included in the "official" unemployment rate.[42] Thus, "**discouraged workers**," those who want to work but have given up searching for employment, are not included in the official rates.[43] This presents a more positive picture but belies true unemployment levels.

The **underemployed** are people working part-time or on a temporary or intermittent basis but who desire regular, full-time work; those who are working for lower wages than their skills would justify or in positions requiring considerably lower skills than they possess; and those involuntarily working outside their fields ("occupational mismatch"). **Underemployment** negatively affects workers in a variety of ways. Earnings and benefits are lower when working part-time, temporary, or intermittent jobs. Health benefits, retirement, vacation, and other benefits are less likely and, if they exist, they are less lucrative in such jobs. Working for lower wages than one's skills merit not only negatively affects workers immediately but also results in lower employer contributions to pensions, 401(k) or other salary-driven benefits. Involuntarily working outside one's field can erode skills and decrease competitiveness for future opportunities. In addition to those negative effects, the underemployed experience reduced self-esteem, job attitudes, and likelihood of appropriate employment later.[44]

As mentioned earlier, Black unemployment rates are consistently and considerably higher than those of Whites. In 2009, 4.2% of Whites and 7.3% of Blacks with a bachelor's degree or more were considered "officially" unemployed. Blacks remain unemployed longer than Whites as well. In 2008, the mean duration of unemployment was 21.7 weeks for Blacks versus 16.7 weeks for Whites.[45] Blacks are also more likely to be underemployed and discouraged workers than Whites.[46] In 2008, Blacks comprised 11% of the labor force but 28% of the discouraged workers.[47] Given the demoralizing effects of discrimination and underemployment, one could speculate about the numbers of discouraged Blacks who are overlooked by the official employment figures, the negative ramifications for them, and the opportunities missed by prospective employers and society as a whole.

[42]Bureau of Labor Statistics. (2009). Current Population Survey. How the Government Measures Unemployment. Bureau of Labor Statistics, http://www.bls.gov/cps/cps_htgm.htm#nilf, accessed December 17, 2010.

[43]Herring, C., & Fasenfest, D. (1999); Tipps, H. C., & Gordon, H. A. (1985). "Inequality at Work: Race, Sex, and Underemployment." *Social Indicators Research*, 16: 35–49; Ullah, P. (1987). "Unemployed Black Youths in a Northern City." In D. Fryer & P. Ullah (Eds.), *Unemployed People*. Milton Keynes, UK: Open University Press, pp. 110–147; Winefield, A. H., Winefield, H. R., Tiggemann, M., & Goldney, R. D. (1991). "A Longitudinal Study of the Psychological Effects of Unemployment and Unsatisfactory Employment on Young Adults." *Journal of Applied Psychology*, 76: 424–431.

[44]See Tipps & Gordon (1985); Ullah (1987); Winefield, Winefield, Tiggemann & Goldney (1991).

[45]Bureau of Labor Statistics. (2009). *Labor Force Characteristics by Race and Ethnicity. Report 1020*. http://www.bls.gov/cps/cpsrace2008.pdf, accessed January 14, 2010.

[46]Herring & Fasenfest (1999); Tipps & Gordon (1985); Ullah (1987).

[47]Bureau of Labor Statistics (2009).

TABLE 4.4 *Mean Total Money Earnings in 2008 by Educational Attainment for Population 25 Years and Over*

	Total*	High School		Bachelor's
		Graduate, Including GED	Some College, No Degree	
All races male	$56,036	$39,835	$46,703	$75,595
All races female	$35,760	$25,851	$30,007	$45,688
Women's % of men's	64%	65%	64%	60%
White male, non-Hispanic	$61,863	$42,579	$49,154	$79,584
White female, non-Hispanic	$37,492	$26,619	$30,703	$45,950
White women's % of men's	61%	63%	62%	58%
Black male	$39,935	$33,492	$36,523	$53,108
Black female	$32,076	$24,493	$29,131	$44,360
Black women's % of men's	80%	73%	80%	84%
Asian male	$64,395	$37,206	$45,925	$69,288
Asian female	$43,246	$24,422	$27,992	$49,800
Asian women's % of men's	67%	66%	61%	72%
Hispanic male (any race)	$37,080	$33,332	$40,090	$58,789
Hispanic female (any race)	$26,753	$23,405	$28,432	$40,947
Hispanic women's % of men's	72%	70%	71%	70%

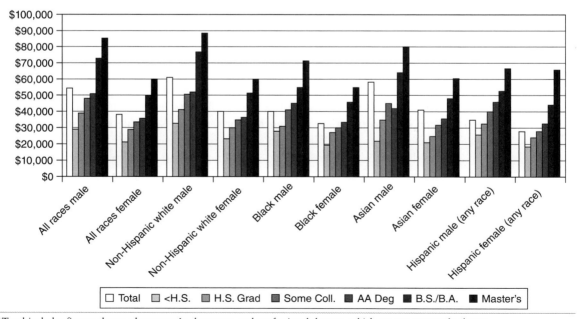

*Total includes figures shown plus master's, doctorate, and professional degrees, which are not separately shown.

Source: U.S. Census Bureau. PINC-03. "Educational Attainment—People 25 Years Old and Over, by Total Money Earnings in 2008, Work Experience in 2008, Age, Race, Hispanic Origin, and Sex." http://www.census.gov/hhes/www/cpstables/032009/perinc/new03_000.htm.

■ RESEARCH ON THE EMPLOYMENT EXPERIENCES OF AFRICAN AMERICANS

The previous section compared the education, employment, and earnings of African Americans to those of other racial and ethnic groups. Clearly, the levels of education, employment, and earnings of Blacks have increased markedly in the past decades. However, the returns gained from their education and their higher unemployment and underemployment suggest that Blacks still experience discrimination in organizations. In this section, we consider empirical evidence of discrimination in access and treatment, name-based discrimination (a form of access discrimination), and other overt racial discrimination in organizations. Recall that **access discrimination** occurs when people are denied employment opportunities, or "access" to jobs, based on their race, sex, age, or other factors unrelated to productivity. **Treatment discrimination** occurs when people are employed but are treated differently once employed, receiving fewer job-related rewards, resources, or opportunities than they should receive based on job-related criteria.[48] As discussed in Chapter 3, both access and treatment discrimination are prohibited by Title VII of the Civil Rights Act; however, research and discrimination settlements indicate both still occur, as discussed in the following sections.

Access Discrimination

African Americans frequently experience access discrimination based on stereotypes, prejudice, stated instructions to discriminate, skin tone (with those with darker skins faring worse than those with lighter skins),[49] or even because their names "sound Black." Several recent field studies using equally matched Black and White applicants have found evidence of access discrimination in a variety of settings. Multiple audit studies using Black, Latino, and White job seekers with matched educational credentials (fields of study, degrees, schools attended, and grade point averages) found that Blacks and Latinos fared worse than White applicants about 20% of the time.[50] In a study using well-matched applicants, Marianne Bertrand and Sendhil Mullainathan (University of Chicago and MIT,

---

[48]Greenhaus, J. H., Parasuraman, S., & Wormley, W. M. (1990). "Effects of Race on Organizational Experiences, Job Performance Evaluations, and Career Outcomes. *Academy of Management Journal*, 33: 64–86.

[49]Harrison, M. S., & Thomas, K. M. (2009). "The Hidden Prejudice in Selection: A Research Investigation on Skin Color Bias." *Journal of Applied Social Psychology*, 39(1): 134–168.

[50]Bendick, M., Jr., Jackson, C., & Reinoso, V. (1994). "Measuring Employment Discrimination through Controlled Experiments." *Review of Black Political Economy*, 23: 25–48; Bendick, M., Jr., Jackson, C., Reinoso V., and Hodges L. (1991). "Discrimination against Latino Job Applicants: A Controlled Experiment." *Human Resource Management*, 30: 469–484; Fix, M., & Struyk, R. (Eds.) (1991). *Clear and Convincing Evidence*. Washington, D.C.: The Urban Institute.

respectively) found that applicants with names that are common to Blacks, such as LaKisha and Jamal, were 50% less likely to be called for interviews than were applicants with names that are common to Whites, such as Emily and Greg. Additional "Black-sounding" names used in the study were Aisha, Keisha, Tamika, Tanisha, LaToya, Kenya, LaTonya, Ebony, Darnell, Hakim, Jermaine, Kareem, Leroy, Rasheed, Tremayne, and Tyrone. Other "White-sounding" names used were Allison, Anne, Carrie, Jill, Laurie, Kristen, Meredith, Sarah, Brad, Brendan, Geoffrey, Brett, Jay, Matthew, Neil, and Todd.

Applicants with "White-sounding" names needed to send out ten résumés to receive one callback, while those with "Black-sounding" names had to send out fifteen résumés—a 50% difference in callbacks. Having higher-quality résumés (e.g., more credentials) improved Whites' likelihood of being called but did not increase callbacks for Blacks. In other words, increasing credentials did not matter if the applicant had a "Black-sounding" name. Having a "White-sounding" name resulted in as many additional callbacks as did having eight more years of experience on a résumé.[51] Like the Bertrand and Mullainathan research, several other audit studies have found evidence that people with distinctively Black names were less likely to be called for interviews.

Roland Fryer and Steven Levitt of Harvard University investigated naming patterns among Blacks in California between 1961 and 2000.[52] During that time, "distinctively Black" names began to appear more frequently, and Fryer and Levitt sought to investigate the factors associated with such naming practices. In a carefully constructed study they found that those with distinctively Black names are "increasingly associated with mothers who are young, poor, unmarried, and have low education."[53] Fryer and Levitt proposed that employers may be exercising **statistical discrimination**, using the distinctiveness of the names as proxies for potential productivity and skills of applicants with such names. Given the evidence from Bertrand and Mullainathan's study, in which the résumés were identical aside from the applicants' names, it seems that statistical discrimination based on names would increase organizations' recruitment and selection costs, as well as result in unfair treatment of applicants with "Black names."

In one of the few investigations that have focused on the effects on hiring practices of firm size and applicant race, Harry Holzer, former chief economist with the U.S. Department of Labor, investigated

[51]Bertrand, M., & Mullainathan, S. (2004). "Are Emily and Greg More Employable than LaKisha and Jamal? A Field Experiment on Labor Market Discrimination." *American Economic Review,* 94: 991–1011.

[52]Fryer, R. G., & Levitt, S. D. (2004). "The Causes and Consequences of Distinctively Black Names." *Quarterly Journal of Economics,* 119(3): 767–804.

[53]Ibid., p. 787.

employers in four large U.S. cities: Atlanta, Boston, Detroit, and Los Angeles.[54] Company size was broken down into the categories of 1–14, 15–49, 50–99, and 100–499, and 500 or more employees. Holzer found that small companies hire much smaller percentages of Black employees than larger companies do and that they hire a significantly smaller percentage of the Blacks who apply. Holzer suggested that large firms are more likely to have affirmative action programs and to have experienced compliance reviews, which may account for some of these differences. Larger firms are also more likely to have formal hiring practices and structured interviews, which leave less room for subjective and possibly discriminatory employment decisions. Holzer noted that the demand for Black labor in the United States would be at least 40% higher if Blacks' hiring rates in small companies were similar to their hiring rates in large firms. Recall that Blacks' unemployment levels are consistently about two times those for Whites; hiring practices may provide some explanations for these differences. Researchers estimate that about 25% of business establishments have no minority workers and another 25% have less than 10% minorities. To have an equal racial distribution across employment contexts, nearly 50% of Black workers would have to change jobs.[55]

In none of the studies using testers, mailed-in résumés, or analyses of other data would applicants have been aware that access discrimination had occurred. All that applicants would have known is they were not called for an interview or were not hired. This reinforces the idea noted in Chapter 2 that those who experience discrimination do not generally sue— many times they do not even know that discrimination has occurred. Research Summary 4.1 reports on a study of access discrimination that documented employers' decision making regarding White convicted felons and Blacks with no criminal record. The results were replicated in a later study that included Latino, Black, and White applicants applying for low-wage jobs. Black and Latino applicants without records were no more successful than Whites with a felony.[56]

Since Title VII has been in effect for more than forty years, a legitimate question is why overt and covert discrimination, that prevent people from obtaining jobs and organizations from obtaining the benefits of a diverse workforce, are so tenacious. New forms of racism may help explain these issues.

[54]Holzer, H. (1998). "Why Do Small Establishments Hire Fewer Blacks than Larger Ones?" *Journal of Human Resources*, 33(4): 896–915.

[55]Robinson, C. L., Taylor, T., Tomaskovic-Devey, D., Zimmer, C., & Irwin, M. (2005). "Studying Race or Ethnic and Sex Segregation at the Establishment Level: Methodological Issues and Substantive Opportunities Using EEO-1 Reports." *Work and Occupations*, 32: 5–38.

[56]Pager, D., Bonikowski, B., & Western, B. (2009). "Discrimination in a Low-Wage Labor Market: A Field Experiment." *American Sociological Review*, 74: 777–799.

RESEARCH SUMMARY 4.1	*Which Do Employers Prefer—A White Convicted Felon or a Black Person with a Clean Record?*

Numerous studies have reported racial disparities between equally qualified Blacks and Whites in access to credit, insurance, and employment. To investigate the effects of a criminal record and race on job search outcomes, Devah Pager sent pairs of well-matched Black and White men to apply for advertised entry-level jobs in Milwaukee, Wisconsin. The paired applicants were well-groomed, well-spoken, college-educated men with identical résumés. The only difference was that one man in each pair said that he had served a prison sentence for cocaine possession.

As expected, employers called the applicants back for interviews at different rates, and Whites were favored. The callback rates were Blacks with criminal record (5%), Blacks with no record (14%), Whites with a record (17%), and Whites without a record (34%). Within-group differences indicated that the ratio of callbacks for nonoffenders relative to ex-offenders was 2 to 1 for Whites and 3 to 1 for Blacks. Thus, the negative effect of having a criminal record on employment opportunities is 40% larger for Blacks than for Whites. Since there is evidence that, when compared with Whites, Blacks are more likely to be arrested, and convicted if arrested, these disparities have even more negative implications.

Reports of the testers' interactions with the managers provide interesting insights. In one case, the hiring manager told the White tester with a record that he liked hiring people who had just been released from prison, as they tended to be harder workers and motivated to avoid returning to prison. In three cases, Black testers were asked even before submitting their applications whether they had a criminal history, but no Whites were asked up front whether they had a criminal history.

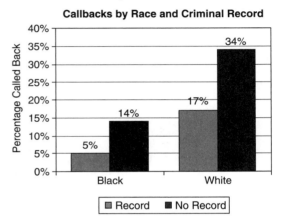

Callbacks by Race and Criminal Record

QUESTIONS TO CONSIDER

1. The testers in these studies were well-educated, well-spoken applicants. What would you expect the results to be for applicants with less education and ability to communicate?

2. Disparities in powder versus crack cocaine sentencing receive a great deal of attention. What are some potential consequences of those disparities, given the results of this study?

Source: Pager, D. (2003). "The Mark of a Criminal Record." *American Journal of Sociology*, 108: 937–975.

"New" or "modern" racism. As discussed in Chapter 3, new forms of racism include beliefs that racism is a thing of the past and that Blacks have attained excessive, unfair gains through programs such as affirmative action. New racists do not display overt racism but when provided with a rationale, use business justifications as excuses to deny employment to Blacks. In a laboratory study, Art Brief and his colleagues investigated whether explicit instructions from "company officials" to discriminate against Blacks would be followed.[57] The business justifications provided were that the company president believed it was important to (1) continue the good relationships built by the previous (White) job incumbent, (2) keep the marketing teams as homogeneous as possible, or (3) match the newly hired employee to the race of the majority of clients in the assigned territory base. Study participants who had high scores on the **new racism** scale were likely to avoid hiring qualified Blacks when provided with this "business justification." In nearly 40% of the cases, those participants chose an *unqualified White* instead of a *qualified Black*.

Treatment Discrimination

Even though there is considerable evidence of access discrimination, and Blacks have higher unemployment than comparably educated Whites, many Blacks are employed and have stable employment histories. How do Blacks fare once they have obtained employment? Does equal opportunity step in after employment and result in fairness in earnings, promotions, job placement, and other rewards? From a review of research and EEOC litigation, the answer, in some cases, is apparently not.

To stringently examine race effects in performance ratings, Kraiger and Ford performed a meta-analysis of research conducted over a fifteen-year period. A meta-analysis is a statistical method of integrating results of findings from multiple studies to determine if there are underlying patterns of relationships. Seventy-four studies conducted both in the field and in the laboratory were included in the analysis. All of the studies included White managers but only fourteen involved Black managers. Results indicated that being the same race as one's supervisor produced significantly higher ratings for employees who were similar in race. Because Whites are much more likely to be managers than Blacks, the "similarity" effect tends to advantage White employees and disadvantage Black employees. Kraiger and Ford also found that these race effects were substantial in the field but not in the lab. Training had no effect in reducing same-race bias, but race effects did decline as the percentage of Blacks in the workgroup increased.[58]

In another study that included several work-related outcome variables, Greenhaus, Parasuraman, and Wormley investigated whether

[57]Brief, A. P., Buttram, R. T., Reizenstein, R. M., Pugh, S. D., Callahan, J. D., McCline, R. L., & Vaslow, J. B. (1997). "Beyond Good Intentions: The Next Step toward Racial Equality in the American Workplace." *Academy of Management Executive,* 11(4): 59–72.

[58]Kraiger, K., & Ford, J. K. (1985). "A Meta-Analysis of Ratee Race Effects in Performance Ratings." *Journal of Applied Psychology,* 70: 56–65.

treatment discrimination negatively affects the job satisfaction, career progress, performance evaluations, and organizational experiences of Blacks.[59] Jeff Greenhaus and his colleagues surveyed 828 managers and their immediate supervisors in the communications, banking, and electronics industries. The sample of managers was matched in terms of age, company tenure, job function, and organizational level; 45% of the managers were Black and 55% were White. More than 93% of the supervisors to whom the managers reported were White. Managers responded to questions about their job and career satisfaction, job discretion, perceived organizational acceptance or isolation, supervisory support, and mentoring. Their supervisors responded to questions about the managers' promotability and job performance. Results indicated that Black managers were more likely to have reached a career plateau (e.g., to have stayed in one position without being promoted), to report less job discretion and less organizational acceptance, and to receive less favorable assessments of promotability from their supervisors. Overall, supervisors rated the performance of Blacks lower than the performance of Whites—4% of the variance in performance ratings was explained by the race of the manager. Because wages are closely tied to performance evaluations (as they should be when the evaluations are accurate and unbiased), lower performance evaluations of Blacks may help explain their lower wages, particularly when differences accumulate over time.

The treatment discrimination identified by researchers in empirical studies is supported by the formal discrimination lawsuits brought against actual, well-known companies. In one case, the Coca-Cola Company settled a lawsuit that alleged systematic discrimination against Black employees, agreeing to a record $192.5 million settlement. Black employees alleged that they were consistently at the bottom of pay scales, earning $26,000 less per year than Whites in comparable jobs, and that they were denied promotions they deserved.[60] In another major settlement, Texaco agreed to a $140 million cash settlement to compensate Black plaintiffs in a class action lawsuit. Texaco executives had made disparaging racial comments that were recorded and released to the public during the lawsuit.[61]

The Glass Ceiling and Walls

The **glass ceiling** is an invisible barrier preventing women, people of color, and people with disabilities from progressing beyond a certain level in

[59]Greenhaus et al. (1990).
[60]Winter, G. (2000, November 17). "Coke Bias Settlement Sets Record," *The Dallas Morning News*, New York Times News Service.
[61]Roberts, B., & White, J. (1998). *Roberts v. Texaco: A True Story of Race in Corporate America.* New York: Avon Books.

organizations.[62] Although many think that the glass ceiling begins at the level near the top management level or at the executive level, empirical evidence shows the ceiling to be actually quite low, beginning at the first-line management and supervisory levels and continuing onward to the top.[63] African Americans are almost nonexistent at the level of Fortune 500 chief executive officer (CEO), numbering between three and six individuals within the last decade.

Glass walls are invisible barriers that confine minorities and women to certain positions within organizations. Blacks are often concentrated in communications, community relations, and human resources positions, rather than in marketing, finance, and operations, which are more likely to lead to higher-level executive jobs. Typically staff, instead of line, positions, these jobs do not involve finance or key decision making, and thus Blacks are prevented from obtaining the breadth of skills needed to advance past certain levels.[64]

Glass ceilings and walls can be created and strengthened through overt and clearly discriminatory practices, as well as by practices that seem less innocuous on the surface. Such practices include:

- assigning less challenging work (leading to less development of skills and thus affecting qualifications for the future);
- failure to provide constructive performance feedback (for fear of being perceived as racist, which leads to failure to identify and achieve necessary improvement); or
- assignment to certain (minority) neighborhoods and clients (on the basis of presumed "fit" or connection or other employees' unwillingness to work there), which can negatively impact employees' earnings and career progress.

Negative Health Effects of Discrimination

In the previous section, we reported research findings indicating that Blacks may have more negative organizational experiences and lower job satisfaction than Whites. Egregious racial harassment at work can also affect the health of Blacks negatively. Documented reports exist of nooses

[62]This chapter considers the effects of the glass ceiling on Blacks; see other chapters for its effects on different groups.

[63]Hurley, A. J., Fagenson-Eland, E. A., & Sonnenfeld, J. A. (1997). "Does Cream Always Rise to the Top? An Investigation of Career Attainment Determinants." *Organizational Dynamics*, 26(2), 65–71; Maume, D. J., Jr. (1999, November). "Glass Ceilings and Glass Escalators: Occupational Segregation and Race and Sex Differences in Managerial Promotions. *Work and Occupations*, 26(4): 483–509; Maume, D. J., Jr. (2004). "Is the Glass Ceiling a Unique Form of Inequality?" *Work and Occupations*, 31(2): 250–274.

[64]Collins, S. M. (1997). "Race Up the Corporate Ladder: The Dilemmas and Contradictions of First-Wave Black Executives." In C. Herring (Ed.), *African Americans and the Public Agenda*. Thousand Oaks, CA: Sage Publications, pp. 87–101.

(representing lynching), racist graffiti, being called "boy" or being asked if they eat "monkey meat," and other harassment at such reputable companies as Lockheed Martin, Northwest Airlines, and Earl Schieb.[65] These negative experiences affect Blacks' health via hypertension and increased risk of heart attack. In addition, lack of autonomy and advancement, job segregation, negative stereotyping, and perceived discrimination have been associated with depression, stress, and high blood pressure for Blacks.[66] These health implications make diversity issues even more important to African Americans and to their employers.

To prepare their children for and help minimize the effects of the bias, stereotyping, and discrimination that they are likely to encounter, Black parents may engage in **racial socialization**. Racial socialization consists of behaviors, communications, and interactions concerning their cultural heritage and the appropriate responses to racial hostility and discrimination that Black parents model and explain to Black children.[67] The messages instill racial pride, including information about the successes and accomplishments of Blacks, countering negative messages, bolstering self-esteem, and increasing a sense of a shared or collective Black identity.[68] Thus, racial socialization can help mitigate some of the negative effects of discrimination, but determining the right amount of socialization and how much focus to place on discrimination without destroying motivation is difficult.

Immigrant Blacks and Their Descendants and Native-born Blacks—Similarities and Differences

The majority of the 40 million U.S. foreign-born population is White (17 million) or Asian (9 million). About 3 million foreign-born are Black,

[65]Bernstein, A. (2001, July 31). "Racism in the Workplace." *Business Week Online,* http://www.businessweek.com/magazine/content/01_31/b3743084.htm, accessed December 17, 2010; The U.S. Equal Employment Opportunity Commission, Litigation Settlements—August 2004. http://archive.eeoc.gov/litigation/settlements/settlement08-04.html, accessed December 17, 2010; The U.S. Equal Employment Opportunity Commission, Litigation Settlements, September 2004. http://www.eeoc.gov/eeoc/newsroom/release/12-30-04.cfm, accessed December 17, 2010.

[66]Mays, V. M., Coleman, L. M., & Jackson, J. S. (1996). "Perceived Race-Based Discrimination, Employment Status, and Job Stress in a National Sample of Black Women: Implications for Health Outcomes." *Journal of Occupational Health Psychology,* 1: 319–329; Pascoe, E. A., & Richman, L. S. (2009). "Perceived Discrimination and Health: A Meta-Analytic Review." *Psychological Bulletin,* 135(4): 531–554.

[67]Brown, D. L. (2008). African American Resiliency: Examining Racial Socialization and Social Support as Protective Factors. *Journal of Black Psychology,* 34: 32–50.

[68]Bell, M. P., Heslin, P., & Fletcher, P. (2010). "Daring to Care About Hidden Unemployment: Discrimination and Discouragement in Minority Communities." Paper presented at the meeting of the Academy of Management, Montreal, Canada; Bennett, M. D. (2006). "Cultural Resources and School Engagement Among African American Youths: The Role of Racial Socialization and Ethnic Identity." *Children & Schools,* 28(4): 197–206; Harris-Britt, A., Valrie, C. R., Kurtz-Costes, B., & Rowley, S. J. (2007). "Perceived Racial Discrimination and Self-esteem in African American Youth: Racial Socialization as a Protective Factor. *Journal of Research on Adolescence,* 17: 660–682.

nearly 8% of the total foreign-born population. In contrast to native-born Hispanics and Asians, who are often erroneously identified as immigrants, immigrant Blacks are often perceived to be native-born. Even when immigrants self-identify as West Indian or Haitian American, others often regard them simply as "Black." However, second-generation immigrants sometimes still construct and enforce an ethnic identity.[69]

As discussed in Chapter 2, a way to easily identify others as different in order to single them out for differential treatment is required. This initial identification is simply "Black" for Black immigrants and their descendants. But in some cases, self-identification differs from the identity of those whose ancestors were enslaved in America.[70] For recent Black immigrants, self-identification as immigrants and their experiences in the homeland may shape their expectations. Immigrants from countries where Blacks are the numerical majority and experience some level of occupational and financial status may not have the same expectations of differential race-based treatment and powerlessness in America as native-born Blacks.[71] Descendants of Black immigrants often have different expectations from those of their parents, however, having observed and experienced first-hand the significance of being Black in the United States.[72] While first-generation Black immigrants believe that discrimination exists, they are more likely to see it as something that can be overcome. Later generations hold to those beliefs less strongly.

In her research on Black identities among West Indian immigrants, Mary Waters found that employers sometimes felt West Indian employees differed from other (native) Blacks, touting their work ethic. Employer beliefs and treatment intertwine with class to shape first- and second-generation immigrants' experiences and outcomes.[73] Country of origin, education, and language (native English or not) are also strong influences. In a study on employment and earnings of native and immigrant Blacks and Whites, Butcher found that native and immigrant Blacks had similar earnings and both earned less than their White counterparts.[74] Jamaican-born Blacks had higher earnings, African-born Blacks had higher education levels, and immigrants with less education had higher employment rates than native-born Blacks.

---

[69]Waters, M. C. (1994). "Ethnic and Racial Identities of Second-Generation Black Immigrants in New York City." *International Migration Review*, 28(4): 795–820.
[70]Waters, M. C. (2001). *Black Identities: West Indian Immigrant Dreams and American Realities*. New York: Russell Sage Foundation.
[71]Ibid., p. 309.
[72]Tormala & Deaux (2006).
[73]Waters (1994).
[74]Butcher, K. (1994). "Black Immigrants in the United States: A Comparison with Native Blacks and Other Immigrants." *Industrial and Labor Relations Review*, 47(2): 265–284.

Through the lens of diversity, the influence of race is clear. For individual Blacks, native-born, immigrant, or descendants of immigrants, their identifiability as "Black" is a strong influence on various life experiences. Racial profiling by police is based on skin color, not country of origin. Guinean immigrant Amadou Diallo, an unarmed man who had committed no crime, was shot nineteen times in New York City by four undercover police officers. Researchers have found that in simulated studies both community members and police officers are more likely to shoot Blacks than Whites but that police officers' discriminatory responses can be changed through extensive training.[75]

African American Women at Work

Misperceptions abound about the employment experiences of women of color, particularly Black women. On the one hand, Black women are often perceived as unwilling to work, preferring instead to draw welfare to support their many children. On the other hand, some think that employers prefer Black women over White women or Black men because they are counted under affirmative action programs as both minority and female ("two-fers"). Analyses of the participation rates and income of Black women shed some light on the inaccuracies of both perceptions.

Almost throughout all of U.S. history, Black women have been more likely to work outside the home than women of all other groups, in sharp contrast to perceptions that they do not work. As we have discussed, Black women have the highest rates of participation in the labor force among all women. In part, this higher participation rate reflects the greater likelihood of Black women being unmarried and of being dependent upon their own earnings. In addition, married Black women are more likely to be employed because of their husbands' lower earnings compared to White men.

Misperceptions about Black women's propensity to miss work because of being "single mothers" of many children also disadvantage Black women. Irene Browne and Ivy Kennelly's investigation of the effects of stereotypes on Black women's employment experiences found that employers' negative perceptions about Black women persisted despite evidence contradicting those perceptions. They found that employers expected Black women to miss work more because of their children.

[75]Correll, J., Park, B., Judd, C. M., Wittenbrink, B., Sadler, M. S., & Keesee, T. (2007). "Across the Thin Blue Line: Police Officers and Racial Bias in the Decision to Shoot." *Journal of Personality and Social Psychology*, 92(6): 1006–1023; Smith, B. W. (2004). "Structural and Organizational Predictors of Homicide by Police." *Policing: An International Journal of Police Strategies and Management*, 27: 539–557.

When they did not and were reliable workers, employers attributed this to being "desperate" for income rather than to their having a "true work ethic."[76]

Misperception: Blacks have considerably more children than Whites.

Reality: Although birthrates for Black women are slightly higher, both Black and White women are likely to have about 2 children.

Racial and sexual harassment of Black women. Researchers have found that Black (and other minority) women are especially likely to be subjected to racialized sexual discrimination and harassment.[77] Davis and others propose that the sexual abuse and powerlessness Black women endured as slaves continue to spill over into egregious harassment in organizations today.[78] Black women, including Mechelle Vinson in the well-known case against Meritor Savings Bank, represented a disproportionate number of litigants in early sexual harassment cases and continue to be overrepresented.[79] As the following report shows, Whirlpool Corporation was found liable for such harassment in one particularly disturbing case.

Whirlpool Corp. To Pay Over $1 Million For Harassing Black Female Worker, Judge Rules In Bench Trial[80]

EEOC Said Company Tolerated Verbal Harassment Culminating in Physical Assault

A final court judgment of $1,073,261 was awarded against Whirlpool Corporation in a race and sex discrimination lawsuit on behalf of Carlota Freeman, an

---

[76]Browne, I., & Kennelly, I. (1999). "Stereotypes and Realities: Images of Black Women in the Labor Market." In I. Browne (Ed.), *Latinas and African American Women at Work: Race, Gender, and Economic Inequality*. New York: Russell Sage Foundation, pp. 302–326.

[77]Cho, S. K. (1997). "Converging Stereotypes in Racialized Sexual Harassment: Where the Model Minority Meets Suzie Wong," *Journal of Gender Race & Justice*, 1: 177–211; Hernández, T. K. (2001). "Sexual Harassment and Racial Disparity: The Mutual Construction of Gender and Race." *Journal of Gender Race & Justice*, 183(4): 186–187.

[78]Davis, A. D. (2004). "Slavery and the Roots of Sexual Harassment." In C. A. MacKinnon & R. B. Siegel (Eds.), *Directions in Sexual Harassment Law*. New Haven, CT: Yale University Press, pp. 457–479.

[79]Ibid.

[80]Adapted from EEOC press release, "Whirlpool Corp to Pay over $1 Million for Harassing Black Female Worker, Judge Rules in Bench Trial." http://www.eeoc.gov/eeoc/newsroom/release/12-29-09.cfm, accessed October 12, 2010.

African American former employee at the company's La Vergne, Tenn.–based facility. The EEOC alleged that the appliance manufacturing giant failed to protect Freeman from persistent harassment by a White male coworker and that Freeman was ultimately physically assaulted and injured by him. Freeman was awarded $773,261 in back pay and front pay and $300,000 in compensatory damages—the maximum allowed under federal law. The evidence showed that:

- Freeman reported escalating offensive verbal conduct and gestures by the male coworker before he physically assaulted her;
- four levels of Whirlpool's management were aware of the escalating harassment;
- Whirlpool failed to take effective steps to stop the harassment; and,
- Freeman suffered devastating permanent mental injuries that will prevent her from working again as a result of the assault and Whirlpool's failure to protect her.

Although Whirlpool argued that its posted policy prohibiting harassment absolved the company from liability, the court pointed out that the managers and supervisors charged with enforcing the policy did not do so, and thus the company remained liable. According to the EEOC Acting Chairman Ishimaru, "It is deeply disturbing that such a large and sophisticated company would allow this sort of abuse to go unchecked—even up to the point where serious physical injuries are inflicted on one of its employees."

News reports provide additional and more troubling details of the racialized sexual harassment endured by Carlota Freeman.[81] After enduring months of abuse and a physical assault at work, Freeman took a leave of absence and, after being diagnosed with post-traumatic stress disorder, eventually quit. The judge in the case wrote that "the facts show a failure of every level of management at Whirlpool," from the harasser's direct supervisor, through to the Manager and Director of Human Resources.[82] These failures occurred despite Whirlpool having a sexual harassment policy. Policies alone are not sufficient to eliminate sexual harassment.

---

[81]Lind, J. R. (2009). "Whirlpool to Pay Big in La Vergne Harassment Case." http://nashvillepost.com/news/2009/12/22/whirlpool_ordered_to_pay_big_in_la_vergne_harassment_case, accessed March 18, 2011.
[82]Ibid.

Discrimination against Customers

The previous sections have described discriminatory acts against job applicants and employees that have negative implications for promoting diversity in organizations, including decreases in the potential for creativity, resource acquisition, problem solving, and flexibility. Individual Blacks as well suffer from the negative effects of unemployment and low earnings. If discrimination against employees becomes widely known, an organization's ability to market to diverse customer groups may also be harmed through negative publicity and boycotts. As we have mentioned, Black buying power was more than $910 billion in 2009 and is projected to grow, and so discrimination against customers can also have a direct negative impact on an organization's ability to market to Blacks. Some of the organizations that have been charged with discrimination against Black customers are the Adams Mark hotels, Dillard's, Denny's, Shoney's, Cracker Barrel, Bloomingdale's, Walmart, and Eddie Bauer. Allegations include making unfounded accusations of theft, unauthorized physical searches, being ignored, refusals of service, and/or inordinate wait times for service.[83] In one case, the Cracker Barrel restaurant chain agreed to pay $8.7 million to settle lawsuits filed by Black employees and customers alleging discrimination in job assignments and denial of service, placing customers in segregated seating areas, and serving them food taken from the trash.[84]

Two beliefs appear to be driving discrimination against Black customers: (1) Blacks are more likely to be shoplifters, and (2) Blacks are less likely to have money to spend. Profiling potential shoplifters using demographic characteristics is simply not a good practice; there is no "typical" shoplifter and race is not a predictor of shoplifting.[85] Shoplifters vary by race, sex, age, and socioeconomic status (as is apparent when successful actors are convicted of shoplifting). Rather than watching Blacks and ignoring everyone else, businesses could adopt the more effective approach of monitoring suspicious behavior, such as wearing heavy clothing when it is warm, looking around quickly, or having a baby stroller but no baby. Lastly, given that Blacks in the United States earn over $600 billion each year and spend nearly $23 billion on clothes and

[83]See Harris, A., Henderson, G., & Williams, J. (2005). "Courting Customers: Assessing Consumer Racial Profiling and Other Marketplace Discrimination," *Journal of Public Policy & Marketing*, 24(1): 163–171.
[84]"Cracker Barrel to Pay $8.7 Million to End Suits." *Dallas Morning News*, September 10, 2004, p. 2D, U.S. and World Briefs.
[85]Dabney, D. A., Hollinger, R. C., & Dugan, L. (2004). "Who Actually Steals? A Study of Covertly Observed Shoplifters." *Justice Quarterly*, 21: 693–728; Klemke, L. (1982). "Exploring Juvenile Shoplifting." *Sociology and Social Research*, 67: 59–75; Lo, L. (1994). "Exploring Teenage Shoplifting Behavior." *Environment and Behavior*, 26(5): 613–639.

$3 billion on electronics, treating Blacks as potential shoplifters rather than customers may cause them to spend their money elsewhere.

Research Summary 4.2 describes an empirical study detailing discrimination against Blacks in new-car pricing, a unique form of customer discrimination.

In addition to higher car prices, discrimination in loan rates and mortgage terms against Blacks (and Latinos) contributes to them being disproportionately represented among foreclosures. Compared with similarly qualified Whites (e.g., credit history, down payment, residential location), Blacks were more likely to receive subprime loans and to receive loans with prepayment penalties and other unfavorable terms.[86] In 2010, Prime Lending, one of the nation's top twenty FHA lenders, agreed to settle a lawsuit brought by the U.S. Department of Justice alleging discrimination against African American borrowers. Between 2006 and 2009, while originating more than $5.5 billion in loans, Prime Lending charged Blacks higher interest rates for home loans than rates charged to similarly situated Whites. The company gave employees wide discretion to increase their commissions by adding fees to loans, which increased interest rates paid by borrowers and had a disparate impact on Black borrowers. Prime Lending agreed to pay $2 million to the affected customers, to implement loan pricing policies, to train employees, and to monitor loans to ensure discrimination does not occur in the future.[87] Policies, training, and monitoring are effective tools in reducing many types of discrimination.

■ RECOMMENDATIONS

The instances of discrimination and harassment presented in this chapter are discouraging, but for organizations committed to equality and inclusion, successful efforts to combat them are possible. The existence of access discrimination *before* employment and treatment discrimination *after* employment emphasizes the need for organizational leaders to make diversity a paramount goal in the post- as well as pre-employment stages. Not only are efforts to recruit and hire people from diverse backgrounds

[86]Avery, R. B., Brevoort, K. P., & Canner G. B. (2007). "The 2006 HMDA Data." *Federal Reserve Bulletin*, 93: 73–109. Avery, R. B., Brevoort, K. P., & Canner, G. B. (2008). "The 2007 HMDA Data." *Federal Reserve Bulletin*, 94: 107–146; Quercia, R. G., Stegman, M. A., & Davis, W. R. (2007). "The Impact of Predatory Loan Terms on Subprime Foreclosures: The Special Case of Prepayment Penalties and Balloon Payments." *Housing Policy Debate*, 18: 311–346; Rugh, & Massey, (2010). "Racial Segregation and the American Foreclosure Crisis." *American Sociological Review*, 75(5): 629–651.

[87]"Justice Department Reaches Settlement with National Mortgage Lender to Resolve Allegations of Lending Discrimination," http://www.justice.gov/opa/pr/2010/December/10-crt-1406.html, accessed December 12, 2010.

Why Pay More? Race (and Gender) Discrimination in New Car Pricing

Do Black men and women and White women pay more for cars? Many newspaper articles and hidden television investigations have suggested that they do. What does sound empirical research suggest? Ian Ayres and Peter Siegelman's study published in *The American Economic Review*, "Race and Gender Discrimination in Bargaining for a New Car," provides empirical evidence that indeed Blacks and White women are charged more for new cars than White men are.

Three hundred testers who were matched in terms of age, educational level, attire, and attractiveness and who were trained to negotiate similarly went to Chicago-area car dealerships ostensibly to buy a car. White male, White female, Black male, and Black female testers used identical bargaining strategies after having received two days of formal training, in which they memorized the bargaining script and participated in negotiation role plays. To avoid bias, the testers were told only that the study involved how sellers negotiate for cars and did not know that other testers would also visit the same dealerships.

Findings strongly support race bias in initial pricing and negotiations. Initial offers to White male testers were about $1,000 over dealer costs. Initial offers to Black males were over $900 greater than those made to White males. Initial offers to Black women and White women were $320 and $110, respectively, over initial offers to White men. Differences between initial offers to Black men and women and White men were significant at the 0.05 level; however, differences between White women and White men were not statistically significant.

For all testers prices were lowered during negotiations, but dealer concessions exacerbated the advantages already present in the offers to White males. When these concessions were factored in, a stronger pattern of discrimination was apparent in the final offers when compared with the initial offers. Specifically, Black men, Black women, and White women were offered final prices of $1,100, $410, and $92, respectively, more than White men. Ayres and Siegelman point out that although Black men were quoted the highest initial offer, they received the lowest average concession. In all, testers' race and sex were strongly related to both the initial offer and the final price offered. Perhaps most disturbing, in almost 44% of cases, the *initial offers* made to White men were lower than the *final offers* made to other testers.

It is impossible to unequivocally explain these results. Some suggest that sellers may expect White men to be more serious, sophisticated customers and non-Whites and White women to be less savvy customers. Others suggest that dealers may believe the latter groups are willing to pay higher markups than White men. Regardless of the theoretical explanations for the disparate treatment, the bottom line is the financial cost to Black consumers.

QUESTIONS TO CONSIDER

1. *If the results of this study, with dealers' names and identification, were to be released to the public, what would the likely outcome be for those dealers? How might competing dealerships capitalize on such a disclosure?*

2. *What can individual dealers do to avoid customer discrimination, given the need to maximize profit? Is a profit-maximization strategy consistent with discriminatory dealer behavior in the long term?*

3. *What are some specific steps that individual new car purchasers can take to avoid dealer discrimination in pricing?*

4. *If such discrimination in large purchases is common, what are the short- and long-term economic effects likely to be for Blacks and*

White women, who earn less than White men, and for Black families, which earn less than White families?

Source: Ayres, I. & Siegelman, P. (1995). "Race and Gender Discrimination in Bargaining for a New Car." *The American Economic Review*, 85 (3): 304–321.

important, efforts to ensure that they are treated fairly after employment are also critical to successful diversity programs.

Recommendations for Blacks

What are some successful strategies that individual Blacks can implement that may increase positive employment outcomes? First, they should obtain as much education as possible. Across racial and ethnic groups, education increases earnings and decreases the likelihood of being unemployed.[88] Second, seeking employment in an affirmative action firm appears to be helpful. Given Holzer's findings about the negative relationships between establishment size and the hiring of Blacks, one strategy might be to seek employment in larger firms. Larger firms are also more likely to have formal hiring programs, which could include recruiter training in attending to job-related criteria in the selection process, structured interviews, and control and monitoring. Avoiding race-segregated firms should also help increase earnings.

Given the research evidence about access discrimination, Blacks may have to search harder, longer, and smarter for an appropriate position. Although data on access, treatment, and earnings discrimination can be de-motivating, knowing about it explains reasons for receiving no calls for interviews despite individual qualifications. Instead of internalizing the rejection, which may be demoralizing and result in dropping out of the labor market, persistence and strategy in searching are required.[89] Both are also completely under one's control.

Recommendations for Black women. Because sex and race segregation combine to lower Black women's wages, avoiding segregated work will likely increase the return on educational investment.[90] Next, as for everyone, earnings increase with additional education. As mentioned earlier, any degree past high school will generally increase earnings.

[88]Day, & Newburger (2002, July).
[89]See Focal Issue 4.2 for information about "discouraged" workers.
[90]Reskin, B. F. (1999). "Occupational Segregation by Race and Ethnicity among Women Workers." In I. Browne (Ed.), *Latinas and African American Women at Work: Race, Gender, and Economic Inequality*. New York: Russell Sage Foundation, pp. 183–204.

Black women should also consider working for unionized and/or affirmative action firms. Black women who work for unionized firms earn nearly 40% more than those who work for nonunionized firms. Blacks and women who work for affirmative action firms have higher earnings and are more likely to work in higher-status positions (e.g., professional, managerial, or technical) than those who work for nonaffirmative action firms.[91] Black women should also negotiate salary offers, rather than accept the first offer made; even a modest increase in starting salary builds over time.[92] Federal, state, and local government resources, professional organizations, and Web sites on salary ranges by education and experience are helpful, as are being well aware and confident about one's abilities and worth and not being afraid to negotiate, emphasizing one's education, skills, and experience. Finally, be aware that sex and race discrimination are illegal and there are resources to help if targeted by them.

Entrepreneurship is also an option that many women and people of color are pursuing given limited opportunities and discrimination. Entrepreneurship allows for flexibility, leadership, autonomy, and the ability to provide a diversity-friendly workplace for others. As shown in Individual Feature 4.1, Dr. Regina Benjamin, prior to becoming Surgeon General, used her education and skills to open a nonprofit medical clinic to serve the poor.

Recommendations for Organizational Change

Individuals of any race and ethnic background in positions of power or at any other level can also take steps to eliminate discrimination. Knowledge of the phenomena of access and treatment discrimination, of preference for Whites (even those less qualified or with criminal backgrounds), differential returns on levels of education, and other issues involved in inequitable treatment should provide a strong impetus to work for change. In addition to the clear moral issues, one can view efforts to prevent discrimination against Black employees and customers as bottom-line issues. Some specific suggestions follow:

- Be aware of personal stereotypes and biases and make conscious efforts to challenge and address them.
- As a manager or supervisor with hiring or performance management responsibilities, pay careful attention to relevant information and ignore irrelevant, race-biased stereotypes.

---

[91]Herring, C. (1997). "African Americans, the Public Agenda, and the Paradoxes of Public Policy: A Focus on the Controversies Surrounding Affirmative Action." In C. Herring (Ed.), *African Americans and the Public Agenda: The Paradoxes of Public Policy*. Thousand Oaks, CA: Sage Publications, pp. 3–26.
[92]See Chapter 9 for evidence of women's reluctance to negotiate salary offers compared to men and their lower success rates when negotiating.

Regina Benjamin, M.D., M.B.A., and U.S. Surgeon General

Regina Benjamin became the eighteenth Surgeon General of the U.S. Public Health Service in 2009, the first African American woman to occupy that position. Born in 1956 in Mobile, Alabama, Benjamin earned a bachelor of science degree in chemistry at Xavier University in New Orleans, an M.D. from the University of Alabama in Birmingham, and an M.B.A. from Tulane. Benjamin attended Morehouse School of Medicine and completed her family residency in Macon, Georgia. She has been awarded five honorary doctorates. In 2002, she became president of the State of Alabama Medical Association, making her the first African American female president of such a state society in the United States.

Benjamin has spent much of her career working for the poor and uninsured. She started a nonprofit clinic in a small fishing village on the Gulf Coast of Alabama to help its uninsured residents, often putting up her own money to cover expenses. She would tell pharmacies to send her patients' bills to her when the patients couldn't afford their medicine. When she had trouble treating increasing numbers of Southeast Asian immigrants in the fishing community because they could not communicate with each other, she went to a Vietnamese pool hall in town to find an interpreter.

Benjamin understands the needs of the poor and uninsured and strongly promotes wellness programs and preventive medicine. Family illness and early death have strongly influenced Benjamin's interest in prevention. Her father died with diabetes and high blood pressure, and her mother died from lung cancer because she began smoking at a young age, trying to be like her twin brother. Benjamin's uncle is now on oxygen to help him breathe. Dr. Benjamin's own brother died of complications from HIV at age 44.

Benjamin is recognized as a compassionate, caring, and committed doctor, working to improve the lives and longevity of the U.S. population. In recognition of her work, Benjamin has received a "genius grant" from the MacArthur Foundation, a Nelson Mandela Award for Health and Human Rights, and the *pro Ecclesia et Pontifice* from Pope Benedict XVI for distinguished service, the highest award given to laity by the pope.

QUESTIONS TO CONSIDER

1. *Dr. Benjamin has amassed many "firsts." What do these firsts mean for people similar to and different from Benjamin?*

2. *Benjamin attended some historically Black universities (HBCUs) as well as some predominantly White schools. Critics have argued that there is no longer a need for HBCUs. Are their claims valid? Why or why not?*

3. *Critics have pointed out that Benjamin appears to be overweight. If accurate, what does her weight have to do with her qualifications for the role of Surgeon General? What does Benjamin have to say about her weight? Investigate.*

Sources: Biography of the Surgeon General. http://www.surgeongeneral.gov/about/biographies/biosg.html, accessed October 12, 2010; Hunter, D., & Neergaard, L. (2009, July 13). "Regina Benjamin, Obama's Pick for Surgeon General." Huffington Post, http://www.huffingtonpost.com/2009/07/13/regina-benjamin-obamas-pi_n_230547.html, accessed October 12, 2010; Lloyd, J. (2009, July 14). "Surgeon General pick 'would do anything to heal.'" *USAToday*, p. 13B.

- Remove name and sex-identifying information (e.g., use initials or numbers) from résumés and applicants in the initial stages of selection. Guard it carefully to ensure fairness afterwards.
- Challenge unfair behavior when it is exhibited by others. People may be discriminating intentionally, but it is also possible they are unaware of the roles of stereotypes and misperceptions in behavior and would be receptive to learning about these influences and how to combat them.
- As an executive, implement procedural changes that include training, policies, and monitoring to increase fairness.

Organizational decision makers are subject to the same stereotypes and misperceptions as the general population and, as discussed in the Whirlpool case earlier, may also be complicit in discrimination and harassment. Having formal hiring programs may reduce reliance on and attending to nonjob factors in the hiring process. What training, control, and monitoring procedures exist to minimize the costly effects of stereotypes on organizational practices? If a firm is not officially an affirmative action employer, investigating measures used by affirmative action employers may be helpful (e.g., benchmarking). Where appropriate, the recruitment, training and development, and other human resources programs used by affirmative action firms may serve as models. Internal analysis of hiring, promotion, compensation, and termination figures should be conducted regularly. Is there evidence of access or treatment discrimination? Are procedures in place and monitored to avoid selection of Whites with lower qualifications than Blacks? Are structured interviews used for selection?

Multiple people, from diverse backgrounds, should be involved in the hiring process. We have learned from empirical research that heterogeneous groups generate more, and better, solutions to problems; we can expect a heterogeneous selection team to do a better job with selection as well. It could also be less likely to discriminate and more likely to have members who would resist and reject stereotypes.

What are the performance evaluation, promotion, and advancement rates of employees by race, ethnicity, and sex? Do these rates appear to co-incide with qualifications of employees (education, tenure, and other attributes)? Is there evidence of a glass ceiling or walls in the organization? Where are Blacks (and other non-dominant groups) employed? Are there barriers to the entry of minorities and women into line positions? Are there differences among employees in rates of turnover? If so, are organizational factors, such as treatment discrimination, partly responsible for such turnover? According to Cox and Blake,[93] this is a distinct possibility. Exit interviews may provide invaluable information. Attention to these matters may allow firms to capitalize on the advantages of having a diverse workforce while avoiding the (however unlikely) possibility of being charged with discrimination.

Consumer/Customer Service Recommendations

From a consumer perspective, African Americans (and all consumers) would be well advised to be savvy shoppers. Conducting thorough online and in-person searches for high-cost consumer goods, loan rates, and so on, that are possibly negotiable is simply good practice. Knowing what a fair price is and seeking out reputable organizations or dealers known to be diversity friendly can help decrease the likelihood of experiencing discrimination as a customer. Dealerships that post flat prices charged to all customers may be preferable. African Americans, women, and others who are ignored or overcharged should choose to do business elsewhere and spread the word about negative (and positive) experiences. Others who have a distaste for discrimination toward any racial or ethnic group may also choose to do so.

Organizational leaders should make concerted efforts to ensure all customers are treated fairly. Salespeople should be trained to avoid discrimination against and stereotyping of customers. Leaders should take customer surveys (from purchasers as well as from those who shop but do not buy) and pay attention to the data gathered. Internal audits can determine if there is evidence of disparate treatment of customers based on demographic factors. Using mystery shoppers of different races can provide valuable information. Customer complaints should also be investigated and addressed. By prioritizing and attending to these matters before problems arise, organizations can build customer loyalty, generate future business, and avoid a host of negative outcomes.

Summary

This chapter has focused on the experiences of African Americans with diversity issues. African Americans in the United States, whose unique background involves discrimination deriving from their status as descendants of slaves or as more recent immigrants, vary in their education and employment but share many negative employment experiences. Fewer Blacks obtain college degrees than Whites and Asians, but more do than Latinos. Blacks at all educational levels, particularly Black

---

[93]Cox, T. & Blake, S. (1991). "Managing Cultural Diversity: Implications for Organizational Competitiveness. Academy of Management Executive: 5(3): 45–56.

women, receive lower returns on their educational investment than Whites; Blacks also experience access and treatment discrimination in organizations as job applicants and employees as well as discrimination as customers. Negative organizational experiences are associated with negative health effects for Blacks, which should provide both personal and organizational motivation to continue to emphasize fairness and equity in employment. Finally, we considered individual and organizational strategies to reduce discrimination, increase fairness and equity, and improve the climate for diversity in organizations.

KEY TERMS

Access discrimination — when people are denied employment opportunities, or "access" to jobs, based on their race, sex, age, or other factors not related to productivity.

Discouraged workers — people who have become so discouraged about the lack of employment opportunities that they have stopped looking for jobs and have dropped out of the workforce.

Glass ceiling — an invisible barrier that prevents women, minorities, and people with disabilities from advancing past a certain level in organizations.

Glass walls — invisible barriers that confine minorities and women to certain types of positions within organizations.

New racism — beliefs that racism no longer exists and that Blacks (or other racial groups) have attained excessive, unfair gains through programs such as affirmative action, resulting in

discrimination when opportunity or rationale to do so arises.

Racial socialization — behaviors, communications, and interactions concerning their cultural heritage and the appropriate responses to racial hostility and discrimination that Black parents model and explain to Black children.

Statistical discrimination — using observable characteristics (e.g., race, sex, age) as proxies for information about the productivity of workers.

Treatment discrimination — when people are employed but are treated differently once employed, receiving fewer job-related rewards, resources, or opportunities than they should receive based on job-related criteria.

Underemployed, Underemployment — the employment of workers at less than their full potential, including those working part-time, temporary, or intermittent jobs but desiring regular full-time work, those working for lower wages than their skills would indicate or in positions requiring considerably lower skills than they possess, and those involuntarily working outside of their fields.

QUESTIONS TO CONSIDER

1. What factor(s) caused the experiences of European and African newcomers to the United States in the period from the 1600s through the 1800s to be so different?
2. What does empirical research say about access and treatment discrimination against Blacks?
3. In Brief's empirical study of "new racism," unqualified Whites were

preferred over qualified Blacks. What role might pervasive stereotypes about Blacks play in decision makers' failure to promote clearly qualified Blacks, even those who have been working for organizations for a while and have demonstrated their competencies? What can be done about this?

4a. In the Bertrand and Mullainathan study of name-based discrimination, job applicants with "Black-sounding" names were granted interviews significantly fewer times than those with "White-sounding" names. Speculate on what might happen to a Black applicant who had a "White-sounding" name and was called for an interview. At what point(s) might prejudice eliminate the applicant from the selection process? What benefit(s) might accrue to such an applicant from being called for the interview? What are some specific things that organizations might do to reduce the likelihood of name-based discrimination in the selection process? How would they know if these steps were working?

4b. Do you know any Blacks with any of the "White-sounding" names used in the study or others more commonly associated with Whites? Do you know of any Whites with any of the "Black-sounding" names used in the study or others more commonly associated with Blacks? Discuss their interview and employment experiences with them.

5a. How do you think most African American customers respond when treated unfairly in a store (e.g., being passed over for service)? If an African American customer were to complain to store management about disparate treatment by an employee, what would you suggest the manager do to retain

the customer? How should the manager respond to the employee?

5b. How do you think most White customers would respond if they were served before Black customers who had arrived first in a store or restaurant? Would the White customers notice that the Black customers had been skipped? What would they do? How would they react if the Black customer complained? Have you observed (or experienced) such an event?

6. What is the racial and ethnic composition of the U.S. Army, Air Force, Navy, and Marines? How many Blacks as a proportion of the Army are in officer positions? Choose one other military organization and answer the same question.

7. How can underemployment affect the quality of a person's future employment? Explain.

ACTIONS AND EXERCISES

1. Observe employment of African Americans in your community in a particular place (such as a store, restaurant, office) in which there are White employees also. What do you observe that is relevant to diversity in organizations?

2. Conduct library or Internet research on the negative effects of discrimination on the health and well-being of African Americans. What does this research say about this relationship? What can individual Blacks do to minimize these health effects?

3. Use a calculator to make a chart projecting the effects of discrimination in initial salaries offered to Blacks and Whites and annual salary increases for

two equally qualified, college-educated new hires.

a. Make columns for starting salaries of $30,000 and $33,000, respectively, for the new employees. Assume the Black applicant earns a 4% increase per year and the White applicant earns a 6% increase per year, based on their performance evaluations.[94] What are the salary differences after ten years? After twenty years?

b. Make another column, based on the assumption that the White applicant receives promotions every three years and the Black applicant is promoted every five years. For promotions, assume a salary increase of an additional 10%. What are the salary differences after ten and twenty years given the differences in initial salaries, in increases, and in promotion rates?

c. What effects would such salary disparities have on each employee's and the employer's contributions to the employees' Social Security, tax-deferred savings plans, and retirement plans?

d. Research Summary 4.2, "Why Pay More? Race (and Gender) Discrimination in New Car Pricing," considers effects of discrimination against Blacks in car pricing. Speculate on the effects of lower initial starting salaries, lower salary increases, and fewer promotions, combined with high prices for consumer goods, mortgages, and insurance, on a person's ability to increase wealth.

4. For your private consideration, make a list of at least five common stereotypes about African Americans.

a. Beside each stereotype, write the name of a real African American person who *does not* fit this stereotype. Look first among friends, family members, or yourself, if applicable. If you cannot think of a person you know, use a public figure or celebrity.

b. Beside each common stereotype about African Americans, write the name of a real person, preferably one you know, who is *not* African American who has exhibited the stereotyped characteristic.

c. How many times did you use a friend, family member, or yourself, if applicable, instead of a public figure or celebrity? What is the effect in addressing stereotypes of knowing someone personally, and somewhat well, who is African American? How conscious an effort would one have to make to avoid behaving on the basis of these stereotypes?

5. Go to the EEOC Web site (www.eeoc. gov) to find current press releases involving access and treatment discrimination against Blacks. Assuming you are a powerful manager hired by the CEO, implement a plan at the offending organization to prevent this kind of thing from happening in the future. Provide at least five specific steps to be taken and five specific measures of success.

---

[94]Recall from Greenhaus et al. (1990) and Kraiger & Ford (1985) that Blacks receive lower performance evaluations and are rated as less promotable.

Latinos/Hispanics

CHAPTER
5

Chapter Objectives

After completing this chapter, readers should have a greater understanding of Hispanics and diversity in organizations. Specifically considered are:

- ❏ *the historical background and current status of Hispanics in the United States.*
- ❏ *the effects on diversity issues of higher population growth rates among Hispanics.*
- ❏ *diversity in race, education, participation rates, employment, and income levels among Hispanics in the United States.*
- ❏ *employment experiences of Hispanics, focusing on those of Latinas, immigrants, and managers and professionals.*
- ❏ *relationships between Latinos and Blacks.*
- ❏ *experiences of Hispanics with police misconduct and racial profiling.*
- ❏ *aspects of the growing Latino consumer market.*
- ❏ *individual and organizational measures that can be used to improve organizational experiences of Hispanics.*

Key Facts

The category Hispanic includes people with different origins and having distinct education, income, and employment experiences in the United States.

Hispanics can be White, Black, Asian, Native American, or other races, and race is contextual and variable among Hispanics.

Sixty percent of the Hispanic population in the United States is native-born. Many Hispanics are second-, third-, and fourth-generation Americans.

Strict "English-only" rules are generally not defensible under Title VII of the Civil Rights Act.

Access and treatment discrimination against Hispanics has been clearly documented; but, in some cases, Hispanic workers are preferred over Black (and sometimes White) workers.

Employers who express preferences for Hispanic immigrant workers pay less than those who do not express such preferences.

Introduction and Overview

Hispanics are the fastest-growing minority group in the United States; as of July 1, 2009, there were 48.4 million Hispanics in the country, up from 41.3 million just five years earlier. Hispanics include people from various races, including Blacks, Whites, American Indians, and Asians whose ancestors have resided in Central and South America for generations and who are native Spanish speakers. Although many are White, Hispanics are included in the "people of color" category, further confounding race, ethnicity, color, and minority group status. Many Latinos view their race as being cultural, often variable, and contextual.[1] The fluid continuum of race for Hispanics is different from the concept of race in the United States, which may cause confusion and identity issues for Hispanic immigrants. In addition, the confounding of race with ethnicity among Hispanics sometimes creates double jeopardy, in which they experience discrimination based on skin color as well as ethnicity.

This chapter considers the unique perspectives of Hispanics in the United States, recognizing their long history in the country, their struggles for civil rights, misperceptions and stereotypes about them, and their numerous contributions to diversity in organizations. As we will see, the diversity-related experiences of Hispanics vary by race, skin color, country of birth, English language fluency, and education.

Terminology

The U.S. Census Bureau describes Hispanics as people who identify themselves as having Mexican, Puerto Rican, Cuban, or other Spanish origin or culture, regardless of race. In this chapter, we interchange use of the Census term *Hispanic* with *Latino*, and when referring to women, we use the term *Latinas*. When comparing populations, unless specified, we generally use the terms *White* and *non-Hispanic White*, *Black* and *non-Hispanic Black* interchangeably, although, as discussed later, the distinctions between "race" and "ethnicity" are not universally agreed upon.[2]

When reporting research or historical events, the terms used in the referenced publication or those used during the historical period, including *Chicano* or *Chicana*, *Puerto Rican*, *Mexican* or *Mexican American*, *Cuban*, or *Peruvian* are used. As much as possible, we strive for accuracy, acknowledging the great diversity among this group and people's preferences for different terms.[3] People of Mexican, Cuban, and Puerto Rican descent are covered, along with selected research on Hispanics from other areas. Space constraints prevent detailed coverage of Hispanics from all backgrounds; readers are encouraged to continue their own investigations. •

▌ History of Hispanics in the United States

This section separately considers the history of people from Mexico, Puerto Rico, and Cuba in the United States. These three groups,

[1] Rodriguez, C. (2000). *Changing Race: Latinos, the Census, and the History of Ethnicity in the United States*. New York: New York University Press. See also Gallegos, P. V., & Ferdman, B. M. (2007). "Identity Orientations of Latinos in the United States: Implications for Leaders and Organizations." *The Business Journal of Hispanic Research*, 1(1): 26–41.

[2] Hitlin, S., Brown, J. S., & Elder, Jr., G. H. (2007). "Measuring Latinos: Racial vs. Ethnic Classification and Self-Understandings." *Social Forces*, 86(2): 587–611.

[3] See, for example, Ferdman, B. M., & Gallegos, P. I. (2001). "Racial Identity Development and Latinos in the United States." In C. L. Wijeyesinghe & B. W. Jackson, III (Eds.), *New Perspectives on Racial Identity Development*. New York: New York University Press; Gutierrez, O. R., Jr. (2005). "'Hispanic' vs. 'Latino': Why It Matters." *DiversityInc.com*, accessed August 17, 2005.

respectively, represent the largest group of Hispanic Americans (who also have the longest history in the United States), those with a clear dual-homeland and identity, and those who have been most economically successful after arriving in the United States.

Mexicans

The earliest known ancestors of Mexican Americans have a long history in what is now the United States, as indigenous people residing in the Southwest and large parts of Mexico long before the arrival of European Americans.[4] With the arrival of the Spaniards in the area in 1519, the colonization of "New Spain" and conquest of the indigenous people began.[5] Many mestizos were born as a result of intermarriages between Spaniards and indigenous women. Cultures and religions blended over the next centuries, as New Spain fought for freedom from Spanish rule. During the same period, the United States concluded the Louisiana Purchase and other treaties with Spain regarding land ownership. New Spain won its freedom in 1821, but disputes with the United States over Texas boundaries and rule continued. After the Mexican–American War, Mexicans residing in Texas were given the option of remaining on their now U.S. land and becoming Americans. Many chose to remain in the country, becoming Mexican Americans.[6]

Being declared Mexican Americans did not guarantee these people equal rights, however. Early on, Mexicans were classified as White for Census purposes, yet they were sometimes barred from restaurants and other businesses, harassed, and even lynched.[7] Between 1929 and 1939, many Mexican Americans were repatriated to Mexico under a program authorized by President Herbert Hoover. Estimates of the numbers of people involved range between 500,000 and 2 million, including many legal immigrants and U.S. citizens, who were sent ("back") to Mexico in an effort to free up jobs during the Depression. Some went voluntarily; others were forced to go by police and other authorities, leaving behind homes and possessions because of the sudden and forced nature of the repatriation. Ironically, many of those repatriated had never even been to Mexico.[8]

[4] Saenz, R. (1999). "Mexican Americans." In A. G. Dworkin & R. J. Dworkin (Eds.), *The Minority Report,* 3rd ed. Fort Worth, TX: Harcourt Brace Publishers, pp. 209–229.
[5] Ibid.
[6] Ibid.
[7] McLemore, D. (2004). "The Forgotten Carnage." *Dallas Morning News,* November 28, cover story.
[8] Fox, B. (2004). "Hispanics Deported in 1931 Seek Reparations." *Dallas Morning News* (Associated Press story), September 12, p. 33A.

Mexicans began large-scale migration to the United States again during World War II, and many who returned learned then that they were already U.S. citizens, by birth. As did the many Japanese who were interned (see Chapter 6), Mexicans often did not speak of the repatriation, but continued to distrust police and government authorities. Some purposely did not speak Spanish to help avoid identification and did not pass on the language to their offspring, which may explain why many of that generation do not know the language.

The well-known 1954 Supreme Court case of *Brown v. Board of Education* of Topeka that declared segregated schools illegal was preceded, in 1946, by *Mendez v. Westminster School District* in Orange County, California.[9] In the Mendez case, the segregation of Mexican children into Mexican schools was declared illegal. The judge ruled in favor of the Mexican plaintiffs because the separate education codes in California specifically called for separation of Chinese, Japanese, and American Indian children but made no reference to Mexican children. Despite the ruling, many California schools remained segregated. Texas schools were also segregated, under a provision of the 1876 constitution. The Texas segregation was intended to exclude Blacks but resulted in the separation of Mexican children as well. In some communities, there were White, Black, and Mexican schools, with the latter two being clearly "unequal."[10]

Mexicans in the United States also experienced residential segregation and segregation in public accommodations and businesses (e.g., theaters, pools). During World War II, Mexican American soldiers served valiantly but returned to their "second-class" citizenship status on coming back to the United States.[11] Like Blacks returning from the war (see Chapter 4), Mexican American soldiers became increasingly unwilling to accept such disparate treatment. A Mexican American physician, Dr. Hector Garcia, founded the G.I. Forum in an attempt to gain rights for Mexicans. The G.I. Forum worked against poll taxes (required for voting), to enroll Mexican children in schools, and to obtain medical benefits for Mexican veterans. The refusal to bury Felix Longoria, a soldier who had been killed in the war, in the White cemetery in Three Rivers, Texas, outraged the Mexican community. In response to the protests of the G.I. Forum, then Senator Lyndon Baines Johnson arranged for Longoria to be buried in

----

[9] Wollenberg, C. (1976). *All Deliberate Speed: Segregation and Exclusion in California Schools, 1855–1975.* Berkeley, CA: University of California Press.
[10] Valencia, R. R. (2000). "Inequalities and the Schooling of Minority Students in Texas: Historical and Contemporary Conditions." *Hispanic Journal of Behavioral Sciences*, 22: 445–459.
[11] Saenz (1999).

Arlington National Cemetery.[12] Later, as U.S. president, Johnson signed the Civil Rights Act into law.

In addition to veterans' rights, many involved in the Chicanos' quest for equality were pursuing workers' rights. César Chávez (founder of the United Farm Workers), Corky Gonzales, José Angel Gutierrez, Dolores Huerta, and Eliseo Medina are some of the people who worked for farm workers' rights, using strikes and boycotts to reduce wage discrimination, among other benefits. The Chicano movement emerged during the 1960s and 1970s, the same period in which strong and vocal Black, American Indian, and women's movements emerged. The Chicano movement took pride in the group's culture and emphasized members' Indian and Mexican heritage, dismissing the negative connotation of the term *Chicano*.[13] As we will discuss, Mexican Americans have obtained many rights, but some remain elusive, particularly for immigrants.

Puerto Ricans

About 9% of Hispanics are of Puerto Rican descent. Puerto Rico was seized by the United States in 1898 during the Spanish–American War. The Jones Act of 1917 extended citizenship to Puerto Ricans, who are thereby citizens at birth, whether born in the United States or in Puerto Rico. After the end of the war and the passage of the Jones Act, migrations of Puerto Ricans to the mainland seeking work significantly increased. Much of this migration, referred to as "the Great Migration," was facilitated by government-supervised contracts.[14] In the 1970s, many economically displaced Puerto Ricans began returning to the island, but high unemployment propelled many to return to the mainland in a circular migratory process.[15] When Stateside, most Puerto Ricans reside in New York City and surrounding areas. Many spend time in both New York and Puerto Rico, traveling frequently and easily between the two. This legal circular migration is unique among Hispanics and is made possible by the dual citizenship of Puerto Ricans.

Despite their dual citizenship and ease of physical movement between the mainland and the island, Puerto Ricans face social, cultural, economic,

---

[12] Saenz, R. (1999). See also "Justice for My People: the Hector Garcia Story." http://www .justiceformypeople.org/drhector.html, accessed October 24, 2010.

[13] Saenz (1999).

[14] Aranda, E. M. (2008). "Class Backgrounds, Modes of Incorporation, and Puerto Ricans' Pathways into the Transnational Professional Workforce." *American Behavioral Scientist*, 52(3): 426–456.

[15] Ibid.

and political barriers to inclusion that are similar to those experienced by other Hispanic immigrants.[16] Puerto Ricans are diverse in race and many are bilingual—Puerto Rico's official languages are English and Spanish. Puerto Rico has a history of slavery (abolished in 1873), racial segregation, and classism, which remain concerns for Puerto Ricans on the island and in the states today.

The average education and occupational attainment levels of Puerto Ricans are low, and they have high rates of unemployment and poverty. According to Tienda's analysis of Census data, Puerto Ricans have lower status than other Hispanics (e.g., Mexicans, Cubans) in the "ethnic" hiring queue.[17] As with other non-dominant groups, there is diversity in the experiences of Puerto Ricans, with some being well-educated and having high occupational status. As discussed in Individual Feature 5.1, Supreme Court Justice Sonia Sotomayor is of Puerto Rican descent.

Cubans

Cubans began arriving in the United States in large numbers in January 1959, when Fidel Castro obtained government power in Cuba by force. Castro had promised democracy and other freedoms, but the promised benefits did not materialize. During the remainder of 1959 through the mid-1970s, Cubans fled from political and economic instability in Cuba and from what appeared to be the beginnings of Communist rule. During 1960, an estimated 60,000 Cubans arrived in the United States, with at least 50% landing in Miami.[18] By the mid-1970s, more than 500,000 Cubans had fled to the United States.[19] At present, about half of the U.S. Cuban population lives in Miami.[20]

Early émigrés were often wealthy or middle class and able to bring money and property with them when they fled. Later émigrés were often destitute, as Castro began limiting what could be taken out of the country. Although they arrived without money or possessions, many in this group were professionals, including physicians, lawyers, teachers, and engineers. Most of the refugees were White Cubans, because some Black Cubans feared the racial unrest and discrimination that were rampant in

---

[16] Ibid.

[17] Tienda, M. (1989). "Puerto Ricans and the Underclass Debate." *Annals of the American Academy of Political Science, 501*(1): 105–119.

[18] Gay, K. (2000). *Leaving Cuba: From Pedro Pan to Elian.* Brookfield, CT: Twenty-first Century Books.

[19] Ibid.

[20] Facts for Features, Hispanic Heritage Month 2010: September 15–October 15. http://www.census.gov/newsroom/releases/archives/facts_for_features_special_editions/cb10-ff17.html, accessed October 16, 2010.

INDIVIDUAL FEATURE 5.1	*Supreme Court Justice Sonia Sotomayor*

Associate Supreme Court Justice Sonia Sotomayor, born in the Bronx, New York, in 1954, is a Latina of Puerto Rican descent. She grew up in a public housing project in the South Bronx, where her mother, a nurse, and father, who passed away when Sotomayor was only 9, instilled in her a love of learning and a belief in the power of education.

Sotomayor earned a bachelor's degree in 1976 from Princeton University, graduating summa cum laude. She studied law at Yale Law School and served as an editor of the *Yale Law Journal*, earning her law degree in 1979 and then working for five years as assistant district attorney in the New York County district attorney's office. In 1991, President George H. W. Bush nominated Sotomayor to the U.S. District Court, Southern District of New York, and she served in that role from 1992 to 1998. Next, she served as a judge on the U.S. Court of Appeals for the Second Circuit from 1998 to 2009.

President Barack Obama nominated Sotomayor to the Supreme Court on May 26, 2009, and she assumed this role on August 8, 2009. After her nomination, critics claimed her 2001 comment that a "wise Latina" would make different decisions than a White male judge was racist and problematic for a potential Supreme Court justice. As discussed in Chapter 3, researchers have found that male and female and White and minority judges do come to different decisions, in part based on their lived experiences. In one study of rulings in racial harassment cases, Black and White judges ruled against plaintiffs 54% and 79% of the time, respectively. In sex discrimination cases, female judges are more likely to rule for plaintiffs than male judges. Given the diversity of the population, and disturbing differences in deferred adjudication discussed in Research Summary 5.3, the need for judges from diverse backgrounds is an important aspect of judicial fairness.

Sources: Biographies of current justices of the Supreme Court. http://www.supremecourt.gov/about/biographies.aspx, accessed March 29, 2010; http://www.huffingtonpost.com/charles-h-green/sotomayor-was-right-the-f_b_245216.html; http://www.whitehouse.gov/the_press_office/Background-on-Judge-Sonia-Sotomayor/, accessed March, 19, 2011.

the United States during that time. Of the relatively few Afro-Cubans who did flee Cuba, most headed North instead of remaining in Florida in an attempt to avoid racism and unrest in the South.[21]

The federal government helped Cubans find a place in U.S. society and assisted professionals with retraining and recertification, scholarships, business loans, and permanent residential status.[22] Cubans have capitalized on these benefits, unprecedented and unparalleled for other immigrants, becoming financially and economically more successful than all other Hispanic immigrants and many others in U.S. history. As we will discuss, Cuban Americans have higher incomes and education levels than other Latinos, in some ways more closely mirroring

---

[21] Ibid.
[22] Ibid.

those of non-Hispanic Whites than of other Latinos and other minority group members.

■ RELEVANT LEGISLATION

Executive orders for affirmative action apply to Hispanics, as does Title VII of the Civil Rights Act. Title VII is relevant because of its prohibition against discrimination on the basis of race and national origin. Hispanics may be of any race, and many U.S. Hispanics are immigrants.

English-only Rules

English-only rules sometimes specifically target Hispanics, some of whom speak only Spanish. The Equal Employment Opportunity Commission (EEOC) regards such rules as justified only when needed for safe or efficient operation of the organization. Some situations in which English-only rules are justified include:

- for communications with customers, coworkers, or supervisors who only speak English
- in emergencies or other situations in which employees must speak a common language for safety reasons
- for cooperative work assignments in which speaking English promotes efficiency
- to enable supervisors who only speak English to monitor the performance of employees who speak with coworkers or customers as part of their job duties.[23]

English-only rules are not generally acceptable for break or lunch times or other nonwork periods. Employers' fears, insecurities, and biases are not legitimate criteria for implementing such rules, as apparently occurred in the Central Station Casino case.

Central Station Casino to Pay $1.5 Million in EEOC Settlement for National Origin Bias[24]

Hispanic Employees Verbally Harassed, Subjected to Speak-English-only Rules

Anchor Coin, doing business as Colorado Central Station Casino, Inc. (CCSC), agreed to settle a national origin discrimination lawsuit for $1.5 million and

---

[23] http://www.eeoc.gov/policy/docs/national-origin.html#VC, accessed October 21, 2010.
[24] Adapted from EEOC press release at http://www.eeoc.gov/eeoc/newsroom/release/archive/7-18-03a.html, accessed October 15, 2010.

other relief. The EEOC filed the suit on behalf of a class of Hispanic employees of the casino's housekeeping department who were verbally harassed and subjected to unlawful English-only rules.

The EEOC alleged that the human resources director, despite their objections, instructed several managers and supervisors to implement a blanket English-only language policy in the housekeeping department. The human resources director also instructed them to discipline any housekeeping employee who violated the policy. The housekeeping department had the highest concentration of Hispanic employees, and although some employees there were bilingual, others spoke only Spanish.

According to the EEOC, the reason given for implementing the restrictive language policy was that a non-Spanish-speaking employee thought that other employees were talking about her in Spanish, and that CCSC needed the policy for undefined "safety reasons." Following the new policy, management told the housekeeping staff that English was the official language of the casino and that Spanish could no longer be spoken. According to the litigation, managers chastised employees for speaking Spanish at any time, saying, "English-English-English" or "English-only." Other managers and non-Hispanic employees would shout "English, English" at the Hispanic employees when encountering them in the halls, resulting in the Hispanic employees being embarrassed and suffering emotional distress.

In the course of the suit, CCSC's claim of a "business necessity" basis for its misguided and discriminatory language policy was eroded by its own management witnesses who referred to the unlawful policy as unnecessary, wrong, and "stupid." At least one management witness testified that in his opinion the language policy arose out of the human resources director's insecurity, anger, and hurt feelings stemming from her perception that housekeeping employees were speaking about her in Spanish. As part of the settlement, CCSC denies all allegations contained in the suit. In addition to the monetary relief for the affected employees, the company will notify all its employees that it has no blanket English-only policy and provide training to ensure that discrimination does not occur.

Instead of banning non-English languages, as discussed later in the chapter, organizations might institute English, Spanish, and other important language classes for monolingual speakers, recognizing that multiple language fluency is an asset that can improve employee interactions and customer service.

▌ POPULATION

In 2009, there were 48.4 million Hispanics in the United States, representing about 16% of the total population. In the 1990 census, the nation's Hispanic population was 22.4 million.[25] The proportion of Hispanics in the United States is growing rapidly as a result of higher Hispanic immigration and birth rates when compared with other groups. As shown in Table 5.1,

TABLE 5.1 *Detailed Hispanic Origin, 2008*

	Number in Millions	**%**
Mexican	30.75	65.7
Puerto Rican	4.15	8.9
All Other Spanish/Hispanic/Latino	1.78	3.8
Cuban	1.63	3.5
Salvadoran	1.56	3.3
Dominican	1.33	2.8
Guatemalan	0.99	2.1
Colombian	0.88	1.9
Spaniard	0.63	1.3
Honduran	0.61	1.3
Ecuadorian	0.59	1.3
Peruvian	0.52	1.1
Nicaraguan	0.35	0.8
Venezuelan	0.21	0.4
Argentinean	0.20	0.4
Panamanian	0.15	0.3
Chilean	0.13	0.3
Costa Rican	0.12	0.3
Bolivian	0.09	0.2
Uruguayan	0.06	0.1
Other Central American	0.04	0.1
Other South American	0.02	0.0
Paraguayan	0.02	0.0
Total	46.82	100.0

Source: Adapted from Pew Hispanic Center, Statistical Portrait of Hispanics in the United States, 2008; their tabulations of 2008 American Community Survey. Accessed from: http://pewhispanic.org/files/factsheets/hispanics2008/Table%206.pdf, October 24, 2010.

---

[25] Facts for Features, Hispanic Heritage Month 2010: September 15–October 15.

the great majority of Hispanics in the United States are of Mexican origin, more than seven times as many as Puerto Ricans, who are the next largest group of Hispanics. Cubans, Salvadorans, and Dominicans are also populous groups. Forty-seven percent of U.S. Hispanics live in California and Texas, and 46% of the population of New Mexico is Hispanic—the highest of any state.[26] Hispanics are the largest minority group in twenty-one states, which are Arizona, California, Colorado, Connecticut, Florida, Idaho, Iowa, Kansas, Massachusetts, Nebraska, Nevada, New Hampshire, New Jersey, New Mexico, Oregon, Rhode Island, Texas, Utah, Vermont, Washington, and Wyoming.[27]

Hispanics are a youthful population, with a median age of 27.4 years, compared with 36.8 years for the population as a whole. Of all U.S. children under age five, 26% are Hispanic; 22% of children younger than 18 are Hispanic.[28] As the youthful population ages, more and more Hispanics will become potential workers. Organizational efforts to attract and retain Hispanic workers (e.g., Cox and Blake's resource acquisition) will become increasingly important.

Population by Race for Hispanics and Non-Hispanics

The meaning of *race* in terms of Hispanics is contextual, variable, and more complex than simply Black or White. As Table 5.2 shows, more than 30% of Hispanics report belonging to "some other race," with an additional 3.9% reporting two or more races.

Since the 1970 census, Americans have been able to state their Hispanic ethnicity, along with their race, and many write in "Hispanic" instead of choosing from the categories provided (e.g., White, Black, American Indian and Alaska Native, Asian). Research published by the Lewis Mumford Center notes important differences in this group, who are sometimes referred to as "Hispanic Hispanics" or "other race" Hispanics.[29] Table 5.3 lists national origins of Hispanics by race; Cubans are most likely to report themselves as White (85.4% versus 4.7% Black), Dominicans are least likely to do so, with 24.3% reporting White, 12.7% Black, and 63.1% classified as other or Hispanic Hispanic.[30]

---

[26] Facts for Features, Hispanic Heritage Month 2010: September 15–October 15.
[27] Ibid.
[28] Ibid.
[29] Logan, J. R. (2003). "How Race Counts for Hispanic Americans." Lewis Mumford Center. http://mumford.albany.edu/census/BlackLatinoReport/BlackLatinoReport.pdf, accessed October 21, 2010.
[30] Ibid. Table 3.

TABLE 5.2 *Racial Self-Identification among Hispanics and Non-Hispanics: 2008*

	Total		Hispanics		Non-Hispanics	
	Number	**%**	**Number**	**%**	**Number**	**%**
One race	297,073,242	97.7	45,010,544	96.1	252,062,698	98.0
White	228,220,501	75.1	29,256,845	62.5	198,963,659	77.3
Black or African American	37,646,898	12.4	872,561	1.9	36,774,337	14.3
American Indian and Alaska Native	2,456,397	0.8	454,410	1.0	2,001,987	0.8
Asian	13,405,682	4.4	178,612	0.4	13,227,070	5.1
Native Hawaiian and Other Pacific Islander	423,643	0.1	24,455	0.1	399,188	0.2
Some other race	14,920,118	4.9	14,223,661	30.4	696,457	0.3
Two or more races	6,986,486	2.3	1,811,932	3.9	5,174,554	2.0
Total	304,059,728	100.0	46,822,476	100.0	257,237,252	100.0

Source: Pew Hispanic Center, Statistical Portrait of Hispanics in the United States, 2008. Table 3. Racial Self-Identification among Hispanics and Non-Hispanics: 2008, accessed from http://pewhispanic.org/files/factsheets/hispanics2008/Table%203.pdf, October 24, 2010. Pew Hispanic Center tabulations from 2008 American Community Survey.

TABLE 5.3 *National Origins of Hispanics by Race (Percent)*

	White Hispanic	**Hispanic Hispanic**	**Black Hispanic**
Mexican	49.3%	49.7%	1.1%
Puerto Rican	49.0	42.8	8.2
Cuban	85.4	9.8	4.7
Dominican	24.3	63.1	12.7
Central American	42.1	53.9	4.1
South American	61.1	37.4	1.6
All others	48.6	48.2	3.2
Total	49.9	47.4	2.7

Source: Logan, J. R. (2003). "How Race Counts for Hispanic Americans." Lewis Mumford Center. http://mumford.albany.edu/census/BlackLatinoReport/BlackLatinoReport.pdf, accessed October 24, 2010.

▌ EDUCATION, EMPLOYMENT, AND EARNINGS

Education

Table 4.1 (Chapter 4) showed that Hispanics lag behind others in educational attainment. While only 67.3% of Hispanics (any race) had at least a high school degree in 2008, 87.1% of Whites and 83.0% of Blacks, respectively have at least a high school degree. Most strikingly, nearly 38% of Hispanics aged 25 and older did not complete high school (not shown). In comparison, 17% of Blacks, 13% of Whites, and 11% of Asians aged 25 and older did not complete high school. These low levels of educational attainment have significant implications for organizations, as Hispanics become a larger proportion of the U.S. population and of job applicants and employees. These factors affect recruitment and selection, training (including English as a second language for employees, and Spanish for managers, supervisors, and peers) and development, and compensation.

Although the average education levels of Hispanics are relatively low, there are many differences within the Hispanic population, including level of educational attainment. While about half of Mexicans have earned at least a high school diploma, 67% of Puerto Ricans and 71% of Cubans do. Nearly 19% of Cubans have at least a college degree, compared with less than 8% of Mexicans (not shown in Table 4.1).[31]

Misperception: Hispanics have low education levels.

Reality: Education levels of Hispanics differ by country of origin.

Research indicates that the educational performance of Latinos at the high school level is positively affected by the presence of Latino administrators and teachers.[32] At the college level, the presence of Latino teachers should also improve outcomes for Latinos. By increasing the numbers of business faculty of Latinos and others of color, the PhD Project, described in Organizational Feature 5.1, contributes to the greater representation of Latinos among business students and therefore as potential employees. The importance of Latino educational attainment to organizational competitiveness is evident from the number of corporate sponsors of the PhD Project, including the founding sponsor, KPMG.

Employment

Hispanic men have the highest employment participation rates of all men, with more than 80% in the workforce. In contrast, Latinas are least likely to be in the workforce relative to other women, with a 56.2% participation rate (see Table 4.2). In both years shown in Table 5.4, unemployment for Hispanics (of any race) varied by education level; it

[31] Ramirez, R., & de la Cruz, G. P. (2003). "The Hispanic Population in the United States: March 2002." *Current Population Reports*. U.S. Census Bureau: Washington, D.C., pp. 20–545.
[32] Ross, A. D., Rouse, S. M., & Bratton, K. A. (2010). "Latino Representation and Education: Pathways to Latino Student Performance." *State Politics and Policy Quarterly*, 10(1): 69–95.

ORGANIZATIONAL FEATURE 5.1	*The PhD Project: Increasing Diversity through Holistic Means*

As their proportions in the workforce increase, the lower educational levels among Latinos, Blacks, and Native Americans compared to those of non-Hispanic Whites are an important diversity concern. The PhD Project is an organization designed to improve workforce diversity by improving the diversity of faculty at business schools by attracting underrepresented minorities to doctoral programs. The rationale for this approach was that having more diversity at the front of the classroom would increase the amount of diversity among students in the classroom. In 1994, the PhD Project estimated that fewer than 300 of the 22,000 business school faculty in the United States were from underrepresented minority groups. With the help of the PhD Project, the number of Latinos, Blacks, and Native Americans on certain business school faculties increased from 294 to 686 between 1994 and 2004.

The PhD Project believes that increasing the diversity of business school faculty will

a. encourage more underrepresented minorities to pursue business degrees.
b. improve the performance and completion rate of underrepresented minorities by providing role models and more natural mentors.
c. better prepare all business students for today's multicultural society and work environment.

Recognizing the importance of diversity to organizational success, many universities and well-known corporations have joined in supporting the PhD Project. Sponsors include PhD Project founder KPMG Foundation, the Graduate Management Admission Council, Citigroup Foundation, Ford Motor Company, Daimler/Chrysler Corporation Fund, GE Foundation, Abbott Labs, JP Morgan Chase, Hewlett-Packard, and numerous other companies. These sponsors believe that participating in the PhD Project signals to its employees and to universities commitment to diversity in the workforce.

The PhD Project provides peer support and assists selected students in obtaining scholarships and funding to obtain a PhD. Doctoral students involved in the PhD Project have higher rates of completion of their degrees and are more likely to work in academic positions than other students. There are currently more than 400 PhD Project students in doctoral programs around the nation.

_____

Sources: http://phdproject.com/index.html, accessed January 1, 2005; "In Just 10 Years, the PhD Project Has More Than Doubled the Corps of Minority Business School Faculty." Press Releases, Ned Steele Communications; http://phdproject.com/10thanniversary.pdf, accessed January 1, 2005.

QUESTIONS TO CONSIDER

1. *The PhD Project estimates that, on average, fewer than one Black, Latino, or Native American business faculty member exists at universities in the United States. If you are a university student, or have studied at that level, how many Black, Latino, or Native American faculty do/did you have? Estimate or investigate the actual proportion of Black, Latino, or Native American faculty at a university (that is not a historically Black university) with which you are familiar.*

2. *What are the potential effects on White students and on students of color of a severe underrepresentation of Blacks, Latinos, or Native Americans among university-level faculty?*

3. **What are the benefits for White students and students of color of having minority faculty members?**

4. **The PhD Project assumes that having more faculty of color will increase the probability that students of color will attend**

and complete college, reducing the education gap between Whites and Blacks, Latinos, and Native Americans. Investigate the changes in college completion rates for these groups between 1995 and the present.

is higher than that of Blacks and Asians but lower than that of non-Hispanic Whites. For example, in 2003, at the highest educational level, Latino unemployment is higher, at 4.1, than the widely reported overall average of 3.1 and higher than unemployment for Whites (2.8), but lower than that of Asians (4.4) and Blacks (4.5). At the high school graduate level, the Latino unemployment of 5.9 is higher than the average of all groups (5.5), Whites (4.8), and Asians (5.6), but lower than the rate for Blacks (9.3). In 2009, a striking difference is that during the recession of that year, Hispanic unemployment at the lowest education level is slightly lower than non-Hispanic White unemployment; both are lower than the average rate for the population.[33] As discussed later in the chapter, this apparent preference for Hispanic workers may be evidence of ulterior motives on the part of employers.

TABLE 5.4 *Unemployment Level by Educational Attainment by Race: 2003 and 2009*

	Total		White		Black		Asian		Latino	
	2003	2009	2003	2009	2003	2009	2003	2009	2003	2009
Less than high school	8.8	14.6	7.8	13.9	13.9	21.3	9.5	8.4	8.2	13.7
High school graduate, incl. GED	5.5	9.7	4.8	9.0	9.3	14.0	5.6	7.5	5.9	10.4
Some college, no degree	5.2	8.6	4.5	7.9	8.6	12.1	6.4	8.9	5.8	9.6
Associate's degree	4.0	6.8	3.6	6.2	6.2	10.3	5.2	7.5	5.3	8.5
Bachelor's degree and higher	3.1	4.6	2.8	4.2	4.5	7.3	4.4	5.6	4.1	5.7

Bachelor's degree and higher includes persons with bachelor's, master's, professional, and doctoral degrees. Persons whose ethnicity is identified as Latino may be of any race.

Sources: For 2009, Bureau of Labor Statistics (2009). "Employment Status of the Civilian Noninstitutional Population 25 Years and Over by Educational Attainment, Sex, Race, and Hispanic or Latino Ethnicity." http://www.bls.gov/cps/cpsaat7.pdf, accessed October 29, 2010. For 2003, Bureau of Labor Statistics (2003). "Employment Status of the Civilian Noninstitutional Population 25 Years and Over by Educational Attainment, Sex, Race, and Hispanic or Latino Ethnicity." http://www.bls.gov/cps/cpsaat7.pdf, accessed October 22, 2004.

....

[33] Because the population of Hispanics includes White Hispanics (62.5% of Hispanics report being White), this confounds the rate of Hispanic unemployment.

TABLE 5.5 *Socioeconomic Characteristics of Hispanic Groups and Non-Hispanic Blacks, 2000*

	Foreign-born (%)	Speak Other Language (%)	Years of Education	Median Income	Unemployed (%)	Below Poverty (%)
White Hispanic	38.8	75.7	11.0	$39,900	8.0	24.1
Hispanic Hispanic	43.8	82.6	9.9	$37,500	9.5	27.7
Black Hispanic	28.2	60.8	11.7	$35,000	12.3	31.5
Hispanic Total	40.9	78.6	10.5	$38,500	8.8	26.0
Non-Hispanic Black	6.4	6.3	12.5	$34,000	11.0	29.7

Source: Logan, J. R. (2003). "How Race Counts for Hispanic Americans." Lewis Mumford Center. http://mumford.albany.edu/census/BlackLatinoReport/BlackLatinoReport.pdf, accessed October 24, 2010.

Earnings

Table 4.4 showed that as with unemployment by race and Hispanic origin, the earnings picture for Hispanics and non-Hispanics is complex. Overall average earnings for Hispanic men are lower than those of White, Black, and Asian men, reflecting the disproportionate amount of Hispanic men with low levels of education. For those with a high school diploma, the mean earnings of Hispanic men are lower than those of other men. As education levels increase, however, the earnings of Hispanic men begin to exceed those of Black men. Results for Hispanic women are also unexpected, although not as extreme. At the lowest education levels, the earnings of Latinas lag those of all other women. At the highest level, Latinas earn slightly more than non-Hispanic White and Black women. Median earnings (not shown) reflect the same patterns.

Although the 2009 data broken down by Hispanic race are not available, Table 5.5 presents socioeconomic characteristics of Hispanic groups in 2000 that contributed to differences in earnings, unemployment, and poverty and may provide some explanatory clues as to the unexpected level of mean earnings of Hispanics with more education. As Table 5.5 shows, the median earnings for White Hispanics are highest, followed by Hispanic Hispanics, and Black Hispanics. Table 5.5 also provides insight into other differences among Hispanics based on race, discussed in the following section.

■ ORGANIZATIONAL EXPERIENCES OF HISPANICS

The earnings and employment experiences of Latinos are strongly affected by their education, English language fluency, nativity, sex, race, and skin color. Research indicates that they sometimes face treatment and access discrimination by employers, customer discrimination, racial profiling, and police misconduct. We consider some of these factors in the following sections.

Race and Hispanic Ethnicity and Employment Outcomes

As we have discussed, there are Black Hispanics, White Hispanics, those who self-report as "some other race," and others. A research report by the Lewis Mumford Center for Comparative Urban and Regional Research suggests that race divides U.S. Hispanics in ways similar to how it divides non-Hispanics.[34] As shown in Table 5.5, Hispanics who are White have higher incomes and lower unemployment and poverty rates than Black and other-race Hispanics. Although they have more education on average than White Hispanics, Black Hispanics fare considerably worse than White Hispanics in terms of income, poverty, unemployment, and residential segregation. White Hispanics are also less residentially segregated than other Hispanics—they are more likely to live among White non-Hispanics and to marry non-Hispanic Whites. Levels of intermarriage with Whites are one measure of the strength of discrimination against particular groups.[35] Those interested in race, ethnicity, and diversity in organizations are well advised to consider race when investigating the experiences and opportunities of U.S. Hispanics.

Access and Treatment Discrimination

As with African Americans, many researchers have found evidence of access and treatment discrimination against Hispanics. In one paired test conducted in Washington, D.C., White and Hispanic testers called or sent résumés to apply for nearly 500 advertised jobs.[36] The applicants were well-matched, with the Hispanic applicants having slightly higher qualifications. Their names provided clues to their ethnicity (e.g., Juanita Ybarra Alvarez versus Julie Anne Mason). The mailed résumés contained an additional clue in that Latinos had attended high school in Texas and

---

[34] Logan, J. R. (2003). For additional research on race and Hispanic origin, see Gomez, C. (2000). "The Continual Significance of Skin Color: An Exploratory Study of Latinos in the Northeast." *Hispanic Journal of Behavioral Sciences*, 22: 94–103; Telles, E. E., & Murguia, E. (1990). "Phenotype Discrimination and Income Differences among Mexican Americans." *Social Science Quarterly*, 73: 120–122.

[35] See Dworkin, A. G., & Dworkin, A. (1999). "What Is a Minority?" In A. G. Dworkin & R. J. Dworkin (Eds.), *The Minority Report*. Fort Worth, TX: Harcourt Brace Publishers, pp. 11–27; Herring, C. (1999). "African Americans in Contemporary America: Progress and Retrenchment." In A. G. Dworkin & R. J. Dworkin (Eds.), *The Minority Report*. Fort Worth, TX: Harcourt Brace Publishers, pp. 181–208.

[36] Bendick, M., Jr., Jackson, C., Reinoso, V., & Hodges, L. (1991). "Discrimination against Latino Job Applicants: A Controlled Experiment." *Human Resource Management*, 30(4): 469–484.

White applicants in Michigan. Clear patterns in access discrimination emerged. At times, Hispanics were told there was no job available, yet when the White applicant called fifteen minutes later, she or he was scheduled for an interview. Hispanic applicants were also less likely to be asked about their previous work experience and other qualifications. In all, in more than 22% of the cases, Hispanic applicants were less likely to advance in the selection process. During most of the phone calls, the applicants spoke with a receptionist or secretary, which emphasizes the importance of training and monitoring decisions and behaviors of everyone (not just managers and supervisors) who will have any influence on the selection decision, including those with whom initial contact is made.

Multiple targets and types of discrimination and harassment. As is evident in the following description of the case against Mercury Air Centers, discrimination and harassment frequently have multiple targets and perpetrators, often from diverse backgrounds. Rutgers law professor T. K. Hernández has examined Latino **inter-ethnic employment discrimination**, which she defined as discrimination among non-White racial and ethnic groups, and found it to be more common than expected.[37]

Mercury Air Centers to Pay $600,000 for National Origin, Race, and Sex Harassment in EEOC Suit[38]

Salvadoran Airport Employee Was Promoted Despite Harassment of Filipino, Guatemalan, and Mexican Male Workers, Federal Agency Charged

Aircraft services provider Mercury Air Centers, Inc. will pay $600,000 and furnish other relief to settle a national origin, race, and sex harassment lawsuit filed by the EEOC. According to the EEOC, the seven victims—including one Filipino male and six Hispanic males—endured a barrage of harassing comments on the part of a Salvadoran male coworker. The EEOC claims that a Filipino line technician was regularly referred to in derogatory racial terms, as a "stupid Chinese," and subjected to offensive statements about Filipinos. The alleged harasser derided the Guatemalan victims with derogatory remarks regarding their national origin, including references to them as "stupid Guatemaltecos" and stating that Guatemalans are useless and inferior to Salvadorans. Prior to learning the actual national origin of one of the Guatemalan victims, the alleged harasser also called him a "stupid Mexican."

---

[37] Hernández, T. K. (2007). "Latino Inter-Ethnic Employment Discrimination and the 'Diversity Defense.'" *Harvard Civil Rights–Civil Liberties Law Review*, 42(2): 259–316.
[38] Adapted from EEOC press release at http://www.eeoc.gov/eeoc/newsroom/release/8-9-2010.cfm, accessed October 16, 2010.

The EEOC contends that the alleged harasser also repeatedly hurled offensive racial and sexual remarks toward the claimants and at least two African American employees, which included usage of the N-word and requests for sexual favors. He also allegedly grabbed his genitals in their presence and engaged in unwanted sexual touching. Despite complaints regarding this inappropriate behavior, the EEOC alleged that Mercury Air Centers' management officials failed to fully investigate or address the alleged harassment, and instead promoted the man to a supervisory position.

The settlement includes total monetary relief of $600,000 to be paid to at least seven employees along with a group of unidentified class members. The company also agreed to a two-year consent decree that calls for the appointment of an equal employment opportunity (EEO) officer to ensure compliance with antidiscrimination laws, along with an antidiscrimination policy, training, procedures, and reporting requirements to the EEOC.

According to the district director of the EEOC's Los Angeles District Office, "as the American workforce becomes increasingly more diverse, the potential for interminority and same-sex discrimination also rises. Employers must be mindful not to downplay such forms of discrimination, which can be just as demoralizing to the workforce as more traditional civil rights violations."

According to Hernández, minorities, through inter-ethnic discrimination, are "complicit in maintaining racial hierarchy in the workplace."[39] She emphasizes that the mere presence of a diverse workforce does not mean there is equality, inclusion, and absence of discrimination, as evident in the Mercury Air Centers case.[40] Organizational leaders should attend to the possibility of a continued racial hierarchy, such as the glass ceiling or walls for members of certain groups (but not for others), even in workplaces that are diverse by the numbers.[41] When such hierarchies exist, taking concerted and overt measures to dismantle them is imperative to promoting diversity *and* inclusion. Further, researchers have found that in addition to the direct negative effects on the targets of ethnic harassment, bystanders who observed ethnic harassment (but who were not directly

[39] Hernández (2007), p. 264.
[40] Hernández (2007).
[41] Cocchiara, F. K., Connerley, M. L., & Bell, M. P. (2010). "'A GEM' for Increasing the Effectiveness of Diversity Training." *Human Resource Management*, 49(4): 1093–1111; Thomas, D. A., & Ely, R. J. (1996). "Making Differences Matter: A New Paradigm for Managing Diversity." *Harvard Business Review*, 74(5): 79–90.

targeted by it) had negative occupational, health-related, and psychological consequences similar to those of the direct target.[42] Aside from the moral and social concerns associated with such harassment, individual and organizational costs, including job satisfaction and turnover, should provide further impetus for eliminating such harassment.

Hispanic Immigrants at Work

There are more Hispanic immigrants in the United States than any other group of immigrants. About 40% of the Hispanic population is foreign-born and nearly half (47%) of all immigrants in the United States are Hispanic.[43] For Latinos, being an immigrant is associated with lower education and lower wages but, ironically, not with lower employment levels. Immigrants' relatively high employment levels in part reflects their willingness to work in jobs viewed as undesirable by other workers. These jobs are often low-wage, dangerous jobs, with little or no opportunity for advancement and with other negative attributes. Both documented and undocumented Hispanic immigrants are disproportionately represented in dangerous industries.[44] In recognition of the danger involved in many Hispanic immigrants' jobs (e.g., construction, meat packing), the Occupational Safety and Health Administration (OSHA) is working to improve workplace safety, providing safety materials and training in Spanish and working to educate workers of their rights.[45]

Misperception: Immigrant workers are preferred because they have a higher work ethic than native-born Americans.

Reality: Immigrants are often preferred because they often will work for lower wages and are less likely to complain about mistreatment than native-born Americans.

Despite being preferred over native-born workers in some cases, immigrants experience various types of discrimination and exploitation.

[42] Low, K. S. D., Radhakrishnan, P., Schneider, K. T., & Rounds, J. (2007). "The Experiences of Bystanders of Workplace Ethnic Harassment." *Journal of Applied Social Psychology*, 37(10): 2261–2297.

[43] Facts for Features, Hispanic Heritage Month 2010: September 15–October 15.

[44] Statement of John L. Henshaw, Assistant Secretary of Labor for Occupational Safety and Health before the Subcommittee on Employment, Safety, and Training Committee on Health, Education, Labor, and Pensions, United States Senate. http://www.osha.gov/pls/oshaweb/owadisp.show_document?p_table=testimonies&p_id=286, accessed October 24, 2010.

[45] http://www.osha.gov/pls/oshaweb/owadisp.show_document?p_table=NEWS_RELEASES&p_id=17994, accessed October 24, 2010.

In one large study of documented immigrants, researchers found—after controlling for human capital characteristics including education, type of employment in home country, and English language proficiency—that immigrants with the lightest skin color earned an average of 17% more than comparable immigrants with the darkest skin color.[46] The study included immigrants to the United States from various places (e.g., Canada, China, Ethiopia, India, Nigeria, Peru, Philippines, Russia, the United Kingdom, and Vietnam). The advantages of lighter skin among immigrants, regardless of racial category, are similar to those that some research indicates are experienced by Blacks in the United States.[47]

Along with discrimination based on skin color, immigrant workers, particularly undocumented ones, endure exploitation through low wages, additional hours with no overtime, sexual harassment and assault, and various other abuses. Denise Segura has documented the experiences of Chicanas, noting the particular issues that undocumented workers face that make them susceptible to threats of deportation or being reported to the Immigration and Naturalization Service if they complain about abuse.[48] In their book *Stories Employers Tell*, Philip Moss and Chris Tilly describe employers' stated preferences for Latino workers and their praise of the "immigrant work ethic." One employer specifically explained that he viewed hiring Latinos as contributing to his organization's competitive advantage: "We have to have a competitive edge, and our edge is that our prices are lower.... All of my guys, practically, start at five dollars an hour." He went on to say, "some of the competitors that we deal with pay $15 per hour."[49] Some employers' preferences for immigrant workers are clearly related to immigrants' tolerance of lower wages. Moss and Tilly's findings indicated that, overall, employers who preferred Hispanic or Asian immigrants over native-born American workers paid noticeably lower wages. In organizations where at least one manager praised the immigrant work ethic, the wage penalty was 39 cents per hour. When half or more managers praised immigrant workers, the wage penalty was 96 cents per hour.

Employers are able to exploit immigrant workers more easily than native-born workers because of immigrants' fears of deportation and little

[46] Hersch, J. (2008). "Profiling the New Immigrant Worker: The Effects of Skin Color and Height." *Journal of Labor Economics*, 26(2): 345–385.

[47] Keith, V. M., & Herring, C. (1991). "Skin Tone and Stratification in the Black Community." *American Journal of Sociology*, 97(3): 60–78.

[48] Segura, D. A. (1992). "Chicanas in White-Collar Jobs: 'You Have to Prove Yourself More.'" *Sociological Perspectives*, 35: 163–182.

[49] Moss, P., & Tilly, C. (2001). *Stories Employers Tell: Race, Skill, and Hiring in America*. New York: Russell Sage Foundation, p. 117.

government attention to the matter.[50] In 2005, Walmart Stores, Inc. agreed to settle the largest case to that date involving immigrant labor. The U.S. government alleged that Walmart knowingly hired undocumented immigrants from Mexico, Eastern Europe, and other countries, even though the hiring was done through contractors rather than by Walmart directly. The $11 million settlement was almost four times as large as the largest previous settlement involving hiring undocumented immigrants but still allegedly amounted to less than one hour's sales at Walmart.[51] An additional civil suit filed by some former workers alleged that the workers, undocumented immigrants, were not paid for overtime, even though they often worked seven days per week.

Joseph Healey assessed the conflict between concern over immigration and willingness to benefit from and participate in it:

Two points seem clear in the midst of the frequently intense and continuing debate over immigration. First, prejudice and racism are part of what motivates people to oppose immigration, and second, immigrants, legal and illegal, continue to find work with Anglo employers and niches in American society in which they can survive. The networks that have delivered cheap immigrant labor for the low-wage sector continue to operate as they have for more than a century. Frequently, the primary beneficiaries of this long-established system are not the immigrants, but employers who benefit from a cheaper, more easily exploited workforce and American consumers who benefit from lower prices in the marketplace. (p. 174)[52]

The EEOC's "Justice, Safety, and Equality in the Workplace" initiative seeks to combat the "exploitation of Latino immigrants through increased education, outreach, and enforcement of the nation's anti-discrimination and labor laws."[53] In recognition of their large immigrant populations, the program began in Houston, Texas, and expanded to Dallas two years later. The EEOC works with the Wage and Hour Division of the U.S. Department of Labor, OSHA, the Office of Federal Contract Compliance Programs (OFCCP), police departments, and community groups to accomplish its goals.

[50] Solis, D., & Mittelstadt, M. (2005). "Walmart to Settle Immigrant Case." *Dallas Morning News*, March 19. Section D, p. 1.
[51] Ibid.
[52] Healey, J. F. (2004). *Diversity and Society: Race, Ethnicity, and Gender.* Thousand Oaks, CA: Pine Forge Press, pp. 157–188.
[53] EEOC (2003). "EEOC to Offer a New Source of Assistance for Immigrant Community in Dallas." www.eeoc.gov/press/6-6-03.html, accessed October 28, 2010.

Latinos and Blacks at Work

Preferences for immigrants over native-born workers often disadvantage Black workers when they are no longer considered for jobs now filled by Hispanic immigrants.[54] This creates hostility between two groups who are both considered "minority" groups in the United States, even though both experience discrimination at times and are both non-dominant groups. Despite similarities, many differences exist in the experiences of Blacks and Hispanics, particularly between Blacks and White Hispanics. As discussed in the previous section, Latino immigrants in many cases are preferred over Black employees, in part due to perceptions that Latinos are hard workers and that Blacks are not and also partly due to employers' preference for workers who are more easily exploited.[55] These and other differences serve to divide non-dominant group members and are counterproductive in the quest for equality and inclusion for all workers.[56]

In October 2010, Tyson Foods agreed to pay damages in the Department of Labor's finding that the company had discriminated against 157 Black and 375 White applicants for laborer positions at its bacon processing plant in Texas.[57] Tyson agreed to pay $560,000 in back pay and interest and to make job offers to fifty nine of the eligible applicants as positions became available. Ironically, that agreement followed a 2008 case in which a Labor Department judge found systematic hiring discrimination against Hispanic applicants in an affiliated Tyson company in Wisconsin.[58] As is evident from those two contrasting cases, Hispanic applicants are at times perceived as more desirable employees (laborers) than Blacks and sometimes than Whites. At other times, Hispanic applicants are seen as less desirable.

Latinos who are also Black or mixed race further complicate analyses of Latino and Black relationships and experiences. Whereas the Black–White racial divide is pervasive in the United States, as mentioned earlier, the divide is more complex among Hispanics. In the United States, Black and darker skinned Dominicans, Puerto Ricans, and other Hispanics face

[54] Shih, J. (2002). "'... Yeah, I Could Hire This One, But I Know It's Gonna Be a Problem': How Race, Nativity, and Gender Affect Employers' Perceptions of the Manageability of Job Seekers." *Ethnic and Racial Studies*, 25(1): 99–119.

[55] Moss & Tilly (2001), p. 117.

[56] Jordan, M. (2006, January 24). "Blacks vs. Latinos at Work: More African Americans Claim They Are Passed Over for Hispanics in Hiring." *Wall Street Journal*, p. B1. See also the discussion of the "model minority" stereotype, which pits Asians against Blacks and Hispanics (Chapter 6).

[57] "U.S. Labor Department Settles Hiring Discrimination Case with Tyson Refrigerated Processed Meats in Vernon, Texas." http://www.dol.gov/opa/media/press/ofccp/ofccp20101461.htm, accessed October 21, 2010.

[58] Ibid.

"intense stigmatization, prejudice, and discrimination to which all people of African origin are subjected."[59] Black Hispanics are more likely to live among and intermarry with non-Hispanic Blacks than are White or other-race Hispanics. However, while they sometimes appear and are treated as simply "Black," Black Hispanics' experiences and identity may be quite different from those of non-Hispanic Blacks and non-Black Hispanics, again emphasizing the need to avoid overgeneralization and categorization on visible factors.[60]

Latinas at Work

As discussed earlier, the participation rates of Latinas in the workforce are lowest among non-Hispanic White, Black, and Asian women. Although Latinas are less likely to be in the workforce than other women, the majority of Latinas (more than 56%) are indeed in the workforce. Nearly 9 million of them were in the workforce in 2008, a 53% increase since 1998.[61] These participation rates and the large number of workers make inclusion of the unique perspective of Latinas an important diversity concern.

Misperception: Due to strong cultural traditions, Latinas are unlikely to work outside the home.

Reality: Nearly 60% of Latinas work outside the home, rates similar to the participation rates of other women.

As women and as minorities, Latinas in formal organizations are subject to multiple forms of disadvantage. They tend to work in female-dominated positions with other women of color, and the larger the proportion of women of color, the lower the wages overall.[62] Between 1990 and 2001, the employment of Latinas in the private sector increased from 2.9% to 4.7%. Crop production employs 18.5% of Hispanic women (and 61.8% of all Hispanics).[63] In the Southwest,

[59] Duany, J. (1998). "Reconstructing Racial Identity: Ethnicity, Color, and Class Among Dominicans in the United States and Puerto Rico." *Latin American Perspectives,* 25(3): 147–172, text quoted from p. 148.
[60] Hernández (2007).
[61] U.S. Department of Labor. "Employment Status of Women and Men in 2008." http://www.dol.gov/wb/factsheets/Qf-ESWM08.htm, accessed October 21, 2010.
[62] Baker, S. G. (1999). "Mexican-Origin Women in Southwestern Labor Markets." In I. Brown (Ed.), *Latinas and African American Women at Work.* New York: Russell Sage Foundation, pp. 244–269.
[63] "Women of Color Make Gains in Employment and Jobs Status: Stubborn Patterns Still Persist Among African American, Hispanic, Asian, and Native American Women." http://www.eeoc.gov/eeoc/newsroom/release/7-31-03a.cfm, accessed October 30, 2010.

RESEARCH SUMMARY 5.1	*Employment Hardship among Mexican-Origin Women*

Employment hardship includes joblessness, involuntary part-time work, and working poverty. Underemployment is also an aspect of employment hardship and is associated with low wages and no medical and pension benefits. In a longitudinal study, Roberto De Anda of Portland State University investigated the prevalence of employment hardship among Mexican-origin women compared with non-Hispanic White women. The sample included 60,000 households, of which 3,000 were of Mexican origin; data were collected in 1992, 1996, and 2000, during a period of economic expansion.

De Anda controlled for factors that could contribute to employment hardship, including length of residence in the United States and characteristics of the jobs themselves. After controlling for those factors, De Anda found that Mexican-origin women were 1.7 times more likely than non-Hispanic White women to experience employment hardship. These disparities existed at lower (e.g., less than high school) and higher (some college or college degree) educational levels and varied by job sector. For women

in the least-skilled occupations, Mexican-origin women were 3.1 times as likely as White women to experience employment hardship. De Anda also found that 20% of the Mexican-origin women in his sample were in poverty, despite working, and one-third experienced employment hardship.

Young Mexican women (16 to 29 years old) were more likely to be participating in the labor force than young White women but faced a higher risk of employment hardship. Because employment hardship works to reduce one's likelihood of future adequate employment, De Anda expressed concern about young Mexican women's prospects for improvement in the future. He found that Mexican-origin women who had been in the United States for more than ten years had employment outcomes similar to those of Mexican-origin women who were born in the United States. Both fared better than did women who had arrived in the country more recently.

Source: De Anda, R. M. (2005). "Employment Hardship Among Mexican-Origin Women." *Hispanic Journal of Behavioral Sciences*, 27: 43–59.

Latinas (primarily Mexican Americans) work in agriculture and food processing, in housekeeping departments of hotels and motels, and in other service jobs. In the Northeast, Latinas (primarily Puerto Ricans and Dominicans) often work in the garment industry, although these jobs are declining and many workers are being displaced. As Table 4.4 shows, Latinas earn about 72% of what Hispanic men earn. Research Summary 5.1 discusses the employment hardship experienced by many Latinas of Mexican origin.

Along with hardship in employment, Latinas are sometimes targeted by virulent sexual harassment, similar to the racialized sexual harassment that occurs against Black women, discussed in Chapter 4. These behaviors perpetrated by high- and low-level managers, supervisors, and coworkers who prey on women whom they believe are most vulnerable. In a case against Nine West and Jones Apparel, the EEOC alleged that two high-level managers at the company's headquarters subjected Hispanic females to sexual solicitation, explicit jokes and comments, groping, and insulting remarks about their Hispanic origin.[64] Nine West agreed to a $600,000 settlement, but ABM Industries agreed to pay nearly ten times as much to settle its egregious sexual harassment of Hispanic women.

ABM Industries Settles EEOC Sexual Harassment Suit for $5.8 Million[65]

Class of Hispanic Janitorial Workers Sexually Harassed, One Raped by Supervisor, Federal Agency Charged

According to ABM's Web site, www.abm.com, ABM Janitorial Services is a *Fortune* 1000 provider of commercial cleaning services, operating in branches nationwide. ABM Industries, Inc. and subsidiaries ABM Janitorial Services, Inc. and ABM Janitorial Services Northern California, Inc. will pay $5.8 million and provide other relief to a class of twenty-one Hispanic female janitorial workers, settling an egregious sexual harassment lawsuit filed by the EEOC.

The sexual harassment began around 2001, with the most severe forms involving sexual assaults of some women beginning in 2005 throughout California's Central Valley region. The EEOC asserted that the twenty-one class members were victims of varying degrees of unwelcome touching, explicit sexual comments, and requests for sex by fourteen male coworkers and supervisors, one of whom was a registered sex offender. Some of the harassers allegedly often exposed themselves, groped female employees' private parts from behind, and even raped at least one of the victims, the EEOC said. The EEOC's suit charged that ABM failed to respond to the employees' repeated complaints of harassment, which made for a dangerous and sexually hostile work environment. Many of the harassers continued to work despite the complaints.

The EEOC filed suit against ABM in 2007, and the settlement was reached in 2010. Aside from the monetary relief, the three-year consent decree settling the suit requires ABM to:

- designate an outside equal employment opportunity monitor to ensure the effectiveness of ABM's investigations and complaint policies and procedures, and assist in antiharassment training to employees;

---

[64] "Nine West, Jones Apparel to Pay $600,000 to Settle National Origin and Sex Bias Suit." http://www.eeoc.gov/press/5-22-06b.html, accessed October 23, 2010.

[65] Adapted from EEOC press release at http://www.eeoc.gov/eeoc/newsroom/release/9-2-10.cfm, accessed December 19, 2010.

- ensure that investigators of harassment complaints are trained thoroughly to investigate internal complaints of discrimination, harassment, and retaliation;
- establish a toll-free telephone hotline to receive complaints of harassment and retaliation;
- provide antiharassment training to its employees in both English and Spanish and to include a video message from the chief executive officer emphasizing zero tolerance for harassment and retaliation;
- ensure that employees are not subjected to harassment and retaliation, among other things.

Bilingualism: An Uncompensated Skill

As discussed in Research Summary 5.2, communication proficiency and education are the strongest predictors of the representation of Latinos in managerial and professional occupations. More than 40% of Hispanics

---

RESEARCH SUMMARY 5.2	*Causes of Hispanic Underrepresentation in Managerial and Professional Occupations*

Hispanics are underrepresented in managerial and professional occupations relative to their representation in the U.S. population. Although the proportion of Hispanics in the population is increasing, their representation in management and professional occupations has not kept pace. In fact, between 1990 and 2000, Hispanic underrepresentation in management increased from 3.9% to 5.0%, and in professional occupations, the underrepresentation increased from 4.0% to 6.1%.

Kusum Mundra and her colleagues sought to investigate the causes of this underrepresentation and the possible contributions of human capital barriers (e.g., education, English language proficiency, and work experience) and economic and spatial barriers (e.g., travel time to work). Data analyses indicated that education, age, sex, English proficiency, marital status, type of employer, travel time to work, and year of entry into the United States affected people's likelihood of being in a managerial or professional occupation, regardless of race or ethnicity. Education was the strongest factor for Whites and

the second strongest factor for Hispanics. English language proficiency was the strongest predictor of working in a managerial or professional job for Hispanics, and the third-strongest predictor for Whites, reflecting the importance to everyone of communications skills in obtaining higher positions.

The underrepresentation of Hispanics in managerial and professional occupations is increasingly problematic as Hispanics' share of the population increases. Because fluency in English and education most strongly contributed to having a managerial or professional position for Hispanics, the authors recommended organizations become involved in increasing and expanding educational opportunities for Hispanics. English as a second-language training and tuition reimbursement and time off for pursuit of a college degree were suggested as possible mechanisms for doing so.

Source: Mundra, K., Moellmer, A., & Lopez-Aqueres, W. (2003). "Investigating Hispanic Underrepresentation in Managerial and Professional Occupations." *Hispanic Journal of Behavioral Sciences,* 25: 513–529.

are foreign-born, which has implications for English fluency, English-only rules at work, and the need for bilingual managers and employees. In 2008, 35 million U.S. residents spoke Spanish at home—12% of U.S. residents, and 76% of all Hispanics aged 5 and older. More than half of those who speak Spanish at home report speaking English "very well," however.[66]

Bilingual employees are often called upon to assist monolingual English speakers with their work tasks, and this may cause problems for those who are bilingual in completing their own work tasks. In her analysis of this irony, Mary Romero notes:

> Bilingual employees are frequently pulled away from their regular jobs to translate conversations between monolingual English-speaking employees and non-English-speaking clients/customers. Yet the English-speaking employees' need for assistance does not lead to questions about their ability to do their jobs, and the bilingual abilities of racial/ethnic [employees] are rarely considered criteria for higher salary or promotion. Generally, the need for bilingual skills is ignored as a job criterion. The deficiencies of monolingual employees are simply covered up by the availability of bilingual employees to translate.... Employers have refused to recognize language as a marketable skill and have refused to provide wage differentials to compensate for the skill. Instead, bilingual employees find themselves in a double bind: They must take on the additional work of translators, yet they are evaluated poorly because they cannot accomplish as much of their regular work as expected because they are constantly called away to serve as translators. (p. 244)[67]

This uncompensated translation results in some Latinos not divulging their bilingualism to their employers. The rapid growth of the Hispanic population makes it increasingly important to recognize the need for more bilingual employees and bilingualism as a compensable skill. Rather than resisting bi- and multilingualism as un-American, employers should recognize its existence and embrace it. Encouraging multilingualism among all workers (not just Latinos) and hiring and compensating multilingual workers are positive steps.

Misperception: Hispanics should learn English, since English is the "official" language in most of the United States.

Reality: Fluency in multiple languages is an asset for everyone.

---

[66] Ibid.
[67] Romero, M. (1997). "Epilogue." In E. Higginbotham & M. Romero (Eds.), *Women and Work: Exploring Race, Ethnicity, and Class.* Thousand Oaks, CA: Sage Publications, pp. 235–248.

Compared to many other nations, the monolingualism of the majority of the U.S. population is uncommon. Multilingual countries include Canada, China, India, Ireland, New Zealand, and South Africa, among others. In areas that have no official multilingual policy, many of the population are nonetheless multilingual. For example, many Swiss speak English, French, Spanish, and German. Although there is no official language for the United States as a whole, twenty-three states have identified English as the official language. In three states, there are two official languages: Hawaii (English, Hawaiian), Louisiana (English, French), and New Mexico (English, Spanish).

Although bilingualism among Hispanics is a valuable asset, the *requirement* that employees speak Spanish can only be used for selection when it is a legitimate business necessity. In a case filed against a Houston, Texas, Mexican restaurant, the EEOC alleged that the company used speaking Spanish as a pretext for discriminatory employment practices, in violation of Title VII.[68] The restaurant, Ostioneria Michoachan, hired an African American male and a Vietnamese female as food servers, both of whom were well qualified. Ostioneria's management fired them after learning during their orientation that neither of them spoke Spanish. Along with those two former servers, the EEOC included a class of non-Hispanic applicants whom the company had refused to hire because of their inability to speak Spanish. According to the EEOC, the requirement that its "servers speak Spanish makes no sense, since its customers are quite diverse." As indicated by this case, employers must not use bilingualism to discriminate against otherwise qualified applicants when the job does not mandate it.

Racial Profiling, Police Misconduct, and Differential Judicial Treatment against Hispanics

Racial profiling by law enforcement officers has received considerable attention in the media; 22 million people in the United States report that they have experienced profiling.[69] Racial profiling has also been identified in Canada.[70] Profiling in the United States most frequently is directed

---

[68] "EEOC Sues Houston Restaurant for Race and National Origin Discrimination." http://www.eeoc.gov/eeoc/newsroom/release/9-30-09b.cfm, accessed October 22, 2010.

[69] Amnesty International (2004). *Threat and Humiliation: Racial Profiling, Domestic Security, and Human Rights in the U.S.* New York: Amnesty International USA.

[70] Wortley, S., & Tanner, J. (2003). "Data, Denials, and Confusion: The Racial Profiling Debate in Toronto." *Canadian Journal of Criminology and Criminal Justice*, 45(3): 367–390; Wortley, S., & Tanner, J. (2005). "Inflammatory Rhetoric? Baseless Accusations? A Response to Gabor's Critique of Racial Profiling Research in Canada." *Canadian Journal of Criminology and Criminal Justice*, 47(3): 581–609.

TABLE 5.6 *Florida Highway Patrol Officer Characteristics and Hit Rate*

Officer Race	% of Force	% of Searches Conducted	% Hit Rate
White	73	88	20
Black	15	4	26
Latino	11	8	24

Source: Close, B. R., & Mason, P. L. (2007). "Searching for Efficient Enforcement: Officer Characteristics and Racially Biased Policing." *Review of Law & Economics*, 3(2): 1–59.

against people of color, including Latinos, Blacks, Asians, Native Americans, and, more recently, Arabs.[71] In their study of the relationships between officer characteristics and biased policing, Close and Mason found differences in the search behavior of White, Black, and Latino Florida Highway Patrol Officers over a two-year period involving nearly 1.3 million traffic stops. While Black and Latino residents were not more likely to be stopped, when they were stopped, they were more likely to be searched. White officers conducted proportionately more searches yet were less successful in finding evidence of criminal activity than Black and Latino officers, who conducted far fewer searches proportionately (Table 5.6). African American and Latino drivers were more likely to be searched, although they were no more likely to have contraband than Whites.[72] The evidence suggests that patrol officers' hit rates could be improved through less emphasis on the driver's race and ethnicity as cues to criminal activity.

In addition to racial profiling, other forms of police misconduct have been documented, including dishonesty among police officers and informants, planting real and fake drugs and guns, and assaulting innocent people. Many of those victimized by police misconduct are Latino immigrants. In Los Angeles, Rafael Perez, a police officer facing trial for stealing six pounds of seized cocaine, agreed to a plea deal in exchange for a reduced sentence that would expose criminal activity among the Los Angeles police. Perez revealed how Los Angeles police "routinely lied in arrest reports, shot and killed or wounded unarmed suspects and innocent bystanders, planted guns on suspects after shooting them, fabricated evidence, and framed defendants," the majority of whom were young Hispanic men.[73] Due to the information provided by Perez, more than 100 defendants had their convictions vacated and dismissed.

[71] Amnesty International (2004).
[72] Close, B. R., & Mason, P. L. (2007). "Searching for Efficient Enforcement: Officer Characteristics and Racially Biased Policing." *Review of Law & Economics*, 3(2): 1–59.
[73] Gross, S. R., Jacoby, K., Matheson, D., Montgomery, N., & Patil, S. (2005). "Exonerations in the United States: 1989 through 2003." *The Journal of Criminal Law and Criminology*, 95: 524–560.

Another form of police misconduct was revealed when rumors of a "fake-drug scandal" began to surface in the city of Dallas, Texas.[74] Paid "informants" targeted innocent Latinos, and then undercover officers Mark De La Paz and Eddie Herrera planted what appeared to be cocaine in the targets' vehicles. What appeared to be cocaine was gypsum, commonly used in making sheetrock, and could easily have been identified had drug testing taken place. Because drug testing did not occur until the trials, those targeted were jailed for months and years or, as occurred in several cases, deported. Many of those arrested were auto mechanics, day laborers, and construction workers, with no prior criminal records, who spoke little English and had little money to mount a defense.[75] Yvonne Gwyn, a 52-year-old grandmother from Honduras, who is a naturalized U.S. citizen and was running her own auto detail shop, was one of those arrested and jailed.[76] When investigations revealed that the cocaine was gypsum, more than 80 innocent people were released. One informant in the Dallas case earned $210,000 in one year, making him the highest-paid informant that year.[77] Former officer De La Paz was convicted of lying in a search warrant and sentenced to five years in prison.

Poor management procedures, lack of supervision, and considerable professional incentives to make drug busts set the stage for the abuses that occurred in both Los Angeles and Dallas. The vulnerability and devaluation of Latino immigrants also facilitated the abuse, which are reminiscent of the drug scandal in the small town of Tulia, Texas, that resulted in 15% of the Black population being arrested on drug charges, which were eventually dropped.[78] These examples are relevant to the issue of diversity in organizations in that they reflect the role of organizations in facilitating unequal treatment of people based on their race, ethnicity, and class and to the need to pay attention when these kinds of behaviors are exhibited toward the diverse public. They also raise questions about the veracity and fairness of other arrests and convictions. As discussed in Research Summary 5.3, Latinos and Blacks in Florida are less likely to receive withheld adjudication, a legal benefit that would allow them to avoid the stigma of being convicted felons and the associated negative employment and social costs.

[74] See Gross et al. (2005); Donald, M. (2002). "Dirty or Duped? Who's to Blame for the Fake-Drug Scandal Rocking Dallas Police? Virtually Everyone." *Dallasobserver.com*. http://www.dallasobserver .com/2002-05-02/news/dirty-or-duped/ accessed September 19, 2005.

[75] Donald (2002).

[76] Ibid.

[77] Ibid.

[78] Stecklein, J. (2009, July 19). "Tulia Drug Busts: 10 Years Later." *Amarillo Globe*. http://amarillo. com/stories/071909/new_news1.shtml, accessed October 24, 2010.

| RESEARCH SUMMARY 5.3 | Convicted Felon, or Not? Differences by Race and Ethnicity |

Considerable criminology research documents the existence of disparities in arrests, convictions, and sentencing for Latinos and Blacks when compared with those of Whites allegedly involved in criminal activity, particularly drug activity. Under certain circumstances, Florida law allows judges to use their discretion and withhold adjudication, which prevents those involved in criminal activity from being labeled a convicted felon. A felony conviction is associated with many negative consequences—even after serving time and being released, such a conviction prevents people from obtaining employment, voting, serving on juries, and holding political office.

Given the documented disparities in sentencing by race and ethnicity, Stephanie Bontrager and her colleagues set out to investigate possible disparities in withholding adjudication based on race and ethnicity. During a three-year period, 91,477 men were sentenced to probation. Overall, 57% received withheld adjudication, with Hispanics, Whites, and Blacks, receiving it, respectively, in 62%, 58%, and 48% of cases. The perceived advantages of Hispanics in sentencing changed after researchers controlled for individual-level factors, contextual variables, and "concentrated disadvantage," factors including such things as the person's age, seriousness of case, legal residency, prior supervision violation, and seriousness of crime; rates of drug arrests, crime rates, and overall arrest rates in the county; percentage of population that was Black and percentage that was Hispanic; and people living in poverty, people on welfare, and families headed by a single mother. After controlling for these factors, Blacks remained least likely to have adjudication withheld, followed by Hispanics and then Whites. Blacks and Hispanics involved in drug and violent crimes were least likely to receive deferred adjudication, consistent with perceptions of threat of drug or violent crimes associated with Blacks and Hispanics.

Because they are less likely to have adjudication withheld, Hispanics and Blacks have less opportunity than Whites to retain certain civil rights, gain citizenship, or obtain employment. Avoiding the stigma of a felony conviction could—all other things being equal—diminish the prospects of recidivism and increase the prospects of a successful return to productive life. Since deferred adjudication is at judges' discretion, these results make a strong case for promoting diversity in the judiciary, as does evidence of differential decision making of male and female and White and minority judges.

Source: Bontrager, S., Bales, W., & Chiricos, T. (2005). "Race, Ethnicity, Threat, and the Labeling of Convicted Felons." *Criminology*, 43: 589–622.

Latinos and Blacks experience sentencing disparities in the courts compared to sentences imposed on Whites. In addition, there are disparities in sentencing based on Hispanic country of origin and immigrant status. In her review of sentences imposed in U.S. federal courts, Melissa Logue found that Mexican Hispanics received harsher sentences than Hispanics who were not of Mexican origin.[79] Mexican

....

[79] Logue, M. A. (2009). "'The Price of Being Mexican': Sentencing Disparities Between Noncitizen Mexican and Non-Mexican Latinos in the Federal Courts." *Hispanic Journal of Behavioral Sciences*, 31(4): 423–445.

immigrants also received harsher sentences than native-born Mexican Americans. Although all Hispanic immigrants received harsher penalties than native-born Hispanics, the immigrant penalty was greatest for Mexican immigrants. Logue speculated that Mexican immigrants' harsher penalties were related to widespread publicity about immigrants and fears of Mexican immigrants taking jobs and committing crimes. The public's perceptions about the proportion of crimes committed by immigrants (and minorities) and their representation in the population are quite distorted and shape the public's attitudes.[80] Among Whites, the more inaccurate their beliefs about the size of the minority population, the more negative their attitudes toward immigrants, Blacks, and Hispanics, which emphasizes the need for education.[81]

▌ LATINOS AS CUSTOMERS

The Marketing Advantage

As we have discussed so far, Latinos are a large and rapidly growing proportion of the U.S. population. As potential employees and customers, Latinos are a force to be reckoned with. Hispanic buying power increased from $504 billion in 2000 to $978 billion in 2009 and will grow to a projected $1.3 trillion in 2014.[82] *People en Español*'s fourth annual Hispanic Opinion Tracker (HOT) reported important differences between the consumption behavior of Hispanics and that of the general population.[83] In phone interviews with 6,000 Hispanics and 2,000 non-Hispanics aged 18 and over, 55% of the Hispanics were Hispanic dominant—those who prefer to speak Spanish and have a strong desire to maintain their Hispanic culture. Of the remaining 45%, 23% were bicultural and bilingual but were culturally more Hispanic. Another 22% identified with their Latino heritage but were more similar to the general population in consumer attitudes. In all, over three-fourths of the Hispanic population reported being bilingual, bicultural, and identifying with their Hispanic heritage. In the HOT survey, Hispanics reported spending an average of $1,992 on clothing and accessories compared to $1,153 for general customers in the twelve months prior to the collection of survey data. Hispanics were also more likely to report strong enthusiasm about

---

[80] Alba, R., Rumbaut, R. G., & Marotz, K. (2005). "A Distorted Nation: Perceptions of Racial/Ethnic Group Sizes and Attitudes Toward Immigrants and Other Minorities." *Social Forces*, 84(2): 901–919.
[81] Ibid.
[82] *Marketing News* (2005, July 15), 39(12): 23.
[83] Wentz, L. (2005, July 18). "Survey: Hispanics 'Passionate' about Shopping." *Advertising Age*, 76(29): 29.

shopping (56%) than was the general population (39%). About 75% of the Hispanics reported preferring to pay cash for their purchases, and only 15% used credit cards, which is significantly lower than the 40% who use credit cards in the general population.

Organizations wishing to tap into the Hispanic market are using such sources as *People en Español* and Univision. Univision refers to itself as "the leading Spanish-language media company serving the rapidly growing Hispanic population in the United States"[84] By focusing on Latinos, Univision has been able to capitalize on the growing market and become a top-ranked network. In 2005, the ABC network began offering prime-time shows in Spanish and English, an acknowledgment of the growing proportion of Latinos in the United States.[85] Prior to that time, only the "George Lopez" sitcom was broadcast in both English and Spanish. ABC's entertainment chief stated that the company wanted to "move beyond toe-dipping and really dive in" to the market for Latino customers. The network now provides both dubbing and closed captioning for some of its most popular shows. Latinos who did not speak English and who had previously been unable to view prime-time shows were enthusiastic in these test screenings.

Discrimination against Hispanic Customers

In contrast to these signs of welcoming and pursuing Hispanic customers, researchers have also documented discrimination that sometimes targets Hispanics as undesirable customers or potential shoplifters. In their article on customer racial profiling and other marketplace discrimination, Ann-Marie Harris, Geraldine Henderson, and Jerome Williams describe one egregious case of discrimination that occurred in a Conoco convenience store and gas station in Fort Worth, Texas.[86] The store employee cursed the Hispanic customers and referred to one as an "Iranian Mexican …, whatever you are."[87] The employee then threw the customers' purchases on the floor and, over the store loudspeaker, told them to "go back to where you came from you poor Mexicans …" in an escalating verbal assault. The customers' complaints to Conoco were ignored, even though the clerk admitted she had done what the customers alleged. Although the courts are often unfriendly to customer complaints of discrimination, the costs of negative publicity and lost business may be potentially higher

---

[84] www.univision.com.
[85] "ABC to Offer Primetime Shows in Spanish." *DiversityInc.com.*
[86] See Harris, A., Henderson, G., & Williams, J. (2005, Spring). "Courting Customers: Assessing Consumer Racial Profiling and Other Marketplace Discrimination." *Journal of Public Policy & Marketing*, 24(1): 163–171.
[87] Ibid., p. 168.

than those of a lawsuit or damage award. As discussed in Chapter 1, discrimination against customers can result in lost business from customers personally targeted by unfair treatment or from other customers when they learn of discriminatory treatment based on race or ethnicity. Both members of the targeted group and members of other racial and ethnic groups may find such behavior unacceptable and choose to do business elsewhere.

▌ RECOMMENDATIONS FOR INDIVIDUALS

Like other groups, individual Latinos should obtain as much education as they can. Although the returns on an investment in education differ by race and national origin, education increases everyone's earnings and the likelihood of employment. Latinos should also carefully investigate prospective employers. What is the demographic composition of the employees? Are Hispanics and other non-dominant group members represented in management, supervisory positions, or other positions of power? Who are the potential role models and mentors? Can allies be found among other minority groups? Rather than practicing inter-ethnic discrimination, resist stereotyping and recognize the value in equality for all.

Hispanic women, like other minority women, face barriers based on race and sex stereotyping and discrimination. Education, persistence, and careful choice of employers can be very helpful. Hispanic women should consider working for organizations with unions; research indicates that although Hispanic women are least likely to be unionized, minority women who are unionized make 38.6% more than those who are not.[88] Sexual harassment should be documented if it occurs, and women should not be afraid to speak up and seek help from resources outside the organization if necessary.

Personal efforts to ensure English fluency are critical to Latinos for whom English is a second language. As discussed earlier, bilingualism is increasingly valuable in today's workplace, for both Hispanics and non-Hispanics. Those who are bilingual should actively pursue positions in which bilingualism is valued and compensated. In addition, people of all races and ethnic backgrounds who are monolingual should consider learning another language, in recognition of the fact that bilingualism is a valuable skill, certain to increase in market value. Latinos who are

---

[88] Hartmann, H., Allen, K., & Owens, C. (1999). *Equal Pay for Working Families: National and State Data on the Pay Gap and Its Costs*. Washington, D.C.: AFL-CIO and Institute for Women's Policy Research, cited in Caiazza, A., Shaw, A., & Werschkul, M. (2003), *Women's Economic Status in the States: Wide Disparities by Race, Ethnicity, and Region*. Washington, D.C.: Institute for Women's Policy Research. http://www.iwpr.org/pdf/R260.pdf, accessed October 21, 2010.

bilingual should seek employment in organizations that recognize and value bilingualism as a compensable skill. More organizations are providing extra pay for bilingual skills that are used in the course of employment. Latinos should also ensure that young family members learn Spanish, rather than ceasing speaking Spanish and letting that part of one's heritage disappear. Languages are learned easiest by the young, and fluency in multiple languages is human capital that can provide many returns.

Because of the large proportion of Latino immigrants and their relatively below-average education levels, it is possible that those most in need of these individual recommendations will not be able to implement them. Readers interested in workplace fairness and equity are encouraged to pursue these goals for those who are not able to do it for themselves. Serving as a mentor, an English as a second-language (ESL) tutor, or a friend and advocate for those who are devalued is beneficial to those who serve as well as to the recipients.

■ RECOMMENDATIONS FOR ORGANIZATIONS

Zero tolerance for discrimination and harassment based on race and ethnicity should specifically include unfair treatment of Latinos. Because Latinos may be immigrants or may speak little English, they are sometimes singled out for virulent discrimination and harassment. Proactive fairness policies would help eliminate or reduce such discrimination. Thorough investigation and discipline as appropriate are important in curbing harassment.

Along with prohibiting unfair treatment based on ethnicity, organizational leaders should take proactive measures to ensure fairness for Latino applicants and employees. Recruitment at high schools and universities with large Latino populations, referrals from Latino employees, and targeted advertising in Latino media should be helpful in increasing representation of Latino employees.

Organizational leaders should consider providing ESL classes for non-English-speaking workers. One such program is *Sed de Saber* ("Thirst to Know"), offered through a partnership of the MultiCultural Foodservice and Hospitality Alliance and Coca-Cola, Inc. *Sed de Saber* is an ESL program designed specifically for adults. Vocational ESL classes are also suggested as important ways to help non-English-speaking workers obtain job-related skills while learning English.[89] These programs may also reduce turnover and improve safety and customer satisfaction while also improving workers' skills, self-esteem, and loyalty.

---

[89] See Huerta-Macias, A. (2002). *Workforce Education for Latinos*. Westport, CT: Greenwood Publishing Group.

Along with helping employees to learn English, leaders should encourage English-speaking managers, supervisors, and employees to learn Spanish, a measure that employers of large numbers of Latinos are finding productive, relatively simple, rewarding, and positive in employee relations.[90] Employers in the restaurant industry are learning Spanish as a means to help reduce turnover, improve training, and connect with employees who do not speak English. While ESL classes are useful for employees, high turnover in certain industries makes having managers and supervisors who speak Spanish (and who have lower turnover) far more effective. Organizations should provide incentives and opportunities for managers to learn Spanish and reward those who already speak Spanish, rather than taking it for granted. Being bilingual is a job-related compensable skill and should be treated as such.

As discussed in the chapter, managers' stated preferences for Latinos because of their "strong work ethic" are sometimes actually stating their preferences for workers who are more likely to accept low wages and unfair treatment. From the point of view of legal and ethical considerations, employers should provide no less than minimum wages, appropriate payment for overtime, Social Security contributions, and safe working conditions for all workers—period. Organizations will likely find that fair treatment of all workers is a good investment, even when wage rates are low. For low-wage, low-skilled workers, fair treatment, efforts to help them improve their language skills, and efforts to learn their language may translate into resource acquisition and cost advantages, reducing turnover, improving recruitment, and increasing productivity.

Employers should be aware that Hispanics are diverse in education, English language fluency, background, and experiences. Although many Hispanics are recent immigrants and some have limited English language fluency, most Hispanics are native-born, many are fluent in English, and some do not even speak Spanish. As with any group, it is important to avoid making assumptions and job-related decisions about individuals based on their group membership rather than on their individual qualifications.

From a customer perspective, the Latino market is strong and growing. Organizations wishing to tap into the market should consider the preferences of Latino consumers and make use of bilingual advertisements, customer service, and managers. Rather than simply seeing Latinos as a market to be exploited, they should be seen as valuable and valued customers.

---

[90] Berta, D. (2005, June 6). "English-Speaking Managers Learn to Use Spanish in Workplace." *Nation's Restaurant News*, 39(26): 6–22.

Summary

In this chapter, we have considered the diverse backgrounds, English language fluency, educational levels, and experiences of Hispanics in the United States. Readers are encouraged to remember that organizational experiences of Hispanics are based in part on their race, ethnicity, and skin color but also on their immigrant or native status, education, occupation, industry, and geographic location. Hispanics are far from being a monolithic group, as is apparent from the diversity in the demographics, education, earnings, and unemployment among Hispanics.

Recommendations for individuals focused on education, careful selection of employers, and English language fluency. We suggested that bilingualism is a positive attribute for Hispanics and non-Hispanics as well and that organizations should encourage and compensate it among employees. Recommendations for organizations focused on including Hispanic workers, valuing them as customers, and reducing workplace exploitation and discrimination against those who experience it.

Key Terms

Employment hardship — joblessness, involuntary part-time work, and working poverty.

Inter-ethnic discrimination — discrimination practiced by non-White racial and ethnic groups against other minorities.

Questions to Consider

1. Prior to reading this chapter, were you aware of the repatriation of Mexicans during the 1930s, lynching, and the Latinos' fight for civil rights?

2. Given the Hispanic buying power discussed in this chapter, what might retailers do to capitalize on the Hispanic consumer market?

3. What would your recommendations be for dealing with the behavior of the Conoco clerk in the incident at Fort Worth, Texas? What measures would you recommend to prevent such discrimination against Hispanic customers in the future?

4. What specific steps can organizations take to ensure that bilingual workers' skills are compensated when these skills are job relevant, to encourage bilingualism among employees, and to reduce resistance to Spanish speakers?

5. What can organizations that pay low wages for low-skill work do to ensure that workers are treated fairly? What is the role of the perception that immigrant workers are "better off than if they were in _____ " in justifying paying them low wages? How pervasive do you think this perception is? What can be done to educate people about discrimination against immigrant workers?

6. What should law enforcement agencies do to curb discrimination against minorities? What can the public do?

Actions and Exercises

1. Investigate and report on the change in the Hispanic population of your local community or state in the past twenty years.

2. Observe employment of Hispanics in your community in a particular place (such as a store, restaurant, and office) in which there are also non-Hispanic White, Black, Asian, or employees of

other backgrounds. What do you observe that is relevant to diversity in organizations?

3. If you are not Hispanic, do you know well someone who is Hispanic? In what capacity do you know him or her (e.g., personal friend, manager, classmate, neighbor)? Do you know his or her ethnic origin (e.g., Mexico, Cuba, Central America)? Is he or she bilingual? Have you discussed race, ethnicity, or other diversity issues with this person? Explain.

4. Investigate the repatriation of Mexican Americans. Have efforts to secure reparations for those affected been successful?

5. Conduct research to find several Hispanics in positions of power in corporations, politics, or academics. Describe their positions, educational background, experience, and other relevant factors that have contributed to their successes.

6. Investigate current instances of racial profiling and police misconduct against people of color. What are your findings?

7. In Chapter 4, Devah Pager's research documented employers' preferences for Whites with criminal records over Blacks without criminal records. Are these preferences also likely for Latinos? How might the failure of Latinos and Blacks to obtain withheld adjudication or similar benefits in other states exacerbate employers' existing preferences for Whites? What effect might questionable arrests and convictions, coupled with lower likelihood of obtaining withheld adjudication, have on the employment levels and earnings of Latinos and Blacks?

Asians/Asian Americans

CHAPTER 6

Chapter Objectives

After completing this chapter, readers should have a greater understanding of the roles of Asian Americans in organizational diversity. Specifically, they should be able to:

❏ *discuss the history of and diversity among Asians in the United States.*

❏ *explain participation rates, employment, and income levels of Asians.*

❏ *examine research on the employment-related experiences of Asians.*

❏ *compare similarities and differences among Asian Americans and between Asians and other minority groups.*

Key Facts

The category Asian American includes people from many different backgrounds who have disparate education, income, and employment experiences in the United States.

Asians with college degrees earn about 13% less per year than Whites with college degrees.

At higher educational levels, Asians are more likely to be unemployed than Whites, but at lower educational levels, Asians are less likely to be unemployed than Whites.

Although Asians are overrepresented in technical fields, they are less likely to be in management than other minority group members.

Despite being preferred over other minorities in some employment contexts, Asians also experience access and treatment discrimination.

Many Asian-owned small businesses succeed only through long hours and the unpaid labor of family members; many others fail despite these factors.

Introduction and Overview

Asians are perhaps the most understudied and most diverse minority group in the United States. Asian Americans differ in culture, language, experiences, and background, particularly those who are recent immigrants and those who are American-born. Despite these differences, Asian Americans are often *perceived* as the **model minority** group, who through hard work, determination, and strong cultural values have been able to achieve educational and financial success, in contrast to other minority groups, who are *perceived* as having done little to improve themselves. At times, such ideas have served to pit minority groups against each other and get in the way of an accurate understanding of the issues important to all people of color. What are the facts about Asians in America? How much in common do Asians of different origins share, with each other and with other minority groups, in terms of education, income, and occupation? In what ways are they different? We consider these and other questions in this chapter.

We begin with a historical review of Asians in the United States, which, as for other racial and ethnic groups, will provide important and possibly unfamiliar insights into their status today. The remainder of this chapter covers our standard topic areas, research summaries, and the focal issues for Asian Americans and includes separate sections on Chinese, Indians, and Southeast Asians. Space constraints prevent detailed coverage of all Asian groups; readers are encouraged to conduct their own investigations.

Terminology

The term *Asian American* refers to a heterogeneous group of people having origins in the Asia Pacific region. According to the current classifications of the U.S. Census Bureau, the category Asians includes people from the Far East, Southeast Asia, or the Indian subcontinent, including Cambodia, China, India, Japan, Korea, Malaysia, Pakistan, the Philippine Islands, Thailand, and Vietnam, among many other areas. Reflecting the fluidity of the concept of "race" as mentioned in previous chapters, racial classifications of people of Asian descent have changed multiple times in the U.S. Census. In 1860, a category for Chinese was first included, and one for Japanese was added in 1870. Between 1910 and 1970, data for other Asian groups were collected periodically. In 1970, Asian Indians were classified as White, and Vietnamese were included in the "other" racial category.

In the past, the U.S. Census Bureau has used the broad category "Asians and Pacific Islanders," which included Native Hawaiians and other Pacific Islanders along with Chinese, Koreans, and many other Asian groups. Due to the small numbers of Native Hawaiians, the categories were separated in 1997 into "Asians" and "Native Hawaiians or other Pacific Islanders" (NHOPI); prior to this change, specific data were sometimes collected on Asian and Pacific Islanders. Thus, in this book, the term *Asians and Pacific Islanders* (API) is sometimes used to ensure accuracy in this discussion. *Asian/Asian American* are generally used interchangeably. Where possible and appropriate, specific references to ethnic origin are made to help clarify differences among people in this diverse category.

Researchers have found that when given a choice in self-identification as Asian American, Asian, ethnic American (e.g., Chinese American, Korean American), or ethnic origin alone (e.g., Chinese, Korean), 34% and 33% of respondents, respectively, chose the latter two categories.[1] Fully 67% preferred these categories over Asian or Asian American. However, when probed, 60% of respondents accepted the term *Asian American*, reflecting the fluidity and malleability of ethnic identity and the influence of others on self-perceptions. ●

---

[1]Lien, P., Conway, M., & Wong, J. (2003). "The Contours and Sources of Ethnic Identity Choices Among Asian Americans." *Social Science Quarterly*, 84: 461–482.

▌ History of Asians in the United States

Asian Americans have long been part of the U.S. history and have contributed to the country's development in many ways. Many Americans of Filipino, Japanese, and Chinese ancestry have been in the United States for several generations; most Southeast Asians are much more recent immigrants or refugees who have fled their countries because of war and fear for their lives. Because entrance criteria (e.g., education, occupation) for refugees are less stringent than requirements for immigrants, Southeast Asian refugees often enter the country with fewer skills and assets, which has long-term effects on their future in the United States.[2]

Filipinos first arrived in what is now the United States around 1763, when Filipino crewmen who had been forced into service jumped ship in Louisiana and escaped into the bayous. They made their homes there and developed Filipino communities. By the late nineteenth century, Filipinos had become thoroughly incorporated into Louisiana life.[3] Chinese immigrants began arriving in the United States in the 1850s, seeking work and opportunity. Early migrants labored in agriculture, in the fishing industry, in domestic service and laundry work, in mining during the California gold rush, and on the railways. Some researchers have suggested that Chinese laborers were replacements for the African slave trade, which had become illegal in the 1840s.[4] One major contribution of Chinese railroad workers was the completion of the first transcontinental railroad in May 1869, during the construction of which Chinese workers were paid less than White European American workers. The railroad made it possible for East Coast laborers to more easily move westward, which fostered stiff labor market competition and fueled anti-Chinese rioting and lynching during the 1870s and 1880s.[5] The Chinese Exclusion Act of 1882 severely and purposefully restricted the entry of Chinese laborers into the United States for many decades; it was the first federal legislation to bar immigrants based on national origin.

Although the first Japanese immigrants arrived in May 1843, the years between 1884 and 1924 are recognized as the period during which the ancestors of most present-day Japanese Americans began arriving in the United States. Economic and political unrest in Japan, coupled with labor shortages and Western expansion, led to migration from Japan to

[2]Gold, S., & Kibria, N. (1993). "Vietnamese Refugees and Blocked Mobility." *Asian and Pacific Migration Journal*, 2(1): 27–56.

[3]Espina, M. (1988). *Filipinos in Louisiana*. New Orleans, LA: LaBorde & Sons.

[4]Lin, J. (1999). "Chinese Americans: From Exclusion to Prosperity?" In A. G. Dworkin & R. J. Dworkin (Eds.), *The Minority Report*, 3rd ed. Fort Worth, TX: Harcourt Brace Publishers, pp. 321–342.

[5]Lin (1999); Takaki, R. (2008). *A Different Mirror*. Boston: Back Bay Books; Zia, H. (2000). *Asian American Dreams: The Emergence of an American People*. New York: Farrar, Straus, and Giroux.

Hawaii and California during the late nineteenth century.[6] Between 1884 and 1908, more than 150,000 Japanese laborers migrated to Hawaii, a number that increased after passage of the Chinese Exclusion Act. Many Japanese workers labored long hours for low pay on Hawaiian sugar plantations, and many paid for their passage to Hawaii by agreeing to work a three-year period with little or no pay, similar to the indentured servants of colonial times. Like the Chinese, the Japanese people faced hostility and exclusionary legislation. The 1908 Gentleman's Agreement and the 1924 National Origins Act were aimed at limiting Japanese worker immigration.[7] In 1922, the U.S. Supreme Court ruled that Japanese, along with others of Asian descent, were ineligible for naturalized citizenship.

The internment of more than 120,000 Japanese Americans during World War II is recognized as an act having devastating effects. After the Japanese attack on Pearl Harbor in December 1941, panic and paranoia erupted about Japanese Americans who were living in the United States. In February 1942, President Franklin Roosevelt signed Executive Order 9066 authorizing the evacuation and internment of anyone considered a threat to national security. Included were all who had at least one-eighth Japanese ancestry—more than 100,000 Japanese Americans. Many of the evacuees sent to the ten internment camps throughout the United States were native-born American citizens; two-thirds were citizens and three-quarters were under age 25.[8] Branded as "enemy aliens," the detainees' privacy, possessions, and freedom were taken away. Ironically, while Japanese American soldiers fought on the U.S. side during the war, some had family members who were detained in the "relocation centers" (which have also been referred to as concentration camps). One battalion included Japanese American soldiers who had been drafted from the relocation centers to serve in the war.[9] Researchers have argued that racism was a key factor behind the rationale to order the evacuation of 90% of Japanese Americans, for very few German or Italian Americans were sent to the relocation centers.[10]

After three years, the centers closed and Japanese Americans were allowed to return home, but many homes and considerable property had been lost, stolen, or destroyed during their internment. Estimates suggest that Japanese Americans lost $3.7 billion (in 1995 dollars) during that

....

[6]Fujiwara, J. H., & Takagi, D. Y. (1999). "Japanese Americans: Stories About Race in America." In A. G. Dworkin & R. J. Dworkin (Eds.), *The Minority Report*, 3rd ed. Fort Worth, TX: Harcourt Brace Publishers, pp. 297–320.

[7]Ibid.

[8]Schaefer, R. T. (2002). *Racial and Ethnic Groups, Census 2000 Update*, 8th ed. Upper Saddle River, NJ: Pearson Education.

[9]Fujiwara & Takagi (1999).

[10]See Schaefer (2002), p. 370.

time. In 1988, the Civil Liberties Act authorized payments of $20,000 tax free to each of the 66,000 surviving internees. The payments were deemed too little and too late for many survivors, yet they were larger than those paid to some other groups that have suffered U.S. government–sanctioned injustice.

People from Southeast Asia began coming to the United States in large numbers as a result of the Vietnam war. Many spoke no English and arrived with few possessions, making their transition extremely difficult. Initially, the U.S. government carefully orchestrated the settlement of Southeast Asian refugees, placing them in disparate cities across the country. Many refugees resettled to warmer climates, to areas in which family members had been settled, or to areas with stronger mechanisms in place (such as public assistance and language training) to assist them. As a result, California, Texas, and Washington have significant numbers of Southeast Asians, along with Asians from other areas, primarily in large cities.

▌ Relevant Legislation

In the past, restrictive immigration laws limited the entry of Asians into the United States. The Chinese Exclusion Act, mentioned earlier, severely restricted Chinese immigration between 1882 and 1943, when it was repealed. It was replaced with a quota system, which allowed only 105 Chinese to enter the United States each year. Other restrictions and quotas, including the National Origins Act of 1924, severely limited other Asians' entry and their ability to become naturalized citizens. Many such laws were enacted specifically to limit the number of Asian workers, who competed with European-born laborers. The Immigration and Nationality Act of 1965 eliminated race, national origin, or ancestry quotas, leading to a substantial increase in the number of immigrants from Asian countries in the years since.[11]

As discussed in previous chapters, Title VII of the Civil Rights Act of 1964, as amended, is the key legislation relevant to people of color and their employment experiences. Although immigration quotas have been eliminated, Asians still experience employment discrimination based on race and national origin, both of which are prohibited by Title VII. Executive orders for affirmative action also apply to people of Asian descent when they are underutilized. As we will discuss, Asians are often

---

[11]Mosisa, A. T. (2002). "The Role of Foreign-Born Workers in the U.S. Economy." *Monthly Labor Review*, 125(2): 3–14.

confined to certain job categories, experience the glass ceiling, and receive lower returns on their educational investments than Whites.

Asians and the Civil Rights Movement

The civil rights movement in the United States is primarily associated with Blacks, but discrimination in employment, education, housing, and other areas led some Asians (specifically, Japanese, Chinese, and Filipinos), Latinos, and American Indians to also participate.[12] In many cases, people of color (and Whites) often worked side by side to advance common civil rights. One Chinese man noted that "what Martin Luther King, Jr. is doing is going to benefit Chinese Americans"; others picketed with signs saying "Minorities unite! Fight for Democratic rights!"[13] More recently, issues arising from employment discrimination, hate crimes, racial profiling by police, and customer discrimination continue to underscore similarities between the experiences of Asians and those of other people of color. Helen Zia, a Chinese American writer and activist discussed in Individual Feature 6.1, has worked tirelessly to achieve fairness and equity for Asian Americans and other non-dominant groups.

Selected EEOC Cases

Cases drawn from the EEOC Web site detail charges and settlements involving employment discrimination against Asians from various backgrounds and in distinct occupations.[14]

In November 2007, a high-end suburban Illinois retirement facility agreed to pay $125,000 to settle a discrimination lawsuit alleging that it terminated its director of nursing because of her national origin (Filipino) and race (Asian). The federal district court approved a two-year consent decree requiring the facility to provide training regarding antidiscrimination laws to all its employees; post a notice informing its employees of the consent decree; report to the EEOC

[12]Louie, S. (2001). "When We Wanted It Done, We Did It Ourselves." In S. Louie & G. Omatsu (Eds.), *Asian Americans: The Movement and the Moment*. Los Angeles: UCLA Asian American Studies Center Press, pp. xv–xxv. See also Widener, D. (2003). "Perhaps the Japanese Are to Be Thanked? Asia, Asian Americans, and the Construction of Black California." *Positions*, 11(1): 135–182. For an investigation of housing discrimination against Asians, see Turner, M. A., Ross, S. L., Bednarz, B. A., Herbig, C., & Lee, S. J. (2003). *Discrimination in Metropolitan Housing Markets: Phase 2—Asians and Pacific Islanders*. Washington, D.C.: The Urban Institute. http://www.huduser.org/publications/pdf/phase2_final.pdf, accessed November 2, 2010.
[13]Lee, C. (2001). "Untitled Photo Essay." In S. Louie & G. Omatsu (Eds.), *Asian Americans: The Movement and the Moment*. Los Angeles: UCLA Asian American Studies Center Press, pp. 130, 131.
[14]All cases are drawn nearly verbatim from "Significant EEOC Race/Color Cases." http://www.eeoc.gov/eeoc/initiatives/e-race/caselist.cfm, accessed October 31, 2010.

INDIVIDUAL FEATURE 6.1	*Helen Zia*

Helen Zia, a Chinese American journalist and activist, has made a difference in the lives of countless people by her tireless commitment to equity and justice. Zia was born in New Jersey in 1952, educated at Princeton, and has worked as an autoworker in Detroit, as executive editor of *Ms.* magazine, as a writer, and as a civil rights and community activist.

A member of one of the earliest Princeton classes that included women, Zia attributes her admission both to graduating at the top of her high school class and to the civil rights movement. While at Princeton, Zia worked for equality for oppressed groups. There she joined a multiracial coalition to denounce racism and the Vietnam war. She also worked on Asian women's issues and became painfully aware of the focus on race as a Black and White issue, neglecting Asians.

Zia first came onto the media radar after Vincent Chin's brutal murder in Detroit in June 1982. Chin, a second-generation Chinese American, was attacked by two unemployed White autoworkers who ostensibly blamed the Japanese for taking away Americans' auto jobs. The men supposedly thought Chin was Japanese and beat him into a coma with a baseball bat; he died four days later. The assailants were sentenced to three years' probation and a $3,780 fine but served no jail time. Outraged at the injustice, Zia and other activists formed a coalition, American Citizens for Justice (ACJ), to seek justice for the heinous crime and the sentencing insult to the Chinese American community.

In addition to her work with ACJ, Zia has been an outspoken voice about other issues involving race, sex, and sexual orientation. Her work has been widely published in numerous respected newspapers and magazines, including *The Nation, Essence,* the *New York Times,* and the *San Francisco Chronicle.* Her book, *Asian American Dreams: The Emergence of an American People*, is a compelling account of the history of Asian Americans in the United States and of Zia's own discovery of what it meant to be an Asian American and a feminist in a patriarchal society.[15]

Source: Chinese American Forum. (2002, January). "Helen Zia: A Dedicated Civil Rights Advocate for Chinese/Asian Americans." 17(3): 5–8.

QUESTIONS TO CONSIDER

1. Prior to reading this selection, had you heard of Helen Zia? With which famous Asian Americans are you familiar?

2. Zia learned that many people see race as Black and White, while neglecting Asians. How prevalent is that perspective today? How does this perspective affect Asians in the United States? How prevalent is the opinion that diversity issues are primarily race issues? How does this perspective affect other diversity issues?

any complaints of discrimination made by its employees; and take affirmative steps to recruit Asian nurses. *EEOC v. Presbyterian Homes,* Case No. 07 C 5443 (N.D. Ill. Nov. 28, 2007)

[15]Zia, H. (2000). *Asian American Dreams: The Emergence of an American People*. New York: Farrar, Straus, and Giroux.

In March 2007, MBNA-America agreed to pay $147,000 to settle a Title VII lawsuit alleging discrimination and harassment based on race and national origin. According to the lawsuit, an Asian Indian employee was subjected to ethnic taunts, such as being called "dot-head" and "Osama Bin Laden," was physically attacked by a coworker with a learning disability who believed he was Osama's brother, and was denied training and promotional opportunities afforded to his White coworkers. *EEOC v. MBNA-America* (E.D. Pa. Mar. 2007)

In January 2006, the Commission settled for $200,000 a case against Bally North America filed on behalf of a former manager of its Honolulu store who was harassed and fired due to her Asian race and Chinese national origin. *EEOC v. Bally North America, Inc.*, No. 05-000631 (D. Haw. Jan. 2006)

In August 2007, a San Jose body shop agreed to pay $45,000 to settle a sexual and racial harassment lawsuit filed by the EEOC, in which a male auto body technician of Chinese and Italian ancestry was taunted daily by his foreman with sexual comments, racial stereotypes and code words, including calling him "Bruce Lee." The company also agreed to establish an internal complaint procedure, disseminate an antiharassment policy, and train its workforce to prevent future harassment. *EEOC v. Monterey Collision Frame and Auto Body, Inc.*, No. 5:06-cv-06032-JF (N.D. Cal. consent decree filed August 30, 2007)

In May 2006, the Commission won a Title VII case filed on behalf of Asian Indian legal aliens who were victims of human trafficking, enslavement, and job segregation because of their race, national origin, and dark-skinned color. *Chellen & EEOC v. John Pickle Co., Inc.*, 434 F.Supp.2d 1069 (N.D. Okl. 2006)

In light of the volume of discrimination involving Asian Americans, the EEOC has implemented a program called The Information Group for Asian American Rights (TIGAAR) that is designed to help educate Asian American employers and employees who may be unfamiliar with employment laws, rights, and responsibilities. TIGAAR is a partnership between the EEOC, the U.S. Department of Labor, local government entities, and numerous community and advocacy groups. It uses radio, television, billboards, and videos to encourage employers to voluntarily comply with employment laws and to educate employees about their rights in the workplace. Inclusion of both Asian American employers and employees will help spread the word to affected parties. A 2005 Gallup Poll study conducted in conjunction with the fortieth anniversary of the U.S. Equal Opportunity Commission indicated that 31% of Asians, 26% of African Americans, 12% of Whites, and 18% of Hispanics reported experiencing workplace discrimination within the prior year.[16] Although Asians were most likely to report discrimination, only 3% of race discrimination claims were filed by Asians, indicating continued need to inform Asians of their rights and responsibilities at work.

▌ POPULATION

There were 15.5 million U.S. residents of Asian descent who reported themselves as Asian alone or Asian in combination with some other race(s) in 2008. Asians now comprise 5% of the U.S. population. Asians and Latinos are now the fastest-growing groups in the United States due to their higher birth and immigration rates. Between 2008 and 2050, the Asian and NHOPI populations are projected to increase by 162% and 132%, respectively, compared with a 44% increase for the population as a whole.[17] Asian Indians are the fastest-growing group of Asians. The median age of single-race Asians is 35.8, and the age for NHOPI is 29.8, compared with the population as a whole (36.8). As discussed in previous chapters, groups with younger average ages will make up proportionately more of the new entrants to the workforce in the future.

Of the 15.5 million Asian U.S. residents, 3.62 million (23%) are of Chinese descent, followed by 3.09 million Filipinos (20%), 2.73 million Asian Indians (16%), 1.73 million Vietnamese (10%), 1.61 million Koreans (10%), and 1.30 million (10%) Japanese (see Figure 6.1).

FIGURE 6.1 *Asian Population* by Detailed Group: 2008*

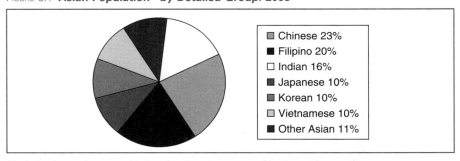

- ■ Chinese 23%
- ■ Filipino 20%
- □ Indian 16%
- ■ Japanese 10%
- ■ Korean 10%
- □ Vietnamese 10%
- ■ Other Asian 11%

*Includes those who report "Asian alone" or Asian in combination with any other group.

Source: Facts for Features, Asian/Pacific Heritage Month, May 2010. http://www.census.gov/newsroom/releases/archives/facts_for_features_special_editions/cb10-ff07.html, accessed October 31, 2010.

[16]Yen, H. (2005, December 8). "Poll: Nearly 1 Out of 6 Workers Claim Bias." Associated Press. WashingtonPost.com. http://www.washingtonpost.com/wp-dyn/content/article/2005/12/08/AR2005120801083_pf.html, accessed December 10, 2005.

[17]Facts for Features, Asian/Pacific Heritage Month, May 2010. http://www.census.gov/newsroom/releases/archives/facts_for_features_special_editions/cb10-ff07.html, accessed October 31, 2010.

Nearly 70% of all Asians in the United States are foreign-born, but this varies by ethnic origin: 40% of Japanese in the United States are foreign-born and about 75% each of Asian Indians, Vietnamese, Koreans, and Pakistanis are foreign-born.[18] Overall, 43% of the foreign-born Asian population entered the United States between 1990 and 2000.[19] More than half (52%) of the Asians who were born outside the United States have been naturalized. This contrasts with 38% of people born elsewhere.

Misperception: Asian Americans are "perpetual outsiders."

Reality: Asians are more likely to be naturalized citizens than other immigrants.

At 5.1 million (in 2008), California has the largest population of Asian Americans, followed by 1.5 million in New York. Hawaii, where 54% of the population is of Asian descent, has the largest proportion of Asian American residents.[20] The largest groups of Asians reside in Honolulu, Los Angeles, New York City, San Francisco, and San Jose, cities that have a high cost of living, which, as we discuss later, affects Asians' earnings relative to other groups that are more geographically dispersed.

▌ EDUCATION, EMPLOYMENT, AND EARNINGS

As a group, Asian Americans have more education than other racial/ethnic groups in the United States. As Table 6.1 shows, more than 52% of Asians of all categories have college degrees, compared to about 30%, 20%, and 13%, respectively, of Whites, Blacks, and Hispanics.[21] On the other hand, Asians are also more likely not to have completed high school than Whites (13.2% versus 10.0%, not shown in the table), which is additional evidence of the great diversity among people of Asian backgrounds.

Misperception: Asian Americans are well-educated.

Reality: Some Asians are well-educated, while others are poorly educated, representing a bimodal distribution of educational attainment.

---

[18]Reeves, T. J., & Bennett, C. E. (2004). *We the People: Asians in the United States, Census 2000 Special Reports*. U.S. Census Bureau. http://www.census.gov/prod/2004pubs/censr-17.pdf, accessed November 1, 2010.
[19]Ibid.
[20]Ibid. Hawaii is the only state in which the majority group is of Asian descent.
[21]Ibid.

TABLE 6.1 *Educational Attainment by Race, Hispanic Origin, and Sex for Population 25 Years and Older (in percentages): 2008*

		High School Graduate or More	College Graduate or More
All Races	Male	85.9	30.1
	Female	87.2	28.8
	Total	86.6	29.4
White	Male	86.3	30.5
	Female	87.8	29.1
	Total	87.1	29.8
Black	Male	81.8	18.7
	Female	84.0	20.4
	Total	83.0	19.6
Asian and Pacific Islander	Male	90.8	55.8
	Female	86.9	49.8
	Total	88.7	52.6
Hispanic*	Male	60.9	12.6
	Female	63.7	14.1
	Total	62.3	13.4

*Persons of Hispanic origin may be of any race.

Source: Educational attainment for males and females by race drawn from Table 225. "Educational Attainment by Race, Hispanic Origin, and Sex: 1970 to 2008."
Total figures drawn from Tables 224 and 226. "Educational Attainment by Selected Characteristics: 2008." U.S. Census Bureau, Current Population Survey. http://www.census.gov/prod/2009pubs/10statab/educ.pdf, accessed October 13, 2010.

Asian immigrants generally fall into two educational categories—highly educated and poorly educated, with relatively few having moderate levels of education.[22] Many Asian immigrants arrive in the United States with high degrees of education, reflecting what is termed a *brain drain*, in which those who are well-educated leave one country to seek greater opportunities and income in other countries. Being well-educated and skilled generally increases the likelihood of gaining entry and employment in the United States. As Table 6.2 shows, the distribution of education among Asians is not symmetrical: 64.4% of Asian Indians, but only 13.8% of Vietnamese and 9.2% of Cambodians/Hmongs/Laotians have completed college.[23] Fewer of the latter groups have college degrees

[22]Mosisa (2002).
[23]Le, C. N. (2005). "Socioeconomic Statistics and Demographics." *Asian-Nation: The Landscape of Asian America*. http://www.asian-nation.org/demographics.shtml, accessed December 19, 2010.

than Blacks and Latinos. In 2003, Asian Americans filed a "friend of the court" brief in support of affirmative action in education regarding the University of Michigan's admission program, which took into account whether applicants were from an underrepresented minority, along with other factors. Signers of the brief included the Asian American Legal Defense and Education Fund, Chinese for Affirmative Action, Filipinos for Affirmative Action, the Southeast Asia Resource Action Center, and the National Association for the Education and Advancement of Cambodian, Laotian, and Vietnamese Americans. Opposing the view that such diversity programs harm Asians, the brief stated:

> The reality is that Asian Pacific Americans continue to suffer from racial discrimination in many aspects of life. In certain contexts, such as employment or public contracting, the effects of such discrimination are sufficiently egregious that Asian Pacific Americans should be specifically included in affirmative action programs to ensure diversity. In other contexts … Asian Pacific Americans will receive fair treatment even if not expressly included in affirmative action programs because the flexibility of programs such as Michigan's takes into account the unique backgrounds and distinctive experiences of Asian Pacific American applicants.[24]

For many Asians, education levels are related to their country of birth; U.S. natives or voluntary immigrants tend to have more education, while refugees (those fleeing their homelands) are more likely to have low levels of education. Asians who are native-born and some immigrants are more likely to have advanced degrees and to speak English fluently, while refugees are more likely to have low education levels and limited language skills. Table 6.2 shows that significant differences among Asians exist in education, income, and likelihood of poverty or of receiving public assistance. Asian Indians' education and income exceed that of Whites in many categories, but the experiences of Cambodians, Hmongs, Laotians, and Vietnamese are quite different and more closely resemble those of Blacks and Latinos than those of Asian Indians or Whites. For all Asian groups combined, in 2009 12.5% of Asian families lived in poverty while 9.4% of White, non-Hispanics did.[25]

---

[24]Brief of Amici Curiae National Asian Pacific American Legal Consortium, Asian Law Caucus, Asian Pacific American Legal Center, et al. in Support of Respondents. http://www.napaba.org/uploads/napaba/02-14-2003_Grutter_&_Gratz_Brief.pdf, accessed July 5, 2005.

[25]DeNavas-Walt, C., Proctor, B. D., & Smith, J. C. (2010). *Income, Poverty, and Health Insurance Coverage in the United States: 2009.* U.S. Census Bureau, Current Population Reports, p60–238. Washington, D.C.: U.S. Government Printing Office.

TABLE 6.2 *Socioeconomic Statistics and Demographics for Selected Racial/Ethnic Groups (2000 Census)*

	Whites	Blacks	Latinos	Asian Indians	Cambodians, Hmongs, or Laotians	Chinese	Koreans	Vietnamese	Pacific Islanders	Filipinos	Japanese
Less than high school	15.3	29.1	48.5	12.6	52.7	23.6	13.8	37.8	21.7	13.1	9.5
College degree	25.3	13.6	9.9	64.4	9.2	46.3	43.6	13.8	13.6	42.8	40.8
Median family income in 2000s*	$48.5	$33.3	$36.0	$69.5	$43.9	$58.3	$48.5	$51.5	$50.0	$65.4	$61.6
Median personal income in 2000s*	$23.6	$16.3	$14.4	$26.0	$16.0	$20.0	$16.3	$16.0	$19.1	$23.0	$26.0
Living in poverty	9.4	24.9	21.4	8.2	22.5	13.1	15.5	13.8	16.7	6.9	8.6
Public assistance	1.3	4.5	3.5	0.9	9.9	1.8	1.6	4.8	4.4	1.6	0.9

*The median income is the income at which half the population in a category is below and half the population is above. Median incomes are generally lower than mean incomes.

Note: All measures are percentages except income.

Source: Adapted from Le, C. N. (2010). "Socioeconomic Statistics & Demographics." *Asian-Nation: The Landscape of Asian America.* http://www.asian-nation.org/demographics.shtml, accessed November 1, 2010.

Participation and Occupations

In 2008, about 3% more Asian men were participating in the workforce than men overall, but Asian women were slightly less likely to participate than White women. By 2018, both Asian and White men's participation rates will have declined in about the same proportions, but 1.6% fewer Asian women will be participating compared with White women (see Table 4.2).

Asians are concentrated in managerial and professional specialty occupations, which include job titles such as managers, executives, administrators, physicians, nurses, lawyers, architects, engineers, scientists, and teachers (Figure 6.2). Asian Americans represent 15% of the nation's physicians and surgeons but slightly more than 4% of the nation's population.[26] At 39.3%, Asian representation in managerial and professional specialty occupations exceeds that of Whites by

FIGURE 6.2 *Occupation Distribution of the White and API-Employed Civilian Labor Force 2002*

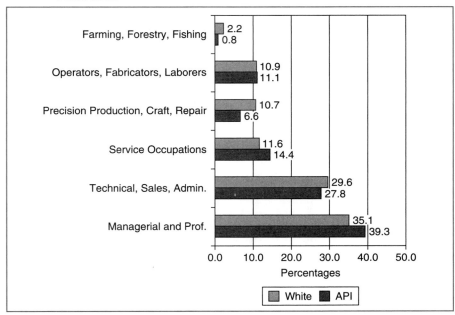

Source: "The Asian and Pacific Islander Population in the United States: March 2002" (PPL-163), Table 11. Major Occupation Group of the Employed Civilian Population 16 Years and Over by Sex, and Race and Hispanic Origin: March 2002. http://www.census.gov/population/socdemo/race/api/ppl-163/tab11.txt, accessed November 2, 2010.

[26]Asian Pacific American Population Census Facts for Heritage Month May 2004. http://www.imdiversity.com/villages/asian/reference/census_apa_stats_2004.asp, accessed July 5, 2005.

4.2 percentage points. On the other hand, the representation of Whites in precision production, craft, and repair occupations exceeds that of Asians by 4.1 percentage points. Asians are slightly more likely than Whites to work in service occupations (14.4% compared to 11.6%).

▌ ASIANS AS THE "MODEL MINORITY"

Despite many researchers' efforts to refute the stereotype of Asians as the "model minority," the perception endures and is fairly widely held. Many people view the success of these Asians as due to hard work and determination, in contrast to Blacks, Latinos, and American Indians. One writer stated in a *Newsweek* magazine article that Asians were "outwhiting the whites," exceeding Whites in education and income.[27] This distorted picture often fuels animosity toward Asians from other minority groups and from Whites and ignores differences among Asians in education, income, and employment and understates the barriers and discrimination that Asians face. Many times, discrimination against Asians occurs concurrently with discrimination against other minorities, as shown in the following EEOC cases.

In February 2007, EEOC obtained a $5 million settlement resolving two consolidated class action employment discrimination lawsuits against a global engine systems and parts company, asserting that the company engaged in illegal discrimination against African Americans, Hispanics, and Asians at its Rockford and Rockton, Illinois, facilities with respect to pay, promotions, and training. *EEOC v. Woodward Governor Company*, No. 06-cv-50178 (N.D. Ill. Feb. 2007)

In August 2006, a major national public works contractor paid $125,000 to settle race, gender, national origin, and religious discrimination and retaliation lawsuits brought by EEOC on behalf of a class of Black, Asian, and female electricians who were subjected to daily harassment due to their race, national origin, and/or gender by their immediate foremen, racial and otherwise offensive graffiti in plain sight at the workplace, and retaliation for complaining. *EEOC v. Amelco*, No. C 05-2492 MEJ (N.D. Cal. Aug. 22, 2006)

In November 2004, the Commission settled for $50 million a lawsuit filed against Abercrombie & Fitch on behalf of a class of African Americans, Asian Americans, Latinos, and women allegedly subjected to discrimination in

------

[27]"Success Story: Outwhiting the Whites." (1971, June 21). *Newsweek*, pp. 24–25.

TABLE 6.3 *Mean Total Money Earnings in 2008 for White, Non-Hispanic Men and Women and Asian Men and Women*

	Asian (alone) male	White (alone) male, non-Hispanic	Asian (alone) female	White (alone) female, non-Hispanic
High school graduate, including GED	$37.2	$42.6	$24.4	$26.6
Some college, no degree	$45.9	$49.2	$28.0	$30.7
Bachelor's degree	$69.3	$79.6	$49.8	$46.0
Master's degree	$80.2	$91.3	$61.8	$54.5
Doctorate degree	$117.4	$116.4	$66.4	$72.4
Professional degree	$141.3	$155.6	$84.6	$86.9

Source: U.S. Census Bureau. PINC-03. "Educational Attainment—People 25 Years Old and Over, by Total Money Earnings in 2008, Work Experience in 2008, Age, Race, Hispanic Origin, and Sex." http://www.census.gov/hhes/www/cpstables/032009/perinc/new03_000.htm, accessed November 12, 2010.

recruitment, hiring, assignment, promotion, and discharge based on race, color, national origin, and sex. Abercrombie & Fitch also agreed to improve hiring, recruitment, training, and promotions policies; revise marketing material; and select a Vice President of Diversity and diversity recruiters. *EEOC v. Abercrombie & Fitch Stores, Inc.*, No. CV-04-4731 (N.D. Cal. Nov. 10, 2004)

Earnings disparities between Asians and Whites also call into doubt the idea that all Asians are successful and free from discrimination. Table 6.3 shows that comparisons between White and Asian men and women are complex. At the lower educational levels, Whites' earnings exceed those of Asians. At the bachelor's degree level, White men earn greater than $10,000 per year more than Asian men, but Asian women earn nearly $4,000 more than White women. Except at the doctorate degree level, White men continue to earn more than Asian men, while White women with doctorate and professional degrees earn more than Asian women. Further, although Asians have higher earnings than Whites in some cases, many Asians live in high-cost areas (Honolulu, Los Angeles, New York, and San Francisco); 95% of all API live in metropolitan areas, compared to 78% of Whites.[28] In addition, Asian family incomes are based on more workers than White family incomes. In metropolitan

[28]Reeves, T. J., & Bennett, C. E. (2003). "The Asian and Pacific Islander Population in the United States: March 2002." Current Population Reports, P20-540. U.S. Census Bureau, Washington, D.C. http://www.census.gov/prod/2003pubs/p20-540.pdf, accessed December 19, 2010.

areas, API are eight times more likely to live in crowded household conditions than Whites.[29]

Misperception: Asians have higher incomes than Whites.

Reality: Asians tend to live in high-cost areas and have more family members contributing to family income, making their earnings appear higher than they actually are.

Yen Espiritu has said the idea of Asians being model minorities is one that tells "only half-truths, masking the plight of disadvantaged subgroups and glossing over the problems of underemployment, misemployment, and unemployment" that Asians face.[30] Many others echo Espiritu's sentiments about the inaccuracies and questionable motivations behind calling Asians "model minorities"referring to these inaccuracies as the **model minority myth**.[31] The unspoken message is that because Asians are hardworking, successful, and free from discrimination, other minority groups should do as Asians do. As discussed in Focal Issue 6.1, Asians at times do face overt racist behavior and recognize and resist being portrayed as a "voiceless model minority."

One important factor in determining how well people have avoided discrimination and how successful they are is to measure the return on their investments in education. As discussed earlier, Asian Americans are, overall, the most highly educated group in the United States, so one might expect their earnings to exceed those of every other racial and ethnic group, but this is not always the case, as Table 6.3 shows. Unemployment and type of occupation are other indicators of a group's success. As Table 6.4 shows, White unemployment at all levels is the lowest and Black unemployment is generally the highest. Asian unemployment is more similar to that of Blacks and Latinos than to that of Whites. Well-educated Asian Americans are likely to be employed; those with less education, particularly

---

[29]Ro, M. (2000). "Overview of Asians and Pacific Islanders in the United States and California." http://www.communityvoices.org/Uploads/om3gfk55hhzyvrn00n4nerbf_20020828090003.pdf, accessed December 19, 2010.

[30]Espiritu, Y. L. (1999). "The Refugees and the Refuge: Southeast Asians in the United States." In A. G. Dworkin & R. J. Dworkin (Eds.), *The Minority Report*, 3rd ed. Fort Worth, TX: Harcourt Brace Publishers, pp. 343–363.

[31]For discussions of the model minority myth, see Cheng, C. (1997). "Are Asian American Employees a Model Minority or Just a Minority?" *Journal of Applied Behavioral Science*, 33: 277–290. Le, C. N. (2010). "The Model Minority Image." *Asian-Nation: The Landscape of Asian America*. http://www.asian-nation.org/model-minority.shtml, accessed November 2, 2010; Takaki (2008); Gold & Kibria (1993); Hurh, W. M., & Kim, K. C. (1989). "The Success Image of Asian Americans—Its Validity, and Its Practical and Theoretical Implications." *Ethnic and Racial Studies*, 12(4): 512–538.

FOCAL ISSUE 6.1	Jersey Guys' Disc Jockeys Make Racist Anti-Asian Statements on Air

On April 25, 2005, two disc jockeys (DJ) of New Jersey radio station NJ 101.5, Craig Carton and Ray Rossi, astounded and offended many listeners by making anti-Asian remarks on air. The discussion began with negative comments about a Korean American named Jun Choi who was running for mayor of Edison, New Jersey. Carton asked, "Would you really vote for someone named Jun Choi?" One DJ noted that concern about the Asian vote from both Choi and his opponent in the election, Jim Spadoro, was "part of a larger problem … forgetting that we're Americans." The on-air show deteriorated from there, with derogatory comments about Chinese, Asians, Indians, and references to the DJs' previous negative comments about Arabs. Carton and Rossi complained that there were too many Asians in New Jersey casinos, suggesting that there should be "Asian-only" rooms there because of Asians' lack of knowledge of the games and their "little beady pocketbooks" stuffed with wads of $100 bills. "Ching chong, ching chong, ching chong" was interspersed with laughter and comments that the DJs had "nothing against them [Asians]," who were "very good people … very nice people."[32]

Many people were outraged by the anti-Asian comments, and complaints poured in to the radio station, which was reportedly caught off guard by the volume of complaints. Both the National Association for the Advancement of Colored People (NAACP) and the Anti-Defamation League joined Asian groups in expressing outrage at the broadcast. Hyundai Motors America indefinitely suspended its advertisements from the station.

Cingular Wireless withdrew advertising from the Jersey Guys' afternoon programming spots. In commenting on the vocal response from the Asian American community, Veronica Jung, executive director of the Korean American League for Civic Action, stated that "we will no longer be the voiceless model minority. We represent significant buying power and a large consumer base, and we'll use that weight." The radio station refused to comment on the amount lost in advertising revenues.

Choi won the election and was sworn in as Edison mayor on January 1, 2006.

QUESTIONS TO CONSIDER

1. *When Michelle Kwan, Chinese American Olympic skater (native of Torrance, California), came in second in an Olympic event, a major news headline read "American Beats Kwan." Four years later, after another skating loss, other news outlets reported that Kwan had been beaten by an "American," repeating the earlier terminology and again alienating and aggravating Asian Americans. As is evident from the comments of the Jersey Guys, Asian Americans are often seen as outsiders, even when they are native-born or naturalized citizens. Why might this perception persist?*

2. *Aside from apologies, what specific responses are appropriate from organizations when actions such as those of the Jersey Guys take place?*

3. *Which of Cox and Blake's six reasons for valuing diversity are relevant to this issue?*

---

[32] Quotes taken from "Transcript of the Jersey Guys on the Edison Mayoral Race NJ 101.5." http://www.sepiamutiny.com/sepia/archives/TranscripttheJerseyGuys.pdf, accessed November 2, 2010.

TABLE 6.4 *Unemployment Level by Educational Attainment and Race/Ethnicity (percent of population 25 and over: 2008, 2009)*

2008	Total	Men	Women	White	Black	Asian	Hispanic[*]
Less than high school	9.0	8.8	9.4	8.2	14.5	6.4	8.2
High school graduate	5.7	5.9	5.3	5.1	9.3	4.3	6.2
Some college, no degree	5.1	5.0	5.1	4.5	8.0	3.8	5.4
Associate degree	3.7	3.8	3.7	3.3	6.2	3.8	4.1
Bachelor's and higher	2.8	2.5	2.7	2.4	4.0	2.8	3.4

Bachelor's and higher includes persons with bachelor's, master's, professional, and doctoral degree.

2009	Total	Men	Women	White	Black	Asian	Hispanic[*]
Less than high school	14.6	14.9	14.2	13.9	21.3	8.4	13.7
High school graduate	9.7	11.0	8.0	9.0	14.0	7.5	10.4
Some college, no degree	8.6	9.3	8.0	7.9	12.1	8.9	9.6
Associate degree	6.8	7.9	5.9	6.2	10.3	7.5	8.5
Bachelor's and higher	4.6	4.7	4.5	4.2	7.3	5.6	5.7

Bachelor's and higher includes persons with bachelor's, master's, professional, and doctoral degree.

*Persons whose ethnicity is Hispanic are classified by ethnicity as well as by race.

Sources: http://www.bls.gov/cps/cpsaat7.pdf, accessed October 12, 2010; U.S. Census Bureau. PINC-03. "Educational Attainment—People 25 Years Old and Over, by Total Money Earnings in 2008, Work Experience in 2008, Age, Race, Hispanic Origin, and Sex." http://www.census.gov/hhes/www/cpstables/032009/perinc/new03_000.htm, accessed November 12, 2010.

immigrants, often work for low wages or are unemployed, in poverty, and often recipients of public assistance.[33] When employed, many immigrant women work in the garment industries; men often work in restaurants, frequently at substandard wages under poor working conditions and with excessive hours. Asian immigrants without education and language skills may be locked into these dead-end positions.

Underemployment affects educated Asian Americans as it does other minority groups. Despite often having higher education than Whites, Asians are underrepresented in senior management and executive ranks. Asians hold less than 0.5% of senior management positions in the United

[33]Borjas, G. J., & Trejo, S. J. (1991). "Immigrant Participation in the Welfare System." *Industrial and Labor Relations Review*, 44(2): 195–211; Jensen, L. (1988). "Patterns of Immigration in Public Assistance Utilization, 1970–1980." *International Migration Review*, 22(1): 51–83. See also Bean, F. D., Van Hook, J. V. W., & Glick, J. E. (1997). "Country of Origin, Type of Public Assistance, and Patterns of Welfare Recipiency Among U.S. Immigrants and Natives." *Social Science Quarterly*, 78: 432–451.

States.[34] They are frequently perceived as technically astute and good at math, which are "positive" stereotypes but likely also to contribute to their underrepresentation in higher-level positions in organizations. Asians are also often stereotyped as passive, nonconfrontational, and lacking in communication and language skills—regardless of whether they are native English speakers. These common misperceptions work to prevent Asians from advancing in organizations and often confine them to positions in which little communication, leadership, and decision making are required. Such positions often have few advancement opportunities, creating a glass ceiling for Asians.[35] For example, although Asians are overrepresented in technical fields, they are less likely than other minority group members to be in management in these fields.[36]

▌ ASIAN AMERICAN ENTREPRENEURS

An accurate perception of Asian Americans is that they are more likely to start their own businesses than other minority groups. Some researchers suggest that a higher level of entrepreneurship among Asians is in part due to their having encountered the glass ceiling. Others propose that limited skills and informal networks among some Asian immigrants make them more likely to start small businesses but that they suffer numerous and expensive social costs as a result of entrepreneurship. It is likely that both ideas have some merit and that the theories apply to different groups of Asians with different skills.[37] Well-educated, more highly skilled Asian entrepreneurs may start their own businesses in response to discrimination or they may be professionals who originally intended to start professional businesses in the United States (e.g., consulting or technical, medical, or legal enterprises). Asian entrepreneurs with few language skills, low education, and few other opportunities may also start small businesses.

There are 1.1 million Asian-owned businesses in the United States, employing 2.2 million people and generating over $326 billion in revenues

---

[34]Minami, D. (1995). Untitled. In *Perspectives on Affirmative Action*. Los Angeles: Asian Pacific American Public Policy Institute, p. 11. Korn/Ferry International, New York. (1990). *Executive Profile: A Decade of Change in Corporate Leadership*, p. 23. See also Brief of Amici Curiae National Asian Pacific American Legal Consortium, Asian Law Caucus, Asian Pacific American Legal Center, et al., in Support of Respondents.

[35]Woo, D. (2000). *Glass Ceiling and Asian Americans: New Face of Workface Barriers*. Walnut Creek, CA: Alta Mira Press.

[36]National Science Foundation, Division of Science Resource Statistics. (2004). *Women, Minorities, and Persons with Disabilities in Science and Engineering*, NSF 04-317 (Arlington, VA). http://www.nsf.gov/statistics/wmpd/pdf/nsf07315.pdf, accessed November 2, 2010.

[37]For a detailed discussion of theories about Asian entrepreneurship, see Le, C. N. (2010). "Asian Small Businesses." *Asian-Nation: The Landscape of Asian America*. http://www.asian-nation.org/small-business.shtml, accessed November 2, 2010.

FIGURE 6.3 *Distribution of Asian- and Pacific Islander-Owned Firms*

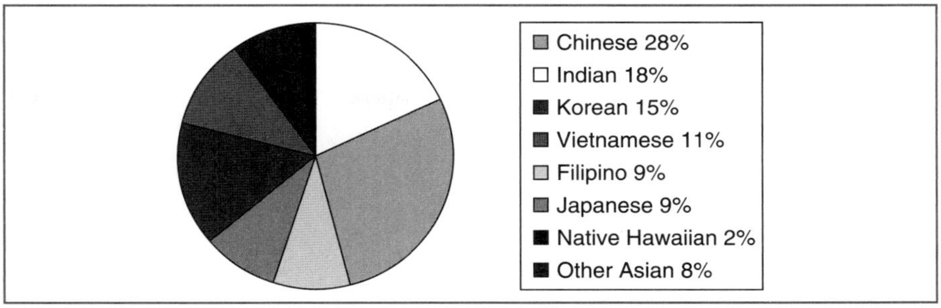

- Chinese 28%
- Indian 18%
- Korean 15%
- Vietnamese 11%
- Filipino 9%
- Japanese 9%
- Native Hawaiian 2%
- Other Asian 8%

Source: U.S. Census Bureau. (2001). "Asian- and Pacific Islander-Owned Businesses: 1997." http://www.census.gov/prod/2001pubs/cenbr01-7.pdf, accessed June 9, 2005.

in a wide variety of industries.[38] Among Asians, those of Chinese, Indian, Korean, and Vietnamese ancestry are most likely to have their own firms (Figure 6.3). Asians from different backgrounds tend to own different kinds of businesses. For example, three of four API-owned hotels and motels are owned by Asian Indians; two of three API-owned fishing, hunting, and trapping firms are owned by Vietnamese; and Koreans own half of the API-owned apparel and accessory stores.[39] Most Asian-owned firms are in the service industries (44%), and 21% are in the retail trade industry. Although there are more than twice as many firms in the service industries as in the retail trade industries, both generate 22% of the total receipts of API-owned firms.

As with small businesses in general, many Asian-owned firms struggle for survival and may fail within the first few years. Although 5% of Asian-owned firms have receipts of $1 million or more, nearly 30% have receipts under $10,000 each year. Researchers have documented long hours of unpaid or extremely low-wage labor among family members of Asian business owners as part of the reason they survive.[40] Edna Bonacich's thought-provoking article argues that many immigrant small business owners are pawns in a capitalistic society (see Research Summary 6.1).

Misperception: Asian business owners are highly successful.

Reality: Some Asian business owners are highly successful, while others marginally succeed due to long hours and the unpaid labor of family members.

---

[38]Facts for Features, Asian/Pacific Heritage Month, May 2010.
[39]U.S. Census Bureau. (2001). "Asian- and Pacific-Islander Owned Businesses: 1997." http://www.census.gov/prod/2001pubs/cenbr01-7.pdf, accessed June 9, 2005.
[40]Espiritu (1999).

RESEARCH SUMMARY 6.1	*Successful Small Business Owners or Unsuspecting Pawns?*

Edna Bonacich, emeritus professor of sociology and ethnic studies at the University of California, Riverside, conducted much research on experiences of Korean immigrant entrepreneurs. Bonacich documents the expensive individual and social costs of immigrant entrepreneurship that often go unreported and unrecognized.

Small businesses are often concentrated in areas that have been abandoned by major retailers (and employers), employ workers (often other immigrants or minority group members) at below minimum wage, and are often unregulated by government entities.[41] Capitalist producers of goods sold or made in small businesses earn profits from those entities without investing in them. Low-wage workers do not organize to demand higher wages because of familial relationships, lack of knowledge, and lack of other opportunities. The small size of most entities hides them from government oversight that would help protect the workers. Ethnic small business owners whose businesses are in minority communities are referred to as *middlemen*, minorities who serve communities that White business owners have abandoned. As middlemen, these business owners at times experience hostility and frustration from African American and Latino customers as well as conflicts with their White suppliers and landlords.[42]

Bonacich and her colleague Ivan Light studied Korean immigrant entrepreneurs in Los Angeles, carefully investigating the reasons behind their entrepreneurship and their personal and professional experiences as a result of entrepreneurship.

Bonacich concluded that immigrant entrepreneurship comes at high costs to the immigrants and to society at large. These costs include:

a. family breakdown, including neglected children, due to excessive hours spent working, spousal (wife) abuse, and marital discord, due to wives having to contribute long (unpaid) hours in support of the business, yet still being expected to maintain the home.

b. expression of anti-immigrant feelings and hostility by customers and clients (e.g., by Black and Latino customers against Korean entrepreneurs, although all three are victims) and other immigrant competitors.

c. lowered labor standards for society as a whole because of labor exploitation that includes long hours at very low wages and unpaid child and family labor.

"Large corporations such as supermarkets have abandoned these neighborhoods, but the producers of the goods sold by immigrant shops continue to get the profits out of the ghetto and the barrio through immigrant firms," says Bonacich.[43] She further states that when firms are small and dispersed, this limits the ability of employees to unionize and the ability of government agencies to enforce labor standards, making abuses more likely.[44]

Pyong Gap Min and other researchers have echoed Bonacich's concerns about entrepreneurship in the Korean community. Min's research indicates that 67% of husbands and 59% of wives who work in Korean businesses work six

[41]See also Wilson, W. J. (1996). *When Work Disappears: The World of the New Urban Poor*. New York: Knopf.

[42]Min, P. G. (1996). *Caught in the Middle: Korean Communities in New York and Los Angeles*. Berkeley: University of California Press.

[43]Bonacich, E. (1988). "The Social Costs of Immigrant Entrepreneurship." *Amerasia Journal*, 14(1): 119–128, p. 121.

[44]Ibid.

or seven days per week.[45] The experiences of Vietnamese small business owners documented by Steven Gold and Nazli Kibria are similar to those reported by Bonacich.[46] They report extremely low wages among small business owners, family members, and other employees, no benefits, high rates of business failure, and stiff competition from other ethnic-owned small businesses.

_____

Source: Bonacich, E. (1988). "The Social Costs of Immigrant Entrepreneurship." *Amerasia Journal*, 14(1): 119–128.

QUESTIONS TO CONSIDER

1. *How familiar are you with small businesses owned by Asian immigrants? If you are* *familiar with such businesses, how does what you perceive about their level of profitability, hours worked, and employees compare with what Bonacich reported?*

2. *Many small businesses are staffed entirely or almost entirely by people of the same race or ethnicity of the owners—indeed they are very homogeneous. Is such homogeneity of employees in violation of Title VII of the Civil Rights Act? Why or why not?*

3. *What does the most recently available U.S. Census Bureau data say about the ownership, numbers, types, size, and profitability of Asian-owned businesses?*

▌ RESEARCH ON EXPERIENCES OF ASIAN AMERICANS AT WORK

Along with the "positive" stereotypes about Asian Americans (e.g., good at math, technically astute, hardworking, highly educated, wealthy) are the negative stereotypes—that Asians lack leadership qualities and communication skills and are arrogant. Many of these stereotypes are partially due to animosity arising from Asians' perceived success in education and business.[47] Some researchers who have studied their treatment in the media have found that Asians are likely to be portrayed as affluent, highly educated, and technologically proficient.[48] Media stereotypes of Asian women as docile, submissive, or exotic contribute to their experiences with racialized sexual harassment, Black and Hispanic women also experience, as previously discussed.[49] Because many other Americans say they do not know any Asians, stereotypes and media representations are the bases for how they perceive this group.

....

[45]Min, P. G. (1997). "Korean Immigrant Wives' Labor Force Participation, Marital Power, and Status." In E. Higginbotham & M. Romero (Eds.), *Women and Work: Exploring Race, Ethnicity, and Class.* Thousand Oaks, CA: Sage Publications, pp. 176–191.

[46]Gold & Kibria (1993).

[47]For example, see "Committee of 100: American Attitudes Toward Chinese Americans and Asian Americans." (2004, Summer). *The Diversity Factor*, 12(3): 38–44.

[48]Paek, H. J., & Shah, H. (2003). "Racial Ideology, Model Minorities, and the 'Not-So-Silent Partner:' Stereotyping of Asian Americans in U.S. Magazine Advertising." *Howard Journal of Communications*, 14(4): 225–244.

[49]Cho, S. (1997). "Converging Stereotypes in Racialized Sexual Harassment: Where the Model Minority Meets Suzie Wong." *Journal of Gender, Race, & Justice*, 1: 177–211.

Compared to Blacks, little empirical research has been done to investigate the organizational experiences of Asian Americans. What research exists indicates that Asians' report experiences with discrimination and the glass ceiling similar to those of other minority groups. The differential treatment takes the form of access and treatment discrimination. For example, Asians sometimes face treatment discrimination when they are steered to particular jobs deemed appropriate for people who are technically strong but have limited English skills and when they are denied management positions due to a perceived lack of leadership skills. Asians' limited representation in state, local, and the federal government, college and university administration and professional school faculty, the judiciary system, and corporations provide evidence of the glass ceiling for Asians.[50] Research Summary 6.2 reports on Asians' experiences with workplace discrimination that are similar to those reported by Blacks and Latinos. Asians' attitudes toward affirmative action in employment are also more similar to the attitudes of Blacks and Latinos than Whites. Rather than buying into inter-ethnic discrimination, minorities should recognize their similarities in experiences and goals.

International Feature 6.1 considers the population, employment, and workplace experiences of Asians in Britain. A study conducted in New Zealand investigating the effects of Chinese, Indian, or Anglo-Saxon names found effects for those with Chinese and Indian names similar to the effects of Black-sounding names in the United States (see Chapter 4).[51] Study participants, primarily practicing managers, chose applicants to be on short lists of candidates and rated them in terms of suitability for the position. The applicants were all highly qualified for the positions in question, but Chinese applicants were least likely to be placed on the short list and received the lowest suitability ratings, below Indian applicants. Applicants with Anglo-Saxon names received more favorable ratings than candidates with ethnic names. Chinese applicants with anglicized names (such as Polly Wong) received lower ratings from European raters than they did from Asian raters. Overall, ethnic candidates were significantly underrepresented in the final short lists and received significantly lower suitability ratings, despite equal qualifications.

[50]For a discussion, see Brief of Amici Curiae National Asian Pacific American Legal Consortium, Asian Law Caucus, Asian Pacific American Legal Center, et al., in Support of Respondents.

[51]Wilson, M., Gahlout, P., Liu, L., & Mouly, S. (2005). "A Rose by Any Other Name ... : The Effect of Ethnicity and Name on Access to Employment." *The University of Auckland Business Review*, 7(2): 55–68.

RESEARCH SUMMARY 6.2	*Asian Americans, Discrimination, and Attitudes toward Affirmative Action in Employment: Empirical Research Evidence*

The topic of Asian Americans' attitudes toward affirmative action commonly comes up in debates about affirmative action, with some writers arguing that Asians support it and others arguing that Asians are against it. Still others present both sides of the story; for example, Michael Fletcher's article in the *Washington Post* debated whether affirmative action was "a barrier or a boon" for Asian Americans.[52] Fletcher's and many popular press articles confound affirmative action in education with affirmative action in employment, both of which strive to help underrepresented groups but which do so by very different mechanisms. Even so, it is clear that some Asians are supportive of affirmative action measures, while others are against it. For example, 61% of Asian Americans voted against California's Proposition 209, an anti-affirmative action effort. Many Asians supported Washington state's Initiative 200, which was modeled after Proposition 209. One Seattle physician felt that "Asian Americans lose their competitive edge because of affirmative action"; another stated that "there has been an attempt to use us (Asians) as a wedge, but the fact is that we are direct beneficiaries of affirmative action."[53]

As with other issues discussed in the media, empirical research may help clarify the inconsistencies. The majority of research assessing employees' experiences with workplace discrimination and attitudes toward affirmative action has focused on Whites and Blacks, however. A lesser amount of research has sampled Latinos, and even fewer studies have included Asian Americans. Although some studies have included Asians in their "minorities" category, this prevents separate analysis of each group's perspective and masks differences between them.

One study specifically assessed Asians' attitudes and compared them with those of Whites, Blacks, and Latinos. The researchers also compared attitudes of Asian U.S. citizens with those of Asian noncitizens, recognizing the potential for differences in experiences, perspectives, and beliefs between these groups. The survey asked questions about the specific attributes commonly associated with affirmative action programs, such as whether they improve job opportunities of women and minorities, reduce discrimination in historically segregated jobs, and create a lot of paperwork for employers. Overall, Asians (both groups) held significantly more positive beliefs about affirmative action than Whites, in every instance. In addition, for some attributes of affirmative action, Asian noncitizens held significantly more positive attitudes than Asian U.S. citizens. The former were more likely to think that affirmative action in employment helps to give everyone qualified an equal chance, create greater awareness of discrimination, and produce a more diverse workforce. They were also less likely to have negative views about attributes of affirmative action programs than Asian U.S. citizens, such as that they frequently operate as quotas or cause employers to hire people who are less qualified.

Study participants' overall impression of affirmative action and their experiences with discrimination were also measured. In all, Whites' attitudes toward affirmative action were most

---

[52]Fletcher, M. A. (1998). "For Asian Americans, a Barrier or a Boon?" *Washington Post*, June 20, 1998. Reprinted in F. J. Crosby & C. VanDeVeer (Eds.), *Sex, Race, and Merit: Debating Affirmative Action in Education and Employment*. Ann Arbor: The University of Michigan Press.

[53]Ibid.

negative, Blacks' attitudes were most favorable, followed by Asians and Latinos, whose attitudes were statistically similar and moderately favorable. Asians reported experiencing workplace discrimination at rates similar to Latinos and Blacks and significantly less than reported by Whites.

As Asians grow as a percentage of the population, it is expected that more research will investigate their workplace experiences. In addition to distinctions between Asian citizens and those who are not citizens, differences among Asians of different ancestry (e.g., Filipino, Chinese, Korean, and Indian) and various educational and occupational levels should also be investigated.

___

Source: Bell, M. P., Harrison, D. A., & McLaughlin, M. E. (1997). "Asian American Attitudes Toward Affirmative Action: Implications for the Model Minority Myth." *Journal of Applied Behavioral Science*, 33: 356–377.

QUESTIONS TO CONSIDER

1. *Why have attitudes of Asian Americans toward affirmative action in employment been studied so little?*

2. *What issues likely contribute to attitudinal differences between Asian U.S. citizens and those who are not citizens?*

3. *What factors may influence differences in experiences with discrimination between minority groups?*

4. *As discussed earlier in this chapter, many Asian Americans also support affirmative action in education. Why might perceptions that Asians do not benefit from affirmative action in employment and that they are harmed by affirmative action in education be so prevalent?*

Asian American Women at Work

As discussed in previous chapters, women of color face unique obstacles related to their sex and race or ethnicity in their organizational experiences. Asian American women are no exception to the double whammy resulting from multiple minority group statuses; they earn less than Asian men in every earnings category.

More Asian women work in the computer and electronic product manufacturing industry than in any other single industry; they also work in retail industries like clothing and health and personal care stores, which are often family-owned or immigrant businesses. Hospitals, nursing, and residential care facilities employ 6.9% of Asian women.[54] Many Asian women occupy lower-paid, lower-status positions and experience discrimination in these industries. Featured Case 6.1 describes egregious discrimination against Asian registered nurses in a nursing and residential care facility.

Asian immigrant women are particularly likely to work in family-owned businesses, computer manufacturing, or the garment industry, often for long hours, at low wages, and with no benefits. Some assemble circuit

___

[54]Women of Color: Their Employment in the Private Sector, Equal Employment Opportunity Commission, http://www.eeoc.gov/eeoc/statistics/reports/womenofcolor/womenofcolor.pdf, accessed November 2, 2010.

INTERNATIONAL FEATURE 6.1	*Asians in the United Kingdom*

Asians have resided in the United Kingdom for centuries and are significant contributors to its history and successes. For a long time, the United Kingdom has placed stringent limits on immigration, although records reveal that Asian merchants, politicians, suffragettes, teachers, students, military personnel, and others have resided there for many years. England's deliberate effort to restrict entry of Asian seamen through the Special Restriction Order of 1925 is viewed as a precursor to the area's current demographic and social conditions, including "institutional racism" against Asians in Britain today.[55]

As of the Census conducted in 2001, there were about 60 million people in the United Kingdom; 92.1% were White, 2% Black, 1.8% Indian, 1.3% Pakistani, 1.2% mixed, and 1.6% other (Chinese, Bangladeshi, and other Asian).[56] The Race Relations Act of 1968, as amended in 1976, prohibits "open and direct" and indirect race-based discrimination in employment, housing, and public services in the United Kingdom.

Educational levels and employment experiences of Asians in the United Kingdom vary greatly, and education and employment of Indians and Chinese are significantly different from the experiences of Pakistanis and Bangladeshis. In some cases, Chinese and Indian earnings, employment levels, and occupational status approach those of Whites. In contrast, Pakistanis and Bangladeshis have lower earnings and higher unemployment. Whereas Indians and Chinese in the United Kingdom are likely to be from established

immigrant communities, Pakistanis and Bangladeshis are more recent immigrants and are less established. The latter often work in low-wage positions in declining industries and are residentially segregated.

The experiences of Asians and other ethnic minorities with discrimination in employment, harassment, exclusion, hate crimes, and racial profiling by police are gaining increased attention in the British media, among the public, and among lawmakers. Overall, unemployment for Asians is considerably higher than for Whites. In one study, unemployment levels ranged between 13% for Indians and 33% for Bangladeshis compared to 8.8% for Whites. In addition, at comparable education levels, Asian unemployment is significantly higher than that of Whites. Asians are more likely to be in declining industries or those involving manual labor, such as manufacturing, or to be self-employed.[57]

As in other areas, some women of color in the United Kingdom are particularly marginalized in employment. White, Black, Indian, and Chinese women have similar rates of workforce participation (about 60%), compared with less than 30% for Pakistani and Bangladeshi women. When employed, Pakistani or Bangladeshi women earn 56 cents to the dollar earned by White men.[58]

Sources: Jones, T. (1993). *Britain's Ethnic Minorities* Muhammad, A. (1998). *Between Cultures: Continuity and Change in the Lives of Young Asians*. London: Routledge.

[55]See Visram, R. (2002). *Asians in Britain: 400 Years of History*. London: Pluto Publishers.

[56]*The World FactBook*. United Kingdom. http://www.cia.gov/cia/publications/factbook/geos/uk.html, accessed July 11, 2005.

[57]Muhammad, A. (1998). *Between Cultures: Continuity and Change in the Lives of Young Asians*. London: Routledge.

[58]"UK Blacks, Asian Women Being Ostracized: Report." *Hindustan Times*, February 17, 2005.

| FEATURED CASE 6.1 | *Woodbine Healthcare Center's Treatment of Filipino Registered Nurses* |

The EEOC headline reads, "EEOC Announces $2.1 Million Settlement of Wage Discrimination Suit for Class of Filipino Nurses," and the text details a case against Woodbine Healthcare Center, a nursing home in Gladstone, Missouri. The lawsuit alleged that Woodbine discriminated against sixty-five Filipino registered nurses (RNs) in multiple ways, including wages, job assignment, and other terms and conditions of employment.

Woodbine had petitioned the Immigration and Naturalization Service (INS) for permission to employ foreign RNs because of a shortage of RNs in the local area. In its petition, Woodbine gave the INS assurances that the Filipinos would be hired as RNs and paid the same wages U.S. RNs were paid. After receiving permission to hire the Filipino nurses, however, Woodbine did not do as agreed. The Filipino nurses were paid about $6.00 per hour less than U.S. nurses and many were assigned to work as aides and technicians instead of RNs. Two Filipino nurses filed discrimination lawsuits, and the EEOC found their claims to be meritorious and of "general public importance," and certified it as a class action suit. Woodbine agreed to a $2.1 million settlement, including $1.2 million in back pay and $470,000 in interest to the nurses and $430,000 in fees and expenses to the women's attorneys. Woodbine sent each nurse a letter of apology for "being misassigned into a lower-paying and less responsible position than that of a registered nurse, and being treated differently from the U.S. employees in other ways."

At the same time as the EEOC lawsuit, Woodbine also had problems with the U.S. Department of Labor, which had investigated Woodbine for prevailing-wage discrimination violations against the Filipino nurses. As a result of its investigation, Woodbine had to pay $700,000 in

back pay and penalties for those violations. In all, the discrimination against the Filipino nurses cost Woodbine $2.8 million.

Source: "EEOC Announces $2.1 Million Settlement of Wage Discrimination Suit for Class of Filipino Nurses." http://www.eeoc.gov/press/3-2-99.html, accessed June 18, 2005.

QUESTIONS TO CONSIDER

1. *Woodbine had petitioned the INS to hire Filipinos as RNs, committing to pay them the same wages but did not do so. What factors may have led to this failure?*

2. *Some of the Filipino RNs were assigned to work as nursing aides and technicians instead of RNs. Shortages of RNs are widely reported in U.S. media. Are there comparable shortages of nursing aides and technicians? What skills are required for the latter jobs?*

3. *Woodbine had trouble with the EEOC and the Department of Labor. What factors cause organizations to fail to comply with multiple types of employment-related laws? What can organizations do to avoid this?*

4. *One common issue in discrimination against non-native English speakers is claims of language problems. If the Filipino nurses were unable to adequately communicate in English, what could Woodbine have done to avoid illegal discrimination? What safeguards should an organization put in place to ensure any communication difficulties are real rather than imagined?*

5. *Researchers have documented discrimination against medical professionals by*

patients who wish to be treated only by Whites.[59] An EEOC case against Georgetowne Place, a senior community, stated that for nine years the former general manager had used elaborate marks on applications to identify minorities so as to avoid hiring them. She claimed that residents "preferred White employees, and did not want minorities to come in their rooms."[60] In another case, management at Linden Grove Health Care Center complied with a family's request that no "colored girls" work with the resident, did not address frequent use of racial slurs by residents and employees, assigned nursing staff to work shifts, lunch times, and lunch rooms by race, and denied promotions to experienced, highly qualified Blacks.[61]

a. If patient discrimination played a role in what happened to the Filipino nurses at Woodbine, what should Woodbine management have done?

b. What proportion of nursing professionals are women of color? Speculate on unnecessary recruitment and selection costs associated with refusal to hire women of color for such jobs.

c. In the Georgetowne Place case, minorities were rejected for at least nine years. What are the likely effects of discrimination on unemployment, poverty, and morale of those people?

boards and cables for one penny per component.[62] Such work may be piecework, and workers may have difficulty keeping up with production rates. But in spite of the possibility of race and sex discrimination, many Asian women do have successful careers, such as Indra Nooyi, president and chief financial officer of PepsiCo (Individual Feature 6.2).

■ FOCUS ON SELECTED ASIAN AMERICANS: CHINESE, INDIANS, AND SOUTHEAST ASIANS

Chinese

China has the largest population in the world, and people from China make up the largest subgroup of people with Asian ancestry in the United States. As discussed earlier in the chapter, the Chinese Exclusion Act and, later, quotas severely and purposely restricted Chinese immigration. Since 1965, however, Chinese immigration to the United States has increased tremendously. There are now more than 3.6 Asians of Chinese descent in

---

[59]For example, see Diamond, T. (1992). *Making Gray Gold: Narratives of Nursing Home Care.* Chicago: University of Chicago Press; DasGupta, T. (1996). *Racism and Paid Work.* Toronto: Garamond.
[60]"Georgetowne Place to Pay $650,000 to Settle EEOC Race Discrimination Lawsuit." (June 22, 2005). http://www.eeoc.gov/eeoc/newsroom/release/6-22-05.cfm, accessed November 2, 2010.
[61]EEOC Litigation Settlement Reports, May 2005. EEOC v. Central Park Lodges Long Term Care, Inc., d/b/a Linden Grove Health Care Center, NO. 04-5627 RBL (W.D. Wash. May 13, 2005).
[62]See Ro (2000) for a discussion of manufacturing and garment work among Asian immigrants.

INDIVIDUAL FEATURE 6.2	*Indra Nooyi, Chairman and Chief Executive Officer, PepsiCo*

Indra Nooyi was named president and chief financial officer of PepsiCo in May 2001 and president and CEO on October 1, 2006, and she assumed the role of chairman on May 2, 2007. PepsiCo is one of the largest producers of convenience foods and beverages, having revenues of over $60 billion and 285,000 employees worldwide.

PepsiCo includes Frito-Lay North America, PepsiCo Beverages North America, PepsiCo International, and Quaker Foods North America. Nooyi is responsible for PepsiCo's corporate functions, including finance, strategy, procurement, and information technology. *Fortune* magazine has described her as a "skilled strategist" responsible for engineering "billions of dollars in acquisition deals." She played an integral role in the purchase of Tropicana and the merger with Quaker Foods.

Prior to joining PepsiCo in 1994, Nooyi held positions at the Boston Consulting Group, where she directed international corporate strategy projects, and was in senior management at Motorola. She holds a master's degree in public and private management from Yale, a master's degree in finance and marketing from the Indian Institute of Management in Calcutta, and a degree in chemistry, physics, and mathematics from Madras Christian College in India.

Fortune credits PepsiCo with having the most diverse team of top leaders. PepsiCo consistently rates high in lists of top companies for minorities, African American women, Latinas, women executives, and supplier diversity as rated by various entities.

Sources: Allers, K. L., Hira, N. A., Tkaczyk, C., Mero, J., Forte, T., & Soehendro, M. (2005, August 22). "From Business and Academia to Hollywood and the Beltway, Meet the People with the Most Clout." *Fortune*, 152(4): 89–99; http://www.pepsico.com/Download/Indra_Nooyi_bio.pdf, accessed November 2, 2010.

the United States, including about 2.0 million people who speak a Chinese language at home.

Chinese Americans differ in income, education, and occupational success. On the one hand, many immigrants are well-educated and are often wealthy professionals or business owners. On the other hand, many immigrants have low incomes, are uneducated, and impoverished. The tourist meccas of the Chinatowns in major metropolitan cities obscure the poverty and substandard housing and working conditions of some Chinese immigrants.[63] Many immigrant women work in the garment industry (i.e., sweatshops) or restaurants; those with strong English language skills work in clerical positions while the men work in the low-wage restaurant sector.[64] Exploitation of Asian immigrant workers takes the form of low wages and long hours. A respondent in one study stated

[63]See Loo, C., & Ong, P. (1987). "Slaying Demons with a Sewing Needle: Feminist Issues for Chinatown's Women." In R. Takaki (Ed.), *From Different Shores: Perspectives on Race and Ethnicity in America*. New York: Oxford University Press, pp. 186–191.
[64]Takaki (2008).

that "Asians are very good workers," especially compared with Blacks and Whites, who "wouldn't do the type of job" he offered, due to lack of "stamina" or "humility to do that type of job."[65]

As shown in Table 6.2, nearly 50% of Chinese in the United States have a college degree, which is considerably more education than most people in the country have obtained. The median family income for Chinese families is $58,300, which exceeds the median family income of Whites. It should be noted that Chinese Americans are concentrated in the West and the Northeast, which contributes to their higher incomes over other groups. Indicative of the diversity of experiences among Asian Americans is the fact that 13.1% of Chinese live in poverty, compared to 9.4% of Whites.[66]

Asian Indians

In the U.S. Census, Asian Indians were once categorized as "White," which is another example of the fluidity of racial categories. Asian Indians have a wide variety of skin tones, and as with Blacks, skin tone has historical significance within and outside the Indian community.

Before 1965, when the Immigration and Nationality Act was passed, few Asian Indians resided in the United States. Since then, the U.S. population of Asian Indians has grown; between 1980 and 2000, the number of Asian Indians in the country increased from less than 400,000 to nearly 2 million. Asian Indians are now 16% of the Asian population in the United States.

The higher earnings and education of Asian Indians strongly contribute to the high average earnings of Asians overall. Asian Indians have considerably more education than all other racial and ethnic groups in the United States, including Whites. As discussed earlier, more than 64% of Asian Indians have at least a college degree, compared with about 30% of Whites. At one point, 11% of Asian Indian men and 8% of the Asian Indian women in the United States were physicians.[67]

Greater opportunities in the United States help fuel the migration of well-educated or affluent people from India, China, and other less developed countries to the United States. However, even highly educated Indians face discrimination and exclusion, making their return on their educational investment lower than the return of highly educated Whites.

---

[65]Moss, P., & Tilly, C. (2001). *Stories Employers Tell: Race, Skill, and Hiring in America*. New York: Russell Sage Foundation, p. 119.
[66]Le, C. N. (2010). "Socioeconomic Statistics and Demographics." *Asian-Nation: The Landscape of Asian America*. http://www.asian-nation.org/demographics.shtml, accessed November 2, 2010.
[67]Healey, J. F. (2004). *Diversity and Society*. Thousand Oaks, CA: Pine Forge Press.

In addition, in the aftermath of the 2001 terrorist attacks in the United States, Asian Indians and other darker-skinned Asians have faced severe discrimination and harassment at work based on religion and national origin (see Chapter 12).

Southeast Asians

Southeast Asians, including Vietnamese, Laotians, Hmongs, Cambodians, and others from the area, began arriving in the United States in the mid-1970s.[68] As the newest groups of Asians, Southeast Asians are the least established. They are more likely to have limited English proficiency than other Asians and non-Asians, with over 40% of Vietnamese, Cambodians, Laotians, and Hmongs reporting limited proficiency. Southeast Asians are slightly less likely to have completed college than Blacks and Latinos and have similar levels of income, which are lower than those of other Asian Americans and Whites. C. N. Le's analyses of 2000 Census data indicate that 13.8% of Vietnamese have college degrees, compared with 13.6% of Blacks, 40.8% of Japanese, and 25.3% of Whites.[69] In the 2000 Census, the proportion of Asians of Vietnamese, Cambodian, Hmong, or Laotian descent receiving public assistance was higher than the proportion of Blacks receiving such assistance (Table 6.2).

As a result of low education and lack of opportunities in other organizations, many immigrants open small businesses. Readers may be familiar with doughnut shops, dry cleaners, and "mom-and-pop" stores owned by Southeast Asians. As discussed in Research Summary 6.1, many of the businesses owned by ethnic immigrant entrepreneurs are "profitable" at high personal and social costs, yet they are the only source of income for immigrant families.

▌ RECOMMENDATIONS FOR INDIVIDUALS AND ORGANIZATIONS

Because Asian Americans are often viewed as well-educated, successful, and free from discrimination, both they and organizations that may employ them are faced with an unusual situation. The "positive" stereotypes contribute to Asians being overlooked as minority group members and seen as not needing assistance and efforts to ensure fairness. The stereotype of Asians as passive contributes to their overrepresentation in technical positions and underrepresentation in management, particularly when their

[68]Espiritu (1999).
[69]Le (2005).

educational levels are taken into account. Individuals should make known their desire to be considered for management and other promotional opportunities. If they indeed tend to avoid speaking up, they should recognize that doing so may be required for advancement.[70] As is true for women in general (see Chapter 9), it is possible to learn to exhibit behaviors that do not come naturally or, more likely, that were not learned earlier in life. Like everyone else, it is important to obtain as much education as possible in a preferred field, to avoid being steered to a technical or mathematical field by others' expectations.

Organizational leaders, management, and human resources staff should acknowledge that not all Asian Americans are well-educated and that all may be subject to exclusion and differential organizational treatment. When underrepresented in particular job categories, or when evidence of the glass ceiling exists, efforts should be made to include Asians in nondiscrimination policies and affirmative action programs. If Asians do not express interest in advancement or managerial positions, organizations should recognize that this may reflect cultural differences in self-promotion. Asians should be asked about their interest in positions, included in assessment center activities, and provided with mentors, just as other high-performing employees.

Organizations should be aware that some discrimination against Asians occurs because of perceptions that they have done too well or that there is a language barrier. Organizational leaders should work to ensure that these barriers do not impede Asian Americans' progress. Many Asians were born in the United States and are native English speakers but experience differential treatment based on an imagined lack of fluency in English. A culture of inclusion, rather than exclusion, and zero tolerance for unfair treatment would be as beneficial to Asians as to other non-dominant groups.

SUMMARY

In this chapter, we have considered the diversity among Asians, the perceptions of Asians as a "model minority" group, and the similarities and differences between Asians and other minority group members and Whites. Asian Americans are a large and diverse group of people with distinct organizational experiences, education levels, opportunities, and incomes. Like many other minority group members, Asians have contributed to the United States in many ways and have also experienced individual, organizational, and societal racism, discrimination, and exclusion.

[70]Hyun, J. (2005). *Breaking the Bamboo Ceiling: Career Strategies for Asians*. New York: HarperCollins.

Many of the organizational experiences of Asian Americans vary by country of origin and education level.

Although Asians have the highest education levels of any racial/ethnic group overall, some groups of Asians are poorly educated and suffer the poverty and low earnings typical of minorities with limited education and skills. These differences are partly a consequence of the large variation within the category of Asian American. Indeed, their categorization obscures important differences among the people who make up this group. Native U.S. Asians and a subset of immigrants are well-educated and have high earnings, but like many other minorities, their incomes as compared to their education are still lower than the incomes of Whites. Another subset of immigrants, particularly recent immigrants, have little education and very low earnings. Researchers have documented experiences of both groups with discrimination, harassment, and stereotyping.

This chapter provided recommendations for individuals and organizations in addressing the unique diversity issues faced by Asian Americans. Because Asians are one of the fastest-growing populations in the United States, and more than half the world's population, it is imperative that they be recognized as important contributors to the future of diversity in organizations around the world.

KEY TERMS

Model minority — a minority group whose members are *perceived* as having achieved success through hard work and determination and who are *perceived* as being suitable models for other minorities to emulate.

Model minority myth — the erroneous perception that U.S. Asians are free from concerns that plague other minorities (e.g., poverty, discrimination, un- and under employment) and have all succeeded through hard work, determination, and commitment to education.

QUESTIONS TO CONSIDER

1. Japanese Americans served in World War II while their family members were held in relocation centers. As discussed in Chapter 4, African Americans served in World War II but rode in the back of busses and drank from separate "colored-only" water fountains while German prisoners of war drank from "Whites-only" fountains; Latinos returning from war faced considerable hostility and violence. What ironies currently exist for people of color in the U.S. military in the present?

2. Prior to reading this chapter, were you aware of the Chinese Exclusion Act and the internment of Japanese Americans? If yes, how much did you know?

3. What are some potential negative individual and organizational consequences for Asian Americans being perceived as a "model minority"?

4. Prior to reading this chapter, what would you have estimated to be the distribution of education, earnings, and poverty for Asian Americans? Were you aware of the wide variety in Asians' education, earnings, and poverty?

5. If you are not Asian American, do you know someone well who is Asian American? What is your relationship to this person (e.g., personal friend, manager, classmate, neighbor)? What are this person's Asian roots (e.g.,

Japan, China, India)? How much time have you spent with him or her? Have you discussed race, ethnicity, or other diversity issues? Explain.

ACTIONS AND EXERCISES

1. Go to U.S. government Web sites (e.g., http://www.census.gov, http://www.dol.gov, and others) to investigate the most current earnings, education level, and incidence of poverty for Asian Americans from five different backgrounds of your choice (e.g., India, Japan, Korea, Thailand, and Vietnam). Document your findings. What would be the result of viewing any one of these groups as representative of all Asian Americans?

2. Search the EEOC Web site (http://www.eeoc.gov) for recent discrimination charges and settlements involving Asian Americans. What are the details of the cases (e.g., who was involved, what happened, and what was the outcome)?

3. Chapter 15 describes the EEOC case and settlement of charges against Abercrombie & Fitch (ANF), a retail store that discriminated against Asian American applicants and employees (and other people of color). If there is an ANF near where you live, visit and document the race and ethnicity of the employees. If there is no ANF nearby, conduct this exercise at another high-end specialty store. Compare what you observe with the population of Asians in your area (available from the U.S. Census Web site).

   a. Conduct an informal census of employees in several places: fast-food restaurant, sit-down restaurant, discount store (e.g., Target, Walmart), department store (e.g., Macy's, Filene's, Marshall Fields), government office, bank, or other locations in which many employees are visible. Document the number of employees overall and the number of Asian American employees visible. Compare your findings with the population of Asians in your area.

   b. Watch television for two nights for thirty minutes to one hour each night. Document the program, type of commercial, and the numbers of Asian American characters on the programs and commercials.

   c. What similarities and differences are apparent among the people in Questions 2, 3a, and 3b?

4. Research from the Department of Housing and Urban Development using paired testers indicates that at times Asian Americans experience housing discrimination (renting and home buying) that is similar to that experienced by Blacks, Hispanics, and American Indians. Search the HUD Web site for such studies and review them. Speculate on reasons for this discrimination.

5. Conduct research to find several Asian Americans in positions of power in corporations, politics, or universities. Describe their jobs, educational background, experience, and other relevant factors that have contributed to their success.

6. Sixty percent of Hispanics in the United States are native-born, and 70% of Asians in the country are foreign-born. Speculate on the reasons for the greater and more widespread antipathy toward Hispanics, compared to that toward Asians.

Whites/European Americans

CHAPTER 7

Chapter Objectives

After completing this chapter, readers should have a greater understanding of Whites/Caucasians and their role in organizational diversity. Specifically, they should be able to:

- ❏ *explain the history of White ethnic groups in the United States.*

- ❏ *discuss participation rates, employment, and income levels of White men and women.*

- ❏ *describe differences in income by education levels between Whites and other racial and ethnic groups.*

- ❏ *explain the similarities and differences between employment experiences of White men and women.*

- ❏ *describe the fluidity in groups deemed "White" in the United States and aspects of "White privilege" and the "myth of meritocracy."*

- ❏ *discuss individual and organizational measures that can be employed to include Whites in the study of diversity and to obtain their commitment to diversity in organizations.*

Key Facts

Whites are less likely to be laid off than minorities, even when taking into account individual and organizational factors.

Although women of all races and minorities of both sexes now comprise a greater share of the labor force, White men and White women continue to hold a disproportionate share of managerial jobs.[1]

The population growth rate for non-Hispanic Whites is lower than that for all minority groups.

White women have higher workforce participation rates than Asian and Hispanic women but lower participation than Black women.

Even Whites who do not personally practice discrimination and exclusion are advantaged by systemic discrimination and exclusion that disadvantages people of color.

[1]Stainback, K., & Tomaskovic-Devey, D. (2009). "Intersections of Power and Privilege: Long-Term Trends in Managerial Representation." *American Sociological Review*, 74: 800–820.

Introduction and Overview

In this chapter, we consider the experiences of non-Hispanic Whites as they relate to diversity in organizations.[2] Whites are the largest and most dominant racial group, yet their experiences are often not directly or purposefully studied as a racial group in diversity research. Despite this, Whites have unique experiences and contributions to make that warrant their direct inclusion in diversity studies. White women have benefited considerably from affirmative action yet they still face the glass ceiling and walls and receive a lower return on their educational investment when compared with White men. They also face sex segregation, sexual harassment, and overt sex discrimination. As relatives of White men, White women have the opportunity to relate their experiences as non-dominant group members. White men who value diversity are, as members of the most dominant group, most likely to be in positions to effect change. Having multiple group memberships themselves (e.g., race, sex, age, sexual orientation, religion), they may also have a personal stake in the pursuit of diversity. Because they often share family income with White women, many White men also experience the negative effects of sex discrimination against women.

Consistent with the organization of chapters on other racial and ethnic groups, this chapter covers history, relevant legislation (including evidence of discrimination and harassment against Whites), research, and the other standard topics. Yet the unique position of Whites as the dominant and preferred group in the United States (and many other countries) must also be emphasized and acknowledged. As we will discuss, Whites disproportionately occupy the highest-paid, highest-status positions in organizations, are less likely to be laid off than minorities,[3] and generally experience "White privilege" and other unearned, often invisible advantages based on race.[4] They receive employment advantages and preferences based on similarity to key decision makers, the benefit of favorable stereotypes (or of negative stereotypes about other potential workers, which have the same effect), and the automatic cueing that is based on race. They also receive advantages as customers and clients, such as lower prices and the assumption that they are not potential shoplifters (both discussed in Chapter 4). They are not targeted by police for racial profiling (Chapter 5), are more likely to get deferred adjudication (Chapter 5), receive better treatment by employers than Blacks and Latinos even when convicted of drug charges (and even when the Blacks and Latinos are not [Chapter 4]), and receive the other benefits detailed in the research evidence offered in previous chapters. When members of one group are disadvantaged and excluded based on race or ethnicity (or sex or age), another group is, as a consequence, advantaged.

Despite these unearned advantages for Whites as a racial group, not every White person enjoys every unearned privilege. As discussed in this chapter and in Chapter 9, White women are disadvantaged relative to White men; women experience sexual harassment, the glass ceiling, and the effects of erroneous stereotypes and assumptions about their competence. White men who are gay and open about their sexual orientation can face harsh sanctions from employers. Socioeconomic status (and economic and educational privilege) also leads to key differences in

---

[2]We use the term *Whites* throughout the chapter to mean Whites not of Hispanic origin.

[3]Elvira, M. M., & Zatzick, C. D. (2002). "Who's Displaced First? The Role of Race in Layoff Decisions." *Industrial Relations*, 41(2): 329–361.

[4]McIntosh, P. (2004). "White Privilege and Male Privilege: A Personal Account of Coming to See Correspondences Through Work in Women's Studies (1988)." In J. F. Healey & E. O'Brien (Eds.), *Race, Ethnicity, and Gender*. Thousand Oaks, CA: Pine Forge Press, pp. 294–301; McNamee, S. J., & Miller, R. K., Jr. (2004). *The Meritocracy Myth*. Rowman & Littlefield Publishing Group.

outcomes and experiences among Whites from different class backgrounds.[5] As emphasized in this chapter, Whites' personal experiences with discrimination, harassment, and exclusion are not only relevant to the experiences of others but also make Whites, because they are members of the dominant group and in positions of power, important allies in the quest for equality and inclusion for *all* workers.

Terminology

The U.S. Census Bureau describes "White" as a person having European origins or who is from the Middle East or North Africa, including those who state their race as "White" or report themselves to be Irish, German, Italian, Lebanese, Near Easterner, Arab, or Polish. In this book we primarily use the term *White*, but at times we use as well *Anglo*, *Caucasian*, *European American*, or *non-Hispanic White*. ●

▍ HISTORY OF WHITES IN THE UNITED STATES

In contrast to the majority of the other racial and ethnic groups we have profiled, anyone educated in the United States has likely encountered the history of U.S. Whites in an "American history" course. In the past, a common complaint about such courses was that they effectively and, at times, purposely excluded people of color or represented them in a derogatory manner. In recent decades, the content of such courses has changed to include wider and more accurate coverage of American Indians, Blacks, Latinos, and Asians in the United States, but discussion of the experiences of different White ethnic groups remains limited. In this chapter, we consider some of these ethnic groups, compare their experiences with those of people of color, and discuss the racial and ethnic identity of Whites in the present.

As we have mentioned in other chapters, some White ethnic groups faced considerable overt discrimination and exclusion in their early years in the United States. Nearly 40 million Europeans (including Irish, Greek, Germans, Italians, and Poles) migrated to the United States between the 1820s and the 1920s. Clashes between Irish, German, Polish, and Italian immigrants, conflicts over work, and residential segregation were common. There was a pecking order for Whites, with the earliest immigrants, the English, at the top, followed by Germans, Irish, Italians, and Poles. The English viewed later White immigrants as dirty, immoral, unintelligent, and dishonest (terms quite similar to those used for Blacks and immigrants of color), and sought to avoid interacting with them at work and in the home.[6]

As Blacks migrated from the South to the North seeking better jobs and greater opportunities, many of the European ethnic groups perceived

---

[5]Wray, M. (2006). *Not Quite White*. Durham, NC, and London: Duke University Press.
[6]Wray (2006).

them to be a threat to their status and livelihoods. Sociologist Joseph Healey states:

Ironically, however, the newly arriving African Americans helped White ethnic groups to become upwardly mobile … The arrival of African Americans from the South actually *aided* the European immigrants and their descendants in their rise up the social class structure. Whites in the dominant group became less vocal about their contempt for the White ethnic groups as their alarm over the presence of Blacks increased. The greater antipathy of the White community toward African Americans made the immigrants less undesirable and thus hastened their admittance to the institutions of the larger society. (p. 79)[7]

White ethnic groups encouraged and capitalized on the fear and antipathy of high-status Whites toward Blacks, using it to "become insiders, or Americans, by claiming their membership as Whites" designating Blacks as the "other."[8] Because the ethnicity of White ethnic groups is largely invisible, it was considerably easier for White immigrants and their descendants to become insiders than it was for native-born Blacks.

The Past Transiency and Current Meaning of "Race" for Whites

In a thought-provoking book, Karen Brodkin considers the transformation of Jews in America from a separate race to White and in the process provides interesting insights into the social constructions of race in America.[9] Brodkin documents the initial employment discrimination by the original Whites (English and Northern Europeans) against White ethnic groups who arrived in the United States later, including Irish, Italians, Poles, Greeks, the French, and Jews. White ethnic groups were segregated from one another; certain jobs were reserved for members of one ethnic group and other jobs for other groups. Italians were perceived as likely to engage in criminal activity, a stereotype that remains to some extent (e.g., mobsters).[10] Irish Catholics, many of whom had fled Ireland in the face of religious persecution, faced open hostility and exclusion. In response, they formed social, political, and labor organizations to resist discrimination and played key roles in the

[7]Healey, J. F. (2004). *Diversity and Society*. Thousand Oaks, CA: Pine Forge Press.
[8]Takaki, R. (1993). *A Different Mirror*. Boston: Back Bay Books, p. 151.
[9]Brodkin, K. (1998). *How Jews Became White Folks & What That Says About Race in America*. New Brunswick, NJ: Rutgers University Press; Ignatiev, N. (1995). *How the Irish Became White*. New York: Routledge.
[10]Schaefer, R. T. (2002). *Racial and Ethnic Groups: Census 2000 Update*, 8th ed. Upper Saddle River, NJ: Pearson Education.

formation of the American Federation of Labor.[11] The exclusion and discrimination faced by Irish Catholics was instrumental in their efforts to shape "ethnic politics" in the United States.[12] Jews, fleeing persecution elsewhere, were excluded from many jobs and denied service by some organizations. Albert Einstein's views on race and racism in America, discussed in Individual Feature 7.1, were reportedly influenced by his experiences with racism as a Jewish person in Germany.

As does Robert Healey, Brodkin suggests that White ethnic groups "became White" in several ways: through overt actions of the government, their own recognition that the way to become American was to assert their Whiteness (in contrast to Blacks), intermarriage with Whites from other groups that diluted the group differences, and through the invisibility of their ethnicity. Healey, Brodkin, and other researchers have documented the inconsistency in categorizations of groups as White and non-White over time and institution.[13] Prior to the 1850 Census, racial categorizations included "free Whites." After 1850, the category was changed to "Whites," because all Whites were indeed free.[14] The 1930 Census distinguished between immigrant Whites and native Whites and recorded immigrants' country of origin.[15] By the 1940 Census, however, distinctions between native and immigrant Whites were no longer recorded, allowing immigrants to become further incorporated into the "White" category, although some overt discrimination against certain ethnic groups remained. Feature 7.1 describes the internment of Italians and Germans during World War II, a largely unknown aspect of the remaining discrimination against certain ethnic groups during that period.

More recently, the U.S. Census has shuttled Mexicans, Middle Easterners, and East Indians (Asian Indians) between the White and non-White categories.[16] Berkeley Law professor Ian Haney Lopez has detailed how Court rulings based on "common knowledge" and "legal precedent" wavered in terms of who was or was not White.[17] Syrians are White, Syrians are not White; Asian Indians are not White, Asian Indians are

[11]Kennedy, R. E., Jr. (1999). "Irish Catholic Americans: A Successful Case of Pluralism." In A. G. Dworkin & R. J. Dworkin (Eds.), *The Minority Report*, 3rd ed. Fort Worth, TX: Harcourt Brace Publishers, pp. 395–414.

[12]Ibid.

[13]Lopez, I. F. H. (1996). *White by Law: The Legal Construction of Race*. New York: New York University Press.

[14]Rodriguez, C. (2000). *Changing Race: Latinos, the Census, and the History of Ethnicity in the United States*. New York: New York University Press, p. 71.

[15]Brodkin, K. (2004). "How Jews Became White." In J. F. Healey & E. O'Brien (Eds.), *Race, Ethnicity, and Gender*. Thousand Oaks, CA: Pine Forge Press, pp. 283–294; Brodkin, K. (1998).

[16]Brodkin (1998), p. 74.

[17]Lopez, I. F. H. (1996), p. 203, Table 1: The Racial Prerequisite Cases, 1878–1909.

INDIVIDUAL FEATURE 7.1	*Albert Einstein, Genius and Antiracist*

Albert Einstein (1879–1955) is viewed by many as perhaps the smartest person to ever live, with the name "Einstein" often used as a synonym for *genius*. Winner of the 1921 Nobel Prize in physics, Einstein is widely known for his theory of relativity and for his contributions to the study of quantum physics. In 2000, *Time* magazine named Einstein the person of the century for his intellectual contributions. His passionate resistance to racism and his civil rights activism, however, are virtually unknown. References to his antiracist stance and activism are almost completely absent from nearly all the books and publications about his life and work. This absence is attributed to the media and biographers' desire to avoid controversy, to avoid tarnishing Einstein's "feel-good" image, and to the strength of his views about what he called the "worst disease" in America, a "disease of White people," which he did not "intend to be quiet about."[18] Since his death, the silence surrounding his views on racism has been deafening.

In *Einstein on Race and Racism*, Fred Jerome and Rodger Taylor detail some of Einstein's close relationships with key Black activists, his co-chairing of the American Crusade to End Lynching (ACEL), the FBI's files on him, and the peculiar silence about this aspect of Einstein's life and work. Jerome and Taylor cite a 1932 letter from Einstein, published in *The Crisis* magazine, written "to American Negroes."[19] In part, the letter stated that "it seems to be a universal fact that minorities, especially when their individuals are recognizable because of physical differences, are treated by majorities among whom they live as an inferior class." Einstein encouraged Blacks to engage in purposeful activism and educational enlightenment to work toward emancipation and encouraged others to recognize and assist Blacks in their work. Einstein perceived the treatment of Blacks in the United States as a mockery of the principle that "all men are created equal." He referred to Blacks as the "stepchildren" of the United States, a country that "still has a heavy debt to discharge for all the troubles and disabilities it has laid on the Negro's shoulders, for all that his fellow-citizens have done and to some extent still are doing to him."[20]

Einstein also discouraged discrimination against and restriction of immigrants. He argued that unemployment is "*not* decreased by restricting immigration" (emphasis in original), but that it "depends on faulty distribution of work among those capable of work. Immigration increases consumption as much as it does demand on labor...."[21] Some who oppose immigration today continue to argue that immigrants take jobs from "Americans."

Einstein believed that the only remedies to racism are "enlightenment and education" and did his part to help. Jerome and Taylor's book contributes to our knowledge about Albert Einstein's other, virtually ignored, work of genius.

QUESTIONS TO CONSIDER

1. *Prior to reading this section, were you aware of Albert Einstein's strong antiracist stance?*

[18]Jerome, F., & Taylor, R. (2005). *Einstein on Race and Racism*. Piscataway, NJ: Rutgers University Press, p. 91.
[19]Ibid., p. 136.
[20]Ibid., p. 73.
[21]Ibid.

2. Some have suggested that because Einstein was Jewish and also experienced discrimination, he was more antiracist than he otherwise might have been. Is this a likely cause of Einstein's perspective? Explain.

Source: Jerome, F., & Taylor, F. (2005). *Einstein on Race and Racism.* Piscataway, NJ: Rutgers University Press.

White; Arabians are White, Arabians are not White; and other such irrational decisions were rendered in cases in which people tried to "prove" their Whiteness in order to become U.S. citizens.

In addition to helping with becoming American, being White is associated with many other advantages; some of these are considered in Research Summary 7.1. One advantage is the ability of Whites to behave badly without such behavior being attributed to all Whites. Because Whites are the dominant and majority group, they are less likely to be viewed as homogeneous (e.g., in-group heterogeneity and out-group homogeneity—see Chapter 2). As examples, Timothy McVeigh was a young White man convicted for the 1995 bombing of the U.S. federal building in Oklahoma City; Eric Rudolph, another young White man, was responsible for the 1996 Olympic Park bombing in Atlanta and bombings of an abortion clinic and a gay nightclub. But these two high-profile cases did not result in a belief that young White men as a group are terrorists.

History of Whites as Allies of Diversity

As discussed in previous chapters, throughout the history of the United States, Whites have participated in the quest for equality for Blacks, American Indians, Latinos, and Asians—as abolitionists, hosts, and workers in the Underground Railroad for runaway slaves, participants in boycotts, marches, and sit-ins, and as educators and researchers. From John Brown, Henry David Thoreau, and Harriet Beecher Stowe to Michael Schwerner and Andrew Goodman, Whites worked (and sometimes died) along with people of color. Despite their differences with Black women activists, White female suffragists often pursued rights for Blacks along with women's rights to vote. Currently, many White allies of diversity support equality for racial-, sexual-, religious-, ability-, and other types of minorities. As discussed in Chapter 1, because White men are more likely to occupy decision-making positions in organizations and have more authority and credibility in many areas, their commitment to equity and fairness is vital. The lifelong commitment to justice of Morris Dees, of the Southern Poverty Law Center, is described in Individual Feature 7.2.

| FEATURE 7.1 | *The Internment of Italians and Germans in World War II* |

Many people are unaware that more than 100,000 Japanese Americans were interned during World War II under Executive Order 9066. Even fewer are aware that Italians and Germans were also evacuated and held in relocation centers during the same period. Estimates suggest that 2,100 Italians were interned and between 10,000 and 14,000 Italians and Germans were arrested for being "enemy aliens" during the war.[22] Although far fewer Americans of Italian and German descent were interned than Japanese, their story is no less important to those who suffered and their descendants. In the past two decades, the internment story of Italian Americans has gone from being told primarily through word of mouth in the Italian community to one more widely known and shared. An exhibit called "Una Storia Segreta" documents surprise evacuations to unknown cities, sons in the military returning home to find their parents evacuated, having to change the Italian family name to avoid being recognized as Italian, and other humiliations.

In New York City, San Francisco, Washington, D.C., and other major cities in which many Italians resided, mandatory curfews were imposed and Italians were forced to carry bright pink enemy alien passbooks and were searched almost at will. Property that was deemed dangerous (e.g., flashlights, radios, cameras, and firearms) was seized. On the West Coast, Italian, German, and Japanese aliens were removed from "prohibited zones."

Geoffrey Dunn details some of the events of the evacuations and internments in the Santa Cruz area. He and others provide cogent theories of why the Japanese, but not Italians or Germans, were singled out for large-scale, mass evacuations: racism, economics, and the comparative Japanese lack of political strength. Because people of German and Italian descent were more widely assimilated, more involved in politics (e.g., elected as mayors of large cities), and had widespread public recognition (e.g., baseball's Joe DiMaggio), internment of Germans and Italians was limited. According to Dunn, then California Attorney General Earl Warren (who went on to become chief justice of the Supreme Court) stated that "when we are dealing with the Caucasian race we have methods that will test the loyalty of them ... but when we deal with the Japanese, we are on an entirely different field."[23]

In October 1942, Italians were removed from the "enemy aliens" classification and allowed to return to prohibited zones. Restrictions for Germans were lifted in January 1943. As they returned to their homes and resumed their businesses, life for the Italian and German Americans returned to some semblance of normalcy.

QUESTIONS TO CONSIDER

1. Prior to reading this selection, were you aware that Italians and Germans had

---

[22]Fox, S. C. (1988). "General John DeWitt and the Proposed Internment of German and Italian Aliens During World War II." *Pacific Historical Review*, 57(November): 407–438; Exhibition announcement for "Prisoners in Our Own Home: The Italian American experience as America's Enemy Aliens." (2004). http://qcpages.qc.edu/calandra/community/commenemy.html, accessed November 14, 2010; Dunn, G. (1994). "Male Notte: The Untold Story of Italian Relocation During World War II." *Santa Cruz County Historical Journal* (1): 83–89.
[23]Dunn (1994).

been evacuated and relocated as enemy aliens during World War II?

2. *Aside from differences in the numbers of people affected, why do you think that the Italian and German relocation experience has received such little attention when compared with that of the Japanese?*

3. *Why might Caucasians have been perceived as more loyal than the Japanese?*

Sources: Fox, S. (1990). *The Unknown Internment: An Oral History of the Relocation of Italian Americans during World War II.* Boston: Twayne; Scherini, R. D. (1991/1992). "Executive Order 9066 and Italian Americans: The San Francisco Story." *California History,* Winter: 367–377.

▌ RELEVANT LEGISLATION

As with the other racial and ethnic groups covered thus far in this book, the primary legislation protecting Whites from discrimination in employment is Title VII of the Civil Rights Act. Although often thought of as being solely for people of color, Title VII prohibits discrimination on the basis of race and national origin and thus is applicable to Whites. Indeed, Title VII is used considerably less by Whites than by people of color, simply because Whites are far less likely to be targeted by intentional employment discrimination (e.g., disparate treatment). Whites are also much more likely to be in positions of power as managers, executives, supervisors, and others with hiring, firing, promotional, and other responsibilities, than are members of other groups, making disparate treatment by non-Whites against Whites unlikely. In addition, although Whites are often underrepresented in jobs primarily occupied by people of color, such jobs are likely to be lower paid and less desirable than those commonly performed by Whites. Claims of disparate impact or underutilization of Whites in such jobs would seem illogical—why would Whites generally aspire to work in jobs that are lower paid and less desirable, with fewer opportunities for advancement? Lastly, despite Whites' often expressed resistance to affirmative action, executive orders concerning affirmative action have benefited White women more than other groups, as discussed in Chapter 3.

Myth: Title VII protects only minorities from racial discrimination.

Reality: Title VII prohibits discrimination against Whites, including White males.

Following are examples of EEOC cases that involved racial discrimination or harassment directed at Whites.[24]

---

[24]Aside from the correction of minor grammatical errors and word deletions for brevity, the text of the cases is quoted directly from http://www.eeoc.gov/eeoc/initiatives/e-race/caselist.cfm, accessed November 3, 2010.

| RESEARCH SUMMARY 7.1 | *"White Privilege" and the "Myth of Meritocracy"* |

Dr. Peggy McIntosh is associate director of the Wellesley College Center for Research on Women. Through her work in women's studies, and her awareness of male privilege as a result of women's disadvantages, Dr. McIntosh began thinking about the privilege that Whites experience at the expense of non-Whites. Although men may acknowledge that women are *disadvantaged* in society, most men are unwilling to acknowledge that men are *advantaged* at women's expense. She argues that while some men may concede that male privilege exists in broad institutional and societal forms, those same men will deny any *personal* advantages stemming from male privilege.

As she considered the strength of men's denial of unearned privileges, McIntosh began to recognize the existence of her own advantages, as a White woman, at the expense of non-Whites. Similar to men's unwillingness to accept unearned privilege, McIntosh notes the difficulty in acknowledging unearned advantages based on white skin color: "I think Whites are carefully taught not to recognize White privilege, as males are taught not to recognize male privilege."[25] Part of her (and men's) unwillingness to deny privilege is that to acknowledge privilege would make plain the "myth of meritocracy ... one's life is not what one makes it; many doors open for certain people through no virtues of their own."[26]

In their book on the subject, Stephen McNamee and Robert Miller include several nonmerit factors that strongly influence people's success in life. They include "the effects of inheritance as unequal starting points in the race to get ahead," knowing the right people and being able to fit in with them (social and cultural capital), unequal access to educational opportunities, and discrimination. According to McNamee and Miller, "by excluding entire categories of people from equal access to opportunity, discrimination has reduced competition and increased the chances of others to get ahead who mistakenly conclude that their success is based exclusively on their own individual 'merit.'"[27] Historical preferences for Whites, in particular White men, by organizational decision makers have systematically advantaged Whites at the expense of others.[28] By excluding women and minorities from union membership, training programs, and high status, high paid jobs, employer discrimination provided systematic advantages for White men and fostered perceptions that only they were qualified for those positions.

McIntosh began documenting and analyzing her everyday experiences that were part of the unearned advantages she experienced as a consequence of being White. She amassed forty-six unearned advantages that have been widely reported in women's studies and the gender and diversity literature. The

[25]McIntosh (2004), p. 297.
[26]McIntosh (2004), p. 298.
[27]McNamee, S. J., & Miller, R. K., Jr. (2004). *The Meritocracy Myth*. Lanham, MD: Rowman & Littlefield Publishing Group, p. 17.
[28]Brodkin, K. (2004). "How Jews Became White." In J. F. Healy & E. O'Brien (Eds.), *Race, Ethnicity, and Gender*. Thousand Oaks, CA: Pine Forge Press, pp. 282–294. See also Jacques, R. (1997). "The Unbearable Whiteness of Being: Reflections of a Pale, Stale Male." In P. Prasad, A. Mills, M. Elmes, & A. Prasad (Eds.), *Managing the Organizational Melting Pot: Dilemmas of Workplace Diversity*. Thousand Oaks, CA: Sage Publications, pp. 80–106.

following have specific, clear relevance to diversity in organizations:[29]

- I can go shopping alone most of the time, fairly well assured that I will not be followed or harassed by store detectives.
- I can be pretty sure that my children's teachers and employers will tolerate them if they fit school and workplace norms; my chief worries about them do not concern others' attitudes toward their race.
- I can be reasonably sure that if I ask to talk to "the person in charge," I will be facing a person of my race.
- I can go home from most meetings of organizations I belong to feeling somewhat tied in, rather than isolated, out of place, outnumbered, unheard, held at a distance, or feared.
- I can be pretty sure that an argument with a colleague of another race is more likely to jeopardize her chances for advancement than to jeopardize mine.
- I can take a job with an affirmative action employer without having coworkers on the job suspect that I got it because of my race.
- I can be pretty sure of finding people who would be willing to talk with me and advise me about my next steps, professionally.
- I can be late to a meeting without having the lateness reflect on my race.
- I can choose public accommodation without fearing that people of my race cannot get in or will be mistreated in the places I have chosen.
- If I have low credibility as a leader, I can be sure that my race is not the problem.

These privileges touch upon many of the factors discussed in this book, including discrimination against customers, racial profiling, stereotyping, perceptions that people of color are unqualified, and others that are familiar to many non-Whites but generally unfamiliar to Whites. These and the remaining privileges McIntosh compiled provide a thought-provoking view of everyday life and events through different lenses. Although she used the term *privilege* to describe these unearned advantages, McIntosh views the term as misleading. *Privilege* is generally seen to be a positive term, yet what she describes "simply *confers dominance*, gives permission to control, because of one's race or sex" (emphasis in original).[30] McIntosh further notes that being White in the United States opens many doors for Whites, whether or not individual Whites personally approve of the way that dominance is conferred on members of their group. When Whites remain oblivious to White advantage, the **myth of meritocracy** is allowed to continue, thus perpetuating the system of White privilege. In discussing White, heterosexual, male privilege, Roy Jacques (a White, heterosexual male) similarly notes that passively receiving privileges does not make one a bad person, but failing to question and resist privileges are "moral and ethical" issues.[31]

McIntosh argues that racism not only involves "individual acts of meanness" but also "invisible systems conferring racial dominance." Whites are taught not to recognize these invisible systems of privilege that advantage Whites in the same way that men are taught not to recognize systems that advantage men. Because of the role of systems (e.g., institutional discrimination) in promoting advantages for one group over others, focusing on one's own attitudes (e.g., deciding not to behave in a discriminatory manner) is but one aspect of addressing inequality. Those in power

---

[29]Privileges are quoted from McIntosh (2004), pp. 296–298. Original numbers for the privileges presented are: 5, 16, 24, 27, 28, 35, 37, 39, 40, and 43.
[30]McIntosh (2004), p. 299.
[31]Jacques (1997).

can continue to ignore systemic influences on inequality or they can work to weaken and reconstruct power systems so that the "normal" privileges can also be enjoyed by other groups.

Sources: McIntosh, P. (2004). "White Privilege and Male Privilege: A Personal Account of Coming to See Correspondences Through Work in Women's Studies (1988)." In J. F. Healey & E. O'Brien (Eds.), *Race, Ethnicity, and Gender*. Thousand Oaks, CA: Pine Forge Press, pp. 294–312; McNamee, S. J., & Miller, R. K., Jr. (2004). *The Meritocracy Myth*. Lanham, MD: Rowman & Littlefield Publishing Group. See also Jacques, R. (1997). "The Unbearable Whiteness of Being: Reflections of a Pale, Stale Male." In P. Prasad, A. Mills, M. Elmes, & A. Prasad (Eds.), *Managing the Organizational Melting Pot: Dilemmas of Workplace Diversity*. Thousand Oaks, CA: Sage Publications, pp. 80–106; Kendall, F. E. (2006). *Understanding White Privilege: Creating Pathways to Authentic Relationships Across Race*. New York: Taylor & Francis; Wildman, S. M. (Ed.) (1996). *Privilege Revealed: How Invisible Preference Undermines America*. New York: New York University Press; Scheurich, J. J. (1993). "Toward a White Discourse on White Racism." *Educational Researcher*, 22(8): 5–10.

QUESTIONS TO CONSIDER

1. *What other White privileges can you think of that have specific relevance to diversity in organizations?*

2. *If you are a member of a non-dominant racial or ethnic group, how many of the privileges listed resonate with you? Which ones?*

3. *If you are White, how many of the privileges listed had you recognized prior to reading this selection? Which ones are most sobering or surprising to you?*

4. *Belief in meritocracy and that people can "pull themselves up by their bootstraps" is common in the United States. Had you considered "the myth of meritocracy" prior to reading this selection? What do you think of the possibility that by discriminating against minorities, society and organizations provide advantages for Whites? In what ways does failure to acknowledge the consequences of discrimination contribute to Whites' feelings of their own individual qualifications and "merit?"*

5. *The expression* qualified minorities *is sometimes used in selection searches. How much is the term* qualified Whites *used? (*Qualified women? *Qualified men?)*

6. *What things might be on a list of "male" privileges—unearned advantages that men experience—relative to diversity in organizations?*

7. *Recall from Chapter 4 that most wealth is inherited. What things might be on a list of privileges provided by wealth.*

Race Discrimination against Whites

- The EEOC concluded that a White complainant was subjected to racial harassment over a period of two years by both managers and coworkers who used various racially derogatory terms when referring to complainant. Evidence showed that management generally condoned racially related comments made by African American supervisors and coworkers who frequently voiced a "Black versus White" mentality at the work place. The Commission ordered the agency to pay the complainant $10,000 in compensatory damages and to provide training to all management and staff at the facility. See *Brown v. United States Postal Service*, EEOC Appeal No. 0720060042.

Morris Dees is a White man with sandy blond hair and blue eyes and a passion for justice. Dees was born in 1936 in Alabama, where he lived during his formative years, witnessing the consequences of prejudice and racial injustice. Trained as a lawyer, Dees had founded a successful book publishing company when, in 1967, after much soul-searching, he acknowledged that working for justice and equality was his appointed path. "I was a good lawyer wasting my time trying to make a few more million dollars," Dees said, and decided instead to specialize in civil rights law.

In 1969, Dees sold his publishing company to Times Mirror (the parent company of the *Los Angeles Times*) and began to take on controversial cases important to civil rights and justice. He sued to integrate the all-White Young Men's Christian Association (YMCA) in Montgomery, Alabama, and to prevent the state of Alabama from building another university in an Alabama city that already had a predominantly Black university. Dees soon recognized the need for a nonprofit organization that would seek justice for minorities and the poor, and along with his law partner Joseph Levin, Jr. and civil rights activist Julian Bond founded the Southern Poverty Law Center (SPLC) in 1971.

The SPLC has been instrumental in many cases of importance to people in the United States, including cases involving challenges to segregation, employment discrimination, the death penalty, hate groups, and the confederate flag. The SPLC has pursued worker safety, tax equity, medical services for the poor, improved prison conditions, parity in education for the poor, and equity for immigrants. Some of the cases involved employer abuses of workers and detriments to their health, government-sanctioned abuse and neglect of mentally ill patients, charges of murder against people who killed in self-defense, and denial of public education to homeless children. In one case, the SPLC defended a female inmate charged with murdering a prison guard who was found dead in her cell without his pants. The woman said the guard had tried to rape her and semen and an ice pick were found on his body. In another death row case, the SPLC won an acquittal for a 16-year-old boy who had been convicted of rape and sentenced to death in Louisiana. Scientific evidence, available at the time he was first convicted but purposely withheld, helped in his later acquittal. The SPLC was instrumental in gaining equitable rights for women in the military and their dependents and for women in law enforcement. In some of its most highly recognized cases, the SPLC was successful in gaining judgments against various groups that had targeted Blacks, Vietnamese fishermen, Jews, and nonviolent Black and White protesters. Some of the SPLC's most influential cases have been heard by the U.S. Supreme Court.

A quarter-century after it was founded, the Southern Poverty Law Center continues to work for justice for disenfranchised groups of all backgrounds. Organizations around the United States recognize the role Dees plays in seeking and obtaining justice for the disenfranchised. He has received the American Bar Association's Young Lawyers Distinguished Service Award and the Roger Baldwin Award from the American Civil Liberties Union. The Trial Lawyers for Public Justice named him Trial Lawyer of the Year in 1987. In 1990, Dees received the Martin Luther King, Jr. Memorial Award from the National Education Association. In 1993, he received the Humanitarian Award from the University of Alabama. He has been awarded at least twenty-five honorary degrees and speaks at colleges and universities around the country, exhorting others to seek justice.

Sources: http://www.splcenter.org/center/history/dees.jsp; Dees, M. (1991). *A Season for Justice*. New York: Charles Scribner's Sons, accessed April 9, 2011.

- The EEOC affirmed an Administrative Judge's (AJ) finding that a White registered nurse had been subjected to racial harassment and constructive discharge. The AJ found that for approximately two and one-half years Black Health Technicians refused to comply with the White nurse's orders while following the orders of African American nurses; that one Health Technician told complainant that she would not take orders from a White nurse; and that Technicians screamed, banged on doors, and blocked complainant's exit when complainant asked for assistance. The AJ found that the harassment ultimately led to proposed disciplinary action and complainant's constructive discharge. The agency was ordered to reinstate complainant to a Registered Nurse position in a different work area, with back pay and benefits, pay complainant $10,000 in compensatory damages, and provide training to her former unit. *Menard v. Department of Veterans Affairs*, EEOC Appeal No. 07A40004, request for reconsideration denied, EEOC Request No. 05A50175.
- The EEOC received a favorable jury verdict in its Title VII lawsuit against the Great Atlantic & Pacific Tea Company (A&P) alleging that a Black senior manager terminated a White manager because of his race. The jury concluded the White manager was discharged solely because of his race and awarded approximately $85,000 in monetary relief. *EEOC v. Great Atlantic & Pacific Tea Co.*, C.A. No. 1:05-cv-01211-JFM.

Discrimination against Whites in Favor of Hispanics

- A Statesville, NC grocery store, agreed to settle for $30,000 a lawsuit alleging that it had fired a White, non-Hispanic meat cutter based on his race and national origin and replaced him with a less-qualified Hispanic employee. In addition, the store has agreed to distribute a formal, written antidiscrimination policy, train all employees on the policy and employment discrimination laws, and send reports to the EEOC on employees who are fired or resign. *EEOC v. West Front Street Foods LLC, d/b/a Compare Foods*, No 5:08-cv-102.
- The EEOC filed a lawsuit against a Charlotte, NC supermarket chain, alleging that it fired or forced long-term Caucasian and African American employees to resign and replaced them with Hispanic workers after it took over a particular facility. The supermarket chain paid $40,000 to settle the case. In addition, the consent decree required the company to distribute a formal, written antidiscrimination policy; provide periodic training to all its employees on the policy and on Title VII's prohibition against national origin and race discrimination; send periodic reports to the EEOC concerning employees who

are fired or resign; and post a "Notice to Employees" concerning this lawsuit. *EEOC v. E&T Foods, LLC, d/b/a Compare Foods*, Civil Action No 3:06-cv-318.

- A Mississippi-based drilling company agreed to pay $50,000 to settle a Title VII lawsuit, alleging that four employees, three White and one Black, experienced racial harassment and retaliation while assigned to a remote drilling rig in Texas. The harassment included being subjected to racial taunts and mistreatment from Hispanic employees and supervisors and having their safety threatened because the supervisors conducted safety meetings in Spanish only and refused to interpret for them in English. Told that they needed to learn Spanish because they were in South Texas, the employees said that instead of addressing their complaints of discrimination, they were fired. The company agreed to establish an effective antidiscrimination policy and to provide antidiscrimination training to its employees. *EEOC v. E&D Services, Inc.*, No. SA-08-CA-0714-NSN.

Termination of Whites for Refusing to Comply with Discrimination against Minorities

- The EEOC obtained a $317,000 settlement in a Title VII case alleging that an extended-stay hotel business discharged and otherwise retaliated against a district manager (DM) for six properties in Georgia, Alabama, and Virginia because she complained about race discrimination. The DM, a White female, e-mailed Defendant's Chief Operating Officer in expressing her concerns about the exclusion of African Americans and other racial minorities from management positions. Despite being considered a stellar performer, following her e-mail, the DM was reprimanded, threatened with a performance improvement plan, accused of being disloyal to the company, and terminated. The 24-month consent decree applies to all of Defendant's facilities in Georgia and includes requirements that Defendant create and institute a non-retaliation policy, advise all employees that it will not retaliate against them for complaining about discrimination, instruct all management and supervisory personnel about the terms of the decree, and provide them with annual training on Title VII's equal employment obligations, including non-retaliation. *EEOC v. InTown Suites Management, Inc.*, No. 1:03-CV-1494-RLV (N.D. Ga. Nov. 21, 2005).

- A Warren, Michigan, automotive supplier paid $190,000 to settle a race discrimination and retaliation lawsuit in which the EEOC alleged that the supplier repeatedly overlooked qualified non-White employees, including a group of Black employees and a Bangladeshi employee, for promotions to the maintenance department. In addition, a White employee who opposed this type of race discrimination and complained that managers in the maintenance department were using racial slurs allegedly was fired shortly after the company learned of his complaints. *EEOC v. Noble Metal Processing, Inc.*, No. 2:08-CV-14713.

As discussed in other chapters, discrimination against members of one group is commonly accompanied by discrimination against members of other groups, including Whites, in some cases. Recall from Chapters 5 and 6 the exploitation and abuse of Latino and Asian immigrant workers and the pretext of preferring the immigrant work ethic as a cloak for such exploitation. When native-born workers are excluded under such pretexts, this is illegal. White immigrant workers also experience direct exploitation and abuse. In some of the Walmart cases, those who were exploited came from Lithuania, Poland, Russia, Uzbekistan, and other Eastern European countries in addition to Mexico. The *New York Times* reported the story of one man from Prague who worked every night for eight months with no overtime pay, no contributions to Social Security, and no health insurance. During a raid of Walmart stores on October 23, 2003, the man was arrested along with 250 other janitors and deported.[32] In *Nickel and Dimed*, an investigation of the work and living experiences of low-wage workers, Barbara Ehrenreich describes a young Polish immigrant's exploitation as a dishwasher in a restaurant.[33]

▌ POPULATION

As of 2008, about 66% of the U.S. population (nearly 200 million people) was non-Hispanic White. The White population is declining as a percentage of the total as a result of immigration and higher birth rates among people of color. When the collection of Census data first began in 1790, 80.7% of the population was White and 19.3% was Black (92% were slaves). In 1930 and 1940, the White population was the largest proportion, 89.8%, and although it is still the largest, it has declined to the current level.[34] As mentioned in Chapter 1, Johnston and Packer's reports of

[32]Greenhouse, S. (2003, November 5). "Illegally in the U.S., and Never a Day Off at Walmart." *New York Times*, Section A, p. 1.

[33]Ehrenreich, B. (2001). *Nickel and Dimed: On (Not) Getting by in America*. New York: Metropolitan Books.

[34]Gibson, C., & Jung, K. (2002). *Historical Census Statistics on Population Totals by Race, 1790 to 1990, and by Hispanic Origin 1970 to 1990 for the United States, Regions, Divisions, and States.* Table 1. United States Race and Hispanic Origin. 1790 to 1990, http://www.census.gov/population/www/documentation/twps0076/twps0076.html, accessed November 14, 2010.

the changing racial and ethnic composition of the U.S. population, particularly the declining proportion of non-Hispanic Whites in the workforce, stimulated considerable interest in diversity in organizations.

According to the Census Bureau, the term *White* refers to those whose origins were any of the original peoples of Europe, the Middle East, or North Africa and includes those who labeled themselves Irish, German, Italian, Lebanese, Arab, and Polish, among others. As of 2003, 25% of the Whites reporting an ethnicity were German, 18% were Irish, 15% were English, and 9% were Italian. People from other groups represented 5% or less of the White population reporting an ethnicity. Perhaps as a reflection of their lack of knowledge of their original ancestry, 7% of Whites who reported an ethnicity wrote "United States" or "American."

■ EDUCATION, EARNINGS, AND EMPLOYMENT

As previous chapters have revealed, the average educational levels of Whites are higher than those of Blacks and Hispanics but generally lower than those of Asians. While about 30% of Whites have at least a bachelor's degree, more than 50% of Asians do (including Asian immigrants; see Table 6.1). While Whites generally have higher earnings and lower unemployment, by education level and overall, this is not always the case, as shown in Table 7.1.

The most recently available data shows that unemployment at the associate's, bachelor's, and higher degree levels ranged from lowest to

TABLE 7.1 *Mean Total Money Earnings in 2008 for Non-Hispanic Whites and Asians by Sex and Education Level*

	Asian (alone) Male	White (alone) Male, Non-Hispanic	Asian (alone) Female	White (alone) Female, Non-Hispanic	Asian (alone) Both Sexes	White (alone) Both Sexes
High school graduate, including GED	$37.2	$42.6	$24.4	$26.6	$30.7	$35.5
Some college, no degree	$45.9	$49.2	$28.0	$30.7	$37.8	$40.4
Bachelor's degree	$69.3	$79.6	$49.8	$46.0	$59.8	$63.4
Master's degree	$80.2	$91.3	$61.8	$54.5	$72.0	$72.2
Doctorate degree	$117.4	$116.4	$66.4	$72.4	$101.5	$100.3
Professional degree	$141.3	$155.6	$84.6	$86.9	$117.1	$131.3

Source: U.S. Census Bureau, PINC-03. Educational Attainment—People 25 Years Old and Over, by Total Money Earnings in 2008, Work Experience in 2008, Age, Race, Hispanic Origin, and Sex. http://www.census.gov/hhes/www/cpstables/032009/perinc/new03_000.htm, accessed November 15, 2010.

Table 7.2 *Unemployment Level by Selected Educational Attainment by Race (2009)*

	Total (%)	White (%)	Black (%)	Asian (%)	Hispanic (%)
Less than high school	14.6	13.9	21.0	8.4	13.7
High school graduate	9.7	9.0	14.0	7.5	10.4
Some college, no degree	8.6	7.9	12.1	8.9	9.6
Associate degree	6.8	6.2	10.3	7.5	8.5
Bachelor's and higher	4.6	4.2	7.3	5.6	5.7

Source: http://www.bls.gov/cps/cpsaat7.pdf, accessed October 12, 2010.

highest among Whites, Asians, Hispanics, and Blacks (see Table 7.2).[35] Consistent with this pattern, in a study of the role of race in layoff decisions for nearly 9,000 employees in a financial firm, Marta Elvira and Christopher Zatzick found that Whites were less likely to be laid off than non-Whites, and Asians were less likely to be laid off than Blacks and Hispanics.[36] These differences persisted even after controlling for differences in business unit, occupation, and job level, and individuals' performance rating and tenure. The researchers also found similar patterns of racial differences in promotions, raises, and performance ratings, although the differences were significant only for Blacks. These findings are consistent with other research that indicates a racial hierarchy ordered preferentially as Whites, Asians, Hispanics, and Blacks. This hierarchy can be modified somewhat by residential integration, intermarriage, and other social contact, though Whites' prejudice toward Asians and Hispanics is reduced in these ways more than their prejudice toward Blacks.[37] Elvira and Zatzick recommended that personnel decisions be closely monitored, with attention to disparities among racial minorities.[38]

Income differences between White men and White women reveal gender-based disparities that are present across racial and ethnic groups but that are exaggerated because White men's incomes are generally higher than the incomes of minority men. For White men and women at all educational levels, women's earnings are about 70% of men's. Contributing to the male/female earnings gap is the fact that White women work fewer hours even when working full-time and have shorter tenure than White men (see also Chapter 9).

....

[35]Recall from Chapters 5 and 6 employers' expressed preferences for immigrants is often associated with their paying lower wages (and other exploitation).
[36]Elvira & Zatzick (2002).
[37]Dixon, J. C. (2006). "The Ties That Bind and Those That Don't: Toward Reconciling Group Threat and Contact Theories of Prejudice." *Social Forces*, 84(4): 2179–2204; Yancey, G. (2003). *Who Is White? Latinos, Asians, and the New Black/nonblack Divide*. London: Lynne Rienner Publishers.
[38]Elvira & Zatzick (2002).

■ RESEARCH ON WHITES AND DIVERSITY

Although often unstated, by default most of the research done in management, psychology, and sociology has focused on the experiences of Whites. Whites are the numerical majority and so race differences in experiences, outcomes, and opportunities were not generally considered by most researchers for a long time. Consequently, because they were a much smaller proportion of the population, minorities' experiences as they related to common management topics (e.g., job satisfaction, turnover) were simply subsumed in the data for all workers. In a 1990 publication, Taylor Cox and Stella Nkomo pointed out the absence of race as a variable in organizational behavior research, noting the invisibility of men and women of color (as contrasted with the unspoken visibility of Whites).[39] Since their call for more research on the subject, hundreds of articles on management topics (e.g., organizational behavior, human resources, strategy) have included race and ethnicity as variables. Most of this research has focused on people of color, using Whites as the "norm" and comparing minorities to Whites. Researchers have reported differences between Whites and minorities in terms of income, promotions, performance evaluations, training, opportunities for mentoring, and job-related attitudes (e.g., job satisfaction, attitudes toward affirmative action programs, and organizational commitment). In previous chapters, we have considered some of that research, Whites' advantages in most job-related outcomes, and many of the differences between Whites and minorities in job-related attitudes. In the following sections, we focus on differences between White men and women and the meaning of ethnicity for Whites.

Similarities and Differences in the Experiences of White Women and Men

As we have discussed in previous chapters, race and sex affect one's opportunities, experiences, and outcomes in organizations. Patriarchal systems disadvantage White women as they do other women. The Naturalization Law of 1790 specifically allowed only White men to become citizens. Male immigrants of color were denied citizenship and White women experienced differential treatment as well. In many cases, White women were unable to own property, enter into contracts, or make decisions about themselves or, if married, about their children. Although they were White, they were also women and subject to patriarchal systems

---

[39]Cox, T., & Nkomo, S. (1990). "Invisible Men and Women: A Status Report on Race as a Variable in Organization Behavior Research." *Journal of Organizational Behavior*, 11: 419–431.

and ideals. As a result, Black men, at least in theory, obtained the right to vote in 1870, fifty years before White women did.[40]

Because White women generally marry White men, married White women's current economic status benefits from White men's higher earnings and occupational status, making their individual disadvantages less obvious than those of women of color. When viewed as individuals, however, White women's earnings and occupational status indicate similarities between their experiences and those of other non-dominant groups. Currently, White women work, as do women of color, in female-dominated jobs and encounter the glass ceiling and walls. When compared with White men, White women are more likely to work part-time and to work fewer hours when working full-time. Women have been called the "51% minority" and "the oppressed majority" as a reflection of their lower status in organizations and society.

As mentioned in Chapter 6, a Gallup Poll study found that 12% of Whites reported experiencing some form of discrimination within the prior year. Women were considerably more likely to report discrimination—22% compared to 3% of men.[41]

Discrimination in job placement and steering (female-dominated jobs) is a less visible but no less strong force affecting White women's earnings and outcomes. The most common jobs for White women—including clerical jobs and elementary school teaching—are sex segregated; these are jobs that are "chosen" but that also reflect strong gender role socialization and they pay less than many male-dominated jobs.[42] Many of the women featured in key sex discrimination cases described in other chapters are White, like Ann Hopkins and Lilly Ledbetter, whose cases went to the Supreme Court.

Myth: Because they are White, White women experience few disadvantages at work.

Reality: Although White women are the least disadvantaged of all women, they are disadvantaged relative to White men, occupying lower-level, lower-status, and lower-paid occupations and gaining lower returns on their educational investments.

[40]The theoretical right to vote did not guarantee Black men the actual right to vote, however; property requirements, poll taxes, literacy requirements, threats of lynching, and other obstacles prevented Blacks from voting well into the 1900s until the passage of the Voting Rights Act of 1965.
[41]Yen, H. (2005, December 8). "Poll: Nearly 1 Out of 6 Workers Claim Bias." *The Associated Press.*
[42]Department of Labor. (2008). *20 Leading Occupations of Employed Women.* Bureau of Labor Statistics, Annual Averages 2008. http://www.dol.gov/wb/factsheets/20lead2008.htm#, accessed November 15, 2010.

The Meaning of Ethnicity for Whites

Research on ethnic identity development indicates that those with high ethnic identity have positive attitudes toward their own and others' ethnicities. One study found that Whites with high racial identity development—measured as displaying acceptance, appreciation, and respect for racial differences and active involvement in cross-racial interactions—were most comfortable with Blacks.[43] Donna Chrobot-Mason has found support for the relationship between White ethnic identity development and the ability to work with and fairly manage dissimilar others.[44] Chrobot-Mason hypothesized that Whites who perceived themselves as members of a White ethnic group would be better at managing diverse employee groups due to their high ethnic identity. In her study investigating the effect of White managers' ethnic identity on minority employees' perceptions of support, 20% of the White managers reported their ethnicity as something other than White/American, such as Italian American or German American, in response to an open-ended question. Chrobot-Mason found that when both White managers and minority employees had developed high ethnic identity, the managers were perceived as more supportive, through listening, encouraging, guiding, being a role model, and fostering a relationship of mutual trust. The difference between those who genuinely self-identify as a member of an ethnic group and those whose ethnic ties are symbolic is worth noting. Herbert Gans has described the latter as **symbolic ethnicity**, which is invoked at will but has little meaning in a person's everyday life, an example being those from Irish backgrounds who emphasize and celebrate St. Patrick's Day, but whose ethnicity has little meaning at other times.[45] Symbolic ethnics are less likely to achieve the diversity-related benefits identified by Chrobot-Mason.

Caryn Block, Loriann Roberson, and Debra Neuger investigated the racial identity development of White adults. They found a complex relationship between levels of racial identity and attitudes toward interracial

[43]Claney, D., & Parker, W. M. (1989). "Assessing White Racial Consciousness and Perceived Comfort with Black Individuals: A Preliminary Study." *Journal of Counseling and Development*, 67: 449–451.

[44]Chrobot-Mason, D. (2004). "Managing Racial Differences: The Role of Majority Managers' Ethnic Identity Development on Minority Employee Perceptions of Support." *Group and Organization Management*, 29(1): 5–31.

[45]Rubin, L. B. (2004). "Is This a White Country, or What?" In J. F. Healey & E. O'Brien (Eds.), *Race, Ethnicity, and Gender*. Thousand Oaks, CA: Pine Forge Press, pp. 301–310.

situations at work.[46] Participants' levels of identity development were related to their beliefs in the existence of discrimination against Blacks, the need for affirmative action, and the existence of **reverse discrimination** against Whites and to their support for or resistance to measures taken to increase equity and levels of comfort interacting with Blacks at work or in work-related social settings. Block and her colleagues emphasized the importance of measuring Whites' levels of identity development prior to implementing diversity training, because the type of training needed (e.g., awareness of the existence of inequities and the need for efforts to reduce them versus skills training) would vary based on employees' level of identity.

Perceptions of "Quotas" and "Reverse Discrimination"

Research consistently shows that the attitudes of White men and women are most negative toward affirmative action programs, which are valuable for increasing diversity in organizations and which have benefited White women more than minorities.[47] Faye Crosby's book *Affirmative Action Is Dead: Long Live Affirmative Action* examines research on resistance to affirmative action and the continued need for such programs in the United States.[48] Frequent use of the term *quotas* by the media, politicians, and even some researchers in reference to affirmative action and other diversity efforts contributes to misperceptions that quotas are legal and commonly used.

Myth: Affirmative action frequently results in quotas and reverse discrimination.

Reality: Quotas are largely illegal and reverse discrimination is uncommon.

As discussed in previous chapters, employers implementing affirmative action use flexible goals and timetables, not "quotas," to reduce imbalances in the representation groups (e.g., among women, Blacks, Latinos, or Asians). These efforts may include enlarging the pool of applicants by using different recruitment sources, the training and development of current employees, or other legal means. The goals and

[46]Block, C. J., Roberson, L., & Neuger, D. A. (1995). "White Racial Identity Theory: A Framework for Understanding Reactions Toward Interracial Situations in Organizations." *Journal of Vocational Behavior*, 46: 71–88.

[47]Corcoran, M. (1999). "The Economic Progress of African American Women." In I. Brown (Ed.), *Latinas and African American Women at Work: Race, Gender, and Economic Inequality*. New York: Russell Sage Foundation, pp. 35–60.

[48]Crosby, F. (2004). *Affirmative Action Is Dead: Long Live Affirmative Action*. New Haven, CT: Yale University Press.

timetables are flexible, and if they are not met after legitimate efforts, there is no penalty.

Whites also tend to think that reverse discrimination, the act of giving preference to members of protected classes to the extent that others feel they are experiencing discrimination, is far more common than minorities think it is. How common is "reverse discrimination" in organizations? Although we have reiterated that most people do not sue when they feel they have experienced discrimination, one gauge of the prevalence of reverse discrimination would be the relative number of lawsuits in which it is alleged. Richard Schaefer reports that "fewer than 100 of the more than 3,000 discrimination opinions in federal courts from 1990 to 1994 even raised the issue of reverse discrimination, and reverse discrimination was actually established in only six cases."[49] As discussed previously, multiple audits conducted in major U.S. cities confirm the greater likelihood of Whites being preferred over similarly qualified Blacks and Latinos.[50]

Another measure of the existence of reverse discrimination would be fewer Whites in positions of high power, status, and income compared to minorities and women. As we have mentioned, White men's occupation of those positions far exceeds their representation in the population. White males make up a disproportionate number of high-level executives in *Fortune* 500 companies, university administrators and professors, physicians and surgeons, politicians, and many other high-status positions. Although White men constitute less than 40% of the population, more than 90% of corporate executives at the highest level are White men. A legitimate question would be to ask if these disproportions came about because White men are more meritorious than other groups and whether they would persist after forty years of reverse discrimination.

In a study that directly assessed trends in managerial representation after the passage of the Civil Rights Act and the year 2000, Stainback and Tomaskovic-Devey found a higher proportion of White men were managers in the private sector in 2000 than in 1966.[51] As shown in Table 7.3, 11% of White men were managers and White men were nearly 91% of all managers in 1966; in 2000, nearly 15% of White men were managers and White men were 57% of all managers. White women, who comprised 28% of all managers in 2000, gained the greatest share of managerial

---

[49]Schaefer, R. T. (2002), p. 96. See original article: "Reverse Discrimination Complaints Rare, a Labor Study Reports." *The New York Times*, March 31, 1995, p. A10.
[50]See Bendick, M., Jr., Jackson, C., & Reinoso, V. (1994). "Measuring Employment Discrimination through Controlled Experiments." *Review of Black Political Economy*, 23: 25–48; Bendick, M., Jr., Jackson, C., Reinoso V., and Hodges L. (1991). "Discrimination Against Latino Job Applicants: A Controlled Experiment." *Human Resource Management*, 30: 469–484; Fix, M., & Struyk, R. (Eds.). (1991). *Clear and Convincing Evidence*. Washington, D.C.: The Urban Institute.
[51]Stainback & Tomaskovic-Devey (2009).

TABLE 7.3 **Trends in the Labor Force Size, Percent Managerial, and Race–Sex Composition of the Private Sector EEO-Reporting Firms, 1966, 1980, 1990, and 2000**

	1966	1980	1990	2000
Total Labor Force				
Employment	19,285,338	28,807,871	30,659,160	37,102,233
Percent managerial jobs	7.19	10.15	10.40	9.68
White Male				
Percent of labor force	62.27	48.47	42.19	37.62
Percent of all managers	90.97	75.69	65.35	57.14
Percent who are managers	10.50	15.85	16.11	14.70
White Female				
Percent of labor force	25.51	32.27	34.68	32.32
Percent of all managers	7.14	16.56	24.24	27.79
Percent who are managers	2.01	5.21	7.27	8.32
Black Male				
Percent of labor force	6.33	6.40	6.22	6.66
Percent of all managers	0.70	2.97	3.08	3.74
Percent who are managers	0.80	4.71	5.16	5.43
Black Female				
Percent of labor force	2.54	5.48	6.83	7.88
Percent of all managers	0.18	1.27	2.21	3.11
Percent who are managers	0.52	2.35	3.37	3.82

Source: Adapted from Table 1, Trends in the Labor Force Size, Percent Managerial, and Race–Sex Composition of the Private Sector EEO-Reporting Firms, 1966 to 2000. Stainback, K., & Tomaskovic-Devey, D. (2009). "Intersections of Power and Privilege: Long-Term Trends in Managerial Representation." *American Sociological Review*, 74: 800–820.

jobs; in 1966, 2% of all White women were managers and more than 8% were managers in 2000. The researchers concluded that White men's representation has changed very little in the older and more desirable (higher-paid, higher-status) sectors of the economy and that gains for White women, Black women, and Black men have been disproportionately higher represented in positions where they manage similar others. Black women's gains are most likely to be in the growing (lower-paid, lower-status) service sectors where they manage other Black women.[52]

Race, quality of education and grades, and "fit." Evidence from empirical research also questions the veracity of claims that minorities and women are now advantaged over Whites and males. In one study of the near absence of Blacks in corporate law firms, researchers found that Blacks with

[52]Ibid, p. 816.

average grades were significantly less likely to be hired than Whites with the same grades.[53] To be hired and to excel at elite firms was far easier for Whites who attended average schools than for Blacks who attended such schools. Whites with average performance at average schools possessed substitutes for educational qualifications, such as "personality" and "fit." The authors proposed that stereotypes and unconscious biases in such firms advantage Whites over equally qualified Blacks.

Race, sex, interview assessments and offer decisions. In a study involving 311 pairs of recruiters and applicants, Caren Goldberg assessed the effects of similarity in race and sex on interview assessments and offer decisions.[54] The recruiters were managers and human resources professionals in a variety of industries, including banking, telecommunications, manufacturing, services, and retail. Goldberg found that White recruiters preferred White applicants, rating them higher in interview assessments and making more job offers to them. Black recruiters did not favor Black applicants, however. Goldberg suggested that her findings regarding Whites, but not Blacks, preferring similar others are consistent with high-status group members seeking to maintain their status by overvaluing in-group members (see also Chapter 2). The results for sex similarity indicated that male recruiters preferred female candidates, but female recruiters showed no preference for male or female applicants. Data analyses indicated that the physical attractiveness of female applicants affected male recruiters' ratings of them.[55]

Race, sex, performance ratings, and salary increases. In a study of the relationships between performance ratings and salary increases, Professor Emilio Castilla of Massachusetts Institute of Technology found that women and minorities received lower salary increases than White men even with the same performance.[56] Because Castilla controlled for factors other than race, ethnicity, and sex that could contribute to differences in salary increases, any differences could then be attributed to race, ethnicity, and sex (i.e., discrimination). Castilla's sample of nearly 9,000 employees worked in a large service organization in the United States and received performance evaluations at least once per year by their immediate supervisor. Over a six-year period, there were no differences in starting

[53]Wilkins, D. B., & Gulati, G. M. (1996). "Why Are There So Few Black Lawyers in Corporate Law Firms? An Institutional Analysis." *California Law Review*, 84: 496–625.

[54]Goldberg, C. (2005). "Relational Demography and Similarity Attraction in Interview Assessments: Are We Missing Something?" *Group and Organization Management*, 30: 597–624. Goldberg also assessed effects of age similarity on interview assessments and offer decisions but found no differences.

[55]Chapter 14 considers the effects of appearance on organizational outcomes.

[56]Castilla, E. J. (2008). "Gender, Race, and Meritocracy in Organizational Careers." *American Journal of Sociology*, 113(6): 1479–1526.

salaries based on race, sex, or other ascriptive characteristics (e.g., age and nationality); comparably skilled employees, regardless of their demographic characteristics, received similar initial salaries. Over time, however, employees who were carefully matched in terms of human capital characteristics, job experience and performance, job class, work unit, and supervisor but different in demographic characteristics earned different dollar amounts of salary increases. These differences resulted in significantly smaller salary growth for women and minorities. Castilla speculated that this **performance-reward discrimination** occurred when employers consciously or unconsciously undervalue the work of minorities in reward situations. This type of discrimination highlights the importance of internal monitoring to identify practices that may be discriminatory.

Effects of Increasing Diversity on Dominant Group Members

In a field study of more than 1,700 people working in 151 groups, Tsui, Egan, and O'Reilly found that increasing organizational diversity was associated with lowered psychological attachment among Whites and males but not among women and minorities.[57] They speculated that increasing diversity may require changes in behavioral norms, such as in language or behavior (e.g., in case of the presence of more women, this could require changes in sexist language or behavior that may be offensive to women). Such changes could be taxing, stressful, or resisted by the dominant group. Tsui and her colleagues also suggested that increased numbers of women and minorities in formerly homogenous groups may signal a lowering of job status to Whites and males. This perceived lowering of status may result in decreased attachment to the organization. The researchers suggested that future research should more closely examine the effects of increasing diversity on majority group members, rather than solely focusing on minority group members.

Myth: Women and minorities have difficulty fitting in when organizations become more diverse.

Reality: In some ways, increasing diversity can be more difficult for Whites and males—members of higher-status groups—than for women and minorities.

---

[57]Tsui, A. S., Egan, T. D., & O'Reilly, C. A. (1992). "Being Different: Relational Demography and Organizational Attachment." *Administrative Science Quarterly*, 37: 549–579.

▌ RECOMMENDATIONS FOR INDIVIDUALS

Whites play distinctive roles in organizational diversity. As members of the dominant racial group, Whites have more power to make changes than do people of color. As members of the dominant group, they may also erroneously view increasing diversity as a lowering of their individual power even though, overall, diversity is beneficial to everyone. Along with other groups, Whites should view diversity as a potential source of competitive advantage—something to be embraced rather than feared. By working toward diversity proactively, organizations will be able to increase competitiveness through cost savings and through gains in resource acquisition, system flexibility, marketing, creativity, and problem-solving, among other areas. This increased competitiveness will result in more opportunities for all, rather than in fewer opportunities and advantages for Whites.

As subjects of discrimination and disadvantages while also being members of the dominant group, White women are in a unique situation. White women in positions of power have an opportunity to make changes through their own positional and organizational power. In addition, because their spouses and other male relatives are generally White men, White women have the power to influence the beliefs and behaviors of White men, with whom they can share experiences that may help men view discrimination, the glass ceiling, and at-work harassment and exclusion as real and pervasive problems, rather than a few isolated or unique incidents. White men may view White women as more believable and trustworthy sources of diversity-related information than people of color. White women should also acknowledge their advantages over women of color, rather than expect women of color to see themselves solely as women working for women's equality. Many women of color view their race, rather than their sex, as their primary impediment to fairness.

White men and women, even those whose ancestors did not own slaves or who do not practice discrimination, should recognize the privileges associated with Whiteness in the United States. Whites should acknowledge and work to dismantle systems of unfair advantage and to share the advantages construed as "normal" for Whites among other racial groups. Whites should also actively work to dispel myths and stereotypes about non-dominant group members. When working for equality, Whites, particularly White men, are viewed as more credible than people of color.

Whites are members of the dominant racial and ethnic group, but they may also belong to non-dominant groups at some points in their lives. White men may be older, be gay, be Jewish, be overweight, or have a disability. White women experience sex discrimination and harassment and may also be older, be lesbian, be members of a non-dominant religious group, have a disability, or have some other non-dominant group status.

Although Whites' racial dominance likely pervades their learning about and understanding of diversity, active efforts to apply to their racial privileges what they have learned from membership in any non-dominant group would be worthwhile.

Because Whites are more likely to be executives, managers, and organizational leaders than others, they are in influential positions to create climates favorable to diversity.[58] The favorable environment and the diversity-supportive behaviors they model are likely to be also modeled by subordinates, contributing to a positive diversity climate. Bill Proudman and Michael Welp joined forces in running "The White Men's Caucus," which presents "White Men as Full Diversity Partners" workshops that are specifically designed to engage White men in diversity initiatives. Employees at clients such as Shell Oil and Detroit Edison report being enlightened about White male privilege, the dominance of White male cultures in organizations, and other diversity issues to which they were previously oblivious. One client realized the need for White men "to get more involved in diversity. We tend to think of it as other people's issues," rather than being relevant to White men as well as to minorities, women, and other non-dominant groups.[59] Frank McCloskey, inaugural vice president of diversity at Georgia Power, who is profiled in Individual Feature 7.3, is one White man who is involved in diversity work, and is genuinely committed to fairness, equality, and inclusion.

One way that Whites in positions of power can get more involved and be more effective in diversity work is by serving as mentors for non-dominant group members. Mentoring can be helpful in facilitating the entry of non-dominant group members into positions of power, providing access to resources and insights, to the "unwritten rules" of leadership, to information on power systems and organizational dynamics, and to a host of other benefits. Historically, White men have been advantaged by mentoring and networking systems (the "good old boy" network), when compared to women and minorities. Active mentoring by Whites in power can open doors to more employees and more widely distribute some of the many benefits of mentoring to both mentor and mentee.

▌ Recommendations for Organizations

As we have discussed, for diversity programs to be successful in organizations, it is imperative that Whites be actively involved. Whites, who are most likely to be in positions of power, are vital allies in diversity efforts. Organizational leaders must recognize that some Whites may resist diversity

---

[58]See the focus feature in Chapter 9 on Sharon Allen, chairman of the board of Deloitte Touche, USA.
[59]Atkinson, W. (2001). "Bringing Diversity to White Men." *HR Magazine*, 46(9): 76–83.

INDIVIDUAL FEATURE 7.3	*Frank McCloskey, Vice-President of Diversity, 2000–2010, Georgia Power*

Frank McCloskey, former vice president of diversity at Georgia Power is a White, heterosexual, Christian male who was a three-year letterman in football at Georgia Tech. He is one example of how White men can authentically be committed to fairness, equality, and inclusion. In a thirty-eight-year career spent primarily in operations, McCloskey became Georgia Power's first vice president of diversity in 2000, a position he held until retiring in 2010. He was charged with developing a long-term management and organizational culture change strategy affecting diversity and inclusion.[60] Recognized by the Society for Human Resource Management as one of the 100 Global Diversity Thought Leaders, McCloskey has received the Willie O'Ree National Hockey League "Black Ice" Diversity Award, the Rainbow Push Coalition Keep Hope Alive Equal Opportunity Award, and the American Institute for Managing Diversity 25th Anniversary Diversity Leader Award. He is past chair of the Atlanta Urban League, Leadership Atlanta, the Korea–Southeast U.S. Chamber of Commerce, and currently serves on the Anti-Defamation League Board of Directors.

McCloskey believes corporations must require leadership and work environments to be better than what is currently modeled in society. In this time of global competition, U.S. corporations must take the lead to close the educational and poverty gap across racial and ethnic lines. This is necessary in order to build a future talent pipeline and sustain corporate business models.

McCloskey also feels that the myth of "postracial" America, the unabated political divisiveness, and the at times irrational fear and fervor of many often well-intended people have combined to dramatically set back race relations and social justice. McCloskey believes we are at either a "break" or "breakthrough" point in our country's history. "Whites have the moral responsibility and power to change the current state and the direction we are heading. Our country can only expand and remain mighty if all of our citizens are free from injustice, educated, and fully participating in and benefiting from wealth creation."[61]

QUESTIONS TO CONSIDER

1. *McCloskey believes that corporations must "take the lead to close the educational and poverty gap across racial and ethnic lines" to build a future talent pipeline and sustain corporate business models. Do you agree that the racial and ethnic disparities in educational attainment discussed in this book may negatively affect corporations? If so, in what specific ways might corporations get involved with alleviating such disparities? Why might individual investors support corporations' involvement in such efforts?*

2. *What is the relationship between a country's success and the ability of all its citizens to be free from injustice, educated, and participating in and benefiting from wealth creation?*

3. *McCloskey believes that change must first begin in one's immediate circle of*

[60]http://www.insightintodiversity.com/index.php?option=com_content&view=article&id=212:frank-mccloskey&catid=15:editorial-board&Itemid=36, accessed November 15, 2010; http://www.georgiapower.com/community/diversity_flash.asp, accessed November 15, 2010.
[61]Personal communication, July 20, 2010, November 16, 2010.

influence—the family—and recommends adults be careful not to unintentionally teach children subtle forms of bias and prejudice.[62] To what kinds of unintentional forms of bias and prejudice are children introduced by well-meaning adults who believe themselves to be unprejudiced?

because they feel excluded, that focusing on diversity is a waste of resources, or that the organization is already diverse and supportive to people of color and women. Including Whites as active participants in the diversity process is a key step to reducing some resistance. Education about the advantages to everyone of increased diversity and about the existence of the glass ceiling and walls, sexual harassment, and other barriers to diversity is also important. Whites should be assured that diversity is not an "us or them" situation, but is valuable to everyone. In our recommendations for individuals, we suggested mentoring as a way that individual Whites in power could assist with diversity efforts. Institutions should facilitate mentoring of non-dominant group members through organizationally sanctioned mentoring programs, mentoring training, and recognition for mentors.

Goldberg's finding that White, but not Black, managers and human resources professionals serving as recruiters for a variety of organizations rated racially similar others more highly and were more likely to make job offers to them indicates that interviewer ratings and job offers should be carefully monitored. Castilla's findings that starting salaries for women and minorities were similar to those offered to White males but that salary increases for women and minorities differed from those of White males despite the same performance ratings underscore the need for organizational attention to the outcomes of processes designed to be meritocratic. Not only should employers pay attention to initial salaries and to biases in performance evaluation ratings for different demographic groups, they should also monitor salary increases and promotions in terms of equivalent ratings. Because research indicates that formalization of human resource practices reduces gender and race discrimination in earnings, practices should be formalized and monitored as much as possible.[63]

[62]Personal communication, July 20, 2010.

[63]Anderson, C. D., & Tomaskovic-Devey, D. (1995). "Patriarchal Pressures: An Exploration of Organizational Processes That Exacerbate and Erode Gender Earnings Inequality." *Work and Occupations*, 22(3): 328–357; Elvira, M. M., & Graham, M. E. (2002). "Not Just a Formality: Pay System Formalization and Sex-Related Earnings Effects." *Organization Science*, 13(6): 601–617; Konrad, A. M., & Linnehan, F. (1995). "Formalized HRM Structures: Coordinating Equal Employment Opportunity or Concealing Organizational Practices?" *Academy of Management Journal*, 38: 787–820; Reskin, B. (2000). "The Proximate Causes of Employment Discrimination." *Contemporary Sociology*, 29(2): 319–328.

SUMMARY

In this chapter, we have considered the contributions of Whites to diversity in organizations and the history of Whites in the United States, including hostility and exclusion practiced by White ethnic groups and the transition from non-White to White status of some of those groups. We also presented research on the relationship between Whites' perceptions of themselves as members of an ethnic group and their ability to effectively manage non-White group members. We considered differences in the experiences of White women and White men and of Whites who belong to other non-dominant groups (such as religious minorities, sexual minorities, or people with disabilities).

As the dominant group, Whites play a key role in efforts to achieve organizational diversity. Historically, many Whites have aligned themselves with the goals of diversity and they continue to do so. We suggested ways for individual Whites to participate in and contribute to diversity in organizations and for organizations to facilitate Whites' inclusion.

KEY TERMS

Myth of meritocracy — the idea that societal resources are distributed exclusively or primarily on the basis of individual merit.

Performance-reward discrimination — the act of giving different amounts of rewards (e.g., salary increases) to members of different groups who have similar performance evaluations.

Reverse discrimination — the act of giving preference to members of protected classes to the extent that others feel they are experiencing discrimination.

Symbolic ethnicity — a form of ethnicity that has little impact on one's daily life and is invoked at will.

QUESTIONS TO CONSIDER

1. Many Whites argue that their resistance to affirmative action and diversity programs is due in part to their families' history of not owning slaves or their not having practiced discrimination.[64] What are some ways in which Whites who have not done these things nonetheless benefited from and been advantaged by slavery and discrimination?

2. How does the visibility (identifiability) of groups such as Blacks and Asians contrast with the invisibility of White ethnics in shaping their organizational experiences?

3. Recall from Chapter 4 that many of the Whites who participated in Blacks' struggle for civil rights were Jewish. How were the organizational experiences of Jews and Blacks in the United States similar and dissimilar?

4. Is the transition of Jews and Irish from the non-White to White category surprising to you? Brodkin also discusses the transformations of Mexicans to White then back again. Were you

---

[64]For discussions of advantages, disadvantages, oblivion, and consciousness of privilege versus discrimination, see McIntosh (1998).

aware of these changes? In addition to those listed in this chapter, what other changes in race occurred within the U.S. Census categorizations?

5. Recall the study by Castilla that found similar starting salaries but differential salary growth for women and minorities compared to White men even when performance ratings were the same. What are some possible negative consequences for the organization if these salary differences become widely known? What specific steps would you recommend to avoid "performance-reward" discrimination?

6a. If you are not White, do you know someone well who is White? In what capacity do you know this person (e.g., personal friend, manager, classmate, neighbor)? Do you know this person's ethnic origin (e.g., Italian, Irish, German)? How much time have you spent with him or her? Have you thought about this person as having a race or an ethnicity? Have you discussed race, ethnicity, or other diversity issues with him or her? Explain.

6b. If you are White, do you know your ethnic origin? How much of a role does your ethnic origin play in your everyday life, experiences, and opportunities? Can outside observers discern your ethnic origin by looking at you?

6c. How does the ethnicity of Whites differ from visible ethnic differences in its effect on a person's experiences and opportunities?

7. Individual Whites may report experiences with reverse discrimination, despite little research evidence to support it. How do such experiences affect support of or resistance toward diversity efforts? What might help such individuals to be supportive of diversity efforts, despite believing they had experienced discrimination?

ACTIONS AND EXERCISES

1. Search the EEOC Web site (http://www.eeoc.gov) for the most recent three or six months for cases of discrimination charges and settlements against Whites. In any month that you find a case involving discrimination against Whites, document the events surrounding this case. What proportion of cases involved race-based discrimination against Whites?

2. Although "quotas" are generally illegal in the United States, many people believe they are legal and common. Prepare an argument to dispel the idea of reverse discrimination basing it on education and earnings and representation in senior and executive management of White men, White women, Black men, and Black women.

3a. Conduct an informal census of employees in several places: a fast-food restaurant, a sit-down restaurant, a discount store (e.g., Target, Walmart), department store (e.g., Macy's, Filene's, Marshall Fields), government office, bank, or other locations in which many employees are visible. Document the number of employees overall and the number of White employees visible. What is the race and sex of the store manager? Estimate the proportion of the employees who are

White in each place. How many managers and assistant managers are White? How many are White and male?

3b. Choose two nights to watch television for thirty minutes to one hour each night. Document the program, type of commercial, and the numbers of White characters in the programs and commercials. In what roles are they portrayed?

3c. What similarities and differences are apparent between the people in parts a and b?

4. From your data in Exercises 3a and 3b, speculate on the ethnicity of the White employees (3a) or characters (3b). What factors did you use in your speculation? Compare the difficulty in speculating on the ethnicity of the Whites with identifying them by race and sex.

5. Use a calculator to make a chart projecting the effects of performance-reward disparities (Castilla's study, discussed in the chapter) in salary growth for White men, White women, and people of color.

a. Make columns for starting salaries of $30,000 for the new employees. Use different annual salary increase estimates (e.g., 1%, 3%, 5%, or other estimates) for each demographic group. What are the salary differences after 10 years? After 20 years?

b. What effects would such disparities in salary growth have on each employee's and the employer's contributions to the employees' Social Security, tax-deferred savings plans, and retirement plans?

c. What effects would such disparities have on other outcomes for these groups (e.g., housing opportunities, investments, children's education)?

American Indians, Alaska Natives, and Multiracial Group Members

CHAPTER 8

Chapter Objectives

After completing this chapter, readers should have a greater understanding of American Indians, Alaska Natives, and multiracial group members in the United States. Specifically, they should be able to:

❑ explain the historical background and current status of American Indians, Alaska Natives, and multiracial group members in the United States.

❑ discuss education, workforce participation rates, employment, and income levels of American Indians and Alaska Natives in the United States.

❑ explain the diversity among multiracial group members and issues unique to them.

❑ identify similarities in experiences of native people in the United States and New Zealand.

❑ explain legislation related to employment experiences of American Indians, Alaska Natives, and multiracial group members.

❑ make recommendations for inclusion of these groups in diversity efforts.

Key Facts

The 4.9 million people of American Indian and Alaskan Native descent comprise 1.6% of the U.S. population.

About 12% of the American Indian and Alaskan Native population lives on reservations or trust lands.

Fourteen percent of American Indians and Alaska Natives have at least a bachelor's degree—fewer than all racial and ethnic groups except Hispanics.

American Indians and Alaska Natives have the worst or nearly the worst unemployment, poverty, and health insurance rates in the United States.

In the 2000 Census, for the first time, people could report belonging to two or more races, and nearly 7 million people did so. By 2010, 9 million people did so, a 32% increase.

Ninety-three percent of multiracial people are of two races and 6% are of three races.

Multirace people are younger than single-race people; over 40% of multiracials are under 18, compared with 25% of single-race people.

Introduction and Overview

This chapter considers American Indian, Alaskan Native (AI/AN), and multiracial group members and their experiences related to diversity in organizations. We consider these groups in combination for several reasons. First, as the original inhabitants of the United States, American Indians and Alaska Natives preceded any racial or ethnic *diversity* to speak of in the country. Second, because they are a relatively small portion of the population, both groups are often overlooked in studies of diversity in organizations, yet their place in the history of diversity in the United States should not be ignored. Next, multiracial group members—people who report belonging to two or more racial backgrounds—could perhaps be considered the "newest" minority groups, at least in terms of their ability to identify themselves as such in the U.S. Census records. Beginning with the 2000 Census, respondents had the option to self-identify using two or more races for the first time since Census data collection began. This has provided more information about the increasing racial diversity of the United States and allowed recognition of the variety of identities in the population.

The chapter begins with a brief discussion of the history, population, education, earnings, and employment of American Indians and Alaska Natives. We next discuss some of the limited research on the organizational experiences of AI/AN in the United States. A feature on the Māori of New Zealand reveals striking similarities to the experiences of native people in the United States. Next considered are the history and population of U.S. multiracial group members.[1]

Terminology

The term *American Indian* is used to refer to the descendants of the people indigenous to what is now the mainland United States (the lower 48) and is consistent with the usage of many other researchers, the Office of American Indian Trust, and the U.S. Census Bureau when referring to that specific population. Although *Native American* is often construed as more appropriate, *American Indian* is often used by group members themselves and is considered broadly acceptable.[2] Further, the term *Native American* has been used to include American Indians, Alaska Natives, Native Hawaiians, and sometimes Chamorros and American Samoans, but the latter three groups are not the focus of this chapter.[3] Thus, here we use the term *American Indians* or *American Indians and Alaska Natives* (AI/AN) as appropriate. Much of the research investigates experiences of American Indians exclusively, and in those cases, we refer only to *American Indians*. At times, data on American Indians and Alaska Natives are included in an "other" category, as described. Lastly, we use the terms *nation* as well as *tribe* in referring to different groups of American Indians, respecting variations in the preferred terminology among Indians themselves and among researchers.[4]

When referring to persons of more than one racial background, we use the term *multiracial*. This includes biracial people as well as those with more than two identified racial backgrounds. Although some researchers have limited their studies to people with White/Black heritage, we do not do so.[5] However, we do acknowledge the importance to one's diversity-related outcomes of the specific combination of multiracial categories (e.g., Black/White, Asian/White) and their identifiability (which

---

[1] The diversity of people included in the multiracial group category prevents coherent discussions of their earnings, education, and unemployment, so we have not made the attempt.

[2] Wildenthal, B. H. (2003). *Native American Sovereignty on Trial*. Santa Barbara, CA: ABC-CLIO.

[3] Ibid.

[4] See Massey, G. M. (2004). "Making Sense of Work on the Wind River Indian Reservation." *American Indian Quarterly*, 28(3/4): 786–816, footnote 1.

[5] Rockquemore, K. A., & Brunsma, D. L. (2002). *Beyond Black*. Thousand Oaks, CA: Sage Publications.

enables people to be categorized, stereotyped, and singled out for differential treatment). Researchers studying multiracial individuals and their similarities to Whites and Blacks suggest that Asian/White and Hispanic/White multiracial individuals exhibit less so- cial distance from Whites than Blacks and have pro- posed that this may be evidence of a trend toward more of a Black/non-Black U.S. social divide and less of the White/non-White divide that has long existed.[6] ●

■ HISTORY OF AMERICAN INDIANS IN NORTH AMERICA

Many people in the United States are familiar with American Indians only through television shows, movies, and sports teams. These media images often reinforce perceptions of Indians as savage enemies, although there have been attempts recently to portray Indians more accurately and fairly. Feature 8.1 considers the debate over stereotyping, insensitivity, and the use of American Indian images as mascots and sports symbols.

American Indians, the original inhabitants of North America, were already present when Columbus made the European discovery of America. After an initial period of what appeared to be peaceful coexistence, relations between American Indians and Europeans began to decline. Historical records document the violence against and near extermination of American Indians. In 1830, the Indian Removal Act, passed under President Andrew Jackson, authorized the expulsion of 14,000 Indians from lands in the southeastern portion of the country to Arkansas and Oklahoma. Thousands of Indians died on the "Trail of Tears" westward, continuing the decline in population begun by war, disease, and the annihilation of buffalo.

The U.S. Census did not count American Indians until 1860, and then only if they were not living on reservations. With the 1890 Census, all American Indians, both on and outside reservations were included in the data.[7] Estimates of the number of American Indians in the United States at first European contact run from 1 million to 8 million, a very wide range.[8] In 1890, the first complete Census count officially recorded 248,000 American Indians, far fewer than even the lowest of the estimates of the original Indian population.[9]

After their conquest and near extermination of the Indians, European Americans focused attention on assimilating them into American society.

[6] Lee, J., & Bean, F. D. (2007). "Reinventing the Color Line: Immigration and America's New Racial/Ethnic Divide." *Social Forces*, 86(2): 561–586.
[7] U.S. Census Bureau. (1993). "We the … first Americans." Washington, D.C.: U.S. Department of Commerce.
[8] Thornton, R. (2004). "Trends Among American Indians in the United States." In J. F. Healey & E. O'Brien (Eds.), *Race, Ethnicity, and Gender*. Thousand Oaks, CA: Pine Forge Press, pp. 195–210.
[9] U.S. Census Bureau (1993).

FEATURE 8.1	*American Indians as Sports Symbols and Mascots*

In the 1970s, Oklahoma, Marquette, Stanford, Dartmouth, and Syracuse discontinued using Indian mascots.[10] Debate over the use of American Indian mascots has waxed and waned since then, with some viewing it as insensitive and offensive with others viewing it as harmless.

In 2001, the U.S. Commission on Civil Rights issued a statement on the use of Native American images and nicknames as sports symbols.[11] The commission opined that the use of such symbols is insensitive and implies that stereotyping is acceptable, a "dangerous lesson in a diverse society." Arguing that the use of stereotypical images of American Indians could create a hostile educational environment for Indian students, the commission cited Indians' low rates of high school and college graduation. The Civil Rights Commission rejected arguments that such images honor American Indians and stimulate interest in Indian cultures. Instead, according to the commission, the images prevent people from learning about real American Indians and their current issues.

Researchers investigating the consequences of Indian mascots on AI students have found that students indicated positive associations with the mascots but reported depressed self-esteem, lower sense of community worth, and fewer expectations for self-achievement. Along with the Civil Rights Commission, the National Association for the Advancement of Colored People, the United Methodist Church, and the National Collegiate Athletic Association (NCAA) have also called for institutions to cease using Indian mascots and sports symbols. Taking a strong stance, the NCAA voted to penalize eighteen schools if they continued using American Indian nicknames, mascots, or images, generating heated debates, threats, and considerable media attention. Prohibited were the use of American Indian imagery and nicknames, performance of mascots at NCAA tournament games, and use of Indian images on athletes', cheerleaders', and band uniforms.[12]

The Florida State University (FSU) Seminoles and the University of Illinois Fighting Illini were on the original list of eighteen schools targeted by the NCAA. University administrators, alumni, supporters, and politicians from Florida were outraged at the proposed sanctions and vowed to pursue all legal avenues available to fight the NCAA's decision. In both states, legislation was introduced to solidify the use of the Indian symbols and mascots, although the legislation did not pass. After reviewing statements of apparent support for continued use of the symbols from Seminoles in Florida and Oklahoma, the NCAA decided to allow FSU to use the Seminole mascot and symbols, removing FSU from the list of restricted schools. However, some American Indians continue to protest the use of such images, focusing on the political pressures placed on the Florida Seminoles to grant their approval of the use of the mascot.[13]

According to NCAA Senior Vice President Bernard Franklin, "The decision of a namesake sovereign tribe, regarding when and how its name and imagery can be used, must be respected even when others may not agree."[14]

[10] Saraceno, J. (2005, August 10). "Some Colleges Have a Lot to Learn about Racism." *USAToday*, p. 2C.

[11] United States Commission on Civil Rights. http://aistm.org/2001usccr.htm, accessed August 24, 2010.

[12] Associated Press (2005, August 19). " NCAA: Tribes Must OK Use of Their Names." http://www.msnbc.msn.com/id/8838557/, accessed August 14, 2010.

[13] American Indian Sports Team Mascots. http://aistm.org/1indexpage.htm, accessed August 14, 2010.

[14] Associated Press (2005, August 23). "Florida State Threatened to Sue over Postseason Ban." http://sports.espn.go.com/ncaa/news/story?id=2141197, accessed August 14, 2010.

Franklin said that the NCAA will handle reviews from other schools on a case-by-case basis and that the NCAA remains committed to ensuring an atmosphere of respect and sensitivity for those participating in and attending its championships.

In contrast to FSU, Illinois discontinued in 2007 its use of Chief Illiniwek, the mascot well known to students, alumni, and supporters. Although the decision making was contentious, the board of trustees' vote was implemented campuswide. A statement by the university's Office of Inclusion and Intercultural Relations stated that "the continued use of Chief Illiniwek is an obstacle to fulfilling our mission of promoting a diverse and welcoming environment that supports full inclusion for all members of the University community. We strive to respect the human dignity of all individuals and communities.... Therefore, the retirement of Chief Illiniwek is in the best interest of our community."

QUESTIONS TO CONSIDER

1. *Colleges and schools are unique organizations, with diverse students, alumni, and faculty, and the general public as customers and constituents. How might the use of an American Indian name and mascot affect individuals from these groups of customers and constituents? What should be done to effectively address disputes that will inevitably arise when a decision is made to continue using or to discontinue using a particular mascot?*

2. *Compare the use of the Seminole and other American Indian mascots to the "Fighting Irish" mascot at the University of Notre Dame.*

3. *How might the size of the American Indian population be related to continued use of AI images and mascots? How might the size of the population be related to people not knowing any "real" Indians? How might AI images and mascots affect such people?*

4. *What factors make elected officials introduce laws calling for continued use of certain mascots? What do you think about this practice?*

Many American Indian children were forced to attend American schools where they were forbidden to speak their native languages as part of attempts to "civilize" them. The language and religious practices lost through attempts to convert American Indians to Christianity resulted in the disappearance of many cultural values and customs.[15]

Throughout the nineteenth century and into the twentieth, laws were passed and court decisions rendered regarding the rights and fates of American Indians in the United States. Assimilation, tribal termination, and self-determination were the stated purposes of various of these decisions.[16] For example, the 1924 Indian Citizenship Act gave citizenship to Indians born in the United States.[17] In 1953, laws were passed to terminate Indian tribes, causing more than 100 tribes to cease to be

[15] Wildenthal (2003).

[16] Deloria, V., Jr., & Lytle, C. M. (1983). *American Indians, American Justice.* Austin, TX: University of Texas Press.

[17] Recall that for long periods of time, only White men in the United States were allowed to become citizens.

recognized. Most recently, the pendulum has swung the other way, toward the goal of self-determination, with American Indians again allowed certain rights of self-governance and decision making. The 1978 Indian Child Welfare Act, which restricted the removal of Indian children from their families by the courts, the American Indian Religious Freedom Act (1978), and the Tribal Self-Governance Act of 1994 were significant steps toward self-determination.

▌ POPULATION

After the decimation experienced in the 1700s and 1800s, the American Indian population began to recover during the 1900s due to declining mortality rates and increasing fertility rates. Increases in self-identification have also contributed to the growth of this population.[18] As of July 1, 2008, 4.9 million people in the United States were classified as American Indians and Alaska Natives, alone or in combination with one or more other races, comprising 1.6% of the U.S. population.[19] Although they are counted as a single group for Census purposes, the AI/AN population is diverse in language, religion, culture, beliefs, values, and geographic location.[20] In addition, estimates suggest that 60% of American Indians marry those who are not Indians, which contributes to the diversity among those with AI ancestry and to increases in the multiracial category.[21]

The self-reporting aspect of data collection for the U.S. Census allows flexibility when claiming a racial identity. If a respondent reports that he or she is American Indian, the data is counted as valid, even though the identification may change, even within the same year. For example, only 42% of the people who identified as American Indian did so on both the 1990 Census and the follow-up reinterview survey later that year. In comparison, 96% of Whites and 91% of Blacks reported the same racial identity in both surveys. One-quarter American Indian ancestry and/or tribal membership has generally been required for recognition by the Bureau of Indian Affairs. Among Indian nations, there is wide variation

---

[18] Deloria & Lytle (1983). See also Eschbach, K., Supple, K., & Snipp, C. M. (1998). "Changes in Racial Identification and the Educational Attainment of American Indians, 1970–1990." *Demography*, 35(1): 35–43.
[19] Facts for Features. "American Indian and Alaska Native Heritage Month: November 2009." http://www.census.gov/newsroom/releases/pdf/cb09-ff20.pdf, accessed August 16, 2010.
[20] Green, D. E. (1999). "Native Americans." In A. G. Dworkin & R. J. Dworkin (Eds.), *The Minority Report*, 3rd ed. Fort Worth, TX: Harcourt Brace Publishers, pp. 255–277; Wildenthal (2003).
[21] Thornton, R. (2004). "Trends Among American Indians in the United States." In J. F. Healey & E. O'Brien (Eds.), *Race, Ethnicity, and Gender*. Thousand Oaks, CA: Pine Forge Press, pp. 195–225.

in the degree of Indian ancestry required for people to be officially recognized as American Indian.[22] In 2003, there were 562 federally recognized American Indian tribes in the United States. "Recognized" tribes have certain rights and privileges, including funding and services from the Bureau of Indian Affairs and the power of self-government (e.g., the right to make and enforce laws, tax, establish membership, license and regulate activities, and exclude people from tribal territories).

Nearly 30% of American Indians and Alaska Natives speak a language other than English at home.[23] The most common language is Navajo, spoken by 178,014 people. More than half a million American Indians live on reservations or trust lands, including 175,200 residing on Navajo lands in Arizona, New Mexico, and Utah. California has the most American Indian residents—687,400—followed by Oklahoma with 398,200 and Arizona with 322,200.

Misperception: The majority of American Indians live on reservations.

Reality: About 12% of Indians live on reservations.

American Indians and Alaska Natives are a youthful people, significantly younger than the general population, and thus will compose a larger portion of the workforce as these youths age. Nearly one-third of the 4.9 million AI/AN are under age 18. Eight percent of the AI/AN population are in the 14 to 17 age range, which is the largest proportion in this age category of all racial and ethnic groups. As examples, 6% of Latinos and 5% of Whites fall into the 14- to 17-year-old age group. The median age of the AI/AN population is 29.7, younger than the U.S. population as a whole, at 36.8.[24] In general, indigenous people in various other countries are younger than their fellow countrymen, including the Māori of New Zealand, as discussed in International Feature 8.1.

Fifty-seven percent of AI/AN now live in metropolitan areas, which is a smaller proportion than any other racial group but a larger proportion than at any time in the past. Until 1990, more than half of the AI/AN population lived outside metropolitan areas. This growth in metropolitan population reflects concerted efforts to move American Indians to places having more employment opportunities than rural or reservation lands. In the 1950s, U.S. government relocation programs contributed to the large-scale migration of American Indians from reservations that had

---

[22] Ibid.
[23] Facts for Features (2009).
[24] Facts for Features (2009).

INTERNATIONAL FEATURE 8.1

Māori: Native New Zealanders

Māori are people indigenous to New Zealand who inhabited the country prior to any other racial or ethnic group. At the time of their first European contact, in 1769, an estimated 100,000 Māori lived in New Zealand. By 1896, the population of Māori had declined to about 42,000, but in the 2006 Census, there were more than 600,000 people of Māori ancestry in New Zealand, comprising nearly 18% of its total population.

The New Zealand Census captures people of Māori ancestry in three ways: Māori only, Māori ethnic group, and Māori ancestry. Some of the people who identified with the Māori ethnic group in the 2006 Census reported uncertainty about whether they did or did not have Māori ancestry. As with determining who is Native American in the United States, determining Māori ancestry is important for constitutional and legal reasons in New Zealand.[25]

Māori are growing faster than the general population and are projected to make up a larger proportion of the population in the future. Between 1991 and 2001, the New Zealand European population (Pakeha) grew by 2.1%, while the New Zealand Māori population grew by 21.1%.[26] Higher Māori growth rates are due to higher fertility rates, births between non-Māori and Māori, and a younger population (who are at the childbearing age) than the general population.[27] In 2001, Māori children under age 15 made up 25% of all New Zealand children, and their percentage is projected to grow to 28% by 2021, compared with 15% of Māori in the general population. The large proportion of Māori children makes full inclusion of Māori in educational and employment opportunities in New Zealand particularly important.

Māori have lower education, employment, and income than non-Māori and higher levels of poverty, incarceration, and unemployment rates. Māori are two to three times as likely to be unemployed as are Pakeha and are more likely to be long-term unemployed. As are minorities in the United States, Māori tend to be residentially segregated, which contributes further to the polarization and disadvantages of non-dominant groups.[28]

The New Zealand 1977 Human Rights Act prohibits discrimination in organizational policies and practices against minorities and indigenous people, women, people with disabilities, sexual minorities, religious minorities, and other non-dominant group members.[29] Diversity issues, including discrimination against non-dominant groups, changing demographics, equity in employment, and other issues are of importance to New Zealand researchers as well as to those in other countries.

QUESTIONS TO CONSIDER

1. *How do the past and current experiences of Māori in New Zealand compare with those of American Indians in the United States?*

2. *How effective is the New Zealand Human Rights Act? Investigate.*

[25] Cormack, D. (n.d.). "The Māori Population." http://www.hauora.māori.nz/downloads/hauora_chapter02_web.pdf, accessed August 24, 2010.

[26] Johnston, R. J., Poulsen, M. F., & Forrest, J. (2003). "The Ethnic Geography of New Zealand: A Decade of Growth and Change, 1991–2001." *Asia Pacific Viewpoint*, 44(2): 109–130.

[27] See Cormack (n.d.).

[28] Johnston et al. (2003).

[29] The Human Rights Commission. http://www.hrc.co.nz/index.php?p=13814, accessed August 24, 2010; Jones, D., Pringle, J., & Shepherd, D. (2000). "'Managing Diversity' Meets Aoetearoa/New Zealand." *Personnel Review*, 29: 364–380.

few economic opportunities to cities that had greater opportunities for employment.[30] The migration resulted in more job opportunities, but less cohesion, fewer relationships with other American Indians and family members, and other problems for American Indians.

▍ EDUCATION, EMPLOYMENT, AND EARNINGS

As shown in Table 8.1, 14% of American Indians aged 25 and older have a college degree and 76% have at least a high school diploma. These education levels are higher than those for persons of Hispanic ethnicity but lower than those of Asians, Whites, and Blacks. The workforce participation rates of American Indians are about 3% lower than those of the total population. American Indian men participate at a rate about 5% lower than rates for all men, and American Indian women participate at a rate about 2% lower than rates for all women.[31]

Overall, employment and earnings for AI/AN are significantly lower than those of Whites and similar to those of Blacks and Hispanics, and the poverty rates for AI/AN are higher than for all groups except

TABLE 8.1 *Educational Attainment of Population 25 Years and Over: 2008*

	High School Graduate or More (%)	College Degree or More (%)
All Groups	86.6	29.4
Non-Hispanic White	87.1	29.8
Black	83.0	19.6
Asian	88.7	52.6
Hispanic	62.3	13.3
American Indian/Alaska Native	76.0	14.0

Notes: Total for All Groups includes other races not shown separately. Persons of Hispanic origin may be of any race. White, Black, and Asian include respondents reporting one race only. Asians do not include Pacific Islanders.

Sources: Data for all figures except American Indians from: Table 224. Educational Attainment by Race and Hispanic Origin: 1970 to 2008. http://www.census.gov/compendia/statab/2010/tables/10s0224.pdf, accessed August 24, 2010; American Indians: Facts for Features. "American Indian and Alaska Native Heritage Month: November 2009." http://www.census.gov/newsroom/releases/archives/facts_for_features_special_editions/cb09-ff20.html, accessed August 24, 2010.

[30] Green (1999), p. 265.
[31] U.S. Census Bureau (1993); "American Indians and Alaska Natives." (1999). Washington, D.C.: Office of American Indian Trust, Department of the Interior.

TABLE 8.2 *Poverty and Lack of Health Insurance by Race and Hispanic Origin: 2008*

	Poverty (%)	Without Health Insurance (%)
All	13.2	15.4
Non-Hispanic White	8.6	10.8
Black	24.7	19.1
Hispanic (any race)	23.2	30.7
Asian*	11.8	17.6
American Indian/Alaska Native	24.2	31.7

*Does not include Native Hawaiian/Other Pacific Islanders.

Sources: Data for all races except American Indian/Alaska Natives taken from DeNavas-Walt, C., Proctor, B. D., & Smith, J. C. (2009). U.S. Census Bureau, Current Population Reports, P60-236, *Income, Poverty, and Health Insurance Coverage in the United States: 2008*. U.S. Government Printing Office: Washington, D.C.; American Indians/Alaska Natives data from: American Indians: Facts for Features. "American Indian and Alaska Native Heritage Month: November 2009." http://www.census.gov/newsroom/releases/archives/facts_for_features_special_editions/cb09-ff20.html, accessed August 24, 2010.

Blacks.[32] Of people who are AI/AN alone (one race), 24.2% live in poverty, compared with 8.6% of non-Hispanic Whites. As shown in Table 8.2, AI/AN have the worst or nearly the worst poverty and health insurance rates in the United States. An Urban Institute study investigating the status of American families concluded that overall, AI/AN "seem to fare the worst of all the racial and ethnic groups."[33]

Although the Census and much other data present summary figures for AI/AN as a group, there are important differences among AI/AN members in terms of education, employment, earnings, values, beliefs, and traditions. Those who work with, recruit, or employ American Indians and Alaska Natives are encouraged to investigate the attributes of the specific population and, more important, the individual applicant or employee. Further, people who have lived primarily on reservation or trust lands will have extremely different experiences, expectations, and backgrounds than those who have primarily (or totally) lived elsewhere or for whom being Indian is not a strong source of their identity.[34] Education, employment, and earnings of AI/AN differ depending on residence, appearance, and language, among other things. Those who live on or near reservations, closely identify with the culture, speak a native

[32] Ibid.

[33] Staveteig, S., & Wigton, A. (2000). *Racial and Ethnic Disparities: Key Findings from the National Survey of America's Families*. Washington, D.C.: The Urban Institute, p. 4.

[34] Massey (2004).

language, and participate in religious and cultural traditions may have experiences similar to those of other people of color.[35]

The issues of membership in the AI/AN population, fluidity and motivations for self-identifying, and variation among experiences between AI/AN living on reservations and elsewhere have all been subjects of debate. A common perception about AI/AN is that their share of gaming wealth associated with casinos on or near reservations is significant. In actuality, such wealth is an important source of revenue for a very small proportion of tribes. In those cases, gaming operations have increased employment opportunities and economic development for the associated nations. For some reservations in rural, isolated places (which are the majority), casinos and gaming revenues and associated financial benefits are nonexistent.[36] In addition, some tribes view gaming as contrary to their values and refuse to participate in it, even given prospects of financial gain.[37]

Misperception: American Indians reap significant benefits from tribal casino operations.

Reality: Some Indian nations have benefited significantly from gaming revenues, but many have not. American Indians and Alaska Natives have some of the highest poverty rates in the United States.

▌ RELEVANT LEGISLATION

Employment of AI/AN on reservation or trust lands is generally governed by tribal regulations rather than federal, state, or local laws. Some federal laws specifically exclude reservations and trust lands. To ensure compliance with appropriate laws, employers are encouraged to consult labor law experts in the local area about tribal regulations and governance. Outside reservation or trust property, American Indians and Alaska Natives are covered under federal legislation prohibiting employment discrimination on the basis of race and national origin, specifically Title VII of the Civil Rights Act of 1964. As apparent in the first English-only case ever filed on behalf of American Indians by the Equal Employment Opportunity Commission (EEOC), which follows, AI/AN do experience discrimination in employment.

---

[35] See Eschbach et al. (1998) for a discussion of race as an ascribed characteristic or a reflection of situational ethnicity and how changes in racial identification affected changes in the reported outcomes of American Indians.
[36] Ibid.
[37] Thornton (2004).

EEOC SUES ARIZONA DINER FOR NATIONAL ORIGIN BIAS AGAINST NAVAJOS AND OTHER NATIVE AMERICANS[38]

First-Ever English-Only Lawsuit by Commission on Behalf of Native Americans

PHOENIX—The U.S. Equal Employment Opportunity Commission (EEOC) announced that it filed a national origin discrimination lawsuit under Title VII of the Civil Rights Act of 1964 on behalf of Native American employees who were subjected to an unlawful English-only policy precluding them from speaking Navajo in the workplace and terminating them for refusing to sign an agreement to abide by the restrictive language policy. The lawsuit, the first-ever English-only suit by the commission on behalf of Native Americans, was filed by the EEOC's Phoenix District Office against RD's Drive-In, a diner located in Page, Arizona—a community adjacent to the Navajo reservation.

… The suit, *EEOC v RD's Drive-In*, CIV 02 1911 PHX LOA, states that RD's posted a policy stating: "*The owner of this business can speak and understand only English. While the owner is paying you as an employee, you are required to use English at all times. The only exception is when the customer cannot understand English. If you feel unable to comply with this requirement, you may find another job.*"

… This policy, in an early form, prohibited employees from speaking Navajo in the workplace. Two employees, Roxanne Cahoon and Freda Douglas, refused to agree to the policy because they believed it to be discriminatory. As a result, they were asked to leave their employment by RD's. In addition, at least two other employees resigned prior to being terminated because they could not agree to the policy. The vast majority of the employees working at the time spoke Navajo.

Also of specific relevance to American Indians is Title VII's prohibition against discrimination based on religion and requirements for reasonable accommodations of the religious practices of applicants and employees. American Indian religious beliefs are different from the beliefs dominant in the United States. Some American Indian practices are long in duration and may necessitate time off from work. As discussed in Chapter 12, allowing flexible personal holidays for all employees, rather than limiting holidays to Christmas, Thanksgiving, and others preferred by the

---

[38] Adapted from EEOC press release at http://www.eeoc.gov/press/9-30-02-c.html, accessed August 16, 2010.

dominant group, lets people celebrate and worship as and when it is appropriate for them. In addition, for certain Indians, wearing their hair uncut is part of their spiritual or religious beliefs and should be accommodated. As for the practices of those who hold to other belief systems, reasonable accommodation of strongly held religious beliefs or practices should be made for them.

▌ RESEARCH ON AMERICAN INDIANS AT WORK

Comparatively little research has investigated the organizational experiences of American Indians. This lack may be partly attributed to the relatively small proportion of American Indians in the population and therefore working in formal organizations as well as to the invisibility of some American Indians' ancestry. In one of the few relevant studies, researchers found a correlation between perceived discrimination and depressive symptoms. However, for nearly 300 adult American Indians living in the Midwest, perceived social support and participation in traditional cultural practices served as buffer against discrimination.[39] In an analysis of data from the General Social Surveys, Charles Weaver found that American Indians were less likely to feel secure in their jobs and were less satisfied with their present financial situation than Whites. No differences were found in job satisfaction, preferred job attributes, and perceptions about opportunities for advancement.[40]

▌ AMERICAN INDIAN AND ALASKAN NATIVE WOMEN

Researchers have detailed many disadvantages experienced by American Indian and Alaskan Native women that are directly correlated with their race and gender status. These include high rates of infant mortality, victimization by violence, involuntary sterilization, and questionable removal of children from their homes.[41] As with many other non-White women, AI/AN women do not fare well in terms of education, workforce participation, unemployment, and income. These factors severely limit their self-sufficiency and constrain their life chances. AI/AN women earn less and are more likely

[39] Whitbeck, L. B., McMorris, B. J., Hoyt, D. R., Stubben, J. D., & LaFromboise, T. (2002). "Perceived Discrimination, Traditional Practices, and Depressive Symptoms." *Journal of Health and Social Behavior*, 43(4): 400–418.

[40] Weaver, C. (2003). "Work Attitudes of American Indians." *Journal of Applied Social Psychology*, 33(2): 432–443.

[41] Allen, P. G. (2004). "Angry Women Are Building: Issues and Struggles Facing American Indian Women Today." In J. F. Healey & E. O'Brien (Eds.), *Race, Ethnicity, and Gender*. Thousand Oaks, CA: Pine Forge Press, pp. 217–220.

to live in poverty than Black, Asian, and White women, particularly when they live on reservations.[42] AI/AN women earn about 58% of the median annual earnings of White men, and researchers suggest that AI/AN women are "systematically paid less than their male counterparts under similar circumstances."[43] AI/AN women are most likely to be employed as sales, clerical, or service workers; as managers, they are most likely to work in gas stations, general merchandise stores, and in social assistance positions.[44]

Although their average workforce participation rates, unemployment levels, and incomes are worse than those of many other women, many American Indian women are well-educated and have successful careers. Wilma Mankiller, discussed in Individual Feature 8.1, was the first woman chief of the Cherokee Nation, a position she held from 1985 to 1995.

In an award-winning study, Helen Muller reported the distinct experiences of American Indian women managers from several different tribes in the Southwest.[45] All of the women in the sample of twenty managers spoke English, and all but one were bilingual or had some level of fluency in a tribal language (subordinate bilingualism). Fifteen of the women in the sample had at least a bachelor's degree. The women worked in a variety of jobs, including industrial development manager, education specialist, director of a human services agency, tribal administrator, and materials manager, among others, and they managed between 1 and 800 people. The women reported living in two worlds, which required them to be able to navigate between "distinctive yet interconnected worlds." Interactions in these "two worlds" included those with customers, employees, peers, supervisors, and competitors. Because the traditional Navajo culture (which was used as the comparison culture) differed from Anglo culture in ways of interacting and learning, association, authority, importance of work, time orientation, spirituality, and natural resources, the AI women managers developed complex strategies and "switching techniques" to work successfully in both worlds. Recall from Cox and Blake that flexibility, biculturalism, and bilingualism are positive consequences of diversity among employees that can increase an organization's competitiveness.[46]

---

[42] Caiazza, A., Shaw, A., and Werschkul, M. 2004. Women's Economic Status in the States: Wide Disparities by Race, Ethnicity, and Region. The Status of Women in the States. Washington, D.C.: The Institute for Women's Policy Research.

[43] Snipp, C. M. (1992). "Sociological Perspectives on American Indians." *Annual Review of Sociology*, 18: 351–371.

[44] EEOC. (2003). "Women of Color: Their Employment in the Private Sector." http://www.eeoc.gov/eeoc/statistics/reports/womenofcolor/womenofcolor.pdf, accessed December 28, 2010.

[45] Muller, H. (1998). "American Indian Women Managers: Living in Two Worlds." *Journal of Management Inquiry*, 7(1): 4–28.

[46] Cox, T., & Blake, S. (1991). "Managing Cultural Diversity: Implications for Organizational Competitiveness." *Academy of Management Executive*, 5(3): 45–56.

INDIVIDUAL FEATURE 8.1	*Wilma Mankiller, Chief of the Cherokee Nation, 1985–1995*

Wilma Mankiller was born in 1945 in Tahlequah, Oklahoma. Her father was a full-blooded Cherokee and her mother was of Dutch and Irish heritage. As chief of the Cherokee Nation, the second-largest Indian nation, Mankiller managed a $75 million budget, comparable to budgets of major corporations.

Mankiller spent her formative years in San Francisco, where her family moved in 1956 as part of the U.S. government relocation program for American Indians. Adjustment to life in San Francisco was hard for the Mankiller family. Wilma and her siblings were teased about their last name, their accent, and their clothing. Wilma noted that Blacks, Latinos, and American Indians were targets of prejudice and discrimination, and it was in San Francisco that Mankiller's pursuit of justice began.

Mankiller learned from the activities of Black and Mexican Americans, including Huey Newton, Bobby Seale, and César Chávez, who worked for change in California during her youth. In what was a life-changing event, Mankiller participated in the occupation of Alcatraz prison in 1969. American Indians from numerous tribes, along with celebrities and activists, occupied the prison to draw attention to the history of abuses, broken treaties, and current discrimination and inequity faced by Indians.

In 1977, Mankiller returned to live in Oklahoma and began working for the Cherokee Nation. She first worked as an economic stimulus coordinator, helping American Indians obtain education and then be reintegrated into their communities. Her next position was as a program development specialist, and she excelled in writing grants and obtaining revenue for the tribe.

At the same time, Mankiller returned to college to finish her degree in social work at the University of Arkansas at Fayetteville, near her home in Oklahoma. In 1983, Mankiller agreed to run for deputy chief of the Cherokee Nation, second in command. She was surprised that her most vociferous opposition was based purely on sex. Some claimed her running for office was an "affront to God," while others said that having a women run the tribe would make the "Cherokees the laughingstock of the tribal world."[47] With every outrageous comment, Mankiller became more certain her decision to run for office was the right one.

Mankiller was elected and took office as deputy chief in August of 1983. In 1985, she became chief of the Cherokee Nation, the first woman in modern history to serve as chief of an American Indian tribe. In 1991, Mankiller was elected for a third term. During her terms as chief, Mankiller focused on education, health care, and economic development for the Cherokee Nation. She acknowledged the tremendous responsibility of the chief's role and encouraged young women to "take risks, to stand up for the things they believe in, and to step up and accept the challenge of serving in leadership roles."[48] Mankiller was awarded an honorary doctorate from Yale University.

Wilma Mankiller died on April 6, 2010, but her legacy lives on.

Source: Mankiller, W., & Wallis, M. (1993). *Mankiller: A Chief and Her People*. New York: St. Martin's Press.

[47] Mankiller, W., & Wallis, M. (1993). *Mankiller: A Chief and Her People*. New York: St. Martin's Press.
[48] Ibid., p. 250.

■ MULTIRACIAL GROUP MEMBERS

We now turn to the investigation of multiracial groups. We begin with an introduction to the population and its history and then discuss legislation relevant to it. We conclude with a focus on Amerasians, a distinct group of multiracial people with a unique history.

Introduction and History

As we have mentioned, the 2000 Census provided the first opportunity for people to state their membership in two or more racial categories, and nearly 7 million people did so. The opportunity to self-identify in this manner may have been new, but multirace people had long been a large portion of the population, regardless of how they self-identified or were identified by others. Previous chapters on African Americans, Latinos, Whites, and Asian Americans have considered some of the fluidity in how race and ethnicity have been recorded in the United States. Since the U.S. Census Bureau began collecting such data, different groups have been included or excluded from certain racial categories but the option of being included in more than one category at the same time did not exist until 2000. Indeed, **miscegenation** was formally illegal in the country until 1967, when the U.S. Supreme Court ruled that state laws prohibiting interracial marriages were unlawful. Despite these laws, the mixing of races was occurring long before the Supreme Court's decision or the option to identify as multiracial in the U.S. Census. Most of the debate around miscegenation had focused on White and Black unions, and such unions are still less likely to occur than those between Whites and other groups.

In an article on legal trials involving racial determination, Ariela Gross described past cases in which people of mixed racial ancestry were attempting to prove or disprove their race. In some cases, issues of inheritance (Blacks could not own property), freedom (Whites could not be held as slaves), or ability to serve as witnesses (Blacks could not be witnesses) were at stake. The presence of American Indians in the population when slavery was legal further confused attempts to determine who was Black when dark skin and wiry hair could be attributed to being Indian rather than being Black.[49] Historical records indicate that some Indian tribes allowed slave ownership and some specifically forbade it.[50] Many Blacks who escaped slavery found refuge among Indians who refused to return them to slavery. In some cases, the presence of Black

---

[49] Gross, A. J. (1998). "Litigating Whiteness: Trials of Racial Determination in the Nineteenth-Century South." *Yale Law Journal*, 108(1): 109–188.
[50] Katz, W. L. (1997). *Black Indians*. New York: Aladdin Paperbacks.

Indians on Indian reservations threatened their tax-exempt status and was viewed suspiciously and nervously by Whites.[51]

Blacks and Racial Determination

The *one-drop rule* was used throughout much of U.S. history to decide who was Black. That is, anyone with one known Black ancestor was usually deemed to be Black (rather than another race or multiracial) regardless of the number or proportion of non-Black ancestors. During certain periods, the labels *mulatto, quadroon,* and *octoroon* were used to refer to people who were, respectively, one-half, one-quarter, or one-eighth Black. Unless evidence of their Black ancestry was invisible and, importantly, they chose to let it remain so (e.g., **passing**), such people were deemed to be, and treated as, Black.

Children that White slave owners and their sons conceived with slaves were considered slaves rather than family members.[52] Pulitzer nominee and sociologist Joe Feagin describes the rapes of Black women and molestation of Black children that contributed to the physical appearance of Blacks today.[53] Feagin cites the story of the lineage of Patricia Williams, a Black law professor at Columbia University. Her great-, great-grandmother Sophie was purchased at age 11 by her great-, great-grandfather, 35-year-old Austin Miller, a lawyer. The next year, 12-year-old Sophie bore Miller's daughter Mary—who was Patricia Williams's great-grandmother. Mary became a house servant to Miller's White children, who were her siblings.[54] Evidence suggests that Thomas Jefferson, third president of the United States, and Sally Hemings, one of Jefferson's slaves, had a lengthy "relationship." Researchers note the difficulty Black females faced in resisting sexual advances or rape by slave owners or employers.[55] Hemings, who was at least half-White herself and possibly the half-sister of Jefferson's wife, conceived several children who lived as slaves at Monticello.[56] Jefferson freed three of those believed to be his children, and Hemings was freed by Jefferson's White daughter

---

[51] Ibid.

[52] See Ball, E. (1998). *Slaves in the Family.* New York: Farrar, Straus, and Giroux.

[53] Feagin, J. R. (2004). "Slavery Unwilling to Die: The Historical Development of Systemic Racism." In J. F. Healey & E. O'Brien (Eds.), *Race, Ethnicity, and Gender.* Thousand Oaks, CA: Pine Forge Press, pp. 92–108.

[54] Ibid., pp. 97–98.

[55] See, for example, Feagin (2004). Women of color remain disproportionately represented among targets of sexual harassment, discussed in Chapters 4, 5, and 6.

[56] See Gordon-Reed, A. (1997). *Thomas Jefferson and Sally Hemings: An American Controversy.* Charlottesville, VA: University of Virginia Press; Jordan, D. P. (2000). "Statement on the TJMF Research Committee Report on Thomas Jefferson and Sally Hemings." http://www.monticello.org/sites/default/files/inline-pdfs/jefferson-hemings_report.pdf, accessed March 19, 2011.

after his death. The descendants of Hemings and Jefferson are believed to have passed into the White population. More recently, one-time arch segregationist South Carolina Senator Strom Thurmond was reported to have fathered a child at age 22 with a 16-year-old who worked in his parents' home.[57] In late 2003, after Thurmond's death, his family acknowledged Essie Mae Washington-Williams as Thurmond's daughter.[58] Washington-Williams lived life as a Black as do her children and grandchildren, despite their identifiable multiracial ancestry.

In a case involving a man whose great-grandfather was Black, the U.S. Supreme Court agreed that "separate but equal" facilities for Whites and Blacks were not unconstitutional.[59] The plaintiff in the case was Homer Plessy, and aside from his great-grandfather, Plessy's other ancestors were all known to be White. In some states, Plessy would also have been White by law because of the preponderance of White ancestors. At seven-eighths White, Plessy looked White but lived as Black and volunteered to test the separate but equal law in Louisiana. Having been advised that Plessy would be entering and sitting in the "White" section of the train (otherwise, given his appearance, Plessy would have gone unnoticed), the conductor had him ejected, arrested, and fined. In what became a landmark case, the courts ruled that segregated, but ostensibly equal, facilities did not violate the Constitution. This Supreme Court ruling stood for five decades, with lasting negative consequences for Blacks and the country.

Regardless of their self- and other identification as being Black, estimates suggest that 70% of the Black population in the United States have some non-Black ancestors. The wide range of skin colors and hair textures attests to the diversity of racial and ethnic background among Blacks. Many well-known Black activists have acknowledged multiracial ancestry, including Martin Luther King, Jr. (whose grandmother was Irish), Malcolm X, WEB DuBois, and Frederick Douglass. Other fairly well-known multiracial people include Halle Berry, Lynda Carter, Ann Curry, Cameron Diaz, Derek Jeter, Norah Jones, Alicia Keyes, Soledad O'Brien, Lou Diamond Phillips, Jimmy Smits, Tiger Woods, and Thandie Newton. President Barack Obama, former Illinois state senator and U.S. senator, who is of multiracial ancestry but self-identifies and is identified by others as Black, is featured in Individual Feature 8.2.

[57] Washington-Williams, E., & Stadiem, W. (2005). *Dear Senator*. New York: HarperCollins Publishers.

[58] Mattingly, D. (2003, December 16). "Strom Thurmond's Family Confirms Paternity Claim." *CNN Washington Bureau*. http://www.cnn.com/2003/US/12/15/thurmond..paternity/, accessed August 29, 2010.

[59] *Plessy v. Ferguson*. 163 U.S. 537 (1896).

INDIVIDUAL FEATURE 8.2	*Barack Obama, 44th President of the United States*

President Barack Obama was born in Honolulu, Hawaii, in 1961 to Ann Dunham, a White woman from Kansas, and Barack Obama, Sr., a Black man from Kenya. His parents named him Barack, meaning "blessed." After his parents' divorce, Obama was reared by his mother and her parents and primarily lived in Hawaii. He was elected U.S. senator from Illinois in 2004, and in 2008 was elected president of the United States, a momentous event.

Obama received his undergraduate education at Columbia University, where he studied political science and international relations. In 1985, he moved to Chicago where he worked for a nonprofit organization helping to create jobs and improve living conditions in some of Chicago's worst neighborhoods. Obama later entered law school at Harvard, where he was the first Black president of the *Harvard Law Review* and graduated magna cum laude. After law school, Obama practiced civil rights law, working on key employment discrimination cases in federal and state courts.

In 1996, Obama was elected to the Illinois State Senate, where he pursued benefits for the working poor, for people who could not afford health insurance, and for AIDS prevention and care programs. Obama was influential in the passage of Illinois' death penalty reform laws, which were motivated by the fact that many innocent people were on death row. In 2004, he was elected the third Black U.S. senator in history. In the Senate, he focused on promoting economic growth and bringing good jobs to Illinois, his home state. He served on the Veterans' Affairs Committee and investigated discrepancies in disability pay among veterans. In 2005, *Time* magazine named Obama as one of the 100 most influential Americans.

As discussed in Chapter 3, ten days after his inauguration in 2009, President Obama signed the Lilly Ledbetter Fair Pay Act, attempting to reduce gender-based pay disparities that systematically disadvantage women workers. Obama stated: "It is fitting that with the very first bill I sign—the Lilly Ledbetter Fair Pay Restoration Act—we are upholding one of this nation's first principles: that we are all created equal and each deserve a chance to pursue our own version of happiness."[60]

Source: Obama, B. (1995). *Dreams from My Father: A Story of Race and Inheritance*. New York: Times Books.

QUESTIONS TO CONSIDER

1. *What does President Obama's self-identification and widespread recognition as Black say about race in America?*

2. *When President Obama completed his 2010 U.S. Census form, his self-identification as Black made news. Why do you think this is so?*

3. *Is the election of President Obama evidence of a "postracial" America? If so, why? If not, what would be evidence of a "postracial" America?*

4. *Aside from the Fair Pay Act, what are some diversity-related measures (laws, appointments, etc.) that occurred since President Obama's 2008 election?*

---

[60] "Obama Signs Lilly Ledbetter Act." http://voices.washingtonpost.com/44/2009/01/29/obama_signs_lilly_ledbetter_ac.html, accessed December 28, 2010.

▌ POPULATION

Many people celebrated having the option in the Census 2000 to self-identify as multiracial, rejecting the category of "other" as an inaccurate reflection of their heritage. Of the nearly 7 million people who reported belonging to two or more races at that time, 32% identified themselves as Hispanic as well, compared to 13% of the general population identifying as Hispanic alone. By 2010, 9 million people reported having a multiracial heritage.[61] The great majority of multiracial people are of two races (93%), and 6% are of three races. The largest to smallest proportions of particular multiracial groups are Native Hawaiian and other Pacific Islanders (54%), American Indians or Alaska Natives (40%), Asians (14%), Blacks (5%), and Whites (2.5%).

Multiracial group members tend to be younger than single-race people. Forty-two percent of multiracials are under 18, compared with 25% of those reporting a single race. Recall from Chapter 6 that Hispanics are younger than non-Hispanics, and that they are more likely to be multiracial than the general population. Because they are younger than the general population, a greater proportion of multiracials will be entering and participating in the future labor force than the one-race population. One might expect multiracial people to have different attitudes toward diversity issues than single-race people. People who reported multiple races are most likely to live in California, where nearly 25% of them reside. California is the only state with more than 1 million people in the multiracial population. In all, 40% of multiracial people live in the West, 27% in the South, 18% in the Northeast, and 15% in the Midwest.[62]

As interracial relationships increase, the proportion of the population that is multiracial will also increase. The first time that more Americans reported approval of interracial marriage (48%) than disapproval (42%) was in 1991, twenty-four years after the Supreme Court overruled laws forbidding intermarriage. At that time Blacks, younger people, those with more education, and people living in the West viewed interracial marriage more favorably than Whites, older people, those with less education, and those living in the South, Midwest, and East. Seventy percent of Blacks approved of interracial marriage, and 44% of Whites did. For those under age 30, 64% approved, compared with 61% of those 50 and older who disapproved of such marriages. Seventy percent of college graduates approved of interracial marriage; 66% of those who did not finish high school disapproved. In the West, 60% of people

---

[61] Jones, N. A., & Smith, A. S. (2001). "The Two or More Races Population: 2000." U.S. Census Bureau. http://www.census.gov/prod/2001pubs/c2kbr01-6.pdf, accessed August 16, 2010. See also http://2010.census.gov/2010census/data/index.php, accessed April 9, 2011.
[62] Ibid.

approved of interracial marriage, compared with only 33% in the South.[63] In 2009, a Louisiana justice of the peace with twenty-five years tenure refused to marry an interracial couple, citing his concern for the interracial children they would produce.[64]

▌ RELEVANT LEGISLATION

As it does for other racial and ethnic groups, Title VII prohibits discrimination against multiracial group members. Research evidence indicates that multiracial people sometimes receive negative treatment from members of various racial groups because of their multiracialism.[65] They may also experience negative organizational outcomes because one of their racial memberships is not visible.[66] Given the importance of identifiability to categorization, stereotyping, and differential treatment, unclear racial identification and inability to categorize multiracial group members may pose unique issues for them.

▌ AMERASIANS

Amerasians are a distinctive group of multiracial people. Although the term **Amerasian** formally includes children born of American servicemen and Asian women (e.g., Vietnamese, Japanese, Korean), it is most commonly used to refer to children born of American servicemen and Vietnamese women during the Vietnam War. During that war, tens of thousands of Amerasian children were fathered by American servicemen, of various racial and ethnic backgrounds. Because of the stigma associated with being fatherless or being fathered by an American (whose country was at war with Vietnam), Vietnamese Amerasians often experienced extreme discrimination, teasing, assault by other children, and societal persecution. Referred to as "children of the dust," many were not educated and lived in extreme poverty in Vietnam.

---

[63] Gallup, G., Jr., & Newport, F. (1991, August). "For First Time, More Americans Approve of Interracial Marriage than Disapprove." *The Gallup Poll Monthly*, pp. 60–63.

[64] Deslatte, M. (2009). "Keith Bardwell Quits: Justice of the Peace Who Refused to Give Interracial Couple Marriage License Resigns." http://www.huffingtonpost.com/2009/11/03/keith-bardwell-quits-just_n_344427.html, accessed March 19, 2011. "Governor Calls for Firing of Justice in Interracial Marriage Case," http://articles.cnn.com/2009-10-16/us/louisiana.interracial.marriage_1_interracial-marriages-keith-bardwell-marriage-license?_s=PM:US, accessed March 19, 2011.

[65] See Rockquemore, K. A., & Brunsma, D. L. (2002). *Beyond Black*. Thousand Oaks, CA: Sage Publications.

[66] See Clair, J., Beatty, J., & MacLean, T. L. (2005). "Out of Sight but Not Out of Mind: Managing Invisible Social Identities in the Workplace." *Academy of Management Review*, 30: 78–95; Ragins, B. R. (2008). "Disclosure Disconnects: Antecedents and Consequences of Disclosing Invisible Stigmas Across Life Domains." *Academy of Management Review*, 33: 194–215.

The Vietnamese Amerasian Homecoming Act of 1987 formalized attempts to bring many Amerasians and their families to the United States. Between 20,000 and 25,000 Amerasians were resettled in this country, but few reunited with their fathers.[67] Due to their lack of education in Vietnam, many resettled Amerasians are illiterate in Vietnamese and English, which impedes their integration into American society. Most live in metropolitan areas around other members of the Vietnamese community, who, as discussed in Chapter 6, are some of the lower-earning, least-educated groups of Asian Americans.

▮ RECOMMENDATIONS FOR INDIVIDUALS AND ORGANIZATIONS

In the following section, we make recommendations for individual American Indians, Alaska Natives, and multiracial group members as well as for organizations who are or will be dealing with these groups.

American Indians and Alaska Natives

We have acknowledged the unique role of American Indians and Alaska Natives in the history and diversity of the United States. Efforts by the government and organizations to increase the education, workforce participation, and employment of AI/AN have been somewhat successful. As with any group, greater education is associated with increases in participation, employment, and earnings. Most AI/AN now live outside reservations and trust lands, but research has found that those who are linked to their traditional culture fare better than those who are not. Thus, it is important for individuals to make an effort to continue relationships with their native traditions and culture.

Organizations should make concerted efforts to support AI/AN, and American Indians should be included in diversity plans. Although a relatively small portion of the population, their numbers in certain areas of the country are significant. In addition, their unique status as indigenous people who once were the only inhabitants of the United States makes omitting them from diversity efforts particularly untenable. The thirty tribal and federally charted American Indian colleges in the United States may be a good source of American Indian job applicants. Nearly all of these schools, like Haskell Indian Nations University, the Institute of American Indian Arts, and Northwest Indian College, are fully accredited by the appropriate regional accrediting agencies. In addition to education,

---

[67] McKelvey, R. S. (1999). *The Dust of Life: America's Children Abandoned in Vietnam*. Seattle, WA: University of Washington Press.

the colleges focus on meeting the cultural and social needs of students.[68] Other universities that have sizable populations of AI/AN are also good places to recruit employees. Such schools include the University of New Mexico, New Mexico State University, and the University of Arizona. New Mexico State University has been recognized for the number of graduate degrees it awards to American Indians.[69]

Once AI/AN have been recruited and hired, organizational efforts to retain them are key. Factors that may be exclusionary and discriminatory to AI/AN should be investigated. Barriers unique to the organizational environment and to the specific AI/AN population should be identified and removed. An example of these barriers is English-only rules, as discussed earlier. Organizations should be aware that many Indians view work as one part of other important aspects of life, rather than the most important aspect of life.[70] Other employees can learn from AI/AN about the importance of life outside of work. Rather than imposing the work-related values of others upon AI/AN, their values, as with those of all other racial and ethnic groups, should be acknowledged.

Multiracial Group Members

As the multiracial population increases, more is being done to ensure they are treated fairly in organizations. Multiracial group members whose multiple group membership is clearly visible may experience disparate treatment specifically due to that membership. Being asked "what are you?" or being called disparaging names because of a multiracial inheritance are examples of such pointed discrimination. Those who appear to be members of only one group (rather than multiracial) may also experience many negative outcomes due to their invisible identity.[71] For example, multiracials who look White may hear negative comments, stereotypes, and disparaging remarks about people of color. They may be fearful of having photos of their family or extended family on their desks at work or of bringing a family member to an organization's social event. Recall that in the South only 33% of people surveyed approved of interracial marriage; 54% disapproved.

A culture of nondiscrimination would help avoid "inadvertent" discrimination against invisibly multiracial people (as well as gays and lesbians who are not "out" at work). Such a culture would also increase the likelihood that

[68] Cunningham, A. F., & Parker, C. (1998). "Tribal Colleges as Community Institutions and Resources." *New Directions for Higher Education*, 102: 45–55.

[69] Frosch, J. (2005). "New Mexico State University Serves American Indian Graduate Students." New Mexico State University News Releases. http://www.nmsu.edu/~ucomm/Releases/2005/august/am_indian_students.htm, accessed August 16, 2010.

[70] Massey (2004). See also Muller (1998).

[71] See, for example, Ragins (2008) and Rockquemore & Brunsma (2002).

those who are not out would feel comfortable enough to be so. Invisible identities and questions and worries about disclosure are stressful.[72] Care should be taken to avoid grouping multiracials with only one group in which they have membership (e.g., Black, Latino) while ignoring the other aspects of their identity. As has the U.S. Census Bureau, allow people to define their own group memberships. Although President Obama's multiracial heritage is discussed in Individual Feature 8.2, his self-identification as Black is respected.

SUMMARY

This chapter has considered American Indians and Alaska Natives and multiracial group members as contributors to diversity in organizations. These two groups, the original inhabitants of the country and the group recently allowed to self-identify as members of two or more races, are different from the non-dominant groups considered in previous chapters. AI/AN are often overlooked in studies of diversity, although they display such factors of diversity in group membership (e.g., nation), age, and lower education and levels of employment.

We next considered multiracial people, an increasingly important and diverse group in the United States. Nearly 7 million people self-identify as multiracial, a number that will only increase in the future. Multiracial people as a whole are younger than single-race people, and the numbers (and approval) of interracial relationships and marriage are increasing. As a unique minority group, multiracial people face unusual diversity issues, including invisibility of one or more of their heritages and pointed harassment and discrimination based on their multiple identities.

The chapter considered relevant legislation, research, and issues confronting AI/AN and multiracials. We also offered recommendations for individuals and organizations for these less-studied, but historically and increasingly important, non-dominant groups.

KEY TERMS

Amerasian — a child born of American servicemen and Asian women, in particular Vietnamese, Japanese, and Korean.

Miscegenation — mixture of races; *especially* marriage, cohabitation, or sexual intercourse between a White person and a member of another race.[73]

Multiracial — a person who self-identifies as having ancestry including two or more races.

Passing — usually refers to light-skinned Blacks or others of color pretending to be and being perceived as Whites; also relevant to gays and lesbians who pretend to be and are perceived as heterosexual and to others whose non-dominant group membership goes unnoticed and undisclosed.

---

[72] Ragins (2008).
[73] Merriam-Webster Online. http://www.merriam-webster.com/dictionary/miscegenation, accessed August 16, 2010.

QUESTIONS TO CONSIDER

1a. If you are not American Indian or Alaska Native, what has your exposure to them been? Do you know any personally? If so, how do you know them? How well? What beliefs about American Indians were you aware of prior to reading this chapter?

1b. If you are American Indian or Alaska Native, how do your work experiences compare with those presented in the chapter?

2a. If you are not multiracial, what has your exposure been to multiracial people? Do you know any? Have you talked with them about being multiracial and about their diversity-related experiences?

2b. If you are multiracial, is being so an important part of your identity? Did any section of the chapter have particular resonance for you?

 3. Homer Plessy of the separate but equal case was seven-eighths White and could have "passed" for White, based on his appearance. What role does the invisibility of someone's race or ethnicity play in their treatment, experiences, and identity?

4a. Professional golfer Tiger Woods emphasizes his White, Asian, Black, and American Indian heritage. Were Woods unknown as a professional golfer, what assumptions would likely be made about his race by (a) a police officer prone to racial profiling, (b) a Black person, (c) an Asian, (d) a White, (e) an American Indian?

4b. The chapter listed several other fairly well-known multiracial people. Are you familiar with any of them? If so, were you aware that they are multiracial? Were you aware of their particular multiracial heritage? If not, what was your impression of the racial or ethnic group to which each belongs? If they were not famous, speculate on the racial or ethnic group to which they would be perceived to belong based on their identifiability (e.g., Dworkin & Dworkin) and on their experiences based on people's perceptions. If they are partnered (married or in a long-term relationship), what is the racial background of the person with whom they are partnered?

ACTIONS AND EXERCISES

1. Excluding American Indian schools, find a college or university not identified in this chapter that is known for the diversity of its students. What are the demographic characteristics of the student body (e.g., race, ethnicity, sex, and age)? What are the characteristics of the school (e.g., size of student body, location, and any other relevant factors)?

2. Investigate the demographic characteristics of the student body at the university in which you are studying or once studied. Do you know of any AI/AN students who attend or attended school with you? If so, is their AI/AN background visible? Do they "pass" at times? If a close friend or acquaintance, discuss their heritage and experiences with them.

3. Investigate the history of American Indians in your state and their current status (including population,

workforce participation, education levels, income, and poverty rates).

4. Estimates suggest that 70% of Blacks in the United States are of multiracial heritage. Were you aware of this? Begin noticing the variation in skin color, features, and hair texture among Blacks. Choose five Blacks whom you know, with whom you come in contact, or who are well-known people and document the visible variations in their skin tone, features, and hair texture. What do you observe?

5. Choose an indigenous people in a particular country (except the United States and New Zealand). Document their original and current population, education level, employment, and workforce participation. How do their education, employment, and participation levels compare to those of the dominant group in that country?

6. If you have access to the film *In Whose Honor? American Indian Mascots in Sports* (http://www.inwhosehonor.com/) by Jay Rosenstein, watch it. What are your thoughts about American Indians as mascots after having watched the film?

Sex and Gender

CHAPTER 9

Chapter Objectives

After completing this chapter, readers should understand sex and gender in the context of diversity in organizations. Specifically they should be able to:

- ❏ *compare women's and men's participation rates, employment, and income levels within and across racial and ethnic groups.*

- ❏ *discuss the role of gender role socialization in men's and women's occupations and opportunities.*

- ❏ *explain the effects of sex segregation, sex discrimination, and sexual harassment on women's careers and discuss selected cases related to them.*

- ❏ *discuss methods that can be used to improve organizational climates for gender equity.*

Key Facts

In many countries, women comprise more than half of the population and about half of the workforce.

Women working full-time, year-round earn less than 80 cents to the dollar earned by men working full-time, year-round. Part-time work further exaggerates the wage gap.

The gap between the earnings of younger women and younger men is considerably smaller than the gap between the earnings of older women and older men.

Women and men who deviate from gender norms are penalized in society and organizations.

Minority women and younger women are disproportionately targets of sexual harassment compared to White women and older women.

Men comprise about 16% of sexual harassment targets, yet men who complain of harassment are often not taken seriously.

Introduction and Overview

Sex and gender issues are critical aspects of diversity in organizations, affecting women and men from all races, ethnicities, ages, and abilities. Sexual harassment and discrimination, the wage gap in pay, and sex segregation are commonly recognized as women's concerns. Indeed these issues constrain women's progress and opportunities in organizations in myriad ways. Even so, although men are significantly less likely to personally experience these constraints, sex discrimination and other gender-based diversity issues also affect them. All men have mothers, wives, daughters, sisters, or female friends, making women's concerns personal for many men as well as for the women they care about. Many men with working wives experience the negative effects of women's lower wages and job rewards on family incomes. Children in single-parent homes are very likely to be living with working mothers; equal pay for working women affects both male and female children. Sex discrimination and harassment negatively affect the workplace as a whole, harming both women and men. Both women and men have prescribed gender roles, violations of which are often met with strong sanctions (consider the man who wishes to work as a child care worker but is denied employment because he is male and the woman who wishes to be a truck driver and is harassed and denied training because of her sex). Women, and increasingly men, face work and family issues as they cope with work, children, and, sometimes, parents or other relatives who need care. Men coping with work and family issues may face harsher sanctions than women—the expectation for them is that their work should take priority over family, and they may experience more negative penalties than women, who are expected to have work and

family issues. These and other reasons make sex and gender issues important to both women and men.

Women, who have been called "the 51% minority,"[1] comprise over half of the population and half of the workforce in the Canada, France, United States, and many other nations.[2] Longer life spans and the changing nature of jobs (e.g., the shift from manufacturing to service jobs) make women likely to be an increasing share of the workforce in many nations. Despite their high proportion in the U.S. workforce (and that of many other nations), women are overrepresented in lower-level, lower-paid jobs and underrepresented in higher-level, higher-paid jobs. In contrast, men are overrepresented in higher-level, higher-paid jobs and underrepresented in lower-level, lower-paid jobs.

Even though women have worked throughout history, they are inaccurately thought of as relatively new entrants to the workforce. In the eighteenth through twentieth centuries, women were part of the agricultural labor force and worked in manufacturing industries. In addition, slave women worked in plantation homes and in the fields alongside slave men and then performed their own domestic duties afterward. As discussed in Chapter 4, Black women continue to participate in the workforce at higher rates than other women.

Traditionally, women's work has been devalued, which plays a key role in sex discrimination and harassment, sex segregation of jobs, and the glass ceiling. Women are frequently viewed as uncommitted workers and as lacking the skills for leadership, management, and decision making, which are desirable in the context of work. In contrast, men are widely thought of as providers for their families, committed, capable workers, and as having strong leadership and managerial skills—attributes that are desirable in the work context.

[1]Dunn, D. (1999). "Women: The Fifty-One Percent Minority." In A. G. Dworkin & R. J. Dworkin (Eds.), *The Minority Report*. Orlando, FL: Harcourt Brace Publishers, pp. 415–435.
[2]Bureau of Labor Statistics, "International Labor Comparison, 2009." http://www.bls.gov/fls/intl_labor_force_charts.htm#lfpr, accessed September 3, 2010.

Terminology

Before continuing the investigation of sex and gender issues in the workplace, it is important to clarify differences between the terms. Although used interchangeably, they are not actually the same. Sex is construed as biological; males have XY chromosomes and females have XX chromosomes (although a small proportion of people have different combinations of chromosomes).[3]

Title VII specifically prohibits discrimination because of "sex," but, as we discuss later, the courts have ruled that discrimination due to the violation of roles associated with one's sex (e.g., gender roles) is also illegal. Gender refers to perceptions of how men and women and boys and girls *should* behave. Both sex and gender are important influences on individuals' outcomes.

▍ RELEVANT LEGISLATION

Legislation particularly relevant to sex and gender at work includes:

- The Equal Pay Act of 1963
- Title VII of the Civil Rights Act of 1964
- Executive orders for affirmative action
- The Pregnancy Discrimination Act of 1978
- EEOC Guidelines on Sexual Harassment of 1980
- The Family and Medical Leave Act of 1993
- The Lilly Ledbetter Fair Pay Act of 2009

These acts (and guidelines) were introduced in Chapter 3; in this chapter we discuss their details as they relate specifically to sex and gender.[4] A look at the chronology of the acts provides insights into the status of women and the issues they faced both at the time the acts were passed and, to some extent, in the present. In 1963, the Equal Pay Act attempted to address overt sex-based pay disparities. In 1964, Title VII prohibited discrimination against women in employment, including in hiring, firing, promotions, and other employment matters. Executive orders for affirmative action included women, going further than the passive prohibition against discrimination in Title VII and requiring certain employers to take active efforts to ensure women had equal opportunity to work. Once women were working and had some level of protection against discrimination as well as the assurance of proactive efforts to increase their employment, the next two pieces of legislation addressed discrimination on the basis of pregnancy and sexual harassment. This type of discrimination was already prohibited by Title VII; that an amendment and formal guidelines were necessary fourteen and sixteen years later, respectively, indicates these issues continued to be serious, pervasive problems.

----

[3]De La Chappelle, A. (1972). "Analytic Review: Nature and Origin of Males with XX Sex Chromosomes." *American Journal of Human Genetics*, 24: 71–105.

[4]Consistent with Chapter 3, we refer to guidelines issued by the EEOC and to executive orders as "acts."

The Family and Medical Leave Act (FMLA) provides job security while allowing women (and men) to take time off for family needs and to be assured of a job afterward. It is relevant to sex and gender at work because family responsibilities disproportionately affect working women, women with children earn less than women without children, and men who wish to participate in family care are often perceived as violating their gender roles and experience negative organizational outcomes as a result. Most recently, the Lilly Ledbetter Fair Pay Act was passed in 2009, nearly fifty years after the Equal Pay Act and Title VII prohibited pay discrimination based on sex. This act states that each paycheck that delivers discriminatory compensation restarts the 180-day clock for filing a claim (or the 300-day clock in places having a state or local law prohibiting such pay discrimination). Thus, women who are unaware of pay discrimination are less likely to run out of time to file a claim once they find out about it. We will discuss some cases concerning laws relevant to sex and gender later in this chapter.

The following sections discuss population, education, participation, and income data for men and women. We then consider several phenomena that are related to sex and gender in organizations: gender role socialization, sex discrimination, sexual harassment, and the glass ceiling (and other boundaries). A separate section investigates where and how sex, race, and ethnicity issues intersect. Finally, we consider two unique gender issues. While it is impossible to cover all issues relevant to sex and gender in organizations, these topics provide a broad representation of the myriad factors affecting women and men in organizations and the differences in their organizational experiences and may stimulate readers to investigate further.

▌ POPULATION

As shown in Table 1.1, the population of females and males represent about 51% and 49%, respectively, of the more than 300 million people in the United States. As shown in Table 9.1, the age distribution of females is different from that of males, and this distribution has implications for valuing women in the workforce. At younger ages, boys outnumber girls. Until age 18, there are slightly more than 105 males to females. Between ages 18 and 24, there are about equal numbers of men and women. In all age groups after that, women outnumber men, and the gap widens with age. Between ages 25 and 64—prime working years—there are about 3 million more women than men. Therefore, more adult women than men are potential employees, and women's longer life expectancies also affect the proportion of older workers who may be female (which compounds the multiple effects of diversity). The large number of women in those years has implications for employers and their human resources and diversity practices.

Table 9.1 *Sex Ratios by Age: 2002 (Males per 100 Females)*

Age Group	Sex Ratio
85 years and over	46.3
75 to 84 years	67.2
65 to 74 years	83.5
55 to 64 years	91.6
45 to 54 years	95.6
35 to 44 years	97.2
30 to 34 years	98.1
25 to 29 years	99.9
18 to 24 years	100.1
5 to 17 years	105.1
Under 5 years	104.1

Source: U.S. Census Bureau, Current Population Survey, March 2002.

▌ EDUCATION

Overall, U.S. men have slightly more education than women, although that varies by level of education, as shown in Table 9.2. For adults age 25 and over a greater percentage of women have completed high school than men, but a greater proportion of men have completed college and obtained advanced degrees than women. However, while White and Asian men have more education than their **co-ethnic** women, Black and Hispanic women have more education than their co-ethnic men.

For younger adults, those aged 25 to 29, the number of women earning advanced degrees compared with men has changed drastically. In 1960, 78% of advanced degree holders in this age group were men (not shown). By 2009, 58% of young advanced degree holders were women. More education is correlated with higher earnings and, for women, a greater likelihood of participating in the workforce due to the opportunity costs of not working and ability to afford quality child care, if needed. Unfortunately, higher education does not automatically translate into similarly high earnings for women when compared with men, as discussed in the following section.

▌ PARTICIPATION AND EARNINGS

As Table 9.3 shows, men's earnings exceed women's at all educational levels, with White men's earnings being the highest of all groups in nearly every category. When comparisons are made between women and their

TABLE 9.2 *Educational Attainment of the Population (25 Years and Over) by Sex, Race, and Hispanic Origin (1960–2008)*

| | **High School Graduate or More** | | | | | | | | | |
| | **All Races (%)** | | **White (%)** | | **Black (%)** | | **Asian and Pacific Islander (%)** | | **Hispanic (%)** | |
	Male	**Female**	**Male**	**Female**	**Male**	**Female**	**Male**	**Female**	**Male**	**Female**
1960	39.5	42.5	41.6	44.7	18.2	21.8	45.4	53.1	n/a	n/a
1970	51.9	52.8	54.0	55.0	30.1	32.5	61.3	63.1	37.9	34.2
1980	67.3	65.8	69.6	68.1	50.8	51.5	78.8	71.4	45.4	42.7
1990	77.7	77.5	79.1	79.0	65.8	66.5	84.0	77.2	50.3	51.3
2000	84.2	84.0	84.8	85.0	78.7	78.3	88.2	83.4	56.6	57.5
2008	85.9	87.2	86.3	87.8	81.8	84.0	90.8	86.9	60.9	63.7

| | **College Graduate or More** | | | | | | | | | |
| | **All Races (%)** | | **White (%)** | | **Black (%)** | | **Asian and Pacific Islander (%)** | | **Hispanic (%)** | |
	Male	**Female**	**Male**	**Female**	**Male**	**Female**	**Male**	**Female**	**Male**	**Female**
1960	9.7	5.8	10.3	6.0	2.8	3.3	13.1	9.0	n/a	n/a
1970	13.5	8.1	14.4	8.4	4.2	4.6	23.5	17.3	7.8	4.3
1980	20.1	12.8	21.3	13.3	8.4	8.3	39.8	27.0	9.4	6.0
1990	24.4	18.4	25.3	19.0	11.9	10.8	44.9	35.4	9.8	8.7
2000	27.8	23.6	28.5	23.9	16.3	16.7	47.6	40.7	10.7	10.6
2008	30.1	28.8	30.5	29.1	18.7	20.4	55.8	49.8	12.6	14.1

Source: U.S. Census Bureau, U.S. Census of Population, 1960, 1970, and 1980, Summary File 3; and Current Population Reports and data published on the Internet.

co-ethnic men at the same educational levels, earnings disparities are also apparent. For all racial and ethnic groups, at all educational levels, men earn more than women. These earnings differences are in part due to sex segregation of jobs, which we discuss later in the chapter, and to women's greater likelihood of working part-time or fewer full-time hours than men, as discussed in greater detail in Chapter 10.

Participation Rates

Females represent 51% of the population and about half the workforce. As discussed in earlier chapters, there are differences in participation rates among women of different groups. About 60% of women of every racial and ethnic background work outside the home, compared to about 73%

TABLE 9.3 *Mean Total Money Earnings in 2008 by Educational Attainment for Population 25 Years and Over*

	Total*	H.S. Graduate, Including GED	Some College, No Degree	Bachelor's	Master's
All races male	$56,036	$39,835	$46,703	$75,595	$88,824
All races female	$35,760	$25,851	$30,007	$45,688	$54,839
Women's % of men's	64%	65%	64%	60%	62%
White male, non-Hispanic	$61,863	$42,579	$49,154	$79,584	$91,310
White female, non-Hispanic	$37,492	$26,619	$30,649	$45,950	$54,528
White women's % of men's	61%	63%	62%	58%	60%
Black male	$39,935	$33,492	$36,523	$53,108	$66,079
Black female	$32,076	$24,493	$29,131	$44,360	$53,185
Black women's % of men's	80%	73%	80%	84%	80%
Asian male	$64,395	$37,206	$45,925	$69,288	$80,194
Asian female	$43,246	$24,422	$27,992	$49,800	$61,810
Asian women's % of men's	67%	66%	61%	72%	77%
Hispanic male (any race)	$37,080	$33,332	$40,090	$58,789	$93,280
Hispanic female (any race)	$26,753	$23,405	$28,432	$40,947	$55,487
Hispanic women's % of men's	72%	70%	71%	70%	59%

Earnings as a Percent of Non-Hispanic White Men's Earnings

	Total	H.S. Graduate, Including GED	Some College, No Degree	Bachelor's	Master's
Non-Hispanic White male	100%	100%	100%	100%	100%
Non-Hispanic White females	61%	63%	62%	58%	60%
All females	58%	61%	61%	57%	60%
Black females	52%	58%	59%	56%	58%
Asian females	70%	57%	57%	63%	68%
Hispanic females	43%	55%	58%	51%	61%

Earnings as a Percent of Non-Hispanic White Women's Earnings

	Total	H.S. Graduate, Including GED	Some College, No Degree	Bachelor's	Master's
Non-Hispanic White females	100%	100%	100%	100%	100%
All females	95%	97%	98%	99%	101%
Black females	86%	92%	95%	97%	98%
Asian females	115%	92%	91%	108%	113%
Hispanic females	71%	88%	93%	89%	102%

*Total includes figures shown plus master's, doctorate and professional degrees, which are not separately shown. Percentage calculations are the author's.

Source: U.S. Census Bureau. PINC-03. "Educational Attainment—People 25 Years Old and Over, by Total Money Earnings in 2008, Work Experience in 2008, Age, Race, Hispanic Origin, and Sex." http://www.census.gov/hhes/www/cpstables/032009/perinc/new03_000.htm, accessed November 30, 2010. Percentage calculations are the author's.

TABLE 9.4 *1998 and 2008 Actual and 2018 Projected Participation Rates by Race/Ethnicity and Sex (%)*

	1998		2008		2018 Projection	
	Men	**Women**	**Men**	**Women**	**Men**	**Women**
All groups	74.9	59.8	73.0	59.5	70.6	58.7
White, non-Hispanic	75.0	59.9	72.4	59.8	70.7	59.0
Black	69.0	62.8	66.7	61.3	65.7	61.2
Hispanic	79.8	55.6	80.2	56.2	78.2	56.4
Asian	75.5	59.2	75.3	59.4	73.8	57.4
All other groups[1]	—	—	71.4	60.1	70.1	63.3

[1]The "All other groups" category includes (1) those classified as being of multiple racial origin and (2) the race categories of (2a) American Indian and Alaska Native or (2b) Native Hawaiian and Other Pacific Islanders. Dash indicates no data collected for category.

Source: Employment Projections Program, U.S. Department of Labor, U.S. Bureau of Labor Statistics. http://www.bls.gov/emp/ep_table_303.htm, accessed September 4, 2010.

of men, as shown in Table 9.4. As Chapter 10 will discuss, however, the most well-educated women participate at about the same average rate as men (of all education levels).

Sex Segregation

Sex segregation, which occurs when members of one sex constitute 70% or more of the incumbents in a job or occupation, characterizes women's employment and is a significant contributor to the male/female wage gap. In the United States and many other societies, most jobs are segregated by sex; women tend to work primarily with other women, and men tend to work with other men. A report on sex segregation around the world suggested that half of all workers seek jobs that are at least 80% sex segregated.[5] Seventy-two percent of women are employed in four occupational groups: administrative support, professional specialty, service workers, and executive, administrative, and managerial positions. Women are "crowded" into seven occupations, including such low-paying jobs as receptionist and cashier. Although "men's" jobs are also segregated by sex, there are seven times as many male-dominated jobs as female-dominated jobs,[6] and male-dominated jobs pay more than female-dominated jobs. That child care workers earn less than garbage truck drivers speaks of the societal devaluation of women's work.

Occupations that are male dominated include protective services (e.g., police and firefighters), crafts (e.g., carpenters, electricians, and plumbers),

[5]Anker, R. (1998). *Gender and Jobs: Sex Segregation of Occupations in the World.* Geneva: International Labor Organization.
[6]Padavic, I., & Reskin, B. (2002). *Women and Men at Work,* 2nd ed. Chapter 4, footnote 5, p. 95. Thousand Oaks, CA: Pine Forge Press.

and transport (e.g., truck, bus, and taxi drivers).[7] Well-known men's jobs include construction worker, police officer, firefighter, physician, engineer, and airline pilot. Working in a male-dominated job positively affects one's income (of both men and women); working in a female-dominated job negatively affects one's income (of both men and women).

Further complicating the relationship between sex segregation and wages is the fact that while working in male-dominated jobs raises women's wages over wages of women who work in female-dominated jobs, women in male-dominated jobs still earn less than men in these jobs.

TABLE 9.5 *Twenty Leading Occupations of Employed Women, 2009 Annual Averages (Employment in Thousands)*

Occupation	Total Employed Women	% Women	Women's Median Weekly Earnings	Men's Median Weekly Earnings	Men's Earnings Advantage
Total, 16 years and older (all employed women)	66,208	47.4	$657	$819	$162
Secretaries and administrative assistants	3,074	96.8*	619	666	47
Registered nurses	2,612	92.0*	1,035	1,090	55
Elementary and middle school teachers	2,343	81.9*	891	1,040	149
Cashiers	2,273	74.4*	361	442	81
Nursing, psychiatric, and home health aides	1,770	88.5*	430	519	89
Retail salespersons	1,650	51.9	443	624	181
First-line supervisors/managers of retail sales workers	1,459	44.1	597	770	173
Waiters and waitresses	1,434	71.6*	363	419	56
Maids and housekeeping cleaners	1,282	89.8*	371	444	73
Customer service representatives	1,263	67.9	587	617	30
Child care workers	1,228	95.1*	364	—	**
Bookkeeping, accounting, and auditing clerks	1,205	92.3*	627	671	44
Receptionists and information clerks	1,168	91.5*	516	537	21

[7]Jacobs, J. (1999). "The Sex Segregation of Occupations." In G. N. Powell (Ed.), *The Handbook of Gender and Work*. Thousand Oaks, CA: Sage, pp. 125–141.

TABLE 9.5 *Twenty Leading Occupations of Employed Women, 2009 Annual Averages (Employment in Thousands) (Continued)*

Occupation	Total Employed Women	% Women	Women's Median Weekly Earnings	Men's Median Weekly Earnings	Men's Earnings Advantage
First-line supervisors/ managers of office and administrative support	1,163	71.3*	705	837	132
Managers, all others	1,106	34.1	1,037	1,292	255
Accountants and auditors	1,084	61.8	902	1,190	288
Teacher assistants	921	91.6*	474	453	−21***
Cooks	831	41.5	371	400	29
Office clerks, general	821	82.0*	594	647	53
Personal and home care aides	789	85.2*	406	424	18

*Sex-segregated; at least 70% female.
**There are too few male child care workers to calculate the median, but median earnings for both sexes are $367, suggesting male child care workers earn more than female child care workers.
***Teacher assistants are the only one of the twenty leading occupations for women in which women earn more than men.

Source: U.S. Department of Labor, Bureau of Labor Statistics, Annual Averages 2009.

In contrast, when men are employed in female-dominated jobs, their average earnings are higher than women working in these jobs. As shown in Table 9.5, in nearly all of the twenty leading occupations of working women, men outearn women. About 92% of registered nurses are female and the median weekly earnings for female nurses is $1,035, but for male nurses it is $1,090. Almost 82% of elementary and middle school teachers are female, and the median weekly earnings for women ($891) are less than those for men ($1,040). These earnings may be partly due to male nurses and teachers having different specialties (e.g., trauma versus obstetrics or math versus English), yet the question of *why* men and women focus on different specialties and the valuation of specialty-based pay differentials remains.

Income

Despite the forty-year existence of the Equal Pay Act and Title VII prohibiting discrimination on the basis of sex, women still earn significantly less than men. In the United States, each year during the month of April many women call attention to "Equal Pay Day," noting that it takes over three more months of working for women to earn what men earned in the previous year. The female-to-male earnings ratio has increased from a low of about 60% in the 1970s to a high of 74% in 1996 and has declined slightly since then. Despite increases in women's education and participation, the pay gap exists in countries all over the world.[8]

In addition to sex segregation, women's earnings are negatively affected by women's likelihood of working fewer hours per week than men, even when employed "full-time." Clearly, the laws prohibiting discrimination are insufficient to eliminate income disparities between men and women. What are the other factors?

▌ GENDER ROLE SOCIALIZATION

Gender role socialization is one prominent reason for the persistence of sex discrimination, women's lower wage levels, sex segregation, and other unequal gender-based treatment. Gender role socialization is the process by which social institutions—including families, friends, organizations, and the media—form and shape expectations of acceptable behaviors for men and women. It affects women's treatment in organizations (by managers and peers), career "choices" and paths, and women's responsibilities outside of work (which are related to organizational progress and success). Socialization neutralizes the effectiveness of antidiscrimination and equal pay legislation by setting up different career "choices" for men and women. Recall from Chapter 3 that the Equal Pay Act requires men and women who work in the same jobs, in the same organization, and who have similar skills, performance, and tenure to be paid equally. Because of sex segregation and the role of "choice" in the jobs occupied by men and women, the Equal Pay Act and other laws against pay discrimination are constrained.

What is the role of "choice" in men's and women's work? From early in life, males and females receive clear messages about what "girls" and "boys" do and should do.[9] These messages encompass dress, behavior, occupations, and countless other "choices" people make throughout life. Research indicates that expectant parents who know the sex of their unborn babies speak more softly to girls in the womb than to boys in the womb. Parents describe baby girls as delicate and soft and speak gently to them; they describe baby boys in more masculine, stronger terms and speak differently to them.[10] Through socialization and observation, children learn that acceptable and

---

[8]Arulampalam, W., Booth, A. L., & Bryan, M. L. (2007). "Is There a Glass Ceiling Over Europe? Exploring the Gender Pay Gap Across the Wage Distribution." *Industrial and Labor Relations Review*, 60: 163–186.

[9]For a thought-provoking discussion of the role of schools in socialization, see Orenstein, P. (2002). "Shortchanging Girls: Gender Socialization in Schools." In P. Dubeck & D. Dunn (Eds.), *Workplace, Women's Place: An Anthology,* 2nd ed. Los Angeles: Roxbury Publishers, pp. 38–46.

[10]Smith, C., & Lloyd, B. B. (1978). "Maternal Behavior and Perceived Sex of Infant." *Child Development,* 49: 1263–1265; Smith, D. (2000). *Women at Work: Leadership for the Next Century.* Upper Saddle River, NJ: Prentice Hall.

TABLE 9.6 *Comparison of Average Annual Earnings and Percent Female in the Teaching Profession*

Occupation	% Female	Wages
Elementary school (includes kindergarten)	84.8/86.8 (public/private)	$49,220/$33,160 (public/private)
Secondary school	59.3/52.4 (public/private)	$50,020/$39,890 (public/private)
Instructor	20.2	$56,934/$44,666 (public/private)
Assistant professor	21.4	$59,433/$59,042 (public/private)
Associate professor	16.8	$70,289/$71,867 (public/private)
Full professor	12.8	$94,723/$106,056 (public/private)

Source: American Association of University Professors. "Average Salaries for College Faculty Members: 2007 to 2009." Annual Report on the Economic Status of the Profession. Washington, D.C.: AAUP.

appropriate jobs for women are elementary school teaching, nursing, and secretarial work—jobs that involve nurturing, care, and support. Research indicates that jobs involving nurturance pay $0.74 per hour less than jobs not requiring nurturance, contributing to the wage gap.[11] Table 9.6 provides examples of the wages for female- and male-dominated jobs at all levels of teaching. The higher one goes in the educational hierarchy (in position, status, and compensation), the higher the wages are and the fewer the women at the lectern.[12] Not shown in the Table 9.6 is how university positions are also gendered, which exacerbates male–female wage differences in the teaching profession. Departments having more men (e.g., engineering, business) pay more than those having fewer men (e.g., liberal arts).

For young women, a lifetime of gender role socialization and seeing those similar to themselves in certain jobs may result in their preparing for female-dominated positions without even considering similar, more lucrative, male-dominated positions as career choices. Many women may not be consciously aware that providing well for one's family and job flexibility are not mutually exclusive; however, they do require deliberate,

[11]England, P., Christopher, K., & Reid, L. L. (1999). "Gender, Race, Ethnicity, and Wages." In I. Browne (Ed.), *Latinas and African American Women at Work*. New York: Russell Sage Foundation, pp. 139–182.
[12]Dunn (1999). See also Mason, M. A., & Goulden, M. (2004). "Marriage and Baby Blues: Redefining Gender Equity in the Academy." *The Annals of the American Academy of Political and Social Science*, 596: 252–253.

conscious thought. A young woman who is interested in being a paralegal might choose to be an attorney; a future nurse might choose to be a certified nursing assistant, physician's assistant, or physician. However, in addition to investing more time and money in school, choosing to deviate from expected career paths may come with other costs.

Girls and boys who deviate from their appropriate gender roles are penalized by parents, teachers, society, and employers. The ground-breaking case of *Ann Hopkins v. Price Waterhouse*, described in Featured Case 9.1, is one such instance in which a woman was penalized for not acting enough like a woman. A male exhibiting female-type behaviors (e.g., "sissy") is often perceived more negatively than a female who exhibits male-type behaviors (e.g., "tomboy"). Females are discouraged from exhibiting aggression and are encouraged to cooperate and to consider the feelings of others in decision making. "Acting like a girl" is used derisively in normal conversation, communicating messages that doing so is a negative for both boys and girls.[13] Males are expected to be aggressive, argumentative, and competitive, and these expectations are reinforced in school through books and teachers and in society.[14] Ironically, a greater willingness to cooperate, seek consensus, and reach common goals is an asset in today's complex global organizations, yet such skills are less valued because women hold them.

In addition to their influence on personal career "choices" that women and men make, gender roles also influence managers and decision makers in organizations when making selection, placement, and pay decisions. A simple example of gender steering is a woman and a man applying for jobs at an office without specifying the position of interest. The woman may be given a typing or clerical test, while the man may be interviewed for a management trainee position. Secretaries generally make less money than managers and have considerably fewer opportunities for advancement. At a hotel, a man with little education may be hired to park cars and deliver luggage, while a similarly educated woman may be hired in housekeeping, cleaning rooms. Although both are low-skill, low-status positions, with little opportunity for advancement, the man stands to make extra money through tips and through fast turnover of customers, but the woman does not because of having a fixed number of rooms to clean and because many people do not leave tips for hotel maids.

As discussed in Chapter 2, stereotypes are types of schemas in which perceptions about people fall into categories related to sex, race, age, and

---

[13]Acting, throwing, crying, or other behaviors "like a girl" are commonly referred to derisively.
[14]Evans, L., & Davies, K. (2000). "No Sissy Boys Here: A Content Analysis of the Representation of Masculinity in Elementary School Reading Textbooks." *Sex Roles*, 42(3/4): 255–274; Harper, S. R., Harris, F., III, & Mmeje, K. (2005). "A Theoretical Model to Explain the Overrepresentation of College Men Among Campus Judicial Offenders: Implications for Campus Administrators." *NASPA Journal*, 42: 565–588.

FEATURED CASE 9.1	Ann Hopkins v. Price Waterhouse: *Wear Makeup, Jewelry, and Carry a Purse!*[15]

In August 1982, eighteen years after the passage of Title VII of the Civil Rights Act prohibiting sex discrimination, Ann Hopkins was nominated for partner at Price Waterhouse (PW) accounting and consulting firm. Of the 88 candidates being considered, Ann was the only woman, and only 7 of the approximately 2,600 PW partners worldwide were women. Hopkins had worked for PW for four years, demonstrating excellent performance, successfully managing difficult accounts, and earning more revenue than any of the other candidates being considered for partner that year.

After consideration by the full partners, 47 of the 88 candidates were offered partnerships, 21 were rejected, and Hopkins and 19 others were put "on hold" for possible consideration the next year. Although Hopkins learned that other candidates who had been ranked similarly had been admitted as partners, she continued to work for PW, participating in developmental activities that would ostensibly improve her chances for being made a partner the next year. Thomas Beyer, a partner who had supported her candidacy and considered himself her friend, gave Hopkins some ideas to increase her chances of obtaining partnership in the future. Beyer said she should "soften her image," curse less, avoid drinking beer at lunch, wear makeup and jewelry, style her hair, and carry a purse instead of a briefcase. In other words, Hopkins was told to act more like a woman.

When it became clear that she would not be nominated for partner the following year, Hopkins left PW, started a management consulting firm, and sued PW for sex discrimination. After many years of judgments and appeals, Hopkins won back pay and a partnership at PW. Hopkins was the first person ever to be admitted to partner by a court order. The court stated that for employers to penalize women for behaving aggressively when job requirements necessitate aggressiveness for successful job performance places women in a bind. Such women are "out of a job if they behave aggressively and out of a job if they don't."[16] This influential decision clarified the illegality of using compliance with gender roles in job decisions.

QUESTIONS TO CONSIDER

1. *How might the prospect of five years of litigation affect many plaintiffs considering a lawsuit?*

2. *Instead of telling Hopkins to act more like a woman, what should Beyer have done to address the apparent discrimination against her in the candidacy process?*

3. *Speculate on the chances Hopkins would have had to make partner had she worn lots of makeup and jewelry and behaved demurely?*

---

[15]Details from this case were drawn from Gentile, M. C. (1996). *Managerial Excellence Through Diversity*. Prospect Heights, IL: Waveland Press; Babcock, L., & Laschever, S. (2003). *Women Don't Ask*. Princeton, NJ: Princeton University Press; Hopkins, A. B. (1996). *So Ordered: Making Partner the Hard Way*. Amherst, MA: University of Massachusetts Press.
[16]Babcock & Laschever (2003), p. 111.

other categories. When a certain schema is activated during the selection process, employers may make decisions on the basis of that schema. Applicants more closely associated with the schema, having female-congruent or male-congruent attributes, as appropriate, are more likely to be selected.[17] William Darity and Patrick Mason (1998) used evidence from audit studies and court cases to document employers' discriminatory actions based on applicant sex (and race). They attributed employers' actions to preferences for certain types of employees in certain jobs according to the stereotypical beliefs they held.[18] In a unique study of hiring bias, orchestras which auditioned musicians behind screens so that judges could not see whether the musicians were male or female hired more women players than those which conducted auditions in which the musicians could be seen.[19]

In 2010, Walmart agreed to pay nearly $12 million to settle a sex discrimination lawsuit that alleged the company engaged in systemic discrimination against women applicants for warehouse positions. The EEOC alleged that between 1998 and 2005, Walmart's distribution center in London, Kentucky, regularly hired male applicants for warehouse positions but denied jobs to equally or more qualified female applicants. Moreover, according to the EEOC, Walmart used gender stereotypes and told applicants order-filling positions were "not suitable for women and that they hired mainly 18- to 25-year-old males" for such positions.[20] Such decisions by employers, along with the "choices" of women, contribute to sex segregation of jobs. Featured Case 9.2 provides two examples of employers' perceptions about appropriate and inappropriate jobs for women and the consequences of acting on those perceptions.

In addition to employers' acting based on sex stereotypes, when current employees make referrals of friends and family for job openings, they may screen references based on gender, referring women to jobs seen as "women's jobs" and men to "men's jobs." As no employer is involved in these actions, this type of screening is not viewed as illegal, yet it still perpetuates sex segregation and resulting wage inequality. If used as the sole or primary source of applicants, it could result in illegal discrimination.

---

[17]Perry, E., Davis-Blake, A., & Kulik, C. (1994). "Explaining Gender-Based Selection Decisions: A Synthesis of Contextual and Cognitive Approaches." *Academy of Management Review*, 19(4): 786–820. See also Terborg, J. R., & Ilgen, D. R. (1975). "A Theoretical Approach to Sex Discrimination in Traditionally Masculine Occupations." *Organizational Behavior and Human Performance*, 13(3): 352–376.

[18]Darity, W. A., & Mason, P. L. (1998). "Evidence on Discrimination in Employment: Codes of Color, Codes of Gender." *The Journal of Economic Perspectives*, 12(2): 63–90.

[19]Golden, C., & Rouse, C. (2000). "Orchestrating Impartiality: The Impact of 'Blind' Auditions on Female Musicians." *American Economic Review*, 90: 715–741.

[20]"Walmart to Pay More Than $11.7 Million to Settle EEOC Sex Discrimination Suit." http://www.eeoc.gov/eeoc/newsroom/release/3-1-10.cfm, accessed September 3, 2010.

Performance Food Group (PFG), a food service distributor in the Baltimore–Washington area, refused to hire women as delivery drivers. One year, PFG hired forty-four men and one woman as drivers. The company's transportation manager told the lone woman driver that her performance would determine whether any other women would be hired as drivers. Unfortunately, for all future women who hoped to be drivers at PFG, the woman had difficulties and quit. Later that same month, another woman (who would ultimately become the "charging party") saw PFG's advertised vacancy seeking delivery drivers and applied for the position. Although she had a commercial driver's license, prior delivery experience, and met all posted criteria for the job, the charging party (CP) was told that PFG would not be hiring any women because of a past bad experience with a female driver. The manager instead offered CP a lower-paying warehouse position, which she declined and instead took her case to the EEOC.

During the investigation of the case, an e-mail corroborating the company's position about not hiring women drivers surfaced. The e-mail, from the company's president and addressed to the transportation manager and HR manager, stated that "I think we have experience that tells us female drivers will not work out." The president concluded that making an offer to women as drivers was "inappropriate."

During the course of the lawsuit, PFG extended unconditional job offers to the charging party and six other women applicants. PFG also agreed to develop defined, uniform, and objective job-related qualifications for the driver and helper positions and to implement consistent job application, recordkeeping, and record retention procedures. The company agreed to affirmatively recruit qualified females for driver and helper positions and paid $350,000 in damages to seven class members.

In a very similar case, Ameripride Services, a linen supply company with nearly 200 facilities in the United States and Canada, discriminated against women applicants for customer service representative/route sales driver positions in Idaho. Ameripride advertised for applicants, stating that a Class B commercial license was required. The charging party in the case had a Class B license and six years of commercial driving experience and was selected for a second interview. During that interview, however, the area manager discouraged the charging party from pursuing the position, telling her that all the drivers were men and that they had a tendency to use foul language. The area manager also told the charging party that she looked more like a secretary and encouraged her to consider applying for a secretarial position that would open soon. Although the charging party and two other women applicants had superior qualifications, the area manager hired a man who did not have a Class B license or commercial driving experience. Under the settlement, Ameripride agreed to pay $110,000 to the charging party and another woman who was rejected.

Source: "EEOC Litigation Settlement Report, June 2004." http://archive.eeoc.gov/litigation/settlements/settlement06-04.html, accessed September 3, 2010, "EEOC Litigation Settlement Report, June 2005." http://archive.eeoc.gov/litigation/settlements/settlement06-05.html, accessed September 3, 2010.

QUESTIONS TO CONSIDER

1. Speculate about the manner in which the forty-four men hired by PFG may have treated the lone woman, who ultimately quit PFG. How likely is it that she was helped or trained?

2. The CEO of PFG used one bad experience with a woman driver as a rationale to avoid hiring any other women drivers.
  a. How large a psychological burden might this have placed on the lone woman driver?
  b. Of the forty-four men hired, is it likely that one of them was unsuccessful? If so, why were different standards applied to male and female failures?

3. PFG had a formal job description and the complaining party had met all job requirements as listed in the job description, yet she was not hired.
  a. Speculate on why "male" was not used as a job requirement, since the hiring managers and PFG believed women were incapable of performing the job.
  b. What might be the effects on employers' recruitment and selection costs be of (1) having and (2) using a legitimate job description?

4. Use http://www.salary.com, other salary-estimating Web sites, or Bureau of Labor Statistics actual salaries to estimate wage differences between a licensed truck driver and a warehouse worker. What is the difference in annual earnings and in percentages between these two positions? Estimate the differences in lifetime earnings at an annual salary increase rate of 3%. Estimate differences in Social Security and 401(k) payments to be matched by PFG between the two positions over a thirty-year career.

▌ Sex Discrimination

As discussed in Chapter 3, Title VII of the Civil Rights Act of 1964 prohibits discrimination on the basis of sex in employment-related matters. Although such discrimination has been prohibited for over forty years, intentional and unintentional discrimination still occurs, with some frequency.

Disparate treatment on the basis of sex occurs when an applicant or employee, typically a woman, is intentionally treated differently than males are treated. Although such blatant, overt discrimination is less common than in the past, it is far from obsolete. As an example, Featured Case 9.3 describes the recent EEOC settlement involving the Phoenix Suns professional basketball team and their sports entertainment firm regarding overt sex discrimination because of their stated requirement for men applicants only.

Disparate or **adverse impact** can occur when an employer's apparently neutral policy or practice negatively affects a person's (typically women's) employment opportunities. Examples are some height and weight requirements, many of which were instituted in the late 1960s and 1970s after the passage of Title VII as organizations tried to implement legitimate job specifications. At the time, many job incumbents were White males; using the average height and weight of current job incumbents as standards for future employees would automatically disadvantage women as a group, who tend to be smaller than men on average, as well as Asian,

FEATURED CASE 9.3	*Phoenix Suns and Sports Magic Sex Discrimination Settlement: A Newspaper Advertisement Seeks "Male" Employees*

Nearly fifty years after sex discrimination was prohibited by law, companies continue to practice overt discrimination. In a blatantly discriminatory newspaper ad that was published in Phoenix-area newspapers, including the *Arizona Republic*, the *Mesa Tribune*, and the *New Times*, the Phoenix Suns professional basketball team and Sports Magic Team sought "males with athletic ability and talent" for half-time and community performances by the "Zoo Crew." The Suns are part of the National Basketball Association and Sports Magic Team is a firm that organizes the Suns' half-time entertainment and promotions by the Zoo Crew.

Prior to the Suns' and Sports Magic's decision to seek only men for the positions, Kathryn Tomlinson had worked as a member of the Zoo Crew, performing acrobatics and other tricks during games, attending community events, and interacting with the public during basketball season. After the decision to hire only men, Tomlinson and another woman took their discrimination claim to the EEOC, which took the case. The Phoenix Suns and Sports Magic agreed to pay over $100,000 to settle the discrimination charges. In addition to the monetary settlement, the Phoenix Suns also agreed to strengthen policies prohibiting sex discrimination, to train personnel, to establish safeguards to ensure discriminatory advertisements were not disseminated in the future, and to apologize to Tomlinson.

Requirements for a particular sex may be legitimate when sex is a bona fide occupational qualification (BFOQ).[21] Assumptions about physical abilities or customer preferences for a certain sex do not qualify as BFOQs.

QUESTIONS TO CONSIDER

1. **Why might the Phoenix Suns and Sports Magic have decided to seek "males with athletic ability and talent"?**

2. **Is it possible that the organizations involved were unaware of legislation prohibiting sex discrimination? Do you think they considered that their actions might be illegal?**

3. **What potential benefits might the Suns and Sports Magic have gained by seeking "people" (rather than males) with athletic ability and talent as members of the Zoo Crew?**

4. **How do the attributes of cheerleaders for professional sports teams differ from those of the Zoo Crew? Is requiring cheerleaders to be women discriminatory?**

Source: "EEOC Resolves Sex Discrimination Lawsuit Against NBA's Phoenix Suns and Sports Magic for $104,500." http://www.eeoc.gov/eeoc/newsroom/release/archive/10-9-03b.html, accessed September 4, 2010.

Native American, or Latino men, who tend to be smaller than White (and Black) men. Although height and weight requirements by themselves are not discriminatory, employers must ensure that they are truly related to successful job performance (rather than simply to the norm for job incumbents) and that no other nondiscriminatory measure is feasible.

---

[21]See Chapter 3 for a discussion of what constitutes a BFOQ based on sex.

Employers may find that unintended positive outcomes result from efforts to remove discriminatory barriers to employment of people of different sizes.

Firefighting often comes to mind when people think of jobs in which they would prefer to have larger workers. "I'd prefer a firefighter to be big enough to be able to carry me out of a burning building" captures some of such apparently rational thinking. However, closer consideration calls into question its legitimacy. The normal, daily job of firefighters is more likely to include responding to false alarms and paramedic calls than rescues involving carrying someone who is unconscious and dead weight. Given the wide range of adult sizes, it is highly unlikely that any single adult would be able to carry any other adult for a significant distance, without assistance. Further, when considering the need to access small basement or bathroom windows, the benefit of having a smaller-sized firefighter (of any sex) seems apparent.

Another job commonly construed as needing large-sized incumbents is police officer. "I want a police officer to be strong enough to take down criminals" is a common perspective. Again, when considering the daily job functions of most police officers (such as directing traffic, writing tickets, completing paperwork) and the limited number of times that greater physical strength is needed to subdue suspects (rather than legitimate authority, pepper spray, or other nonlethal weapons), large size seems less critical. When taking into account the benefits of having women police officers interview and assist victims of certain crimes, the benefit of attributes and skills other than simply physical strength becomes apparent.

Misperception: Most women are physically unable to perform jobs such as police officer and firefighter.

Reality: Without a partner or special equipment, many men are unable to perform tasks believed to be commonly performed by firefighters and police officers. In addition, most job tasks of police officers and firefighters do not involve strength or size, and certain functions may be performed more successfully by a woman (interviewing rape and child molestation victims) or a small person of either sex (crawling into tight spaces).

For firefighting, police work, and other historically male-dominated jobs, a critical look at job requirements can be advantageous for employers as well as female applicants. Pairing male and female officers or those of smaller and larger statures can provide many unforeseen positive consequences, along with the widening of the applicant pool to more qualified people. In addition, constraining the applicant pool through unnecessary "job requirements" can result in higher recruitment, selection, and compensation costs to employers. Jobs can be redesigned and equipment replaced to open positions to a larger proportion of the workforce, providing benefits to employers, applicants, and society.[22]

In some situations, testing constrains the job pool even though some excluded applicants could have performed the job without job redesign or special equipment. In one case, Dial Corporation began using a strength test purportedly to reduce injuries in its Armour Star meat-packing plant in Iowa.[23] The test required repeated lifting of 35 pounds to a height of 65 inches. Although women had successfully performed the jobs before the test was implemented, only 40% of female applicants passed it, while nearly all male applicants did. One plaintiff, Paula Liles, successfully passed the test but was still rejected because she had to stand on her toes during parts of it; she was told she was too short (62 inches). The courts ruled that the test was both intentional and disparate impact discrimination against women that was not justified by business necessity. Liles and the other fifty-one plaintiffs shared a $3.4 million settlement that included compensatory and punitive damages. Each plaintiff also received a job offer from Dial, and at least fourteen accepted. In response to the judgment, Liles said, "I have done physical labor all my life, and I was able to perform the job at Dial. Dial was the highest paying employer in the area, and I felt that I was being rejected because of my sex and my height." The EEOC attorney said that the test was based on "stereotypes rather than actual ability."[24]

▌ SEXUAL HARASSMENT

As discussed in Chapter 3, sexual harassment is unwelcome conduct of a sexual nature in the workplace and is a form of sex discrimination. The courts have recognized two forms of sexual harassment: quid pro quo and hostile environment. In quid pro quo harassment, managers, supervisors, or others with authority make sexual demands and submission to or rejection of those demands is used as a basis for employment decisions (such as promotion, termination). In hostile environment harassment, unwelcome sexual conduct has the "purpose or effect of unreasonably interfering with job performance, or creating an intimidating, hostile, or

---

[22]Padavic & Reskin (2002).

[23]"DialOrdered to Pay More Than $3 Million in EEOC Sex Discrimination Case." http://www.eeoc.gov/press/9-29-05.html, accessed September 4, 2010.

[24]Ibid.

offensive working environment."[25] The latter kind of harassment is most commonly perpetrated by coworkers and peers and is less clear-cut than is quid pro quo harassment. Hostile environment harassment includes such things as jokes, photographs of scantily clad women (or men), and comments that some may view as normal and harmless but others may view as offensive and harassing. The EEOC and researchers suggest that organizations should clarify what constitutes harassment and identify harassing behaviors in regular, mandatory training programs.

Sexual Harassment of Women

Sexual harassment is a common experience for working women around the world. Studies conducted in Australia, Austria, Brazil, Canada, China, Hong Kong, India, Israel, Mexico, New Zealand, Norway, Portugal, Spain, Turkey, the United Kingdom, and various other places found pervasive sexual harassment with common negative individual and organizational outcomes. Estimates suggest that between 25% and 75% of women and 15% of men will be harassed in their working lives.[26] In the U.S. military, 47% of female officers, 60% of enlisted women, and 96.8% of women attending elite military institutions report having been harassed.[27]

As with other cases of discrimination, most people who are harassed do not sue or file formal complaints. In the United States, the 13,000 new charges of sexual harassment filed with the EEOC each year, on average, are but a fraction of the estimated yearly instances of harassment. A brief scan of the Equal Employment Opportunity Commission Web site reveals numerous instances of egregious sexual harassment.[28] In one such case against ABM Industries, a *Fortune* 1000 provider of commercial cleaning services, twenty-one Hispanic women were verbally and physically harassed and groped by fourteen male coworkers and supervisors (one of whom was a registered sex offender) over a period of years. At least one woman was sexually assaulted. ABM agreed to settle the case for $5.8 million and to provide other relief to the aggrieved parties.[29]

---

[25]EEOC Guidelines on Discrimination Because of Sex, 29, C. F. R. Section 1604. 11(a). 1995.
[26]Gutek, B. A., & Koss, M. P. (1993). "Changed Women and Changed Organizations: Consequences of and Coping with Sexual Harassment." *Journal of Vocational Behavior*, 42: 28–48; U. S. Merit Systems Protection Board. (1988). *Sexual Harassment in the Federal Workplace: An Update.* Washington, D.C.: U.S. Government Printing Office.
[27]Department of Defense. (2004). "Report on the Status of Female Members of the Armed Forces." http://www.dtic.mil/dacowits/tablerearch_subpage.html, accessed December 24, 2010.
[28]http://www.eeoc.gov/.
[29]"ABM Industries Settles EEOC Sexual Harassment Lawsuit for $5.8 Million." http://www.eeoc.gov/eeoc/newsroom/release/9-2-10.cfm, accessed September 4, 2010.

Many of the complaining parties in these and other cases were terminated or constructively discharged. In addition to the real possibility of job loss, harassment targets experience various negative physical and psychological outcomes, including stress, symptoms of posttraumatic stress disorder, nervousness, and fear. Sexual harassment negatively affects job satisfaction, morale, productivity, turnover, and absence and increases the targets' intentions to quit. These negative physical, psychological, and organizational outcomes of sexual harassment have been repeatedly documented in international research.[30] In addition to the negative effects on the direct targets of harassment, researchers have found that men and women who perceive the organization to be lax about harassment have a lower sense of well-being and are more likely to withdraw socially.[31] Researchers have also linked sexual harassment to greater conflict in work teams and subsequent lower productivity.[32] Women who are harassed tend to be younger, unmarried, and in lower-status, lower-level jobs than women who are not harassed. Because all over the world women's jobs and positions are generally lower in status, power, and authority than men's, this likely contributes to the nearly universal sexual harassment of women.

In one study, Barbara Gutek and her colleagues found that sexual harassment and sexualization of the work environment, such as sexual jokes, comments, or innuendoes, and a general lack of professionalism are associated. Gutek's sample was a broad spectrum of workers in the city of Los Angeles.[33] Other researchers have also found that the nature of the work environment and expectations are related to sexual harassment; in places where work roles are clear and where workers are generally treated respectfully, sexual harassment is less likely to occur.[34] Sexual harassment is frequently experienced by women who enter male-dominated fields. Researchers have found that women in blue-collar trade and transit

---

[30]Fitzgerald, L. F., Drasgow, R., Hulin, C. L., Gelfand, M. J., & Magley, V. J. (1997). "Antecedents and Consequences of Sexual Harassment in Organizations: A Test of an Integrated Model." *Journal of Applied Psychology*, 82: 578–589; Gelfand, M. J., Fitzgerald, L. F., & Drasgow, F. (1995). "The Structure of Sexual Harassment: A Confirmatory Analysis Across Cultures and Settings." *Journal of Vocational Behavior*, 47: 167–177; Shaffer, M. A., Joplin, J. R. W., Bell, M. P., Lau, T., & Oguz, C. (2000). "Gender Discrimination and Job-Related Outcomes: A Cross-Cultural Comparison of Working Women in the United States and China." *Journal of Vocational Behavior*, 57(4): 395–427; Wasti, S. A., Bergman, M. E., Glomb, T. M., & Drasgow, F. (2000). "Test of the Cross-Cultural Generalizability of a Model of Sexual Harassment." *Journal of Applied Psychology*, 85: 766–789.
[31]Miner-Rubino, K., & Cortina, L. M. (2007). "Beyond Targets: Consequences of Vicarious Exposure to Misogyny." *Journal of Applied Psychology*, 92(5): 1254–1269.
[32]Raver, J. L., & Gelfand, M. J. (2005). "Beyond the Individual Victim: Linking Sexual Harassment, Team Processes, and Team Performance." *Academy of Management Journal*, 48: 387–400.
[33]Gutek, B. A., Cohen, A. G., & Konrad, A. M. (1990). "Predicting Social-Sexual Behavior at Work: A Contact Hypothesis." *Academy of Management Journal*, 33: 560–577.
[34]O'Hare, E. A., & O'Donohue, W. (1998). "Sexual Harassment: Identifying Risk Factors." *Archives of Sexual Behavior*, 27: 561–580.

positions, autoworkers, lawyers, police officers, and firefighters experience more peer harassment than women working in female-dominated fields.[35] In one nationwide survey of women firefighters, 85% reported mistreatment at work, including hostility, sexual harassment, and being placed in unnecessary danger on fire scenes.[36] For those who believe that women are incapable of performing certain male-dominated jobs, women's failure may serve to confirm negative expectations, but such failure may be a result of harassment and lack of training rather than women's abilities.[37] As with any newcomer of any sex to a job, training and (positive) socialization are critical to success. Lack of training and harassment in *any* job predict failure (for men, women, people of color, etc.), and in certain jobs they can be life-threatening. Featured Case 9.4 describes a dangerous case of sex-based hostility toward a woman truck driver at Federal Express. Organizational intervention, through education, training, monitoring, and a zero tolerance policy for harassment, can help women successfully enter and remain in male-dominated fields, reducing sex segregation, increasing women's wages, and improving the climate for diversity and inclusion.

Sexual Harassment of Men

The EEOC reports that about 16% of its sexual harassment charges are filed by men, most of whom report being targeted by other men.[38] Men who are harassed may be even less willing to complain than are women who are harassed, due to the prevailing belief that they should be flattered if harassed by women or that they are gay if harassed by men.

In 1998, the Supreme Court issued an important decision on same-sex harassment, clarifying its illegality. Prior to this decision, court rulings had differed as to whether such harassment was covered under Title VII or whether the sexuality of the harasser was relevant. In 1991, Joseph Oncale was working on an oil platform in the Gulf of Mexico for Sundowner

---

[35]Gruber, J. E., & Bjorn, L. (1982). "Blue-Collar Blues: The Sexual Harassment of Women Autoworkers." *Work and Occupations*, 93: 271–298; LaFontaine, E., & Tredeau, L. (1986). "The Frequency, Sources, and Correlates of Sexual Harassment in Traditional Male Occupations." *Sex Roles*, 1(5): 433–442; Rosenberg, J., Perlstadt, H., & Philips, W. R. (1993). "Now That We Are Here: Discrimination, Disparagement, and Harassment at Work and the Experience of Women Lawyers." *Gender and Society*, 7: 415–433.

[36]Hulett, D., Bendick, M., Jr., Thomas, S., & Moccio, F. (2008). "Enhancing Women's Inclusion in Firefighting in the USA." *International Journal of Diversity in Organizations, Communities, & Nations*, 8: 1–24.

[37]See also Padavic & Reskin (2002).

[38]"EEOC Sues Kraft Foods North America for Same-Sex Harassment of Men." http://www.eeoc.gov/press/10-25-02.html, accessed September 4, 2010.

| FEATURED CASE 9.4 | *Federal Express Pays Over $3.2 Million to Woman Truck Driver* |

Marion Shaub was the only female tractor-trailer driver at the Middletown, Pennsylvania, facility of Federal Express (FedEx). Shaub alleged that she was constantly subjected to antifemale remarks and threats from her male coworkers. After she made numerous complaints about the gender-based hostility and harassment at work, Shaub alleged that the brakes on her truck were sabotaged and that her coworkers refused to help with the loading of her truck. After Shaub was fired in October 2000, she sued FedEx under Title VII. In early 2004, a federal jury found FedEx liable for a sex-based hostile environment and retaliation, awarding Shaub $391,400 in back and front pay, $350,000 in compensatory damages, and $2.5 million in punitive damages. The Civil Rights Act of 1991 allows for punitive damages in cases of intentional discrimination such as that experienced by Shaub.

QUESTIONS TO CONSIDER

1. *Why might Shaub's coworkers have been so hostile toward her?*

2. **What signal would Shaub's experiences at FedEx send to other women desiring to be truck drivers?**

3. **What could Federal Express have done to circumvent the harassment prior to Shaub or other women being hired as drivers?**

4. **What should FedEx have done in response to Shaub's initial complaints?**

5. **What should FedEx do to prevent this kind of thing from happening in the future?**

6. **If Shaub had an accident while driving and been injured or killed or injured or killed others because the brakes on her truck had been sabotaged, what consequences might FedEx have faced?**

Source: "Federal Express to Pay Over $3.2 Million to Female Truck Driver for Sex Discrimination, Retaliation." www.eeoc.gov/press/2-25-04.html, accessed September 3, 2010.

Offshore Services along with seven other men. On several occasions, two of Oncale's supervisors physically assaulted him in a sexual manner, threatened to rape him, and subjected him to humiliating sex-related behavior. When Oncale complained to Sundowner's Safety Compliance clerk, the clerk called him a heterosexist name and characterized the supervisors were simply "picking on" people, behavior they had displayed toward others as well. Oncale said he resigned his position to avoid being raped and filed a lawsuit against Sundowner. The first court to hear the case ruled that because both Oncale and the harassers were male, Oncale had no cause of action, and this ruling was confirmed on appeal.[39] The Supreme Court agreed to hear the case and ruled in Oncale's favor, seven years after the harassment occurred. Thus, prohibitions against discrimination because of sex do not require the parties to be of different sexes.

[39]http://www.law.cornell.edu/supct/html/96-568.ZO.html, accessed March 1, 2011.

Those who experience sexual harassment, regardless of their sex or that of the perpetrator, have legal rights and recourse.

■ THE GLASS CEILING AND OTHER BOUNDARIES

The invisible barrier that prevents women, people of color, and people with disabilities from progressing beyond a certain level in organizations is termed the **glass ceiling**.[40] The glass ceiling is often thought to begin near the level of top management, including executive positions; however, the ceiling is actually quite low.[41] Relatively few women or minorities advance past first- or second-level management positions in organizations, leading researchers to suggest that the term **sticky floors** more accurately reflects this phenomenon. In other words, women are far closer to the bottom rungs of the ladder to the top rather than on the rungs approaching the ceiling.

In the Canada, the United Kingdom, United States, and most other nations, women rarely reach the executive suite or even middle-to-upper management. Despite the forty years in which legislation prohibiting sex discrimination has existed in the United States, only 12% of women are corporate officers, only about 6% hold the highest corporate titles, and only 4% occupy the highest-earning positions, even though they comprise about half the workforce. In 2010, only fifteen of the CEOs of *Fortune* 500 companies were women.[42] The higher in the organizational hierarchy from the first level of management, the fewer the number of women. The experiences of Sharon Allen beyond the glass ceiling, from entry level to chairman of the board of Deloitte & Touche, USA, are discussed in Individual Feature 9.1.

In a recent case, the EEOC alleged that Outback Steakhouse discriminated against thousands of women at hundreds of its restaurants nationwide.[43] Female employees were denied job assignments that were required for promotion to top management, particularly kitchen management experience. Without such experience, women hit a glass ceiling and could not get promoted into the higher-level, profit-sharing management positions.

---

[40]This chapter considers the effects of the glass ceiling on women; see chapters on Blacks (Chapter 4), Latinos (Chapter 5), Asians (Chapter 6), and people with disabilities (Chapter 14) for a consideration of its effects on members of these groups.

[41]Hurley, A. E., Fagenson-Eland, E. A., & Sonnenfeld, J. A. (1997). "Does Cream Always Rise to the Top? An Investigation of Career Attainment Determinants." *Organizational Dynamics,* 26(2): 65–71.

[42]"Fortune 500 2010: Top Women CEOs—Fortune on CNNMoney.com." http://money.cnn.com/magazines/fortune/fortune500/2010/womenceos/, accessed September 3, 2010.

[43]"Outback Steakhouse to Pay $19 Million for Sex Bias Against Women In 'Glass Ceiling' Suit By EEOC" http://www.eeoc.gov/eeoc/newsroom/release/12-29-09a.cfm, accessed September 14, 2010.

INDIVIDUAL FEATURE 9.1	*Sharon Allen, Chairman of the Board, Deloitte & Touche, USA, LLP*

Deloitte & Touche, USA, LLP, provides audit, advisory, and other services to its clients, including more than half of the world's largest companies. When Sharon Allen was named chairman of the board of Deloitte & Touche, USA, she became the first woman ever elected to such a position and the highest-ranking woman in Deloitte's history. An accounting graduate of the University of Idaho, Allen joined the company in 1973 and was named chairman of the board in May 2003.

Glass ceiling research notes the dearth of women on boards, the near absence of women chairing boards, and the unlikelihood of executive women being married or having children compared to men executives. Allen has defied the odds, serving on Deloitte's board, chairing the board, remaining married to her high school sweetheart, and being an actively involved mother, going to soccer games like many other mothers.

At one time, women at Deloitte were overlooked for assignments working with high-profile clients, in part because women had higher turnover than men. Fearing that the clients would be left in the lurch when this happened, the high-profile accounts that led to promotions were not given to women. Women saw that they were not getting the significant accounts and left. Deloitte responded by developing the "Women's Initiative" to help ensure that women had the opportunity to compete for certain positions and were not overlooked. Allen believes that the Women's Initiative provided her with the visibility to be selected that she might not otherwise have had and makes it her personal responsibility to help others who might be overlooked. At present, Deloitte has the highest percentage of women partners, principals, and directors among similar companies and plans to increase those numbers.

Allen supports Deloitte's efforts to increase the diversity of partners and helps develop a corporate culture that allows for family time, which she believes provides a recruiting advantage. Deloitte's Women's Initiative received a 2010 Catalyst Award, honoring seventeen years of commitment to and innovation in the advancement of women.

QUESTIONS TO CONSIDER

1. **Deloitte's Women's Initiative was formed to address its problems with women leaving the company. How likely is it that presumptions about women's turnover prevent them from getting key assignments and thus contribute to their turnover?**

2. **Ensuring that women "are appropriately represented on each short list for succession into important client service and firm leadership positions" helps them to be able to compete for jobs. How is this similar to affirmative action?**

3. **Some high-level executive women have partners whose careers take a subordinate position. Is this the case with Sharon Allen? Investigate.**

Sources: Cole, Y. (2005, March 11). "Chairman of the Board and Then Some: Deloitte's Sharon L. Allen." *DiversityInc*, 42–50; "Sharon Allen Chairman of the Board, Deloitte & Touche, USA, LLP." http://www .deloitte.com/view/en_US/us/About/Leadership/sharon-allen/6694f16bc31fb110VgnVCM100000ba42f00aRCRD .htm, accessed September 3, 2010; "Deloitte's Women's Initiative Receives 2010 Catalyst Award." http://www.deloitte.com/view/en_US/us/press/Press-Releases/3f84d1724fda6210VgnVCM200000 bb42f00aRCRD.htm, accessed September 3, 2010.

In addition to the $19 million settlement, Outback agreed to institute an online application system for employees interested in management and other supervisory positions and to employ an outside consultant for at least two years, who would determine compliance with the terms of the settlement and monitor whether women are being provided equal opportunities for promotion.

Women's persistent overrepresentation in lower-level jobs and under-representation in higher-level jobs, in a wide range of industries, cannot simply be attributed to lack of education, qualifications, or desire to advance. In their study of nearly 1,000 senior managerial appointments, Karen Lyness and Christine Schrader found that women's new appointments were more similar to their previous positions than men's were. They also found that women's moves were less likely to involve a promotion to a higher level, women were less likely than men to move from staff positions to line positions, and, when they did move to line jobs, women were more likely to move to line jobs that had had prior female incumbents.[44] Lateral moves and staff jobs are characteristics of glass barriers that constrain women's opportunity to advance to the executive suite.

The term **glass walls** refers to invisible horizontal barriers that constrain women, people of color, and people with disabilities to certain occupations and positions within organizations. Glass walls confine members of these (and other non-dominant) groups to staff (supportive) versus line positions (decision making with profit-and-loss responsibility). Occupations heavily dominated by women and people of color include human resources, communications, diversity/affirmative action, and public relations, which are positions that rarely advance to the top management level. In contrast, Whites and men are dominant in areas such as finance, marketing, and operations, from which executives and chief executive officers are most often selected. Glass walls prevent those constrained by them from obtaining the breadth of experience and exposure required for advancement.[45]

The term **glass escalator** refers to men's rapid ascent into management and higher-level positions after entering female-dominated occupations. This anomaly may reflect the well-known general preference for men as managers and leaders and the idea of "think manager, think male." Using large-scale data on income, managerial attainment, and career progress, David Maume, of the University of Cincinnati, has documented empirical evidence of the glass ceiling for women and people of color and the glass

[44]Lyness, K., & Schrader, C. A. (2006). "Moving Ahead or Just Moving? An Examination of Gender Differences in Senior Corporate Management Appointments." *Group and Organization Management,* 31: 651–676.

[45]Smith, D. (2000). *Women at Work: Leadership for the Next Century.* Upper Saddle River, NJ: Prentice Hall; Lopez, J. A. (1992, March 3). "Study Says Women Face Glass Walls as Well as Ceilings." *Wall Street Journal,* B1–B2.

escalator for White men.[46] Maume found that Black men and women and White women waited longer for the managerial promotions they received and that, for White men especially, the percentage of women in the occupation positively affected the men's chances of moving into a supervisory position. After twelve years of working in a female-dominated position, 44%, 17%, 15%, and 7% of White men, Black men, White women, and Black women, respectively, will have been promoted into management.[47] Other U.S. and international researchers as well have found compelling evidence of glass escalators.[48]

▌ Sex, Race, and Ethnicity

Previous sections in this chapter have considered women's experiences compared with men's experiences. A thorough consideration of sex, race, and ethnicity must also incorporate within-group differences, that is, differences between women and men in various racial and ethnic groups. Numerous researchers have documented problems associated with categorizing "women" into one group, in that doing so obscures the many important differences between and among women of various racial and ethnic backgrounds and ignores the multiple effects of racism and sexism.[49] Because of the clear dominance of White men in earnings, organizational status, and level, White men and men of color are placed into the same group ("men") far less than women are categorized. The following sections consider these issues.

White Women and Women of Color

As members of the dominant racial group, White women share some workplace advantages with White men relative to women of color (and, in some ways, relative to men of color). Differences among women exist in education, participation rates, and employment levels, but generally,

---

[46]Maume, D. J., Jr. (November 1999). "Glass Ceilings and Glass Escalators: Occupational Segregation and Race and Sex Differences in Managerial Promotions." *Work and Occupations,* 26(4): 483–509.

[47]Padavic & Reskin (2002).

[48]For example, Hultin, M. (2003). "Some Take the Glass Escalator, Some Hit the Glass Ceiling?" *Work and Occupations,* 30(1): 30–61; Goldberg, C. B., Finkelstein, L. M., Perry, E. L., & Konrad, A. M. (2004). "Job and Industry Fit: The Effects of Age and Gender Matches on Career Progress Outcomes." *Journal of Organizational Behavior,* 25: 807–829; Williams, C. L. (1992). "The Glass Escalator: Hidden Advantages for Men in Non-Traditional Occupations." *Social Problems,* 39: 253–267.

[49]See Ferdman, B. M. (1999). "The Color and Culture of Gender in Organizations: Attending to Race and Ethnicity." In G. N. Powell (Ed.), *Handbook of Gender and Work.* Thousand Oaks, CA: Sage Publications, pp. 17–34.

White women are advantaged relative to women of color. Claims in the popular press that women of color are advantaged relative to White women because of their double minority status (e.g., racial and sexual) fuel misperceptions. Rather than being a source of double advantage, being a woman and a person of color instead multiplies disadvantages stemming from multiple race and gender stereotypes, discrimination, and segregation.

An organizational analysis of data regarding affirmative action, organizational status, employment level and income, and returns on educational investment provides evidence contradicting the myth of the employment advantage of being a woman of color. At a societal level, women of color occupy the lowest-paid, lowest-status jobs of any group, including jobs such as housekeepers (both in homes and in hotels/motels), nursing aides, and cashiers. For example, in New Orleans, hotel maids are likely to be African American and Central American (Hispanic) Blacks; in Texas, they are Mexican, Central, or South Americans; in Seattle, many are Asian Americans; in New York and Miami, many maids are Puerto Ricans. Although European American women also work in female-dominated jobs, they are far less likely to be hotel maids than women of color and instead are more likely to be nurses, elementary school teachers, secretaries, or managers.[50] This is in part due to White women's higher education levels and in part due to close interpersonal and familial relationships with White men, who are the key decision makers and who may feel more comfortable with White women than with women of color in certain jobs.[51] As shown in Table 9.3, the earnings of women of color are lower than those of non-Hispanic White women in most educational categories.

Misperception: Women of color receive employment preference over White women because of their status as sexual and racial minorities.

Reality: White women have benefited most from affirmative action programs, are more likely to be in management than women of color.[52]

---

[50]Reskin, B. (1999). "Occupational Segregation by Race and Ethnicity Among Women Workers." In I. Browne (Ed.), *Latinas and African American Women at Work*. New York: Russell Sage Foundation, pp. 183–204.

[51]Department of Labor. (2008a). *20 Leading Occupations of Employed Women*. Bureau of Labor Statistics, Annual Averages 2008. http://www.dol.gov/wb/factsheets/20lead2008.htm#, accessed February 7, 2010.

[52]Corcoran, M. (1999). "The Economic Progress of African American Women." In I. Brown (Ed.), *Latinas and African American Women at Work: Race, Gender, and Economic Inequality*. New York: Russell Sage Foundation, pp. 35–60.

The combination of gender and racial segregation at work creates multiple disadvantages for women of color.[53] In addition to discrimination in hiring, they sometimes experience discrimination and harassment based on both race and sex from managers and peers. For example, as in the class action case against ABM discussed earlier, in which Hispanic women experienced egregious sexual harassment, a Chicago-area company agreed to pay four Black female production workers $155,000 in back pay and attorneys' fees for the sexual harassment they experienced. The EEOC alleged that supervisors and coworkers exposed their buttocks and genitals to the plaintiffs, referred to them using sexually derogatory terms coupled with racist terms, and twice opened the restroom door and threw water on a Black woman as she used the restroom.[54]

∎ UNIQUE GENDER ISSUES

The following section considers two unique issues concerning gender and diversity in organizations: gender and poverty and women and pay negotiations. Numerous other unique gender issues exist, such as differences in managerial women's and men's likelihood of being parents, gender differences in health care, and countless others. Space constraints prevent treatment of every issue; readers are encouraged to continue their own exploration of unique gender issues.

Gender and Poverty

Worldwide, women earn about 66% of men's earnings and they are about 50% more likely to live in poverty than men are.[55] In 2007, 13.8% of women and 11.1% of men lived in poverty in the United States, and for all racial and ethnic groups, American women are more likely than men to live in poverty.[56] Black, Hispanic, and American Indian women are at least twice as likely to live in poverty as White women, in part due to White women's greater likelihood of being partnered with higher-

---

[53]Caiazza, A., Shaw, A., & Werschkul, M. (2004). "The Status of Women in the United States." Institute for Women's Policy Research, Washington, D.C. http://www.iwpr.org/States2004/PDFs/National.pdf, accessed August 16, 2010. Corcoran, M. (1999); Bound, J., & Dresser, L. (1999). "Losing Ground: The Erosion of the Relative Earnings of African American Women During the 1980s." In I. Brown (Ed.), *Latinas and African American Women at Work: Race, Gender, and Economic Inequality*. New York: Russell Sage Foundation, pp. 61–104.
[54]"EEOC Litigation Settlements Monthly Reports." December 2002. http://archive.eeoc.gov/litigation/settlements/settlement12-02.html, accessed September 4, 2010.
[55]United Nations. "The Feminization of Poverty." http://www.un.org/womenwatch/daw/followup/session/presskit/fs1.htm, accessed September 4, 2010.
[56]Cawthorne, A. (2008). "The Straight Facts on Women in Poverty." Center for American Progress. http://www.americanprogress.org/issues/2008/10/pdf/women_poverty.pdf, accessed September 4, 2010.

earning White men.[57] Although poverty is often associated with single parenting, only 25% of all adult women who live in poverty are single mothers, and 54% of all poor adult women have no dependent children.[58] Many researchers have studied the "feminization of poverty" and its effects on women and children.[59]

Women's lower rates of participation in the workforce, their higher employment in part-time work, and the wage gap negatively affect women (and their families) in the present as well as their lifetime earnings and their retirement savings and incomes.[60] Women's longer life expectancies, during which time they may deplete their lower retirement savings, have long-term financial implications. Readers may be able to easily think of older women whose current poor financial situation reflects intermittent or no work outside the home, part-time work, or, as is common for women of color, a lifetime of full-time work in lower-paying, female-dominated jobs or of being paid in cash, with no contributions to Social Security from their employers. The roles played by socialization in women's job "choices" and discrimination in women's employment opportunities and earnings must not be ignored as factors underlying the social issue of poverty.

Negotiating Pay

Socialization and gender roles negatively affect working women during salary negotiations as well. Carnegie Mellon economist Linda Babcock and Sara Laschever documented women's failure to negotiate pay, promotions, and raises.[61] This failure, they propose, is a result of women's lifelong conditioning to graciously accept what is offered, regardless of whether it differs from what they desire or from what is fair and just. Babcock and Laschever report several empirical studies indicating that both women's failure to negotiate for what they deserve and employers' view that women deserve and will settle for less contribute to the wage gap. Babcock and Laschever suggest that women should be taught to assert their needs and wishes more and that society should learn to accept rather than penalize women who ask for what they want and deserve. Parents, teachers, and other adults can help young women to learn to ask for what they want. And adult women, who know that violating gender

[57]Caiazza et al. (2004).
[58]Cawthorne (2008).
[59]The feminization of poverty as a worldwide problem is discussed at http://www.un.org/womenwatch/daw/followup/session/presskit/fs1.htm, accessed September 4, 2010. See also Caiazza et al. (2004).
[60]Caiazza et al. (2004), p. 10.
[61]Babcock & Laschever (2003).

differences when asking for what one deserves can be very costly, can learn to do what for them may be uncomfortable but is worth the effort.

It is also important to consider the possibility that even when women do negotiate, they face more resistance than men and are less successful in increasing their salaries.[62] Contrary to Babcock and Laschever's findings, other researchers found that women were not less likely than men to negotiate salary offers, but when they did negotiate, they were less likely to receive as much.[63] (In a similar vein, recall from Chapter 4 that White men's initial offers and final negotiated prices for automobiles were lower than prices quoted to members of other groups.)

As part of the effort to achieve organizational diversity, managers should make comparable, fair salary offers to men and women with similar qualifications and skills rather than act on the assumption that women don't or shouldn't ask as a rationale to pay them less. There is no long-term benefit from unfair treatment of any group of workers (or customers) in a competitive, increasingly diverse society. Paying women less than they deserve can result in dissatisfaction and quitting, causing organizations to lose valued workers and to experience other costs associated with dysfunctional turnover.

▌ RECOMMENDATIONS FOR INDIVIDUALS AND ORGANIZATIONS

Knowledge of sex and gender issues is an important first step in making changes to address them. Everyone should share what he or she knows about gender disparities with friends, family, and coworkers. Ignorance of the long-term, significant, often negative effects of these issues perpetuates adherence to strict gender roles, denial of the continued need for such programs as affirmative action, and failure to work for change. To reduce salary differences arising from lower levels of education, individual women should complete college and obtain advanced degrees, if possible. To avoid pay disparities associated with sex segregation, women should consciously choose careers that utilize their interests and skills but that also pay well. Men should encourage individual women to do so and provide them with interpersonal social support and, when working with such women, intra-organizational support. Parents and employers can

---

[62]Belliveau, M. (2005). "An Offer You Should Refuse: Gender Differences in Job Candidate Counteroffers." Paper presented at annual Academy of Management meeting, Honolulu; Marks, M., & Harold, C. (2009). "Who Asks and Who Receives in Salary Negotiation." *Journal of Organizational Behavior* doi:10.1002/job.671; Gerhart, B., & Rynes, S. (1991). "Determinants and Consequences of Salary Negotiations by Male and Female MBA Graduates." *Journal of Applied Psychology,* 76: 256–262.

[63]Gerhart & Rynes (1991); Marks & Harold (2009).

encourage male and female children to pursue nontraditional occupations and interests. Individuals already employed in sex-segregated occupations can improve their earnings and opportunities by researching and applying to organizations that value women workers, by additional education and training, and possibly through career change or enhancement. What schools, for example, pay elementary school teachers well? How much more do teachers with a graduate degree earn compared to those with an undergraduate degree? How much more does an R.N. earn compared to an L.P.N., or does an M.D. earn compared to an R.N.? What current skills are transferable to better-paying jobs? What can be done to encourage more pay equality for jobs done by women that are devalued by society?

Women and men managers should mentor women employees, helping them gain job and organization-appropriate skills for advancement. Both should recognize the value of women's leadership, consensus, and team-building skills and encourage their use while also encouraging men to learn and apply those skills.[64] Women should be encouraged to use skills traditionally associated with men, such as task orientation and assertiveness.[65] Women and men should question sexist behaviors, comments, and innuendoes that occur in their personal and organizational lives.

Organizations have a powerful influence on sex discrimination and harassment, the existence of glass ceilings, walls, and sticky floors, intra-firm sex segregation, and other gender and diversity issues. Committed organizational leadership and vigilance are critical in shaping behaviors and, ultimately, attitudes. Researchers suggest one important and effective systemic change to accomplish is the establishment of formalized pay structures. In their investigation of earnings differences between men and women, Marta Elvira and Mary Graham found in a sample of more than 8,000 employees of a large financial services organization that less-formalized pay structures (e.g., cash incentive bonuses) resulted in greater salary differences than those in more formalized pay systems (e.g., merit raises and base salary).[66] Elvira and Graham concluded that incentive bonuses "may widen the earnings gap between women and men, and have implications for the design of pay structures in organizations," findings that support those of Castilla, discussed in Chapter 7.[67] Castilla pointed out the need for careful attention to pay differences emerging over time between dominant and non-dominant group members and found

[64]Rosener, J. B. (1995). *America's Competitive Secret: Women Managers*. London: Oxford University Press.
[65]Nelson, T. D. (2002). *The Psychology of Prejudice*. Boston, MA: Allyn & Bacon.
[66]Elvira, M. M., & Graham, M. E. (2002). "Not Just a Formality: Pay System Formalization and Sex-related Earnings Effects." *Organization Science*, 13(6): 601–617.
[67]Ibid., p. 601.

differences in pay increases and salary growth for women and minorities compared to White men, despite equal performance ratings.

The presence of women in managerial and leadership positions is of particular importance when dealing with gender issues in organizations. Again, due to space constraints, the following discussion is limited to the two areas of curbing sexual harassment and removing the glass ceiling; readers are encouraged to further investigate other issues involved in sex discrimination.

Curbing Sexual Harassment

Women constitute 85% of harassment targets and are perpetrators in about 7% of harassment cases. Of the men who experience harassment (about 16% of cases), most are harassed *by other men*. Thus, both quid pro quo and hostile environment harassment are less likely when there are women in managerial and supervisory roles. Because women are less likely to perpetrate harassment than are men, quid pro quo harassment is less likely when there are significant numbers of women managers. Having women as managers should also reduce hostile environment harassment. Research indicates that women reporting to male supervisors experience more harassment than women working for women managers and that women with male supervisors perceived their employers to be more tolerant of sexual harassment.[68] Researchers have also found that women and men view hostile environment harassment differently. Certain behaviors that men view as inoffensive, women view as offensive and harassing. These differences suggest that women as managers would view harassing behaviors similar to other, nonmanagerial women. With appropriate support and a zero tolerance policy, managerial women may, therefore, be well equipped to recognize and curb harassment in their departments and organizations.

The best prescription for sexual harassment may be one of prevention, rather than remedial efforts after harassment has occurred.[69] All employees should receive regular training that clarifies acceptable and unacceptable workplace behavior, reporting channels, and appropriate responses. Sexual harassment training has been shown to increase understanding of

---

[68]Hulin, C. L., Fitzgerald, L. F., & Drasgow, F. (1996). "Organizational Influences on Sexual Harassment." In M. S. Stockdale (Ed.), *Sexual Harassment in the Workplace,* Vol. 5. Thousand Oaks, CA: Sage Publications, pp. 127–150; Piotrkowski, C. S. (1998). "Gender Harassment, Job Satisfaction, and Distress Among Employed White and Minority Women." *Journal of Occupational Health Psychology,* 3: 33–43.

[69]For a discussion of the merits and attributes of a preventive program, see Bell, M. P., Quick, J. C., & Cycycota, C. (2002). "Assessment and Prevention of Sexual Harassment: Creating Healthy Organizations." *International Journal of Selection and Assessment,* 21: 160–167.

what constitutes harassment and reduce uncertainty about what is and what is not harassment.[70] Managers and supervisors should be made aware of their responsibilities for harassment prevention. The organization's sexual harassment policy should be widely and clearly communicated, such that the organization's position on harassment is clear to those who would harass and those who might be harassed. Charges of harassment and informal complaints should be promptly investigated and addressed, with appropriate sanctions as indicated. Chapter 3 provided other details about sexual harassment charges, lawsuits, settlements, and prevention.

Breaking the Glass Ceiling

Rather than focusing on helping women "break through" the ceiling, with its implication of personal failure on the part of women who do not advance, dismantling the formidable institutional obstacles—systemic barriers—to the advancement of women must be the objective. These barriers include the good-old-boys' network, through which information about key positions and assignments is disseminated and employment decisions are made; perceptions that women's leadership styles are inconsistent with management tasks; lip service to, but no accountability for, advancing women; selection, appraisal, compensation, and promotion systems that advantage men; cultural discouragement (e.g., cultures that reward face time over performance and gendered organizational cultures); and sex discrimination and harassment, which serve to remove women from organizations.[71] Executive-level women report having to repeatedly outperform men to be considered for high-level positions and having to reestablish credibility with each new assignment.[72] Organizational commitment must precede an in-depth organizational analysis of these factors and others unique to the organization that impede women's progress, and the analysis must be followed up by interventions for change, monitoring, and continued analysis, as in the Outback case discussed earlier. Putting systems online that allow applicants to apply and be considered for promotions may also be helpful.

[70]Antecol, H., & Cobb-Clark, D. (2003). "Does Sexual Harassment Training Change Attitudes? A View from the Federal Level." *Social Science Quarterly*, 84(4): 826–843.

[71]Mattis, M. C. (2002). "Best Practices for Retaining and Advancing Women Professionals and Managers." In R. C. Burke & D. L. Nelson (Eds.), *Advancing Women's Careers*. Oxford, UK: Blackwell Publishers, pp. 309–332.

[72]Ragins, B. R., Townsend, B., & Mattis, M. (1998). "Gender Gap in the Executive Suite: CEOs and Female Executives Report on Breaking the Glass Ceiling." *Academy of Management Executive*, 12: 28–42.

Women managers may be particularly well equipped to assist in dismantling the glass ceiling. Researchers have found that having more women in management helped other women to advance into top management and that fewer women in management is correlated with an increase in intentions to quit and actual turnover. A few women in power, in combination with men in power who also support gender equity and see value in diversity, may thus make significant progress.

SUMMARY

Most adult women and men work outside the home, including women with children. Women who work full-time, year-round earn about three-fourths the income of men working full-time, year-round. Women overall have slightly less education than men, although younger women have more education than men, which should affect the male/female wage gap and workforce participation rates in the future. Men and women work in different occupations, and this segregation contributes to the pay gap. Laws passed since the 1960s have improved women's employment, status, and pay, yet many disparities remain. Organizational efforts to reduce gender inequity and commitment to gender diversity are vital to continued progress.

KEY TERMS

Co-ethnic — from the same race or ethnic group.

Disparate impact — when an apparently neutral, evenly applied, practice has a negative effect on the employment of members of protected classes.

Disparate treatment — when an applicant or employee is intentionally treated differently than others are treated based on their group membership.

Gender role socialization — the process by which social institutions, including families, friends, organizations, and the media, form and shape expectations of acceptable behaviors for men and women.

Glass ceiling — an invisible barrier that prevents women, minorities, and people with disabilities from advancing past a certain level in organizations.

Glass escalator — the rapid advancement of men working in female-dominated occupations into management, particularly White men.

Glass walls — invisible barriers that confine minorities and women to certain types of positions within organizations.

Sex segregation — when members of one sex constitute 70% or more of the incumbents of a job.

Sticky floors — when women are clustered in staff roles or in low-level management or below, rather than approaching the glass ceiling.

QUESTIONS TO CONSIDER

1. What is the role of socialization in women's and men's "choice" of occupations and how do these

relationships affect sex segregation and the wage gap?

2. What are some specific individual and organizational steps that could help reduce sex segregation?

3. How are the participation rates, workplace experiences, income, occupations, and poverty of White women and women of color similar and dissimilar? Why are erroneous perceptions about the similarities and differences among these groups so pervasive?

4. Prior to reading this chapter, had you heard of the "glass escalator"? Are you aware of a situation in which a man is the manager or supervisor of a group of women employees?

5. What can individual women do to reduce the influence of sex and gender discrimination on their careers?

ACTIONS AND EXERCISES

1. Interview a person who is employed in a sex-atypical occupation (e.g., a male dental hygienist or female professor of business in a tenure-track position). What factors affected his or her career decision? What background experiences and/or educational requirements were needed to qualify for this particular job? What were the reactions of families, friends, and coworkers? What diversity-related experiences have stood out for this person at work?

2. Conduct a survey of at least ten working professionals. How many men versus women negotiated their starting salary? How many were successful in their negotiations? How much was the increase in salary, if any, after the negotiations? Are any differences apparent after comparing the results for men and women?

3. Create an informal organization chart of the organization in which you work or for which you can gather information. Is there evidence of the glass ceiling, walls, and/or escalators in this organization?

4. Begin observing women in organizations. What evidence do you observe of gender and race-based segregation? Where are women clustered? Are women of color in different positions than White women?

Work and Family

CHAPTER 10

Chapter Objectives

After completing this chapter, readers should have a greater understanding of work and family as an aspect of diversity. Specifically, they should be able to:

❏ *explain changes in workforce participation rates for women with children.*

❏ *discuss legislation and litigation related to work and family.*

❏ *compare parental policies in the United States with those in selected other countries.*

❏ *discuss the effects of having children on the career progress of men and women.*

❏ *explain why family issues, including child and elder care, are relevant to employers.*

❏ *suggest measures organizations may implement to assist employees to cope with work and family issues.*

[1]U.S. Department of Labor. (2009). *Women in the Labor Force: A Databook.* Report 973, Table 6, http://www.bls.gov/cps/wlf-databook.pdf, accessed September 14, 2010.
[2]Glover, S. L., & Crooker, K. J. (1995). "Who Appreciates Family-Friendly Policies: The Impact of Family-Friendly Policies on Organizational Attachment of Parents and Non-Parents." *Personnel Psychology,* 48(2): 247–271; Honeycutt, T. L., & Rosen, B. (1997). Family-Friendly Human Resource Policies, Salary Levels, and Salient Identity as Predictors of Organizational Attraction. *Journal of Vocational Behavior,* 50: 271–290.

Key Facts

Since 1975, labor force participation of U.S. women with children under age 18 has increased from 47% to 71%.[1]

On average, working mothers experience a 5% wage penalty per child.

Women spend seventeen years caring for children and eighteen years caring for aging parents, primarily during their prime working years.

About half of employees are not covered by the Family and Medical Leave Act.

Being "family friendly" is viewed positively by both parents and nonparents; both are more attached to family-friendly organizations.[2]

Over 2.6 million grandparents, the majority of whom are employed, have primary responsibility for their grandchildren under age 18.

Although they have fewer support mechanisms than parents, employed grandparents caring for their grandchildren experience work and family concerns that may be more difficult than those experienced by parents.

Introduction and Overview

In this chapter, we consider several factors related to work and family, including child and elder care, equal pay, pregnancy discrimination, flexible schedules, paid and unpaid leave, and flexible family units. Although these issues do not cover all possible work and family concerns, one or more are relevant to nearly everyone at some point in his or her career. Work and family affect us all.

Historically, men have been viewed as economic providers and women as caretakers of the home. As more women have entered and remained in the workforce, awareness that work and family are not separate and independent spheres has increased. Employers' perceptions about ways that families affect employees' work lives and motivations to work, and employees' perceptions of how their work lives affect their families, are critical in shaping employees' experiences at work. Organizations that help employees to navigate work and family issues effectively are advantaged in recruiting and retaining people who are currently facing these issues as well as those who are not (but likely will be at some point in the future). Researchers have also found correlations between employers' work-family initiatives and stock prices.[3] Organizations in which work and family are viewed as inevitably in conflict often alienate workers with families, which has negative cost and resource acquisition reasons (e.g., Cox and Blake). Consider the possible effects on employees of hostile, irrational statements like the following:

- In *Moore v. Alabama State University* (1997), a supervisor remarked to a pregnant employee while pointing to her extended abdomen: "I was going to put you in charge of the office, but look at you now."[4]

- In *Knussman v. Maryland* (1999, 2001), a state trooper was told he could not take parental leave unless his wife were "in a coma or dead." He was also told that parental leave was for women because "God made women to have babies."[5]

- In *Wells v. City of Montgomery* (2006), a male policeman was passed over for promotion three times because he took leave under the FMLA to care for his three children. A supervisor told him, "Congratulations for taking the most time off for having a baby and not actually having the baby."[6]

The topic of work and family is broad, but the majority of research focuses on issues involving working parents, particularly women, and the negative effects of children on women's earnings, career progress, and full-time work status. Research has focused as well on the organizational measures implemented to ameliorate these effects. In addition, we also examine the positive relationships between having children and men's earnings and employment. We also consider the growing trend of grandparents (many of whom are employed) caring for grandchildren. Lastly, the fact that the U.S. population is aging and employees are increasingly likely to be responsible for both their parents and children leads us to investigate caring for elders while also working.

[3]Arthur, M. M., & Cook, A. (2004). "Taking Stock of Work-Family Initiatives: How Announcements of 'Family-Friendly' Human Resource Decisions Affect Shareholder Value." *Industrial & Labor Relations Review*, 57: 599–613.
[4]Ibid.
[5]Ibid.
[6]Cited in Williams, J. C., & Boushey, H. (2010). "The Three Faces of Work-Family Conflict." Center for American Progress. http://www.worklifelaw.org/pubs/ThreeFacesofWork-FamilyConflict.pdf, accessed September 7, 2010.

▌ HISTORY OF WORK AND FAMILY

The belief that a woman's place is in the home while a man's place is outside the home, earning a living for the family, has shaped the history of work and family in the U.S. culture. In the past, many organizations openly paid men more than the few women they employed, following a "family wage" philosophy. Pay disparities were justified by the belief that, unlike men, women did not have (but were) dependents, a point of view widely accepted until the 1960s.[7]

Minority, poor, and unmarried women have worked outside the home for a long time; much of the outcry about "working women" came about when married, middle-class White women began to join the workforce in increasing numbers.[8] The research focus on middle-class Whites in the past (and to some extent in the present) has exacerbated misperceptions about women's commitment to work.[9] Despite differences among various groups, about 60% of women (compared to about 74% of men) of every racial and ethnic group participate in the workforce. The idea that women do not or should not work does not reflect the reality that women work because they want and need to do so. Representing women as "stay-at-home moms" or as "opting out" of the workforce is an inaccurate picture of the overwhelming majority of women and mothers in the United States and many other countries.[10] Economic pressures, the rise in single parenthood, and the psychological benefits associated with work make women's continued participation in the workforce increasingly likely and normal, rather than unlikely and abnormal. The task for organizations is to ensure that people have the opportunity to work, advance, and be paid fairly without penalty due to their sex or parental status.

▌ RELEVANT LEGISLATION

Federal legislation particularly relevant to work and family issues includes the Equal Pay Act, Title VII of the Civil Rights Act, the Pregnancy

[7]Kramer, L. (1991). *The Sociology of Gender*. New York: St. Martin's Press.

[8]Gerstel, N., & McGonagle, K. (2002). "Job Leaves and the Limits of the Family and Medical Leave Act." In P. J. Dubeck & D. Dunn (Eds.), *Workplace/Women's Place: An Anthology,* 2nd ed. Los Angeles: Roxbury Publishers, pp. 205–215.

[9]Dietz, J. (2010). "Introduction to the Special Issue on Employment Discrimination Against Immigrants." *Journal of Managerial Psychology,* 25: 104–112; Eby, L. T., et al. (2005). "Work and Family Research in IO/OB: Content Analysis and Review of the Literature (1980–2002)." *Journal of Vocational Behavior,* 66: 124–197; Jonsen, K., Maznevski, M. L., & Schneider, S. C. (2011). "Diversity and Its Not So Diverse Literature: An International Perspective." *International Journal of Cross-Cultural Management,* 11(1): 35–62.

[10]Williams, J. C. (2006). "One Sick Child Away from Being Fired: When 'Opting Out' Is Not an Option," San Francisco: Hastings College of Law. http://www.uchastings.edu/site_files/WLL/onesick-child.pdf, accessed September 9, 2010.

Discrimination Act (PDA), the Family and Medical Leave Act (FMLA), and the Lilly Ledbetter Fair Pay Act. The first equal employment legislation to be enforced by the EEOC is the Equal Pay Act of 1963; it is significant to working women who are completely or partially responsible for supporting their families. Title VII offers protection to women who may experience disparate treatment because of misperceptions about their roles as women (and/or as mothers), and to men as well, who may also experience gender discrimination for exercising their responsibilities as fathers or sons in caring for elderly parents. The PDA protects women from discrimination due to pregnancy, but it is also of interest to men, in that it protects their pregnant wives or partners from exclusion from medical and benefits plans that cover other temporary medical issues. The FMLA covers all employees, providing time off, job security, and continuation of benefits during a personal illness; the illness of a spouse, parent, or child; or the birth, adoption, or placement of a foster child. The Lilly Ledbetter Fair Pay Act is the most recently passed legislation relevant to work and family.

Each of these laws has been used by employees to address discriminatory treatment by organizations. In this section, we consider the particular relevance of each one to work and family issues. As in previous chapters, we emphasize that fear of litigation is insufficient to motivate organizations to avoid or address discrimination; that most of the aggrieved parties do not appeal to the EEOC; and that, for a variety of reasons, those who do are unlikely to have their claims accepted for regulatory action or to prevail in litigation. Even so, the flagrant acts of discrimination and harassment that occur despite the laws reinforce their importance and the very real need for them. Compliance with legislation is one of many important steps organizations that value diversity must take.

Equal Pay Act and Title VII

The Equal Pay Act and Title VII are often used concurrently by plaintiffs faced with sex-based pay discrimination in organizations. The former addresses only compensation, while the latter is useful in counteracting discrimination in all employment-related matters, including compensation. Reports of litigation document the existence of overt sex-based pay discrimination (disparate treatment), retaliation for complaining about it, and paying men more than women on the presumptions that men have a family to support or are the heads of households.[11] From the employers' perspective, having a family is often perceived as a positive for men and a negative for women. They often view women as *less* committed to work

---

[11]www.eeoc.gov.

because of commitments to family, and men as *more* committed to work because of family obligations. When children arrive, employers often expect women to cut back on work hours to care for them and men to work longer and harder to provide for them.

But, like men, many women work to support themselves and their families financially and do not decrease commitment to work because of having children and families. The percentage of married couples with children under 18 with both parents employed was 59% in 2009. Although this figure was down from 63% in 2007, the decrease was due in large part to more men losing their jobs during the recession while wives continued (or resumed) working. Despite data like these to the contrary, the perceptions of men as breadwinners and women as unwilling, uncommitted workforce participants are tenacious.

As discussed in Chapter 3, the Equal Pay Act has been somewhat successful in reducing male and female pay disparities, but its effectiveness has been limited by sex segregation. It has been used successfully by many women in situations where men are also employed doing the same or substantially similar work. Three such cases brought by the EEOC in the 1990s were against organizations that paid higher wages and benefits to men than to women in the same jobs. Organizations engaging in such pay discrimination have used terminology like "family" and "head-of-household" allowances to justify the disparities. Tree of Life Christian Schools agreed to pay almost $100,000 to nineteen women who were denied the "family allowances" given to men. In similar cases, two other schools agreed to $48,000 and $80,000 settlements for female teachers who had been denied "head-of-household" allowances.[12] In a case against a nursing home company, the EEOC alleged that female licensed practical nurses (LPNs) were paid less than male LPNs "based on a presumption that men needed a higher salary to support their families."[13] The $40,000 settlement was divided among twelve women and one man whose pay had been reduced in an attempt to cover up the sex-based discrimination.

Pregnancy Discrimination Act of 1978

Recall that the PDA prohibits employers from discrimination because of pregnancy and related medical conditions but does not require pregnancy-related benefits or leave. Pregnancy discrimination is of most interest to women of child-bearing age, but it also applies to the wives or partners of men if they are covered under the male's medical insurance.

---

[12]Highlights of Equal Pay Act Cases. Fiscal Year 1993. http://archive.eeoc.gov/epa/anniversary/epa-highlights.html, accessed September 14, 2010.
[13]Ibid.

These women are protected from pregnancy discrimination enacted under the employers' medical plans. Before passage of the PDA, employers commonly required pregnant women to take leaves of absence or to resign, openly refused to hire pregnant women, and treated pregnancy differently than other medical conditions in terms of leaves and medical benefits.

In 2010, the EEOC received 6,119 charges of pregnancy discrimination and resolved 6,293 (including charges from previous years), but aggrieved parties are unlikely to prevail in pregnancy discrimination cases. Only 25.4% of the resolved cases were resolved with merit, compared to 58.3% judged as having no reasonable cause and 16.3% being closed for administrative reasons. However, as is evident by the $161 million in monetary benefits awarded to aggrieved parties between 1997 and 2009, and another $18 million in 2010, pregnancy discrimination continues to be a significant issue.

Selected Pregnancy Discrimination Cases

EEOC v. Berge Ford, Inc. and Auto Care Center, LLC[14]
No. CIV 02-943 PHX SRB (D. Ariz. June 10, 2004)

The Phoenix District Office alleged that a Mesa, Arizona auto dealership and its parent company violated Title VII/PDA when it fired the charging party because she was pregnant. Prior to her termination, CP had been working for Berge Ford for three to four months as a general services technician; her duties included cleaning, picking up trash, monitoring the front desk, and driving Berge's customer shuttle. Phoenix alleged that the defendants had no problems with CP's job performance, but when they learned she was pregnant they fired her in fear that she might become ill (since she had been experiencing morning sickness) while driving Berge vehicles and expose defendants to liability.

EEOC v. O'Reilly Automotive, Inc., dba O'Reilly Auto Parts[15]
No. 03-1347-WEB (D. Kan. June 16, 2004)

The St. Louis District Office brought this Title VII/PDA case alleging that one of the nation's largest specialty retailers of automotive aftermarket parts, tools, and supplies discharged charging party, an assistant manager at an auto parts store, because she was pregnant. CP's doctor had imposed a 30-pound lifting

---

[14]*EEOC Litigation Settlement Reports—June 2004.* http://archive.eeoc.gov/litigation/settlements/settlement06-04.html, accessed September 14, 2010.
[15]Ibid.

restriction, and although the store manager and district manager agreed that CP could continue working despite the restriction, defendant's Human Resources staff in its Springfield, Missouri headquarters decided she could not work. After CP exhausted her leave under the Family & Medical Leave Act, she was terminated since she was still pregnant and had lifting restrictions. Defendant had permitted other employees with temporary medical conditions to work even though they had lifting restrictions.

Although the PDA does not require that employers provide leave or medical coverage for pregnancy and related conditions, it does require that employers treat pregnancy similarly to other temporary medical conditions. If the employer provides medical benefits, pregnancy benefits should be at the same level, with the same deductibles, co-pay, and other benefits as those provided for other medical conditions. Women who are pregnant must be allowed to continue working as long as they are able to perform their jobs. Women who are temporarily unable to perform their jobs must be treated the same as any other employee with a temporary disability.[16] For example, an employer could provide modified tasks, alternative assignments, disability leave, or unpaid leave.

In the O'Reilly Automotive case, even if pregnancy discrimination were not illegal, the HR staff should have considered the costs associated with attracting and retaining competent, committed workers such as they apparently had in the pregnant employee whom they terminated. Pregnancy is a temporary, short-lived condition; had the employee's weight restrictions been accommodated, her positive employment history could have continued when the pregnancy was over.

Researchers have documented both hostile and benevolent reactions toward pregnant women. Both of the cases we summarized happened in male-dominated environments. In a study assessing reactions toward pregnant women, Michelle Hebl and colleagues found that pregnant women were particularly likely to experience hostility when applying for masculine-type jobs (e.g., corporate lawyer, janitor, surgeon, or farm machinery sales representative) compared to feminine-type jobs (e.g., family lawyer, maid, pediatrician, furniture sales representative).[17] In one study, researchers had women wearing a pregnancy prosthesis pose as job applicants or customers at retail stores. Store employees were more likely

[16]EEOC. "Pregnancy Discrimination." http://www.eeoc.gov/laws/types/pregnancy.cfm, accessed September 14, 2010.
[17]Hebl, M. R., King, E. B., Glick, P., Singletary, S. L., & Kazama, S. (2007). "Hostile and Benevolent Reactions Toward Pregnant Women: Complementary Interpersonal Punishments and Rewards That Maintain Traditional Roles." *Journal of Applied Psychology*, 92(6): 1499–1511.

to be rude to the applicants wearing the prosthesis but benevolent—overly friendly toward and touching—to pregnant customers.[18]

Multiple studies have found that pregnant women who work for family-supportive organizations plan to work later into their pregnancies and return to work sooner after childbirth and are more committed to their organizations. The ability to choose not to work overtime, the length of leave allowed, and supportive coworkers and supervisors also play a part in pregnant women's job satisfaction and their return to work after childbirth.[19]

The Family and Medical Leave Act of 1993

As mentioned, the FMLA allows employees to take up to twelve weeks unpaid leave when ill; on the birth, adoption, or placement of a foster child; or to care for a sick child, parent, or spouse. When on leave, employees' benefits are continued and they are guaranteed the same or a substantially similar job on returning from the leave. Although this act is positive in many regards and is an improvement over having no family leave legislation, the FMLA still fails to meet many of the needs of workers with families. The most obvious inadequacies are that the leave is unpaid, many family members or others in familial-type relationships are not included, and, due to employer-size restrictions and other requirements, about half of working Americans are not covered.

In 2010, in what was called a "win for all families no matter what they look like," the Department of Labor broadened its description of who could be considered a son or daughter under the FMLA to ensure that employees who assume the role of caring for a child had rights to family leave regardless of the legal or biological relationship.[20] This was viewed as a victory for same-sex families with children, grandparents caring for grandchildren, and others assuming parental roles for children. According to Secretary of Labor Hilda L. Solis, "the Labor Department's action today sends a clear message to workers and employers alike: All families, including LGBT families, are protected by the FMLA."[21] This is a good step for those considered sons and daughters, but the limitation of

---

[18]Ibid.

[19]Lyness, K. S., Thompson, C. A., Francesco, A. M., & Judiesch, M. K. (1999). "Work and Pregnancy: Individual and Organizational Factors Influencing Organizational Commitment, Time of Maternity Leave, and Return to Work." *Sex Roles*, 41: 485–508; Glass, J., & Riley, L. (1998). "Family Responsive Policies and Employee Retention Following Childbirth." *Social Forces*, 76(4): 1401–1446; Holtzman, M., & Glass, J. (1999). "Explaining Changes in Mothers' Job Satisfaction Following Childbirth." *Work and Occupations*, 26(3): 365–404.

[20]U.S. Department of Labor (2010, June 22). News release. http://www.dol.gov/opa/media/press/whd/whd20100877.htm, accessed September 7, 2010.

[21]Ibid.

FMLA to married partners is still problematic for unmarried same-sex partners, who would be able to care for each other's children, but not for each other. As a result, some organizations have specifically included family leave coverage for domestic partners; effective January, 2011, the city of Fort Worth, Texas, did so.[22]

For California residents, even more of the inadequacies of the federal provisions of the FMLA were remedied with the California Family Rights Act (2002).[23] Under the act, eligible workers are entitled to six weeks paid leave to care for a newborn, an adopted, or a foster child or to care for a seriously ill parent, child, spouse, or registered domestic partner. The act allowed payments of up to 55% of weekly wages up to a maximum benefit, which in 2010 was $987 per week. This act acknowledges that workers with new children or family health problems need income and that domestic partners are part of families.

Lilly Ledbetter Fair Pay Act of 2009

On January 29, 2009, President Obama signed the Lilly Ledbetter Fair Pay Act, the first legislation passed under his administration. In signing the bill, the president emphasized that "equal pay is by no means just a women's issue—it's a family issue" clearly relevant to working women and their families, who also suffer from pay discrimination.[24] The Fair Pay Act supersedes a 2007 Supreme Court decision that required compensation discrimination charges to be filed within 180 days (or 300 days in some cities and states) of a discriminatory pay decision. It restores the pre-Ledbetter position of the EEOC that with every paycheck that delivers discrimination, a new clock starts. This allows women who experience sex-based pay discrimination more time to file, even when pay discrimination remains unknown for an extended period.[25]

▌ POPULATION, PARTICIPATION, AND EDUCATION

Because the topic of work and family issues covers men and women from all races, ethnic backgrounds, incomes, and ages, generalizations about population size, workforce participation, employment levels, education,

[22]"Fort Worth's New Domestic Partners' Insurance Plan Begins Jan 1," http://www.star-telegram.com/2010/12/25/2727425/fort-worths-new-domestic-partners.html, accessed December 26, 2010.

[23]http://www.paidfamilyleave.org/learn/basics.html, accessed September 14, 2010.

[24]The White House Blog, "Not Just a Woman's Issue." http://www.whitehouse.gov/blog/2010/01/29/not-just-a-womens-issue, accessed September 16, 2010.

[25]Notice concerning the Lilly Ledbetter Fair Pay Act of 2009. http://www.eeoc.gov/laws/statutes/epa_ledbetter.cfm, accessed September 16, 2010.

and income are impossible to sort out by group membership. However, the historical (and somewhat inaccurate) view of women solely as homemakers makes the participation rates of women and mothers one important and easily measured factor. Since 1975, the labor force participation of all women with children under age 18 has increased from 47% to 71%.[26] Women with children under age 3 are also likely to be employed outside the home; about 56% of such women work. Women who are single parents are even more likely to be in the workforce: 76% of such women with children under age 18 work outside the home. Single mothers also work more hours than married mothers do.

Misperception: The majority of women with small children leave the workforce to be "stay-at-home" moms.

Reality: Most women, with or without children of any age, married or unmarried, work outside the home.

Education level is an additional factor that affects women's propensity to be in the workforce even if they have very young children. Among mothers of children under 1 year old, 66.5% with college degrees work, and 73.6% of women with graduate or professional degrees (e.g., J.D. and M.D.) work, compared to 52% of all women with children under 1 year old.[27] Women with higher educational levels face higher opportunity costs of staying home (such as lost income and promotional and developmental opportunities) than women with lower educational levels. Women with more education are more financially able to purchase quality child care and other services (e.g., laundry, house cleaning) that they might themselves provide were they not in the workforce. Feature 10.1 discusses in more detail the education, career aspirations, and workplace strategies of these women, along with media misrepresentations of them.

In 2000, 19% of all families included employed husbands with wives who did not work outside the home, considerably fewer than the 26% of

[26]U.S. Department of Labor. (2009). *Women in the Labor Force: A Databook.* Report 973, Table 6. http://www.bls.gov/cps/wlf-databook.pdf, accessed September 14, 2010; U.S. Bureau of Labor Statistics. "Employment Status of Mothers with Own Children Under 3 Years Old by Single Year of Age of Youngest Child and Marital Status, 2008–09 Annual Averages." http://www.bls.gov/news.release/famee.t06.htm, accessed September 14, 2010.

[27]For education by employment data: Bachu, A., & O'Connell M. (1995). *Fertility of American Women. Current Population Reports.* P20-526. Washington, DC: U.S. Census Bureau. For participation rates for women with children under age 1: U.S. Bureau of Labor Statistics. Table 6, "Employment Status of the Population by Sex, Marital Status, and Presence and Age of Own Children Under 18, 2008–09 Annual Averages." http://www.bls.gov/news.release/famee.t06.htm, accessed September 14, 2010.

FEATURE 10.1	*Education, Career Aspirations, and Work: The Media versus the Data*

A troubling trend in publications and media reports is the suggestion that women, including college-educated and executive women, are less interested in careers than men, preferring instead to be homemakers. Readers may also have personal knowledge of a woman who has left the workforce to be a "stay-at-home mom," which may increase their perceptions that this phenomenon is more frequent than it actually is. What do U.S. Census data and large-scale empirical studies suggest about women and work?

Women of all education levels participate in the workforce and highly educated women are more likely to be in the workforce than women with less education. Education is also correlated with organizational level; the more education a person has, the more money she or he earns, and the higher organizational position that person is likely to attain. Relationships among education, earnings, and employment for men and women and people of all backgrounds are clear. Although returns on educational investment differ for men, women, and people of color and Whites, more educated people of all demographic backgrounds earn more and are more likely to be in the workforce than people with similar backgrounds who have less education. The opportunity costs and inability to use one's investments in human capital that are associated with being out of the workforce, and the ability to afford quality child care, if needed, make educated women more likely to be in the workforce than to leave it in large numbers, as the media have suggested. Women with less education have lower earnings, lower opportunity costs associated with not working, less investment in their education, and less ability to afford quality child care when compared with well-educated women. On the other hand, having a high-earning spouse does enable some women (and a few men) to leave the workforce to rear children, which complicates the relationships between parenting, education, earnings, and workforce participation and further confuses observers without access to research and large-scale data.[28]

What are the expectations of well-educated women for their future careers, workforce participation, and family roles? Alison Konrad, a professor at the Ivey Business School in Western Ontario, has published several empirical studies of women's preferences in job attributes when compared with those of men. In a longitudinal study of M.B.A.s, Konrad found that while women accurately predicted that family demands would affect them at work more than men, women still desired and pursued fulfilling careers, interesting work, and high salaries. For these women, flexibility and control over hours were important. Konrad suggested that organizations wishing to attract, motivate, and retain such highly qualified workers should add flexibility to their career and job offerings.[29]

QUESTIONS TO CONSIDER

1. *What employment-related problems for working women may be caused by perceptions that women often stop working to be "stay-at-home moms"?*

---

[28]Song, Y. (2007). "The Working Spouse Penalty/Premium and Married Women's Labor Supply." *Review of Economics of the Household*, 5: 279–304.

[29]Konrad, A. M. (2003). "Family Demands and Job Attribute Preferences: A 4-Year Longitudinal Study of Women and Men." *Sex Roles: A Journal of Research.* 49(1/2): 35–46.

2. *Does an individual's experience with or personal knowledge of a woman who has left the workforce to stay at home influence the perceptions that many or most women do so?*

3. *What specific recommendations would you make to an organization for it to attract,*

motivate, and retain women and men with child and elder care issues? How would you convince the organization that implementing these recommendations would be a good idea?

households that were maintained by single mothers.[30] For many of these divorced, never married, or widowed mothers, who are the sole or primary source of income for their families, work is not generally an option. Perceptions of single mothers as uncommitted workers do not accurately characterize women who work as providers for their families. In addition, in 2006, 20% of women past child-bearing age did not have children, up from 10% in 1980.[31] Children do not affect the workforce participation of these women, yet because they are women, perceptions that family and child care needs will come before their commitment to work are still likely to affect them negatively.

Misperception: Women work to supplement their husbands' incomes.

Reality: Nearly half of all women are unmarried and 26% of women in married couples earn at least $5,000 more than their employed husbands. When unemployed husbands are included, 34% of women earn more than their husbands.[32]

In summary, in contrast to perceptions that women, particularly mothers, do not work outside the home, the majority of women do, including those with small children. Employers should be careful to avoid basing assumptions about women's ability and willingness to participate in the workforce on whether they are married or currently have or are likely to have children in the future. Women work for the same reasons that men do—to support themselves and, where relevant, their families and children.

▌ EARNINGS

In this section, we consider differential earnings for men and women who are parents. As discussed earlier, having children creates perceptions that

[30]Padavic, I., & Reskin, B. (2002). *Women and Men at Work*, 2nd ed. Thousand Oaks, CA: Pine Forge Press.

[31]Dye, Jane Lawler. (2008). *Fertility of American Women: 2006*. Current Population Reports, P20-558. Washington, DC: U.S. Census Bureau.

[32]U.S. Department of Labor (2008, December). *Women in the Labor Force: A Databook*. http://www.bls.gov/cps/wlf-table25-2009.pdf, accessed September 4, 2010.

men are more committed to work and that women are less committed to work (and more committed to family). These ideas are partially driven by gendered views of men as providers and women as caretakers of the home. These perceptions also correlate with lower earnings for women who are parents compared with those who are not and higher earnings for men who are parents compared with men who are not. Multiple studies using data from the National Longitudinal Survey of Youth (NLSY) have found significant gender differences in earnings and promotion based on marital status and the presence of young children. Beginning its data collection in 1979 using people who were aged 14 to 21 at the time, the NLSY has continued sampling that population. In one study, researchers using data collected in 1979, 1989, and 1996 found that married men were more likely to have been promoted than single men, but married women were less likely to have been promoted than single women. Further, having preschool-aged children was associated with higher promotion rates for men but with lower promotion rates for women. Overall, never-married, childless women had the highest rates of promotion.[33]

In another study, Michelle Budig and Paula England found that women with children earned 7% less per child. Because women with more children have fewer years of experience than those with fewer (or no) children, Budig and England controlled for any negative effects that being out of the workforce rearing children would have on wages. Indeed, part-time work, employment breaks, and having accumulated fewer years of job experience helped to explain a portion of the wage penalty, but a 5% wage penalty for mothers remained even after the researchers controlled for those factors.[34]

The wage penalty may be partly due to perceptions that mothers are less competent than others. In the litigation of *Trezza v. The Hartford Inc.* (1998), a senior vice president was quoted as complaining to the plaintiff about the "incompetence and laziness of women who are also working mothers."[35] Such perceptions may be common; in a study measuring perception of competence of certain groups, mothers were rated by working professionals and by college students similarly to the elderly, blind, and retarded. In contrast,

[33]Cobb-Clark, D., & Dunlop, Y. (1999). "The Role of Gender in Job Promotions." *Monthly Labor Review*, 122(12): 32–38.

[34]Budig, M. J., & England, P. (2001, April). "The Wage Penalty for Motherhood." *American Sociological Review*, 66: 204–225.

[35]Williams, J., & Segal, N. (2002). "The New Glass Ceiling: Mothers—and Fathers—Sue for Discrimination." http://www.wcl.american.edu/gender/workfamily/chilly_climate0211.pdf, accessed September 7, 2010. See also Williams, J. C., & Cooper, H. C. (2004). "The Public Policy of Motherhood." *Journal of Social Issues*, 60(4): 849–865.

business women and women without children are perceived as highly competent.[36]

Researchers have found that male and female managers perceive women as less promotable, poorer performers who fit their jobs less well—because of their having greater work/family conflict than men.[37] These perceptions affect women's likelihood of being promoted. In addition to managers' *perceptions* about men's and women's work/family conflicts, differences in earnings and rates of promotion may also reflect actual behaviors of men and women. Overall, men who become fathers increase their time spent at work, while women who become mothers, particularly married women, decrease their time spent at work. In 2008, while men worked an average of 41.3 hours per week, women worked 36.1—both numbers constitute full-time work, but for hourly wage workers, fewer hours mean lower earnings.[38]

Part-time Work and Earnings

In addition to fewer hours spent in full-time work, part-time work also contributes to lower earnings. Although we have stressed that women, including mothers, do work, more married mothers of dependent children work part-time than single mothers, women without children, and men. Part-time work is one way in which some women address child care needs and greater responsibilities for home and family than men assume. While 89% of men usually work full-time and 11% work part-time, 75% of women usually work full-time and 25% work part-time.[39] Part-time work is associated with fewer job rewards, lower wages, fewer benefits, and shorter career ladders, which are costly to women. Some of the disadvantages of part-time work have long-lasting, significantly negative effects. Seventy-three percent of full-time workers have health insurance through their employers, but only 17% of part-time workers do. Sixty-four percent of full-time workers are included in pension plans, compared with 21% of part-time workers.[40] Recall from Chapter 9 some of the other factors associated with the feminization of poverty.

----

[36]See Cuddy, A. J. C., Fiske, S. T., & Glick, P. (2004). "When Professionals Become Mothers, Warmth Doesn't Cut the Ice." *Journal of Social Issues*, 60(4): 701–718; Fiske, S. T., Cuddy, A. J. C., Glick, P., & Xu, J. (2002). "A Model of (Often Mixed) Stereotype Content: Competence and Warmth Respectively Follow from Perceived Status and Competition." *Journal of Personality and Social Psychology*, 82(6): 878–902; Heilman, M., & Okimoto, T. G. (2008). "Motherhood: A Potential Source of Bias in Employment Decisions." *Journal of Applied Psychology*, 93: 189–198.

[37]Hoobler, J. M., Wayne, S. J., & Lemmon, G. (2009). "Bosses' Perceptions of Family-Work Conflict and Women's Promotability: Glass Ceiling Effects." *Academy of Management Journal*, 52: 939–957.

[38]U.S. Labor Department. (2009, September). *Annual Averages of Women in the Labor Force, a Databook*. Report 1018, Table 21, "Employed Persons by Full- and Part-time Status and Sex, 1970–2008."

[39]Ibid., Table 20.

[40]U.S. General Accounting Office. (2000). "Contingent Workers: Incomes and Benefits Lag Behind Those of the Rest of the Workforce," HEHS-00-76. http://www.gao.gov/new.items/he00076.pdf, accessed September 14, 2010.

Rather than simply offering part-time work as a means of helping working women cope with family needs, organizations can also address wage, benefit, and promotion disparities, lessening the negative impact on women who decide to work part-time. Further, rather than applying any statistic to individual members of a group, or making the assumption that mothers will want to work part-time, employers should instead consider the behaviors of individual employees rather than their sex or marital or parental status in determining raises, promotions, and other rewards.

Some organizations offer flexible scheduling, paid and unpaid leave, job sharing, telecommuting, referral services, and on-site child care as well as part-time work to help employees address work and family needs. Flexible scheduling and leaves are considered in the following sections.

▌ FLEXIBLE SCHEDULES

Flexible schedules, or "flextime," increase the ability of employees to meet both their work and family needs. Although the specifics depend on each employer's rules, generally, in flex-scheduling, employees may vary their start and stop times on a daily, weekly, monthly, or on an as-needed basis, as long as they work a certain minimum number of hours in a specific time period. For example, flextime may allow workers to start and end the work day earlier or later, such as starting at 6 a.m. and ending at 3 p.m. or starting at 9 a.m. and ending at 6 p.m. In a dual-career couple, if both parents used flexible scheduling, one parent could take children to school while the other headed to work early. The parent who arrives at his or her job later in the morning would work later in the evening, while the other parent would leave early to pick the children up from school.

Along with regular flexible scheduling (e.g., 6 a.m. to 3 p.m. or 9 a.m. to 6 p.m. as a regular schedule), some companies also allow flexible flex-scheduling. This even more flexible plan allows workers to vary start and stop times daily if needed, which gives employees the ability to deal with day-to-day emergencies (such as the arriving two hours late because the car wouldn't start) without unplanned absences or being considered tardy. Tardiness, absenteeism, intentions to quit, and turnover are lower and job satisfaction is higher in organizations that allow employees flexibility in scheduling.[41]

[41]Beauregard, T. A., & Henry, Lesley C. (2009) "Making the Link Between Work-Life Balance Practices and Organizational Performance." *Human Resource Management Review*, (19): 9–22; Glover & Crooker, (1995). Narayanan, V. K., & Nath, R. (1982). "A Field Test of Some Attitudinal and Behavioral Consequences of Flexitime." *Journal of Applied Psychology*, 67: 214–218; Pierce, J. L., & Newstrom, J. W. (1983). "The Design of Flexible Work Schedules and Employee Responses: Relations and Process." *Journal of Occupational Behavior*, 4: 247–262.

Flexible scheduling can reduce some of the stress in dealing with work and family issues, but it is not a possibility for many jobs, such as those employing few workers to open a store or other business, teaching, or other place- and time-specific positions in which many people work. As we have discussed, in the United States and much of the world, in most families, women assume the larger proportion of family responsibilities than men. Thus, flexible scheduling would most benefit women in their attempts to integrate work and family. Ironically, men are more likely to work in jobs that allow flexible scheduling than women (see Table 10.1). Consider the female- and male-dominated positions of secretary and executive or elementary school teacher and professor. While the executive may be able to come in late or leave early, the secretary has particular time periods in which she must be at her desk answering phones or greeting clients or customers.[42] The professor's time and place requirements are considerably less restrictive than those for elementary school teachers.[43]

Table 10.1 provides evidence of differences in access to flexible scheduling by sex. Overall, 28.1% of men and 26.7% of women work in jobs with flexible scheduling. White men and women are most likely to have such jobs, and Hispanic and Black men are least likely to work in such jobs. More striking are disparities in access to flexible scheduling for men and women with children. While nearly 30% of men with children under 18 have access to flexible schedules, less than 26% of women do. Access to flexible scheduling also varies by type of job, with managerial and professional workers having more flexibility than others. Workers with lower earnings are more likely to have informal child care arrangements than workers with higher earnings, which are more likely to fall through (causing missed work and related consequences for the worker and employer).[44] Higher earners are more able to pay exorbitant late fees charged at some child care centers. Overall, it seems that workers most in need of flexible scheduling are least likely to have access to it.

Another negative that can arise from a form of flexible scheduling occurs when the employer mandates a flexible scheduling plan and employees have to comply with these variable, or nonstandard, schedules. Under this scheme, employers do not provide a set schedule for workers

---

[42]Because 97% to 98% of secretaries and receptionists are women, "she" is used to refer to them here.
[43]The gendered organizational climate for those in tenure-track positions is noted, however. Williams, J. C., Alon, T., & Bornstein, S. (2006). "Beyond the 'Chilly Climate': Eliminating Bias Against Women and Fathers in Academe." *The NEA Higher Education Journal, Thought in Action*, 22: 79–96.
[44]Williams (2006); Williams, J. C. (2010). *Reshaping the Work-Family Debate: Why Men and Class Matter*. Cambridge: Harvard University Press.

TABLE 10.1 *Access to Flexible Schedules for Full-Time Wage and Salary Workers by Selected Characteristics, May 2004*[45]

Age	Women with Access to Flexible Work Schedules (%)	Men with Access to Flexible Work Schedules (%)
16 years and over	26.7	28.1
16 to 24 years	26.1	20.7
25 to 54 years	27.0	28.7
55 years and over	24.8	30.5
Race and Hispanic Ethnicity		
White	27.8	29.4
Black	20.9	18.5
Asian	22.4	31.3
Hispanic ethnicity (any race)	21.2	16.6
Marital Status		
Married, spouse present	25.9	29.7
Never married	28.9	24.9
Other marital status	25.9	26.6
Presence and Age of Children		
With no own children under 18	27.1	27.1
With own children under 18	25.8	29.6
With own children 6 to 17, none younger	25.5	29.1
With own children under 6	26.4	30.2

Note: Excludes all self-employed persons.

Source: Adapted from Flexible Schedules: Full-Time Wage and Salary Workers by Selected Characteristics, May 2004, Table 30 of *Women in the Labor Force, a Data Book.* (2009, February). Report 1018. U.S. Department of Labor, U.S. Bureau of Labor Statistics.

and instead schedule them on an as-needed basis, calling them in or sending them home when work demands increase or decrease. Inability to arrange child care in advance can make such jobs nearly impossible to hold, further disadvantaging low-wage workers and decreasing the possibility that they will be able to work successfully. When an hourly worker is sent

[45]Persons with flexible schedules are able to vary or make changes in their beginning and ending hours of work, whether or not they have a formal flextime program on their job.

home because of low workload (e.g., low customer traffic in a store), she or he is unlikely to obtain a reduced price or a refund for the child care that was arranged. Mandatory overtime with little or no advance notice is particularly troublesome for those with child or parental care responsibilities and sometimes results in termination of those unable to comply.[46]

Flexible Schedules for Singles

Employers should not presume that singles—employees without partners and who do not have children—should be more willing to work excessive hours or unreasonable schedules, travel consistently, or perform duties that would not be expected or asked of employees with family needs.[47] All employees (regardless of their family status) could make use of flexible work schedules, leaves, and other benefits primarily associated with families.[48] Outside of parenting responsibilities, religious, community, school, or other nonwork commitments can make flexible scheduling highly desirable to all employees. Single employees repay employers who offer such benefits to them through greater willingness to provide extra help, such as helping peers or taking over work for absent employees, when needed.[49]

▌ Unpaid and Paid Leaves

As the previous section pointed out, Whites and men are most likely to have access to flexible scheduling to assist them in addressing work and family needs. Access to leave under the FMLA is also differentially available to different populations. The FMLA is applicable to employers having fifty or more employees; women and Hispanics are more likely to work for the smallest employers (having ten or fewer employees).[50] Naomi Gerstel and Katherine McGonagle reported that 39% of people making $20,000 or less and 66% of people making $50,000 or more worked for firms that fit FMLA criteria; lower earners were significantly

[46]Williams (2006).

[47]ten Brummelhuis, L. L., & Van Der Lippe, T. (2010). "Effective Work-Life Balance Support for Various Household Structures," *Human Resource Management*, 49(2): 173–193.

[48]Ibid.

[49]Ibid.

[50]Holzer, H. (1998). "Why Do Small Establishments Hire Fewer Blacks than Larger Ones?" *Journal of Human Resources*, 33(4): 896–915.

less likely to be working for firms covered by the FMLA.[51] Overall, about half of U.S. workers are not covered by the FMLA.[52] As important as questions about which groups of employees are more likely to have access to family leave under the FMLA are questions about whether employees take leave when it is available, what the career outcomes are for employees who do take leave, and what employers can do to help employees deal with needs for leave.

Many employees who have access to and need for family leave do not take it even when it is available to them partly because such leaves are unpaid. In some European countries (e.g., Sweden) and in a few states (e.g., California), some family or maternity leaves provide all or a portion of employees' salary for certain periods of time. Under the FMLA, however, leaves are unpaid, even though the health emergencies or childbirth that necessitate time off from work make having income even more important.

Career Outcomes for Employees Who Take Leaves of Absence

Michael Judiesch and Karen Lyness investigated, from the point of view of human capital and gendered organizational theories, the effects of leaves of absence on rewards and promotions for 11,815 managers in a financial services organization.[53] **Human capital** theorists argue that while on leave people fail to accumulate valuable "human capital," such as job knowledge, training, and expertise and that this negatively affects their subsequent job performance and, thus, their career progress. In **gendered organizational cultures** managers reward those who set aside personal and family commitments and are dedicated to their jobs. Both theories suggest that people who take family leave will suffer career penalties as a result of doing so.

Only 5% of the nearly 12,000 managers in the Judiesch and Lyness study had taken leaves of absence, but those who did were less likely to be subsequently promoted and received lower salary increases than those who did not take leave. As an example, a 35-year-old manager who had taken a leave of absence would have had a 36% probability of promotion and would have received $7,799 in increases. In contrast, a manager who had similar qualifications and time on the job but had not taken a leave of absence would have

[51]Gerstel, N., & McGonagle, K. (2002). "Job Leaves and the Limits of the Family and Medical Leave Act." In P. Dubeck & D. Dunn (Eds.), *Workplace, Women's Place*, 2nd ed. Los Angeles: Roxbury Publishers, pp. 205–215; American Association of University Women. http://www.aauw.org/takeaction/policyissues/familymedical_leave.cfm, accessed September 14, 2010.

[52]Commission on Family and Medical Leave. (1996). "A Workable Balance: Report to Congress on Family and Medical Leave Policies." http://digitalcommons.ilr.cornell.edu/cgi/viewcontent.cgi?article=1002&context=key_workplace&sei-redir=1#search="51Commission+on+Family+and+Medical+Leave+(1996).+â••A+Workable+Balance:+Report+to+Congress", accessed September 14, 2010.

[53]Judiesch, M. K., & Lyness, K. S. (1999). "Left Behind? The Impact of Leaves of Absence on Managers' Career Success." *Academy of Management Journal, 42(6): 641–651.*

had a 44% probability of promotion and would have received $8,462 in salary increases. In a study of Australian employees of a public sector agency, researchers found that employees who took leaves of absence were penalized career-wise, and these penalties were viewed as legitimate, despite the employer's statement of support for work and family initiatives.[54] Because women are more likely to take leaves of absence than men, women's promotions and earnings are most negatively affected by taking leaves.

▋ SAME-SEX COUPLES IN FAMILY RELATIONSHIPS

Important differences exist in the levels of workforce participation in families with same-sex partners compared with heterosexual partners. In contrast to some families headed by married, heterosexual couples, in which women are more likely to work fewer than forty hours, both partners in most families headed by lesbian and gay male couples work full-time. A study of workplace attitudes toward lesbian mothers suggests that stereotypical perceptions of lesbians and views that lesbians are unlikely to be mothers result in their being preferred over heterosexual women as employees. In part, this may be due to the expectation that lesbians will not get married and stop working to rear children (which, as discussed earlier, is a common misperception about heterosexual women). Lesbians indeed earn more than heterosexual women and lesbian mothers are perceived as more competent than heterosexual mothers.[55]

It is frequently true (although becoming less so) that organizations do not recognize and support the familial relationships of same-sex partners. In some situations, gays and lesbians may not have disclosed their sexual orientation at work. In other cases, even when someone is out at work, organizational policies may not include same-sex partner benefits. Lack of such benefits negatively affects same-sex partnerships: through medical costs if one partner is not covered by another plan, lack of coverage for a surviving partner through pension plans, and inability to take family leave to care for nonmarital partners. As discussed in Chapter 11, Google includes same-sex partners among the family members that the company considers covered by the FMLA.[56]

----

[54]McDonald, P., Bradley, L., & Brown, K. (2008). "Visibility in the Workplace: Still an Essential Ingredient for Career Success?" *The International Journal of Human Resource Management,* 19(12): 2198–2215.

[55]Peplau, L. A., & Fingerhut, A. (2004). "The Paradox of the Lesbian Worker." *Journal of Social Issues,* 60(4): 719–735.

[56]Bernard, T. S. (2010, June 30). "The Tax Treatment of Domestic Partner Benefits." *New York Times,* http://bucks.blogs.nytimes.com/2010/06/30/the-tax-treatment-of-domestic-partner-benefits/, accessed July 22, 2010.

▌ Men, Work, and Family

Much of this chapter has focused on work and family issues as they affect women, because women are in fact disproportionately involved in working outside the home while concurrently performing more of the household and child care tasks associated with families. However, increasing numbers of men desire to and do participate in family and child care. As discussed in the previous section, for gay couples, gender-role stereotypes that prescribe certain responsibilities to men and others to women are significantly diminished; both partners participate in housework and child care. Husbands in heterosexual couples contribute more to child care and housework when their wives work full-time and when their wives contribute a larger proportion of the family income.[57] More male participation in family and home care is beneficial to husbands, wives, their relationships, and children, who grow up with less rigid gender-role stereotypes.[58]

Misperception: Women are better at family and home care than men.

Reality: Family and home care is learned behavior; participation by men is good for men, women, and children.

Unfortunately, many of the men who participate in caring for their children experience negative reactions for doing so from their employers and peers at work. In conjunction with the gendered organizational cultures that value and reward employees who put work first and other things (including family) second, men who participate in family care are harshly penalized, as are women. Stereotypical gender roles and perceptions about what men and women should do create expectations that men should have wives who take care of the family responsibilities, freeing men to focus on organizational demands.

Reflective of their gendered organizational culture and women's greater responsibilities for child care, researchers in Japan recently found that flextime, maternity leave, child care leave, and nursing care leave were significantly related to the job turnover of women (but not men).[59]

---

[57]Coltrane, S. (1996). *Family Man: Fatherhood, Housework, and Gender Equity*. New York: Oxford University Press.
[58]Ibid.; Chafetz, J. (1997). "I Need a 'Traditional Wife.'" In D. Dunn (Ed.), *Workplace/Women's Place*. Los Angeles: Roxbury Publishers, pp. 116–124.
[59]Yanadori, Y., & Kato, T. (2009). "Work and Family Practices in Japanese Firms: Their Scope, Nature and Impact on Employee Turnover." *International Journal of Human Resource Management*, 20(2): 439–456.

Some research suggests that men who participate in family care may be more strongly sanctioned than women who do so because of perceptions that women are expected to care for families while men are not. This may be particularly likely for men who work in lower-status, male-typed jobs.[60] These negative perceptions of what men "should do" are outdated and problematic in the face of the increasing numbers of men who play and desire to play an active role in child rearing.

▌ BEYOND THE FAMILY: SOCIETY, ORGANIZATIONS, AND FAMILY ISSUES

Relationships among society, organizations, and the family are closely intertwined. In her book *The Sociology of Gender*, Laura Kramer described this relationship well:

> ... even if the members of a household reject broader social norms and arrange their own divisions of labor and responsibility, these individuals will find their choices limited to some degree by larger social arrangements outside their control. For example, as long as the average man earns 40% more than the average women, economic factors rather than personal preferences will guide the choice of which parent will take an unpaid parental leave from work. Social policies regarding parental leave, sex disparities in earnings, the practice of mandatory overtime, and the availability of quality child care all inhibit particular families as they try to arrange their lives as best suits their members.[61]

As an example, when considering the need to take unpaid family leave, gender differences in earnings play a role. In most married-couple families, men earn more than women. In such families, twelve weeks without pay would more negatively affect the family income if the man, rather than the woman, took leave. According to Kramer's arguments, even in families that resist gender-role stereotyping, if a child were ill and required a parent to take leave, the lower-earning parent, who is more likely to be the woman, would take leave. Further, were family leave available for employees to care for parents-in-law, it is likely that many women would also take unpaid family leave to care for in-laws as well as for their own parents because of gender disparities in earnings. In this case, the exclusion of parents-in-law from the FMLA reduces the likelihood that the gender-based expectation of women as caregivers and

---

[60]Williams & Boushey (2010).
[61]Kramer, L. (1991), p. 168. As shown in Table 13.3, the average wage gap for full-time workers is now closer to 30% than in 1991.

women's lower earnings would lead to their taking leave to care for parents-in-law. Relieving working women of this responsibility (and the associated negative employment outcomes of taking leave) is a positive outcome of the stipulation, but it may also negatively affect families' incomes and not respect true care-giving desires.

Another societal, organizational, and family concern is the need of working parents for quality child care. Multiple studies document the relationship between the quality of child care and children's current and future well-being. Despite this, without child care subsidies from the U.S. government (as exist for public schools for children in kindergarten through college), care for the youngest children is often haphazard and of low quality. When child care arrangements fall through (a friend, relative, neighbor, or provider with unreliable transportation, for example), poor workers are faced with the dilemma of missing work and being fired or, in the extreme, leaving young children home alone or in a car outside work, often with deadly consequences.[62] Recent headlines publicizing the dilemmas of single women who have such child care emergencies but fear job loss attest to the need to develop public and organizational policies to address work-family conflicts. Researchers have also documented relationships between mothers' satisfaction with child care, their financial concerns, and job satisfaction, further emphasizing the relevance of these issues to organizational costs.[63]

Misperception: Relationships within families are independent of organizations and society.

Reality: Society and organizations significantly affect relationships within families.

▌ FAMILY POLICIES IN SELECTED COUNTRIES

The United States lags other developed nations by a great deal in its efforts to help the population manage work and family concerns, as shown in Table 10.2. The relatively recent implementation of the FMLA (1993) provides less than half of U.S. workers with a small amount of

[62]Moredock, W. (2007, August 8). "South Carolina Shares Blame with Sametta Heyward." *Charleston City Paper,* http://www.charlestoncitypaper.com/charleston/south-carolina-shares-blame-with-sametta-heyward/Content?oid=1110883, accessed September 15, 2010; Williams (2006).
[63]Poms, L. W., Botsford, W. E., Kaplan, S. A., Buffardi, L. C., & O'Brien, A. S. (2009). "The Economic Impact of Work and Family Issues: Child Care Satisfaction and Financial Concerns of Employed Mothers." *Journal of Occupational Health Psychology,* 14(4): 402–413.

Table 10.2 *Selected Characteristics of Family Policies in Selected Countries*

	Maternity Leave Policies	Paternity Leave
Canada	17 weeks unpaid, job-protected leave; additional 35 weeks unpaid, job-protected leave if combined with maternity leave, to care for newborn or newly adopted child. If employee paid into Employee Insurance Fund, depending on job tenure and earnings, portion of earnings will be paid during entire leave.	37 weeks unpaid, job-protected leave to care for newborn or newly adopted child. If employee paid into Employee Insurance Fund, depending on job tenure and earnings, portion of earnings will be paid during entire leave.
United Kingdom	26 weeks, with most mothers usually qualifying for paid leave. Additional unpaid leave available for up to 26 weeks.	1 or 2 weeks; most fathers qualify for paid paternity leave. Additional 26 weeks paternity leave (some paid) available if mother returns to work.
United States	Up to 12 weeks unpaid, same or similar job-protected leave.	Up to 12 weeks unpaid, same or similar job-protected leave.
Netherlands	16 weeks, 100% salary under Sickness Benefits Act. If pregnancy results in "incapacity for work" 100% of salary for up to 1 year during illness. Otherwise, additional parental leave for 13 weeks at 100% of salary, and 26 weeks unpaid leave.	2 days, 100% salary for childbirth. Also parental leave for 13 weeks at 100% salary.
Norway	3 weeks prior to birth, 6 weeks after, 100% salary; may also take 44 weeks at 100% salary or 54 weeks at 80% salary, shared with father.	6 weeks, 100% salary; may also take 44 weeks at 100% salary or 54 weeks at 80% salary, shared with mother.
Italy	5 months, 100% salary; additional 6 months at 30% pay possible.	3 months at 80% salary.
Russia	10 weeks before birth, 10 weeks after, with payments as specified by law.	10 weeks after birth.
Sweden	7 weeks before and 7 weeks after delivery at 100% salary, followed by parental leave of 56 weeks at 100% (if 20% paid by employer) or 80% of salary, 12 weeks at low flat rate and 12 weeks unpaid, 8 weeks lost if not taken by father.	2 weeks, 100% salary; parental leave of 56 weeks at 100% (if 20% paid by employer) or 80% of salary, 12 weeks at low flat rate and 12 weeks unpaid, 8 weeks lost if not taken by father.
Australia	52 weeks, unpaid.	12 weeks unpaid if primary caregiver; otherwise, 1 week unpaid.

Source: Adapted from "Family Leave in the U.S., Canada, & Global," *Catalyst 2009.* http://www.catalyst.org/file/155/qt_family_leave.pdf, accessed September 16, 2010.

unpaid time off for family needs, including pregnancy and parenting. Lower-wage workers, women, and some minorities are more likely to work for smaller organizations that are not covered by the FMLA, to be ineligible because they do not meet the required number of hours worked per year, or to be unable to afford time off without pay.

In the United States, less than half of all working women receive any paid leave during the first twelve weeks after pregnancy, and only

7% of employers offer paid paternity leave.[64] In contrast, many other developed countries have long offered mandatory paid maternity and parental leaves of more than twelve weeks. Compared to the United States, it appears that some countries view parenting as a social responsibility that benefits everyone and thus provide support for those who parent. Some of those countries have responded to very low birth rates by increasing maternity and paternity leaves and benefits; reducing penalties for having children increases the likelihood that citizens will have them. Facilitating women's contributions to the economy benefits everyone as well.

In 1942, in response to the need for women workers while men were away serving in the military, the U.S. government passed the Lanham Act, which subsidized child care across the country during the war for mothers working in defense industries. After the war ended, however, 2,800 of the 3,000 centers that had been opened were closed, leaving 1.5 million children without services.[65] At present, many countries offer government subsidized or funded child care for young children, much like public schools do in the United States for older children. In Finland, Denmark, Sweden, Belgium, and France, one-third to one-half of all infants and almost all preschool-aged children have access to publicly supported child care.[66] In the United States, only 1% of infants and 14% of preschool-aged children are offered publicly supported child care; on the other hand, the costs of public education for older children (kindergarten through college) are highly subsidized by taxes. As one reflection of the differences in maternity and parental leave and access to child care, 89% of mothers in Finland and 57% of mothers in the United States are employed.[67]

■ ELDER CARE

Although most research on work and family focuses on children and child care, elder care is growing in importance as a work and family issue. People can choose whether to become parents, but everyone has or has had parents and other elderly loved ones. Indeed, as the U.S. population ages

---

[64]Gornick, J. C., & Meyers, M. K. (2003). *Families That Work: Policies for Reconciling Parenthood and Employment*. New York: Russell Sage Foundation.

[65]Frohmann, A. (1978). "Day Care and the Regulation of Women's Workforce Participation." *Catalyst*, 1(2): 5–17.

[66]Martin, G. T., Jr. (1991). "Family, Gender, and Social Policy." In L. Kramer (Ed.), *The Sociology of Gender*. New York: St. Martin's Press, pp. 323–345; Gornick, J. C., Meyers, M. K., & Ross, K. E. (1998). "Public Policies and the Employment of Mothers: A Cross-National Study." *Social Science Quarterly*, 79(1): 35–54.

[67]Ibid.

and life spans increase, more people find themselves caring for both their children and their aging elders; such individuals are called **the sandwich generation.** The National Alliance for Caregiving and American Association of Retired Persons (AARP) estimate that 44 million adults provide unpaid care to another adult and 26 million of them work or have worked while doing so.[68] Similar to child care, women participate in elder care more than men, often caring for their own aging parents as well as for their spouse or partner's parents. Women working full-time are four times as likely as men working full-time to be primary care givers to elderly relatives, spending an average of seventeen years caring for children and eighteen years aiding aging parents.[69] These years are all or nearly all of a working woman adult's employment years. In response to elder caregiving needs, caregivers may come in late, leave early, miss work, take leaves of absence, retire early, or transfer to part-time jobs.[70]

Employees with elder care needs are increasingly requesting assistance from their employers.[71] Major corporations such as Bank of America, Blue Cross/Blue Shield, and Wells Fargo offer assistance with elders, including care referrals, help with finding and financing in-home care services and long-term care insurance. Wells Fargo's progressive program includes the employee's spouse, parents, parents-in-law, grandparents, and grandparents-in-law as eligible dependents.[72] Unlike the FMLA, Wells Fargo acknowledges people's real responsibilities toward a larger group of elders and loved ones than solely parents.

▌ PARENTING AGAIN: GRANDPARENTS CARING FOR GRANDCHILDREN

Although older adults are often cared for by their children, they sometimes become **parents again.** The term *parenting again* refers to those grandparents who become responsible for their grandchildren due to teen pregnancy, substance abuse or imprisonment of the parents, child abuse, neglect, and

---

[68]"Adult Caregivers Looking for Elder Care Benefit Packages." (2005, February 11). http://www .bizjournals.com/jacksonville/stories/2005/02/14/focus2.html, accessed September 14, 2010; "Caregiving in the United States." (2004). National Alliance for Caregiving and American Association of Retired Persons. http://www.caregiving.org/data/04execsumm.pdf, accessed September 14, 2010.

[69]Martin, G. T., Jr. (1991). "Family, Gender, and Social Policy." In L. Kramer (Ed.), *The Sociology of Gender.* New York: St. Martin's Press, pp. 323–345.

[70]"Caregiving in the U.S.". (2004). http://www.caregiving.org/data/04execsumm.pdf, accessed April 10, 2011.

[71]"Adult Caregivers Looking for Elder Care Benefit Packages." (2005, February 11). http://www .bizjournals.com/jacksonville/stories/2005/02/14/focus2.html, accessed September 14, 2010.

[72]Ibid.

abandonment, or death of the child's parents. These grandparents may have legal custody of their grandchildren or they may be caring for the children without having custody. At some point, nearly 11% of all grand-parents care for their grandchildren for at least six months.[73] In 2008, 2.6 million people indicated they had primary responsibility for co-resident grandchildren younger than 18, an increase from the 2000 Census.[74] Sixty-two percent (1.6) million of these grandparents are in the labor force and 38% of the grandparents had been caring for their grandchildren for more than five years, creating lengthy work-family conflicts for them.

The circumstances leading to children being cared for by a grand-parent often cause those children to have special emotional, physical, and psychological needs that may negatively affect grandparents at work. These special needs (and other normal needs of children) can be more disruptive for grandparents than for parents. In one study, 40% of grandparents missed or were late to work or had to leave work suddenly because of grandchildren.[75] These are issues similar to those experienced by working parents but may be exacerbated by the grandparents' reduced access to parental assistance, lower tolerance by employers, and more difficulty in obtaining subsequent employment after job loss than (younger) parents. As discussed in Chapter 13, when older workers lose their jobs, it takes them longer to become re-employed than younger workers.

■ RECOMMENDATIONS FOR INDIVIDUALS

At some point in their lives, most people are faced with one or more of the work and family issues that have been considered in this chapter. Although societal and organizational constraints affect everyone, edu-cated, conscious choice in decision making about work and family can play an important role in navigating work and family issues successfully. For example, to help deal with these issues, Chafetz suggests "reducing standards" for household cleanliness, purchasing services one would

[73]Fuller-Thomson, E., Minkler, M., & Driver, D. (1997). "A Profile of Grandparents Raising Grand-children in the United States." *Gerontologist*, 37(3): 406–411.

[74]Facts for Features. Grandparents Day 2010: September 12. http://www.census.gov/newsroom/releases/pdf/cb10ff-16_grandparent.pdf, accessed September 14, 2010; Simmons, T., & Dye, J. L. (2003). *Grandparents Living with Grandchildren: 2000*. Washington, DC: U.S. Census Bureau.

[75]Pruchno, R. (1999). "Raising Grandchildren: The Experience of Black and White Grandmothers." *The Gerontologist*, 39: 209–221. For additional research on the characteristics and experiences of custodial grandparents, see Ruiz, D., Zhu, C., & Crowther, M. (2003). "Not on Their Own Again: Psychological, Social, and Health Characteristics of Custodial African American Grandmothers." *Journal of Women and Aging*, 15(2): 167–187.

normally perform (e.g., laundry, grocery shopping), and refusing to comply with demands of "greedy employers."[76]

Refusing to comply with demands of employers might prove detrimental to continued employment, but making an educated choice from among all possible employers would be a useful strategy. After assessing individual life plans and goals, people should actively seek employment in organizations that offer programs such as flexible scheduling, child and elder care assistance, paid parental leaves, and other family-friendly programs as appropriate to their current or expected needs in the future. If one lives in a nontraditional family, for example, investigating companies that provide benefits for nonmarital partners, leave time when a partner is ill, and other relevant programs is recommended. Women and men wishing for equity in parenting, household, and child care roles can resist gendered notions of who is responsible for what.

Because women are often stereotyped as uncommitted workers and as likely to leave the workforce when or if children arrive, they should make sure that their plans for work and continued development and opportunity at work are known. The widely held misperceptions that women with children do not work can and do negatively affect women who fully intend to continue working despite having children. If a woman intends to continue working full-time, she should be aware that perceptions may negatively affect her opportunities and outcomes unless she makes concerted, purposeful efforts and engages in behaviors designed to combat them. She should recognize that working while parenting and parenting while working are the norm, rather than the exception. Expectations for a "balance" at all times are not reasonable. During certain periods, work will take precedence over family; at other times, family needs will take precedence over work. Realistic expectations, dependable partners, care providers, and back-up helpers, along with carefully chosen employers and job assignments, make coping with work and family more successful.

If a woman does decide to temporarily reduce hours, she should begin working part-time or take a leave and make an effort to remain connected to decision makers and key activities at work. Remaining connected will make the return to full-time work easier and more successful.

∎ Recommendations for Organizations

As discussed earlier in the chapter, career and job satisfaction, organizational commitment, coming back from maternity leave, absence, and turnover are related to organizational work/family policies. People who

---

[76]Chafetz (1997).

work for organizations that are family friendly are more loyal, attached, and committed to their organizations and have greater job satisfaction. Both parents and those without children or experiences with work and family conflicts appreciate the organizational support provided by work-family policies. In addition to the lower costs associated with reduced absence and turnover, being more attractive to job applicants (e.g., resource acquisition) as a result of being family friendly, and being viewed positively by external organizational stakeholders for good work-family policies, firms that undertake new initiatives and established policies experience increases in share prices.[77]

Organizations can implement several policies to assist employees in successfully coping with work and family, including:

- recognizing the role that policies *and* supportive supervisor/manager behavior play; policies without commitment are ineffective.[78]
- building flexibility and choice for employees into scheduling, work location, part-time work, travel, and overtime.
- eliminating the practice of inconsistent scheduling and overtime that prevents employees from being able to obtain child and elder care.
- providing job guarantees for those taking maternity and family leave that exceeds twelve weeks and providing child care subsidies for qualified employees.
- implementing procedures to provide some income for employees needing family leave.
- assisting employees who opt for part-time work or leaves of absence to remain connected to the organization and to return to full-time work.
- allowing employees to decide which people constitute their family and providing the same time off, leaves, and other benefits as are provided for legally recognized families.
- recognizing that there is and should be life outside of work for employees, whether single or married, parents or not.[79]

---

[77]See Cook, A. (2009). "Connecting Work-Family Policies to Supportive Work Environments." *Group and Organization Management*, 34: 206–240; ten Brummelhuis, L. L., & Van Der Lippe, T. (2010); Arthur, M. (2003). "Work-Family Initiatives and Share Price Reaction: An Institutional Perspective." *Academy of Management Journal*, 46: 497–505.

[78]Thompson, C. A., Beauvais, L. L., & Lyness, K. S. (1999). "When Work-Family Benefits Are Not Enough: The Influence of Work-Family Culture on Benefit Utilization, Organizational Attachment, and Work-Family Conflict." *Journal of Vocational Behavior*, 54: 392–415.

[79]See Casper, W. J., Weltman, D., & Kwesiga, E. (2007). "Beyond Family-Friendly: The Construct and Measurement of Singles-Friendly Work Culture." *Journal of Vocational Behavior*, 70: 478–501; Hamilton, E. A., Gordon, J. R., & Whelan-Berry, K. S. (2005). "We're Busy Too: Understanding the Work-Life Conflict of Never Married Women Without Children." Paper presented at the annual meeting of the Academy of Management, Honolulu.

SUMMARY

In contrast to perceptions and reports in the popular press, the majority of women participate in the workforce, including women with children. On average, women work fewer hours when working full-time and are more likely to work part-time than men. Fewer hours contribute to women's lower wages, but even when hours are taken into account, women experience a 5% wage penalty per child. Part-time work has fewer benefits, security, and access to pensions, resulting in long-term negative effects for women. Current issues in work and family include different family relationships, such as same-sex partnerships, grandparents rearing grandchildren, and extended families; employers should let employees determine who makes up a "family" for them. Flexible scheduling and family leave can help employees cope with their particular work and family needs, and the availability of flexible scheduling positively affects employees' commitment to their employers and career satisfaction.

Individuals should not have to try to make the impossible choice between work and family. The more employers are able to assist employees to be effective workers and family members, the better for employees, employers (including many of the Cox and Blake reasons for valuing diversity), and society (including the future workforce—children) as a whole. Men, women, and organizations should resist gender-role stereotyping. Participation in family care and life outside of work is normal for both sexes and is beneficial to men, women, organizations, and society.

KEY TERMS

Gendered organizational culture — an organizational culture that rewards employees who are dedicated to their jobs and set aside personal and family commitments for job responsibilities.

Human capital — factors such as education, job knowledge, training, and expertise that positively affect job performance and earnings.

Sandwich generation — people rearing children while also caring for or assisting with care of their elderly parents.

Parents again — grandparents caring for grandchildren, with or without having formal custody.

QUESTIONS TO CONSIDER

1. Why do you think perceptions are so pervasive and persistent that women do not work or are uncommitted workers when they do work? Do you know women who are uncommitted workers? Do you know men who are uncommitted workers? Do you know women and men who are highly committed workers? Consider similar questions about perceptions of women and men as incompetent.

2. Negative perceptions about the competence of women who are mothers were evident in the research and the court cases discussed in the chapter. What factors contribute to these negative perceptions?

3. Carefully review the comparisons of workers' access to flexible schedules by

race, ethnicity, and sex in Table 10.1. What clear differences exist?

4. What are some possible reasons for state-subsidized K–12 and college education but not child care in the United States?

Actions and Exercises

1. Interview two working parents with children under 12 (if applicable, answer one set of these questions yourself). Ask questions related to work and family, such as who provides child care after school hours (or all day, if required), how having children affects their work, how their employer reacts to child-related absences, and so forth. What is the age, race, and sex of each interviewee? Compare the answers of both interviewees and document your findings.

2. If you know a grandparent who is responsible for his or her grandchildren, interview that person and ask the same questions as in question 1 above. Document and compare your findings for both parents and the grandparent.

3. Search the EEOC Web site (http://www.eeoc.gov) for the most recent pregnancy discrimination cases. Summarize the most egregious case and settlement. What kind of organization was involved? How might the situation have been avoided?

4. Investigate and document the work-family programs of three organizations, including your current employer or an organization for which you'd like to work. How are they similar and different?

5. Prepare a presentation to convince an employer to offer family-friendly programs. Include such things as impacts on absence, turnover, organizational commitment, job satisfaction, and other relevant items. What else should you include?

6. Conduct research (library, Internet, or estimates from users of the relevant services) to construct a table containing the following information for the city in which you live:
   a. Annual costs of care for a child under age 5
   b. Annual costs of care for a school-aged child between 5 and 11 needing after-school care and daily summer care or camps
   c. Annual costs for house-cleaning every other week
   d. Annual costs for laundry services for a family of four
   e. Annual costs associated with eating out three nights per week at a moderately priced family restaurant
   f. Mean and median annual income for households in the United States or in the city in which you live, if available
   g. Ratio of the sum of items a–e to item f

Sexual Orientation

CHAPTER 11

Chapter Objectives

After completing this chapter, readers should have a greater understanding of work and family as an aspect of diversity. Specifically, they should be able to:

❏ *discuss the experiences of sexual minorities in organizations, in particular, gays and lesbians.*

❏ *explain similarities and differences between sexual minorities and other non-dominant groups.*

❏ *compare population estimates, education, and income levels of gays and lesbians with those of heterosexual men and women.*

❏ *examine misperceptions about sexual minorities at work, negative outcomes associated with being closeted, and benefits of full inclusion of sexual minorities.*

❏ *suggest individual and organizational measures that can be employed to include sexual minorities as valued employees, customers, and constituents.*

Key Facts

No federal laws currently prohibit sexual orientation discrimination in private workplaces in the United States, but many cities, states, and organizations do prohibit such discrimination.

Regardless of their sexual orientation, employees are more committed to organizations in which sexual orientation discrimination is not tolerated.

Organizations with inclusive GLBT (gay, lesbian, bisexual, and transgender) policies financially outperform competitors with less inclusive policies.[1]

[1]Wang, P., & Schwarz, J. (2010). "Stock Price Reactions to GLBT Nondiscrimination Policies." *Human Resource Management*, 49(2): 195–216.

Introduction and Overview

The issue of sexual orientation is an emotionally charged one; it arouses feelings similar to, yet also very different from, those aroused by other diversity issues. The experiences of sexual minorities with discrimination, harassment, exclusion, and hate crimes are similar in many ways to those of other minority groups. Although sexual minorities have not suffered slavery, near annihilation, or lynching, certain factors create problems for gays that are not experienced by other non-dominant group members. For example, members of other minority groups (Blacks or women) are not viewed as having chosen their group membership. Nor are members of other minority groups commonly faced with the dilemma of informing others of their group membership; race, sex, and age range are more likely to be obvious to observers.

A key difference between the difficulties posed by the invisibility of **sexual orientation** and the difficulties of being Black was pointed out by a Black lesbian who observed, "you don't have to tell your mother you're Black."[2] As discussed in Chapter 4, through racial socialization, many Black parents discuss race-based prejudice and discrimination with their children from an early age, which can help them adjust and cope. Parents of gays and lesbians may not even be aware that their children are gay,[3] and even if they know their child is gay, heterosexual parents do not have the personal experience with antigay prejudice and discrimination to help children learn to adjust. Thus, compared with Blacks and other minority group members, gays and lesbians often do not learn to deal with anti-gay discrimination from family and friends; families and friends may well harbor anti-gay sentiment.

The invisibility of sexual orientation creates other concerns, and at the same time some advantages, for many who are gay or lesbian.[4] Being in the closet may appear to be easier than risking discrimination, harassment, ostracism, and being fired, but it comes with many negative consequences, including stress and anxiety related to continual fear of disclosure.[5] We discuss these consequences later in the chapter.

Terminology

The American Psychological Association defines **sexual orientation** as a component of sexuality "characterized by enduring emotional, romantic, sexual, and/or affectional attractions to individuals of a particular gender."[6] The three commonly recognized sexual orientations are heterosexual, homosexual, and bisexual. As the dominant group, heterosexuals are least likely to experience differential treatment based on their sexual orientation when compared with homosexuals and bisexuals.

Research on sexual orientation often considers people who are gay, lesbian, bisexual, and transgender (GLBT) as one group; however, many of the individual and organizational experiences of bisexual

---

[2]Correll, S. (1999). "Lesbian and Gay Americans." In A. G. Dworkin & R. J. Dworkin (Eds.), *The Minority Report,* 3rd ed. Fort Worth, TX: Harcourt Brace Publishers, pp. 436–456.

[3]Racial socialization refers to Black parents preparing their children for the racial bias, stereotyping, and discrimination they will experience.

[4]Human Rights Campaign (2009). "At the Intersection." http://www.hrc.org/documents/HRC_Equality_Forward_2009.pdf, accessed December 28, 2010.

[5]Ragins, B. R. (2008). "Disclosure Disconnects: Antecedents and Consequences of Disclosing Invisible Stigmas Across Life Domains." *Academy of Management Review,* 33: 194–215.

[6]"Examining the Employment Non-Discrimination Act (ENDA): The Scientists Perspective." http://www.apa.org/pi/lgbt/resources/employment-nondiscrimination.aspx, accessed August 12, 2010.

and, especially, transgender people are unique.[7] Many of the concepts that we consider in the chapter do apply to all sexual minorities (e.g., desire for equity and fairness), but when reporting specific research, we will use accurate terminology for the population studied. In this book, the term **sexual minorities** is used to include people who are gay, lesbian, bisexual, or transgender, although other researchers have used the term to refer to only a subset of nonheterosexuals, again reflecting disparities in terminology in the research.[8] **Gender identity** or **expression** refers to a person's internal sense of gender (which may or may not be the same as the denotation of "male" or "female" assigned at birth), as well as how a person behaves, appears, or presents with regard to societal expectations of that person.[9]

Homophobia is the fear of homosexuals; **heterosexism** is "an ideological system that denies, denigrates, and stigmatizes any nonheterosexual behavior, relationship, identity, or community" and is similar to racism and sexism.[10,11] Researchers have suggested that heterosexism more commonly affects the workplace experiences of sexual minorities than homophobia.[12] Heterosexist organizational policies implicitly assume workers are heterosexual, for example, requiring marriage to qualify for benefits, not acknowledging that some committed partners are unable to marry in most states. Heterosexist attitudes are reflected in the view that gays and lesbians are "flaunting" their sexual orientation by bringing a same-sex partner to a company event, ignoring the fact that heterosexuals "flaunt" their sexual orientation by bringing an opposite-sex partner.[13]

▍ HISTORY OF GAY RIGHTS IN THE UNITED STATES

The earliest known gay rights organization, The Society for Human Rights, was formed in 1924 in Chicago.[14] The Mattachine Society, the

[7]See Lubensky, M. E., Holland, S. L., Wiethoff, C., & Crosby, F. J. (2004). "Diversity and Sexual Orientation: Including and Valuing Sexual Minorities in the Workplace." In M. Stockdale & F. Crosby (Eds.), *The Psychology and Management of Workplace Diversity*. Malden, MA: Blackwell, pp. 206–223; Dietch, E. A., Butz, R. M., & Brief, A. P. (2004). "Out of the Closet and Out of a Job? The Nature, Import, and Causes of Sexual Orientation Discrimination in the Workplace." In R. W. Griffin & A. O'Leary-Kelly (Eds.), *The Dark Side of Organizational Behavior*. San Francisco, CA: Jossey-Bass, pp. 187–234.

[8]Lubensky et al. (2004).

[9]http://www.hrc.org/documents/HRC_Corporate_Equality_Index_2010.pdf, accessed June 12, 2010.

[10]Weinberg, G. (1972). *Society and the Healthy Homosexual*. New York: St. Martin's Press.

[11]Herek, G. M. (1993). "The Context of Anti-Gay Violence: Notes on Cultural and Psychological Heterosexism." In L. D. Farnets & D. C. Kimmel (Eds.), *Psychological Perspectives on Lesbian and Gay Male Experiences*. New York: Columbia University Press, pp. 89–107.

[12]For example, Herek, G. M. (1984). "Beyond 'Homophobia': A Social Psychological Perspective on Attitudes Toward Lesbians and Gay Men." *Journal of Homosexuality*, 10: 1–21. See also Ragins, B. R., & Wiethoff, C. (2005). "Understanding Heterosexism at Work: The Straight Problem." In R. L. Dipboye & A. Colella (Eds.), *Discrimination at Work*. Mahwah, NJ: Lawrence Erlbaum Associates, pp. 177–201.

[13]See Kaplan, M., & Lucas, J. (1996). "Heterosexism as a Workforce Diversity Issue." In E. Y. Cross & M. B. White (Eds.), *The Diversity Factor: Capturing the Competitive Advantage of a Changing Workforce*. Chicago IL: Irwin.

[14]Infoplease. (2005). "The American Gay Rights Movement: A Timeline." *Information Please® Database*, ©2005 Pearson Education, Inc. http://www.infoplease.com/ipa/A0761909.html, accessed July 4, 2010.

first national gay rights organization, was organized in 1951, followed by the Daughters of Bilitis, a national lesbian organization founded in 1956. Activism and resistance to discrimination based on sexual orientation continued through the 1950s and 1960s. In June of 1969, when police raided Stonewall, a gay bar in Greenwich Village, patrons resisted and began rioting instead of dispersing as was their normal practice after a raid. Riots and protests went on for three days, turning the gay rights movement into a widespread and vocal protest for equality.[15] Hate crimes, overt prejudice, discrimination, exclusion, and changing attitudes have continued to fuel the gay rights movement into the present.

Ironically, on the fortieth anniversary of the Stonewall riots, in 2009, a police raid at the Rainbow Lounge in Fort Worth, Texas, included brutal beatings of bar patrons that resulted in suspensions of three police officers. The raid was conducted by eight officers and two agents from the Texas Alcohol Beverage Commission (TABC) who entered the bar at about 1 a.m. and began arresting people allegedly for public intoxication.[16] Many patrons suffered broken bones, and one was hospitalized for a week with a fractured skull. Eyewitness accounts contradicted police reports that the violence was precipitated by the actions of bar patrons.[17] The internal review that resulted in three police officers being suspended for a total of five days outraged the gay community and its allies. In contrast, the two agents from the TABC and their supervisor were fired and the agency ordered diversity training for all employees throughout the state.[18]

The Rainbow Lounge event and the others in which the rights of the gay community have been violated are similar to events that violated the rights of other non-dominant group members. Many have drawn these parallels and called for unity in the fight against discrimination based on race, sex, class, and sexual orientation. Unity, however, is not always achieved.[19]

---

[15]Ibid. See also Schaefer, R. T. (2002). *Racial and Ethnic Groups,* 8th ed. Upper Saddle River, NJ: Prentice Hall.

[16]McKinley, J. C. (2009). "A Raid at a Club in Texas Leaves a Man in the Hospital and Gay Advocates Angry." *New York Times.* http://www.nytimes.com/2009/07/05/us/05texas.html, accessed June 10, 2010.

[17]Nash, T. (2009). "What They Saw at the Rainbow Lounge." http://www.dallasvoice.com/artman/publish/article_11500.php, accessed June 10, 2010; Gordon, S. (2009). "Three Officers Suspended in Rainbow Lounge Raid." http://www.nbcdfw.com/news/local-beat/Three-Officers-Suspended-in-Rainbow-Lounge-Raid-69298017.html, accessed June 10, 2010.

[18]Gordon (2009).

[19]Human Rights Campaign (2009); "Talk About It." http://www.hrc.org/issues/13235.htm, accessed December 28, 2010.

▌ POPULATION

The wide range of estimates on the number of gays and lesbians in the population reflects a difficulty of collecting data on sexual orientation that does not often exist for other minorities. Whereas surveys commonly ask one's race, sex, ethnicity, or age, they do not ask one's sexual orientation. Recent estimates suggest that 4% to 17% of people in the United States—between 12 and 53 million people—are gay or lesbian.[20] Both the lower and the higher estimates indicate that significant numbers of people are gay or lesbian. At 4% of the population, gays and lesbians would be similar to the percentage of Asian Americans; at 17%, there would be more gays and lesbians than African Americans and Latinos. Either way, or at any number in between, sexual minorities are a large proportion of the population and of consumers, employees, and job applicants. In addition to the ethical problems posed, ignoring the needs of sexual minorities and discriminating against them can result in a host of negative outcomes for the individuals and organizations. On the other hand, practicing inclusion and fairness toward sexual minorities can be of benefit to individuals and organizations.

▌ EDUCATION AND INCOME LEVELS

Although possibly as a result of sampling, gays and lesbians appear to have higher levels of education than heterosexuals, which contributes somewhat to higher earnings.[21] About a quarter of both gay men and lesbians have college degrees, compared with about 17% of heterosexual men and women.[22] As we have discussed in earlier chapters, education and earnings are highly correlated, and this holds for gays, lesbians, and heterosexuals. However, the returns for sexual minorities compared with heterosexuals on investments in education are not consistent; lesbians appear to earn more than comparably educated heterosexual women, but gay males appear to earn less than comparably educated heterosexual men.[23]

In one study investigating earnings differences between gays and lesbians and heterosexuals, Lee Badgett found that gay males earned

---

[20]Gonsiorek, J. C., & Weinrich, J. D. (1991). "The Definition and Scope of Sexual Orientation." In J. C. Gonsiorek & J. D. Weinrich (Eds.), *Homosexuality: Research Implications for Public Policy.* Newbury Park, CA: Sage; see also Lubensky et al. (2004).

[21]Antecol, H., Jong, A., & Steinberger, M. (2008). "The Sexual Orientation Wage Gap: The Role of Occupational Sorting and Human Capital." *Industrial and Labor Relations Review,* 61: 518–543.

[22]Black, D., Gates, G., Sanders, S., & Taylor, L. (2000). "Demographics of the Gay and Lesbian Population in the United States: Evidence from Available Systematic Data Sources." *Demography,* 37(2): 139–154.

[23]Ibid.

between 11% and 27% less than heterosexual men. Using a national random sample, Badgett considered people with comparable experience, education, occupation, marital status, and region of residence and did not find statistically significant earnings differences between lesbians and heterosexual women.[24] More recent studies have also found that gay males earn less than heterosexual men, but that lesbian women do tend to earn more than heterosexual women, in contrast to Badgett's earlier findings. This may be due to lesbians being less likely to choose "typically female" majors in school and gay men being somewhat more likely to have "typically female" majors.[25] As discussed in Chapter 9, female-dominated jobs pay less than jobs that are not. As a result, lesbian and bisexual women's earnings are between 17% and 23% higher than the earnings of heterosexual women.[26] When in partnered relationships, the disparity between lesbians' and heterosexual women's earnings is even greater; lesbians with partners earn considerably more than heterosexual women with partners. In addition to type of work, lesbians' higher earnings may be due in part to their greater attachment to the labor market. Partnered lesbians also share more equitably in household responsibilities and are less likely to have children than women in heterosexual couples, which may also affect earnings.[27]

Compared to Badgett's earlier estimate of an 11% to 17% wage gap between gay men and heterosexual men, Black and colleagues found that gay and bisexual men earn between 30% and 32% less than heterosexual men.[28] This earnings disparity may be due to some gay men choosing or being channeled into positions believed appropriate based on their sexual orientation (e.g., art designer instead of architect), although some research disputes that idea.[29] Generally, among non-Hispanic White men, 34% choose fields of study that are "typically female," compared with 44% of gay men choosing such majors.[30] As we have considered in previous chapters, there is a wage penalty for working in female-dominated jobs. In addition, in one study published in the *Journal of Applied Psychology*, researchers found that both gays and lesbians who worked with other gays and lesbians had lower earnings than those whose coworkers were

[24]Badgett, M. V. L. (1995). "The Wage Effects of Sexual Orientation Discrimination." *Industrial and Labor Relations Review*, 48(4): 726–739.
[25]Black, D. A., Sanders, S. G., & Taylor, L. J. (2007). "The Economics of Lesbian and Gay Families." *Journal of Economic Perspectives*, 21(2): 53–70.
[26]Blanford, J. M. (2003). "The Nexus of Sexual Orientation and Gender in the Determination of Earnings." *Industrial and Labor Relations Review*, 56(4): 622–643.
[27]Black et al. (2007).
[28]Ibid.
[29]Antecol et al. (2008).
[30]Black et al. (2007).

primarily heterosexual or equally balanced.[31] They suggested that gays and lesbians may be channeled into jobs deemed appropriate for them or that they may choose work groups with other gays in hopes of finding more supportive coworkers.

■ RELEVANT LEGISLATION

Gallup polls indicate that the great majority of Americans believe that gays and lesbians should have equal employment opportunities; only 11% believe that discrimination based on sexual orientation is acceptable.[32] Despite this, no uniform federal legislation prohibits sexual orientation discrimination in the workplace. Thus, in most states, a person can be fired for being (or being perceived as) gay, lesbian, or transgender.

The Human Rights Campaign (HRC), an organization working for lesbian, gay, bisexual, and transgender rights, has documented cases in which people who had been performing satisfactorily were fired because of their sexual orientation. Reasons given for some terminations were frank—being gay is not acceptable in the organization, the district manager does not like homosexuals, or other such reasons. Other terminations were effected under the guise of failing to meet performance standards, having a poor attitude, tardiness, or other behaviors for which heterosexual employees were not disciplined. Although legislation has not eliminated discrimination on the basis of sex, race, age, disability, and religion, the absence of widespread laws prohibiting sexual orientation discrimination implies that it is acceptable. As discussed in Chapter 3, legislation alone is insufficient to ensure diversity, equality, and inclusion, but the absence of legislation can also be an impediment. For sexual orientation specifically, researchers have found that in states lacking sexual orientation legislation, HR professionals rated gay male applicants as less hireable than (presumably) straight applicants. Researchers also found that antidiscrimination legislation was correlated with decreased prejudice toward gay men.[33]

Executive Order 11478 (enacted in 1998) prohibits sexual orientation discrimination in federal civilian workplaces, but this prohibition has not been extended to other employers. The proposed Employment

[31]Ragins, B. R., & Cornwell, J. M. (2001). "Pink Triangles: Antecedents and Consequences of Perceived Workplace Discrimination against Gay and Lesbian Employees." *Journal of Applied Psychology*, 86: 1244–1261.

[32]Human Rights Campaign (2001). "Documenting Discrimination." http://www.hrc.org/documents/documentingdiscrimination.pdf, accessed August 12, 2010.

[33]Barron, L. (2009). "Promoting the Underlying Principle of Acceptance: The Effectiveness of Sexual Orientation Employment Antidiscrimination Legislation." *The Journal of Workplace Rights*, 14(2): 251–268.

Nondiscrimination Act (ENDA) would do so and would prohibit sexual orientation discrimination in all employment matters except in certain circumstances (e.g., religious schools and churches). Many *Fortune 500* corporations support ENDA, as do many small- and medium-sized organizations. Despite considerable corporate support, widespread individual support, and some political support, however, the U.S. Congress has thus far failed to pass ENDA as a federal law. Many states and cities have passed legislation prohibiting sexual orientation discrimination, including California, Connecticut, Hawaii, Minnesota, New Jersey, Washington, D.C., and numerous others. In the District of Columbia, for example, sexual orientation discrimination is included in the provisions of the Human Rights Act of 1977, which, as mentioned in Chapter 15, also prohibits discrimination on the basis of personal appearance and other factors not covered under federal laws. Thus, in the District of Columbia, the home of the federal government, sexual orientation discrimination by employers, employment agencies, and labor unions is prohibited.

Title VII, even though it does not cover discrimination on the basis of sexual orientation, has been used in sexual orientation discrimination cases when these have involved sexual harassment and gender-based stereotyping. As discussed in Chapter 9, same-sex sexual harassment was not viewed as harassment by the courts until the 1998 U.S. Supreme Court ruling in *Oncale v. Sundowner* that harassment may occur between people of the same sex. In cases of gender-based stereotyping, courts have ruled illegal discrimination due to acting outside of one's gender role, such as what happened to Ann Hopkins (see Chapter 9). Gays and lesbians have found relief under Title VII although sexual orientation discrimination alone is not expressly prohibited by that law.

Even though legislation prohibiting sexual orientation discrimination does not exist, many employers have incorporated sexual orientation into their nondiscrimination policies. Nearly all (49) of the *Fortune 50* and 473 (almost 95%) of the *Fortune 500* include sexual orientation in their policies of nondiscrimination.[34] Cracker Barrel's reversal of its overt policy of sexual orientation discrimination is discussed in Organizational Feature 11.1.

Another critical gauge of an organization's stance on sexual orientation discrimination is whether equal benefits for same-sex partners are offered to employees. The issues of partner benefits, HIV/AIDS at work, some of the determinants of attitudes toward gays and lesbians, and the consequences of being out or closeted at work are discussed in the following sections.

---

[34]Equality Forum. http://www.equalityforum.com/fortune500/, accessed June 22, 2010.

ORGANIZATIONAL FEATURE 11.1	*Cracker Barrel Reverses Its Antigay Stance but Diversity Problems Remain*

Cracker Barrel, which now has a Diversity Outreach group that promotes the company's commitment to inclusion, at one time instituted a policy that called for termination of employees "whose sexual preferences fail to demonstrate normal heterosexual values which have been the foundation of families in our society."[35] The policy, which Cracker Barrel later referred to as a "well-intentioned overreaction to the perceived values" of its customers, set off a storm of negative publicity in the United States. At least eleven workers were fired because of being gay, which is not illegal under federal law nor was it illegal in the states in which the terminations occurred. Some employees' termination slips clearly stated being gay as the reason for dismissal.

Boycotts of Cracker Barrel were coupled with powerful shareholder activism to bring about a change in the official policy. Ten years of activism, with each year seeing increasing support among shareholders, finally worked. The New York City Employees Retirement System (NYCERS), controlling 189,000 shares of Cracker Barrel's stock, was the most vocal and powerful shareholder pressing for a change. NYCERS and other shareholders represented 58% of outstanding shareholders supporting a nondiscrimination policy. Eventually, Cracker Barrel's board voted to add *sexual orientation* to its nondiscrimination policy. The official Web site of Cracker Barrel's parent company (CBRL group) now says that, "CBRL Group, INC. will not tolerate any form of discrimination, harassment, or retaliation affecting its employees or applicants due to race, color, religion, sex, sexual orientation, national origin, age, marital status, medical condition, or disability."[36] The statement also prohibits discrimination against customers on the basis of similar factors.

Cracker Barrel has also had other diversity troubles, including more than 100 allegations of discrimination against African American customers. Black customers reported excessive wait times, racial slurs, being seated in smoking sections with other Black customers even when requesting the nonsmoking section and when nonsmoking tables were vacant, and being followed around the store. A U.S. Justice Department inquiry included interviews of 150 employees, 80% of whom said they had experienced or witnessed discriminatory treatment of Black customers and suggested this behavior was directed, participated in, or condoned by management.[37] The department found evidence of discriminatory conduct in about fifty stores in seven states. Although admitting to no wrongdoing, CBRL agreed to an $8.7 million settlement. CBRL also agreed to improve its employee diversity training and to create a new department to investigate discrimination complaints, among other changes.

QUESTIONS TO CONSIDER

*1. **What are the similarities and differences between the race and sexual orientation concerns at Cracker Barrel?***

---

[35]Cracker Barrel Corporate Site. http://www.crackerbarrel.com/about-outreach.cfm?doc_id=674, accessed June 9, 2010.
[36]Ibid.
[37]"Justice Department Settles Race Discrimination Lawsuit against Cracker Barrel Restaurant Chain." (2004, May 3). U.S. Attorney's Office, Northern District of Georgia.

2. What does the Cracker Barrel Web site say about its "Pleasing People" goal?

3. What kinds of messages are sent by an agreement to an $8.7 million settlement but no admission of wrongdoing?

Sources: Human Rights Campaign. http://www.hrc.org; French, R. (2005, June 21). "Cracker Barrel Fights Stigma of Discrimination." Associated Press, *Detroit News*. http://www.htrends.com/article17189Cracker_Barrel_fights_stigma_of_discrimination.html, accessed December 27, 2010; Schmit, J., & Copeland, L. (2004, May 7). "Cracker Barrel Customer Says Bias Was 'Flagrant'." *USAToday*. http://www.usatoday.com/money/companies/2004-05-07-cracker-barrel_x.htm, accessed December 27, 2010.

▌ PARTNER BENEFITS

Although many people think of medical benefits when assessing whether an organization's benefits are equitable with respect to same-sex partners, the HRC considers a broader array of benefits that are offered by employers. The HRC Corporate Equality Index surveys companies on their equality of offerings for bereavement leave, family and medical leave, COBRA (legally required) benefits continuation, supplemental life insurance, relocation assistance, adoption assistance, retiree medical coverage, employer-provided life insurance, automatic pension benefits for same-sex partners in the event of an employee's death, and employee discounts. Of the 590 companies most recently rated by the HRC, the average rating was 86%. Eleven of the *Fortune* top twenty companies received 100% ratings.[38] In their study of the effects of higher Corporate Equality Index ratings from HRC, Wang and Schwarz found that companies with the more progressive GLBT nondiscrimination policies had higher stock performance than companies that were otherwise equivalent but had less progressive policies.[39] Not offering partner and family benefits to a subset of the employee population sends clear messages to employees that the family life and well-being of heterosexuals (but not homosexuals) are important to the organization, and that retirement and income security are important for heterosexual employees and their dependents and survivors (but not for homosexuals and their dependents and survivors).

As companies have begun to recognize the importance of equality of benefits for all employees, regardless of sexual orientation, the proportion offering domestic partner health benefits continues to increase. The majority of *Fortune* 500 companies now provide them.[40]

---

[38]Human Rights Campaign. *Corporate Equality Index 2010*. http://www.hrc.org/documents/HRC_Corporate_Equality_Index_2010.pdf? accessed March 19, 2011.
[39]Wang & Schwarz (2010).
[40]Ibid.

Some well-known companies that offer some partner benefits include American Airlines, Hewlett-Packard, Prudential, Kodak, Merrill Lynch, and Imation. Employers have often expressed fears of the increased costs associated with offering domestic partner health benefits as a reason for avoiding doing so. Evidence suggests that few employees request domestic partner benefits, and when they do, costs are generally consistent with an increase in the number of plan participants, instead of being proportionately higher. Partnered gays and lesbians are likely to be employed; U.S. Census data reveal that just over 86% of men and women in same-sex couples are employed.[41] In part due to high rates of employment and unwillingness to disclose, fewer than 2%, on average, of the entire employee population enrolls for partner benefits when they are offered.[42] Partly because in same-sex partnerships both partners are likely to be employed and may already have medical coverage through their own employers, and partly because of privacy concerns, rates of enrollment for domestic partner benefits are low. When same-sex partners do sign up for benefits, they tend to be younger than other enrollees (which reduces insurance costs). Because they are also significantly less likely to parent, gays and lesbians are also less likely to incur the high costs associated with pregnancy, childbirth, adoption, and insurance for newborn and young children.[43]

Misperception: Offering same-sex partner benefits incurs considerable additional health insurance costs for employers, especially due to risks of AIDS.

Reality: Adding same-sex benefits increases costs to employers between 1% and 3%; costs are proportionate to any increase in the number of plan participants.

To address negative tax consequences for employees who receive benefits for same-sex partners, some companies have begun to offer tax "gross-ups," which are an additional year-end lump-sum payment to reimburse employees whose health benefits for same-sex domestic partners are treated as taxable income in the United States. These gross-ups eliminate an otherwise invisible tax inequality faced by employees with same-sex domestic partners that heterosexual married couples to not have. Companies such as Barclays, Google, Cisco, and Kimpton Hotels provide gross-ups; benefits advisors propose that doing so will serve as a

[41]Leppel, K. (2009). "Labour Force Status and Sexual Orientation." *Economica*, 76(301): 197–207.
[42]See Human Rights Campaign for further discussion.
[43]Black et al. (2007).

competitive advantage for organizations.[44] Google also recently added same-sex couples to the family members that the company considers covered by the Family and Medical Leave Act.[45] In response to the Rainbow Lounge raid discussed earlier, the city of Fort Worth, Texas, formed a Diversity Task Force that recommended providing family leave to employees with domestic partners, expanding the city's health plan to include domestic partners, and allowing domestic partners to be designated as survivors to receive monthly pension benefits.[46] As discussed in Organizational Feature 11.2, however, even organizations with inclusive sexual orientation policies must still be vigilant about all aspects of their diversity climate.

■ HIV/AIDS AT WORK: UNFOUNDED FEARS

As mentioned, fears of incurring excessive costs due to HIV/AIDS are sometimes offered as a rationale for not providing domestic partner benefits. The fear of contracting HIV/AIDS may also affect many people's resistance to working with or employing gay men, but there are fallacies associated with both fears. First, although HIV/AIDS is strongly perceived as a gay male disease, heterosexuals and people who use injectable drugs comprise a significant portion of the population with HIV/AIDS. In the United States, revised data collection procedures have shown that an estimated 53% of the new HIV/AIDS infections for the most currently available year were the result of male-to-male sexual contact.[47] Thus, nearly half of new infections were for other reasons. Second, the risk of contracting HIV/AIDS while at work is very small.

Misperception: HIV/AIDS is a gay male disease.

Reality: Estimates indicate that nearly half of the new HIV/AIDS infections result from heterosexual contact or the injection of drugs.[48]

[44]Bernard, T. S. (2010, June 30). "The Tax Treatment of Domestic Partner Benefits." *New York Times. http://bucks.blogs.nytimes.com/2010/06/30/the-tax-treatment-of-domestic-partner-benefits/*, accessed July 22, 2010.
[45]Ibid.
[46]"Fort Worth's New Domestic Partners' Insurance Plan Begins Jan. 1." http://www.star-telegram.com/2010/12/25/2727425/fort-worths-new-domestic-partners.html, accessed December 27, 2010.
[47]Centers for Disease Control and Prevention. "HIV Incidence." http://www.cdc.gov/hiv/topics/surveillance/incidence.htm, accessed June 12, 2010.
[48]Ibid.

ORGANIZATIONAL FEATURE 11.2	*Hewlett-Packard's Sexual Orientation Policies Amid Charges of Discrimination—A Study in Contrasts?*

The Hewlett-Packard Web site says that the company believes "diversity and inclusion are key drivers of creativity, innovation, and invention." Some of the inclusive practices that HP has implemented to support its goals are a nondiscrimination policy, electronic job posting, harassment-free work environment, domestic partner benefits, employee network groups, flexible work hours, and a safe and pleasant work environment. HP includes "race, creed, color, religion, gender, sexual orientation, gender identity/expression, national origin, disability, age (and) covered veteran status" in its nondiscrimination policy.

In addition to including sexual orientation and gender identity/expression in its non-discrimination policy, HP has offered domestic partner benefits to its employees since 1997. Offering benefits to domestic partners is said to be part of "HP's ongoing efforts to create an inclusive environment," which also enhances HP's ability to attract and retain top talent.[49] Under the policy, domestic partners may be of the same sex or opposite sex. To qualify for most benefits, the employee must submit a declaration of domestic partnership. The domestic partnership must be a committed relationship that has lasted for at least six months and in which partners live together and share financial responsibility for the household. If criteria are met, medical, dental, retiree medical, long-term care, and life insurance are available. HP's plan allows for twelve weeks of unpaid leaves of absence to care for a domestic partner with a serious health condition, with job security. Children of domestic partners are eligible for HP's employee scholarship program.

If a domestic partnership ends, HP must be notified within thirty days and, the former domestic partner (and his or her dependents) must be removed from the benefits plans. A six-month waiting period is required before a new domestic partner becomes eligible for benefits.

Despite having comprehensive non-discrimination policies, HP has experienced allegations of discrimination from members of multiple groups. Terry Garrett, a Black man with more than twenty years' tenure with HP and typically rated as "good" to "very good" in his performance, filed a lawsuit alleging race and age discrimination and constructive discharge. Garrett had also begun participating in a diversity program aimed at promoting the hiring of people of color and fostering relationships with minority firms. Although the program was endorsed by HP, Garrett alleged that management was unsupportive of his participation, even telling him that they "were tired of hearing about 'that diversity stuff.'" After multiple judgments, appeals, and reversals, the courts ruled in Garrett's favor.[50]

In another case, a former HP executive sought class action status in a lawsuit alleging discrimination against women and older employees. In 2008, Carter's salary was more than $200,000 with about the same amount in bonuses; her pay was reduced to $153,400 in April of 2010. Carter alleged that once her supervisor (a woman) retired, her new male managers began

---

[49]"State of the Workplace for Lesbian, Gay, Bisexual and Transgender Americans 2004." http://www.hrc.org/Template.cfm?Section=Get_Informed2&Template=/ContentManagement/ContentDisplay.cfm&ContentID=27214, accessed July 2, 2005.
[50]01-1022, *Garrett v. Hewlett-Packard Company*, September 25, 2002. http://ca10.washburnlaw.edu/cases/2002/09/01-1022.htm, accessed June 25, 2010.

trying to drive her from HP by micromanaging or ignoring her.[51]

QUESTIONS TO CONSIDER

1. *One important purpose of a company Website is to communicate positive information about the company. How might the seven inclusive practices listed earlier be perceived by people who are gay or lesbian? How might the practices be perceived by other employees?*

2. *Electronic job posting can be viewed as a means to ensure that every applicant has a fair chance, based on his or her qualifications, to be considered for a job. How might electronic job posting be viewed positively by workers from all backgrounds?*

3. *How do the requirements for coverage for domestic partners, such as length of the relationship, compare with requirements for married couples? Do companies usually require a waiting period after dissolution of a marriage (divorce) before a new spouse can become eligible for benefits? What factors may have influenced the inclusion of these stipulations?*

4. *Why do you think that HP offers domestic partner benefits to opposite-sex partners as well as to same-sex partners?*

5. *What kinds of things might explain the race and sex discrimination issues that were described, given the existence of HP's stated nondiscrimination policies? What else should be done within HP to address issues such as this?*

Sources: http://www.hp.com/hpinfo/abouthp/diversity/nondisc.html, accessed July 25, 2010; Human Rights Campaign. (2005). Hewlett-Packard Co.—Domestic Partner Benefits Program.

Employers should take specific steps through education to alleviate unfounded fears of transmission: HIV/AIDS is not spread through casual contact, such as those behaviors that occur at work; and for people working in professions in which blood and bodily fluids are handled, safe-handling procedures minimize the risk of transmission. Education about HIV/AIDS offered as part of an employer's health and wellness programs should not focus on gay men or other specific populations at relatively higher risk, but rather on prevention for all employees.

Misperception: Working with coworkers or customers with HIV/AIDS puts people at high risk of infection.

Reality: HIV/AIDS is transmitted through sharing of blood and bodily fluids, primarily through unprotected sex or the sharing of needles in intravenous drug use. In most occupations, the risk of transmission of HIV/AIDS is very small.

---

[51]"Longtime Boise HP Exec Claims discrimination." http://www.idahostatesman.com/2010/06/17/1234577/longtime-boise-hp-exec-claims.html, accessed June 25, 2010.

Employees and managers should be trained regarding HIV/AIDS and the law. Coworkers who refuse to work with someone who has, is perceived as having, or is associated with someone who has HIV/AIDS can be fired. HIV/AIDS is a protected disability under the Americans with Disabilities Act (ADA), and employers are prohibited from discriminating against people with HIV/AIDS. In one such case, Cirque du Soleil agreed to a $600,000 settlement for firing an employee who was HIV positive. The charging party, Matthew Cusick, was awarded the $300,000 maximum punitive damages allowable under the ADA, plus $200,000 in lost wages, $60,000 in front pay, and $40,000 in attorneys' fees. The settlement also required Cirque du Soleil to appoint an Equal Employment Opportunity Commission (EEOC) officer to oversee its annual training on the laws enforced by the EEOC, with an emphasis on HIV/disability discrimination.[52]

■ DETERMINANTS OF ATTITUDES TOWARD GAYS AND LESBIANS

Several factors are consistently related to attitudes toward sexual minorities: sex, education, marital status, and religious fundamentalism. Those who are more highly educated, unmarried, female, and less religious have more favorable attitudes than others. Race is an inconsistent predictor of attitudes toward sexual minorities. Some researchers have found that African Americans have more negative attitudes about homosexuality than Whites; other researchers have found that attitudes of Whites and Blacks toward homosexuality were similar when differences in religiosity were controlled.[53] Heterosexual men have more negative attitudes toward gays and lesbians, particularly toward gay men. People who believe that sexual orientation is biologically determined, rather than a choice, have more favorable attitudes toward gays and lesbians.[54]

■ CODES OF SILENCE: NOT JUST THE U.S. MILITARY

The U.S. military is a unique organization employing 1.4 million people who are more diverse in race, ethnicity, and sex than ever before.[55] An

[52]"Cirque Du Soleil to Pay $600,000 for Disability Discrimination Against Performer with HIV," http://www.eeoc.gov/eeoc/newsroom/release/4-22-04.cfm, accessed December 28, 2010.
[53]Herek, G. M., & Capitanio, J. P. (1996). "'Some of My Best Friends': Intergroup Contact, Concealable Stigma, and Heterosexuals' Attitudes Toward Gay Men and Lesbians." *Personality and Social Psychology Bulletin*, 22: 412–424. See also Herek, G. M., & Capitanio, J. P. (1995). "Black Heterosexuals' Attitudes Toward Lesbians and Gay Men in the United States." *Journal of Sex Research*, 32(2): 95–106.
[54]Wood, P. B., & Bartkowski, J. P. (2004). "Attribution Style and Public Policy Attitudes Toward Gay Rights." *Social Science Quarterly*, 85: 58–74.
[55]Segal, D. R., & Segal, M. W. (2004). "America's Military Population." *Population Bulletin*, 59(4): 1–44. Population Reference Bureau. Washington, D.C.

estimated 2.5% of military personnel are believed to be gay male (2%) or lesbian (5%).[56] Diversity in sexual orientation remains controversial, despite votes to repeal the official "don't ask, don't tell, don't pursue, don't harass" policy. The policy, commonly known only as "don't ask, don't tell" (DADT), was passed in 1993 under President Bill Clinton. President Clinton's initial plans to repeal the ban on gays in the military were met with such virulent resistance that DADT was passed as a compromise of sorts.

Under the policy, more than 13,000 gays and lesbians were discharged from the military, at an estimated cost of between $250 million and $1.2 billion.[57] These discharge rates were higher than before the implementation of the policy, indicating that pursuit was occurring. Media reports and discharge testimony indicate that many of those discharged were successfully and dependably performing in key positions, such as linguists and nuclear warfare experts. The discharges therefore represent a tremendous loss of investment in training, education, and key skills of military personnel.[58] Of the 6,300 discharged between during a five-year period, only 75 were officers.[59] Women (particularly those aged 18 to 25) were more likely to be discharged than men, indicating the existence of multiple aspects of this type of discrimination. Although women make up about 15% of the military overall, 29% of those who were discharged under the policy were women. Some reports suggest these discharges occurred after "witch hunts" and for refusing men's sexual advances.[60]

Efforts to repeal DADT emphasized that fears of reduced cohesion, reduced enlistment of heterosexuals, and violations of the right to privacy of heterosexual personnel were unfounded.[61] The FBI, CIA, NASA, and the Secret Service, as well as numerous foreign militaries lifted bans on the service of gays and lesbians, without ill effects.[62] Police forces in large

[56]Ibid.

[57]Human Rights Campaign, Service Members Legal Defense Network, and American Veterans for Equal Rights. (2004). "Documenting Courage: Gay, Lesbian, Bisexual and Transgender Veterans Speak Out." http://www.hrc.org/documents/Courage.pdf http://www.hrc.org/documents/Courage.pdf, accessed August 1, 2010.

[58]Ibid.

[59]Fouhy, B. (2004, June 21). "Military Discharged 770 Last Year for Being Gay: Hundreds Held High Level Job Specialties that Required Years of Training." *San Diego Union Tribune.*

[60]Human Rights Campaign, Service Members Legal Defense Network, and American Veterans for Equal Rights (2004).

[61]See Segal & Segal (2004).

[62]Human Rights Campaign. (2004). "The State of the Workplace for Lesbian, Gay, Bisexual, and Transgender Americans 2003." http://www.hrc.org/Template.cfm?Section=Get_Informed2&Template=/ ContentManagement/ContentDisplay.cfm&ContentID=18678, accessed March 25, 2005. See also Belkin, A. (2003). "Don't Ask, Don't Tell: Is the Gay Military Ban Based on Military Necessity?" *Parameters,* 33(2): 107–119.

INDIVIDUAL FEATURE 11.1	*Lupe Valdez, Sheriff, Dallas County, Texas*

Lupe Valdez was elected the sheriff of Dallas County, Texas, in November 2004 and re-elected in 2008. In Dallas County, the sheriff is the only countywide law enforcement official. With a salary of more than $140,000 and over 1,300 deputies to manage, Valdez is a powerful law enforcement figure in one of the largest counties in Texas. She is bilingual and earned a graduate degree in criminology and criminal justice from the University of Texas at Arlington and an undergraduate degree in business from what is now Southern Nazarene University.

Valdez was the first woman ever elected as Dallas County Sheriff. In a state noted for Republican governors and presidents, Valdez is a Democrat—the first Democrat to be elected Dallas County Sheriff in twenty-five years. She is also Latina and grew up picking crops from Texas to Michigan. Valdez and her family often slept and ate in the car to save money and to avoid being turned away at hotels and restaurants. The family eventually settled in her mother's hometown of San Antonio, where Valdez recalls seeing a fellow student hit with a ruler for speaking Spanish in school. Valdez attended college in Oklahoma and later was a captain in the U.S. Army Reserves,

serving as an officer in the military police and in army intelligence. She was an agent for the U.S. Customs service until she retired to run for sheriff.

Perhaps most notable in an election year in which same-sex marriage was a hot issue, Valdez is a lesbian. Valdez ran a campaign that emphasized integrity, which was quite effective after years of scandals had plagued the sheriff's office. Apparently, voters were more concerned with integrity than with Valdez being a lesbian. In response to charges that she would promote a "gay agenda," Valdez emphasizes that her job as sheriff provides no opportunity to influence legislation. Although she has always been open about her sexual orientation, Valdez notes that "it has nothing to do with being sheriff." It does, according to one author, say a lot "about the new politics of sexual orientation in Texas," in which voters viewed her sexual orientation as not being relevant.[63]

_____

Sources: Blumenthal, R. (2004, November 10). "An Improbable Victor Becomes a Texas Sheriff." *New York Times*. Section A, Column 1, National Desk, p. 16; Olsson, K. (2005, January). "The Gay Non-Issue." *Texas Monthly*, p. 82; http://lupevaldez.com.

cities have used advertisements in gay publications to recruit officers; for their police forces, being gay or lesbian does not preclude success as an officer.[64] As discussed in Individual Feature 11.1, Lupe Valdez, sheriff of Dallas County, Texas, has served successfully in the military and in law enforcement.

[63]Olsson, K. (2005, January). "The Gay Non-Issue." *Texas Monthly*, p. 82.
[64]Correll, S. J. (1999). "Lesbian and Gay Americans." In A. G. Dworkin & R. J. Dworkin (Eds.), *The Minority Report*, 3rd ed. Fort Worth TX: Harcourt Brace Publishers, pp. 436–456.

▌ Out at Work?

Although not formalized, many organizations have codes of silence similar to DADT regarding sexual minority status.[65] One advertisement in *DiversityInc* spoke of the silencing of sexual minorities, and highlights the everyday problems gays and lesbians experience when closeted at work:

I wonder if people really want to know how I spent my weekend.

When they ask me, I sometimes avoid the question.

When I focus too much on what people might think, I'm not being true to myself.

When I am true to myself, I worry that people will only see what I am rather than who I am. *(PriceWaterhouseCoopers advertisement in* DiversityInc, *May/June 2009, p. 1).*

Innocuous questions such as what someone did on the weekend can cause sexual minorities considerable unnecessary stress that heterosexuals do not face. Some gay and lesbian employees endure a continual "nightmare" of monitoring phone calls, social network postings, and other everyday activities.[66] When employees are forced to hide important aspects of their identity, this can lead to hopelessness, disengagement, and withdrawal.[67] In line with Cox and Blake's ideas, costs associated with this silencing, including turnover and lowered productivity, may be tremendous.

Many gays and lesbians expect, and are often subject to, discrimination, harassment, or termination if they are open at work about their sexual orientation.[68] Unlike women and many people of color, sexual

---

[65]"Don't Ask, Don't Tell—Don't Call Home?" http://www.cnn.com/2009/POLITICS/12/23/gay.military .communication/index.html, accessed June 12, 2010; Bell, M. P., Özbilgin, M., Beauregard, T. A., & Surgevil, O. (2011). "Voice, Silence, and Diversity in 21st Century Organizations." *Human Resource Management*, 50(1): 1–16.

[66]Ibid.

[67]Bell et al. (2011); Brinsfield, C. T., Edwards, M. S., & Greenberg, J. (2009). "Voice and Silence in Organizations: Historical Review and Current Conceptualizations." In J. Greenberg & M. S. Edwards (Eds.), *Voice and Silence in Organizations*. Bingley, UK: Emerald Group Publishing, pp. 1–33; Brenner, B. R., Lyons, H. Z., & Fassinger, R. E. (2010). "Can Heterosexism Harm Organizations? Predicting the Perceived Organizational Citizenship Behaviors of Gay and Lesbian Employees." *The Career Development Quarterly*, 58: 321–335.

[68]See Levine, M. P., & Leonard, R. (1984). "Discrimination against Lesbians in the Work Force." *Signs: Journal of Women in Culture and Society*, 9: 700–710; Kronenberger, G. K. (1991). "Out of the Closet." *Personnel Journal*, 70: 40–44; Graham, M. A. (1986). "Out of the Closet and into the Courtroom." *Employment Relations Today*, 13: 167–173; Ragins, B. R., & Cornwell, J. M. (2001). "Pink Triangles: Antecedents and Consequences of Perceived Workplace Discrimination against Gay and Lesbian Employees." *Journal of Applied Psychology*, 86: 1244–1261; Huffman, A. N., Watrous-Rodriguez, K. M., & King, E. G. (2008). "Supporting a Diverse Workforce: What Type of Support Is Most Meaningful for Lesbian and Gay Employees?" *Human Resource Management*, 47: 237–253.

minorities have the option of disclosing or not disclosing their sexual orientation.[69] By not disclosing (e.g., **passing**), sexual minorities can avoid some of the negative consequences associated with being out at work, and at some point in their work lives, many gays pass as a strategy for avoiding discrimination.[70] Not disclosing, however, is also associated with significant negative consequences. Being continually on guard at work, the effort to avoid letting information about one's sexual orientation "slip" in conversation, or constructing (imaginary) heterosexual partners is extremely taxing. Researchers have suggested this requires "a great deal of psychological effort and perpetual vigilance."[71] As a result, gays and lesbians may distance themselves from coworkers, resulting in dysfunctional team and communication processes.[72] When passing, gays and lesbians are likely to hear many negative comments and stereotypes about members of their group, as do other invisible minorities.

In one study on relationships between being out at work and job-related psychological outcomes, Nancy Day and Patricia Schoenrade found that employees who were out at work had higher affective commitment and job satisfaction and viewed top management as being more supportive. Employees who were out had lower role ambiguity, role conflict, and conflict between work and home.[73] Other researchers have found that perceptions of workplace discrimination were negatively related to the likelihood of being out at work. People who perceived sexual orientation discrimination in their workplace had more negative job attitudes and lower satisfaction, and thought they had less opportunity for promotion.[74] In another study, Brenner and colleagues found that heterosexism that had the effect of preventing people from being out was negatively related to employees' willingness to undertake organizational citizenship behaviors, such as helping others and complying with company rules and regulations even when no one was looking.[75] As discussed in Individual Feature 11.2, some gays recommend being open about one's

[69]Ragins (2008).
[70]See Woods, J. D. (1993). *The Corporate Closet: The Professional Lives of Gay Men in America.* New York: The Free Press.
[71]Dietch, E. A., Butz, R. M., & Brief, A. P. (2004). "Out of the Closet and Out of a Job? The Nature, Import, and Causes of Sexual Orientation Discrimination in the Workplace." In R. W. Griffin & A. O-Leary-Kelly (Eds.), *The Dark Side of Organizational Behavior.* San Francisco, CA: Jossey-Bass, pp. 187–234. For a discussion of specific strategies gays and lesbians may use to avoid concealment, see also Chrobot-Mason, D., Button, S. B., & DiClementi, J. D. (2001). "Sexual Identity Management Strategies: An Exploration of Antecedents and Consequences." *Sex Roles,* 45: 321–336.
[72]Chrobot-Mason et al. (2001); Brenner et al. (2010).
[73]Day, N. E., & Schoenrade, P. (1997). "Staying in the Closet Versus Coming Out: Relationships Between Communication About Sexual Orientation and Work Attitudes." *Personnel Psychology,* 50(1): 147–163.
[74]Ragins & Cornwell (2001).
[75]Brenner et al. (2010).

INDIVIDUAL FEATURE 11.2	*Pascal Lepine, President of Atypic Multimedia Marketing and the Chambre du Commerce Gaie Du Québec*

Pascal Lepine is president of the successful multimedia marketing firm Atypic and of the Chambre de Commerce Gaie Du Québec in Montreal. Atypical himself, Lepine, at 28, is viewed as a role model for young gays entering the workforce. When Lepine began work, he was dismayed to find no gay role models; now he is doing his part to ensure young gays do have gay role models in the workforce.

Lepine believes that networking is the key to running a successful business, and thus he and the Chambre de Commerce Gaie Du Québec have partnered with McGill University to help gay and lesbian students as they start their careers. Chamber members network with students as prospective employers; students network with members. McGill's director of career and placement students, Gregg Blachford, who is also gay, holds career workshops for gay and lesbian students. Blachford encourages students to be open about their sexual orientation, because being open helps them build supportive networks of

other gays and lesbians. Being closeted takes work and erodes confidence out of fear of slipping up and being found out. Both Lepine and Blachford view being gay as an advantage and that being gay helps people be more positive toward diversity. "Sometimes, when you've been marginalized in society, you're more open to others who are marginal. You're open to diversity and seeing the negative effects of discrimination against others."

_____

Sources: Whittaker, S. (2005, April 18). "Coming Out, Moving Up." *The Gazette* (Montreal), Bottom Line, p. B2.

QUESTIONS TO CONSIDER

1. *Do you agree with the perspective that gays and lesbians and others who have been marginalized are more likely to embrace diversity? Why or why not?*

2. *How might people who have been marginalized work together for diversity and inclusion? Why might they not do so?*

sexual orientation at work, building supportive networks and serving as role models for others.

▮ RECOMMENDATIONS FOR INDIVIDUALS

Although we have considered many negative aspects of discrimination and unfair treatment of sexual minorities, we also examined many positive aspects and many companies' supportive policies. Like other non-dominant group members, sexual minorities should take an active role in their employment searches and careers to minimize discrimination and unfairness and to maximize positive outcomes. In job seeking, they should determine which organizations include sexual orientation in their non-discrimination policies and offer equality in partner benefits. Such overtly inclusive actions are strong statements about the organization's commitment to fairness for sexual minorities. This information is usually available on company Web sites or through organizations such as the Human Rights Campaign.[76] Each year, the HRC publishes thorough reports on inclusive organizations, their benefits offerings, whether they include sexual minorities in their nondiscrimination policies, and other information useful to GLBT and heterosexuals concerned about fairness issues.

Sexual minorities should consider using referrals from friends and allies. Referrals are excellent sources of job information; as insiders, referrals know whether the company culture is supportive or hostile toward sexual minorities. If out at work, gay males should carefully assess their initial starting salaries and salary increases throughout their careers. Being proactive, knowledgeable, and willing to seek other employment options when faced with unfair treatment is a good idea for everyone. Individuals should make conscious career choices and resist being channeled into jobs that others perceive as appropriate for those who are gay, unless these occupational choices happen to coincide with personal career interests.

As in other quests for equality, straight allies have a key role to play, providing referrals to welcoming companies. Allies can also set the stage for nondiscrimination, model inclusive behavior, and help create safe and inclusive climates at work.

▌ RECOMMENDATIONS FOR ORGANIZATIONS

Including sexual orientation in an organization's nondiscrimination policy and offering equality in benefits for domestic partners are two important ways to support sexual orientation diversity. As we have discussed, multiple studies have found that a supportive climate, including nondiscrimination policies, and top management support are related to increased commitment and job satisfaction of sexual minorities.[77] Organizations with supportive climates may experience many of the positive outcomes proposed by Cox and Blake, including advantages in cost, resource acquisition, creativity, and marketing. For example, when energy spent worrying about concealing one's sexual orientation on the job can instead be spent on productive and creative work, many individual and organizational benefits ensue. In terms of marketing advantages, gays and lesbians have strong buying power and are responsive to organizational fairness. Market researchers estimate that gays and lesbians in the United

[76]http://www.hrc.org.
[77]Day, N. E., & Schoenrade, P. (2000). "The Relationship Among Reported Disclosure of Sexual Orientation, Anti-Discrimination Policies, Top Management Support, and Work Attitudes of Gay and Lesbian Employees." *Personnel Review*, 29: 346–363; Burton, S. B. (2001). "Organizational Efforts to Affirm Sexual Diversity: A Cross-Level Examination." *Journal of Applied Psychology*, 86(1), 17–28.

States have more than $835 billion in buying power and are loyal to companies that have a good record with them.[78] Many heterosexual allies of GLBT will also choose to patronize companies that emphasize fairness. Researchers have also found that benefits of inclusion extend to both small and large organizations.[79] Recall that in a recent study, Peng Wang and Joshua Schwarz discovered that firms with high Corporate Equality Ratings of inclusiveness (as rated by HRC) outperformed otherwise equivalent firms that were less inclusive.[80]

Negative outcomes are possible as well from being supportive of GLBT. While overt racism, sexism, and ageism are less widespread than in the past, overt heterosexism is still fairly common. Some employee resistance can be circumvented through training, education, and discipline of those who would persist in discrimination and exclusion. Misperceptions about "special rights" being afforded to sexual minorities should be dispelled, as should fears about the risks of transmission of HIV/AIDS. One relevant question about whether gays and lesbians should be afforded equal rights in organizations has to do with whether their sexual orientation affects their job performance. Recalling that *employment discrimination* occurs when personal characteristics of applicants and workers that are unrelated to productivity are valued in the labor market can reiterate the effects of sexual orientation discrimination on performance.[81] Just as with other invisible minorities, discrimination and fear of discrimination can affect performance by causing worry (about discrimination, ostracism, or being fired or "outed" at work).[82] Removing those fears through organizational policies of nondiscrimination and inclusion and zero tolerance for discrimination and harassment would reduce these impediments to performance.

Management or coworker preferences for heterosexual employees do not justify discrimination and it should not be tolerated. Although care must also be taken not to trample on the belief systems of other employees, those who view homosexuality as morally wrong should not be allowed to disrupt carefully constructed policies of inclusion and non-discrimination. Organizations concerned with fairness and equity for all employees should keep in mind that carefully created, widely communicated

[78]Iwata, E. (2006, November 2). "More Marketing Aimed at Gay Consumers." *USAToday*, p. B3; Witeck Combs Communications (2007, January 25). "Buying Power of U.S. Gays and Lesbians to Exceed $835 Billion in 2011." http://www.witeckcombs.com/news/releases/20070125_buyingpower.pdf, accessed March 19, 2011.

[79]Day, N. E., & Greene, P. G. (2008). "A Case for Sexual Orientation Diversity Management in Small and Large Organizations." *Human Resource Management*, 47: 637–654; Wang & Schwarz (2010).

[80]Wang & Schwarz (2010).

[81]Ehrenberg, R. G., & Smith, R. S. (1982). *Modern Labor Economics: Theory and Public Policy.* Glenview, IL: Scott, Foresman and Company, p. 394.

[82]Examining the Employment Non-Discrimination Act (ENDA).

policies of inclusion and zero tolerance for discrimination are upheld by the courts.[83] External customers and stakeholders may also resist measures to reduce sexual orientation discrimination. As discussed in Chapter 1, Disney faced vociferous, lengthy boycotts as a result of its nondiscriminatory position toward gays and lesbians. In developing and implementing policies related to sexual orientation, leaders should be prepared for resistance and committed to their plans. They must make decisions and organizational policies based on belief systems, mission, and long-term goals regarding diversity and inclusion.

SUMMARY

Sexual orientation is an increasingly important aspect of diversity. Gays and lesbians are estimated to be between 4% and 17% of the U.S. population, the large difference in estimates reflecting the difficulties associated with collecting data on sexual orientation. Employment discrimination against sexual minorities is not prohibited by federal law in the United States and in many other places. The lack of federal protections for gays and lesbians may signal to some that discrimination on the basis of sexual orientation is acceptable. Codes of silence and other problems are the result in many organizations. The Human Rights Campaign regularly assesses organizations' progress toward equal treatment for sexual minorities. Many organizations do now include sexual orientation in their nondiscrimination policies and offer equal benefits to domestic partners, which bodes well for the future.[84]

KEY TERMS

Gender identity or expression — a person's internal sense of their gender, as well as how a person behaves, appears, or presents with regard to societal expectations of that person.

Heterosexism — attitudes and behaviors denigrating and stigmatizing to non-heterosexuals.

Homophobia — the fear of homosexuals.

Passing — refers to gays and lesbians who pretend to be and are perceived as being heterosexual, to light-skinned Blacks or others of color pretending to be and being perceived as Whites, and to others whose non-dominant group membership goes unnoticed and undisclosed.

Sexual minorities — nonheterosexuals, including gay males, lesbians, bisexuals, and transgender people.

Sexual orientation — a component of sexuality characterized by enduring emotional, romantic, sexual, and/or affectional attractions to individuals of a particular gender.

[83]See the case *Peterson v. Hewlett-Packard* discussed in Chapter 12.
[84]Corporate Equality Index. (2010)

QUESTIONS TO CONSIDER

1. Some states and cities have legislation prohibiting discrimination based on sexual orientation, weight, appearance, and other factors that are not covered under federal legislation. What factors may affect the passage of such legislation in some areas but not in others? Is sexual orientation discrimination prohibited in the city or state in which you live?

2. When the U.S. armed forces were first integrated there was tremendous opposition, but integration has been accomplished. How similar and different is the opposition to the open service of gays and lesbians in the military to that for the integrated service of Blacks and Whites?

3. What is the official policy on partner benefits and sexual orientation discrimination in the organization in which you work or are interested in working? With or without non-discrimination policies, what is the climate toward GLBT in the organization?

4. How is the invisibility of sexual orientation similar to or different from the invisibility of religion?

5. In Individual Feature 11.2, Pascal Lepine proposes that gays and lesbians may also be more open to others who have also been marginalized in society. In what kinds of situations have devalued, disenfranchised, and marginalized groups in the United States supported each other's causes? When have they undermined or resisted each other's causes?

ACTIONS AND EXERCISES

1. Conduct research to identify at least two people who are gay or lesbian who are not actors or entertainers, but who are somewhat public figures. How difficult was it to find these two people? What did you learn about them?

2. Investigate the number of states in which sexual orientation discrimination is currently illegal in the United States.

3. If you are not gay, interview a close friend or relative who is openly gay about his or her experiences at work. If you are gay, how do your experiences compare with those reported in the chapter?

Religion

CHAPTER 12

Chapter Objectives

After completing this chapter, readers should have a greater understanding of religion as an aspect of diversity in organizations. Specifically, they should be able to:

❏ *discuss religion as an aspect of diversity.*

❏ *explain legislation related to religious diversity and selected legal cases involving religious discrimination.*

❏ *compare relationships between religious organizations and gender diversity among organizational leaders.*

❏ *discuss ways in which employers can accommodate religious practices of employees and applicants.*

❏ *examine ways employers can deal with conflicts among employees' different religious beliefs.*

Key Facts

An estimated 84% of the world's population is part of a religion.

In the United States, employers are required to make reasonable accommodations for employees' religious practices, much as they make reasonable accommodations for people with disabilities.

Harassment of Middle Easterners, Asian Indians, Sikhs, and others believed or known to be Muslims increased significantly in the United States after September 11, 2001, and has not returned to previous levels.

Women clergy experience a "stained glass ceiling" in religious organizations that is similar to the glass ceiling in other organizations.

Employees may post religious sayings in their workspaces, as long as they are of a size that is reasonable for personal viewing, but posting large religious sayings that target specific groups (e.g., gays) can be grounds for dismissal.

Introduction and Overview

In this chapter, we consider religion as an aspect of diversity. Religion is specifically protected from employment discrimination in the United States by Title VII of the Civil Rights Act. Despite this, religious discrimination continues to occur. In some cases, managers and supervisors discriminate by refusing to hire people who wear religious attire. In other cases, it is coworkers who discriminate and harass others on the basis of religion or, even when there is no overt discrimination, simply prefer to work with those having the same religious beliefs (e.g., shared social identity).[1] Organizational practices can also be either discriminatory, such as requiring all employees to regularly work on Saturday and Sunday, or inclusive, allowing religious expression that does not infringe on the rights of others. For some employees, the acceptance of religious expression at work is related to job satisfaction.[2] Religion is related to mental and physical health and coping, all of which are important for individuals and the organizations that employ them.

Despite its historical and current importance and clear relevance to diversity in organizations, less research and media attention have been directed toward religion compared to other protected areas.[3] In recent years, however, religious diversity has attracted more scrutiny, partly due to fears of terrorism, which have increased overt discrimination against Muslims or those perceived to be Muslims. In addition to prohibiting religious discrimination in employment, Title VII outlaws harassment and requires employers to make reasonable accommodations to allow employees to observe their religious practices.

We begin the chapter with a brief account of the history of religious diversity in the United States. We then review the population of different religious groups and U.S. laws related to religion. Our standard topics of education, earnings, and workforce participation rates are not germane to religious diversity and are not included, but because they often occur concurrently, we consider the relationship between religious discrimination and discrimination based on national origin in this chapter. The diversity of religions in the United States prevents detailed explorations of all of them, and so we focus on Arabs (most of whom are Christians) and Muslims because of the hostility toward and misperceptions about members of these groups since September 11. We also examine the "stained glass ceiling" that constrains women pastors and conflicts between religious and sexual orientation diversity. As we have done in other chapters, we provide suggestions to individuals and organizations for achieving diversity and inclusion.

Terminology

Religion involves the feelings, thoughts, and behaviors that arise from a search for the sacred, along with the rituals or prescribed behaviors of the search (such as prayer or worship services) that receive validation and support from an identifiable group of people.[4] **Religious discrimination** cant, employee, or customer unfavorably because of his or her religious beliefs. **Religiosity** is the degree to which an individual practices a religion or the strength of his or her connection with, adherence to, or conviction about the beliefs, practices, or precepts of a religion.[5] Thus, people of the same faith may have different levels of religiosity, and this may influence their behaviors at work and their interactions with others of different faiths. ●

[1]King, J. E., Stewart, M. M., & McKay, P. F. (2010). "Religiosity, Religious Identity, and Bias Towards Workplace Others." Academy of Management Conference Best Papers Proceedings. Montreal, Canada.

[2]King, J. E., & Williamson, I. (2005). "Workplace Religious Expression, Religiosity and Job Satisfaction: Clarifying a Relationship." *Journal of Management, Spirituality and Religion*, 2(2): 173–198.

[3]King, J. E. (2008). "(Dis)Missing the Obvious: Will Mainstream Management Research Ever Take Religion Seriously?" *Journal of Management Inquiry*, 17(3): 214–224.

[4]King et al. (2010).

[5]Ibid.

■ History of Religious Diversity in the United States

Since the colonies were founded, the United States has been a Protestant nation and Protestant beliefs have predominated in the country's government, courts, and many organizations.[6] The pledge of allegiance includes the phrase "one nation, under God"; "In God we trust" is visible on U.S. currency. Some of the Protestant subgroups that have long histories in the United States are the Baptists, Methodists, Lutherans, and Presbyterians.

Other religious groups in the United States have been significantly less numerous than the Protestants, yet they have still played important roles. These groups include Roman Catholics, Jews,[7] Muslims, Buddhists, and Hindus, among many others. The arrival of Irish and French Catholics "curdled the blood" of Protestant colonialists, who viewed Catholicism "as a religious and political threat."[8] The first Jews arrived in 1654 from Europe, where they had experienced isolation and expulsion.[9] In 1776, 2,500 Jews lived in the United States, and by 1870, there were 200,000 Jews, mostly of German origin.[10] Many other religious minorities came to the United States seeking, but not always finding, refuge from religious persecution elsewhere. For example, during certain periods in U.S. history, Jews could not hold political office and Catholics could not practice their faith or hold office and were heavily taxed.[11] Signs in storefronts commonly notified Jews and Catholics (and Blacks) that they were unwelcome. In addition to persecution by Protestants, non-dominant religions themselves practiced religious discrimination.

■ Population and Variations among Beliefs

As in the past, the majority of the U.S. population continues to identify themselves as Christian—about 76% (a decline, however, from 86% in 1990).[12] As Table 12.1 shows, the largest single group of Christians is Catholics (25.1%), followed by Baptists (15.8%). Slightly more than 1% of the adults in the United States report being Jewish (1.2%), 0.5% are Buddhists, and 0.6% are Muslim. A growing proportion of the U.S.

---

[6]Smith, T. W., & Kim, S. (2005). "The Vanishing Protestant Majority." *Journal for the Scientific Study of Religion,* 44(2): 211–223.
[7]Jews are an ethnic group that experiences religious as well as ethnic discrimination.
[8]Archdeacon, T. J. (1983). *Becoming American.* New York: Free Press, p. 21.
[9]Schaefer, R. T. (2002). *Racial and Ethnic Groups,* 8th ed. Princeton, NJ: Prentice Hall.
[10]Ibid.
[11]Archdeacon (1983).
[12]Kosmin, B. A., & Keysar, A. (2009). *American Religious Identification Survey (ARIS 2008).* The Graduate Center, City University of New York.

Table 12.1 *Comparison of Religious Self-Identification, 1990, 2001, 2008*

Christian Groups	Percent		
	1990	2001	2008
Catholic	26.2	24.5	25.1
Baptist	19.3	16.3	15.8
Other Christian*	40.7	35.9	35.1
Total Christian	86.2	76.7	76.0
Other Religious Groups			
Jewish	1.8	1.4	1.2
Eastern Religions	0.4	1.0	0.9
Muslim	0.3	0.5	0.6
Other Non-Christians	0.1	0.8	1.2
Total Other Religions	3.3	3.7	3.9
No Religion Groups	**8.2**	**14.1**	**15.0**
Don't Know/Refused	**2.3**	**5.4**	**5.2**

*Includes Methodist, Lutheran, Presbyterian, Non-Denominational Christian, Pentecostal, among others.

Source: Adapted from Kosmin, B. A., & Keysar, A. (2009). *American Religious Identification Survey (ARIS 2008).* Summary Report. Hartford, CT: Trinity College. http://www.americanreligionsurvey-aris .org/reports/ARIS_Report_2008.pdf, accessed July 31, 2010.

population reports no stated religious preference, up from 8.2% in 1990 to 15.0% in 2008.[13]

Because the U.S. population is overwhelmingly Christian but a nontrivial one-quarter is not, there is a potential for conflict between groups. In addition, even though most Americans are Christian, there is a diversity of beliefs among Christian organizations, often over women's roles and, as we discuss later, sexual orientation. Religious organizations themselves are some of the most homogenous of organizational types, having primarily male leadership and little racial and ethnic diversity. Only an estimated 1% of Blacks, for example, worship in primarily White religious organizations.[14]

■ RACE, ETHNICITY, AND RELIGION

The American Religious Identification Survey (ARIS) provides insightful data on the variation in religious and secular identification by race,

[13]Ibid.
[14]Schaefer (2002).

ethnicity, age, and sex.[15] Blacks (81%), Whites (77%), Hispanics (75%), and Asians (62%) are most to least likely to regard themselves as religious or very religious. Asians (30%), Whites (17%), Hispanics (16%), and Blacks (11%) are most to least likely to view themselves as secular or somewhat secular. Women are more religious than men, with 78% reporting being religious or very religious, compared to 72% of men. Older adults are more religious than younger adults; 78% of people aged 35 to 64 are religious or very religious, compared to 70% of those aged 18 to 34. We consider relationships between reported religiosity and attitudes toward sexual minorities later in the chapter.

ARIS highlights the "multilayered nature of social identity" as it relates to religion, particularly for Hispanics and Jews.[16] The majority of Hispanics (57%) are Catholics, but 22% are Protestants, 12% report no religion, and 5% identify themselves as belonging to some other religion.[17] Thus, the common assumption that Hispanics are Catholics is erroneous for a significant portion of the Hispanic population.

Among American Jews, "Jewish identity" reflects religious, ethnic, and cultural elements, and not everyone who is Jewish identifies with all three. Of the population that self-identifies as Jewish, 53% identify with Judaism as a religion, while 47% identify with Judaism because their parents were Jewish, they were raised Jewish, or for some other reason. As discussed in Chapter 7, at one point, Jews in the United States were viewed as a separate "race." Overt actions taken by the government, such as providing veterans' educational and housing benefits to Jews, helped them to be regarded as Whites, although they still experience discrimination at times.[18,19]

▍ RELEVANT LEGISLATION

In the United States, laws require that individuals with different beliefs recognize the rights of others to their own religious practices and to a nondiscriminatory workplace. Title VII defines religious discrimination as treating an applicant or employee unfavorably because of his or her

---

[15]Kosmin, B. A., Mayer, E., & Keysar, A. (2001). *American Religious Identification Survey (2001).* The Graduate Center, City University of New York. http://www.gc.cuny.edu/faculty/research_briefs/aris/key_findings.htm, accessed August 1, 2010.
[16]Kosmin, B. A., et al. (2001). "Religion and Identity: Hispanics and Jews." *American Religious Identification Survey.*
[17]Ibid.
[18]Brodkin, K. (1998). *How Jews Became White Folks & What That Says About Race in America.* Piscataway, NJ: Rutgers University Press.
[19]Ragins, B. R. (2008). "Disclosure Disconnects: Antecedents and Consequences of Disclosing Invisible Stigmas Across Life Domains." *Academy of Management Review,* 33(1): 199–215.

religious beliefs.[20] Title VII prohibits employers of fifteen or more people from discriminating against employees or applicants in hiring, firing, and other terms and conditions of employment because of their religious beliefs or practices. The law protects people who belong to organized religions, those who have sincerely held religious, ethical, or moral beliefs, and those who hold no religious beliefs.

EEOC Guidelines on Religious Exercise and Religious Expression in the Federal Workplace

To help employers deal with the many and varied issues that may arise concerning religious diversity, the EEOC has issued guidelines on religious exercise and religious expression.[21] The guidelines were written for federal workplaces but are quite useful to private employers as well. They provide recommendations for handling such issues as the display of religious materials, wearing religious jewelry, inviting coworkers to religious services, harassment, and accommodations. The focus of the EEOC's guidelines on religious exercise is treating "all employees with the same respect and consideration, regardless of their religion (or lack thereof)."

The EEOC has listed multiple areas in which employers (not just the Federal government) must try to avoid religious discrimination (Table 12.2). The following sections discuss these areas and provide examples of actual lawsuits filed and won by the EEOC against employers for discrimination.

Discrimination in Work Situations and Harassment

A case of religious discrimination in a work situation occurred when two customer service technicians for AT&T who had regularly attended the annual Jehovah's Witnesses Convention were denied their requests for leave.[22] Both men had sincerely held religious beliefs that required them to attend the convention each year, and they had attended each of the previous years they had worked at AT&T. Although they submitted written requests for one day of leave six months in advance, the men were suspended and then fired for going

---

[20]Equal Employment Opportunity Commission. http://www.eeoc.gov/laws/types/religion.cfm, accessed July 31, 2010.
[21]"Guidelines on Religious Exercise and Religious Expression in the Federal Workplace." http://clinton2.nara.gov/WH/New/html/19970819-3275.html, accessed August 1, 2010.
[22]"AT&T to Pay $756,000 for Religious Bias against Jehovah's Witnesses." http://www.eeoc.gov/eeoc/newsroom/release/10-23-07.cfm, accessed August 1, 2010.

Table 12.2 *Clarifying Religious Discrimination (EEOC)*

Discrimination in Work Situations—discrimination regarding any aspect of employment, including hiring, firing, pay, job assignments, promotions, layoffs, training, fringe benefits, and any other term and condition of employment.

- Harassment—offensive remarks about a person's religious beliefs that are so frequent or severe as to create a hostile or offensive work environment or result in a person being fired or demoted. Harassment can be perpetrated by a manager, supervisor, coworker, client, or customer.

- Reasonable Accommodation—Title VII requires reasonable accommodation of an employee's religious beliefs or practices unless doing so would cause more than a minimal burden on business operations (e.g., undue hardship). Some common religious accommodations include flexible scheduling, voluntary shift substitutions, job reassignments, and modification of work policies or practices.

  - Undue hardship—employers are not required to make accommodations that are costly, compromise workplace safety, decrease efficiency, infringe on the rights of other employees, or require other employees to do more than their share of work.

- Dress and Grooming Practices—requires employers, without undue hardship, to allow changes in dress or grooming practices that an employee follows for religious reasons, including such things as wearing certain hairstyles, head coverings, or certain clothing.

- Employment Policies/Practices—employees cannot be forced to participate (or not participate) in certain religious activities as a condition of employment.

Source: Equal Employment Opportunity Commission. "Religious Discrimination." http://www.eeoc .gov/laws/types/religion.cfm, accessed July 31, 2010.

to the convention. A jury awarded the men, who had six and eight years of service with AT&T, $756,000 in back pay and compensatory damages for religious discrimination.

In another recent case, two Jewish brothers who worked for Administaff were subjected to egregious verbal and physical harassment.[23] (Administaff is a nationwide company that provides full human resources services to small- and medium-sized businesses.) Over a two-year period, Scott and Joey Jacobson were called numerous anti-Semitic slurs by managers and coworkers. At one point, a swastika was drawn on Scott's work vehicle. Scott was also thrown into a trash bin while managers watched on a surveillance camera and laughed. Administaff agreed to pay $115,000 to settle the case.

[23]"Administaff to Pay $115,000 for Religious Bias." http://www.eeoc.gov/eeoc/newsroom/release/ 3-17-10.cfm, accessed August 1, 2010.

Employers are encouraged to have an antiharassment policy that explicitly includes religious harassment and to have an effective procedure for reporting harassment. Employees who report harassment should be assured of a prompt, fair investigation; freedom from retaliation for having complained; and appropriate consequences for harassers.

Reasonable Accommodations

Under Title VII, covered employers must make reasonable accommodations to allow employees to observe their normal religious practices. Reasonable accommodations include such things as flexible scheduling, job reassignments and lateral transfers, and modifying workplace practices when doing so does not pose an undue hardship on the organization's legitimate business interests. Undue hardship varies by employer, and there are no set rules for which practice or request is deemed an instance of undue hardship. If, for an individual employer, accommodating an employee's religious beliefs would result in excessive administrative costs, diminished efficiency or safety, or an excessive burden for coworkers, a claim of undue hardship would be warranted. Excessive administrative costs would be different for a small employer having thirty employees and an organization employing thousands of workers. Similarly, accommodating an employee's request for a particular day off to observe his or her religious practices in an organization that operates twenty-four hours per day, seven days a week, would be a different situation for an organization that is open fewer hours and days per week.

Misperception: A request for Saturdays off to worship is undue hardship for retailers.

Reality: A Saturday Sabbath could be traded for a Sunday work day in organizations that are open seven days per week.

Flexible scheduling. Three years after she was fired for refusing to work on Sundays in her job in a public library in a Kentucky town, Connie Rehm won her job back. Rehm, a practicing Christian, had been working for the library for twelve years when the library adopted Sunday hours. During the three years between filing the lawsuit and winning the court case, the library offered Rehm a settlement. Apparently, the library's position was "to deal with it as a financial matter" and make it go away, but Rehm wanted her job back because it allowed her to serve the community. In addition to getting her beloved job back, the jury awarded

Rehm $53,712 in damages to cover her lost wages, minus what she earned at other jobs after being fired.[24]

Because Christianity is the dominant religion in the United States, and the large numbers of people professing Christianity, employers may be reluctant to accommodate employees who wish not to work on Sundays. However, many Christian employees, even those who attend Sunday services, are willing to work on that day. For those who do wish to be off for the entire day, employers should, as with members of any other religion, attempt to accommodate their religious beliefs. At the same time, employers must also be careful to avoid responding more favorably to Christians' requests for accommodation, assuming all employees are Christian, or disbelieving Christians' claim of religious harassment and discrimination. Researchers have documented overt stereotyping, harassment, and discrimination against Christians at work, despite their numerical majority in the U.S. population.[25]

Pre-employment scheduling inquiries. According to the EEOC, employers have a duty to accommodate prospective employees as well as current employees. Job advertisements often specify the days and hours of work required, and applicants' availability to work during those hours is used to prequalify them. However, an employer may not use an applicant's need for a religious accommodation to exclude the applicant unless doing so would result in undue hardship.[26] After making a contingent offer, the employer can inquire into the need for a religious accommodation and then determine whether such an accommodation is possible. From a diversity perspective, the key idea is that people with varying religious observances and practices need to work, and when a scheduling accommodation can be made, employing these people will be beneficial to them, to employers (e.g., resource acquisition), and to society.

Accommodations for dress or grooming. Khadija Ahdaoui was fired from her job as a housekeeper at Ivy Hall Assisted Living when she

[24]Fields, D. (2006). "Woman Wins Religious Discrimination Case." http://blaisebaptist.com/templates/System/details.asp?id=36001&PG=xCast&LID=996&CID=2888, accessed August 1, 2010.

[25]Lyons, B. J., Wessel, J., Ghumman, S., & Ryan, A. M. (2010). "Stereotypes and Identity Management Strategies of Christians in the Workplace." Paper presented at the 2010 meeting of the Academy of Management. Montreal; Moran, C. D. (2007). "The Public Identity Work of Evangelical Christians." *Journal of College Student Development,* 48(4): 418–434. For discrimination against Christians in New Zealand, see Lips-Wiersma, M., & Mills, C. (2002). "Coming Out of the Closet: Negotiating Spiritual Expression in the Workplace." *Journal of Managerial Psychology,* 17: 183–202.

[26]Title 29—Labor, Chapter XIV—Equal Employment Opportunity Commission Part 1605—Guidelines on Discrimination Because of Religion, 1605.2, Reasonable accommodation without undue hardship as required by Section 701(j) of Title VII of the Civil Rights Act of 1964. http://www.access.gpo.gov/nara/cfr/waisidx_06/29cfr1605_06.html, accessed August 1, 2010.

refused to stop wearing a hijab (head scarf) on the job.[27] As part of her Muslim beliefs, Khadija wore the hijab outside her home. Although the company denied any liability or wrongdoing, it agreed in a settlement with the EEOC to pay $43,000 and to provide equal employment opportunity training, report any further religious discrimination complaints, and post an antidiscrimination notice.

Claims and Selected Cases under Title VII

In 2010, the EEOC received 3,790 claims alleging religious discrimination, a more than 10% increase from the prior year. As with other claims of discrimination, the claimant is unlikely to prevail: 22.4% of resolved charges were merit resolutions. Nonetheless, $10.0 million was recovered for plaintiffs and others who were affected.[28] The EEOC received 11,304 charges of national origin discrimination and resolved 12,404 charges; 20.6% were merit resolutions and $29.6 million was recovered for affected parties.[29]

As Table 12.3 shows, since the terrorist acts of September 11, 2001, settlements with the EEOC for employment discrimination based on religion, ethnic origin, or national origin have increased from pre-9/11 levels, peaking at $48.1 million in 2001. In October 2001, the EEOC issued specific statements regarding such discrimination, reiterating that it was

TABLE 12.3 **EEOC Settlements for Religious and National Origin Discrimination 1999–2010 (millions of dollars)**

	1999	2000	2001	2002	2003	2004	2005	2006	2007	2008	2009	2010
Religion monetary settlements	$3.1	$5.5	$14.1*	$4.3	$6.6	$6.0	$6.1	$5.7	$6.4	$7.5	$7.6	$10.0
National origin monetary settlements	$19.7	$15.7	$48.1*	$21.0	$21.3	$22.3	$19.4	$21.2	$22.8	$25.4	$25.7	$29.6

*The peak of $14.1 and $48.1 million in religion and national origin settlements occurred in 2001, reflecting a large number of discrimination and harassment charges and settlements that occurred after 9/11.

Sources: The U.S. Equal Employment Opportunity Commission. "Religion-Based Charges FY 1997–FY 2009." http://www.eeoc.gov/eeoc/statistics/enforcement/religion.cfm, accessed January 12, 2011; "National Origin-Based Charges FY 1997–FY 2009." http://www.eeoc.gov/eeoc/statistics/enforcement/origin.cfm, accessed January 12, 2011.

[27]"Ivy Hall Assisted Living Pays $43,000 to Settle Religious Discrimination Suit." http://www.eeoc.gov/eeoc/newsroom/release/12-18-09.cfm, accessed August 1, 2010.

[28]"Religious Discrimination." http://www.eeoc.gov/eeoc/statistics/enforcement/religion.cfm, accessed August 1, 2010.

[29]"National Origin-Based Charges FY 1997–FY 2010." http://www.eeoc.gov/eeoc/statistics/enforcement/origin.cfm, accessed January 12, 2010.

prohibited by Title VII of the Civil Rights Act of 1964. Employers and unions were encouraged to be "particularly sensitive" to discrimination against or harassment of persons who are, or are perceived to be, Muslim, Arab, Afghani, Middle Eastern, or South Asian (e.g., Pakistani, Indian).[30] Despite prohibitions against harassment on the basis of religion, ethnicity, and national origin, the cases filed with the EEOC indicate that they still occur, often concurrently.

■ THE DIVERSITY AMONG ARAB AMERICANS AND MUSLIMS IN THE UNITED STATES

The Arab-American Institute (AAI) estimates that there are 3.5 million Americans with some Arab heritage. Eighty percent of people of Arab descent in America are U.S. citizens, nearly two-thirds are Christian (predominantly Catholic), and 24% are Muslims.[31] The Muslims are from various racial and ethnic groups: 34% are Asian, 27% are African American, 15% are White, 10% are Hispanic, and 14% report other racial/ethnic origins.[32] Consistent with other blanket generalizations applied to groups, anti-Arab and anti-Muslim stereotypes are often based on erroneous assumptions.

Misperception: Most Arab Americans are Muslims.

Reality: The majority of Arab Americans are Christians.

Racial Profiling of Arabs (or People Who Look as though They Might Be Arab)

The irrational subheading above appropriately captures the confusion of surrounding attitudes and actions associated with profiling. As discussed in previous chapters, **profiling** is using someone's real or perceived demographic characteristic to single the person out for scrutiny. The profiling of African Americans and Latinos is a concern in the United States, and since the 2001 terrorist attacks on the U.S. Pentagon and the World Trade Center, the profiling of Arabs, Muslims, and people who look as though they might be either or both has also become of

---

[30]Equal Employment Opportunity Commission. "Employment Discrimination Based on Religion, Ethnicity, or Country of Origin." http://www.eeoc.gov/facts/fs-relig_ethnic.html, accessed March 7, 2005.
[31]Arab American Institute. "Demographics." http://www.aaiusa.org/demographics.htm, accessed August 1, 2010.
[32] *American Religious Identification Survey (2001).*

concern.[33] The expression "flying while Brown" refers to the numerous instances in which law-abiding Middle Easterners (often long-term residents or U.S. citizens) were repeatedly questioned or even removed from planes.

As with other forms of discriminatory behavior toward customers, profiling can be expensive and counterproductive. American Airlines, Delta, Continental, Northwestern, and United have all been accused of discriminating against customers of Middle Eastern descent. In response to the widely reported profiling, the CEO of Delta Airlines insisted that employees' behavior should be based on customers' conduct rather than on their race or national origin.[34] Other forms of discrimination against Muslim customers, such as refusal of service, have also been documented.

▌ RELIGION AS AN INVISIBLE IDENTITY

In the absence of identifiable attire, members of many religions are invisible, which, as for sexual orientation, comes with privileges and problems. The experience of a Jewish business school professor who ignored a warning not to take a job at a particular university highlights the negative effects of passing for religious minorities:

She told me they'd fire me once they found out that I'm Jewish. I thought she was so old school, until my first day on the job. The ex-Dean told me that he moved from a neighborhood because "there were too many Jews there."
I decided not to tell anyone I was Jewish. But then my colleagues became my friends, and one day I found myself putting up Christmas ornaments before they came over. I was denying who I was in my very own home. So I decided to come out of the "Jewish closet" at work. I found out later that the Provost kept a list of Jewish faculty. He added me to the list.[35]

The invisibility of the professor's religion provided the opportunity to remain closeted, yet doing so came with the negative consequence of denying an important aspect of his identity. Like racial minorities and gays and lesbians who "pass," religious minorities suffer the stress and worry that their stigmatized identity may be found out, along with guilt and confusion about the denial. Religious minorities may have common

[33]Heumann, M., & Cassak, L. (2003). *Good Cop, Bad Cop: Racial Profiling and Competing Views of Justice.* New York: Peter Lang Publishers. See also Bennett, W., Dilulio, J., & Walters, J. (1996). *Body Count.* New York: Simon & Schuster.
[34]Polakow-Suransky, S. (2001, November). "Flying While Brown." *The American Prospect,* 12(20).
[35]Ragins, B. R. (2008). "Disclosure Disconnects: Antecedents and Consequences of Disclosing Invisible Stigmas Across Life Domains." *Academy of Management Review,* 33(1): 199–215.

in-group status with those in the majority, such as race or sex, but at times, religious differences are more salient than areas of commonality.

■ WOMEN'S ROLES IN ORGANIZED RELIGION

One important source of differences in beliefs within and among religions is their attitude toward allowing women to be ordained as clergy or to otherwise serve in leadership positions. As discussed in Chapter 3, religious organizations are exempted from certain U.S. laws prohibiting discrimination. When doctrines relegate women to subservient roles and when the organization is strictly religious (and not operating for secular purposes), it is not generally illegal to discriminate against women in hiring, placement, promotion, compensation, or other job-related matters. The two largest Christian groups in the United States, Catholics and Baptists, do not allow women to serve in the highest leadership positions of their organizations. Some other religious groups that do not allow women to serve as clergy are the Church of Jesus Christ of the Latter-day Saints, Orthodox Judaism, and the Church of God in Christ.[36] Although they are dissimilar in key beliefs about faith, they are in agreement on women's unsuitability as clergy.

However, many religious organizations do ordain women. The Episcopal, Presbyterian, and Methodist churches are some of those that allow women to be ordained. The numbers of ordained women have increased significantly since the 1970s, when the ordination of women first began to take hold. More than one in eight clergy in the United States are now female.[37] However, through what is referred to as the **stained glass ceiling**, women clergy are often confined to junior, associate, or co-pastor positions in smaller, less prestigious congregations and have lower earnings than male clergy."[38]

In their article "Clergy and the Politics of Gender," Melissa Deckman and her colleagues analyzed attitudinal and behavioral aspects of male and female clergy in mainline Protestant organizations and found clear differences.[39] Women were more likely to support political and social

---

[36]Schaefer (2002).
[37]"Women as Clergy: The Status of Women in Society and Religion." http://www.religioustolerance. org/femclrg6.htm, accessed August 1, 2010.
[38]Schaefer (2002); see also Nesbitt, P. (1997). "Clergy Feminization: Controlled Labor or Transformative Change?" *Journal for the Scientific Study of Religion,* 36: 585–598; Sullins, P. (2000). "The Stained Glass Ceiling. Career Attainment for Women Clergy." *Sociology of Religion,* 61(3): 243–267; Purvis, S. B. (1995). *The Stained Glass Ceiling: Churches and Their Women Pastors.* Louisville, KY: Westminster John Knox Press.
[39]Deckman, M. M., Crawford, S. E. S., Olson, L. R., & Green, J. C. (2003). "Clergy and the Politics of Gender." *Journal for the Scientific Study of Religion,* 42: 621–631.

issues such as abortion, gay rights, and women's rights. Women clergy were significantly more likely to work in race relations programs and domestic violence counseling, to minister to gay people, and to provide support to people living with HIV/AIDS. The researchers proposed that challenges women clergy face "might embolden them to take political action, particularly to fight on behalf of the rights of devalued, disenfranchised minority groups."[40]

Individual Feature 12.1 focuses on Pastor Jacquelyn Donald-Mims, a minister who is concerned with social and economic issues in the community of the multicultural, multiracial church she pastors.

▌ RELIGION AND DIVERSITY IN SEXUAL ORIENTATION AT WORK

As we have discussed, religious diversity has become increasingly important as the U.S. population has become more diverse in race and origin. At the same time, the pressure on organizations to practice inclusion and to prohibit discrimination on the basis of sexual orientation has also intensified. Because many religions in the United States hold that homosexuality is morally wrong, inclusive organizations must attend to the rights of sexual minorities to a nondiscriminatory work environment while not requiring others to profess "valuing" homosexuality or other behaviors contradictory to their religious beliefs. How can the rights of employees who are sexual minorities and those who strongly believe that homosexuality is immoral both be protected? When do attempts at inclusion go too far? When does religious freedom go too far?

Recent research indicates that religious fundamentalism, rather than religiosity alone or membership in any particular religion, is most strongly related to negative attitudes toward sexual (and often racial) minorities.[41] In one study of Christians, Muslims, Jews, and Hindus, people from any of these religions who had strongly fundamentalist beliefs were more negative toward homosexuals than people who did not have strong fundamentalist beliefs.[42]

----

[40]Deckman et al. (2003), p. 629.
[41]See Altameyer, B., & Hunsberger, B. (1992). "Authoritarianism, Religious Fundamentalism, Quest, and Prejudice." *The International Journal for the Psychology of Religion,* 2(2): 113–133; Duck, R. J., & Hunsberger, B. (1999). "Religious Orientation and Prejudice: The Role of Religious Proscription, Right-Wing Authoritarianism, and Social Desirability." *The International Journal for the Psychology of Religion,* 9(3): 157–179; Laythe, B., Finkel, D., & Kirkpatrick, L. A. (2001). "Predicting Prejudice from Religious Fundamentalism and Right-Wing Authoritarianism: A Multiple-Regression Approach." *Journal for the Scientific Study of Religion,* 40(1): 1–10.
[42]Husberger, B. (1996). "Religious Fundamentalism, Right-Wing Authoritarianism, and Hostility Toward Homosexuals in Non-Christian Religious Groups." *International Journal for the Psychology of Religion,* 6(1): 39–49.

INDIVIDUAL FEATURE 12.1	*Pastor Jacquelyn Donald-Mims, D. Min., Imani Community Church*

Jacquelyn Donald-Mims founded Imani Community Church in Austin, Texas, in 1995, an African Methodist Episcopal church. Imani's objective is to appeal to all with an "interdenominational, multiracial embrace, open to all races, classes, and cultures." In an article entitled "Women Clergy Come into Their Own in Protestant Churches," Donald-Mims writes about women in the ministry: "Christian church tradition worships an inclusive savior but unfortunately has historically denied recognition of women's divine calling. Today, female clergy represent a growing and influential presence."[43] Donald-Mims believes we are witnessing a change in the hierarchy that has traditionally "put men and clergy at the top and women and laity at the bottom."[44] This change is accompanied by not only upheaval, but also rewards.

One of the rewards of women in the ministry is inclusion. Imani Community Church is a Christian inclusive church that focuses on those who are "un-churched" and "de-churched" or feel estranged in Austin's diverse community. Donald-Mims is a member of Austin Area Interreligious Ministries (AAIM), which is an interfaith group of about 150 faith communities, including the various Catholic and Protestant Christian denominations, Buddhist, Hindu, Jewish, Mennonite, Muslim, Scientologist, and Sikh, among many others. She participates in AAIM events designed to focus attention on "long neglected divisions among people of faith." Such divisions include social issues such as racism, classism, and police treatment of minorities, including questionable fatal shootings. Donald-Mims

believes that cultural proficiency, embraced by everyone in the community, is important in eradicating stereotypes. Strength emanates from the unity of religious leaders, both strong and weak. Together, leaders must "speak truth to power" and hold law enforcement and civic leaders accountable for what happens throughout the communities, rather than myopically protecting only their own individual jurisdictions. Along with social issues, Donald-Mims sees helping people deal with economic issues as key aspects of her ministry.

Donald-Mims has earned five degrees: the Doctor of Ministry degree at United Theological Seminary, Dayton, Ohio; the Master of Divinity at Perkins School of Theology at Southern Methodist University, Dallas; the Master of Theological Studies at University of Dallas; the Master of Business Administration at Georgia State University, Atlanta; and the Bachelor of Science at Tuskegee University in Alabama. Prior to entering the ministry, Donald-Mims had a successful career as a financial manager and executive in a large corporation, where she mentored numerous women and minorities. A dual-career wife and mother, Donald-Mims is married to an intellectual property lawyer and has one son.

Sources: http://www.imanichurch.com; Flynn, E. (2005, July 13). "Uniting in Spirit: Clerics Gather to Address Austin's Racial, Economic Divisions." *American-Statesman*; http://www.statesman.com/metrostate/content/metro/stories/07/13clergy.html, accessed September 21, 2005; Jacquelyn Donald-Mims, personal communication, September 21, 2005.

[43]Donald-Mims, J. (2005, February 28). "Women Clergy Come into Their Own in Protestant Churches." Austin Area Interreligious Ministries.

[44]Donald-Mims has also authored a book about women clergy entitled *Move over Men: God Calls Women into the Pulpit* (1998). Austin, TX: Devon Publishers.

Misperception: Christians have stronger negative reactions toward sexual minorities than people from other religious groups.

Reality: People from various religious who are strong fundamentalists have the most negative reactions toward sexual minorities.

Not everyone who has strongly held religious beliefs will behave negatively toward gays and lesbians, or resist sexual orientation diversity at work, however. Two cases exemplify potential conflicts arising from religious beliefs, sexual orientation, and an organization's diversity practices. In one case, *Peterson v. Hewlett-Packard Co.,* the company was vindicated. In the other case, AT&T Broadband was found liable for religious discrimination.[45]

Conflicts between Religion and Sexual Orientation: Two Cases with Different Outcomes

Richard Peterson and Hewlett-Packard.[46] Richard Peterson, a devout Christian, had worked successfully for Hewlett-Packard (HP) for twenty-one years in its Boise, Idaho, office. HP is noted for its diversity efforts, such as same-sex (and heterosexual) partner benefits and a non-harassment policy that includes sexual orientation, among other things. As part of its overall workforce diversity campaign, HP began displaying diversity posters. The posters were photos of HP employees who represented different aspects of diversity (e.g., Black, Hispanic, gay). Peterson objected to the poster that displayed a gay male, and in response to that poster, Peterson posted Bible scriptures condemning homosexuality on his cubicle. The scriptures were written in a sufficiently large type to be seen by Peterson's coworkers, by customers, and by others in the office area.

Peterson's supervisors removed the Bible passages because they were inconsistent with HP's nonharassment policy. In at least four discussions with HP management, Peterson acknowledged that he meant for the scriptures to be hurtful and to condemn homosexual behavior. He also claimed that HP's diversity program was intended to target Christian employees. Peterson suggested that he would remove the scriptures if the

---

[45]Although both cases involve Christians, people from other faiths also may take issue with homosexuals, particularly those with strong fundamentalist beliefs.

[46]http://www.danpinello.com/Peterson.htm, accessed, August 12, 2010; "Court Rules for HP in Religious Discrimination Case." *Sacramento Business Journal*, January 7, 2004.

"gay" posters were removed. When he refused any other compromise, management gave Peterson time off with pay to reconsider. After the paid time off, Peterson returned to work, posted the scriptures again, and was fired.

Peterson went to the EEOC to complain of religious discrimination, received a right to sue notice, and filed a lawsuit against HP. In his lawsuit, Peterson alleged that Christians were targeted by HP's diversity policy, that its goals were to change Christians' beliefs to support homosexuality, and that HP was on a crusade to change moral values in Idaho under the guise of diversity. He alleged HP had treated him differently than other employees and failed to reasonably accommodate his religious beliefs. The courts assessed HP's behavior, including a three-day meeting to deliberately and consciously make decisions about the company's diversity program and allowing Peterson to post antihomosexual bumper stickers on his car that was regularly parked in the company's parking lot. HP did not forbid Peterson to park his car, but did ask him to exhibit respect for his coworkers.

The district court ruled for HP, noting that the only accommodation that was acceptable to Peterson, removing the posters or allowing his targeted, large-type scriptures to remain, required HP to endure undue hardship. Upon appeal, the appeals court also ruled for HP, rejecting Peterson's religious discrimination claims.

Albert Buonanno and AT&T.[47] Albert Buonanno, a devout Catholic, worked for AT&T Broadband in Denver. Buonanno was described as a model employee, who befriended and helped others, including transgender and gay employees. As part of AT&T's diversity program, Buonanno was told that he needed to sign an agreement stating he would "value" fellow employees and their behaviors. Buonanno stated that he could tolerate other religions and love and appreciate other people but could not "value" homosexuality or other religious beliefs.

When Buonanno was fired for refusing to sign the document, he sued AT&T under Title VII of the Civil Rights Act, alleging religious discrimination. He asked for compensatory damages to cover his lost wages and contributions to his 401k plan, emotional distress, interest, and punitive damages (available in cases of intentional discrimination). The judge focused on how AT&T handled Buonanno's firing and ruled in his favor, awarding all but punitive damages. She acknowledged that although deleting portions of the company handbook could make uniform application of company policies more difficult, a reasonable accommodation could have been made for Buonanno's closely held religious beliefs.

---

[47]Hudson, K. (2004, April 6). "Diversity Suit Loss for Cable Titan." *Denver Post*.

Resolving Conflicts

As these two cases indicate, the courts do assess reasonableness of accommodation requests and undue hardship. People's different beliefs about religion and sexual orientation require careful employer attention to fairness and equity for all parties in a careful balancing act. HP's purposefully designed diversity policy and thoughtful consideration of Richard Peterson's rights allowed HP to prevail in a religious discrimination lawsuit. In contrast, AT&T's failure to carefully consider and reasonably accommodate Buonanno's simple request resulted in its loss in a religious discrimination lawsuit.

Managers and supervisors must avoid being judgmental about those who have strongly held religious beliefs regarding sexual orientation. Employees have the right to their beliefs about homosexuality, but they do not have the right to denigrate or harass coworkers based on sexual orientation when doing so is prohibited by organizational policy. Even if sexual orientation discrimination is not specifically prohibited by organizational policy, respectful behaviors should be required of all employees. In addition, employees with closely held religious beliefs have responsibilities to comply with organizational regulations to the extent that they do not trample on the employees' religious rights. Where an organization requires respectful behavior toward each other, employees should comply. In the HP and AT&T cases described, both Christian men had strongly held beliefs. Peterson chose to go against organizational policy in an unreasonable manner. In contrast, Buonanno chose to go against an organizational policy that was unreasonable.

An unusual situation involving conflicts between an employee's Christian religious beliefs and job requirements occurred at Eckerd's in Denton, Texas. Gene Herr, a pharmacist at Eckerd's, was fired because he refused to fill a prescription for the "morning-after" contraceptive pill for a woman who had been raped, citing religious grounds. If taken within seventy-two hours of intercourse, the morning-after pill prevents contraception in most cases. According to news reports, an unnamed rape victim took her prescription for the pill to Eckerd's in Denton, Texas. There, Gene Herr and two other unnamed pharmacists reportedly refused to fill the prescription. Herr called his associate pastor to see what he thought and learned that the associate pastor agreed with his decision.[48] Herr returned to the counter and told the woman that if she had conceived as a result of the rape, the prescription would take the child's life, and thus he couldn't fill the prescription.

[48]Tapper, J., & Date, J. (2004). "Can Pharmacists Withhold Birth Control?" http://abcnews.go.com/WNT/story?id=131591, accessed July 31, 2010.

Eckerd's has a policy that no pharmacist can refuse to fill a prescription solely on moral or religious grounds; therefore, Herr and the other two pharmacists were fired. Although he had worked for Eckerd's for five years and had refused to fill that prescription for several other women, Herr was reportedly unaware of the policy prior to his termination. Texas law prohibits doctors, nurses, staff, or employees of hospitals or health care centers from being forced to participate in an abortion; however, Eckerd's is none of those facilities.[49] In another, less urgent situation, also in Texas, a CVS pharmacist refused to fill the birth control prescription for a customer, Julee Lacey. The pharmacist told Lacey that she did not believe in birth control and therefore would not fill the prescription. The CVS policy is not to force pharmacists to do things that will violate their religious beliefs; thus the pharmacist retained her job. Lacey, a married mother of two and a Christian herself, found another pharmacy.[50]

As with the cases involving sexual orientation and religion, these two situations demonstrate the diversity of religious beliefs, within the same religion, and different consequences for the employee. Given the complexity of religious beliefs, organizations must pay careful attention to religion as an aspect of diversity.

■ RECOMMENDATIONS FOR INDIVIDUALS

Individuals should be aware of their rights to fairness in the workplace with respect to religion. Employers should allow employees to observe religious practices, so long as this does not cause undue hardship to the employer. In requesting an accommodation, individuals should decide in advance what things would help the employer to comply. If a time is required to pray during work hours, employees should plan to make up the time before or after normal hours. Posting religious sayings is not illegal, but such postings should be for one's own edification, rather than for sending a message to others. A reasonable size for such postings and nonoffensive language are allowed under EEOC guidelines.

Employees should also carefully watch their own behavior for actions that could be construed as discriminatory or unfair. Simple things such as language can be offensive. For example, a statement that someone was "Jewed down" is derogatory and may be offensive to Jews and non-Jews alike. People should also try not to make assumptions about someone's

---

[49]Associated Press. (2004, February 24). "Denial of Rape Victim's Pills Raises Debate." http://www
.msnbc.msn.com/id/4359430/, accessed August 12, 2010; CNN. "Pharmacist Fired for Denying
'Morning-After' Pill." http://www.cnn.com, accessed February 12, 2004.
[50]Tapper & Date (2004).

religious beliefs or practices based on his or her outward appearance, race, or national origin. As with other aspects of diversity, people should make a conscious attempt to be aware and avoid denigrating someone's religion.

Individual job applicants and employees should decide what they will and will not do and what is reasonable or fair to ask of employers. They should figure out a way to help employers help them. What is a *reasonable* accommodation? Lastly, they should be willing to assess whether their beliefs sufficiently conflict with an organization's legitimate position on certain issues (e.g., the morning-after pill) to decide to work elsewhere.

■ RECOMMENDATIONS FOR ORGANIZATIONS

Although the U.S. population is predominantly Christian, about 74 million people hold other, or no, religious beliefs. To avoid religious discrimination, organizational leaders should recognize the diversity of religious beliefs in the United States. As is apparent from this chapter, the issue of religious diversity is complex and different from many of the other aspects of diversity we have discussed.[51] Organizations should implement procedures that ensure people of various religious groups are treated equitably and organizational functioning is not impaired. They can provide a certain number of holidays that employees may use to decide which days they will be away from work. Some employees may choose to be off on Good Friday, while others may take Rosh Hashanah or certain days of Ramadan. For most employers, there is sufficient diversity in religious beliefs in the United States to ensure an appropriate number of employees on various holidays.

Employers should also carefully scrutinize their requirements in terms of appearance that may result in religious discrimination. Is the requirement necessary to successful operation of the business? Can a reasonable accommodation be made? For most organizations and most religions, different beliefs and certain requirements for appearance do not preclude the ability to perform most jobs.

The interaction between religious and sexual orientation diversity is complex. Some religious doctrines teach that homosexuality is morally wrong, and people who strongly hold to these beliefs may regard non-heterosexual behaviors negatively. However, as was the situation with Albert Buonanno (the AT&T case), negative beliefs do not always

[51]King, J. E., Bell, M. P., & Lawrence, E. (2009). "Religion as an Aspect of Workplace Diversity: An Examination of the U.S. Context and a Call for International Research." *Journal of Management, Spirituality & Religion,* 6(1): 43–57.

translate into discriminatory behaviors. Rather than trying to change employees' religious beliefs, leaders should model and require respectful treatment of all employees and customers. When organizational policies conflict with employees' religious beliefs, they can ensure that employees are aware of the policies and that an appropriate accommodation may be available. When employees flagrantly resist legitimate, carefully constructed policies of inclusion and fairness, termination may be warranted.

Even though termination may be justified, organizations should work to create cultures of inclusion regarding religion. They should be willing to reassess policies that may impact people of various religious beliefs differently. What is "normal" for the majority may not be normal for others. How might inclusive policies be good for the organization in other ways? For example, flexibility in scheduling and breaks to allow employees to worship may help those who are in school as well as those who need time to pray. Might an acceptable solution be reached without violating company policies on diversity and inclusion?

SUMMARY

In this chapter, we have explored religion as an aspect of diversity. The increasing variety of religious groups in the United States makes religious diversity a particularly interesting and unique aspect of organizational diversity. Title VII prohibits religious discrimination and requires employers to make reasonable accommodations for the religious practices of job applicants and employees. We discussed litigation concerning Arabs and Muslims, or those perceived to be Arabs or Muslims, related to discrimination based on religion and national origin. We also examined issues unique to religious diversity, such as the treatment of sexual minorities and the ordination of women, and provided recommendations for both individuals and employers regarding religious diversity and possible ways to accommodate it.

KEY TERMS

Profiling — using people's real or perceived demographic characteristic to single them out for scrutiny.

Religion — the feelings, thoughts, and behaviors that arise from a search for the sacred, along with the rituals or prescribed behaviors of the search that receive validation and support from an identifiable group of people.

Religiosity — the degree to which an individual practices a religion or the strength of his or her connection with, adherence to, or conviction about the beliefs, practices, or precepts of a religion.

Religious discrimination — treating a job applicant, an employee, or a customer unfavorably because of his or her religious beliefs.

Stained glass ceiling — an invisible barrier that keeps women clergy from advancing past associate, junior, and co-pastor positions and confines them to lower-status positions in religious organizations.

characterizations of minority group as proposed by Dworkin and Dworkin? What implications do these mistakes have for perpetrators of profiling and hate crimes and for their targets?

QUESTIONS TO CONSIDER

1. How is the "stained glass ceiling" similar to and different from the regular "glass ceiling"?
2. Title VII requires that employers make reasonable accommodations for employees' or applicants' religious beliefs that do not cause undue hardship. How frequent do you think requests for religious accommodation are?
3. Given that the majority of Arabs in the United States are Christians, why is the perception that they are Muslims so widespread?
4. This chapter considers the profiling of people who look as though they might be Arab but aren't. How do mistakes such as these relate to the "identifiability"

ACTIONS AND EXERCISES

1. By attending a service (or watching from outside as people leave), investigate the racial variation at a religious service in the area in which you live. Compare your observed proportions with the racial composition of the area's population. What is apparent from this nonscientific study of diversity among members of religious organizations?
2. If you know a woman who is a minister or can locate one, interview her about her experiences. How did she become a minister? What route did she take? Did she have a male minister as a mentor? What interesting diversity-related stories does she tell?

Age

CHAPTER 13

Chapter Objectives

After completing this chapter, readers should understand age as an aspect of diversity in organizations. Specifically, they should be able to:

❏ *define ageism and age stereotyping and discuss their meaning for older and younger workers.*

❏ *explain why younger workers as well as older workers should be included in conceptualizations of age as an aspect of diversity.*

❏ *discuss misperceptions about the performance and abilities of older and younger workers.*

❏ *explain age-related legislation and discuss selected cases of employment discrimination against older workers and younger workers.*

❏ *discuss the effects of discrimination and harassment on young workers and the goals of the EEOC's Youth@Work initiative.*

Key Facts

For the first time in history, there are four generations in the workforce.

Although older workers are widely perceived to perform at lower levels than younger workers, this perception is not supported by research.

Older workers are less likely to be laid off but it takes them longer to obtain another job than younger workers.

Younger workers are sometimes targeted by egregious sexual harassment, and many do not know their rights.

Discrimination and stereotypes on the basis of age affect older and younger workers.

Introduction and Overview

In this chapter, we consider age as an aspect of diversity, focusing on ageism, age-based misperceptions about the contributions and performance of workers, and the need to value contributions of all workers, regardless of age. **Ageism** is defined as prejudice, stereotypes, and discrimination directed at a person because of his or her age.[1] **Age stereotypes** are judgments about individual employees based upon their age rather than on their actual knowledge, skills, or abilities.[2] As is evident by the definitions, ageism and age stereotypes are not limited to older workers, contrary to common belief. Thus, the perspectives and experiences of both younger and older workers are included in this chapter. The increasing proportion of older workers, the declining ratio of younger workers entering the workforce, and the greater racial and ethnic diversity of younger workers make both younger and older workers important to an understanding of age diversity in organizations.

Age is a unique aspect of diversity, having attributes that differentiate it from things such as race, sex, and ethnicity. First, at some point, those who are young cease to be young and become old and those who are now old were once young.[3] This change in status contrasts with the permanence and stability of race and ethnicity and (in most cases) gender.[4] Although cosmetics, hair coloring, or cosmetic surgery may be of some help in avoiding the appearance of aging, people's general age range remains fairly apparent to observers and the process of aging remains certain for everyone who lives. The inevitability of this change in status also makes age discrimination seem particularly strange in comparison with other forms of discrimination. Those who hold prejudices and discriminate against other groups will generally not become a member of the devalued groups; there is no risk of suffering their fate. Whites will not become Black, chromosomal men will not become chromosomal women, and Native Americans will not become Asians. With aging, however, unless people die young (which most would not choose), everyone will become a member of the devalued group. Although this fact would appear to provide a rationale against age discrimination, age discrimination is common.

Second, when compared to race, ethnicity, and sex, the concepts of "older" and "younger" are more complex than perceptions of other attributes. When does one become an older worker? At what age does one become older and thus less likely to be hired, trained, or promoted? At what age do employees become old enough such that negative perceptions (e.g., irresponsible, lazy) about them as younger workers end? At what age do positive perceptions (e.g., trainable, energetic) about younger workers cease and perceptions shift to the negative (e.g., too old to learn, set in their ways)? Clearly, there are no definitive answers to these questions. Perceptions of young, old, younger, and older vary by perceiver, employee/applicant, organization, industry, and position. As much as possible, and where appropriate, in this chapter we explain the relevant age or age range.

When are younger workers preferred and older workers disadvantaged? Consider the following apparent contradictions. Consistent with general perceptions, in many situations, younger workers are viewed as more desirable than older workers.

---

[1]Nelson, T. D. (2002). *The Psychology of Prejudice*. Boston: Allyn & Bacon.

[2]Posthuma, R. A., García, M. F., & Campion, M. A. (forthcoming). "Age Stereotypes and Workplace Age Discrimination: A Framework for Future Research." In Jerry W. Hedge and Walter C. Borman (Eds.), *Oxford Handbook of Work and Aging*. New York: Oxford University Press.

[3]Nelson (2002), p. 190.

[4]But, for discussions on changes in people's self-reported race or ethnicity over time, see Passel, J., & Berman, P. (1986). "Quality of 1980 Census Data for American Indians." *Social Biology*, 33: 163–182; or Snipp, C. M. (1989). *American Indians: The First of This Land*. New York: Russell Sage.

On the other hand, the great majority of managers, executives, and higher-status workers are older, rather than younger, workers. Even so, young managers and executives are often actively pursued and viewed as being on the "fast track." The youngest workers, aged 14 to 17, experience sexual harassment at higher rates than older workers, which may be due to perceptions that they lack knowledge and are vulnerable. These apparent contradictions may be explained in part by the idea that there is a "prime age." **Prime age** refers to the age range of the most preferred employees—those who are between 25 and 35—which suggests that this group is favored over those who are both younger and older.[5]

The world's population is aging, and older people are working longer than ever before. Because these older workers often have more corporate memory and experience than others, organizations that fail to recognize the value in providing opportunities for older workers will be disadvantaged. In addition, there are fewer younger workers entering the workforce than in the past, and younger workers are more diverse in race and ethnicity than ever before. In this chapter, we consider the value that people of all ages bring to organizations.

▌ HISTORICAL BACKGROUND

During the early and mid-1900s, many employees remained with one employer for most of their adult work lives. This stability in employment (for the most desired workers) persisted through the 1950s. During the 1960s, however, employers' refusal to hire older workers, which was legal, and enforcement of mandatory retirement resulted in protests and resistance from older workers. Like Blacks, women, and Latinos who obtained civil and employment rights, older workers also worked to obtain greater employment rights through their vocal and purposeful struggles that contributed to the passage of the Age Discrimination in Employment Act (ADEA) in 1967. Organizations such as the Gray Panthers and the American Association of Retired Persons (AARP) continue to work for equal rights for workers of various ages.[6]

▌ RELEVANT LEGISLATION FOR OLDER WORKERS

The ADEA prohibits employment-related discrimination against employees and job applicants who are at least 40 years of age by employers of twenty or more people, including state and local governments, employment agencies, and labor unions. The stated purpose of the ADEA is

---

[5]Loretto, W., Duncan, C., & White, P. (2002.) "Ageism and Employment: Controversies, Ambiguities, and Younger People's Perceptions." *Ageing and Society*, 20: 279–302. See also Duncan, C., & Loretto, W. (2004). "Never the Right Age? Gender and Age-Based Discrimination in Employment." *Gender, Work, and Organization*, 11(1): 95–115.

[6]Gray Panthers is a national organization of intergenerational activists dedicated to social change. For information, see http://www.graypanthers.org/. AARP is an advocacy and information group focusing on the population that is at least age 50. For information, see http://www.aarp.org.

"to promote employment of older persons based on their ability rather than age (and) to prohibit arbitrary age discrimination in employment,"[7] which acknowledges the effects of age stereotyping on employment opportunities of older workers. It is *perceptions* that older people are unable to perform that have greater negative effects on older employees and applications, rather than the actual performance decrements associated with aging.

In 2010, the EEOC received 23,264 age discrimination charges, resolved 24,800 charges (including charges from prior years), and obtained $93.6 million (nearly 30% more than in 2009) in settlements for plaintiffs and other aggrieved parties. Since inception of the ADEA, most litigants have been White men who had worked in managerial and professional jobs.[8] As with other protected groups, however, those who experience age discrimination are unlikely to sue or to win if they should sue. While in 2010 17.4% of charges were resolved with merit, 65.8% were deemed to have no reasonable cause.[9]

Originally, the ADEA prohibited discrimination against persons aged 40 to 65, consistent with the assumption that people retired by age 65. In 1978, the age limit moved to 70, and in 1986, the upper limit was removed entirely. The removal of the upper age limit reflected the fact that many workers are capable of performing well and still desire or must for financial reasons work past age 70.

In 1990, the Older Workers Benefit Protection Act (OWBPA) further amended the ADEA. The OWBPA allows employers to lower the benefits offered to older workers as long as the cost of providing those benefits is the same as providing (higher) benefits for younger workers. As is the case of requiring reasonable accommodations *without undue hardship* for employment of people with disabilities under the ADA, the OWBPA is evidence of lawmakers' intention to protect workers while not unduly burdening employers.

As discussed in Chapter 2, it is illegal in the United States to discriminate against those aged 40 or over in favor of those under 40. It is also illegal to discriminate against persons who are considerably over 40 in favor of those who are also over 40 but younger (e.g., preferring 45-year-olds over 58-year-olds). Intentional age discrimination, creating a disparate impact in layoffs, and allowing a hostile environment (e.g., age-related comments, jokes) are all prohibited, thus requiring careful attention to decisions, attitudes, and behavior at work. As an example, although the ADEA does not prohibit employers from asking age or date

---

[7]The Age Discrimination in Employment Act of 1967, the U.S. Equal Employment Opportunity Commission, http://www.eeoc.gov/policy/adea.html, accessed November 30, 2010.

[8]For discussion, see Gregory, R. F. (2002). *Age Discrimination in the American Workplace: Old at a Young Age*. Piscataway, NJ: Rutgers University Press.

[9]Age Discrimination, the U.S. Equal Employment Opportunity Commission, http://www.eeoc.gov/types/age.html, accessed November 30, 2010.

of birth, doing so may create the appearance of age discrimination. Employers are instead advised to ask if applicants are *over 18* or the required age minimum for a particular job. Similarly, employers are advised to ask applicants if they are high school graduates instead of requesting the *date of high school graduation*, which could be used to closely estimate age.

In 2004, the U.S. Supreme Court further solidified the idea that the ADEA is designed specifically to protect older workers from discrimination in employment, even to the detriment of younger workers. In *General Dynamics Land Systems, Inc., v. Cline*, workers who were between 40 and 49 sued General Dynamics because it provided full medical benefits for retirees over 50, but not for those who were older than 40 but not yet 50. After seven years of litigation and appeals, the Court ruled for the company, determining that favoring relatively older workers over 40 was allowable under the ADEA. The ruling in *General Dynamics v. Cline* clearly indicates that the ADEA is meant to protect employment rights of older workers. As with any other protected group of workers, however, the ADEA does not forbid disciplining or terminating older workers for cause, including poor performance. Consistency of treatment is vital, and employers must be certain older workers are treated similarly to (or more favorably than) younger workers to avoid disparate treatment.

When age is a bona fide occupational qualification (BFOQ), failing to hire, discharging, or forcing retirement on certain selected types of employees is not illegal. Included are executives, firefighters, law enforcement officers, and others working in positions involving public safety or transportation. Employers may force those executives who have reached age 65 and would receive at least $44,000 in retirement earnings to retire. Employers may also set maximum ages for hiring and mandatory ages for retirement of firefighters, law enforcement officers, and public safety or transportation personnel (e.g., bus drivers or air traffic controllers). When employers use age as a BFOQ, the burden of proof that the conditions of business necessity are met rests on the employer. The employer must also demonstrate that substantially everyone who reaches a certain age is limited in the ability to perform the job and that distinguishing among those who could perform the job would be impractical. Even actions that are "legitimate" due to BFOQs should be carefully scrutinized by organizations pursuing diversity and inclusion. Doing so can be beneficial for individual employees and applicants, the organizations that employ them, and society.

Selected EEOC Cases Involving Older Age Discrimination Claims

Following are selected EEOC cases that include substantial allegations of egregious age discrimination. These cases involve organizations from various industries and parts of the United States and include instances of disparate impact of reductions in force on older workers, hiring less qualified younger workers, refusing to train older workers, and other discriminatory actions.

Kodak Subsidiary to Pay $272,000 for Age Bias[10]

EEOC Settles Suit with Qualex for Targeting Older Workers During RIF

Qualex, Inc., a wholly owned subsidiary of Eastman Kodak, agreed to pay $272,000 to settle an age discrimination lawsuit brought by the U.S. EEOC. The lawsuit alleged that Qualex, a photo processing company, and its parent company, Eastman Kodak, violated federal law by targeting older workers for termination through a reduction in force (RIF). According to the EEOC's lawsuit, Qualex subjected Teresa Cristelli and other workers aged 40 or older to age discrimination through an inequitable RIF, in violation of the Age Discrimination in Employment Act (ADEA). The average age of those who lost their jobs from the RIF was over 50, and far exceeded the average age of employees retained.

"Employers must be very careful in making layoff decisions to ensure they do not violate employment discrimination laws," said EEOC Acting Chairman Stuart J. Ishimaru. "Contrary to some stereotypes, older workers are productive, hard-working employees who can contribute to an employer's bottom line through their knowledge and experience."

Under the settlement with Qualex, Cristelli will receive $200,000, and three other former employees identified by the EEOC will receive payments ranging from $12,000 to $30,000. In addition to the monetary payments, the consent decree resolving the litigation enjoins Qualex from violating the Older Workers Benefit Protection Act when it seeks waivers and releases in exchange for severance payments; mandates training of management on ADEA requirements; requires the issuance of a new antidiscrimination policy and the posting of a notice regarding the settlement; and allows the EEOC to monitor future severance agreements during RIFs.

Partly as a consequence of the U.S. recession that began in 2007 and resulting layoffs, more age discrimination claims were filed with the

---

[10]Adapted from "Kodak Subsidiary to Pay $272,000 for Age Bias." http://www.eeoc.gov/eeoc/newsroom/release/3-24-09a.cfm, accessed November 6, 2010.

EEOC in 2008 and 2009 than ever before. Employer vigilance to avoid age discrimination and disparate impact is particularly required during reductions in force. In addition to the legal costs and moral issues associated with targeting older workers, experienced workers may help organizations remain competitive during periods of contraction.

As discussed in the following Nassau County case, constructively discharging older workers through transfers or undesirable work assignments is prohibited by law.

Nassau County Police Dept. to Pay $450,000 for Age Bias[11]

EEOC Says County Attempted to Force Out Senior Marine Bureau Police Officers

NEW YORK—The U.S. Equal Employment Opportunity Commission (EEOC) today announced that Nassau County on Long Island will pay $450,000 and agree to significant injunctive relief to settle an age discrimination lawsuit on behalf of several police officers in the Marine Bureau.

In its lawsuit, the EEOC asserted that Nassau County discriminated against Lawrence Coleman, Arthur D'Alessandro, Robert Macaulay, and Joseph Petrella (charging parties) in violation of the Age Discrimination in Employment Act (ADEA) by transferring them out of their Marine Bureau positions and into precincts that were less desirable and replacing them with younger officers.

As a result of the discriminatory transfers, Coleman and Macaulay were constructively discharged and D'Alessandro and Petrella continued to work in precincts that were less favorable to them. The charging parties' files contained numerous positive commendations from the public throughout their employment with Nassau County and no negative performance evaluations.

The consent decree resolving the litigation provides $450,000 in total for the charging parties as well as injunctive relief, including antidiscrimination training for more than 400 supervisors and managers in the Nassau County Police Department.

In contrast to the decision makers in Nassau County, some police forces are deliberately seeking older officers to relieve shortages, relaxing age and fitness standards, and at the same time getting officers with

[11]Adapted from "Nassau County Police Dept. to pay $450,000 for Age Bias." http://www.eeoc.gov/eeoc/newsroom/release/10-23-08.cfm, accessed November 7, 2010.

different positive attributes.[12] As a result of shortages in personnel, departments around the country are altering age and fitness requirements that excluded otherwise competent applicants. As a result, they are finding "officers who are wiser, more worldly, and cooler-headed in a crisis," more "mature and measured," "less hotheaded and less trigger-happy," and "creative problem-solvers."[13] Seeking some of these benefits, Boston raised its age limit for hiring new officers from 32 to 40, and Houston raised its limit from 36 to 44. These higher limits allow retired military who have relevant experience and skills, but who might previously have been past the minimum age, to qualify. As we have discussed in previous chapters in terms of women police officers and firefighters, there are often additional, unexpected benefits to be gained from finding ways to avoid excluding potentially good workers.

▌ LEGAL PROTECTIONS FOR YOUNGER WORKERS

Younger workers are a significant portion of the current and future workforce in the United States, where the legal working age is 14. An estimated 2.8 million 16- and 17-year-olds were employed in 2000, and 80% of all teenagers will work at some point during their high school years.[14] Presently in the United States, there are no specific federal laws that protect workers who are younger than 40, even though younger age discrimination and stereotyping frequently occur. However, some states and some countries do have broad prohibitions against age discrimination based on any age (younger or older). As in many other areas, local and state laws prohibiting age discrimination vary and at times are more stringent than federal laws; employers should focus on avoiding non-job-related discrimination rather than on compliance with laws.

Australia's Age Discrimination Act, enacted in 2004, prohibits treating a person unfavorably because of his or her age (or differently than a person of another age group would be treated under similar circumstances).[15] As discussed in International Feature 13.1, this act

---

[12]"Youth, Fitness No Longer Police Prerequisites." http://www.msnbc.msn.com/id/19116778/, accessed November 6, 2010. Also note the implicit stereotyping of younger officers in these statements, however.

[13]Ibid.

[14]Nester, R. (2003, Winter). "Protecting Young Workers." *Job Safety & Health Quarterly*, 14(2). http://www.osha.gov/Publications/JSHQ/winter2003html/youngwork.htm, accessed December 30, 2010.

[15]"All About Age Discrimination." http://www.hreoc.gov.au/age/, accessed November 7, 2010.

INTERNATIONAL FEATURE 13.1	*Australia's Age Discrimination Act*

The Age Discrimination Act (ADA) went into effect in Australia in 2004. The Australian ADA is designed to reduce, and ultimately eliminate, both younger and older age discrimination. According to the Australian Human Rights Commission, "Young, old and everyone in between—Australians of all ages have a right to be treated fairly and have the same opportunities as everyone else." Under Australia's law, age discrimination occurs when an opportunity is denied to a person because of his or her age and age is irrelevant to the person's ability to take advantage of the opportunity. Education, employment, accommodation (housing), and goods, services, or facilities are considered opportunities under the act.

The Australian ADA describes direct and indirect discrimination, which are similar to disparate treatment and disparate impact discrimination in the United States. In direct discrimination, a person is treated less favorably because of his or her age than a person of another age group would be treated under similar circumstances. For example, it is illegal to assume that younger workers will be less mature and responsible than older workers and therefore refuse to hire them.

Indirect discrimination occurs when a requirement, condition, or practice used for all parties negatively affects people of a particular age or age group. For example, it is unlawful to require strength and agility tests that disadvantage older applicants or employees when the levels of strength or agility are not prerequisites to successful job performance.

All employers, regardless of size, may be found liable for discrimination unless they have taken "all reasonable" steps to reduce liability. Reasonable steps vary by employer, but include implementation of proactive antidiscrimination measures. Complaints under the act are made through Australia's Human Rights and Equal Opportunity Commission (HREC). Complaints must be in writing and are investigated, and the HREC attempts to conciliate disagreements. When agreements are not reached, the complaining party may take the complaint to Australian courts. The HREC also provides education for employers on how to avoid age discrimination.

Source: "All About Age Discrimination." http://www.hreoc.gov.au/age/, accessed November 5, 2010.

covers hiring, terms and conditions of employment, and dismissal. Similar legislation prohibiting any age discrimination took effect in the United Kingdom in December 2006. The state of Michigan's Elliott-Larsen Civil Rights Act also prohibits discrimination on the basis of any age as well as other categories of discrimination not covered under federal law (such as weight—see Chapter 15). Elliott-Larsen can be used by both younger and older workers who experience age discrimination, but, so far, high-profile cases have involved older workers. Because there is currently no federal legislation prohibiting age discrimination against younger workers, there are no specific EEOC cases in this category. However, there are cases involving young workers and their experiences with sexual and gender harassment at work and these are presented later in this chapter.

■ POPULATION, PARTICIPATION RATES, AND EMPLOYMENT

Table 13.1 shows that growth rates for the younger segment of the population are slower than those of the older segment. This creates concerns about the financial stability of retirement systems and the supply of employees as older workers exit the workforce. Between 2000 and 2008, the number of people aged 45 to 64 grew 25%, whereas the number of people aged 25 to 44 declined by 2%.

Most people aged 16 and older are employed, with an overall participation rate of more than 66% in 1982 and 1992, and 67.2% projected by 2012. Workforce participation peaks between ages 35 and 44; 81.2% and 85.1% of this group worked in 1982 and 1992, respectively; and 86% of people aged 35 to 44 are projected to be working in 2012. After age 44, participation drops steadily, although a greater percentage of older workers are remaining in the workforce now than in the past. In 1982 and 1992, about 16% of workers aged 65 to 74 were still working, but the U.S. Department of Labor projects this rate to be nearly 24% by 2012. The increase in older workers remaining in the workforce reflects changes in technology that lessen the physical demands of work, inflation, increases in the cost of medical care, and other economic changes.

Misperception: People over 65 no longer want to work.

Reality: Many people over 65 want to work for personal, psychological, and financial reasons.

TABLE 13.1 *Annual Estimates of the U.S. Population by Selected Age Groups, July 2000 and 2008*

Age Range	July 2008	July 2000	% Change
Under 5 years	21,005,852	19,186,365	9
5 to 13 years	36,004,639	37,048,925	–3
14 to 17 years	16,931,357	16,120,320	5
18 to 24 years	29,757,219	27,307,593	9
Total population under 24	103,699,067	99,663,203	4
25 to 44 years	83,432,695	85,021,424	–2
45 to 64 years	78,058,246	62,410,319	25
Total population from 25 to 64	161,490,941	147,431,743	10
65 years and over	38,869,716	35,076,990	11
Total population	304,059,724	282,171,936	8

Source: Population Division, U.S. Census Bureau. Table 1: "Annual Estimates of the Resident Population by Sex and Five-Year Age Groups for the United States: April 1, 2000 to July 1, 2008" (NC-EST2008-01). http://www.census.gov/popest/national/asrh/NC-EST2008-sa.html, accessed November 5, 2010.

The population is also aging in many nations around the world. The AARP reports that with 27.4% of the population at age 50 or over, the U.S. population is younger than that of Japan (38.2%), Germany (35.4%), Italy (36.3%), and Sweden (36.1).[16] The aging of populations in both developed and developing nations has focused attention on the needs of an older population, including employment. Despite the increased workforce participation of older workers due to the recession that began in 2007, increasing age is still a major cause of their exit from the labor force.[17] An aging population means that ensuring fairness and equality for both older people who wish to continue work and younger people is important to diversity in organizations.

An Intergenerational Workforce

According to the Society for Human Resource Management (SHRM), having an intergenerational workforce offers organizations a competitive advantage.[18] For the first time in history, there are four generations in the workforce: traditionalists, baby-boomers, Generation X, and Millennials. The SHRM study counts traditionalists, born 1922 to 1945, as 8% of the workforce, baby-boomers, born 1946 to 1964, as 44%, Generation X, born 1965 to 1980, as 34%, and Millennials, born 1981 to 2000, as 14%. Other researchers use somewhat different terminology and birth-dates (e.g., veterans instead of traditionalists, born 1925 to 1942, and Generation Y instead of Millennials, born after 1982).[19] Concerned with ensuring these different generations can interact successfully at work, many organizations are investing in training and mentoring programs to help them learn to do so.[20]

Although differences in work values among different generations have been widely discussed, some research suggests these differences are more perceived than real, similar to the arguments about work value differences between men and women.[21] As with other groups, resisting stereotyping

---

[16]"AGEing in Europe: Realizing and Promoting the Contributions of Older People." http://www .aarpinternational.org/resourcelibrary/resourcelibrary_show.htm?doc_id=546892, accessed December 30, 2010.

[17]Toossi, M. (2009). "Labor Force Projections to 2018: Older Workers Staying More Active." Bureau of Labor Statistics. http://www.bls.gov/opub/mlr/2009/11/art3full.pdf, accessed November 7, 2010.

[18]Society for Human Resource Management. (2009). *The Multigenerational Workforce: Opportunity for Competitive Success*. Alexandria, VA.

[19]Parry, E., & Urwin, P. (2011). "Generational Differences in Work Values: A Review of Theory and Evidence." *International Journal of Management Reviews*, 12(1): 1–18.

[20]For ideas on helping generations work together, see Cappelli, P., & Novelli, B. (2010). *Managing the Older Worker*. Boston, MA: Harvard Business Review Press.

[21]Ibid.

and categorization is important. In their review of survey data from 1.4 million people collected between the 1930s and 2006, Jean Twenge and Stacy Campbell did find evidence of differences in psychological traits (rather than work values) across groups. Millennials demonstrated higher self-esteem, narcissism, anxiety, and depression, a lower need for social approval, more external locus of control, and women with more agentic traits.[22] Potential generational differences aside, in evaluating leaders, each generation ranks honesty, competence, and loyalty as key qualities.[23]

▌ EDUCATION

Although there are fewer younger workers as a percentage of the population, younger workers are obtaining more education than previous generations obtained. As shown in Table 13.2, about 19.3% of people aged 65 to 69 have a bachelor's degree or more, compared to 27.4% of persons aged 25 to 29. Among younger people, women are now considerably more likely than men to hold advanced degrees; 58% of the advanced degree holders aged 25 to 29 are women (see Table 13.3). These figures have changed tremendously from fifty years before, when men were considerably more likely to have earned advanced degrees. These disparities in education by gender highlight the importance of avoiding discrimination against women and of attending to reasons fewer young men today are pursuing higher education than young women and at lower rates than in the past.

Further analysis of the younger population also sheds light on the future status of the older population. Figure 13.1 shows that nearly 13% of women, but less than 7% of men, among 22-year-olds have earned a bachelor's degree or higher. While 29.1% of women aged 22 are enrolled in college, only 25.2% of men are. The current educational advantages of men over women will continue to decrease in the future. More needs to be done to close the gender wage gap and remove the glass ceiling and glass walls to ensure that these highly educated women will receive opportunities to contribute that are commensurate with their education. Organizations could interest themselves in what these young women study and encourage and support them in fields nontraditional for women (such as science and engineering).

---

[22]Twenge, J. M., & Campbell, S. M. (2008). "Generational Differences in Psychological Traits and Their Impact on the Workplace." *Journal of Managerial Psychology*, 23(8): 862–877.
[23]Ibid., p. 4.

TABLE 13.2 *Summary Measures of the Educational Attainment of the Population 25 Years and Over: 2007 by Age Group*

Characteristic	Number in 000s	High School or More (%)	Some College or More (%)	Bachelor's Degree or More (%)	Advanced Degree (%)
Population	197,892	84.5	54.4	27.5	10.1
Age Group					
25 to 29	20,624	86.1	57.3	27.4	6.3
30 to 34	19,363	86.4	59.5	31.0	10.4
35 to 39	21,173	87.2	59.9	31.9	11.1
40 to 44	22,238	87.3	57.4	29.0	9.9
45 to 49	22,922	87.4	56.5	27.7	9.9
50 to 54	21,003	88.1	58.1	28.9	11.3
55 to 59	18,115	88.0	59.8	31.0	13.2
60 to 64	14,615	84.8	54.3	28.3	13.0
65 to 69	37,841	74.0	39.3	19.3	8.4
Sex					
Men	95,390	83.9	53.8	28.2	10.7
Women	102,502	85.0	54.8	26.7	9.6
Race and Origin					
White alone	152,051	87.0	56.6	29.1	10.7
Non-Hispanic White alone	138,468	89.4	58.8	30.5	11.3
Black alone	22,172	80.1	45.8	17.3	5.8
Asian alone	9,046	85.8	68.0	49.5	19.6
Hispanic (any race)	24,823	60.6	32.4	12.5	3.9

Source: Adapted from Crissey, S. R. (2009). "Educational Attainment in the United States: 2007." *Current Population Reports*. Table 1. "Educational Attainment for the Population Aged 25 and Over by Age, Sex, Race and Hispanic Origin, and Nativity Status: 2007." U.S. Census Bureau, Washington, D.C.

Previous chapters have mentioned that the racial/ethnic educational gap is decreasing, but non-Hispanic Whites and Asians still obtain more education than Blacks and Latinos. Changing the factors that lead more Blacks and Latinos to drop out of high school (Figure 13.1) and fewer to enroll in and complete college is important not only to their future but to organizational and national competitiveness. One factor that may contribute to lower persistence of Blacks and Latinos in high school is teacher expectations. Harriet Tenenbaum and Martin Ruck conducted four meta-analyses of studies involving differences between Whites and minorities in terms of teachers' expectations; their referral rates to special education, discipline, or gifted placement; the positive and neutral speech they direct

TABLE 13.3 *Percentage of Young (ages 25–29) Advanced Degree Holders by Sex*

	Total	Percent Men	Percent Women
1960	416,000	78	22
1970	783,000	73	27
1980	1,474,000	58	42
1990	1,384,000	53	47
2000	994,000	42	58
2009	1,579,000	42	58

Note: Data from 1960 to 1980 pertain to those with five or more years of college. Data for 2000 and 2009 pertain to those with a master's, professional, or doctoral degree.

Source: "Census Bureau Reports Nearly 6 in 10 Advanced Degree Holders Age 25–29 Are Women." 2010. http://www.census.gov/newsroom/releases/archives/education/cb10-55.html, accessed November 6, 2010.

FIGURE 13.1 *School Enrollment Status of Young Adults Ages 20 to 22 During 2000–2007 by Sex, Race, and Hispanic or Latino Ethnicity*

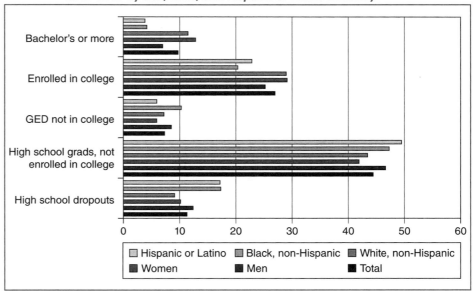

Source: Bureau of Labor Statistics. Table 1: "School Enrollment Status of Young Adults During the October When Ages 20 to 22 in 2000–2007 by Sex, Race, and Hispanic or Latino Ethnicity." http://www.bls.gov/news.release/nlsyth.t01.htm, accessed November 8, 2010.

at students; and their negative speech.[24] Teachers held the highest expectations for Asian American students, and more positive expectations for Whites compared to Latino and Black students. Teachers made more positive referrals and fewer negative ones for White students and directed more positive and neutral speech toward White students compared to Black and Latino students and were more likely to recommend Blacks and Latinos for special education and disciplinary action. The researchers proposed that teachers' different expectations for students may lead to differential academic performance and are likely to contribute to a less than fair classroom climate and limited educational opportunities for Black and Latino students in particular.[25] As discussed in Chapter 5, the PhD Project is an organization designed to help increase the persistence of Black and Latino business students by increasing the numbers of Black and Latino faculty in colleges of business.

■ RESEARCH ON EMPLOYMENT EXPERIENCES OF OLDER WORKERS

Although there is evidence that in many contexts older workers are preferred over younger workers (e.g., high-level or executive management), empirical research also documents negative experiences of older workers in employment situations. Older workers are often perceived to be incompetent, unable and unwilling to learn, accident and injury prone, and performing at a lower level than younger workers, even though evidence does not support these perceptions.

Mary Kite and her colleagues published a meta-analysis of effect sizes found in studies that included attitudes toward older and younger adults.[26] For 232 effect sizes, Kite and her colleagues found that younger adults were consistently rated more favorably than older adults in competence, attractiveness, and behavior. Presentation of information about the targeted adult reduced, but did not eliminate, the differences in perceptions of younger versus older adults. Specifically, information on employment history and health status reduced the bias against older adults.

Rather than attitudes about younger and older workers' competence, Caren Goldberg and her colleagues assessed differences in actual job promotions and salaries based on age and sex of workers and job gender

[24]Tenenbaum, H. R., & Ruck, M. D. (2007). "Are Teachers' Expectations Different for Racial Minority Than for European American Students? A Meta-Analysis." *Journal of Educational Psychology*, 99(2): 253–273.
[25]Ibid., p. 271.
[26]Kite, M. E., Stockdale, G. D., Whitley, B. E., Jr., & Johnson, B. T. (2005). "Attitudes Toward Older and Younger Adults: An Updated Meta-Analytic Review." *Journal of Social Issues*, 61: 241–266.

context.[27] Their sample was composed of 232 MBA alumni from a public institution in the northeastern United States. The researchers found complex interactions in which younger workers earned lower salaries, but older workers received fewer promotions. Older men had more salary advantages relative to younger men than older women had relative to younger women. They also found evidence of glass escalators, as men in feminine-typed jobs earned more than those in masculine-typed jobs.

These studies indicate that attitudes toward the competence of older and younger workers do not always agree with the promotions and salaries of those workers. Depending on the nature of the job and the organizational context, stereotypical perceptions about workers' competence may or may not result in unfair behaviors toward them.

Age, Accidents, and Injuries at Work

Research results on age, accidents, and injuries at work indicate that risks of injury and accidents vary by industry, employee age, and sex. Despite common misperceptions, it is younger and newly hired employees, rather than older and longer-tenured employees, who appear to be more likely to have accidents or to be injured at work. The youngest workers, aged 15 to 24, are 75% more likely to be injured at work than people in other age groups, and young men are most likely to be injured.[28] Reasons for this greater risk of injury include lack of experience, training, and supervision and overconfidence and overenthusiasm on the part of young workers. Proper training and supervision can help reduce the rate of accidents and injury at work for workers of all ages.

Misperception: Older workers are more likely to have accidents and be injured at work than younger workers.

Reality: Younger workers are more likely to have accidents and be injured at work than older workers.

Training and Development

One particular concern for older workers is access to training and development. Older workers are sometimes denied training and development

[27]Goldberg, C. B., Finkelstein, L. M., Perry, E. L., & Konrad, A. M. (2004). "Job and Industry Fit: The Effects of Age and Gender Matches on Career Progress Outcomes." *Journal of Organizational Behavior*, 25: 807–829.

[28]http://www.acc.co.nz, accessed January 1, 2011. See also Salminen, S. (2004). "Have Young Workers More Injuries Than Older Ones? An International Literature Review." *Journal of Safety Research*, 35: 513–521.

opportunities because of two key misperceptions about the length of time of their remaining in the workforce and their ability and desire to learn. Because older workers are perceived as being near to retirement, many people believe that training older workers is not a good investment of employers' resources. In contrast, and consistent with changes in ideas about the benefits of long tenure with one employer, younger workers are more likely to turn over than older workers.

Misperception: Older workers will retire soon after being trained; therefore, employers should not invest training dollars in them.

Reality: Younger workers have higher turnover rates than older workers.

The second misperception, that older workers are unwilling and unable to learn new technologies, is also unsupported by research. Evidence does indicate that older workers learn *differently* than younger workers, preferring self-paced learning over rote memorization on a rigid time schedule.[29] Despite their inaccuracy, perceptions that they are not good training investments negatively affect the likelihood that older workers will be selected for training at work. Reports from the Department of Labor indicate that people aged 55 to 64 were one-third as likely to receive training as people aged 35 to 44.[30] A study in Hong Kong also found that organizations were more willing to train younger workers than older workers.[31] When workers are older than others in their department or than their managers, they are also less likely to receive training.[32] The intergenerational nature of current employees in many organizations makes the possibility of workers being older than their managers and peers likely, and organizations need to ensure they are not denied training, which can be counterproductive for both the affected employees and their employers.

Given the relationships between training and development, performance, promotion, and job retention, denying training to older workers can negatively affect them significantly. Since perceptions that older

[29]For a discussion, see Shore, L. M., & Goldberg, C. B. (2005). "Age Discrimination in the Workplace." In R. L. Dipboye & A. Colella (Eds.), *Discrimination at Work: The Psychological and Organizational Bases*. Mahwah, NJ: Lawrence Erlbaum Associates.

[30]Department of Labor report cited in Maurer, T. J., & Rafuse, N. E. (2001). "Learning, Not Litigating: Managing Employee Development and Avoiding Claims of Age Discrimination." *Academy of Management Executive*, 15: 110–121.

[31]Heywood, J. S., Ho, L., & Wei, X. (1999). "The Determinants of Hiring Older Workers: Evidence from Hong Kong." *Industrial and Labor Relations Review*, 52: 444–459.

[32]Cleveland, J. N., & Shore, L. M. (1992). "Self- and Supervisory Perspectives on Age and Work Attitudes and Performance." *Journal of Applied Psychology*, 77: 469–484; Shore, L. M., Cleveland, J. N., & Goldberg, C. (2003). "Work Attitudes and Decisions as a Function of Manager Age and Employee Age." *Journal of Applied Psychology*, 88: 529–537.

workers are unwilling and unable to learn and are not good training investments are inaccurate, organizations would be well advised to make training and development decisions based on criteria other than age. Some companies purposely hire older employees, seeking benefits such as lower turnover and absenteeism, lower inventory damage and theft, and higher profits. International Feature 13.2 discusses the strategies and experiences of one such company, B&Q hardware.

Bridge Employment and Layoffs

Bridge employment occurs when workers have retired from long-term jobs but have not fully withdrawn from the workforce.[33] These midlife bridge workers contribute to organizations and the economy in many ways. Because they are retirees, bridge workers may be more flexible than other workers in terms of scheduling, assignments, compensation and benefits, and other important attributes. Along with flexibility, their expertise and job knowledge make them valuable contributors. Organizations often hire bridge workers to address worker shortages, needs for part-time workers, and skills losses due to mass retirements and layoffs.

There is considerable discussion about the effects of layoffs on older workers, yet younger workers and those with little seniority tend to be hardest hit during economic downturns. During the economic downturn that began in 2001, workers aged 16 to 19 experienced five times the job losses experienced by those over 25. Workers between 20 and 24 were two times as likely to experience job loss as those over 25.[34] However, younger workers who lost their jobs found comparable employment faster than older workers, taking 18.4 weeks compared to 25.5 weeks.[35] This may be partly attributed to the likelihood that younger workers are employed in lower-level jobs, which are more prevalent (and thus easier to find), than older workers.

Misperception: Compared with younger workers, older workers are often targeted in layoff situations.

Reality: Younger workers are more likely to be laid off, but when laid off they find other employment faster than older workers.

[33]Kim, S., & Feldman, D. C. (2000). "Working in Retirement: The Antecedents of Bridge Employment and Its Consequences for Quality of Life in Retirement." *Academy of Management Journal*, 43: 1195–1210.

[34]Ibid.

[35]Rix, S. E. (2004). "Update on the Older Worker: 2003." AARP Public Policy Institute. www.aarp .org, accessed December 30, 2010.

| INTERNATIONAL FEATURE 13.2 | *B&Q Hardware Stores Find Hiring Older Workers Profitable* |

B&Q PLC is the largest "do-it-yourself" (DIY) company in the United Kingdom, with over 320 stores and 36,000 employees, many of whom are *older workers*, whom the company considers to be persons at least 50 years old. In the late 1980s, B&Q started its age diversity efforts, deciding to try hiring older workers to help address problems it was having with recruitment and turnover. The initial response to B&Q's recruitment ads was tremendous—600 people applied for the fifty positions advertised.

Customers had requested employees who could help them with their DIY and decorating needs, and B&Q found knowledgeable plumbers, electricians, and decorators through its recruitment programs targeted at those over 50. B&Q realized that older people were more likely to own their own homes, to have experience with DIY projects, and to enjoy gardening and DIY as hobbies than the younger workers who predominantly staffed the company's stores. The two-year performance review of B&Q's Macclesfield store, which was purposely staffed entirely by people at least 50, was significantly higher than that of other stores. The Macclesfield store had more satisfied customers, 18% higher profits, turnover that was six times lower, and absenteeism that was 39% lower.

B&Q has taken other steps to increase employment of older workers. Compulsory retirement was discontinued in 1989, and workers can shape their hours and work roles as appropriate to their needs. B&Q employs a diversity manager and has training and development programs for older workers (including fast-track management trainee positions). The company has had two employees turn 90 while working for B&Q!

Flexible work programs are important to B&Q's ability to attract an age-diverse workforce. Flexible work schedules are available to all employees and are also used by employees of different ages to balance work with school, care responsibilities, or other interests. According to B&Q's CEO, "we are committed to promoting age diversity in B&Q, by valuing and respecting the contributions which people make whatever their age, actively challenging the general acceptance of ageism at work and seeking to eliminate age stereotyping from the field of employment."

———————

Sources: James, M. (2004, January). "The Value of Experience." *Corporate Sector Review,* 47; B&Q's Age Diversity Policy." http://www.diy.com/diy/jsp/corporate/pdfs/age.pdf, accessed November 5, 2010; http://www.thematuremarket.com/SeniorStrategic/B&Q_older_worker_policy-10301-5.html, accessed November 5, 2010.

QUESTIONS TO CONSIDER

1. Given the experience of B&Q with targeted hiring of workers over 50, why don't more companies experiencing similar problems with turnover and absenteeism use a similar hiring strategy?

2. This chapter has focused on the need to avoid age bias and discrimination against both younger and older workers.

a. Given B&Q's success with targeted hiring of workers over 50, what steps could be taken to ensure that younger workers who would also be good workers are not excluded?

b. What effect might having a mix of workers over 50 along with workers in the 18 to 24 age group have on overall turnover, absenteeism, shortage, and customer satisfaction?

c. What are some specific steps that an organization might use to best capitalize on a mixed-age employee base?

Older Women at Work

Research suggests that older women experience even more prejudice and discrimination at work than older men. Women are perceived to become old at younger ages than men and being old is viewed more negatively for women than it is for men.[36] In work and nonwork contexts, older men are sometimes viewed as striking and attractive, while older women are more likely to be viewed as dumpy and unattractive. These general perceptions affect perceptions of older men and women as employees as well. Executives are often men in their mid-50s and 60s, but very few women occupy such positions. One study found that older men were perceived as having more intellectual competence while older women were viewed as being more nurturing.[37] Intellectual competence, but not nurturance, is likely to be associated with executives.

Journalist Christine Craft's story of her experiences with age and sex discrimination in the media is documented in her book *Too Old, Too Ugly, Not Deferential to Men*.[38] More recently, Marny Midkiff, who had worked at the Weather Channel for sixteen years, alleged that she was fired (at age 41) because the network wanted younger meteorologists. To bolster her lawsuit, Midkiff showed video excerpts from a staff meeting in which the network's programming chief, Terry Connelly, referred to their female newscasters as "matronly." Ironically, as he spoke, Connelly stood in front of a "diversity" poster.[39] Arguments about the media's sale of attractiveness instead of journalistic education, skills, and experience are sometimes offered as explanations for choosing people with certain looks to read the news. As discussed in Chapter 15, when perceived attractiveness is based on age (sex, race, and ethnicity), diversity and discrimination concerns are legitimate, as discussed in Organizational Feature 13.1.

Preferences for younger and male workers most severely disadvantage older women, many of whom may desire (or financially need) to be in the workforce. As Chapter 9 considered, because women tend to marry older men, have longer life spans, and are more likely to have spent time outside the workforce (e.g., not contributing to retirement savings or pension growth), older women are much more likely to be living in poverty than older men. For example, between ages 55 and 64, 10.3% of women and

[36]Deutsch, F. M., Zalenski, C. M., & Clark, M. E. (1986). "Is There a Double Standard of Aging?" *Journal of Applied Social Psychology*, 16: 771–785.
[37]Canetto, S. S., Kaminski, P. L., & Felicio, D. M. (1995). "Typical and Optimal Aging in Women and Men: Is There a Double Standard?" *International Journal of Aging and Human Development*, 40: 187–207.
[38]Craft, C. (1988). *Too Old, Too Ugly, Not Deferential to Men*. New York: Prima Publishing of St. Martin's Press.
[39]Flint, J. (2005). "A Former Weathercaster Files Charges of Age Bias." CareerJournal.com. *The Wall Street Journal* online. http://www.careerjournal.com, accessed February 10, 2005.

ORGANIZATIONAL FEATURE 13.1	*L'Oréal*

"EEOC Sues L'Oréal for Age Discrimination and Retaliation"[40]

"L'Oréal Receives Diversity Best Practices 2004 Global CEO Leadership Award"[41]

What are the details behind these headlines that appeared about a year apart? On the one hand, the EEOC alleged that L'Oréal had engaged in age discrimination and retaliation. On the other hand, L'Oréal received a best practices award for diversity.

At the time the EEOC filed its lawsuit, L'Oréal was the world's largest cosmetics company, employing more than 50,000 people representing 100 nationalities. Women made up one-third of the company's management and 55% of its research and development scientists. L'Oréal USA was the company's largest subsidiary, with over 8,000 employees. Women and minorities comprised 60% and 16%, respectively, of management at L'Oréal USA, which equaled or exceeded their representation in many other U.S. companies.

The EEOC alleged that L'Oréal USA had engaged in age discrimination and retaliation against Joyce Head, who had been a senior director at the company. The EEOC said that a newly hired vice president of sales told Head that she was "too old to move to New York" and "too old for a VP sales position," and that she needed a makeover "to fit in with L'Oréal's youthful image." According to the EEOC report, Head had sales of $30 million the prior year and at times had generated 70% of her department's business. Despite her performance, Head was terminated after she reported the VP's negative age comments to L'Oréal's Human Resources department.

In stark contrast to the EEOC's allegations, L'Oréal was awarded the inaugural Diversity Best Practices 2004 Global CEO Leadership Award. Diversity Best Practices (DBP) is a member-based service for facilitating the exchange among companies and government entities of best practices concerning diversity issues and to help them build up diversity management and resources. DBP members included L'Oréal, the recipient of the organization's first award, which reportedly recognizes the world's most progressive companies and their leaders for embracing diversity in markets, workforces, and communities. L'Oréal was honored for creating a corporate culture that embraces and drives diversity throughout the company. In response to being named the award winner, L'Oréal's CEO stated that the company "fosters and values diversity," including age diversity.

Head's lawsuit was settled in 2004 for an undisclosed amount, but L'Oréal's diversity troubles continued five years later in Paris, when it was found guilty of racial discrimination.[42] Apparently, code words for French people born to White French parents were used in recruiting, which limited the hiring of Black, Arab, and Asian applicants.

---

[40]"EEOC Sues L'Oréal for Age Discrimination and Retaliation." (2003, September 30). http://www.eeoc.gov/press/9-30-03d.html, accessed November 6, 2010.

[41]The Diversity Best Practices Global Leadership Award in 2004. http://www.loreal.com/_en/_ww/html/our-company/our-involvments/2004.aspx, accessed November 6, 2010.

[42]Sage, A. (2009). "French Cosmetics Giant L'Oréal Guilty of Racial Discrimination." *The Times.* http://business.timesonline.co.uk/tol/business/industry_sectors/consumer_goods/article6572173.ece, accessed November 6, 2010.

QUESTIONS TO CONSIDER

1. **What factors may explain the apparent contradiction between the EEOC litigation and the Diversity Business Practices Global Leadership Award received by L'Oréal?**

2a. **If the award, DBP, and the EEOC's charges are legitimate, what factors might explain the apparent disconnect between L'Oréal's overall values and the behavior of the newly hired vice president of sales, who allegedly discriminated against Head? What could L'Oréal have done in response to Head's complaints that might have circumvented the lawsuit?**

2b. **Many companies are recognized for positive diversity efforts while at the same time being charged with discrimination or harassment. What recommendations would you make to help companies deal with these contradictions, both internally with employees and externally with the media and constituents? Since simply ruling out organizations as potential employers on the basis of lawsuits or bad press is not reasonable, what recommendations would you make to individuals when sorting out in which organizations to seek employment, given contradictions such as these?**

8.4% of men live in poverty; for those 65 and older, 12.4% of women and 7.0% of men live in poverty.[43] For older women, employment discrimination may increase their likelihood of living in poverty even when they are able to and want to work, as was the case with Gloria Rose's desire to work for Red Rock Tours.

Red Rock Western Jeep Tours Settles Age Discrimination Case

Sedona Tour Operator Unlawfully Fired 75-Year-Old Because of Age, Federal Agency Charged

Red Rock Western Jeep Tours, Inc., was ordered to pay $35,000 to settle an age discrimination lawsuit filed by the EEOC. In the lawsuit, the EEOC charged that Red Rock, which operates jeep tours in Sedona, Arizona, fired Gloria Rose, a reservationist, because of her age. According to the EEOC, Rose was hired and told to return a "new hire" packet, which contained various forms such as tax and direct deposit forms. When Rose returned the forms the next day, a supervisor met with her and, among other things, asked Rose for her age. Rose responded that she was 75 years old. After that meeting, and not hearing from the company for several days, Rose sent an e-mail inquiring as to when her start date would be. Red Rock responded

---

[43]Smith, D. (2003). "The Older Population in the United States: March 2002." http://www.census.gov/prod/2003pubs/p20-546.pdf, accessed November 6, 2010; Weiss, L. (2009). "Unmarried Women Hit Hard by Poverty," http://www.americanprogress.org/issues/2009/09/census_women.html, accessed November 6, 2010.

that the general manager and supervisor did not think Rose was "the right person" for the job. Rose responded with an e-mail inquiring as to how they could make that determination without actually seeing her work product and informed the company that she believed she had been discriminated against on the basis of her age.

After receiving the e-mail, Red Rock then decided to hire Rose, only to terminate her after only two days of work, the EEOC said. The EEOC alleged that Red Rock replaced Rose by substantially younger employees. As part of the decree settling the suit, Red Rock is mandated to adopt an antidiscrimination policy and to provide antidiscrimination training for all of its employees involved in the hiring process. Red Rock is also enjoined from engaging in any further age discrimination or retaliation.

■ Research on Employment Experiences of Younger Workers

In contrast to the large amount of empirical research on the employment experiences of older workers, relatively little comparable work has been done on experiences of younger workers.[44] This lack may reflect widespread perceptions that younger workers are generally advantaged compared to older workers. Perceptions that younger workers are irresponsible, disloyal, and immature are also common, however, and a small number of studies have documented reports of younger workers' experiences with age discrimination. Wendy Loretto, Colin Duncan, and Phil White found that 35% of their sample felt their age had been a factor, both positive and negative, in their employment experiences. Some of the workers reported that they had gotten a job because of their youth but then were paid less than other workers in similar jobs because they were young.[45] In another study, one quarter of the respondents aged 16 to 24 reported having experienced age discrimination.[46]

Anecdotal evidence and reports in the popular press also suggest younger workers experience discrimination based on perceptions that they are unqualified for the positions they hold. Michael Sisler, hired as a bank vice president making $70,000, believed he was fired when management

---

[44]As younger workers are now the new "minority" age group in the workforce, more research may consider their experiences. As an example, see Kwesiga, E. (2005). "Ain't You Too Young to Be the Boss: When Age Discrimination Targets Younger Employees." Paper presented at the annual Academy of Management meeting, Honolulu.

[45]Loretto, W., Duncan, C., & White, P. (2000). "Ageism and Employment: Controversies, Ambiguities, and Young People's Perceptions." *Ageing and Society,* 20: 279–302.

[46]Age Concern. (1998). *Age Discrimination: Make It a Thing of the Past.* London: Author.

learned he was only 25. Sisler filed a discrimination charge under New Jersey's law prohibiting age discrimination and the case was settled before trial.[47] A 27-year-old attorney reported that in front of a courtroom full of observers and opposing counsel the sitting judge asked if this was "bring your kids to work day" and whether his father would be arguing the case for him.[48] Young college professors report having to dress maturely or wear beards or glasses in an attempt to look older than they are.

Younger workers as managers of older workers may face unique problems. Some researchers have found that younger managers receive lower ratings from older subordinates than from younger subordinates.[49] Younger workers may be reluctant to direct and discipline those old enough to be their parents or grandparents, and older workers may be unwilling to be supervised by those young enough to be their children or grandchildren. Organizations that expect and prepare for these strains and train both parties can expect fewer problems and more successful relationships.

Sexual Harassment of Teen Workers and the EEOC's Youth@Work Initiative

In addition to overt age discrimination in hiring, pay, and termination, the high rates of younger workers' experience with sexual harassment may be related to their age and vulnerability. As Chapters 3 and 9 pointed out, sexual harassment is a serious problem, with negative consequences for its targets and for the organizations that employ them. The experience of sexual harassment (and other forms of discrimination) may affect young workers' future earnings, work lives, and career decisions in critical ways.

A review of the EEOC Web site provides a disturbing picture of the experiences of young workers—in particular, with sexual harassment at work. Well-known companies that have incurred EEOC settlements involving young workers include certain locations of Longhorn Steakhouse, Taco Bell, Chili's, Radisson Inn, Church's Chicken, Burger King, and Babies "R" Us. Harassment targets involved included employees as young as 14, summer employees, and students working as part of a class

---

[47]Armour, S. (2003, October 7). "Young Workers Say Their Age Holds Them Back." *USAToday.* http://www.usatoday.com/money/workplace/2003-10-07-reverseage_x.htm, accessed November 7, 2010.
[48]Ibid.
[49]Collins, M. H., Hair, J. F., Jr., & Rocco, T. S. (2009). "The Older-Worker–Younger-Supervisor Dyad: A Test of the Reverse Pygmalion Effect." *Human Resource Development Quarterly*, 20(1): 21–41.

project. Consider the following egregious cases taken from the EEOC Web site:

- **EEOC v. Rare Hospitality Int'l, Inc., d/b/a Longhorn Steakhouse**[50]
  No. 8:02-CV-177OT30-TBM (M.D. Fl. Dec. 30, 2003)

  The Miami District Office filed this Title VII sexual harassment and retaliatory discharge suit against defendant, a national restaurant chain that operates two steak restaurants in Tampa, Florida. The suit alleged that, for nine months, defendant's 36-year-old assistant manager subjected charging party, a 16-year-old student working as a hostess as part of a high school on-the-job training class requirement, to physical and verbal sexual conduct, which included breast grabbing, other inappropriate touching, and remarks about wanting to have sex with her. Two other female employees were subjected to sexually offensive conduct by the assistant manager. Despite charging party's and the other female the employees' complaints, the harassment continued. The suit also alleged that in retaliation for complaining to management about the harassment, charging party's hours were reduced and she was eventually terminated.

  The case settled when the parties entered into a three-year consent decree that requires Defendant to pay monetary relief totaling $200,000. Specifically, Defendant will pay $2,500 in lost wages and $147,500 in compensatory damages to the charging party and $30,000 and $20,000 in compensatory damages to the other two affected women.

- **EEOC v. L&L Wings, Inc.**[51]
  No. 5:02-CV-856-BO(3) (E.D.N.C. December 3, 2002)

  The Charlotte District Office alleged in this Title VII lawsuit that defendant, an owner/operator of a chain of retail stores which sell beachwear and accessories, subjected four female summer sales associates, ages 16 to 18, to a sexually hostile working environment and discharged one of them because of her sex. The Store Manager and the Assistant Manager repeatedly made comments about the claimants' bodies, questioned them about their sexual activities, touched their legs and buttocks and propositioned them for sex. Two of the claimants quit their jobs after only four days of work due to the

----

[50]Adapted from EEOC Litigation Settlements—December 2003. http://archive.eeoc.gov/litigation/settlements/settlement12-03.html, accessed November 6, 2010.
[51]Adapted from EEOC Litigation Settlements—December 2002. http://archive.eeoc.gov/litigation/settlements/settlement12-02.html, accessed November 7, 2010.

harassment and a third was discharged on her fourth day of work. The fourth claimant was employed for less than two months and quit after she was sexually assaulted by the Store Manager.

The case was resolved through a consent decree which provides for a total payment of $115,000 to the four female claimants ($40,000 to one of the claimants and $25,000 to each of the other three claimants).

- **EEOC v. Babies "R" Us, Inc.**[52]
  No. 02-CV-989 (WGB) (D. N.J. January 10, 2003)

In this Title VII lawsuit, the Philadelphia District Office alleged that defendant subjected charging party, an 18-year-old male sales clerk, to a hostile working environment because of his sex. Throughout his employment, charging party was the target of daily unwelcome and derogatory comments (such as "fag," "faggot" and "happy pants") that mocked him because he did not conform to societal stereotypes of how a male should appear or behave. He was also grabbed and held by co-workers and had his pants forcibly removed. Despite knowledge by defendant's supervisors of the verbal and physical harassment, no action was taken to stop the unlawful conduct. As a result of the ongoing harassment, charging party was forced to quit his job.

The case was resolved through a consent decree which provides for payment of $205,000 to charging party representing $30,000 in backpay and $175,000 in compensatory damages.

As discussed in Chapter 9, sexual harassment of any worker at any age is associated with numerous negative physical and psychological outcomes. Such harassment of young workers has the potential to significantly reduce their future outcomes and occupational choices, particularly if the harassment occurs in their first or very early working experiences. The rise in complaints by younger workers of sexual harassment led to the EEOC's Youth@Work initiative, launched in 2004, which is designed to educate young workers about their rights to fair and inclusive work environments. As part of the initiative, the EEOC offers free outreach events at high schools, youth organizations, and businesses that hire young workers that provide case scenarios involving discrimination and suggested response strategies. Because some of the EEOC cases involved young people both as perpetrators of harassment and as harassment

---

[52]Adapted from EEOC Litigation Settlements—January 2003. http://archive.eeoc.gov/litigation/settlements/settlement01-03.html, accessed November 7, 2010.

targets, education may serve to educate both populations, neither of whom may have had any sexual harassment, discrimination, or other diversity-related training.[53]

According to the EEOC, one goal of Youth@Work is to protect and promote equal employment opportunity, thereby creating positive initial employment experiences for young workers, helping them as they "enter and navigate the professional world." Because they are "the next generation of managers, business leaders, and entrepreneurs, young workers will carry the information they learn from our agency with them throughout their professional careers."[54] An understanding of key diversity issues is of particular importance to young workers; not only will such education promote fairness and inclusion, it will also help younger workers reduce the effects of harassment and discrimination on their own careers.

Long-term Consequences of Harassment of Young Workers

Quitting, being fired, or fleeing to another career may shape people's career paths, earnings, and future in many undesirable ways. Quitting or being fired from one's first job can negatively affect one's ability or desire to seek another position. In addition, other types of discrimination may result in underemployment and its consequences, such as lower earnings and low or no health benefits, retirement, or vacation. As would be expected, research indicates that young adults who are underemployed experience declines in their self-esteem, job attitudes, and likelihood of appropriate later employment.[55]

Along with sexual harassment, two other major factors are key to younger workers' experiences with issues of diversity: discrimination and gender role socialization (see Table 13.4 and Chapter 9). These experiences, which are associated with sex segregation, un- and underemployment, termination, and numerous other negative factors for employees of all ages, are particularly significant to the youngest workers.[56] As the EEOC proposes, young workers' early career experiences can strongly influence their current and future behaviors and careers. Given

---

[53]For limited sexual harassment policy accessibility, see Lichty, L. F., Torres, J. M. C., Valenti, M. T., & Buchanan, N. T. (2008). "Sexual Harassment Policies in K-12 Schools: Examining Accessibility to Students and Content." *Journal of School Health*, 78(11): 607–614.

[54]Equal Employment Opportunity Commission. (2004). http://www.eeoc.gov/press/12-15-04.html, accessed November 5, 2010.

[55]Winefield, A. H., Winefield, H. R., Tiggemann, M., & Goldney, R. D. (1991). "A Longitudinal Study of the Psychological Effects of Unemployment and Unsatisfactory Employment on Young Adults." *Journal of Applied Psychology*, 76: 424–431.

[56]These concepts were introduced in previous chapters.

TABLE 13.4 *Relationships between Key Diversity Issues and Career Outcomes for Young Workers*

Diversity Concern	Career Outcome
• Harassment	• Segregation
• Sexual/gender	• Low wages
• Racial	• Low status
• Disability	• Low advancement opportunity
	• Un- and underemployment
	• Termination
	• Constructive discharge
	• Intention to quit/quitting
	• Stress
	• Lowered commitment
• Discrimination	• Segregation
• Sex	• Sex
• Race	• Race
• Disability	• Un- and underemployment
	• Glass ceiling and walls
	• Low wages
	• Lowered motivation
	• Intention to quit/quitting
• Gender role socialization	• Sex segregation
	• Sex-appropriate career planning, training (e.g., teaching, firefighting), and job steering
	• Sex stereotyping
	• Sanctions for role violations

the increasing importance of diversity to organizations, ensuring a positive effect on future managers, leaders, and employees is critical. The effect of experiences young workers have with age and other diversity issues and early education cannot be stressed enough.

▌ RECOMMENDATIONS FOR INDIVIDUALS

Older and younger workers are likely to be aware of existing stereotypes about people in their age groups. As with all stereotypes, taking steps to combat them does not mean one is at fault or responsible for their existence. Consciously working against stereotypes may enable a person to obtain or keep a job. Since older workers are sometimes assumed to be unwilling and unable to learn, enrolling in and completing training at work and outside of work may be useful. When managers or supervisors control access to company-provided training, older workers should make their interest in such training widely known. If tuition reimbursement is available as a company benefit, older workers should make use of it. Tuition reimbursement is not usually limited to younger workers, nor is admission to colleges and universities.

Employees face the clear dilemma of providing sufficient educational and employment information on résumés without also providing information that could result in their being excluded from consideration based on age. Omitting specific graduation dates on résumés that would allow estimating one's age (e.g., such as date of college or high school graduation) can reduce the possibility of older age discrimination prior to being interviewed. On the other hand, including the dates of recently completed training and degree programs may improve perceptions of (and actual) job qualifications.

The stereotypical view of younger workers as irresponsible and lazy may result in access discrimination that prevents them from being hired. Younger workers may be able to demonstrate responsibility by earning good grades, completing school within a reasonable period, working reliably at previous jobs, consistently participating in extracurricular activities, or similar positive behaviors. Once hired, younger workers should make a conscious effort to behave responsibly and maturely at work. Any negative (e.g., immature, irresponsible) behavior may activate preexisting age-based stereotypes more than would the same behavior exhibited by an older worker.

Younger workers should not confuse education with company- or job-specific knowledge. They should also not fear asking for advice or seeking a more tenured mentor within an organization. On the other hand, when in management or leadership positions, younger workers should not be fearful of exercising authority and directing workers who are older.

Sexual and gender harassment of young workers is of particular concern. Younger workers appear to be unfairly targeted for this type of discrimination, and they must not be afraid to complain, both at work and at home (and school if appropriate), about harassment. The EEOC's Youth@Work initiative provides helpful information on what employees and employers can do to reduce discrimination and harassment of young workers.

▌ RECOMMENDATIONS FOR ORGANIZATIONS

This chapter has documented existing stereotypes and misperceptions about both older and younger workers. These fallacies lead to discrimination and unfair treatment at work and can reduce organizational functioning. If some managers and supervisors do not want to hire older workers and others do not want to hire younger workers, complex, expensive, dysfunctional recruitment and selection could result. The shortage of younger workers and the aging of the population make employment fairness toward both groups of workers critical to employers' ability to attract and retain an adequate supply of workers in the future.

In their article "Learning, Not Litigating: Managing Employee Development and Avoiding Claims of Age Discrimination," Todd Maurer and Nancy Rafuse have given useful suggestions for employers seeking to avoid discrimination against older workers in training and development.[57] The suggestions are appropriate for avoiding both older and younger age discrimination:

- Explicitly state age-neutral policies.
- Scrutinize policies and practices for signs of age bias. Have zero tolerance for age bias.
- Rely on job-relevant criteria, not stereotypical assumptions.
- Train decision makers about age stereotypes and their potential effects on decisions and behavior.

As with race, ethnicity, sex, or other factors, decision makers should not make assumptions about individual workers based on their group memberships. Similar to methods used to combat perceptions that women or minorities are not qualified, employers should publicize the job-related qualifications of both younger and older hires. They should acknowledge the young manager's previous experience or relevant educational background and emphasize the older hire's recent completion of a graduate degree or relevant job experience. Conscious efforts to address age stereotypes and adherence to zero tolerance for age-based discrimination are vital. If the concerns are that workers are "overqualified" or will retire soon, the employer might ask whether there are potential benefits to having an "overqualified" worker; whether fewer years of outstanding service are more valuable than a longer period of mediocre service by a less-qualified applicant; and whether having older workers serving as experienced mentors and guides would be valuable to the organization.[58]

The importance of fairness to young workers, their future careers, and future influence on diversity issues should provide organizations with sufficient motivation to treat younger workers fairly, even in the absence of legislation requiring it. With or without widespread federal protections

[57]Maurer & Rafuse (2001).
[58]Naomi Hardy, Regional HR Manager, TGH US, personal communication, August 4, 2010.

against discrimination, young workers should be assured of fair organizational treatment, freedom from harassment and discrimination, and recourse if it does occur.

SUMMARY

In this chapter, we have considered age as an aspect of diversity, including both younger and older workers. Although discrimination against older workers is more common and pervasive, younger workers also experience age-based stereotyping and discrimination. We discussed the ADEA and other legislation related to age discrimination along with worldwide population changes that underscore the need to treat workers from all age groups fairly, even in the absence of legislation. Fewer younger workers are being added to the workforce than in the past and there is more racial and ethnic diversity among younger workers than ever before. Younger workers tend to have more education than older workers, and younger women are gaining more education than younger men. Black and Latino young adults are less likely to attend and complete college, which has individual, organizational, and societal implications. Financial concerns and changing jobs mean that older workers are working longer than in the past and comprise a larger share of the workforce. More than 50% of the U.S. workforce is over age 40 and protected by federal nondiscrimination legislation, yet younger workers, now the minority age group, have no similar protections. We also considered age-based stereotypes, research evidence, and suggestions for age-based fairness for both older and younger workers.

KEY TERMS

Ageism — prejudice, stereotypes, and discrimination directed at a person because of his or her age.

Age stereotypes — judgments about individual employees based upon their age rather than on their actual knowledge, skills, or abilities.

Bridge employment — the employment of retired older workers who continue working for the same or other companies, in full- or part-time positions, for a period of time.

Prime age — the ages ranging between 25 and 35, often viewed as the most desirable for workers.

QUESTIONS TO CONSIDER

1. What possible effects could a large proportion of people aged 45 to 64 and a smaller proportion of people under 45 in the current workforce have on organizations' ability to attract and retain a competent and motivated workforce? How might discrimination against younger and older workers combined affect employers, given the shifting age distribution?
2. In addition to the suggestions provided in this chapter, what other things might organizations do to counter employees' age-based stereotypes?

3. How might the lack of broad federal legislation prohibiting age discrimination against younger workers contribute to their experiences of discrimination and harassment at work?
4. Marny Midkiff's programming chief at the Weather Channel reportedly stood by a diversity poster as he made disparaging age- and gender-related comments about the appearance of women anchors. What signal does this send about the genuineness of the Weather Channel's commitment to diversity?

ACTIONS AND EXERCISES

1. Conduct an investigation of the age-related employment experiences of your family and friends. Is there evidence of younger or older age favoritism or discrimination, or both? Explain.
2a. Conduct an informal census of employees in several places: casual restaurant, bank, department store, university, or other locations where many employees are visible. Document the number of older and younger employees and the positions they appear to hold. Estimate the ages of each person. How do your data fit with what you have read in this chapter? What conclusions did you reach?
2b. Choose two nights to watch television for thirty minutes to one hour each. Document the type of program, commercials, and the numbers of older and younger characters by sex on the programs and commercials.
2c. What similarities and differences are apparent between the people in questions 2a and 2b?
3. Conduct research to see what, if any, additional legislation has been passed regarding younger age discrimination in the United States and other countries.

Physical and Mental Ability

After completing this chapter, readers should have an understanding of physical and mental disability as aspects of diversity. Specifically, they should be able to:

❏ *discuss the proportion of people who have disabilities in the United States and the implications for diversity in organizations.*

❏ *explain the purposes and provisions of legislation related to employment of people with disabilities.*

❏ *discuss earnings and employment experiences of people with disabilities.*

❏ *compare perceptions about people with disabilities to their actual work performance.*

❏ *describe selected cases involving disability discrimination.*

❏ *discuss ways in which efforts to avoid discrimination against people with disabilities can improve working conditions for them and for other workers as well.*

Nearly one in five Americans—about 54 million people—have a disability.

Many disabilities are invisible.

Although people with disabilities want to work, they are more likely to be unemployed and have lower earnings than people without disabilities.

People with disabilities have similar rates of absence and levels of performance as people without disabilities.

Most workers with disabilities require no special accommodations.

Introduction and Overview

The number of people with disabilities is increasing in the United States. Nearly one in five people, or 54 million, are now affected, making this population more numerous than "minority" racial and ethnic groups, but they receive considerably less attention.[1] Older people are more likely to have disabilities than younger people, thus, as the U.S. population ages, the proportion of people with a disability is likely to grow. People are working for more years than in the past, making the likelihood of acquiring a disability during one's work years greater than ever. An aging population, a greater propensity to acquire a disability with age, and working longer make the employment experiences of people with disabilities an increasingly important issue for organizations.

People with disabilities are more likely to be un- or underemployed than people without disabilities, in part because of stereotypes and negative perceptions of their employability and abilities.[2] It is commonly believed that they are more likely to miss work, perform at a lower level, and require employers to spend a lot of money on special accommodations. However, people with disabilities have rates of absence, turnover, and performance that are comparable to those without disabilities (and sometimes better). Furthermore, according to the Job Accommodation Network, 70% of workers with disabilities do not require special accommodations, and even if accommodations are required, they are generally inexpensive—71% cost under $500 and 20% cost nothing.[3] As with other nondominant groups, inaccurate, but commonly held,

negative beliefs about people with disabilities result in overt and covert employment discrimination against them. This discrimination negatively affects the individuals and their families, the organizations that would benefit from employing them, and society.

Although in some ways similar to other aspects of diversity considered thus far, physical and mental disabilities involve many more complexities. For example, people are generally considered to be immutably male or female, Black, White, or Asian, and, despite the social constructions of gender and race, there is little public disagreement about these categories.[4] Disabilities, however, vary in time of onset, type, severity, effects on functioning, and permanence, and whether they exist at all is sometimes debated by employers and insurance companies. Some disabilities at times cause periods of lowered functioning, but not always (e.g., multiple sclerosis). Some have few effects on functioning but elicit strong negative reactions from others that may affect interactions and acceptance at work (e.g., visible impairments, HIV). Certain disabilities are clearly visible (e.g., wheelchair use) resulting in instant categorization while others are not (such as hearing impairments).[5] A number of disabilities may be completely cured (e.g., cancer); others are permanent (e.g., paraplegia). Some disabilities may not affect a person's capabilities; others may cause them to decline permanently. Some disabilities can be improved with therapy (e.g., ability to speak after a stroke).

Although some are present at birth and many are acquired later, disabilities can affect everyone at some point in life. People may not have a family member who is of a different race, but many have

---

[1]U.S. Census Bureau. "Facts for Features: 20th Anniversary of Americans with Disabilities Act." http://www.census.gov/newsroom/releases/pdf/cb10ff-13.pdf, accessed September 16, 2010.

[2]Bricout, J. C., & Bentley, K. J. (2000). "Disability Status and Perceptions of Employability by Employers." *Social Work Research*, 24(2): 87–96.

[3]Job Accommodation Network. (1999). *Accommodation Benefit/Cost Data*. Morgantown, WV: Job Accommodation Network of the President's Committee on Employment of People with Disabilities.

[4]It is not as well known that Latinos may be of any race.

[5]Recall from Chapter 2 that when differences are immediately recognizable, it allows for immediate categorization, which, under the right circumstances, can lead to discrimination.

one or more family members with a disability. Even so, people may feel fearful or uncomfortable about disabilities or illnesses, which can lead to some employment discrimination. They may also project a family member's limitations onto others with disabilities, even though the type of disability, level of functioning, and work versus home contexts may be completely different. ●

▌ HISTORY

Current beliefs about people with disabilities—that they are incompetent, unable to work, and to be feared—are similar to those that have existed throughout history. In ancient times, people with disabilities were viewed as undesirable, defective, or marked. People who could not walk were carried about and had to beg for a living; people with leprosy were banished from villages and towns. The United States once ran a leper colony in Carville, Louisiana (now a research facility). Reports are that in Nazi Germany children with physical and mental disabilities were euthanized.[6] Schools for the blind and deaf isolated children with sensory impairments from other children, much as segregated schools separated children by race. (Schools for the blind and deaf were themselves separated by race; Blacks who were blind or deaf went to different schools from Whites so impaired.) Words like *cripple*, *deaf and dumb*, *crazy*, and *retard* reflect commonly held perceptions about the abilities of those with physical or mental disabilities and are reminders of the power of language.

As early as 1929, President Franklin D. Roosevelt attempted to expand opportunities for people with mental and physical disabilities. Roosevelt, a paraplegic due to polio he contracted as an adult, advocated that governments and individuals should play a role in helping people with disabilities to obtain the best assistance and care possible. Ironically, Roosevelt, who used a wheelchair, had an agreement with the media never to be photographed in it so as not to appear handicapped. Currently, in part due to activism, resistance, and legislation prohibiting discrimination and requiring accessibility, greater opportunities are being afforded to people with disabilities.

▌ RELEVANT LEGISLATION

Chapter 3 described the major U.S. federal laws regarding the rights of people with disabilities in the workplace, including Section 501 of the Rehabilitation Act of 1973 (RA), Title I of the Americans with Disabilities

[6]Shevell, M. I. (1999). "Neurosciences in the Third Reich: From Ivory Tower to Death Camps." *Canadian Journal of Neurological Sciences*, 26: 132–138.

Act of 1990 (ADA), and the Americans with Disabilities Amendments Act (2008). In 2010, 25,165 charges of disability discrimination were received by the EEOC, 24,401 were resolved (some from prior years), and $76.1 million was recovered for affected parties. While 21.5% of charges were deemed meritorious, 62.2% were deemed to have no reasonable cause.[7]

The express purpose of the ADA is "to provide a clear and convincing national mandate for the elimination of discrimination against individuals with disabilities, (and to) provide clear, strong, consistent, enforceable standards for addressing discrimination against individuals with disabilities."[8] One important difference between the ADA and its precursor, the RA, is that in addition to prohibiting discrimination, the RA requires the federal government to take affirmative action for the hiring, placement, and advancement of people with disabilities. The ADA prohibits private employers and state and local governments having fifteen or more employees for twenty or more weeks per year, employment agencies, and labor unions from discriminating against qualified persons in employment matters such as hiring, firing, advancement, compensation, and job training, and other terms, conditions, and privileges of employment. Federal employees are covered under the RA; because the acts are substantially similar in purpose and definitions, the remainder of the chapter focuses on the ADA.[9]

Under the ADA, a person with a disability is one who has a **physical or mental impairment** that substantially limits one or more **major life activities,** has a record of such impairment, or is regarded as having such an impairment. A physical impairment is any physiological disorder or condition, cosmetic disfigurement, or anatomical loss affecting at least one of the body's systems (i.e., neurological, musculoskeletal, sensory, respiratory, cardiovascular, or others). An impairment could also be any mental or psychological disorder, such as mental retardation, organic brain syndrome, emotional or mental illness, and specific learning disabilities. A person is considered **substantially limited** when he or she is unable to perform one or more "major life activities" or is significantly restricted in the manner or length of performance of major life activities that most people in the population can perform. The major life activities are such things as personal care, manual tasks, walking, seeing, speaking, hearing, breathing, learning, and working. As is apparent from the breadth of the definition, many people who have problems performing these tasks can be

---

[7]"Americans with Disabilities Act of 1990 (ADA) Charges (includes concurrent charges with Title VII, ADEA, and EPA) FY 1997–2010 FY." http://www.eeoc.gov/eeoc/statistics/enforcement/ada-charges .cfm, accessed January 12, 2011.

[8]"Titles I and V of the Americans with Disabilities Act." http://www.eeoc.gov/laws/statutes/ada.cfm, accessed March 21, 2011.

[9]http://www.eeoc.gov/types/ada.html, accessed November 7, 2010.

regarded as having a disability. Job applicants or employees who have, or have a history of, these impairments are covered under the ADA, and even those who have been erroneously classified as having a substantially limiting impairment. Such a person may have an impairment that in fact does not limit his or her life activities but is treated as though it does.

Perceptions about physical and mental impairment are particularly significant when attempting to address employment discrimination and are particularly relevant to the study of diversity in organizations. In other words, if someone is perceived to have a disability or perceived as unable to perform a job because of a disability, the person comes under the provisions of the ADA, regardless of whether the perceptions are accurate. The EEOC's specific wording is:

These parts of the definition reflect a recognition by Congress that *stereotyped assumptions* about what constitutes a disability and *unfounded concerns* about the limitations of individuals with disabilities form major discriminatory barriers, not only to those persons presently disabled, but also to those persons either previously disabled, misclassified as previously disabled, or mistakenly perceived to be disabled. To combat the effects of these *prevalent misperceptions*, the definition of an individual with a disability precludes discrimination against persons who are *treated as if* they have a substantially limiting impairment, even if in fact they have no such current incapacity (emphasis added).[10]

These strong statements speak to the pervasiveness of the perceptions that people with disabilities are incapable of successful work performance and recognize that what people believe about others, whether or not accurate, affects how those others are treated. Recall from Chapter 1 that the definition of *diversity* includes "real" and "perceived" differences that can strongly affect people's opportunities to work. In Featured Case 14.1, a young woman plaintiff was discriminated against on the basis of her hearing impairment, although she had successfully worked at a similar job.

The Americans with Disabilities Amendments Act, passed in September 2008, emphasizes that the definition of disabilities should be construed broadly and should not generally require extensive examination.[11] This makes it easier for those seeking protection under the ADA to establish their disability. The law expands the meaning of "major life activities" to include activities that had not been recognized in the past and makes clear that an episodic impairment, such as multiple sclerosis, or one in remission,

[10]"Section 902 Definition of the Term Disability." http://www.eeoc.gov/policy/docs/902cm.html, accessed November 7, 2010.
[11]http://www.eeoc.gov/laws/statutes/adaaa_info.cfm, accessed October 7, 2010.

| FEATURED CASE 14.1 | *A Staffing Company and Its Client Refuse to Hire an Experienced Deaf Applicant* |

The ADA prohibits discrimination in hiring by both employers and employment agencies. One case involving a temporary staffing employment agency, Mitchell Temporary, and Dakota Pork Industries, a meat processing company, provides evidence of the need for such protections. The complaining party (CP), a deaf woman, applied for positions directly with Dakota Pork and Mitchell Temporary, which provided workers to Dakota Pork. Although she had prior meat processing experience, and both Mitchell and Dakota Pork hired workers during the same period when the CP applied, she was never hired. Also during that same time, Mitchell hired the CP's brother (who did not have a disability) to work at Dakota Pork. He was hired less than an hour after the CP was told there were no jobs available!

The EEOC's suit resulted in financial settlements worth $125,000 for the CP and agreements by both defendants to change their hiring practices. Defendants also agreed to adopt hiring goals for deaf or hearing-impaired applicants.

QUESTIONS TO CONSIDER

1. *What type of working conditions likely exist in a meat processing plant? What skills do workers there likely possess?*

2. *What kinds of recruitment, selection, and retention costs could Dakota Pork be experiencing that are associated with refusing to hire experienced applicants who desired to work at the company?*

3. *Since Dakota Pork hired the complaining party's brother less than one hour after telling the complaining party there were no jobs available, it is possible that the company was unaware of the ADA. How likely is this? How likely is it that Mitchell Temporary was unaware of the ADA? Aside from overt discrimination on the basis of the complaining party's disability, why else might the complaining party have been told there were no jobs available?*

Source: The U.S. Equal Employment Opportunity Commission, Litigation Settlements, August 2004. *EEOC v. Industries.* http://archive.eeoc.gov/litigation/settlements/settlement08-04.html, accessed November 9, 2010.

---

such as cancer, is a disability if it would substantially limit a major life activity when active.

Essential and Marginal Functions

How does an organization know if an applicant with a disability is qualified? A qualified person is one who can perform the **essential functions** of the job in question, with or without a **reasonable accommodation**. Essential functions are those that are the basis for the existence of a job; if these functions were not required, there would be no need for the job. In the context of human resources, they are the job functions used to focus the recruitment and selection efforts. What are the most important things that an applicant should be able to do?

Marginal functions are those that are secondary to the job; the applicant often does them, but even if they are not performed, the job would still be required. A qualified applicant or employee must be able to perform the essential, but not marginal, functions, with or without a reasonable accommodation. As an example, a receptionist's essential functions would include such things as answering phones and greeting customers. A receptionist might regularly order and drive a car to pick up a monthly birthday celebration cake, but doing so is not critical to the performance of the receptionist job. Many impairments generally have little effect on applicants' or employees' ability to work; it is the fear of incurring costs in the future that result in illegal employer actions, such as occurred in the following case.

EEOC v. Phillips Edison & Co.

The Baltimore District Office filed this ADA action, alleging that the defendant, a commercial real estate company specializing in acquiring retail shopping centers, fired an employee with multiple sclerosis (MS) because it feared increased insurance costs. The defendant had initially hired charging party (CP) through an employment agency as a temporary administrative assistant. One month after she began work, the company's vice president offered her a permanent position to occur automatically after she completed 500 hours under the contract with the employment agency. CP accepted the job offer and shortly thereafter informed the vice president that she had MS. After she completed her trial period, CP inquired as to why she did not receive a paycheck directly from defendant. The CEO told her he was going to wait to hire her permanently and that she should continue submitting her time to the temp agency. Thereafter, she heard a recorded phone conversation in which the CEO commented to an investor about increasing healthcare costs and the fact that he had a decent employee who came as a temp seeking full-time employment but had MS, and the difficult ethical issues this presented for a small company. A week later, the CEO fired CP allegedly because of constant tardiness and a backlog of work. The case was resolved by consent decree that requires defendant to pay CP $61,000 and provide her with a positive letter of reference.[12]

Attempts to minimize future medical costs by not hiring people with disabilities are prohibited by the ADA, and, as in the Phillips Edison case, can wind up costing the employer even more. With an episodic type of disability, such as MS, the applicant could work successfully and be

---

[12]"EEOC Litigation Settlements, June 2004." http://archive.eeoc.gov/litigation/settlements/settlement 06-04.html, accessed November 9, 2010.

productive for many years with or without an accommodation. The potential for employee illness is a risk and cost of doing business and employers should not attempt to minimize it through illegal discrimination.

Reasonable Accommodations

In some cases, a reasonable accommodation must be made so that a person can perform the essential job functions. What is a reasonable accommodation, and how does one determine if something is reasonable or not? A reasonable accommodation is one that the employer can implement to enable the qualified person to perform essential job functions without causing **undue hardship** to the employer. If providing an accommodation would require significant difficulty or expense relative to the employer's size, financial resources, and/or the nature and structure of the organization, then the employer would face undue hardship and would not have to provide the accommodation. Thus, undue hardship varies by employer; what is reasonable for a large, multinational corporation may be undue hardship for a fifty-member local firm with limited revenues, profits, and employees.

Research indicates that most employees with disabilities do not require accommodations, but for those who do, many of the accommodations (20%) cost nothing and most (71%) cost $500 or less.[13] As with other equal opportunity legislation, the purpose is to reduce discrimination against, and increase employment opportunities for, persons and groups historically excluded, without unduly burdening employers in doing so. As evident from Feature 14.1, many accommodations result in benefits to other employees and are also beneficial to the organization in many ways. By being open to other methods of accomplishing tasks, along with allowing individuals with disabilities to work, an organization may improve its effectiveness.

An additional point about making reasonable accommodations to enable people with disabilities to work is that managers often do so for people without disabilities, without thought or fanfare. Allowing an employee who is a student to tailor his or her work schedule around classes is a reasonable accommodation. Allowing the employee to take time off to study for exams and make up the time on weekends or after the school term is an accommodation. Allowing an employee who is a "night person" to work between noon and 9 p.m. and providing extra security is an accommodation. Accommodating employees (whether they have a disability or not) is often easy and inexpensive, generates goodwill, and increases retention and productivity.

----

[13]Job Accommodation Network (1999).

FEATURE 14.1	*Examples of Reasonable Accommodations and Estimated Costs*

1. *Circumstances:* An employee had difficulty using a telephone because of a hearing impairment that requires the use of hearing aids.
   Accommodation: A telephone amplifier that works along with the employee's hearing aids is purchased at a cost of $48.00.
2. *Circumstances:* An employee with a learning disability worked in the mail room but had difficulty remembering which streets belong to which zip codes.
   Accommodation: A card system is now filed by street name, alphabetically, with the zip code. This will help the employee increase output. Cost: $150.00.
   Other benefits: This accommodation also improved performance of other employees and reduced misdirected mail by 20% in the first six months.
3. *Circumstances:* A large grocery store was considering hiring an applicant with Down syndrome and a mild hearing loss as a stock person. The store manager was concerned that the applicant might not be able to hear the paging loudspeaker system that is used to call stockers to specific areas in the store for work assignments.
   Accommodation: A vibrating personal pager, worn on the wrist or belt, was purchased for the applicant's use. When signaled, the applicant goes immediately to the front office for specific instructions of where to go to do what is needed in the store. Cost: $350.
   Other benefits: Store management is now considering purchasing several vibrating pagers for use by key employees when the loudspeaker is inoperable or when there are many customers in the store, making the loudspeaker difficult for everyone to hear.
4. *Circumstances:* A police officer with dyslexia spent hours completing forms at the end of each day, sometimes missing deadlines.
   Accommodation: The police officer was provided with a tape recorder, which she uses to dictate her reports. The secretary now types this police officer's reports from dictation, and for other officers from their written reports.

Cost of tape recorder: $69.00.
Other benefits: The tape recorder is so effective that recorders will be provided to other officers as the budget permits, freeing officers to perform other tasks with the time they would have spent writing reports.

5. *Circumstances:* A person who used a wheelchair could not sit at his office desk because it was too low and his knees would not go under it.
   Accommodation: The employee brought some scrap wood from home, and the desk was raised with stable wood blocks, allowing a proper amount of space for the wheelchair to fit under it. Cost: $0.
   Other benefits: When the office furniture is replaced, as it is every three years, appropriately scaled furniture will be purchased for the employee. Cost: No additional costs for regular furniture replacement.
6. *Circumstances:* An applicant for a housekeeping position at a large hotel chain has a hearing and speaking impairment.
   Accommodation: The applicant was provided with an interpreter who used American Sign Language to conduct the interview. Cost: Free service provided by a local organization.
7. *Circumstances:* An employee with HIV is extremely tired in the afternoons and unable to concentrate.
   Accommodation: A futon is put in an empty office and the employee can nap for twenty minutes to an hour, making up the time later in the day. Cost: $100.
   Other benefits: Other employees (working students, pregnant women, parents, and older workers) needing a "power" nap also use the futon when it is available and have requested more be added. A "nap room" with multiple futons for power naps will be considered in the next budget cycle.
8. *Circumstances:* An employee with multiple sclerosis is sometimes unable to walk rapidly to weekly meetings in a building across the worksite where he works and is sometimes late for his weekly presentation to upper management.

Accommodation: Meetings are now scheduled in the conference room in the employee's building. Cost: $0.

Other benefits: Upper management is now more accessible to employees who work in different buildings and now does more "management by walking around."

9. *Circumstances:* Because one of her arms is considerably shorter than the other one, an applicant for a job at a large retailer had difficulty typing her answers into the computers used for the application process.

Accommodation: The applicant was given a paper application to write with her preferred writing hand and her answers were scanned into the system. Cost: Nothing.

10. *Circumstances:* A morbidly obese employee is unable to move rapidly from the teller window in a bank's drive-through to the front line to serve walk-in customers.

Accommodation: Job redesign allows the obese teller to be one of two tellers to work the drive-through during peak hours and to work solely in a front line during other times. Cost: $0.

Other benefits: This accommodation improves customer service in the drive-through line as customers no longer have to wait for busy tellers to break from the front line to go to the drive-through.

Note: Scenarios 1 to 5 drawn and adapted from Job Accommodation Network. http://www.jan.wvu.edu/media/LowCostSolutions.html, accessed November 24, 2004.

Medical Examinations

There are strict guidelines for employers about questions they may ask of job applicants, requirements for medical exams, and identification of a disability.[14] Only after making a contingent job offer may employers ask applicants to answer medical questions or take a medical exam. Instead of asking whether an employee has a disability, employers should describe the job and ask if applicants—not just those with visible disabilities—can perform the job. If any applicant is asked to take a medical exam, all applicants should be asked to do so. This way, employers are focusing on the performance of the job, not whether an applicant appears to have a disability that may make him or her unable to perform well. Because many impairments are invisible, asking about the ability to perform the job is good practice and avoids discrimination against people perceived to have disabilities.

▌ POPULATION, EDUCATION, AND EMPLOYMENT

As we have mentioned, nearly 20% of the population—54 million people— have a disability.[15] The proportion varies by age and sex: 5% of those aged 5 to 17 have a disability and 10% of those aged 18 to 64, the working years,

---

[14]http://www.eeoc.gov/laws/types/disability.cfm, accessed November 11, 2010.
[15]U.S. Census Bureau, Facts for Features (2010).

have a disability. Women are slightly more likely to have a disability than men (12.4% versus 11.7%), partly because women have longer life spans.

As Table 14.1 shows, 27 million people aged 16 to 64 have a disability, but only 22.4% are participating in the labor force—working or looking for work.[16] Of those participating, 14.5% are unemployed, compared to 9.0% of the population without a disability. As with the general population, unemployment rates for people with disabilities vary by race and ethnicity: 8.3% of Whites and 7.2% of Asians with a disability are unemployed, as are 14.5% of Blacks and 11.9% of Hispanics. With accommodations and fewer unfounded stereotypes about their abilities, many of these people who are unemployed or who have dropped out of the labor force because they are unable to find employment would be able to work successfully.

TABLE 14.1 *Employment Status of the Civilian Noninstitutional Population by Disability Status and Selected Characteristics, 2009 Annual Averages*

Characteristic	Civilian Noninstitutional Population (in millions)	Participation Rate (%)	Unemployment Rate (%)
Total, 16 years and over	235.8	65.4	9.3
Persons with a disability	27.0	22.4	14.5
Age 16 to 64	14.8	35.2	15.6
White	22.0	23.0	13.3
Black	3.5	18.1	22.1
Asian	0.6	18.9	11.6
Hispanic	2.5	22.7	19.0
Persons with no disability	208.8	70.9	9.0
Age 16 to 64	183.0	77.8	9.2
White	168.9	71.4	8.3
Black	24.7	68.7	14.5
Asian	10.2	68.9	7.2
Hispanic	30.4	71.6	11.9

Source: Bureau of Labor Statistics. Table 1: "Employment Status of the Civilian Noninstitutional Population by Disability Status and Selected Characteristics, 2009 Annual Averages." http://www.bls.gov/news.release/disabl.t01.htm, accessed November 9, 2010.

[16]Bureau of Labor Statistics. Table 1: "Employment Status of the Civilian Noninstitutional Population by Disability Status and Selected Characteristics, 2009 Annual Averages." http://www.bls.gov/news.release/disabl.t01.htm, accessed November 9, 2010.

Table 14.2 *Education of People Aged 16 to 64 with and without Work Disabilities: 2004*

	With a Work Disability (%)	Without a Work Disability (%)	Difference (%)
Less than 12th	25.8	17.6	+8.2
High school diploma only	37.6	29.6	+8.0
Associate's degree or some college	24.7	27.6	−2.9
Bachelor's degree or more	11.8	25.2	−13.4

Source: Table 1. "Selected Characteristics of Civilians 16 to 74 Years Old with a Work Disability by Educational Attainment and Sex: 2004." http://www.census.gov/hhes/www/disability/cps/cps104.html, accessed November 9, 2010.

Misperception: People with disabilities prefer to collect disability checks than to work.

Reality: People with disabilities want to work, even though having a disability is a strong predictor of unemployment.

Table 14.2 shows that 25.8% of people with a work disability have less than a high school diploma, 37.6% have a high school diploma, 24.7% have an associate's degree or some college, and 11.8% have a bachelor's degree or higher. These numbers are lower than those of the U.S. population without a work disability; fewer of the nondisabled population did not finish high school and more completed college or obtained advanced degrees. The number of people with disabilities with a high school degree or less is 16% higher, and 16% fewer people with disabilities have completed some college or more. These lower levels of educational achievement may be a reflection of the barriers faced by people with disabilities in obtaining education, even when their disabilities are not learning related.

When comparing earnings and employment of people at the same level of education with and without work disabilities, those with disabilities have lower employment and earnings. Table 14.3 reports 2007 earnings for people with and without disabilities who worked during the year. Because people with disabilities are considerably more likely to work intermittently and part-time and people without disabilities are more likely to work full time, year-round earnings disparities are actually greater than are apparent from the table.

TABLE 14.3 *Comparison of Earnings All Workers with and without Work Disabilities for Persons Aged 16 to 64: 2007*

	Mean Earnings with a Work Disability	Mean Earnings without a Work Disability
12th grade or less, no diploma	$13,473	$18,656
High school diploma	$19,400	$31,903
Associate's degree or some college	$25,847	$35,204
Bachelor's degree or more	$42,158	$66,524

Source: Table 3. "Work Experience and Mean Earnings in 2007—Work Disability Status of Civilians 16 to 74 Years Old by Educational Attainment and Sex." http://www.census.gov/hhes/www/disability/cps/cps307.html, accessed November 9, 2010.

▌ EMPLOYMENT EXPERIENCES OF PEOPLE WITH DISABILITIES

The previous section described differences in education, earnings, and employment for people with and without disabilities. Despite the disparities, 10% more of the people with disabilities who were able to work were employed in 2000 than in 1986. Thus, the ADA appears to be having a positive effect on the employment of these people. As Chapter 3 stated, the majority of claims filed under the ADA are deemed to have no reasonable cause. However, many claims are considered meritorious and result in settlements and damage awards against small, medium, and large employers. These cases, coupled with the persistent unemployment of people with disabilities despite their desires and ability to work, are evidence that discrimination against people with disabilities still occurs. Organizational Focus 14.1 considers the experiences of people with several different disabilities when they were employed or seeking jobs at Walmart.

Intellectual Disabilities

People are considered to have an intellectual disability when their IQ is below 70 or 75; when they have significant limitations in conceptual, social, and practical skills needed for everyday life; and when the disability originated before age 18. About 2.5 million people in the United States have an intellectual disability, and as with other types of disabilities, these disabilities can impede their ability to work. Only 31% of those with intellectual disabilities are employed, although many more want to work. The EEOC has proposed the following examples of jobs that might be appropriate for people with these disabilities: animal caretakers, laundry

| ORGANIZATIONAL FEATURE 14.1 | *Applicants and Employees with Disabilities and Employment at Walmart: Persistent Problems, Expensive Settlements, and Negative Publicity* |

Walmart Stores, Inc., America's largest retailer, is at the center of a long-lived, tangled web of litigation, consent decrees, motions for contempt, and settlements involving the EEOC and applicants and employees with disabilities. In 1995, Jeremy Fass and William Darnell, who are both deaf, applied for work at a Tucson Walmart store. They were denied employment, and in 1997, the Arizona Center for Disability Law (ACDL), a nonprofit public interest law firm, and the EEOC filed suit. (See Figure 14.1.) In January 2000, Walmart agreed to the terms of a consent decree regarding Fass and Darnell's case that included:

- offering them positions and providing them a sign language interpreter for training and orientation and in other regular meetings.
- paying each young man $66,250 plus profit sharing and reimbursement for out-of-pocket medical expenses that would have been covered by health insurance benefits had each been hired in 1995.
- providing them corporate service (start) dates of September 1, 1995 and payment of their $57,500 attorneys' fees and litigation expenses.
- making corporate-wide changes in the hiring and training of persons who are deaf or hearing impaired.

FIGURE 14.1 **Walmart's Disability Troubles**

Entry Date	Caption
January 7, 2000	Walmart settles employment discrimination claim of two applicants who are deaf; also agrees to make corporate-wide changes in hiring and training.
May 10, 2001	EEOC files contempt motion against Walmart for violating consent decree in disability bias case.
June 14, 2001	Judge slaps Walmart with major sanctions for violating court order in EEOC disability bias case. Retail giant to pay $750,200 in fines, produce TV ad, reinstate deaf worker, and provide ADA training.
June 21, 2001	Walmart violates disabilities act again; EEOC files 16th ADA suit against retail giant.
September 20, 2001	Walmart agrees to air TV ad and pay $427,500 after court finds retailer in contempt.
October 23, 2001	Walmart TV ad tells the story of two deaf men's employment discrimination claim against the retail giant.
December 17, 2001	Comprehensive EEOC–Walmart settlement resolves disability lawsuit.

Sources: "Wal-Mart TV Ad Tells the Story of Two Deaf Men's Employment Discrimination Claim Against the Retail Giant." http://www.eeoc.gov/press/10-23-01.html, accessed November 9, 2010; "Comprehensive EEOC, Wal-Mart Settlement Resolves Disability Lawsuit." http://www.eeoc.gov/press/12-17-01.html, accessed November 9, 2010; "Wal-Mart Settles Employment Discrimination Claim of Two Applicants Who Are Deaf, Also Agrees to Make Corporate-wide Changes in Hiring and Training." http://www.eeoc.gov/press/1-7-00-b.html, accessed November 9, 2010; "Wal-Mart Violates Disabilities Act Again, EEOC Files Sixteenth Suit Against Retail Giant." http://www.eeoc.gov/press/6-21-01.html, accessed November 9, 2010; "Judge Slaps Wal-Mart with Major Sanctions for Violating Court Order in EEOC Disability Bias Case." http://www.eeoc.gov/press/6-14-01.html, accessed November 9, 2010.

In the spring of 2001, the EEOC returned to court to file a contempt motion against Walmart. The motion alleged that Walmart had violated terms of the consent decree by not creating alternative training materials for nationwide use by the hearing impaired, by not providing training to management on the ADA, and by refusing to allow the EEOC and the ACDL to visit stores to check for compliance. After reviewing the evidence, a judge agreed, awarding more than $750,000 in fines to the ACDL for use in advocacy for employment of people with hearing disabilities. Walmart was required to reinstate William Darnell, who had been hired but quit because of a lack of assistance with training (given his hearing impairment). Walmart also had to produce and air a television ad about its previous problems with people with disabilities.

Walmart's disability-related difficulties with the EEOC continued with the EEOC's sixteenth ADA suit against Walmart, filed in June 2001. Alice Rehberg was a Walmart People Greeter whose disability made her need to sit periodically. According to the suit, Walmart constructively discharged Rehberg by refusing to allow her to sit periodically and failing to follow ADA procedures. Notably, in two of the earlier cases mentioned, juries had levied sizable awards against Walmart for intentionally discriminating against an applicant whose arm had been amputated and another applicant who used a wheelchair. Although one award was the most ever awarded for asking an illegal medical question on an application, Walmart's disability and employment problems subsequently worsened.

In September 2001, Walmart consented to pay $427,500 in contempt fines and to air the television ads agreed to in the Fass and Darnell case. The sixty-second ads featured Fass and Darnell and were close captioned for the hearing impaired. They also featured telephone numbers for the EEOC and the ADCL so that viewers who had questions or felt they had experienced discrimination could seek assistance.

The Walmart/EEOC disability saga paused in December 2001, when Walmart agreed to a $6.8 million consent decree to settle the multiple disability lawsuits that were still outstanding. Under the decree, Walmart agreed to

- provide nationwide training on the ADA and job offers.
- abolish a pre-employment questionnaire that sought information on disabilities prior to conditional job offers being made.
- institute new or revised selection policies.
- provide priority consideration for hiring those applicants who were qualified but had been rejected based on medical or disability-related information obtained through the improper questionnaire.

Questions to Consider

1. *Walmart is the largest retailer in the United States. What role may its size have played in (a) Walmart's persistent issues with disability discrimination and (b) the EEOC's persistence in litigating these cases?*

2. *Walmart agreed to provide priority consideration for hiring applicants who were qualified to work at Walmart but had been rejected based on illegal information obtained through its employment questionnaire. What are the likely qualifications required for most jobs in Walmart stores?*

3. *What might other firms learn from Walmart's experiences regarding application forms, selection decisions, accommodations, management training, and other human resource management issues discussed in this sidebar? Have you seen inappropriate questions on employment applications?*

workers, library assistants, data entry clerks, mail clerks, printers, assemblers, grocery clerks, housekeepers, and automobile detail workers, among others.[17] Along with providing opportunities to work, the high turnover associated with many of these and similar routine jobs could be reduced if people with intellectual disabilities who desired these jobs were given opportunities to work in them. As with all applicants and jobs, it is important to assess job requirements and applicant skills and interests to achieve an appropriate fit.

People with intellectual disabilities sometimes experience egregious discrimination and attacks at work, as the following EEOC case involving a Wendy's restaurant illustrates. In addition to being morally wrong and reprehensible, allowing these kinds of behaviors demonstrates poor business judgment, given the high turnover in such jobs.

- **EEOC v. Spylen of Denville, Inc., dba Wendy's**
  No. 02-4091 (WHW) (D. N.J March 16, 2004)

The Philadelphia District Office alleged in this ADA action that defendant subjected charging party (CP) to a hostile work environment because of his disability, Down syndrome, causing CP's constructive discharge. CP is moderately mentally retarded and is limited in learning, communicating, and caring for himself. The District Office alleged that management staff and coworkers at the Wendy's restaurant where CP worked repeatedly harassed him because of his disability. Coworkers screamed profanities at CP and called him "stupid." He was subjected to physical assaults including pushing, shoving, placing a knife against his stomach, putting ice down his clothes, and throwing water in his face. As a result of this harassment, the CP was forced to resign. The case was resolved through a consent decree providing $90,000 to CP, which (less $9,000 in attorney's fees) is to be used to fund a special needs trust established for CP by his mother. Creation of the trust allows CP to remain eligible for needs-based government benefits notwithstanding receipt of the monetary relief. The decree enjoins defendant from violating the ADA and specifically from creating or tolerating a disability-based hostile work environment and from retaliation.[18]

---

[17]"Questions and Answers About Employees with Intellectual Disabilities in the Workplace and the Americans with Disabilities Act." http://www.eeoc.gov/facts/intellectual_disabilities.html, accessed 07/04/05.

[18]Adapted from EEOC Litigation Settlements—March, 2004. http://archive.eeoc.gov/litigation/settlements/settlement03-04.html, accessed November 9, 2010.

The Glass Ceiling, Walls, and Secondary Job Markets for People with Disabilities

In 1994, the U.S. Glass Ceiling Commission published a comprehensive report on the employment status of people with disabilities.[19] Much like women and minorities, people with disabilities experience a glass ceiling that impedes their advancement beyond certain (low) organizational levels and tend to be segregated into certain job markets. They are underrepresented in management and professional positions and overrepresented in lower-paid service and operator jobs. White males with disabilities work at higher levels and have higher earnings than women and people of color with disabilities. In particular, women of color who have a disability suffer triple jeopardy, facing obstacles due to race, sex, and disability.

Perceptions of Performance Inadequacies

As is apparent in the cases discussed so far, people with disabilities may experience access and treatment discrimination. Research evidence drawn from the rehabilitation counseling, psychology, sociology, management, and legal literatures supports the existence of both forms of discrimination. It appears, however, that much of the discrimination occurs because of people's perceptions that the disability will impede performance, even though these perceptions are often inaccurate.

Misperception: People with disabilities have lower performance than people without disabilities.

Reality: Many disabilities have no effect on job performance.

A study by Adrienne Colella of Tulane University reported that employers' expectations for the work performance of people with disabilities is either the same or lower than for those without disabilities and the expectations vary by disability type.[20] In one experiment, Colella and her colleagues also found that job fit affected ratings of people with disabilities as potential task partners. Where the fit was poor, the expectations for performance were lower than where the fit was good.[21] Mary McLaughlin

[19]Braddock, D., & Bachelder, L. (1994). *The Glass Ceiling and Persons with Disabilities*. Washington, D.C.: Department of Labor.

[20]Colella, A. (1994). "Organizational Socialization of Employees with Disabilities. Critical Issues and Implications for Workplace Interventions." *Journal of Occupational Rehabilitation*, 4: 87–106.

[21]Colella, A., DeNisi, A. S., & Varma, A. (1998). "The Impact of Ratee's Disability on Performance Judgments and Choice as Partner: The Role of Disability–Job Fit Stereotypes and Interdependence of Rewards." *Journal of Applied Psychology*, 83: 102–111.

and her colleagues found that for three different disabilities (AIDS, cerebral palsy, and stroke) only concerns about impacts on performance were consistently negatively related to attitude and perceived fairness of accommodations. Concerns about performance were positively related to the propensity to discriminate against the person with a disability.[22] In other words, the type of disability was less important than were the perceptions that the prospective employee would be unable to perform adequately because of the disability. It is possible that if misperceptions about performance abilities were alleviated, discrimination could also be reduced.

When Employees Acquire a Disability

Because some disabilities are acquired, employers need to take measures to ensure current employees who acquire a disability are allowed to continue working without discrimination. Most accommodations cost nothing, and the remainder are typically inexpensive. Unfortunately, some employers are unaware of their responsibilities under the ADA and may thus run afoul of the law, as occurred at a major Arkansas auto dealership.

EEOC SETTLES ADA LAWSUIT FOR $220,000 AGAINST MAJOR ARKANSAS AUTO DEALERSHIP[23]

LITTLE ROCK, Ark.—The EEOC settled a lawsuit filed under the ADA against Landers Auto Sales, Inc. (Landers), part of the United Auto Group, for discriminating against Steven Hart, a former sales manager who has quadriplegia due to a severe diving accident. The suit alleged that Landers failed to provide reasonable accommodations for Mr. Hart, who is paralyzed and uses a wheelchair; substantially cut his salary; demoted him because of his disability; and retaliated against him for engaging in activity protected by the ADA.

A Consent Decree settling the case provided for a payment of $160,000 to Mr. Hart along with $30,000 in attorneys' fees. As part of the settlement, Larson will also pay for a disabled-accessible Dodge conversion van valued at more than $30,000 that was previously provided to Mr. Hart.

....

[22]McLaughlin, M. E., Bell, M. P., & Stringer, D. Y. (2004). "Stigma and Acceptance of Coworkers with Disabilities: Understudied Aspects of Workforce Diversity." *Group and Organization Management*, 29: 302–333.

[23]Adapted from EEOC press release at http://www.eeoc.gov/eeoc/newsroom/release/8-31-00.cfm, accessed November 11, 2010.

Landers also agreed to provide comprehensive training for management employees in the requirements of the ADA and post a notice informing its workforce that it will not tolerate disability discrimination. Landers is enjoined from retaliating against any employees who participated in this action and prohibits the company from engaging in any employment practice that discriminates against employees on the basis of disability, including failing to provide reasonable accommodations to employees with disabilities. Landers also agreed to maintain a wheelchair-accessible workplace, including accessible doors, parking facilities, work areas, computers, telephones, and restrooms.

DuPont and the Employment of People with Disabilities

In contrast to cases in which an employee acquires a disability and organizations may be unfamiliar with employing people with disabilities, DuPont has a long history of hiring people with disabilities. As part of this long history, since 1958 DuPont has also conducted surveys to assess their performance, attendance, and safety records. In *Equal to the Task II*, DuPont reported that workers with disabilities had above-average or average ratings of performance, attendance, and safety in 90%, 86%, or 97% of cases, respectively. These ratings were comparable to those of employees without disabilities and are similar to the ratings reported in the study conducted a decade earlier. At DuPont, workers with disabilities have proven themselves "equal to the task" for decades.

In a surprising twist, a disability discrimination case involving DuPont clearly demonstrated the need for widespread vigilance against employment discrimination. The EEOC alleged that DuPont violated the ADA by terminating Laura Barrios, who has severe physical impairments. Despite successfully working for the company for eighteen years (with the disability), Barrios was forced to take a lengthy and painful "functional capacity exam" that was not related to her sedentary job as a secretary. Although she passed the exam, Barrios was still terminated "due to her alleged inability to walk well enough to evacuate" in case of an emergency. During the trial, however, the human resources manager acknowledged that Barrios could walk well enough to safely evacuate the building. A jury found DuPont liable for malicious intentional disability discrimination, and the final award to Barrios was $591,000, which included the maximum allowable $300,000 for punitive damages.[24] Barrios stated, "I tried

----

[24]"Judge Upholds Jury Verdict Against DuPont for $591,000 in Disability Bias Suit by EEOC." http://www.eeoc.gov/press/6-9-05a.html, accessed November 9, 2010.

to prove to them that I could safely evacuate the plant site, but they would not let me prove it. All I wanted was to do my job."[25] As for people in general, for people with disabilities meaningful work is a determinant of life satisfaction and well-being.

■ CUSTOMERS WITH DISABILITIES

After years of neglect, many retailers and marketing groups are recognizing the market potential of consumers with disabilities. The aging population, greater access to work (and income), and public concern over the absence of people with disabilities in consumer advertising are attracting more attention to this neglected population.[26] As with other populations discussed in previous chapters, thinking of people with disabilities as desired and valuable customers and using inclusive marketing materials can provide organizations with some of the benefits discussed by Cox and Blake (e.g., marketing). In addition, in the United States, the federal government provides tax incentives (credits or deductions) to organizations that remove access barriers from their facilities, provide accessible services, or take other steps to improve accessibility for customers with disabilities.[27] Compliance with laws related to rights of access and accommodation can help organizations reach the growing market of consumers with disabilities, while also making restaurants, stores, and other public venues more comfortable for consumers without disabilities. Many of the aging baby boomers do not themselves have a disability but could benefit from larger print in reading materials, wider aisles in stores and restaurants, and other "seamlessly" accessible improvements.[28] As with the provision of reasonable accommodation to employees, accommodating consumers with disabilities can provide other unexpected benefits.

---

[25]"EEOC Obtains $1.2 Million Jury Verdict Against DuPont for Disability Discrimination." http://www.eeoc.gov/press/10-25-04.html, accessed November 9, 2010.

[26]Baker, S. M., & Kaufman-Scarborough, C. (2001). "Marketing and Public Accommodation: A Retrospective on Title III of the Americans with Disabilities Act." *Journal of Public Policy & Marketing*, 20(2): 297–304; Burnett, J. J., & Baker, H. B. (2001). "Assessing the Travel-Related Behaviors of the Mobility-Disabled Consumer." *Journal of Travel Research*, 40(1): 4–11; Haller, B., & Ralph, S. (2001). "Profitability, Diversity, and Disability Images in Advertising in the United States and Great Britain." *Disability Studies Quarterly*, 21(2): 1–16; Kaufman-Scarborough, C. (1998). "Retailers' Perceptions of the Americans with Disabilities Act: Suggestions for Low-Cost, High-Impact Accommodations for Disabled Shoppers." *Journal of Consumer Marketing*, 15(2): 94–110.

[27]http://www.ada.gov/taxincent.htm, accessed November 11, 2010.

[28]http://www.ada.gov/olderaccess.htm, accessed November 12, 2010.

▮ RECOMMENDATIONS FOR INDIVIDUALS

As we have recommended to members of other underutilized populations, our first suggestion for individuals with disabilities wishing to increase their employment opportunities and outcomes is to obtain as much education as possible. The Glass Ceiling Commission reports cite research indicating that people with disabilities who have higher levels of education obtain jobs faster, earn more, and progress farther than those with low levels of education.[29] Individuals should seek positions in larger firms and in those firms that have formal diversity and/or affirmative action programs. Organizations with formal programs should provide more opportunities, training, and development. Individuals should seek positions that are well-suited to their interests and abilities. Because the perception of job fit reduces discrimination, people should be aware of accommodations that will enable them to work successfully and not be afraid to ask for them or to seek outside assistance to obtain them.

People without disabilities should try to treat people with disabilities with fairness and equity. Being aware of the employment obstacles they face and the diversity both among them and in their disabilities is one step in improving their opportunities for fairness at work. Not all disabilities are visible, and having one type of disability (e.g., hearing impairment) does not mean a person also has another type of disability (e.g., mental impairment). People should at all times be careful about how they express themselves; common speech includes derogatory terms that refer to many disabilities. Most people would try to avoid openly racist or sexist remarks at work, but words like "retarded," "cripple," or "crazy" are sometimes common. Not only could someone with a disability be offended, so also could many others who do not have disabilities.

▮ RECOMMENDATIONS FOR ORGANIZATIONS

The U.S. Department of Labor, the National Institute on Disability and Rehabilitation Research, the National Organization on Disability, the Job Accommodation Network, the U.S. Department of Justice, and countless other organizations are available to help employers employ and fully utilize workers and serve customers with disabilities. Employers may also consult state and local organizations for assistance. Following, specific recommendations first consider research on changing negative attitudes. Second, ways in which employers can help applicants and employees with disabilities are

[29]Braddock & Bachelder (1994).

discussed, focusing on human resource management issues, consistent with the ADA's prohibition against discrimination in all employment-related matters. Lastly, accommodations for people with disabilities are discussed.

Changing Negative Attitudes at Work

What can be done to change the negative attitudes some people have about interacting with, working with, or hiring those with disabilities? Multiple researchers have identified ways of successfully changing these attitudes. In one study, using an established theory of attitude change, the negative attitudes toward persons with disabilities were changed by means of behavioral suggestions, which focused on reducing the tension and anxiety often associated with interactions between persons with and without disabilities.[30] Researchers have also found that providing facts about people with disabilities improved attitudes toward them.[31] In another study of business leaders with responsibility for hiring, attitudes toward people with disabilities were improved after a one-day training seminar.[32] The seminar included a video about hiring people with disabilities, a three-hour simulation experience, small group discussions, interacting with a panel of persons with disabilities, and listening to employers describe their experiences in hiring workers with disabilities. Training for all employees, including managers, supervisors, executives, and staff, that includes data on the performance, attendance, and safety records of people with disabilities should also be helpful.

Human Resources Needs

Once overall training has been conducted, organizations should ensure all human resources functions are free of barriers. The first requirement is a valid, written job description prior to advertising and interviewing for a position, which makes clear what the essential and marginal functions are. Such a job description can help decision makers avoid discrimination against qualified individuals with disabilities or falling victim to other biases (e.g., similarity error) that may disadvantage people based on their demographic status and reduce organizational effectiveness. To help ensure that people with disabilities are treated fairly as applicants and employees, the job description should be used for all phases of the human resources process.

[30]Evans, J. H. (1976). "Changing Attitudes Toward Disabled Persons: An Experimental Study." *Rehabilitation Counseling Bulletin*, 19: 572–579.
[31]Hunt, C. S., & Hunt, B. (2004). "Changing Attitudes Toward People with Disabilities: Experimenting with an Educational Intervention." *Journal of Managerial Issues*, 16: 266–281.
[32]Perry, D. C., & Apostal, R. A. (1986, October–December). "Modifying Attitudes of Business Leaders Toward Disabled Persons." *Journal of Rehabilitation*, 54(4): 35–38.

Recruitment. Numerous organizations can provide recruitment assistance to organizations seeking to employ workers with disabilities. The Employer Assistance Referral Network (earnworks.com), the Marriott Foundation's Bridges program (see Organizational Feature 14.2), and the Job Accommodation Network are three of many reputable sources. In addition, some university career centers provide assistance, particularly if the university has large numbers of students with disabilities or is specifically designed to focus on their needs (e.g., the University of Texas at Arlington or Gallaudet University, respectively).

Selection. The job description and structured interviews should be used when selecting applicants who are capable of successful job performance, with or without reasonable accommodations. Having and using a job description can help organizations make appropriate selection decisions in all situations (not just of applicants with disabilities). Tests and other methods used in selection must be related to successful performance of the job and should be required of all applicants—not just those with disabilities. Medical exams can only be required after a conditional job offer has been made, only if required for all applicants, and only if necessary for successful job performance.

Compensation and benefits. People with disabilities should be compensated based on the worth of the job and based on the education, experience, and skills they possess. Disability should not be considered in compensation; disability-based discrimination in compensation is illegal under the ADA.

Training and development. People with disabilities should be given the same opportunities for training and development as those without disabilities. If accommodations are needed to facilitate training, such as for hearing-impaired employees, these should be provided. Failure to provide a sign-language interpreter for training new hires was one of the problems at Walmart (see Organizational Feature 14.1 earlier), which could have been very easily remedied.

Performance evaluation. The performance of people with disabilities should be evaluated regularly, just as it should for people without disabilities. Performance standards, for the essential job functions, should be the same for both groups. Vague performance standards may disadvantage people with disabilities and are a liability for organizations.[33] On the other hand, some researchers have suggested that people with disabilities

---

[33]Braddock & Bachelder (1994).

ORGANIZATIONAL FEATURE 14.2	*Marriott's Spirit to Serve and Bridges to Employment Program: Helping Employers and People with Disabilities*

Marriott International, Inc., is a leading hospitality company that operates more than 2,600 hotels and resorts, employing over 128,000 people worldwide. For the past several years, Marriott has been recognized by *Working Mother, Latina Style, DiversityInc., Computerworld,* and *Fortune* magazines as one of the top places to work. Marriott has also been acclaimed as one of the best corporate citizens, receiving a Corporation of the Year award, and in 2002, J. W. Marriott, Jr., won the Lifetime Achievement Award for "his exemplary commitment to recognizing and including women, minorities, and people with disabilities in the hospitality industry.

Marriott has been a pioneer in the employment of people with disabilities. In the 1980s, prior to the passage of the ADA, Marriott employed adults with Down syndrome as housekeepers at Marriott hotels, paying them $7.00 per hour for forty hours per week, well above minimum wage at the time.[34] Marriott embraces a "spirit to serve" philosophy, through which the company attempts to make a difference in the lives of others, including employees, customers, business partners, and the community. This philosophy is reflected in the commitment to employ people with disabilities at Marriott and in the company's work to facilitate employment of youth with disabilities at other companies around the United States.

The Marriott Foundation for People with Disabilities, a public charity, established the Bridges from School to Work program in 1989 to enhance employment opportunities for youth with disabilities.[35] The Bridges program is guided by three key principles:

- To consistently establish successful employment opportunities, the business needs of employers must take precedence.
- People with disabilities can be employees with capabilities; focusing on their skills and interests is more important than being preoccupied with what they can't do.
- The future needs everyone.

Since the first Bridges program was pilot tested in Maryland in 1990, more than 6,000 young people completing special education programs have been employed by over 1,500 different employers who participate in the program. Bridges now operates in the Atlanta, Chicago, District of Columbia, Los Angeles, Philadelphia, and San Francisco.

The Bridges model considers the perspectives and needs of employers and youths, job analyses, and the skills, interests, and preparation of youths to make effective job matches.

Bridges establishes strong relationships with prospective and current employers. Through these relationships, fears and negative perceptions about employment of people with disabilities can be allayed, workplaces made more welcoming, and chances for success increased. The employers' needs for particular skills are considered paramount, with particular attention being paid to requirements for successful job performance. Potential student participants are identified by school administrators and teachers. Interested students then apply and are considered for

---

[34]"The New Workforce. Special Report." *Businessweek Online*, March 20, 2000 Issue. http://www.businessweek.com/2000/00_12/b3673022.htm, accessed November 9, 2010.
[35]"Marriott Foundation for People with Disabilities." http://marriott.com/foundation/facts.mi?WT_Ref=mi_left, accessed November 9, 2010.

participation in the program. Selected students and their parents are trained and coached in the attitudes and behaviors expected at work, appropriate attire, and other important factors that will facilitate success. Importantly, students' interests and skills are assessed, along with the students' individual characteristics. These skills, interests, and characteristics are matched with employers' needs, with special attention being paid to needs for accommodation and support. Eighty-nine percent of students who successfully complete the program receive offers of ongoing employment—a figure that likely exceeds other internship-type programs.

Marlee Matlin, an actress and director who is hearing impaired, is one of the well-known participants in Marriott's Bridges program. When she was 21, Matlin received the Best Actress Oscar and attributes some of her success to participation in Bridges. Matlin notes that without the opportunity to participate in Bridges, she doesn't know where she would be. She encourages others to give opportunities to people whom they might not normally consider.

Sources: "About Bridges." http://marriott.com/foundation/facts.mi?WT_Ref=mi_left, accessed November 9, 2010; http://www.marleematlinsite.com/, accessed November 9, 2010.

receive inflated ratings because of supervisors' desire to be kind.[36] But as with people from other underrepresented groups, failure to rate performance accurately and to provide constructive and developmental feedback keeps employees from improving and advancing. People with disabilities should be rated accurately and negative feedback provided as appropriate.

Managers and coworkers with hiring responsibility should be trained about stereotypes and misperceptions of people with disabilities. The fact should be made clear that the performance and rates of absence from work of those with disabilities are comparable and sometimes better than those of people without disabilities. The job descriptions provided should be used in the hiring, training, promoting, and evaluation of the performance of all employees.

Complaint mechanisms. Internal resources, such as an "open-door policy" or an ombudsman, should be available to employees with disabilities who experience discrimination or to others who know that discrimination is occurring. What happened to Laura Barrios at DuPont demonstrates that continued vigilance is needed to ensure workers are treated fairly, even in a company known for supportive behaviors. Although Barrios had worked successfully for nearly two decades, the actions of a few people resulted in her termination. When discrimination occurs, having several avenues for redress available can help the individual, peers, and the organization.

------

[36]Czajka, J. M., & DeNisi, A. S. (1988). "Effects of Emotional Disability and Clear Performance Standards on Performance Ratings." *Academy of Management Journal*, 31: 394–404.

Accommodations

As we have discussed, most people with disabilities do not require special accommodations, and for those who do, most of these are inexpensive or cost nothing. In addition, federal tax incentives are often available to fund accommodations, depending on the employer's size and number of employees. The Omnibus Budget Reconciliation Act (1990) provides for credits of up to $5,000 per year for providing accommodations. (Tax laws change frequently, however, so an organization will need to seek advice from a tax professional.)

SUMMARY

People with disabilities are a valuable, growing, but underutilized portion of the population. Nearly 20% of Americans have a disability, a number expected to increase as the U.S. population ages and works longer. Like many other groups, people with disabilities are more likely to be un- or underemployed and to have lower earnings than people without disabilities. Access and treatment discrimination against people with disabilities are common problems, but much of this discrimination is based on unfounded perceptions that people with disabilities will be unable to perform effectively or be absent from work more often than others. In fact, the performance and attendance of people with disabilities is comparable to that of others. Concerted efforts can change these misperceptions. When treated fairly, people with disabilities can help organizations maintain a stable, productive workforce, which is beneficial to the individual employees and society as well.

KEY TERMS

Essential functions — job functions that are the basis for the existence of the job.

Major life activities — functions such as self-care, performing manual tasks, walking, seeing, speaking, hearing, breathing, learning, and working.

Marginal functions — job functions that are secondary in importance to essential functions.

Physical or mental impairment — any physiological disorder or condition, cosmetic disfigurement, or anatomical loss affecting at least one of the body's systems (i.e., neurological, musculoskeletal, sensory, respiratory, cardiovascular, or others), or any mental or psychological disorder, such as mental retardation, organic brain syndrome, emotional or mental illness, and specific learning disabilities.

Reasonable accommodation — a change that can be implemented to enable a qualified person with a disability to perform essential job functions without unduly burdening the employer.

Substantially limited — the inability to perform one or more of major life activities that most people in the general population can perform, or a significant restriction in the manner or length of performance of major life activities that most people in the population can perform.

Undue hardship — significant difficulty or expense relative to the employer's size, financial resources, and/or nature and structure of the organization.

QUESTIONS TO CONSIDER

1. What are *reasonable accommodations*? How does a company determine what is "reasonable" and what is not?
2. What similarities exist between perceptions about the competence and performance of workers with disabilities and older workers?
3. In the $561,000 DuPont disability discrimination judgment, even if Ms. Barrios had been unable to walk, what steps could have been taken to assist her if the need to evacuate the building arose? Speculate on reasons this case was not resolved before Ms. Barrios was terminated or after she filed her discrimination charge with the EEOC but before the jury trial.
4. How can recommendations for employment equity for people with disabilities be helpful in ensuring equity for other non-dominant group members?

ACTIONS AND EXERCISES

1. Observe people with visible disabilities in your community in one particular place (such as a university, store, restaurant, office, or television commercial). Are you able to observe many people with visible disabilities? Is the proportion of people you observed close to the 20% of the population who have a disability? What does this exercise indicate about invisible disabilities?
2. Conduct library or Internet research on the positive effects of work on people's health and well-being. Discuss the applicability of employment to the health and well-being of people with disabilities.
3. This chapter included examples of cases in which a person with a disability was clearly qualified to work, and many of the companies involved are those that should have had knowledge of the ADA. Choose one of these industries and investigate annual turnover and costs of turnover. Speculate on the cost and productivity benefits that might be realized if people with disabilities were sought out as applicants and employees.
4. Investigate resources in your community that facilitate employment of people with disabilities.

Weight and Appearance

CHAPTER 15

Chapter Objectives

After completing this chapter, readers should understand weight and appearance as factors in organizational diversity. Specifically, they should be able to:

- ❏ *discuss increasing weight levels in the United States and in other populations around the world.*

- ❏ *discuss legislation relevant to discrimination on the basis of weight and appearance.*

- ❏ *explain how weight and appearance are relevant aspects of diversity and consider whether the obese should be a protected class.*

- ❏ *discuss legitimate health consequences of obesity and employers' concerns about increased health care and other costs associated with obesity.*

- ❏ *discuss how seemingly legitimate requirements concerning appearance may result in illegal discrimination.*

- ❏ *develop methods that can be used to increase acceptance of people of varying dimensions and appearance, with or without the enactment of legislation.*

Key Facts

Over two-thirds of the U.S. population is overweight or obese.

In most states, people can be fired for being fat.

Overweight women earn about 20% less than women who are not overweight.

Overweight people are more likely to be absent and have higher medical and benefits-related costs than people who are not heavy, but an individual who is overweight is not necessarily in poorer health than someone who is thin.

Medical professionals have stereotypes about overweight people similar to those held by the general population, and this may contribute to the fewer preventive care services received by overweight people.

Requiring that employees have a neat and professional appearance is generally legal, but requirements that discriminate against people from different racial, ethnic, and religious groups are not.

Introduction and Overview

In this chapter, we consider weight and appearance as aspects of diversity. *Appearance* is the overall umbrella term that refers to one's outward form. Weight, height, race, sex, physical disfigurement, beauty, makeup, hairstyle, and attire are some of the attributes of appearance that are important to one's organizational experiences and outcomes. We begin our discussion with weight in this chapter because increasing numbers of people in the United States and worldwide are overweight, because overwhelmingly negative stereotypes about those who are overweight exist, and because there are clear relationships between excess weight and health. Although some societies value corpulence, in a wide variety of contexts thinness is preferable, for the most part, to being heavy. Preferences for thinner and dislike for fatter people have been found among adolescents, children, parents, students, practicing managers, medical personnel, and even those who themselves are fat.[1]

Like sex, race, and age, weight and appearance are visible on the surface, and with these factors, stereotypical assumptions based on weight and appearance are often immediate and unconscious. On the other hand, some aspects of weight and appearance are unlike those of other visible factors. One difference is that weight and other physical attributes related to appearance vary among all people and among every race, ethnicity, sex, age, and ability. Another distinction is that while people are not considered responsible for their race, sex, age, or ethnicity, they are commonly held responsible for their weight. People who feel guilt and responsibility for their weight may try to lose excess weight through diet and exercise or even undergo major, dangerous surgery. Plastic surgery, hair coloring and bleach, and cosmetics are also used by many people trying to change other aspects of their physical appearance. People are far less likely to feel guilt, responsibility, or the need to change their race or sex. The most important difference about the guilt and personal responsibility felt by those who are perceived as unattractive or overweight is that it may make them more likely to accept, rather than resist, unfair organizational treatment and discrimination. (See Dworkin and Dworkin's discussion of group awareness and resistance of discrimination by minority group members in Chapter 2.)

Even though overweight is not confined to certain demographic groups, Blacks, Latinos, American Indians, older people, and the poor are more likely to be overweight than Whites, younger people, and those who are more affluent. Excess weight also has different effects on employment outcomes for people from different groups. Overweight women suffer more interpersonal discrimination and more negative employment consequences than overweight men, for example.[2]

Those who are overweight are often assumed to be lazy, unmotivated, and lacking in discipline—attributes that are undesirable in employment (and other) contexts. Employers' preference for workers who are motivated, disciplined, and not lazy is logical and understandable. However, refusal to hire applicants who are overweight does not guarantee that those hired instead will have desirable attributes, particularly job competence. Even so, because of the negative perceptions about the attributes of overweight people, those who are overweight often experience lower selection rates and salaries, placement in positions with little or no customer contact, and more frequent, harsher discipline at work.

---

[1]Crandall, C. S. (1991). "Do Heavy-Weight Students Have More Difficulty Paying for College?" *Personality and Social Psychology Bulletin*, 17(6): 606–611; Crandall, C. S., & Biernat, M. (1990). "The Ideology of Anti-Fat Attitudes." *Journal of Applied Social Psychology*, 23: 227–243; Wadden, T. A., & Stunkard, A. J. (1985). "Social and Psychological Consequences of Obesity." *Annals of Internal Medicine*, 103: 1062–1067.

[2]Puhl, R. M., Andreyeva, T., & Brownell, K. D. (2008). "Perceptions of Weight Discrimination: Prevalence and Comparison to Race and Gender Discrimination in America." *International Journal of Obesity*, 1–9.

In addition to negative perceptions about the personal attributes of those who are overweight, excess weight is associated with negative health effects, such as diabetes, hypertension, high cholesterol, and certain types of cancers. These conditions are associated with higher rates of absence from work and higher medical costs, which seem to be legitimate reasons for discrimination based on weight and which pose a dilemma for employers trying to create inclusive cultures. The clear relationship between excess weight and higher absence and medical costs further differentiates weight-related discrimination from race, sex, or age discrimination, which are not as easy to blame for higher organizational costs.

Appearance preferences or requirements that disadvantage women, people of color, and people with visible physical disabilities are also relevant to the issue of diversity in organizations. While some requirements are legitimate, if they are improperly applied or ill-conceived, they may result in disparate treatment or disparate impact discrimination. Preferences sometimes favor those who are young, physically attractive, slim, White, or with Caucasian features, and disadvantage those who have other characteristics. As discussed later in this chapter, the retailer Abercrombie & Fitch has been sued by applicants of color alleging such discrimination. Similarly, organizations requiring women to wear makeup or dress in a feminine manner may be practicing illegal gender discrimination. And, when requirements for "professional appearance" are used to discriminate against people who are overweight, this can result in unnecessary resource acquisition costs, since the majority of the U.S. population is overweight or obese.

Terminology

The factors of weight and appearance share visibility, stereotypes, commonality to people of various backgrounds, and lack of broad legal protections prohibiting discrimination. This chapter discusses these similarities as well as issues solely relevant to weight. As much as possible, we consider weight and appearance separately but also discuss them together when they interact. After clarifying terminology and definitions, we begin our discussion with evidence about the population and employment of persons who are overweight and follow with a discussion of relevant legislation. We discuss population first to emphasize the large number of people who are overweight and who are not protected from weight-based employment discrimination. We then continue as appropriate with the other standard topics we have included in other chapters.

Weight.   In this chapter, when referring to specific research or to the population in certain categories, we use specific, accurate terminology. In other cases, we use the terms *overweight*, *obese*, and *fat* somewhat interchangeably. We respectfully use the term fat, a non-judgmental adjective—a descriptor, like "tall" or "thin".[3] Fat is the preferred term of activists, who argue that the terms *overweight* and *obese* assume there is a *normal* weight—an assumption they dispute.[4] Many of the ranges in the tables included were obtained from insurance companies, using middle-class Whites as the standard.[5] What is "normal" for middle-class Whites may be far from "normal" for other people, and as discussed later in this chapter, the health consequences of overweight appear to vary by race and ethnicity. Further, fat activists also argue that contrary to common perceptions, one can be fat while also being healthy and that being thin does not necessarily mean one is healthy, particularly when thinness is obtained at the cost of anorexia, bulimia, or smoking.

Although what is "normal" is debatable, fluid, and sometimes irrational, there are criteria that are

---

[3]Ibid.

[4]Solovay, S. (2000). *Tipping the Scales of Justice: Fighting Weight-Based Discrimination*. Amherst, NY: Prometheus Books.

[5]Kristen, K. (2002). "Addressing the Problem of Weight Discrimination in Employment." *California Law Review*, 9: 57–109.

FEATURE 15.1	*Calculating Your Body Mass Index*

The National Institutes of Health (NIH) identifies the following BMI ranges for underweight to obese for those aged 20 or older.

- Underweight = <18.5
- Normal weight = 18.5–24.9
- Overweight = 25–29.9
- Obese = 30 or greater

To calculate your BMI, use your height and weight and the formula below.

English Formula

Body mass index can be calculated using pounds and inches with this equation

$$BMI = \frac{Weight\ in\ pounds}{(Height\ in\ inches) \times (Height\ in\ inches)} \times 703$$

For example, a person who weighs 220 pounds and is 6 feet 3 inches tall has a BMI of 27.5.

$$BMI = \frac{220\ pounds}{(75\ inches) \times (75\ inches)} \times 703 = 27.5$$

Metric Formula

Body mass index can also be calculated using kilograms and meters (or centimeters).

$$BMI = \frac{Weight\ in\ kilograms}{(Height\ in\ meters) \times (Height\ in\ meters)}$$

or

$$BMI = \frac{Weight\ in\ kilograms}{(Height\ in\ centimeters) \times (Height\ in\ centimeters) \times 10,000}$$

For example, a person who weighs 99.79 kilograms and is 1.905 meters (190.50 centimeters) tall has a BMI of 27.5.

$$BMI = \frac{99.79\ kilograms}{(1.905\ meters) \times (1.905\ meters)} = 27.5$$

Source: Centers for Disease Control. (2004). "Body Mass Index Formula for Adults." http://www.cdc.gov/nccdphp/dnpa/bmi/bmi-adult-formula.htm, accessed August 14, 2010.

commonly used to gauge levels of fat. Various sources categorize overweight and obesity differently, using percentages of body fat compared to lean muscle mass, weight and height, or excess weight compared to those who are of "normal" weight. The U.S. Centers for Disease Control (CDC) defines obesity as being 20% above the recommended weight for the height and weight for one's sex, and morbid obesity as occurring when a person is 100 pounds over the recommended weight for his or her height.[6] An applicable international standard is the World Health Organization's (WHO) measurement of overweight and obesity by the *body mass index* (BMI). As shown in Feature 15.1, the BMI uses weight in kilograms divided by the square of height, resulting in respective ranges of BMI for normal, overweight, and obese of 17 to 24.9, 25 to 29.9, and 30 or more. The NIH uses slightly different ranges: <18.5, underweight; 18.5 to 24.9, normal weight; 25.0 to 29.9, overweight; 30.0 to 39.9, obese; and, 40 or more, morbidly obese.

As these different criteria show, determining what constitutes normal, overweight, obese, and morbidly obese is debatable. On the other hand,

[6]See Roehling, M. V. (1999). "Weight-Based Discrimination in Employment: Psychological and Legal Aspects." *Personnel Psychology*, 52: 969–1016; Kristen (2002); Ziolkowski, S. M. (1994). "The Status of Weight-Based Employment Discrimination Under the Americans with Disabilities Act After *Cook v. Rhode Island Department of Mental Health, Retardation, and Hospitals.*" *Boston Law Review*, 74: 667–686.

the CDC, the WHO, and the NIH all agree that on a continuum, the classifications of normal, overweight, obese, and morbidly obese represent the lowest to the highest excess weight with the least to the most negative health implications. However, for the average person, exactly where he or she falls on an inexact continuum is not the critical issue. Further, many who are quite healthy and fit (e.g., tall, muscular athletes) would be construed as overweight or obese using BMI classifications.

Appearance. Researchers use many terms in reference to one's outward form, including *appearance*, *attractiveness*, *unattractiveness*, and *beauty*. Unlike well-known (although debatable) standards for determining degrees of overweight, standards of beauty are less well defined. Even so, research suggests that there is agreement on attractiveness and beauty across cultures, periods of time, races, and ethnicities.[7] People tend to agree on what is attractive and believe that attractive people are more intelligent, sociable, and popular (all of which are positive in employment and other contexts). In the United States and in many other societies, weight is closely related to perceptions of attractiveness and appearance, with excess weight often used as a negative qualifier (e.g., "such a pretty face"). Along with our focus on weight, in this chapter, we consider aspects of appearance such as physical attractiveness, beauty, height, attire, makeup, hairstyle, beards, and physical disfigurement. ●

▮ POPULATION

The prevalence of obesity and overweight is increasing in the United States, Mexico, parts of Europe, and many other places around the world. The increased girth is partially a result of changes in transportation, activities, and quantities and types of food consumed in the twentieth century. Work has changed from labor-intensive to sedentary, and convenience has become increasingly important. People are riding more than walking and participating in sedentary work and leisure activities more than active ones (e.g., desk work versus farming or manual labor, watching television or playing video games versus playing sports). During the same period when physical activity began to decrease, people began eating more processed, fried, fatty, and fast foods instead of fresh vegetables, fruits, and home-cooked foods, contributing further to weight gain.

....

[7]See Cleveland, J. N., Stockdale, M., & Murphy, K. R. (2000). "Physical Attractiveness, Interpersonal Relationships, and Romance at Work." In J. N. Cleveland, M. Stockdale, & K. R. Murphy (Eds.), *Women and Men in Organizations: Sex and Gender Issues at Work.* Mahwah, NJ: Lawrence Erlbaum Associates, pp. 67–76; Cunningham, M. R., Roberts, A. R., Barbee, A. P., Druen, P. B., & Wu, C.-H. (1995). "'Their Ideas of Beauty Are, on the Whole, the Same as Ours': Consistency and Variability in the Cross-Cultural Perception of Female Physical Attractiveness." *Journal of Personality and Social Psychology*, 68(2): 261–279; Hamermesh, D. S., & Biddle, J. E. (1994). "Beauty and the Labor Market." *American Economic Review*, 84: 1174–1194; Marin, G. (1984). "Stereotyping Hispanics: The Differential Impact of Research Method, Label, and Degree of Contact." *Intercultural Journal of Intercultural Relations*, 8: 17–27; Shaffer, D. R., Crepaz, N., & Sun, C. R. (2000). "Physical Attractiveness Stereotyping in Cross-Cultural Perspective: Similarities and Differences Between Americans and Taiwanese." *Journal of Cross-Cultural Psychology*, 31: 557–582.

Despite the very real contributions of changes in transportation, work, leisure activities, and food consumption to increases in weight, numerous other factors are associated with weight. Research indicates that weight is also controlled by social, behavioral, cultural, physiological, metabolic, and genetic factors.[8] Different people may consume the same amounts of food but gain or lose different amounts of weight due to their physiological, metabolic, and genetic makeup. In one study of 4,500 adoptees who had been separated from their biological parents early in life, the weight of the adoptees was strongly related to the weight of the biological parents, which supports the strong biological basis of weight.[9]

Misperception: Overweight people are overweight because they eat too much and exercise too little.

Reality: Strong genetic components are associated with size and weight; the combinations of genetics, eating, and exercise determine one's ultimate size.

More than 1 billion people of the world's population are overweight and at least 300 million people are obese. Between 1995 and 2000, the number of obese adults in the world increased by 50%, from 200 to 300 million. In the United States, about 68% of adults now fall into the combined category of obese and overweight, nearly twice the percentage of those who were overweight about three decades ago.[10]

The prevalence of obesity and overweight varies by race, ethnicity, and sex. Blacks, Hispanics, and American Indians are more likely to carry excess weight than non-Hispanic Whites. However, because of differences in lean body mass and fatty tissues, researchers urge caution in interpreting racial and ethnic differences in the prevalence of obesity and overweight.[11] When compared with Whites at the same BMI, Blacks tend to have higher lean mass, lower fat mass, and lower relative health risks associated with a given BMI

[8]*Clinical Guidelines on the Identification, Evaluation, and Treatment of Overweight and Obesity in Adults.* (1998). National Institutes of Health. http://www.ncbi.nlm.nih.gov/books/NBK2003/pdf/TOC. pdf, accessed December 30, 2010; WHO. (2003). "Obesity and Overweight." In *Fact Sheet 2002.* http://www.who.int/hpr/NPH/docs/gs_obesity.pdf, accessed August 14, 2010; Angier, N. (1994). "Researchers Link Obesity in Humans to Flaw in Genes." *New York Times*, A1, A8.

[9]See Stunkard, A. J., Thorkild, I. A., Sorensen, C. H., Teasdale, T. W., Chakraborty, R., Schull, W. J., & Schulsigner, F. (1986). "An Adoption Study of Human Obesity." *New England Journal of Medicine*, 314(4): 193–198; Stunkard, A. J., Harris, J. R., Pedersen, N. L., & McClearn, G. E. (1990). "The Body-Mass Index of Twins Who Have Been Reared Apart." *New England Journal of Medicine*, 322(21): 1483–1487.

[10]Flegal, K. M., Carroll, M. D., Ogden, C. L., & Curtin, R. (2010). "Prevalence and Trends in Obesity Among US Adults, 1999–2008." *JAMA*, 303(3): 235–241.

[11]Ibid.

level.[12] Because of these differences, some researchers suggest using different ranges for different ethnic groups.

Obesity affects people in both the developed world and developing countries; an estimated 115 million people in developing countries are obese. Obesity levels range from lows of about 5% in parts of China, Japan, and Africa to more than 75% in Samoa and other areas of the South Pacific, where many view fat as desirable or a sign of wealth.[13] Marked increases in overweight and obesity are also occurring in children in parts of the developed and developing world. In the United States, the numbers of obese and overweight youths have more than doubled in the past three decades. In Thailand, for example, the percentage of overweight youngsters increased about 25% in just two years.[14] One study in Tianjin, a city in northern China, found one in five children to be overweight, which was attributed to increasing hours spent watching television, similar to studies of adults that found an association between watching television and excess weight.[15] Researchers found that 15.8% of those watching TV more than three hours per day were obese, compared with 10.8% of children who watched TV for less than one hour per day.[16]

Fat children are more likely to have diseases formerly associated with adults, including high blood pressure, high cholesterol, and Type 2 diabetes, than children who are not overweight.[17] Increasing numbers of overweight children will lead to more fat adults in the future as those youths age: 70% to 80% of overweight adolescents will be overweight adults, resulting in longer-term, more severe health problems for them.[18] Although increased health problems are indeed important, overweight children view social discrimination as the most immediate consequence of their size.[19] Social discrimination and very real employment discrimination will also affect them in the future.

[12]Ibid.

[13]Brewis, A. A., McGarvey, S. T., Jones, J., & Swinburn, B. A. (1998). "Perceptions of Body Size in Pacific Islanders." *International Journal of Obesity*, 22(2): 185–190; see also Sobal, J., & Stunkard, A. J. (1989). "Socioeconomic Status and Obesity: A Review of the Literature." *Psychological Bulletin*, 105(2): 260–275.

[14]WHO (2003).

[15]Fernandez, I. D., Su, H., Winters, P. C., & Liang, H. (2010). "Association of Workplace Chronic and Acute Stressors with Employee Weight Status." *Journal of Occupational and Environmental Medicine*, 52(18): S34–S41; Jeffrey, R. W., & French, S. A. (1998). "Epidemic Obesity in the United States: Are Fast Foods and Television Contributing?" *American Journal of Public Health*, 88: 277–280.

[16]http://news.xinhuanet.com/english/2004-08/19/content_1825612.htm, accessed August 14, 2010.

[17]U.S. Department of Health and Human Services (n.d.) "The Surgeon General's Call to Action to Prevent and Decrease Overweight and Obesity." http://www.surgeongeneral.gov/topics/obesity/calltoaction/fact_adolescents.htm, accessed August 14, 2010.

[18]WHO (2003).

[19]U.S. Department of Health and Human Services (n.d.).

▌ EDUCATION, EMPLOYMENT LEVELS, TYPES, AND INCOME

Because men and women from all races, ethnic backgrounds, and ages can be overweight, generalization about their education, employment, and income is difficult. People of various weights will have similar and different education levels, employment levels, types, and income levels. What is clear from numerous studies, however, is that as with members of other non-dominant groups, there are fewer fat people at higher levels and disproportionately more fat people at lower levels. Fat people are also more likely to be unemployed and to remain unemployed longer than people who are not fat. They are less likely to be hired than normal-weight or thin people are, even when their qualifications are similar.[20] If they are hired, fat people often earn less and are sometimes more likely to be assigned to jobs where they are not seen. They receive lower performance evaluations and are more likely to be disciplined than workers who are not fat. All things being equal, fat workers fare worse than those who are not fat, particularly fat women, as discussed in Research Summary 15.1.[21]

In a carefully controlled laboratory study, Regina Pingitore and colleagues found disturbing evidence of weight-based discrimination in hiring.[22] Videotapes of the same professional actors made up and dressed to appear normal or overweight were shown to 320 participants who rated the perceived personality attributes of the applicants and their willingness to hire them. The normal-weight female applicant was 5 feet 6½ inches and weighed 142 pounds and was dressed and made up to appear to weigh 170 in the overweight video. The normal-weight male applicant was about 5 feet 9 inches and weighed 162 pounds but was dressed and made up to appear to weigh about 194 pounds. A professional makeup artist used the size and proportions of actual overweight people, prostheses, and larger clothing to make the "applicants" look about 20% overweight. Excess weight explained 35% of the variance in decisions to hire or not hire an applicant, and overweight female applicants were less likely to be hired than overweight male applicants. Pingitore and colleagues did not find that fat applicants were more likely to be placed in nonvisible jobs, however.[23]

[20]Larkin, J. C., & Pines, H. A. (1979), "No Fat Persons Need Apply." *Sociology of Work and Occupations*, 6: 312–327; Pingitore, R., Dugoni, B. L., Tindale, R. S., & Spring, B. (1994). "Bias Against Overweight Job Applicants in a Simulated Employment Interview." *Journal of Applied Psychology*, 79: 949–959.

[21]See Solovay (2000), Kristen (2002), and Ziolkowski (1994) for research summaries; Jasper, C. R., & Klassen, M. L. (1990), "Perceptions of Salespersons' Appearance and Evaluation of Job Performance." *Perceptual and Motor Skills*, 71: 563–566; Bellizzi, J. A., & Hasty, R. W. (1998). "Territory Assignment Decisions and Supervisory Unethical Selling Behavior: The Effects of Obesity and Gender as Moderated by Job-Related Factors." *Journal of Personal Selling and Sales Management*, 18: 35–49; Bellizzi, J. A., & Hasty, R. W. (2000). "Does Successful Work Experience Mitigate Weight and Gender-Based Employment Discrimination in Face-to-Face Industrial Selling?" *Journal of Business and Industrial Marketing*, 15(6): 384–398.

[22]Pingitore et al. (1994).

[23]Ibid.

Fat Women Fare Worse Than Fat Men!

Multiple studies indicate that fat women experience more negative outcomes than fat men. In one study conducted by Steven Gortmaker and colleagues, using over 10,000 randomly selected participants, overweight women had completed fewer years of formal education, had higher rates of poverty, and earned almost $7,000 per year less than slim women.[24] Register and Williams found that young women who were at least 20% over their "ideal" weights earned 12% less than women who were not fat. No effects were found for fat men, however.[25] Rebecca Puhl and her colleagues at Yale University found that the most overweight women had much higher rates of discrimination; women with 30 to 35 BMI were three times more likely to report discrimination than men.[26]

José Pagán and Alberto Dávila's study using the National Longitudinal Survey of Youth indicated that fat women were segregated into lower-paying occupations but fat men were more well represented across occupations. Fat women earned less than thin women, but fat men did not earn less than thin men.[27] Researchers have also found both fat men and fat women to be less likely to be married than their thinner counterparts, although women again fare worse than men (20% less likely versus 11% less likely to be married).[28]

QUESTIONS TO CONSIDER

1. **Why are the work-related effects of overweight different for men and women?**

2. **Researchers have debated whether people are fat because they are poor or are poor because they are fat. How might each affect the other? Explain.**

Effects of Attractiveness of Appearance on Employment and Income

In contrast to the negative perceptions of those who are fat, people often attribute positive attributes to people who are attractive. These stereotypical perceptions translate into employment and income advantages for attractive people. Numerous researchers have investigated the effects of attractiveness on perceptions of applicant competence and qualifications, hiring decisions, placement, job type, initial salary and salary growth, and

[24]Gortmaker, S. L., Must, A., Perrin, J., Sobol, A. M., & Dietz, W. H. (1993). "Social and Economic Consequences of Overweight in Adolescence and Young Adults." *New England Journal of Medicine*, 329: 1008–1112.

[25]Register, C. A., & Williams, D. R. (1990). "Wage Effects of Obesity Among Young Workers." *Social Science Quarterly*, 71(1): 130–141.

[26]Puhl et al. (2008).

[27]Pagán, J. A., & Dávila, A. (1997). "Obesity, Occupational Attainment, and Earnings." *Social Science Quarterly*, 78, 756–770.

[28]Gortmaker et al. (1993).

promotion and advancement.[29] In both field studies of actual employees and lab studies with simulations, and longitudinal and cross-sectional studies, attractive people are advantaged over those who are not as attractive in the United States and other nations. Although the magnitude of the effects of attractiveness on the job outcomes varies, overall, attractive people fare considerably better in employment and income than less or unattractive people. In a meta-analysis of sixty-eight experimental studies that investigated the relationships between physical attractiveness and job-related outcomes, attractiveness was found to be positively related to hiring, performance evaluations, and promotion, for both men and women.[30]

Attractive women may find themselves in a quandary, however. When does attractiveness help and when does it hurt? At what levels and positions is attractiveness positive or negative? It appears that for lower-level and female-dominated positions, attractiveness improves women's employment opportunities and income. However, for promotional opportunities or in male-dominated or management positions, being too attractive or appearing too feminine can backfire, reducing perceptions of competence and qualifications and reducing the likelihood of selection.[31]

Height is also related to employment outcomes and has different effects for men and women. Height has been found to positively affect men's likelihood of being hired but to have limited effect on performance ratings once hired.[32] Another study found that being taller affected starting salaries of men but not women.[33] In a study of more than 2,000

[29]Cash, T. F., Gillen, P., & Burns, S. D. (1977). "Sexism and 'Beautyism' in Personnel Consultant Decision-Making." *Journal of Applied Psychology*, 62: 301–310; Dipboye, R. L., Arvey, R. D., & Terpstra, D. E. (1977). "Sex and Physical Attractiveness of Raters and Applicants as Determinants of Resume Evaluations." *Journal of Applied Psychology*, 63: 288–294; Drogosz, L. M., & Levy, P. E. (1996). "Another Look at the Effects of Appearance, Gender, and Job Type on Performance-Based Decisions." *Psychology of Women Quarterly*, 20(3): 437–445; Frieze, I. H., Olson, J. E., & Russell, J. (1991). "Attractiveness and Income for Men and Women in Management." *Journal of Applied Social Psychology*, 21: 1039–1057; Hamermesh, D. S., & Biddle, J. E. (1994). "Beauty and the Labor Market." *American Economic Review*, 84: 1174–1194.

[30]Heilman, M. E., & Saruwatari, L. R. (1979). "When Beauty Is Beastly: The Effects of Appearance and Sex on Evaluations of Job Applicants for Managerial and Non-managerial Jobs." *Organizational Behavior and Human Decision Processes*, 23(3): 360–372; Hosoda, M., Stone-Romero, E. F., & Coats, G. (2003). "The Effects of Physical Attractiveness on Job-Related Outcomes: A Meta-Analysis of Experimental Studies." *Personnel Psychology*, 52: 431–463; Johnson, S. K., Podratz, K. E., Dipboye, R. L., & Gibbons, E. (2010). "Physical Attractiveness Biases in Ratings of Employment Suitability: Tracking Down the 'Beauty is Beastly' Effect." *Journal of Social Psychology*, 150(3): 301–318.

[31]See Hatfield, E., & Sprecher, S. (1986). *Mirror, Mirror…: The Importance of Looks in Everyday Life*. Albany: State University of New York Press.

[32]Hensley, W. E., & Cooper, R. (1987). "Height and Occupational Success: A Review and Critique." *Psychological Reports*, 60: 843–849.

[33]Frieze, I. H., Olson, J. E., & Good, D. C. (1990). "Perceived and Actual Discrimination in the Salaries of Male and Female Managers." *Journal of Applied Social Psychology*, 20: 46–67.

U.S. participants, both men and women who were taller than average had higher earnings, but men received greater returns on height than women did.[34] Other samples have produced similar results.[35] In a comprehensive longitudinal U.S. study with 8,590 people, Timothy Judge and Daniel Cable found that height was significantly related to earnings for both men and women and that advantages for tall people were stable over the course of their careers.[36] International Feature 15.1 discusses a British study on the effects of beauty and height on labor market outcomes.

■ LEGISLATION RELEVANT TO WEIGHT AND APPEARANCE

Is it illegal to prefer those who are tall, thin, or attractive over others? In general, it is not, unless doing so also disadvantages people with other protected attributes (such as race, sex, age, disability, or religion). In one study with a representative sample of U.S. adults, researchers found that more of the 2,300 adults surveyed reported weight or height discrimination than those who reported race and sex discrimination.[37] In this section, legislation and some cases related to weight are discussed, followed by appearance legislation and related cases.

The ADA and Weight

Presently in the United States, no federal legislation prohibits discrimination based on weight alone; however, in certain cases, such discrimination may be illegal under the Americans with Disabilities Act (ADA). As previous chapters have pointed out, under the ADA, people who actually have or who are *perceived* to have a disability (regardless of whether this perception is accurate) are protected from employment discrimination.[38] Therefore, if an employer assumes that an applicant's weight will impede his or her ability to perform a job and makes a negative employment decision on the basis of this perception, the applicant could have a claim under the ADA.

....

[34]Loh, E. S. (1993). "The Economic Effects of Physical Appearance." *Social Science Quarterly*, 74: 420–438.

[35]Harper, B. (2000). "Beauty, Stature, and the Labour Market: A British Cohort Study." *Oxford Bulletin of Economics and Statistics* (Special Issue), 62: 771–800; Sargent, J. D., & Blanchflower, D. G. (1994). "Obesity and Stature in Adolescence and Earnings in Young Adulthood: Analysis of a British Birth Cohort." *Archives of Pediatrics and Adolescent Medicine*, 148: 681–687.

[36]Judge, T. A., & Cable, D. M. (2004). "The Effect of Physical Height on Workplace Success and Income: A Preliminary Test of a Theoretical Model." *Journal of Applied Psychology*, 89: 428–441.

[37]Puhl et al. (2008).

[38]Roehling, M. V., Posthuma, R. A., & Dulebohn, J. (2007). "Obesity-Related 'Perceived Disability' Claims: Legal Standards and Human Resource Implications." *Employee Relations Law Journal*, 32: 30–51.

INTERNATIONAL FEATURE 15.1	*Research Translation of Beauty, Stature, and the Labor Market: A British Cohort Study*

The majority of research on the effects of physical attractiveness, weight, and height on labor market outcomes has been conducted in the United States. A study by Professor Barry Harper of London Guildhall University reported findings strikingly similar to those found in U.S. studies. Unattractive, overweight, or short people are penalized in the labor market and effects vary by gender.

Harper's sample was drawn from the National Child Development Study, a longitudinal sample that followed more than 11,000 participants who were born in March 1958. Harper's final sample included 4,160 males and 3,541 females. Their attractiveness at ages 7 and 11 was rated by teachers, who also provided measures of intelligence and sociability—both of which may also affect labor market outcomes. Height and weight were measured by interviewers, except at age 23, when it was self-reported.

Harper found that it was unattractiveness, rather than attractiveness, that affected earnings and the likelihood of being employed. Men who were rated as unattractive at both ages 7 and 11 experienced a 15.9% earnings penalty. Women rated as unattractive at both ages earned 10.9% less than others. The shortest men and women—those in the bottom 10% of the height distribution for their sex—earned, respectively, 4.3% and 5.1% less than those not in the bottom of the distribution.

Relatively tall men (about 6 feet) earned nearly 6% more than men of average height, but the tallest men (more than 6 feet) experienced no earnings premium. Taller women of any height did not experience a premium; height benefits accrued to men only. On the other hand, obese women, but not men, were penalized. Obese women in the top 20% of the weight distribution for their sex suffered a 5.3% earnings penalty. Harper also found that unattractive or short people were less likely to be employed than others in the sample. Because he had controlled for differences in productivity, sociability, intelligence, and other factors that may have contributed to earnings differences, Harper concluded that the majority of the earnings penalty experienced by those short, unattractive, or obese resulted from employer discrimination.

QUESTIONS TO CONSIDER

1. *How might height affect employers' perceptions about applicants or employees?*

2. *What specific recommendations would you make to help employers avoid height discrimination?*

Source: Harper, B. (2000). "Beauty, Stature, and the Labour Market: A British Cohort Study." *Oxford Bulletin of Economics and Statistics* (Special Issue), 62: 771–800.

Misperception: It is illegal to fire someone because he or she is overweight.

Reality: It is generally not illegal to fire someone because of his or her weight, except in specific cities or states where laws prohibit doing so, or when the person is perceived as having or has a disability. Firing someone simply because he or she is overweight may not be illegal, but is probably not good business sense.

Aside from employers' assumptions, those who are morbidly obese are specifically covered under the ADA. As noted earlier, a person is considered morbidly obese when his or her weight is two times or 100 pounds over the recommended weight for height or the person has a BMI of 40 or more. Relatively few people meet these criteria, however, and a person can be extremely obese without meeting the technical criteria for protection under the ADA. Perhaps more important than the relatively small proportion of people who are morbidly obese is the fact that very few people make weight discrimination claims. As discussed in previous chapters, most people who perceive they have been discriminated against do not sue. The unwillingness to file a claim may be greater for those who are overweight. Unlike women and minorities who do not generally feel ashamed or to blame for their sex or race, those who are overweight may feel this way about their weight and may be more reluctant to address unfair treatment. Further, when overweight people have brought litigation in response to discrimination, the courts have been reluctant to rule in their favor (see Solovay, 2000, for a discussion). The low risk of litigation and the social acceptability of and cost-based rationale for weight-based discrimination make other avenues for reducing weight discrimination even more imperative. One important case involving weight-based discrimination, *Cook v. Rhode Island Department of Mental Health, Retardation, and Hospitals,* is discussed in Featured Case 15.1.

State and Local Statutes Prohibiting Weight and Appearance Discrimination

In the face of the limited protections under the ADA, some cities, states, and localities have taken it upon themselves to prohibit weight-based and appearance-related discrimination. The state of Michigan and the cities of Santa Cruz and San Francisco, California, Madison, Wisconsin, and Washington, D.C. are a few of the small number of locales with such prohibitions. The statutes use terminology like *appearance, height and weight, personal appearance, outward appearance, hair style, manner of dress,* and other broad terms, which should encourage employers to closely scrutinize their appearance requirements. Washington's Human Rights Act describes *personal appearance* as "the outward appearance of any person, irrespective of sex, with regard to bodily condition or characteristics, manner of style of dress, and manner of style of personal grooming, including, but not limited to hair style and beards."[39] This and similar acts emphasize that requiring a professional and clean appearance is not prohibited when these are necessary

---

[39]http://www.ohr.dc.gov/ohr/cwp/view,a,3,q,491858,ohrNav,|30953l.asp, accessed August 14, 2010.

FEATURED CASE 15.1	*Bonnie Cook: Fat, but Clearly Competent*

At 5 feet 2 inches and 320 pounds, Bonnie Cook was morbidly obese when she applied for a position at the Ladd Center of the State of Rhode Island's Department of Mental Health, Retardation, and Hospitals (MHRH). As part of the hiring process, Cook was given a prehire medical exam, which indicated that although she was morbidly obese, this did not appear to limit her ability to do the job, thus Cook passed the physical examination. Even so, MHRH refused to hire Cook, stating that her weight would compromise her ability to be able to evacuate patients in emergencies and would make her more likely to become ill, be absent, and file workers' compensation claims. Although problematic in and of themselves, these statements were particularly unusual *because Cook had worked successfully for MHRH twice before, from 1978 to 1980 and from 1981 to 1986, when her weight was about the same!* MHRH acknowledged that Cook had been a satisfactory worker when she was previously employed. Further reflecting their arbitrary and senseless behavior, MHRH offered to hire Cook if she reduced her weight to 300 pounds or less.

Cook took MHRH and the state of Rhode Island to court for its discriminatory behavior, suing under the Rehabilitation Act of 1973 (the precursor to the ADA). Cook stated that her weight was due to a medical condition and that she ate properly and exercised. Regardless of Cook's inability to control her weight, the courts saw as more important that MHRH perceived her as having a disability and disregarded her previously demonstrated ability to do the job. The courts ruled in Cook's favor, finding that MHRH's discrimination against Cook was illegal, awarding her $100,000 in compensatory damages and the job for which she had applied.

QUESTIONS TO CONSIDER

1. **Why do you think MHRH refused to rehire Bonnie Cook after she had successfully worked for it twice before?**

2. **What might MHRH do to avoid this kind of situation in the future?**

Source: Solovay, S. (2000), *Tipping the Scales of Justice: Fighting Weight-Based Discrimination.* Amherst, NY: Prometheus Books.

for reasonable business purposes and are consistently applied. Michigan's Elliott-Larsen Civil Rights Act forbids employers who have at least one employee from discrimination based on weight (and other factors).[40]

Should Size Discrimination Be Prohibited by Federal Law?

Some researchers and fat activists have argued persuasively that the facts of overt discrimination (in employment, housing, public accommodations, and other areas) and inability to control weight warrant inclusion of the overweight and obese as a protected class. This would make weight-based

---

[40]Elliott-Larsen Civil Rights Act. http://www.michigan.gov/documents/act_453_elliott_larsen_8772_7.pdf, accessed August 14, 2010.

employment discrimination illegal in most circumstances.[41] As discussed in Featured Case 15.2, Jennifer Portnick's claim against Jazzercise was successful because of legislation prohibiting size discrimination. Portnick's attorney, Sandra Solovay, noted that Jennifer was lucky to be living in San Francisco, one of a very few places in which size discrimination is illegal. She pointed out, "on one side of the bridge you can be protected from weight discrimination and on the other side you're vulnerable," speaking of San Francisco and Oakland, two California cities separated by the Bay Bridge.[42] Ziolkowski has argued that because of the pervasiveness of weight discrimination, the increased risks for health conditions associated with excess weight, and the difficulty in losing weight and maintaining weight loss, it is possible that weight should be a federally protected class, similar to sex, race, ethnicity, and disability.[43] For those who maintain that weight is controllable (unlike sex, race, and age) and therefore deserves no special protection, the issue of whether controllability should be used as a disqualifier for protection must be carefully analyzed. Some disabilities, such as cancer due to smoking or hearing impairment due to listening to loud music, could be construed as preventable, yet persons so disabled are protected from employment discrimination. Further, as with other arguments supportive of diversity in organizations, employers should be encouraged to make job-related decisions on the ability to perform the job in question. Assuming that fat applicants are unfit and unqualified can rule out nearly two-thirds of the population who may also be highly competent employees.

Organizations must also consider the risks of disparate treatment or impact on protected classes as a result of employment actions based on weight, appearance, and perceived attractiveness. Appearance declines and weight gain are more likely as one ages; Black, Latina, and Native American women tend to be heavier than White women. These and other relationships among appearance, weight, age, race, and sex require that employers pay careful attention to their selection preferences and decisions. They should also emphasize legitimate job requirements and use highly structured interviews to help reduce discrimination.

▌ EFFECTS OF WEIGHT ON HEALTH AND ON COSTS TO EMPLOYERS

Although some overweight people are quite healthy, the correlation between excess weight and various severe health problems is clear. Being

[41]Solovay (2000).

[42]Brown, P. L. (2002, May 8). "240 pounds, Persistent and Jazzercise's Equal." *New York Times.* http://www.nytimes.com/2002/05/08/us/240-pounds-persistent-and-jazzercise-s-equal.html, accessed December 30, 2010.

[43]Ziolkowski (1994).

FEATURED CASE 15.2	*Jennifer Portnick: Clearly Fit, but Not Up to Jazzercise Appearance Standards*

Although 5 feet 8 inches and 240 pounds, Jennifer Portnick's ability to perform high-impact aerobics was not in question. Portnick exercised six days per week and had been doing high-impact aerobics, as a student and a teacher, for fifteen years. Portnick performed aerobics so well that her Jazzercise teacher encouraged her to seek Jazzercise certification so that she could teach for the Jazzercise organization. To do so, Portnick had to obtain permission to try out for certification, but, because of her size, Jazzercise management would not allow her to try out. Jazzercise told Portnick that she needed to lose weight and to cut down on carbohydrates. Reflecting the erroneous position that being heavy and being fit are mutually exclusive, Jazzercise management told Portnick that "Jazzercise sells fitness" and that a Jazzercise applicant needed to look leaner than the public.[44]

Portnick sued Jazzercise under San Francisco's ordinance that prohibits discrimination on the basis of weight and height. This law is also called the *fat and short law* by critics. The case went to mediation and was settled when Jazzercise changed its mind about the need to appear fit. The company acknowledged that it is possible for people of varying weights to be fit.[45]

In addition to one's right to be judged on competence rather than appearance, Portnick's supporters viewed Jazzercise's position as narrow-minded and counterproductive, particularly given the increasing size of the U.S. population. Although overweight people may be self-conscious in a "normal" aerobics class, they may be comfortable and confident in a class taught by a "fat-but-fit" instructor. Instead of Jazzercise, Portnick began teaching aerobics at the YMCA, which viewed her cardiovascular fitness, despite her size, as a tremendous opportunity to reach the sedentary.[46]

QUESTIONS TO CONSIDER

1. *What are the likely responses to having an aerobics instructor, such as Jennifer Portnick, larger than the "normal"-weight students at a health club? What are the likely responses from the general public to the Jazzercise settlement?*

2. *Is being "fat and fit" possible? If so, how could this be reconciled with the documented higher costs associated with heavier employees?*

3. *The YMCA viewed Portnick's size as an opportunity to reach the sedentary. How might this opportunity be realized?*

overweight increases the likelihood of developing Type 2 diabetes and hypertension. Overweight is also associated with certain types of cancers, including those of the colon, breast, prostate, endometrium, and kidney. Carrying excess pounds is associated with arthritis and other joint ailments that contribute to disabilities in adults, to reproductive health

....

[44]Fernandez, E. (2002, May 7). "Exercising Her Right to Work: Fitness Instructor Wins Weight-Bias Fight." *San Francisco Chronicle*; "Jazzercise Settlement Redefines Who's Fit." http://abcnews.go.com/GMA/story?id=126114&page=1, accessed January 1, 2011.
[45]Brown (2002).
[46]Ibid.

problems in women, and to depression. Estimates suggest that overweight will soon surpass smoking as the primary cause of preventable deaths in the United States as fewer people smoke and more people are overweight.

Table 15.1 presents the mean costs of overweight and obesity for employees at General Motors. The negative health effects of excess weight result in increased medical, benefit, and absence costs for other employers as well. Some estimates suggest that obese and overweight workers use nearly 40 million work days and cost employers 15%, 20%, and 55% more, respectively, in prescription drug, long-term disability, and short-term disability costs, with greater costs as the weight level increases.[47] As obesity increases among the population worldwide, these costs can only be expected to increase, providing further incentives for many employer-sponsored weight and health management programs.

Aside from the legitimate reasons for pursuing weight loss, people who exercise and eat properly yet remain overweight can be healthier than slim people who do not exercise or eat healthy foods. Fat people who exercise and eat properly may also be healthier than those who lose and regain weight in fruitless "yo-yo" dieting attempts. For most people, losing weight and maintaining weight loss are very difficult, despite ardent, repeated attempts. As anyone who has ever dieted repeatedly can attest, continued attempts to lose weight appear to make weight loss increasingly difficult to achieve and maintain, while also resulting in other negative health effects.[48] Glenn Gaesser's book, *Big Fat Lies: The Truth About Your Weight and Your Health*, provides compelling support for focusing on health, exercise, and avoidance of weight gain rather than on futile attempts to lose weight.[49]

TABLE 15.1 *Mean Costs of Overweight and Obesity at General Motors*

BMI	BMI Category	Percent of Workers	Medical and Drug Costs
18.5–24.9	Normal	25.2	$3,593
25.0–29.9	Overweight	40.4	$3,705
30.0–34.9	Obese	21.8	$5,032
>34.9	Obese to morbidly obese (BMI ≥ 40)	11.7	$5,965

Source: Adapted from Grossman R. J. (2004, March). "Countering a Weight Crisis." *HR Magazine*, p. 45.

[47]U.S. Department of Health and Human Services (n.d.); Wolf, A. M., & Colditz, G. A. (1998). "Current Estimates of the Economic Cost of Obesity in the United States." *Obesity Research*, 6: 97–106.
[48]Gaesser, G. (2000). *Big Fat Lies: The Truth About Your Weight and Your Health*. Carlsbad, CA: Gurze Books.
[49]Ibid.

Misperception: People who diet and lose weight are healthier than those who do not.

Reality: Maintaining a stable weight, even if it is a somewhat less healthy weight, is healthier than losing and regaining excess weight multiple times.

■ Is It the Fat, the Health, or the Stigma of Overweight?

Overweight people are more likely to miss work than others, and insuring those who are fat is more expensive than insuring those who are not fat. Those with anorexia and bulimia are also more likely to miss work and have related increased insurance costs, as do smokers. Cancer and numerous other illnesses are also more likely to cause absence and be expensive to insure. Those who are fat, however, are unique in their experiences with overt hostility, negative comments, and lack of protection from discrimination on the job. Further, unlike anorexia, bulimia, cancers, and many other illnesses that cause employers additional expense, obesity is clearly visible. Few would question employers' preferences for workers who are energetic, disciplined, and self-controlled. More legitimately, people might ask themselves whether all overweight people are lazy, undisciplined, and lacking in self-control and whether all thin or normal-weight people are energetic, disciplined, and self-controlled. Few would answer these questions affirmatively. In fact, common perceptions about the personality attributes of fat workers—that they are less conscientious, agreeable, and outgoing—are largely inaccurate.[50]

A thin applicant or employee might be thin due to anorexia, bingeing and purging, or smoking, none of which exemplifies energy, discipline, or self-control. As discussed in Feature 15.2, costs of thinness can also be very high. Further, multiple studies using different populations have found that people who are excessively thin (BMI < 18) have higher mortality rates than people who have BMI ranges of 20 to 22.[51] These higher rates of mortality occur after controlling for previous illness, smoking, or being elderly (and its associated weight loss).

[50]Roehling, M. V., Roehling, P. V., & Dunn, H. (2008). "Investigating the Validity of Stereotypes About Overweight Employees: The Investigation of Body Weight and Normal Personality Traits." *Group Organization Management*, 33(4): 392–424.

[51]See, for example, Thorogood, M., Appleby, P. N., Key, T. J., & Mann, J. (2003). "Relation Between Body Mass Index and Mortality in an Unusually Slim Cohort." *Journal of Epidemiology and Community Health*, 57: 130–133.

FEATURE 15.2	*Costs of Thinness*

Eating disorders such as anorexia nervosa and bulimia nervosa are increasingly common weight-related health issues that receive less attention than obesity and overweight. Anorexia and bulimia involve disordered eating behavior, such as eating very little for extended periods of time or eating extreme amounts in a short period of time, coupled with measures to binge or purge oneself of the food consumed. Both anorexia and bulimia are associated with intense fear of weight gain, inappropriate behavior to prevent weight gain, often including misusing laxatives, diuretics, or enemas, and excessive exercising.

Anorexia is essentially self-starvation. In response to being starved, the body slows down its processes to conserve energy. Negative health effects associated with anorexia include dry, brittle bones (osteoporosis), muscle loss and weakness, hair loss, severe dehydration (sometimes resulting in kidney failure), and disrupted menstrual cycles. Bulimia involves recurrent episodes of binge eating, sometimes accompanied by purging. The binge-eating episodes may last for hours or days, followed by guilt, disgust, and shame. Those suffering from bulimia are likely to be average or above average weight. Negative health effects resulting from bulimia include swelling of the stomach or pancreas, tooth decay (resulting from vomiting), abnormal heart rhythms, and muscle spasms.

Anorexia and bulimia cross racial, ethnic, age, and gender lines; however, young women are significantly more likely to develop them than others. Estimates suggest that between 0.5% and 3.7% of females will suffer from anorexia at some point in life and that between 1.1% and 4.2% will have bulimia at some point. The mortality rate for those with anorexia is 5.6% per decade, or twelve times higher than the death rate due to all causes for young women in the population. The most common causes of death due to anorexia are cardiac arrest, electrolyte imbalance, and suicide. After battling anorexia for many years, Karen Carpenter, a popular singer from the 1970s and 1980s, died at age 32. French actress and model Isabelle Caro, whose emaciated body appeared in an anti-anorexia ad died at age 28 in December 2010.[52] Mary-Kate Olsen, Jane Fonda, and Sally Field have also reportedly suffered from eating disorders.

QUESTIONS TO CONSIDER

1. Why do the negative health effects associated with thinness and attempts to be thin receive relatively little attention when compared with obesity?

2. Investigate mortality rates for obese young women. How do these rates compare with those for young women suffering from anorexia or bulimia?

Sources: Spearing, M. (2001). "Eating Disorders: Facts About Eating Disorders and the Search for Solutions." National Institute of Mental Health. http://www.nimh.nih.gov/publicat/eatingdisorders.cfm, accessed August 9, 2010; Soriano, C. G. (2004, June 22). "Mary-Kate Olsen Seeks Treatment for Eating Disorder." *USAToday*. http://www.usatoday.com/life/people/2004-06-22-olsen-treatment_x.htm, accessed August 9, 2010.

---

[52]"Isabelle Caro Dies After Anorexia Struggle." http://www.guardian.co.uk/society/2010/dec/30/isabelle-caro-dies-model-anorexia, accessed January 1, 2011.

Misperception: Thinness is always healthier than heaviness.

Reality: Excessive thinness and excessive weight are both unhealthy.

The widespread dislike for fatness, its clear visibility, its perceived association with many negative personal attributes, and the lack of widespread sanctions for discrimination on the basis of fat all contribute to continued discrimination. Research on stigma provides some clues to understanding fat discrimination. **Stigma** theory suggests that those whose attributes deviate from the typical, normal, or preferred attributes of others in a situation may be *stigmatized* and this stigmatization will result in various negative outcomes.[53] Since two-thirds of the U.S. population is now overweight or obese, the "typical" or "normal" person is no longer thin. Stigmatization appears instead to result from deviance from *preferred attributes* rather than common or normal attributes. As discussed earlier, women suffer more negative consequences for being overweight than do men. Several authors suggest this is partly a response to media images that portray nearly all women as unrealistically thin and ignore larger (normal) women, resulting in greater preferences for thin women.[54] Even "plus-sized" models are often smaller than the "average" woman. Since the images of women's thinness are so pervasive and so strongly equated with beauty, women who deviate from these images are penalized by society, including employers and health care providers.

Obesity Discrimination in Health Care

As discussed in the previous section, excess weight is associated with numerous health problems. Although not every overweight person is unhealthy, overweight people use more health care services compared to those who are not overweight, but, ironically, they are less likely to receive preventive care than others. Obese women are more likely to delay having breast exams, gynecological exams, and Pap smears, even when the sample is controlled for age, race, income, education, smoking, and health insurance.[55] Medical professionals hold many of the same negative perceptions that discriminating employers hold about the character and attributes of those who

[53]Goffman, E. (1963). *Stigma: Notes on the Management of Spoiled Identity.* Englewood Cliffs, NJ: Prentice Hall.
[54]Wolf, N. (1991). *The Beauty Myth.* New York: William Morris & Co.; Goodman, C. (1995). *The Invisible Woman: Confronting Weight Prejudice in America.* Carlsbad, CA: Gurze Books.
[55]Fontaine, K. R., Faith, M. S., Allison, D. B., & Cheskin, L. J. (1998). "Body Weight and Health Care Among Women in the General Population." *Archives of Family Medicine,* 7: 381–384.

are overweight, and differential treatment of obese patients by medical professionals may contribute to the obese delaying important preventive care.

In one study, 33% of physicians reported responding negatively to obese patients and associated obesity with poor hygiene, noncompliance, and dishonesty. In another study, 63% of nurses agree that obesity could be prevented by self-control, and 43% and 22%, respectively, felt the obese were overindulgent and lazy. Nearly half (48%) of the nurses said they felt uncomfortable caring for obese patients, and 31% said they preferred not to do so.[56] Medical students in one study reported negative attitudes about obese patients, and those attitudes did not change after the students spent eight weeks working with obese patients. Researchers speculated that overweight people may be hesitant to obtain preventive care exams because of negative body image. When this reluctance is combined with physicians' unwillingness to serve overweight people, that may contribute to very dangerous health consequences.

▌ APPEARANCE: CASES AND LEGISLATION

When appearance or attractiveness requirements discriminate against people with disabilities, older people, or certain racial groups, violations of the ADA, the ADEA, or Title VII may have occurred. In prohibiting race, ethnic, sex, religious, age, and disability discrimination, these acts require organizations to assess carefully the legality of preferences for certain "looks" or other attributes. According to these laws, the "look" preferred by management at Abercrombie & Fitch resulted in illegal discrimination against women and people of color, as discussed in Organizational Feature 15.1.

Recall that the ADA prohibits discrimination if a person is *perceived as* being limited by a disability, regardless of whether that person is actually limited by a disability. According to the EEOC, one such case in which appearance preferences resulted in illegal discrimination occurred at a McDonald's in Northport, Alabama. Samantha Robichaud had a cosmetic disfigurement, called a port wine stain, which covered the majority of her face. Robichaud began working at McDonald's as a cook but said she accepted that position with the assurance she would have the opportunity to be promoted into management. To obtain such promotions, McDonald's requires employees to be cross-trained and rotated into several of the jobs at the restaurant, including serving customers at the counter. Robichaud worked at the front counter for a while but was removed because of her appearance. She was later told that she would

[56]Puhl, R., & Brownell, K. D. (2001). "Bias, Discrimination, and Obesity." *Obesity Research*, 9(12): 788–805.

ORGANIZATIONAL FEATURE 15.1	*Multiple Diversity Concerns at Abercrombie & Fitch*

Abercrombie & Fitch (ANF), an upscale retailer known for its attractive "All-American" salespeople, has been accused of discriminating against applicants who are not blonde and blue-eyed, even though the company has a stated nondiscrimination policy. While preferring applicants of a certain appearance is not illegal in and of itself, when doing so eliminates nearly all people of a particular race or ethnicity, this can be illegal. According to charges filed by former employees and applicants, and some that have been confirmed by former managers, ANF discriminated against Latinos, Asian Americans, and Blacks in hiring, firing, and job placement. Reports indicated that minorities were told there were no jobs when jobs were available, were steered to nonvisible jobs (such as stocking), or were fired or transferred and replaced with White employees.

One Latino, Eduardo Gonzalez, applied for work at ANF in a mall near Stanford University, where he was a student. Gonzalez noticed that all the sales staff on duty were White and said that the manager encouraged him to work in the stockroom or in another nonsales position. Researchers refer to this behavior as **race-coded job channeling**, whereby employers who prefer Whites for certain positions and minorities for others steer applicants to the preferred jobs, regardless of the applicants' interests, skills, or experience.[57] Gonzalez left ANF and instead was hired at Banana Republic.

Asian Americans have also reported suspicious treatment by ANF. Another Stanford student, Anthony Ocampo, a Filipino American, had worked for ANF during the Christmas holidays. When he applied at a different ANF the following summer, Ocampo was reportedly told he was not hired because there were already too many Filipinos working there. Jennifer Lu was a student at University of California, Irvine when she worked for ANF. According to Lu, corporate representatives from ANF came to inspect the store, pointed to one of the ANF posters that depicted a White male model, and told the store manager to make the store look like the poster. Soon thereafter, Lu (who had more than three years of service) and four other Asian American employees were terminated and an African American was transferred to the night shift at a different store. Class action lawsuits were filed against ANF in California and New Jersey.

Not only has ANF had employment-related diversity problems, it has also had problems related to choice of merchandise. After complaints from customers about "racist fashion," ANF removed offensive T-shirts from its shelves, one depicting two Asian men and the words "Wong Brothers Laundry Service—Two Wongs Can Make It White," perpetuating stereotypes of Asians. Customers in San Francisco picketed ANF stores and planned boycotts around the country. A diverse buying team or store-level associates might have recognized the potential for trouble with those particular shirts before they reached the shelves.

Articles about these issues appeared in the *San Francisco Chronicle*, in the *Miami Herald*, in the *New York Times,* in *Black Enterprise*, in Associate Press reports distributed nationwide, and on CNN and CBS news, generating negative publicity from coast to coast. The NAACP Legal Defense

[57]Pager, D., Bonikowski, B., & Western, B. (2009). "Discrimination in a Low-Wage Labor Market: A Field Experiment." *American Sociological Review*, 74: 777–799.

and Educational Fund, the Mexican-American Legal Defense and Educational Fund, and the Asian Pacific American Legal Centers joined forces with the plaintiffs' attorneys in this effort.[58]

ANF's diversity concerns may have negatively affected its ability to market to its target consumers, a point noted in an article on young buyers' tastes. According to David Morrison, founder and CEO of a firm that analyzes shopping habits of people from 18 to 35 years old, "to the college-age shopper, Abercrombie is 'so over.'" In Morrison's opinion, "Abercrombie lost it when they became a little 'too white' with their advertising. They lost and alienated a lot of people who didn't see themselves or their friends represented."[59]

ANF also lost in the settlement of the class action lawsuit, agreeing to pay $40 million to the affected applicants and employees and $10 million to monitor compliance attorneys' fees. The company is enjoined from discriminating against African Americans, Asian Americans, and Latinos based on their race, color, and national origin; from discriminating against women due to their sex; and from denying promotional opportunities to minorities and women. ANF agreed to implement new policies and programs to prevent future discrimination, hire a vice president of diversity, hire up to twenty-five diversity recruiters, provide training to all its managers, and ensure its marketing materials reflect diversity.[60]

ANF chairman and CEO Mike Jeffries said that the company decided to settle the suit because a long dispute would have been harmful to the company and distracting to managers. Jeffries denied that the company had engaged in discriminatory practices and stated that they currently "have, and always have had, no tolerance for discrimination."[61] Despite those statements, ANF's problems with discrimination claims continued. Two years after the original settlement, the EEOC again sued the company, alleging they discriminated against a 17-year-old Muslim woman by refusing to hire her because she wore a hijab, in violation of the company's "Look Policy," which prohibited head coverings.[62]

QUESTIONS TO CONSIDER

1. *Chapters 4 and 5 discuss the "youthfulness" of African Americans and Latinos when compared to Caucasians. What are the potential ramifications of ANF's exclusion of these groups as employees and models?*

2. *How might having buyers from different racial and ethnic backgrounds have circumvented the marketing "blunders" and lost business associated with the offensive merchandise at ANF?*

3. *How may the company's denial of discrimination, even after settling the first lawsuit, have negatively impacted the effectiveness of measures to stop discrimination in hiring and advancement at ANF?*

[58]Holmes, T. E. (n.d.) "Abercrombie & Fitch's Discrimination Woes." http://www.blackenterprise.com/ExclusiveskOpen.asp?id=387, accessed September 27, 2004.

[59]Wellington, E. (2004, October 14). "The Old College Buy: Company Tracks Students' Tastes and Finds Good News for Burt's Bees, Bad News for Nike." *Fort Worth Star Telegram*, Section 8E.

[60]"EEOC Agrees to Landmark Resolution of Discrimination Case Against Abercrombie & Fitch." http://www.eeoc.gov/press/11-18-04.html, accessed January 1, 2011; Chavez, P. (2004, November 16). "Abercrombie & Fitch to Pay $40 Million to Settle Discrimination Case." *Mercury News.* www.mercurynews.com/mld/mercurynews/news/10189859.htm, accessed November 18, 2004.

[61]Chavez (2004).

[62]"Abercrombie & Fitch Sued by EEOC for Religious Discrimination Against Muslim Teen Applicant." http://www.eeoc.gov/eeoc/newsroom/release/9-17-09b.cfm, accessed August 2, 2010.

4. How does the experience of Asian Americans in California with employment discrimination at ANF contrast with the perception of Asian Americans as a group that does not experience employment-related discrimination?

5. Choose a retail store in your area or use a catalog to document (in one visit) the racial, gender, and age composition of the sales associates (or models, if a catalog). What diversity-related factors are visible from your report?

Sources: Greenhouse, S. J. (2003, June 17). "Clothing Chain Accused of Discrimination." *New York Times*; Chin A. (2002, April 23). "Why Abercrombie and Fitch Still Doesn't Get It." http://www.modelminority.com/joomla/index.php?option=com_content&view=article&id=65: why-abercrombie-and-fitch-still-doesnt-get-it&catid=44: media&Itemid=56, accessed August 9, 2010; "Lieff Cabraser and Civil Rights Organizations Announce Abercrombie & Fitch Charged with Employment Discrimination in Federal Class Action Lawsuit." http://www.afjustice.com/press_release_01.htm, accessed August 9, 2010; Holmes, T. E. (n.d.). "Abercrombie & Fitch's Discrimination Woes." http://www.blackenterprise.com/Exclusivesek Open.asp?id=387, accessed September 27, 2004; Leung, R. (2004, November 24). "The Look of Abercrombie & Fitch." http://www.cbsnews.com/stories/2003/12/05/60minutes/main587099.shtml, accessed August 8, 2010.

never be able to receive a management position because of her appearance. The EEOC in Birmingham, Alabama, found Robichaud's case to be meritorious and, after failing to reach a conciliation agreement with the restaurant, filed its first suit involving facial disfigurement in Alabama.[63]

Other situations involving questionable appearance requirements concern employers' restrictions against facial hair, preferences for hair color of a person's ethnic origin, suggestions that women wear makeup or certain hairstyles, and limitations on religious apparel at work. Such requirements may constitute religious, racial, ethnic, or gender discrimination. Restrictions against beards have been challenged by African American men, who sometimes experience a painful condition called *pseudofolliculitis barbae,* or "razor bumps," as a result of shaving. As discussed in Chapter 12, requirements that women not wear head coverings can result in religious discrimination. Other companies accused of appearance-related discriminatory conduct include Federal Express, Enterprise Rent-A-Car, Alamo Rent-A-Car, Price Waterhouse, and Jean Louis David Salons.

■ RECOMMENDATIONS FOR INDIVIDUALS AND ORGANIZATIONS

Considerations for Employers: Weight

The increasing numbers of people who are overweight and obese in the United States and around the world; the very real, expensive costs and health risks associated with excess weight; and the discrimination against

---

[63]"EEOC Sues McDonald's Restaurant for Disability Bias Against Employee with Facial Disfigurement." http://www.eeoc.gov/press/3-7-03.html, accessed August 14, 2010.

those who are overweight create an unusual situation for employers. Should overweight people be denied employment because they are more likely to miss work and are more expensive for organizations to insure? Although weight discrimination is not usually illegal, employers should consider several factors when developing an approach to combat weight-related discrimination. First, they should consider the legitimacy of health, absence, and cost-related concerns for their specific employee population. Are similar concerns expressed regarding other health issues? Do people with other health issues that are viewed as controllable (e.g., pregnancy, smoking-related lung cancer) receive similar treatment?

Employers should view the negative consequences of weight discrimination through the same preventive lenses used to consider other discrimination. Adding size, weight, and appearance to the company's zero tolerance policy would signal to all employees that discrimination and harassment on the basis of these factors are unacceptable. Fat jokes, comments, and overt discrimination would be strongly sanctioned, as would racist, sexist, or ageist behaviors. Decision makers must be aware that the broad social acceptability of fat discrimination and general dislike for fatness may make efforts to reduce discrimination more difficult, requiring more concerted, rigorous, and sincere efforts.

Those who are fat report experiencing extreme hostility, rudeness, and harassment by hiring managers, coworkers, and peers. As an example, when he arrived for an interview, one overweight applicant was not spoken to by the interviewing manager. Instead, the manager told the secretary to "get this fat (expletive) out of my office!"[64] Another heavy applicant was forced to stand throughout the interview, for fear he would break the chairs. An article in *Working Woman* magazine reported that a woman who was thinner at the time of a job interview said that on her first day of work she was told she had "put on a lot of weight!" since the interview. Throughout her miserable employment tenure, the woman was told to wear dark clothing and coached on her appearance, despite successful job performance and an otherwise professional (although fat) appearance.[65] Clearly, these behaviors are unacceptable in any business environment and should not be tolerated. Although fat discrimination is not currently illegal, respectful, professional behavior should be mandatory at work, in school, and in other professional environments.

Finally, because the majority of the U.S. population is overweight or obese, if potential workers are continually screened out due to their weight,

[64]Fraser, L. (1994). "The Office F Word: Job Discrimination Against Fat People." *Working Woman*, 53–54(6): 88–91.
[65]Ibid.

recruitment and selection costs could become extremely high. If fat employees are given positions with low visibility, disciplined more harshly, and experience other negative outcomes at work, employer costs related to turnover, absence, and low morale could exceed or rival those related to higher medical and benefit costs for fat workers. As with other diversity-related issues, employers should focus their decision making and actions on job-related issues and take measures to ensure that fat discrimination that is not clearly job related is minimized. In addition, no one should overlook the social and ethical concerns of hostile treatment toward those who are overweight or obese.

Employers may be able to assist *all* workers with health-related issues by encouraging wellness rather than focusing on weight loss, which may be futile and could perpetuate fat discrimination. Wellness would include healthy behaviors, such as proper eating, exercise, moderate drinking, avoiding smoking, and reducing stress (which contributes to hypertension and weight gain). Employers should offer healthy foods in vending machines and cafeterias, provide bonuses for smoking cessation, and encourage regular participation in exercise programs and other healthy behaviors. Companies could subsidize health club memberships or provide workout equipment and training at work, allowing employees paid breaks to exercise. By focusing on health, rather than weight, employers may create a healthier workplace overall, for all employees.

Lastly, the medical profession should adopt a zero tolerance approach toward discrimination. Not only is discrimination by medical professionals morally wrong, it could also contribute to the worsening of the health of those who are overweight or even be life-threatening.

Considerations for Employees: Weight

Whether one is currently thin, "normal," overweight, or obese, the issue of weight as an aspect of diversity has relevance for everyone. We all have the potential to gain weight and experience some of the negative social, employment, and health consequences associated with being heavy. This is particularly true as a function of age because as people enter middle age, the likelihood of growing heavier increases. With age also comes the greater likelihood of acquiring a disability, which may also contribute to weight gain. No one is immune to the intolerance and prejudice associated with weight issues and disparate treatment on the basis of weight.

When faced with or observing weight-based stereotyping or discrimination, employees should address the issue with valid information about weight and the characteristics of those who are overweight. Many people are unaware that weight is a combination of lifestyle choices and genetics and that different metabolic rates may result in some people being heavier than others, regardless of similar activity levels and food consumed. As with many other inaccurate stereotypes, people's belief that being fat is solely a result of laziness and lack of discipline may be changed with knowledge. Statements about legitimate health issues as a reason for weight-based discrimination in employment can be countered with statements about the other "voluntary" issues discussed in this chapter, such as smoking, or invisible health issues related to other voluntary behaviors that are not so vehemently disdained and acutely obvious.

Those who are overweight should consider and model the behaviors of other non-dominant groups in the face of overt social and employment discrimination. They should take care not to internalize society's negative beliefs about fat people. Members of other non-dominant groups (e.g., women, Blacks) do not generally feel self-blame and loathing toward their sex or gender. Instead, in response to differential power and treatment, they have sought, and obtained, greater acceptance and understanding of their differences and contributions and some reduction of discriminatory behaviors. Those who are overweight should also take care to monitor their health; with exercise and proper eating, they may be healthy in spite of excess weight.

Recommendations to Individuals and Organizations for Minimizing Appearance Discrimination

Because there are so many distinct issues related to appearance discrimination, broad recommendations focus on ensuring that employer preferences are job related and that decisions are made only on job-related factors. While requirements for neatness and cleanliness are reasonable and legal, requirements that women wear makeup and carry a purse instead of a briefcase (e.g., Ann Hopkins) are not. Employers should carefully scrutinize the potential of their appearance preferences and requirements to cause various types of discrimination, as they can be based on race, class, and gender in ways that are not related to job performance.

Applicants and employees should be aware that organizations are legally able to prescribe many aspects of appearance at work. Professional standards and uniform appearance alone are not generally illegal, particularly when consistently applied. When no specific racial, ethnic, gender, religious, or disability discrimination results from the requirements, employer rights to a consistent appearance for employees may supersede employees' rights to wear certain clothing. For example, after filing suit and exhausting multiple appeals under Madison, Wisconsin's policy prohibiting appearance discrimination, an employee learned that her dismissal for wearing an eyebrow ring to her job at Sam's Club was not illegal. Sam's dress code, which specifically prohibited nose rings or other facial jewelry, was deemed to be consistent with the organization's conservative, Spartan, "no-frills" approach. When both employees and employers apply logic and reason, many appearance disputes could be avoided.

SUMMARY

In this chapter, we have considered weight and appearance as diversity issues. Weight, a subcategory of appearance, has many implications for people's experiences in organizations. Nearly two-thirds of the U.S. population is overweight or obese, and the prevalence of these conditions is increasing around the world. Discrimination against those who are overweight, based on perceptions that overweight people are lazy and unmotivated, negatively affects their employment outcomes. We have examined research documenting discriminatory employment experiences, including differences in rates of employment and unemployment, job assignments, compensation, and performance evaluations. We discussed the lack of universal legislation prohibiting weight discrimination and the legitimate health costs of overweight (some borne by employers) and made suggestions for employers and employees seeking to reduce weight discrimination in their organizations.

Many other aspects of appearance, including hairstyle, attire, makeup, height, and physical disfigurement, also affect people's organizational experiences. Although employer preferences for certain types of appearance are not necessarily illegal, such preferences, when ill-conceived or misapplied, may result in illegal discrimination. Employers should be careful to ensure that appearance requirements are job related and that attractiveness does not overshadow job competence in selection,

promotion, retention, and other job-related decision making.

KEY TERMS

Race-coded job channeling — steering applicants to certain jobs based on employer preferences for Whites in certain positions and minorities in others, regardless of the applicants' interests, skills, or experience.

Stigma — a negative discrepancy between the real or perceived attributes of an individual and the *expectations* for typical or normal individuals in a particular context.

QUESTIONS TO CONSIDER

1. What are the employment and income-related effects of being overweight for women? For men?
2. The association between excess weight and higher absence and medical and benefit costs is clear. What is the meaning of this relationship regarding weight discrimination for the many individuals who are fat and for organizational policymakers? How should organizations address weight-based discrimination, given these clear, costly associations?
3. Fat is commonly believed to be the result of laziness and gluttony rather than a combination of factors. How do these perceptions affect the experiences

and treatment of overweight people in organizations? What can be done about these perceptions?

4. What laws are relevant to weight and appearance discrimination? How might seemingly legitimate appearance requirements result in illegal discrimination? What should organizations do to minimize the likelihood of such discrimination?

5. There are significant, long-term, negative health effects associated with anorexia and bulimia, yet neither receives the attention and focus that excess weight does. Why should employers be concerned about the negative health effects associated with under- and overweight?

ACTIONS AND EXERCISES

1. If you are personally overweight or have a close friend/family member who is overweight, consider your or their employment or interviewing experiences. Ask yourself or your friend/family member about them. How have they been similar to or different from the experiences of those who are overweight described in this chapter?

2a. Conduct an informal census of employees in several places: fast-food restaurant, sit-down restaurant, discount store, department store, government office, bank, or other locations in which many employees are visible. Document the number of employees and the number of those who appear a little, a lot, and very overweight/obese. What is the race, ethnicity, and sex of the obese workers? Are any of the overweight employees working in positions of power (e.g., managers, supervisors)?

2b. Choose two nights to watch television for thirty minutes to one hour each. Document the program, type of commericals, and the numbers of overweight/obese or physically unattractive characters on the programs and commercials. What is the race, ethnicity, and sex of those characters/actors?

2c. What similarities and differences are apparent between the people in questions 2a and 2b?

2d. Watch newscasters several times and during different broadcasts. Report on their appearance (including weight, race, sex, attire, and other appearance attributes).

3. Investigate health and medical costs associated with alcoholism, anorexia, bulimia, smoking, and/or other illnesses perceived as controllable with self-discipline. Compare these costs to those associated with obesity.

4. Compare the look allegedly preferred by ANF to the approach used by the United Colors of Benetton to advertising and staffing. What "look" accurately represents the present population of the United States?

5. What recommendations would you make to help large organizations with recognized diversity programs to reduce the likelihood of inadvertent discrimination by managers trying to follow procedures for dress codes?

SECTION III
Global Vision

Yuri Arcurs/Shutterstock.com

Chapter 16   *International Diversity and Facing the Future*

International Diversity and Facing the Future

After completing this chapter, readers should be able to:

- ❏ *explain issues concerning dominant and non-dominant groups around the world.*

- ❏ *discuss why inequity based on sex and gender, disability, sexual orientation, and poverty is common in many countries.*

- ❏ *analyze historical and current factors to help identify and assess the specific diversity issues in any country.*

- ❏ *make specific recommendations for individuals, organizations, and society to increase equality and inclusion for non-dominant group members.*

- ❏ *explain why the diversity of the U.S. population, globalization, and increased competitiveness make attending to equality and inclusion in the United States and including the contributions of its entire population imperative, rather than optional.*

Key Facts

Diversity issues are relevant to work and organizations in countries around the world.

Workforces in many nations are changing due to changes in birth and mortality rates, immigration, age distributions, external pressures, and competition.

Specific diversity concerns vary by location, but differences in education, participation, and employment levels can be used to help identify non-dominant groups in a particular location.

Discrimination based on sex, sexual orientation, and disability exists virtually everywhere and is an underlying feature of persistent poverty.

Diversity in organizations is an aspect of societal changes and is increased or impeded by individual, organizational, and societal factors.

Past and present diversity issues in the United States make its urgent attention to diversity vital to its future success and competitiveness.

Introduction and Overview

In the first chapter of this book, diversity was defined as real or perceived differences among people that affect their interactions and relationships.[1] With this as a foundation and a focus on different groups in the U.S. population, the following fourteen chapters covered theories of diversity; legislation concerning diversity; Blacks, Latinos, Asians, Whites, American Indians, Alaska Natives, and multiracial group members; sex and gender; work and family; sexual orientation; religion; age; physical and mental ability; and weight and appearance as specific aspects of diversity. These are the issues that are currently most important in the United States, which is where most of the furor about *increasing* diversity began and is the source of most of the published research on diversity.

Each chapter included information on non-U.S. diversity research, laws, or other issues, but this chapter goes further, exploring diversity from an international viewpoint. Researchers and scholars outside the United States have emphasized the limited relevance to other countries of the U.S. experience with diversity[2] and how little "diversity" there is in diversity research.[3] Yet, diversity as "real or perceived differences among people that affect their interactions and relationships" does fit within an international context. Discrimination, dominance, marginalization, and the colonization of people based on race, ethnicity, gender, religion, sexual orientation, and numerous other factors occur all over the world. From the viewpoint of power, dominance, discrimination, and control of resources, the fact that diversity issues (regardless of the chosen terminology) are

universal becomes clearer. As we investigate diversity from an international viewpoint, we maintain the perspective that diversity is increasingly inevitable and is of value to individuals, organizations, and society everywhere.

Misperception: Diversity is a U.S. concept.

Reality: When viewed as the existence of non-dominant and dominant groups and from issues of power, discrimination, and control of resources between them, the universality of these concerns is clear.

Why is encouraging diversity and inclusion important worldwide? The current and future workforce in many nations is changing greatly as a result of changes in birth and mortality rates, immigration, age distributions, advances in health care, external pressures, and competition. As in the United States, the growth of the workforce in Canada, the United Kingdom, and Mexico is small when compared to previous periods. In Spain, Italy, Germany, France, Japan, and South Africa, declines in the population of working adults are projected for 2010 through 2050. The need to allow or, indeed, encourage active, full participation in the workforce is particularly vital in these countries.

Further, although the majority of the laws, cases, and examples discussed in earlier chapters are from the United States, the overall premise of diversity and inclusion via multiple avenues is common in many places.[4] Many of the topics covered in each chapter are substantially similar regardless of where they occur. For example, sex and gender strongly influence one's education, workforce participation, income, treatment, occupation, and status within organizations

---

[1]Dobbs, M. F. (1996). "Managing Diversity: Lessons from the Private Sector." *Public Personnel Management*, 25(September): 351–368.

[2]See, for example, Jones, D., Pringle, J., & Shepherd, D. (2000). "'Managing Diversity' Meets Aotearoa/New Zealand." *Personnel Review*, 29(3): 364–380.

[3]Jonsen, K., Maznevski, M. L., & Schneider, S. C. (2011). "Diversity and Its Not So Diverse Literature: An International Perspective." *Cross Cultural Management*, 11(1): 35–62.

[4]Strachan, G., Burgess, J., & Henderson, L. (2007). "Equal Employment Opportunity Legislation and Policies: The Australian Experience." *Equal Opportunities International*, 26(6): 525–540.

in Australia, China, England, Japan, New Zealand, Pakistan, the United States, and most places that one could name. Work and family considerations, including the availability and cost of child care, social policies, income, and institutional support, are important to people wherever they live and work. Differences in people's religious beliefs affect them everywhere, and employer discrimination based on religion occurs in many countries. The racial profiling of minorities discussed in previous chapters is also a problem in Canada, where Blacks and, to a lesser extent, Asians are more likely to be stopped and searched (and thus arrested and convicted) than similarly behaving Whites.[5] Discrimination based on color and preferences for White or lighter-skinned people are common in Brazil, India, Mexico, South Africa, and many other countries.[6] And there are numerous other similarities, such as wage discrimination, un- and underemployment, and occupational segregation of non-dominant racial and ethnic groups, in many countries. In many places, there are employment-related laws that focus on diversity issues (e.g., equal employment for women, minority, or disenfranchised groups) although who is targeted varies by country.

On the other hand, within each region there are numerous unique issues and concerns, which are based on that region's particular historical, cultural, religious, and other differences. For example, in Saudi Arabia, religious beliefs severely impede women's participation in the workforce. In Japan, most women hold temporary jobs, rather than the lifetime jobs that are common for Japanese men. The Burakumin people in Japan have experienced historical discrimination and exclusion based on their class, and this continues today.[7] Similarly, India maintains a system of caste-based discrimination that disadvantages the majority of its population due to their caste rather than their individual abilities and competencies.[8] Migrants and ethnic minorities in Australia experience discrimination in various forms despite current diversity policies.[9] Given the size of the world and the number of countries, each with distinct concerns, a truly comprehensive study of diversity worldwide is a nearly impossible undertaking. Even so, there is value in understanding issues that are common around the world.

It is not possible to include here the history of multiple groups in every country, as we did in previous chapters for groups in the United States. However, knowing that country-specific history, culture, and laws affect diversity everywhere will allow readers to address and value diversity, regardless of context. Armed with this knowledge, readers will be better equipped to investigate, understand, and apply ways to best incorporate the diversity of a particular area. A "Western" view of diversity is not at all appropriate to every culture; indeed, a U.S. point of view is not appropriate for Canada, nor is a Canadian point of view appropriate for the United States, although both are Western countries. What is applicable is the recognition that diversity issues affect individuals, and thus organizations, differently around the world and so they should be investigated within the context of where they occur. Figure 16.1 presents some of the factors to consider in identifying the dominant and non-dominant groups and areas of concern in

[5]Wortley, S., & Tanner, J. (2003). "Data, Denials, and Confusion: The Racial Profiling Debate in Toronto." *Canadian Journal of Criminology and Criminal Justice*, 45(3): 367–390; Wortley, S., & Tanner, J. (2005). "Inflammatory Rhetoric? Baseless Accusations? A Response to Gabor's Critique of Racial Profiling Research in Canada." *Canadian Journal of Criminology and Criminal Justice*, 47(3): 581–609.

[6]Glenn, E. N. (2009). *Shades of Difference: Why Skin Color Matters*. Stanford, CA: Stanford University Press.

[7]De Vos, G. A., & Wagatsuma, A. (1966). *Japan's Invisible Race: Caste in Culture and Personality*. Berkeley: University of California Press; Gottlieb, N. (1998). "Discriminatory Language in Japan: Burakumin, the Disabled, and Women." *Asian Studies Review*, 22(2): 157–173.

[8]As in the United States, historical differences in treatment, access, and opportunity lead to differences in education, health, wealth and poverty, and other factors that influence individuals.

[9]Syed, J., & Kramar, R. (2010). "What Is the Australian Model for Managing Cultural Diversity?" *Personnel Review*, 39(1): 96–115.

FIGURE 16.1 *Considerations Useful for Identifying Non-Dominant Group Members and Diversity Issues*

- Historical differential treatment
- Identifiability, power, discrimination, and group awareness[10]
- Distribution of wealth
- Employment, unemployment, and underemployment rates
- Participation rates
- Occupational levels, types, and representation in management and executive positions
- Income and earnings distributions
- Literacy
- Educational attainment
- Return on educational investment
- Residential and employment segregation
- Rates of intermarriage with the dominant group
- Poverty rates
- Health and longevity
- Racial profiling and incarceration rates
- Legal protections
- Political participation[11]

countries around the world, although not every factor is relevant to each group in every country.

We begin our exploration of international diversity by documenting that discrimination and differential treatment are worldwide phenomena; we then consider sex and gender, disabilities, sexual orientation, and poverty as important factors. In each section, we focus on a particular factor in a specific region. Throughout, we use research drawn from the International Labour Organization (ILO), an international body set up to help workers in 178 member states. Members of the ILO include varied developing and developed countries such as Albania, Australia, Austria, Bahrain, Cambodia, Canada, Finland, France, Hungary, Kenya, Nicaragua, St. Lucia, Swaziland, Switzerland, the United Kingdom, the United States, and Zambia. We next consider the future and make some recommendations for change to improve opportunities for equity and inclusion for all workers as the twenty-first century continues. As much as possible, we recognize variance between the dominant and non-dominant groups, the colonized and the colonizers, and other important distinctions.

Coming full circle, this chapter (and book) ends with a return to the factors unique to the diversity situation in the United States, emphasizing its urgency of attending to diversity, given the distinctive history and great diversity among U.S. inhabitants as compared to other countries. With its history of slavery, immigration, religious freedom, and its often expressed (but not always practiced) welcome of diversity, the United States is potentially the most diverse nation of all. Its history generates more potential for division but also more opportunities than in many other countries. While many countries have permitted slavery or

[10]From Dworkin, A. G., & Dworkin, R. J. (1999). *The Minority Report*, 3rd ed. Orlando, FL: Harcourt Brace Publishers, pp. 11–27.
[11]Hausmann, R., Tyson, L. D., & Zahidi, S. (2010). *The Global Gender Gap Report 2010*. Geneva: World Economic Forum. http://www.weforum.org/pdf/gendergap/report2010.pdf, accessed November 23, 2010.

indentured servitude, nearly annihilated their indigenous peoples, and have subordinated women, none had and continues to have the unique combination of factors the United States does. Given its history and the current diversity of its population, no longer does the United States have the option to discriminate, exclude, and limit the contributions of an increasingly diverse population if it is to compete in an increasingly global world without boundaries. Thus, we make recommendations specific to the United States in the final section of this chapter and book. ●

▌ DISCRIMINATION AND DIFFERENTIAL TREATMENT AS WORLDWIDE PHENOMENA

The ILO's "Declaration on Fundamental Principles and Rights at Work" is viewed as a "commitment by governments, employers' and workers' organizations to uphold basic human values—values that are vital to our social and economic lives."[12] One of the four values addressed in the ILO's declaration is the elimination of workplace discrimination. As discussed throughout this book, discrimination is a formidable impediment to diversity in organizations. The ILO's posture on people's rights to freedom from employment discrimination confirms the existence of discrimination and differential treatment worldwide. Targets vary by region, but discrimination exists everywhere and "denies opportunities for individuals and robs societies of what those people can and could contribute."[13]

The need to eradicate discrimination and to make other conscious efforts to include and value the perspectives of all workers has been a consistent theme in this book. The ILO also takes the position we have discussed in previous chapters, that eradicating discrimination would benefit individuals, organizations, the economy, and society. Many countries have instituted antidiscrimination or equal opportunity legislation (see Table 16.1).[14] The emotional, psychological, and economic rewards of workplace fairness for individuals are apparent. For organizations, as we have pointed out, diversity can provide benefits related to cost, resource acquisition, marketing, creativity, problem solving, and system flexibility. The ability to hire from a larger pool of workers, rather than excluding workers based on characteristics not related to their productivity, is beneficial for organizations. Avoiding lawsuits, boycotts, and lost business are also positives for organizations, wherever they are. For

----

[12]ILO. (2003). "Declaration on Fundamental Principles and Rights at Work." http://www.ilo.org/dyn/declaris/DECLARATIONWEB.INDEXPAGE, accessed November 21, 2010.

[13]http://www.ilo.org/declaration/principles/eliminationofdiscrimination/lang–en/index.htm, accessed November 21, 2010.

[14]Table 16.1 provides a limited summary of laws in selected areas. Readers are encouraged to investigate the laws in specific countries of interest.

TABLE 16.1 *Various Equal Employment Opportunity Legislation in Selected Countries*

Country	Act(s)	Provisions
Argentina	Anti-discrimination Act, No. 23.592, 1988	Prohibits sex discrimination. Sanctions any person who impedes, obstructs, limits, or in any way undermines constitutional rights or guarantees on the basis of sex.
Australia	Disability Discrimination Act; Sex Discrimination Act, as amended; Equal Opportunity for Women Act; various others	Prohibit discrimination on the basis of age, criminal record, disability, sex (including pregnancy, potential pregnancies), sexual orientation, same-sex couples, various others.
Canada	Canadian Human Rights Act; various others	Prohibit discrimination based on race and color, national or ethnic origin, religion, age, sex, sexual orientation, marital or family status, physical and mental ability, and other areas. An act requiring equal pay for men and women in same jobs has also been passed.
France	Constitution, Penal Code of 1994	Criminalize discrimination based on race, religion, or ethnicity.
Germany	Various laws	Prohibit sex discrimination, harassment, unequal pay, pregnancy and maternity discrimination.
Hungary	Act CXXV 362/2004 of 22 December 2003, Equal Treatment and Promotion of Equal Opportunities	Prohibits direct or indirect negative discrimination, harassment, unlawful segregation, and retribution based on sex, racial origin, color, nationality, national or ethnic origin, mother tongue, disability, state of health, religious or ideological conviction, family status, motherhood (pregnancy) or fatherhood, sexual orientation, sexual identity, age, social origin, financial status, among other protected areas.
South Africa	Employment Equity Act (amended)	Applies to a broad spectrum of employers; prohibits "unfair discrimination" and requires affirmative action; covers Africans, coloureds, Indians, people with disabilities, and women.
United Kingdom	Equal Pay Directive; Equal Treatment Directive; various others	Prohibit discrimination on the basis of age, race, sex, pregnancy, parental status, marital or family status, among other protected areas.

The language of the legislation may vary, and all protected areas are not listed. In addition to employment-related laws, many laws refer to housing, accommodation, and other areas.

society, the benefits of eliminating discrimination and valuing diversity are immense—they can reduce poverty worldwide, increase life spans, and create stronger economies, among other countless positive outcomes. People who have the opportunity to work, contribute, and receive fair treatment and remuneration become, again quoting the ILO, "creators of life and communities ... caregivers and receivers ... workers, consumers, and entrepreneurs ... savers, investors, producers and employers ... inventors and generators of knowledge ... as citizens and organizers."[15] On a societal level, these outcomes are lasting and sustaining.

Having argued that diversity is indeed a worldwide concern, we now consider specifically from a global perspective three of the topics from the preceding chapters: sex and gender, disabilities, and sexual orientation. In addition, we investigate poverty and class, in recognition of the unique contribution of discrimination and differential treatment to poverty in countries around the world.

▌ SEX AND GENDER: THE STATUS OF WOMEN AROUND THE WORLD

Volumes of research from various disciplines attest to women's low occupational status worldwide. The ILO views disparities in access to education and women's disproportionate share of home and child care as contributors to discrimination against women.[16] Females often receive less education than males, and, as discussed throughout this book, education is closely associated with earnings and the likelihood of being employed. In part as a consequence of less education, women are less likely to be employed, and when employed they tend to earn less than men, worldwide. In addition, women work fewer hours than men and are more likely to live in poverty than men. On the other hand, even with similar or more education, women's earnings and status are generally lower than men's. With more, less, or equal amounts of education, discrimination and segregation contribute to women's lower occupational status and earnings all over the world.

Population and Participation Rates

Due to the need for more workers, lower birthrates, and changes in attitudes toward women's employment and in social policies concerning child care, women around the world are participating in the workforce at

---

[15]"Working Out of Poverty." (2003). Report of the Director-General, International Labour Conference, 91st session, p. 23.

[16]http://www.ilo.org/declaration/principles/eliminationofdiscrimination/lang–en/index.htm, accessed November 21, 2010.

higher rates than ever before. These factors, coupled with men's declining participation rates, have resulted in women becoming a larger proportion of the worldwide workforce than at any time in the past. In some countries, women now participate at about 80% of the rate than men do. However, in other areas, such as the Middle East, Arabia, North Africa, and South Asia, women participate at about 40% or less of the male rate.[17]

Sexual Harassment, Segregation, Discrimination, and Other Inequities

Sex discrimination and harassment, sex segregation, wage inequity, and the glass ceiling are eerily common problems faced by women around the world.[18] Sex segregation of jobs is common and women are considerably less likely to be in high-status or managerial positions than their proportions in the population and workforce participation would suggest. Women's concentration in low-status, often powerless, positions contributes to the prevalence of sexual harassment. Researchers have found evidence of sexual harassment in Australia, Austria, Belgium, Brazil, Canada, China, Denmark, France, Italy, Japan, Mexico, the Netherlands, New Zealand, Northern Ireland, Norway, Spain, Sweden, and the United Kingdom.[19] Table 16.2 presents the ILO's key facts about sexual harassment in various places worldwide.

The ILO reports that women most likely to be targeted for sexual harassment are young, financially dependent, divorced or never married, and migrant. Recall from previous chapters the egregious harassment of immigrant and young workers in the United States. Men most likely to be harassed are young, gay, and members of ethnic or racial minority groups.[20] In multiple studies of working women, Louise Fitzgerald and

---

[17]ILO. (2005). "Women's Employment: Global Trends and ILO responses." http://www.ilo.org/dyn/gender/docs/RES/399/F1503666968/Womens%20Employment%20-%20Global%20Trends%20and%20ILO%20Respon.pdf, accessed November 22, 2010.

[18]Shaffer, M. A., Joplin, J. R. W., Bell, M. P., Oguz, C., & Lau, T. (2000). "Gender Discrimination and Job-Related Outcomes: A Cross-Cultural Comparison of Working Women in the United States and China." *Journal of Vocational Behavior*, 57: 395–427; Muli, K. (1995). "Help Me Balance the Load: Gender Discrimination in Kenya." In J. Peters & A. Wolper (Eds.), *Women's Rights, Human Rights: International Feminist Perspectives*. London: Routledge, pp. 78–81.

[19]Fitzgerald, L. F., & Hesson-McInnis, M. (1989). "The Dimensions of Sexual Harassment: A Structural Analysis." *Journal of Vocational Behavior*, 35: 309–326; Gelfand, M. J., Fitzgerald, L. F., & Drasgow, F. (1995). "The Structure of Sexual Harassment: A Confirmatory Factor Analysis Across Cultures and Settings." *Journal of Vocational Behavior*, 47: 164–177. For reports on research evidence of sexual harassment in North American and European countries, see Gruber, J. E. (1997). "An Epidemiology of Sexual Harassment: Evidence from North America and Europe." In W. O'Donohue (Ed.), *Sexual Harassment*. Boston: Allyn & Bacon, pp. 84–98.

[20]ILO. (n.d.). "Sexual Harassment Fact Sheet." http://www.ilo.org/wcmsp5/groups/public/—ed_norm/—declaration/documents/publication/wcms_decl_fs_96_en.pdf, accessed November 21, 2010.

TABLE 16.2 **The ILO's Key Facts about Sexual Harassment in Various Places Worldwide**

Hong Kong	Nearly 25% of workers surveyed in Hong Kong in 2007, one-third of whom were men, reported experiencing sexual harassment. While 20% of women who were harassed reported it, only 6.6% of men who were harassed did so because they felt too embarrassed to face "ridicule."
Italy	According to a 2004 report, 55.4% of Italian women aged 14–59 reported having experienced sexual harassment. One out of three female workers had been subjected to sexual intimidation (a form of quid pro quo harassment) for career advancement, with 65% having been blackmailed weekly by the same harasser, typically a supervisor or coworker. More than half of the women subjected to sexual intimidation had quit.
European Union	In the EU, 40%–50% of women have reported some form of workplace sexual harassment.
Australia	According to a survey carried out by the Australian Equal Opportunity Commission in 2004, 18% of interviewees aged between 18 and 64 years said they had experienced sexual harassment in the workplace. Less than 37% of those who experienced sexual harassment were likely to report the abuse.
South Africa	A case decided in 2004 was the first time an employer was held liable for sexual harassment by one of its employees. The company was ordered to pay the victim, a woman working as a security guard, compensation for unfair dismissal and sexual harassment.
India	The case of *Vishaka v. State of Rajasthan* brought a shift in the legal definition of sexual harassment by the Supreme Court. Previously identified as "Eve teasing," sexual harassment was deemed to be a violation of women's human rights. The judgment also outlined guidelines for sexual harassment prevention and redress.

Source: Adapted from ILO. (n.d.). "Sexual Harassment Fact Sheet." http://www.ilo.org/wcmsp5/groups/public/—ed_norm/—declaration/documents/publication/wcms_decl_fs_96_en.pdf, accessed November 21, 2010.

her colleagues have found that sexual harassment is similar in structure, type, and negative consequences for women, regardless of where the harassment occurs.[21] As discussed in Chapter 9, sexual harassment results in negative physical, psychological, career, and financial consequences for those who are harassed, as well as in high costs for the organizations in which they work. Absence and turnover, lowered productivity, reduced creativity, and damaged reputations are among a few of the organizational costs. These outcomes are quite similar to those described by the ILO.[22]

Wage Inequity and the Glass Ceiling

The glass ceiling phenomenon discussed in Chapter 9 exists in both developed and developing countries. In industrialized nations, women occupy

[21]See, for example, Fitzgerald, L. F., Drasgow, R., Hulin, C. L., Gelfand, M. J., & Magley, V. J. (1997). "Antecedents and Consequences of Sexual Harassment in Organizations: A Test of an Integrated Model." *Journal of Applied Psychology*, 82: 578–589; Shaffer et al. (2000); Wasti, S. A., Bergman, M. E., Glomb, T. M., & Drasgow, F. (2000). "Test of the Cross-Cultural Generalizability of a Model of Sexual Harassment." *Journal of Applied Psychology*, 85(5): 766–778.
[22]ILO. (n.d.).

at most 10% of the highest positions. In Canada, for example, 10% of executives are women, compared with 43% in middle management. In the United Kingdom, women occupy 9.6% of executive positions. In terms of the wage gap, women working full-time in the United States earn about 75% of men's earnings; in Russia, the ratio is about 72%; while in France and Australia, women earn between 80% and 90% of men's earnings. Worldwide, women earn 66% of what men earn.[23]

Focus: "Think Manager, Think Male" Worldwide?

One of the reasons behind women's lack of advancement is people's perception that characteristics associated with successful managers are those associated with men, rather than women. The "think manager, think male" phenomenon was first identified by Virginia Schein in 1973. In more than three decades since then, researchers have confirmed the existence of this perception in the United States as well as in Britain, China, Germany, and Japan.[24] American men continue to perceive men as having requisite managerial characteristics, while women now view both men and women as having characteristics of successful managers. In China and Japan, however, both men and women view men, but not women, as likely to have qualities associated with successful managers. As discussed in Organizational Feature 16.1, the Royal Dutch Shell company treats gender as one of three common diversity issues that it focuses on worldwide.

■ PEOPLE WITH DISABILITIES

The ILO includes people with disabilities among the *marginalized, disadvantaged,* or *vulnerable* groups in society—terms that are also relevant to other non-dominant groups.[25] Workers with disabilities around the world face un- and underemployment, lower wages, misperceptions about competence, and overt and covert employment

---

[23]ILO (2005).

[24]See Schein, V. E. (1973). "The Relationship Between Sex Role Stereotypes and Requisite Management Characteristics." *Journal of Applied Psychology*, 57: 95–100; Heilman, M. E., Block, C. J., Martell, R. F., & Simon, M. C. (1989). "Has Anything Changed? Current Characterizations of Men, Women, and Managers." *Journal of Applied Psychology*, 74: 935–943; Schein, V. E., Mueller, R., Lituchy, T., & Liu, J. (1996). "Think Manager—Think Male: A Global Phenomenon?" *Journal of Organizational Behavior*, 17(1): 33–41.

[25]ILO (2002). "Disability and Poverty Reduction Strategies." Working Paper. The Disability Programme, InFocus Programme on Skills, Knowledge, and Employability. International Labour Office: Geneva. http://www.ilo.org/public/english/employment/skills/disability/download/discpaper.pdf, accessed November 22, 2010.

ORGANIZATIONAL FEATURE 16.1	*Global Diversity and Inclusion at Shell*

Royal Dutch Shell, or "Shell" as it is more commonly known, is a group of energy and petrochemicals companies with $13 billion in earnings. Because Shell employs more than 101,000 employees in over ninety countries and territories, attention to diversity and inclusion is necessarily important. According to Shell CEO Peter Voser, embedding diversity and inclusion within Shell's structure, people, processes, and culture will result in customers, employees, partners, and other stakeholders choosing Shell more often.

Shell defines "diversity" as the ways in which people differ, including visible differences, such as age and gender, and invisible differences, such as religion and sexual orientation, among other areas. For Shell, "inclusion" means a culture in which differences are valued and people feel involved, respected, and connected. Some of the ways in which Shell pursues diversity and inclusion are through educational offerings, recruitment, retention, development, and mentoring across diverse groups.

According to Josefine van Zanten, vice president of diversity and inclusion, it is important for Shell to focus on what diversity means in a global context rather than try to apply lessons learned from specific issues in one particular country to other areas, where they may not even be relevant. She recognizes that while "there are companies that have their U.S. policies and try to go global with them, when you export U.S. D&I policies, you may create unforeseen hurdles." Thus, Shell considers the different pressing needs for each region and also attends to common denominators

across regions. In the United States, for example, Shell focuses on the myriad diversity-related laws and court rulings that are unique to the United States. In Malaysia, government-mandated stipulations regarding the proportion of Bumi Putras in leadership positions require specific attention. In Canada, there is a focus on aborigines. Laws in Norway require that there must be *at least* 40% women and *at least* 40% men on corporate boards, and this requires close monitoring. In Nigeria, although there are no specific governmental mandates, Shell recognized differences in utilization across different tribal groups and now checks for equity in this area.

Along with country-specific issues, gender, nationality, and inclusion are the common denominators that Shell attends to around the world.[26] In terms of gender, Shell has a target of increasing the proportion of women in senior management to at least 20%. This goal seems low at first glance but reflects the entrenched male dominance in the industry and an unspoken goal of exceeding the "token" level of women's representation, as identified by Rosabeth Moss Kanter.[27] According to Kanter, extremely low proportions of women have very limited effectiveness (a point that can also be extrapolated to other underrepresented minorities). The "tipping point" occurs when women have at least 20% representation. Since the goal was set in 2005, the proportion of women in senior management at Shell has increased by over 50%, from about 9% to more than 13% women in senior management in 2010. In her communications with stakeholders,

---

[26]Shell also targets disability, sexual orientation, and generations (age differences) but does not attend to such differences as thinking styles (although the company recognizes that differences in thinking styles will appear as a result of higher levels of gender, ethnic, and national diversity and a more inclusive environment).

[27]Kanter, R. M. (1977). "Some Effects of Proportions on Group Life: Skewed Sex Ratios and Responses to Token Women." *American Journal of Sociology*, 82(5): 965–990.

van Zanten emphasizes that Shell does not use "quotas." "Some of this is very cultural; what we see is that the language and wording of 'quota' raises very high emotions. People are concerned that 'quota' means you lower the bar and you dilute the talent pool—even if this has proven to be untrue." Rather than quotas, Shell uses targets and actions, including putting women on short lists for promotions, which increases visibility and begins the conversation about them but does not ensure they are selected. While acknowledging that the bar at Shell is very high, van Zanten points out that "best" does not necessarily mean clones of current management. "Best" can be viewed in many ways, and van Zanten tries to open minds to other possibilities of what it may mean.

In terms of nationality, van Zanten says that Shell's goal is to have local employees fill more than half the senior management positions in every country in which it operates. Success with this goal will help achieve company diversity goals, reduce expatriation, and provide opportunities for employees in the home countries. With core operations in places such as Brazil, China, India, Oman, Qatar, and UAE, Shell also contributes significantly to the local communities by hiring local employees in senior management.

In terms of inclusion, Shell knows that inclusion is correlated to employee engagement and innovation, and this is why the company keeps a strong focus on this "softer," to use van Zanten's word, yet equally important element of the "Diversity and Inclusion" equation. According to van Zanten, while Shell is making progress on diversity, the company is "acutely aware that the challenge is inclusion. If you recruit people in and they walk out the door 2 years later it's not very helpful. People need to feel they can speak up, have their opinions, and that they are not asked to conform. Inclusion is when you accept people for who they are and listen to their content versus the underrepresented groups they represent."

To assess how included employees feel, in Shell's annual People Survey, employees respond to the following five core items:

- Where I work we are treated with respect.
- I am free to speak my mind without fear of negative consequences.
- My organization has a working environment in which different views and perspectives are valued.
- My organization has a working environment that is free from harassment and discrimination.
- The decisions leaders in my organization make concerning employees are fair.

Shell's goal is to have no significantly different results among subgroups of employees (e.g., among men and women).

Personal, interpersonal (group), and organizational levels of change are used to build and sustain an environment that respects and values difference for all those who attend D&I courses. At the personal level, employees learn about themselves, including their attitudes, behavior, assumptions, beliefs, and biases surrounding diversity. The interpersonal level includes building diverse and inclusive relationships through listening, understanding, and identifying and challenging assumptions and behaviors that limit and exclude. The organizational level leads the change process, including building the diversity and inclusion plan; building tools, processes, and systems; and developing goals, measures, and accountability. This level also includes modeling desired behavior, providing resources, and identifying and removing barriers to diversity and inclusion. These three levels work together to create sustainable change.

Recognition from sources in numerous different countries indicates that Shell is successful in its pursuit of diversity and inclusion:

- United Kingdom: Shell was listed by the UK's *Times* newspaper among the top fifty employers for women for two consecutive years.

- Chile: Shell was recognized by the Chilean government for good practices on diversity and nondiscrimination.
- United States: Shell received a 100% Corporate Equality Index rating from the Human Rights Campaign, an organization focused on equality and inclusion for gay, lesbian, bisexual, and transgender employees.

Despite these accolades and recognition, van Zanten says, "This is a long-term journey, and to reach our goals, we need to constantly review progress and work to embed diversity and inclusion values across the whole organization. What matters, I believe, is that we keep working at it, learning as we move along the D&I journey."

QUESTIONS TO CONSIDER

1. *Choose a different global organization to compare with Shell. Use that company's Web site and other sources to gather information on its diversity practices. How do the two companies compare?*

2. *Along with the traditional male dominance in the energy and petrochemicals field, what factors might contribute to the low representation of women in senior management at Shell? What recommendations would you make to Shell to help address those factors?*

3. *Many organizations with comprehensive diversity programs have histories of discrimination claims, litigation, judgments, and settlements. Does Shell have such a history? Investigate and document your findings.*

4. *Do you know a person who works at Shell? What is his or her perception of the sincerity of Shell's diversity commitment? What is the perception of the success of Shell's diversity programs and policies from that person's view? What problem areas are there at Shell? What else needs to be done?*

5. *What aspects of Cox and Blake's six reasons for valuing diversity covered and Cox's Interactional Model (Featured Case 1.1) can you identify in the information given about Shell?*

Sources: "Diversity and Inclusion at Shell" brochure; Shell Annual Report. http://www.annualreportandform20f.shell.com/2009/servicepages/downloads/files/all_shell_20f_09.pdf, accessed November 23, 2010; Josefine van Zanten, Shell Vice-President of Diversity and Inclusion, personal communication, July 15 and 27, 2010.

discrimination. The numbers of people with a disability have increased due to longer life spans, new types of illnesses (e.g., HIV/AIDS), injuries from wars and conflicts, substance abuse, and illnesses associated with child labor. While some countries prohibit employment discrimination on the basis of disability, many do not. We consider the population and participation of people with disabilities and disability legislation in the following sections.

Population and Participation

Estimates from the ILO and the World Health Organization suggest that more than 600 million people worldwide have disabilities and 386 million of them are of working age.[28] Greater un- and underemployment and lower earnings of these people compared to people without disabilities are common all over the world. When compared to other marginalized groups, the differences for people with disabilities are even more extreme. This situation requires specific attention, in recognition of their uniquely marginalized roles.[29]

Legislation

The ILO views employment fairness toward people with disabilities as "a human rights issue," with access to decent work being one of those basic rights. The ILO has carefully compared laws in Canada, France, Germany, the Netherlands, New Zealand, Sweden, the United Kingdom, and the United States. In countries in which the laws are more carefully designed and monitored (e.g., by controlling hiring, conditions of employment, and dismissal of workers with disabilities), there is more employment equity than in countries that use the "laissez-faire" approach.[30] France, Germany, and Sweden use recruitment grants, public subsidies, and special incentives to promote employment of people with disabilities, which are more effective. Strategies to improve job retention for people with disabilities are helpful to employers in controlling the escalating cost of payments to workers with disabilities who are out of the workforce. By encouraging and assisting workers with disabilities to return to the workforce, both employers and individuals benefit.[31]

In 1983 and 2001, the ILO issued recommendations for the employment of people with disabilities and for managing disabilities in the workplace. It promotes equal opportunity and employment through training and development, funding and disseminating research, and establishing policy guidelines and manuals for employers. Employers wishing to hire and retain people with disabilities may turn to the ILO and their local governments for recommendations.

Focus: Disabled People's Experiences in the Workplace in England

The purpose of the United Kingdom's Disability Discrimination Act (DDA) of 1995, as amended in 2005, is to end discrimination based on

---

[28]ILO. (2002). "Managing Disability in the Workplace." Geneva: International Labor Office. http://www.ilo.org/public/english/employment/skills/disability/download/codeeng.pdf, accessed November 22, 2010.

[29]ILO. (2002)."Disability and Poverty Reduction Strategies." http://www.ilo.org/wcmsp5/groups/public/—ed_emp/—ifp_skills/documents/publication/wcms_107921.pdf, accessed March 23, 2011.

[30]ILO. (1998). "Worker Disability Problems Rising in Industrialized Countries." Press Releases. http://www.ilo.org/public/english/bureau/inf/pr/1998/19.htm, accessed August 24, 2005.

[31]ILO. (2002). "Managing Disability in the Workplace."

disability.[32] The United Kingdom defines as disabled a person having a physical or mental impairment that has a "substantial and long-term" adverse effect on the person's ability to perform normal daily activities. As with the U.S. ADA, the DDA requires employers to make reasonable adjustments to enable people with disabilities to work. Although the fact that the act exists is positive, managerial attitudes toward people with disabilities and structural barriers limit its effectiveness.[33] These barriers impede access to employment and the ability to remain employed. In the United Kingdom, unemployment among people with disabilities is considerably higher than it is for people without disabilities.[34]

■ SEXUAL ORIENTATION

Gays and lesbians face discrimination and harassment in much of the world. Reports suggest that more than 4,000 lesbians and gay men have been executed in Iran since 1979.[35] In July 2005, two Iranian teens were hanged in a public square because of their sexual orientation. One study done in Estonia, Latvia, and Lithuania documented such discrimination against sexual minorities in the workplace, in service organizations, and in religious institutions such that many respondents reported a desire to move to other countries.[36]

Legislation Prohibiting Sexual Orientation Discrimination

Because sexual minorities may face discrimination and harassment in various situations, many remain closeted or work in informal labor markets. Although no federal legislation in the United States prohibits employment discrimination based on sexual orientation, several countries do have such laws, including Canada, Denmark, Finland, France, Hungary, Iceland, Ireland, Israel, the Netherlands, New Zealand, Norway, Slovenia, South Africa, Spain, Sweden, and other countries. The strength of these laws and the entities targeted vary; some apply only to national governments or to public or private organizations. Without genuine commitment, laws do little to help those experiencing discrimination.

[32]Disability Discrimination Act. (1995). http://www.legislation.gov.uk/ukpga/1995/50/contents, accessed November 23, 2010; Newton, R., Ormerod, M., & Thomas, P. (2007). "Disabled People's Experiences in the Workplace Environment in England," *Equal Opportunities International*, 26(6): 610–623.
[33]Newton et al. (2007).
[34]Disability Rights Commission. (2006, March). Disability Briefing, DRC, London, cited in Newton et al. (2007).
[35]Ireland, D. (2005). "Iran Executes Two Gay Teenagers." http://direland.typepad.com/direland/2005/07/iran_executes_2.html, accessed November 23, 2010.
[36]Platovas, E., & Simonko, V. (2002). *Sexual Orientation Discrimination in Lithuania, Latvia, and Estonia*. Lithuanian Gay League Publisher: http://www.gay.lt/lgl/sod.pdf, accessed March 23, 2011.

Focus: Anti-Gay Sentiment among Youth in Belgium and Canada

A large-scale study of the determinants of anti-gay attitudes among nearly 10,000 16-year-olds in Belgium and Canada documented distinct factors among participants.[37] The researchers found that girls were significantly more supportive of GLBT rights, and parents' education levels (particularly mothers') were strongly related to support for GLBT rights. Although they did not assess religious fundamentalism, which, as noted in Chapter 12, is strongly related to negativity toward GLBTs, the researchers did find that Muslim males had the most negative attitudes. Immigrants were also less supportive of GLBT rights than were natives.

▮ POVERTY

The ILO condemns persistent poverty as a "moral indictment of our times."

For individuals, poverty is a vicious cycle of poor health, reduced working capacity, low productivity, and shortened life expectancy … it leads to the trap of inadequate schooling, low skills, insecure income, early parenthood, ill health, and an early death.[38]

As discussed in Feature 16.1, a sobering indictment of poverty in the United States arose in the aftermath of the 2005 Hurricane Katrina in New Orleans, Louisiana. Similarly, in France in late 2005 French youths of North African origin engaged in widespread rioting in response to discrimination, unemployment, and poverty.

In the United States, many tend to blame those who are poor for their situations, often failing to acknowledge the role of discrimination and systemic exclusion and attributing poverty instead to personal failures and laziness—poor people could do better if they simply tried.[39] Like the meritocracy myth that allows people to believe they alone are responsible for having achieved their wealth and positions, the predicament of the poor or otherwise disadvantaged is seen as a direct result of their choices.

[37]Hooghe, M., Claes, E., Harrell, A., Quintelier, E., & Dejaeghere, Y. (2010). "Anti-Gay Sentiment Among Adolescents in Belgium and Canada: A Comparative Investigation into the Role of Gender and Religion." *Journal of Homosexuality*, 57: 384–400.
[38]"Working Out of Poverty," p. 1.
[39]For example, see Cozzaredi, C., Tagler, M. J., & Wilkinson, A. V. (2001). "Attitudes Toward the Poor and Attributions for Poverty." *Journal of Social Issues*, 57(2): 207–228.

FEATURE 16.1	*Poverty as a Diversity Concern*

Poverty is a specific area of emphasis for the ILO, which points out that poverty remains widespread in the developing world and some transition countries.[40] However, it is not limited to developing and transition countries—it is deep and widespread in some developed nations as well. The horror of the unnecessary loss of lives as a result of Hurricane Katrina in the southeastern United States awakened the country to long-denied and ignored, yet long-lasting and stable, distinctions based on class, poverty, and race. At the time Katrina hit, 26.9% of the population in the region lived in persistent poverty although the U.S. poverty rate was 12.7%. Many affected by the disaster were working poor, employed in restaurants, hotels, and casinos, or driving cabs, trolleys, and limousines for affluent tourists, partygoers, and conventioneers.

Despite mandatory evacuation orders, persistent poverty left tens of thousands of people, largely Blacks, unable to flee the natural disaster and vulnerable to its destruction. Without cars, credit cards, or money to rent hotel rooms out of town, the persistently poor went to the Louisiana Superdome (a large sports facility) and Convention Center for shelter. After the hurricane and in the midst of unprecedented flooding, their poverty left these victims vulnerable to the further, human-made destruction of insensitivity and neglect.

In the United States, the poor and disenfranchised live in public housing projects in communities near toxic waste dumps in Chicago, Memphis, and Cleveland; near cancer-causing refineries in Baton Rouge and Houston; and in flood-prone areas of Tucson, Dallas, and New Orleans, and struggle to make ends meet.[41] Every day, in cities all around the United States, poverty, persistent segregation, poor housing, and separate and unequal schools contribute to preventable disease, violence, and suicide.[42] Although widely perceived as an urban problem, many people in poverty live in rural areas, also struggling to make ends meet and in poor living conditions.[43] Regardless of their location, those affected by poverty are disproportionately minorities, with 25.8% of Blacks, 25.3% of Hispanics, 23.6% of American Indians, 12.5% of Asians, and 12.3% of Whites living at or below the poverty line in 2009.[44] Although minorities are disproportionately poor, Whites are the majority of the U.S. poor numerically. Media representations, however, portray significantly more Blacks as poor and support other erroneous perceptions—such that the poor primarily live in cities and that they are lazy. One study found that only 30% of the poor adults in media representations were depicted as working or in job training, although 50% of the poor work full- or part-time.[45]

---

[40]"Working Out of Poverty," p. 22.

[41]Ash, M., & Fetter, T. R. (2004). "Who Lives on the Wrong Side of the Environmental Tracks? Evidence from the EPA's Risk-Screening Environmental Indicators Model." *Social Science Quarterly*, 85: 441–462.

[42]See, for example, Barnes, S. L. (2005). *The Cost of Being Poor: A Comparative Study of Life in Poor Urban Neighborhoods in Gary, Indiana.* Albany: State University of New York Press.

[43]Tickamyer, A. R., & Duncan, C. M. (1990). "Poverty and Opportunity Structure in Rural America." *Annual Review of Sociology*, 16: 67–86.

[44]Table 4. "People and Families in Poverty by Selected Characteristics: 2008 and 2009." http://www.census.gov/hhes/www/poverty/data/incpovhlth/2009/table4.pdf, accessed November 23, 2010.

[45]Clawson, R. A., & Trice, R. (2000). "Poverty as We Know It: Media Portrayals of the Poor." *Public Opinion Quarterly*, 64: 53–64.

Erroneous perceptions aside, being poor has similar consequences worldwide—from poor health to inadequate schooling to early death in Africa, Brazil, England, India, Mexico, and the United States—everywhere one would venture to look. Favelas, barrios, projects, shanty towns, slums, and the backwoods are where the impoverished can be found. Although who is impoverished varies by where one is in the world, persistent poverty is a universal diversity concern. The ILO views "discrimination based on race, caste, ethnic origin, skin colour, religion, gender, sexual orientation, health status and disability" as an "underlying feature" of persistent poverty.[46]

In France, the motto *liberté, égalité, fraternité* ("liberty, equality, fraternity") has little meaning to immigrants of color and their French descendants. As in the United States, in France, unemployment, underemployment, and poverty among the foreign-born, who are often racial and ethnic minorities, is considerably higher than among the natives, and this is consistent across education levels.[47] As the ILO suggests, discrimination against immigrants in Europe is correlated with higher poverty.[48]

QUESTIONS TO CONSIDER

1. *Given equal education and opportunity, why is it easier for Whites in the United States to escape poverty and discrimination than it is for people of color?*

2. *Why is it easier for men to avoid or escape poverty than it is for women?*

3. *The ILO proposes that discrimination is an underlying feature of poverty. How are discrimination in employment and poverty related for workers around the world? Discuss.*

4. *In this and previous chapters, the un- and underemployment of non-dominant group members were documented. How do such employment patterns negatively affect the productivity of a country?*

However, nearly 9 million of the poor in the United States are *working poor*, earning too little to escape poverty. Blacks and Hispanics are more than twice as likely as Whites and women are more likely than men to be working poor. Of occupations requiring less education, people working in service fields (disproportionately women and minorities) are more likely to be working poor than those working in male-dominated fields (e.g., farming, forestry, and fishing, or natural resource, construction, and maintenance).[49] As discussed in previous chapters, job "choice," gender-role socialization, employer channeling and steering, and race and sex discrimination affect proportions of different groups represented in higher paid versus lower paid jobs.

[46]Ibid., p. 68.

[47]"French Muslims Face Job Discrimination." (2005, November 2). http://news.bbc.co.uk/2/hi/europe/4399748.stm, accessed November 23, 2010.

[48]See also Kogan, I. (2000). "A Study of Employment Careers of Immigrants in Germany." Working paper, No. 66. Mannheim Centre for European Social Research (MZES), Mannheim, Germany.

[49]"A Profile of the Working Poor, 2008." (2010). U.S. Department of Labor, U.S. Bureau of Labor Statistics. http://www.bls.gov/cps/cpswp2008.pdf, accessed January 2, 2011.

The ILO acknowledges the relationship between discrimination and poverty and proposes that people living in persistent poverty

draw from enormous reservoirs of courage, ingenuity, persistence, and mutual support to keep on the treadmill of survival. Simply coping with poverty demonstrates the resilience and creativity of the human spirit.... Imagine where their efforts could take them with the support and possibilities to move up a ladder of opportunity. Our common responsibility is to help put it there.[50]

Misperception: Most people who live in persistent poverty are lazy and unmotivated.

Reality: Most people living in poverty survive through enormous courage, persistence, and resilience.

Valuing, pursuing, and embracing diversity can help place a ladder of opportunity at the feet of those previously ignored but who have enormous reservoirs of skills and assets, be they poor, minority group members, women, sexual minorities, people with disabilities, or other non-dominant group members. At the same time, valuing, pursuing, and embracing diversity can be beneficial for the organizations that employ previously devalued workers and for the societies in which they live.

❚ FACING THE FUTURE: THE BROAD REACH OF DIVERSITY IN ORGANIZATIONS

As the world population becomes increasingly diverse, so should organizations. Organizations themselves differ in their size, structure, earnings, design, and purpose, and included in the category are various entities such as schools, churches, governments, nonprofits, retailers, service providers, co-ops, farms, and countless others in which people earn a living and interact. The success, or failure, of organizations will be greatly influenced by the ability to attract, retain, and maximize the contributions of people from all backgrounds and from around the world, by the ability to market to diverse customers, to engage diverse constituents, and to encourage the full participation of every worker and potential worker. In this section, we offer recommendations for organizations to encourage full participation of all potential workers. Returning to the original hypothesis that

50"Working Out of Poverty," p. 1.

diversity and inclusion provides organizations with a variety of competitive advantages, we then go on to consider how these potential benefits reach beyond the organization in which they occur.

As the world becomes more connected globally, discrimination, harassment, and exclusion based on race, ethnicity, sexual orientation, religion, age, family status, physical or mental ability, weight, appearance, and other irrelevant factors will be increasingly unwise, unprofitable, and unacceptable. At the same time, as the world's population becomes more diverse, this will bring new challenges, threats, and opportunities, including the propensities to stereotype and discriminate, to hoard rather than to help, and to fight for resources believed to be scarce. Rather than stereotyping, hoarding, and fighting, those who understand the value of diversity expect that including the ideas and input of more and more diverse contributors would result in the sharing of more resources. Organizations and their leaders should welcome the challenges of diversity, minimize the threats, and capitalize on the opportunities resulting from it.

Attending to "diversity in organizations" is necessary, but not sufficient, to increase organizational diversity. Organizations cannot be separated from the individuals who comprise them and the society in which they exist, nor are individuals and society distinct from the organizations in which they participate. Diversity among individuals in the population should result in diversity in organizations. But absent concrete actions to ensure that it does, historical evidence and the current status of many groups clearly indicate that it will not.

The ideas proposed by Cox and Blake, which have been central to the discussion of why diversity should be valued and pursued, are only part of the picture. When organizations pursue diversity solely to obtain cost, resource acquisition, marketing, creativity, problem solving, system flexibility, and other advantages, they will help some individuals improve their circumstances. Indeed, for these individuals, an organization's self-interested pursuit of diversity is personally helpful. And if sufficient numbers of individuals in a group are helped, the group's overall position will improve to some extent. However, these are superficial and shallow changes, incapable of supporting long-term, sustainable progress. For long-term change to occur, a fundamental shift in views on the value of diversity and the reasons to pursue it must occur. Rather than seeing diversity solely as a means of gaining competitive advantage, what is required is changed views of ourselves, our prejudices and biases, our personal attitudes, and our behaviors. It involves willingness to pursue and to advance societal changes that will reduce widespread inequity among people of the world. Diversity in organizations is but one aspect of such societal changes.

▊ RECOMMENDATIONS FOR CHANGE AT A SOCIETAL LEVEL

Governments of many countries have implemented legislation prohibiting discrimination against and encouraging the employment of non-dominant groups. Previous chapters have examined legislation in the United States. Similar legislation prohibiting discrimination exists in countries such as Australia, Canada, China, England, India, Mexico, New Zealand, South Africa, Sweden, and numerous others. Some legislation has been more successful than others in reducing disparities, but clearly more needs to be done. The persistence of discrimination, segregation, and exclusion makes obvious the insufficiency of legislation. However, without legislation, circumstances would likely be even worse. At a minimum, laws signal the need to pursue equity for all people. But strong measures are needed, rather than a "laissez-faire" approach that holds no consequences for continued disparity nor offers incentives to comply.

In addition to legislation, governmental actions are needed to improve the education of non-dominant groups. Education is an important part of preparedness for equity, and without education, inequity is certain to persist. Governments must work to ensure all residents have a certain minimum level of education in quality, safe schools. The digital divide between Whites and people of color, and rich and poor, must be eliminated. Everyone should have access to computers and the power of the Internet as part of their education. As much as possible, in order to improve the opportunities for women, family-friendly policies should be implemented. Rather than viewing child care and rearing as an individual or personal responsibility and a societal burden, children should be thought of as the future of a society.

▊ RECOMMENDATIONS FOR CHANGE AT AN ORGANIZATIONAL LEVEL

In this section, we synthesize and expand upon some of the recommendations from previous chapters suggested to help organizations in their pursuit of a diverse workforce and offer some additional recommendations. Although we have considered diversity issues relevant to a variety of formal organizations in a variety of ways (e.g., customer discrimination in restaurants or stores), the recommendations in this section focus on organizations as employers. They are based on problems considered in the previous chapters, are drawn from the human resources and diversity literature, and are generally applicable to many organizations anywhere in the world. Some of the recommendations are in the form of questions rather than specific prescriptions, in recognition of the differences inherent in organizations' human resources practices. Answering these questions and formulating others that are relevant to one's own organization and specific industry and locations will improve understanding of the specific situation for a particular organization and affect any recommendations. What is the population of employees, applicant pool, customers, clients, and constituents? What are their key concerns with respect to diversity? What legislation exists in the particular location? Is there evidence of discrimination that needs attention, even in the absence of legislation?

Management Commitment to Diversity in Organizations

Diversity literature documents the miserable failure of ill-conceived diversity initiatives, training programs, and other "diversity" measures. Prior to embarking upon a diversity program, the commitment of top management is imperative. One key step is the appointment of a leader at the executive level who is responsible for and has the authority to make changes. Some of these responsibilities would include assessing the organization's diversity climate, developing and implementing organization-specific diversity objectives and goals and then measuring progress against them, and addressing concerns, comments, and suggestions of employees, customers, and constituents.

In addition to a key diversity executive with power to effect change, genuine commitment from other executives is also required for success. When leaders view diversity as an imperative, whether due to its competitive advantages or moral and ethical aspects, diversity is more likely. However, not only is *top* management commitment to diversity necessary, commitment from *all* management in an organization is also required. Without the commitment of managers and supervisors throughout an organization, diversity efforts will not be successful. Senior managers and executives, middle managers, first-line managers, assistant managers, and supervisors all play important roles in ensuring that all employees have an opportunity to work and contribute to organizational success. As the first line of decision making, first-level managers and supervisors have the power to obstruct or facilitate diversity. They are the ones who make fair selection decisions, encourage working parents to have a healthy work–life balance, facilitate employees' quest to learn multiple languages, provide reasonable accommodations for applicants with disabilities and for those with specific religious preferences, and so on. First-line, mid-level, and executive-level management can all foster or impede diversity.

Diversity-supportive behaviors at all levels of management are observed by employees, and employees are most likely to come into contact with low-level managers on a regular basis. How do such managers behave regarding diversity in the organization? Are they sincere about eradicating sexual, racial, and other harassment? Do they make sexist, racist, ageist, heterosexist, and other "-ist" comments and decisions? Are business meetings held in inappropriate or potentially offensive locations (e.g., strip bars, Hooters)? Are older workers given or denied training opportunities? The performance of diversity-supportive aspects of managers' jobs should be rated along with other job criteria. The adage that "if it's not measured, it doesn't matter" is particularly true for diversity efforts.

Changes in Human Resource Practices

Job criteria and the selection team. To facilitate diversity in the selection process, management and human resources should start with clear job criteria—what competencies are desired of a successful candidate? How will these competencies be identified and compared among candidates? Are the desired competencies clearly related to successful job performance (i.e., valid)? What is the demographic makeup of the recruitment and selection team? What measures are in place to ensure that all candidates are viewed fairly? Are there post-hiring analyses of candidates' demographic backgrounds and their hiring success in order to check for potential unfairness? As discussed throughout this book, applicants may not even be aware of discrimination or unfairness and are unlikely to sue. Although avoiding lawsuits is not a sufficient rationale for pursuing diversity, taking these steps will increase the likelihood of a diverse employee population, which should be the real stimulus.

Recruiting. What efforts can be taken to ensure that qualified applicants from a variety of backgrounds are included in the candidate pool? Schools that are highly diverse in race, ethnicity, sexual orientation, and physical (and, as appropriate, mental) ability are good places to begin. Referrals from employees who are members of the target population are likely to be demographically similar to those making the referral. Incentives should be offered for referrals who are hired and retained.

Advertising in publications geared toward certain groups, for example, *Latina Style*, *Ebony*, and the AARP magazine would increase the pool of Hispanics, Blacks, and older applicants in the United States. Companies outside the United States could seek appropriate country-specific outlets that target different groups.

Selection. Once the pool of qualified applicants is generated, efforts must be made to ensure that certain candidates are not unfairly eliminated as the selection process continues. In attempting to increase diversity among university faculty, for example, is research in areas related to race, ethnicity, gender, and diversity devalued because it is not considered "mainstream"? Is the academic quality of such publications discounted because of the research topic? Do corporate organizations recruit candidates at "historically black colleges and universities"? or American Indian universities, or are they deemed less qualified than those from other universities? What steps can be taken to reduce these misperceptions? Are the schools at which corporations recruit accredited by recognized authorities? Have the employees involved in hiring and selecting and the employee population as a whole been informed of such accreditation? Are managers and employees aware of ingrained preferential treatment of certain groups? Do misperceptions exist about the qualifications of non-dominant and dominant group members? If either or both are perceived as having been hired due to non-job-related qualifications (e.g., being a person of color or being White; being a woman or being a man), how might publicizing the qualifications of all hires reduce such misperceptions?

Training and development. Are all employees provided opportunities to participate in job-related training and development? Are older workers steered away from training? By participating in training and development, workers prepare for advancement opportunities.

Do all workers participate in substantive diversity learning (e.g., training and education)? Research indicates that poorly designed or implemented diversity training can have negative consequences, such as backlash and unmet expectations. Are diversity learning programs of high quality and well implemented and relevant? Do such programs include short-term as well as long-term education? Diversity training is not a "quick fix" to long-term issues, particularly given institutional and systemic sexism, racism, ageism, and other "isms." People need help unlearning and divesting themselves of stereotypical beliefs about others. Do diversity learning programs help to eradicate stereotypes?

Do programs include sound data on the hiring, retention, promotion, and advancement of all groups? If an organization fears to disseminate such data, that suggests inadequate attention to diversity. Is there something to hide? Do employees resist attending diversity learning programs or do they understand their importance? Is there tolerance for joking and kidding in sexual harassment training? Are managers and supervisors periodically updated about changes in EEOC guidelines and regulations?

Mentoring. Mentoring is valuable in helping dominant and non-dominant group members succeed in organizations. Dominant group members are advantaged by their similarity to leaders and executives; forming mentoring relationships without organizational assistance is simpler for them than for non-dominant group members. Successful mentoring programs pair a protégée with a mentor who is genuinely interested in seeing the protégée grow and advance. Dominant group members tend to have greater access to social networks that share valuable job- and organization-related information. A formal mentoring program can provide access to such networks to non-dominant group members also.

Promotion and advancement. The promotion and advancement rates of employees should be regularly monitored. Are promotion rates for non-dominant and dominant group members similar? Since measures to recruit, select, train, and develop should be carefully monitored to ensure fairness and equity, both non-dominant and dominant group members would ideally experience similar rates of advancement. If they do not, reasons for differential rates should be investigated. Are women assumed to be less interested in advancement opportunities because of perceptions they are more focused on their families? Are groups with strong family ties believed to be unwilling to relocate for promotional opportunities due to these ties? Are men with children viewed as more committed workers and thus advantaged because of that perception (regardless of its veracity)?

Are non-dominant group employees held to different standards than dominant group candidates? What mechanisms are in place to determine whether differential standards exist and to address and remove them if they do? Is the performance of all employees regularly and fairly assessed? Are poor performers advised and counseled to facilitate improvement? Is there evidence of "the norm to be kind" when evaluating employees with disabilities?[51] If employees are not given negative performance feedback when warranted, they will not be able to improve. If performance is unfairly scrutinized, employees will notice it and it will serve to depress motivation and increase dissatisfaction and turnover.

Affinity and employee resource groups. Many organizations sponsor **affinity or employee resource groups**, in which people who are similar in some way or share similar concerns formally and informally gather as employees. American Airlines, for example, has affinity groups for Blacks, Latinos, gays and lesbians, and other non-dominant group members (and allies). Shell has affinity groups for women, Latinos, Blacks, Asians, and other groups. Verizon and Lockheed have similar groups. The existence of affinity groups in an organization may signal support for and commitment to diversity among employees and constituents. Affinity groups that are social in nature should not be confused with formal mentoring programs that provide more instrumental support and assist non-dominant groups in actual career progress.

....

[51]Colella, A., & Stone, D. L. (2005). "Workplace Discrimination toward Persons with Disabilities: A Call for Some New Research Directions." In R. L. Dipboye & A. Colella (Eds.), *Discrimination at Work: The Psychological and Organizational Bases*. Mahwah, NJ: Lawrence Erlbaum Associates, pp. 227–253.

Equitable benefits. When same-sex and domestic partner benefits are offered, that is an important signal to gay and lesbian employees. Although particularly important to gays and lesbians, offering such benefits sends a strong signal to heterosexual employees about the value the organization places on diversity and its sincerity in pursuit of it. In addition, when also offered to heterosexuals domestic partner benefits are also useful to heterosexuals who are in committed relationships but who remain unmarried.

Although organizations are not required to provide benefits for any employee, inclusion of all employees in benefit offerings indicates that all are valued. In addition to same-sex and domestic partner benefits, are employees allowed to indicate who is part of their family? Are care-giving responsibilities toward grandchildren, grandparents, and fictive (but no less important) kin recognized? The fear of excessive costs associated with recognizing different family members is similar to the fear of hiring women in child-bearing years or of hiring workers with disabilities—largely unfounded. As discussed in Chapter 11, costs associated with offering domestic partner benefits are similar to those involved with any increase in plan participants. The costs of such benefits will likely be offset by reduced costs in turnover, lower resource acquisition costs, greater commitment and productivity, and the intangible benefits resulting from treating employees equitably.

Other Employment Considerations

The preceding sections have considered ways in which organizations can work to increase diversity among employees. The recommendations are in no way exhaustive, and management is encouraged to investigate its particular organization and to assess its strengths and weaknesses in terms of diversity when developing an organization-specific plan. Are women fairly represented at various levels but not people of color? Are men of color well represented but Whites and minorities underrepresented? Are certain groups overrepresented in technical fields and underrepresented elsewhere? A commitment to diversity will ensure that the appropriate questions are asked, the answers evaluated, and steps taken to continue to work toward fairness and equity for all applicants, employees, customers, and prospective customers.

Diversity for Service Providers

The previous sections focused on organizations as employers. We now consider organizations in their other roles, particularly as service providers dealing with diverse customers and clients. Previous chapters gave evidence of the disparate treatment of customers, such as assuming Black customers had stolen merchandise they had paid for or following them in stores, expecting them to steal. Customers of color have also reported being ignored in stores while Whites are offered help in finding merchandise and excessive wait times for restaurant service. Hotels, restaurants, retailers, colleges, and universities have also treated certain customer groups unfairly. Although there have been some large and expensive lawsuits in the United States (e.g., Denny's, Shoney's, Eddie Bauer, and Dillard's), as we have discussed in previous chapters, most customers do not sue. Costs associated with lost business and goodwill are more likely and more expensive than lawsuits, judgments, and settlements.

As institutions with strong societal influence, service providers must take a strong and proactive stand for diversity. Employees at all levels should receive education on common biases and stereotypes they may hold about members of certain groups. Customer complaints should be taken seriously and addressed. Mystery shoppers (diners, hotel guests, students, etc.) can provide valuable information on the treatment of customers of different backgrounds. Are all customers greeted pleasantly when they enter an establishment? Are Black and female customers quoted higher prices for goods than White males? Are certain customers routinely seated at the least desirable tables in restaurants? In hospitals and nursing homes, are there multilingual and multicultural doctors, nurses, social workers, clergy, and counselors who are aware of cultural differences in beliefs about medical treatment, life, and death?

Law enforcement agencies. Law enforcement agencies play a critical role in diversity. The hiring and retention of women and those who are bilingual (to reach large populations of non-English speakers) is one role. Racial profiling is another, for the profiling of Black, Latino, Asian, and, in some areas, American Indian young men is a widespread problem in the United States. Men of color are disproportionately more likely to be stopped and searched, based on perceptions they are more likely to have done something criminal, and they are more likely to be arrested than those who are not stopped and searched. When arrest records are used as a screening mechanism for certain jobs, racial profiling can take an expensive, long-lasting, life-changing toll. To avoid discrimination and reduce the effect of biased stops and arrests, many employers require that convictions, rather than arrests, be used as the deciding factor for exclusion. But the pool of people convicted is drawn from those arrested, and poor and minority group members are more likely to be convicted when arrested and to receive harsher sentences.[52] Focusing on convictions does

[52]See Beckett, K., & Sasson, T. (2004). *The Politics of Injustice: Crime and Punishment in America*, 2nd ed. Thousand Oaks, CA: Sage Publications; Dees, M. (with Fiffer, S.). (1991). *A Season for Justice: The Life and Times of Civil Rights Lawyer Morris Dees*. New York: Scribners.

not address racial profiling. Committed law enforcement agencies must get to the heart of that matter. The public, of all racial and ethnic backgrounds, must demand that they do.

Colleges and universities. Because they are training grounds for future employees, managers, and leaders, colleges and universities are in a unique position to shape diversity in organizations and in society. The study of diversity should be an integral part of every college and graduate student's curriculum to equip them as future managers and leaders in a diverse society. As discussed in this book, many researchers have documented the ways in which exposure to diverse classmates and to diversity curricula benefits students. Diversity issues are relevant to each one of us, throughout our lives and careers. Students need to understand the historical background of diversity, the current status of dominant and nondominant groups, legislation, why stereotyping occurs and how to avoid it, and why diversity learning is important to individual and organizational success. For the 70% of the U.S. population who does not receive college degrees,[53] inclusion of diversity training in lower level education (e.g., high school) would exponentially increase the beneficial outcomes.

The Role of the Media

The media must take an active stance against the promulgation of stereotypes that impede diversity and harm society. Selling a story and generating high ratings are not important in the overall scheme. If responsible journalism becomes a general priority, the programming will sell. Like other organizations that take steps to ensure diversity among employees, the media must make sincere and concerted efforts to foster diversity. The first step is eradicating discriminatory news reports, television shows, movies, and commercials. Another step would be inclusive programming and discontinuing programming that fosters stereotyping and bias. Granted that entertainment is one goal of programming, but critical analysis and thought can be employed as well to promote and support diversity and equity.

▌ RECOMMENDATIONS FOR CHANGE AT AN INDIVIDUAL LEVEL

Blacks, Latinos, Asians, American Indians and Alaska Natives, multiracial group members, and other non-Whites, women, people with disabilities,

---

[53]Table 224. "Educational Attainment by Race and Hispanic Origin: 1970-2008." http://www.census.gov/compendia/statab/2010/tables/10s0224.pdf, accessed November 30, 2010.

those who are overweight or obese, sexual minorities, and religious minorities are the non-dominant group members that we have discussed in terms of the United States. The Māori in New Zealand, Asians in Britain, the Burakumin in Japan, ethnic Chinese in Indonesia, Blacks and Coloreds in South Africa, Koreans in Japan, North Africans in France, women, people with disabilities, sexual minorities, immigrants, and the "untouchables" in India are some of the numerous non-dominant groups who experience discrimination and differential treatment in countries around the world. Racism, sexism, heterosexism, ableism, classism, and other "isms" are alive and well, but there are some things that individuals can do to minimize the negative effects of such discrimination. As many chapters have proposed, whenever possible, individuals should work to obtain as much education as possible and to prepare themselves to seize every opportunity when it arises—education, fluency in multiple languages, and job flexibility are just some of the ways in which an individual can circumvent discrimination.

Although race, sex, and often class segregation of jobs is prevalent around the world, non-dominant group members should try to avoid segregated jobs and occupations. They should investigate an organization's posture on diversity during the job search process. Is there evidence of a glass ceiling and walls? Are non-dominant group members confined to staff, rather than line, jobs? Are non-dominant group members represented at all levels of the organization? Find and talk with people who work there. What is the diversity climate of the organization *truly* like?

People should not deny their identity and individuality, neither should they be afraid of being viewed as a "token" or "affirmative action hire." Such perceptions reflect on the perceiver, rather than on the perceived. People should be careful to avoid internalizing low expectations and reject stereotypes about their own and others' groups. They should resist discrimination against other non-dominant group members—working for fairness for everyone, even when doing so does not appear to be a personal issue. They should not assume that all dominant group members are against diversity; many allies can be found among the dominant group.

In addition to seizing opportunities when available, individuals should work to make opportunities for themselves and others. Like increasing numbers of non-dominant group members, they can consider starting a business and letting it be a beacon, modeling support for diversity and providing opportunities for others. Individuals should seek a mentor and serve as a mentor. They can ask what one person can do to make a difference, and then do it when that is possible and avoid being a passive observer or complainer. Activism can help give people a sense of power while also helping to change situations.

Dominant group members should recognize their unearned advantages and be aware of their membership in many groups and the fluidity of some of these memberships (e.g., age, physical and mental ability). They should recognize the value in diversity and pursue it, working to foster diversity and resisting stereotyping and discrimination. They should not see the situation as "us" against "them," a competition for a slice of a small and finite pie. Instead, dominant group members should view diversity as fostering more and greater opportunities for everyone, but only when everyone has the opportunity to contribute. In an increasingly global community, "us" is everyone, and without the contributions of everyone, long-term success for anyone is at risk.

▌ CAPITALIZING ON THE STRENGTH OF DIVERSITY IN THE UNITED STATES

At the beginning of this chapter, we considered the idea that diversity issues are not specific to the United States. At this point, however, a discussion of the experiences unique to the United States is appropriate: the annihilation of or banishment to reservations of American Indians, the enslavement of Blacks and continued discrimination against them, the anti-Chinese legislation and sentiment of the past and the past restriction of citizenship to "White men" only, the internment of the Japanese during World War II, the current relative paucity of women in the political system and the absence of women from the highest elected offices (e.g., president and vice president) compared to other developed nations (e.g., England, India), the peculiar employment of undocumented immigrants but stated disdain for illegal immigration, and many other examples. The diversity issues in the United States are uniquely its own, even though it shares numerous aspects of these issues (e.g., gender, sexual orientation, disability, and poverty) with many other countries.

The history of the United States and its stated belief in welcoming diverse others make its standing distinct. Indeed, people seeking opportunities and refuge from racial, ethnic, religious, and other persecution often turn to the United States. Because of this and the increasing connectedness of the world, the United States is in a particularly unique and precarious position—unique in that no other nation has its history and experience with diversity, and precarious in that if its diverse population is not given opportunities to contribute, the United States may be left behind in an increasingly competitive and global world.

The United States no longer has the "luxury" of ignoring, excluding, devaluing, failing to adequately educate, and segregating large populations of workers. If women continue to be 51% of the population and live longer than men, as "minorities" grow to become the majority, as older workers need and desire to work longer, as more people acquire and live longer with disabilities, as religious diversity increases, and as more people work and have families, all potential workers must be encouraged to contribute to the country's success. The United States needs women as scientists, engineers, computer programmers, and truck drivers, not just as kindergarten teachers, nurses, and secretaries only—limiting them to a few job categories and competing for low wages in these limited categories. It needs Blacks, Latinos, and American Indians as scientists, engineers, programmers, managers, and entrepreneurs, not just in the low-wage positions they currently disproportionately occupy, or, worse still, unemployed at twice the rate of Whites and many having given up looking for work. The United States needs to allow people with disabilities to work— their stability, their education, their willingness to work must not be ignored. It needs to provide everyone with the opportunity to obtain at least a high school education, rather than allowing large proportions of the fastest-growing groups to remain uneducated. The United States needs a population that is multilingual rather than one in which the majority of people are monolingual and many resist languages other than English. It needs to let older workers who are willing and able to work continue to provide their technical and managerial expertise and to let sexual minorities feel comfortable being "out" in the workplace rather than worrying about being "out-ed" and thus failing to contribute as they otherwise would.

In sum, in an increasingly competitive world the United States simply cannot afford to do without potential contributors or to limit their contributions. As national boundaries grow increasingly dim, as mergers, acquisitions, cross-cultural relationships, and international business become the norm, intranational infighting and discrimination are increasingly absurd.

In addition to the organizational, societal, and individual recommendations we have presented, what else can be done to encourage diversity? Increased, not decreased, attention should be paid to the pursuit of diversity. The playing field is not level—indeed there has been significant retrenchment in recent years. The education, employment, opportunities, and earning power of many non-dominant groups have actually declined through resistance to diversity measures and the recent recession. Harassment for religious and sexual orientation is significant, as are racial profiling, hate crimes, and hostility toward immigrants. Intellectual leaders and a government with a view to the country's future must work to educate the population that diversity is not about "us" versus "them" and a finite set of resources. Rather, by embracing diversity, and pursuing education, equity, fairness, and opportunities for all, the contributions of all of the more than 300 million potential contributors will create an infinite set of possibilities.

Summary

This chapter has focused on three areas: diversity issues in the international context, recommended changes for the future, and the imperative need for attending to diversity issues in the United States. We discussed the universal relevance of ensuring diversity around the world, specifically in the areas of sex and gender, disabilities, sexual orientation, and poverty. We also explored the relationships among individual, organizational, and societal diversity, emphasizing that they are intertwined. Finally, we considered the unique position of the United States and its particular need and opportunity to embrace and foster diversity in organizations, given the diversity of its population.

This chapter concludes with the hope that readers have learned a great deal about diversity in organizations and its relevance to individuals and society and are inspired to pursue diversity—perhaps for competitive advantage, but more important, as a moral imperative. When everyone, regardless of race, sex, ethnicity, age, sexual orientation, physical and mental ability, family status, or other non-job-related attributes, has opportunities to work in a variety of jobs, to obtain promotions and advancement at work, to shop without being followed and drive without being profiled, and to obtain education, housing, loans, service in restaurants, and other "normal" privileges, individuals, organizations, and societies will be more able to contribute to the well-being of us all in the world in which we live.

Key Terms

Affinity or employee resource groups — informal social organizations at work composed of demographically or otherwise similar members.

Questions to Consider

1. Aside from the topics discussed in this chapter (sex and gender, workers with disabilities, sexual orientation, and poverty), what other areas are of universal relevance to diversity in organizations, regardless of one's location in the world?
2. What can dominant groups in each society do to foster diversity? What can the non-dominant do? What can you do?
3. Figure 16.1 lists some of the factors useful in identifying specific diversity concerns in any country. What others would you add to the list?
4. Why is diversity a particularly important concern for the United States?

Actions and Exercises

1. Choose a country other than the United States and document the key diversity concerns for that country. Which groups are dominant and which are non-dominant? What are the workforce participation rates, earnings, and employment differences among the groups? Does the country have legislation covering those groups? How is diversity in the country you chose similar to or different from diversity in the United States?
2. Assume you are starting a business in the country you chose in #1. Which diversity-related factors would you emphasize most or be most concerned about, based on the information you obtained in #1 above?

Name Index

A

Acuna, R., 28
Ahdaoui, Khadija, 385
Alba, R., 179
Albright, M., 54
Allen, K., 181
Allen, P. G., 269
Allen, Sharon, 250, 308
Allers, K. L., 216
Allison, D. B., 478
Alon, T., 336
Altameyer, B., 390
Anastasio, P. A., 49
Anderson, C. D., 252
Ando, F., 113
Andreyeva, T., 460
Angier, N., 464
Anker, R., 290
Antecol, H., 317, 357, 358
Apostal, R. A., 452
Appleby, P. N., 476
Aranda, E. M., 151
Archdeacon, T. J., 379
Armour, S., 422
Arthur, M. M., 322, 349
Arulampalam, W., 293
Arvey, R. D., 468
Ash, M., 507
Astor, G., 112
Atkinson, W., 250
Avery, D. R., 15
Avery, R. B., 137

B

Babcock, L., 296, 313, 314
Bacharach, S. B., 22
Bachelder, L., 6, 447, 451, 453
Bachu, A., 330
Back, A., 116
Badgett, M. V. L., 357, 358

Baker, H. B., 450
Baker, S. G., 170
Baker, S. M., 450
Baldonado, Michael, 80
Baldor, L. C., 115
Bales, W., 178
Ball, E., 273
Barbee, A. P., 463
Barnes, S. L., 507
Barreto, M., 56
Barrios, Laura, 449, 455
Barron, L., 359
Bartkowski, J. P., 367
Bean, F. D., 205, 259
Beaton, A. M., 57
Beatty, J., 277
Beauregard, T. A., 370
Beauvais, L. L., 349
Beckett, K., 517
Bednarz, B. A., 192
Belkin, A., 368
Bell, M. P., 19, 21, 86, 95, 131, 165, 370, 396, 448, 498
Belliveau, M., 314
Bellizzi, J. A., 466
Bendick, M., Jr., 124, 163, 245, 305
Benjamin, Dr. Regina - U. S. Surgeon General, 140, 141
Bennett, C. E., 196, 202
Bennett, M. D., 131
Bennett, W., 388
Bentley, K. J., 432
Bergman, M. E., 304, 499
Berman, P., 400
Bernard, T. S., 340, 364
Bernstein, A., 131
Berta, D., 183
Bertrand, M., 124, 125
Beyer, Thomas, 296
Biddle, J. E., 463, 468
Biernat, M., 460
Bin Laden, Osama, 194
Bjorn, L., 305
Black, D. A., 357, 358, 363

Blake, S., 12, 19, 22, 23, 25, 27, 64, 157, 450, 510
Blanford, J. M., 358
Blau, F. D., 113
Block, C. J., 86, 243, 500
Block, R., 71
Boldry, J. G., 51, 52
Bonacich, E., 207, 208, 209
Bond, Julian, 235
Bonikowski, B., 126, 480
Bonilla-Silva, E., 55, 56
Bontrager, S., 178
Booth, A. L., 293
Borjas, G. J., 205
Borman, Walter C., 400
Bornstein, S., 336
Botsford, W. E., 343
Bouamama, Youssef, 99
Bound, J., 312
Boushey, H., 322, 342
Braddock, D., 6, 447, 451, 453
Bradley, L., 340
Bratton, K. A., 159
Brenner, B. R., 370, 371
Brett, J. F., 22
Brevoort, K. P., 137
Brewis, A. A., 465
Bricout, J. C., 432
Brief, A. P., 86, 355, 371
Brinsfield, C. T., 370
Brodkin, K., 86, 114, 226, 227, 232, 381
Brown, D. L., 131
Brown, I., 7, 170, 244
Brown, J. S., 148
Brown, John, 229
Brown, K., 340
Brown, P. L., 473, 474
Brown, R., 57
Browne, I., 110, 133, 134, 294, 311, 312
Brownell, K. D., 460, 479
Brunsma, D. L., 258, 277, 279
Bryan, M. L., 293
Buchanan, N. T., 425
Budig, M. J., 333

523

Subject Index

Page numbers followed by *f* indicate figures; and those followed by *t* indicate tables.